Library of America, a nonprofit organization,
champions our nation's cultural heritage
by publishing America's greatest writing in
authoritative new editions and providing resources
for readers to explore this rich, living legacy.

MAXINE HONG KINGSTON

Maxine Hong Kingston

THE WOMAN WARRIOR
CHINA MEN
TRIPMASTER MONKEY
HAWAI'I ONE SUMMER
OTHER WRITINGS

Viet Thanh Nguyen, *editor*

THE LIBRARY OF AMERICA

Maxine Hong Kingston: The Woman Warrior,
China Men, Tripmaster Monkey, Hawai'i One Summer
& Other Writings
is published in memory of

OU SHEE ENG
(Born 1899, Chu Lin Village, in the Sun Woy district of
China; died Seattle, Washington, 1981)

who, when few women were taught to read, was a
voracious reader in Chinese all her life and shared this
skill with women in Seattle's Chinatown by reading
aloud the letters they received from home

with a gift from

**her granddaughter Elana Eng Lim and husband
Randy Lim, and their sons, Justin and Jordon Lim.**

Contents

THE WOMAN WARRIOR

Memoirs of a Girlhood Among Ghosts

To Mother and Father

Contents

No Name Woman

"YOU MUST not tell anyone," my mother said, "what I am about to tell you. In China your father had a sister who killed herself. She jumped into the family well. We say that your father has all brothers because it is as if she had never been born.

"In 1924 just a few days after our village celebrated seventeen hurry-up weddings—to make sure that every young man who went 'out on the road' would responsibly come home—your father and his brothers and your grandfather and his brothers and your aunt's new husband sailed for America, the Gold Mountain. It was your grandfather's last trip. Those lucky enough to get contracts waved goodbye from the decks. They fed and guarded the stowaways and helped them off in Cuba, New York, Bali, Hawaii. 'We'll meet in California next year,' they said. All of them sent money home.

"I remember looking at your aunt one day when she and I were dressing; I had not noticed before that she had such a protruding melon of a stomach. But I did not think, 'She's pregnant,' until she began to look like other pregnant women, her shirt pulling and the white tops of her black pants showing. She could not have been pregnant, you see, because her husband had been gone for years. No one said anything. We did not discuss it. In early summer she was ready to have the child, long after the time when it could have been possible.

"The village had also been counting. On the night the baby was to be born the villagers raided our house. Some were crying. Like a great saw, teeth strung with lights, files of people walked zigzag across our land, tearing the rice. Their lanterns doubled in the disturbed black water, which drained away through the broken bunds. As the villagers closed in, we could see that some of them, probably men and women we knew well, wore white masks. The people with long hair hung it over their faces. Women with short hair made it stand up on end. Some had tied white bands around their foreheads, arms, and legs.

7

"At first they threw mud and rocks at the house. Then they threw eggs and began slaughtering our stock. We could hear the animals scream their deaths—the roosters, the pigs, a last great roar from the ox. Familiar wild heads flared in our night windows; the villagers encircled us. Some of the faces stopped to peer at us, their eyes rushing like searchlights. The hands flattened against the panes, framed heads, and left red prints.

"The villagers broke in the front and the back doors at the same time, even though we had not locked the doors against them. Their knives dripped with the blood of our animals. They smeared blood on the doors and walls. One woman swung a chicken, whose throat she had slit, splattering blood in red arcs about her. We stood together in the middle of our house, in the family hall with the pictures and tables of the ancestors around us, and looked straight ahead.

"At that time the house had only two wings. When the men came back, we would build two more to enclose our courtyard and a third one to begin a second courtyard. The villagers pushed through both wings, even your grandparents' rooms, to find your aunt's, which was also mine until the men returned. From this room a new wing for one of the younger families would grow. They ripped up her clothes and shoes and broke her combs, grinding them underfoot. They tore her work from the loom. They scattered the cooking fire and rolled the new weaving in it. We could hear them in the kitchen breaking our bowls and banging the pots. They overturned the great waist-high earthenware jugs; duck eggs, pickled fruits, vegetables burst out and mixed in acrid torrents. The old woman from the next field swept a broom through the air and loosed the spirits-of-the-broom over our heads. 'Pig.' 'Ghost.' 'Pig,' they sobbed and scolded while they ruined our house.

"When they left, they took sugar and oranges to bless themselves. They cut pieces from the dead animals. Some of them took bowls that were not broken and clothes that were not torn. Afterward we swept up the rice and sewed it back up into sacks. But the smells from the spilled preserves lasted. Your aunt gave birth in the pigsty that night. The next morning when I went for the water, I found her and the baby plugging up the family well.

"Don't let your father know that I told you. He denies her.

Now that you have started to menstruate, what happened to her could happen to you. Don't humiliate us. You wouldn't like to be forgotten as if you had never been born. The villagers are watchful."

Whenever she had to warn us about life, my mother told stories that ran like this one, a story to grow up on. She tested our strength to establish realities. Those in the emigrant generations who could not reassert brute survival died young and far from home. Those of us in the first American generations have had to figure out how the invisible world the emigrants built around our childhoods fit in solid America.

The emigrants confused the gods by diverting their curses, misleading them with crooked streets and false names. They must try to confuse their offspring as well, who, I suppose, threaten them in similar ways—always trying to get things straight, always trying to name the unspeakable. The Chinese I know hide their names; sojourners take new names when their lives change and guard their real names with silence.

Chinese-Americans, when you try to understand what things in you are Chinese, how do you separate what is peculiar to childhood, to poverty, insanities, one family, your mother who marked your growing with stories, from what is Chinese? What is Chinese tradition and what is the movies?

If I want to learn what clothes my aunt wore, whether flashy or ordinary, I would have to begin, "Remember Father's drowned-in-the-well sister?" I cannot ask that. My mother has told me once and for all the useful parts. She will add nothing unless powered by Necessity, a riverbank that guides her life. She plants vegetable gardens rather than lawns; she carries the odd-shaped tomatoes home from the fields and eats food left for the gods.

Whenever we did frivolous things, we used up energy; we flew high kites. We children came up off the ground over the melting cones our parents brought home from work and the American movie on New Year's Day—*Oh, You Beautiful Doll* with Betty Grable one year, and *She Wore a Yellow Ribbon* with John Wayne another year. After the one carnival ride each, we paid in guilt; our tired father counted his change on the dark walk home.

Adultery is extravagance. Could people who hatch their own

chicks and eat the embryos and the heads for delicacies and boil the feet in vinegar for party food, leaving only the gravel, eating even the gizzard lining—could such people engender a prodigal aunt? To be a woman, to have a daughter in starvation time was a waste enough. My aunt could not have been the lone romantic who gave up everything for sex. Women in the old China did not choose. Some man had commanded her to lie with him and be his secret evil. I wonder whether he masked himself when he joined the raid on her family.

Perhaps she encountered him in the fields or on the mountain where the daughters-in-law collected fuel. Or perhaps he first noticed her in the marketplace. He was not a stranger because the village housed no strangers. She had to have dealings with him other than sex. Perhaps he worked an adjoining field, or he sold her the cloth for the dress she sewed and wore. His demand must have surprised, then terrified her. She obeyed him; she always did as she was told.

When the family found a young man in the next village to be her husband, she stood tractably beside the best rooster, his proxy, and promised before they met that she would be his forever. She was lucky that he was her age and she would be the first wife, an advantage secure now. The night she first saw him, he had sex with her. Then he left for America. She had almost forgotten what he looked like. When she tried to envision him, she only saw the black and white face in the group photograph the men had had taken before leaving.

The other man was not, after all, much different from her husband. They both gave orders: she followed. "If you tell your family, I'll beat you. I'll kill you. Be here again next week." No one talked sex, ever. And she might have separated the rapes from the rest of living if only she did not have to buy her oil from him or gather wood in the same forest. I want her fear to have lasted just as long as rape lasted so that the fear could have been contained. No drawn-out fear. But women at sex hazarded birth and hence lifetimes. The fear did not stop but permeated everywhere. She told the man, "I think I'm pregnant." He organized the raid against her.

On nights when my mother and father talked about their life back home, sometimes they mentioned an "outcast table" whose business they still seemed to be settling, their voices tight. In a commensal tradition, where food is precious, the powerful older people made wrongdoers eat alone. Instead of letting them start separate new lives like the Japanese, who could become samurais and geishas, the Chinese family, faces averted but eyes glowering sideways, hung on to the offenders and fed them leftovers. My aunt must have lived in the same house as my parents and eaten at an outcast table. My mother spoke about the raid as if she had seen it, when she and my aunt, a daughter-in-law to a different household, should not have been living together at all. Daughters-in-law lived with their husbands' parents, not their own; a synonym for marriage in Chinese is "taking a daughter-in-law." Her husband's parents could have sold her, mortgaged her, stoned her. But they had sent her back to her own mother and father, a mysterious act hinting at disgraces not told me. Perhaps they had thrown her out to deflect the avengers.

She was the only daughter; her four brothers went with her father, husband, and uncles "out on the road" and for some years became western men. When the goods were divided among the family, three of the brothers took land, and the youngest, my father, chose an education. After my grandparents gave their daughter away to her husband's family, they had dispensed all the adventure and all the property. They expected her alone to keep the traditional ways, which her brothers, now among the barbarians, could fumble without detection. The heavy, deep-rooted women were to maintain the past against the flood, safe for returning. But the rare urge west had fixed upon our family, and so my aunt crossed boundaries not delineated in space.

The work of preservation demands that the feelings playing about in one's guts not be turned into action. Just watch their passing like cherry blossoms. But perhaps my aunt, my forerunner, caught in a slow life, let dreams grow and fade and after some months or years went toward what persisted. Fear at the enormities of the forbidden kept her desires delicate, wire and bone. She looked at a man because she liked the way the hair was tucked behind his ears, or she liked the question-mark line of a long torso curving at the shoulder and straight at the hip. For warm eyes or a soft voice or a slow walk—that's all—a few hairs, a line, a brightness, a sound, a pace, she gave up family.

She offered us up for a charm that vanished with tiredness, a pigtail that didn't toss when the wind died. Why, the wrong lighting could erase the dearest thing about him.

It could very well have been, however, that my aunt did not take subtle enjoyment of her friend, but, a wild woman, kept rollicking company. Imagining her free with sex doesn't fit, though. I don't know any women like that, or men either. Unless I see her life branching into mine, she gives me no ancestral help.

To sustain her being in love, she often worked at herself in the mirror, guessing at the colors and shapes that would interest him, changing them frequently in order to hit on the right combination. She wanted him to look back.

On a farm near the sea, a woman who tended her appearance reaped a reputation for eccentricity. All the married women blunt-cut their hair in flaps about their ears or pulled it back in tight buns. No nonsense. Neither style blew easily into heart-catching tangles. And at their weddings they displayed themselves in their long hair for the last time. "It brushed the backs of my knees," my mother tells me. "It was braided, and even so, it brushed the backs of my knees."

At the mirror my aunt combed individuality into her bob. A bun could have been contrived to escape into black streamers blowing in the wind or in quiet wisps about her face, but only the older women in our picture album wear buns. She brushed her hair back from her forehead, tucking the flaps behind her ears. She looped a piece of thread, knotted into a circle between her index fingers and thumbs, and ran the double strand across her forehead. When she closed her fingers as if she were making a pair of shadow geese bite, the string twisted together catching the little hairs. Then she pulled the thread away from her skin, ripping the hairs out neatly, her eyes watering from the needles of pain. Opening her fingers, she cleaned the thread, then rolled it along her hairline and the tops of her eyebrows. My mother did the same to me and my sisters and herself. I used to believe that the expression "caught by the short hairs" meant a captive held with a depilatory string. It especially hurt at the temples, but my mother said we were lucky we didn't have to have our feet bound when we were seven. Sisters used to sit on their beds and cry together, she said, as their mothers or their slaves removed the bandages for a few minutes each night and let the blood gush back into their veins. I hope that the man my aunt loved appreciated a smooth brow, that he wasn't just a tits-and-ass man.

Once my aunt found a freckle on her chin, at a spot that the almanac said predestined her for unhappiness. She dug it out with a hot needle and washed the wound with peroxide.

More attention to her looks than these pullings of hairs and pickings at spots would have caused gossip among the villagers. They owned work clothes and good clothes, and they wore good clothes for feasting the new seasons. But since a woman combing her hair hexes beginnings, my aunt rarely found an occasion to look her best. Women looked like great sea snails—the corded wood, babies, and laundry they carried were the whorls on their backs. The Chinese did not admire a bent back; goddesses and warriors stood straight. Still there must have been a marvelous freeing of beauty when a worker laid down her burden and stretched and arched.

Such commonplace loveliness, however, was not enough for my aunt. She dreamed of a lover for the fifteen days of New Year's, the time for families to exchange visits, money, and food. She plied her secret comb. And sure enough she cursed the year, the family, the village, and herself.

Even as her hair lured her imminent lover, many other men looked at her. Uncles, cousins, nephews, brothers would have looked, too, had they been home between journeys. Perhaps they had already been restraining their curiosity, and they left, fearful that their glances, like a field of nesting birds, might be startled and caught. Poverty hurt, and that was their first reason for leaving. But another, final reason for leaving the crowded house was the never-said.

She may have been unusually beloved, the precious only daughter, spoiled and mirror gazing because of the affection the family lavished on her. When her husband left, they welcomed the chance to take her back from the in-laws; she could live like the little daughter for just a while longer. There are stories that my grandfather was different from other people, "crazy ever since the little Jap bayoneted him in the head." He used to put his naked penis on the dinner table, laughing. And one day he brought home a baby girl, wrapped up inside his brown western-style greatcoat. He had traded one of his sons, probably my father, the youngest, for her. My grandmother made him trade back. When he finally got a daughter of his own, he doted on her. They must have all loved her, except perhaps my father, the only brother who never went back to China, having once been traded for a girl.

Brothers and sisters, newly men and women, had to efface their sexual color and present plain miens. Disturbing hair and eyes, a smile like no other threatened the ideal of five generations living under one roof. To focus blurs, people shouted face to face and yelled from room to room. The immigrants I know have loud voices, unmodulated to American tones even after years away from the village where they called their friendships out across the fields. I have not been able to stop my mother's screams in public libraries or over telephones. Walking erect (knees straight, toes pointed forward, not pigeon-toed, which is Chinese-feminine) and speaking in an inaudible voice, I have tried to turn myself American-feminine. Chinese communication was loud, public. Only sick people had to whisper. But at the dinner table, where the family members came nearest one another, no one could talk, not the outcasts nor any eaters. Every word that falls from the mouth is a coin lost. Silently they gave and accepted food with both hands. A preoccupied child who took his bowl with one hand got a sideways glare. A complete moment of total attention is due everyone alike. Children and lovers have no singularity here, but my aunt used a secret voice, a separate attentiveness.

She kept the man's name to herself throughout her labor and dying; she did not accuse him that he be punished with her. To save her inseminator's name she gave silent birth.

He may have been somebody in her own household, but intercourse with a man outside the family would have been no less abhorrent. All the village were kinsmen, and the titles shouted in loud country voices never let kinship be forgotten. Any man within visiting distance would have been neutralized as a lover—"brother," "younger brother," "older brother"— one hundred and fifteen relationship titles. Parents researched birth charts probably not so much to assure good fortune as to circumvent incest in a population that has but one hundred surnames. Everybody has eight million relatives. How useless then sexual mannerisms, how dangerous.

As if it came from an atavism deeper than fear, I used to add "brother" silently to boys' names. It hexed the boys, who would or would not ask me to dance, and made them less scary and as familiar and deserving of benevolence as girls.

But, of course, I hexed myself also—no dates. I should have stood up, both arms waving, and shouted out across libraries, "Hey, you! Love me back." I had no idea, though, how to make attraction selective, how to control its direction and magnitude. If I made myself American-pretty so that the five or six Chinese boys in the class fell in love with me, everyone else—the Caucasian, Negro, and Japanese boys—would too. Sisterliness, dignified and honorable, made much more sense.

Attraction eludes control so stubbornly that whole societies designed to organize relationships among people cannot keep order, not even when they bind people to one another from childhood and raise them together. Among the very poor and the wealthy, brothers married their adopted sisters, like doves. Our family allowed some romance, paying adult brides' prices and providing dowries so that their sons and daughters could marry strangers. Marriage promises to turn strangers into friendly relatives—a nation of siblings.

In the village structure, spirits shimmered among the live creatures, balanced and held in equilibrium by time and land. But one human being flaring up into violence could open up a black hole, a maelstrom that pulled in the sky. The frightened villagers, who depended on one another to maintain the real, went to my aunt to show her a personal, physical representation of the break she had made in the "roundness." Misallying couples snapped off the future, which was to be embodied in true offspring. The villagers punished her for acting as if she could have a private life, secret and apart from them.

If my aunt had betrayed the family at a time of large grain yields and peace, when many boys were born, and wings were being built on many houses, perhaps she might have escaped such severe punishment. But the men—hungry, greedy, tired of planting in dry soil, cuckolded—had had to leave the village in order to send food-money home. There were ghost plagues, bandit plagues, wars with the Japanese, floods. My Chinese brother and sister had died of an unknown sickness. Adultery, perhaps only a mistake during good times, became a crime when the village needed food.

The round moon cakes and round doorways, the round tables of graduated size that fit one roundness inside another, round windows and rice bowls—these talismans had lost their power to warn this family of the law: a family must be whole, faithfully keeping the descent line by having sons to feed the old and the dead, who in turn look after the family. The villagers came to show my aunt and her lover-in-hiding a broken house. The villagers were speeding up the circling of events because she was too shortsighted to see that her infidelity had already harmed the village, that waves of consequences would return unpredictably, sometimes in disguise, as now, to hurt her. This roundness had to be made coin-sized so that she would see its circumference: punish her at the birth of her baby. Awaken her to the inexorable. People who refused fatalism because they could invent small resources insisted on culpability. Deny accidents and wrest fault from the stars.

After the villagers left, their lanterns now scattering in various directions toward home, the family broke their silence and cursed her. "Aiaa, we're going to die. Death is coming. Death is coming. Look what you've done. You've killed us. Ghost! Dead ghost! Ghost! You've never been born." She ran out into the fields, far enough from the house so that she could no longer hear their voices, and pressed herself against the earth, her own land no more. When she felt the birth coming, she thought that she had been hurt. Her body seized together. "They've hurt me too much," she thought. "This is gall, and it will kill me." Her forehead and knees against the earth, her body convulsed and then released her onto her back. The black well of sky and stars went out and out and out forever; her body and her complexity seemed to disappear. She was one of the stars, a bright dot in blackness, without home, without a companion, in eternal cold and silence. An agoraphobia rose in her, speeding higher and higher, bigger and bigger; she would not be able to contain it; there would be no end to fear.

Flayed, unprotected against space, she felt pain return, focusing her body. This pain chilled her—a cold, steady kind of surface pain. Inside, spasmodically, the other pain, the pain of the child, heated her. For hours she lay on the ground, alternately body and space. Sometimes a vision of normal comfort obliterated reality: she saw the family in the evening gambling at the dinner table, the young people massaging their elders' backs. She saw them congratulating one another, high joy on the mornings the rice shoots came up. When these pictures burst, the stars drew yet further apart. Black space opened.

She got to her feet to fight better and remembered that old-fashioned women gave birth in their pigsties to fool the jealous, pain-dealing gods, who do not snatch piglets. Before the next spasms could stop her, she ran to the pigsty, each step a rushing out into emptiness. She climbed over the fence and knelt in the dirt. It was good to have a fence enclosing her, a tribal person alone.

Laboring, this woman who had carried her child as a foreign growth that sickened her every day, expelled it at last. She reached down to touch the hot, wet, moving mass, surely smaller than anything human, and could feel that it was human after all—fingers, toes, nails, nose. She pulled it up on to her belly, and it lay curled there, butt in the air, feet precisely tucked one under the other. She opened her loose shirt and buttoned the child inside. After resting, it squirmed and thrashed and she pushed it up to her breast. It turned its head this way and that until it found her nipple. There, it made little snuffling noises. She clenched her teeth at its preciousness, lovely as a young calf, a piglet, a little dog.

She may have gone to the pigsty as a last act of responsibility: she would protect this child as she had protected its father. It would look after her soul, leaving supplies on her grave. But how would this tiny child without family find her grave when there would be no marker for her anywhere, neither in the earth nor the family hall? No one would give her a family hall name. She had taken the child with her into the wastes. At its birth the two of them had felt the same raw pain of separation, a wound that only the family pressing tight could close. A child with no descent line would not soften her life but only trail after her, ghostlike, begging her to give it purpose. At dawn the villagers on their way to the fields would stand around the fence and look.

Full of milk, the little ghost slept. When it awoke, she

hardened her breasts against the milk that crying loosens. Toward morning she picked up the baby and walked to the well.

Carrying the baby to the well shows loving. Otherwise abandon it. Turn its face into the mud. Mothers who love their children take them along. It was probably a girl; there is some hope of forgiveness for boys.

"Don't tell anyone you had an aunt. Your father does not want to hear her name. She has never been born." I have believed that sex was unspeakable and words so strong and fathers so frail that "aunt" would do my father mysterious harm. I have thought that my family, having settled among immigrants who had also been their neighbors in the ancestral land, needed to clean their name, and a wrong word would incite the kins-people even here. But there is more to this silence: they want me to participate in her punishment. And I have.

In the twenty years since I heard this story I have not asked for details nor said my aunt's name; I do not know it. People who can comfort the dead can also chase after them to hurt them further—a reverse ancestor worship. The real punishment was not the raid swiftly inflicted by the villagers, but the family's deliberately forgetting her. Her betrayal so maddened them, they saw to it that she would suffer forever, even after death. Always hungry, always needing, she would have to beg food from other ghosts, snatch and steal it from those whose living descendants give them gifts. She would have to fight the ghosts massed at crossroads for the buns a few thoughtful citizens leave to decoy her away from village and home so that the ancestral spirits could feast unharassed. At peace, they could act like gods, not ghosts, their descent lines providing them with paper suits and dresses, spirit money, paper houses, paper automobiles, chicken, meat, and rice into eternity—essences delivered up in smoke and flames, steam and incense rising from each rice bowl. In an attempt to make the Chinese care for people outside the family, Chairman Mao encourages us now to give our paper replicas to the spirits of outstanding soldiers and workers, no matter whose ancestors they may be. My aunt remains forever hungry. Goods are not distributed evenly among the dead.

My aunt haunts me—her ghost drawn to me because now, after fifty years of neglect, I alone devote pages of paper to her, though not origamied into houses and clothes. I do not think she always means me well. I am telling on her, and she was a spite suicide, drowning herself in the drinking water. The Chinese are always very frightened of the drowned one, whose weeping ghost, wet hair hanging and skin bloated, waits silently by the water to pull down a substitute.

White Tigers

WHEN WE Chinese girls listened to the adults talking-story, we learned that we failed if we grew up to be but wives or slaves. We could be heroines, swordswomen. Even if she had to rage across all China, a swordswoman got even with anybody who hurt her family. Perhaps women were once so dangerous that they had to have their feet bound. It was a woman who invented white crane boxing only two hundred years ago. She was already an expert pole fighter, daughter of a teacher trained at the Shao-lin temple, where there lived an order of fighting monks. She was combing her hair one morning when a white crane alighted outside her window. She teased it with her pole, which it pushed aside with a soft brush of its wing. Amazed, she dashed outside and tried to knock the crane off its perch. It snapped her pole in two. Recognizing the presence of great power, she asked the spirit of the white crane if it would teach her to fight. It answered with a cry that white crane boxers imitate today. Later the bird returned as an old man, and he guided her boxing for many years. Thus she gave the world a new martial art.

This was one of the tamer, more modern stories, mere introduction. My mother told others that followed swordswomen through woods and palaces for years. Night after night my mother would talk-story until we fell asleep. I couldn't tell where the stories left off and the dreams began, her voice the voice of the heroines in my sleep. And on Sundays, from noon to midnight, we went to the movies at the Confucius Church. We saw swordswomen jump over houses from a standstill; they didn't even need a running start.

At last I saw that I too had been in the presence of great power, my mother talking-story. After I grew up, I heard the chant of Fa Mu Lan, the girl who took her father's place in battle. Instantly I remembered that as a child I had followed my mother about the house, the two of us singing about how Fa Mu Lan fought gloriously and returned alive from war to settle in the village. I had forgotten this chant that was once mine, given me by my mother, who may not have known its power to remind. She said I would grow up a wife and a slave, but she taught me the song of the warrior woman, Fa Mu Lan. I would have to grow up a warrior woman.

The call would come from a bird that flew over our roof. In the brush drawings it looks like the ideograph for "human," two black wings. The bird would cross the sun and lift into the mountains (which look like the ideograph "mountain"), there parting the mist briefly that swirled opaque again. I would be a little girl of seven the day I followed the bird away into the mountains. The brambles would tear off my shoes and the rocks cut my feet and fingers, but I would keep climbing, eyes upward to follow the bird. We would go around and around the tallest mountain, climbing ever upward. I would drink from the river, which I would meet again and again. We would go so high the plants would change, and the river that flows past the village would become a waterfall. At the height where the bird used to disappear, the clouds would gray the world like an ink wash.

Even when I got used to that gray, I would only see peaks as if shaded in pencil, rocks like charcoal rubbings, everything so murky. There would be just two black strokes—the bird. Inside the clouds—inside the dragon's breath—I would not know how many hours or days passed. Suddenly, without noise, I would break clear into a yellow, warm world. New trees would lean toward me at mountain angles, but when I looked for the village, it would have vanished under the clouds.

The bird, now gold so close to the sun, would come to rest on the thatch of a hut, which, until the bird's two feet touched it, was camouflaged as part of the mountainside.

The door opened, and an old man and an old woman came out carrying bowls of rice and soup and a leafy branch of peaches.

"Have you eaten rice today, little girl?" they greeted me.

"Yes, I have," I said out of politeness. "Thank you."

("No, I haven't," I would have said in real life, mad at the Chinese for lying so much. "I'm starved. Do you have any cookies? I like chocolate chip cookies.")

"We were about to sit down to another meal," the old woman said. "Why don't you eat with us?"

They just happened to be bringing three rice bowls and three pairs of silver chopsticks out to the plank table under the pines. They gave me an egg, as if it were my birthday, and tea, though they were older than I, but I poured for them. The teapot and the rice pot seemed bottomless, but perhaps not; the old couple ate very little except for peaches.

When the mountains and the pines turned into blue oxen, blue dogs, and blue people standing, the old couple asked me to spend the night in the hut. I thought about the long way down in the ghostly dark and decided yes. The inside of the hut seemed as large as the outdoors. Pine needles covered the floor in thick patterns; someone had carefully arranged the yellow, green, and brown pine needles according to age. When I stepped carelessly and mussed a line, my feet kicked up new blends of earth colors, but the old man and old woman walked so lightly that their feet never stirred the designs by a needle.

A rock grew in the middle of the house, and that was their table. The benches were fallen trees. Ferns and shade flowers grew out of one wall, the mountainside itself. The old couple tucked me into a bed just my width. "Breathe evenly, or you'll lose your balance and fall out," said the woman, covering me with a silk bag stuffed with feathers and herbs. "Opera singers, who begin their training at age five, sleep in beds like this." Then the two of them went outside, and through the window I could see them pull on a rope looped over a branch. The rope was tied to the roof, and the roof opened up like a basket lid. I would sleep with the moon and the stars. I did not see whether the old people slept, so quickly did I drop off, but they would be there waking me with food in the morning.

"Little girl, you have now spent almost a day and a night with us," the old woman said. In the morning light I could see her earlobes pierced with gold. "Do you think you can bear to stay with us for fifteen years? We can train you to become a warrior."

"What about my mother and father?" I asked.

The old man untied the drinking gourd slung across his back. He lifted the lid by its stem and looked for something in the water. "Ah, there," he said.

At first I saw only water so clear it magnified the fibers in the walls of the gourd. On the surface, I saw only my own round reflection. The old man encircled the neck of the gourd with his thumb and index finger and gave it a shake. As the water shook, then settled, the colors and lights shimmered into a picture, not reflecting anything I could see around me. There at the bottom of the gourd were my mother and father scanning the sky, which was where I was. "It has happened already, then," I could hear my mother say. "I didn't expect it so soon." "You knew from her birth that she would be taken," my father answered. "We'll have to harvest potatoes without her help this year," my mother said, and they turned away toward the fields, straw baskets in their arms. The water shook and became just water again. "Mama. Papa," I called, but they were in the valley and could not hear me.

"What do you want to do?" the old man asked. "You can go back right now if you like. You can go pull sweet potatoes, or you can stay with us and learn how to fight barbarians and bandits."

"You can avenge your village," said the old woman. "You can recapture the harvests the thieves have taken. You can be remembered by the Han people for your dutifulness."

"I'll stay with you," I said.

So the hut became my home, and I found out that the old woman did not arrange the pine needles by hand. She opened the roof; an autumn wind would come up, and the needles fell in braids—brown strands, green strands, yellow strands. The old woman waved her arms in conducting motions; she blew softly with her mouth. I thought, nature certainly works differently on mountains than in valleys.

"The first thing you have to learn," the old woman told me, "is how to be quiet." They left me by streams to watch for animals. "If you're noisy, you'll make the deer go without water."

When I could kneel all day without my legs cramping and my breathing became even, the squirrels would bury their hoardings at the hem of my shirt and then bend their tails in a celebration dance. At night, the mice and toads looked at me, their eyes quick stars and slow stars. Not once would I see a three-legged toad, though; you need strings of cash to bait them.

The two old people led me in exercises that began at dawn

and ended at sunset so that I could watch our shadows grow and shrink and grow again, rooted to the earth. I learned to move my fingers, hands, feet, head, and entire body in circles. I walked putting heel down first, toes pointing outward thirty to forty degrees, making the ideograph "eight," making the ideograph "human." Knees bent, I would swing into the slow, measured "square step," the powerful walk into battle. After five years my body became so strong that I could control even the dilations of the pupils inside my irises. I could copy owls and bats, the words for "bat" and "blessing" homonyms. After six years the deer let me run beside them. I could jump twenty feet into the air from a standstill, leaping like a monkey over the hut. Every creature has a hiding skill and a fighting skill a warrior can use. When birds alighted on my palm, I could yield my muscles under their feet and give them no base from which to fly away.

But I could not fly like the bird that led me here, except in large, free dreams.

During the seventh year (I would be fourteen), the two old people led me blindfolded to the mountains of the white tigers. They held me by either elbow and shouted into my ears, "Run. Run. Run." I ran and, not stepping off a cliff at the edge of my toes and not hitting my forehead against a wall, ran faster. A wind buoyed me up over the roots, the rocks, the little hills. We reached the tiger place in no time—a mountain peak three feet three from the sky. We had to bend over.

The old people waved once, slid down the mountain, and disappeared around a tree. The old woman, good with the bow and arrow, took them with her; the old man took the water gourd. I would have to survive bare-handed. Snow lay on the ground, and snow fell in loose gusts—another way the dragon breathes. I walked in the direction from which we had come, and when I reached the timberline, I collected wood broken from the cherry tree, the peony, and the walnut, which is the tree of life. Fire, the old people had taught me, is stored in trees that grow red flowers or red berries in the spring or whose leaves turn red in the fall. I took the wood from the protected spots beneath the trees and wrapped it in my scarf to keep dry. I dug where squirrels might have come, stealing one or two nuts at each place. These I also wrapped in my scarf. It is possible, the old people said, for a human being to live for fifty days on water. I would save the roots and nuts for hard climbs, the places where nothing grew, the emergency should I not find the hut. This time there would be no bird to follow.

The first night I burned half of the wood and slept curled against the mountain. I heard the white tigers prowling on the other side of the fire, but I could not distinguish them from the snow patches. The morning rose perfectly. I hurried along, again collecting wood and edibles. I ate nothing and only drank the snow my fires made run.

The first two days were gifts, the fasting so easy to do, I so smug in my strength that on the third day, the hardest, I caught myself sitting on the ground, opening the scarf and staring at the nuts and dry roots. Instead of walking steadily on or even eating, I faded into dreams about the meat meals my mother used to cook, my monk's food forgotten. That night I burned up most of the wood I had collected, unable to sleep for facing my death—if not death here, then death someday. The moon animals that did not hibernate came out to hunt, but I had given up the habits of a carnivore since living with the old people. I would not trap the mice that danced so close or the owls that plunged just outside the fire.

On the fourth and fifth days, my eyesight sharp with hunger, I saw deer and used their trails when our ways coincided. Where the deer nibbled, I gathered the fungus, the fungus of immortality.

At noon on the tenth day I packed snow, white as rice, into the worn center of a rock pointed out to me by a finger of ice, and around the rock I built a fire. In the warming water I put roots, nuts, and the fungus of immortality. For variety I ate a quarter of the nuts and roots raw. Oh, green joyous rush inside my mouth, my head, my stomach, my toes, my soul—the best meal of my life.

One day I found that I was striding long distances without hindrance, my bundle light. Food had become so scarce that I was no longer stopping to collect it. I had walked into dead land. Here even the snow stopped. I did not go back to the richer areas, where I could not stay anyway, but, resolving to fast until I got halfway to the next woods, I started across the dry rocks. Heavily weighed down by the wood on my back, branches poking maddeningly, I had burned almost all of the fuel not to waste strength lugging it.

Somewhere in the dead land I lost count of the days. It seemed as if I had been walking forever; life had never been different from this. An old man and an old woman were help I had only wished for. I was fourteen years old and lost from my village. I was walking in circles. Hadn't I been already found by the old people? Or was that yet to come? I wanted my mother and father. The old man and old woman were only a part of this lostness and this hunger.

One nightfall I ate the last of my food but had enough sticks for a good fire. I stared into the flames, which reminded me about helping my mother with the cooking and made me cry. It was very strange looking through water into fire and seeing my mother again. I nodded, orange and warm.

A white rabbit hopped beside me, and for a moment I thought it was a blob of snow that had fallen out of the sky. The rabbit and I studied each other. Rabbits taste like chickens. My mother and father had taught me how to hit rabbits over the head with wine jugs, then skin them cleanly for fur vests. "It's a cold night to be an animal," I said. "So you want some fire too, do you? Let me put on another branch, then." I would not hit it with the branch. I had learned from rabbits to kick backward. Perhaps this one was sick because normally the animals did not like fire. The rabbit seemed alert enough, however, looking at me so acutely, bounding up to the fire. But it did not stop when it got to the edge. It turned its face once toward me, then jumped into the fire. The fire went down for a moment, as if crouching in surprise, then the flames shot up taller than before. When the fire became calm again, I saw the rabbit had turned into meat, browned just right. I ate it, knowing the rabbit had sacrificed itself for me. It had made me a gift of meat.

When you have been walking through trees hour after hour—and I finally reached trees after the dead land— branches cross out everything, no relief whichever way your head turns until your eyes start to invent new sights. Hunger also changes the world—when eating can't be a habit, then neither can seeing. I saw two people made of gold dancing the earth's dances. They turned so perfectly that together they were the axis of the earth's turning. They were light; they were molten, changing gold—Chinese lion dancers, African lion dancers in midstep. I heard high Javanese bells deepen in mid-ring to Indian bells, Hindu Indian, American Indian. Before my eyes, gold bells shredded into gold tassels that fanned into two royal capes that softened into lions' fur. Manes grew tall into feathers that shone—became light rays. Then the dancers danced the future—a machine-future—in clothes I had never seen before. I am watching the centuries pass in moments because suddenly I understand time, which is spinning and fixed like the North Star. And I understand how working and hoeing are dancing; how peasant clothes are golden, as king's clothes are golden; how one of the dancers is always a man and the other a woman.

The man and the woman grow bigger and bigger, so bright. All light. They are tall angels in two rows. They have high white wings on their backs. Perhaps there are infinite angels; perhaps I see two angels in their consecutive moments. I cannot bear their brightness and cover my eyes, which hurt from opening so wide without a blink. When I put my hands down to look again, I recognize the old brown man and the old gray woman walking toward me out of the pine forest.

It would seem that this small crack in the mystery was opened, not so much by the old people's magic, as by hunger. Afterward, whenever I did not eat for long, as during famine or battle, I could stare at ordinary people and see their light and gold. I could see their dance. When I get hungry enough, then killing and falling are dancing too.

The old people fed me hot vegetable soup. Then they asked me to talk-story about what happened in the mountains of the white tigers. I told them that the white tigers had stalked me through the snow but that I had fought them off with burning branches, and my great-grandparents had come to lead me safely through the forests. I had met a rabbit who taught me about self-immolation and how to speed up transmigration: one does not have to become worms first but can change directly into a human being—as in our own humaneness we had just changed bowls of vegetable soup into people too. That made them laugh. "You tell good stories," they said. "Now go to sleep, and tomorrow we will begin your dragon lessons."

"One more thing," I wanted to say. "I saw you and how old you really are." But I was already asleep; it came out only a murmur. I would want to tell them about that last moment of my journey; but it was only one moment out of the weeks that I had been gone, and its telling would keep till morning. Besides, the two people must already know. In the next years, when I suddenly came upon them or when I caught them out of the corners of my eyes, he appeared as a handsome young man, tall with long black hair, and she, as a beautiful young woman who ran bare-legged through the trees. In the spring she dressed like a bride; she wore juniper leaves in her hair and a black embroidered jacket. I learned to shoot accurately because my teachers held the targets. Often when sighting along an arrow, there to the side I would glimpse the young man or young woman, but when I looked directly, he or she would be old again. By this time I had guessed from their sexless manner that the old woman was to the old man a sister or a friend rather than a wife.

After I returned from my survival test, the two old people trained me in dragon ways, which took another eight years. Copying the tigers, their stalking kill and their anger, had been a wild, bloodthirsty joy. Tigers are easy to find, but I needed adult wisdom to know dragons. "You have to infer the whole dragon from the parts you can see and touch," the old people would say. Unlike tigers, dragons are so immense, I would never see one in its entirety. But I could explore the mountains, which are the top of its head. "These mountains are also *like* the tops of *other* dragons' heads," the old people would tell me. When climbing the slopes, I could understand that I was a bug riding on a dragon's forehead as it roams through space, its speed so different from my speed that I feel the dragon solid and immobile. In quarries I could see its strata, the dragon's veins and muscles; the minerals, its teeth and bones. I could touch the stones the old woman wore—its bone marrow. I had worked the soil, which is its flesh, and harvested the plants and climbed the trees, which are its hairs. I could listen to its voice in the thunder and feel its breathing in the winds, see its breathing in the clouds. Its tongue is the lightning. And the red that the lightning gives to the world is strong and lucky—in blood, poppies, roses, rubies, the red feathers of birds, the red carp, the cherry tree, the peony, the line alongside the turtle's eyes and the mallard's. In the spring when the dragon awakes, I watched its turnings in the rivers.

The closest I came to seeing a dragon whole was when the old people cut away a small strip of bark on a pine that was over three thousand years old. The resin underneath flows in the swirling shapes of dragons. "If you should decide during your old age that you would like to live another five hundred years, come here and drink ten pounds of this sap," they told me. "But don't do it now. You're too young to decide to live forever." The old people sent me out into thunderstorms to pick the red-cloud herb, which grows only then, a product of dragon's fire and dragon's rain. I brought the leaves to the old man and old woman, and they ate them for immortality.

I learned to make my mind large, as the universe is large, so that there is room for paradoxes. Pearls are bone marrow; pearls come from oysters. The dragon lives in the sky, ocean, marshes, and mountains; and the mountains are also its cranium. Its voice thunders and jingles like copper pans. It breathes fire and water; and sometimes the dragon is one, sometimes many.

I worked every day. When it rained, I exercised in the downpour, grateful not to be pulling sweet potatoes. I moved like the trees in the wind. I was grateful not to be squishing in chicken mud, which I did not have nightmares about so frequently now.

On New Year's mornings, the old man let me look in his water gourd to see my family. They were eating the biggest meal of the year, and I missed them very much. I had felt loved, love pouring from their fingers when the adults tucked red money in our pockets. My two old people did not give me money, but, each year for fifteen years, a bead. After I unwrapped the red paper and rolled the bead about between thumb and fingers, they took it back for safekeeping. We ate monk's food as usual.

By looking into the water gourd I was able to follow the men I would have to execute. Not knowing that I watched, fat men ate meat; fat men drank wine made from the rice; fat men sat on naked little girls. I watched powerful men count their money, and starving men count theirs. When bandits brought their share of raids home, I waited until they took off their masks so I would know the villagers who stole from their neighbors. I studied the generals' faces, their rank-stalks quivering at the backs of their heads. I learned rebels' faces, too, their foreheads tied with wild oaths.

The old man pointed out strengths and weaknesses whenever heroes met in classical battles, but warfare makes a scramble of the beautiful, slow old fights. I saw one young fighter salute his opponent—and five peasants hit him from behind with scythes and hammers. His opponent did not warn him.

"Cheaters!" I yelled. "How am I going to win against cheaters?"

"Don't worry," the old man said. "You'll never be trapped like that poor amateur. You can see behind you like a bat. Hold the peasants back with one hand and kill the warrior with the other."

Menstrual days did not interrupt my training; I was as strong as on any other day. "You're now an adult," explained the old woman on the first one, which happened halfway through my stay on the mountain. "You can have children." I had thought I had cut myself when jumping over my swords, one made of steel and the other carved out of a single block of jade. "However," she added, "we are asking you to put off children for a few more years."

"Then can I use the control you taught me and stop this bleeding?"

"No. You don't stop shitting and pissing," she said. "It's the same with the blood. Let it run." ("Let it walk" in Chinese.)

To console me for being without family on this day, they let me look inside the gourd. My whole family was visiting friends on the other side of the river. Everybody had on good clothes and was exchanging cakes. It was a wedding. My mother was talking to the hosts: "Thank you for taking our daughter. Wherever she is, she must be happy now. She will certainly come back if she is alive, and if she is a spirit, you have given her a descent line. We are so grateful."

Yes, I would be happy. How full I would be with all their love for me. I would have for a new husband my own playmate, dear since childhood, who loved me so much he was to become a spirit bridegroom for my sake. We will be so happy when I come back to the valley, healthy and strong and not a ghost.

The water gave me a close-up of my husband's wonderful face—and I was watching when it went white at the sudden approach of armored men on horseback, thudding and jangling. My people grabbed iron skillets, boiling soup, knives, hammers, scissors, whatever weapons came to hand, but my father said, "There are too many of them," and they put down the weapons and waited quietly at the door, open as if for guests. An army of horsemen stopped at our house; the foot soldiers in the distance were coming closer. A horseman with silver scales afire in the sun shouted from the scroll in his hands, his words opening a red gap in his black beard. "Your baron has pledged fifty men from this district, one from each family," he said, and then named the family names.

"No!" I screamed into the gourd.

"I'll go," my new husband and my youngest brother said to their fathers.

"No," my father said, "I myself will go," but the women held him back until the foot soldiers passed by, my husband and my brother leaving with them.

As if disturbed by the marching feet, the water churned; and when it stilled again ("Wait!" I yelled. "Wait!"), there were strangers. The baron and his family—all of his family—were knocking their heads on the floor in front of their ancestors and thanking the gods out loud for protecting them from conscription. I watched the baron's piggish face chew open-mouthed on the sacrificial pig. I plunged my hand into the gourd, making a grab for his thick throat, and he broke into pieces, splashing water all over my face and clothes. I turned the gourd upside-down to empty it, but no little people came tumbling out.

"Why can't I go down there now and help them?" I cried. "I'll run away with the two boys and we'll hide in the caves."

"No," the old man said. "You're not ready. You're only four-teen years old. You'd get hurt for nothing."

"Wait until you are twenty-two," the old woman said. "You'll be big then and more skillful. No army will be able to stop you from doing whatever you want. If you go now, you will be killed, and you'll have wasted seven and a half years of our time. You will deprive your people of a champion."

"I'm good enough now to save the boys."

"We didn't work this hard to save just two boys, but whole families."

Of course.

"Do you really think I'll be able to do that—defeat an army?"

"Even when you fight against soldiers trained as you are, most of them will be men, heavy footed and rough. You will have the advantage. Don't be impatient."

"From time to time you may use the water gourd to watch your husband and your brother," the old man said.

But I had ended the panic about them already. I could feel a wooden door inside of me close. I had learned on the farm that I could stop loving animals raised for slaughter. And I could start loving them immediately when someone said, "This one is a pet," freeing me and opening the door. We had lost males before, cousins and uncles who were conscripted into armies or bonded as apprentices, who are almost as lowly as slave girls.

I bled and thought about the people to be killed; I bled and thought about the people to be born.

During all my years on the mountain, I talked to no one except the two old people, but they seemed to be many people. The whole world lived inside the gourd, the earth a green and blue pearl like the one the dragon plays with.

When I could point at the sky and make a sword appear, a silver bolt in the sunlight, and control its slashing with my mind, the old people said I was ready to leave. The old man opened the gourd for the last time. I saw the baron's messenger leave our house, and my father was saying, "This time I must go and fight." I would hurry down the mountain and take his place. The old people gave me the fifteen beads, which I was to use if I got into terrible danger. They gave me men's clothes and armor. We bowed to one another. The bird flew above me down the mountain, and for some miles, whenever I turned to look for them, there would be the two old people waving. I saw them through the mist; I saw them on the clouds; I saw them big on the mountaintop when distance had shrunk the pines. They had probably left images of themselves for me to wave at and gone about their other business.

When I reached my village, my father and mother had grown as old as the two whose shapes I could at last no longer see. I helped my parents carry their tools, and they walked ahead so straight, each carrying a basket or a hoe not to overburden me, their tears falling privately. My family surrounded me with so much love that I almost forgot the ones not there. I praised the new infants.

"Some of the people are saying the Eight Sages took you away to teach you magic," said a little girl cousin. "They say they changed you into a bird, and you flew to them."

"Some say you went to the city and became a prostitute," another cousin giggled.

"You might tell them that I met some teachers who were willing to teach me science," I said.

"I have been drafted," my father said.

"No, Father," I said. "I will take your place."

My parents killed a chicken and steamed it whole, as if they were welcoming home a son, but I had gotten out of the habit of meat. After eating rice and vegetables, I slept for a long time, preparation for the work ahead.

In the morning my parents woke me and asked that I come with them to the family hall. "Stay in your nightclothes," my mother said. "Don't change yet." She was holding a basin, a towel, and a kettle of hot water. My father had a bottle of wine, an ink block and pens, and knives of various sizes. "Come with us," he said. They had stopped the tears with which they had greeted me. Forebodingly I caught a smell—metallic, the iron smell of blood, as when a woman gives birth, as at the sacrifice of a large animal, as when I menstruated and dreamed red dreams.

My mother put a pillow on the floor before the ancestors. "Kneel here," she said. "Now take off your shirt." I kneeled with my back to my parents so none of us felt embarrassed. My mother washed my back as if I had left for only a day and were her baby yet. "We are going to carve revenge on your back," my father said. "We'll write out oaths and names."

"Wherever you go, whatever happens to you, people will know our sacrifice," my mother said. "And you'll never forget either." She meant that even if I got killed, the people could use my dead body for a weapon, but we do not like to talk out loud about dying.

My father first brushed the words in ink, and they fluttered down my back row after row. Then he began cutting; to make fine lines and points he used thin blades, for the stems, large blades.

My mother caught the blood and wiped the cuts with a cold towel soaked in wine. It hurt terribly—the cuts sharp; the air burning; the alcohol cold, then hot—pain so various. I gripped my knees. I released them. Neither tension nor relaxation helped. I wanted to cry. If not for the fifteen years of training, I would have writhed on the floor; I would have had to be held down. The list of grievances went on and on. If an enemy should flay me, the light would shine through my skin like lace.

At the end of the last word, I fell forward. Together my parents sang what they had written, then let me rest. My mother fanned my back. "We'll have you with us until your back heals," she said.

When I could sit up again, my mother brought two mirrors, and I saw my back covered entirely with words in red and black files, like an army, like my army. My parents nursed me just as if I had fallen in battle after many victories. Soon I was strong again.

A white horse stepped into the courtyard where I was polishing my armor. Though the gates were locked tight, through the moon door it came—a kingly white horse. It wore a saddle and bridle with red, gold, and black tassels dancing. The saddle was just my size with tigers and dragons tooled in swirls. The white horse pawed the ground for me to go. On the hooves of its near forefoot and hindfoot was the ideograph "to fly."

My parents and I had waited for such a sign. We took the fine saddlebags off the horse and filled them with salves and herbs, blue grass for washing my hair, extra sweaters, dried peaches. They gave me a choice of ivory or silver chopsticks. I took the silver ones because they were lighter. It was like getting wedding presents. The cousins and the villagers came bearing bright orange jams, silk dresses, silver embroidery scissors. They brought blue and white porcelain bowls filled with water and carp—the bowls painted with carp, fins like orange fire. I accepted all the gifts—the tables, the earthenware jugs—though I could not possibly carry them with me, and culled for travel only a small copper cooking bowl. I could cook in it and eat out of it and would not have to search for bowl-shaped rocks or tortoiseshells.

I put on my men's clothes and armor and tied my hair in a man's fashion. "How beautiful you look," the people said. "How beautiful she looks."

A young man stepped out of the crowd. He looked familiar to me, as if he were the old man's son, or the old man himself when you looked at him from the corners of your eyes.

"I want to go with you," he said.

"You will be the first soldier in my army," I told him.

I leapt onto my horse's back and marveled at the power and height it gave to me. Just then, galloping out of nowhere straight at me came a rider on a black horse. The villagers scattered except for my one soldier, who stood calmly in the road. I drew my sword. "Wait!" shouted the rider, raising weaponless hands. "Wait. I have travelled here to join you."

Then the villagers relinquished their real gifts to me—their sons. Families who had hidden their boys during the last conscription volunteered them now. I took the ones their families could spare and the ones with hero-fire in their eyes, not the young fathers and not those who would break hearts with their leaving.

We were better equipped than many founders of dynasties had been when they walked north to dethrone an emperor; they had been peasants like us. Millions of us had laid our hoes down on the dry ground and faced north. We sat in the fields, from which the dragon had withdrawn its moisture, and sharpened those hoes. Then, though it be ten thousand miles away, we walked to the palace. We would report to the emperor. The emperor, who sat facing south, must have been very frightened—peasants everywhere walking day and night toward the capital, toward Peiping. But the last emperors of dynasties must not have been facing in the right direction, for they would have seen us and not let us get this hungry. We would not have had to shout our grievances. The peasants would crown as emperor a farmer who knew the earth or a beggar who understood hunger.

"Thank you, Mother. Thank you, Father," I said before leaving. They had carved their names and address on me, and I would come back.

Often I walked beside my horse to travel abreast of my army. When we had to impress other armies—marauders, columns of refugees filing past one another, boy gangs following their martial arts teachers—I mounted and rode in front. The soldiers who owned horses and weapons would pose fiercely on my left and right. The small bands joined us, but sometimes armies of equal or larger strength would fight us. Then screaming a mighty scream and swinging two swords over my head, I charged the leaders; I released my bloodthirsty army and my straining warhorse. I guided the horse with my knees, freeing both hands for sword-work, spinning green and silver circles all around me.

I inspired my army, and I fed them. At night I sang to them glorious songs that came out of the sky and into my head. When I opened my mouth, the songs poured out and were loud enough for the whole encampment to hear; my army stretched out for a mile. We sewed red flags and tied the red scraps around arms, legs, horses' tails. We wore our red clothes so that when we visited a village, we would look as happy as for New Year's Day. Then people would want to join the ranks. My army did not rape, only taking food where there was an abundance. We brought order wherever we went.

When I won over a goodly number of fighters, I built up my army enough to attack fiefdoms and to pursue the enemies I had seen in the water gourd.

My first opponent turned out to be a giant, so much bigger than the toy general I used to peep at. During the charge, I singled out the leader, who grew as he ran toward me. Our eyes locked until his height made me strain my neck looking up, my throat so vulnerable to the stroke of a knife that my eyes dropped to the secret death points on the huge body. First I cut off his leg with one sword swipe, as Chen Luan-feng had chopped the leg off the thunder god. When the giant stumped toward me, I cut off his head. Instantly he reverted to his true self, a snake, and slithered away hissing. The fighting around me stopped as the combatants' eyes and mouths opened wide in amazement. The giant's spells now broken, his soldiers, seeing that they had been led by a snake, pledged their loyalty to me.

In the stillness after battle I looked up at the mountaintops; perhaps the old man and woman were watching me and would enjoy my knowing it. They'd laugh to see a creature winking at them from the bottom of the water gourd. But on a green ledge above the battlefield I saw the giant's wives crying. They had climbed out of their palanquins to watch their husband fight me, and now they were holding each other weeping. They were two sisters, two tiny fairies against the sky, widows from now on. Their long undersleeves, which they had pulled out to wipe their tears, flew white mourning in the mountain wind. After a time, they got back into their sedan chairs, and their servants carried them away.

I led my army northward, rarely having to sidetrack; the emperor himself sent the enemies I was hunting chasing after me. Sometimes they attacked us on two or three sides; sometimes they ambushed me when I rode ahead. We would always win, Kuan Kung, the god of war and literature riding before me. I would be told of in fairy tales myself. I overheard some soldiers—and now there were many who had not met me—say that whenever we had been in danger of losing, I made a throwing gesture and the opposing army would fall, hurled across the battlefield. Hailstones as big as heads would shoot out of the sky and the lightning would stab like swords, but never at those on my side. "On *his* side," they said. I never told them the truth. Chinese executed women who disguised themselves as soldiers or students, no matter how bravely they fought or how high they scored on the examinations.

One spring morning I was at work in my tent repairing equipment, patching my clothes, and studying maps when a voice said, "General, may I visit you in your tent, please?" As if it were my own home, I did not allow strangers in my tent. And since I had no family with me, no one ever visited inside. Riverbanks, hillsides, the cool sloped rooms under the pine trees—China provides her soldiers with meeting places enough. I opened the tent flap. And there in the sunlight stood my own husband with arms full of wildflowers for me. "You are beautiful," he said, and meant it truly. "I have looked for you everywhere. I've been looking for you since the day that bird flew away with you." We were so pleased with each other, the childhood friend found at last, the childhood friend mysteriously grown up. "I followed you, but you skimmed over the rocks until I lost you."

"I've looked for you too," I said, the tent now snug around us like a secret house when we were kids. "Whenever I heard about a good fighter, I went to see if it were you," I said. "I saw you marry me. I'm so glad you married me."

He wept when he took off my shirt and saw the scar-words on my back. He loosened my hair and covered the words with it. I turned around and touched his face, loving the familiar first.

So for a time I had a partner—my husband and I, soldiers together just as when we were little soldiers playing in the village. We rode side by side into battle. When I became pregnant, during the last four months, I wore my armor altered so that I looked like a powerful, big man. As a fat man, I walked with the foot soldiers so as not to jounce the gestation. Now when I was naked, I was a strange human being indeed— words carved on my back and the baby large in front.

I hid from battle only once, when I gave birth to our baby. In dark and silver dreams I had seen him falling from the sky, each night closer to the earth, his soul a star. Just before labor began, the last star rays sank into my belly. My husband would talk to me and not go, though I said for him to return to the battlefield. He caught the baby, a boy, and put it on my breast. "What are we going to do with this?" he asked, holding up the piece of umbilical cord that had been closest to the baby.

"Let's tie it to a flagpole until it dries," I said. We had both seen the boxes in which our parents kept the dried cords of all their children. "This one was yours, and this yours," my mother would say to us brothers and sisters, and fill us with awe that she could remember.

We made a sling for the baby inside my big armor, and rode back into the thickest part of the fighting. The umbilical cord flew with the red flag and made us laugh. At night inside our own tent, I let the baby ride on my back. The sling was made of red satin and purple silk; the four paisley straps that tied across my breasts and around my waist ended in housewife's pockets lined with a coin, a seed, a nut, and a juniper leaf. At the back of the sling I had sewn a tiny quilted triangle, red at its center against two shades of green; it marked the baby's nape for luck. I walked bowed, and the baby warmed himself against me, his breathing in rhythm with mine, his heart beating like my heart.

When the baby was a month old, we gave him a name and shaved his head. For the full-month ceremony my husband had found two eggs, which we dyed red by boiling them with a flag. I peeled one and rolled it all over the baby's head, his eyes, his lips, off his bump of a nose, his cheeks, his dear bald head and fontanel. I had brought dried grapefruit peel in my saddlebag, and we also boiled that. We washed our heads and hands in the grapefruit water, dabbing it on the baby's forehead and hands. Then I gave my husband the baby and told him to take it to his family, and I gave him all the money we had taken on raids to take to my family. "Go now," I said, "before he is old enough to recognize me." While the blur is still in his eyes and the little fists shut tight like buds, I'll send my baby away from me. I altered my clothes and became again the slim young man. Only now I would get so lonely with the tent so empty that I slept outside.

My white horse overturned buckets and danced on them; it lifted full wine cups with its teeth. The strong soldiers lifted the horse in a wooden tub, while it danced to the stone drums and flute music. I played with the soldiers, throwing arrows into a bronze jar. But I found none of these antics as amusing as when I first set out on the road.

It was during this lonely time, when any high cry made the milk spill from my breasts, that I got careless. Wildflowers distracted me so that I followed them, picking one, then another, until I was alone in the woods. Out from behind trees, springing off branches came the enemy, their leader looming like a genie out of the water gourd. I threw fists and feet at them, but they were so many, they pinned me to the earth while their leader drew his sword. My fear shot forth—a quick, jabbing sword that slashed fiercely, silver flashes, quick cuts wherever my attention drove it. The leader stared at the palpable sword swishing unclutched at his men, then laughed aloud. As if signaled by his laughter, two more swords appeared in midair. They clanged against mine, and I felt metal vibrate inside my brain. I willed my sword to hit back and to go after the head that controlled the other swords. But the man fought well, hurting my brain. The swords opened and closed, scissoring madly, metal zinging along metal. Unable to leave my sky-sword to work itself, I would be watching the swords move like puppets when the genie yanked my hair back and held a dagger against my throat. "Aha!" he said. "What have we here?" He lifted the bead pouch out of my shirt and cut the string. I grabbed his arm, but one of his swords dived toward me, and I rolled out of the way. A horse galloped up, and he leapt on it, escaping into the forest, the beads in his fist. His swords fought behind him until I heard him shout, "I am here!" and they flew to his side. So I had done battle with the prince who had mixed the blood of his two sons with the metal he had used for casting his swords.

I ran back to my soldiers and gathered the fastest horsemen for pursuit. Our horses ran like the little white water horses in the surf. Across a plain we could see the enemy, a dustdevil rushing toward the horizon. Wanting to see, I focused my eyes as the eagles had taught me, and there the genie would be—shaking one bead out of the pouch and casting it at us. Nothing happened. No thunder, no earthquake that split open the ground, no hailstones big as heads.

"Stop!" I ordered my riders. "Our horses are exhausted, and I don't want to chase any farther south." The rest of the victories would be won on my own, slow and without shortcuts.

I stood on top of the last hill before Peiping and saw the roads below me flow like living rivers. Between roads the woods and plains moved too; the land was peopled—the Han people, the People of One Hundred Surnames, marching with one heart, our tatters flying. The depth and width of Joy were exactly known to me: the Chinese population. After much hardship a few of our millions had arrived together at the capital. We faced our emperor personally. We beheaded him, cleaned out the palace, and inaugurated the peasant who would begin the new order. In his rags he sat on the throne facing south, and we, a great red crowd, bowed to him three times. He commended some of us who were his first generals.

I told the people who had come with me that they were free to go home now, but since the Long Wall was so close, I would go see it. They could come along if they liked. So, loath to disband after such high adventures, we reached the northern boundary of the world, chasing Mongols en route.

I touched the Long Wall with my own fingers, running the edge of my hand between the stones, tracing the grooves the builders' hands had made. We lay our foreheads and our cheeks against the Long Wall and cried like the women who had come here looking for their men so long building the wall. In my travels north, I had not found my brother.

Carrying the news about the new emperor, I went home, where one more battle awaited me. The baron who had drafted my brother would still be bearing sway over our village. Having dropped my soldiers off at crossroads and bridges, I attacked the baron's stronghold alone. I jumped over the double walls and landed with swords drawn and knees bent, ready to spring. When no one accosted me, I sheathed the swords and walked about like a guest until I found the baron. He was counting his money, his fat ringed fingers playing over the abacus.

"Who are you? What do you want?" he said, encircling his profits with his arms. He sat square and fat like a god.

"I want your life in payment for your crimes against the villagers."

"I haven't done anything to you. All this is mine. I earned it. I didn't steal it from you. I've never seen you before in my life. Who are you?"

"I am a female avenger."

Then—heaven help him—he tried to be charming, to appeal to me man to man. "Oh, come now. Everyone takes the girls when he can. The families are glad to be rid of them. 'Girls are maggots in the rice.' 'It is more profitable to raise geese than daughters.'" He quoted to me the sayings I hated.

"Regret what you've done before I kill you," I said.

"I haven't done anything other men—even you—wouldn't have done in my place."

"You took away my brother."

"I free my apprentices."

"He was not an apprentice."

"China needs soldiers in wartime."

"You took away my childhood."

"I don't know what you're talking about. We've never met before. I've done nothing to you."

"You've done this," I said, and ripped off my shirt to show him my back. "You are responsible for this." When I saw his startled eyes at my breasts, I slashed him across the face and on the second stroke cut off his head.

I pulled my shirt back on and opened the house to the villagers. The baron's family and servants hid in closets and under beds. The villagers dragged them out into the courtyard, where they tried them next to the beheading machine. "Did you take my harvest so that my children had to eat grass?" a weeping farmer asked.

"I saw him steal seed grain," another testified.

"My family was hiding under the thatch on the roof when the bandits robbed our house, and we saw this one take off his mask." They spared those who proved they could be reformed. They beheaded the others. Their necks were collared in the beheading machine, which slowly clamped shut. There was one last-minute reprieve of a bodyguard when a witness shouted testimony just as the vise was pinching blood. The guard had but recently joined the household in exchange for a child hostage. A slow killing gives a criminal time to regret his crimes and think of the right words to prove he can change.

I searched the house, hunting out people for trial. I came upon a locked room. When I broke down the door, I found women, cowering, whimpering women. I heard shrill insect noises and scurrying. They blinked weakly at me like pheasants that have been raised in the dark for soft meat. The servants who walked the ladies had abandoned them, and they could not escape on their little bound feet. Some crawled away from me, using their elbows to pull themselves along. These women would not be good for anything. I called the villagers to come identify any daughters they wanted to take home, but no one claimed any. I gave each woman a bagful of rice, which they sat on. They rolled the bags to the road. They wandered away like ghosts. Later, it would be said, they turned into the band of swordswomen who were a mercenary army. They did not wear men's clothes like me, but rode as women in black and red dresses. They bought up girl babies so that many poor families welcomed their visitations. When slave girls and daughters-in-law ran away, people would say they joined these witch amazons. They killed men and boys. I myself never encountered such women and could not vouch for their reality.

After the trials we tore down the ancestral tablets. "We'll use this great hall for village meetings," I announced. "Here we'll put on operas; we'll sing together and talk-story." We washed the courtyard; we exorcised the house with smoke and red paper. "This is a new year," I told the people, "the year one."

I went home to my parents-in-law and husband and son. My son stared, very impressed by the general he had seen in the parade, but his father said, "It's your mother. Go to your mother." My son was delighted that the shiny general was his mother too. She gave him her helmet to wear and her swords to hold.

Wearing my black embroidered wedding coat, I knelt at my parents-in-law's feet, as I would have done as a bride. "Now my public duties are finished," I said. "I will stay with you, doing farmwork and housework, and giving you more sons."

"Go visit your mother and father first," my mother-in-law said, a generous woman. "They want to welcome you."

My mother and father and the entire clan would be living happily on the money I had sent them. My parents had bought their coffins. They would sacrifice a pig to the gods that I had returned. From the words on my back, and how they were fulfilled, the villagers would make a legend about my perfect filiality.

My American life has been such a disappointment.

"I got straight A's, Mama."

"Let me tell you a true story about a girl who saved her village."

I could not figure out what was my village. And it was important that I do something big and fine, or else my parents would sell me when we made our way back to China. In China there were solutions for what to do with little girls who ate up food and threw tantrums. You can't eat straight A's.

When one of my parents or the emigrant villagers said, "Feeding girls is feeding cowbirds," I would thrash on the floor and scream so hard I couldn't talk. I couldn't stop.

"What's the matter with her?"

"I don't know. Bad, I guess. You know how girls are. 'There's no profit in raising girls. Better to raise geese than girls.'"

"I would hit her if she were mine. But then there's no use

wasting all that discipline on a girl. 'When you raise girls, you're raising children for strangers.'"

"Stop that crying!" my mother would yell. "I'm going to hit you if you don't stop. Bad girl! Stop!" I'm going to remember never to hit or to scold my children for crying, I thought, because then they will only cry more.

"I'm not a bad girl," I would scream. "I'm not a bad girl. I'm not a bad girl." I might as well have said, "I'm not a girl."

"When you were little, all you had to say was 'I'm not a bad girl,' and you could make yourself cry," my mother says, talking-story about my childhood.

I minded that the emigrant villagers shook their heads at my sister and me. "One girl—and another girl," they said, and made our parents ashamed to take us out together. The good part about my brothers being born was that people stopped saying, "All girls," but I learned new grievances. "Did you roll an egg on *my* face like that when *I* was born?" "Did you have a full-month party for *me*?" "Did you turn on all the lights?" "Did you send *my* picture to Grandmother?" "Why not? Because I'm a girl? Is that why not?" "Why didn't you teach me English?" "You like having me beaten up at school, don't you?"

"She is very mean, isn't she?" the emigrant villagers would say.

"Come, children. Hurry. Hurry. Who wants to go out with Great-Uncle?" On Saturday mornings my great-uncle, the ex–river pirate, did the shopping. "Get your coats, whoever's coming."

"I'm coming. I'm coming. Wait for me."

When he heard girls' voices, he turned on us and roared, "No girls!" and left my sisters and me hanging our coats back up, not looking at one another. The boys came back with candy and new toys. When they walked through Chinatown, the people must have said, "A boy—and another boy—and another boy!" At my great-uncle's funeral I secretly tested out feeling glad that he was dead—the six-foot bearish masculinity of him.

I went away to college—Berkeley in the sixties—and I studied, and I marched to change the world, but I did not turn into a boy. I would have liked to bring myself back as a boy for my parents to welcome with chickens and pigs. That was for my brother, who returned alive from Vietnam.

If I went to Vietnam, I would not come back; females desert families. It was said, "There is an outward tendency in females," which meant that I was getting straight A's for the good of my future husband's family, not my own. I did not plan ever to have a husband. I would show my mother and father and the nosey emigrant villagers that girls have no outward tendency. I stopped getting straight A's.

And all the time I was having to turn myself American-feminine, or no dates.

There is a Chinese word for the female I—which is "slave." Break the women with their own tongues!

I refused to cook. When I had to wash dishes, I would crack one or two. "Bad girl," my mother yelled, and sometimes that made me gloat rather than cry. Isn't a bad girl almost a boy?

"What do you want to be when you grow up, little girl?"

"A lumberjack in Oregon."

Even now, unless I'm happy, I burn the food when I cook. I do not feed people. I let the dirty dishes rot. I eat at other people's tables but won't invite them to mine, where the dishes are rotting.

If I could not-eat, perhaps I could make myself a warrior like the swordswoman who drives me. I will—I must—rise and plow the fields as soon as the baby comes out.

Once I get outside the house, what bird might call me; on what horse could I ride away? Marriage and childbirth strengthen the swordswoman, who is not a maid like Joan of Arc. Do the women's work; then do more work, which will become ours too. No husband of mine will say, "I could have been a drummer, but I had to think about the wife and kids. You know how it is." Nobody supports me at the expense of his own adventure. Then I get bitter: no one supports me; I am not loved enough to be supported. That I am not a burden has to compensate for the sad envy when I look at women loved enough to be supported. Even now China wraps double binds around my feet.

When urban renewal tore down my parents' laundry and paved over our slum for a parking lot, I only made up gun and knife fantasies and did nothing useful.

From the fairy tales, I've learned exactly who the enemy are. I easily recognize them—business-suited in their modern

American executive guise, each boss two feet taller than I am and impossible to meet eye to eye.

I once worked at an art supply house that sold paints to artists. "Order more of that nigger yellow, willya?" the boss told me. "Bright, isn't it? Nigger yellow."

"I don't like that word," I had to say in my bad, small-person's voice that makes no impact. The boss never deigned to answer.

I also worked at a land developers' association. The building industry was planning a banquet for contractors, real estate dealers, and real estate editors. "Did you know the restaurant you chose for the banquet is being picketed by CORE and the NAACP?" I squeaked.

"Of course I know." The boss laughed. "That's why I chose it."

"I refuse to type these invitations," I whispered, voice unreliable.

He leaned back in his leather chair, his bossy stomach opulent. He picked up his calendar and slowly circled a date. "You will be paid up to here," he said. "We'll mail you the check."

If I took the sword, which my hate must surely have forged out of the air, and gutted him, I would put color and wrinkles into his shirt.

It's not just the stupid racists that I have to do something about, but the tyrants who for whatever reason can deny my family food and work. My job is my own only land.

To avenge my family, I'd have to storm across China to take back our farm from the Communists; I'd have to rage across the United States to take back the laundry in New York and the one in California. Nobody in history has conquered and united both North America and Asia. A descendant of eighty pole fighters, I ought to be able to set out confidently, march straight down our street, get going right now. There's work to do, ground to cover. Surely, the eighty pole fighters, though unseen, would follow me and lead me and protect me, as is the wont of ancestors.

Or it may well be that they're resting happily in China, their spirits dispersed among the real Chinese, and not nudging me at all with their poles. I mustn't feel bad that I haven't done as well as the swordswoman did; after all, no bird called me, no wise old people tutored me. I have no magic beads, no water gourd sight, no rabbit that will jump in the fire when I'm hungry. I dislike armies.

I've looked for the bird. I've seen clouds make pointed angel wings that stream past the sunset, but they shred into clouds. Once at a beach after a long hike I saw a seagull, tiny as an insect. But when I jumped up to tell what miracle I saw, before I could get the words out I understood that the bird was insect-size because it was far away. My brain had momentarily lost its depth perception. I was that eager to find an unusual bird.

The news from China has been confusing. It also had something to do with birds. I was nine years old when the letters made my parents, who are rocks, cry. My father screamed in his sleep. My mother wept and crumpled up the letters. She set fire to them page by page in the ashtray, but new letters came almost every day. The only letters they opened without fear were the ones with red borders, the holiday letters that mustn't carry bad news. The other letters said that my uncles were made to kneel on broken glass during their trials and had confessed to being landowners. They were all executed, and the aunt whose thumbs were twisted off drowned herself. Other aunts, mothers-in-law, and cousins disappeared; some suddenly began writing to us again from communes or from Hong Kong. They kept asking for money. The ones in communes got four ounces of fat and one cup of oil a week, they said, and had to work from 4 A.M. to 9 P.M. They had to learn to do dances waving red kerchiefs; they had to sing nonsense syllables. The Communists gave axes to the old ladies and said, "Go and kill yourself. You're useless." If we overseas Chinese would just send money to the Communist bank, our relatives said, they might get a percentage of it for themselves. The aunts in Hong Kong said to send money quickly; their children were begging on the sidewalks and mean people put dirt in their bowls.

When I dream that I am wire without flesh, there is a letter on blue airmail paper that floats above the night ocean between here and China. It must arrive safely or else my grandmother and I will lose each other.

My parents felt bad whether or not they sent money. Sometimes they got angry at their brothers and sisters for asking. And they would not simply ask but have to talk-story too. The revolutionaries had taken Fourth Aunt and Uncle's store, house, and lands. They attacked the house and killed the grandfather and oldest daughter. The grandmother escaped with the loose cash and did not return to help. Fourth Aunt picked up her sons, one under each arm, and hid in the pig house, where they slept that night in cotton clothes. The next day she found her husband, who had also miraculously escaped. The two of them collected twigs and yams to sell while their children begged. Each morning they tied the faggots on each other's back. Nobody bought from them. They ate the yams and some of the children's rice. Finally Fourth Aunt saw what was wrong. "We have to shout 'Fuel for sale' and 'Yams for sale,'" she said. "We can't just walk unobtrusively up and down the street." "You're right," said my uncle, but he was shy and walked in back of her. "Shout," my aunt ordered, but he could not. "They think we're carrying these sticks home for our own fire," she said. "Shout." They walked about miserably, silently, until sundown, neither of them able to advertise themselves. Fourth Aunt, an orphan since the age of ten, mean as my mother, threw her bundle down at his feet and scolded Fourth Uncle, "Starving to death, his wife and children starving to death, and he's too damned shy to raise his voice." She left him standing by himself and afraid to return empty-handed to her. He sat under a tree to think, when he spotted a pair of nesting doves. Dumping his bag of yams, he climbed up and caught the birds. That was when the Communists trapped him, in the tree. They criticized him for selfishly taking food for his own family and killed him, leaving his body in the tree as an example. They took the birds to a commune kitchen to be shared.

It is confusing that my family was not the poor to be championed. They were executed like the barons in the stories, when they were not barons. It is confusing that birds tricked us.

What fighting and killing I have seen have not been glorious but slum grubby. I fought the most during junior high school and always cried. Fights are confusing as to who has won. The corpses I've seen had been rolled and dumped, sad little dirty bodies covered with a police khaki blanket. My mother locked her children in the house so we couldn't look at dead slum people. But at news of a body, I would find a way to get out; I had to learn about dying if I wanted to become a swords-woman. Once there was an Asian man stabbed next door, words on cloth pinned to his corpse. When the police came around asking questions, my father said, "No read Japanese. Japanese words. Me Chinese."

I've also looked for old people who could be my gurus. A medium with red hair told me that a girl who died in a far country follows me wherever I go. This spirit can help me if I acknowledge her, she said. Between the head line and heart line in my right palm, she said, I have the mystic cross. I could become a medium myself. I don't want to be a medium. I don't want to be a crank taking "offerings" in a wicker plate from the frightened audience, who, one after another, asked the spirits how to raise rent money, how to cure their coughs and skin diseases, how to find a job. And martial arts are for unsure little boys kicking away under fluorescent lights.

I live now where there are Chinese and Japanese, but no emigrants from my own village looking at me as if I had failed them. Living among one's own emigrant villagers can give a good Chinese far from China glory and a place. "That old bus-boy is really a swordsman," we whisper when he goes by, "He's a swordsman who's killed fifty. He has a tong ax in his closet." But I am useless, one more girl who couldn't be sold. When I visit the family now, I wrap my American successes around me like a private shawl; I *am* worthy of eating the food. From afar I can believe my family loves me fundamentally. They only say, "When fishing for treasures in the flood, be careful not to pull in girls," because that is what one says about daughters. But I watched such words come out of my own mother's and father's mouths; I looked at their ink drawing of poor peo-ple snagging their neighbors' flotage with long flood hooks and pushing the girl babies on down the river. And I had to get out of hating range. I read in an anthropology book that Chinese say, "Girls are necessary too"; I have never heard the Chinese I know make this concession. Perhaps it was a saying in another village. I refuse to shy my way anymore through our Chinatown, which tasks me with the old sayings and the stories.

The swordswoman and I are not so dissimilar. May my

people understand the resemblance soon so that I can return to them. What we have in common are the words at our backs. The ideographs for *revenge* are "report a crime" and "report to five families." The reporting is the vengeance—not the beheading, not the gutting, but the words. And I have so many words—"chink" words and "gook" words too—that they do not fit on my skin.

Shaman

ONCE IN a long while, four times so far for me, my mother brings out the metal tube that holds her medical diploma. On the tube are gold circles crossed with seven red lines each— "joy" ideographs in abstract. There are also little flowers that look like gears for a gold machine. According to the scraps of labels with Chinese and American addresses, stamps, and postmarks, the family airmailed the can from Hong Kong in 1950. It got crushed in the middle, and whoever tried to peel the labels off stopped because the red and gold paint came off too, leaving silver scratches that rust. Somebody tried to pry the end off before discovering that the tube pulls apart. When I open it, the smell of China flies out, a thousand-year-old bat flying heavy-headed out of the Chinese caverns where bats are as white as dust, a smell that comes from long ago, far back in the brain. Crates from Canton, Hong Kong, Singapore, and Taiwan have that smell too, only stronger because they are more recently come from the Chinese.

Inside the can are three scrolls, one inside another. The largest says that in the twenty-third year of the National Republic, the To Keung School of Midwifery, where she has had two years of instruction and Hospital Practice, awards its Diploma to my mother, who has shown through oral and written examination her Proficiency in Midwifery, Pediatrics, Gynecology, "Medecine," "Surgary," Therapeutics, Ophthalmology, Bacteriology, Dermatology, Nursing, and Bandage. This document has eight stamps on it: one, the school's English and Chinese names embossed together in a circle; one, as the Chinese enumerate, a stork and a big baby in lavender ink; one, the school's Chinese seal; one, an orangish paper stamp pasted in the border design; one, the red seal of Dr. Wu Pak-liang, M.D., Lyon, Berlin, president and "Ex-assistant étranger à la clinique chirugicale et d'accouchement de l'université de Lyon"; one, the red seal of Dean Woo Yin-kam, M.D.; one, my mother's seal, her chop mark larger than the president's and the dean's; and one, the number 1279 on the back. Dean

Woo's signature is followed by "(Hackett)." I read in a history book that Hackett Medical College for Women at Canton was founded in the nineteenth century by European women doctors.

The school seal has been pressed over a photograph of my mother at the age of thirty-seven. The diploma gives her age as twenty-seven. She looks younger than I do, her eyebrows are thicker, her lips fuller. Her naturally curly hair is parted on the left, one wavy wisp tendrilling off to the right. She wears a scholar's white gown, and she is not thinking about her appearance. She stares straight ahead as if she could see me and past me to her grandchildren and grandchildren's grandchildren. She has spacy eyes, as all people recently from Asia have. Her eyes do not focus on the camera. My mother is not smiling; Chinese do not smile for photographs. Their faces command relatives in foreign lands—"Send money"— and posterity forever—"Put food in front of this picture." My mother does not understand Chinese-American snapshots. "What are you laughing at?" she asks.

The second scroll is a long narrow photograph of the graduating class with the school officials seated in front. I picked out my mother immediately. Her face is exactly her own, though forty years younger. She is so familiar, I can only tell whether or not she is pretty or happy or smart by comparing her to the other women. For this formal group picture she straightened her hair with oil to make a chin-length bob like the others'. On the other women, strangers, I can recognize a curled lip, a sidelong glance, pinched shoulders. My mother is not soft; the girl with the small nose and dimpled underlip is soft. My mother is not humorous, not like the girl at the end who lifts her mocking chin to pose like Girl Graduate. My mother does not have smiling eyes; the old woman teacher (Dean Woo?) in front crinkles happily, and the one faculty member in the western suit smiles westernly. Most of the graduates are girls whose faces have not yet formed; my mother's face will not change anymore, except to age. She is intelligent, alert, pretty. I can't tell if she's happy.

The graduates seem to have been looking elsewhere when they pinned the rose, zinnia, or chrysanthemum on their precise black dresses. One thin girl wears hers in the middle of her chest. A few have a flower over a left or a right nipple. My mother put hers, a chrysanthemum, below her left breast. Chinese dresses at that time were dartless, cut as if women did not have breasts; these young doctors, unaccustomed to decorations, may have seen their chests as black expanses with no reference points for flowers. Perhaps they couldn't shorten that far gaze that lasts only a few years after a Chinese emigrates. In this picture too my mother's eyes are big with what they held—reaches of oceans beyond China, land beyond oceans. Most emigrants learn the barbarians' directness—how to gather themselves and stare rudely into talking faces as if trying to catch lies. In America my mother has eyes as strong as boulders, never once skittering off a face, but she has not learned to place decorations and phonograph needles, nor has she stopped seeing land on the other side of the oceans. Now her eyes include the relatives in China, as they once included my father smiling and smiling in his many western outfits, a different one for each photograph that he sent from America.

He and his friends took pictures of one another in bathing suits at Coney Island beach, the salt wind from the Atlantic blowing their hair. He's the one in the middle with his arms about the necks of his buddies. They pose in the cockpit of a biplane, on a motorcycle, and on a lawn beside the "Keep Off the Grass" sign. They are always laughing. My father, white shirt sleeves rolled up, smiles in front of a wall of clean laundry. In the spring he wears a new straw hat, cocked at a Fred Astaire angle. He steps out, dancing down the stairs, one foot forward, one back, a hand in his pocket. He wrote to her about the American custom of stomping on straw hats come fall. "If you want to save your hat for next year," he said, "you have to put it away early, or else when you're riding the subway or walking along Fifth Avenue, any stranger can snatch it off your head and put his foot through it. That's the way they celebrate the change of seasons here." In the winter he wears a gray felt hat with his gray overcoat. He is sitting on a rock in Central Park. In one snapshot he is not smiling; someone took it when he was studying, blurred in the glare of the desk lamp.

There are no snapshots of my mother. In two small portraits, however, there is a black thumbprint on her forehead, as if someone had inked in bangs, as if someone had marked her.

"Mother, did bangs come into fashion after you had the picture taken?" One time she said yes. Another time when I asked, "Why do you have fingerprints on your forehead?" she said, "Your First Uncle did that." I disliked the unsureness in her voice.

The last scroll has columns of Chinese words. The only English is "Department of Health, Canton," imprinted on my mother's face, the same photograph as on the diploma. I keep looking to see whether she was afraid. Year after year my father did not come home or send for her. Their two children had been dead for ten years. If he did not return soon, there would be no more children. ("They were three and two years old, a boy and a girl. They could talk already.") My father did send money regularly, though, and she had nobody to spend it on but herself. She bought good clothes and shoes. Then she decided to use the money for becoming a doctor. She did not leave for Canton immediately after the children died. In China there was time to complete feelings. As my father had done, my mother left the village by ship. There was a sea bird painted on the ship to protect it against shipwreck and winds. She was in luck. The following ship was boarded by river pirates, who kidnapped every passenger, even old ladies. "Sixty dollars for an old lady" was what the bandits used to say. "I sailed alone," she says, "to the capital of the entire province." She took a brown leather suitcase and a seabag stuffed with two quilts.

At the dormitory the school official assigned her to a room with five other women, who were unpacking when she came in. They greeted her and she greeted them. But no one wanted to start friendships until the unpacking was done, each item placed precisely to section off the room. My mother spotted the name she had written on her application pinned to a headboard, and the annoyance she felt at not arriving early enough for first choice disappeared. The locks on her suitcase opened with two satisfying clicks; she enjoyed again how neatly her belongings fitted together, clean against the green lining. She refolded the clothes before putting them in the one drawer that was hers. Then she took out her pens and inkbox, an atlas of the world, a tea set and tea cannister, sewing box, her ruler with the real gold markings, writing paper, envelopes with the thick red stripe to signify no bad news, her bowl and silver chopsticks. These things she arranged one by one on her shelf. She spread the two quilts on top of the bed and put her slippers side by side underneath. She owned more—furniture, wedding jewelry, cloth, photographs—but she had left such troublesome valuables behind in the family's care. She never did get all of it back.

The women who had arrived early did not offer to help unpack, not wanting to interfere with the pleasure and the privacy of it. Not many women got to live out the daydream of women—to have a room, even a section of a room, that only gets messed up when she messes it up herself. The book would stay open at the very page she had pressed flat with her hand, and no one would complain about the field not being plowed or the leak in the roof. She would clean her own bowl and a small, limited area; she would have one drawer to sort, one bed to make.

To shut the door at the end of the workday, which does not spill over into evening. To throw away books after reading them so they don't have to be dusted. To go through boxes on New Year's Eve and throw out half of what is inside. Sometimes for extravagance to pick a bunch of flowers for the one table. Other women besides me must have this daydream about a carefree life. I've seen Communist pictures showing a contented woman sitting on her bunk sewing. Above her head is her one box on a shelf. The words stenciled on the box mean "Fragile," but literally say, "Use a little heart." The woman looks very pleased. The Revolution put an end to prostitution by giving women what they wanted: a job and a room of their own.

Free from families, my mother would live for two years without servitude. She would not have to run errands for my father's tyrant mother with the bound feet or thread needles for the old ladies, but neither would there be slaves and nieces to wait on her. Now she would get hot water only if she bribed the concierge. When I went away to school my mother said, "Give the concierge oranges."

Two of my mother's roommates, who had organized their corners to their satisfaction, made tea and set a small table with their leftover travel food. "Have you eaten, Lady Scholar?" they invited my mother. "Lady Scholar, come drink tea," they

said to each of the others. "Bring your own cup." This lar-
gess moved my mother—tea, an act of humility. She brought
out meats and figs she had preserved on the farm. Everyone
complimented her on their tastiness. The women told which
villages they came from and the names they would go by. My
mother did not let it be known that she had already had two
children and that some of these girls were young enough to
be her daughters.

Then everyone went to the auditorium for two hours of
speeches by the faculty. They told the students that they would
begin with a text as old as the Han empire, when the prescription for immortality had not yet been lost. Chang Chung-
ching, father of medicine, had told how the two great winds,
yang and *yin*, blew through the human body. The diligent
students would do well to begin tonight memorizing his book
on colds and fevers. After they had mastered the ancient cures
that worked, they would be taught the most up-to-date western discoveries. By the time the students graduated—those
of them who persevered—their range of knowledge would be
wider than that of any other doctor in history. Women have
now been practicing medicine for about fifty years, said one
of the teachers, a woman, who complimented them for adding to their growing number and also for coming to a school
that taught modern medicine. "You will bring science to the
villages." At the end of the program, the faculty turned their
backs to the students, and everyone bowed the three bows
toward the picture of Doctor Sun Yat-sen, who was a western
surgeon before he became a revolutionary. Then they went
to the dining hall to eat. My mother began memorizing her
books immediately after supper.

There were two places where a student could study: the dining hall with its tables cleared for work, everyone chanting
during the common memorization sessions; or the table in her
own room. Most students went to the dining hall for the company there. My mother usually stayed in her room or, when a
roommate wanted the privacy of it also, went to a secret hiding place she had hunted out during the first week of school.
Once in a while she dropped by the dining hall, chanted for
a short while with the most advanced group, not missing a
syllable, yawned early, and said good-night. She quickly built

a reputation for being brilliant, a natural scholar who could glance at a book and know it.

"The other students fought over who could sit next to me at exams," says my mother. "One glimpse at my paper when they got stuck, and they could keep going."

"Did you ever try to stop them from copying your paper?"

"Of course not. They only needed to pick up a word or two, and they could remember the rest. That's not copying. You get a lot more clues in actual diagnosis. Patients talk endlessly about their ailments. I'd feel their pulses knocking away under my very fingertips—so much clearer than the paperdolls in the textbooks. I'd chant the symptoms, and those few words would start a whole chapter of cures tumbling out. Most people don't have the kind of brains that can do that." She pointed at the photograph of the thirty-seven graduates. "One hundred and twelve students began the course at the same time I did."

She suspected she did not have the right kind of brains either, my father the one who can recite whole poems. To make up the lack, she did secret studying. She also gave herself twenty years' headstart over the young girls, although she admitted to only ten, which already forced her to push. Older people were expected to be smarter; they are closer to the gods. She did not want to overhear students or teachers say, "She must be exceedingly stupid, doing no better than anyone else when she is a generation older. She's so dumb, she has to study day and night."

"I studied far in advance," says my mother. "I studied when the breathing coming from the beds and coming through the wood walls was deep and even. The night before exams, when the other students stayed up, I went to bed early. They would say, 'Aren't you going to study?' and I'd say, 'No, I'm going to do some mending,' or, 'I want to write letters tonight.' I let them take turns sitting next to me at the tests." The sweat of hard work is not to be displayed. It is much more graceful to appear favored by the gods.

Maybe my mother's secret place was the room in the dormitory which was haunted. Even though they had to crowd the other rooms, none of the young women would sleep in it. Accustomed to nestling with a bedful of siblings and grannies, they fitted their privacy tighter rather than claim the haunted room as human territory. No one had lived in it for at least five years, not since a series of hauntings had made its inhabitants come down with ghost fear that shattered their brains for studying. The haunted ones would give high, startled cries, pointing at the air, which sure enough was becoming hazy. They would suddenly turn and go back the way they had come. When they rounded a corner, they flattened themselves fast against the building to catch what followed unawares moving steadily forward. One girl tore up the photographs she had taken of friends in that room. The stranger with arms hanging at its sides who stood beside the wall in the background of the photograph was a ghost. The girl would insist there had been nobody there when she took the picture. "That was a Photo Ghost," said my mother when the students talked-story. "She needn't have been afraid. Most ghosts are only nightmares. Somebody should have held her and wiggled her ears to wake her up."

My mother relished these scare orgies. She was good at naming—Wall Ghost, Frog Spirit (frogs are "heavenly chickens"), Eating Partner. She could find descriptions of phenomena in ancient writings—the Green Phoenix stories, "The Seven Strange Tales of the Golden Bottle," "What Confucius Did Not Talk About." She could validate ghost sightings.

"But ghosts can't be just nightmares," a storyteller protested. "They come right out into the room. Once our whole family saw wine cups spinning and incense sticks waving through the air. We got the magic monk to watch all night. He also saw the incense tips tracing orange figures in the dark—ideographs, he said. He followed the glow patterns with his inkbrush on red paper. And there it was, a message from our great-grandfather. We needed to put bigger helpings and a Ford in front of his plaque. And when we did, the haunting stopped immediately."

"I like to think the ancestors are busier than that," my mother said, "or more at rest. Yes, they're probably more at rest. Perhaps it was an animal spirit that was bothering your house, and your grandfather had something to do with chasing it off." After what she thought was a suitably tactful pause, she said, "How do we know that ghosts are the continuance of dead people? Couldn't ghosts be an entirely different species of creature? Perhaps human beings just die, and that's the end. I don't think I'd mind that too much. Which would you rather be? A ghost who is constantly wanting to be fed? Or nothing?"

If the other storytellers had been reassuring one another with science, then my mother would have flown stories as factual as bats into the listening night. A practical woman, she could not invent stories and told only true ones. But tonight the younger women were huddling together under the quilts, the ghost room with its door open steps away.

"Did you hear that?" someone would whisper. And sure enough, whenever their voices stilled simultaneously, a thump or a creak would unmistakably sound somewhere inside the building. The girls would jump closer together giggling.

"That was the wind," my mother would say. "That was somebody who fell asleep reading in bed; she dropped her book." She neither jumped nor giggled.

"If you're so sure," said an impertinent girl, perhaps the one with the disdainful chin, "why don't you go out there and take a look?"

"Of course," said my mother. "I was just thinking about doing that," and she took a lamp and left her friends, impressed, in a dimmer room. She advanced steadily, waking the angular shadows up and down the corridor. She walked to both ends of the hallway, then explored another wing for good measure. At the ghost room, door open like a mouth, she stopped and, stepping inside, swung light into its corners. She saw cloth bags in knobby mounds; they looked like gnomes but were not gnomes. Suitcases and boxes threw shadow stairs up the walls and across the floor. Nothing unusual loomed at her or scurried away. No temperature change, no smell.

She turned her back on the room and slowly walked through one more wing. She did not want to get back too soon. Her friends, although one owes nothing to friends, must be satisfied that she searched thoroughly. After a sufficiently brave time, she returned to the storytellers. "I saw nothing," she said. "There's nothing to be afraid of in the whole dormitory, including the ghost room. I checked there too. I went inside just now."

"The haunting begins at midnight," said the girl with the adamantine chin. "It's not quite eleven."

My mother may have been afraid, but she would be a

dragoness ("my totem, your totem"). She could make herself not weak. During danger she fanned out her dragon claws and riffled her red sequin scales and unfolded her coiling green stripes. Danger was a good time for showing off. Like the dragons living in temple eaves, my mother looked down on plain people who were lonely and afraid.

"I'm so sleepy," my mother said. "I don't want to wait up until midnight. I'll go sleep in the ghost room. Then if anything happens, I won't miss it. I hope I'll be able to recognize the ghost when I see it. Sometimes ghosts put on such mundane disguises, they aren't particularly interesting."

"Aiaa. Aiaa," the storytellers exclaimed. My mother laughed with satisfaction at their cries.

"I'll call out if something bad happens to me," she said. "If you come running all together, you will probably be able to scare any ghost away."

Some of them promised to come; some offered their talismans—a branch from a peach tree, a Christian cross, a red paper with good words written on it. But my mother refused them all. "If I take charms, then the ghost will hide from me. I won't learn what kind of ghost it is, or whether or not a ghost lives in there at all. I'll only bring a knife to defend myself and a novel in case I get bored and can't sleep. You keep the charms; should I call for help, bring them with you." She went to her own room and got weapon and book, though not a novel but a textbook.

Two of her roommates walked her to the ghost room. "Aren't you afraid?" they asked.

"What is there to be afraid of?" she asked. "What could a ghost do to me?" But my mother did pause at the door. "Listen," she said, "if I am very afraid when you find me, don't forget to tweak my ears. Call my name and tell me how to get home." She told them her personal name.

She walked directly to the back of the room, where the boxes formed a windowseat. She sat with the lamp beside her and stared at her yellow and black reflection in the night glass. "I am very pretty," she thought. She cupped her hands to the window to see out. A thin moon pricked through the clouds, and the long grass waved. "That is the same moon that they see in New Society Village," she thought, "the same stars."

("That is the same moon that they see in China, the same stars though shifted a little.")

When she set the lamp next to the bed, the room seemed darker, the uncurtained window letting in the bare night. She wrapped herself well in her quilt, which her mother had made before dying young. In the middle of one border my grandmother had sewn a tiny satin triangle, a red heart to protect my mother at the neck, as if she were her baby yet.

My mother read aloud; perhaps the others could hear how calmly. The ghost might hear her too; she did not know whether her voice would evoke it or disperse it. Soon the ideographs lifted their feet, stretched out their wings, and flew like blackbirds; the dots were their eyes. Her own eyes drooped. She closed her book and turned off the lamp.

A new darkness pulled away the room, inked out flesh and outlined bones. My mother was wide awake again. She became sharply herself—bone, wire, antenna—but she was not afraid. She had been pared down like this before, when she had travelled up the mountains into rare snow—alone in white not unlike being alone in black. She had also sailed a boat safely between land and land.

She did not know whether she had fallen asleep or not when she heard a rushing coming out from under the bed. Cringes of fear seized her soles as something alive, rumbling, climbed the foot of the bed. It rolled over her and landed bodily on her chest. There it sat. It breathed airlessly, pressing her, sapping her. "Oh, no. A Sitting Ghost," she thought. She pushed against the creature to lever herself out from underneath it, but it absorbed this energy and got heavier. Her fingers and palms became damp, shrinking at the ghost's thick short hair like an animal's coat, which slides against warm solidity as human flesh slides against muscles and bones. She grabbed clutches of fur and pulled. She pinched the skin the hair grew out of and gouged into it with her fingernails. She forced her hands to hunt out eyes, furtive somewhere in the hair, but could not find any. She lifted her head to bite but fell back exhausted. The mass thickened.

She could see the knife, which was catching the moonlight, near the lamp. Her arm had become an immensity, though, too burdensome to lift. If she could only move it to the edge of the bed, perhaps it would fall off and reach the knife. As if feeding on her very thoughts, the ghost spread itself over her arm.

A high ringing sound somewhere had grown loud enough so that she heard it, and she understood that it had started humming at the edge of her brain before the ghost appeared. She breathed shallowly, panting as in childbirth, and could not shout out. The room sang, its air electric with the ringing; surely someone would hear and come help.

Earlier in the night, on the other side of the ringing, she could hear women's voices talking. But soon their conversations had ceased. The school slept. She could feel that the souls had gone travelling; there was a lightness not in the dormitory during the day. Without looking at the babies on her back or in their cribs, she had always been able to tell—after the rocking and singing and bedtime stories and keeping still not to startle them—the moment when they fell asleep. A tensing goes out of their bodies, out of the house. Beyond the horror in the ghost room, she felt this release throughout the dormitory. No one would come to see how she was doing.

"You will not win, Boulder," she spoke to the ghost. "You do not belong here. And I will see to it that you leave. When morning comes, only one of us will control this room, Ghost, and that one will be me. I will be marching its length and width; I will be dancing, not sliding and creeping like you. I will go right out that door, but I'll come back. Do you know what gift I will bring you? I'll get fire, Ghost. You made a mistake haunting a medical school. We have cabinets full of alcohol, laboratories full. We have a communal kitchen with human-sized jars of oil and cooking fat, enough to burn for a month without our skipping a single fried meal. I will pour alcohol into my washbucket, and I'll set fire to it. Ghost, I will burn you out. I will swing the bucket across the ceiling. Then from the kitchen my friends will come with the lard; when we fire it, the smoke will fill every crack and corner. Where will you hide, Ghost? I will make this room so clean, no ghost will ever visit here again.

"I do not give in," she said. "There is no pain you can inflict that I cannot endure. You're wrong if you think I'm afraid of you. You're no mystery to me. I've heard of you Sitting Ghosts before. Yes, people have lived to tell about you. You kill babies, you cowards. You have no power over a strong woman. You are no more dangerous than a nesting cat. My dog sits on my feet more heavily than you can. You think this is suffering? I can make my ears ring louder by taking aspirin. Are these all the tricks you have, Ghost? Sitting and ringing? That is nothing. A Broom Ghost can do better. You cannot even assume an interesting shape. Merely a boulder. A hairy butt boulder. You must not be a ghost at all. Of course. There are no such things as ghosts.

"Let me instruct you, Boulder. When Yen, the teacher, was grading the provincial exams one year, a thing with hair as ugly as yours plopped itself on his desk. (That one had glaring eyes, though, so it wasn't blind and stupid like you.) Yen picked up his ferule and hit it like a student. He chased it around the room. (It wasn't lame and lazy.) And it vanished. Later Yen taught us, 'After life, the rational soul ascends the dragon; the sentient soul descends the dragon. So in the world there can be no ghosts. This thing must have been a Fox Spirit.' That must be just what you are—a Fox Spirit. You are so hairy, you must be a fox that doesn't even know how to transform itself. You're not clever for a Fox Spirit, I must say. No tricks. No blood. Where are your hanged man's rotting noose and icy breath? No throwing shoes into the rafters? No metamorphosis into a beautiful sad lady? No disguises in my dead relatives' shapes? No drowned woman with seaweed hair? No riddles or penalty games? You are a puny little boulder indeed. Yes, when I get my oil, I will fry you for breakfast."

She then ignored the ghost on her chest and chanted her lessons for the next day's classes. The moon moved from one window to the other, and as dawn came, the thing scurried off, climbing quickly down the foot of the bed.

She fell asleep until time for school. She had said she was going to sleep in that room, and so she did.

She awoke when the students came tumbling into the room. "What happened?" they asked, getting under the quilt to keep warm. "Did anything happen?"

"Take my earlobes, please," said my mother, "and pull them back and forth. In case I lost any of my self, I want you to call me back. I was afraid, and fear may have driven me out of my body and mind. Then I will tell you the story." Two friends clasped her hands while a third held her head and took each earlobe between thumb and forefinger, wiggling them and chanting, "Come home, come home, Brave Orchid, who has fought the ghosts and won. Return to To Keung School, Kwangtung City, Kwangtung Province. Your classmates are here waiting for you, scholarly Brave Orchid. Come home. Come home. Come back and help us with our lessons. School is starting soon. Come for breakfast. Return, daughter of New Society Village, Kwangtung Province. Your brother and sisters call you. Your friends call you. We need you. Return to us. Return to us at the To Keung School. There's work to do. Come back, Doctor Brave Orchid, be unafraid. Be unafraid. You are safe now in the To Keung School. All is safe. Return."

Abundant comfort in long restoring waves warmed my mother. Her soul returned fully to her and nestled happily inside her skin, for this moment not travelling in the past where her children were nor to America to be with my father. She was back among many people. She rested after battle. She let friends watch out for her.

"There," said the roommate, giving her ear a last hearty tug, "you are cured. Now tell us what happened."

"I had finished reading my novel," said my mother, "and still nothing happened. I was listening to the dogs bark far away. Suddenly a full-grown Sitting Ghost loomed up to the ceiling and pounced on top of me. Mounds of hair hid its claws and teeth. No true head, no eyes, no face, so low in its level of incarnation it did not have the shape of a recognizable animal. It knocked me down and began to strangle me. It was bigger than a wolf, bigger than an ape, and growing. I would have stabbed it. I would have cut it up, and we would be mopping blood this morning, but—a Sitting Ghost mutation—it had an extra arm that wrested my hand away from the knife.

"At about 3 A.M. I died for a while. I was wandering, and the world I touched turned into sand. I could hear wind, but the sand did not fly. For ten years I lost my way. I almost forgot about you; there was so much work leading to other work and another life—like picking up coins in a dream. But I returned. I walked from the Gobi Desert to this room in the To Keung

School. That took another two years, outwitting Wall Ghosts en route. (The way to do that is to go straight ahead; do not play their side-to-side games. In confusion they will instantly revert to their real state—weak and sad humanity. No matter what, don't commit suicide, or you will have to trade places with the Wall Ghost. If you are not put off by the foot-long lolling tongues and the popped-out eyes of the hanged ones or the open veins or the drowned skin and seaweed hair—and you shouldn't be because you're doctors—you can chant these poor souls on to light.)

"No white bats and no black bats flew ahead to guide me to my natural death. Either I would die without my whole life or I would not die. I did not die. I am brave and good. Also I have bodily strength and control. Good people do not lose to ghosts.

"Altogether I was gone for twelve years, but in this room only an hour had passed. The moon barely moved. By silver light I saw the black thing pulling shadows into itself, setting up magnetic whorls. Soon it would suck in the room and begin on the rest of the dormitory. It would eat us up. It threw boulders at me. And there was a sound like mountain wind, a sound so high it could drive you crazy. Didn't you hear it?"

Yes, they had. Wasn't it like the electric wires that one sometimes heard in the city? Yes, it was the sound of energy amassing.

"You were lucky you slept because the sound tears the heart. I could hear babies crying in it. I could hear tortured people screaming, and the cries of their relatives who had to watch."

"Yes, yes, I recognize that. That must have been the singing I heard in my dream."

"It may be sounding even now, though too strangely for our daytime ears. You cannot hit the ghost if you sweep under the bed. The ghost fattens at night, its dark sacs empty by daylight. It's a good thing I stopped it feeding on me; blood and meat would have given it strength to feed on you. I made my will an eggshell encasing the monster's fur so that the hollow hairs could not draw. I never let up willing its size smaller, its hairs to retract, until by dawn the Sitting Ghost temporarily disappeared.

"The danger is not over. The ghost is listening to us right

now, and tonight it will walk again but stronger. We may not be able to control it if you do not help me finish it off before sundown. This Sitting Ghost has many wide black mouths. It is dangerous. It is real. Most ghosts make such brief and gauzy appearances that eyewitnesses doubt their own sightings. This one can conjure up enough substance to sit solidly throughout a night. It is a serious ghost, not at all playful. It does not twirl incense sticks or throw shoes and dishes. It does not play peekaboo or wear fright masks. It does not bother with tricks. It wants lives. I am sure it is surfeited with babies and is now coming after adults. It grows. It is mysterious, not merely a copy of ourselves as, after all, the hanged men and seaweed women are. It could be hiding right now in a piece of wood or inside one of your dolls. Perhaps in daylight we accept that bag to be just a bag"—she pointed with the flat of her palm as if it balanced a top—"when in reality it is a Bag Ghost." The students moved away from the bag in which they collected their quilting scraps and pulled up their feet that were dangling over the edge of the bed.

"You have to help me rid the world of this disease, as invisible and deadly as bacteria. After classes, come back here with your buckets, alcohol, and oil. If you can find dog's blood too, our work will go fast. Act unafraid. Ghost chasers have to be brave. If the ghost comes after you, though I would not expect an attack during the day, spit at it. Scorn it. The hero in a ghost story laughs a nimble laugh, his life so full it splatters red and gold on all the creatures around him."

These young women, who would have to back up their science with magical spells should their patients be disappointed and not get well, now hurried to get to classes on time. The story about the ghost's appearance and the coming ghost chase grew, and students snatched alcohol and matches from the laboratories.

My mother directed the arrangement of the buckets and burners into orderly rows and divided the fuel. "Let's fire the oil all at once," she said. "Now."

"Whup. Whup." My mother told the sound of new fire so that I remember it. "Whup. Whup."

The alcohol burned a floating blue. The tarry oil, which someone had bought from her village witch, fumed in black clouds. My mother swung a big bucket overhead. The smoke curled in black boas around the women in their scholars' black gowns. They walked the ghost room, this circle of little black women, lifting smoke and fire up to the ceiling corners, down to the floor corners, moving clouds across the walls and floors, under the bed, around one another.

"I told you, Ghost," my mother chanted, "that we would come after you." "We told you, Ghost, that we would come after you," sang the women. "Daylight has come yellow and red," sang my mother, "and we are winning. Run, Ghost, run from this school. Only good medical people belong here. Go back, dark creature, to your native country. Go home. Go home." "Go home," sang the women.

When the smoke cleared, I think my mother said that under the foot of the bed the students found a piece of wood dripping with blood. They burned it in one of the pots, and the stench was like a corpse exhumed for its bones too soon. They laughed at the smell.

The students at the To Keung School of Midwifery were new women, scientists who changed the rituals. When she got scared as a child, one of my mother's three mothers had held her and chanted their descent line, reeling the frighted spirit back from the farthest deserts. A relative would know personal names and secrets about husbands, babies, renegades and decide which ones were lucky in a chant, but these outside women had to build a path from scraps. No blood bonded friend to friend (though there were things owed beggars and monks), and they had to figure out how to help my mother's spirit locate the To Keung School as "home." The calling out of her real descent line would have led her to the wrong place, the village. These strangers had to make her come back to them. They called out their own names, women's pretty names, haphazard names, horizontal names of one generation. They pieced together new directions, and my mother's spirit followed them instead of the old footprints. Maybe that is why she lost her home village and did not reach her husband for fifteen years.

When my mother led us out of nightmares and horror movies, I felt loved. I felt safe hearing my name sung with hers and my father's, my brothers' and sisters', her anger at children who hurt themselves surprisingly gone. An old-fashioned woman would have called in the streets for her sick child. She'd hold its little empty coat unbuttoned, "Come put on your coat, you naughty child." When the coat puffed up, she'd quickly button up the spirit inside and hurry it home to the child's body in bed. But my mother, a modern woman, said our spells in private. "The old ladies in China had many silly superstitions," she said. "I know you'll come back without my making a fool of myself in the streets."

Not when we were afraid, but when we were wide awake and lucid, my mother funneled China into our ears: Kwangtung Province, New Society Village, the river Kwoo, which runs past the village. "Go the way we came so that you will be able to find our house. Don't forget. Just give your father's name, and any villager can point out our house." I am to return to China where I have never been.

After two years of study—the graduates of three-week and six-week courses were more admired by the peasants for learning at such wondrous speeds—my mother returned to her home village a doctor. She was welcomed with garlands and cymbals the way people welcome the "barefoot doctors" today. But the Communists wear a blue plainness dotted with one red Mao button. My mother wore a silk robe and western shoes with big heels, and she rode home carried in a sedan chair. She had gone away ordinary and come back miraculous, like the ancient magicians who came down from the mountains.

"When I stepped out of my sedan chair, the villagers said, 'Ahhh,' at my good shoes and my long gown. I always dressed well when I made calls. Some villagers would bring out their lion and dance ahead of me. You have no idea how much I have fallen coming to America." Until my father sent for her to live in the Bronx, my mother delivered babies in beds and pigsties. She stayed awake keeping watch nightly in an epidemic and chanted during air raids. She yanked bones straight that had been crooked for years while relatives held the cripples down, and she did all this never dressed less elegantly than when she stepped out of the sedan chair.

Nor did she change her name: Brave Orchid. Professional

women have the right to use their maiden names if they like. Even when she emigrated, my mother kept Brave Orchid, adding no American name nor holding one in reserve for American emergencies.

Walking behind the palanquin so that the crowd took her for one of themselves following the new doctor came a quiet girl. She carried a white puppy and a rice sack knotted at the mouth. Her pigtails and the puppy's tail ended in red yarn. She may have been either a daughter or a slave.

When my mother had gone to Canton market to shop, her wallet had unfolded like wings. She had received her diploma, and it was time to celebrate. She had hunted out the seed shops to taste their lichees, various as wines, and bought a sack that was taller than a child to bedazzle the nieces and nephews. A merchant had given her one nut fresh on its sprig of narrow leaves. My mother popped the thin wood shell in her curled palm. The white fruit, an eye without an iris, ran juices like spring rivers inside my mother's mouth. She spit out the brown seed, iris after all.

She had bought a turtle for my grandfather because it would lengthen his life. She had dug to the bottom of fabric piles and explored the shadows underneath awnings. She gave beggars rice and letter-writers coins so that they would talk-story. ("Sometimes what I gave was all they had, and stories.") She let a fortuneteller read the whorls on her fingerprints; he predicted that she would leave China and have six more children. "Six," he said, "is the number of everything. You are such a lucky woman. Six is the universe's number. The four compass points plus the zenith and the nadir are six. There are six low phoenix notes and six high, six worldly environments, six senses, six virtues, six obligations, six classes of ideograph, six domestic animals, six arts, and six paths of metempsychosis. More than two thousand years ago, six states combined to overthrow Ch'in. And, of course, there are the hexagrams that are the *I Ching*, and there is the Big Six, which is China." As interesting as his list of sixes was, my mother hurried on her way; she had come to market to buy herself a slave.

Between the booths and stores, whoever could squeeze a space—a magician who could turn dirt into gold, twenty-five acrobats on one unicycle, a man who could swim—displayed

his or her newest feat for money. From the country the villagers brought strange purple textiles, dolls with big feet, geese
with brown tufts on their heads, chickens with white feathers and black skin, gambling games and puppet shows, intricate ways to fold pastry and ancestors' money, a new boxing
stance.

Herders roped off alleys to pen their goats, which stared out
of the dimness with rectangular pupils. Whisking a handful
of grass, my mother coaxed them into the light and watched
the tiny yellow windows close and open again as the goats
skipped backward into the shade. Two farmers, each leading
this year's cow, passed each other, shouting prices. Usually my
mother would have given herself up to the pleasure of being in
a crowd, delighting in the money game the people would play
with the rival herders, who were now describing each other's
cows—"skinny shoulder blades," "lame legs," "patchy hair,"
"ogre face." But today she hurried even when looking over the
monkey cages stacked higher than her head. She paused only
a while in front of the ducks, which honked madly, the down
flying as some passer-by bumped into their cages. My mother
liked to look at the ducks and plan how she would dig a pond
for them near the sweet potato field and arrange straw for their
eggs. She decided that the drake with the green head would
be the best buy, the noblest, although she would not buy him
unless she had money left over; she was already raising a nobler
duck on the farm.

Among the sellers with their ropes, cages, and water tanks
were the sellers of little girls. Sometimes just one man would
be standing by the side of the road selling one girl. There
were fathers and mothers selling their daughters, whom they
pushed forward and then pulled back again. My mother
turned her face to look at pottery or embroidery rather than
at these miserable families who did not have the sense to leave
the favored brothers and sisters home. All the children bore
still faces. My mother would not buy from parents, crying and
clutching. They would try to keep you talking to find out what
kind of mistress you were to your slaves. If they could just hear
from the buyer's own mouth about a chair in the kitchen, they
could tell each other in the years to come that their daughter
was even now resting in the kitchen chair. It was merciful to

give these parents a few details about the garden, a sweet feeble grandmother, food.

My mother would buy her slave from a professional whose little girls stood neatly in a row and bowed together when a customer looked them over. "How do you do, Sir?" they would sing. "How do you do, Madam?" "Let a little slave do your shopping for you," the older girls chorused. "We've been taught to bargain. We've been taught to sew. We can cook, and we can knit." Some of the dealers merely had the children bow quietly. Others had them sing a happy song about flowers.

Unless a group of little girls chanted some especially clever riddle, my mother, who distrusts people with public concerns, braggarts, went over to the quiet older girls with the dignified bows. "Any merchant who advertises 'Honest Scales' must have been thinking about weighing them," she says. Many sellers displayed the sign "Children and Old Men Not Cheated."

There were girls barely able to toddle carrying infant slaves tied in slings to their backs. In the undisciplined groups the babies crawled into gutters and the older girls each acted as if she were alone, a daughter among slaves. The one- to two-year-old babies cost nothing.

"Greet the lady," the dealer commanded, just as the nice little girls' mothers had when visitors came.

"How do you do, Lady," said the girls.

My mother did not need to bow back, and she did not. She overlooked the infants and toddlers and talked to the oldest girls.

"Open your mouth," she said, and examined teeth. She pulled down eyelids to check for anemia. She picked up the girls' wrists to sound their pulses, which tell everything.

She stopped at a girl whose strong heart sounded like thunder within the earth, sending its power into her fingertips. "I would not have sold a daughter such as that one," she told us. My mother could find no flaw in the beat; it matched her own, the real rhythm. There were people jumpy with silly rhythms; broken rhythms; sly, secretive rhythms. They did not follow the sounds of earth-sea-sky and the Chinese language.

My mother brought out the green notebook my father had given her when he left. It had a map of each hemisphere on the inside covers and a clasp that shut it like a pocketbook. "Watch carefully," she said. With an American pencil, she wrote a word, a felicitous word such as "longevity" or "double joy," which is symmetrical.

"Look carefully," she said into the girl's face. "If you can write this word from memory, I will take you with me. Concentrate now." She wrote in a plain style and folded the page a moment afterward. The girl took the pencil and wrote surely; she did not leave out a single stroke.

"What would you do," my mother asked, "if you lost a gold watch in a field?"

"I know a chant on the finger bones," said the girl. "But even if I landed on the bone that says to look no more, I would go to the middle of the field and search in a spiral going outward until I reached the field's edge. Then I would believe the chant and look no more." She drew in my mother's notebook the field and her spiraling path.

"How do you cast on yarn?"

The girl pantomimed her method with her large hands.

"How much water do you put in the rice pot for a family of five? How do you finish off weaving so that it doesn't unravel?"

Now it was time to act as if she were very dissatisfied with the slave's answers so that the dealer would not charge her extra for a skillful worker.

"You tie the loose ends into tassels," said the girl.

My mother frowned. "But suppose I like a finished border?"

The girl hesitated. "I could, uh, press the fibers under and sew them down. Or how about cutting the fibers off?"

My mother offered the dealer half the price he named. "My mother-in-law asked me to find a weaver for her, and obviously she and I will have to waste many months training this girl."

"But she can knit and cook," said the dealer, "and she can find lost watches." He asked for a price higher than her suggestion but lower than his first.

"I knit and cook and find things," said my mother. "How else do you suppose I think of such ingenious questions? Do you think I would buy a slave who could outwork me in front of my mother-in-law?" My mother walked off to look at a group of hungry slaves across the street. When she returned, the dealer sold her the girl with the finding chant at my mother's price.

"I am a doctor," she told her new slave, when they were out of the dealer's hearing, "and I shall train you to be my nurse."

"Doctor," said the slave, "do you understand that I do know how to finish off my weaving?"

"Yes, we fooled him very well," said my mother.

The unsold slaves must have watched them with envy. I watch them with envy. My mother's enthusiasm for me is duller than for the slave girl; nor did I replace the older brother and sister who died while they were still cuddly. Throughout childhood my younger sister said, "When I grow up, I want to be a slave," and my parents laughed, encouraging her. At department stores I angered my mother when I could not bargain without shame, poor people's shame. She stood in back of me and prodded and pinched, forcing me to translate her bargaining, word for word.

On that same day she bought at the dog dealer's a white puppy to train as her bodyguard when she made night calls. She tied pretty red yarn around its tail to neutralize the bad luck. There was no use docking the tail. No matter at what point she cut, the tip would have been white, the mourning color.

The puppy waved its red yarn at the nurse girl, and she picked it up. She followed my mother back to the village, where she always got enough to eat because my mother became a good doctor. She could cure the most spectacular diseases. When a sick person was about to die, my mother could read the fact of it a year ahead of time on the daughters-in-law's faces. A black veil seemed to hover over their skin. And though they laughed, this blackness rose and fell with their breath. My mother would take one look at the daughter-in-law who answered the door at the sick house and she'd say, "Find another doctor." She would not touch death; therefore, untainted, she brought only health from house to house. "She must be a Jesus convert," the people from the far villages said. "All her patients get well." The bigger the talk, the farther the distances she travelled. She had customers everywhere.

Sometimes she went to her patients by foot. Her nurse-slave carried an umbrella when my mother predicted rain and a parasol when she predicted sun. "My white dog would be standing at the door waiting for me whenever I came home," she said.

When she felt like it, my mother would leave the nurse-slave to watch the office and would take the white dog with her.

"What happened to your dog when you came to America, Mother?"

"I don't know."

"What happened to the slave?"

"I found her a husband."

"How much money did you pay to buy her?"

"One hundred and eighty dollars."

"How much money did you pay the doctor and the hospital when I was born?"

"Two hundred dollars."

"Oh."

"That's two hundred dollars American money."

"Was the one hundred and eighty dollars American money?"

"No."

"How much was it American money?"

"Fifty dollars. That's because she was sixteen years old. Eight-year-olds were about twenty dollars. Five-year-olds were ten dollars and up. Two-year-olds were about five dollars. Babies were free. During the war, though, when you were born, many people gave older girls away for free. And here I was in the United States paying two hundred dollars for you."

When my mother went doctoring in the villages, the ghosts, the were-people, the apes dropped out of trees. They rose out of bridge water. My mother saw them come out of cervixes. Medical science does not seal the earth, whose nether creatures seep out, hair by hair, disguised like the smoke that dispels them. She had apparently won against the one ghost, but ghost forms are various and many. Some can occupy the same space at the same moment. They permeate the grain in wood, metal, and stone. Animalcules somersault about our faces when we breathe. We have to build horns on our roofs so that the nagging once-people can slide up them and perhaps ascend to the stars, the source of pardon and love.

On a fine spring day the villagers at a place my mother had never visited before would wave peach branches and fans, which are emblems of Chung-li Ch'uan, the chief of the Eight Sages and keeper of the elixir of life. The pink petals would fall on my mother's black hair and gown. The villagers would set off firecrackers as on New Year's Day. Only if it had really been New Year's, she would have had to shut herself up in her own house. Nobody wanted a doctor's visit in the first days of the year.

But at night my mother walked quickly. She and bandits were the only human beings out, no palanquins available for midwives. For a time the roads were endangered by a fantastic creature, half man and half ape, that a traveller to the west had captured and brought back to China in a cage. With his new money, the man had built the fourth wing to his house, and in the courtyard he grew a stand of bamboo. The ape-man could reach out and touch the thin leaves that shaded its cage.

This creature had gnawed through the bars. Or it had tricked its owner into letting it play in the courtyard, and then leapt over the roof of the new wing. Now it was at large in the forests, living off squirrels, mice, and an occasional duck or piglet. My mother saw in the dark a denser dark, and she knew she was being followed. She carried a club, and the white dog was beside her. The ape-man was known to have attacked people. She had treated their bites and claw wounds. With hardly a rustle of leaves, the ape-man leapt live out of the trees and blocked her way. The white dog yelped. As big as a human being, the ape-thing jumped up and down on one foot. Its two hands were holding the other foot, hurt in the jump. It had long orange hair and beard. Its owner had clothed it in a brown burlap rice sack with holes for neck and arms. It blinked at my mother with human eyes, moving its head from shoulder to shoulder as if figuring things out. "Go home," she shouted, waving her club. It copied her waving with one raised arm and made complex motions with its other hand. But when she rushed at it, it turned and ran limping into the forest. "Don't you scare me again," she yelled after its retreating buttocks, tailless and hairless under the shirt. It was definitely not a gorilla; she has since seen some of those at the Bronx Zoo, and this ape-man was nothing like them. If her father had not brought Third Wife, who was not Chinese, back from his travels, my mother might have thought this orange creature with the great nose was a barbarian from the west. But my grandfather's Third Wife was black with hair so soft that it would not hang, instead blowing up into a great brown puffball. (At first she talked constantly, but who could understand her? After a while she never talked anymore. She had one son.) The owner of the ape-man finally recaptured it by luring it back into its cage with cooked pork and wine. Occasionally my mother went to the rich man's house to look at the ape-man. It seemed to recognize her and smiled when she gave it candy. Perhaps it had not been an ape-man at all, but one of the Tigermen, a savage northern race.

My mother was midwife to whatever spewed forth, not being able to choose as with the old and sick. She was not squeamish, though, and deftly caught spewings that were sometimes babies, sometimes monsters. When she helped the country women who insisted on birthing in the pigpen, she could not tell by starlight and moonlight what manner of creature had made its arrival on the earth until she carried it inside the house. "Pretty pigbaby, pretty piglet," she and the mother would croon, fooling the ghosts on the lookout for a new birth. "Ugly pig, dirty pig," fooling the gods jealous of human joy. They counted fingers and toes by touch, felt for penis or no penis, but not until later would they know for sure whether the gods let them get away with something good.

One boy appeared perfect, so round in the cool opal dawn. But when my mother examined him indoors, he opened up blue eyes at her. Perhaps he had looked without protection at the sky, and it had filled him. His mother said that a ghost had entered him, but my mother said the baby looked pretty.

Not all defects could be explained so congenially. One child born without an anus was left in the outhouse so that the family would not have to hear it cry. They kept going back to see whether it was dead yet, but it lived for a long time. Whenever they went to look at it, it was sobbing, heaving as if it were trying to defecate. For days the family either walked to the fields or used the night soil buckets.

As a child, I pictured a naked child sitting on a modern toilet desperately trying to perform until it died of congestion. I had to flick on the bathroom lights fast so that no small shadow would take a baby shape, sometimes seated on the edge of the bathtub, its hopes for a bowel movement so exaggerated. When I woke at night I sometimes heard an infant's grunting and weeping coming from the bathroom. I did not go to its rescue but waited for it to stop.

I hope this holeless baby proves that my mother did not prepare a box of clean ashes beside the birth bed in case of a girl. "The midwife or a relative would take the back of a girl baby's head in her hand and turn her face into the ashes," said my mother. "It was very easy." She never said she herself killed babies, but perhaps the holeless baby was a boy.

Even here on Gold Mountain grateful couples bring gifts to my mother, who had cooked them a soup that not only ended their infertility but gave them a boy.

My mother has given me pictures to dream—nightmare babies that recur, shrinking again and again to fit in my palm. I curl my fingers to make a cradle for the baby, my other hand an awning. I would protect the dream baby, not let it suffer, not let it out of my sight. But in a blink of inattention, I would mislay the baby. I would have to stop moving, afraid of stepping on it. Or before my very eyes, it slips between my fingers because my fingers cannot grow webs fast enough. Or bathing it, I carefully turn the right-hand faucet, but it spouts hot water, scalding the baby until its skin tautens and its face becomes nothing but a red hole of a scream. The hole turns into a pinprick as the baby recedes from me.

To make my waking life American-normal, I turn on the lights before anything untoward makes an appearance. I push the deformed into my dreams, which are in Chinese, the language of impossible stories. Before we can leave our parents, they stuff our heads like the suitcases which they jam-pack with homemade underwear.

When the thermometer in our laundry reached one hundred and eleven degrees on summer afternoons, either my mother or my father would say that it was time to tell another ghost story so that we could get some good chills up our backs. My parents, my brothers, sisters, great-uncle, and "Third Aunt," who wasn't really our aunt but a fellow villager, someone else's third aunt, kept the presses crashing and hissing and shouted out the stories. Those were our successful days, when so much laundry came in, my mother did not have to pick tomatoes. For breaks we changed from pressing to sorting.

"One twilight," my mother began, and already the chills travelled my back and crossed my shoulders; the hair rose at the nape and the back of the legs, "I was walking home after doctoring a sick family. To get home I had to cross a footbridge. In China the bridges are nothing like the ones in Brooklyn and San Francisco. This one was made from rope, laced and knotted as if by magpies. Actually it had been built by men who had returned after harvesting sea swallow nests in Malaya. They had had to swing over the faces of the Malayan cliffs in baskets they had woven themselves. Though this bridge pitched and swayed in the updraft, no one had ever fallen into the river, which looked like a bright scratch at the bottom of the canyon, as if the Queen of Heaven had swept her great silver hairpin across the earth as well as the sky."

One twilight, just as my mother stepped on the bridge, two smoky columns spiraled up taller than she. Their swaying tops hovered over her head like white cobras, one at either hand-rail. From stillness came a wind rushing between the smoke spindles. A high sound entered her temple bones. Through the twin whirlwinds she could see the sun and the river, the river twisting in circles, the trees upside down. The bridge moved like a ship, sickening. The earth dipped. She collapsed to the wooden slats, a ladder up the sky, her fingers so weak she could not grip the rungs. The wind dragged her hair behind her, then whipped it forward across her face. Suddenly the smoke spindles disappeared. The world righted itself, and she crossed to the other side. She looked back, but there was nothing there. She used the bridge often, but she did not encounter those ghosts again.

"They were Sit Dom Kuei," said Great-Uncle. "Sit Dom Kuei."

"Yes, of course," said my mother. "Sit Dom Kuei."

I keep looking in dictionaries under those syllables. "Kuei" means "ghost," but I don't find any other words that make sense. I only hear my great-uncle's river-pirate voice, the voice of a big man who had killed someone in New York or Cuba, make the sounds—"Sit Dom Kuei." How do they translate?

When the Communists issued their papers on techniques for combating ghosts, I looked for "Sit Dom Kuei." I have not found them described anywhere, although now I see that my

mother won in ghost battle because she can eat anything—
quick, pluck out the carp's eyes, one for Mother and one for
Father. All heroes are bold toward food. In the research against
ghost fear published by the Chinese Academy of Science is
the story of a magistrate's servant, Kao Chung, a capable eater
who in 1683 ate five cooked chickens and drank ten bottles of
wine that belonged to the sea monster with branching teeth.
The monster had arranged its food around a fire on the beach
and started to feed when Kao Chung attacked. The swan-
feather sword he wrested from this monster can be seen in the
Wentung County Armory in Shantung today.

Another big eater was Chou Yi-han of Changchow, who
fried a ghost. It was a meaty stick when he cut it up and cooked
it. But before that it had been a woman out at night.

Chen Luan-feng, during the Yuan Ho era of the T'ang dynasty (A.D. 806–820), ate yellow croaker and pork together,
which the thunder god had forbidden. But Chen wanted to
incur thunderbolts during drought. The first time he ate, the
thunder god jumped out of the sky, its legs like old trees. Chen
chopped off the left one. The thunder god fell to the earth,
and the villagers could see that it was a blue pig or bear with
horns and fleshy wings. Chen leapt on it, prepared to chop its
neck and bite its throat, but the villagers stopped him. After
that, Chen lived apart as a rainmaker, neither relatives nor the
monks willing to bring lightning upon themselves. He lived in
a cave, and for years whenever there was drought the villagers
asked him to eat yellow croaker and pork together, and he did.

The most fantastic eater of them all was Wei Pang, a scholar-
hunter of the Ta Li era of the T'ang dynasty (A.D. 766–779).
He shot and cooked rabbits and birds, but he could also eat
scorpions, snakes, cockroaches, worms, slugs, beetles, and
crickets. Once he spent the night in a house that had been
abandoned because its inhabitants feared contamination from
the dead man next door. A shining, twinkling sphere came
flying through the darkness at Wei. He felled it with three true
arrows—the first making the thing crackle and flame; the second dimming it; and the third putting out its lights, sputter.
When his servant came running in with a lamp, Wei saw his arrows sticking in a ball of flesh entirely covered with eyes, some
rolled back to show the dulling whites. He and the servant

pulled out the arrows and cut up the ball into little pieces. The servant cooked the morsels in sesame oil, and the wonderful aroma made Wei laugh. They ate half, saving half to show the household, which would return now.

Big eaters win. When other passers-by stepped around the bundle wrapped in white silk, the anonymous scholar of Hanchow took it home. Inside were three silver ingots and a froglike evil, which sat on the ingots. The scholar laughed at it and chased it off. That night two frogs the size of year-old babies appeared in his room. He clubbed them to death, cooked them, and ate them with white wine. The next night a dozen frogs, together the size of a pair of year-old babies, jumped from the ceiling. He ate all twelve for dinner. The third night thirty small frogs were sitting on his mat and staring at him with their frog eyes. He ate them too. Every night for a month smaller but more numerous frogs came so that he always had the same amount to eat. Soon his floor was like the healthy banks of a pond in spring when the tadpoles, having just turned, sprang in the wet grass. "Get a hedgehog to help eat," cried his family. "I'm as good as a hedgehog," the scholar said, laughing. And at the end of the month the frogs stopped coming, leaving the scholar with the white silk and silver ingots.

My mother has cooked for us: raccoons, skunks, hawks, city pigeons, wild ducks, wild geese, black-skinned bantams, snakes, garden snails, turtles that crawled about the pantry floor and sometimes escaped under refrigerator or stove, catfish that swam in the bathtub. "The emperors used to eat the peaked hump of purple dromedaries," she would say. "They used chopsticks made from rhinoceros horn, and they ate ducks' tongues and monkeys' lips." She boiled the weeds we pulled up in the yard. There was a tender plant with flowers like white stars hiding under the leaves, which were like the flower petals but green. I've not been able to find it since growing up. It had no taste. When I was as tall as the washing machine, I stepped out on the back porch one night, and some heavy, ruffling, windy, clawed thing dived at me. Even after getting chanted back to sensibility, I shook when I recalled that perched everywhere there were owls with great hunched shoulders and yellow scowls. They were a surprise for my mother from my father. We children used to hide under the beds with our fingers in our ears to shut out the bird screams and the thud, thud of the turtles swimming in the boiling water, their shells hitting the sides of the pot. Once the third aunt who worked at the laundry ran out and bought us bags of candy to hold over our noses; my mother was dismembering skunk on the chopping block. I could smell the rubbery odor through the candy.

In a glass jar on a shelf my mother kept a big brown hand with pointed claws stewing in alcohol and herbs. She must have brought it from China because I do not remember a time when I did not have the hand to look at. She said it was a bear's claw, and for many years I thought bears were hairless. My mother used the tobacco, leeks, and grasses swimming about the hand to rub our sprains and bruises.

Just as I would climb up to the shelf to take one look after another at the hand, I would hear my mother's monkey story. I'd take my fingers out of my ears and let her monkey words enter my brain. I did not always listen voluntarily, though. She would begin telling the story, perhaps repeating it to a homesick villager, and I'd overhear before I had a chance to protect myself. Then the monkey words would unsettle me; a curtain flapped loose inside my brain. I have wanted to say, "Stop it. Stop it," but not once did I say, "Stop it."

"Do you know what people in China eat when they have the money?" my mother began. "They buy into a monkey feast. The eaters sit around a thick wood table with a hole in the middle. Boys bring in the monkey at the end of a pole. Its neck is in a collar at the end of the pole, and it is screaming. Its hands are tied behind it. They clamp the monkey into the table; the whole table fits like another collar around its neck. Using a surgeon's saw, the cooks cut a clean line in a circle at the top of its head. To loosen the bone, they tap with a tiny hammer and wedge here and there with a silver pick. Then an old woman reaches out her hand to the monkey's face and up to its scalp, where she tufts some hairs and lifts off the lid of the skull. The eaters spoon out the brains."

Did she say, "You should have seen the faces the monkey made"? Did she say, "The people laughed at the monkey screaming"? It was alive? The curtain flaps closed like merciful black wings.

"Eat! Eat!" my mother would shout at our heads bent over bowls, the blood pudding awobble in the middle of the table.

She had one rule to keep us safe from toadstools and such: "If it tastes good, it's bad for you," she said. "If it tastes bad, it's good for you."

We'd have to face four- and five-day-old leftovers until we ate it all. The squid eye would keep appearing at breakfast and dinner until eaten. Sometimes brown masses sat on every dish. I have seen revulsion on the faces of visitors who've caught us at meals.

"Have you eaten yet?" the Chinese greet one another.

"Yes, I have," they answer whether they have or not. "And you?"

I would live on plastic.

My mother could contend against the hairy beasts whether flesh or ghost because she could eat them, and she could not-eat them on the days when good people fast. My mother was not crazy for seeing ghosts nor was she one of those the women teased for "longing" after men. She was a capable exorcist; she did not "long" ("mong" in Cantonese). The village crazy lady was somebody else, an inappropriate woman whom the people stoned.

It was just after this stoning that my mother left China. My father had made the money for the fare at last, but he sent for her instead of returning, one more postponement of home, this time because of the Japanese. By 1939 the Japanese had taken much of the land along the Kwoo River, and my mother was living in the mountains with other refugees. (I used to watch my mother and father play refugees, sleeping sitting up, huddled together with their heads on each other's shoulder, their arms about each other, holding up the blanket like a little tent. "Aiaa," they'd sigh. "Aiaa." "Mother, what's a refugee? Father, what's a refugee?") The Japanese, though "little," were not ghosts, the only foreigners considered not ghosts by the Chinese. They may have been descended from the Chinese explorers that the First Emperor of Ch'in (221–210 B.C.) had deployed to find longevity medicine. They were to look for an island beyond the Eastern Ocean, beyond the impassable wind and mist. On this island lived phoenixes, unicorns, black apes, and white stags. Magic orchids, strange trees, and plants of jasper grew on Penglai, a fairy mountain, which may have been Mount Fuji. The emperor would saw off the explorers' heads if they returned without the herbs of immortality. Another ancestor of the Japanese is said to be an ape that raped a Chinese princess, who then fled to the eastern islands to have the first Japanese child. Whichever the case, they were not a totally alien species, connected as they were even to royalty. Chinese without sons stole the boy babies of Japanese settlers who left them bundled up at the ends of the potato rows.

Now the villagers were watching for Japanese airplanes that strafed the mountainsides every day. "If you see a single plane, you needn't be afraid," my mother taught us. "But watch for planes in threes. When they spread apart, you know they're going to drop bombs. Sometimes airplanes covered the sky, and we could not see and we could not hear." She warned us because it was the same war still going on years after she crossed the ocean and had us. I huddled under my blankets when Pan Am and United Air Lines planes flew overhead, the engines sounding like insects at first and getting louder and louder.

In the mountains my mother set up a hospital in a cave, and she carried the wounded there. Some villagers had never seen an airplane before. Mothers stopped up their babies' mouths so their crying would not attract the planes. The bombing drove people insane. They rolled on the ground, pushed themselves against it, as if the earth could open a door for them. The ones who could not stop shaking after the danger passed would sleep in the cave. My mother explained airplanes to them as she wiggled their ears.

One afternoon peace and summer rested on the mountains. Babies napped in the tall grass, their blankets covering the wildflowers with embroidered flowers. It was so quiet; the bees hummed and the river water played the pebbles, the rocks, and the hollows. Cows under the trees whisked their tails; goats and ducks followed the children here and there; and the chickens scratched in the dirt. The villagers stood about in the sunshine. They smiled at one another. Here they all were together idle above their fields, nobody hoeing, godlike; nobody weeding, New Year's in summer. My mother and the women her age talked about how similar this day was to the orderly days long ago when they walked up the mountain to collect firewood, only now they could dally without the mothers-in-law scolding.

The village crazy lady put on her headdress with the small mirrors, some of them waving quickly on red stalks. In her crazy lady clothes of reds and greens, she greeted the animals and the moving branches as she carried her porcelain cup to the river. Although her bindings had come loose, her tiny feet made her body sway pleasantly, her shoes like little bridges. She knelt singing at the river and filled her cup. Carrying the brimming water in two careful hands, she undulated toward a clearing where the light of the afternoon seemed to be concentrated. The villagers turned to look at her. She dipped her fingertips into the water and flung droplets into grass and air. Then she set the cup down and pulled out the long white undersleeves of her old-fashioned dress. She began to move in fanning circles, now flying the sleeves in the air, now trailing them on the grass, dancing in the middle of the light. The little mirrors in her headdress shot rainbows into the green, glinted off the water cup, caught water drops. My mother felt as if she were peering into Li T'ieh-kuai's magic gourd to check the fate of an impish mortal.

One villager whispered away the spell, "She's signaling the planes." The whisper carried. "She's signaling the planes," the people repeated. "Stop her. Stop her."

"No, she's only crazy," said my mother. "She's a harmless crazy lady."

"She's a spy. A spy for the Japanese."

Villagers picked up rocks and moved down the hill.

"Just take away the mirrors," my mother called. "Just take her headdress."

But the tentative first stones were already falling around the crazy lady. She dodged them; she tried to catch them, laughing, at last, people to play with.

The rocks hit harder as the villagers came within stoning range. "Here. Here. I'll get her mirrors," said my mother, who had come running down the mountain into the clearing.

"Give me your headdress," she ordered, but the woman only shook her head coquettishly.

"See? She's a spy. Get out of the way, Doctor. You saw the way she flashed the signals. She comes to the river every day before the planes come."

"She's only getting drinking water," said my mother. "Crazy people drink water too."

Someone took the crazy lady's cup and threw it at her. It broke at her feet. "Are you a spy? Are you?" they asked her.

A cunning look narrowed her eyes. "Yes," she said, "I have great powers. I can make the sky rain fire. Me. I did that. Leave me alone or I will do it again." She edged toward the river as if she were about to run, but she wouldn't have been able to get away on her tiny feet.

A large stone rammed her head, and she fell in a flutter of sleeves, the ornaments jumping about her broken head. The villagers closed in. Somebody held a fragment of glass under her nostrils. When it clouded, they pounded her temples with the rocks in their fists until she was dead. Some villagers remained at the body beating her head and face, smashing the little mirrors into silver splinters.

My mother, who had turned her back and walked up the mountain (she never treated those about to die), looked down at the mass of flesh and rocks, the sleeves, the blood flecks. The planes came again that very afternoon. The villagers buried the crazy lady along with the rest of the dead.

My mother left China in the winter of 1939, almost six months after the stoning, and arrived in New York Harbor in January, 1940. She carried the same suitcase she had taken to Canton, this time filled with seeds and bulbs. On Ellis Island the officials asked her, "What year did your husband cut off his pigtail?" and it terrified her when she could not remember. But later she told us perhaps this lapse was for the best: what if they were trying to trap him politically? The men had cut their pigtails to defy the Manchus and to help Sun Yat-sen, fellow Cantonese.

I was born in the middle of World War II. From earliest awareness, my mother's stories always timely, I watched for three airplanes parting. Much as I dream recurringly about shrinking babies, I dream that the sky is covered from horizon to horizon with rows of airplanes, dirigibles, rocket ships, flying bombs, their formations as even as stitches. When the sky seems clear in my dreams and I would fly, if I look too closely, there so silent, far away, and faint in the daylight that people who do not know about them do not see them, are shiny silver machines, some not yet invented, being moved, fleets always being moved from one continent to another, one planet to another. I must figure out a way to fly between them.

But America has been full of machines and ghosts—Taxi Ghosts, Bus Ghosts, Police Ghosts, Fire Ghosts, Meter Reader Ghosts, Tree Trimming Ghosts, Five-and-Dime Ghosts. Once upon a time the world was so thick with ghosts, I could hardly breathe; I could hardly walk, limping my way around the White Ghosts and their cars. There were Black Ghosts too, but they were open eyed and full of laughter, more distinct than White Ghosts.

What frightened me most was the Newsboy Ghost, who came out from between the cars parked in the evening light. Carrying a newspaper pouch instead of a baby brother, he walked right out in the middle of the street without his parents. He shouted ghost words to the empty streets. His voice reached children inside the houses, reached inside the children's chests. They would come running out of their yards with their dimes. They would follow him just a corner too far. And when they went to the nearest house to ask directions home, the Gypsy Ghosts would lure them inside with gold rings and then boil them alive and bottle them. The ointment thus made was good for rubbing on children's bruises.

We used to pretend we were Newsboy Ghosts. We collected old Chinese newspapers (the Newsboy Ghost not giving us his ghost newspapers) and trekked about the house and yard. We waved them over our heads, chanting a chant: "Newspapers for sale. Buy a newspaper." But those who could hear the insides of words heard that we were selling a miracle salve made from boiled children. The newspapers covered up green medicine bottles. We made up our own English, which I wrote down and now looks like "eeeeeeeeee." When we heard the real newsboy calling, we hid, dragging our newspapers under the stairs or into the cellar, where the Well Ghost lived in the black water under a lid. We crouched on our newspapers, the San Francisco *Gold Mountain News*, and plugged up our ears with our knuckles until he went away.

For our very food we had to traffic with the Grocery Ghosts, the supermarket aisles full of ghost customers. The Milk Ghost drove his white truck from house to house every other day. We hid watching until his truck turned the corner, bottles rattling in their frames. Then we unlocked the front door and the screen door and reached for the milk. We were regularly visited by the Mail Ghost, Meter Reader Ghost, Garbage Ghost. Staying off the streets did no good. They came nosing at windows—Social Worker Ghosts; Public Health Nurse Ghosts; Factory Ghosts recruiting workers during the war (they promised free child care, which our mother turned down); two Jesus Ghosts who had formerly worked in China. We hid directly under the windows, pressed against the baseboard until the ghost, calling us in the ghost language so that we'd almost answer to stop its voice, gave up. They did not try to break in, except for a few Burglar Ghosts. The Hobo Ghosts and Wino Ghosts took peaches off our trees and drank from the hose when nobody answered their knocks.

It seemed as if ghosts could not hear or see very well. Momentarily lulled by the useful chores they did for whatever ghostly purpose, we did not bother to lower the windows one morning when the Garbage Ghost came. We talked loudly about him through the fly screen, pointed at his hairy arms, and laughed at how he pulled up his dirty pants before swinging his hoard onto his shoulders. "Come see the Garbage Ghost get its food," we children called. "The Garbage Ghost," we told each other, nodding our heads. The ghost looked directly at us. Steadying the load on his back with one hand, the Garbage Ghost walked up to the window. He had cavernous nostrils with yellow and brown hair. Slowly he opened his red mouth, "The . . . Gar . . . bage . . . Ghost," he said, copying human language. "Gar . . . bage . . . Ghost?" We ran, screaming to our mother, who efficiently shut the window. "Now we know," she told us, "the White Ghosts can hear Chinese. They have learned it. You mustn't talk in front of them again. Someday, very soon, we're going home, where there are Han people everywhere. We'll buy furniture then, real tables and chairs. You children will smell flowers for the first time."

"Mother! Mother! It's happening again. I taste something in my mouth, but I'm not eating anything."

"Me too, Mother. Me too. There's nothing there. Just my spit. My spit tastes like sugar."

"Your grandmother in China is sending you candy again," said my mother. Human beings do not need Mail Ghosts to send messages.

I must have tinkered too much wondering how my invisible grandmother, illiterate and dependent on letter writers, could give us candy free. When I got older and more scientific, I received no more gifts from her. She died, and I did not get "home" to ask her how she did it. Whenever my parents said "home," they suspended America. They suspended enjoyment, but I did not want to go to China. In China my parents would sell my sisters and me. My father would marry two or three more wives, who would spatter cooking oil on our bare toes and lie that we were crying for naughtiness. They would give food to their own children and rocks to us. I did not want to go where the ghosts took shapes nothing like our own.

As a child I feared the size of the world. The farther away the sound of howling dogs, the farther away the sound of the trains, the tighter I curled myself under the quilt. The trains sounded deeper and deeper into the night. They had not reached the end of the world before I stopped hearing them, the last long moan diminishing toward China. How large the world must be to make my grandmother only a taste by the time she reaches me.

When I last visited my parents, I had trouble falling asleep, too big for the hills and valleys scooped in the mattress by child-bodies. I heard my mother come in. I stopped moving. What did she want? Eyes shut, I pictured my mother, her white hair frizzy in the dark-and-light doorway, my hair white now too, Mother. I could hear her move furniture about. Then she dragged a third quilt, the thick, homemade Chinese kind, across me. After that I lost track of her location. I spied from beneath my eyelids and had to hold back a jump. She had pulled up a chair and was sitting by the bed next to my head.

I could see her strong hands in her lap, not working fourteen pairs of needles. She is very proud of her hands, which can make anything and stay pink and soft while my father's became like carved wood. Her palm lines do not branch into head, heart, and life lines like other people's but crease with just one atavistic fold. That night she was a sad bear; a great sheep in a wool shawl. She recently took to wearing shawls and granny glasses, American fashions. What did she want, sitting there so large next to my head? I could feel her stare—her eyes two lights warm on my graying hair, then on the creases at the sides of my mouth, my thin neck, my thin cheeks, my thin arms. I felt her sight warm each of my bony elbows, and I flopped about in my fake sleep to hide them from her criticism. She sent light at full brightness beaming through my eyelids, her eyes at my eyes, and I had to open them.

"What's the matter, Mama? Why are you sitting there?"

She reached over and switched on a lamp she had placed on the floor beside her. "I swallowed that LSD pill you left on the kitchen counter," she announced.

"That wasn't LSD, Mama. It was just a cold pill. I have a cold."

"You're always catching colds when you come home. You must be eating too much *yin*. Let me get you another quilt."

"No, no more quilts. You shouldn't take pills that aren't prescribed for you. 'Don't eat pills you find on the curb,' you always told us."

"You children never tell me what you're really up to. How else am I going to find out what you're really up to?" As if her head hurt, she closed her eyes behind the gold wire rims. "Aiaa," she sighed, "how can I bear to have you leave me again?"

How can I bear to leave her again? She would close up this room, open temporarily for me, and wander about cleaning and cleaning the shrunken house, so tidy since our leaving. Each chair has its place now. And the sinks in the bedrooms work, their alcoves no longer stuffed with laundry right up to the ceiling. My mother has put the clothes and shoes into boxes, stored against hard times. The sinks had been built of gray marble for the old Chinese men who boarded here before we came. I used to picture modest little old men washing in the mornings and dressing before they shuffled out of these bedrooms. I would have to leave and go again into the world out there which has no marble ledges for my clothes, no quilts made from our own ducks and turkeys, no ghosts of neat little old men.

The lamp gave off the sort of light that comes from a television, which made the high ceiling disappear and then suddenly drop back into place. I could feel that clamping down and see how my mother had pulled the blinds down so low that the bare rollers were showing. No passer-by would detect a daughter in this house. My mother would sometimes be a large animal, barely real in the dark; then she would become a mother again. I could see the wrinkles around her big eyes, and I could see her cheeks sunken without her top teeth.

"I'll be back again soon," I said. "You know that I come back. I think of you when I'm not here."

"Yes, I know you. I know you now. I've always known you. You're the one with the charming words. You have never come back. 'I'll be back on Turkeyday,' you said. Huh."

I shut my teeth together, vocal cords cut, they hurt so. I would not speak words to give her pain. All her children gnash their teeth.

"The last time I saw you, you were still young," she said. "Now you're old."

"It's only been a year since I visited you."

"That's the year you turned old. Look at you, hair gone gray, and you haven't even fattened up yet. I know how the Chinese talk about us. 'They're so poor,' they say, 'they can't afford to fatten up any of their daughters.' 'Years in America,' they say, 'and they don't eat.' Oh, the shame of it—a whole family of skinny children. And your father—he's so skinny, he's disappearing."

"Don't worry about him, Mama. Doctors are saying that skinny people live longer. Papa's going to live a long time."

"So! I knew I didn't have too many years left. Do you know how I got all this fat? Eating your leftovers. Aiaa, I'm getting so old. Soon you will have no more mother."

"Mama, you've been saying that all my life."

"This time it's true. I'm almost eighty."

"I thought you were only seventy-six."

"My papers are wrong. I'm eighty."

"But I thought your papers are wrong, and you're seventy-two, seventy-three in Chinese years."

"My papers are wrong, and I'm eighty, eighty-one in Chinese years. Seventy. Eighty. What do numbers matter? I'm dropping dead any day now. The aunt down the street was resting on her porch steps, dinner all cooked, waiting for her husband and son to come home and eat it. She closed her eyes for a moment and died. Isn't that a wonderful way to go?"

"But our family lives to be ninety-nine."

"That's your father's family. My mother and father died very young. My youngest sister was an orphan at ten. Our parents were not even fifty."

"Then you should feel grateful you've lived so many extra years."

"I was so sure you were going to be an orphan too. In fact, I'm amazed you've lived to have white hair. Why don't you dye it?"

"Hair color doesn't measure age, Mother. White is just another pigment, like black and brown."

"You're always listening to Teacher Ghosts, those Scientist Ghosts, Doctor Ghosts."

"I have to make a living."

"I never do call you Oldest Daughter. Have you noticed that? I always tell people, 'This is my Biggest Daughter.'"

"Is it true then that Oldest Daughter and Oldest Son died in China? Didn't you tell me when I was ten that she'd have been twenty; when I was twenty, she'd be thirty?" Is that why you've denied me my title?

"No, you must have been dreaming. You must have been making up stories. You are all the children there are."

(Who was that story about—the one where the parents are throwing money at the children, but the children don't pick it up because they're crying too hard? They're writhing on the floor covered with coins. Their parents are going out the door for America, hurling handfuls of change behind them.)

She leaned forward, eyes brimming with what she was about to say: "I work so hard," she said. She was doing her stare—at what? My feet began rubbing together as if to tear each other's skin off. She started talking again, "The tomato vines prickle my hands; I can feel their little stubble hairs right through my gloves. My feet squish-squish in the rotten tomatoes, squish-squish in the tomato mud the feet ahead of me have sucked. And do you know the best way to stop the itch from the tomato hairs? You break open a fresh tomato and wash yourself with it. You cool your face in tomato juice. Oh, but it's the potatoes that will ruin my hands. I'll get rheumatism washing potatoes, squatting over potatoes."

She had taken off the Ace bandages around her legs for the night. The varicose veins stood out.

"Mama, why don't you stop working? You don't have to work anymore. Do you? Do you really have to work like that? Scabbing in the tomato fields?" Her black hair seems filleted with the band of white at its roots. She dyed her hair so that the farmers would hire her. She would walk to Skid Row and stand in line with the hobos, the winos, the junkies, and the Mexicans until the farm buses came and the farmers picked out the workers they wanted. "You have the house," I said. "For food you have Social Security. And urban renewal must have given you something. It was good in a way when they tore down the laundry. Really, Mama, it was. Otherwise Papa would never have retired. You ought to retire too."

"Do you think your father wanted to stop work? Look at his eyes; the brown is going out of his eyes. He has stopped talking. When I go to work, he eats leftovers. He doesn't cook new food," she said, confessing, me maddened at confessions. "Those Urban Renewal Ghosts gave us moving money. It took us seventeen years to get our customers. How could we start all over on moving money, as if we two old people had another seventeen years in us? Aa"—she flipped something aside with her hand—"White Ghosts can't tell Chinese age."

I closed my eyes and breathed evenly, but she could tell I wasn't asleep.

"This is terrible ghost country, where a human being works her life away," she said. "Even the ghosts work, no time for acrobatics. I have not stopped working since the day the ship landed. I was on my feet the moment the babies were out. In China I never even had to hang up my own clothes. I shouldn't have left, but your father couldn't have supported you without me. I'm the one with the big muscles."

"If you hadn't left, there wouldn't have been a me for you

two to support. Mama, I'm really sleepy. Do you mind letting me sleep?" I do not believe in old age. I do not believe in getting tired.

"I didn't need muscles in China. I was small in China." She was. The silk dresses she gave me are tiny. You would not think the same person wore them. This mother can carry a hundred pounds of Texas rice up- and downstairs. She could work at the laundry from 6:30 A.M. until midnight, shifting a baby from an ironing table to a shelf between packages, to the display window, where the ghosts tapped on the glass. "I put you babies in the clean places at the laundry, as far away from the germs that fumed out of the ghosts' clothes as I could. Aa, their socks and handkerchiefs choked me. I cough now because of those seventeen years of breathing dust. Tubercular handkerchiefs. Lepers' socks." I thought she had wanted to show off my baby sister in the display window.

In the midnight unsteadiness we were back at the laundry, and my mother was sitting on an orange crate sorting dirty clothes into mountains—a sheet mountain, a white shirt mountain, a dark shirt mountain, a work-pants mountain, a long underwear mountain, a short underwear mountain, a little hill of socks pinned together in pairs, a little hill of handkerchiefs pinned to tags. Surrounding her were candles she burned in daylight, clean yellow diamonds, footlights that ringed her, mysterious masked mother, nose and mouth veiled with a cowboy handkerchief. Before undoing the bundles, my mother would light a tall new candle, which was a luxury, and the pie pans full of old wax and wicks that sometimes sputtered blue, a noise I thought was the germs getting seared.

"No tickee, no washee, mama-san?" a ghost would say, so embarrassing.

"Noisy Red-Mouth Ghost," she'd write on its package, naming it, marking its clothes with its name.

Back in the bedroom I said, "The candles must have helped. It was a good idea of yours to use candles."

"They didn't do much good. All I have to do is think about dust sifting out of clothes or peat dirt blowing across a field or chick mash falling from a scoop, and I start coughing." She coughed deeply. "See what I mean? I have worked too much. Human beings don't work like this in China. Time goes slower there. Here we have to hurry, feed the hungry children before we're too old to work. I feel like a mother cat hunting for its kittens. She has to find them fast because in a few hours she will forget how to count or that she had any kittens at all. I can't sleep in this country because it doesn't shut down for the night. Factories, canneries, restaurants—always somebody somewhere working through the night. It never gets done all at once here. Time was different in China. One year lasted as long as my total time here; one evening so long, you could visit your women friends, drink tea, and play cards at each house, and it would still be twilight. It even got boring, nothing to do but fan ourselves. Here midnight comes and the floor's not swept, the ironing's not ready, the money's not made. I would still be young if we lived in China."

"Time is the same from place to place," I said unfeelingly. "There is only the eternal present, and biology. The reason you feel time pushing is that you had six children after you were forty-five and you worried about raising us. You shouldn't worry anymore, though, Mama. You should feel good you had so many babies around you in middle age. Not many mothers have that. Wasn't it like prolonging youth? Now wasn't it? You mustn't worry now. All of us have grown up. And you can stop working."

"I can't stop working. When I stop working, I hurt. My head, my back, my legs hurt. I get dizzy. I can't stop."

"I'm like that too, Mama. I work all the time. Don't worry about me starving. I won't starve. I know how to work. I work all the time. I know how to kill food, how to skin and pluck it. I know how to keep warm by sweeping and mopping. I know how to work when things get bad."

"It's a good thing I taught you children to look after your-selves. We're not going back to China for sure now."

"You've been saying that since nineteen forty-nine."

"Now it's final. We got a letter from the villagers yesterday. They asked if it was all right with us that they took over the land. The last uncles have been killed so your father is the only person left to say it is all right, you see. He has written saying they can have it. So. We have no more China to go home to."

It must be all over then. My mother and father have stoked each other's indignation for almost forty years telling stories about land quarrels among the uncles, the in-laws, the grandparents. Episodes from their various points of view came weekly in the mail, until the uncles were executed kneeling on broken glass by people who had still other plans for the land. How simply it ended—my father writing his permission. Permission asked, permission given twenty-five years after the Revolution.

"We belong to the planet now, Mama. Does it make sense to you that if we're no longer attached to one piece of land, we belong to the planet? Wherever we happen to be standing, why, that spot belongs to us as much as any other spot." Can we spend the fare money on furniture and cars? Will American flowers smell good now?

"I don't want to go back anyway," she said. "I've gotten used to eating. And the Communists are much too mischievous. You should see the ones I meet in the fields. They bring sacks under their clothes to steal grapes and tomatoes from the growers. They come with trucks on Sundays. And they're killing each other in San Francisco." One of the old men caught his visitor, another old fellow, stealing his bantam; the owner spotted its black feet sticking out of his guest's sweater. We woke up one morning to find a hole in the ground where our loquat tree had stood. Later we saw a new loquat tree most similar to ours in a Chinese neighbor's yard. We knew a family who had a sign in their vegetable patch: "Since this is not a Communist garden but cabbages grown by private enterprise, please do not steal from my garden." It was dated and signed in good handwriting.

"The new immigrants aren't Communists, Mother. They're fugitives from the real Communists."

"They're Chinese, and Chinese are mischievous. No, I'm too old to keep up with them. They'd be too clever for me. I've lost my cunning, having grown accustomed to food, you see. There's only one thing that I really want anymore. I want you here, not wandering like a ghost from Romany. I want every one of you living here together. When you're all home, all six of you with your children and husbands and wives, there are twenty or thirty people in this house. Then I'm happy. And your father is happy. Whichever room I walk into overflows with my relatives, grandsons, sons-in-law. I can't turn around without touching somebody. That's the way a house should be." Her eyes are big, inconsolable. A spider headache spreads out in fine branches over my skull. She is etching spider legs into the icy bone. She pries open my head and my fists and crams into them responsibility for time, responsibility for intervening oceans.

The gods pay her and my father back for leaving their parents. My grandmother wrote letters pleading for them to come home, and they ignored her. Now they know how she felt.

"When I'm away from here," I had to tell her, "I don't get sick. I don't go to the hospital every holiday. I don't get pneumonia, no dark spots on my x-rays. My chest doesn't hurt when I breathe. I can breathe. And I don't get headaches at 3:00. I don't have to take medicines or go to doctors. Elsewhere I don't have to lock my doors and keep checking the locks. I don't stand at the windows and watch for movements and see them in the dark."

"What do you mean you don't lock your doors?"

"I do. I do. But not the way I do here. I don't hear ghost sounds. I don't stay awake listening to walking in the kitchen. I don't hear the doors and windows unhinging."

"It was probably just a Wino Ghost or a Hobo Ghost looking for a place to sleep."

"I don't want to hear Wino Ghosts and Hobo Ghosts. I've found some places in this country that are ghost-free. And I think I belong there, where I don't catch colds or use my hospitalization insurance. Here I'm sick so often, I can barely work. I can't help it, Mama."

She yawned. "It's better, then, for you to stay away. The weather in California must not agree with you. You can come for visits." She got up and turned off the light. "Of course, you must go, Little Dog."

A weight lifted from me. The quilts must be filling with air. The world is somehow lighter. She has not called me that endearment for years—a name to fool the gods. I am really a Dragon, as she is a Dragon, both of us born in dragon years. I am practically a first daughter of a first daughter.

"Good night, Little Dog."

"Good night, Mother."

She sends me on my way, working always and now old, dreaming the dreams about shrinking babies and the sky covered with airplanes and a Chinatown bigger than the ones here.

At the Western Palace

Wꜰᴇɴ ꜱʜᴇ was about sixty-eight years old, Brave Orchid took a day off to wait at San Francisco International Airport for the plane that was bringing her sister to the United States. She had not seen Moon Orchid for thirty years. She had begun this waiting at home, getting up a half-hour before Moon Orchid's plane took off in Hong Kong. Brave Orchid would add her will power to the forces that keep an airplane up. Her head hurt with the concentration. The plane had to be light, so no matter how tired she felt, she dared not rest her spirit on a wing but continuously and gently pushed up on the plane's belly. She had already been waiting at the airport for nine hours. She was wakeful.

Next to Brave Orchid sat Moon Orchid's only daughter, who was helping her aunt wait. Brave Orchid had made two of her own children come too because they could drive, but they had been lured away by the magazine racks and the gift shops and coffee shops. Her American children could not sit for very long. They did not understand sitting; they had wandering feet. She hoped they would get back from the pay t.v.'s or the pay toilets or wherever they were spending their money before the plane arrived. If they did not come back soon, she would go look for them. If her son thought he could hide in the men's room, he was wrong.

"Are you all right, Aunt?" asked her niece.

"No, this chair hurts me. Help me pull some chairs together so I can put my feet up."

She unbundled a blanket and spread it out to make a bed for herself. On the floor she had two shopping bags full of canned peaches, real peaches, beans wrapped in taro leaves, cookies, Thermos bottles, enough food for everybody, though only her niece would eat with her. Her bad boy and bad girl were probably sneaking hamburgers, wasting their money. She would scold them.

Many soldiers and sailors sat about, oddly calm, like little boys in cowboy uniforms. (She thought "cowboy" was what

97

you would call a Boy Scout.) They should have been crying hysterically on their way to Vietnam. "If I see one that looks Chinese," she thought, "I'll go over and give him some advice." She sat up suddenly; she had forgotten about her own son, who was even now in Vietnam. Carefully she split her attention, beaming half of it to the ocean, into the water to keep him afloat. He was on a ship. He was in Vietnamese waters. She was sure of it. He and the other children were lying to her. They had said he was in Japan, and then they said he was in the Philippines. But when she sent him her help, she could feel that he was on a ship in Da Nang. Also she had seen the children hide the envelopes that his letters came in.

"Do you think my son is in Vietnam?" she asked her niece, who was dutifully eating.

"No. Didn't your children say he was in the Philippines?"

"Have you ever seen any of his letters with Philippine stamps on them?"

"Oh, yes. Your children showed me one."

"I wouldn't put it past them to send the letters to some Filipino they know. He puts Manila postmarks on them to fool me."

"Yes, I can imagine them doing that. But don't worry. Your son can take care of himself. All your children can take care of themselves."

"Not him. He's not like other people. Not normal at all. He sticks erasers in his ears, and the erasers are still attached to the pencil stubs. The captain will say, 'Abandon ship,' or, 'Watch out for bombs,' and he won't hear. He doesn't listen to orders. I told him to flee to Canada, but he wouldn't go."

She closed her eyes. After a short while, plane and ship under control, she looked again at the children in uniforms. Some of the blond ones looked like baby chicks, their crew cuts like the downy yellow on baby chicks. You had to feel sorry for them even though they were Army and Navy Ghosts.

Suddenly her son and daughter came running. "Come, Mother. The plane's landed early. She's here already." They hurried, folding up their mother's encampment. She was glad her children were not useless. They must have known what this trip to San Francisco was about then. "It's a good thing I made you come early," she said.

Brave Orchid pushed to the front of the crowd. She had to be in front. The passengers were separated from the people waiting for them by glass doors and walls. Immigration Ghosts were stamping papers. The travellers crowded along some conveyor belts to have their luggage searched. Brave Orchid did not see her sister anywhere. She stood watching for four hours. Her children left and came back. "Why don't you sit down?" they asked.

"The chairs are too far away," she said.

"Why don't you sit on the floor then?"

No, she would stand, as her sister was probably standing in a line she could not see from here. Her American children had no feelings and no memory.

To while away time, she and her niece talked about the Chinese passengers. These new immigrants had it easy. On Ellis Island the people were thin after forty days at sea and had no fancy luggage.

"That one looks like her," Brave Orchid would say.

"No, that's not her."

Ellis Island had been made out of wood and iron. Here everything was new plastic, a ghost trick to lure immigrants into feeling safe and spilling their secrets. Then the Alien Office could send them right back. Otherwise, why did they lock her out, not letting her help her sister answer questions and spell her name? At Ellis Island when the ghost asked Brave Orchid what year her husband had cut off his pigtail, a Chinese who was crouching on the floor motioned her not to talk. "I don't know," she had said. If it weren't for that Chinese man, she might not be here today, or her husband either. She hoped some Chinese, a janitor or a clerk, would look out for Moon Orchid. Luggage conveyors fooled immigrants into thinking the Gold Mountain was going to be easy.

Brave Orchid felt her heart jump—Moon Orchid. "There she is," she shouted. But her niece saw it was not her mother at all. And it shocked her to discover the woman her aunt was pointing out. This was a young woman, younger than herself, no older than Moon Orchid the day the sisters parted. "Moon Orchid will have changed a little, of course," Brave Orchid was saying. "She will have learned to wear western clothes." The woman wore a navy blue suit with a bunch of dark cherries at the shoulder.

"No, Aunt," said the niece. "That's not my mother."

"Perhaps not. It's been so many years. Yes, it is your mother. It must be. Let her come closer, and we can tell. Do you think she's too far away for me to tell, or is it my eyes getting bad?"

"It's too many years gone by," said the niece.

Brave Orchid turned suddenly—another Moon Orchid, this one a neat little woman with a bun. She was laughing at something the person ahead of her in line said. Moon Orchid was just like that, laughing at nothing. "I would be able to tell the difference if one of them would only come closer," Brave Orchid said with tears, which she did not wipe. Two children met the woman with the cherries, and she shook their hands. The other woman was met by a young man. They looked at each other gladly, then walked away side by side.

Up close neither one of those women looked like Moon Orchid at all. "Don't worry, Aunt," said the niece. "I'll know her."

"I'll know her too. I knew her before you did."

The niece said nothing, although she had seen her mother only five years ago. Her aunt liked having the last word.

Finally Brave Orchid's children quit wandering and drooped on a railing. Who knew what they were thinking? At last the niece called out, "I see her! I see her! Mother! Mother!" Whenever the doors parted, she shouted, probably embarrassing the American cousins, but she didn't care. She called out, "Mama! Mama!" until the crack in the sliding doors became too small to let in her voice. "Mama!" What a strange word in an adult voice. Many people turned to see what adult was calling, "Mama!" like a child. Brave Orchid saw an old, old woman jerk her head up, her little eyes blinking confusedly, a woman whose nerves leapt toward the sound anytime she heard "Mama!" Then she relaxed to her own business again. She was a tiny, tiny lady, very thin, with little fluttering hands, and her hair was in a gray knot. She was dressed in a gray wool suit; she wore pearls around her neck and in her earlobes. Moon Orchid *would* travel with her jewels showing. Brave Orchid momentarily saw, like a larger, younger outline around this old woman, the sister she had been waiting for. The familiar dim halo faded, leaving the woman so old, so gray. So old. Brave Orchid pressed against the glass. *That* old lady? Yes, that old lady facing the ghost who stamped her papers without questioning her was her sister. Then, without noticing her family, Moon Orchid walked smiling over to the Suitcase Inspector Ghost, who took her boxes apart, pulling out puffs of tissue. From where she was, Brave Orchid could not see what her sister had chosen to carry across the ocean. She wished her sister would look her way. Brave Orchid thought that if *she* were entering a new country, she would be at the windows. Instead Moon Orchid hovered over the unwrapping, surprised at each reappearance as if she were opening presents after a birthday party.

"Mama!" Moon Orchid's daughter kept calling. Brave Orchid said to her children, "Why don't you call your aunt too? Maybe she'll hear us if all of you call out together." But her children slunk away. Maybe that shame-face they so often wore was American politeness.

"Mama!" Moon Orchid's daughter called again, and this time her mother looked right at her. She left her bundles in a heap and came running. "Hey!" the Customs Ghost yelled at her. She went back to clear up her mess, talking inaudibly to her daughter all the while. Her daughter pointed toward Brave Orchid. And at last Moon Orchid looked at her—two old women with faces like mirrors.

Their hands reached out as if to touch the other's face, then returned to their own, the fingers checking the grooves in the forehead and along the side of the mouth. Moon Orchid, who never understood the gravity of things, started smiling and laughing, pointing at Brave Orchid. Finally Moon Orchid gathered up her stuff, strings hanging and papers loose, and met her sister at the door, where they shook hands, oblivious to blocking the way.

"You're an old woman," said Brave Orchid.

"Aiaa. *You're* an old woman."

"But you are really old. Surely, you can't say that about me. I'm not old the way you're old."

"But *you* really are old. You're one year older than I am."

"Your hair is white and your face all wrinkled."

"You're so skinny."

"You're so fat."

"Fat women are more beautiful than skinny women."

The children pulled them out of the doorway. One of Brave

Orchid's children brought the car from the parking lot, and the other heaved the luggage into the trunk. They put the two old ladies and the niece in the back seat. All the way home— across the Bay Bridge, over the Diablo hills, across the San Joaquin River to the valley, the valley moon so white at dusk— all the way home, the two sisters exclaimed every time they turned to look at each other, "Aiaa! How old!"

Brave Orchid forgot that she got sick in cars, that all vehicles but palanquins made her dizzy. "You're so old," she kept saying. "How did you get so old?"

Brave Orchid had tears in her eyes. But Moon Orchid said, "You look older than I. You *are* older than I," and again she'd laugh. "You're wearing an old mask to tease me." It surprised Brave Orchid that after thirty years she could still get annoyed at her sister's silliness.

Brave Orchid's husband was waiting under the tangerine tree. Moon Orchid recognized him as the brother-in-law in photographs, not as the young man who left on a ship. Her sister had married the ideal in masculine beauty, the thin scholar with the hollow cheeks and the long fingers. And here he was, an old man, opening the gate he had built with his own hands, his hair blowing silver in twilight. "Hello," he said like an Englishman in Hong Kong. "Hello," she said like an English telephone operator. He went to help his children unload the car, gripping the suitcase handles in his bony fingers, his bony wrists locked.

Brave Orchid's husband and children brought everything into the dining room, provisions for a lifetime move heaped all over the floor and furniture. Brave Orchid wanted to have a luck ceremony and then to put things away where they belonged, but Moon Orchid said, "I've got presents for everybody. Let me get them." She opened her boxes again. Her suitcase lids gaped like mouths; Brave Orchid had better hurry with the luck.

"First I've got shoes for all of you from Lovely Orchid," Moon Orchid said, handing them out to her nieces and nephews, who grimaced at one another. Lovely Orchid, the youngest aunt, owned either a shoe store or a shoe factory in Hong Kong. That was why every Christmas she sent a dozen pairs, glittering with yellow and pink plastic beads, sequins, and turquoise blue flowers. "She must give us the leftovers," Brave Orchid's children were saying in English. As Brave Orchid ran back and forth turning on all the lights, every lamp and bulb, she glared sideways at her children. They would be sorry when they had to walk barefoot through snow and rocks because they didn't take what shoes they could, even if the wrong size. She would put the slippers next to the bathtub on the linoleum floors in winter and trick her lazy children into wearing them.

"May I have some scissors? Oh, where are my scissors?" said Moon Orchid. She slit the heel of a black embroidered slipper and pulled out the cotton—which was entangled with jewels. "You'll have to let me pierce your ears," she told her nieces, rubbing their earlobes. "Then you can wear these." There were earrings with skewers like gold krisses. There was a jade heart and an opal. Brave Orchid interrupted her dashing about to rub the stones against her skin.

Moon Orchid laughed softly in delight. "And look here. Look here," she said. She was holding up a paper warrior-saint, and he was all intricacies and light. A Communist had cut a wisp of black paper into a hero with sleeves like butterflies' wings and with tassels and flags, which fluttered when you breathed on him. "Did someone really cut this out by hand?" the children kept asking. "Really?" The eyebrows and mustache, the fierce wrinkles between the eyes, the face, all were the merest black webs. His open hand had been cut out finger by finger. Through the spaces you could see light and the room and each other. "Oh, there's more. There's more," said Moon Orchid happily. She picked up another paper cutout and blew on it. It was the scholar who always carries a fan; her breath shook its blue feathers. His brush and quill and scrolls tied with ribbon jutted out of lace vases. "And more"—an orange warrior-poet with sword and scroll; a purple knight with doily armor, holes for scales; a wonderful archer on a red horse with a mane like fire; a modern Communist worker with a proud gold hammer; a girl Communist soldier with pink pigtails and pink rifle. "And this is Fa Mu Lan," she said. "She was a woman warrior, and really existed." Fa Mu Lan was green and beautiful, and her robes whirled out as she drew her sword.

"Paper dolls," said Brave Orchid to her children. "I'd have

thought you were too old to be playing with dolls." How greedy to play with presents in front of the giver. How impolite ("untraditional" in Chinese) her children were. With a slam of her cleaver, she cracked rock candy into jagged pieces. "Take some," she urged. "Take more." She brought the yellow crystals on a red paper plate to her family, one by one. It was very important that the beginning be sweet. Her children acted as if this eating were a bother. "Oh, all right," they said, and took the smallest slivers. Who would think that children could dislike candy? It was abnormal, not in the nature of children, not human. "Take a big piece," she scolded. She'd make them eat it like medicine if necessary. They were so stupid, surely they weren't adults yet. They'd put the bad mouth on their aunt's first American day; you had to sweeten their noisy barbarous mouths. She opened the front door and mumbled something. She opened the back door and mumbled something.

"What do you say when you open the door like that?" her children used to ask when they were younger.

"Nothing. Nothing," she would answer.

"Is it spirits, Mother? Do you talk to spirits? Are you asking them in or asking them out?"

"It's nothing," she said. She never explained anything that was really important. They no longer asked.

When she came back from talking to the invisibilities, Brave Orchid saw that her sister was strewing the room. The paper people clung flat against the lampshades, the chairs, the tablecloths. Moon Orchid left fans unfolded and dragons with accordion bodies dangling from doorknobs. She was unrolling white silk. "Men are good at stitching roosters," she was pointing out bird embroidery. It was amazing how a person could grow old without learning to put things away.

"Let's put these things away," Brave Orchid said.

"Oh, Sister," said Moon Orchid. "Look what I have for you," and she held up a pale green silk dress lined in wool. "In winter you can look like summer and be warm like summer." She unbuttoned the frogs to show the lining, thick and plaid like a blanket.

"Now where would I wear such a fancy dress?" said Brave Orchid. "Give it to one of the children."

"I have bracelets and earrings for them."

"They're too young for jewelry. They'll lose it."

"They seem very big for children."

"The girls broke six jade bracelets playing baseball. And they can't endure pain. They scream when I squeeze their hands into the jade. Then that very day, they'll break it. We'll put the jewelry in the bank, and we'll buy glass and black wood frames for the silk scrolls." She bundled up the sticks that opened into flowers. "What were you doing carrying these scraps across the ocean?"

Brave Orchid took what was useful and solid into the back bedroom, where Moon Orchid would stay until they decided what she would do permanently. Moon Orchid picked up pieces of string, but bright colors and movements distracted her. "Oh, look at this," she'd say. "Just look at this. You have carp." She was turning the light off and on in the goldfish tank, which sat in the rolltop desk that Brave Orchid's husband had taken from the gambling house when it shut down during World War II. Moon Orchid looked up at the grandparents' photographs that hung on the wall above the desk. Then she turned around and looked at the opposite wall; there, equally large, were pictures of Brave Orchid and her husband. They had put up their own pictures because later the children would not have the sense to do it.

"Oh, look," said Moon Orchid. "Your pictures are up too. Why is that?"

"No reason. Nothing," said Brave Orchid. "In America you can put up anybody's picture you like."

On the shelf of the rolltop desk, like a mantel under the grandparents' photos, there were bowls of plastic tangerines and oranges, crepe-paper flowers, plastic vases, porcelain vases filled with sand and incense sticks. A clock sat on a white runner crocheted with red phoenixes and red words about how lucky and bright life is. Moon Orchid lifted the ruffles to look inside the pigeon holes. There were also pen trays and little drawers, enough so that the children could each have one or two for their very own. The fish tank took up half the desk space, and there was still room for writing. The rolltop was gone; the children had broken it slat by slat when they hid inside the desk, pulling the top over themselves. The knee hole had boxes of toys that the married children's children played with now. Brave Orchid's husband had padlocked one large bottom cabinet and one drawer.

"Why do you keep it locked?" Moon Orchid asked. "What's in here?"

"Nothing," he said. "Nothing."

"If you want to poke around," said Brave Orchid, "why don't you find out what's in the kitchen drawers so you can help me cook?"

They cooked enough food to cover the dining room and kitchen tables. "Eat!" Brave Orchid ordered. "Eat!" She would not allow anybody to talk while eating. In some families the children worked out a sign language, but here the children would speak English, which their parents didn't seem to hear.

After they ate and cleaned up, Brave Orchid said, "Now! We have to get down to business."

"What do you mean?" said her sister. She and her daughter held one another's hands.

"Oh, no. I don't want to listen to this," said Brave Orchid's husband, and left to read in bed.

The three women sat in the enormous kitchen with the butcher's block and two refrigerators. Brave Orchid had an inside stove in the kitchen and a stove outside on the back porch. All day long the outside stove cooked peelings and gristle into chicken feed. It horrified the children when they caught her throwing scraps of chicken into the chicken feed. Both stoves had been turned off for the night now, and the air was cooling.

"Wait until morning, Aunt," said Moon Orchid's daughter. "Let her get some sleep."

"Yes, I do need rest after travelling all the way from China," she said. "I'm here. You've done it and brought me here." Moon Orchid meant that they should be satisfied with what they had already accomplished. Indeed, she stretched happily and appeared quite satisfied to be sitting in that kitchen at that moment. "I want to go to sleep early because of jet lag," she said, but Brave Orchid, who had never been on an airplane, did not let her.

"What are we going to do about your husband?" Brave Orchid asked quickly. That ought to wake her up.

"I don't know. Do we have to do something?"

"He does not know you're here."

Moon Orchid did not say anything. For thirty years she had been receiving money from him from America. But she had never told him that she wanted to come to the United States. She waited for him to suggest it, but he never did. Nor did she tell him that her sister had been working for years to transport her here. First Brave Orchid had found a Chinese-American husband for her daughter. Then the daughter had come and had been able to sign the papers to bring Moon Orchid over.

"We have to tell him you've arrived," said Brave Orchid.

Moon Orchid's eyes got big like a child's. "I shouldn't be here," she said.

"Nonsense. I want you here, and your daughter wants you here."

"But that's all."

"Your husband is going to have to see you. We'll make him recognize you. Ha. Won't it be fun to see his face? You'll go to his house. And when his second wife answers the door, you say, 'I want to speak to my husband,' and you name his personal name. 'Tell him I'll be sitting in the family room.' Walk past her as if she were a servant. She'll scold him when he comes home from work, and it'll serve him right. You yell at him too."

"I'm scared," said Moon Orchid. "I want to go back to Hong Kong."

"You can't. It's too late. You've sold your apartment. See here. We know his address. He's living in Los Angeles with his second wife, and they have three children. Claim your rights. Those are *your* children. He's got two sons. *You* have two sons. You take them away from her. You become their mother."

"Do you really think I can be a mother of sons? Don't you think they'll be loyal to her, since she gave birth to them?"

"The children will go to their true mother—you," said Brave Orchid. "That's the way it is with mothers and children."

"Do you think he'll get angry at me because I came without telling him?"

"He deserves your getting angry with him. For abandoning you and for abandoning your daughter."

"He didn't abandon me. He's given me so much money. I've had all the food and clothes and servants I've ever wanted.

And he's supported our daughter too, even though she's only a girl. He sent her to college. I can't bother him. I mustn't bother him."

"How can you let him get away with this? Bother him. He deserves to be bothered. How dare he marry somebody else when he has you? How can you sit there so calmly? He would've let you stay in China forever. *I* had to send for your daughter, and *I* had to send for you. Urge her," she turned to her niece. "Urge her to go look for him."

"I think you should go look for my father," she said. "I'd like to meet him. I'd like to see what my father looks like."

"What does it matter what he's like?" said her mother. "You're a grown woman with a husband and children of your own. You don't need a father—or a mother either. You're only curious."

"In this country," said Brave Orchid, "many people make their daughters their heirs. If you don't go see him, he'll give everything to the second wife's children."

"But he gives us everything anyway. What more do I have to ask for? If I see him face to face, what is there to say?"

"I can think of hundreds of things," said Brave Orchid. "Oh, how I'd love to be in your place. I could tell him so many things. What scenes I could make. You're so wishy-washy."

"Yes, I am."

"You have to ask him why he didn't come home. Why he turned into a barbarian. Make him feel bad about leaving his mother and father. Scare him. Walk right into his house with your suitcases and boxes. Move right into the bedroom. Throw her stuff out of the drawers and put yours in. Say, 'I am the first wife, and she is our servant.'"

"Oh, no, I can't do that. I can't do that at all. That's terrible."

"Of course you can. I'll teach you. 'I am the first wife, and she is our servant.' And you teach the little boys to call you Mother."

"I don't think I'd be very good with little boys. Little American boys. Our brother is the only boy I've known. Aren't they very rough and unfeeling?"

"Yes, but they're yours. Another thing I'd do if I were you, I'd get a job and help him out. Show him I could make his life easier; how I didn't need his money."

"He has a great deal of money, doesn't he?"

"Yes, he can do some job the barbarians value greatly."

"Could I find a job like that? I've never had a job."

"You could be a maid in a hotel," Brave Orchid advised. "A lot of immigrants start that way nowadays. And the maids get to bring home all the leftover soap and the clothes people leave behind."

"I would clean up after people, then?"

Brave Orchid looked at this delicate sister. She was such a little old lady. She had long fingers and thin, soft hands. And she had a high-class city accent from living in Hong Kong. Not a trace of village accent remained; she had been away from the village for that long. But Brave Orchid would not relent; her dainty sister would just have to toughen up. "Immigrants also work in the canneries, where it's so noisy it doesn't matter if they speak Chinese or what. The easiest way to find a job, though, is to work in Chinatown. You get twenty-five cents an hour and all your meals if you're working in a restaurant."

If she were in her sister's place, Brave Orchid would have been on the phone immediately, demanding one of those Chinatown jobs. She would make the boss agree that she start work as soon as he opened his doors the next morning. Immigrants nowadays were bandits, beating up store owners and stealing from them rather than working. It must've been the Communists who taught them those habits.

Moon Orchid rubbed her forehead. The kitchen light shined warmly on the gold and jade rings that gave her hands completeness. One of the rings was a wedding ring. Brave Orchid, who had been married for almost fifty years, did not wear any rings. They got in the way of all the work. She did not want the gold to wash away in the dishwater and the laundry water and the field water. She looked at her younger sister whose very wrinkles were fine. "Forget about a job," she said, which was very lenient of her. "You won't have to work. You just go to your husband's house and demand your rights as First Wife. When you see him, you can say, 'Do you remember me?'"

"What if he doesn't?"

"Then start telling him details about your life together in China. Act like a fortuneteller. He'll be so impressed."

"Do you think he'll be glad to see me?"

"He better be glad to see you."

As midnight came, twenty-two hours after she left Hong Kong, Moon Orchid began to tell her sister that she really was going to face her husband. "He won't like me," she said.

"Maybe you should dye your hair black, so he won't think you're old. Or I have a wig you can borrow. On the other hand, he should see how you've suffered. Yes, let him see how he's made your hair turn white."

These many hours, her daughter held Moon Orchid's hand. The two of them had been separated for five years. Brave Orchid had mailed the daughter's young photograph to a rich and angry man with citizenship papers. He was a tyrant. Mother and daughter were sorry for one another. "Let's not talk about this anymore," said Moon Orchid. "We can plan tomorrow. I want to hear about my grandchildren. Tell me about them. I have three grandchildren, don't I?" she asked her daughter.

Brave Orchid thought that her niece was like her mother, the lovely, useless type. She had spent so much time trying to toughen up these two. "The children are very smart, Mother," her niece was saying. "The teachers say they are brilliant. They can speak Chinese and English. They'll be able to talk to you."

"My children can talk to you too," said Brave Orchid. "Come. Talk to your aunt," she ordered.

Her sons and daughters mumbled and disappeared—into the bathroom, the basement, the various hiding places they had dug throughout the house. One of them locked herself in the pantry-storeroom, where she had cleared off a shelf for a desk among the food. Brave Orchid's children were antisocial and secretive. Ever since they were babies, they had burrowed little nests for themselves in closets and underneath stairs; they made tents under tables and behind doors. "My children are also very bright," she said. "Let me show you before you go to sleep." She took her sister to the living room where she had a glass case, a large upside-down fish tank, and inside were her children's athletic trophies and scholarship trophies. There was even a beauty contest trophy. She had decorated them with runners about luck.

"Oh my, isn't that wonderful?" said the aunt. "You must

be so proud of them. Your children must be so smart." The children who were in the living room groaned and left. Brave Orchid did not understand why they were ashamed of the things they could do. It was hard to believe that they could do the things the trophies said they did. Maybe they had stolen them from the real winners. Maybe they had bought cups and medallions and pretended they'd won them. She'd have to accuse them and see how they reacted. Perhaps they fooled the Ghost Teachers and Ghost Coaches, who couldn't tell smart Chinese from dumb Chinese. Her children certainly didn't seem like much.

She made some of the children sleep on the floor and put Moon Orchid and her daughter in their room. "Will my mother be living at your house or my house?" her niece asked Brave Orchid.

"She's going to live with her own husband." Brave Orchid was firm. She would not forget about this subject in the morning.

The next day, immediately after breakfast, Brave Orchid talked about driving to Los Angeles. They would not take the coast route along mountainsides that dropped into the sea— the way her children, who liked carnival rides, would want to go. She would make them take the inland route, flat and direct.

"The first thing you've got to ask your husband," she said, "is why he never came back to China when he got rich."

"All right," said Moon Orchid. She was poking about the house, holding cans up to her ear, trailing after the children.

"He probably has a car," Brave Orchid persisted. "He can drive you places. Should he tell you to go away, turn around at the door and say, 'May I come and watch your television now and then?' Oh, wouldn't that be pathetic? But he won't kick you out. No, he won't. You walk right into the bedroom, and you open the second wife's closet. Take whatever clothes you like. That will give you an American wardrobe."

"Oh, I can't do that."

"You can! You can! Take First Sister-in-Law as your example." Their only brother had had a first wife in the village, but he took a second wife in Singapore, where he went to make his gold. Big Wife suffered during the Revolution. "The

Communists will kill me," she wrote to her husband, "and you're having fun in Singapore." Little Wife felt so sorry for her, she reminded her husband that he owed it to Big Wife to get her out of China before it was too late. Little Wife saved the passage fare and did the paper work. But when Big Wife came, she chased Little Wife out of the house. There was nothing for their husband to do but build a second house, one for each wife and the children of each wife. They did get together, however, for yearly family portraits. Their sons' first and second wives were also in the pictures, first wives next to the husbands and second wives standing among the children. "Copy our sister-in-law," Brave Orchid instructed. "Make life unbearable for the second wife, and she'll leave. He'll have to build her a second house."

"I wouldn't mind if she stays," said Moon Orchid. "She can comb my hair and keep house. She can wash the dishes and serve our meals. And she can take care of the little boys." Moon Orchid laughed. Again it occurred to Brave Orchid that her sister wasn't very bright, and she had not gotten any smarter in the last thirty years.

"You must make it plain to your husband right at the start what you expect of him. That is what a wife is for—to scold her husband into becoming a good man. Tell him there will be no third wife. Tell him you may go visiting anytime you please. And I, the big sister, may visit your house for as long as I please. Let him know exactly how much money you expect for allowance."

"Should I ask for more or less money now that I'm here?"

"More, of course. Food costs more here. Tell him that your daughter, who is the oldest, must inherit his property. You have to establish these things at the start. Don't begin meek."

Sometimes Moon Orchid seemed to listen too readily—as if her sister were only talking-story. "Have you seen him in all these years?" she asked Brave Orchid.

"No. The last time I saw him was in China—with you. What a terrible, ugly man he must be not to send for you. I'll bet he's hoping you'd be satisfied with his money. How evil he is. You've had to live like a widow for thirty years. You're lucky he didn't have his second wife write you telling you he's dead."

"Oh, no, he wouldn't do that."

"Of course not. He would be afraid of cursing himself."

"But if he is so ugly and mean, maybe I shouldn't bother with him."

"I remember him," said her daughter. "He wrote me a nice letter."

"You couldn't remember him," said her mother. "You were an infant when he left. He never writes letters; he only sends money orders."

Moon Orchid hoped that the summer would wear away while her sister talked, that Brave Orchid would then find autumn too cold for travel. Brave Orchid did not enjoy travelling. She found it so nauseating that she was still recovering from the trip to San Francisco. Many of the children were home for the summer, and Moon Orchid tried to figure out which one was which. Brave Orchid had written about them in her letters, and Moon Orchid tried to match them up with the descriptions. There was indeed an oldest girl who was absent-minded and messy. She had an American name that sounded like "Ink" in Chinese. "Ink!" Moon Orchid called out; sure enough, a girl smeared with ink said, "Yes?" Then Brave Orchid worried over a daughter who had the mark of an unlucky woman; yes, there was certainly a girl with an upper lip as curled as Brigitte Bardot's. Moon Orchid rubbed this niece's hands and cold feet. There was a boy Brave Orchid said was thick headed. She had written that when he crawled as a baby his head was so heavy he kept dropping it on the floor. Moon Orchid did indeed see a boy whose head was big, his curls enlarging it, his eyebrows thick and slanted like an opera warrior's. Moon Orchid could not tell whether he was any less quick than the others. None of them were articulate or friendly. Brave Orchid had written about a boy whose oddity it was to stick pencil stubs in his ears. Moon Orchid sneaked up on the boys and lifted their hair to look for pencil stubs. "He hangs upside down from the furniture like a bat," his mother wrote. "And he doesn't obey." Moon Orchid didn't find a boy who looked like a bat, and no stubs, so decided that that boy must be the one in Vietnam. And the nephew with the round face and round eyes was the "inaccessible cliff." She immediately recognized the youngest girl, "the raging billows." "Stop following me around!" she shouted at her aunt. "Quit hanging over my neck!"

"What are you doing?" Moon Orchid would ask. "What are you reading?"

"Nothing!" this girl would yell. "You're breathing on me. Don't breathe on me."

It took Moon Orchid several weeks to figure out just how many children there were because some only visited and did not live at home. Some seemed to be married and had children of their own. The babies that spoke no Chinese at all, she decided, were the grandchildren.

None of Brave Orchid's children was happy like the two real Chinese babies who died. Maybe what was wrong was that they had no Oldest Son and no Oldest Daughter to guide them. "I don't see how any of them could support themselves," Brave Orchid said. "I don't see how anybody could want to marry them." Yet, Moon Orchid noticed, some of them seemed to have a husband or a wife who found them bearable.

"They'll never learn how to work," Brave Orchid complained.

"Maybe they're still playing," said Moon Orchid, although they didn't act playful.

"Say good morning to your aunt," Brave Orchid would order, although some of them were adults. "Say good morning to your aunt," she commanded every morning.

"Good morning, Aunt," they said, turning to face her, staring directly into her face. Even the girls stared at her—like cat-headed birds. Moon Orchid jumped and squirmed when they did that. They looked directly into her eyes as if they were looking for lies. Rude. Accusing. They never lowered their gaze; they hardly blinked.

"Why didn't you teach your girls to be demure?" she ventured.

"Demure!" Brave Orchid yelled. "They *are* demure. They're so demure, they barely talk."

It was true that the children made no conversation. Moon Orchid would try to draw them out. They must have many interesting savage things to say, raised as they'd been in the wilderness. They made rough movements, and their accents were not American exactly, but peasant like their mother's, as if they had come from a village deep inside China. She never saw the girls wear the gowns she had given them. The young, raging one, growled in her sleep, "Leave me alone." Sometimes when the girls were reading or watching television, she crept up behind them with a comb and tried to smooth their hair, but they shook their heads, and they turned and fixed her with those eyes. She wondered what they thought and what they saw when they looked at her like that. She liked coming upon them from the back to avoid being looked at. They were like animals the way they stared.

She hovered over a child who was reading, and she pointed at certain words. "What's that?" she tapped at a section that somebody had underlined or annotated. If the child was being patient, he said, "That's an important part."

"Why is it important?"

"Because it tells the main idea here."

"What's the main idea?"

"I don't know the Chinese words for it."

"They're so clever," Moon Orchid would exclaim. "They're so smart. Isn't it wonderful they know things that can't be said in Chinese?"

"Thank you," the child said. When she complimented them, they agreed with her! Not once did she hear a child deny a compliment.

"You're pretty," she said.

"Thank you, Aunt," they answered. How vain. She marveled at their vanity.

"You play the radio beautifully," she teased, and sure enough, they gave one another puzzled looks. She tried all kinds of compliments, and they never said, "Oh, no, you're too kind. I can't play it at all. I'm stupid. I'm ugly." They were capable children; they could do servants' work. But they were not modest.

"What time is it?" she asked, testing what kinds of minds they had, raised away from civilization. She discovered they could tell time very well. And they knew the Chinese words for "thermometer" and "library."

She saw them eat undercooked meat, and they smelled like cow's milk. At first she thought they were so clumsy, they spilled it on their clothes. But soon she decided they themselves smelled of milk. They were big and smelled of milk; they were young and had white hair.

When Brave Orchid screamed at them to dress better, Moon

Orchid defended them, sweet wild animals that they were. "But they enjoy looking like furry animals. That's it, isn't it? You enjoy looking like wild animals, don't you?"

"I don't look like a wild animal!" the child would yell like its mother.

"Like an Indian, then. Right?"

"No!"

Moon Orchid stroked their poor white hair. She tugged at their sleeves and poked their shoulders and stomachs. It was as if she were seeing how much it took to provoke a savage.

"Stop poking me!" they would roar, except for the girl with the cold hands and feet.

"Mm," she mused. "Now the child is saying, 'Stop poking me.'"

Brave Orchid put her sister to work cleaning and sewing and cooking. Moon Orchid was eager to work, roughing it in the wilderness. But Brave Orchid scolded her, "Can't you go any faster than that?" It infuriated Brave Orchid that her sister held up each dish between thumb and forefinger, squirted detergent on the back and front, and ran water without plugging up the drain. Moon Orchid only laughed when Brave Orchid scolded, "Oh, stop that with the dishes. Here. Take this dress and hem it." But Moon Orchid immediately got the thread tangled and laughed about that.

In the mornings Brave Orchid and her husband arose at 6 A.M. He drank a cup of coffee and walked downtown to open up the laundry. Brave Orchid made breakfast for the children who would take the first laundry shift; the ones going to summer school would take the afternoon and night shifts. She put her husband's breakfast into the food container that she had bought in Chinatown, one dish in each tier of the stack. Some mornings Brave Orchid brought the food to the laundry, and other days she sent it with one of the children, but the children let the soup slosh out when they rode over bumps on their bikes. They dangled the tiers from one handlebar and the rice kettle from the other. They were too lazy to walk. Now that her sister and niece were visiting, Brave Orchid went to the laundry later. "Be sure you heat everything up before serving it to your father," she yelled after her son. "And make him coffee after breakfast. And wash the dishes." He would eat with his father and start work.

She walked her sister and niece to the laundry by way of Chinatown. Brave Orchid pointed out the red, green, and gold Chinese school. From the street they could hear children's voices singing the lesson "I Am a Person of the Middle Nation." In front of one of the benevolent associations, a literate man was chanting the *Gold Mountain News*, which was taped to the window. The listening crowd looked at the pictures and said, "Aiaa."

"So this is the United States," Moon Orchid said. "It certainly looks different from China. I'm glad to see the Americans talk like us."

Brave Orchid was again startled at her sister's denseness. "These aren't the Americans. These are the overseas Chinese."

By the time they got to the laundry, the boiler was screaming hot and the machines were ready. "Don't touch or lean against any machine," Brave Orchid warned her sister. "Your skin would fry and peel off." In the midst of the presses stood the sleeve machine, looking like twin silver spaceships. Brave Orchid's husband fitted the shirt sleeves over it with a karate chop between the shoulder blades. "You mustn't back into that," said Brave Orchid.

"You should start off with an easy job," she said. But all the jobs seemed hard for Moon Orchid, who was wearing stockings and dress shoes and a suit. The buttons on the presses seemed too complicated for her to push—and what if she caught her hands or her head inside a press? She was already playing with the water jets dancing on springs from the ceiling. She could fold towels, Brave Orchid decided, and handkerchiefs, but there would be no clean dry clothes until afternoon. Already the temperature was going up.

"Can you iron?" Brave Orchid asked. Perhaps her sister could do the hand-finishing on the shirts when they came off the machines. This was usually Brave Orchid's husband's job. He had such graceful fingers, so good for folding shirts to fit the cardboard patterns that he had cut from campaign posters and fight and wrestling posters. He finished the shirts with a blue band around each.

"Oh, I'd love to try that," Moon Orchid said. Brave Orchid gave her sister her husband's shirts to practice on. She showed her how family clothes were marked with the ideograph "middle," which is a box with a line through its center. Moon Orchid tugged at the first shirt for half an hour, and she folded it crooked, the buttonholes not lined up with the buttons at all. When a customer came in, her ironing table next to the little stand with the tickets, she did not say "hello" but giggled, leaving the iron on the shirt until it turned yellow and had to be whitened with peroxide. Then she said it was so hot she couldn't breathe.

"Go take a walk," Brave Orchid said, exasperated. Even the children could work. Both girls and boys could sew. "Free Mending and Buttons," said the lettering on the window. The children could work all of the machines, even when they were little and had to stand on apple crates to reach them.

"Oh, I can't go out into Gold Mountain myself," Moon Orchid said.

"Walk back toward Chinatown," suggested Brave Orchid.

"Oh, come with me, please," Moon Orchid said.

"I have to work," said her sister. Brave Orchid placed an apple crate on the sidewalk in front of the laundry. "You sit out here in the cool air until I have a little time." She hooked the steel pole to the screw that unrolled the awning. "Just keep turning until the shadow covers the crate." It took Moon Orchid another half-hour to do this. She rested after every turn and left the pole hanging.

At noon, when the temperature inside reached one hundred and eleven degrees, Brave Orchid went out to the sidewalk and said, "Let's eat." She had heated the leftovers from breakfast on the little stove at the back of the laundry. In back there was also a bedroom for the nights when they finished packaging too tired to walk home. Then five or six people would crowd into the bed together. Some slept on the ironing tables, and the small children slept on the shelves. The shades would be pulled over the display windows and the door. The laundry would become a cozy new home, almost safe from the night footsteps, the traffic, the city outside. The boiler would rest, and no ghost would know there were Chinese asleep in their laundry. When the children were sick and had to stay home from school, they slept in that bedroom so that Brave Orchid could doctor them. The children said that the boiler, jumping up and down, bursting steam, flames shooting out the bottom, matched their dreams when they had a fever.

After lunch, Brave Orchid asked her husband if he and the children could handle the laundry by themselves. She wanted to take Moon Orchid out for some fun. He said that the load was unusually light today.

The sisters walked back to Chinatown. "We're going to get some more to eat," said Brave Orchid. Moon Orchid accompanied her to a gray building with a large storefront room, overhead fans turning coolly and cement floor cool underfoot. Women at round tables were eating black seaweed gelatin and talking. They poured Karo syrup on top of the black quivering mass. Brave Orchid seated Moon Orchid and dramatically introduced her, "This is my sister who has come to Gold Mountain to reclaim her husband." Many of the women were fellow villagers; others might as well have been villagers, together so long in California.

"Marvelous. You could blackmail him," the women advised. "Have him arrested if he doesn't take you back."

"Disguise yourself as a mysterious lady and find out how bad he is."

"You've got to do some husband beating, that's what you've got to do."

They were joking about her. Moon Orchid smiled and tried to think of a joke too. The large proprietress in a butcher's apron came out of the kitchen lugging tubs full of more black gelatin. Standing over the tables and smoking a cigarette, she watched her customers eat. It was so cool here, black and light-yellow and brown, and the gelatin was so cool. The door was open to the street, no passers-by but Chinese, though at the windows the venetian blinds slitted the sunlight as if everyone were hiding. Between helpings the women sat back, waving fans made out of silk, paper, sandalwood, and pandanus fronds. They were like rich women in China with nothing to do.

"Game time," said the proprietress, clearing the tables. The women had only been taking a break from their gambling. They spread ringed hands and mixed the ivory tiles click-clack for the next hemp-bird game. "It's time to go," said Brave Orchid, leading her sister outside. "When you come to America, it's a chance to forget some of the bad Chinese habits. A person could get up one day from the gambling table and find her life over." The gambling women were already caught up in their game, calling out good-byes to the sisters.

They walked past the vegetable, fish, and meat markets—not as abundant as in Canton, the carp not as red, the turtles not as old—and entered the cigar and seed shop. Brave Orchid filled her sister's thin hands with carrot candy, melon candy, and sheets of beef jerky. Business was carried out at one end of the shop, which was long and had benches against two walls. Rows of men sat smoking. Some of them stopped gurgling on their silver or bamboo water pipes to greet the sisters. Moon Orchid remembered many of them from the village; the cigar store owner, who looked like a camel, welcomed her. When Brave Orchid's children were young, they thought he was the Old Man of the North, Santa Claus.

As they walked back to the laundry, Brave Orchid showed her sister where to buy the various groceries and how to avoid Skid Row. "On days when you are not feeling safe, walk around it. But you can walk through it unharmed on your strong days." On weak days you notice bodies on the sidewalk, and you are visible to Panhandler Ghosts and Mugger Ghosts.

Brave Orchid and her husband and children worked hardest in the afternoon when the heat was the worst, all the machines hissing and thumping. Brave Orchid did teach her sister to fold the towels. She placed her at the table where the fan blew most. But finally she sent one of the children to walk her home.

From then on Moon Orchid only visited the laundry late in the day when the towels came out of the dryers. Brave Orchid's husband had to cut a pattern from cardboard so Moon Orchid could fold handkerchiefs uniformly. He gave her a shirt cardboard to measure the towels. She never could work any faster than she did on the first day.

The summer days passed while they talked about going to find Moon Orchid's husband. She felt she accomplished a great deal by folding towels. She spent the evening observing the children. She liked to figure them out. She described them aloud. "Now they're studying again. They read so much. Is it because they have enormous quantities to learn, and they're trying not to be savages? He is picking up his pencil and tapping it on the desk. Then he opens his book to page 168. His eyes begin to read. His eyes go back and forth. They go from left to right, from left to right." This makes her laugh. "How wondrous—eyes reading back and forth. Now he's writing his thoughts down. What's *that* thought?" she asked, pointing.

She followed her nieces and nephews about. She bent over them. "Now she is taking a machine off the shelf. She attaches two metal spiders to it. She plugs in the cord. She cracks an egg against the rim and pours the yolk and white out of the shell into the bowl. She presses a button, and the spiders spin the eggs. What are you making?"

"Aunt, please take your finger out of the batter."

"She says, 'Aunt, please take your finger out of the batter,'" Moon Orchid repeated as she turned to follow another niece walking through the kitchen. "Now what's this one doing? Why, she's sewing a dress. She's going to try it on." Moon Orchid would walk right into the children's rooms while they were dressing. "Now she must be looking over her costumes to see which one to wear." Moon Orchid pulled out a dress. "This is nice," she suggested. "Look at all the colors."

"No, Aunt. That's the kind of dress for a party. I'm going to school now."

"Oh, she's going to school now. She's choosing a plain blue dress. She's picking up her comb and brush and shoes, and she's going to lock herself up in the bathroom. They dress in bathrooms here." She pressed her ear against the door. "She's brushing her teeth. Now she's coming out of the bathroom. She's wearing the blue dress and a white sweater. She's combed her hair and washed her face. She looks in the refrigerator and is arranging things between slices of bread. She's putting an orange and cookies in a bag. Today she's taking her green book and her blue book. And tablets and pencils. Do you take a dictionary?" Moon Orchid asked.

"No," said the child, rolling her eyeballs up and exhaling loudly. "We have dictionaries at school," she added before going out the door.

"They have dictionaries at school," said Moon Orchid, thinking this over. "She knows 'dictionary.'" Moon Orchid stood at the window peeping. "Now she's shutting the gate. She strides along like an Englishman."

The child married to a husband who did not speak Chinese translated for him, "Now she's saying that I'm taking a machine off the shelf and that I'm attaching two metal spiders to it. And she's saying the spiders are spinning with legs intertwined and beating the eggs electrically. Now she says I'm hunting for something in the refrigerator and—ha!—I've found it. I'm taking out butter—'cow oil.' 'They eat a lot of cow oil,' she's saying."

"She's driving me nuts!" the children told each other in English.

At the laundry Moon Orchid hovered so close that there was barely room between her and the hot presses. "Now the index fingers of both hands press the buttons, and—ka-lump—the press comes down. But one finger on a button will release it—ssssss—the steam lets loose. Sssst—the water squirts." She could describe it so well, you would think she could do it. She wasn't as hard to take at the laundry as at home, though. She could not endure the heat, and after a while she had to go out on the sidewalk and sit on her apple crate. When they were younger the children used to sit out there too during their breaks. They played house and store and library, their orange and apple crates in a row. Passers-by and customers gave them money. But now they were older, they stayed inside or went for walks. They were ashamed of sitting on the sidewalk, people mistaking them for beggars. "Dance for me," the ghosts would say before handing them a nickel. "Sing a Chinese song." And before they got old enough to know better, they'd dance and they'd sing. Moon Orchid sat out there by herself.

Whenever Brave Orchid thought of it, which was every day, she said, "Are you ready to go see your husband and claim what is yours?"

"Not today, but soon," Moon Orchid would reply.

But one day in the middle of summer, Moon Orchid's daughter said, "I have to return to my family. I promised my husband and children I'd only be gone a few weeks. I should return this week." Moon Orchid's daughter lived in Los Angeles.

"Good!" Brave Orchid exclaimed. "We'll all go to Los Angeles. You return to your husband, and your mother returns to hers. We only have to make one trip."

"You ought to leave the poor man alone," said Brave Orchid's husband. "Leave him out of women's business."

"When your father lived in China," Brave Orchid told the children, "he refused to eat pastries because he didn't want to eat the dirt the women kneaded from between their fingers."

"But I'm happy here with you and all your children," Moon Orchid said. "I want to see how this girl's sewing turns out. I want to see your son come back from Vietnam. I want to see if this one gets good grades. There's so much to do."

"We're leaving on Friday," said Brave Orchid. "I'm going to escort you, and you will arrive safely."

On Friday Brave Orchid put on her dress-up clothes, which she wore only a few times during the year. Moon Orchid wore the same kind of clothes she wore every day and was dressed up. Brave Orchid told her oldest son he had to drive. He drove, and the two old ladies and the niece sat in the back seat.

They set out at gray dawn, driving between the grape trees, which hunched like dwarfs in the fields. Gnomes in serrated outfits that blew in the morning wind came out of the earth, came up in rows and columns. Everybody was only half awake. "A long time ago," began Brave Orchid, "the emperors had four wives, one at each point of the compass, and they lived in four palaces. The Empress of the West would connive for power, but the Empress of the East was good and kind and full of light. You are the Empress of the East, and the Empress of the West has imprisoned the Earth's Emperor in the Western Palace. And you, the good Empress of the East, come out of the dawn to invade her land and free the Emperor. You must break the strong spell she has cast on him that has lost him the East."

Brave Orchid gave her sister last-minute advice for five hundred miles. All her possessions had been packed into the trunk.

"Shall we go into your house together," asked Brave Orchid, "or do you want to go by yourself?"

"You've got to come with me. I don't know what I would say."

"I think it would be dramatic for you to go by yourself. He opens the door. And there you are—alive and standing on the porch with all your luggage. 'Remember me?' you say. Call him by his own name. He'll faint with shock. Maybe he'll say, 'No. Go away.' But you march right in. You push him aside and go in. Then you sit down in the most important chair, and you take off your shoes because you belong."

"Don't you think he'll welcome me?"

"She certainly wasn't very imaginative," thought Brave Orchid.

"It's against the law to have two wives in this country," said Moon Orchid. "I read that in the newspaper."

"But it's probably against the law in Singapore too. Yet our brother has two, and his sons have two each. The law doesn't matter."

"I'm scared. Oh, let's turn back. I don't want to see him. Suppose he throws me out? Oh, he will. He'll throw me out. And he'll have a right to throw me out, coming here, disturbing him, not waiting for him to invite me. Don't leave me by myself. You can talk louder than I can."

"Yes, coming with you would be exciting. I can charge through the door and say, 'Where is your wife?' And he'll answer, 'Why, she's right here.' And I'll say, 'This isn't your wife. Where is Moon Orchid? I've come to see her. I'm her first sister, and I've come to see that she is being well taken care of.' Then I accuse him of murderous things; I'd have him arrested—and you pop up to his rescue. Or I can take a look at his wife, and I say, 'Moon Orchid, how young you've gotten.' And he'll say, 'This isn't Moon Orchid.' And you come in and say, 'No. I am.' If nobody's home, we'll climb in a window. When they get back we'll be at home; you the hostess, and I your guest. You'll be serving me cookies and coffee. And when he comes in I'll say, 'Well, I see your husband is home. Thank you so much for the visit.' And you say, 'Come again anytime.' Don't make violence. Be routine."

Sometimes Moon Orchid got into the mood. "Maybe I could be folding towels when he comes in. He'll think I'm so clever. I'll get to them before his wife does." But the further they came down the great central valley—green fields changing to fields of cotton on dry, brown stalks, first a stray bush here and there, then thick—the more Moon Orchid wanted to turn back. "No. I can't go through with this." She tapped her nephew on the shoulder. "Please turn back. Oh, you must turn the car around. I should be returning to China. I shouldn't be here at all. Let's go back. Do you understand me?"

"Don't go back," Brave Orchid ordered her son. "Keep going. She can't back out now."

"What do you want me to do? Make up your minds," said the son, who was getting impatient.

"Keep going," said Brave Orchid. "She's come this far, and we can't waste all this driving. Besides, we have to take your cousin back to her own house in Los Angeles. We have to drive to Los Angeles anyway."

"Can I go inside and meet my grandchildren?"

"Yes," said her daughter.

"We'll see them after you straighten out things with your husband," said Brave Orchid.

"What if he hits me?"

"I'll hit *him*. I'll protect you. I'll hit him back. The two of us will knock him down and make him listen." Brave Orchid chuckled as if she were looking forward to a fight. But when she saw how terrified Moon Orchid was, she said, "It won't come to a fight. You mustn't start imagining things. We'll simply walk up to the door. If he answers, you'll say, 'I have decided to come live with you in the Beautiful Nation.' If *she* answers the door, you'll say, 'You must be Little Wife. I am Big Wife.' Why, you could even be generous. 'I'd like to see our husband, please,' you say. I brought my wig," said Brave Orchid. "Why don't you disguise yourself as a beautiful lady? I brought lipstick and powder too. And at some dramatic point, you pull off the wig and say, 'I am Moon Orchid.'"

"That is a terrible thing to do. I'd be so scared. I am so scared."

"I want to be dropped off at my house first," said the niece. "I told my family I'd be home to make lunch."

"All right," said Brave Orchid, who had tried to talk her niece into confronting her father five years ago, but all she had done was write him a letter telling him she was in Los Angeles. He could visit her, or she could visit him if he wanted to see her, she had suggested. But he had not wanted to see her.

When the car stopped in front of her daughter's house, Moon Orchid asked, "May I get out to meet my grandchildren?"

"I told you no," said Brave Orchid. "If you do that you'll stay here, and it'll take us weeks to get up our courage again. Let's save your grandchildren as a reward. You take care of this other business, and you can play with your grandchildren without worry. Besides, you have some children to meet."

"Grandchildren are more wonderful than children."

After they left the niece's suburb, the son drove them to the address his mother had given him, which turned out to be a skyscraper in downtown Los Angeles.

"Don't park in front," said his mother. "Find a side street. We've got to take him by surprise. We mustn't let him spot us ahead of time. We have to catch the first look on his face."

"Yes, I think I would like to see the look on his face."

Brave Orchid's son drove up and down the side streets until he found a parking space that could not be seen from the office building.

"You have to compose yourself," said Brave Orchid to her sister. "You must be calm as you walk in. Oh, this is most dramatic—in broad daylight and in the middle of the city. We'll sit here for a while and look at his building."

"Does he own that whole building?"

"I don't know. Maybe so."

"Oh, I can't move. My knees are shaking so much I won't be able to walk. He must have servants and workers in there, and they'll stare at me. I can't bear it."

Brave Orchid felt a tiredness drag her down. She had to baby everyone. The traffic was rushing, Los Angeles noon-hot, and she suddenly felt carsick. No trees. No birds. Only city. "It must be the long drive," she thought. They had not eaten lunch, and the sitting had tired her out. Movement would strengthen her; she needed movement. "I want you to stay here with your aunt while I scout that building," she instructed her son. "When I come back, we'll work out a plan." She walked around the block. Indeed, she felt that her feet stepping on the earth, even when the earth was covered with concrete, gained strength from it. She breathed health from the air, though it was full of gasoline fumes. The bottom floor of the building housed several stores. She looked at the clothes and jewelry on display, picking out some for Moon Orchid to have when she came into her rightful place.

Brave Orchid rushed along beside her reflection in the glass. She used to be young and fast; she was still fast and felt young. It was mirrors, not aches and pains, that turned a person old, everywhere white hairs and wrinkles. Young people felt pain.

The building was a fine one; the lobby was chrome and glass, with ashtray stands and plastic couches arranged in semicircles. She waited for the elevator to fill before she got in, not wanting to operate a new machine by herself. Once on the sixth floor she searched alertly for the number in her address book.

How clean his building was. The rest rooms were locked, and there were square overhead lights. No windows, though. She did not like the quiet corridors with carpets but no windows. They felt like tunnels. He must be very wealthy. Good. It would serve a rich man right to be humbled. She found the door with his number on it; there was also American lettering on the glass. Apparently this was his business office. She hadn't thought of the possibility of catching him at his job. Good thing she had decided to scout. If they had arrived at his house, they would not have found him. Then they would have had to deal with *her*. And she would have phoned him, spoiled the surprise, and gotten him on her side. Brave Orchid knew how the little wives maneuvered; her father had had two little wives.

She entered the office, glad that it was a public place and she needn't knock. A roomful of men and women looked up from their magazines. She could tell by their eagerness for change that this was a waiting room. Behind a sliding glass partition sat a young woman in a modern nurse's uniform, not a white one, but a light blue pantsuit with white trim. She sat before an elegant telephone and an electric typewriter. The wallpaper in her cubicle was like aluminum foil, a metallic background for a tall black frame around white paint with dashes of red. The wall of the waiting room was covered with burlap, and there were plants in wooden tubs. It was an expensive waiting room. Brave Orchid approved. The patients looked well dressed, not sickly and poor.

"Hello. May I help you?" said the receptionist, parting the glass. Brave Orchid hesitated, and the receptionist took this to mean that she could not speak English. "Just a moment," she said, and went into an inner room. She brought back another woman, who wore a similar uniform except that it was pink trimmed in white. This woman's hair was gathered up into a bunch of curls at the back of her head; some of the curls were fake. She wore round glasses and false eyelashes, which gave her an American look. "Have you an appointment?" she asked in poor Chinese; she spoke less like a Chinese than Brave Orchid's children. "My husband, the doctor, usually does not take drop-in patients," she said. "We're booked up for about a month." Brave Orchid stared at her pink-painted finger-nails gesticulating, and thought she probably would not have given out so much information if she weren't so clumsy with language.

"I have the flu," Brave Orchid said.

"Perhaps we can give you the name of another doctor," said this woman, who was her sister-in-law. "This doctor is a brain surgeon and doesn't work with flu." Actually she said, "This doctor cuts brains," a child making up the words as she went along. She wore pink lipstick and had blue eyelids like the ghosts.

Brave Orchid, who had been a surgeon too, thought that her brother-in-law must be a clever man. She herself could not practice openly in the United States because the training here was so different and because she could never learn English. He was smart enough to learn ghost ways. She would have to be clever to outwit him. She needed to retreat and plan some more. "Oh, well, I'll go to another doctor, then," she said, and left.

She needed a new plan to get her sister and brother-in-law together. This nurse-wife was so young, and the office was so rich with wood, paintings, and fancy telephones, that Brave Orchid knew it wasn't because he couldn't get the fare to-gether that he hadn't sent for his old wife. He had abandoned her for this modern, heartless girl. Brave Orchid wondered if the girl knew that her husband had a Chinese wife. Perhaps she should ask her.

But no, she mustn't spoil the surprise by giving any hints. She had to get away before he came out into the corridor, perhaps to go to one of the locked rest rooms. As she walked back to her sister, she noted corners and passageways, broom closets, other offices—ambush spots. Her sister could crouch behind a drinking fountain and wait for him to get thirsty. Waylay him.

"I met his second wife," she said, opening the car door.

"What's she like?" asked Moon Orchid. "Is she pretty?"

"She's very pretty and very young; just a girl. She's his nurse. He's a doctor like me. What a terrible, faithless man. You'll have to scold him for years, but first you need to sit up straight. Use my powder. Be as pretty as you can. Otherwise you won't be able to compete. You do have one advantage, however. Notice he has her be his worker. She is like a servant, so you have room to be the wife. She works at the office; you work at the house. That's almost as good as having two houses. On the other hand, a man's real partner is the hardest worker. You couldn't learn nursing, could you? No, I guess not. It's almost as difficult as doing laundry. What a petty man he turned out to be, giving up responsibility for a pretty face." Brave Orchid reached for the door handle. "Are you ready?"

"For what?"

"To go up there, of course. We're at his office, and I think we ought to be very direct. There aren't any trees to hide you, no grass to soften your steps. So, you walk right into his office. You make an announcement to the patients and the fancy nurses. You say, 'I am the doctor's wife. I'm going to see my husband.' Then you step to the inner door and enter. Don't knock on any doors. Don't listen if the minor wife talks to you. You walk past her without changing pace. When you see him, you say, 'Surprise!' You say, 'Who is that woman out there? She claims to be your wife.' That will give him a chance to deny her on the spot."

"Oh, I'm so scared. I can't move. I can't do that in front of all those people—like a stage show. I won't be able to talk." And sure enough, her voice was fading into a whisper. She was shivering and small in the corner of the seat.

"So. A new plan, then," said Brave Orchid, looking at her son, who had his forehead on the steering wheel. "You," she said. "I want you to go up to his office and tell your uncle that there has been an accident out in the street. A woman's leg has been broken, and she's crying in pain. He'll have to come. You bring him to the car."

"Mother."

"Mm," mused Brave Orchid. "Maybe we ought to put your aunt in the middle of the street, and she can lie down with her leg bent under her." But Moon Orchid kept shaking her head in trembling no's.

"Why don't you push her down in the intersection and pour ketchup on her? I'll run over her a little bit," said her son.

"Stop being silly," she said. "You Americans don't take life seriously."

"Mother, this is ridiculous. This whole thing is ridiculous."

"Go. Do what I tell you," she said.

"I think your schemes will be useless, Mother."

"What do you know about Chinese business?" she said. "Do as I say."

"Don't let him bring the nurse," said Moon Orchid.

"Don't you want to see what she looks like?" asked Brave Orchid. "Then you'll know what he's giving up for you."

"No. No. She's none of my business. She's unimportant."

"Speak in English," Brave Orchid told her son. "Then he'll feel he has to come with you."

She pushed her son out of the car. "I don't want to do this," he said.

"You'll ruin your aunt's life if you don't. You can't understand business begun in China. Just do what I say. Go."

Slamming the car door behind him, he left.

Moon Orchid was groaning now and holding her stomach. "Straighten up," said Brave Orchid. "He'll be here any moment." But this only made Moon Orchid groan louder, and tears seeped out between her closed eyelids.

"You want a husband, don't you?" said Brave Orchid. "If you don't claim him now, you'll never have a husband. Stop crying," she ordered. "Do you want him to see you with your eyes and nose swollen when that young so-called wife wears lipstick and nail polish like a movie star?"

Moon Orchid managed to sit upright, but she seemed stiff and frozen.

"You're just tired from the ride. Put some blood into your cheeks," Brave Orchid said, and pinched her sister's withered face. She held her sister's elbow and slapped the inside of her arm. If she had had time, she would have hit until the black and red dots broke out on the skin; that was the tiredness coming out. As she hit, she kept an eye on the rearview mirror. She saw her son come running, his uncle after him with a black bag in his hand. "Faster. Faster," her son was saying. He opened the car door. "Here she is," he said to his uncle. "I'll see you later." And he ran on down the street.

The two old ladies saw a man, authoritative in his dark western suit, start to fill the front of the car. He had black hair and no wrinkles. He looked and smelled like an American. Suddenly the two women remembered that in China families married young boys to older girls, who baby-sat their husbands their whole lives. Either that or, in this ghost country, a man could somehow keep his youth.

"Where's the accident?" he said in Chinese. "What is this? You don't have a broken leg."

Neither woman spoke. Brave Orchid held her words back. She would not let herself interfere with this meeting after long absence.

"What is it?" he asked. "What's wrong?" These women had such awful faces. "What is it, Grandmothers?"

"Grandmother?" Brave Orchid shouted. "This is your wife. I am your sister-in-law."

Moon Orchid started to whimper. Her husband looked at her. And recognized her. "You," he said. "What are you doing here?"

But all she did was open and shut her mouth without any words coming out.

"Why are you here?" he asked, eyes wide. Moon Orchid covered her face with one hand and motioned no with the other.

Brave Orchid could not keep silent. Obviously he was not glad to see his wife. "I sent for her," she burst out. "I got her name on the Red Cross list, and I sent her the plane ticket. I wrote her every day and gave her the heart to come. I told her how welcome she would be, how her family would welcome her, how her husband would welcome her. I did what you, the husband, had time to do in these last thirty years."

He looked directly at Moon Orchid the way the savages looked, looking for lies. "What do you want?" he asked. She shrank from his stare; it silenced her crying.

"You weren't supposed to come here," he said, the front seat a barrier against the two women over whom a spell of old age had been cast. "It's a mistake for you to be here. You can't belong. You don't have the hardness for this country. I have a new life."

"What about me?" whispered Moon Orchid.

"Good," thought Brave Orchid. "Well said. Said with no guile."

"I have a new wife," said the man.

"She's only your second wife," said Brave Orchid. "This is your real wife."

"In this country a man may have just one wife."

"So you'll get rid of that creature in your office?" asked Brave Orchid.

He looked at Moon Orchid. Again the rude American eyes. "You go live with your daughter. I'll mail you the money I've always sent you. I could get arrested if the Americans knew about you. I'm living like an American." He talked like a child born here.

"How could you ruin her old age?" said Brave Orchid.

"She has had food. She has had servants. Her daughter went to college. There wasn't anything she thought of that she couldn't buy. I have been a good husband."

"You made her live like a widow."

"That's not true. Obviously the villagers haven't stoned her. She's not wearing mourning. The family didn't send her away to work. Look at her. She'd never fit into an American household. I have important American guests who come inside my house to eat." He turned to Moon Orchid, "You can't talk to them. You can barely talk to me."

Moon Orchid was so ashamed, she held her hands over her face. She wished she could also hide her dappled hands. Her husband looked like one of the ghosts passing the car windows, and she must look like a ghost from China. They had indeed entered the land of ghosts, and they had become ghosts.

"Do you want her to go back to China then?" Brave Orchid was asking.

"I wouldn't wish that on anyone. She may stay, but I do not want her in my house. She has to live with you or with her daughter, and I don't want either of you coming here anymore."

Suddenly his nurse was tapping on the glass. So quickly

that they might have missed it, he gestured to the old women, holding a finger to his mouth for just a moment: he had never told his American wife that he had a wife in China, and they mustn't tell her either.

"What's happening?" she asked. "Do you need help? The appointments are piling up."

"No. No," he said. "This woman fainted in the street. I'll be up soon."

They spoke to each other in English.

The two old women did not call out to the young woman. Soon she left. "I'm leaving too now," said the husband.

"Why didn't you write to tell her once and for all you weren't coming back and you weren't sending for her?" Brave Orchid asked.

"I don't know," he said. "It's as if I had turned into a different person. The new life around me was so complete; it pulled me away. You became people in a book I had read a long time ago."

"The least you can do," said Brave Orchid, "is invite us to lunch. Aren't you inviting us to lunch? Don't you owe us a lunch? At a good restaurant?" She would not let him off easily.

So he bought them lunch, and when Brave Orchid's son came back to the car, he had to wait for them.

Moon Orchid was driven back to her daughter's house, but though she lived in Los Angeles, she never saw her husband again. "Oh, well," said Brave Orchid. "We're all under the same sky and walk the same earth; we're alive together during the same moment." Brave Orchid and her son drove back north, Brave Orchid sitting in the back seat the whole way.

Several months went by with no letter from Moon Orchid. When she had lived in China and in Hong Kong, she had written every other week. At last Brave Orchid telephoned long distance to find out what was happening. "I can't talk now," Moon Orchid whispered. "They're listening. Hang up quickly before they trace you." Moon Orchid hung up on Brave Orchid before the minutes she had paid for expired.

That week a letter came from the niece saying that Moon Orchid had become afraid. Moon Orchid said that she had overheard Mexican ghosts plotting on her life. She had been creeping along the baseboards and peeping out windows. Then she had asked her daughter to help her find an apartment at the other end of Los Angeles, where she was now hiding. Her daughter visited her every day, but Moon Orchid kept telling her, "Don't come see me because the Mexican ghosts will follow you to my new hiding place. They're watching your house."

Brave Orchid phoned her niece and told her to send her mother north immediately, where there were no Mexicans, she said. "This fear is an illness," she told her niece. "I will cure her." ("Long ago," she explained to her children, "when the emperors had four wives, the wife who lost in battle was sent to the Northern Palace. Her feet would sink little prints into the snow.")

Brave Orchid sat on a bench at the Greyhound station to wait for her sister. Her children had not come with her because the bus station was only a five-block walk from the house. Her brown paper shopping bag against her, she dozed under the fluorescent lights until her sister's bus pulled into the terminal. Moon Orchid stood blinking on the stairs, hanging tightly to the railing for old people. Brave Orchid felt the tears break inside her chest for the old feet that stepped one at a time onto the cold Greyhound cement. Her sister's skin hung loose, like a hollowed frog's, as if she had shrunken inside it. Her clothes bagged, not fitting sharply anymore. "I'm in disguise," she said. Brave Orchid put her arms around her sister to give her body warmth. She held her hand along the walk home, just as they had held hands when they were girls.

The house was more crowded than ever, though some of the children had gone away to school; the jade trees were inside for the winter. Along walls and on top of tables, jade trees, whose trunks were as thick as ankles, stood stoutly, green now and without the pink skin the sun gave them in the spring.

"I am so afraid," said Moon Orchid.

"There is no one after you," said Brave Orchid. "No Mexicans."

"I saw some in the Greyhound station," said Moon Orchid.

"No. No, those were Filipinos." She held her sister's earlobes and began the healing chant for being unafraid. "There are no Mexicans after you," she said.

"I know. I got away from them by escaping on the bus."

"Yes, you escaped on the bus with the mark of the dog on it."

In the evening, when Moon Orchid seemed quieter, her sister probed into the cause of this trouble.

"What made you think anyone was after you?"

"I heard them talking about me. I snuck up on them and heard them."

"But you don't understand Mexican words."

"They were speaking English."

"You don't understand English words."

"This time, miraculously, I understood. I decoded their speech. I penetrated the words and understood what was happening inside."

Brave Orchid tweaked her sister's ears for hours, chanting her new address to her, telling her how much she loved her and how much her daughter and nephews and nieces loved her, and her brother-in-law loved her. "I won't let anything happen to you. I won't let you travel again. You're home. Stay home. Don't be afraid." Tears fell from Brave Orchid's eyes. She had whisked her sister across the ocean by jet and then made her scurry up and down the Pacific coast, back and forth across Los Angeles. Moon Orchid had misplaced herself, her spirit (her "attention," Brave Orchid called it) scattered all over the world. Brave Orchid held her sister's head as she pulled on her earlobe. She would make it up to her. For moments an attentiveness would return to Moon Orchid's face. Brave Orchid rubbed the slender hands, blew on the fingers, tried to stoke up the flickerings. She stayed home from the laundry day after day. She threw out the Thorazine and vitamin B that a doctor in Los Angeles had prescribed. She made Moon Orchid sit in the kitchen sun while she picked over the herbs in cupboards and basement and the fresh plants that grew in the winter garden. Brave Orchid chose the gentlest plants and made medicines and foods like those they had eaten in their village.

At night she moved from her husband's room and slept beside Moon Orchid. "Don't be afraid to sleep," she said. "Rest. I'll be here beside you. I'll help your spirit find the place to come back to. I'll call it for you; you go to sleep." Brave Orchid stayed awake watching until dawn.

Moon Orchid still described aloud her nieces' and nephews' doings, but now in a monotone, and she no longer interrupted herself to ask questions. She would not go outside, even into the yard. "Why, she's mad," Brave Orchid's husband said when she was asleep.

Brave Orchid held her hand when she appeared vague. "Don't go away, Little Sister. Don't go any further. Come back to us." If Moon Orchid fell asleep on the sofa, Brave Orchid sat up through the night, sometimes dozing in a chair. When Moon Orchid fell asleep in the middle of the bed, Brave Orchid made a place for herself at the foot. She would anchor her sister to this earth.

But each day Moon Orchid slipped further away. She said that the Mexicans had traced her to this house. That was the day she shut the drapes and blinds and locked the doors. She sidled along the walls to peep outside. Brave Orchid told her husband that he must humor his sister-in-law. It was right to shut the windows; it kept her spirit from leaking away. Then Moon Orchid went about the house turning off the lights like during air raids. The house became gloomy; no air, no light. This was very tricky, the darkness a wide way for going as well as coming back. Sometimes Brave Orchid would switch on the lights, calling her sister's name all the while. Brave Orchid's husband installed an air conditioner.

The children locked themselves up in their bedrooms, in the storeroom and basement, where they turned on the lights. Their aunt would come knocking on the doors and say, "Are you all right in there?"

"Yes, Aunt, we're all right."

"Beware," she'd warn. "Beware. Turn off your lights so you won't be found. Turn off the lights before they come for us."

The children hung blankets over the cracks in the doorjambs; they stuffed clothes along the bottoms of doors. "Chinese people are very weird," they told one another.

Next Moon Orchid removed all the photographs, except for those of the grandmother and grandfather, from the shelves, dressers, and walls. She gathered up the family albums. "Hide these," she whispered to Brave Orchid. "Hide these. When they find me, I don't want them to trace the rest of the family. They use photographs to trace you." Brave Orchid wrapped the pictures and the albums in flannel. "I'll carry these far away where no one will find us," she said. When Moon Orchid wasn't looking, she put them at the bottom of a storage box in the basement. She piled old clothes and old shoes on top. "If they come for me," Moon Orchid said, "everyone will be safe."

"We're all safe," said Brave Orchid.

The next odd thing Moon Orchid did was to cry whenever anyone left the house. She held on to them, pulled at their clothes, begged them not to go. The children and Brave Orchid's husband had to sneak out. "Don't let them go," pleaded Moon Orchid. "They will never come back."

"They will come back. Wait and see. I promise you. Watch for them. Don't watch for Mexicans. This one will be home at 3:30. This one at 5:00. Remember who left now. You'll see."

"We'll never see that one again," Moon Orchid wept.

At 3:30 Brave Orchid would remind her, "See? It's 3:30; sure enough, here he comes." ("You children come home right after school. Don't you dare stop for a moment. No candy store. No comic book store. Do you hear?")

But Moon Orchid did not remember. "Who is this?" she'd ask. "Are you going to stay with us? Don't go out tonight. Don't leave in the morning."

She whispered to Brave Orchid that the reason the family must not go out was that "they" would take us in airplanes and fly us to Washington, D.C., where they'd turn us into ashes. Then they'd drop the ashes in the wind, leaving no evidence.

Brave Orchid saw that all variety had gone from her sister. She was indeed mad. "The difference between mad people and sane people," Brave Orchid explained to the children, "is that sane people have variety when they talk-story. Mad people have only one story that they talk over and over."

Every morning Moon Orchid stood by the front door whispering, whispering. "Don't go. The planes. Ashes. Washington, D.C. Ashes." Then, when a child managed to leave, she said, "That's the last time we'll see him again. They'll get him. They'll turn him into ashes."

And so Brave Orchid gave up. She was housing a mad sister who cursed the mornings for her children, the one in Vietnam too. Their aunt was saying terrible things when they needed blessing. Perhaps Moon Orchid had already left this mad old body, and it was a ghost bad-mouthing her children. Brave

Orchid finally called her niece, who put Moon Orchid in a California state mental asylum. Then Brave Orchid opened up the windows and let the air and light come into the house again. She moved back into the bedroom with her husband. The children took the blankets and sheets down from the doorjambs and came back into the living room.

Brave Orchid visited her sister twice. Moon Orchid was thinner each time, shrunken to bone. But, surprisingly, she was happy and had made up a new story. She pranced like a child. "Oh, Sister, I am so happy here. No one ever leaves. Isn't that wonderful? We are all women here. Come. I want you to meet my daughters." She introduced Brave Orchid to each inmate in the ward—her daughters. She was especially proud of the pregnant ones. "My dear pregnant daughters." She touched the women on the head, straightened collars, tucked blankets. "How are you today, dear daughter?" "And, you know," she said to Brave Orchid, "we understand one another here. We speak the same language, the very same. They understand me, and I understand them." Sure enough, the women smiled back at her and reached out to touch her as she went by. She had a new story, and yet she slipped entirely away, not waking up one morning.

Brave Orchid told her children they must help her keep their father from marrying another woman because she didn't think she could take it any better than her sister had. If he brought another woman into the house, they were to gang up on her and play tricks on her, hit her, and trip her when she was carrying hot oil until she ran away. "I am almost seventy years old," said the father, "and haven't taken a second wife, and don't plan to now." Brave Orchid's daughters decided fiercely that they would never let men be unfaithful to them. All her children made up their minds to major in science or mathematics.

A Song for a Barbarian Reed Pipe

What my brother actually said was, "I drove Mom and Second Aunt to Los Angeles to see Aunt's husband who's got the other wife."

"Did she hit him? What did she say? What did he say?"

"Nothing much. Mom did all the talking."

"What did she say?"

"She said he'd better take them to lunch at least."

"Which wife did he sit next to? What did they eat?"

"I didn't go. The other wife didn't either. He motioned us not to tell."

"I would've told. If I was his wife, I would've told. I would've gone to lunch and kept my ears open."

"Ah, you know they don't talk when they eat."

"What else did Mom say?"

"I don't remember. I pretended a pedestrian broke her leg so he would come."

"There must've been more. Didn't Aunt get in one nasty word? She must've said something."

"No, I don't think she said anything. I don't remember her saying one thing."

In fact, it wasn't me my brother told about going to Los Angeles; one of my sisters told me what he'd told her. His version of the story may be better than mine because of its barrenness, not twisted into designs. The hearer can carry it tucked away without it taking up much room. Long ago in China, knot-makers tied string into buttons and frogs, and rope into bell pulls. There was one knot so complicated that it blinded the knot-maker. Finally an emperor outlawed this cruel knot, and the nobles could not order it anymore. If I had lived in China, I would have been an outlaw knot-maker.

Maybe that's why my mother cut my tongue. She pushed my tongue up and sliced the frenum. Or maybe she snipped it with a pair of nail scissors. I don't remember her doing it, only her telling me about it, but all during childhood I felt sorry for the baby whose mother waited with scissors or knife in hand for it to cry—and then, when its mouth was wide open like a baby bird's, cut. The Chinese say "a ready tongue is an evil."

I used to curl up my tongue in front of the mirror and tauten my frenum into a white line, itself as thin as a razor blade. I saw no scars in my mouth. I thought perhaps I had had two frena, and she had cut one. I made other children open their mouths so I could compare theirs to mine. I saw perfect pink membranes stretching into precise edges that looked easy enough to cut. Sometimes I felt very proud that my mother committed such a powerful act upon me. At other times I was terrified—the first thing my mother did when she saw me was to cut my tongue.

"Why did you do that to me, Mother?"

"I told you."

"Tell me again."

"I cut it so that you would not be tongue-tied. Your tongue would be able to move in any language. You'll be able to speak languages that are completely different from one another. You'll be able to pronounce anything. Your frenum looked too tight to do those things, so I cut it."

"But isn't 'a ready tongue an evil'?"

"Things are different in this ghost country."

"Did it hurt me? Did I cry and bleed?"

"I don't remember. Probably."

She didn't cut the other children's. When I asked cousins and other Chinese children whether their mothers had cut their tongues loose, they said, "What?"

"Why didn't you cut my brothers' and sisters' tongues?"

"They didn't need it."

"Why not? Were theirs longer than mine?"

"Why don't you quit blabbering and get to work?"

If my mother was not lying she should have cut more, scraped away the rest of the frenum skin, because I have a terrible time talking. Or she should not have cut at all, tampering with my speech. When I went to kindergarten and had to speak English for the first time, I became silent. A dumbness—a shame—still cracks my voice in two, even when I want to say "hello" casually, or ask an easy question in front of the check-out counter, or ask directions of a bus driver. I stand frozen, or I hold up the line with the complete, grammatical sentence that comes squeaking out at impossible length. "What did you say?" says the cab driver, or "Speak up," so I have to perform again, only weaker the second time. A telephone call makes my throat bleed and takes up that day's courage. It spoils my day with self-disgust when I hear my broken voice come skittering out into the open. It makes people wince to hear it. I'm getting better, though. Recently I asked the postman for special-issue stamps; I've waited since childhood for postmen to give me some of their own accord. I am making progress, a little every day.

My silence was thickest—total—during the three years that I covered my school paintings with black paint. I painted layers of black over houses and flowers and suns, and when I drew on the blackboard, I put a layer of chalk on top. I was making a stage curtain, and it was the moment before the curtain parted or rose. The teachers called my parents to school, and I saw they had been saving my pictures, curling and cracking, all alike and black. The teachers pointed to the pictures and looked serious, talked seriously too, but my parents did not understand English. ("The parents and teachers of criminals were executed," said my father.) My parents took the pictures home. I spread them out (so black and full of possibilities) and pretended the curtains were swinging open, flying up, one after another, sunlight underneath, mighty operas.

During the first silent year I spoke to no one at school, did not ask before going to the lavatory, and flunked kindergarten. My sister also said nothing for three years, silent in the playground and silent at lunch. There were other quiet Chinese girls not of our family, but most of them got over it sooner than we did. I enjoyed the silence. At first it did not occur to me I was supposed to talk or to pass kindergarten. I talked at home and to one or two of the Chinese kids in class. I made motions and even made some jokes. I drank out of a toy saucer when the water spilled out of the cup, and everybody laughed, pointing at me, so I did it some more. I didn't know that Americans don't drink out of saucers.

I liked the Negro students (Black Ghosts) best because they laughed the loudest and talked to me as if I were a daring talker too. One of the Negro girls had her mother coil braids over her ears Shanghai-style like mine; we were Shanghai twins except that she was covered with black like my paintings. Two Negro kids enrolled in Chinese school, and the teachers gave them Chinese names. Some Negro kids walked me to school and home, protecting me from the Japanese kids, who hit me and chased me and stuck gum in my ears. The Japanese kids were noisy and tough. They appeared one day in kindergarten, released from concentration camp, which was a tic-tac-toe mark, like barbed wire, on the map.

It was when I found out I had to talk that school became a misery, that the silence became a misery. I did not speak and felt bad each time that I did not speak. I read aloud in first grade, though, and heard the barest whisper with little squeaks come out of my throat. "Louder," said the teacher, who scared the voice away again. The other Chinese girls did not talk either, so I knew the silence had to do with being a Chinese girl.

Reading out loud was easier than speaking because we did not have to make up what to say, but I stopped often, and the teacher would think I'd gone quiet again. I could not understand "I." The Chinese "I" has seven strokes, intricacies. How could the American "I," assuredly wearing a hat like the Chinese, have only three strokes, the middle so straight? Was it out of politeness that this writer left off strokes the way a Chinese has to write her own name small and crooked? No, it was not politeness; "I" is a capital and "you" is lower-case. I stared at that middle line and waited so long for its black center to resolve into tight strokes and dots that I forgot to pronounce it. The other troublesome word was "here," no strong consonant to hang on to, and so flat, when "here" is two mountainous ideographs. The teacher, who had already told me every day how to read "I" and "here," put me in the low corner under the stairs again, where the noisy boys usually sat.

When my second grade class did a play, the whole class went to the auditorium except the Chinese girls. The teacher, lovely and Hawaiian, should have understood about us, but instead left us behind in the classroom. Our voices were too soft or nonexistent, and our parents never signed the permission slips anyway. They never signed anything unnecessary. We opened the door a crack and peeked out, but closed it again quickly. One of us (not me) won every spelling bee, though.

I remember telling the Hawaiian teacher, "We Chinese can't sing 'land where our fathers died.'" She argued with me about politics, while I meant because of curses. But how can I have that memory when I couldn't talk? My mother says that we, like the ghosts, have no memories.

After American school, we picked up our cigar boxes, in which we had arranged books, brushes, and an inkbox neatly, and went to Chinese school, from 5:00 to 7:30 P.M. There we chanted together, voices rising and falling, loud and soft, some boys shouting, everybody reading together, reciting together and not alone with one voice. When we had a memorization test, the teacher let each of us come to his desk and say the lesson to him privately, while the rest of the class practiced copying or tracing. Most of the teachers were men. The boys who were so well behaved in the American school played tricks on them and talked back to them. The girls were not mute. They screamed and yelled during recess, when there were no rules; they had fistfights. Nobody was afraid of children hurting themselves or of children hurting school property. The glass doors to the red and green balconies with the gold joy symbols were left wide open so that we could run out and climb the fire escapes. We played capture-the-flag in the auditorium, where Sun Yat-sen and Chiang Kai-shek's pictures hung at the back of the stage, the Chinese flag on their left and the American flag on their right. We climbed the teak ceremonial chairs and made flying leaps off the stage. One flag headquarters was behind the glass door and the other on stage right. Our feet drummed on the hollow stage. During recess the teachers locked themselves up in their office with the shelves of books, copybooks, inks from China. They drank tea and warmed their hands at a stove. There was no play supervision. At recess we had the school to ourselves, and also we could roam as far as we could go—downtown, Chinatown stores, home—as long as we returned before the bell rang.

At exactly 7:30 the teacher again picked up the brass bell that sat on his desk and swung it over our heads, while we charged down the stairs, our cheering magnified in the stairwell. Nobody had to line up.

Not all of the children who were silent at American school found voice at Chinese school. One new teacher said each of us had to get up and recite in front of the class, who was to listen. My sister and I had memorized the lesson perfectly. We said it to each other at home, one chanting, one listening. The teacher called on my sister to recite first. It was the first time a teacher had called on the second-born to go first. My sister was scared. She glanced at me and looked away; I looked down at my desk. I hoped that she could do it because if she could, then I would have to. She opened her mouth and a voice came out that wasn't a whisper, but it wasn't a proper voice either. I hoped that she would not cry, fear breaking up her voice like twigs underfoot. She sounded as if she were trying to sing though weeping and strangling. She did not pause or stop to end the embarrassment. She kept going until she said the last word, and then she sat down. When it was my turn, the same voice came out, a crippled animal running on broken legs. You could hear splinters in my voice, bones rubbing jagged against one another. I was loud, though. I was glad I didn't whisper. There was one little girl who whispered.

You can't entrust your voice to the Chinese, either; they want to capture your voice for their own use. They want to fix up your tongue to speak for them. "How much less can you sell it for?" we have to say. Talk the Sales Ghosts down. Make them take a loss.

We were working at the laundry when a delivery boy came from the Rexall drugstore around the corner. He had a pale blue box of pills, but nobody was sick. Reading the label we saw that it belonged to another Chinese family, Crazy Mary's family. "Not ours," said my father. He pointed out the name to the Delivery Ghost, who took the pills back. My mother muttered for an hour, and then her anger boiled over. "That ghost! That dead ghost! How dare he come to the wrong house?" She could not concentrate on her marking and pressing. "A mistake! Huh!" I was getting angry myself. She fumed. She made her press crash and hiss. "Revenge. We've got to avenge this wrong on our future, on our health, and on our lives. Nobody's going to sicken my children and get away with it." We brothers and sisters did not look at one another. She would do something awful, something embarrassing. She'd already been hinting that during the next eclipse we slam pot lids together to scare the frog from swallowing the moon.

(The word for "eclipse" is *frog-swallowing-the-moon.*) When we had not banged lids at the last eclipse and the shadow kept receding anyway, she'd said, "The villagers must be banging and clanging very loudly back home in China."

("On the other side of the world, they aren't having an eclipse, Mama. That's just a shadow the earth makes when it comes between the moon and the sun."

"You're always believing what those Ghost Teachers tell you. Look at the size of the jaws!")

"Aha!" she yelled. "You! The biggest." She was pointing at me. "You go to the drugstore."

"What do you want me to buy, Mother?" I said.

"Buy nothing. Don't bring one cent. Go and make them stop the curse."

"I don't want to go. I don't know how to do that. There are no such things as curses. They'll think I'm crazy."

"If you don't go, I'm holding you responsible for bringing a plague on this family."

"What am I supposed to do when I get there?" I said, sullen, trapped. "Do I say, 'Your delivery boy made a wrong delivery'?"

"They know he made a wrong delivery. I want you to make them rectify their crime."

I felt sick already. She'd make me swing stinky censers around the counter, at the druggist, at the customers. Throw dog blood on the druggist. I couldn't stand her plans.

"You get reparation candy," she said. "You say, 'You have tainted my house with sick medicine and must remove the curse with sweetness.' He'll understand."

"He didn't do it on purpose. And no, he won't, Mother. They don't understand stuff like that. I won't be able to say it right. He'll call us beggars."

"You just translate." She searched me to make sure I wasn't hiding any money. I was sneaky and bad enough to buy the candy and come back pretending it was a free gift.

"Mymotherseztagimmesomecandy," I said to the druggist. Be cute and small. No one hurts the cute and small.

"What? Speak up. Speak English," he said, big in his white druggist coat.

"Tatatagimme somecandy."

The druggist leaned way over the counter and frowned. "Some free candy," I said. "Sample candy."

"We don't give sample candy, young lady," he said.

"My mother said you have to give us candy. She said that is the way the Chinese do it."

"What?"

"That is the way the Chinese do it."

"Do what?"

"Do things." I felt the weight and immensity of things impossible to explain to the druggist.

"Can I give you some money?" he asked.

"No, we want candy."

He reached into a jar and gave me a handful of lollipops. He gave us candy all year round, year after year, every time we went into the drugstore. When different druggists or clerks waited on us, they also gave us candy. They had talked us over. They gave us Halloween candy in December, Christmas candy around Valentine's day, candy hearts at Easter, and Easter eggs at Halloween. "See?" said our mother. "They understand. You kids just aren't very brave." But I knew they did not understand. They thought we were beggars without a home who lived in back of the laundry. They felt sorry for us. I did not eat their candy. I did not go inside the drugstore or walk past it unless my parents forced me to. Whenever we had a prescription filled, the druggist put candy in the medicine bag. This is what Chinese druggists normally do, except they give raisins. My mother thought she taught the Druggist Ghosts a lesson in good manners (which is the same word as "traditions").

My mouth went permanently crooked with effort, turned down on the left side and straight on the right. How strange that the emigrant villagers are shouters, hollering face to face. My father asks, "Why is it I can hear Chinese from blocks away? Is it that I understand the language? Or is it they talk loud?" They turn the radio up full blast to hear the operas, which do not seem to hurt their ears. And they yell over the singers that wail over the drums, everybody talking at once, big arm gestures, spit flying. You can see the disgust on American faces looking at women like that. It isn't just the loudness. It is the way Chinese sounds, chingchong ugly, to American ears, not beautiful like Japanese sayonara words with the consonants and vowels as regular as Italian. We make guttural peasant noise and have Ton Duc Thang names you can't remember. And the Chinese can't hear Americans at all; the language is too soft and western music unhearable. I've watched a Chinese audience laugh, visit, talk-story, and holler during a piano recital, as if the musician could not hear them. A Chinese-American, somebody's son, was playing Chopin, which has no punctuation, no cymbals, no gongs. Chinese piano music is five black keys. Normal Chinese women's voices are strong and bossy. We American-Chinese girls had to whisper to make ourselves American-feminine. Apparently we whispered even more softly than the Americans. Once a year the teachers referred my sister and me to speech therapy, but our voices would straighten out, unpredictably normal, for the therapists. Some of us gave up, shook our heads, and said nothing, not one word. Some of us could not even shake our heads. At times shaking my head no is more self-assertion than I can manage. Most of us eventually found some voice, however faltering. We invented an American-feminine speaking personality, except for that one girl who could not speak up even in Chinese school.

She was a year older than I and was in my class for twelve years. During all those years she read aloud but would not talk. Her older sister was usually beside her; their parents kept the older daughter back to protect the younger one. They were six and seven years old when they began school. Although I had flunked kindergarten, I was the same age as most other students in our class; my parents had probably lied about my age, so I had had a head start and came out even. My younger sister was in the class below me; we were normal ages and normally separated. The parents of the quiet girl, on the other hand, protected both daughters. When it sprinkled, they kept them home from school. The girls did not work for a living the way we did. But in other ways we were the same.

We were similar in sports. We held the bat on our shoulders until we walked to first base. (You got a strike only when you actually struck at the ball.) Sometimes the pitcher wouldn't bother to throw to us. "Automatic walk," the other children would call, sending us on our way. By fourth or fifth grade, though, some of us would try to hit the ball. "Easy out," the other kids would say. I hit the ball a couple of times. Baseball was nice in that there was a definite spot to run to after hitting the ball. Basketball confused me because when I caught the ball I didn't know whom to throw it to. "Me. Me," the kids would be yelling. "Over here." Suddenly it would occur to me I hadn't memorized which ghosts were on my team and which were on the other. When the kids said, "Automatic walk," the girl who was quieter than I kneeled with one end of the bat in each hand and placed it carefully on the plate. Then she dusted her hands as she walked to first base, where she rubbed her hands softly, fingers spread. She always got tagged out before second base. She would whisper-read but not talk. Her whisper was as soft as if she had no muscles. She seemed to be breathing from a distance. I heard no anger or tension.

I joined in at lunchtime when the other students, the Chinese too, talked about whether or not she was mute, although obviously she was not if she could read aloud. People told how *they* had tried *their* best to be friendly. *They* said hello, but if she refused to answer, well, they didn't see why they had to say hello anymore. She had no friends of her own but followed her sister everywhere, although people and she herself probably thought I was her friend. I also followed her sister about, who was fairly normal. She was almost two years older and read more than anyone else.

I hated the younger sister, the quiet one. I hated her when she was the last chosen for her team and I, the last chosen for my team. I hated her for her China doll hair cut. I hated her at music time for the wheezes that came out of her plastic flute.

One afternoon in the sixth grade (that year I was arrogant with talk, not knowing there were going to be high school dances and college seminars to set me back), I and my little sister and the quiet girl and her big sister stayed late after school for some reason. The cement was cooling, and the tetherball poles made shadows across the gravel. The hooks at the rope ends were clinking against the poles. We shouldn't have been so late; there was laundry work to do and Chinese school to get to by 5:00. The last time we had stayed late, my mother had phoned the police and told them we had been kidnapped by bandits. The radio stations broadcast our descriptions. I had to get home before she did that again. But sometimes if you loitered long enough in the schoolyard, the other children would have gone home and you could play with the equipment before the office took it away. We were chasing one another through the playground and in and out of the basement, where the playroom and lavatory were. During air raid drills (it was during the Korean War, which you knew about because every day the front page of the newspaper printed a map of Korea with the top part red and going up and down like a window shade), we curled up in this basement. Now everyone was gone. The playroom was army green and had nothing in it but a long trough with drinking spigots in rows. Pipes across the ceiling led to the drinking fountains and to the toilets in the next room. When someone flushed you could hear the water and other matter, which the children named, running inside the big pipe above the drinking spigots. There was one playroom for girls next to the girls' lavatory and one playroom for boys next to the boys' lavatory. The stalls were open and the toilets had no lids, by which we knew that ghosts have no sense of shame or privacy.

Inside the playroom the lightbulbs in cages had already been turned off. Daylight came in x-patterns through the caging at the windows. I looked out and, seeing no one in the schoolyard, ran outside to climb the fire escape upside down, hanging on to the metal stairs with fingers and toes.

I did a flip off the fire escape and ran across the schoolyard. The day was a great eye, and it was not paying much attention to me now. I could disappear with the sun; I could turn quickly sideways and slip into a different world. It seemed I could run faster at this time, and by evening I would be able to fly. As the afternoon wore on we could run into the forbidden places—the boys' big yard, the boys' playroom. We could go into the boys' lavatory and look at the urinals. The only time during school hours I had crossed the boys' yard was when a flatbed truck with a giant thing covered with canvas and tied down with ropes had parked across the street. The children had told one another that it was a gorilla in captivity; we couldn't decide whether the sign said "Trail of the Gorilla" or "Trial of the Gorilla." The thing was as big as a house. The teachers couldn't stop us from hysterically rushing to the fence and clinging to the wire mesh. Now I ran across the boys' yard clear to the Cyclone fence and thought about the hair that I had seen sticking out of the canvas. It was going to be summer soon, so you could feel that freedom coming on too.

I ran back into the girls' yard, and there was the quiet sister all by herself. I ran past her, and she followed me into the girls' lavatory. My footsteps rang hard against cement and tile because of the taps I had nailed into my shoes. Her footsteps were soft, padding after me. There was no one in the lavatory but the two of us. I ran all around the rows of twenty-five open stalls to make sure of that. No sisters. I think we must have been playing hide-and-go-seek. She was not good at hiding by herself and usually followed her sister; they'd hide in the same place. They must have gotten separated. In this growing twilight, a child could hide and never be found.

I stopped abruptly in front of the sinks, and she came running toward me before she could stop herself, so that she almost collided with me. I walked closer. She backed away, puzzlement, then alarm in her eyes.

"You're going to talk," I said, my voice steady and normal, as it is talking to the familiar, the weak, and the small. "I am going to make you talk, you sissy-girl." She stopped backing away and stood fixed.

I looked into her face so I could hate it close up. She wore black bangs, and her cheeks were pink and white. She was baby soft. I thought that I could put my thumb on her nose and push it bonelessly in, indent her face. I could poke dimples into her cheeks. I could work her face around like dough. She stood still, and I did not want to look at her face anymore; I hated fragility. I walked around her, looked her up and down the way the Mexican and Negro girls did when they fought, so tough. I hated her weak neck, the way it did not support her head but let it droop; her head would fall backward. I stared at the curve of her nape. I wished I was able to see what my own neck looked like from the back and sides. I hoped it did not look like hers; I wanted a stout neck. I grew my hair long to hide it in case it was a flower-stem neck. I walked around to the front of her to hate her face some more.

I reached up and took the fatty part of her cheek, not dough, but meat, between my thumb and finger. This close, and I saw no pores. "Talk," I said. "Are you going to talk?"

Her skin was fleshy, like squid out of which the glassy blades
of bones had been pulled. I wanted tough skin, hard brown
skin. I had callused my hands; I had scratched dirt to blacken
the nails, which I cut straight across to make stubby fingers.
I gave her face a squeeze. "Talk." When I let go, the pink
rushed back into my white thumbprint on her skin. I walked
around to her side. "Talk!" I shouted into the side of her head.
Her straight hair hung, the same all these years, no ringlets or
braids or permanents. I squeezed her other cheek. "Are you?
Huh? Are you going to talk?" She tried to shake her head,
but I had hold of her face. She had no muscles to jerk away.
Her skin seemed to stretch. I let go in horror. What if it came
away in my hand? "No, huh?" I said, rubbing the touch of
her off my fingers. "Say 'No,' then," I said. I gave her another pinch and a twist. "Say 'No.'" She shook her head, her
straight hair turning with her head, not swinging side to side
like the pretty girls'. She was so neat. Her neatness bothered
me. I hated the way she folded the wax paper from her lunch;
she did not wad her brown paper bag and her school papers. I
hated her clothes—the blue pastel cardigan, the white blouse
with the collar that lay flat over the cardigan, the homemade
flat, cotton skirt she wore when everybody else was wearing
flared skirts. I hated pastels; I would wear black always. I
squeezed again, harder, even though her cheek had a weak
rubbery feeling I did not like. I squeezed one cheek, then the
other, back and forth until the tears ran out of her eyes as if I
had pulled them out. "Stop crying," I said, but although she
habitually followed me around, she did not obey. Her eyes
dripped; her nose dripped. She wiped her eyes with her pa-
pery fingers. The skin on her hands and arms seemed pow-
dery-dry, like tracing paper, onion skin. I hated her fingers. I
could snap them like breadsticks. I pushed her hands down.
"Say 'Hi,'" I said. "'Hi.' Like that. Say your name. Go ahead.
Say it. Or are you stupid? You're so stupid, you don't know
your own name, is that it? When I say, 'What's your name?'
you just blurt it out, o.k.? What's your name?" Last year the
whole class had laughed at a boy who couldn't fill out a form
because he didn't know his father's name. The teacher sighed,
exasperated, and was very sarcastic, "Don't you notice things?
What does your mother call him?" she said. The class laughed

at how dumb he was not to notice things. "She calls him father of me," he said. Even we laughed, although we knew that
his mother did not call his father by name, and a son does not
know his father's name. We laughed and were relieved that
our parents had had the foresight to tell us some names we
could give the teachers. "If you're not stupid," I said to the
quiet girl, "what's your name?" She shook her head, and some
hair caught in the tears; wet black hair stuck to the side of the
pink and white face. I reached up (she was taller than I) and
took a strand of hair. I pulled it. "Well, then, let's honk your
hair," I said. "Honk. Honk." Then I pulled the other side—
"ho-o-n-nk"—a long pull; "ho-o-n-n-nk"—a longer pull. I
could see her little white ears, like white cutworms curled underneath the hair. "Talk!" I yelled into each cutworm.

I looked right at her. "I know you talk," I said. "I've heard
you." Her eyebrows flew up. Something in those black eyes
was startled, and I pursued it. "I was walking past your house
when you didn't know I was there. I heard you yell in English
and in Chinese. You weren't just talking. You were shouting.
I heard you shout. You were saying, 'Where are you?' Say that
again. Go ahead, just the way you did at home." I yanked
harder on the hair, but steadily, not jerking. I did not want
to pull it out. "Go ahead. Say, 'Where are you?' Say it loud
enough for your sister to come. Call her. Make her come help
you. Call her name. I'll stop if she comes. So call. Go ahead."

She shook her head, her mouth curved down, crying. I could
see her tiny white teeth, baby teeth. I wanted to grow big
strong yellow teeth. "You do have a tongue," I said. "So use
it." I pulled the hair at her temples, pulled the tears out of her
eyes. "Say, 'Ow,'" I said. "Just 'Ow.' Say, 'Let go.' Go ahead.
Say it. I'll honk you again if you don't say, 'Let me alone.' Say,
'Leave me alone,' and I'll let you go. I will. I'll let go if you say
it. You can stop this anytime you want to, you know. All you
have to do is tell me to stop. Just say, 'Stop.' You're just asking
for it, aren't you? You're just asking for another honk. Well
then, I'll have to give you another honk. Say, 'Stop.'" But she
didn't. I had to pull again and again.

Sounds did come out of her mouth, sobs, chokes, noises
that were almost words. Snot ran out of her nose. She tried to
wipe it on her hands, but there was too much of it. She used

her sleeve. "You're disgusting," I told her. "Look at you, snot streaming down your nose, and you won't say a word to stop it. You're such a nothing." I moved behind her and pulled the hair growing out of her weak neck. I let go. I stood silent for a long time. Then I screamed, "Talk!" I would scare the words out of her. If she had had little bound feet, the toes twisted under the balls, I would have jumped up and landed on them—crunch!—stomped on them with my iron shoes. She cried hard, sobbing aloud. "Cry, 'Mama,'" I said. "Come on. Cry, 'Mama.' Say, 'Stop it.'"

I put my finger on her pointed chin. "I don't like you. I don't like the weak little toots you make on your flute. Wheeze. Wheeze. I don't like the way you don't swing at the ball. I don't like the way you're the last one chosen. I don't like the way you can't make a fist for tetherball. Why don't you make a fist? Come on. Get tough. Come on. Throw fists." I pushed at her long hands; they swung limply at her sides. Her fingers were so long, I thought maybe they had an extra joint. They couldn't possibly make fists like other people's. "Make a fist," I said. "Come on. Just fold those fingers up; fingers on the inside, thumbs on the outside. Say something. Honk me back. You're so tall, and you let me pick on you.

"Would you like a hanky? I can't get you one with embroidery on it or crocheting along the edges, but I'll get you some toilet paper if you tell me to. Go ahead. Ask me. I'll get it for you if you ask." She did not stop crying. "Why don't you scream, 'Help'?" I suggested. "Say, 'Help.' Go ahead." She cried on. "O.K. O.K. Don't talk. Just scream, and I'll let you go. Won't that feel good? Go ahead. Like this." I screamed, not too loudly. My voice hit the tile and rang it as if I had thrown a rock at it. The stalls opened wider and the toilets wider and darker. Shadows leaned at angles I had not seen before. It was very late. Maybe a janitor had locked me in with this girl for the night. Her black eyes blinked and stared, blinked and stared. I felt dizzy from hunger. We had been in this lavatory together forever. My mother would call the police again if I didn't bring my sister home soon. "I'll let you go if you say just one word," I said. "You can even say, 'a' or 'the,' and I'll let you go. Come on. Please." She didn't shake her head anymore, only cried steadily, so much water

coming out of her. I could see the two duct holes where the
tears welled out. Quarts of tears but no words. I grabbed her
by the shoulder. I could feel bones. The light was coming in
queerly through the frosted glass with the chicken wire embedded in it. Her crying was like an animal's—a seal's—and
it echoed around the basement. "Do you want to stay here all
night?" I asked. "Your mother is wondering what happened
to her baby. You wouldn't want to have her mad at you. You'd
better say something." I shook her shoulder. I pulled her hair
again. I squeezed her face. "Come on! Talk! Talk! Talk!" She
didn't seem to feel it anymore when I pulled her hair. "There's
nobody here but you and me. This isn't a classroom or a playground or a crowd. I'm just one person. You can talk in front
of one person. Don't make me pull harder and harder until
you talk." But her hair seemed to stretch; she did not say a
word. "I'm going to pull harder. Don't make me pull anymore, or your hair will come out and you're going to be bald.
Do you want to be bald? You don't want to be bald, do you?"

Far away, coming from the edge of town, I heard whistles
blow. The cannery was changing shifts, letting out the afternoon people, and still we were here at school. It was a sad
sound—work done. The air was lonelier after the sound died.

"Why won't you talk?" I started to cry. What if I couldn't
stop, and everyone would want to know what happened?
"Now look what you've done," I scolded. "You're going to
pay for this. I want to know why. And you're going to tell me
why. You don't see I'm trying to help you out, do you? Do you
want to be like this, dumb (do you know what dumb means?),
your whole life? Don't you ever want to be a cheerleader? Or
a pompon girl? What are you going to do for a living? Yeah,
you're going to have to work because you can't be a housewife.
Somebody has to marry you before you can be a housewife.
And you, you are a plant. Do you know that? That's all you
are if you don't talk. If you don't talk, you can't have a personality. You'll have no personality and no hair. You've got to
let people know you have a personality and a brain. You think
somebody is going to take care of you all your stupid life? You
think you'll always have your big sister? You think somebody's
going to marry you, is that it? Well, you're not the type that
gets dates, let alone gets married. Nobody's going to notice

you. And you have to talk for interviews, speak right up in front of the boss. Don't you know that? You're so dumb. Why do I waste my time on you?" Sniffling and snorting, I couldn't stop crying and talking at the same time. I kept wiping my nose on my arm, my sweater lost somewhere (probably not worn because my mother said to wear a sweater). It seemed as if I had spent my life in that basement, doing the worst thing I had yet done to another person. "I'm doing this for your own good," I said. "Don't you dare tell anyone I've been bad to you. Talk. Please talk."

I was getting dizzy from the air I was gulping. Her sobs and my sobs were bouncing wildly off the tile, sometimes together, sometimes alternating. "I don't understand why you won't say just one word," I cried, clenching my teeth. My knees were shaking, and I hung on to her hair to stand up. Another time I'd stayed too late, I had had to walk around two Negro kids who were bonking each other's head on the concrete. I went back later to see if the concrete had cracks in it. "Look. I'll give you something if you talk. I'll give you my pencil box. I'll buy you some candy. O.K.? What do you want? Tell me. Just say it, and I'll give it to you. Just say, 'yes,' or, 'O.K.,' or, 'Baby Ruth.'" But she didn't want anything.

I had stopped pinching her cheek because I did not like the feel of her skin. I would go crazy if it came away in my hands. "I skinned her," I would have to confess.

Suddenly I heard footsteps hurrying through the basement, and her sister ran into the lavatory calling her name. "Oh, there you are," I said. "We've been waiting for you. I was only trying to teach her to talk. She wouldn't cooperate, though." Her sister went into one of the stalls and got handfuls of toilet paper and wiped her off. Then we found my sister, and we walked home together. "Your family really ought to force her to speak," I advised all the way home. "You mustn't pamper her."

The world is sometimes just, and I spent the next eighteen months sick in bed with a mysterious illness. There was no pain and no symptoms, though the middle line in my left palm broke in two. Instead of starting junior high school, I lived like the Victorian recluses I read about. I had a rented hospital bed in the living room, where I watched soap operas on t.v., and my family cranked me up and down. I saw no one but my family, who took good care of me. I could have no visitors, no other relatives, no villagers. My bed was against the west window, and I watched the seasons change the peach tree. I had a bell to ring for help. I used a bedpan. It was the best year and a half of my life. Nothing happened.

But one day my mother, the doctor, said, "You're ready to get up today. It's time to get up and go to school." I walked about outside to get my legs working, leaning on a staff I cut from the peach tree. The sky and trees, the sun were immense—no longer framed by a window, no longer grayed with a fly screen. I sat down on the sidewalk in amazement—the night, the stars. But at school I had to figure out again how to talk. I met again the poor girl I had tormented. She had not changed. She wore the same clothes, hair cut, and manner as when we were in elementary school, no make-up on the pink and white face, while the other Asian girls were starting to tape their eyelids. She continued to be able to read aloud. But there was hardly any reading aloud anymore, less and less as we got into high school.

I was wrong about nobody taking care of her. Her sister became a clerk-typist and stayed unmarried. They lived with their mother and father. She did not have to leave the house except to go to the movies. She was supported. She was protected by her family, as they would normally have done in China if they could have afforded it, not sent off to school with strangers, ghosts, boys.

We have so many secrets to hold in. Our sixth grade teacher, who liked to explain things to children, let us read our files. My record shows that I flunked kindergarten and in first grade had no IQ—a zero IQ. I did remember the first grade teacher calling out during a test, while students marked X's on a girl or a boy or a dog, which I covered with black. First grade was when I discovered eye control; with my seeing I could shrink the teacher down to a height of one inch, gesticulating and mouthing on the horizon. I lost this power in sixth grade for lack of practice, the teacher a generous man. "Look at your family's old addresses and think about how you've moved," he said. I looked at my parents' aliases and their birthdays, which variants I knew. But when I saw Father's occupations I exclaimed, "Hey, he wasn't a farmer, he was a . . ." He had been a gambler. My throat cut off the word—silence in front of the most understanding teacher. There were secrets never to be said in front of the ghosts, immigration secrets whose telling could get us sent back to China.

Sometimes I hated the ghosts for not letting us talk; sometimes I hated the secrecy of the Chinese. "Don't tell," said my parents, though we couldn't tell if we wanted to because we didn't know. Are there really secret trials with our own judges and penalties? Are there really flags in Chinatown signaling what stowaways have arrived in San Francisco Bay, their names, and which ships they came on? "Mother, I heard some kids say there are flags like that. Are there? What colors are they? Which buildings do they fly from?"

"No. No, there aren't any flags like that. They're just talking-story. You're always believing talk-story."

"I won't tell anybody, Mother. I promise. Which buildings are the flags on? Who flies them? The benevolent associations?"

"I don't know. Maybe the San Francisco villagers do that; our villagers don't do that."

"What do our villagers do?"

They would not tell us children because we had been born among ghosts, were taught by ghosts, and were ourselves half ghosts. They called us a kind of ghost. Ghosts are noisy and full of air; they talk during meals. They talk about anything.

"Do we send up signal kites? That would be a good idea, huh? We could fly them from the school balcony." Instead of cheaply stringing dragonflies by the tail, we could fly expensive kites, the sky splendid in Chinese colors, distracting ghost eyes while the new people sneak in. Don't tell. "Never tell."

Occasionally the rumor went about that the United States immigration authorities had set up headquarters in the San Francisco or Sacramento Chinatown to urge wetbacks and stowaways, anybody here on fake papers, to come to the city and get their files straightened out. The immigrants discussed whether or not to turn themselves in. "We might as well," somebody would say. "Then we'd have our citizenship for real."

"Don't be a fool," somebody else would say. "It's a trap. You go in there saying you want to straighten out your papers, they'll deport you."

"No, they won't. They're promising that nobody is going to go to jail or get deported. They'll give you citizenship as a reward for turning yourself in, for your honesty."

"Don't you believe it. So-and-so trusted them, and he was deported. They deported his children too."

"Where can they send us now? Hong Kong? Taiwan? I've never been to Hong Kong or Taiwan. The Big Six? Where?" We don't belong anywhere since the Revolution. The old China has disappeared while we've been away.

"Don't tell," advised my parents. "Don't go to San Francisco until they leave."

Lie to Americans. Tell them you were born during the San Francisco earthquake. Tell them your birth certificate and your parents were burned up in the fire. Don't report crimes; tell them we have no crimes and no poverty. Give a new name every time you get arrested; the ghosts won't recognize you. Pay the new immigrants twenty-five cents an hour and say we have no unemployment. And, of course, tell them we're against Communism. Ghosts have no memory anyway and poor eyesight. And the Han people won't be pinned down.

Even the good things are unspeakable, so how could I ask about deformities? From the configurations of food my mother set out, we kids had to infer the holidays. She did not whip us up with holiday anticipation or explain. You only remembered that perhaps a year ago you had eaten monk's food, or that there was meat, and it was a meat holiday; or you had eaten moon cakes or long noodles for long life (which is a pun). In front of the whole chicken with its slit throat toward the ceiling, she'd lay out just so many pairs of chopsticks alternating with wine cups, which were not for us because there were a different number from the number in our family, and they were set too close together for us to sit at. To sit at one of those place settings a being would have to be about two inches wide, a tall wisp of an invisibility. Mother would pour Seagram's 7 into the cups and, after a while, pour it back into the bottle. Never explaining. How can Chinese keep any traditions at all? They don't even make you pay attention, slipping in a ceremony and clearing the table before the children notice specialness. The adults get mad, evasive, and shut you up if you ask. You get no warning that you shouldn't wear a white ribbon in your hair until they hit you and give you the sideways glare for the rest of the day. They hit you if you wave brooms around or drop chopsticks or drum them. They hit you if you wash your hair on certain days, or tap somebody with a ruler, or step over a brother whether it's during your menses or not. You figure out what you got hit for and don't do it again if you figured correctly. But I think that if you don't figure it out, it's all right. Then you can grow up bothered by "neither ghosts nor deities." "Gods you avoid won't hurt you." I don't see how they kept up a continuous culture for five thousand years. Maybe they didn't; maybe everyone makes it up as they go along. If we had to depend on being told, we'd have no religion, no babies, no menstruation (sex, of course, unspeakable), no death.

I thought talking and not talking made the difference between sanity and insanity. Insane people were the ones who couldn't explain themselves. There were many crazy girls and women. Perhaps the sane people stayed in China to build the new, sane society. Or perhaps our little village had become odd in its isolation. No other Chinese, neither the ones in Sacramento, nor the ones in San Francisco, nor Hawaii speak like us. Within a few blocks of our house were half a dozen crazy women and girls, all belonging to village families.

There was the woman next door who was chatty one moment—inviting us children to our first "sky movie"—and shut up the next. Then we would see silver heat rise from her body; it solidified before our eyes. She made us afraid, though she said nothing, did nothing. Her husband had to drive home fast in the middle of the show. He threw the loudspeaker out the window. She sat like stone in the front seat; he had to open the door for her and help her out. She slammed the door. After they went inside, we could hear doors slamming throughout their house. They did not have children, so it was not children slamming doors. The next day, she disappeared, and people would say she had been taken to Napa or Agnew. When a woman disappeared or reappeared after an absence, people whispered, "Napa." "Agnew." She had been locked up before. Her husband rented out the house and also went away. The last time he had left town, he had been single. He had gone back to China, where he had bought her and married her. Now while she was locked up in the asylum, he went, people said, to the Midwest. A year or two passed. He returned to Napa to drive her home. As a present, he had brought with him from the Midwest a child, half Chinese and half white. People said it was his illegitimate son. She was very happy to have a son to raise in her old age, although I saw that the boy hit her to get candy and toys. She was the one who died happy, sitting on the steps after cooking dinner.

There was Crazy Mary, whose family were Christian converts. Her mother and father had come to the Gold Mountain leaving Mary, a toddler, in China. By the time they made enough money to send for her, having replaced the horse and vegetable wagon with a truck, she was almost twenty and crazy. Her parents often said, "We thought she'd be grown but young enough to learn English and translate for us." Their other children, who were born in the U.S., were normal and could translate. I was glad that I was born nine months after my mother emigrated. Crazy Mary was a large girl and had a big black mole on her face, which is a sign of fortune. The black mole pulls you forward with its power; a mole at the back of the head pulls you back. She seemed cheerful, but pointed at things that were not there. I disliked looking at her; you never knew what you were going to see, what rictus would shape her face. Or what you would hear—growls, laughs. Her head hung like a bull's, and her eyes peeked at you out of her hair. Her face was a white blur because she was indoors so much and also because I tried not to look at her directly. She often had rice on her face and in her hair. Her mother cut her hair neatly around her ears, stubble at the back of her neck. She wore pajamas, a rough brown sweater buttoned crooked, and a big apron, not a work apron but a bib. She wore slippers, and you could see her thick ankles naked, her naked heels and tendons. When you went to her house, you had to keep alert because you didn't want her to come at you from around a corner, her hands loose. She would lurch out of dark corners; houses with crazy girls have locked rooms and drawn curtains. A smell came from her which would not have been unpleasant had it belonged to someone else. The house smelled of her, camphoraceous. Maybe they tied camphor on her pulse to cure her. Our mother used to tie dried prunes stuffed with camphor to our wrists. We got very embarrassed at school when the rags came loose and their contents fell out in clumps and grains. Crazy Mary did not improve, and so she too was locked up in the crazyhouse. She was never released. Her family said she liked it there.

There was a slough where our mother took us to pick orange berries. We carried them home in pots and bags to cook in an egg soup. It was not a wild slough, although tules, cattails and foxtails still grew, also dill, and yellow chamomile, fat and fuzzy as bees. People had been known to have followed the hobo paths and parted the tall stalks to find dead bodies—hobos, Chinese suicides, children. Red-winged blackbirds, whose shoulders were the same color as the berries, perched on a wood bridge, really a train trestle. When a train heaved across it, the black steam engine swollen to bursting like the boiler at the laundry, the birds flew up like Halloween.

We were not the only people who picked in the slough; a witchwoman also went there. One of my brothers named her Pee-A-Nah, which does not have a meaning. Of all the crazy ladies, she was the one who was the village idiot, the public one. When our mother was with us, she would chase the witchwoman away. We'd stand beside and behind our mother, who would say to her, "Leave us alone now" or "Good morning," and Pee-A-Nah would go away. But when we were by ourselves, she chased us. "Pee-A-Nah!" we'd scream. We'd run, terrified, along the hobo paths, over the trestle, and through the streets. Kids said she was a witch capable of witch deeds, unspeakable boilings and tearings apart and transformations if she caught us. "She'll touch you on the shoulder, and you'll not be you anymore. You'd be a piece of glass winking and blinking to people on the sidewalk." She came riding to the slough with a broom between her legs, and she had powdered one cheek red and one white. Her hair stood up and out to the sides in dry masses, black even though she was old. She wore a pointed hat and layers of capes, shawls, sweaters buttoned at the throat like capes, the sleeves flying behind like sausage skins. She came to the slough not to harvest the useful herbs and berries the way we did, but to collect armfuls of cattails and tall grasses and tuber flowers. Sometimes she carried her broomstick horse like a staff. In the fall (she would be such a sight in the fall) she ran "faster than a swallow," her cattails popping seed, white seed puffs blowing after her, clouds of fairies dancing over her head. She streamed color and flapped in layers. She was an angry witch, not a happy one. She was fierce; not a fairy, after all, but a demon. She did run fast, as fast as a child, although she was a wrinkled woman, an outburst that jumped at us from bushes, between cars, between buildings. We children vowed that we would never run home if she came after one of us. No matter what she did to us, we had to run in the opposite direction from home. We didn't want her to know where we lived. If we couldn't outrun her and lose her, we'd die alone. Once she spotted my sister in our yard, opened the gate, and chased her up the stairs. My sister screamed and cried, banging on the door. Our mother let her in quickly, looking frightened as she fumbled at the latches to lock out Pee-A-Nah. My sister had to be chanted out of her screaming. It was a good thing Pee-A-Nah had a short memory because she did not find our house again. Sometimes when a bunch of tules and reeds and grasses mixed and blew and waved, I was terrified that it was she, that she was carrying them or parting them. One day we realized that we had not seen her for a while. We forgot her, never seeing her again. She had probably been locked up in the crazyhouse too.

I had invented a quill pen out of a peacock feather, but stopped writing with it when I saw that it waved like a one-eyed slough plant.

I thought every house had to have its crazy woman or crazy girl, every village its idiot. Who would be It at our house? Probably me. My sister did not start talking among nonfamily until a year after I started, but she was neat while I was messy, my hair tangled and dusty. My dirty hands broke things. Also I had had the mysterious illness. And there were adventurous people inside my head to whom I talked. With them I was frivolous and violent, orphaned. I was white and had red hair, and I rode a white horse. Once when I realized how often I went away to see these free movies, I asked my sister, just checking to see if hearing voices in motors and seeing cowboy movies on blank walls was normal, I asked, "Uh," trying to be casual, "do you talk to people that aren't real inside your mind?"

"Do I *what*?" she said.

"Never mind," I said fast. "Never mind. Nothing."

My sister, my almost-twin, the person most like me in all the world, had said, "*What?*"

I had vampire nightmares; every night the fangs grew longer, and my angel wings turned pointed and black. I hunted humans down in the long woods and shadowed them with my blackness. Tears dripped from my eyes, but blood dripped from my fangs, blood of the people I was supposed to love.

I did not want to be our crazy one. Quite often the big loud women came shouting into the house, "Now when you sell this one, I'd like to buy her to be my maid." Then they laughed. They always said that about my sister, not me because I dropped dishes at them. I picked my nose while I was cooking and serving. My clothes were wrinkled even though we owned a laundry. Indeed I was getting stranger every day. I affected a limp. And, of course, the mysterious disease I had had might have been dormant and contagious.

But if I made myself unsellable here, my parents need only wait until China, and there, where anything happens, they would be able to unload us, even me—sellable, marriageable. So while the adults wept over the letters about the neighbors gone berserk turning Communist ("They do funny dances; they sing weird songs, just syllables. They make us dance; they make us sing"), I was secretly glad. As long as the aunts kept disappearing and the uncles dying after unspeakable tortures, my parents would prolong their Gold Mountain stay. We could start spending our fare money on a car and chairs, a stereo. Nobody wrote to tell us that Mao himself had been matched to an older girl when he was a child and that he was freeing women from prisons, where they had been put for refusing the businessmen their parents had picked as husbands. Nobody told us that the Revolution (the Liberation) was against girl slavery and girl infanticide (a village-wide party if it's a boy). Girls would no longer have to kill themselves rather than get married. May the Communists light up the house on a girl's birthday.

I watched our parents buy a sofa, then a rug, curtains, chairs to replace the orange and apple crates one by one, now to be used for storage. Good. At the beginning of the second Communist five-year plan, our parents bought a car. But you could see the relatives and the villagers getting more worried about what to do with the girls. We had three girl second cousins, no boys; their great-grandfather and our grandfather were brothers. The great-grandfather was the old man who lived with them, as the river-pirate great-uncle was the old man who lived with us. When my sisters and I ate at their house, there we would be—six girls eating. The old man opened his eyes wide at us and turned in a circle, surrounded. His neck tendons stretched out. "Maggots!" he shouted. "Maggots! Where are my grandsons? I want grandsons! Give me grandsons! Maggots!" He pointed at each one of us, "Maggot! Maggot! Maggot! Maggot! Maggot! Maggot!" Then he dived into his food, eating fast and getting seconds. "Eat, maggots," he said. "Look at the maggots chew."

"He does that at every meal," the girls told us in English.

"Yeah," we said. "Our old man hates us too. What assholes."

Third Grand-Uncle finally did get a boy, though, his only great-grandson. The boy's parents and the old man bought him toys, bought him everything—new diapers, new plastic pants—not homemade diapers, not bread bags. They gave him a full-month party inviting all the emigrant villagers; they deliberately hadn't given the girls parties, so that no one would notice another girl. Their brother got toy trucks that were big enough to climb inside. When he grew older, he got a bicycle and let the girls play with his old tricycle and wagon. My mother bought his sisters a typewriter. "They can be clerk-typists," their father kept saying, but he would not buy them a typewriter.

"What an asshole," I said, muttering the way my father muttered "Dog vomit" when the customers nagged him about missing socks.

Maybe my mother was afraid that I'd say things like that out loud and so had cut my tongue. Now again plans were urgently afoot to fix me up, to improve my voice. The wealthiest villager wife came to the laundry one day to have a listen. "You better do something with this one," she told my mother. "She has an ugly voice. She quacks like a pressed duck." Then she looked at me unnecessarily hard; Chinese do not have to address children directly. "You have what we call a pressed-duck voice," she said. This woman was the giver of American names, a powerful namer, though it was American names; my parents gave the Chinese names. And she was right: if you squeezed the duck hung up to dry in the east window, the sound that was my voice would come out of it. She was a woman of such power that all we immigrants and descendants of immigrants were obliged to her family forever for bringing us here and for finding us jobs, and she had named my voice.

"No," I quacked. "No, I don't."

"Don't talk back," my mother scolded. Maybe this lady was powerful enough to send us back.

I went to the front of the laundry and worked so hard that I impolitely did not take notice of her leaving.

"Improve that voice," she had instructed my mother, "or else you'll never marry her off. Even the fool half ghosts won't have her." So I discovered the next plan to get rid of us: marry us off here without waiting until China. The villagers' peasant minds converged on marriage. Late at night when we walked home from the laundry, they should have been sleeping be-hind locked doors, not overflowing into the streets in front of the benevolent associations, all alit. We stood on tiptoes and on one another's shoulders, and through the door we saw spotlights open on tall singers afire with sequins. An opera from San Francisco! An opera from Hong Kong! Usually I did not understand the words in operas, whether because of our obscure dialect or theirs I didn't know, but I heard one line sung out into the night air in a woman's voice high and clear as ice. She was standing on a chair, and she sang, "Beat me, then, beat me." The crowd laughed until the tears rolled down their cheeks while the cymbals clashed—the dragon's copper laugh—and the drums banged like firecrackers. "She is play-ing the part of a new daughter-in-law," my mother explained. "Beat me, then, beat me," she sang again and again. It must have been a refrain; each time she sang it, the audience broke up laughing. Men laughed; women laughed. They were having a great time.

"Chinese smeared bad daughters-in-law with honey and tied them naked on top of ant nests," my father said. "A hus-band may kill a wife who disobeys him. Confucius said that." Confucius, the rational man.

The singer, I thought, sounded like me talking, yet every-one said, "Oh, beautiful. Beautiful," when she sang high.

Walking home, the noisy women shook their old heads and sang a folk song that made them laugh uproariously:

> Marry a rooster, follow a rooster.
> Marry a dog, follow a dog.
> Married to a cudgel, married to a pestle,
> Be faithful to it. Follow it.

I learned that young men were placing ads in the *Gold Mountain News* to find wives when my mother and father started answering them. Suddenly a series of new workers showed up at the laundry; they each worked for a week before they disappeared. They ate with us. They talked Chinese with my parents. They did not talk to us. We were to call them "Elder Brother," although they were not related to us. They were all funny-looking FOB's, Fresh-off-the-Boat's, as the Chinese-American kids at school called the young immigrants. FOB's wear high-riding gray slacks and white shirts with the sleeves rolled up. Their eyes do not focus correctly— shifty-eyed—and they hold their mouths slack, not tight-jawed masculine. They shave off their sideburns. The girls said *they'd* never date an FOB. My mother took one home from the laundry, and I saw him looking over our photographs. "This one," he said, picking up my sister's picture.

"No. No," said my mother. "This one," my picture. "The oldest first," she said. Good. I was an obstacle. I would protect my sister and myself at the same time. As my parents and the FOB sat talking at the kitchen table, I dropped two dishes. I found my walking stick and limped across the floor. I twisted my mouth and caught my hand in the knots of my hair. I spilled soup on the FOB when I handed him his bowl. "She can sew, though," I heard my mother say, "and sweep." I raised dust swirls sweeping around and under the FOB's chair—very bad luck because spirits live inside the broom. I put on my shoes with the open flaps and flapped about like a Wino Ghost. From then on, I wore those shoes to parties, whenever the mothers gathered to talk about marriages. The FOB and my parents paid me no attention, half ghosts half invisible, but when he left, my mother yelled at me about the dried-duck voice, the bad temper, the laziness, the clumsiness, the stupidity that comes from reading too much. The young men stopped visiting; not one came back. "Couldn't you just stop rubbing your nose?" she scolded. "All the village ladies are talking about your nose. They're afraid to eat our pastries because you might have kneaded the dough." But I couldn't stop at will anymore, and a crease developed across the bridge. My parents would not give up, though. "Though you can't see it," my mother said, "a red string around your ankle ties you to the person you'll marry. He's already been born, and he's on the other end of the string."

At Chinese school there was a mentally retarded boy who followed me around, probably believing that we were two of a kind. He had an enormous face, and he growled. He laughed from so far within his thick body that his face got confused about what the sounds coming up into his mouth might be, laughs or cries. He barked unhappily. He didn't go to classes but hung around the playgrounds. We suspected he was not a boy but an adult. He wore baggy khaki trousers like a man's. He carried bags of toys for giving to certain children. Whatever you wanted, he'd get it for you—brand-new toys, as many as you could think up in your poverty, all the toys you never had when you were younger. We wrote lists, discussed our lists, compared them. Those kids not in his favor gave lists to those who were. "Where do you get the toys?" I asked. "I . . . own . . . stores," he roared, one word at a time, thick tongued. At recess the day after ordering, we got handed out to us coloring books, paint sets, model kits. But sometimes he chased us—his fat arms out to the side; his fat fingers opening and closing; his legs stiff like Frankenstein's monster, like the mummy dragging its foot; growling; laughing-crying. Then we'd have to run, following the old rule, running away from our house.

But suddenly he knew where we worked. He found us; maybe he had followed us in his wanderings. He started sitting at our laundry. Many of the storekeepers invited sitting in their stores, but we did not have sitting because the laundry was hot and because it was outside Chinatown. He sweated; he panted, the stubble rising and falling on his fat neck and chin. He sat on two large cartons that he brought with him and stacked one on top of the other. He said hello to my mother and father, and then, balancing his heavy head, he lowered himself carefully onto his cartons and sat. My parents allowed this. They did not chase him out or comment about how strange he was. I stopped placing orders for toys. I didn't limp anymore; my parents would only figure that this zombie and I were a match.

I studied hard, got straight A's, but nobody seemed to see that I was smart and had nothing in common with this monster, this birth defect. At school there were dating and dances, but not for good Chinese girls. "You ought to develop yourself socially as well as mentally," the American teachers, who took me aside, said.

I told nobody about the monster. And nobody else was talking either; no mention about the laundry workers who appeared and disappeared; no mention about the sitter. Maybe I was making it all up, and queer marriage notions did not occur to other people. I had better not say a word, then. Don't give them ideas. Keep quiet.

I pressed clothes—baskets of giants' BVD's, long underwear even in summertime, T-shirts, sweat shirts. Laundry work is men's clothes, unmarried-men's clothes. My back felt sick because it was toward the monster who gave away toys. His lumpishness was sending out germs that would lower my IQ. His leechiness was drawing IQ points out of the back of my head. I maneuvered my work shifts so that my brothers would work the afternoons, when he usually came lumbering into the laundry, but he caught on and began coming during the evening, the cool shift. Then I would switch back to the afternoon or to the early mornings on weekends and in summer, dodging him. I kept my sister with me, protecting her without telling her why. If she hadn't noticed, then I mustn't scare her. "Let's clean house this morning," I'd say. Our other sister was a baby, and the brothers were not in danger. But the were-person would stalk down our street; his thick face smiled between the lettering on the laundry window, and when he saw me working, he shouldered inside. At night I thought I heard his feet dragging around the house, scraping gravel. I sat up to listen to our watchdog prowl the yard, pulling her long chain after her, and that worried me too. I had to do something about that chain, the weight of it scraping her neck fur short. And if she was walking about, why wasn't she barking? Maybe somebody was out there taming her with raw meat. I could not ask for help.

Every day the hulk took one drink from the watercooler and went once to the bathroom, stumbling between the presses into the back of the laundry, big shoes clumping. Then my parents would talk about what could be inside his boxes. Were they filled with toys? With money? When the toilet flushed, they stopped talking about it. But one day he either stayed in the bathroom for a long time or went for a walk and left the boxes unguarded. "Let's open them up," said my mother, and she did. I looked over her shoulder. The two cartons were stuffed with pornography—naked magazines, nudie postcards and photographs.

You would think she'd have thrown him out right then, but my mother said, "My goodness, he's not too stupid to want to find out about women." I heard the old women talk about how he was stupid but very rich.

Maybe because I was the one with the tongue cut loose, I had grown inside me a list of over two hundred things that I had to tell my mother so that she would know the true things about me and to stop the pain in my throat. When I first started counting, I had had only thirty-six items: how I had prayed for a white horse of my own—white, the bad, mournful color—and prayer bringing me to the attention of the god of the black-and-white nuns who gave us "holy cards" in the park. How I wanted the horse to start the movies in my mind coming true. How I had picked on a girl and made her cry. How I had stolen from the cash register and bought candy for everybody I knew, not just brothers and sisters, but strangers too and ghost children. How it was me who pulled up the onions in the garden out of anger. How I had jumped headfirst off the dresser, not accidentally, but so I could fly. Then there were my fights at Chinese school. And the nuns who kept stopping us in the park, which was across the street from Chinese school, to tell us that if we didn't get baptized we'd go to a hell like one of the nine Taoist hells forever. And the obscene caller that phoned us at home when the adults were at the laundry. And the Mexican and Filipino girls at school who went to "confession," and how I envied them their white dresses and their chance each Saturday to tell even thoughts that were sinful. If only I could let my mother know the list, she—and the world—would become more like me, and I would never be alone again. I would pick a time of day when my mother was alone and tell her one item a day; I'd be finished in less than a year. If the telling got excruciating and her anger too bad, I'd tell five items once a week like the Catholic girls, and I'd still be through in a year, maybe ten months. My mother's most peaceful time was in the evenings when she starched the white shirts. The laundry would be clean, the gray wood floors sprinkled and swept with water and wet sawdust. She would be wringing shirts at the starch tub and not running about. My father and sisters and brothers would be at their own jobs mending, folding, packaging. Steam would be rising from the starch, the air cool at last. Yes, that would be the time and place for the telling.

And I wanted to ask again why the women in our family have a split nail on our left little toe. Whenever we asked our parents about it, they would glance at each other, embarrassed. I think I've heard one of them say, "She didn't get away." I made up that we are descended from an ancestress who stubbed her toe and fell when running from a rapist. I wanted to ask my mother if I had guessed right.

I hunkered down between the wall and the wicker basket of shirts. I had decided to start with the earliest item—when I had smashed a spider against the white side of the house: it was the first thing I killed. I said, clearly, "I killed a spider," and it was nothing; she did not hit me or throw hot starch at me. It sounded like nothing to me too. How strange when I had had such feelings of death shoot through my hand and into my body so that I would surely die. So I had to continue, of course, and let her know how important it had been. "I returned every day to look at its smear on the side of the house," I said. "It was our old house, the one we lived in until I was five. I went to the wall every day to look. I studied the stain." Relieved because she said nothing but only continued squeezing the starch, I went away feeling pretty good. Just two hundred and six more items to go. I moved carefully all the next day so as not to do anything or have anything happen to me that would

make me go back to two hundred and seven again. I'd tell a
couple of easy ones and work up to how I had pulled the quiet
girl's hair and how I had enjoyed the year being sick. If it was
going to be this easy, maybe I could blurt out several a day,
maybe an easy one and a hard one. I could go chronologically,
or I could work from easy to hard or hard to easy, depending
on my mood. On the second night I talked about how I had
hinted to a ghost girl that I wished I had a doll of my own
until she gave me a head and body to glue together—that she
hadn't given it to me of her own generosity but because I had
hinted. But on the fifth night (I skipped two to reward myself)
I decided it was time to do a really hard one and tell her about
the white horse. And suddenly the duck voice came out, which
I did not use with the family. "What's it called, Mother"—the
duck voice coming out talking to my own mother—"when a
person whispers to the head of the sages—no, not the sages,
more like the buddhas but not real people like the buddhas
(they've always lived in the sky and never turned into people like the buddhas)—and you whisper to them, the boss of
them, and ask for things? They're like magicians? What do you
call it when you talk to the boss magician?"

"'Talking-to-the-top-magician,' I guess."

"I did that. Yes. That's it. That's what I did. I talked-to-the-
top-magician and asked for a white horse." There. Said.

"Mm," she said, squeezing the starch out of the collar and
cuffs. But I had talked, and she acted as if she hadn't heard.

Perhaps she hadn't understood. I had to be more explicit.
I hated this. "I kneeled on the bed in there, in the laundry
bedroom, and put my arms up like I saw in a comic book"—
one night I heard monsters coming through the kitchen, and
I had promised the god in the movies, the one the Mexicans
and Filipinos have, as in "God Bless America," that I would
not read comic books anymore if he would save me just this
once; I had broken that promise, and I needed to tell all this
to my mother too—"and in that ludicrous position asked for
a horse."

"Mm," she said, nodded, and kept dipping and squeezing.

On my two nights off, I had sat on the floor too but had not
said a word.

"Mother," I whispered and quacked.

"I can't stand this whispering," she said looking right at me, stopping her squeezing. "Senseless gabbings every night. I wish you would stop. Go away and work. Whispering, whispering, making no sense. Madness. I don't feel like hearing your craziness."

So I had to stop, relieved in some ways. I shut my mouth, but I felt something alive tearing at my throat, bite by bite, from the inside. Soon there would be three hundred things, and too late to get them out before my mother grew old and died.

I had probably interrupted her in the middle of her own quiet time when the boiler and presses were off and the cool night flew against the windows in moths and crickets. Very few customers came in. Starching the shirts for the next day's pressing was probably my mother's time to ride off with the people in her own mind. That would explain why she was so far away and did not want to listen to me. "Leave me alone," she said.

The hulk, the hunching sitter, brought a third box now, to rest his feet on. He patted his boxes. He sat in wait, hunching on his pile of dirt. My throat hurt constantly, vocal cords taut to snapping. One night when the laundry was so busy that the whole family was eating dinner there, crowded around the little round table, my throat burst open. I stood up, talking and burbling. I looked directly at my mother and at my father and screamed, "I want you to tell that hulk, that gorilla-ape, to go away and never bother us again. I know what you're up to. You're thinking he's rich, and we're poor. You think we're odd and not pretty and we're not bright. You think you can give us away to freaks. You better not do that, Mother. I don't want to see him or his dirty boxes here tomorrow. If I see him here one more time, I'm going away. I'm going away anyway. I am. Do you hear me? I may be ugly and clumsy, but one thing I'm not, I'm not retarded. There's nothing wrong with my brain. Do you know what the Teacher Ghosts say about me? They tell me I'm smart, and I can win scholarships. I can get into colleges. I've already applied. I'm smart. I can do all kinds of things. I know how to get A's, and they say I could be a scientist or a mathematician if I want. I can make a living and take care of myself. So you don't have to find me a keeper who's too dumb to know a bad bargain. I'm so smart, if they say write ten pages, I can write fifteen. I can do ghost things even better than ghosts can. Not everybody thinks I'm nothing. I am not going to be a slave or a wife. Even if I am stupid and talk funny and get sick, I won't let you turn me into a slave or a wife. I'm getting out of here. I can't stand living here anymore. It's your fault I talk weird. The only reason I flunked kindergarten was because you couldn't teach me English, and you gave me a zero IQ. I've brought my IQ up, though. They say I'm smart now. Things follow in lines at school. They take stories and teach us to turn them into essays. I don't need anybody to pronounce English words for me. I can figure them out by myself. I'm going to get scholarships, and I'm going away. And at college I'll have the people I like for friends. I don't care if their great-great-grandfather died of TB. I don't care if they were our enemies in China four thousand years ago. So get that ape out of here. I'm going to college. And I'm not going to Chinese school any-more. I'm going to run for office at American school, and I'm going to join clubs. I'm going to get enough offices and clubs on my record to get into college. And I can't stand Chinese school anyway; the kids are rowdy and mean, fighting all night. And I don't want to listen to any more of your stories; they have no logic. They scramble me up. You lie with stories. You won't tell me a story and then say, 'This is a true story,' or, 'This is just a story.' I can't tell the difference. I don't even know what your real names are. I can't tell what's real and what you make up. Ha! You can't stop me from talking. You tried to cut off my tongue, but it didn't work." So I told the hardest ten or twelve things on my list all in one outburst.

My mother, who is champion talker, was, of course, shout-ing at the same time. "I cut it to make you talk more, not less, you dummy. You're still stupid. You can't listen right. I didn't say I was going to marry you off. Did I ever say that? Did I ever mention that? Those newspaper people were for your sister, not you. Who would want you? Who said we could sell you? We can't sell people. Can't you take a joke? You can't even tell a joke from real life. You're not so smart. Can't even tell real from false."

"I'm never getting married, never!"

"Who'd want to marry you anyway? Noisy. Talking like a duck. Disobedient. Messy. And I know about college. What makes you think you're the first one to think about college? I was a doctor. I went to medical school. I don't see why you have to be a mathematician. I don't see why you can't be a doctor like me."

"I can't stand fever and delirium or listening to people coming out of anesthesia. But I didn't say I wanted to be a mathematician either. That's what the ghosts say. I want to be a lumberjack and a newspaper reporter." Might as well tell her some of the other items on my list. "I'm going to chop down trees in the daytime and write about timber at night."

"I don't see why you need to go to college at all to become either one of those things. Everybody else is sending their girls to typing school. 'Learn to type if you want to be an American girl.' Why don't you go to typing school? The cousins and village girls are going to typing school."

"And you leave my sister alone. You try that with the advertising again, and I'll take her with me." My telling list was scrambled out of order. When I said them out loud I saw that some of the items were ten years old already, and I had outgrown them. But they kept pouring out anyway in the voice like Chinese opera. I could hear the drums and the cymbals and the gongs and brass horns.

"You're the one to leave your little sisters alone," my mother was saying. "You're always leading them off somewhere. I've had to call the police twice because of you." She herself was shouting out things I had meant to tell her—that I took my brothers and sisters to explore strange people's houses, ghost children's houses, and haunted houses blackened by fire. We explored a Mexican house and a redheaded family's house, but not the gypsies' house; I had only seen the inside of the gypsies' house in mind-movies. We explored the sloughs, where we found hobo nests. My mother must have followed us.

"You turned out so unusual. I fixed your tongue so you could say charming things. You don't even say hello to the villagers."

"They don't say hello to me."

"They don't have to answer children. When you get old, people will say hello to you."

"When I get to college, it won't matter if I'm not charming. And it doesn't matter if a person is ugly; she can still do schoolwork."

"I didn't say you were ugly."

"You say that all the time."

"That's what we're supposed to say. That's what Chinese say. We like to say the opposite."

It seemed to hurt her to tell me that—another guilt for my list to tell my mother, I thought. And suddenly I got very confused and lonely because I was at that moment telling her my list, and in the telling, it grew. No higher listener. No listener but myself.

"Ho Chi Kuei," she shouted. "Ho Chi Kuei. Leave then. Get out, you Ho Chi Kuei. Get out. I knew you were going to turn out bad. Ho Chi Kuei." My brothers and sisters had left the table, and my father would not look at me anymore, ignoring me.

Be careful what you say. It comes true. It comes true. I had to leave home in order to see the world logically, logic the new way of seeing. I learned to think that mysteries are for explanation. I enjoy the simplicity. Concrete pours out of my mouth to cover the forests with freeways and sidewalks. Give me plastics, periodical tables, t.v. dinners with vegetables no more complex than peas mixed with diced carrots. Shine floodlights into dark corners: no ghosts.

I've been looking up "Ho Chi Kuei," which is what the immigrants call us—Ho Chi Ghosts. "Well, Ho Chi Kuei," they say, "what silliness have you been up to now?" "That's a Ho Chi Kuei for you," they say, no matter what we've done. It was more complicated (and therefore worse) than "dogs," which they say affectionately, mostly to boys. They use "pig" and "stink pig" for girls, and only in an angry voice. The river-pirate great-uncle called even my middle brother Ho Chi Kuei, and he seemed to like him best. The maggot third great-uncle even shouted "Ho Chi Kuei!" at the boy. I don't know any Chinese I can ask without getting myself scolded or teased, so I've been looking in books. So far I have the following translations for *ho* and/or *chi*: "centipede," "grub," "bastard carp," "chirping insect," "jujube tree," "pied wagtail," "grain sieve," "casket sacrifice," "water lily," "good frying," "non-eater," "dustpan-and-broom" (but that's a synonym for "wife"). Or perhaps I've romanized the spelling wrong and it is *Hao* Chi Kuei, which could mean they are calling us "Good Foundation Ghosts." The immigrants could be saying that we were born on Gold Mountain and have advantages. Sometimes they scorn us for having had it so easy, and sometimes they're delighted. They also call us "Chu Sing," or "Bamboo Nodes." Bamboo nodes obstruct water.

I like to look up a troublesome, shameful thing and then say, "Oh, is that all?" The simple explanation makes it less scary to go home after yelling at your mother and father. It drives the fear away and makes it possible someday to visit China, where I know now they don't sell girls or kill each other for no reason.

Now colors are gentler and fewer; smells are antiseptic. Now when I peek in the basement window where the villagers say they see a girl dancing like a bottle imp, I can no longer see a spirit in a skirt made of light, but a voiceless girl dancing when she thought no one was looking. The very next day after I talked out the retarded man, the huncher, he disappeared. I never saw him again or heard what became of him. Perhaps I made him up, and what I once had was not Chinese-sight at all but child-sight that would have disappeared eventually without such struggle. The throat pain always returns, though, unless I tell what I really think, whether or not I lose my job, or spit out gaucheries all over a party. I've stopped checking "bilingual" on job applications. I could not understand any of the dialects the interviewer at China Airlines tried on me, and he didn't understand me either. I'd like to go to New Society Village someday and find out exactly how far I can walk before people stop talking like me. I continue to sort out what's just my childhood, just my imagination, just my family, just the village, just movies, just living.

Soon I want to go to China and find out who's lying—the Communists who say they have food and jobs for everybody or the relatives who write that they have not the money to buy salt. My mother sends money she earns working in the tomato fields to Hong Kong. The relatives there can send it on to the remaining aunts and their children and, after a good harvest, to the children and grandchildren of my grandfather's two minor wives. "Every woman in the tomato row is sending money home," my mother says, "to Chinese villages and Mexican villages and Filipino villages and, now, Vietnamese villages, where they speak Chinese too. The women come to work whether sick or well. 'I can't die,' they say, 'I'm supporting fifty,' or 'I'm supporting a hundred.'"

What I'll inherit someday is a green address book full of names. I'll send the relatives money, and they'll write me stories about their hunger. My mother has been tearing up the letters from the youngest grandson of her father's third wife. He has been asking for fifty dollars to buy a bicycle. He says a bicycle will change his life. He could feed his wife and children if he had a bicycle. "We'd have to go hungry ourselves," my mother says. "They don't understand that we have ourselves to feed too." I've been making money; I guess it's my turn. I'd like to go to China and see those people and find out what's a cheat story and what's not. Did my grandmother really live to be ninety-nine? Or did they string us along all those years to get our money? Do the babies wear a Mao button like a drop of blood on their jumpsuits? When we overseas Chinese send money, do the relatives divide it evenly among the commune? Or do they really pay 2 percent tax and keep the rest? It would be good if the Communists were taking care of themselves; then I could buy a color t.v.

Here is a story my mother told me, not when I was young, but recently, when I told her I also am a story-talker. The beginning is hers, the ending, mine.

In China my grandmother loved the theater (which I would not have been able to understand because of my seventh-grade vocabulary, said my mother). When the actors came to the village and set up their scaffolding, my grandmother bought a large section up front. She bought enough room for our entire family and a bed; she would stay days and nights, not missing even the repeating scenes.

The danger was that the bandits would make raids on households thinned out during performances. Bandits followed the actors.

"But, Grandmother," the family complained, "the bandits will steal the tables while we're gone." They took chairs to plays.

"I want every last one of you at that theater," my grandmother raved. "Slavegirls, everybody. I don't want to watch that play by myself. How can I laugh all by myself? You want me to clap alone, is that it? I want everybody there. Babies, everybody."

"The robbers will ransack the food."

"So let them. Cook up the food and take it to the theater. If you're so worried about bandits, if you're not going to concentrate on the play because of a few bandits, leave the doors open. Leave the windows open. Leave the house wide open. I order the doors open. We are going to the theater without worries."

So they left the doors open, and my whole family went to watch the actors. And sure enough, that night the bandits struck—not the house, but the theater itself. "Bandits aa!" the audience screamed. "Bandits aa!" the actors screamed. My family ran in all directions, my grandmother and mother holding on to each other and jumping into a ditch. They crouched there because my grandmother could run no farther on bound feet. They watched a bandit loop a rope around my youngest aunt, Lovely Orchid, and prepare to drag her off. Suddenly he let her go. "A prettier one," he said, grabbing somebody else. By daybreak, when my grandmother and mother made their way home, the entire family was home safe, proof to my grandmother that our family was immune to harm as long as they went to plays. They went to many plays after that.

I like to think that at some of those performances, they heard the songs of Ts'ai Yen, a poetess born in A.D. 175. She was the daughter of Ts'ai Yung, the scholar famous for his library. When she was twenty years old, she was captured by a chieftain during a raid by the Southern Hsiung-nu. He made her sit behind him when the tribe rode like the haunted from one oasis to the next, and she had to put her arms around his waist to keep from falling off the horse. After she became pregnant, he captured a mare as his gift to her. Like other captive soldiers until the time of Mao, whose soldiers volunteered, Ts'ai Yen fought desultorily when the fighting was at a distance, and she cut down anyone in her path during the madness of close combat. The tribe fought from horseback, charging in a mass into villages and encampments. She gave birth on the sand; the barbarian women were said to be able to birth in the saddle. During her twelve-year stay with the barbarians, she had two children. Her children did not speak Chinese. She spoke it to them when their father was out of the tent, but they imitated her with senseless singsong words and laughed.

The barbarians were primitives. They gathered inedible reeds when they camped along rivers and dried them in the sun. They dried the reeds tied on their flagpoles and horses' manes and tails. Then they cut wedges and holes. They slipped feathers and arrow shafts into the shorter reeds, which became nock-whistles. During battle the arrows whistled, high whirling whistles that suddenly stopped when the arrows hit true. Even when the barbarians missed, they terrified their enemies by filling the air with death sounds, which Ts'ai Yen had thought was their only music until one night she heard music tremble and rise like desert wind. She walked out of her tent and saw hundreds of the barbarians sitting upon the sand, the sand gold under the moon. Their elbows were raised, and they were blowing on flutes. They reached again and again for a high note, yearning toward a high note, which they found at last and held—an icicle in the desert. The music disturbed Ts'ai Yen; its sharpness and its cold made her ache. It disturbed her so that she could not concentrate on her own thoughts. Night after night the songs filled the desert no matter how many dunes away she walked. She hid in her tent but could not sleep through the sound. Then, out of Ts'ai Yen's tent, which was apart from the others, the barbarians heard a woman's voice singing, as if to her babies, a song so high and clear, it matched the flutes. Ts'ai Yen sang about China and her family there. Her words seemed to be Chinese, but the barbarians understood their sadness and anger. Sometimes they thought they could catch barbarian phrases about forever wandering. Her children did not laugh, but eventually sang along when she left her tent to sit by the winter campfires, ringed by barbarians.

After twelve years among the Southern Hsiung-nu, Ts'ai Yen was ransomed and married to Tung Ssu so that her father would have Han descendants. She brought her songs back from the savage lands, and one of the three that has been passed down to us is "Eighteen Stanzas for a Barbarian Reed Pipe," a song that Chinese sing to their own instruments. It translated well.

CHINA MEN

Contents

On Discovery

ONCE UPON a time, a man, named Tang Ao, looking for the Gold Mountain, crossed an ocean, and came upon the Land of Women. The women immediately captured him, not on guard against ladies. When they asked Tang Ao to come along, he followed; if he had had male companions, he would've winked over his shoulder.

"We have to prepare you to meet the queen," the women said. They locked him in a canopied apartment equipped with pots of makeup, mirrors, and a woman's clothes. "Let us help you off with your armor and boots," said the women. They slipped his coat off his shoulders, pulled it down his arms, and shackled his wrists behind him. The women who kneeled to take off his shoes chained his ankles together.

A door opened, and he expected to meet his match, but it was only two old women with sewing boxes in their hands. "The less you struggle, the less it'll hurt," one said, squinting a bright eye as she threaded her needle. Two captors sat on him while another held his head. He felt an old woman's dry fingers trace his ear; the long nail on her little finger scraped his neck. "What are you doing?" he asked. "Sewing your lips together," she joked, blackening needles in a candle flame. The ones who sat on him bounced with laughter. But the old women did not sew his lips together. They pulled his earlobes taut and jabbed a needle through each of them. They had to poke and probe before puncturing the layers of skin correctly, the hole in the front of the lobe in line with the one in back, the layers of skin sliding about so. They worked the needle through—a last jerk for the needle's wide eye ("needle's nose" in Chinese). They strung his raw flesh with silk threads; he could feel the fibers.

The women who sat on him turned to direct their attention to his feet. They bent his toes so far backward that his arched foot cracked. The old ladies squeezed each foot and broke many tiny bones along the sides. They gathered his toes, toes over and under one another like a knot of ginger root. Tang Ao wept with pain. As they wound the bandages tight and tighter around his feet, the women sang footbinding songs to distract him: "Use aloe for binding feet and not for scholars."

During the months of a season, they fed him on women's food: the tea was thick with white chrysanthemums and stirred the cool female winds inside his body; chicken wings made his hair shine; vinegar soup improved his womb. They drew the loops of thread through the scabs that grew daily over the holes in his earlobes. One day they inserted gold hoops. Every night they unbound his feet, but his veins had shrunk, and the blood pumping through them hurt so much, he begged to have his feet re-wrapped tight. They forced him to wash his used bandages, which were embroidered with flowers and smelled of rot and cheese. He hung the bandages up to dry, streamers that drooped and draped wall to wall. He felt embarrassed; the wrappings were like underwear, and they were his.

One day his attendants changed his gold hoops to jade studs and strapped his feet to shoes that curved like bridges. They plucked out each hair on his face, powdered him white, painted his eyebrows like a moth's wings, painted his cheeks and lips red. He served a meal at the queen's court. His hips swayed and his shoulders swiveled because of his shaped feet. "She's pretty, don't you agree?" the diners said, smacking their lips at his dainty feet as he bent to put dishes before them.

In the Women's Land there are no taxes and no wars. Some scholars say that that country was discovered during the reign of Empress Wu (A.D. 694–705), and some say earlier than that, A.D. 441, and it was in North America.

On Fathers

WAITING AT the gate for our father to come home from work, my brothers and sisters and I saw a man come hastening around the corner. Father! "BaBa!" "BaBa!" We flew off the gate; we jumped off the fence. "BaBa!" We surrounded him, took his hands, pressed our noses against his coat to sniff his tobacco smell, reached into his pockets for the Rainbo notepads and the gold coins that were really chocolates. The littlest ones hugged his legs for a ride on his shoes. And he laughed a startled laugh. "But I'm not your father. You've made a mistake." He took our hands out of his pockets. "But I'm not your father." Looking closely, we saw that he probably was not. We went back inside the yard, and this man continued his walk down our street, from the back certainly looking like our father, one hand in his pocket. Tall and thin, he was wearing our father's two-hundred-dollar suit that fit him just right. He was walking fast in his good leather shoes with the wingtips.

Our mother came out of the house, and we hung on to her while she explained, "No, that wasn't your father. He did look like BaBa, though, didn't he? From the back, almost exactly." We stood on the sidewalk together and watched the man walk away. A moment later, from the other direction, our own father came striding toward us, the one finger touching his hat to salute us. We ran again to meet him.

THE FATHER FROM CHINA

FATHER, I have seen you lighthearted:
"Let's play airplane," you said. "I'll make you a toy airplane." You caught between your thumb and finger a dragonfly. You held it by the abdomen. Its fast wings blurred, but when its motor paused, I saw that the wings were networks of cellophane. Its head bulged with eyes, below which the rest of its face was crowded. "You hold it," you said. Around its belly you slipped a lasso of thread, which you tightened, crinkled its shell, pinched a waist, and the tail bent downward slightly. Then you tied the other end of the string around my finger, and said, "Let go." The tying hadn't hurt it one bit; the dragonfly whirled up and flew in circles at the extent of the string, which I pulled toward me and cast away, controlling my pet airplane. It flew lower, and I turned with it not to get entangled. Suddenly the dragonfly dropped and dangled, but all we had to do was shake it, and it flew again. After a while, though I poked and prodded, it did not go any more. You watched for five more dragonflies to alight until each sister and brother had had a turn.

Upon hearing about the sage of the Ming period who shook himself and turned into a red dragonfly, I remembered our airplane, which was not red. The sunlight had iridized the black into blues and greens.

On summer nights, when we picked new routes home from the laundry through the Stockton streets, crickets covered the sidewalks and the lighted windows. Bats flew between the buildings, and some got hit by cars; we examined them, spread their wings, looked at their teeth and furry countenances. The bats wafted like burned paper in the searchlights, which lit up tightrope walkers who had strung wires from the tallest rooftops and walked with no nets to and from the courthouse dome. On garbage nights, we children ran ahead and rummaged the department store bins for treasures; in trade, you left our garbage, a bag here and a bag on the next block. But usually we didn't walk the long way on Main Street; we went through Chinatown, Tang People's Street, gray and quiet except for the clicking of gamblers who had left a window open.

Then we passed the Japanese's closed-up house, nobody home for years, and the Filipino Lodge, where we sat on the benches that were held up by tree bark growing over their edges; the Filipinos had gone in for the night. On our own front porch, you snapped on the light, and the moths came swarming. "It's a Hit-lah," you said, swatting one with your newspaper. "Hit-lah," we shouted, and attacked the moths, killed them against the walls and railings, "*Hit*-lah!" and a hit on the first syllable. They were plain no-color butterflies. We killed Hitler moths every summer of The War. It was interesting to grow older and find out that only we called them that, and outside the family, things have other names.

But usually you did not play. You were angry. You scared us. Every day we listened to you swear, "Dog vomit. Your mother's cunt. Your mother's smelly cunt." You slammed the iron on the shirt while muttering, "Stink pig. Mother's cunt." Obscenities. I made a wish that you only meant gypsies and not women in general.

You were tricked twice by gypsies. One unwrapped her laundry right there on the counter. She shook out her purple and rose cloths, held them up, and said, "You've torn my best dress. Oh, look. And the blouse, too. Nothing left but rags. And the skirts. Torn to pieces. Mangled. You'll have to pay for them, you know. Replace them. Oh, my new expensive tablecloth. You're going to have to give me money for new clothes. A wardrobe. Come on. Pay up now. Pay. Pay." She wiggled her fingers through the holes. She had brought dustrags, of course.

"No," you said. "Your clothes be old," you said.

The gypsy strewed her clean, pressed rags and rushed out, but she returned with a sister gypsy—and a cop. The two gypsies talked hard, their earrings leaping with the movements of their jaws. The fan and air-conditioner circulated the smell of their winged hairdos. The policeman, whose navy blue bulk expanded to fill the room, metal and wood clunking, kept saying, "Small claims court." Deportation. So you paid, rang up the No Sale on the cash register and paid. Twice.

"I knew she was up to something," MaMa shouted. "Remember when I sorted her bag, I said, 'How do the gypsies afford to have rags laundered?' I could tell that that Romany demoness was up to no good. She and that other one who acted as witness concocted a big story in English for the police. And you couldn't speak English well enough to counteract it. Fell for it twice. You fell for it twice."

"Kill your Romany mother's cunt," you said between your clenched teeth. "Kill your Romany demoness mother's cunt dead." There is a Cantonese word that sounds almost like "grandmother," *po*, and means a female monster that looms and sags. In the storeroom were a black bag and a white bag, which we never opened. They were big enough for us children to climb like hills and we called them Black Bag Po and White Bag Po. You called the gypsies those names too. "Old bags," you muttered. "Gypsy bag. Smelly pig bag. Sow. Stink pig. Bag cunt."

When the gypsy baggage and the police pig left, we were careful not to be bad or noisy so that you would not turn on us. We knew that it was to feed us you had to endure demons and physical labor.

You screamed wordless male screams that jolted the house upright and staring in the middle of the night. "It's BaBa," we children told one another. "Oh, it's only BaBa again." MaMa would move from bed to bed. "That was just BaBa having a dream. Bad dreams mean good luck." She would leave us puzzling, then what do good dreams mean?

Worse than the swearing and the nightly screams were your silences when you punished us by not talking. You rendered us invisible, gone. MaMa told us to say Good Morning to you whether or not you answered. You kept up a silence for weeks and months. We invented the terrible things you were thinking: That your mother had done you some unspeakable wrong, and so you left China forever. That you hate daughters. That you hate China.

You complained about holiday dumplings: "Women roll dough to knead out the dirt from between their fingers. Women's fingernail dirt." Yet you did eat them. MaMa said, though, that you only lately began eating pastries. "Eating pastries is eating dirt from women's fingernails and from between their fingers." As if women had webs. Finger jams.

MaMa pays you back, with her tomato and potato wages, the money she sends to China. "They're my relatives," she says, "not his."

You say with the few words and the silences: No stories. No past. No China.

You only look and talk Chinese. There are no photographs of you in Chinese clothes nor against Chinese landscapes. Did you cut your pigtail to show your support for the Republic? Or have you always been American? Do you mean to give us a chance at being real Americans by forgetting the Chinese past?

You are a man who enjoys plants and the weather. "It's raining," you said in English and in Chinese when the California drought broke. "It's raining." You make us inordinately happy saying a simple thing like that. "It rains."

What I want from you is for you to tell me that those curses are only common Chinese sayings. That you did not mean to make me sicken at being female. "Those were only sayings," I want you to say to me. "I didn't mean you or your mother. I didn't mean your sisters or grandmothers or women in general."

I want to be able to rely on you, who inked each piece of our own laundry with the word *Center*, to find out how we landed in a country where we are eccentric people.

On New Year's eve, you phone the Time Lady and listen to her tell the minutes and seconds, then adjust all the clocks in the house so their hands reach midnight together. You must like listening to the Time Lady because she is a recording you don't have to talk to. Also she distinctly names the present moment, never slipping into the past or sliding into the future. You fix yourself in the present, but I want to hear the stories about the rest of your life, the Chinese stories. I want to know what makes you scream and curse, and what you're thinking when you say nothing, and why when you do talk, you talk differently from Mother.

I take after MaMa. We have peasant minds. We see a stranger's tic and ascribe motives. I'll tell you what I suppose from your silences and few words, and you can tell me that I'm mistaken. You'll just have to speak up with the real stories if I've got you wrong.

My father was born in a year of the Rabbit, 1891 or 1903 or 1915. The first year of the Republic was 1911. In one of his incarnations, one of the Buddhas was a rabbit; he jumped alive into a fire to feed the hungry.

BaBa was the youngest and the smartest of four brothers. They put their ears to the door of the room where he was being born. At midday the midwife came out carrying a basin of blood; and they did not understand how a baby could be constructed with so much blood left over.

The oldest brother, Dai Bak, Big Uncle, said, "Get some boxes and chairs and come with me." The brothers balanced the teaks and pines in a stack under their parents' window and climbed it like acrobats. By the time they reached the curved sill, the baby had been born. They saw its foot sticking out of a bundle tied to the hook of the rice scale. The baby's bottom plumped out the white cloth. Their mother and father were laughing, and laughed harder when they saw the boys at the window. "BiBi has arrived," their father announced, and simultaneously they heard a baby's cry come from the dumpling, the *dim sum*, the little heart. The brothers clutched one another, they cheered, jumped up and down. "'Jump like a squirrel,'" they sang. "'Bob like a blue jay, tails in the air, tails in the air.' A baby is born. A baby is born." They scrambled down and ran inside to have a look at him. They hung over the headboard, knelt by the bedside, put their heads next to the baby's on their mother's pillow. All day the brothers smiled when they saw one another and the baby.

Grandmother, Ah Po, said, "Your little brother is different from any of you. Your generation has no boy like this one. Come. Look." She unwrapped the baby to show how skinny he was. She uncurled his fists, and his brothers touched the wrinkles inside, looked at their own wrinkles. "Look at the length of his hands and fingers," said Ah Po. "This kind of hand was made for holding pens. This is the boy we'll prepare for the Imperial Examinations." The other boys were built like horses and oxen, made for farmwork. Ah Po let them each sit on the bed and hold the baby in his lap. They felt big and important. Dai Bak, the oldest, remembered also holding the other two; curious how each brother had felt different in his arms, this one so light. "Now when you go out to play, you have a baby to strap on your back," he said to the brother who, up to then, had been the youngest. Grandfather stood at the foot of the bed and was dumfounded that he had four sons, all in his old age.

At the baby's one-month birthday party, Ah Po gave him the Four Valuable Things: ink, inkslab, paper, and brush. The other children had only gotten money. She put the brush in his right fist. Villagers and relatives praised the way he waved it about. Eating bowls of chicken-feet-and-sweet-vinegar soup and pigs'-feet-and-sweet-vinegar soup, they said good words for the future. Ah Po shaved her baby's head except for the crown, though it was only baby fuzz he had growing on his head. The house was ashine with lights and lucky with oranges.

Third Uncle, Sahm Bak, waited until the baby was tucked away in his parents' bedroom for a nap. Then he ducked into that room and pressed himself against the wall so as not to be spotted from the guest hall, the doors never shut in this house. He dropped to his knees, crawled quickly behind and under furniture, and reached the bed. He grabbed two handfuls of the quilt and hoisted himself up, his chubby legs kicking. He saw the baby asleep, curled in a nest of blankets in the middle of the bed. Sahm Bak delighted in drawing the curtains and hiding inside the layers of canopy and mosquito netting; this high bed was his flying boat to the moon, a secret room, a stage for plays, night in the middle of the day. He stood up, captain of his flying boat, and walked over to his baby brother. His feet sank into the quilts. He was wearing a pair of leather shoes his father had brought back from the Gold Mountain. The shoes were too big for him, but he had stuffed the toes. He pushed and pulled the baby free of the blankets, then he jumped on its stomach. The baby was not as soft as the quilts. The unexpected bones and the oversize shoes made Sahm Bak fall. The baby began to cry. Sahm Bak got to his feet quickly. He had to hurry before the noise brought the adults running. He jumped up and down, up and down on the baby's stomach, so bouncy. The baby let out a squeal each time the shoes depressed his stomach. When the adults arrived, the baby was not squalling any more, but was blue. Since being hit and scolded on a birthday would be bad luck, Sahm Bak had to wait until the next day for his punishment; Dai Bak, who should have been more alert watching his brothers, would have to be punished too. The adults sent the guests hastily home with red eggs and ginger to "fill their hands."

For years afterwards, Ah Po would say, "You were so bad, you stomped on him for hours."

"I don't remember doing that," her third son said. "Do you remember my doing that?" he asked you, BaBa.

"No," you said. "I don't remember either."

Sometimes Sahm Bak pretended he was a baby, quietly nudging himself onto his mother's lap, but when she noticed him, she put him on the floor and picked up BaBa, her BiBi, her lap baby. She loved him so much, she licked the snot from his nose.

Grandfather, Ah Goong, plowed fields hour after hour alone, inching along between earth and sky. To amuse himself, he sang girls' songs in an old man's falsetto. He wished for a happy daughter he could anticipate seeing in the evenings after work; she would sing for him and listen to him sing. He tied his ox near some water and took a walk about the village to find out what the neighbors were doing. One family he often visited had had a baby due at the same time as our family. After seeing what he himself had gotten, he went to find out what they'd gotten. His mouth and throat, his skin puckered all over with envy. He discovered why to be envious is "to guzzle vinegar." Theirs was the loveliest dainty of a baby girl. She lay ignored in a yam basket. He gazed at her and sang to her until he had to leave, should he fall farther behind in his plowing. The next time he visited, he brought her a red ribbon, which he fashioned into a bow and arranged by her ear. He laughed at the air it gave her. She wore rags, which sent waves of delicious pity coursing through him. "Poor girl," he said. "Poor, poor girl."

The day his third son stomped on the baby, Ah Goong sneaked away from the commotion. He scooped up party food on the way out. He went to the girl's house. He tucked red packets of money in her faded shirt, no special red dress for her today, no new red jacket, no tiger shoes nor hat with eight boy dolls for tassels. Her family offered him shredded carrots, scant celebration. How sorry he felt for her, how he loved her. She cried, squeezing bitty tears out of her shut lids. His heart and his liver filled with baby tears. Love filled his heart and his liver. He piled grapefruits and oranges in a pyramid for her. He tarried so long that he had to use the outhouse, but he carefully weighed his shit on the outhouse scales so that these neighbors could return a like amount to his fields.

He cut a reed from the New Year narcissus and blew tunes between his thumbs. Though the snowpeas would be fewer at harvest, he brought the girl their blossoms, pinks with purple centers, light blues with dark blue centers, the vine flowering variously as if with colors of different species. She chewed on the flowers and pulled the tendrils apart in her chubby hands. Extravagance. In the summer he fanned her with a sandal-wood fan; he rubbed its ribs with sandpaper, and with one pass, the air thickened with memories of Hawai'i, which is the Sandalwood Mountains. In the autumn the two of them would rattle dry peapods.

"It's only a girl," her parents kept saying. "Just a girl."

"Yes," said Ah Goong. "Pretty little sister. Pretty miss."

Away from her he detached a fuzzy green melon from its nest and tucked it for a moment inside his sweater next to his heart. Whenever he had to leave her, he felt the time until he would see her again extend like an unplowed field, the sun going down and a long country night to come. No, he would not endure it.

He went home and put on the brown greatcoat that he had bought in San Francisco. "Where are you going with that coat in this weather?" asked Ah Po, who did not follow him about the house because of her bound feet; the three maids who fanned her and helped her walk were working in the kitchen. When she walked unassisted or with one maid, she touched the walls gracefully with thumb and little finger spread, index and middle fingers together, fourth finger down. "I'll just take a peek at the baby," he said, "then go out." He picked up his wife's baby and hid him inside his greatcoat. If you had been a little older, BaBa, you might have felt proud, singled out for an excursion that made Ah Goong dance down the road, a bright idea in his head.

He ran into the neighbor's house and unwrapped the baby, first the greatcoat, then the diapers to show the family that this doggy really was a boy. "Since you want a boy and I want a girl," he said, "let's strike a bargain. Let's trade." The family was astounded. They would have let him buy the girl if only he'd asked. They would have had to give her away eventually anyhow. And here was this insane man who did not know the value of what he had. What a senile fool. Take him up on it before he comes to his senses. As if his son's boyness were not enough, he pointed out his attributes. "This boy will be very intelligent," he said. "He's got scholar's hands. And look what a smart forehead he has. He'll win a name for you at the Imperial Examinations. He's very skinny and eats hardly any food."

"Yes, we'll take him," said the neighbors. Ah Goong placed the girl inside his greatcoat. He did not remove the boy's fancy clothes, the gold necklace, the new shoes, nor the jade bracelet that signified that you would not have to do physical labor. He hurried out before her family could change their minds. His heart beat that they would reclaim her at the last minute. The girl wore no jewelry, but with his soul he adopted her, full diapers and all.

He walked slowly, adoring the peachy face. He sat by the side of the road to look at her. He counted her pink toes and promised that no one would break them. He tickled her under the chin. She would make his somber sons laugh. Kindness would soon soften the sides of their mouths. They would kneel to listen to her funny requests. They would beguile her with toys they'd make out of feathers and wood. "I'll make you a doll," he promised her. "I'll buy you a doll." And surely his wife would get used to her soon. The walk home was the nicest time. He showed her, his daughter, how the decorative plants grow wild and the useful plants in rows. "Flower," he said, pointing. "Tree." He rested by the stream for her to listen to its running.

At home, he walked directly to the crib and tucked her in. He drew the quilt over her as a disguise. Then he hung up his greatcoat and returned to the crib, gave the quilt a pat. She was a well-behaved baby and made no noise. He kept strolling past the crib. His happiness increased in her vicinity. "My heart and my liver" he called her. (*Sweetheart* is an English word that emigrants readily learn.)

Ah Po heard the sniffing and squeaking of a baby waking

up. She swayed over to the crib. The baby noises sounded unfamiliar. She screamed when she saw the exchanged baby.

Ah Goong came running. "What's wrong? What's wrong?"
he asked.

"What is this? Where's my baby?" Ah Po yelled.

"It's all right." He patted the baby. "Everything's all right.
He's at the neighbors'. They'll take good care of him."

"What neighbors?" she yelled. "What's he doing at the
neighbors'? Whose is this ugly thing?"

"Oh, no, she isn't ugly. Look at her." He picked her up.

"Where's my baby? You crazy old man. You're insane. You
idiot. You dead man."

"The neighbors have him. I brought this one back in his place."
He held his little girl. "All we have are boys. We need a girl."

"You traded our son for a girl? How could you? Who has my
son? Oh, it's too late. It's too late." She thrust her arms as far
as she could reach; she bent her torso from side to side, backward and forward, a woman six feet tall on toy feet. "Take me
to that family," she cried. "We're trading back." Lunging her
weight at Ah Goong, who hunched his shoulders and caved
in his chest to protect the baby, she pushed him out the door.
She walked in back of him, shoving him while hanging on to
his shoulder. She was not used to dashing about on the roads.
"I'm coming to rescue you, BiBi. Your mother's coming." Ah
Goong clung to his baby as if she were holding him up. "Dead
man," Ah Po raged, "trading a son for a slave. Idiot." He led
her to the neighbors' house, weeping as he walked. "Dead demon." The villagers lined the road to look at Grandfather and
Grandmother making fools of themselves.

Ah Po scolded the girl's family. "Cheating the greedy
pig, huh? Thieves. Swindlers. Taking advantage of an idiot.
Cheaters. Trying to catch a pig, are you? Did you really think
you'd get away with it? Pig catchers. A girl for a boy. A girl for
a boy." The family hung their heads.

She pulled the girl out of Ah Goong's arms and shoved her
at an older child. Her own baby she snatched and held tight.
She sent for her sedan chair and waited for it in the road. She
carried her son herself all the way home, not letting Ah Goong
touch her baby, not letting him ride. He hardly saw the road
for his tears. Poor man.

Perhaps it was that very evening and not after the Japanese bayoneted him that he began taking his penis out at the dinner table, worrying it, wondering at it, asking why it had given him four sons and no daughter, chastising it, asking it whether it were yet capable of producing the daughter of his dreams. He shook his head and clucked his tongue at it. When he saw what a disturbance it caused, he laughed, laughed in Ah Po's irked face, whacked his naked penis on the table, and joked, "Take a look at *this* sausage."

When BiBi was walking upright instead of "in cow position" on all fours, his second brother, Ngee Bak, walked him to the fields. "Come on, BiBi," he said, taking his hand. "Let's go look at what shoots came up overnight." He slowed his steps for the toddler, but walking the veering way children walk, the two boys often turned around and went back the way they came, each one following the other here and there, lifting rocks, prodding bugs, squatting to part the grass and thrill at the small live movements. But a plan kept reappearing in Ngee Bak's mind so that they did eventually arrive at the rice field, which looked like a lake on fire with rows of doubling green flames.

"Isn't it beautiful?" said Ngee Bak, who threw a pebble at the water in front of BiBi. Waterdrops spattered his knees, and laughter gurgled up inside his chest like ripples and like the waterdrops. With both hands, he plucked stones out of the dam. He threw one rock after another and loved the giggles that splashed happily out of his mouth. Then he pushed the mud and rice straw and rocks aside and jumped into the water, kicked it, watched the rings spread and fade. He touched the shoots, grasped them, and pulled, such a satisfying loosening and snapping of roots from the earth. He collected the green rice in his pockets.

Meanwhile, Ngee Bak ran tattletaling to the house, "Come quick. Hurry. Look. Look. Look at BiBi."

Grandfather and Grandmother lifted him out of the water and ordered their oldest son, "Go cut a switch." Dai Bak did not climb a tree for a fresh switch; he hunted in the faggots for a brittle branch that had fallen during a winter storm. He trimmed off the twigs. He knelt at his parents' feet and knocked his forehead on the ground.

"Please beat me, Father and Mother, to teach me a lesson," he requested.

They took turns hitting him across the back and shoulders, not his head because they did not want to damage his brains. "This—will—teach—you—to—teach—your—younger—brother—to—watch—his—younger—brother," a switch with each word. They administered what Tu Fu called "the beating by which he remembered his guilt." There was sap in the branch yet.

"Thank you, Father and Mother," he said when they were done whipping. BiBi and Ngee Bak stood nearby and watched. The two of them listened, thankful he wasn't the oldest, who has the duty of setting a good example. (We American children heard too, and resolved not to "return" to China.)

Instead of acrobatics and shuttlecock, he liked studying. Ah Po kept her boy close. She sewed little scholar's caps and scholar's gowns. She used the leftover black scraps for knee patches on her other sons' pants. Even before BiBi could talk, she fed and lodged itinerant scholars, who stayed the night or week to read to him. They drew giant words and held them over his crib. "How intelligent he looks," they told her. When he was old enough for regular lessons, his brothers sometimes came inside from their chores to rest on the floor at the tutor's feet. Ah Po did not stop them, did not chase them back out. If they overheard some learning, all the better; they would have it to ponder during their years in the fields. Soon the farming brothers' heads nodded; when they suddenly jerked awake, it embarrassed them that the tutor might have seen them bored. One by one they withdrew to slop pigs, draw water, feed chickens before it grew too dark for chickens to eat, dumb fowls.

BaBa was also very good at gambling, but he won so often that his brothers would not play with him. "It's not fair," they complained. "He memorizes the cards and tiles."

"He's lucky," Ah Po bragged, her eyes and her rings glittering as if she were sweeping in the winnings herself. "Lucky."

So instead of gambling in the evenings, BaBa "hummed" poems. He practiced his handwriting at his own corner of the gambling table, which was also the dining table. The words he wrote were as large as his chest, the word *heart* bigger than his own heart, the word *man* almost as big as himself. He had to stand on a chair to write so big, "playing with big words" like the nine-year-old Tu Fu, who wrote enough words "to fill a hard-bottomed bag." A humming came from him continually.

The three older brothers founded a clubhouse inside a grape arbor. By excluding one, they made a secret society. Under the jagged leaves, the three brothers peeked at their little brother kneeling in the dirt. He was scratching the ground with a stick. "He's writing," they whispered. "Even outdoors he's writing. Let's torture him." They scurried out of the vines and circled him while they sang "The Song of the Man of the Green Hill." They schemed that if their mother saw them from the house, she'd think they were only playing with him. "'Poetry addict, poetry addict,'" they sang. "'Poetry addict won't work for rice, shoulders a hoe but forgets to till. Poetry addict won't comb his hair, defends his home with a rusty sword. Poetry addict rude to guests, out of food and forgets to eat. He won't loosen tongue to bring about the fall of seventy cities.'" He scribbled on the ground until his brothers wearied and left him alone.

One autumn morning, when he was about fourteen years old, he left the village to take the qualifying test for the last Imperial Examination ever given. Instead of taking a boat, he walked beneath the trees, useful for inspiration, their branches like open arms forking smaller and smaller until the topmost branches spread into fingers reaching and gesturing, posing and pointing in the wind. The branches formed words too, as did the skeins of geese. "The snow goose of ambition stirs its wings," Tu Fu had said on his way to the tests. "I ride the great snow goose of my ambition." The geese flew with wingtips pointing. The farther BaBa walked from the village, the larger the world grew. He sat by a stream at noon and hummed a poem that ordered the sounds of water.

Toward evening he passed a hermitage with door open and no hermit inside; he passed an inn, and farmhouses where rich families were lighting lanterns. The owls flew with fanning wings into the twilight. He spread his bedroll in a reaped field. The wooden pillow under his neck lifted his thick braid, which Grandmother had woven tight to last for days, and it trailed on the ground. No trees obstructed the simple sky, no building or mountain; no hair blew in his face. He saw only sky, which made him feel simultaneously very big and very small, like one of the stars, like an eye. Each time he awoke, he could tell by the moon's place how long he had slept, and how unevenly.

No one moment was the dawn, but ten thousand blending moments, each one a dawn. The sun edging up did not begin the morning; it was somehow always at its center.

Noticing the foreign ways of fencing, terracing, and ricking, he walked two days. Within sight of the building that had been erected centuries ago specially for examinations, he threw away his village clothes, which were not proper clothing but wrappings and rags, and donned a black silk robe. He walked through the doorposts—fresh red posters on left and right: TO BEGIN THE YEAR, TELL ABOUT THE GREATNESS OF CHINA. MAY ALL THE EARTH'S PEOPLE DRINK WINE. And above the door: COME AND GO IN PEACE, which is a common blessing. So this was the Dragon's Gate, and he was a carp ready to run the falls.

He entered a courtyard, where scholars quietly conversed, not a one of them loud and scolding like the villagers. As he wandered among them, he heard them talk about what happened in books as if it were real. They were a different race from the splay-fingered village men, whose most imaginative talk was about the Gold Mountain. The scholars sprang riddles on one another. One would describe a situation or a relationship and the others, by calculating geomancy, rhymes, metaphors, puns, and radicals and other sections of words, guessed which ideograph it made. They clapped hands and laughed when somebody hit on the answer. Explaining to the ones who didn't get it, they opened their left palms and drew invisible calligraphy on them with the long, tapering index fingers of their right hands.

The camaraderie ended when an official stood at an inner door and called them out of the courtyard one by one. At mid-afternoon, he shouted the name BaBa had invented for himself on the occasion of taking the tests. (His baby name was like Shy Cutie, which would not do here.) It was the first time he heard his adult name said aloud by someone else. If another scholar had answered to that name, one or the other would have renamed himself on the spot, in case the name did not have enough power for two people. An official led BaBa to a cell, where he asked him to undress. The official looked over his naked body for notes written on the skin, combed through his long hair for hidden papers, cut open the seams and hems of his clothes. "I'll bring your dinner at six," he said, and took away BaBa's bedroll and everything in it.

BaBa sat on the cot, sat at the table. He would have enjoyed the luxury of having a window, though he did not need daylight or moonlight to study by. With hands folded behind his back, he paced, brushing the floor with the balls of his feet, and sang his memorizations. A jailer brought food, returned for the utensils, gave him back his bedroll, and locked him up "until time for the first test," he said. He left a teapot, around which BaBa held his hands and caught the rich heat that arose. He decided to stay awake all night. The tea lasted a short while. Fireflies in a jar would have given an appearance of warmth. Back in the village he had read by their light. Steam must have been issuing from his mouth and nose, but he could not see it. Huddling in a blanket, his knees against his chest, he perched on the straight-backed chair, but the blanket turned into a nest for sleeping, and he had to discard it. Muttering the texts, he gave voice and breath to word after word. His attention was a flame; when he saw it turn into a firefly, shrinking, going out, he almost fell off the chair with alarm; for a moment or longer he had fallen asleep. He tried propping himself up by the elbows. His eyes closed, and shapes and colors began turning into dreams. He tried holding his eyelids open with his fingers, but in the dark they might as well have been closed. He understood the blue-eyed Buddha-who-cut-off-his-eyelids. He stood on the chair and stretched—and felt a hook or a ring in a beam directly overhead. So there it was; of course, the poets said it would be there. He looped the end of his pigtail into the ring and tied it tight. Then he sat in his chair to study some more. When he dozed, his own hair jerked his head back up. Hours later, when the pull on his scalp no longer kept him alert, he opened the table drawer, where he found an awl. Like the poets whose blood had been wiped off it, he jabbed the awl into his thigh, held it there, and studied on. At the worst dark of the night, he needed neither ring nor awl. "Aiya!" Out of the disembodying dark came screams of men already driven

mad, footsteps, scufflings, someone yelling, "Ah Ma. Ah Ma."
The poets say that men have used the ring to hang themselves.

At last an official unlocked the cell to give him breakfast. He
searched him again before escorting him to a testing room,
where a panel of scholars sat at a long table. BaBa stood with
his face to the wall and his hands clasped behind him. In this
position he recited by heart from the Three Character Classics,
the Five Classics (*The Book of Changes, The Book of History, The
Book of Poetry, The Book of Propriety, The Spring and Autumn
Annals*), and the Thirteen Classics by Confucius's disciples;
the examiners also threw in some five-word poems. He had
been afraid that nothing would come out of his mouth, but
once the first words, many of which he had kept ready on his
tongue, broke forth, the rest came tumbling out, like water,
like grain. The judges wrote numbers beside his new name.
When he returned to the cell, he felt lighter. On the second
evening he reached the last word of the last book. He fell asleep
that night without having to study for the first time in years.

On the third morning an official returned his Four Valuable
Things. He set brushes, ink, inkslab, and paper on the table
horizontally and vertically, aligned the papers' edges parallel
to the table's edges. He sat with spine straight and ground the
ink blacker and blacker. The blacker his ink, the more patient
the man—the Genie of the Ink, who is no bigger than a fly,
will land in it. A proctor entered and handed BaBa the topics
to write about, and locked the door on his way out. His hand
hollow as if fingers curled around a walnut, an actual walnut
when he was a child, BaBa held the pen perpendicular, ready.
So he was to write alone in a cell instead of among candidates
sitting together in a hall. Poets warned about fake walls and
blinds behind which established scholars hid and made fun
of the candidates—the old men taking the test for the twentieth time and the young men tapping their feet and scratching as they conned words. The ceilings and walls of the cell
seemed opaque enough. He concentrated on remembering the
text. Knowledge fell into place, moved from head, from heart,
down his arm and out the fingers to converge at the tip of
the brush. At a downward pull, he made the first mark in the
upper left side of the first word. The heel of his hand steady
on the table, he drew the strong deliberate stem, then with a

shake he quickened a branch. His fingers lifted on the thin strokes, pulling the brush up for tapering, and pressed down for the heavier, thicker lines, a flick the hook at the bottom. He worked for three days, building each word from top to bottom, left to right, water strokes, dots for flames, tailing gondolas for the boat words, never going back for repairs. He wrote in many styles including The Beauty Adorns Her Hair with Blossoms and The Maid Apes Her Mistress. The seven-hundred-word essays were geometries that demonstrated his knowledge of philosophy and, because this was modern times, of international politics. He dared one poem in the grass style and, with a new brush, one humorous poem that darted down the page like swifts in a clear sky.

He waited for three days to hear his rank among the scholars, who talked about winning and losing. They were at leisure. It was too late to study any more and too early to begin studying for the next try three years hence. Failing wasn't such a shame. Kai Li-shih hid in the gambling houses but became a poet nevertheless. Tu Fu, the Earthly Poet, sang about how he failed his third, fifth, and sixth tries, and about failing on his fortieth birthday. He had even failed a special test arranged in his honor. And he had come from eleven generations of scholars. (BaBa was the only one as far back as the family knew. We were a family of eighty pole fighters and no scholars.) Though the ignorant villagers would tease and mock, there was an honorable tradition of failing the exams. The emperors gave special honorary degrees for perseverance to eighty- and ninety-year-olds who had tried their whole lives. Ah, but winning, a scholar would become one of the philosophers who rules China; everyone would hear of him, everyone would want to befriend him. All things good come to the mandarin scholar. His ancestors would receive titles and degrees. (His descendants would not get anything, and so save the government expenses and trouble.)

BaBa did not win the top honors; he would have had an easier life then and not come to the Gold Mountain. He did not "fly" to Canton or Peiping. He must have been a Learned Scholar or a Righteous Worthy; he won the job of village teacher. Our family painted the rooftree red and trimmed the windows with green and gold.

His new name brought him enough luck, and so he kept it; the name he has now is that name: Think Virtue, my father's name. I hesitate to tell it; I don't want him traced and deported. Even MaMa rarely calls him by name and not this one but other vocatives, like So-and-so's Father. Friends call him Uncle or Brother or Teacher. Anyway, a translation, Think Virtue, is nothing like this name; the English words are like fiction, that is, their sounds are dissimilar from the Chinese sounds. Nobody would call anyone else by a translation, Think Virtue his written name anyway. He is still disguised. Think Virtue—*think* is an ideograph combining the radicals for *field* and *heart*, and *virtue* also has the root *heart* in it; his name looks like two valentines and is not as cerebral as it appears in English.

So he had once had three free days. He spent them talking to the other scholars, making friends, singing, touring the capital. Counting the days walking, you had seven free days.

My maternal grandparents or "outside grandmother" and "outside grandfather"—one of the words in *maternal grandparents* the same as in *foreigner* or *barbarian*—these "outsiders" tracked BaBa down by following the invisible red string that ties his ankle to MaMa's. Year by year the string grew shorter.

The outside grandparents had four daughters, and so one of this grandmother's habits whenever she heard of an interesting boy or young man was to count him. Using the poor people's divining method, she took a pinchful of rice, said his name, and counted the grains to see if she had picked an odd or even number, carefully dropping each speck back into the rice box. Odd meant Yes, this boy was her daughter's true husband; even meant No, wrong boy; *four* sounds like *die*. In addition to counting rice, she confirmed the results by paying an expensive blind fortuneteller to touch a list of young men's names, and he picked out her future son-in-law. He also used the yarrow sticks and the tortoise shell and told the wedding date.

Then these outsiders sent spies to find out if their prospective son-in-law was deformed or leprous or mad or poor or ugly. His family sent counterspies. Some families bribed the neighbors to bruit it about how good looking, intelligent, rich, and good humored their son or daughter was. But BaBa's and MaMa's families did not have to lie; he and she were exceptionally smart, the proof being their literacy. The outside grandfather, like the real one, was an unusual man in that he valued girls; he taught all his daughters how to read and write. The families had about the same amounts of money, earned by the generations going-out-on-the-road to the Gold Mountain.

On her third to the last evening at home, MaMa dressed in white. A lucky old woman, who had a good woman's long life, helped her wash her hair, though this being modern days she only sprinkled water on her head. Dressed in white, MaMa sat behind her bedcurtains to sing-and-weep. "Come and hear the bride cry," the village women invited one another. "Hurry. Hurry. The bride's started singing-and-crying." "Listen. Listen. The bride's singing. The bride's weeping." They sat around the bed to listen as if they were at the opera. The girl children sat too; they would learn the old and new songs. The women called out ideas: "Cry about the years your mother held you prisoner." "And you're ransomed at last." "Scold your mother for not finding you your husband sooner."

"Give me a rifle to shoot my mother down," MaMa wailed. "Mother, you've kept me working at your house. You've hidden me from my husband and family. Mother, I'm leaving you now. I'm aiming my rifle at your stomach and shooting you down."

"Oh-h-h," exclaimed the women. "She's the best crying bride I've ever heard." The drummers banged. The bride's mother stood against the wall and smiled proudly.

"Cry for widows and orphans," the guests suggested. "Cry for boys and men drafted into armies." "And leaving for the Gold Mountain." She cried-and-sang about the three times her father left for the Gold Mountain and how he brought back two stepmothers. "They fried dumplings for their own babies and spattered oil on my feet," she sang. "And my bridegroom will go too out-on-the-road and send me photographs of an old man."

"Sing for a husband for the spinsters." "Sing for a husband for my older sister," said pretty younger sisters who could not jump over the old maids.

"Pull a barrel on top of you, and cry over how heavy a man is." The women cackled at that one.

"Cry for going hungry."

"The men don't make enough money for spending all those years away."

"Scold them for enjoying the barbarian lands more than home." "Scold unfaithful men." "Make up a song for scolding a man when he comes back."

"My husband will pick a plum," she sang. "He'll pick a plum blossom as I become a prune."

The women punctuated her long complaints with clangs of pot lids for cymbals. The rhymes made them laugh. MaMa wailed, her eyes wet, and sang as she laughed and cried, mourned, joked, praised, found the appropriate old songs and invented new songs in melismata of singing and keening. She sang for three evenings. The length of her laments that ended in sobs and laughter was wonderful to hear.

The bridegroom's family sent three thousand wedding cakes, two thousand of the expensive bought kind and one thousand of the homemade cheap kind. They sent either one thousand pigs or one pig and the price of a thousand pigs. The outside grandparents parceled the cakes and hunks of crackly orange-skin pork among their friends and relatives, gave some each evening to the women who came to hear the crying-and-singing, and also sent it by messengers throughout the village.

On the morning of the fourth day, MaMa dressed in her black wedding coat with the embroidered flowers and birds. ("I'm going to order wedding coats from Hong Kong for you," she says. "No. No, thanks," we say.) Layers of veiling hung from her headdress; no one could see her face. Men carried the bridal palanquin through the streets, where a band of dancers and beggars, "the flowery ones," who cannot be turned away on a wedding day, followed. "She rides like a queen above the men," said the wedding guests. "The men are kidnapping her," they also said. Her palanquin was called a "bridge." She would go no more to her parents' house except as a visitor; the visit a woman makes to her parents is a metaphor for rarity.

In the middle of the courtyard of her new home, she sat on

a round wicker tray. Another lucky old woman lifted the veil in back and combed her hair, but actually only touched it with a comb, her hair being already dressed. The wedding guests gasped, wanting to reach out and stop the comb; they had also been uneasy at the hairwashing and at hearing the bad words, *death, army, rifle,* and at seeing the woman riding above the men. There was a suspense, a shock to see the bride dressed in funeral white, to see her feet and butt touch the winnower, which touches food, and to watch the burning of the paper horses like a funeral. The wedding guests held still, waited, then exhaled, laughed, and shouted.

Then the bride went inside the house to meet the groom. Being a very clever bride and having been coached by the married women, when the wedding guests pulled aside the bedcurtains and she saw him for the first time—sitting in his bed "like a Buddha statue," she said; that is, "like a *fut*"—she leapt up on the bed and sat facing him so closely that there was no room for her to kowtow. She quickly served him the tea; the kowtowing-to-the-husband part of the ceremony was skipped.

You were sitting there on your bed when out of nowhere jumped this veiled woman. Your family had reminded you, "Be sure to make her bow her head," but she was already pouring tea while the wedding guests threw popcorn, which fell like a warm snowfall, covering the quilt, landing on her headdress, and catching in your long sleeves. In the kitchen more corn popped like distant gunfire.

Bride and groom arose from the cloud of popcorn and went to the family hall, where Grandfather and Grandmother sat in the two best chairs. The new couple kneeled at their feet and served them tea while they said lucky words about long life and many children and much money. The mother-in-law gave the daughter-in-law jewelry. The bride's sisters served dry tea to the women in the groom's family; dry tea is a cupful of cookie crumbs.

Finally at the feast, the groom and his brothers walked from table to table to drink an entire glass of whiskey at each toast. The bride and her sisters walked to each table to pour and drink tea; the wedding guests loaded her tray with red money. Serving with both hands, she displayed her arms, covered from wrists to elbows with gold and jade bracelets, the right arm showing his family's gifts, the left arm her family's. Many of the bracelets were chains of American quarter eagle gold pieces. Catenaries of gold necklaces strung with gold coins, jade hearts, and gold words adorned her neck. She also wore a gold ring in the shape of two clasping hands that Grandfather had brought from the Gold Mountain.

After the guests left, the bride and groom went to their room, which was fluffy with popcorn, and he saw her face for the first time.

BaBa made a living by being the village teacher. Every day at sunrise, he called the roll in a name chant, which was a sort of hexameter, each student's name filling half a line. Staggering the lessons, he began the older boys copying their textbook and told the six- and seven-year-olds, "Repeat after me." He read Lesson One to them many times, the children chorusing line by line. They copied it while he read a more advanced lesson with an older group.

At 9 A.M. everyone went home for breakfast, which was recess. There was no need for other rest; reading and writing are rest, mere sitting. When all the boys were copying at once, BaBa walked up and down between tables, corrected a brush hold, switched a pen from left hand to right hand, straightened a paper and a spine. He kept a rod tucked under his arm. All seemed to go well the first few days, the students obedient enough, though when sweeping out the schoolhouse he found piles of chewed sunflower seeds in corners.

In the evening, after marking the copybooks, which were almost all poor, he began working on a project he had thought up to give his students an advantage in their education. Instead of having them buy handwriting patterns printed in Canton, he would make one for each boy, using that boy's own special words, including his father's name, which some shy or backward villagers did not tell their children. He ruled sturdy pieces of paper into squares and filled each square with a word that was the epitome of a particular kind of stroke or radical. The students would insert these master sheets into the transparent sleeves of their tracing booklets and follow the lines of their teacher's excellent handwriting. He would finish two or three patterns an evening until every student had one.

Worries, like roosters crowing in the dark, woke BaBa hours before he needed to go to school. He stared at the ceiling, listened, listed things to do, waited until his father and brothers, silent like thieves, stealing an extra hour from the night, got up and walked to the fields, and the women went to the well to catch the first water of dawn, the Glory of the Well, good for the skin. Before sunrise, he walked to the schoolhouse; the closer he came, the louder the birds, whose wakening sounded like children's voices. To his horror, children's voices, their laughter, and the scrape and thud of furniture came from the schoolhouse. A small boy at the door sprang up as he recognized his teacher. The boy ran inside, where scurrying, talking—a door slammed—scuttling stopped completely upon BaBa's entrance. The students were supposed to be studying during the hour before the teacher's arrival, their loud studious voices to accompany the farmers' walk to the fields. The whole village must have heard the chaos. He did not know which boys to punish; they were now chanting the last lines of their various lessons.

When he explained things in the common language, the students should have marveled that they had a teacher who knew the meanings of the texts and not just the rote. Today he would explain some of the "parallelisms"—how the directions, the elements, the humors, the architecture of emperors' palaces and commoners' houses, the weather, the trees, the members of families, the hours of the day, the centuries, the dynasties of China, the winds, all have their correspondences one to another. For example, pre-dawn is the time of the unborn child and of bulbs in the earth. Mid-winter, midnight, and old age are times of sleep and death and harvest in the barns. The students ought to know that at that very moment, they were at a mid-morning in spring, youth, a growing time. It was a year of Approach, when a good man is inexhaustible in his will to learn and teach. He recited the poem that had won first place at the Imperial Examinations: "'Escaping the fire, the second grandfather ran with the pig in his arms, and the fifth son carried the sheep.' The numbers, the relatives, the animals all have important meanings," he said. "The winner explained that he was describing an actual fire at his house."

Eyes blinked and glazed. Heads nodded and jerked. Boys

flipped their pigtails over the tops of their heads and un-
braided the ends; they hid their sleeping eyes behind the hair.
At any moment, they would awaken and go into uproar again.
BaBa retreated. "Read aloud after me," he said, quitting explanations. Sometimes the boys shouted out the end of a line.
He liked them for doing that, though it was just an outburst
against tedium. When their voices dwindled, he looked at the
clock; there was half an hour to fill. "Read aloud by yourselves," he said. Without his leading them, they straggled and
faltered; the smartest boy heard himself solo, and stopped. So
he diverted them to chanting the multiplication tables until
breakfast. Once he placed the rod across the shoulders of a boy
who snored aloud. The rod transmitted a sense of his corpore-
ity, the skin, the muscles, the two wing bones.

BaBa could not eat breakfast, and both his mother and my
mother said, "You have to eat. You can't use your brain all day
without food." He paced, then had to go to school again.

"Writing," he taught, "isn't painting. Get enough ink on the
brush to complete a stroke in one movement. Don't go back
to fill in. No backward painting. If you don't have enough ink,
use the dry brush technique, a very advanced method." He
handed out the one-of-a-kind patterns he had made. "What
do we do with the patterns we spent money on?" the students
asked. While the younger students one by one stood beside
his desk and read aloud, out of the corners of his eyes he saw a
writer splotch his paper; another took dab after dab to form one
stroke; another outlined a word and colored it in; another drib-
bled ink in the wide part of a word, then spread it out. Heavy
hands moving from right to left smeared columns of writing.

At mid-afternoon, he told the students that they had been
working so hard, he would treat them: he'd give them the first
line of a couplet, and they could finish it almost any way they
pleased. He read many examples in order to inspire them. But
boredom drained their eyes. The word *poetry* had hit them
like a mallet stunning cattle. As he recited, two boys were
whispering; he needed to reprimand them, knock their heads
together right now, but a scolding would interrupt the poem.
He pressed onward, his face stiff, eyes glowering, ruining the
mood of the poem, his lips mouthing the words. "Now I'll
give you a first line that establishes the season and place," he

said. "You find the second line. You can write about an animal, a plant, a battle strategy, the climate, a cloud, a finger of the hand, a tree, a feeling, a color, a political rank, a condition of the soil, whatever. You can write about a boat; there are many different kinds."

"Go ahead. Start now," he said when the boys continued to stare.

"What do you want us to do?" asked a boy who had been sighing and yawning throughout the assignment.

"Could you explain that again?" asked another boy, exasperated, rolling his eyes at the teacher's ineptness.

He had fallen into talking about the parallels they hadn't understood earlier, but it was too late; dropping a lesson once started spoils a teacher's authority.

"I don't get it." "We don't understand you." "You don't explain clearly."

"Take a guess," he suggested. "Taking a guess is the same as making up a story."

"That doesn't make sense." "We don't understand." "You're making things up because you don't know the answers."

A flash of lightning broke red across the room. He grit his teeth. He wanted to kill. "Finish the couplet," he said.

"What's that?"

A blood vessel must have broken in his temple, and the red lightning was the blood spurted across his eyes.

"Could you repeat your half of the poem?" someone asked.

"Could you repeat the assignment?" said someone else, whom he ignored.

Controlling his face, he repeated the start of the couplet, and what poetry had been in the line was a mortification in his mouth.

"Explain," said the students.

The boys spoke in the brute vulgate, and he saw that he had made a bad mistake translating literature into the common speech. The students had lost respect for him; if he were so smart, he would not speak like them. Scorn curled their lips and lifted their eyebrows. "Explain," they demanded without standing up for recognition.

The opening line was not even a complex one, very colloquial: "At mid-morning in late spring, when walking west—"

"What?" "What did he say?" The students had not seen his anger, then; it had not shown on his face. They would otherwise not act so dumb. "Explain that again."

Their previous teacher must have spent school time drinking tea and reading novels.

"How do you write *clear* and *bright*?" At last, one of the boys was getting down to work, though he had forgotten two of the simplest and most commonly used ideographs in the language. BaBa wrote the words invisibly on his table. "Slower," said the boy. BaBa wrote with ink on paper. "How do you write *wood*?" the boy asked. BaBa wrapped his hand around the boy's and wrote the tree-like word. "See?" BaBa said. "It looks like a tree." The word written by two people's hands wiggled with impatience and with not wanting to show impatience, the little hand pulling one way and the big hand another.

BaBa kept hearing furtive motion behind him. Just you wait until I give your parents your report cards, he thought. I'll show you. You'll be sorry. ("In China parents beat children for getting beaten by the teacher," said the adults.)

He whirled and hit a boy on the arm. "Work!" he shouted. Neither the boy whose hand he guided nor the one he hit said "Thank you, Teacher."

At last he decided that they had sweated enough over the couplet, which they should have closed instantly. He had meant it as a recreation, a break in the work, just for fun. The boys were forcing him to turn literature into a weapon against them.

During the tracing hour, their heavy heads lolled like cows' heads toward whatever insect of distraction alit. Some boys drew pictures of animals. The younger children squirmed from one buttock to the other, wriggling to join the girls and baby boys playing outside.

At last the day ended. The students could not possibly have reached the last sentence in unison, but all together they closed their books at 4 P.M. as if they had been dismissed. Mid-sentence, mid-word, they slapped their books shut and tricked their teacher into saying, "Well, you may go." Then they charged out the door without bidding "Thank you, Teacher" or "Good afternoon, Teacher."

Suddenly the school was quiet. A dusty peace settled. BaBa sat down at his desk. The greased paper in the windows soaked up the afternoon sun in brownish stains. Most "desks" were only pieces of furniture the farmers could spare. A few show-offs had given their sons heirloom tables knotty with carvings. It was a small room after all, not an unwieldy size. He sprinkled water on the floor and swept it clean—gobs of sunflower seeds again in the corner. He smoothed out the paper wads and read them. He poured the dustpan of sweepings into the stove. Long strands of shedded hair snapped in the fire. As he walked about the room, everything he touched became well ordered. He would oil new paper for the windows, perhaps white paper rather than brown so the students could see better. He would bring a hammer and nails and other tools to-morrow. He would build a fence around the school and dig a garden. Then the students might not want so much to escape. Leaving the door open for light and air, he graded papers and recorded the low grades in a ledger.

His wife was watching for him in the road when he came home late. "I thought you'd been kidnapped by bandits," she said. "It's dangerous to be out after dark. Where would we get the money to ransom you?" He went immediately to dinner. Perhaps the student he hit would have felt it more if he ate better. He was losing weight teaching.

He dreamed that he was teaching mathematics but the numbers did not come out right. The correct answer wavered and changed by itself into an impossible figure; digits kept switching places. The students were yelling, "What's the answer, Teacher?" He abandoned the calculations and, rod raised, went chasing after them. They laughed when he hit them. The rod seemed to press giggles out of them. They hid under their tables. They jumped through the paper windows. "QUIET!" he screamed. He screamed lessons, morals, stories, poems, songs, but the students kept playing and fighting. Parents and the district principal peeked in the holes in the windows and saw that he could not teach. "Go away!" he screamed, and woke himself up.

There came to be small difference between his day life and the nightmares. The students ran amok. They stole vegetables from the neighboring gardens; they played war; they staged shows on top of the tables. He tried locking the door on the late boys and got some satisfaction from their shadows bobbing and passing like puppets at the windows, but they worried him when they disappeared. Where did they go? The school looked like a crazy house, like a Sung Dynasty painting of a classroom showing kids putting boxes over one another's heads, drawing cartoons of their teacher, lying on their backs and spinning chairs and tables with their feet.

As the year went on, BaBa made a habit of staying at school during breakfast so that he would not have to wrench himself away from home twice in one morning. He used the rest period to read his own books before he forgot how. Someone had to enjoy reading in this school. The students ruined his eating; they ruined his sleep. They spoiled the songs of birds. And they were taking his books and calligraphy from him too—no time now for his own reading, no time to practice his own writing. Teaching was destroying his literacy. He was spending his brains picking out flaws and poring over them. School was the very opposite of reading and writing. The books that he taught had lost their subtlety and life, puns dead from slow explanations, philosophy reduced to saws. He could not read without thinking up test questions and paraphrases. He shrank poems to fit the brains of peasant children, who were more bestial than animals; when he used to plow, the water buffalo had let him prop a book between its horns.

One day when the students were throwing paper at one another, he walked over to a wad of it, the students watching, picked it up, and put it inside his desk drawer. He opened a book that had no connection whatsoever to school and read it. There were indeed a few students who took up their own books and read, did as he did; for a while on that one day, he taught by example, which, according to sages, is the most powerful way of teaching. Silently he unfurled a scroll and wrote as he pleased while all around him the class fell apart.

A boy got up from his desk and, since the teacher did not scold him, walked around him, pulled monkey faces, and peered in his ear. Egged on by the others, the wild boy jostled his teacher's elbow; his writing broke into a black smear. He stood up, knocking over the chair, which fell with a silencing bang. The students hushed. He seized the rod—the brush rolling down the scroll—and hit the boy, not carefully on the back but anywhere. The boy rolled up into a ball. BaBa hit harder, but the blows fell as if landing on a cushion. He struck almost as hard as he could, but there was an inconclusiveness. Perhaps if the boy had screamed louder when he hit harder, or if he could himself feel the pain, then he would have had satisfaction. If only the boy would properly kneel. If he could hit with all his might. Suddenly he stopped; it felt like beating a doll. Like a Japanese sensei, he ordered the boy to kneel with his head on the ground just outside the open door, where everyone could see him in shame, but when BaBa checked the doorway, the boy had run away.

"Why do we need to write?" the students asked. "We can pay letter writers." "We aren't going to starve," they said. "We'll go to sea and pick up the free gold on the Gold Mountain."

During the next two years, BaBa had two babies; they closed up the circle of children who harried his day. The boy and girl did keep his wife busy though; she had them to dote on.

BaBa did not learn how hard and often students have to be hit to make them polite. He shot them with an imaginary pistol; he stabbed them with an imaginary knife. Sometimes while standing in front of the bad boys, he pointed the imaginary pistol at his own head, and blew it open; then they would see the insides of his skull and know what their hate had done. He also imagined lifting his arms and flying over their heads, out the door, and into the sky; then they would want to learn how he did it. If the Imperial Examinations had not been canceled, he might have tried for a job away from children, become not a magistrate refereeing quarrels but a scribe or a bookkeeper. Mental work was harder than physical work, although it was not exactly the mind that teaching strained. He yearned for the fields with their quiet surprises, which he had plowed around—the nest with eggs from which he had felt the warmth rise, the big mushroom with nibbles around its crown and the mouse dead underneath, a volunteer lily when the field had been sown to rice.

Grading papers night after night for years, BaBa became susceptible to the stories men told, which were not fabulations like the fairy tales and ghost stories told by women. The Gold

Mountain Sojourners were talking about plausible events less than a century old. Heroes were sitting right there in the room and telling what creatures they met on the road, what customs the non-Chinese follow, what topsy-turvy land formations and weather determine the crops on the other side of the world, which they had seen with their own eyes. Nuggets cobbled the streets in California, the loose stones to be had for the stooping over and picking them up. Four Sojourners whom somebody had actually met in Hong Kong had returned from the Gold Mountain in 1850 with three thousand or four thousand American gold dollars each. These four men verified that gold rocks knobbed the rivers; the very dirt was atwinkle with gold dust. In their hunger the men forgot that the gold streets had not been there when they'd gone to look for themselves.

One night of a full moon, BaBa neglected to grade papers, and joined the talking men and listening women. His oldest brother, Dai Bak, who had already traveled to Cuba and back, told how fish the size of long squash fell with the rain. "In Cuba the sky rains fish—live, edible fish. Fish *this* big fell on the roofs and sidewalks. Their tails and fins were flipping. Thick gray fish, little orange and yellow ones, all different species of fish. I caught a rainbow fish in my frying pan. We had to shovel them off the roofs before the sun rotted them."

"Isn't Havana a seaport?" BaBa asked. "Isn't Cuba an island? Couldn't it have happened that a tornado sucked the seas up into the air, and water fell back down like rain on the land, fish and seaweed and all?"

"No. We were inland, and it wasn't salt water but fresh water sprinkling in raindrops. In fact, they were freshwater trout that fell. And it wasn't storming. I saw fish fall. It rains fish in Cuba." Everyone believed Dai Bak, since he was older than BaBa.

Most of the men had already been to the Gold Mountain and did not ask as at the beginning of going-out-on-the-road, "Does it rain, then, on the other side of the world?"

"I saw plains covered with cattle from horizon to horizon," said Grandfather. "The cowboys herd thousands of head of cattle, not one cowboy leading one cow on a rope like here."

"On the Gold Mountain, a man eats enough meat at one meal to feed a family for a month," said Great Grandfather.

"Yes, slabs of meat." The hungrier the family got, the bigger the stories, the more real the meat and the gold.

Grandfather also said, "The Gold Mountain is lonely. You could get sick and almost die, and nobody come to visit. When you're well, you climb out of your basement again, and nobody has missed you." "Idiot," shouted Grandmother. "What do you know? Don't listen to the idiot. Crazy man. Only an idiot would bring up a bad luck story like that tonight." They acted as if he hadn't said it.

Great Grandfather said, "In Hawai'i the papayas are so big, the children scoop out the seeds and carve faces and light candles inside the shell. The candles grow on trees. You can make black ink from the nuts of that same tree."

"Don't sign contracts," he said. "Go as free working men. Not 'coolies.'" He undid his shirt and showed a white scar that was almost lost in his wrinkles. "We're men, not boy apprentices."

"America—a peaceful country, a free country." America. The Gold Mountain. The Beautiful Nation.

The night grew late. The men talking story, lighting chains of cigarettes, and drinking wine, did not need to sleep in order to have dreams. "Let me show you. Let me show you. My turn. My turn." Even the ones who had only explored the world as far as Canton and Hong Kong had stories. Second Uncle, Ngee Bak, dressed in his Western suit, grabbed an old man's cane and strutted straight through the house. "My name is John Bullyboy," he said, imitating a foreign walk and talk, stiff-legged and arrogant, big nostrils in the air, cane swishing about and hitting chinamen and dogs. He did not swerve for shit in his path. Those playing blindmen bumped into the English demon and knocked him over. The women scolded, "Do we have to remind you that you have to work in the morning? You're making so much noise, you're waking the babies." But the men talked on, and the women went to bed self-righteous and angry; *they* would rise early to feed the chickens and the children; *they* were not childish like men. But the women couldn't sleep for the rumbling laughter, and returned, not to be left out. Grandmother brought out the gold that Great Great Grandfather, Great Grandfather, Grandfather, and the uncles had earned. Hardly diluted by alloys, it gave off red glints in the lantern light. The family took turns hefting the gold, which was heavier than it looked; its density was a miracle in the hand. A chain lowering into the palm coiled and folded on its links like a gold snake. Grandmother boiled gold and they drank the water for strength. Gold blood ran in their veins. How could they not go to the Gold Mountain again, which belonged to them, which they had invented and discovered?

Suddenly a knocking pounded through the house. Someone with a powerful hand was at the front gate in the middle of the night. Talk stopped. Everyone reached for a weapon—a cleaver, a hammer, a scythe. They blew out lights and listened for breathing and footsteps. A lookout shouted down from the coign door, "It's Kau Goong." Great Uncle.

"Kau Goong's come home." They threw open doors. The children were up now too. "Huh!" In strode Kau Goong, Grandmother's brother, an incarnation of a story hero, returning during a night of stories, a six-foot-tall white gorilla with long hair and white eyebrows that pointed upward like an owl's, his mouth jutting like an ape's, saying "Huh!" "Huh! Here I am," he roared. "I've come back." He threw down his bags. "Help yourselves! Ho!" His sister's relatives scrambled for the gifts. Nobody asked where he had won these prizes. He threw off his coat and unbuckled pistols and silver knives. While the family emptied the bags, he cleaned his guns, twirled the cylinders, blew and sighted through the bullet chambers and bores. In better times, he had walked unarmed up to rich people and taken their money. He was the biggest man in the known world, and there was no law.

"It just so happened," said Ah Po, "that when you were on your journey, pirates boarded a passenger boat going upriver and one going downriver, and sacked them both. I'm glad you're safe." Ransoms had been collected and paid.

"Dangerous times," said Kau Goong. He shook his head. "Sixty dollars for an old lady." "Yes, sixty dollars for an old lady." This was a family saying, meaning nobody was safe from kidnappers.

The family divided up used shoes, a coat, a blanket, and some lunches. "These old shoes hardly replace all the loot the bandits took from us," said Ah Po. "You'll have to look harder for those raiders. The last time they came here, I peeked from my hiding place up on the roof, and at that very moment, the full moon shone on a bandit's face. It was a Mah from Duck Doo. Let's raid their village and take our stuff back. Revenge."

Too few boats were plying the rivers. Kau Goong had boarded them as far as the ocean and also far inland, and had found no money, jewels, or silks. "Is this all?" said Ah Po.

"We need to go-out-on-the-road again," Kau Goong roared. "We need to go to the Gold Mountain." And since the Chinese word for "need" and "want" and "will" is one and the same word, he was also saying, "We want to go-out-on-the-road again. We will go to the Gold Mountain."

"Every man who leaves must reach the Gold Mountain, and every man must come home to Han Mountain," said Grandmother and Mother, unable to stop the emigration, and hoping that saying something would make it so. The men re-assured them that, of course, they were Sojourners only, that they meant to come back, not settle in America with new wives. "Didn't I return last time? And the time before that?" they said; "I'm a Gold Mountain Sojourner, only a tourist," and kept other possibilities secret from women.

"One last time out-on-the-road," said the oldest men.

No infant cried out, no fireball flashed a warning, no care-less eater dropped a dish or a chopstick, no sick neighbor knocked asking for medicine, no deer or rooster called in the moonlight, no cloud passed over the full moon. Crickets con-tinued chirping. Nothing unusual happened; all remained in continuance. So, omens favorable, one of the grandfathers said, "Write a list of the men going-out-on-the-road."

BaBa set down the date, which was in 1924, and listed: Grandfather, Second Grandfather, Third Grandfather, Fourth Grandfather, Great Uncle, First Uncle, Second Uncle, and Third Uncle. After Third Uncle's name, he wrote his own name. He wanted to taste the rain fish; he wanted to pocket some gold. He wanted to say good-bye to the students. "You'll have to find a new teacher; I'm going to the Gold Mountain." He would quit school in the middle of a lesson.

"I'll get a legal visa," he said. Words of anguish came up from Ah Po, "But you're only a boy."

The travelers teased him. "Hoo! So he thinks he can walk

about the West posing as a scholar." "He'll saunter up to the
Immigration Demon and say, 'I'm an academician. Hand over
my visa.'" "They'll clap him in jail for lying." "How are you
going to prove that you're a scholar? Open up your skull and
show them your brains?" "Just because he's skinny and too
weak for physical labor, he thinks the white demons will say
he's obviously a scholar. But they can't tell a teacher's body
from a laborer's body."

"I have a diploma."

"Huh. He thinks they make laws to search out scholars to
teach them and rule them. Listen, stupid, nobody gets to be
classified 'Scholar.' You can't speak English, you're illiterate,
no scholar, no visa. 'Coolie.' Simple test."

A kinder uncle reminded him of a father's advice to his son.
"'Son, books can't be turned into food when you're hungry,
nor into clothes when you're cold.'"

At the request of the women, he wrote lists of things to
bring back from the Gold Mountain: Dunhill lighters, Rolex
wristwatches, Seth Thomas clocks, Parker pens, Singer sewing
machines, glass window panes, davenports, highboys, pianos.

"You'll make a lot of money," said MaMa. "You'll come
home rich. You'll fly. You'll show them."

The next day the families unburied their documents—
visas, passports, re-entry permits, American birth certificates,
American citizenship papers—and distributed them. BaBa and
Sahm Bak, Third Uncle, beginners, let it out that they were
interested in purchasing papers and that they were willing to be
adopted by Gold Mountain Sojourners who were legal citizens
of the United States of America. These Americans had declared
the birth of a new son for every year they had been visiting in
China and thereby made "slots" for many "paper sons." When
a Sojourner retired from going-out-on-the-road or died, he
made another slot. Somebody took his place. The last owner of
papers taught their buyer the details about the house, the farm,
the neighborhood, the family that were nominally his now. A
Test Book accompanied the papers; the Sojourners who had
traveled on that set of papers had recorded the questions the
Immigration Demons had asked, and how they had answered.
The men preparing to go wandered in the fields and among the
mud huts and great houses of the village, chanting these facts to

a beat, rhymed them, quizzed one another. They ate sturgeon for mental prowess. They paid big fees to memory experts, and it was like in the old days when the Jesuit priest Matteo Ricci taught how to study for the Imperial Examinations, which were no more. BaBa read Test Books to their new owners, who repeated the words to memorize another man's life, a consistent life, an American life.

BaBa would go with two sets of papers: bought ones and his own, which were legal and should get him into the Gold Mountain according to American law. But his own papers were untried, whereas the fake set had accompanied its owners back and forth many times. These bought papers had a surname which was the same as our own last name—unusual luck: he would be able to keep the family name. He would carry his diplomas, and if they did not work, he would produce the fake papers.

Our family calculated money for passage. They mortgaged a field and also borrowed fifteen hundred dollars from the neighbor in the front house and another fifteen hundred dollars from the neighbor in the back house. (This three thousand dollars must have been in Chinese money.) They promised high interest, and it was also understood that our family, including the descendants, even after the monetary repayment of the debt, would show gratitude to those families, wherever their descendants, forever.

Husbands and wives exchanged stories to frighten one another. The men told about a husband who smeared his cheating wife with honey and tied her naked on an ant hill. The women told how there was once a queen, who, jealous of the king's next wife, had this other woman's arms and legs cut off and her eyes, tongue, and ears cut out. She shoved her through the hole of the outhouse, then showed her to the king, who looked down and said, "What's that?" "It's the human pig," said the queen. The wives, of course, agreed with the American antimiscegenation laws; the men would have to come home, and also they would have to be faithful, preferably celibate.

The villagers unfolded their maps of the known world, which differed: turtles and elephants supported the continents, which were islands on their backs; in other cartographies, the continents were mountains with China the middle mountain, Han Mountain or Tang Mountain or the Wah Republic, a Gold Mountain to its west on some maps and to its east on others. Yet the explorers who had plotted routes to avoid sea monsters and those who had gone in the directions the yarrow fell had found gold as surely as the ones with more scientific worlds. They had met one another as planned in Paris or Johannesburg or San Francisco.

"Bali," said a very great grandfather, pointing at the fabulous island where the holy monkeys live. He had seen the monkeys dance. Hou Yin the Monkey God lives on Bali. A generation of great grandfathers had gone there and brought back wives. Others had remained and turned into monkeys.

"Not me," said First Uncle, Dai Bak. "No big cities in Bali. The money is in the big cities now. I'm going to San Francisco."

"Chicago," said Second Uncle, Ngee Bak. "Right in the middle of North America."

"Canada," said Third Uncle, Sahm Bak. "I hear it's easier to get into Canada."

"I'm going as a worker if I can't go as a teacher," BaBa said. His brothers laughed at him. Those frail hands lifting sledgehammers?

"Don't go," said Ah Po. "You're never coming back." And then she wept, having spoken his life.

The band of Gold Mountain travelers walked to the ocean. Almost a troop themselves, they were not challenged by bandits, rebels, government or warlord armies, or by demons, to whom China belonged now. At the waterfront, the oldest men dickered in demon language for ships, "How much? Dollars? No, too much." BaBa was glad that he was the youngest and had go-betweens.

BaBa never told us about sailing on a ship. He did not say whether he went as a carpenter or crewman or passenger from Canton or Macao or Hong Kong. Did masts and riggings, sails, smokestacks, and bridges block the sky, and at night did the ship's lights wash out the stars? Or could he stand on the deck and again see the sky without anything in the way? He would have had suitcases full of dried food. He would have brought seeds of every kind of vegetable.

The ship docked in Cuba, where the surf foamed like the petticoats of the dancing ladies. This part of the journey was legal. For money, BaBa rolled cigarettes and cigars ("Mexican cigarettes") and worked in the sugarcane fields. He did not see any rain of fish, but promises would be kept on the Gold Mountain mainland.

I tell everyone he made a legal trip from Cuba to New York. But there were fathers who had to hide inside crates to travel to Florida or New Orleans. Or they went in barrels and boxes all the way up the coast to New York harbor. BaBa may have been in charge of addressing those crates, marking them "Fragile" in Chinese and English and Spanish. Yes, he may have helped another father who was inside a box.

I think this is the journey you don't tell me:

The father's friends nailed him inside a crate with no conspicuous air holes. Light leaked through the slats that he himself had fitted together, and the bright streaks jumped and winked as the friends hammered the lid shut above his head. Then he felt himself being lifted as in a palanquin and carried to a darker place. Nothing happened for hours so that he began to lose his bearings—whether or not he was in a deep part of the ship where horns and anchor chains could not be heard, whether or not there had already been a pulling away from land, a plunging into the ocean, and this was steady speed. The father sat against a corner and stretched each limb the diagonal of the box, which was a yard by a yard by a yard. He had padded the bottom with his bedding and clothes. He had stuffed dried food, a jar of water, and a chamber pot in a bag. The box contained everything. He felt caught.

Various futures raced through his mind: walking the plank, drowning, growing old in jail, being thrown overboard in chains, flogged to tell where others were hiding, hung by the neck, returned to China—all things that happened to caught chinamen.

Suddenly—a disturbance—a giant's heart came to life; the ship shook and throbbed. A pulse had started up, and his box vibrated with it. He thought he could hear men running and calling. He must be near the engine room or a deck, near people.

The father's thoughts reached out as if stretching in four

directions—skyward, seaward, back toward land, and forward to the new country. Oh, he did yearn for the open sea. The nerves in his chest and legs jumped with impatience. In the future he had to walk on deck the entire voyage, sleep on it, eat there.

He ought to have brought a knife to cut holes in the wood, or at least to carve more lines into the grain. He wanted to look out and see if his box had dropped overboard and was floating atop water, a transparency that ought not to be able to bear weight; he could have been immersed and this wooden air bubble hanging at a middle depth, or falling through the whale waters. People said that a Dragon King ruled an underwater city in the Yellow River; what larger oceanic unknown—tortoises twenty feet across, open-mouthed fish like the marine monster that swallowed the sutras—swam alongside or beneath him. What eels, sharks, jellies, rays glided a board's-width away? He heard the gruff voices of water lizards calling for the night rain. He must not be afraid; it was sea turtles and water lizards that had formed a bridge for King Mu of Chou.

Because of fear, he did not eat nor did he feel hungry. His bowels felt loose and bladder full, but he squeezed shut ass and sphincter against using the chamber pot. He slept and woke and slept again, and time seemed long and forever. Rocking and dozing, he felt the ocean's variety—the peaked waves that must have looked like pines; the rolling waves, round like shrubs, the occasional icy mountain; and for stretches, lulling grasslands.

He heard voices, his family talking about gems, gold, cobbles, food. They were describing meat, just as they had his last evenings home. "They eat it raw." "All you can eat." The voices must have been the sounds of the ocean given sense by his memory. They were discussing a new world. "Skyscrapers tall as mountains." He would fly an aeroplane above the skyscrapers tall as mountains. "They know how to do things there; they're very good at organization and machinery. They have machines that can do anything." "They'll invent robots to do all the work, even answer the door." "All the people are fat." "They're honest. If they say they'll do something, they do it. A handshake is enough." "They arrive for appointments at the very moment they say they will." "They wrap everything—food, flowers, clothes. You can use the paper over again. Free paper bags." "And westward, there are wild horses. You can eat them or ride them." It alarmed him when the strange talk did not cease at his concentration. He was awake, not dozing, and heard mouth noises, sighs, swallows, the clicking and cluck-ing of tongues. There were also seas when the waves clinked like gold coins, and the father's palm remembered the peculiar heaviness of gold. "Americans are careless; you can get rich picking over what they drop." "Americans are forgetful from one day to the next." "They play games, sports; grown men play ball like children." "All you have to do is stay alert; play a little less than they do, use your memory, and you'll become a millionaire." "They have swimming pools, elevators, lawns, vacuum cleaners, books with hard covers, X-rays." The villag-ers had to make up words for the wonders. "Something new happens every day, not the same boring farming."

The sea invented words too. He heard a new language, which might have been English, the water's many tongues speaking and speaking. Though he could not make out words, the whispers sounded personal, intimate, talking him over, sometimes disapproving, sometimes in praise of his bravery.

"It's me. It's me." A solid voice. Concrete words. "I'm open-ing the box." It was the smuggler, who squeaked the nails out and lifted the lid. He helped the father climb out of the box with firm and generous hands. "You're safe to come out and walk," he said. The size of the room outside the box seemed immense and the man enormous. He brought fresh food from the dining room and fresh water and he talked to the father.

Suddenly they heard a march of footsteps, the leather heels of white demons. Coming steadily toward them. The two men gave each other a look, parted, and ran between the hallways of cargo, ducked behind crates. The door clanked open, shut, and the father heard the footsteps nearing. He made out the sounds of two people pacing, as if searching for a stowaway. Crouched like a rabbit, he felt his heart thud against his own thigh. He heard talking and fervently wished to know whether they were discussing stowaways. He looked for other places to dart, but the crates, lashed with rope, towered above him in straight stacks. He was in a wedge with an opening like a cracked door. The cargo room was small after all, a mere closet, and he could not step from aisle to aisle without being seen; his footsteps would echo on the metal floor. If only there were portholes to jump through or tarpaulins to hide under.

The white demons' voices continued. He heard them speak their whispery language whose sentences went up at the end as if always questioning, sibilant questions, quiet, quiet voices. The demons had but to walk this far and see into the wedge. His friend, the smuggler, could say, "I came to check the ropes," or "The captain ordered me to take inventory." Or "I'm looking for stowaways, and I found one," and deliver him up. But there were no explanations for him, a stowaway chinaman. He would not be able to talk convincingly; he would have to fight. He hardly breathed, became aware of inadequate shallow breaths through his nose.

Then, so close to his face he could reach out and touch it, he saw a white trouser leg turn this way and that. He had never seen anything so white, the crease so sharp. A shark's tooth. A silver blade. He would not get out of this by his own actions but by luck.

Then, blessedness, the trouser leg turned once more and walked away.

He had not been caught. The demons had not looked down. After a time of quiet, the two hiders called to each other and came out hysterical with relief. Oh, they had the luck of rich men. The trousers had practically brushed his face.

"It's time to go back in your box," said the smuggler. A moment before, the father had thought it would be a joy to be back in, but as the lid shut on him again, reluctance almost overwhelmed him. He did not visit outside of the box again. He rode on, coming to claim the Gold Mountain, his own country.

The smuggler came occasionally and knocked a code on the wood, and the stowaway father signaled back. Thus he knew that he had not been forgotten, that he had been visited. This exchange of greetings kept him from falling into the trance that overtakes animals about to die.

At last the smuggler let him out; the ship had docked at a pier in New York. He motioned the father up hatches, across empty decks, around corners to an unguarded gangway. He would not have to swim past patrol boats in the dark. "Come. Come. Hurry," the smuggler guided him. He staggered along on cramped legs; the new air dizzied him. As they were saying good-bye, the smuggler said, "Look," and pointed into the harbor. The father was thrilled enough to see sky and sky-scrapers. "There." A gray and green giantess stood on the gray water; her clothes, though seeming to swirl, were stiff in the wind and the moving sea. She was a statue, and she carried fire and a book. "Is she a goddess of theirs?" the father asked. "No," said the smuggler, "they don't have goddesses. She's a symbol of an idea." He was glad to hear that the Americans saw the idea of Liberty so real that they made a statue of it.

The father walked off the ship and onto the Gold Mountain. He disciplined his legs to step confidently, as if they belonged where they walked. He felt the concrete through his shoes. The noise and size of New York did not confuse him; he fol-lowed a map that his kinsmen had drawn so clearly that each landmark to Chinatown seemed to be waiting to welcome him. He went to the Extending Virtue Club, where people from his own village gave him a bed in a basement; it could have been a grocery shelf or an ironing table or the floor under a store counter. To lie stretched out on any part of the Gold Mountain was a pleasure to him.

Of course, my father could not have come that way. He came a legal way, something like this:

Arriving in San Francisco Bay, the legal father was detained for an indefinite time at the Immigration Station on Angel Island, almost within swimming distance of San Francisco. In a wooden house, a white demon physically examined him, poked him in the ass and genitals, looked in his mouth, pulled his eyelids with a hook. This was not the way a father ought to have been greeted. A cough tickled his chest and throat, but he held it down. The doctor demon pointed to a door, which he entered to find men and boys crowded together from floor to ceiling in bunkbeds and on benches; they stood against the walls and at the windows. These must be the hundred China Men who could enter America, he thought. But the quota was one hundred a year, not one hundred per day, and here were packed more than one hundred, nearer two hundred or three.

A few people made room for him to set down his suitcases. "A newcomer. Another newcomer," they called out. A welcome party made its way to him. "I'm the president of the Self-Governing Association," one of them was telling him in a dialect almost like his. "The most important rule we have here is that we guard one another's chances for immigration." He also asked for dues; the father gave a few dimes toward buying newspapers and phonograph records, an invention that he had never heard before. "Now you're eligible to vote," said the president, who then said that he had won his office by having been on the island the longest, three and a half years. The legal father's heart sank, and rose again; there must be something wrong with this man, not a good man, a criminal to be jailed for so long. "Do you want to spend money on a rubber ball? Vote Yes or No." The legal father voted No. How odd it would be to say to these men, "Play ball. Go ahead. Play with it," as if they were boys and could play. Even the boys wouldn't play. Who can be that lighthearted? He wasn't really going to stay here for more than a day or two, was he? He made his way across the room. Some of the men were gambling, others exercising, cutting one another's hair, staring at their feet or folded hands or the floor. He saw two men handcuffed to each other. Readers chanted San Francisco newspapers, *Young China* and *Chinese World*. The legal father, who was skillful and lucky, joined a game and won forty silver dollars, and gave away one for the rubber ball. He learned who was being deported and who was serving a year's sentence before deportation.

A bell went off like a ship's alarm, but it was a dinner bell. The father followed the others to a dining hall. About ten women were coming out. They were the first women he had seen since China, and they already belonged to husbands. He did not know that he had come to a country with no women. The husbands and wives talked quickly as the guards pushed them past one another. The father saw the man ahead of him hold hands with a woman for a moment and—he saw it—pass her a note. She dropped it. She knelt and, fixing her shoe with one hand, snatched the piece of paper with the other. A big white matron grabbed her arm and took the paper. Though these people were all strangers, the father joined the men who surrounded the matron. They wrested the paper from her and tore it up. The legal father ate some of the shreds. That was the last time the men's and women's mealtimes overlapped. There seemed to be no other immediate consequences; perhaps denial of entry would be the punishment.

The China Men who worked in the kitchen brought food cooked and served in buckets. "Poison," the prisoners grumbled. "A couple of years ago," said the president of the Self-Governing Association, "the demons tried to starve us to death. They were taking the food money for themselves. If it weren't for us rioting, you newcomers wouldn't be eating so much today. We faced bayonets for this food." The legal father wasn't sure he would've wanted any more of the slop they were eating.

The men spent the long days rehearsing what they would say to the Immigration Demon. The forgetful men fingered their risky notes. Those who came back after being examined told what questions they had been asked. "I had to describe all the streets in my village." "They'll ask, 'Do you have any money?' and 'Do you have a job?'" "They've been asking those questions all this week," the cooks and janitors confirmed. "What's the right answer?" asked the legal fathers. "Well, last week they liked 'No job' because it proves you were an aristocrat. And they liked 'No money' because you showed a willingness to work. But this week, they like 'Yes job' and 'Yes money' because you wouldn't be taking jobs away from white workers." The men groaned, "Some help." The demons did not treat people of any other race the way they did Chinese. The few Japanese left in a day or two. It was because their emperor was strong.

Footsteps walked across the ceiling, and bedsprings squeaked above their heads. So there were more of them locked on the second floor. "The women are up there," the father was told. Diabolical, inauspicious beginning—to be trodden over by women. "Living under women's legs," said the superstitious old-fashioned men from the backward villages. "Climbed over by women." It was bad luck even to walk under women's pants on clotheslines. No doubt the demons had deliberately planned this humiliation. The legal father decided that for a start in the new country, he would rid himself of Chinese superstitions; this curse would not count.

He read the walls, which were covered with poems. Those who could write protested this jailing, this wooden house (*wood* rhyming with *house*), the unfair laws, the emperor too weak to help them. They wrote about the fog and being lonely and afraid. The poets had come to a part of the world not made for honor, where "a hero cannot use his bravery." One poet was ready to ride his horse to do mighty American deeds but instead here he sat corraled, "this wooden house my coffin." The poets must have stayed long to carve the words so well. The demons were not going to free him, a scholar, then. Some were not poems exactly but statements. "This island is not angelic." "It's not true about the gold." One man blamed "the Mexican Exclusion Laws" for his imprisonment. The writers were anonymous; no official demon could trace them and penalize them. Some signed surname and village, but they were still disguised; there were many of that name from that village, many men named Lee from Toi Sahn, many a Hong of Sun Woi, and many a Three District Man and Four District No Such Man. There were dates of long stays.

Night fell quickly; at about four o'clock the fog poured down the San Francisco hillsides, covered the bay, and clouded the windows. Soon the city was gone, held fast by black sea and sky. The fog horns mourned. San Francisco might have been a figment of Gold Mountain dreams.

The legal father heard cries and thumps from someone locked in a separate shed. Words came out of the fog, the wind whipping a voice around the Island. "Let me land. Let me out. Let me land. I want to come home."

In the middle of one night when he was the only man awake, the legal father took out his Four Valuable Things, and using spit and maybe tears to mix the ink, he wrote a poem on the wall, just a few words to observe his stay. He wrote about wanting freedom. He did not sign his name; he would find himself a new American name when he landed. If the U.S. government found out his thoughts on freedom, it might not let him land. The next morning the readers sang the new poem for the others to hear. "Who wrote this wonderful poem during the night?" they asked, but the father modestly did not say.

For one another's entertainment, the men rehearsed and staged skits, puppet shows, and heroic parts of operas. They juggled fruit, bottles, and the new rubber ball. The father, who was traveling with the adventures of Yüeh Fei, the Patriot, in six volumes, read aloud the part where Yüeh Fei's mother carved on his back four words: FIRST—PROTECT MY NATION. He held up for all to see the illustrations of warriors in battle. He also carried the poems of Li Po, the best poet, the Heavenly Poet, the Great White Light, Venus. The father sang about a sentry stopping Li Po from entering a city. Li Po was drunk as usual and riding a mule. He refused to give his name to the sentry, but wrote a daring poem that he was a man from whose mouth the emperor had wiped the drool; the emperor's favorite wife had held his inkslab. The impressed sentry granted him entrance. This poem heartened the men; they laughed and clapped at Li Po's cleverness and the sentry's recognition of him and poetry.

"What is a poem exactly?" asked an illiterate man, a Gold Mountain Sojourner who had spent twenty years in America and was on his way back to his family. "Let me give it a try," he said. "A short poem: 'On the Gold Mountain, I met black men black like coal.' Is that a poem?" The literate men were delighted. "Marvelous," they said. "Of course, it's a poem." "A simile. A simile. Yes, a poem." The legal father liked it so much, he remembered it forever.

The legal father learned many people's thoughts because he wrote their letters. They told their wives and mothers how wonderful they found the Gold Mountain. "The first place I came to was The Island of Immortals," they told him to write. "The foreigners clapped at our civilized magnificence when we walked off the ship in our brocades. A fine welcome. They call us 'Celestials.'" They were eating well; soon they would be sending money. Yes, a magical country. They were happy, not at all frightened. The Beautiful Nation was glorious, exactly the way they had heard it would be. "I'll be seeing you in no time." "Today we ate duck with buns and plum sauce," which was true on days when the China Men in San Francisco sent gifts.

Every day at intervals men were called out one by one. The legal father kept himself looking presentable. He wore his Western suit and shined shoes, constantly ready.

One morning the barracks awoke to find a man had hanged himself. He had done it from a railing. At first he looked as if he had been tortured, his legs cut off. He had tied his legs bent at the knees like an actor or beggar playing a man with no legs, and hung himself by pushing over his chair. His body had elongated from hanging all night. The men looked through his papers and found X's across them. When new arrivals looked for beds, nobody told them that a dead, hung man had slept in that one.

Also, the rumor went, a woman upstairs had killed herself by sharpening a chopstick and shoving it through her ear. Her husband had sent for her, and she did not understand why he did not come to take her home.

At last came the legal father's turn to be interrogated. He combed his hair again. He said his good-byes. Inside the interrogation room were several white demons in formal wear; the legal father gauged by the width of lapels and ties that his own suit was not quite stylish. Standing beside the table was a Chinese-looking soldier in American uniform and a demon soldier in the same uniform. This Chinese American was the interpreter. The legal father sat opposite the interrogators, who asked his name, his village, where he was born, his birth date—easy questions.

"Can you read and write?" the white demon asked in English and the Chinese American asked in Cantonese.

"Yes," said the legal father.

But the secretary demon was already writing No since he obviously couldn't, needing a translator.

"When did you cut off your pigtail?" asked the translator.

"In 1911," said the legal father. It was a safe answer, the year he would have picked anyway, not too early before the Republic nor too late, not too revolutionary nor too reactionary. Most people had cut their hair in 1911. He might have cut it for fashion as much as for revolution.

"Do you have relatives who are American citizens?"

The janitor, a China Man, who just then entered the room with dustpan and broom, nodded.

"Yes."

"Who?"

"My grandfather is an American. My father is an American. So I'm an American, also my three older brothers and three uncles—all Americans."

Then came the trap questions about how many pigs did they own in 1919, whether the pig house was made out of bricks or straw, how many steps on the back stoop, how far to the outhouse, how to get to the market from the farm, what were the addresses of the places his grandfather and father and brothers and uncles had lived in America. The interrogators liked asking questions with numbers for answers. Numbers seemed true to them. "Quick. How many windows do you have in your house?" "How many times did your grandfather return to the United States?" "Twice." "Twice?" "Yes, twice. He was here once and returned twice. He was here three times altogether. He spent half his life in America and half in China." They looked into his eyes for lies. Even the Chinese American looked into his eyes, and they repeated his answers, as if doubting them. He squelched an urge to change the answers, elaborate on them. "Do you have any money?" "Yes." "How much?" He wondered if they would charge him higher fees the more money he reported. He decided to tell the truth; lying added traps. Whether or not he spoke the truth didn't matter anyway; demons were capricious. It was up to luck now.

They matched his answers to the ones his relatives and fellow villagers gave. He watched the hands with yellow hair on their backs turn the copies of his grandfather's and father's papers.

They told him to go back to the jail, where he waited for more weeks. The next time he was called to be examined—*searched* the Chinese word—they asked again, "What American relatives do you have?"

"My grandfather and father," he said again, "and also my three brothers and three uncles."

"Your grandfather's papers are illegal," the Chinese American translated. "And your father is also an illegal alien." One by one the demons outlawed his relatives and ancestors, including a Gold Rush grandfather, who had paid a bag of gold dust to an American Citizenship Judge for papers. "There are no such things as Citizenship Judges," said the Immigration Demon and put an X across the paper that had been in the family for seventy-five years. He moved on to ask more trap questions, the directions the neighbors' houses faced and the

number of water buffaloes in 1920, and sent him back to the
barracks.

He waited again. He was examined again, and since he had
an accurate memory, he told them the same number of pigs as
the last two times, the same number of water buffaloes (one),
the same year of cutting his queue, and at last they said, "You
may enter the United States of America." He had passed the
American examination; he had won America. He was not sure
on what basis they let him in—his diploma, his American lin-
eage (which may have turned out to be good after all), his ability to withstand jailing, his honesty, or the skill of his deceits.

This legal father then worked his way across the continent to
New York, the center of America.

Ed, Woodrow, Roosevelt, and Worldster held their bowls
to their mouths and shoveled as fast as they could, chewing
crackly pork and pressed duck in one bite, gulping while jabbing from the center dishes without choosiness. They raced as
if food were scarce and one of them would be left the runt pig.
Woodrow picked up the soup tureen and drank directly from
it. "Uh. Uh," the others protested, but didn't stop gulping to
say "You're cheating."

Worldster threw down his bowl and chopsticks, spit the
bones "p-foo" out on the table, knocked back his shot of whiskey, jumped up—his orange crate hit the floor with a bang—
and shouted, "I won. I won."

But Woodrow, the soup drinker, ran out the door. "Last
one to leave the table loses," he said.

"You're still chewing and swallowing," Worldster yelled.

"Okay," said Ed. "Okay, I lose." His friends cheered him as
he leaned back and sipped his whiskey. "That was a four-and-
a-half-minute dinner," he said, looking at his new gold watch.
"It's a record." They gave their record a cheer.

The last one to finish eating did the dishes. While the others
returned to work in the front of the laundry, Ed set a kettle to
boil, unfolded his newspaper, lit a Lucky Strike, the brand he
had chosen, and poured another glass of whiskey and a cup of
coffee. Reading while drinking and smoking was one of the
great pure joys of existence. He read that a Gold Mountain
Sojourner, upon returning to his village, had gotten bilked by

relatives, most of whom he had never met before. They had flocked to him. They tricked him with an intricate scheme for investing in a bogus Hong Kong housing project for refugees. Another Sojourner put his life savings into a bank that the entire village had set up just to get his money. The Sojourners were quoted as saying they were coming back to America.

Ed scraped the dishes onto the tablecloth, which was layers of newspapers. Then he rolled up the top layer; the table was instantly clean and already covered for the next meal. He sudsed the dishes with laundry soap and put them in a drainer. From the whistling tea kettle, he poured boiling water on them; the water was so hot, the dishes dried before his eyes. It was a method he remembered the slaves in China using. Dishwashing just took common sense; women had made such a to-do about it. The Gold Mountain was indeed free: no manners, no traditions, no wives.

When he joined his partners doing the ironing, his favorite part of laundry work, they were planning "the weekend."

"I want to go tea dancing," said Worldster, "and take driving lessons." He had a thick moustache and tried to look like Clark Gable.

"Let's see the Statue of Liberty at night," said Woodrow, who vowed that he would make a million bucks by 1935.

"I want to go on a date," said Roosevelt, who was looking for a medical school that gave night classes. "A weekend date with a Rockette," he said in English.

"I know where *City Lights* is playing," said Ed. "Also *Little Miss Marker.* You know, someday, when the people from the future see the movies, they'll think people today walked and moved like Charlie Chaplin." Oh, it was wonderful; for a dime the ushers let you stay all day through the intermissions, and the shows ran again and again. "Every Saturday night is a party in this country." Customers were picking up the big bundles—cash for the weekend.

Ed placed shirt after shirt on the stack that was growing beside his ironing board. Friends were fairer than brothers; there was an equality. When Tu Fu left his village, friends cared for him; "we swore brotherhood for eternity," he wrote. How good life was. Ed was young, and he was in New York with three new true friends who sang at their work.

They were singing the Rainy Alley Poet, who lived in Paris and followed black hair in the rain: "'I will follow that gleam though stumbling in the haze, the twilight like a bubble of rose rising in the wine glass, and let my nostalgic eyes become ensnared in memory dark as her hair.'"

"Aiya," breathed Woodrow. "True love. True life. The free pursuit of happiness."

"Aiya. That's me," said Roosevelt, "'ensnared in memory dark as her hair,' except it should be blonde hair. 'Ensnared in memory yellow as her hair!'"

They sang Wang Tu Ching, a Sojourner, who had done all the wonderful things that a young man ought to do in Paris—having affairs, getting French girls pregnant. "'Oh, this endless journey home. I am Chinese, and must not expect happiness but tears and sacrifice. Farewell, Latin Quarter, chestnut trees, bookstalls along the Seine.'" "'Latin Quarter, chestnut trees,'" Ed repeated.

"'I'm madly in love with Europe,'" they sang, "'where I played my reed flute on an empty stomach.'" This was a song by Ai Ch'ing, a fellow Kwangtung man.

They sang an old poet, too, Yüan Mei, who had advocated educating women and written from a woman's point of view: "'For years I've been imagining a boat/Shooting over the waves as fast as any bird/But never taking the traveler away from friends/Always carrying the traveler back to his home.'"

"Oh, that's beautiful," said Roosevelt. He rested under the fan and smoked a cigarette with tears in his eyes. "That's how I feel." The men were thinking not about one another but of lifelong friends.

"And listen to this one," said Ed. "The first wife welcomes her man home: 'If it were not for Second Wife, you would not come home. She is your plum blossom.'"

"Oh, oh," moaned the lonesome men. "Welcomed home by two wives."

They worked very late at night, and after a while did not sing or talk. The two fans whirred, blowing the calendars, the monthly calendars swinging on the walls, and the pages of the daily calendars riffling. Ed's legs ached. At about eleven o'clock, he spoke the bitter verses of "The Laundry Song," by Wen I-to of Chicago:

> *A piece, two pieces, three pieces—*
> *Wash them clean,*
> *Four pieces, five pieces, six—*
> *Iron them smooth.*

No, they were not going to be welcomed home by wives; they would stay here working forever. He thumped his iron on the accents.

> *Years pass and I let drop but one homesick tear.*
> *A laundry lamp burns at midnight.*
> *The laundry business is low, you say,*
> *Washing out blood that stinks like brass—*
> *Only a Chinaman can debase himself so.*
> *But who else wants to do it? Do you want it?*
> *Ask for the Chinaman. Ask the Chinaman.*

The other men were so tired, they only grunted in agreement. At midnight they switched off the lights in the windows, turned the Open sign around to Closed, and pulled down the shades. They worked without interruptions from customers, then made the ironing tables into beds.

Under his desk lamp, Ed did the accounts on his abacus and wrote down the profits in ledgers. Woodrow, who had bought a Kodak with a part of his million, took a picture of him. "You can send this to your wife and tell her you study a lot," he said. When Ed finished the bookkeeping, the others were asleep. In the quiet of the night, he practiced his calligraphy by writing down modern poems for his friends to paste on the walls over their ironing tables. He wrote a letter to his wife, and went to bed.

On Saturday Ed and Woodrow went to Fifth Avenue to shop for clothes. With his work pants, Ed wore his best dress shirt, a silk tie, gray silk socks, good leather shoes with pointed toes, and a straw hat. At a very good store, he paid two hundred dollars cash for a blue and gray pinstripe suit, the most expensive suit he could find. In the three-way mirror, he looked like Fred Astaire. He wore the suit out of the store. Woodrow took a picture of him dancing down the New York Public Library steps next to one of the lions. "I don't see why you have to spend all this money on clothes," said Woodrow, whose entire wardrobe came from the unclaimed laundry. He was the one who had written the sign in English: WE WILL NOT BE RESPONSIBLE FOR CLOTHES UNCLAIMED AFTER 30 DAYS. He shot his cuffs and said, "You must admit I look pretty swanky in these secondhand outfits." The two of them strolled Fifth Avenue and caught sight of themselves in windows and hubcaps. They looked all the same Americans.

Suddenly a band of white demons came up from behind them. One picked off Ed's straw hat and kicked its lid through. Before Ed and Woodrow could decide what to do for the shame on China Men, they saw the whites stomp on other whites' hats. "It must be a custom," said Ed.

That afternoon, the partners trimmed one another's hair with their barber's shears and electric hair clippers. They copied Ed's professional haircut, parted in the middle and the two sides lifted just so in "pompadours." Then all four gentlemen went to a tearoom. Ed regretted having to check his gray felt hat at the door. It looked good with his new suit. Girls liked the way he cocked his head and looked at them sideways with his hat brim tilted at a smart angle. The hatcheck girl also sold them strips of tickets for ten cents apiece. The hostess escorted them to a table, where they ordered cookies, open-faced raw cucumber sandwiches, strawberry parfaits, and tea. They nibbled carefully at their sandwiches, chewed with their mouths shut, sipped tea, and dabbed their lips even though they had not slobbered or made crumbs. They looked around at the couples to decide which dancing girls they were going to ask. "Look at the legs on that one," said Roosevelt. "She must be a Rockette."

"The main difference between them and us Tang People," Woodrow observed, "is the shape of their nostrils, which are oval instead of small, neat, and round like ours."

They were saying those things in Chinese, so weren't being rude. They were sophisticated New York gentlemen, and knew more about American manners than white people. "When I was a waiter," said Worldster, "there were hick tourists who tipped us after every course. Every time we came to the table they tipped us." Since the music took so long stopping, he went over to a couple, tapped the white man on the shoulder, and cut in. "What's your name, sweetheart?" he said like in the movies.

The others waited until the orchestra stopped, then stood and walked out onto the dance floor. "Dance with me?" Ed asked, holding out his tickets. "Sure," the blonde dancing girl of his choice said, smiling, taking several tickets, which was a compliment; he would get to dance with her a lot. He smiled back and said, "Sure." The music did not start up right away. "You like come my table after you dance with me?" he invited. "Of course," she said. "You speak English very well," she said. "Thank you," he said. "You be very beautiful. Pretty. You be pretty. I like you." "How nice," she said. "Thank you. You're very handsome. You're good looking. Do you understand *handsome*?" "Sure. Of course. How nice. Thank you." A fox-trot started, and he put out his hand; she put her hand in it, and he led her, his feet in their new leather shoes, glissading across the waxed wood floor. He saw himself and her in the mirrors, and they looked like the movies. He guided her a little closer with the intimate hand at her waist. He looked down at the gold eyebrows and curving eyelashes and her blue eyes. He pulled their two clasped hands closer so that her gold hair brushed his hand. Her hair was fine and soft, not like hair at all. He dared a dip, and her wonderful hair rippled near the floor and swung back against his other hand. When the music stopped, she said, "You're a very good dancer." "And handsome too?" he asked. She laughed with her beautiful lipsticked mouth.

The others had also brought their blondes over to the table under the potted palm, and they ate the sandwiches, drank tea, and smoked cigarettes. "Is he really a Chinese prince?" Worldster's girl asked. "What's 'prince'?" asked Ed. "A king's son," she said. "A king's son," said Worldster in Chinese. "Oh, yes," said Ed, "in China, we all be prince with so much money. Too much money. But. Now we all the same Americans."

They danced until they had no more tickets. And they danced with as many different blondes as they pleased. And Ed was so handsome that some danced with him for free, vied with one another to dance with him. He became bold enough to ask the friendliest blonde, one who had been studying his eyes, his high cheekbones, and neat nose, who had made him unbutton his sleeve and hold his tan arm against her pink arm, "You like come home with me? Please?"

"No, honey," she said. "No."

Not one of the four of them told any blonde that they were married and were fathers. "See you next week," they said, learning new ways to say good-bye. "See ya." "So long."

On Sunday they rode the ferry boat to Coney Island. Woodrow asked a blonde to take pictures of the four friends with their arms on the railing and their black hair flying in the wind. At the beach, a bathing beauty photographed them in their bathing suits, nobody wearing a jockstrap, which might not yet have come into fashion. Ed had bought a beach robe, "which is different from a bedroom robe," he explained. He sent many pictures to his wife, including one of himself sitting on the sand with his arms around his knees and his sweat shirt tied around his neck; he was smiling and looking out to sea.

On another weekend, Worldster, who had taken flying lessons, rented an aeroplane and invited each of his friends up into the sky. (*Friends* in Chinese connotes play, good times, and youth.) "We're men of the Twentieth Century," he lectured as Ed marveled at the speed and height. "We're modern men, and have to learn to make use of the new machines." He explained how to move the plane right and left and up and down, then said, "You try it," and let go of the controls. Ed flew over rivers, trees, and houses, raced cars, and made the plane go back up when it fell into air pockets. They circled the airport and waggled their wings at Roosevelt and Woodrow down there.

Ed sent his wife pictures of himself in the cockpit; he wore a white scarf flying behind him, goggles, and a leather skullcap with flaps over the ears. He also sent several shots of the plane in the air, an insect against the white sky.

Woodrow bought a car, and Roosevelt a motorcycle. Each of the four friends stood by the car for his picture. They also took pictures of one another leaning into curves on the motorcycle. Ed did not pass the driver's test but drove anyway. "You can drive without a license here," he wrote to people in China. "It's a free country."

In the spring, Ed sent his wife a picture of the four partners with their arms around one another's shoulders, laughing next to a Keep Off the Grass sign. He was wearing another two-hundred-dollar suit, a navy blue one, and a shirt with

French cuffs, which closed with gold cuff links. For a winter picture, he sat on a rock in Central Park in his new gray great-coat and jaunty hat and leather gloves lined with rabbit fur.

In his quiet time at night, he mounted the photographs in a fine leather album. With his first spending money, he had bought a postcard of the Statue of Liberty, the album, picture mounts, white ink, and a pen with a steel nib. He pasted that postcard in his expensive album, then added the other pictures.

Ed's wife wrote often and sometimes sent lichee, which she had picked from the three trees that Ed's father had planted and the twenty trees that Ed's brother had planted. When would he return to plant lichee trees?

Then she wrote that their two children had died. What should she do? "I think you ought to come back right now," she said.

He did much worrying, and hit upon a plan. He would not end his American life but show her how to live one. "Here's what you have to do if I'm to bring you to America," he wrote, though there was a law against her. "I will bring you to America on one condition, and that is, you get a Western education. I'll send you money, which you must only spend on school, not on food or clothes or jewelry or relatives. Leave the village. Go to Hong Kong or Canton and enroll in a Western scientific school. A science school. Get a degree. Send it to me as evidence you are educated, and I'll send you a ship ticket. And don't go to a school for classical literature. Go to a scientific school run by white people. And when you get your degree, I'll send for you to come here to the United States." He would figure out later how to accomplish that.

When next she wrote, she had enrolled in medical school; she was writing him from there. As years passed and sometimes she became discouraged with how long her education was taking and how difficult the work, he wrote encouragement: "If you don't get that degree, I'll not send for you. We will never see each other again." He did not want an ignorant villager for his American wife.

So much time went by, he saved another two hundred dollars, which he spent on a gray suit and a Countess Mara tie.

At last she mailed him her diploma. He spent another few

years saving passage money, and fifteen years after they had last seen one another, he sent for her. Applying for her, he risked having his citizenship again scrutinized. She would enter legally and gracefully, no question of asking a lady to ride the sea in a box or to swim to an unwatched shore.

At dinner one evening, he announced to his partners, "I've sent for my wife, who will be here in January." They were so surprised that they stopped their eating race.

"How did you save enough money?" Worldster asked.

"I guess you'll be moving to your own apartment," said Roosevelt.

"Why do you want to do that?" asked Woodrow.

After writing letters for fifteen years, Ed and his wife ended their correspondence. They were near each other, she on Ellis Island, where there was no mail, and he on Manhattan. When he saw her on the ferry, she was standing surrounded by bundles and bags, no child tugging her coat and no baby in her arms. He recognized her, though she was older. Her hair was slicked against her head with a bun in back, a proper married-lady hairdo. In spite of the law against her, she was landing, her papers in order. Her immigration verified the strength of his citizenship.

"Here you are," he said. "You've come."

"You look like a foreigner," she said. "I can barely recognize you."

"Was it a rough journey?" he asked.

"It was terrible," she exclaimed. "The Japanese were right behind me. When I tried to board the ship from Canton to Hong Kong, the man acted as if my papers were wrong and asked for a seventy-five-dollar bribe. So I ran to another gangplank and found out seventy-five dollars wasn't policy at all; this man wanted a hundred dollars. I had to run back to the first entrance. Then I paid another hundred to get off the ship. It was the last ship out of Canton before the Japanese took the harbor. And I was so seasick, I vomited the whole way across the Atlantic. And what a questioning I got on the Island. They asked me what year you had cut your queue, and a workman shook his head, hawked, and spat. It was a signal. So I said, 'I don't know.' On my way to be locked up again, I said to that workman, 'That was a delicious bun you gave me. Thank you.

I hope you bring me another if you have more.' Get it? It was a code I made up, meaning, 'Thank you for giving me the right answer. Please give me more help,' Oh, I was so scared. If it weren't for him I might not be here."

"Don't worry any more," said Ed. "That's over now. Don't worry any more." Her big eyes had lines aound them. "That's all over now," he said.

"I had to build roads," she said. "Since your father is too crazy to work, and you were away, I had to pay the labor tax for two men. Your father followed me and wept on the road when I left."

"Never mind now," he said. "That's all over now."

They rode the subway to the room he had rented in preparation for her coming. He taught her the name of the subway stop for the laundry. "Easu Bu-odd-way Su-ta-son," she repeated. "That's good," he said. "Remember that, and you can't get lost."

She unpacked jars of seeds. "But we aren't farmers any more," he said. "I'll plant in tin cans and put them out here on the fire escape," she said. "You'll see how many vegetables we can grow in cans."

She showed him a piece of cloth. "Do you recognize this?" she asked. "The Japanese were right behind me, and I had time to take just one keepsake—the trimming on the bed canopy." She had ripped it off and shoved it in her purse. She unfolded it. "This is the only thing we have left from China," she said. "The heirloom." A red phoenix and a red dragon played across the strip of linen; the Chinese words down one end and English words across the top said, "Good morning." She had cross-stitched it herself.

"You could write English even then," he teased her, "and getting ready to come here." "I didn't know what it said," she demurred, "I only copied it from a needlework book."

He took her shopping and bought her a black crepe dress with a bodice of white lace ruffles and buttons of rhinestone and silver. "You look very pretty," he told her. They bought a black coat with a fur collar and a little black-eyed animal head over her shoulder, high heels, silk stockings, black kid gloves, and a picture hat with a wide, wide brim and silk fluttery ribbon. They strolled in their finery along Fifth Avenue.

"I washed all these windows," he told her. "When I first came here, I borrowed a squeegee and rags and a bucket, and walked up and down this street. I went inside each store and asked if they wanted the windows washed. The white foreigners aren't so hard to get along with; they nod to mean Yes and shake their heads to mean No, the same as anybody." New York glittered and shined with glass. He had liked pulling the water off the panes and leaving brief rainbows. While working, he had looked over the displays of all the wonderful clothes to own and wear. He had made the money to pool for starting the laundry. "In the spring," he promised her, "we'll buy you white cotton gloves."

"On the first day of autumn," he told her, "New Yorkers stomp on one another's straw hats. I wear my gray felt one as soon as summer's over. I save the straw for spring. I'm not extravagant. You ought to put your earrings in the safe deposit box at the bank. Pierced ears look a little primitive in this country." He also told her to buy makeup at a drugstore. "American people don't like oily faces. So you ought to use some powder. It's the custom. Also buy some rouge. These foreigners dislike yellow skin."

She also bought a long black rat of hair to roll her own hair over for an upswept hairdo. At a beauty parlor, she had her wavy hair cut and curled tighter with a marcel. She washed, ironed, and wrapped her silk pants and dresses and never wore them again.

He took her to see the Statue of Liberty. They climbed the ladder, she in high heels, up the arm to the torch, then the stairs to the crown. "Now we're inside her chin. This part must be the nose." From the windows of the crown, he showed her his city.

They also went to the top of the Empire State Building, took the second elevator to the very top, the top of the world. Ed loved the way he could look up at the uncluttered sky. They put money in the telescopes and looked for the laundry and their apartment. "So I have been on the tallest building in the world," she said. "I have seen everything. Wonderful. Wonderful. Amazing. Amazing."

"Yes," he said. "Everything's possible on the Gold Mountain. I've danced with blondes." "No, really?" she said.

"You didn't. You're making that up, aren't you? You danced with demonesses? I don't believe it."

Her favorite place to go was the free aquarium, "the fish house," where all manner of creatures swam. Walking between the lighted tanks, she asked, "When do you think we'll go back to China? Do you think we'll go back to China?" "Shh," he said. "Shh." The electric eels glowed in their dark tank, and the talking fish made noises. "There are bigger fish in China," she said.

They went to the movies and saw *Young Tom Edison* with Mickey Rooney. They both liked the scene where the mother took Eh-Da-Son into the barn, but only pretended to thrash him; she faked the slaps and crying and scolding to fool the strict father, the father "the severe parent," according to Confucius, and the mother "the kind parent." ("My bones, my flesh, father and mother," said Tu Fu.) After the movie, Ed explained to his wife that this cunning, resourceful, successful inventor, Edison, was who he had named himself after. "I see," she said. "Eh-Da-Son. Son as in *sage* or *immortal* or *saint*."

They also saw a movie where a big man bridged two mountain peaks with his prone body. He held on to one cliff of a chasm with his fingers and the other with his toes. Hundreds of little people walked across on him.

The four partners no longer had to race to get out of doing the dishes. Ed's wife shopped and cooked. She bought a tiered food carrier, filled each pot with a different accompaniment to rice, and carried it and a pot of soup hot through the subway to the laundry. The first day she did this, she got off at the wrong stop in the underground city. She went from white ghost to white ghost shouting over the trains, which sounded like the Japanese bombing, "Easu Bu-odd-way Su-ta-son?" And a conductor said, "Of course. East Broadway Station. Go that way."

"He understood me," she proudly told the men. "I can speak English very well." She set the table with her homemade meal so they didn't get to buy restaurant take-out food any more. And they did not race but had manners. "Tell me how you started this laundry," she said. Woodrow described their Grand Opening. "Our friends sent stands of flowers tied in wide red ribbons, on which your husband wrote good words in gold ink. We exploded firecrackers out on the sidewalk, right out there on Mott Street. And then the customers came." "Working for ourselves, we can close whenever we please and go do as we like," Ed said.

The partners did not tell her that they hardly ever celebrated holidays. They had learned that holidays do not appear with the seasons; the country does not turn festive just because a rubric day appears on the calendar. The cooking women, the shopping and slicing and kneading and chopping women brought the holidays. The men let holidays pass. If they did not go to the bother of keeping it, a holiday was another free day. It was that free a country. They could neglect attending the big public celebrations such as those at the benevolent associations and New Year's eve at Times Square, and no one minded. Neglecting the planting and harvest days made no difference in New York. No neighbors looked askance. And there were no godly repercussions. They had no graves to decorate for the memorial days of Clarity and Brightness. They did arrange cotton snow, reindeer, a stable scene, and a Santa Claus in the laundry window at Christmas. "We don't want them to break our window or not bring their laundry," Ed explained. His wife brought back the holidays. She made the holidays appear again.

Her arrival ended Ed's independent life. She stopped him from reading while eating. She'd learned at the school of Western medicine, she said, that doing those two actions at once divides the available blood between brain and stomach; one should concentrate. She kept telling Ed to cut down on his smoking. She polished his World's Fair copper souvenir ashtray clean. She cut new covers from brown wrapping paper and shirt cardboards for his books, and resewed the bindings. He inked the new covers with the titles, authors, and volume numbers.

When the partners took the couple to a restaurant, the men wiped their chopsticks and bowls with napkins. "That doesn't really clean them, you know," she said. "All you're doing is wiping the germs around. Germs are little animals invisible to the naked eye." "That must be a superstition from your village, a village superstition," said Worldster. "You ought to give up village superstitions in America." The next day she brought her microscope to the laundry and showed them the germs under their fingernails and on their tongues and in the water.

At one of their dinners, Worldster handed papers to Woodrow and Roosevelt, and the three of them started discussing business.

"What is this?" said Ed.

"Deeds for the business," said Worldster, "contracts for the partnership."

"Where's mine?" said Ed. "What contracts? Why contracts all of a sudden?"

"Where's his?" asked his wife.

"You weren't at the meeting," said Worldster.

"Since when did we have to have contracts?" Ed asked. "We had a spoken partnership. We shook hands. We gave one another our word."

"We wrote it down too," said Worldster. "I guess you have the status of an employee."

"I don't see why you didn't show up for the meeting," said Roosevelt.

"This is all perfectly legal," said Woodrow. "Look—registered with the demon courts." It was in English. There wasn't anything Ed could do. They had ganged up on him and swindled him out of his share of the laundry. "You were always reading when we were working," somebody said.

"What are we going to do?" said his wife, the lines around her eyes and mouth deepening.

"Don't worry," he said. "I've been planning for us to go to California anyway."

So the two of them took a train across the United States, stopping in Chicago to visit some relatives—they saw more of the United States than they had ever seen of China—and went to live in California, which some say is the real Gold Mountain anyway.

The Ghostmate

M ANY TIMES it has happened that a young man walks along a mountain road far from home. He may have passed the Imperial Examinations ("entered the toad palace on the moon") or failed. If he failed, he would be singing a song, "What Does the Scholar Do with His Bagful of Books After Failing?" Or he may not have been a student at all but a farmer at market overnight—or an artisan, whose wife will be pleased with the good money he made on pots or rugs or shoes. Or he carries a satisfying batch of cotton or silk on his back and is heading into town. On the nooning day, sun and leaves dapple his face with shadows and golden coins. The fine road opens before him coming around turns and over rises. Grass and water above and below him, he glimpses the road ahead threading the mountains. Some of the one hundred kinds of birds that fly the sky and nest the earth let him see them, and even the phoenix seems to hover near. A music accompanies him. Released for this day from his past and future, the young traveler feels his freedom. His walk is loose. He cocks his head; the music is real. He laughs at its cacophony, which blasts any worries out of his head. He sings melodies that wind like ribbons into the vistas. His conducting hands lift notes out of the air, stroke them, and let them go. Long streams drop down mountains. Beyond mountains, still higher mountains rise until the peaks fade from human sight. He is climbing a dragon's spine. Green-black trees twist overhead, taller than distant mountains. The man is the size of the far trees.

Suddenly it starts to rain. The naked drought-dwarfs with the one eye on top of their heads run for cover. Thunder and lightning close out the day. The trees howl, bend to earth, and snap back as if giants were stepping on them in their run downhill. The grass flattens against the ground. The wind, though it's only the wind, whips up a sense of danger in him, and the young man hurries along, hoping for a shrine to use as shelter. When he begins to despair of finding any such signs of other people having come this way, a big house appears in the woods, and simultaneously the smell of a strong flower fills his head. Lightning reveals him knocking at the unfamiliar emblems on the outer gate; thick passion flower vines like elephant trunks twist around the carved and lacquered pillars.

The storm dies for a moment as if listening to his knocks. The forms and colors of the clouds change rapidly. A gold, silver, and pink mist covers the house.

An old servant answers, and dogs charge out, barking at him. Sometimes, though, the beautiful lady lives there alone and comes to the gate herself. She is the most beautiful woman he has ever seen. She must have come from the West Lake region, land of the most beautiful women in the world. (Kwangtung women are the second most beautiful.) "Enter, stranger," she says, and later he remembers that the cheerless wind again quieted, the guard dogs subsided, and he heard her voice. In the garden, lumps of peacocks squat on the branches of swaying, laden trees. He follows her on a long path to the inner door; he walks under a horizontal scroll of mountains and sea. The red paper surely means a good house; a spirit woman or a fox would not have it, would she? Walking on through the cool rooms, he follows her retreating back. She is wearing a light-colored dress, her hair a black tail alive down the middle. She turns one corner after another until he wonders if he can find his way out alone. She finally enters a small room and faces him. "Change your wet clothes," she says in a voice that sings. "I'll return with more food." On a stool by the fire he finds clothing and slippers, which fit him. A tureen of hot soup sits on a table, and one bowl has already been poured. The tea steeps. How lucky am I, he thinks; a stranger is owed no more than a drink of water.

"Please eat with me." Her voice startles him because he did not hear her return to the room. She is dressed in the old style. (No matter what year this is, China is old enough for there to have been an old style.) She wears the combs with the long prongs. Her eyebrows are moth's wings joined at the center, and her eyes are like bronze bells with brights and deeps.

Holding her right sleeve with her left hand, she uncovers the complex dishes—duck in sheets, embryonic chicks in soup and in cakes, minces, and stuffings. Steam rises as if a mirage of food floated on the table. The meal lasts for a long while.

He sucks bones thoroughly of marrow. He pushes an almond sliver over all the taste buds in his mouth, the ones along the upper gums, the lower gums, the ones under his tongue, and the corners of his cheeks. Then he bolts meat and rice. He gorges; he indulges his appetite. Food seems to reappear, the bowls bottomless. She pours tea and gives him the tiny cup with her own hands. He accepts it carefully so that his fingers do not oafishly touch hers. He feeds like an aristocrat.

If he knows ceramics and manners, he picks up a piece of tableware and says, "How beautiful." "Yes, hold it up to the light and see the glow," she says. The orange of the firelight suffuses the porcelain. He hears a deer cry outside. She ignores it. She is looking into his face, and her mouth forms a delightful O. She touches his wrist. "Tell me a story about your life," she says. As he talks, feeding her admiration, he understands that he is a special man. Up to now he was only filling his work-habituated hands with the clay from the least fertile part of his land; he made utensils, but she calls him an artist. If he is a failed student, he has his poems to sing to her, and she comforts him so that he is almost glad he lost at the exams. If he won, then what triumph—a position in government service and a beautiful woman—the beginning of a run of victories.

If he is a cobbler, she asks him to sew a pair of shoes for her, challenging him to do it before the storm abates. From the suede she brings him, he cuts pieces as symmetrical as butterflies. Until now he frugally used scraps from the winter coats. After finishing the seams, he nimbly works flowers into the tops and sides. He kneels before her chair, where she sits enthroned, and she steps into the shoes. Her tiny feet in each of his palms, he has the impression that he is holding a fairy dancing on his hands. "I can give you your wishes," she is saying. "I can give you time to study, money to buy gold thread and rare glazes." He laughs, "Spoken like a woman who never has to work. I wish never to have to work at all." What a strange woman. If he were a farmer, would she give him a shovel or a bag of manure as a present?

A farmer whose wife and babies are waiting for him would mean to stay only until the rain stops, only until the end of the slow night. He would memorize each moment and the scrolls and the furniture and the food; his wife would enjoy hearing about this lucky night.

His wife is waiting at home, cooking roots and bark for the children, the adopted daughter or son, the widower uncle, the old folks with no teeth. She is a brave cooking wife. She has never had a romantic dinner for two. He'll have to ask her if she can manage without sweating so, and he doesn't like the calluses on her hands and feet either.

The young husband should have hinted for some leftovers to bring home to his dying grandparents and hungry parents and toilsome wife. When he found out there was going to be free food, he could have sent the rich woman's servant to fetch his family. Instead he feeds like a zoo animal, a pet.

Toward the end of the meal, he asks, "Do you live here alone?"

"I'm a widow," she says, and he feels all the erotic things the words *young widow* arouse in men.

As if she expected just him and no other, his hostess brings him the very fruits, the very poem, the very game he likes best. "I'll leave when the storm flags," he says. "I'll leave after the winning point." The storm heightens. She wins a game, and he wins a game; they have to play again. She tells him the long, long story of how she came to be a young widow. Tears magnify her eyes and brim on the lids, the prisms breaking and melting, wetting the pink cheekbones, the white cheeks, the corners of her mouth. When she talks, the words give her mouth such shapes that he cannot cease watching it. His wife's tears were no more interesting than his own tears; her nose turned red when she cried. One more fascination, and yet one more holds him. Through the windows, there gleams weather fit for travel, but he stays. He becomes drowsy. He will see his wife the next day, for lunch at the latest.

For breakfast the beautiful widow feeds him more foods he has never eaten before, shows him more things he has only known in stories. When he asks if he can pack a few leftovers for his wife, she looks at him gravely, and says, "Let me give you a better present. You must take a lasting gift from me. Tell me about your work, and I can show you how to improve it and make lots of money." She says "lots of money" as if she were a girl imitating adult talk, guessing at his grown-up concerns.

She seems to have come from a world where the inhabitants do not use money. She brings glazes in textures, blues, and greens the potter has not been able to mix, mounds of white lamb's wool to the weaver, paper with deer and willow and mountain watermarks to the poet, rolls of leather and cloth, threads like skeins of rainbows to the cobbler and tailor. To try the new substances, his hands begin their familiar work. They move smoothly now, not encountering bumps or tangles, knots, or nodes. The slips run exactly. Then, of course, he has to wait for the kiln to fire, the ink to dry, the glue to set. The embroidery artist has begun stitching the first of the one hundred birds, that is, two hundred birds, a pair of each kind, composed about a tree. Then, time to eat. Then, time to go to bed again, too late to travel. He should have observed the custom of refusing gifts.

The morning light shows his work to him; he sees in what he has done the possibility of the lightest, smallest shoe, the true poem, the embroidery or painting of the phoenix. He may fathom at this moment how many more pieces he has to make before the masterpiece. He bows to the years he must remain at his work. Each piece draws him on to the next one. Days go by. Nights.

And it is not only the work that holds him but the woman. If he is a tailor, he sews for her; the clothes are her size, and he does not mind that she cannot sew or cook, or that she sometimes laughs inappropriately. With clean tools and rich materials to choose from, he does the most elegant work of his life. He has a new life, a new quotidian. He does not forget the old life, but he remembers it like a bedtime story heard as a child. The beautiful lady pleases him easily; she disappears for a part of each day so that he can work. The student writes his poem about her and looks forward to her listening to it. The potter dedicates his vases to her. He used to make them for his wife, but that was not the same. At first he is very happy. The beautiful lady gives him enough to eat, robes, music from nowhere. "Love me," she says. "I love you," she says. "Do you love me?" Like a salt plum, she makes his mouth water. He and his wife never talked about loving each other. Now whenever he conjures up thoughts about his family, he sees their black and white portraits. "I love you," she says, and he loves this stranger more than mother and father.

But one day there seems a surplus of pots, shoes, scrolls. The embroidery artist has finished his two hundredth bird. When he has completed this much, doesn't he usually go to market?

The beautiful lady, braceleted up to her elbows like a bride, draws her eyebrows and the line connecting them with special care. She feeds him and charms him.

"Tell me you've been happy here," she says. "Tell me you are happy."

"I have been happy here. I have never been happier than here with you. Why are you crying? Why are you looking like that?"

"Stay with me today."

"I'll be gone for just a few hours." Or "I'll be back in just a few days."

"I love this scroll. Let me have it. Don't sell it." "And these shoes." She says, "I love this cup, its lines, its design, its handle. Let me keep it," pulling things out of his pack.

"But I've already given you the best pieces. These are for market."

"But you don't need to go to market any more," she says.

He says, "I don't need to study any more. I'm ready to take the examination again."

"It's harvest time," he says. Or "Time for the planting."

She puts on the same dress she wore when he first saw her. She brings festive food as for Sweethearts' Day, but when he finishes eating, he takes up his pack. "I have to find out," says the student, "if I can beat this year's crop of scholars." Suddenly he yearns for air that does not smell feverish with gardenias. She kneels at his feet and begs him to stay. Perhaps it is now that the deer cries. She stands, opens her robe, opens it like wings, and wraps him inside, enclosing him against her naked body, reminding him how unwifely her breasts and thighs are, how helplessly her body works as his touches it. Unable to remain joined, connected, he breaks from her, and leaves.

On the road, breathing dizzies him. The sky looks as big as it is. He has been seeing window-framed pieces of it for too long. Its immensity dazzles him—blue without end.

His appearance startles the townspeople, who run, pretending they are late for something important, not looking
back. Dogs slink from him. He could leave his bundles on the
street and no thief would touch them because of the phospho-
rescence that would rub off like contagious death. Children
point at him, and the mothers hit them and rush them away.
Confusedly, he arranges his wares on the ground in wait for
shoppers. The vendors on either side of him and the letter
writers across the way dismantle their tables and awnings; not
discussing it, they leave quickly. Even with no competition, he
cannot lure any customers. He picks up his goods and stum-
bles to a better location.

This young man must have had a good family and a loyal
village because as he wanders like a ghost, a villager from his
former life grabs him. "Brother Brother," calls the fellow villager, and the sounds of "Brother Brother" are like a rooster's
crow in the morning. "What's wrong? What's happened to
you? Where have you been all this time? We've missed you.
Aiya! Look at you. You're so thin. Have you been ill? Why, I
can feel your bones. What black bags under your eyes, and why
do you let your hair hang like this? Here, let me braid it for
you. You shouldn't be traveling when you're sick. Let me see
you home." The villager puts his arms around the young man.
The familiar is so comforting that he sobs.

His friend guides him along the mountain road toward the
home village. They are like two bugs in the landscape. The
nearby oaks are gnarling and the far pines standing straight.
The trees hold gray antlers high, already budded with leaves.
Midway home, the young man stops. He seems to hear something, and though he stares straight ahead, the whites under
his irises show. Marionette strings pull him into the tall grass.
He remembers a beautiful lady he met in a previous incarnation or a dream last night.

The closer he comes to where the house had been, the more
the home village becomes the dream. "Look," says his friend.
"A grave."

Where a front door stood is the marker for a noblewoman's
grave. The rain and wind have not quite rubbed the dates and
the strange emblems off. She has been dead for years, centuries.

Fear burns along the young man's spine, and he runs from

the lonely spot where no paths meander, no house looms, no peacocks or dogs stalk among the lilac trees. His friend dashes after him, not to be left by himself at the grave.

The young man walks home with his fellow villager. Sun, air, wind chase away his memory of nightingales singing and night-blooming cereus. The young husband returns to his family. The hero's home has its own magic.

Fancy lovers never last.

THE GREAT GRANDFATHER
OF THE SANDALWOOD
MOUNTAINS

ABOUT A year ago, I mailed fifty dollars to China to a cousin who is black, they say, and not strictly a cousin. "You don't have to send anything," my mother said several times. "It's entirely up to you," which, of course, it wasn't; we'd already been asked. Like his father before him, my maternal grandfather had brought a third wife back from his third trip West, Bali or Hawai'i or South America or Africa. They had one black boy child, who is MaMa's half-brother. He grew up and got married and now has a son, the cousin to whom I sent the fifty dollars. He had written saying that a bicycle costs fifty dollars, and that it would change his life to own one. "I'll make sure in my letter," said MaMa, "to specify that it was you who sent it." "It doesn't matter," I said. "You don't have to do that." I don't want anybody attached to me forever with gratitude.

A few weeks later, a letter came from my black "uncle," the bicycle cousin's father. "Why did you send him money and me nothing?" he wrote. "I'm the father. I deserve the money. If you don't send me my money, I'm going to kill him." Even though they are black Chinese Red Communists living on the other side of the world, and even though they are poor, I do not believe he meant that. He must have only threatened to use his son as a hostage because he thinks us so entirely foreign we would be susceptible to such a threat; he was appealing to us Americans in a language we'd understand. "Furthermore," he said, "you have disrupted the economy and technology of the commune. Send fifty dollars in reparations." We don't feel an obligation to send him anything.

But in case he means what he said and Communists are as wild as the stories about them, I won't tell the name of our village. I don't want anybody arresting my uncle for extortion or confiscating the bicycle. The Chinese American newspapers list names of tourists from the United States and Hong Kong who disappear visiting China.

I am glad to see that the black grandmother ended up with a son and a grandson who are articulate. When she came to China she "jabbered like a monkey," but no one answered her. "Who knows what she was saying anyway?" She fell mute.

263

Many men on my mother's side of the family, even today, even the young men in countries where polygamy has been outlawed, have two wives, two houses, two families. The men in the past had three wives. The first wife, of course, was the important one; the others were "for love."

At a party in Honolulu, I met a dancer just returned from China, where she studied for six months. (Her aunt in China danced the Dark Haired Girl's part in *The White Haired Girl.*) She visited her ancestral village, Chung Sahn, where Sun Yat Sen was born, where the ancestors of most Chinese Americans in Hawai'i came from. She said that all the people were housed and fed. Her uncle's house had been divided into apartments, and he lived in one of them. "Were very many killed during the Revolution—I mean, Liberation?" I asked. She said No. "Nobody in my family," she said. I said, "Most of the men in our family were killed. The relatives write letters asking for money and bicycles." She said, "There are remote parts of the country where people are still ignorant, greedy, and lazy."

A physicist wrote me a letter about his trip to China; he visited his ancestral village, which, it so happens, is also my ancestral village. He had been born there, but emigrated to America as a child. After lecturing at Beijing University, he was given a Volkswagen. Dressed like one of the people and speaking both Mandarin and Cantonese, he traveled about freely. When he arrived at the village, he saw houses from his childhood; the ones that had belonged to families that had sent men to the United States had been decorated with expensive tiles. He met a woman whom he recognized from his childhood as an aunt and went home with her. An automobile and some electrical kitchen appliances were rusting in the yard, stuff brought back from the Gold Mountain; there was no gasoline or electricity in the village. A young man was sitting idle by the door; he was some kind of a cousin. "Stay for dinner," the aunt invited the physicist, but the young man said rudely, "He's too busy to have dinner." The physicist ate at the communal dining room; the commune people also showed him around. Though the land in this area was more fertile than in most other parts of China, he found the farmers less eager to meet production quotas. In the middle of the work day, young men sat talking about how someday soon they would move to the Gold Mountain, where their ancestors, American pioneers, had gone for hundreds of years. The physicist felt that indeed there was something different about the people in our village.

I'd like to go to China if I can get a visa and—more difficult—permission from my family, who are afraid that applying for a visa would call attention to us: the relatives in China would get in trouble for having American capitalist connections, and we Americans would be put in relocation camps during the next witch hunt for Communists. Should I be able to convince my family about the good will of normalization, it's not the Great Wall I want to see but my ancestral village. I want to talk to Cantonese, who have always been revolutionaries, nonconformists, people with fabulous imaginations, people who invented the Gold Mountain. I want to discern what it is that makes people go West and turn into Americans. I want to compare China, a country I made up, with what country is really out there.

I have gone east, that is, west, as far as Hawai'i, where I have stood alongside the highway at the edge of the sugarcane and listened for the voices of the great grandfathers. But the cane is merely green in the sunlight; the tassels waving in the wind make no blurry fuzzy outlines that I can construe as a message from them. The dirt and sun are red and not aglitter with gold motes like in California. Red and green do not readily blend, nothing lurking in the overlaps to bend the eyes. The winds blowing in the long leaves do not whisper words I hear. Yet the rows and fields, organized like conveyor belts, hide murdered and raped bodies; this is a dumping ground. Old Filipino men die in abandoned sheds. Mushrooms and marijuana grow amidst the cane, irrigated by the arches of vaulting water. People with friends on the mainland steal long-distance calls on the field telephones.

Driving along O'ahu's windward side, where sugarcane grew in my great grandfathers' day, I like looking out at the ocean and seeing the pointed island offshore, not much bigger than a couple of houses, nothing else out in that ocean to catch the eye—Mokoli'i Island, but nobody calls it that. I had a shock when I heard it's also named Chinaman's Hat. I had only encountered that slurred-together word in taunts when walking past racists. (They would be the ones loafing on a fence, and they said the chinaman was sitting on a fence ". . . trying to make a dollar out of fifty cents.") But Hawai'i people call us Paké, which is their way of pronouncing Bak-ah, Uncle. They even call Chinese women Paké.

When driving south, clockwise, there is an interesting optical illusion. At a certain point in the road, the sky is covered with Chinaman's Hat, which bulges huge, near. The closer you drive toward what seems like a mountain, the farther it shrinks away until there it is, quite far off, an island, a brim and crown on the water.

At first, I did not say Chinaman's Hat; I didn't call the island anything. "You see the island that looks like a Chinaman's hat?" locals ask, and visitors know right away which one they mean.

I swam out to Chinaman's Hat. We walked partway in low tide, then put on face masks. Once you open your eyes in the water, you become a flying creature. Schools of fish—zebra fish, rainbow fish, red fish—curve with the currents, swim alongside and away; balloon fish puff out their porcupine quills. How unlike a dead fish a live fish is. We swam through spangles of silver-white fish, their scales like sequins. Sometimes we entered cold spots, deserts, darkness under clouds, where the sand churned like gray fog, and sometimes we entered golden chambers. There are summer forests and winter forests down there. Sea cucumbers, holothurians, rocked side to side. A sea turtle glided by and that big shell is no encumbrance in the water. We saw no sharks, though they spawn in that area, and pilot fish swam ahead in front of our faces. The shores behind and ahead kept me unafraid.

Approaching Chinaman's Hat, we flew around and between a group of tall black stones like Stonehenge underwater, and through there, came up onto the land, where we rested with arms out holding on to the island. We walked among the palm trees and bushes that we had seen from the other shore. Large white birds were nesting on the ground under these bushes. We hurried to the unseen side of the island. Even such a tiny island has its windward and leeward. On the ocean side, we found a cave, a miniature pirate's cove with a finger of ocean for its river, a beach of fine yellow sand, a blowhole, brown and lavender cowry shells, not broken, black live crabs side-stepping and red dead crabs drying in the red sun, a lava rock shelf with tide pools as warm as baths and each one with its ecology. A brown fish with a face like a cartoon cow's mugged at me. A white globule quivered, swelled, flipped over or inside out, stretched and turned like a human being getting out of bed, opened and opened; two arms and two legs flexed, and feathery wings, webbing the arms and the legs to the body, unfolded and flared; its thighs tapered to a graceful tail, and its ankles had tiny wings on them—like Mercury; its back was muscled like a comic book superhero's—blue and silver metallic leotards outlined with black racing stripes. It's a spaceman, I thought. A tiny spaceman in a spacesuit. Scooping these critters into another tide pool, I got into theirs, and lying in it, saw nothing but sky and black rock, the ocean occasionally flicking cold spit.

At sunset we built a campfire and sat around it inside a cleft in the hillside. We cooked and ate the fish we caught. We were climbing along a ledge down to the shore, holding on to the face of the island in the twilight, when a howling like wolves, like singing, came rising out of the island. "Birds," somebody said. "The wind," said someone else. But the air was still, and the high, clear sound wound through the trees. It continued until we departed. It was, I know it, the island, the voice of the island singing, the sirens Odysseus heard.

The Navy continues to bomb Kaho'olawe and the Army blasts the green skin off the red mountains of O'ahu. But the land sings. We heard something.

It's a tribute to the pioneers to have a living island named after their work hat.

I have heard the land sing. I have seen the bright blue streaks of spirits whisking through the air. I again search for my American ancestors by listening in the cane.

Ocean people are different from land people. The ocean never stops saying and asking into ears, which don't sleep like eyes. Those who live by the sea examine the driftwood and glass balls that float from foreign ships. They let scores of invisible imps loose out of found bottles. In a scoop of salt water, they revive the dead blobs that have been beached in storms and tides: fins, whiskers, and gills unfold; mouths, eyes, and colors bloom and spread. Sometimes ocean people are given to understand the newness and oldness of the world; then all morning they try to keep that boundless joy like a little sun inside their chests. The ocean also makes its people know immensity.

They wonder what continents contain the ocean on its other side, what people live there. Hong Kong off the coast tugged like a moon at the Cantonese; curiosity had a land mass to fasten upon, and beyond Hong Kong, Taiwan, step by step a leading out. Cantonese travel, and they gamble.

But China has a long round coastline, and the northern people enclosed Peiping, only one hundred miles from the sea, with walls and made roads westward across the loess. The Gulf of Chihli has arms, and beyond, Korea, and beyond that, Japan. So the ocean and hunger and some other urge made Cantonese people explorers and Americans.

Bak Goong, Great Grandfather, came to Hawai'i at the invitation of the Royal Hawaiian Agricultural Society. Their agent, who had been born in our district and spoke like us, came straight into the village and talked about how he got to be a recruiter. Even today the family trusts any insurance, encyclopedia, or gadget salesman who talks like us, our language a music that charms away common sense. The family knew the growing habits of cane; a stand grew in the courtyard. Convoys used to relay lichee and sugarcane from Canton to the Imperial palace. A few times a year, on a holiday or a birthday, Grandmother cut a stalk and divided it into small chunks, one for each person. The sweet taste affected Bak Goong. The recruiter told his fellow villagers, Chinese were the first sugarmakers in Hawai'i; they brought the first millstones and vats in 1802. "Right now," said the agent, "we're offering free passage, free food, free clothing, and housing. In fact, we're advancing you six dollars. Here. See. I have six dollars right here. Here, Grandma. We'll let Po Po hold it; she can return it to me if she wants to. Couldn't you use six dollars before you've even begun to work? You repay it with just six weeks' work.

After six weeks, clear profit. Figure it out. You're joining us at a lucky time. The pay just went up again. You're getting an instant raise. We need every kind of labor. You inexperienced kids can be house servants for two dollars a month. Now, once you secure this fine job, you'll want to protect it, right? You're thinking, What if I get to the Sandalwood Mountains, and they fire me? Well, listen to this. We can't fire you. We protect you against firing. We can't fire you because you sign this three-year contract, and for more protection, this five-year contract." "Mm," said the family. "Of course, there'll be some hardships, but that's life, isn't it? You'll be traveling with a shipload of fellow Chinese, with whom you'll be sharing free housing. You'll have people to discuss things with. We're giving you a dormitory just like going to college. And did you know that the Sandalwood Mountains are very close to the Gold Mountain? You get free passage as far as the Sandalwood Mountains, where you can stay as long as you want, and you invest a little of your profits in passage to California. You'll get there before the Gold Rush is over. Why, in Hawai'i, you're already halfway there. Figure: You start with nothing. You already have six dollars' advance. Three years from today, home with riches."

Impressed by the agent's homely dialect, his suit, his title, and his philosophic bent, Bak Goong muttered what Confucius taught on the occasion of breaking a promise to his captors, "'Heaven doesn't hear an oath which is forced on one,'" and made his X.

He told his family that he would be back in three years. Traveling alone, he watched armies march or straggle by, close calls, he on a cliff, an army in the ravine; he behind a waterfall, an army drinking at the river; he flattened like a shadow on the earth, an army silhouetted against the moon. He spied British demons with big noses and guns. He was walking on dangerous and sick land. In the north, the Yellow River had reversed its course overnight; it reared up, coiled in the air, and slapped down backwards to run the other way, south instead of north. It troughed new watercourses and flooded four provinces before settling on its route. Winds collided. The Yangtze also flooded. Eels hung from ceilings, and red worms curled inside wells and jars. Migrating from lakes of drowned crops and

trees, farmers came to fields of dust where drought cracked the
ground, the land was burned, and there were no fishing boats
on the rivers. New monsters were appearing on the earth,
barbarians everywhere; the British demons opened the sea-
ports to opium and soldiers. A crazy Cantonese (whose name
is pronounced like our own last name but isn't the same at
all), either fooling the Jesus demons or deranged by Christian
education, taught that Mary had given two virgin births, Jesus
and himself. With a sister and two brothers, Jesus Christ's
Younger Brother led sixteen provinces and the Taiping, the
army of the Great Peace, the Long Hairs, in revolt against the
emperor and his British and French armies. The Shao Lin, an
order of fighting monks, famous for their battles against the
Manchus, were emerging again. The Manchus had burned the
Shao Lin Temple, but their five Founding Fathers had escaped
by hiding under a bridge (Pagoda and Bridge their symbols),
then trained successors, who were the teachers of the monks
fighting for the Great Peace. The Miao tribes and the Nien
were also uprising, as were the Moslems of Yunan. The magnetic poles of the world had switched; gravity itself had come
loose. China was changing again, as it does every thirty years
in small cycles and every hundred years in large cycles.

Bak Goong recognized a century-size upheaval; he shook
his head and walked away, turned his back and walked away.
He arrived in Canton without being conscripted, and signed
on a schooner as a crewman to make extra money while traveling. He would jump ship in Hawai'i if he wasn't allowed to
quit there.

The Chinese who had sailed before him had painted a sea
bird on the side of the ship, which protected it from storms.
His first free moment he lowered himself on a rope and painted
eyes on the bow. He tied poles and lines to the rails and caught
fish. The ocean was a bowl with horizon all around. Lucky to
be a crewman.

He met all manner of men, broad faced and sharp faced Han
Men, tall dark ones, white ones, little ones like the Japanese.
One group spoke the language so queerly that he laughed out
loud. He imitated their *thl* sound blown out of the mouth with
big, airy cheeks and spit. "One, two, three, *four*." Sputtering
and spitting as he shouted out the *four*, which has that *thl*, he

called out the rhythm for lifting and hauling. "Do you come from near our village?" a man from the *thl* village asked. "Yes, I also come from the *Four* Districts," said Bak Goong. He mimicked men with staccato consonants and a lone northerner who spoke a soft dialect like English, and he would have talked to the Englishmen too except that he could not hear their sliding, slippery little voices out of the fronts of their pursed mouths. "Their asses must be as tight as their mouths," he said out loud right in front of them.

The Chinese passengers were locked belowdeck though they were not planning to escape. Their fresh air was the whiff and stir when crewmen exchanged the food buckets for the vomit and shit buckets. Some men brought their pigs, which slept under the bottom bunks. The beds looked like stacks of coffins in a death house. "Here we are," said Bak Goong, who had to sleep in this hold too, "emigrating with our pigs our only family."

He gave advice to the boys who were away from their mothers for the first time. "You'll be a rich man in three years," he said. "Three years is forever for a kid, but for a man in his thirties like me, the years pass too quickly. Don't you notice how one year passes faster than the last? The first year abroad will be the worst; then we'll wish that time would slow up for our lives to last longer." (He talked about time as going from up to down, last week being the "upper week" and next week the "lower week," time a sort of ladder that one descends.)

"Be quiet, Dog Vomit," somebody hollered. "Shut up and let me sleep."

"Don't say 'vomit,'" somebody else groaned.

"Try laughing," said Bak Goong. "I'll bet you can't laugh and vomit at the same time." *Laugh* is another word that has the *thl* combination in that queer dialect. "And as for the dark," he advised the children, "it makes the room feel larger, doesn't it?"

"Tobacco shit stops the seasickness," said an opium smoker, who passed his pipe.

"No, no, shit cures colds, not seasickness."

"Let's try it for seasickness."

"Your mother's cunt. You make this room smoky, and I'll throw up all over you."

The berths, come to think of it, were also stacked like beds in an opium house. "Is opium bitter?" asked Bak Goong. "It's not addicting if you just try it once, right?" The tempted men had a discussion on exactly which pipe—the twelfth? the hundredth?—addicted, and how often—once a week? five times a day? once a month?—an addict smoked. "It takes two years of smoking three times a day to learn the opium habit," an addict said confidently.

So Bak Goong gave a tobacco shit man some money and smoked. The silver and wooden water pipes gurgled like rivers; the bowl pipes drew airily. Bak Goong leaned against the wall, and the meaning of life and time and what he was doing on this ship all became clear to him; even his vomity feeling fell into its place in the scheme of the universe. His thoughts branched and flowed and branched again and connected like rivers, veins, roads, ships' lanes. New ideas sparked, and he caught his breath when he saw their connections to old ideas. Circles wheeled by, whirled concentrically, and stilled into a simple light. The bald heads of monks, who sit in circles, bowed toward the center like a hand, a lotus flower, or wood sorrel closing. The world's people arranged themselves in parades, palaces, windows, roads, stadiums, attempting to form this bond. These men in the hold were trying to circumnavigate the world. Men build bridges and streets when there is already an amazing gold electric ring connecting every living being as surely as if we held hands, flippers and paws, feelers and wings. Though he was leaving his good wife and his village, they were connected to him by a gold net or a light; it shimmered when the people and other creatures moved about. Even the demons abovedeck let out a glow. Bak Goong thought he understood the Tao, which is everywhere and in everything, even in our excrement, which is why opium is shit. It seemed that he would have to bring his mind hard to bear in order to discriminate between sleeping and waking, work and play, yours and mine. Wars were laughable; how could a human being remember which side he was on? Fear gives us red to brighten the world, and meanings are for decoration. "Is this true?" he asked, and answered, "Yes." Everything was true. He was Lao Tse's great thinker, who can embrace opposing thoughts at the same moment. He loved the strangers around him as much as he loved his family. He closed his eyes and saw islands in the sea or planets in space or lakes he could dive into or observe. Suffering, happiness, hurt children were similar dots. He felt wise. But after enjoying his wisdom for a while, he noticed that there had been all along a weight or a rock at the bottom of his well-being, the familiar nag of tasks to do. The opium must be wearing off soon; was there a last question he wanted to ask it? "How am I going to withstand pain, plain physical hurt?" An accidental cut could make him say, "I can't bear it." He dug his nails into his arm. How could he take lonely inevitable death? What about death with pain, pain unto death? That his body felt content now did not mean that it had learned a sufficient lesson in the habit of well-being. An urge to touch the ground with bare feet came over him, not to have floorboards or shoes between him and earth. What if his body had to undergo deliberate torture, for example? "Don't hurt," he answered himself, or opium, the reminder, answered him. "Don't give pain. Don't take pain." The ring of light was disbanding, slivers of it returning to the various separate bodies of flesh and bone. How not to take pain? How to have no pain? "Be able," he said. "Be capable." Capable. Opium was merely a rest from constant pain. He said aloud, repeating, "Be capable," to remember this answer for use later when these unwordable feelings were gone. "I am a capable man. An able man," he said, and did feel a touch of dreariness at this mundane answer. He wrapped himself in his quilt and patted his money belt to feel his sugarcane contract crackle. "No pain. Don't give pain. Don't take pain." He did not smoke opium again on the journey because he did not want to become an addict or to spend money.

After three months at sea, Bak Goong smelled in the wind a sweetness like a goddess visiting. Whenever the hatches and doors opened in the right combinations, the men below also smelled it. "It's sandalwood," Bak Goong said, looking for land on the horizon. The smell of boxes and chests of drawers, statues, castanets and fans, incenses and powders must have inspired him to come here. Chinese had followed that essence to India, where sandalwood grew in phoenix-shaped roots in the caves of lions, and to Persia, where it congealed in the

Eastern Ocean as a cicada. And now they followed sandalwood to its home here.

One day Bak Goong opened the hatches for the men below, who stumbled through the passageways and up ladders
to the topdeck, where they blinked in the sunlight. A demon
from shore counted and recounted the China Men. There
were three or four fewer live ones than when they began the
journey. The demon strung a tab about each neck. Bak Goong
climbed down to the longboat, past the weeds that had grown
like skirts on the ship's sides.

On shore among crates, burlap bags, barrels, haystacks, they
waited for their bosses, some of whom were China Men. The
men with no papers signed anything that was handed them;
most made a cross like the ideograph *ten*; "The Word Ten,"
they called their signatures. A pair of horses, which delighted
Bak Goong, pulled a wagon to the dock, but only a few workers rode to those fields close enough to Honolulu to be reached
by roads. Bak Goong's group was to walk, led by a demon boss
on a horse. He bade good-byes to friends he had made on the
ship. Walking after rolling on the sea confused his legs, but
with his seabag across his back, he edged quickly to the front
of the group. He buffered himself in case the demon used his
whip on men.

They walked out of the town and up a mountain road so
narrow that the demon dismounted and led the horse. The
trail led upward among banana trees. Bak Goong ate bananas
to his heart's content, throwing away the peels instead of
scraping their insides and eating the fibers; there were that
many bananas, hands of them, overripe fruit rotting on the
ground. He ate fruit and nuts he had never seen before. And
mangos like in China. He wished he could give his wife some.
With a handful of rice a day, he could live here without working. Five-petaled flowers spun from the trees, pink stars, white
stars, yellow stars, striped red and white stars. At one beautiful
spot, white trumpet flowers hung above his head like hats. He
walked on ground royally carpeted with jacaranda. When the
sun became hot, a tall rain fell and made two rainbows across
the sky, the colors of the top one in the opposite order of the
bottom one. "Aiya," said the men. "Beautiful. Beautiful." "Is
that a good omen or a bad omen?" "How does it happen?"

"It has to be a good omen." The rainbows moved ahead of them. Before they became too wet, the rain stopped; the sun and breeze dried them. Bak Goong memorized all this to tell his wife.

He sucked in deep breaths of the Sandalwood Mountain air, and let it fly out in a song, which reached up to the rims of volcanoes and down to the edge of the water. His song lifted and fell with the air, which seemed to breathe warmly through his body and through the rocks. The clouds and frigate birds made the currents visible, and the leaves were loud. If he did not walk heavy seated and heavy thighed like a warrior, he would float away, snuggle into the wind, and let it slide him down to the ocean, let it make a kite, a frigate bird, a butterfly of him. He would dive head first off the mountain, glide into the airstreams thick with smells, and curve into the ocean. From this mountaintop, ocean before him and behind him, he saw the size of the island. He sang like the heroes in stories about wanderers and exiles, poets and monks and monkeys, and princes and kings out for walks. His arias unfurled and rose in wide, wide arcs.

The men passed a hutment of grass shacks with long yellow thatch weathered and fine, rippling and ruffling in the breeze like the hair of blonde ladies. Roofs had fallen, and the frames showed like bones. The doorways were empty. They did not see brown people come and go.

They descended another side of the mountain and walked along the sea all day, and at last came to the place where they were to work. They had arrived in the middle of the workday, and were to start at once. There was no farm, no sugarcane ready to tend. It was their job to hack a farm out of the wilderness, which they were to level from the ocean to the mountain. To do this, Bak Goong was given a machete, a saw, an ax, and a pickax. The green that had looked like grass at a distance was a tangle of trees so thick that they shut out sunlight. Leaves grew only on their tops and bent backs. They were not tall trees, branch having wrestled branch into a knot that gnarled for miles. It may have been one tree that had replanted itself tighter and tighter. A criminal dropped into the midst of the webwork would be imprisoned forever. Beginning anywhere, Bak Goong chopped into the edge of this strange forest. He could not take hold of the branches because of the thorns on them. Dust shook down. Coughing, alarmed at how quickly he grew hot, tired, and thirsty in the intervals between the water-and-tea man's rounds, he shook a silver ball from the flat glass bottle he carried in his pocket and swallowed it for thirst. He gave pills to the boys working on either side of him. Though he chopped, hacked, and sawed with all his might, the knot of trees did not seem smaller. Black birds with flashes of white wings flew easily straight through the maze.

After work, though he could get sick and die from mixing cold water with hot sweat—open pores draw in the cold—he ran with the others into the ocean, and let it wash him. In the water rushing away from him, he held on to his body and mind with effort. The horizon seemed to be up in the air. He would have gone to sleep right there on the beach, but the ones who had arrived earlier had established an eating system. "Eh, China Man, come eat," the China Men invited. They had already organized the food, decided who would cook and on what terms. "Eh, China Man, come eat," Bak Goong imitated their English. So he got to sit down to a good dinner on plank tables. They passed around candy before dinner; it was a regular welcome party. The few Hawaiian workers passed around salt. Chinese take a bit of sugar to remind them in times of bitter struggle of the sweetness of life, and Hawaiians take a few grains of salt on the tongue because it tastes like the sea, like the earth, like human sweat and tears. Some fishermen and surfers and a demon traveler also ate with them, as did the other great grandfather, Bak Sook Goong, who was not yet related. (They would have called one another Bak and Sook in any case—Uncles.) These strangers ate like a family, drank from the same soup tureen, ate from the same plates of accompaniments to the rice. They did not gobble directly from the center dishes to the mouth but first touched the meat or vegetable to the rice. Bak Goong was lucky to have fallen among the civilized in the wild Sandalwood Mountains. He ate chunks of coconut wet in its milk and the fruit they had gathered on the way that morning. The hot tea on the hot day cooled him.

In the talk-story time after dinner, young men gave advice to young men. There were no old men in the Sandalwood Mountains. "Mind your own business, and work like an ox."

"Don't gamble." "Keep your machete sharp, and hold it like so when you smell a demon near you." "Wrap your queue around your head or tuck it inside your shirt." "If you have the opium habit, you can ask for your wages by the week." Bak Goong congratulated himself on what a good ear he had; he could understand much of what these unusual men were saying. He had traveled to the middle of the ocean and was getting along with the people he found. He spoke to the most foreign, barbarous-looking China Men. When a storyteller lost him with apocopations, he wondered whether a puff of opium would help him understand language more clearly, but "No," he said politely, "I'd not be able to repay you." The men who had come earlier also said that the plantation had a rule that they not talk at work, but this rule was so absurd, he thought he must have misheard tones.

He lay down out in the open. The sights of the day unreeled behind his eyelids—the ocean jumping with silver daggers, fronds shredding in wind, twin rainbows, spinning flowers, the gray mass of the maze tree like all the roads of many lives. How was he to marvel adequately, voiceless? He needed to cast his voice out to catch ideas. I wasn't born to be silent like a monk, he thought, then promptly said. "If I knew I had to take a vow of silence," he added, "I would have shaved off my hair and become a monk. Apparently we've taken a vow of chastity too. Nothing but roosters in this flock."

The next morning at 5 A.M., he was again standing before the fist of trees. The dimness of shapes gave the coming day many possibilities until the sun delineated the pleached trees, the mountains, and another day of toil. He worked for that day and the next and the next without saying anything, but got angry, chopping as if cutting arms and legs. He withstood the hours; he did the work well, but the rule of silence wrought him up whenever a demon rode by. He wanted to talk about how he sawed through trunks and the interlocked branches held the trees upright. He suddenly had all kinds of things to say. He wanted to tell the men who worked beside him about the rewards to look forward to, for example, chewing cane for breakfast; the fibers would clean their teeth like a toothbrush. "You go out on the road to find adventure," he wanted to say, "and what do you find but another farm where the same things happen day after day. Work. Work. Work. Eat. Eat. Eat. Shit and piss. Sleep. Work. Work." He axed a limb at each word. "Actually, I like being bored," he would have said. "Nothing bad is happening, no useless excitement." He wanted to discuss mutes and kings who rip out tongues by the roots.

And one day—he could not help it—he sang about the black mountains reddening and how mighty was the sun that shone on him in this enchanted forest and on his family in China. The sweep of the ocean was so wide, he watched the sun rise and set in it. In the heat of noon, he wished he could shoot out the sun, like Prince I, who dropped nine suns with his bow and arrows. The demons paid his singing no mind. They must have thought he was singing a traditional song when he was really commenting and planning.

"I've solved the talking," he sang to his fellow workers. "If that demon whips me, I'll catch the whip and yank him off his horse, crack his head like a coconut. In an emergency a human being can do miracles—fly, swim, lift mountains, throw them. Oh, a man is capable of great feats of speed and strength."

There was a bang or crack next to his ear. The demon was recoiling his whip. "Shut up, Paké." He heard distinct syllables out of the white demon's moving mouth. "Shut up. Go work. Chinaman, go work. You stay go work. Shut up." He caught every word, which surprised him so much, he forgot to grab the whip. He labored on, muttering, "Shut up. Shut up, you." He found a cut on his shoulder.

The men tried burning instead of cutting the trees. They set fires in the red heat of the sun. Bak Goong felt the fire was the same as his anger; his anger was this size and this red. But only the dead branches and leaves burned. Cutting the burned trees, the men became sooted black. To make them work faster, the demons had a trick of telling the slowest man that he was sick and had to take the day off without pay.

On their own time, after 5 P.M., the workers built two huts for bunkhouses, each with wooden beds laid head to foot one above another like the shelves on ships. They arranged gourds and vines, buckets, and hats on the verandas, which they kept adding to the huts. Bak Goong wove a hammock, and it was as comfortable as his mother's lap.

At the very end of the day, the men exchanged remedies. They scraped one another's backs with spoons to get rid of rheumatism and arthritis. For heat sickness they scraped necks with the edge of a coin cooled in water, the square hole in the middle of the coin giving a good grip. They slapped the insides of one another's elbows and knees, where tiredness collects. They soaked cuts and sores, and rubbed bruises with tobacco and whiskey. Some exercised, and Bak Goong learned some kung fu movements and also some ways of breathing that would strengthen his body and sharpen his brain. They nursed runaways who had escaped from other work camps. Bak Goong showed his scarring shoulder and said, "I will talk again. Listen for me." Boys put rocks under their pillows to stop crying at night. Several people not from the same village believed in "passing fear over fire," which means lifting one who has been badly frightened and passing him over a fire. Some "passed rice over hearts" and some "over heads." Everybody thought that his way of doing things was the way all Chinese were supposed to do them.

Bak Goong worried that he had overlooked a trick clause in his contract and that he would not be paid at all; this was some kind of a slave labor camp. But pay day came. When the demon handed him his money Bak Goong counted it in front of him in Chinese and in business ("pidgin") English. He came out short. "Too little," he complained, holding up his fingers. "Too little bit money. Are you trying to catch a pig?" he asked, which means to cheat, to take advantage of a greedy person.

The paymaster demon said, "Shut up, you. You shut up," clapping a hand over his own mouth several times. Bak Goong had been fined for talking. And sick men had been docked for every day they had been lying lazy in bed. Those who had not recovered from crossing the ocean got an accounting of how much they owed for food and lodging plus passage. The strong workers had money subtracted for broken tools.

The men cursed as they reckoned their pay. "Dead man." "Rotten corpse afloat." "Corpse on the roadside." "Hunchback with a turtle on his back," that is "Cuckold." "Your mother's ass." "Your mother's cunt." "They take my piss and shit away from me to feed their fields. Take my shit." "Eat my shit and piss. Drink piss, white monster. Eat shit." Bak Goong turned his ass at the pig catcher demon's face. He was finding out that the dollar a week wasn't the minimum wage but the maximum to strive for, that hoeing paid less than other jobs. The China Man accountant told them their wages were reduced until the plantation made a bigger profit. If Bak Goong did not give any dinner parties, did not drink or smoke or gamble, he would bring home maybe a hundred dollars after three years. The big talk about a thousand dollars must have been about men who came home old to die after scrimping for thirty years and more.

One day, like a knight rescuing a princess, Bak Goong broke clear through the thicket. The demons bought bullocks; they had longer horns than water buffaloes. He yoked them to the stumps, which they yanked out. But the Hawaiians quit rather than help pull the boulders out of the earth. The remaining workers plowed around groups of big rocks in the middle of the fields. They were the first human beings to dig into this part of the island and see the meat and bones of the red earth. After rain, the mud ran like blood. The maze tree and woodrose sprouted behind the plows.

A team of six men including Bak Goong was sent to a plantation farther up the coast where cane already stood like a green army; the tassels were called "arrows." On the same day as he cleared land, he cut cane twice as tall as a man. The cane and rice growers were trying out the seasons. The workers stripped the long leaves like shucking corn. Dust shook loose, and they breathed it even through their kerchiefs. They cut the stalks close to the ground. The new men tasted the cane in which the sap was running warm. They cut the tips beneath the top three nodes for seed cane. There were seeds in the arrows, but it was faster to plant the nodes. The men seemed small and few wading among the sticky mounds.

The wagoners, who had a good job, drove the cane to the sugar mill on a route along the sea. It was crushed into molasses and boiled into sugar, for which the world was developing an insatiable hunger as for opium.

Bak Goong and his team brought the seed cane and a few bottles of rum back. The land was ready to be sown. They bagged the slips in squares of cloth tied over their shoulders. Flinging the seed cane into ditches, Bak Goong wanted to sing like a farmer in an opera. When his bag was empty, he stepped into the furrow and turned the seed cane so the nodes were to the sides, nodes on either side of the stick like an animal's eyes. He filled the trenches and patted the pregnant earth.

The work changed from watering season to hoeing season. He weeded the ivy that wrapped and would choke the young cane, the ratoons. The vines pulled like rubber. Using a short hoe, he knelt to uproot them, and carried the weeds to the fires at the ends of the rows else they take root where they fell. He worked even in the rain lest he lose money. Then there was a stripping season when he peeled the plants so they would use their strength to make sugar instead of leaves.

The next harvest, the men invented a burning season when they set the cane on fire to burn off the outer leaves instead of stripping by hand. They chose a dry and moderately windy day. Like a savage, Bak Goong ran with brands, torching the cane along the border. During the night watches, fires like furry red beasts lurked and occasionally roared into the black sky, showing it endless, nothing illuminated but smoke as high as the flames climbed. In the day the smoke curled like white snakes in the directions of the winds. Demons in white suits walked gingerly inspecting the char. Then there was clearing and planting, the hoeing, and harvest, and the planting season again.

The cough that had begun when he cut trees and stripped leaves worsened because of breathing the hot sweet smoke and because of the hoeing in the rains. On the hottest days, the coughing made his nose bleed. He stuffed rags in his nostrils and kept working. The blood clotted in the back of his throat, and he spit out gouts. He hawked and spat to entertain the men and to disgust the demons. His cough did come in handy. When the demons howled to work faster, faster, he coughed in reply. The deep, long, loud coughs, barking and wheezing, were almost as satisfying as shouting. He let out scolds disguised as coughs. When the demon beat his horse and dust rose from its brown flanks, he coughed from his very depths. All Chinese words conveniently a syllable each, he said, "Get—that—horse—dust—away—from—me—you—dead—white—demon. Don't—stare—at—me—with—those—glass—eyes. I—can't—take—this—life." He felt better after having his say. He did not even mind the despair, which dispelled upon his speaking it. The suicides who walked into the ocean or jumped off the mountains were not his kindred.

At night the very thought of dust tickled his lungs. In order to sleep, he imagined his lungs warming and becoming two red diamonds.

If the moisture and soil had been natural to cane, the men would not have had to work so hard coaxing it, leading water to it. The weather and soil were just good enough for cane to require constant nursing and effort. There was a scarcity of animals on the island too, and of laborers.

Whenever Bak Goong looked up from the work, the mountains were there above him. They rose, sheer green walls without slope like great stage curtains that could part or rise, and then he would see behind them what really runs the world, whether the gods' faces are kind or evil. The beings on either side of the curtains would have a look at one another—surprise—before they shut again. Perhaps the gods did fly this far from China and landed on this island for a rest in mid-ocean. Perhaps China Men attracted them. On a gray day, the mountains looked like Chinese mountains. But usually they were stark, bright green curtains. After a rainstorm, waterfalls dropped like silver scrolls down each fold. Bak Goong said, "Aiya!" in wonder. He counted over twenty waterfalls before his eyes.

For recreation, because he was a farmer and as antidote for the sameness of the cane, he planted a garden near the huts. Planting as if in his old village, which was like this island in weather and red dirt, he even grew flowers, for which there was no edible use whatsoever. "It's a regular park with coppices and flowers," he said. He ticked off in a chant the cuttings, seeds, and bulbs he had brought across the ocean—pomelo, kumquat, which is "golden luck," tangerines, citron also known as five fingers and Buddha's hand, ginger, bitter melon and other kinds of melon, squashes, peas, beans, narcissus, orchids, and chrysanthemums. To see how his plants had grown and changed overnight gave him eagerness, a reason, and curiosity for getting out of bed in the morning. The transplants another gardener had given him would be standing up. Tomatoes the size of pinheads would have appeared in the centers of the yellow flowers. His orange tree would have

grown a pair of balls. He took his morning piss in his garden. He garnered and ate thinnings for breakfast. "Harvest,"
he said with one skinny luffa in his hand. For free, he found
mushrooms, full-blown white domes and orange puffs in the
grass and fluted wooden ears in the trees. He let at least one of
each kind of plant go to seed and collected their generations.
Harvest gave him a happy sense of order. "Li Shih Min," he
informed the others, "established such order in his kingdom
that criminals came out of jail for harvests and returned for
the winter executions."

On their "day offu," the China Men went into Honolulu to
spend their pay. They could ride cane and mill wagons as far as
they had built roads, and they walked until there was another
road, where they could catch another wagon for a few cents
more. A family could eat for a week on that fare. They dressed
for town in their black silk suits and yellow straw boaters with
the black band and forked streamers; their braids hung between the swallowtails. "I'm going to town," Bak Goong sang
and sang *town* as if Honolulu were his own village. A family
man, he walked the entire way and reached town by noon. He
went directly to the general store, where he bought a money
order for his wife and dictated a letter about how well and
lighthearted he was in this Sandalwood paradise. The leftover
money was his to keep or spend on careful gambling (more for
the companionship than the money), a restaurant meal with a
shot of whiskey, and a yearly picture taken at the photo studio.
Unlike Bak Sook Goong, the other great grandfather, he did
not spend money on Sandalwood Mountain women. He wandered about on the wooden sidewalks creaking underfoot and
sat in the stores. "Come in and sit awhile," the store owners
said as if inviting him into their own houses in China, and he
was a real uncle or brother.

Most of the men were young enough to have their entire
lives changed on a day off. A farmer could come to town,
change his name, and become a merchant. Bak Goong met
men who had forgotten the names of their Chinese family
or the name and location of their Chinese village. They kept
shaking their heads when he named village after village. They
had lost a last piece of paper or a letter with the address on it.
The gambling men played with fate for a new life. They bought

chances. It was no work at all to throw the dice, flip a card, or pick a word in the pigeon lottery. In one Sunday, a lucky man could buy a farm or take a ship home or to California, stand up from the gambling table and walk to the harbor. Or he could sign his years away, mortgage his labor and future, not go home yet, ever. Two poor men gamble and one becomes a rich man. The other becomes a fleaman. A day in town was full of possibilities.

The other great grandfather, Bak Sook Goong, did not spend much of his time off with the men. One day off, when following a stream, he heard the voices and laughter of women, and from behind bushes, saw them in a pool at the foot of a waterfall. Some naked women were bathing. Nude women sitting on the rocks were weaving flowers and leaves into crowns for their drying hair. They were singing, and laughed at the ends of lines, so he knew it had to be a lascivious song. And one of them was looking at him, into his eyes. Instead of covering herself, she held his gaze and washed herself here and there. Then she said something, and the women tugged him out of hiding. They made him bathe with them. "But this is just like stories," he told them, though they did not understand everything he said. "Let me sing you one." He stood garlanded and sang to them about a prince on horseback who came upon naked sisters bathing and singing. "Sun and water double and touch, double and touch," he sang. "Wash up here—and here—and wash down there." He did the movements as he sang, and the beautiful women understood and laughed. The end of that song was that the prince had burst out laughing, and the sisters covered themselves and vanished, but these women asked him to have a picnic with them.

"Come eat, Brother," they said in English. "Sit, Brother. You stay eat. Stay eat, Brother." As he ate with them serving him, he was reminded that this was the right way for a man to live, and how much he missed his family, which was a family of women, two wives and many daughters, also many slaves. He turned to the woman who had looked so boldly at him. "I come live with you?" he asked. "Let me come live with you."

"Yes," she said. "You come live with me." He became the godfather of many Hawaiian children. "Paké godfather," they called him.

When the China Men asked Bak Sook Goong how his family was doing, they continued to mean the one in China, and he answered that way too. After work and on days off, he went to his Hawaiian village.

Bak Goong, meanwhile, helped build a dragon for the many New Years to come. He collected metal and glass shards, seashells, and wood shavings, which he glued and sewed into scales. Once a month, he brought his dragon section to town and added it to the tail, which grew very layered and long. When the clothes he had brought from China and the new clothes he had bought here turned into rags, he worked them into the dragon. The island dragon was more splendid than any village dragon he had left behind. None of the men had seen a longer dragon in China. "This is the longest dragon in the world," they said. Only the men who regularly practiced kung fu were dragon dancers. They argued about which postures and moves were the correct kung fu. They had been taught by different teachers in contradicting traditions. On New Year's the dragon in its fierce dance undulated like the Pacific Ocean, coiled and twisted, leapt and stepped nimbly among the firecrackers. Bak Goong had his picture taken inside the dragon, not in motion but stretched out straight, the dancers' feet in white socks aligned in front of the wooden sidewalks.

Bak Goong spoke kindly and happily at the beginning of the New Year, saying only good things. But some aggravation would make him swear, and no year was perfect.

Once he saw five humpback whales on their New Year's birthing journey pass like spouting islands, backs like wet rocks, alive with moss and lichen. A wind blew leaves across the beach.

In 1856 every great grandfather on every island gave some of his money to throw a Grand Ball for the Sandalwood Mountain king and queen's wedding. Neither Bak Goong nor Bak Sook Goong went to it, but they were represented by wealthy China Men. "He practices quadrilles alone in front of a mirror in his room at night," the plain men gossiped. The ball was held at the courthouse. Four white demons, named with Chinese names and dressed in mandarin gowns, acted as hosts. The queen danced the opening quadrille with a real China Man, the king with a demoness. Six whole sheep and

one hundred and fifty chickens were eaten. The China Men's
Ball was the most elegant ever held in Hawai'i. The newspapers praised the China Men for their dancing and generosity; a
ball was not above their comprehension. Great grandmothers
were to understand that their husbands did not spend $3,700
on a Grand Ball to dance with the blonde Jesus demonesses
or the princesses of the wild people but to prove their civility.

When Bak Goong needed to get off this rock of an island,
he sat at an edge of the ocean where he often watched the sun
pop out on his left, and later drop back in on his right. One
moonless night the winds blowing from Kona met the winds
blowing trade, and the air was still; the fronds hung silent.
Two people were standing in the black water halfway between
him and the horizon, halfway between the sky and earth. A
yellow light shown from them; their random movements repeated in series, a dance. They revolved in the only brightness,
and stopped, hands and feet held like Balinese temple dancers.
Time moved at their rate of motion. It was either two people or one Hindoo with four arms. He heard music draw out
into one long note. The waves going in and out forever was
the same as no motion at all. The ocean remains the same
basic water. Flesh does not evolve into the necessary iron. He
yearned for the sun to blast out of the ocean. He sat for hours
in the exact center of eternity.

Then it all started up again; the couple on the water stirred.
A fisherman and woman suddenly came out of the sea and
walked toward him. "Want to see our catch?" He could barely
answer for staring at their ordinary faces. Between the time
the Hindoo danced and these two stood beside him, he had
seen streaming up to him rows of shining people; they had had
wings flapping light and bare feet and hands glowing. It had
been bright as day.

"You like fish, Brother?" "You like fish, Uncle?" said the human voices coming from flesh and blood bodies. The light was
contained in lanterns the man and woman were carrying and
also came from the rising moon. The two figures were only
an elderly Hawaiian couple he had met before; they had been
nightfishing. They handed him a fish, "Eh, you like fish?" and
walked away along the beach.

Later when he heard people say they had seen the torches

of the dead warriors who walk across the water, he would say, "You saw the Hawaiians nightfishing or checking their lobster traps." But when someone said, "Those are the Hawaiians nightfishing," Bak Goong, a fanciful, fabulous man, said, "It may be dead Hawaiian warriors walking." If a human being crossed the path of the walkers, he could die on the spot, but Bak Goong said that he knew for a fact that this was not true. He mustn't sit so long looking at the ocean, he resolved. The opium must have had a permanent effect; he would not take any more. He asked the tobacco shit men, "How can you tell it hasn't changed you once and for all? Could everything have become permanently exaggerated?" Now that he was in a new land, who could tell what normal was?

Among the cane weeds, he found a new, free opiate: a mushroom with a speckled brown cap that turned purple when picked. It tasted of earth and must, but he did not see much new vision; perhaps he had seen all there was to see. He did not eat it again. Nor did he chew the wood whose Hawaiian name sounded like *ka fa*, "fake flower" in Cantonese. So he had smoked opium, eaten mushroom, and gambled, but he would not become an opium addict or mushroom addict or gambler. He was a talk addict.

On another day off, he got lost while exploring and came upon abandoned huts he had not seen before. The doors and windows gaped. Some huts only had a hole for crawling in and out of. The stones, however, had not tumbled down but sat stacked one on top of another in god shapes or human shapes—he did not know what they meant. There were no rocks wrapped in fresh ti leaves. In case it had been measles or smallpox that had emptied the village, he did not go inside any house.

Suddenly out of the air and lifting the hair on the back of his neck like the wind lifting the grass on the roofs came a howling that was high and long. It's a bird, he reasoned. It's crying in flight. That's why the notes come now here, now there. It's wild dogs on the hillside. But it grew louder and in it he heard sobs, the lamentation of old men and children, thousands of souls wailing in separate voices. He could not make out the quivering words, or it was a language he did not know. "Ghosts," his wife would have said. I'm imagining this, he thought. It's really wild dogs. Or wolves. They sounded hungry. He felt like weeping in sympathy; sorrow filled his chest, but he kept the tears back not to blind himself as he ran out of the village.

A woman standing by the last hut called to him. "This way. This way," she said. "You hear?" he asked. "Yes," she said, but the noise stopped. She stood under plumeria, the star flower, the deadman's flower that grows in graveyards. The hut behind her had been mended, the earth around it swept. She touched his arm; he felt a tiredness come from her and weight his arm. His face nodded toward hers, his head heavy and helpless. Though no icy breath came from her mouth, his chicken skin was proof of the supernatural nearby, and he left quickly, rudely. When he looked back, she had gone inside her hut.

He entered town in an unfamiliar place with the sun setting and no wagons in sight. A police demon stopped him, but English phrases had flown out of his mind. The police demon was about to arrest him, runaway chinamen a menace now, but just then Bak Goong saw a young countryman across the street, someone who could help him. "Sook-ah," he called out. "Sook-ah," that is, "Hey, Father's Younger Brother." "Sook-ah."

"Sugar?" said the police demon. "Sugar plantation? You better hurry. The wagon is leaving soon." He pointed with his nightstick to a street that jumped into recognition. Bak Goong returned on the last wagon.

Old men laugh with tears in their eyes every time they hear or tell the "sugar" story. Another way it goes is like this: A China Man enters a grocery store, where he wants to buy some sugar for New Year's day. But at the counter he can't think of the word. Luckily, a young man walks past the door. "Sook-ah," the older man calls, and the grocer demon gets him a bag of sugar, a good omen for the New Year.

On days off, it was safest to stay on the plantation. There was entertainment to be had without spending money. It was a recreation to sleep like winter gods. Peddlers came bringing medicines and toiletries; they talked story and talked stink about people on the other plantations. The pesky missionary Jesus demons also came nosing and sniffing out Hawaiians and China Men even in the remote valleys. They were like the wandering persuaders in China. Some workers walked about with them, whispering and nodding. Converts got extra days off on demon holidays. "I'm just a pig catcher," they said as they dressed up for church, where they ate free food, "and you get to go inside demon houses." Bak Goong went to Christian church once or twice, but they talked "baptism," and he quit. He asked the converts, "Who's the pig that got caught?" They didn't even talk like China Men any more, the salt gone from their speech. "Thank God," they said instead of "Your mother's cunt."

Jesus demonesses with pale eyebrows and gold eyelashes visited on a Sunday. They spoke a well-intoned Cantonese, which sounded disincarnated coming out of their white faces. They said they had lived in China and respected Chinese. They wanted to come in and talk story. Fingers in black books, they took peeks to see what to say next.

Bak Goong walked about the room to look at these strange women from various angles. No rudeness seemed to discomfit them; when any of the men did some interesting Chinese antic, they complimented him or did not notice. They handed out presents—candy, clothes, toothpaste, combs, soaps, medicines, Jesus pictures, which were grisly cards with a demon nailed to a cross, probably a warning about what happened to you if you didn't convert. In China, Bak Goong had seen pictures of soldiers eating Christians, whose meat looked like drumsticks. The briny men asked the Jesus demonesses, "Would you administer this medicine to me?" They grinned lewdly at one another, but the demonesses did not see Chinese facial expressions. The men brushed up against their yellow hair, reached behind and touched it. They talked about what was under the long dresses; no lady would understand anyway.

A mischievousness came into the room. Bak Goong brewed tea for the ladies. "It's the custom to drink it all," he said, scooping sugar into the cups. The sugar made the demonesses thirstier, and they asked for more tea. The men asked for more stories so that the women stayed and stayed. The listeners did like the one about the baby being born and the childless wise men searching for him and finding him. "Speak English," Bak Goong requested. If anybody talked long enough in a foreign language and he heard enough, he understood. At last the

ladies got up one at a time, and everyone knew they were going to the outhouse to piss.

Later the men rolled on the floor laughing. Bak Goong
told the origin of the joke they'd played: "The Story of Chan
Moong Gut and the Gambling Wives," he announced, and
clanged his pot-lid cymbals. "Chan invited all the rich women
to his house to play cards while their husbands were at work.
He lured them with prizes and pastries. He served them syrup
with just a little water. The sweetness made the ladies drink tea
and go to the urine bucket continually. No, no, don't laugh
yet. There's more. There's more. Chan Moong Gut had wet
the rim of the bucket with red paint. That night their husbands beat the ladies. 'What man did you allow to paint a red
ring around your ass?' the husbands hollered. They spanked
their wives' asses redder. Wait till the white demonesses' husbands see their asses." The men drew rings with lascivious fingers. "You're going to hell," said the demon convert China
Men. "Straight to hell, you demons."

Bak Goong told more stories about Chan Moong Gut,
Fortunate Dream Chan, a trickster who never worked but
lived by his wits gambling and catching pigs. He used to put
chicken shit at the bottom of the rice for the blindman. When
the blindman ate past the nicely mounded top, he said, "Oh,
how wonderfully seasoned. How kind to put sauce in my rice."

"Every morning Chan would shit on his neighbor's doorstep. The first couple of days the neighbor stepped in it when
he went out. After that, he opened the door cautiously and
cleaned it up, cursing all the while. Chan Moong Gut arranged that this neighbor would run into him at market. Chan
was boasting what an undauntable appetite he had. 'I can eat
anything,' he said, tricking the people around him into buying
him food. They were wagering on how much and how fast
he could eat. He was good at sleight of hand, and was hiding
food in his clothes. The neighbor thought of a bet, and he set
the terms himself instead of letting wily Chan do it. 'I'll bet,'
said the neighbor, 'that you can't eat whatever appears on my
doorstep tomorrow morning.' Chan Moong Gut took the bet.
Instead of shitting on the step, however, he arranged bananas
dipped in brown sugar sauce. The neighbor could barely stand
to look, but he felt gratified watching Chan hold his nose and

weep as he ate shit. He was glad to give Chan the money and believed that he had caught a pig." People with the name Chan have asked storytellers to change the trickster's name, or to forget those stories in America.

It wasn't right that Bak Goong had to save his talking until after work when stories would have made the work easier. He grew the habit of clamping his mouth shut in a line, and the sun baked that expression on him. If he opened his mouth, words might tumble forth like coral out of the surf; spit would spout like lava. He still hacked at the cane while coughing: "Take— that—white—demon. Take—that. Fall—to—the—ground— demon. Cut—you—into—pieces. Chop—off—your—legs. Die—snake. Chop—you—down—stinky—demon." His sentences shortened, angry pellets that shot out of him.

He woke one morning and felt a yang wind blow too hot through his body. He forced himself to sit up, not to be left behind among the sick, who were one-third of the workers. He rolled out of bed, stood, and fell. The healthier men were heading out into the humid day. He pulled himself up and dropped into his bunk. Asleep, again and again he seemed to jump out of bed, run sluggishly about gathering his clothes and tools, run through thick air in search of the fields, hear the demon boss in wait for him saying, "Late. You late, Paké," only to wake up and find that nothing had been done, no shoes put on, no breakfast eaten. He slept while the gecko lizards tsked-tsked-tsked at his sloth. He slept while a mushroom grew in a corner of the hut. His garden did not cajole him out of bed.

Each time he awoke, he was lying among the sick men, some breathing with clogged lungs like his, some doubled up holding their stomachs, cripples soaking their limbs. A few men looked bodily healthy but did not move. Somebody seemed to be piling dry leaves near the door and lighting them.

In his fever, he yearned so hard for his family that he felt he appeared in China. He reached out his arms and said, "Wife. Wife, I'm home." But she said, "What are you doing here? What are you doing here without the money? Moneyless and bodiless, you better go back to the Sandalwood Mountains. Go back and pick up your money and your body. Go back where you belong. Go now." He tried to talk to her, but his tongue was heavy and his throat blocked. He awoke certain that he had to cure himself by talking whenever he pleased.

Yin, the cool, was returning a little. Raindrops plunked loudly on the banana and ti leaves. It was what the Hawaiians called a cane-tapping rain. He chuckled with the geckos, their fingers and toes spread like little suctioning stars on the walls and ceilings, where they waited to flick at bugs. They were so sly playing dead, but through their translucent skins he saw their blue hearts beating and their organs swallowing. He shouted to make them leap to the ground. When they hid, he heard their clucking and chuckling. He had learned to recognize some of them individually. He told the sick men around him, "You can't die because then your poor wife will miss you, your family will go hungry awaiting your pay, and your mother will be uncertain forever what became of you. If there were only yourself, you would have the luxury of dying. Uncles and Brothers, I have diagnosed our illness. It is a congestion from not talking. What we have to do is talk and talk.

He lurched out to the rain barrel, poured water down his back and splashed it on his face. His wife would have scolded him for drinking cold water, a Sandalwood Mountain habit he was acquiring. He was carrying water to the sicker men when a demon galloped toward him, boss and horse both with cavernous nostrils wide open. Bak Goong turned toward the fields. The demon pushed sick men out the door. He pulled a boy by the hair. Bak Goong could tell he was saying, "Aha! I caught you malingering, you fake, lazy, sneaky chinaman." He pointed the whip toward the cane. "Go work, Paké. No stay sick." The demons had changed their rules again, no longer sending stragglers back to the huts. Bak Goong put his left arm around the stalks and leaned his face and body against them while his right arm swung at the feet of the cane. He neither sang nor spoke. Unhealthily, he wet handkerchiefs and plastered them on his head.

That evening, he talked an apt story to the silenced men, who had heard it already in the long ago place where there had been mothers and children: "Old Uncles and Young Uncles, I have an appropriate story to tell. It cannot be left unsaid." He recalled a land arranged in layers like clouds or stages, where animals, common men and women, kings and gods held adventures. "Bak-ah, Sook-ah, a long time ago in China, there lived a king who would have given his kingdom for a son. Powerful but childless, sonless, yearning to be a father, he bought ponies of various sizes for his someday son to ride as he grew. He would trot behind his father on tours of the kingdom. Together they would shoot arrows, snare rabbits, and catch fish. Longing to hold his own son to his chest, he felt envious looking at ordinary fathers. He read tea leaves and oil wicks looking for a son. But at last, when his wish was granted and his own only boy was born, the queen and the midwives hesitated to show him the new prince. 'Is it a boy?' he asked. 'It is a boy, isn't it?' He pushed aside the blanket and saw that on either side of the bald head, the prince had little pointed furry ears like a kitten's. 'Oh, no,' said the king. 'Cat ears. The prince has cat ears. We order everyone present never to tell that the prince has cat ears. Keep our secret. Don't tell the people.'

"So the years went by; the prince grew into noble perfection except for the kitty ears. The queen combed his long hair over them. Only in appearance were the ears strange; the prince heard as clearly as anyone else. The subjects exclaimed over his handsomeness. The king never mentioned the cat ears, and so the secret grew large inside his chest and mouth.

"One day when the boy was almost grown, the king could not hold the secret inside himself any more. He walked alone in a winter field, where he scooped out a hole. He shouted into it, 'The king's son has cat ears. The king's son has cat ears.' He shouted until he was empty of his secret, and satisfied, relieved, he pushed the dirt back into the hole and stamped it down.

"In the spring, grass grew in that field, and when the wind blew through it, the people heard words. The sounds swelled through the summer, enunciated until the people knew for sure what the tall grass and the wind said louder and louder: 'The king's son has cat ears. The king's son has cat ears.' It grew into a song. 'The king's son has cat ears.' The news spread throughout the land. It made the people laugh to hear it."

The listening men thought how they would love their baby boy even if he had cat ears; he'd be even cuter with cat ears.

They would brag as they handed out red eggs to the other unfamilied men, who would come to visit the baby. "See?" the fathers would say. "Cat ears. Bet you've never seen anything like them." "Eh, Father," the other China Men would say enviously. "A father, are you?" They'd make much of giving the baby red money.

The next day the men plowed, working purposefully, but they dug a circle instead of straight furrows. They dug a wide hole. They threw down their tools and flopped on the ground with their faces over the edge of the hole and their legs like wheel spokes.

"Hello down there in China!" they shouted. "Hello, Mother." "Hello, my heart and my liver."

"I miss you." "What are you doing right now?" "Happy birthday. Happy birthday for last year too."

"I've been working hard for you, and I hate it."

"Sometimes I forget my family and go to clubs. I drink all night." "I lost all the money again." "I've become an opium addict." "I don't even look Chinese any more." "I'm sorry I ate it all by myself."

". . . and I fell to my knees at the sight of twenty waterfalls." "I saw only one sandalwood tree."

They said any kind of thing. "Blonde demoness." "Polynesian demoness."

"I'm coming home by and by." "I'm not coming home." "I'm staying here in the Sandalwood Mountains."

"I want to be home," Bak Goong said.

"I'm bringing her home," said Bak Sook Goong.

They had dug an ear into the world, and were telling the earth their secrets.

"I want home," Bak Goong yelled, pressed against the soil, and smelling the earth. "I want my home," the men yelled together. "I want home. Home. Home. Home. Home."

Talked out, they buried their words, planted them. "Like cats covering shit," they laughed.

"That wasn't a custom," said Bak Goong. "We made it up. We can make up customs because we're the founding ancestors of this place."

They made such a noise that the demons could have come charging upon them and the hole fill with the sounds of battle.

But the demons hid, the China Men so riled up, who knows what they were up to?

From the day of the shout party, Bak Goong talked and sang at his work, and did not get sent to the punishment fields. In cutting season, the demons no longer accompanied the knife-wielding China Men into deep cane.

Soon the new green shoots would rise, and when in two years the cane grew gold tassels, what stories the wind would tell.

Bak Goong, the great grandfather with a good memory, kept his promises and so chose to go back to China. Bak Sook Goong also went back, though the king and queen of the Sandalwood Mountains had ruled that a China Man who married a Hawaiian would be called Hawaiian, and many another Paké godfather stayed. Bak Sook Goong brought his Sandalwood Mountain wife back with him. She would become sister of his other two wives. He would abandon none of them. So these two great grandfathers made their lives of a piece.

On Mortality

As YOU know, any plain person you chance to meet can prove to be a powerful immortal in disguise come to test you.

Li Fu-yen told a story about Tu Tzu-chun, who lived from A.D. 558 to 618, during the Northern Chou and Sui dynasties. Tu's examiner was a Taoist monk, who made him rich twice, and twice Tu squandered his fortune though it took him two lifetimes to do so. The third time the Taoist gave him money, he bought a thousand li of good land, plowed it himself, seeded it, built houses, roads, and bridges, then welcomed widows and orphans to live on it. With the leftover money, he found a husband for each spinster and a wife for every bachelor in his family, and also paid for the weddings. When he met the Taoist again, he said, "I've used up all your money on the unfortunates I've come across."

"You'll have to repay me by working for me," said the Taoist monk. "I need your help on an important difficult task." He gave Tu three white pills. "Swallow these," he said, pouring him a cup of wine. "All that you'll see and feel will be illusions. No matter what happens, don't speak; don't scream. Remember the saying 'Hide your broken arms in your sleeves.'"

"How easy," said Tu as he swallowed the pills in three gulps of wine. "Why should I scream if I know they're illusions?"

Level by level he descended into the nine hells. At first he saw oxheads, horsefaces, and the heads of generals decapitated in war. Illusions. Only illusions, harmless. He laughed at the heads. He had seen heads before. Soon fewer heads whizzed through the dark until he saw no more of them.

Suddenly his wife was being tortured. Demons were cutting her up into pieces, starting with her toes. He heard her scream; he heard her bones crack. He reminded himself that she was an illusion. *Illusion*, he thought. She was ground into bloodmeal.

Then the tortures on his own body began. Demons poured bronze down his throat and beat him with iron clubs and chains. They mortar-and-pestled and packed him into a pill.

He had to walk over mountains of knives and through fields of knives and forests of swords. He was killed, his head chopped off, rolling into other people's nightmares.

He heard gods and goddesses talking about him, "This man is too wicked to be reborn a man. Let him be born a woman." He saw the entrance of a black tunnel and felt tired. He would have to squeeze his head and shoulders down into that enclosure and travel a long distance. He pushed head first through the entrance, only the beginning. A god kicked him in the butt to give him a move on. (This kick is the reason many Chinese babies have a blue-gray spot on their butts or lower backs, the "Mongolian spot.") Sometimes stuck in the tunnel, sometimes shooting helplessly through it, he emerged again into light with many urgent things to do, many messages to deliver, but his hands were useless baby's hands, his legs wobbly baby's legs, his voice a wordless baby's cries. Years had to pass before he could regain adult powers; he howled as he began to forget the cosmos, his attention taken up with mastering how to crawl, how to stand, how to walk, how to control his bowel movements.

He discovered that he had been reborn a deaf-mute female named Tu. When she became a woman, her parents married her to a man named Lu, who at first did not mind. "Why does she need to talk," said Lu, "to be a good wife? Let her set an example for women." They had a child. But years later, Lu tired of Tu's dumbness. "You're just being stubborn," he said, and lifted their child by the feet. "Talk, or I'll dash its head against the rocks." The poor mother held her hand to her mouth. Lu swung the child, broke its head against the wall.

Tu shouted out, "Oh! Oh!"—and he was back with the Taoist, who sadly told him that at the moment when she had said, "Oh! Oh!" the Taoist was about to complete the last step in making the elixir for immortality. Now that Tu had broken his silence, the formula was spoiled, no immortality for the human race. "You overcame joy and sorrow, anger, fear, and evil desire, but not love," said the Taoist, and went on his way.

On Mortality Again

THE LAST deed of Maui the Trickster, the Polynesian demigod who played jokes, pushed the sky higher, roped the sun with braided pubic hair from his mother, pulled the land up out of the ocean, and brought fire to earth, was to seek immortality for men and women by stealing it from Hina of the Night. He instructed the people, the beasts, the birds, and the elements to be silent. Hunters walked through forests and fishermen waited in this same silence. In silence the snarer caught birds alive, plucked the few red feathers, and released them; the seer read the clouds, heard spirits and did not disturb them. Children learned and worked silently. There was a chant that could hardly be discerned from silence. Maui dived into the ocean, where he found great Hina asleep. Through her vagina like a door, he entered her body. He took her heart in his arms. He had started tunneling out feet first when a bird, at the sight of his legs wiggling out of the vagina, laughed. Hina awoke and shut herself, and Maui died.

THE GRANDFATHER OF THE
SIERRA NEVADA MOUNTAINS

THE TRAINS used to cross the sky. The house jumped and dust shook down from the attic. Sometimes two trains ran parallel going in opposite directions; the railroad men walked on top of the leaning cars, stepped off one train onto the back of the other, and traveled the opposite way. They headed for the caboose while the train moved against their walk, or they walked toward the engine while the train moved out from under their feet. Hoboes ran alongside, caught the ladders, and swung aboard. I would have to learn to ride like that, choose my boxcar, grab a ladder at a run, and fling myself up and sideways into an open door. Elsewhere I would step smoothly off. Bad runaway boys lost their legs trying for such rides. The train craunched past—pistons stroking like elbows and knees, the coal cars dropping coal, cows looking out between the slats of the cattle-cars, the boxcars almost stringing together sentences—Hydro-Cushion, Georgia Flyer, Route of the Eagle—and suddenly sunlight filled the windows again, the slough wide again and waving with tules, for which the city was once named; red-winged blackbirds and squirrels settled. We children ran to the tracks and found the nails we'd placed on them; the wheels had flattened them into knives that sparked.

Once in a while an adult said, "Your grandfather built the railroad." (Or "Your grandfathers built the railroad." Plural and singular are by context.) We children believed that it was that very railroad, those trains, those tracks running past our house; our own giant grandfather had set those very logs into the ground, poured the iron for those very spikes with the big heads and pounded them until the heads spread like that, mere nails to him. He had built the railroad so that trains would thunder over us, on a street that inclined toward us. We lived on a special spot of the earth, Stockton, the only city on the Pacific coast with three railroads—the Santa Fe, Southern Pacific, and Western Pacific. The three railroads intersecting accounted for the flocks of hoboes. The few times that the train stopped, the cows moaned all night, their hooves stumbling crowdedly and banging against the wood.

Grandfather left a railroad for his message: We had to go

somewhere difficult. Ride a train. Go somewhere important. In case of danger, the train was to be ready for us.

The railroad men disconnected the rails and took the steel away. They did not come back. Our family dug up the square logs and rolled them downhill home. We collected the spikes too. We used the logs for benches, edged the yard with them, made bases for fences, embedded them in the ground for walkways. The spikes came in handy too, good for paperweights, levers, wedges, chisels. I am glad to know exactly the weight of ties and the size of nails.

Grandfather's picture hangs in the dining room next to an equally large one of Grandmother, and another one of Guan Goong, God of War and Literature. My grandparents' similarity is in the set of their mouths; they seem to have hauled with their mouths. My mouth also feels the tug and strain of weights in its corners. In the family album, Grandfather wears a greatcoat and Western shoes, but his ankles show. He hasn't shaved either. Maybe he became sloppy after the Japanese soldier bayoneted his head for not giving directions. Or he was born slow and without a sense of direction.

The photographer came to the village regularly and set up a spinet, potted trees, an ornate table stacked with hardbound books of matching size, and a backdrop with a picture of paths curving through gardens into panoramas; he lent his subjects dressy ancient mandarin clothes, Western suits, and hats. An aunt tied the fingers of the lame cousin to a book, the string leading down his sleeve; he looks like he's carrying it. The family hurried from clothes chests to mirrors without explaining to Grandfather, hiding Grandfather. In the family album are group pictures with Grandmother in the middle, the family arranged on either side of her and behind her, second wives at the ends, no Grandfather. Grandmother's earrings, bracelets, and rings are tinted jade green, everything and everybody else black and white, her little feet together neatly, two knobs at the bottom of her gown. My mother, indignant that nobody had readied Grandfather, threw his greatcoat over his nightclothes, shouted, "Wait! Wait!" and encouraged him into the sunlight. "Hurry," she said, and he ran, coat flapping, to be in the picture. She would have slipped him into the group and had the camera catch him like a peeping ghost, but

Grandmother chased him away. "What a waste of film," she said. Grandfather always appears alone with white stubble on his chin. He was a thin man with big eyes that looked straight ahead. When we children talked about overcoat men, exhibitionists, we meant Grandfather, Ah Goong, who must have yanked open that greatcoat—no pants.

MaMa was the only person to listen to him, and so he followed her everywhere, and talked and talked. What he liked telling was his journeys to the Gold Mountain. He wasn't smart, yet he traveled there three times. Left to himself, he would have stayed in China to play with babies or stayed in the United States once he got there, but Grandmother forced him to leave both places. "Make money," she said. "Don't stay here eating." "Come home," she said.

Ah Goong sat outside her open door when MaMa worked. (In those days a man did not visit a good woman alone unless married to her.) He saw her at her loom and came running with his chair. He told her that he had found a wondrous country, really gold, and he himself had gotten two bags of it, one of which he had had made into a ring. His wife had given that ring to their son for his wedding ring. "That ring on your finger," he told Mother, "proves that the Gold Mountain exists and that I went there."

Another of his peculiarities was that he heard the crackles, bangs, gunshots that go off when the world lurches; the gears on its axis snap. Listening to a faraway New Year, he had followed the noise and come upon the blasting in the Sierras. (There is a Buddhist instruction that that which is most elusive must, of course, be the very thing to be pursued; listen to the farthest sound.) The Central Pacific hired him on sight; chinamen had a natural talent for explosions. Also there were not enough workingmen to do all the labor of building a new country. Some of the banging came from the war to decide whether or not black people would continue to work for nothing.

Slow as usual, Ah Goong arrived in the spring; the work had begun in January 1863. The demon that hired him pointed up and up, east above the hills of poppies. His first job was to fell a redwood, which was thick enough to divide into three or four beams. His tree's many branches spread out, each limb like a little tree. He circled the tree. How to attack it? No side looked like the side made to be cut, nor did any ground seem the place for it to fall. He axed for almost a day the side he'd decided would hit the ground. Halfway through, imitating the other lumberjacks, he struck the other side of the tree, above the cut, until he had to run away. The tree swayed and slowly dived to earth, creaking and screeching like a green animal. He was so awed, he forgot what he was supposed to yell. Hardly any branches broke; the tree sprang, bounced, pushed at the ground with its arms. The limbs did not wilt and fold; they were a small forest, which he chopped. The trunk lay like a long red torso; sap ran from its cuts like crying blind eyes. At last it stopped fighting. He set the log across sawhorses to be cured over smoke and in the sun.

He joined a team of men who did not ax one another as they took alternate hits. They blew up the stumps with gunpowder. "It was like uprooting a tooth," Ah Goong said. They also packed gunpowder at the roots of a whole tree. Not at the same time as the bang but before that, the tree rose from the ground. It stood, then plunged with a tearing of veins and muscles. It was big enough to carve a house into. The men measured themselves against the upturned white roots, which looked like claws, a sun with claws. A hundred men stood or sat on the trunk. They lifted a wagon on it and took a photograph. The demons also had their photograph taken.

Because these mountains were made out of gold, Ah Goong rushed over to the root hole to look for gold veins and ore. He selected the shiniest rocks to be assayed later in San Francisco. When he drank from the streams and saw a flash, he dived in like a duck; only sometimes did it turn out to be the sun or the water. The very dirt winked with specks.

He made a dollar a day salary. The lucky men gambled, but he was not good at remembering game rules. The work so far was endurable. "I could take it," he said.

The days were sunny and blue, the wind exhilarating, the heights godlike. At night the stars were diamonds, crystals, silver, snow, ice. He had never seen diamonds. He had never seen snow and ice. As spring turned into summer, and he lay under that sky, he saw the order in the stars. He recognized constellations from China. There—not a cloud but the Silver

River, and there, on either side of it—Altair and Vega, the
Spinning Girl and the Cowboy, far, far apart. He felt his heart
breaking of loneliness at so much blue-black space between
star and star. The railroad he was building would not lead him
to his family. He jumped out of his bedroll. "Look! Look!"
Other China Men jumped awake. An accident? An avalanche?
Injun demons? "The stars," he said. "The stars are here."
"Another China Man gone out of his mind," men grumbled.
"A sleepwalker." "Go to sleep, sleepwalker." "There. And
there," said Ah Goong, two hands pointing. "The Spinning
Girl and the Cowboy. Don't you see them?" "Homesick China
Man," said the China Men and pulled their blankets over their
heads. "Didn't you know they were here? I could have told you
they were here. Same as in China. Same moon. Why not same
stars?" "Nah. Those are American stars."

Pretending that a little girl was listening, he told himself
the story about the Spinning Girl and the Cowboy: A long
time ago they had visited earth, where they met, fell in love,
and married. Instead of growing used to each other, they remained enchanted their entire lifetimes and beyond. They
were too happy. They wanted to be doves or two branches of
the same tree. When they returned to live in the sky, they were
so engrossed in each other that they neglected their work. The
Queen of the Sky scratched a river between them with one
stroke of her silver hairpin—the river a galaxy in width. The
lovers suffered, but she did devote her time to spinning now,
and he herded his cow. The King of the Sky took pity on them
and ordered that once each year, they be allowed to meet. On
the seventh day of the seventh month (which is not the same as
July 7), magpies form a bridge for them to cross to each other.
The lovers are together for one night of the year. On their
parting, the Spinner cries the heavy summer rains.

Ah Goong's discovery of the two stars gave him something
to look forward to besides meals and tea breaks. Every night he
located Altair and Vega and gauged how much closer they had
come since the night before. During the day he watched the
magpies, big black and white birds with round bodies like balls
with wings; they were a welcome sight, a promise of meetings.
He had found two familiars in the wilderness: magpies and
stars. On the meeting day, he did not see any magpies nor

hear their chattering jaybird cries. Some black and white birds flew overhead, but they may have been American crows or late magpies on their way. Some men laughed at him, but he was not the only China Man to collect water in pots, bottles, and canteens that day. The water would stay fresh forever and cure anything. In ancient days the tutelary gods of the mountains sprinkled corpses with this water and brought them to life. That night, no women to light candles, burn incense, cook special food, Grandfather watched for the convergence and bowed. He saw the two little stars next to Vega—the couple's children. And bridging the Silver River, surely those were black flapping wings of magpies and translucent-winged angels and faeries. Toward morning, he was awakened by rain, and pulled his blankets into his tent.

The next day, the fantailed orange-beaked magpies returned. Altair and Vega were beginning their journeys apart, another year of spinning and herding. Ah Goong had to find something else to look forward to. The Spinning Girl and the Cowboy met and parted six times before the railroad was finished.

When cliffs, sheer drops under impossible overhangs, ended the road, the workers filled the ravines or built bridges over them. They climbed above the site for tunnel or bridge and lowered one another down in wicker baskets made stronger by the lucky words they had painted on four sides. Ah Goong got to be a basketman because he was thin and light. Some basketmen were fifteen-year-old boys. He rode the basket barefoot, so his boots, the kind to stomp snakes with, would not break through the bottom. The basket swung and twirled, and he saw the world sweep underneath him; it was fun in a way, a cold new feeling of doing what had never been done before. Suspended in the quiet sky, he thought all kinds of crazy thoughts, that if a man didn't want to live any more, he could just cut the ropes or, easier, tilt the basket, dip, and never have to worry again. He could spread his arms, and the air would momentarily hold him before he fell past the buzzards, hawks, and eagles, and landed impaled on the tip of a sequoia. This high and he didn't see any gods, no Cowboy, no Spinner. He knelt in the basket though he was not bumping his head against the sky. Through the wickerwork, slivers of depths darted like needles, nothing between him and air but thin rattan. Gusts of wind spun the light basket. "Aiya," said Ah Goong. Winds came up under the basket, bouncing it. Neighboring baskets swung together and parted. He and the man next to him looked at each other's faces. They laughed. They might as well have gone to Malaysia to collect bird nests. Those who had done high work there said it had been worse; the birds screamed and scratched at them. Swinging near the cliff, Ah Goong stood up and grabbed it by a twig. He dug holes, then inserted gunpowder and fuses. He worked neither too fast nor too slow, keeping even with the others. The basketmen signaled one another to light the fuses. He struck match after match and dropped the burnt matches over the sides. At last his fuse caught; he waved, and the men above pulled hand over hand hauling him up, pulleys creaking. The scaffolds stood like a row of gibbets. Gallows trees along a ridge. "Hurry, hurry," he said. Some impatient men clambered up their ropes. Ah Goong ran up the ledge road they'd cleared and watched the explosions, which banged almost synchronously, echoes booming like war. He moved his scaffold to the next section of cliff and went down in the basket again, with bags of dirt, and set the next charge.

This time two men were blown up. One knocked out or killed by the explosion fell silently, the other screaming, his arms and legs struggling. A desire shot out of Ah Goong for an arm long enough to reach down and catch them. Much time passed as they fell like plummets. The shreds of baskets and a cowboy hat skimmed and tacked. The winds that pushed birds off course and against mountains did not carry men. Ah Goong also wished that the conscious man would fall faster and get it over with. His hands gripped the ropes, and it was difficult to let go and get on with the work. "It can't happen twice in a row," the basketmen said the next trip down. "Our chances are very good. The trip after an accident is probably the safest one." They raced to their favorite basket, checked and double-checked the four ropes, yanked the strands, tested the pulleys, oiled them, reminded the pulleymen about the signals, and entered the sky again.

Another time, Ah Goong had been lowered to the bottom of a ravine, which had to be cleared for the base of a trestle, when a man fell, and he saw his face. He had not died of shock before hitting bottom. His hands were grabbing at air. His stomach and groin must have felt the fall all the way down. At night Ah Goong woke up falling, though he slept on the ground, and heard other men call out in their sleep. No warm women tweaked their ears and hugged them. "It was only a falling dream," he reassured himself.

Across a valley, a chain of men working on the next mountain, men like ants changing the face of the world, fell, but it was very far away. Godlike, he watched men whose faces he could not see and whose screams he did not hear roll and bounce and slide like a handful of sprinkled gravel.

After a fall, the buzzards circled the spot and reminded the workers for days that a man was dead down there. The men threw piles of rocks and branches to cover bodies from sight.

The mountainface reshaped, they drove supports for a bridge. Since hammering was less dangerous than the blowing up, the men played a little; they rode the baskets swooping in wide arcs; they twisted the ropes and let them unwind like tops. "Look at me," said Ah Goong, pulled open his pants, and pissed overboard, the wind scattering the drops. "I'm a waterfall," he said. He had sent a part of himself hurtling. On rare windless days he watched his piss fall in a continuous stream from himself almost to the bottom of the valley.

One beautiful day, dangling in the sun above a new valley, not the desire to urinate but sexual desire clutched him so hard he bent over in the basket. He curled up, overcome by beauty and fear, which shot to his penis. He tried to rub himself calm. Suddenly he stood up tall and squirted out into space. "I am fucking the world," he said. The world's vagina was big, big as the sky, big as a valley. He grew a habit: whenever he was lowered in the basket, his blood rushed to his penis, and he fucked the world.

Then it was autumn, and the wind blew so fiercely, the men had to postpone the basketwork. Clouds moved in several directions at once. Men pointed at dust devils, which turned their mouths crooked. There was ceaseless motion; clothes kept moving; hair moved; sleeves puffed out. Nothing stayed still long enough for Ah Goong to figure it out. The wind sucked the breath out of his mouth and blew thoughts from his brains. The food convoys from San Francisco brought tents to replace the ones that whipped away. The baskets from China, which the men saved for high work, carried cowboy jackets, long underwear, Levi pants, boots, earmuffs, leather gloves, flannel shirts, coats. They sewed rabbit fur and deer-skin into the linings. They tied the wide brims of their cowboy hats over their ears with mufflers. And still the wind made confusing howls into ears, and it was hard to think.

The days became nights when the crews tunneled inside the mountain, which sheltered them from the wind, but also hid the light and sky. Ah Goong pickaxed the mountain, the dirt filling his nostrils through a cowboy bandanna. He shov-eled the dirt into a cart and pushed it to a place that was tall enough for the mule, which hauled it the rest of the way out. He looked forward to cart duty to edge closer to the entrance. Eyes darkened, nose plugged, his windy cough worse, he was to mole a thousand feet and meet others digging from the other side. How much he'd pay now to go swinging in a bas-ket. He might as well have gone to work in a tin mine. Coming out of the tunnel at the end of a shift, he forgot whether it was supposed to be day or night. He blew his nose fifteen times before the mucus cleared again.

The dirt was the easiest part of tunneling. Beneath the soil, they hit granite. Ah Goong struck it with his pickax, and it jarred his bones, chattered his teeth. He swung his sledge-hammer against it, and the impact rang in the dome of his skull. The mountain that was millions of years old was locked against them and was not to be broken into. The men teased him, "Let's see you fuck the world now." "Let's see you fuck the Gold Mountain now." But he no longer felt like it. "A man ought to be made of tougher material than flesh," he said. "Skin is too soft. Our bones ought to be filled with iron." He lifted the hammer high, careful that it not pull him backward, and let it fall forward of its own weight against the rock. Nothing happened to that gray wall; he had to slam with strength and will. He hit at the same spot over and over again, the same rock. Some chips and flakes broke off. The granite looked everywhere the same. It had no softer or weaker spots anywhere, the same hard gray. He learned to slide his hand up the handle, lift, slide and swing, a circular motion, hammer-ing, hammering, hammering. He would bite like a rat through that mountain. His eyes couldn't see; his nose couldn't smell; and now his ears were filled with the noise of hammering. This rock is what is real, he thought. This rock is what real is, not clouds or mist, which make mysterious promises, and when you go through them are nothing. When the foreman measured at the end of twenty-four hours of pounding, the rock had given a foot. The hammering went on day and night. The men worked eight hours on and eight hours off. They worked on all eighteen tunnels at once. While Ah Goong slept, he could hear the sledgehammers of other men working in the earth. The steady banging reminded him of holidays and harvests; falling asleep, he heard the women chopping mincemeat and the millstones striking.

The demons in boss suits came into the tunnel occasionally, measured with a yardstick, and shook their heads. "Faster," they said. "Faster. Chinamen too slow. Too slow." "Tell us we're slow," the China Men grumbled. The ones in top tiers of scaffolding let rocks drop, a hammer drop. Ropes tangled around the demons' heads and feet. The cave China Men muttered and flexed, glared out of the corners of their eyes. But usually there was no diversion—one day the same as the next, one hour no different from another—the beating against the same granite.

After tunneling into granite for about three years, Ah Goong understood the immovability of the earth. Men change, men die, weather changes, but a mountain is the same as permanence and time. This mountain would have taken no new shape for centuries, ten thousand centuries, the world a still, still place, time unmoving. He worked in the tunnel so long, he learned to see many colors in black. When he stumbled out, he tried to talk about time. "I felt time," he said. "I saw time. I saw world." He tried again, "I saw what's real. I saw time, and it doesn't move. If we break through the mountain, hollow it, time won't have moved anyway. You translators ought to tell the foreigners that."

Summer came again, but after the first summer, he felt less nostalgia at the meeting of the Spinning Girl and the Cowboy. He now knew men who had been in this country for twenty years and thirty years, and the Cowboy's one year away from his lady was no time at all. His own patience was longer. The stars were meeting and would meet again next year, but he would not have seen his family. He joined the others celebrating Souls' Day, the holiday a week later, the fourteenth day of the seventh month. The supply wagons from San Francisco and Sacramento brought watermelon, meat, fish, crab, pressed duck. "There, ghosts, there you are. Come and get it." They displayed the feast complete for a moment before falling to, eating on the dead's behalf.

In the third year of pounding granite by hand, a demon invented dynamite. The railroad workers were to test it. They had stopped using gunpowder in the tunnels after avalanches, but the demons said that dynamite was more precise. They watched a scientist demon mix nitrate, sulphate, and glycerine, then flick the yellow oil, which exploded off his fingertips. Sitting in a meadow to watch the dynamite detonated in the open, Ah Goong saw the men in front of him leap impossibly high into the air; then he felt a shove as if from a giant's unseen hand—and he fell backward. The boom broke the mountain silence like fear breaking inside stomach and chest and groin. No one had gotten hurt; they stood up laughing and amazed, looking around at how they had fallen, the pattern of the explosion. Dynamite was much more powerful than gunpowder. Ah Goong had felt a nudge, as if something kind were moving him out of harm's way. "All of a sudden I was sitting next to you." "Aiya. If we had been nearer, it would have killed us." "If we were stiff, it would have gone through us." "A fist." "A hand." "We leapt like acrobats." Next time Ah Goong flattened himself on the ground, and the explosion rolled over him.

He never got used to the blasting; a blast always surprised him. Even when he himself set the fuse and watched it burn, anticipated the explosion, the bang—*bahng* in Chinese—when it came, always startled. It cleaned the crazy words, the crackling, and bingbangs out of his brain. It was like New Year's, when every problem and thought was knocked clean out of him by firecrackers, and he could begin fresh. He couldn't worry during an explosion, which jerked every head to attention. Hills flew up in rocks and dirt. Boulders turned over and over. Sparks, fires, debris, rocks, smoke burst up, not at the same time as the boom (*bum*) but before that—the sound a separate occurrence, not useful as a signal.

The terrain changed immediately. Streams were diverted, rockscapes exposed. Ah Goong found it difficult to remember what land had looked like before an explosion. It was a good thing the dynamite was invented after the Civil War to the east was over.

The dynamite added more accidents and ways of dying, but if it were not used, the railroad would take fifty more years to finish. Nitroglycerine exploded when it was jounced on a horse or dropped. A man who fell with it in his pocket blew himself up into red pieces. Sometimes it combusted merely standing. Human bodies skipped through the air like puppets and made Ah Goong laugh crazily as if the arms and legs would come together again. The smell of burned flesh remained in rocks.

In the tunnels, the men bored holes fifteen to eighteen inches deep with a power drill, stuffed them with hay and dynamite, and imbedded the fuse in sand. Once, for extra pay, Ah Goong ran back in to see why some dynamite had not gone off and hurried back out again; it was just a slow fuse. When the explosion settled, he helped carry two-hundred-, three-hundred-, five-hundred-pound boulders out of the tunnel.

As a boy he had visited a Taoist monastery where there were nine rooms, each a replica of one of the nine hells. Lifesize sculptures of men and women were spitted on turning wheels. Eerie candles under the suffering faces emphasized eyes poked out, tongues pulled, red mouths and eyes, and real hair, eyelashes, and eyebrows. Women were split apart and men dismembered. He could have reached out and touched the sufferers and the implements. He had dug and dynamited his way into one of these hells. "Only here there are eighteen tunnels, not nine, plus all the tracks between them," he said.

One day he came out of the tunnel to find the mountains white, the evergreens and bare trees decorated, white tree sculptures and lace bushes everywhere. The men from snow country called the icicles "ice chopsticks." He sat in his basket and slid down the slopes. The snow covered the gouged land, the broken trees, the tracks, the mud, the campfire ashes, the unburied dead. Streams were stilled in mid-run, the water petrified. That winter he thought it was the task of the human race to quicken the world, blast the freeze, fire it, redden it with blood. He had to change the stupid slowness of

one sunrise and one sunset per day. He had to enliven the silent world with sound. "The rock," he tried to tell the others.
"The ice." "Time."

The dynamiting loosed blizzards on the men. Ears and toes
fell off. Fingers stuck to the cold silver rails. Snowblind men
stumbled about with bandannas over their eyes. Ah Goong
helped build wood tunnels roofing the track route. Falling
ice scrabbled on the roofs. The men stayed under the snow
for weeks at a time. Snowslides covered the entrances to the
tunnels, which they had to dig out to enter and exit, white
tunnels and black tunnels. Ah Goong looked at his gang
and thought, If there is an avalanche, these are the people
I'll be trapped with, and wondered which ones would share
food. A party of snowbound barbarians had eaten the dead.
Cannibals, thought Ah Goong, and looked around. Food was
not scarce; the tea man brought whiskey barrels of hot tea, and
he warmed his hands and feet, held the teacup to his nose and
ears. Someday, he planned, he would buy a chair with metal
doors for putting hot coal inside it. The magpies did not abandon him but stayed all winter and searched the snow for food.

The men who died slowly enough to say last words said,
"Don't leave me frozen under the snow. Send my body home.
Burn it and put the ashes in a tin can. Take the bone jar when
you come down the mountain." "When you ride the fire car
back to China, tell my descendants to come for me." "Shut
up," scolded the hearty men. "We don't want to hear about
bone jars and dying." "You're lucky to have a body to bury,
not blown to smithereens." "Stupid man to hurt yourself,"
they bawled out the sick and wounded. How their wives would
scold if they brought back deadmen's bones. "Aiya. To be
buried here, nowhere." "But this is somewhere," Ah Goong
promised. "This is the Gold Mountain. We're marking the
land now. The track sections are numbered, and your family
will know where we leave you." But he was a crazy man, and
they didn't listen to him.

Spring did come, and when the snow melted, it revealed the
past year, what had happened, what they had done, where they
had worked, the lost tools, the thawing bodies, some standing with tools in hand, the bright rails. "Remember Uncle
Long Winded Leong?" "Remember Strong Back Wong?"

"Remember Lee Brother?" "And Fong Uncle?" They lost count of the number dead; there is no record of how many died building the railroad. Or maybe it was demons doing the counting and chinamen not worth counting. Whether it was good luck or bad luck, the dead were buried or cairned next to the last section of track they had worked on. "May his ghost not have to toil," they said over graves. (In China a woodcutter ghost chops eternally; people have heard chopping in the snow and in the heat.) "Maybe his ghost will ride the train home." The scientific demons said the transcontinental railroad would connect the West to Cathay. "What if he rides back and forth from Sacramento to New York forever?" "That wouldn't be so bad. I hear the cars will be like houses on wheels." The funerals were short. "No time. No time," said both China Men and demons. The railroad was as straight as they could build it, but no ghosts sat on the tracks; no strange presences haunted the tunnels. The blasts scared ghosts away.

When the Big Dipper pointed east and the China Men detonated nitroglycerine and shot off guns for the New Year, which comes with the spring, these special bangs were not as loud as the daily bangs, not as numerous as the bangs all year. Shouldn't the New Year be the loudest day of all to obliterate the noises of the old year? But to make a bang of that magnitude, they would have to blow up at least a year's supply of dynamite in one blast. They arranged strings of chain reactions in circles and long lines, banging faster and louder to culminate in a big bang. And most importantly, there were random explosions—surprise. Surprise. SURPRISE. They had no dragon, the railroad their dragon.

The demons invented games for working faster, gold coins for miles of track laid, for the heaviest rock, a grand prize for the first team to break through a tunnel. Day shifts raced against night shifts, China Men against Welshmen, China Men against Irishmen, China Men against Injuns and black demons. The fastest races were China Men against China Men, who bet on their own teams. China Men always won because of good teamwork, smart thinking, and the need for the money. Also, they had the most workers to choose teams from. Whenever his team won anything, Ah Goong added to his gold stash. The Central Pacific or Union Pacific won the land on either side of the tracks it built.

One summer day, demon officials and China Man translators went from group to group and announced, "We're raising the pay—thirty-five dollars a month. Because of your excellent work, the Central Pacific Railroad is giving you a four-dollar raise per month." The workers who didn't know better cheered. "What's the catch?" said the smarter men. "You'll have the opportunity to put in more time," said the railroad demons. "Two more hours per shift." Ten-hour shifts inside the tunnels. "It's not ten hours straight," said the demons. "You have time off for tea and meals. Now that you have dynamite, the work isn't so hard." They had been working for three and a half years already, and the track through the Donner Summit was still not done.

The workers discussed the ten-hour shift, swearing their China Man obscenities. "Two extra hours a day—sixty hours a month for four dollars." "Pig catcher demons." "Snakes." "Turtles." "Dead demons." "A human body can't work like that." "The demons don't believe this is a human body. This is a chinaman's body." To bargain, they sent a delegation of English speakers, who were summarily noted as troublemakers, turned away, docked.

The China Men, then, decided to go on strike and demand forty-five dollars a month and the eight-hour shift. They risked going to jail and the Central Pacific keeping the pay it was banking for them. Ah Goong memorized the English, "Forty-five dollars a month—eight-hour shift." He practiced the strike slogan: "Eight hours a day good for white man, all the same good for China Man."

The men wrapped barley and beans in ti leaves, which came from Hawai'i via San Francisco, for celebrating the fifth day of the fifth month (not May but mid-June, the summer solstice). Usually the way the red string is wound and knotted tells what flavors are inside—the salty barley with pickled egg, or beans and pork, or the gelatin pudding. Ah Goong folded ti leaves into a cup and packed it with food. One of the literate men slipped in a piece of paper with the strike plan, and Ah Goong tied the bundle with a special pattern of red string. The time and place for the revolution against Kublai Khan

had been hidden inside autumn mooncakes. Ah Goong looked
from one face to another in admiration. Of course, of course.
No China Men, no railroad. They were indispensable labor.
Throughout these mountains were brothers and uncles with
a common idea, free men, not coolies, calling for fair working
conditions. The demons were not suspicious as the China Men
went gandying up and down the tracks delivering the bundles
tied together like lines of fish. They had exchanged these gifts
every year. When the summer solstice cakes came from other
camps, the recipients cut them into neat slices by drawing the
string through them. The orange jellies, which had a red dye
stick inside soaked in lye, fell into a series of sunrises and sunsets. The aged yolks and the barley also looked like suns. The
notes gave a Yes strike vote. The yellow flags to ward off the
five evils—centipedes, scorpions, snakes, poisonous lizards,
and toads—now flew as banners.

The strike began on Tuesday morning, June 25, 1867. The
men who were working at that hour walked out of the tunnels
and away from the tracks. The ones who were sleeping slept
on and rose as late as they pleased. They bathed in streams
and shaved their moustaches and wild beards. Some went fishing and hunting. The violinists tuned and played their instruments. The drummers beat theirs at the punchlines of jokes.
The gamblers shuffled and played their cards and tiles. The
smokers passed their pipes, and the drinkers bet for drinks
by making figures with their hands. The cooks made party
food. The opera singers' falsettos almost perforated the mountains. The men sang new songs about the railroad. They made
up verses and shouted Ho at the good ones, and laughed at
the rhymes. Oh, they were madly singing in the mountains.
The storytellers told about the rise of new kings. The opium
smokers when they roused themselves told their florid images.
Ah Goong sifted for gold. All the while the English-speaking
China Men, who were being advised by the shrewdest bargain-
ers, were at the demons' headquarters repeating the demand:
"Eight hours a day good for white man, all the same good for
China Man." They had probably negotiated the demons down
to nine-hour shifts by now.

The sounds of hammering continued along the tracks and
occasionally there were blasts from the tunnels. The scabby

white demons had refused to join the strike. "Eight hours a day good for white man, all the same good for China Man," the China Men explained to them. "Cheap John Chinaman," said the demons, many of whom had red hair. The China Men scowled out of the corners of their eyes.

On the second day, artist demons climbed the mountains to draw the China Men for the newspapers. The men posed bare-chested, their fists clenched, showing off their arms and backs. The artists sketched them as perfect young gods reclining against rocks, wise expressions on their handsome noble-nosed faces, long torsos with lean stomachs, a strong arm extended over a bent knee, long fingers holding a pipe, a rope of hair over a wide shoulder. Other artists drew faeries with antennae for eyebrows and brownies with elvish pigtails; they danced in white socks and black slippers among mushroom rings by moonlight.

Ah Goong acquired another idea that added to his reputation for craziness: The pale, thin Chinese scholars and the rich men fat like Buddhas were less beautiful, less manly than these brown muscular railroad men, of whom he was one. One of ten thousand heroes.

On the third day, in a woods—he would be looking at a deer or a rabbit or an Injun watching him before he knew what he was seeing—a demon dressed in a white suit and tall hat beckoned him. They talked privately in the wilderness. The demon said, "I Citizenship Judge invite you to be U. S. citizen. Only one bag gold." Ah Goong was thrilled. What an honor. He would accept this invitation. Also what advantages, he calculated shrewdly; if he were going to be jailed for this strike, an American would have a trial. The Citizenship Judge unfurled a parchment sealed with gold and ribbon. Ah Goong bought it with one bag of gold. "You vote," said the Citizenship Judge. "You talk in court, buy land, no more chinaman tax." Ah Goong hid the paper on his person so that it would protect him from arrest and lynching. He was already a part of this new country, but now he had it in writing.

The fourth day, the strikers heard that the U. S. Cavalry was riding single file up the tracks to shoot them. They argued whether to engage the Army with dynamite. But the troops did not come. Instead the cowardly demons blockaded the food wagons. No food. Ah Goong listened to the optimistic China Men, who said, "Don't panic. We'll hold out forever. We can hunt. We can last fifty days on water." The complainers said, "Aiya. Only saints can do that. Only magic men and monks who've practiced." The China Men refused to declare a last day for the strike.

The foresighted China Men had cured jerky, fermented wine, dried and strung orange and grapefruit peels, pickled and preserved leftovers. Ah Goong, one of the best hoarders, had set aside extra helpings from each meal. This same quandary, whether to give away food or to appear selfish, had occurred during each of the six famines he had lived through. The foodless men identified themselves. Sure enough, they were the shiftless, piggy, arrogant type who didn't worry enough. The donors scolded them and shamed them the whole while they were handing them food: "So you lived like a grasshopper at our expense." "Fleaman." "You'll be the cause of our not holding out long enough." "Rich man's kid. Too good to hoard." Ah Goong contributed some rice crusts from the bottoms of pans. He kept how much more food he owned a secret, as he kept the secret of his gold. In apology for not contributing richer food, he repeated a Mohist saying that had guided him in China: "'The superior man does not push humaneness to the point of stupidity.'" He could hear his wife scolding him for feeding strangers. The opium men offered shit and said that it calmed the appetite.

On the fifth and sixth days, Ah Goong organized his possessions and patched his clothes and tent. He forebore repairing carts, picks, ropes, baskets. His work-habituated hands arranged rocks and twigs in designs. He asked a reader to read again his family's letters. His wife sounded like herself except for the polite phrases added professionally at the beginnings and the ends. "Idiot," she said, "why are you taking so long? Are you wasting the money? Are you spending it on girls and gambling and whiskey? Here's my advice to you: Be a little more frugal. Remember how it felt to go hungry. Work hard." He had been an idle man for almost a week. "I need a new dress to wear to weddings. I refuse to go to another banquet in the same old dress. If you weren't such a spendthrift, we could be building the new courtyard where we'll drink wine

among the flowers and sit about in silk gowns all day. We'll
hire peasants to till the fields. Or lease them to tenants, and
buy all our food at market. We'll have clean fingernails and
toenails." Other relatives said, "I need a gold watch. Send me
the money. Your wife gambles it away and throws parties and
doesn't disburse it fairly among us. You might as well come
home." It was after one of these letters that he had made a
bonus investigating some dud dynamite.

Ah Goong did not spend his money on women. The strikers
passed the word that a woman was traveling up the railroad
and would be at his camp on the seventh and eighth day of
the strike. Some said she was a demoness and some that she
was a Chinese and her master a China Man. He pictured a
nurse coming to bandage wounds and touch foreheads or a
princess surveying her subjects; or perhaps she was a merciful
Jesus demoness. But she was a pitiful woman, led on a leash
around her waist, not entirely alive. Her owner sold lottery
tickets for the use of her. Ah Goong did not buy one. He took
out his penis under his blanket or bared it in the woods and
thought about nurses and princesses. He also just looked at it,
wondering what it was that it was for, what a man was for, what
he had to have a penis for.

There was rumor also of an Injun woman called Woman
Chief, who led a nomadic fighting tribe from the eastern
plains as far as these mountains. She was so powerful that she
had four wives and many horses. He never saw her though.

The strike ended on the ninth day. The Central Pacific announced that in its benevolence it was giving the workers a
four-dollar raise, not the fourteen dollars they had asked for.
And that the shifts in the tunnels would remain eight hours
long. "We were planning to give you the four-dollar raise all
along," the demons said to diminish the victory. So they got
thirty-five dollars a month and the eight-hour shift. They
would have won forty-five dollars if the thousand demon
workers had joined the strike. Demons would have listened to
demons. The China Men went back to work quietly. No use
singing and shouting over a compromise and losing nine days'
work.

There were two days that Ah Goong did cheer and throw
his hat in the air, jumping up and down and screaming Yippee

like a cowboy. One: the day his team broke through the tunnel
at last. Toward the end they did not dynamite but again used
picks and sledgehammers. Through the granite, they heard
answering poundings, and answers to their shouts. It was not
a mountain before them any more but only a wall with people breaking through from the other side. They worked faster.
Forward. Into day. They stuck their arms through the holes
and shook hands with men on the other side. Ah Goong saw
dirty faces as wondrous as if he were seeing Nu Wo, the creator
goddess who repairs cracks in the sky with stone slabs; sometimes she peeks through and human beings see her face. The
wall broke. Each team gave the other a gift of half a tunnel,
dug. They stepped back and forth where the wall had been.
Ah Goong ran and ran, his boots thudding to the very end of
the tunnel, looked at the other side of the mountain, and ran
back, clear through the entire tunnel. All the way through.

He spent the rest of his time on the railroad laying and
bending and hammering the ties and rails. The second day the
China Men cheered was when the engine from the West and
the one from the East rolled toward one another and touched.
The transcontinental railroad was finished. They Yippee'd
like madmen. The white demon officials gave speeches. "The
Greatest Feat of the Nineteenth Century," they said. "The
Greatest Feat in the History of Mankind," they said. "Only
Americans could have done it," they said, which is true. Even
if Ah Goong had not spent half his gold on Citizenship Papers,
he was an American for having built the railroad. A white demon in top hat tap-tapped on the gold spike, and pulled it
back out. Then one China Man held the real spike, the steel
one, and another hammered it in.

While the demons posed for photographs, the China Men
dispersed. It was dangerous to stay. The Driving Out had
begun. Ah Goong does not appear in railroad photographs.
Scattering, some China Men followed the north star in the
constellation Tortoise the Black Warrior to Canada, or they
kept the constellation Phoenix ahead of them to South America
or the White Tiger west or the Wolf east. Seventy lucky men
rode the Union Pacific to Massachusetts for jobs at a shoe
factory. Fifteen hundred went to Fou Loy Company in New
Orleans and San Francisco, several hundred to plantations in

Mississippi, Georgia, and Arkansas, and sugarcane plantations in Louisiana and Cuba. (From the South, they sent word that it was a custom to step off the sidewalk along with the black demons when a white demon walked by.) Seventy went to New Orleans to grade a route for a railroad, then to Pennsylvania to work in a knife factory. The Colorado State Legislature passed a resolution welcoming the railroad China Men to come build the new state. They built railroads in every part of the country—the Alabama and Chattanooga Railroad, the Houston and Texas Railroad, the Southern Pacific, the railroads in Louisiana and Boston, the Pacific Northwest, and Alaska. After the Civil War, China Men banded the nation North and South, East and West, with crisscrossing steel. They were the binding and building ancestors of this place.

Ah Goong would have liked a leisurely walk along the tracks to review his finished handiwork, or to walk east to see the rest of his new country. But instead, Driven Out, he slid down mountains, leapt across valleys and streams, crossed plains, hid sometimes with companions and often alone, and eluded bandits who would hold him up for his railroad pay and shoot him for practice as they shot Injuns and jackrabbits. Detouring and backtracking, his path wound back and forth to his railroad, a familiar silver road in the wilderness. When a train came, he hid against the shaking ground in case a demon with a shotgun was hunting from it. He picked over camps where he had once lived. He was careful to find hidden places to sleep. In China bandits did not normally kill people, the booty the main thing, but here the demons killed for fun and hate. They tied pigtails to horses and dragged chinamen. He decided that he had better head for San Francisco, where he would catch a ship to China.

Perched on hillsides, he watched many sunsets, the place it was setting, the direction he was going. There were fields of grass that he tunneled through, hid in, rolled in, dived and swam in, suddenly jumped up laughing, suddenly stopped. He needed to find a town and human company. The spooky tumbleweeds caught in barbed wire were peering at him, waiting for him; he had to find a town. Towns grew along the tracks as they did along rivers. He sat looking at a town all day, then ducked into it by night.

At the familiar sight of a garden laid out in a Chinese scheme—vegetables in beds, white cabbages, red plants, chives, and coriander for immortality, herbs boxed with boards—he knocked on the back door. The China Man who answered gave him food, the appropriate food for the nearest holiday, talked story, exclaimed at how close their ancestral villages were to each other. They exchanged information on how many others lived how near, which towns had Chinatowns, what size, two or three stores or a block, which towns to avoid. "Do you have a wife?" they asked one another. "Yes. She lives in China. I have been sending money for twenty years now." They exchanged vegetable seeds, slips, and cuttings, and Ah Goong carried letters to another town or China.

Some demons who had never seen the likes of him gave him things and touched him. He also came across lone China Men who were alarmed to have him appear, and, unwelcome, he left quickly; they must have wanted to be the only China Man of that area, the special China Man.

He met miraculous China Men who had produced families out of nowhere—a wife and children, both boys and girls. "Uncle," the children called him, and he wanted to stay to be the uncle of the family. The wife washed his clothes, and he went on his way when they were dry.

On a farm road, he came across an imp child playing in the dirt. It looked at him, and he looked at it. He held out a piece of sugar; he cupped a grassblade between his thumbs and whistled. He sat on the ground with his legs crossed, and the child climbed into the hollow of his arms and legs. "I wish you were my baby," he told it. "My baby." He was very satisfied sitting there under the humming sun with the baby, who was satisfied too, no squirming. "My daughter," he said. "My son." He couldn't tell whether it was a boy or a girl. He touched the baby's fat arm and cheeks, its gold hair, and looked into its blue eyes. He made a wish that it not have to carry a sledgehammer and crawl into the dark. But he would not feel sorry for it; other people must not suffer any more than he did, and he could endure anything. Its mother came walking out into the road. She had her hands above her like a salute. She walked tentatively toward them, held out her hand, smiled, spoke. He did not understand what she said except

"Bye-bye." The child waved and said, "Bye-bye," crawled over his legs, and toddled to her. Ah Goong continued on his way in a direction she could not point out to a posse looking for a kidnapper chinaman.

Explosions followed him. He heard screams and went on, saw flames outlining black windows and doors, and went on. He ran in the opposite direction from gunshots and the yell—*eeha awha*—the cowboys made when they herded cattle and sang their savage songs.

Good at hiding, disappearing—decades unaccounted for—he was not working in a mine when forty thousand chinamen were Driven Out of mining. He was not killed or kidnapped in the Los Angeles Massacre, though he gave money toward ransoming those whose toes and fingers, a digit per week, and ears grotesquely rotting or pickled, and scalped queues, were displayed in Chinatowns. Demons believed that the poorer a chinaman looked, the more gold he had buried somewhere, that chinamen stuck together and would always ransom one another. If he got kidnapped, Ah Goong planned, he would whip out his Citizenship Paper and show that he was an American. He was lucky not to be in Colorado when the Denver demons burned all chinamen homes and businesses, nor in Rock Springs, Wyoming, when the miner demons killed twenty-eight or fifty chinamen. The Rock Springs Massacre began in a large coal mine owned by the Union Pacific; the outnumbered chinamen were shot in the back as they ran to Chinatown, which the demons burned. They forced chinamen out into the open and shot them; demon women and children threw the wounded back in the flames. (There was a rumor of a good white lady in Green Springs who hid China Men in the Pacific Hotel and shamed the demons away.) The hunt went on for a month before federal troops came. The count of the dead was inexact because bodies were mutilated and pieces scattered all over the Wyoming Territory. No white miners were indicted, but the government paid $150,000 in reparations to victims' families. There were many family men, then. There were settlers—abiding China Men. And China Women. Ah Goong was running elsewhere during the Drivings Out of Tacoma, Seattle, Oregon City, Albania, and Marysville. The demons of Tacoma packed all its chinamen into boxcars and sent them to Portland, where they were run out of town. China Men returned to Seattle, though, and refused to sell their land and stores but fought until the army came; the demon rioters were tried and acquitted. And when the Boston police imprisoned and beat 234 chinamen, it was 1902, and Ah Goong had already reached San Francisco or China, and perhaps San Francisco again.

In Second City (Sacramento), he spent some of his railroad money at the theater. The main actor's face was painted red with thick black eyebrows and long black beard, and when he strode onto the stage, Ah Goong recognized the hero, Guan Goong; his puppet horse had red nostrils and rolling eyes. Ah Goong's heart leapt to recognize hero and horse in the wilds of America. Guan Goong murdered his enemy—crash! bang! of cymbals and drum—and left his home village—sad, sad flute music. But to the glad clamor of cymbals entered his friends—Liu Pei (pronounced the same as Running Nose) and Chang Fei. In a joyful burst of pink flowers, the three men swore the Peach Garden Oath. Each friend sang an aria to friendship; together they would fight side by side and live and die one for all and all for one. Ah Goong felt as warm as if he were with friends at a party. Then Guan Goong's archenemy, the sly Ts'ao Ts'ao, captured him and two of Liu Pei's wives, the Lady Kan and the Lady Mi. Though Ah Goong knew they were boy actors, he basked in the presence of Chinese ladies. The prisoners traveled to the capital, the soldiers waving horsehair whisks, signifying horses, the ladies walking between horizontal banners, signifying palanquins. All the prisoners were put in one bedroom, but Guan Goong stood all night outside the door with a lighted candle in his hand, singing an aria about faithfulness. When the capital was attacked by a common enemy, Guan Goong fought the biggest man in one-to-one combat, a twirling, jumping sword dance that strengthened the China Men who watched it. From afar Guan Goong's two partners heard about the feats of the man with the red face and intelligent horse. The three friends were reunited and fought until they secured their rightful kingdom.

Ah Goong felt refreshed and inspired. He called out Bravo like the demons in the audience, who had not seen theater before. Guan Goong, the God of War, also God of War and

Literature, had come to America—Guan Goong, Grandfather Guan, our own ancestor of writers and fighters, of actors and gamblers, and avenging executioners who mete out justice. Our own kin. Not a distant ancestor but Grandfather.

In the Big City (San Francisco), a goldsmith convinced Ah Goong to have his gold made into jewelry, which would organize it into one piece and also delight his wife. So he handed over a second bag of gold. He got it back as a small ring in a design he thought up himself, two hands clasping in a handshake. "So small?" he said, but the goldsmith said that only some of the ore had been true gold.

He got a ship out of San Francisco without being captured near the docks, where there was a stockade full of jailed chinamen; the demonesses came down from Nob Hill and took them home to be servants, cooks, and baby-sitters.

Grandmother liked the gold ring very much. The gold was so pure, it squished to fit her finger. She never washed dishes, so the gold did not wear away. She quickly spent the railroad money, and Ah Goong said he would go to America again. He had a Certificate of Return and his Citizenship Paper.

But this time, there was no railroad to sell his strength to. He lived in a basement that was rumored to connect with tunnels beneath Chinatown. In an underground arsenal, he held a pistol and said, "I feel the death in it." "The holes for the bullets were like chambers in a beehive or wasp nest," he said. He was inside the earth when the San Francisco Earthquake and Fire began. Thunder rumbled from the ground. Some say he died falling into the cracking earth. It was a miraculous earthquake and fire. The Hall of Records burned completely. Citizenship Papers burned, Certificates of Return, Birth Certificates, Residency Certificates, passenger lists, Marriage Certificates—every paper a China Man wanted for citizenship and legality burned in that fire. An authentic citizen, then, had no more papers than an alien. Any paper a China Man could not produce had been "burned up in the Fire of 1906." Every China Man was reborn out of that fire a citizen.

Some say the family went into debt to send for Ah Goong, who was not making money; he was a homeless wanderer, a shiftless, dirty, jobless man with matted hair, ragged clothes, and fleas all over his body. He ate out of garbage cans. He was

a louse eaten by lice. A fleaman. It cost two thousand dollars
to bring him back to China, his oldest sons signing promissory
notes for one thousand, his youngest to repay four hundred to
one neighbor and six hundred to another. Maybe he hadn't
died in San Francisco, it was just his papers that burned; it
was just that his existence was outlawed by Chinese Exclusion
Acts. The family called him Fleaman. They did not understand his accomplishments as an American ancestor, a holding,
homing ancestor of this place. He'd gotten the legal or illegal
papers burned in the San Francisco Earthquake and Fire; he
appeared in America in time to be a citizen and to father citizens. He had also been seen carrying a child out of the fire, a
child of his own in spite of the laws against marrying. He had
built a railroad out of sweat, why not have an American child
out of longing?

The Laws

The United States of America and the Emperor of China cordially recognize the inherent and inalienable right of man to change his home and allegiance, and also the mutual advantage of the free migration and emigration of their citizens and subjects respectively from the one country to the other for purposes of curiosity, of trade, or as permanent residents. ARTICLE V OF THE BURLINGAME TREATY, SIGNED IN WASHINGTON, D. C., JULY 28, 1868, AND IN PEKING, NOVEMBER 23, 1869

The First Years: 1868, the year of the Burlingame Treaty, was the year 40,000 miners of Chinese ancestry were Driven Out. The Fourteenth Amendment, adopted in that same year, said that naturalized Americans have the same rights as native-born Americans, but in 1870 the Nationality Act specified that only "free whites" and "African aliens" were allowed to apply for naturalization. Chinese were not white; this had been established legally in 1854 when Chan Young unsuccessfully applied for citizenship in Federal District Court in San Francisco and was turned down on grounds of race. (He would have been illegal one way or another anyway; the Emperor of China did not give permission for any of his subjects to leave China until 1859.) Debating the Nationality Act, Congressmen declared that America would be a nation of "Nordic fiber."

1878: California held a Constitutional Convention to settle "the Chinese problem." Of the 152 delegates, 35 were not American citizens but Europeans. The resulting constitution, voted into existence by a majority party of Working Men and Grangers, prohibited Chinese from entering California. New state laws empowered cities and counties to confine them within specified areas or to throw them out completely. Shipowners and captains were to be fined and jailed for hiring or transporting them. (This provision was so little respected that the American merchant marine relied heavily on Chinese seamen from the

Civil War years to World War I.) "Mongolians, Indians, and Negroes" were barred from attending public schools. The only California fishermen forced to pay fishing and shellfish taxes were the Chinese, who had brought shrimp nets from China and started the shrimp, abalone, and lobster industries. (The taxes were payable monthly.) Those Chinese over eighteen who were not already paying a miner's tax had to pay a "police tax," to cover the extra policing their presence required. Though the Chinese were filling and leveeing the San Joaquin Delta for thirteen cents a square yard, building the richest agricultural land in the world, they were prohibited from owning land or real estate. They could not apply for business licenses. Employers could be fined and jailed for hiring them. No Chinese could be hired by state, county, or municipal governments for public works. No "Chinese or Mongolian or Indian" could testify in court "either for or against a white man."

At this time San Francisco supplemented the anti-Chinese state laws with some of its own: a queue tax, a "cubic air ordinance" requiring that every residence have so many cubic feet of air per inhabitant, a pole law prohibiting the use of carrying baskets on poles, cigar taxes, shoe taxes, and laundry taxes.

Federal courts declared some of the state and city laws unconstitutional, and occasionally citizens of a county or city repealed an especially punitive ordinance on the grounds that it was wrong to invite the Chinese to come to the United States and then deny them a livelihood. The repealed laws were often reenacted in another form.

1880: The Burlingame Treaty was modified. Instead of being free, the immigration of Chinese laborers to the United States would be "reasonably limited." In return (so as not to bring about limits on American entry into China), the American government promised to protect Chinese from lynchings.

1881: The Burlingame Treaty was suspended for a period of twenty years. (Since 1881 there has been no freedom of travel between China and the United States.) In protest against this suspension and against the refusal to admit Chinese boys to U. S. Army and Naval academies, China ordered scholars studying in the United States to return home. The act suspending the treaty did have two favorable provisions: all Chinese already resident in the United States in 1882 could stay; and they were permitted to leave and reenter with a Certificate of Return.

1882: Encouraged by fanatical lobbying from California, the U. S. Congress passed the first Chinese Exclusion Act. It banned the entrance of Chinese laborers, both skilled and un-skilled, for ten years. Anyone unqualified for citizenship could not come in—and by the terms of the Nationality Act of 1870, Chinese were not qualified for citizenship. Some merchants and scholars were granted temporary visas.

1884: Congress refined the Exclusion Act with An Act to Amend an Act. This raised fines and sentences and further defined "merchants" to exclude "hucksters, peddlers, or those engaged in taking, draying, or otherwise preserving shell or other fish for home consumption or exportation."

1888: The Scott Act, passed by Congress, again forbade the entry of Chinese laborers. It also declared that Certificates of Return were void. Twenty thousand Chinese were trapped outside the United States with now-useless re-entry permits. Six hundred returning travelers were turned back at American ports. A Chinese ambassador, humiliated by immigration officers, killed himself. The law decreed that Certificates of Residence had to be shown on demand; any Chinese caught without one was deported.

1889: Chinese pooled money to fight the various Exclusion Acts in the courts. They rarely won. In *Chae Chan Ping v. The United States*, Chae Chan Ping argued for the validity of his Certificate of Return. The Supreme Court ruled against him, saying that "regardless of the existence of a prior treaty," a race "that will not assimilate with us" could be excluded when deemed "dangerous to . . . peace and security. . . . It matters not in what form aggression and encroachment come, whether from the foreign nation acting in its national character or from vast hordes of its people crowding in upon us." Moreover, said the Court, "sojourners" should not "claim surprise" that any Certificates of Return obtained prior to 1882 were "held at the will of the government, revocable at any time, at its pleasure."

1892: The Geary Act extended the 1882 Exclusion Act for another ten years. It also decreed that Chinese caught illegally in the United States be deported after one year of hard labor.

Chinese Americans formed the Equal Rights League and

the Native Sons of the Golden State in order to fight disen-
franchisement bills. Chinese Americans demanded the right to
have their citizenship confirmed before traveling abroad.

1893: In *Yue Ting v. The United States*, the U. S. Supreme
Court ruled that Congress had the right to expel members of a
race who "continue to be aliens, having taken no steps toward
becoming citizens, and incapable of becoming such under the
naturalization laws." This applied only to Chinese; no other
race or nationality was excluded from applying for citizenship.

1896: A victory. In *Yick Wo v. Hopkins*, the U. S. Supreme
Court overturned San Francisco safety ordinances, saying that
they were indeed designed to harass laundrymen of Chinese
ancestry.

1898: Another victory. The Supreme Court decision in *The
United States v. Wong Kim Ark* stated that a person born in
the United States to Chinese parents is an American. This decision has never been reversed or changed, and it is the law on
which most Americans of Chinese ancestry base their citizenship today.

1900: Deciding *The United States v. Mrs. Cue Lim*, the
Supreme Court ruled that wives and children of treaty merchants—citizens of China, aliens traveling on visas—were allowed to come to the United States.

1904: The Chinese Exclusion Acts were extended indefinitely,
and made to cover Hawai'i and the Philippines as well as the
continental United States. The question of exclusion was not
debated in Congress; instead, the measure passed as a rider
on a routine appropriations bill. China boycotted American
goods in protest.

1906: The San Francisco Board of Education ordered that
all Chinese, Japanese, and Korean children be segregated in
an Oriental school. President Roosevelt, responding to a protest from the Japanese government, persuaded the Board of
Education to allow Japanese to attend white schools.

1917: Congress voted that immigrants over sixteen years of
age be required to pass an English reading test.

1924: An Immigration Act passed by Congress specifically
excluded "Chinese women, wives, and prostitutes." Any
American who married a Chinese woman lost his citizenship;
any Chinese man who married an American woman caused her

to lose her citizenship. Many states had also instituted antimis-cegenation laws. A Supreme Court case called *Chang Chan et al. v. John D. Nagle* tested the law against wives; Chang Chan et al. lost. For the first time, the 1924 Immigration Act distinguished between two kinds of "aliens": "immigrants" were admitted as permanent residents with the opportunity to become citizens eventually; the rest—scholars, merchants, ministers, and tourists—were admitted on a temporary basis and were not eligible for citizenship. The number of persons allowed in the category of immigrant was set by law at one-sixth of one percent of the total population of that ancestry in the United States as of the 1920 census. The 1920 census had the lowest count of ethnic Chinese in this country since 1860. As a result, only 105 Chinese immigrants were permitted each year.

In *Cheuno Sumchee v. Nagle*, the Supreme Court once again confirmed the right of treaty merchants to bring their wives to the United States. This was a right that continued to be denied to Chinese Americans.

1938: A Presidential proclamation lifted restriction on immigration for Chinese and nationals of a few other Asian countries. The Chinese were still ineligible for citizenship, and the quota was "100."

1943: The United States and China signed a treaty of alliance against the Japanese, and Congress repealed the Exclusion Act of 1882. Immigration continued to be limited to the 1924 quota of 105, however, and the Immigration and Nationalization Service claimed to be unable to find even that many qualified Chinese. A "Chinese" was defined as anyone with more than 50 percent Chinese blood, regardless of citizenship or country of residence. At this time Japanese invaders were killing Chinese civilians in vast numbers; it is estimated that more than 10 million died. Chinese immigration into the United States did not rise.

1946: Congress passed the War Bride Act, enabling soldiers to bring Japanese and European wives home, then enacted a separate law allowing the wives and children of Chinese Americans to apply for entry as "non-quota immigrants." Only now did the ethnic Chinese population in the United States begin to approach the level of seventy years previous. (When the first Exclusion Act was passed in 1882, there were some 107,000 Chinese here; the Acts and the Driving Out steadily reduced the number to fewer than 70,000 in the 1920s.)

1948: The Refugee Act passed by Congress this year applied only to Europeans. A separate Displaced Persons Act provided that for a limited time—1948 to 1954—ethnic Chinese already living in the United States could apply for citizenship. During the postwar period, about 10,000 Chinese were permitted to enter the country under individual private bills passed by Congress. Confidence men, like the Citizenship Judges of old, defrauded hopeful Chinese by promising to acquire one of these bills for $1,500.

1950: After the Chinese Communist government took over in 1949, the United States passed a series of Refugee Relief Acts and a Refugee Escapee Act expanding the number of "non-quota immigrants" allowed in. As a condition of entry, the Internal Security Act provided that these refugees swear they were not Communists. (Several hundred "subversives or anarchists" of various races were subsequently deported; some were naturalized citizens who were "denaturalized" beforehand.)

1952: The Immigration and Nationality Act denied admission to "subversive and undesirable aliens" and made it simpler to deport "those already in the country." Another provision of this act was that for the first time Chinese women were allowed to immigrate under the same conditions as men.

1954: Ruling on *Mao v. Brownell*, the Supreme Court upheld laws forbidding Chinese Americans to send money to relatives in China. Before the Communist Revolution, there were no such restrictions in effect; Chinese Americans sent $70 million during World War II. Nor could they send money or gifts through CARE, UNESCO, or church organizations, which provided only for non-Communist countries.

1957: The Refugee Relief Act of 1953 expired in 1956 and was followed by the Act of 1957, which provided for the distribution of 18,000 visas that had remained unused.

1959: Close relatives, including parents, were allowed to enter.

1960: A "Fair Share Refugee Act" allowed certain refugees from Communist and Middle Eastern countries to enter. Close to 20,000 people who were "persecuted because of race, religion, or political beliefs" immigrated before this act was repealed in 1965, when a new act allowed the conditional entry of 10,200 refugees annually.

1962: A Presidential directive allowed several thousand "parolees" to enter the United States from Hong Kong. Relatives of citizens and resident aliens were eligible. President Kennedy gave Congress a special message on immigration, saying, "It is time to correct the mistakes of the past."

1965: A new Immigration and Nationality Act changed the old quota system so that "national origin" no longer means "race" but "country of birth." Instead of being based on a percentage of existing ethnic populations in the United States, quotas were reallocated to countries—20,000 each. But this did not mean that 20,000 Chinese immediately could or did come to the United States. Most prospective immigrants were in Hong Kong, a British colony. Colonies received 1 percent of the mother country's allotment: only 200. "Immediate relatives," the children, spouses, and parents of citizens, however, could enter without numerical limitations. Also not reckoned within the quota limitations were legal residents returning from a visit abroad.

1968: Amendments to the Immigration and Nationality Act provided that immigrants not be allocated by race or nation but by hemispheres, with 120,000 permitted to enter from the Western Hemisphere and 170,000 from the Eastern Hemisphere. This act limits immigration from the Western Hemisphere for the first time in history. The 20,000-per-country quota remained in effect for the Eastern Hemisphere, no per-country limitation for the Western Hemisphere.

1976: The Immigration and Nationality Act Amendments, also called the Western Hemisphere Bill, equalized the provisions of law regulating immigration from the two hemispheres. The House Committee on the Judiciary in its report on this legislation stated, "This constitutes an essential first step in a projected long-term reform of U. S. Immigration law." The 20,000-per-country limit was extended to the Western Hemisphere. The limitation on colonies was raised from 200 to 600.

1978: The separate quotas for the two hemispheres were replaced by a worldwide numerical limitation on immigration of

290,000 annually. On the basis of the "immediate relatives" clause, about 22,000 Chinese enter legally each year, and the rate is increasing. There are also special quotas in effect for Southeast Asian refugees, most of whom are of Chinese ancestry. In the last decade, the ethnic Chinese population of the United States has doubled. The 1980 census may show a million or more.

Alaska China Men

THE CHINA MAN also went to Alaska to strike-it-rich in gold mining. At the top of the world, people wrote in their diaries for entertainment; they recorded the weather and described their health, their daily farming, hunting, and cooking, and the executions they witnessed. Many of them wrote about seeing an old Indian put to death in the middle of a public street: The tribe feasted and drank whiskey. Then while they drummed on walrus hide, the old father calmly brought out a walrus hide thong. A son or a brother came from behind him, noosed his throat, pushed a foot against his back, and broke his neck. There was also a stoning of an Indian woman in Juneau.

The strongest court of law was the miners' meetings, and the code of self-defense was the miners' law. Citizenship was cheaper in Alaska; the Citizenship Judge, who followed the prospectors, only asked for a pinch of gold dust. The white miners voted in 1885 that the chinamen be shipped out for fighting with the Indian miners. Posters and newspapers announced that on a certain day in July, chinamen were to report to the waterfront on Douglas Island. Diaries glowed with the weather: "It was a beautiful sight, and one of the few days when the channel was smooth the day it was done." (Beauty was different in those days, the foliage along the edges of Douglas Island was dead because of the sulphur from the gold mills. After the ore was pounded a hundred and twenty times by nine-hundred-pound pistons, the gold was broken free, and the sulphur was slagged onto the land and into the channel.) Demons came from miles around to see the Driving Out done. There were no fights. The whites stood on the shore with guns and tools; the Indians in their colors paddled fifty war canoes into the channel and rowed away "the entire Chinese population" of one hundred. In Juneau they were put on a schooner to Puget Sound, where they were released.

The area was rid of chinamen except for China Joe, who was a baker in Juneau. He had saved the miners in the Cassiar

335

District from starvation and bad winters by giving bread away. He had opened his stores to everyone. "He was the most loved person in Alaska," a diarist wrote. When he died, Juneau held the largest funeral Alaska had ever seen.

As soon as they touched shore in Puget Sound, the China Men found ways to return and take back their mines, jobs, houses, and girl friends.

So the next year, there had to be another shipping out (unless it only happened once with two versions of the same event and the dates mixed up). This time the white miners went on strike against the Treadwell Mining Company, and ninety Chinese scabs took their jobs. Treadwell blackballed the strikers, who hired rustlers, claim jumpers, trap looters, to get rid of the chinamen. One of these rowdies or bummers wrote in his diary: "The citizens of Juneau did not approve of the mining company's employing them and appealed to us to aid them in getting rid of the orientals which we did in the month of July." The China Men asked Treadwell for guns to defend themselves, but the mining company refused to arm them. Some citizens wrote to the governor to send help: "They are commencing the dynamiting business against the Chinese." The governor himself came. But one day in July 1886, the demons walked the chinamen at gunpoint to the harbor, no Indians with war canoes this time. They were forced to board an old ship, and the ship was set adrift at sea. Some say there were two old schooners. There was no food or water, and the hundred China Men were so crowded together, they could not lie down. After eight days at sea, they steered the ship to Wrangel, a hundred and fifty miles south of Douglas Island. A white man named Captain Carroll gave them water and food and berths on his ship, the *Ancon*. He offered to sail them home, and they said, Yes, they would take him up on that. "Take us home," said the sourdough China Men, "to Douglas Island."

The only China Man not set adrift was China Joe, who owned a laundry and a big garden. He had provided vegetables during the bad winters. As French Pete was probably the name of more than one man, as were Dutch John and Missouri Frank and Arkansas Jim and French Charley, Dago Joe, and Indian Joe—one of the Citizenship Judges himself was named French Pete—perhaps any China Man was China Joe.

THE MAKING OF
MORE AMERICANS

To visit grandfathers, we walked over three sets of railroad tracks, then on sidewalks cracked by grass and tree roots, then a gray dirt path. The roadside weeds waved tall overhead, netting the sunlight and wildflowers. I wore important white shoes for walking to the grandfathers' house.

The black dirt in their yard set off my dazzling shoes—two chunks of white light that encased my feet. "Look. Look," said Say Goong, Fourth Grandfather, my railroad grandfather's youngest brother. "A field chicken." It was not a chicken at all but a toad with alert round eyes that looked out from under the white cabbage leaves. It hopped ahead of my shoes, dived into the leaves, and disappeared, reappeared, maybe another toad. It was a clod that had detached itself from the living earth; the earth had formed into a toad and hopped. "A field chicken," said Say Goong. He cupped his hands, walked quietly with wide steps and caught it. On his brown hand sat a toad with perfect haunches, eyelids, veins, and wrinkles—the details of it, the neatness and completeness of it swallowing and blinking. "A field chicken?" I repeated. "Field chicken," he said. "Sky chicken. Sky toad. Heavenly toad. Field toad." It was a pun and the words the same except for the low tone of *field* and the high tone of *heaven* or *sky*. He put the toad in my hands—it breathed, and its heart beat, every part of it alive— and I felt its dryness and warmth and hind feet as it sprang off. How odd that a toad could be both of the field and of the sky. It was very funny. Say Goong and I laughed. "Heavenly chicken," I called, chasing the toad. I carefully ran between the rows of vegetables, where many toads, giants and miniatures, hopped everywhere. Which one was the toad in my hand? Then suddenly they were all gone. But they clucked. So it isn't that toads look or taste like chickens that they're called chickens; they cluck alike! Dragonflies held still in the air, suddenly darted. Butterflies in pairs flew far away from their partners, then together again. I stepped into a green hallway in the corn and sat in a teepee grown of vines over lattices; from ceilings and walls hung gourds, beans, tomatoes, grapes, and peas, winter melons like fat green prickly piglets, and bitter melons like green mice with tails. But the real marvel was the black dirt, which was clean and not dirty at all.

In one corner of the yard was a pile of horse manure taller than an adult human being. "Aiya! Aiya!" our parents, grandfathers, and neighbors exclaimed, eyes open in wonder as they stood around the pile, neighbors and friends invited especially to view it. "Come here! Come look. Oh, just look at it!"—I could tell that the adults felt what I felt, that I did not feel it alone, but truly. This pile hummed, and it was the fuel for the ground, the toads, the vegetables, the house, the two grandfathers. The flies, which were green and turquoise-black and silvery blue, swirling into various lights, hummed too, like excess sparks. The grandfathers boxed the horse manure, presents for us and their good friends to take home. They also bagged it in burlap. It smelled good.

Say Goong took my hand and led me to a cavernous shed black from the sun in my eyes. He pointed into the dark, which dark seemed solid and alive, heavy, moving, breathing. There were waves of dark skin over a hot and massive something that was snorting and stomping—the living night. In the day, here was where the night lived. Say Goong pointed up at a wide brown eye as high as the roof. I was ready to be terrified but for his delight. "Horse," he said. "Horse." He contained the thing in a word—*horse*, magical and earthly sound. A horse was a black creature so immense I could not see the outlines. Grasping Say Goong's finger, I dared to walk past the horse, and then he pointed again, "Horse." There was a partition, and on the other side of it—another horse. There were two such enormities in the world. Again and again I looked inside the stalls to solve the mystery of what a horse was. On the outside of the shed was horse shit, on the inside, the source of horse shit.

What I could see in its entirety because inanimate was the vegetable wagon, which was really a stagecoach. I climbed up a wheel and into the seat. I opened the compartments, drawers, and many screened doors. A scale hung in back, and in front were reins and two long prongs.

When I heard hooves clippity-clopping down our street, I ran to the upstairs window and saw two grandfathers and the two horses, which were contained between the prongs. They had blinders cupping their eyes. I had discovered the daily shape of horses. My mother opened the window, and she and I made up a song about grandfathers and horses; we sang it to them in the interplaying rhythm of hooves on the street:

> *Third Grandfather and Fourth Grandfather,*
> *Where are you going?*
> *Hooves clippity-clopping*
>   *four by four,*
> *Where are you going?*

"We're going to the north side to sell lettuce," they said. Or, the horses facing another direction, "We're going to the feed store," or "We're going home." "We're going on our route of demonesses." The grandfathers could understand demon talk; they told us how the demonesses praised the tomatoes all the same size. "Allee sem," said the demonesses.

Sometimes under our very windows, the grandfathers fitted nosebags of oats over the horses' muzzles. The water for the horses had run into two buckets from a block of ice that sat melting in the middle of the wagon. The grandfathers sprinkled the vegetables with a watering can while the horses drank. Neighbors who had waited until late in the day for bargains circled the wagon. Through the screens they looked shrewdly at the red, yellow, and green vegetables. The god with the gourd had a gourd like the ones the grandfathers sold. At New Year's, tangerines hung by the branch from the roof, and in the fall, persimmons. In summer the grandfathers sold watermelons, which grew in China too, only there the meat was light pink and nobody we knew had ever tasted it. A railing along the top of the stagecoach kept the sacks of potatoes and yams from rolling off. Our family got what remained for free.

One time I went to the shed to have a look at the horses, and they were gone. "Where are the horses?" I asked. "They're gone," said both my parents with no surprise or emphasis. Not satisfied with the answer, I asked them again and again. Such vastness could not possibly have disappeared so completely. But they said, "They've been gone a long time." I walked inside each bare stall. "Where are the horses? Where are they?" No more horses. "What happened to them?" "They've been gone for a long time." No explanation. Did they trot away down the street without the stagecoach and the grandfathers? Time must have gone by, then, since I'd last come to visit them, though the visits seemed like the same time, no time at all, time just one time, but it must have been later, a last time. I looked inside the first stall, looked again in the other one but found no aliveness there, bright now and not dark with horses. I could see boards and into corners, no vestige of horses, no hay spilling over the troughs, not a single yellow straw sticking out of a crack, floor not covered with straw and horse shit, everything swept clean. Manure pile gone. I have looked for proof of horses, and found it in the family album, which has photographs of horses with blinders, though the men standing in front of the wagons are not the grandfathers but the uncles, the same ones who later had their pictures taken with cars and trucks.

The stagecoach was still there. I sat in the seat, shook the reins, and looked in the distance for Indians and bisons.

One day Sahm Goong, Third Grandfather, came to our house alone, and he said to my mother, "Say Goong is standing in the stable."

"No," said my mother. "He's dead."

"He's in the stable. I saw him. I left him there just now, standing by the wall near the door."

"What was he doing?"

"Just standing there. Not working."

"You know he's dead, don't you?"

"Yes. It must be his ghost standing there. He comes to visit me every day."

"What does he have to say?" she asked.

"Nothing. I talk to him, but he doesn't answer."

"You tell him to go home," said my mother. "Scold him. 'Go home!' Loud. Like that. 'Go home, Say Goong!'" They both called him that even though he was my fourth grandfather and not theirs.

Sahm Goong walked back home. He sat on a crate in the empty stable, the gray floorboards awash with afternoon sun. There in the shade beside the door stood his brother.

"How nice of you to visit me again," said Sahm Goong.

Say Goong did not reply. He was wearing his good clothes,

his new bib overalls, a white shirt, a tie, his cardigan, and his cloth cap, which he had worn when working in the yard or driving the stagecoach. His fine white hair caught the light like a halo.

"Sit down," invited Sahm Goong, but his brother did not want to. He certainly could not be seen through, and he was not floating; he had his feet on the floor. The high work shoes were polished.

Third Grandfather stood up and walked over to Fourth Grandfather, the two of them the same size. They did not touch each other. "I am very well, you know," the live grandfather said. "My health is good. Yes, the rest of the family is fine too. Though there are a lot of girls. We're all well." Say Goong did not say a thing. Sahm Goong walked sideways and examined him in profile; he certainly looked as usual. Then Sahm Goong sat down again, looking a moment into the garden. When he looked back, his brother was still there, no shimmering, no wavering, just as solid and real as ever before. The two brothers stayed with each other until suppertime. Then Sahm Goong went in the house to cook and eat.

After dinner he took his flashlight and went again into the shed. He shone it into the place where the ghost had been. He was still there. He turned off the flashlight so as not to glare it in his face and sat in the dark with his brother. When he felt sleepy, he said, "Good night," and went back up to bed.

The next morning, he ate breakfast, then watered the yard, left the hose trickling. He went into the stable and did not see his brother, but the next time he checked, there he was again. Again he sat with him for a while. Then he got up and looked into the familiar old face. They were alike, two wispy old men, two wispy old brothers.

"Do you need to say something to me?" Sahm Goong asked.

The ghost did not answer.

"You don't have something to tell me then? No message?" Sahm Goong paced about. "What are you doing here?" he asked. "What do you want? You don't have something to tell me? No message? Why are you here?" He waited for a reply. "What do you want?"

But Say Goong's ghost said nothing.

"It's time to go home, then," said Sahm Goong. He said it

louder. "Go home! It's time for you to go home now. What's the use of staying here any more? You don't belong here. There's nothing for you to do here. Go home. Go back to China. Go."

There did seem to be a flickering then. All was still, no sound of bird or toad, no aroused insect, only the humming that could have been the new refrigerator. "Go home," Sahm Goong said sternly. "Go back to China. Go now. To China." His voice was loud in the bare shed.

Say Goong disappeared, as if the vehement voice had filled the space he had been using. He had been startled away, reminded of something. He did not come back again. Later Sahm Goong couldn't say whether he had been looking directly at his brother at the moment of disappearance. He might have looked aside for a second, and when he looked again, Say Goong was gone. A slant of light still came in at the door.

Then Third Grandfather too disappeared, perhaps going back to China, perhaps dead here like his brother. When their descendants came across the country to visit us, we took them to the place where two of our four grandfathers had had their house, stable, and garden. My father pointed out where each thing had stood, "They had two horses, which lived in a stable here. Their house stood over there." The aunts and uncles exclaimed, "Their horses were here, then," and said it again in English to their children. "And their house over there." They took pictures with a delayed-shutter camera, everyone standing together where the house had been. The relatives kept saying, "This is the ancestral ground," their eyes filling with tears over a vacant lot in Stockton.

Third Grandfather had a grandson whom we called Sao Elder Brother to his face, but for a while behind his back, Mad Sao, which rhymes in our dialect. Sao firmly established his American citizenship by serving in the U. S. Army in World War II, then sent for a wife from China. We were amazed at how lovely and kind she was even though picked sight unseen. The new couple, young and modern (*mo-dang*), bought a ranch house and car, wore fashionable clothes, spoke English, and seemed more American than us.

But Sao's mother sent him letters to come home to China.

"I'm growing old," she said or the letter writer said. "If you don't come home now you'll never see me again. I remember you, my baby. Don't wait until you're old before coming back. I can't bear seeing you old like me." She did not know how American he had looked in his army uniform. "All you're doing is having fun, aren't you?" she asked. "You're spending all the money, aren't you? This is your own mother who rocked you to sleep and took care of you when you were sick. Do you remember your mother's face? We used to pretend our rocker was a boat like a peapod, and we were peas at sea. Remember? Remember? But now you send paper boats into my dreams. Sail back to me." But he was having his own American babies yearly, three girls and a boy. "Who will bury me if you don't come back?" his mother asked.

And if she wasn't nagging him to return, she was asking for money. When he sent photographs of the family with the car in the background, she scolded him: "What are you doing feeding these girls and not your mother? What is this car, and this radio? A new house. Why are you building a new house in America? You have a house here. Sell everything. Sell the girls, and mail the profits to Mother. Use the money for ship fare. Why are you spending money on photographs of girls? Send me the money you give the photographers so I can send you *my* picture, the face you've forgotten." She did not know that he owned his own camera. His family was one of the first to own a shower, a lawn, a carport, and a car for passengers rather than for hauling.

"You're doing everything backward," his mother wrote. "I'm starving to death. In the enclosed picture, you can see my bones poking through the skin. You must be turning into a demon to treat a mother so. I have suffered all my life; I need to rest now. I'll die happy if you come home. Why don't you do your duty? I order you to come back. It's all those daughters, isn't it? They've turned your head. Leave them. Come back alone. You don't need to save enough money to bring a litter of females. What a waste to bring girls all the way back here to sell anyway. You can find a second wife here too. A Gold Mountain Sojourner attracts ten thousand rich fat women. Sell those girls, apprentice the boy, and use the money for your passage." Of course, though Mad Sao favored his son, there was no question but that, being very American, he would raise and protect his daughters.

"Let me tell you about hunger," wrote his mother. "I am boiling weeds and roots. I am eating flowers and insects and pond scum. All my teeth have fallen out. An army drafted the ox, and soldiers took the pigs and chickens. There are strangers in the orchard eating the fruit in its bud. I tried to chase them away. 'We're hungry. We're hungry,' they kept explaining. The next people through here will gnaw the branches. The sly villagers are hoarding food, begging it, and hiding it. You can't trust the neighbors. They'd do anything. I haven't eaten meat for so long, I might as well have been a nun who's taken a vegetable vow. You'd think I'd be holy by now and see miracles. What I see are the hungry, who wander lost from home and village. They live by swindling and scheming. Two crazed villagers are stealing a Dragon King statue from each other. It goes back and forth and whoever's doorstep it lands on has to pay for a party. There's no goodness and wisdom in hunger. You're starving me. I see you for what you are—an unfaithful son. Oh, what blame you're incurring. All right, don't bring yourself to me. I don't need a son. But send money. Send food. Send food. I may have been exaggerating before, but don't punish me for playing the boy who cried wolf. This time there really is a wolf at the door." He shut his heart and paid his house mortgage. He did nothing for her, or he did plenty, and it was not enough.

"Now we're eating potato leaves," she wrote. "We pound rice hulls into paste and eat it. At least send money to bury me." (Sao felt the terror in *bury*, the dirt packing the nose, plugging the eyes and mouth.) "I've wasted my life waiting, and what do I get for my sacrifices? Food and a fat old age? No. I'm starving to death alone. I hold you responsible. How can you swallow when you know of me?" Some letters were long and some short. "The beggar children who came to the door on your sister's wedding day were the worst-looking beggars in many years," she wrote. "Give them food? Huh. I should have kidnapped them and sold them. Except that people don't buy children any more, not even boys. There's a baby on the rich family's doorstep every morning. Oh, it's so pathetic. The mother hides behind bushes to watch the rich lady bring the baby inside. There are people eating clay balls and chewing bark. The arbor we sat under is gone, eaten. No more fish in the rivers. Frogs, beetles, all eaten. I am so tired. I can't drive the refugees off our property. They eat the seeds out of the dirt. There'll not be harvest again."

Other relatives wrote letters about their hunger: "We'd be glad to catch a rat but they're gone too," a cousin wrote. "Slugs, worms, bugs, all gone. You think we're dirty and depraved? Anything tastes good fried, but we can't buy oil." "We're chewing glue from hems and shoes," wrote another cousin. "We steal food off graves if people are rich enough to leave some. But who tends the dead any more?" "Starving takes a long time." "No more dogs and cats. No more birds. No mice. No grasshoppers." "We've burned the outhouse for fuel. Didn't need it anyway. Nothing comes out because nothing goes in. What shall we do? Eat shit and drink piss? But there isn't any coming out." "I can't sleep for the hunger. If we could sleep, we'd dream about food. I catch myself opening cupboards and jars even though I know they're empty. Staring into pots." "I searched under my own children's pillows for crumbs." "Soon I won't be able to concentrate on writing to you. My brain is changing. If only the senses would dull, I wouldn't feel so bad. But I am on the alert for food." "There are no children on some streets." "We know which weeds and berries and mushrooms and toads are poisonous from people eating them and dying." "Fathers leave in the middle of the night, taking no food with them." "The dead are luckier."

When the relatives read and discussed one another's hunger letters, they said, "Perhaps it's more merciful to let them die fast, starve fast rather than slow." "It's kinder either to send a great deal of money or none at all," they said. "Do you think people really go into euphoria when they die of hunger? Like saints fasting?"

"How can you leave me to face famine and war alone?" wrote Mad Sao's mother. "All I think about is you and food. You owe it to me to return. Advise me. Don't trick me. If you're never coming home, tell me. I can kill myself then. Easily stop looking for food and die." "The neighbors heard rumors about food inland to the north," she wrote next. "Others are following an army their sons joined. The villagers are moving.

Tell me what to do. Some people are walking to the cities. Tin miners are coming through here, heading for the ocean. They spit black. They can't trade their tin or money for food. Rich people are throwing money into the crowds. I've buried the gold. I buried the money and jewels in the garden. We were almost robbed. The bandit used the old trick of sticking a pot like his head bulging against the curtain, and when I clubbed it, it clanged. At the alarm he fled. I had nothing to steal anyway." Hearing that money couldn't buy food relieved Mad Sao of feeling so guilty when he did not send money.

"Since everyone is traveling back and forth, I might as well stay put here," wrote his mother. "I'm frightened of these hungry eaters and killer soldiers and contagious lepers. It used to be the lepers and the deformed who hid; now the fat people hide."

"Shall I wait for you? Answer me. How would you like to come home and find an empty house? The door agape. You'll not find me waiting when you get here. It would serve you right. The weather has changed; the world is different. The young aren't feeding the old any more. The aunts aren't feeding me any more. They're keeping the food for their own children. Some slaves have run away. I'm chasing my slaves away. Free people are offering themselves as soldiers and slaves."

"I'm too old. I don't want to endure any more. Today I gave my last handful of rice to an old person so dried up, I couldn't tell whether it was man or woman. I'm ready to die." But she wrote again, "The fugitives are begging for burial ground and make a cemetery out of our farm. Let them bury their skinny bodies if they give me a little funeral food. They ask if Jesus demons have settled nearby; they leave the children with them. If you don't have stories that are equally heart-rending, you have nothing better to do with your money than send it to me. Otherwise, I don't want to hear about your mortgage payment or see photographs of your new car. What do you mean mortgage payment? Why are you buying land there when you have land here?"

"If only I could list foods on this paper and chew it up, swallow, and be full. But if I could do that, I could write your name, and you'd be here."

"I keep planning banquets and menus and guests to invite.

I smell the food my mother cooked. The smell of puffed rice cookies rises from tombs. The aunts have left me here with the babies. The neighbors took their children with them. If they find food, they can decide then what to do with the children, either feed them or trade them for the food. Some children carry their parents, and some parents carry their children."

Mad Sao wished that his mother would hurry up and die, or that he had time and money enough to pay his mortgage, raise all his children, and also give his mother plenty.

Before a letter in a white envelope reached us saying that Sao Brother's mother had died, she appeared to him in America. She flew across the ocean and found her way to him. Just when he was about to fall asleep one night, he saw her and sat up with a start, definitely not dreaming. "You have turned me into a hungry ghost," she said. "You did this to me. You enjoyed yourself. You fed your wife and useless daughters, who are not even family, and you left me to starve. What you see before you is the inordinate hunger I had to suffer in my life." She opened her mouth wide, and he turned his face away not to see the depths within.

"Mother," he said. "Mother, how did you find your way across the ocean and here?"

"I am so cold. I followed the heat of your body like a light and fire. I was drawn to the well-fed."

"Here, take this, Mother," he cried, handing her his wallet from the nightstand.

"Too late," she said. "Too late."

With her chasing him he ran to the kitchen. He opened the refrigerator. He shoved food at her.

"Too late."

Curiously enough, other people did not see her. All they saw was Mad Sao talking to the air, making motions to the air, talking to no voice, listening to someone who moved about, someone very tall or floating near the ceiling. He yelled and argued, talked, sobbed. He lost weight from not eating; insomnia ringed his eyes. That's when people began to call him Mad Sao.

He knew how his grandfather had helped Fourth Grandfather by scolding him on his way. "Go home, Mother!" he was heard to scold, very firm, his face serious and his voice loud. "Go home! Go back to China. Go home to China where you belong." He went on with this scolding for days and nights, but it did not work. She never left him for a moment.

"I'm hungry," she cried. "I'm hungry." He threw money at her; he threw food at her. The money and food went through her. She wept continually, most disturbingly loud at night; though he pulled the covers over his ears and eyes, he heard her. "Why didn't you come home? Why didn't you send money?"

"I did send money."

"Not enough."

"It's against the law to send money," he told her—a weak excuse. "But even so, I sent it."

"I'm not a rich man," he said. "It isn't easy in this country either."

"Don't lie to me," she said. She pointed toward the kitchen, where the refrigerator and freezer were filled with food, and at the furniture, the radio, the TV. She pointed with her chin the way Chinese people point.

"Since you're here, Mother," he tried to bribe her, "you may have all the food I have. Take it. Take it."

She could see her surroundings exactly, but though she could see food, she could not eat it.

"It's too late," she mourned, and passed her hand through the footboard of his bed. He drew his feet up. He could not bear it if she should pass her hand through his feet. His wife beside him saw him gesturing and talking, sleepwalking and sleeptalking, and could not calm him.

"I died of starvation," his mother said. She was very thin, her eye sockets hollow like a Caucasian's. "I died of starvation while you ate."

He could not sleep because she kept talking to him. She did not fade with the dawn and the rooster's crowing. She kept a watch on him. She followed him to work. She kept repeating herself. "You didn't come home. You didn't send money."

She said, "I've got things to tell you that I didn't put in letters." "I am going to tell them to you now. Did you know that when children starve, they grow coarse black hairs all over their bodies? And the heads and feet of starving women suddenly swell up. The skin of my little feet split open, and pus and blood burst out; I saw the muscles and veins underneath.

"One day there was meat for sale in the market. But after cooking and eating it, the villagers found out it was baby meat. The parents who had sold their children regretted it. 'We shouldn't have sold her,' they said. The rich people had bought the babies and resold them to butchers."

"Stop it, Mother," he said to the air. "I can't stand any more."

Night after night, she haunted him. Day after day. At last he drove to the bank. She sat in the back seat directly behind him. He took a lump of money out of his savings. Then he ran to a travel agency, his mother chasing him down the street, goading him. "Look, Mother," he was heard to say, sounding happier as he showed her the money and papers. "I'll take you home myself. You'll be able to rest. I'll go with you. Escort you. We're going home. I'm going home. I'm going home at last, just as you asked. I'll take you home. See? Isn't it a wonderful idea I have? Here's a ticket. See all the money I spent on a ticket, Mother? We're going home together." He had bought an oceanliner ticket for one, so it was evident that he knew she was a ghost. That he easily got his passport proves that he was indeed an American citizen and in good standing with the Immigration and Naturalization Service. It was strange that at a time when Americans did not enter China, he easily got a visa also. He became much calmer. He did not suddenly scream any more or cry or throw food and money.

The family told him that there were no such things as ghosts, that he was wasting an enormous amount of savings, that it was dangerous to go to China, that the bandits would hold him hostage, that an army would draft him. The FBI would use our interest in China to prove our un-Americanness and deport all of us. The family scolded him for spending a fortune on a dead person. Why hadn't he mailed her the money when she was alive if he was going to spend it anyway? Why hadn't he gone to see her earlier? "Why don't you give the money to some wretch instead of wasting it on a vacation for yourself, eh?" He reminded them of a ghost story about a spirit that refused ghost money but had to have real money. They shook their heads. When my father saw that Mad Sao would not be swayed, he bought two Parker 51 fountain pens for fifty-five dollars, kept one for himself, and told Mad Sao to deliver the other to a most loved relative in China.

Mad Sao packed a small bag, all the time talking, "See, Mother? We're on our way home now. Both of us. Yes, I'm going home too. Finally going home. And I'm taking you home. We're together again, Mother." He hardly heard the live people around him.

All the way up the gangway, he was waving her on, "This way, Mother," leading her by the hand or elbow. "This way, Mother. This way." He gave her his bed and his deck chair. "Are you comfortable, Mother?" "Yes, Mother." He talked to no other passenger, and did not eat any of the ship's meals, for which he had already paid. He walked the decks day and night. "Yes, Mother. I'm sorry. I am sorry I did that. Yes, I did that, and I'm sorry."

He returned his mother to the village. He went directly to her grave, as if led by her. "Here you are, Mother," he said, and the villagers heard him say it. "You're home now. I've brought you home. I spent passage fare on you. It equals more than the food money I might have sent. Travel is very expensive. Rest, Mother. Eat." He heaped food on her grave. He piled presents beside it. He set real clothes and real shoes on fire. He burned mounds of paper replicas and paper money. He poured wine into the thirsty earth. He planted the blue shrub of longevity, where white carrier pigeons would nest. He bowed his forehead to the ground, knocking it hard in repentance. "You're home, Mother. I'm home too. I brought you home." He set off firecrackers near her grave, not neglecting one Chinese thing. "Rest now, heh, Mother. Be happy now." He sat by the grave and drank and ate for the first time since she had made her appearance. He stepped over the fires before extinguishing them. He boarded the very same ship sailing back. He had not spent any time sightseeing or visiting relatives and old friends except for dropping off the Parker 51. He hurried home to America, where he acted normal again, continuing his American life, and nothing like that ever happened to him again.

Another grandfather we had was Kau Goong, the ex–riverboat pirate, our grandmother's brother. When a neighbor boy called him Kau Goong too, I saw rush across the old man's face, pleasure at being the Great Uncle, a title with loft, but he

said, "I'm not *your* kau goong," scornful of an American boy,
a Ho Chi Kuei, who did not know the titles. Kau Goong was
the longest-lived and biggest human being I had ever seen, and
my mother said that Grandmother was the same size; in fact
this was her younger brother. He had to duck under doorways.
We tied rags around the pipes in the basement to cushion him
when he hit his head; we let strips hang down to warn him. He
carried trunks, stones, trees, the railroad ties. He was lucky,
and won for us a TV set and a vacuum cleaner, which were
raffled off at the Chinese Community Fourth of July Annual
Picnic. He also gave us Nabisco wafers, one entire box for each
kid. This same Great Uncle had been a murderer in Cuba and
a second-story man in New York, a city he climbed the way
King Kong climbed the Empire State Building. That killing
must have been done not in stealth but in hand-to-hand fight,
no weapons but his enormous hands. A second-story man, we
learned, clamps his mouth shut when jumping so he doesn't
bite his tongue off upon landing. At the laundry Kau Goong
worked without pay doing the heaviest work, which was pressing overalls and Levis.

Another of his chores was to walk my youngest sister from
kindergarten. Once when she came home alone, a wino
knocked all afternoon on the doors and windows. She bar-
ricaded herself under the dining table with chairs tight all
around. When we found her in there among the legs, she
was still scared. After that Kau Goong met her at school and
walked her to the laundry.

My brothers remember him as a generous old man; he took
them to a smoking place where men with silver and wood pipes
gave them presents and praised them. The only times he spoke
to me were to scold and to give orders. "Bad girl," he said.

There was a day when he was shouting for me, probably
to do some chore, clean house or wash dishes, rinse the rice,
some routine work, which I suddenly did not want to do. I did
not want to hear him order me to make a phone call or address
an envelope; I would not fill out a form or take something to
the laundry or whatever. I did not want to see him or hear
him or be in his bossy presence. I dashed downstairs into the
basement, where I locked myself into the storeroom, and sat
on the stairs under the cellar door as in *The Wizard of Oz*. I

liked hiding in the dark, which could be anywhere. The cellar door sloped overhead, a room within the storeroom within the basement. I listened to footsteps above the rafters. He would not come down to the basement, where he had to duck the pipes and walk stooped. I was safely tucked away among the bags of old clothes and shoes, the trunks and crates the grown-ups had brought with them from China, the seabags with the addresses in English and Chinese, the tools, the bags and bottles of seeds, the branches of seeds and leaves and pods hanging upside down, and the drying loofahs. Outside the cellar door, the pigeons purred, the chickens squawked, and a turkey and a dog, a rooster, a train made their noises. In the middle of the basement, the swing my father had hung from a beam bounced and squeaked when Kau Goong walked over it; at night ghosts played on that swing.

I thought over useless things like wishes, wands, hibernation. I talked to the people whom I knew were not really there. I became different, complete, an orphan; my partners were beautiful cowgirls, and also men, cowboys who could talk to me in conversations; I named this activity Talking Men.

But today, interrupting the conversations were the stomping and roaring overhead. "Children. Children. Where are you?" He sounded angry. But that was his usual voice. The basement ran the length of the house, and his footsteps went everywhere across the ceiling. He was stomping from room to room, opening and slamming doors, closet doors too. I stretched my legs out on the cement and put one elbow on the highest step, my back against one wall and toes against the other. I belonged here; everything was my size. The air smelled of anise from the drying stalks. Kau Goong was calling out our names one by one. I wondered where my brothers and sisters were; one of them ought to be answering by now. If one of them answered, Kau Goong would forget about me. But I heard no reply. Maybe they were hiding in other places—the ledge along the top of the neighbor's goose pen, which was roofless but tall enough for the lazy geese not to fly away, or under the grape leaves on top of the pigeon coop, or on top of wardrobes, behind the boxes. We had many special places. My brothers and sisters were good at chores too, but Kau Goong mostly called me because I was the oldest and took blames. A long time had passed, and he was still calling. He did not give up; he would not forget about it. We had to be there somewhere; the front door had been open, that was how he had got in, and so somebody had to be home.

The longer he looked, I realized, the less plausibly I'd be able to step out of the basement and say, acting natural, "Yes, Kau Goong, were you calling me?" I tried the appropriate facial expression, erased guile and worry from my face, casually said, "Here I am." But then he would say, "Where have you been?" And then what would I say? I couldn't say, "I was in the bathroom." He had checked every room. I couldn't say, "I was watering the yard," or "I was feeding the chickens and rabbits," because he had made the rounds of the yard too. I had seen his legs at the basement windows.

Then his footsteps came across the kitchen and down the basement stairs. He would know I was in the storeroom—I had latched the door from the inside. Trapped. How dumb. Stupid. If he found me while I was doing something of use like sweeping out the basement or restacking the lumber or roller skating on the concrete or drawing on the walls, then all would have been right, but to be found doing nothing, to be found hiding, I could not explain. He walked past the storeroom door. Through its screen, I saw him from the shoulders to the waist, the rolled-up sleeves over the long arms. He growled; he lumbered past. I darted out of the corner, unlatched the door, and hid again. Even if he opened the door and looked in, maybe I could count on his eyes not being used to the dark. He walked to the end of the basement. He shouted into the corners. He walked over to the pile of sawdust which we used to outline borders when we played Cities, walked around the Texas rice, the onion pile, the potato pile, and the woodpile of boards and railroad ties. The upright stakes were transfixing vampires. Over where there were treasures buried underneath the front stairs (I had buried some myself in cigar boxes), he roared my name several times. I should either stay hidden or come out. Miraculously, he passed the door again without looking inside. I didn't feel sorry for him calling through an empty house, and it was not as if my name were a tether to me, but I got up, opened the door, and said to his big back, "Hello, Kau Goong. Did I hear you calling me?" Then scooted around him and ran up the stairs. "Yes," he said. From the basement he would only be able to see my feet. "Oh, here and there," I mumbled in case he was saying, "Where were you?" "I was just on my way to finish my work," I said, sweeping something into the dustpan I'd grabbed. He did not scold me taking so long to answer. I must have fooled him.

When he was over ninety, and his forehead grown very high, his wife, Great Aunt, wrote to him: "Now we're surely in our old age. Why don't you come back, and let's spend a few years together before we die." But in China he would have to have a hole drilled in his head and warm soapy water slooshed through, brainwashed into a Communist. He would have to stand up night after night without sleep until his brain turned Communist. Great Aunt wrote, however, that the Communists had quit breaking up families; men no longer lived in separate houses from women. Some children had been taught to inform on their parents, but some were only pretending they'd do so. Now that families were reuniting, couldn't the two of them also meet again? "You only have a few years left anyway," she wrote, "so don't be afraid of plane crashes or ships sinking. Haven't you had your life of adventure? Now it's time to come home."

"What are you going to do?" asked my mother, who read him his letters.

"Who knows?" he roared and stomped out of the house to his room at the Benevolent Association, so he wouldn't have to discuss this going back to China.

"What do you think he should do?" MaMa asked. "If he goes back to China, he'll see his wife again. But he may have to suffer Communism and famines. And we'll never see him again." We children thought about Kau Goong finding the way street by street to an ocean, then over the Atlantic or the Pacific, then distinguishing the coast of Asia from Africa. Finding was a power not a one of us had, and we too had to go someday on that same quest, for which our mother had made us memorize the directions in syllables. "If he stays here," MaMa analyzed, "he'll grow old and never see his wife again, but he'll always have food to eat." There was no question of Great Aunt coming here, against the law to leave Communist China, also against the law to enter the United States. "She's so old too," MaMa said. "On the other hand, they saw each other when they were young and not again for the rest of their lifetimes; what difference does it make if they don't see each other a little longer? It would only be a sentimental indulgence." *If, old, but*—terrible words. Gapping, gaping spaces. Two old people with a planet between them, and the planet unfathomable with its hunger and wars and laws.

One day MaMa said, "He ought to go back," and I did not see how she came to this conclusion, what bridges of reasoning she took to arrive at it, why this conclusion was better than the other possibility. It must have been Father who had decided and she was doing the announcing. "You must go back, Kau Goong," she said. "Here you're all alone. What use are you here?" She asked him several times, "What have you decided?" But his growl didn't sound like a Yes or a No. He left the house without talking about the decision he had to make and did not visit again for a week or two.

Then she told us, "Kau Goong has decided he's not going back." *Never, forever*—two more terrible words.

"Why?" I asked. "How did he decide that? Why? How come?"

So Great Aunt, who was also more than ninety years old, saved seventy-five dollars and bribed a farmer, who hid her under the potatoes in his cart, and he smuggled her out of Communist China. "I could hear the border guard talking with the farmer," she wrote. "They even talked about people hiding in sacks—under potatoes. 'Eyes among the eyes,' they said. Then they laughed, and we went on. A donkey drew the cart. I'm now in Hong Kong. You don't have to worry about Communists any more. They're not of any consideration whatsoever. We can spend our old age in Hong Kong. I'll wait for you here." I wondered, if she had been hiding under corn would they have said, "Ears among the ears," whether Chinese also think corn comes in ears.

More weeks passed while the adults thought over this new development. He has to go now, I thought; he cannot leave her alone and old in a foreign country. But Great Uncle, who was standing by the window, the profile of his big head against the glass and peach trees, the long tendons of his neck stretching, his big Adam's apple bobbing, said, "I've decided to stay in California." He said, "California. This is my home. I belong here." He turned and, looking at us, roared, "We belong here."

My mother wrote Great Aunt about the decision. Not much later, Great Aunt wrote that she had bribed another farmer to smuggle her back into China. Another seventy-five dollars. She said she was not going to spend the rest of her life alone in a strange city. Her return was a clue that Red China couldn't have been as horrible as everyone made out.

Not many years after his decision, Great Uncle grew shorter and thinner, though he was still bigger than most people. He did not appear for dinner one day, and he was dead.

We and the old men sat in rows at the funeral. Some of the old men were: the storekeeper who had torn up his accounts and stopped keeping them when he saw he was not getting ahead, the delivery man who whistled on leaves, the hatchet man who sang opera, the artist uncle who said how paper and pencil are cheap and how inexpensive it is to be an artist, the piano player who lived in the basement and played without depressing the keys so as not to disturb the people upstairs, the Old Man of the North disguised as Uncle Camel Face, the uncle who lived with the Mexican lady, and Uncle Bing Sun Who Laughed Twice (which rhymes). They wore their brown or blue jackets and sweaters; some took off their tweed caps, and others kept them on. Only my father wore a matching suit. I thought about myself dying and about parents dying. We were the only children; the old men admired children.

MaMa sat for a moment, then left, hurried back with four dented buckets filled with sand. She stuck incense sticks any old how into the sand and put the buckets around the coffin. She lit the incense and sat down, having filled the room with smells and broken up the symmetry of the demon mortuary. I looked at the mortician demons, who stood in the back of the room, to see if they were going to upbraid her and remove the buckets. The coffin was brown and very long as if it were made with doors nailed together. He was that tall; he was in-side. One old man, then another one, stood up, walked in front of the coffin, and made a speech. They seemed to speak in a higher language than when talking to children; I did not understand most of what they said. Perhaps on this serious occasion, they did not put things into many synonyms until they hit on one a kid could understand. I listened to find out more about Kau Goong's pillages, his plunders, and sackings, and for some details about how he had killed a man, but they did not mention his crimes though he was safe from deportation now. I should have yelled questions at him. I shouldn't have hidden from him. He was almost a hundred years old; Chinese live a long time—to do many things and to make their ages span the legal immigration dates. The old men and a politician told how Kau Goong had come to the Gold Mountain and stayed. He was a Gold Mountain Man. They said "Gold Mountain" a lot, "Gum Sahn" many times. "Long time Califoon," they said in English.

Mad Sao wept. I did not think that men had feelings; it was women who missed people, minded the distances, the time, and cared about whether or not they saw someone again. But Mad Sao was an unusual man.

After the speeches, the mourners got up to go, but when the demons saw everybody leaving, they started nabbing pallbearers. We hadn't known we were to designate some. My parents asked the old men to carry the coffin, my father asking and my mother tugging them by the sleeves. They were doing us a favor saying Yes, not wanting to do it, reluctant to associate with death. The white demons handed them white gloves, which the men shoved their splintery hands into. There must have been a demon taboo against touching a coffin with one's bare hands. Father, Mad Sao, and four men not in our family each took a coffin handle and, fumbling and stumbling, jostled it between the chairs and out the door. It wasn't like the processions in the movies but like moving furniture, some pallbearers facing forward and some backward, bumping out the door and down the steps, then lifting the big coffin into the hearse.

The limousine unfolded inside; jump seats came up out of the floor and the walls. My mother walked around to the windows in back—we were like the children who ride in station wagons—and gave us strips of white paper the size of dollar bills. "Throw this money out the window," she said, but she was unceremonious; I thought it would be better to dole the "money" out, scatter it in intervals along the way, not just dump it. "Use it up," was all she said. We would not have to save any of it. Luxury. We divided the paper evenly amongst us. "Wait until the car starts so that it'll fly," we instructed one another.

When the car moved, we flung out a few white bills, budgeting them so that we would not run out before reaching the cemetery. For lack of adult explanations, we children made up what was happening. "It's for him to spend in heaven," we said. It may have also been for the waif ghosts lining the streets, or it was like a carrot on a stick to entice Kau Goong, who was lingering behind or hovering overhead, to the cemetery. The hearse, the vegetable trucks, the pickup trucks, and Mad Sao's automobile moved in procession through Stockton. We drove to the places where Kau Goong went when he was alive as if we were following him on his rounds, very slowly, as if gathering him in. His ghost was not to stay at the club where he smoked his water pipe or at the school, where he waited to pick us up. We drove to our house and paused there, engines running. Perhaps he'd come for his things—the trunk and wicker baskets that he had brought from China, his water gourd, his ceramic jug, the rags on the pipes, the TV set, the vacuum cleaner—that is, the invisible duplicates of these things, or perhaps he'd left some of his anima in them and was collecting that. "We're taking him on a last look," we explained to one another. "Or we're looking for him." We next drove to Chinatown, where we idled in front of the Benevolent Association. In the window of his room on the second floor, the gauze curtains were slightly parted and still. His room overlooked the square where the hoboes and winos slept under the palm trees. On one side of the square was the Chinese school, whose classrooms were also on the second floor; he had heard us at our lessons and seen us lean on the balconies. On the other side of the square was the Catholic church, where the hoboes and winos were lined up for lunch an hour ahead of time; a cop walked by with his dog, and the poor men stiffened to attention like an army. One of them drank water out of the gutter. Beneath Kau Goong's room was the store where the old men sat out on the sidewalk among the big tin cans full of tofu and bean sprouts and live snails and turtles; the bench between the parking meters was empty, the sitters at the funeral. Next to the store was the closed-up place that used to be our gambling house. Next to that was the herbalist's, and at the corner was the Filipino grocery store. At the other corner was the demon liquor store all lit up no matter what time of day or night; in the window, a black scotty and a white scotty, run by batteries behind the cardboard, wagged their tails and tongues. A loudspeaker mounted above the door played country music loud enough for everyone to hear. Once I was crossing the street and heard machine-gun fire full blast and a grenade and a long scream—"Aaaaaa!"—then the announcer saying, "Another G.I. shot down in battle," more shooting and the scream again, striking me stock-still in the intersection. We did not drive through the middle of Chinatown, which was the one block with the uncles' businesses on both sides of the street. The cars crossed Washington Street, and from the intersection we looked down Chinatown at the grocery stores, the butcher shops, the shoe store, the restaurants, the candy-and-tobacco store. Leaving Skid Row, we drove to the laundry, where we slowed a moment and then sped onto the highway. The wind twisted the white money, pulled it out of our hands, and carried it away. It went whipping and spinning over the alfalfa fields, and caught in the fruit trees and the tumbleweeds.

We stopped at the Chinese cemetery, which is not on a hillside in China but beside Interstate 5 on the flat San Joaquin Valley floor. The pallbearing uncles carried the coffin and lowered it into the grave. We may have been one man short, for a demon helped carry. The mortician demons threw their white gloves into the grave, and so the uncles did too. As she does wherever she goes, my mother brought food, which she arranged on the ground around the grave. It was like birthday food, the whole chicken, pork, beef, vegetables. She filled a shot glass with whiskey; my father poured it into the grave and bowed three times. She refilled the glass and did that too. Then, according to her directions, starting with my oldest brother, who was younger than I, and ending with the girls, each of us kids poured a glass of the amber and fumy whiskey into the blackening dirt and on the coffin, and bowed three times. Whenever we had to do this bowing at political meetings or assemblies at Chinese school, we kids giggled. Now I felt my body slop and shuffle, lean crooked on one foot like an informal American punk—there being something wrong with bowing, something embarrassing, awkward. Not looking at one another, we did some quick nods.

My mother burned Kau Goong's clothes and shoes in the black incinerator at the end of a row of graves. I looked inside the grate; I saw black shoes and red mouths, blood and eyes. She shut the lid before I finished looking. She gave us and the pallbearers red paper with money inside; it was to end the death and begin the luck again.

We went to the big expensive restaurant in the middle of Chinatown, where my parents ordered a moderate amount of food, not like the profusion at wedding banquets. I thought it typical of us to order stingily, but it was only lunch, and we had the grave food left over. As if there were no funeral a moment ago, the adults laughed, talked, ate.

When we got home, we did not burn a pile of leaves and newspapers at the curb. We were modern. We children had seen such piles and women stoking them. When we asked, "Is it so that the ghost won't follow you in? Is it so that you're no longer contagious?" the adults scolded, "It's nothing. Don't talk about it." We went directly indoors, a relief not to be jumping over fire like Indians or Africans or South Seas Islanders in front of the neighbors and passersby.

That was the only time our family went to the cemetery. Other families go every year and even twice a year to bring food, flowers, and paper to their relatives. They eat with or for the dead. "Superstitious backward peasants," my parents say. "We don't have that custom in our family," MaMa says proudly. "Nothing happens to you after you die. You just disappear. No afterlife. Right?" "Right," says BaBa. We treat Kau Goong and any other grandfathers who may be in that cemetery like any American dead.

I had a dream about Kau Goong one morning. MaMa asked, "What did he say?" I couldn't remember and was tempted to make up something extravagant. "Sometimes there's a message," she said. In another family, a grandfather came to one of them in a dream and said that the kids were to bury their parents correctly; after that they would be absolved of all duties to ancestors since they were now Americans.

We had an uncle, a second or third cousin maybe, who went back to China to be a Communist. We called him Uncle Bun, which might have been his name, but could also be a pun,

Uncle Stupid. He was a blood relative and not just a villager. He was very talkative. In fact, he hardly ever stopped talking, and we kids watched the spit foam at the corners of his mouth. He came to the laundry and sat, or if it was very hot, he stood near the door to talk and talk. It was more like a lecture than a conversation. He repeated himself so often that some of what he said seeped into the ears. He talked about wheat germ. "You ought to eat wheat germ," he said, "because wheat germ is the most potent food in the world. Eat it and you'll stay young for a long time; you'll never get sick. You'll be beautiful and tall and strong, also intelligent. The reason for so much unhappiness and strife is that people have been eating wrong. Meat turns them into animals. Wheat germ, which we can digest easier, can help us evolve into better people. Wheat germ is full of vitamins (*why-huh-ming*), and it is very cheap. A, C, thiamine, riboflavin, niacin, calcium, carbohydrates, fats, iron (*eye-yun*)." He was a scientific and up-to-date man who used English scientific terms. In two weighty syllables, both equally accented, a spondee, he said "Wheat Germ." Wheat germ would fatten up my father and also fatten up all the skinny children. Unlike the rest of the men in the family, who were thin and had white hair, this uncle was round and bald with black hair above his ears and around the back of his head. He wore a pearl gray three-piece suit and a necktie with a gold tiepin, the gold chain of his pocket watch linking one vest pocket to the other, the last button of his vest open over his prosperous paunch. He opened his eyes wide to see everything through his round gold-framed eyeglasses.

"Wheat germ—you can put it into any food," he said. "Sprinkle it on the rice and strew it on all the accompaniments. Stir it into milk and juices. Drink it in soups and beverages; it melts right in. Mix it with ice cream and strawberries. Combine it with flour. Combine it with rice. Beat it into cakes and pancakes. Scatter it on fried eggs for a crunchy texture. You can eat it by itself. Eat it by the handful, cooked or raw. Add it to cold food or hot food, sauces and gravies. Rain it on vegetables. Coat fish, meat, and fowl with it. Use it as a binder in meatballs and fishcakes. It goes with anything." Wheat germ. I could not imagine this miracle food, whether it was sweet or salty, what size it was, what it was, what color, whether it tasted

good. Was it a liquid or a solid? Was *germ* the same germ as
in bacteria? "Wheat germ is golden brown," he said, "though
the color blends with whatever you're cooking. A pinch of it
changes regular food into a medicine." It sounded like a fairy-
tale elixir, fairy food. "You cannot taste or detect its presence
in other foods," he said. "Yet you can eat it by itself like cornflakes," which he also pronounced spondaically in his accent,
Coon Flex. "Wheat germ is the heart of the wheat," he said,
"the heart of bread and wheat, which is more nutritious in the
first place than rice. It repairs broken parts and tissues."

"Hum," said my father and mother.

"We ought to buy some, don't you think?" I asked my parents, hating to ask them to spend more money, but we might
be wasting away from the lack of a vital food.

"He's crazy," my mother said. "Anything that necessary has
to have been invented long ago."

He brought us some sample wheat germ, which tasted like
raw peas or raw oats.

Although he was about my father's age, Uncle Bun, like
many of the old men, did not appear to have a job and was
able to afford entire mornings, afternoons, days, and evenings
sitting and chatting while we worked. Maybe his sons sent
money from Chicago. My father did join him talking politics,
a man's topic as gray as newspapers. They talked about Sun
Yat Sen and Chiang Kai Shek and Mao Tse Tung, about their
moves and countermoves, their strategies, the Red Army and
the White Army, and the Japanese maneuvering here, marching there, meeting and retreating, circling, war for years. My
father scoffed at Chiang and Mao, at their ineptness. Their
inconsistencies made him laugh. Since Sun's death, nobody
could unite China.

"The way Chiang solves poverty is to print paper money,"
my father said.

"We have to examine the causes of poverty," said Uncle
Bun. "The world has never experimented to find out if it is
rich enough and big enough to support all its people. It probably is. Look at all the rich people who own too much, and
you can see there's extra food, land, and money. And certainly,
there's always work enough. Only the distribution is wrong;
we have to divide up the goods evenly." We kids divided every

five-cent candy bar and all the chores. "Who really owns the land?" he asked. "The man who farms it with his sweat and piss or the man whose name is on the paper? And shouldn't the worker on the assembly line own his labor and the results of his labor?"

"The farmers should own the land," he answered himself. "The workers should own the factories—and the profits. The rich pigs turn profit into extra cars, ostrich-feather hats, and golf parks. When it ought to be distributed as food among the poor. We have the airplanes and ships and trains for the distribution. The true purpose of the diesel engine is to rush food to everyone on every continent and island. Every child has the right to food."

"And would the owners, landlords, and bosses voluntarily give away their holdings?" asked my father. "And the housewives their slaves?"

"Yes!" shouted Uncle Bun. "Either we educate them, to see the right way, or we, the poor of the earth, will take what's ours by revolution. The takeover by the poor is inevitable. The poor become more and more numerous as the rich become fewer. Haven't you noticed how many poor people there are and how few rich? We will overcome them with our numbers. I get so angry that a boss can deny a worker his job. Why should another man own my muscles and brains and what I make with my hands and my time?" He told again about some fight he had had with the boss at one of his past jobs, his face red and his spit spraying. "How dare he treat me like that? I'm a man and he's a man. In a fair system, the worker would be the more valuable man, and the supervisor serve him and make his job easier."

My father had ideas too but merely an observation here and there that changed from day to day. Uncle Bun said the white demons were not the only oppressors, that upper-class Chinese made their money off lower-class ones; the immigrants got twenty-five cents an hour if they were lucky. No day off. We children made exactly twenty-five cents an hour. "You're in trouble at the cannery if the forelady is Chinese," my mother agreed. "She'll make trouble for you to impress the boss." (*Fo-laydee, chup-bo*—trouble—*bossu, day offu*, Chinese American words.)

"Actually these aren't dreams or plans," Uncle Bun said. "I'm making predictions about ineluctabilities. This Beautiful Nation, this Gold Mountain, this America will end as we know it. There will be one nation, and it will be a world nation. A united planet. Not just Russian Communism. Not just Chinese Communism. World Communism."

He said, "When we don't need to break our bodies earning our daily living any more, and we have time to think, we'll write poems, sing songs, develop religions, invent customs, build statues, plant gardens, and make a perfect world." He paused to contemplate the wonders.

"Isn't that great?" I said after he left.

"Don't get brainwashed," said my mother. "He's going to get in trouble for talking like that. He's going to get us in trouble; the barbarians think that Communists and Chinese are the same."

Even when the uncles were killed during the Revolution and the aunts tortured, Uncle Bun did not change his mind about Communism. "We have to weigh the death of a few against the lives of millions of poor workers and the coming generations," he said.

"A fermentation of dreams," said my father. Uncle Bun should not have said such Communist things against our dead relatives. His fingers followed the gold chain to the gold watch in his vest pocket; he looked at the time and left. BaBa snorted, "Foolish man. Silly man. Long winded." "Long winded," the same metaphor in Chinese and English. "Fermenting dreams," said BaBa. "Dreams fermenting." I heard in his scorn and words how dreams ferment the way yeast and mold do, how dreams are like fungus.

Next time Uncle Bun came over, he said that Mao himself had had to leave his sick wife and child behind on the Long March, his dedication to Communism that strong. With spit flying, Uncle Bun talked about the glory of the Long March. The lame and weak sacrificed their bodies for use as ladders and fords so that others could leap mountains and rivers. Yes, some of his own family—our family—had given their lives too, though unwillingly. He talked about five-year plans. It frightened me that someone could keep something in mind for five years—keeping track for five years.

"Ah, sad, sad America, which does not respect the poor," he said. "The poor are important. And look, look, even if we distribute everything, and it's spread so thin that we're all poor—that's good. Consider the culture we poor have invented—vegetarianism and fasting, pencil sketches, pottery, singing without instruments, mending, saving and reusing things, quilting, patchwork, the poetry written on leaves, rocks, and walls, acrobatics, dancing, and kung fu, which doesn't require expensive sports equipment. Oh, let's value the poor, who in a way are all of us. Even with money, the rich can't buy good food. They eat white bread and poisoned food. What they ought to do is eat wheat germ."

Amazing! His two big ideas—wheat germ and Communism—connected.

His ideas had come together neater and neater as the months and years passed. "Not just China," he said, "and not just America, but the world. We will organize the entire world. End world hunger. And we will have world peace." What scope. What neatness. World peace. How amazingly his ideas connected up.

Then one day, he announced in a whisper, "The milk demon is poisoning me. The grocer demon is poisoning me. They have a plot against me. They put poison in my milk and eggs."

My mother said, "It's impossible to inject poison into eggs. Look how perfect the shells are."

But he said, "Science. Science can do anything."

When he connected his two big ideas, he touched wrong wires to each other, shot off sparks, and shorted out. He had become a paranoiac. "They're trying to poison me," he said, running into the laundry, his red face bursting above the collar and tie. "I've discovered their plot. They think they can get away with it but because of the sharp senses I've developed on wheat germ, I can detect poisons. I smelled the poison, and did not eat or drink it. I've discontinued milk delivery, and I'm going to buy groceries at a different store." He looked canny. "Why do you suppose they're after me?" he asked. "It must be because I've hit on the truth and discovered the plot against the poor. And so they want to get me." He entered rooms as if pursued, stepping in and out of doorways, checking behind him, peeping out of windows, and pressing his back to walls. He continually surveyed the street. "I've noticed a pattern," he said. "They put the poison into white food—eggs, bread, milk, vanilla ice cream, flour, sugar, white beans. They're thinking that the seeming purity of white food would fool me, and it would disguise the poison, but I know that they have developed an invisible dissolvable poison. I'm outsmarting them. I'll shop at a different store every day. I'll keep changing stores."

"He's gone crazy," my mother diagnosed. "He's getting crazier. When he comes to the house, and we're at the laundry, you kids don't let him in."

He became more and more agitated. "I saw the wholesale demon open a bottle of milk. Yes, I saw him lift the lid. He dropped in a pellet of poison. I could tell by the way he cupped his hand. Then he pressed the lid back on. Sleight of hand. Lately the tops of milk bottles have been looser. That's evidence. And today's evidence is that I saw the wholesale demon tampering with the vacuum seal. He placed the bottle in the exact spot where I had picked my last bottle. They're out to get me because—" and he held his breath on "because"—"I am a Communist." "FBI," he whispered. "Secret police. House Un-American Activities Committee. Coconut. Inside the husk. They've even gotten inside the coconut with their scientific know-how."

"His head is a coconut," said BaBa.

Another day Uncle Bun came in, said nothing, sat. His face was red and purple. "How much did you spend for the kids' bikes?" he asked. "Where did you get the extra money? Roller skates. Then bikes." He whirled on my father, poked his face and finger at him. "Where's my money?" he shouted.

"I don't know," said BaBa. "Did you lose your money?"

"Half the money is gone from my savings account," he shouted. He looked as if he were in a fit, his mouth foaming. Breathing, snorting, bursting, he yelled, "Where is it?" His round body expanded.

"You shouldn't be accusing me," said BaBa, and continued ironing. "Banks are very careful," he said. "No one can get your money without your signature and your passbook. Did you lose your passbook and your I.D.'s?"

"No, I didn't lose my passbook and my I.D.'s," said Uncle

Bun, imitating hatefully. "You took them, and you withdrew my money. You disguised yourself as me. They see a chinaman and can't tell it's not me. You know a lot about handwriting, you forger." Then he stopped explaining. "Give me my money," he shouted. He took his glasses off. Red shot out of his eyes. "Give me back my money." He had changed from the jolly roly-poly man; I had not seen him jolly for quite a while. My mother had stopped letting him take the baby for walks, but lately he had not asked to baby-sit her either. "Thief!" he yelled. As in other emergencies, we kids kept working steadily, acting normal so that the rest of the world would return to normal too. I wished that my father would say soft, cajoling words, even pay him some money, but that was part of the fear too, that my father does not give in. "You walked into the bank with my passbook, and you took half, thinking that I wouldn't notice. You thought I was going mad and had forgotten how to add and subtract. You're very good at pen and abacus. I see you. I know you. You did it. Give me back the money, or I'll call the cops. Then you'll be sorry."

He was a hard, perverse man. He might just do that, call the police and get us deported. A man crazy enough to be glad that his relatives had been killed by Communists was capable of treachery.

"Why don't you phone your son long distance in Chicago?" said BaBa. "Tell him what happened. Or why don't you go to Chicago and stay with him until you feel better?"

"I don't see how I'm going to have money for train fare with you siphoning it. How long have you been dipping in, huh? A little at a time or one lump sum? I'm going to the cops."

"Why don't you look at the dates in the passbook?" said my father.

"I'm going to the police station," said Uncle Bun and ran out.

"He may get violent," said my mother. "Don't let him in the house."

He returned to the laundry the next day for further accusations, his open passbook in his hand, pointed at figures, and shouted out numbers. "Proof!" he said. "Proof!" and slapped the little book with the back of his hand.

BaBa took the passbook and studied it. "Look. There are no entries in the withdrawal column."

"Of course not. You didn't do it with this passbook. You did it so that it wouldn't show on this passbook. You told them you had lost the passbook. You filled out a special form."

"I'll go to the bank with you," said BaBa. He was taking Uncle Bun very seriously, setting down his iron, offering to take a break from work for him.

"Just watch it," said Uncle Bun. "When they see the two of us together, they'll put you in jail. They'll know which is really me." Which was very crazy; they looked the opposite of each other. When they returned from the bank, Uncle Bun had stopped talking about missing money.

He did come to our house one day when neither of our parents were home. Unfortunately, the front door was wide open, so we couldn't hide and pretend we were out. It would be embarrassing to tell him why he couldn't come in. Being the oldest, I decided that we children would go outside and talk to him on the porch. It was pleasant out there under the grapevines. We stood between him and the red door and asked him questions to distract him. He usually walked right in. "What exactly is wheat germ?" we asked, but he seemed not as interested in wheat germ as before. "How's shopping at the new grocery store?" "Fine. Fine," he said. "May I have a drink of water?" he asked. "We'll get it," we said, some of us blocking his way while one ran inside, very rude, a guest having to ask for refreshments. He drank the entire glassful quickly. "You must finish all your water," he advised us. "When you have milk, finish all of it. Finish your food. Eat everything. Don't leave scraps. Scraps turn into garbage. Food one moment, garbage the next. Same with paper. Don't blotch it, and if you do, save it for scratch paper. Cross out the mistakes rather than crumple the paper. Make every page count." He did not go berserk, did not break into the house and throw himself against the sofa like a padded cell, did not act like a maniac at all. He sounded like other adults, advising this, advising that, advising eat.

At the laundry, where it would be dangerous to run amok among the hot machines, he announced: "*They* are not *only* hiding the poison in my food. I am on the verge of discovering the *real* plot. Have you noticed—oh, surely, you must have been alarmed by it—you must have seen how many garbage demons there are in this country?" "Yes, there are," said my mother. "Do you see," he asked, "how the white demons are very careful with garbage? And how much garbage there is?"

Now, our family knew a great deal about garbage and how much of it was not garbage at all. On our way home on garbage nights, we visited bins that belonged to the stores and found valuables—mannequin heads and hands, sheet music, hats, magazines, comics, English-language newspapers, a cardboard Eiffel Tower, the black and white scotties, books of rug samples, Christmas card samples, wallpaper, perfectly good boxes. To lower our garbage bill, we left a sack or two of our own garbage—marrowed bones, papers written on front and back, shoes that couldn't be repaired. At the grocery stores, we found carrots and lettuce for our rabbits, the outer leaves for the rabbits. Sometimes we split up to cover the route faster, meeting one another with loot at another corner. So we understood garbage better than most people.

"The white demons are very careful with garbage, aren't they?" said Uncle Bun. "The city pays men to sweep the gutters and pick up paper with a stick and nail. They attach wire baskets to the signal poles, and on other street corners they have tax-paid trash cans right next to the mailboxes. And every week, regularly, on a highly organized schedule, teams of garbage demons come to each house and collect garbage. Truckloads." All this we agreed to seeing, and it did not, after all, seem crazy. You could see what he was talking about for yourself. "Have you ever thought about what they're saving the garbage for?" he asked. "What are they doing with it? Why are they so diligent? Today I saw children put their candy wrappers in their lunchboxes. And the hoboes who pick up cigarette butts and put them in their pockets—do you assume they're going to smoke them later? There has got to be a purpose behind this storing up and bagging and chuting. Have you seen the buildings with chutes? Garbage from every floor plunges to the basement. The government pays armies of collectors to take it somewhere for a purpose."

"They take it to the dump," my mother said. "They leave it there in heaps, which they burn. They take wet garbage from restaurants and feed it to pigs. Or they use it for fertilizer. They re-pulp paper and make newspaper."

"Oh, you think so?" he asked. "Have you ever seen any of

this paper-making? Have you ever followed the garbage truck when it leaves your house? Too early in the morning for you to bother, isn't it? Have you seen any of these restaurant pigs?" Then he left very mysteriously, abruptly.

A few days later he again came running into the laundry. He was highly excited and frightened, as if he were being chased. "I've discovered what they do with the garbage." He was sweating. "They're collecting it for me. They're going to feed it to me. They'll capture me and tie me down and shovel it into my mouth. They're going to make me eat it. All of it. It's all for me. You must see what a big plot it is. Everybody is manufacturing garbage constantly, some knowing the purpose and some just because everyone else is doing it. It all ties in with the poisoning, don't you see? The newspapers and radios are in on it too, telling them to buy, buy, and then they turn everything they buy into garbage as fast as they can. They're preparing and saving for the day when they'll shovel it into my mouth. They've been collecting for years, and I didn't see the plot till now. That day is coming soon. They'll make me eat it."

"Why should they do that to you?" asked my mother.

"Because of my talk about Communism," he said.

"The garbage is not for you," said my father. "The garbage isn't that important. You're not that important. Forget the garbage."

"You should go to a mind doctor," said my mother.

He got offended and left. "You'll be sorry when the day arrives, and you see it all come true. Feeding day."

His stomach got thinner. He refused most food; he ate only greens and browns, leaving not a scrap, not contributing to the garbage that "they" would feed him later. "Paper garbage too," he said. "Paper cups, paper plates, paper napkins, Kleenex, gum and gum wrappers."

At last he said, "I'm going back to China. I've outsmarted them. I know which day the feeding will be on, and I'll leave before then. It was not like this in China. Remember? In fact, they couldn't poison your milk and bread because we didn't drink milk; only babies drank milk. And we didn't eat much bread. We used everything thoroughly in China. Remember? There was hardly any garbage. We ate all the food. Remember how we could see with our own eyes that the hogs ate the peelings? If the human beings didn't eat rinds, the animals did, and the fish bones got plowed into the fields. Remember how paper gatherers collected paper that had writing on it and burned it in word furnaces? Remember we saved the bags and boxes? Why, this—" he picked up a cornflakes box—"we would have treasured a pretty box like this, such bright colors, such sturdy cardboard. We would have opened the flaps carefully and used it to store valuable and useful things in. We'd have taken good care of it, made it last, handed it down. I'm going back to New Society Village."

"But New Society Village isn't there any more," said MaMa. "It's been Communized. You'd have to sleep in a men's barracks and eat in a dining hall with hundreds of strangers. You'd have to eat whatever they cook. The Communists will take away your bank account."

"That's right," he said, and he blinked as if clearing his eyes. "That's the way the world should be."

From that decision on, he acted saner and saner, happier, and stopped talking about the garbage except to say, "I'm returning to China before feeding day." "Returning" is not to say that he necessarily had ever been there before.

He talked about how he was using only a part of his money for passage and giving the rest to the new China. If they were suspicious of his years in America and did not let him in, he would sneak in from Hong Kong.

The day he left, he spoke to my youngest sister, who was about three years old. He bent over so that she could hear and see him very well. "Don't forget me, will you?" he asked. "Remember I used to play with you. Remember I'm the man who sang songs to you and gave you dimes. What's my name?" She laughed that he would ask her such a silly, easy question. Of course, she knew his name. He coaxed her to say it several times for him. "You won't forget? Tell me you won't forget."

"I won't forget," she said. He seemed satisfied to leave, and we never saw him or heard from him again.

For a while I reminded my sister, "Do you remember Uncle Bun, the bald fat man who talked a lot? Do you remember him asking you not to forget him?"

"Oh, yes, the funny man. I remember."

I reminded her periodically. But one day, I noticed that I had not asked her for some time. "Do you remember the funny man who talked a lot, the one who smuggled himself into Red China?"

"Who?" she asked.

"Uncle Bun. Remember?"

"No," she said.

With no map sense, I took a trip by myself to San Francisco Chinatown and got lost in the Big City. Wandering in a place very different from our own brown and gray Chinatown, I suddenly heard my own real aunt calling my name. She was my youngest aunt, my modern aunt just come from Hong Kong. We screamed at each other the way our villagers do, hugged, held hands. "Have you had your rice yet?" we shouted. "I have. I have had my rice." "Me too. I've eaten too," letting the whole strange street know we had eaten, and me becoming part of the street, abruptly not a tourist, the street mine to shout in, never mind if my accent be different. She had been talking with a couple of women, to whom I said, "Hello, Aunt. Hello, Aunt," mumbling because there are different kinds of aunts depending on whether they're older or younger than one's mother. They'd tease you for being too distant, for addressing them as Lady or Mademoiselle, affectations, and also for being familiar.

"Who is this?" the women asked, one of them pointing at me with her chin, the other with her rolled up newspaper. This talking about me in the third person, this pointing at me—I shoved the resentment down my throat. They do not mean disdain—or they *do* mean disdain, but it's their proper way of treating young people. Mustn't dislike them for it.

"This is my own actual niece come to visit me," my aunt said, as if I had planned to run into her all along. The women were to understand that I was not just somebody she called a niece out of politeness, but a blood niece. "Come see my new apartment," she said to me, turned around, and entered the doorway near which we were standing.

I followed her up the stairs, flight after flight, and along a hallway like a tunnel. But her apartment need not be dismal, I thought; these doors could open into surprisingly large, bright, airy apartments with shag carpets. "Our apartment is very small," she warned, her voice leading the way. "Not like a regular house. Not like your mother's big house." So she noticed space; I had thought perhaps people from Hong Kong didn't need room, that Chinese people preferred small spaces. Some early mornings if we went down into our basement, we found two straight-backed chairs facing one another, blankets and shawls still cupped in shapes of the women who had sat there. The cord of the electric heater rose to a ceiling socket. Coffee cups and footstools sat on the floor. Our mother and this aunt had stayed up all night talking again. I might have known from the good times they could have in the basement that it would be the smallest apartment I had seen in my life. The door didn't open up all the way because of a table, which had stuff stored on top and underneath. The half of the table away from the wall was cleared for eating and studying.

"Coffee? Tea?" Auntie asked.

"Coffee," I said. "Black."

"How can you drink it like that? How about some meat? Fish?"

"MaMa has started drinking it black," I said, giving her the news. "MaMa has switched to black at her age."

Big and medium-sized blonde dolls sat and stood on tops of stacks of things. Their pink gauze dresses fluffed against the cellophane windows of their cardboard boxes. They were expensive dolls with little socks and gloves, purses and hats. I felt very relieved that my cousin, who was about ten or twelve years old, did not have to share one doll, the naked kind that one had to make clothes out of scraps for; she had two bride dolls. My relatives were not bad off, not as poor as we used to be. They had luxuries.

Auntie went into the kitchen, which did not have room for another person. I snooped about at the desk in one corner of the living room; looked at the desk calendar and the statu-ettes of the guardians of Happiness, Money, and Long Life, read the appointments pinned among the cut-outs of flow-ers on the wall. It was this aunt who had given my mother a nice set of the guardians mounted on wood and red velvet. There were some Christian pamphlets on a shelf over the desk; I couldn't remember whether this was the aunt who had con-verted to Christianity and was sending my parents tracts and

Bibles or whether it was another aunt in Hong Kong who was sending to both of them. Or maybe she'd been accosted by a missionary working Chinatown. ("Are you a Christian?" my mother asks periodically. "No, of course not." "That's good. Don't be a Christian. What *do* you believe in?" "No religion. Nothing." "Why don't you take the Chinese religion, then?" And a few minutes later, "Yes, you do that," she'd say. "Sure, Mom. Okay.") Next to the telephone were notebooks, pads, very sharp pencils, a pencil sharpener, another luxury. They had shaving lotion and hand lotion, toiletries on the shelf too.

"The bathroom is over there," she shouted as if it were a huge house. I went into the bathroom, which was the closet next to the kitchen, to spy some more. They had built shelves with stores of sale toilet paper and soap, which was in fancy shapes prettily boxed. They aren't so poor, I thought. They are above subsistence; we have been worse off.

I stood by the kitchen door and watched my aunt cut cake. A corner of the floor was stacked with shiny gallon cans without labels. "My husband baked these cakes," she said. *Hus-u-bun*, she called him, a clever solution; some wives get so embarrassed about what to call their husbands, their names and *husband* such intimate words (like *rooster*—or *cock*), that they call him So-and-so's Father. My uncle worked at a famous bakery whose name is stamped on pink boxes that people carry about Chinatown.

"Cake?" asked my aunt. "Pie? Chuck-who-luck? Le-mun?"

"I just ate," I said, which was true, but took a plate anyway. The biggest difference between my aunt and my mother was that my mother would have forced me to eat it. I sat on the sofa, facing the front door. There was another door near the desk; it must have been to the next apartment.

Auntie got herself some chocolate cake and lemon pie and sat next to me. I enjoyed looking at this aunt, who was how my mother would have been if she were the youngest instead of the oldest, the city woman rather than the peasant. She was wearing a white blouse with sharp lapels; I also liked the straight gray skirt and intelligent glasses.

"I saw those hoppies they tell about in the newspaper," she said. "Some of them talked to me. 'Spare change?' That's what they say. 'Spare change?' I memorized it." She held out her hand to show their ways. "'Spare change?' What does 'spare

change' mean?" "They're asking if you have extra money."
"Oh-h, I see," she said, laughing. "'Spare change?' How
witty." She was silly compared to my mother. She giggled
and talked about inconsequentials. "Condo," she would say.
"Cottage cheese. Football? Foosball?"

But here I was alone with her, and no adults to distract her;
maybe I could ask her things, two equal adults, talk the way
Americans talk. Talk grown-up. "Is it hard to endure?" I asked
like an old Chinese lady, but because I was not brave enough
to hear the answer, quickly said on top of it, "Where did you
go? Were you grocery shopping? Going for a walk? Visiting
neighbors?"

"I was coming from the beauty parlor, getting my hair
done," she said, and I wished that I had noticed to compliment
her on how nice she looked, but her hair looked the way she
always wore it, in stiff black curls. "Otherwise, it wouldn't be
this black," she said. "It's really white, you know." She went to
beauty parlors. Another luxury, I enumerated. Leisure.

"Are you working?" I asked because it was odd that she was
having her hair done in the middle of a workday. "Is it your
day offu?"

"No. I'm not working any more."

"What happened to your hotel job? Didn't you have a hotel
job? As a maid?" I said *maid* in English, not knowing the
Chinese word except for *slave*. If she didn't know the word,
she wouldn't hear it anyway. Languages are like that.

"I've been fired," she said.

"Oh, no. But why?"

"I've been very sick. High blood pressure," she said. "And I
got dizzy working. I had to clean sixteen rooms in eight hours.
I was too sick to work that fast." Something else I liked about
this aunt was her use of exact numbers. "Ten thousand rooms
per second," my mother would have said. "Uncountable.
Infinite." Half an hour per unit, including bathrooms. "People
leave the rooms very messy," she said, "and I kept coughing
from the ashes in the ashtrays. I was efficient until I fell sick.
Once I was out for six weeks, but when I came back, the head
housekeeper said I was doing a good job, and he kept me on."
She worked at a famous hotel, not a flop house in Chinatown.
She'd given us miniature cakes of soap whenever she came to

visit. "The head housekeeper said I was an excellent worker." My mother was the same way, caring tremendously how her employer praised her, never so hurt as when a boss reprimanded her, never so proud as when a forelady said she was picking cleanly and fast. "He said I speak English very well," Auntie said. She was proud of that compliment.

"What do you do all day long now that you aren't cleaning hotel rooms?"

"The days go by very slowly. You know, in these difficult times in the Big City mothers can't leave their children alone. The kidnappers are getting two thousand dollars per child. And whoever reports a missing child the FBI turns over to Immigration. So I posted ads, and one in the newspaper too, that I wanted to mind children, but I haven't gotten any customers. When the mothers see the apartment, they say No." Of course. No place to run, no yard, no trees, no toys except to look at the dollies. Being poor in Stockton was better than this Big City poverty; we had trees and sloughs and vegetable gardens and animals. Also there were jobs in the fields. "I could mind four or five children," she said. "I'd make as much money as cleaning the hotel. They don't want me to watch their children because I can't speak English."

"But you do," I said. "You know lots of English." When I could not think of the Chinese for something, she always knew the English word.

She was flattered. "No, I don't," she said. "Now, *you* speak Chinese well," but I was speaking well because I was talking to her; there are people who dry up language.

"You speak like your mother. She used to sound like a city person, but American people speak peasant accents, village accents, so she talks that way now."

"Do my mother and father speak alike?"

"Why, yes," she said, but maybe she couldn't hear the difference; being a city person she lumped the village accents together.

"My own son doesn't talk to me," she said. "What's *nutrition*?"

"It has to do with food and what people ought to eat to keep healthy."

"You mean like cooking? He's going to college to learn how to cook?"

"Well, no. It's planning menus for big companies, like schools and hospitals and the Army. They study food to see how it works. It's the science of food," but I did not feel I was giving an adequate explanation, the only word for *science* I knew was a synonym or derivative of *magic*, something like *alchemy.* "He could work in public health, and that's a field that has lots of jobs right now. He could work for cafeterias and college dormitories, restaurant chains, mass production food plants that make frozen TV dinners, canned foods, cake mixes."

"And *engineering*?" she asked.

"Building things, designing them, like designing bridges and mines and electrical things. Do you know what kind of engineering he's studying?"

"No, they shout at me and tell me I'm too stupid to understand. They hardly come home, and when I ask them what they're doing, they say I'm dumb. Oh, my sons have turned out very bad, and after all I've suffered for them."

I did not want to hear how she suffered, and then I did. I did have a duty to hear it and remember it. She started by telling me how my mother had suffered. "Oh, the suffering," she said. "Think of it. Both of your mother's babies died. How painful it must be to watch your babies die after they can walk and talk and have personalities. Aiya! How hard to endure."

"What did they die of?"

"Firecrackers. The village women exploded firecrackers to scare germs and bad spirits away, but instead they scared away the babies. They filled the air with smoke so the babies couldn't breathe. And then a few years later, it happened again; when you were a baby, you suddenly stopped breathing, and she pounded on the floor for the downstairs neighbor to help. The fire trucks and the police came, and they revived you. She wrote to me about that."

"Probably all babies, having recently been nothing, have a tenuous hold on life," I observed. MaMa would have sat on the floor and held the babies to her or laid them on blankets in the middle of the house. I remembered the floor, the linoleum patterns and smells of it. Under the linoleum I had hidden milk bottle caps, flattening into lovely disks.

In the falling afternoon, I looked out the windows at the

neighbors' windows. For a short while light had pushed through the curtains making little suns and a haze. We faced west and caught the last pale sun. The fog rolled between the buildings, and the foghorns were sounding already. My aunt made no move to switch on the lights. Her eyes were very bright. It aggravated me how easily tears came to women her age, not hardened at all by the years. "I suffered terribly too," she said. I would never be able to talk with them; I have no stories of equal pain.

Now she was telling her part of the story: When she was born, the blind fortuneteller said that she would be alternately very rich and very poor many times but end up rich. Sure enough, they were poor until her father went to the Gold Mountain, whence he traveled three times; each time he got richer and twice brought back wives. He hired teachers for his daughters, who learned to read and write. Between his trips they were poor. He died when she was ten. She was poor from then until she married a rich man. When Communism transformed the villagers, they chased her family out of their house. She hid with her two boys in the pig house. It was winter, and all they had on were cotton clothes. The boys knew better than to cry, learned instantly. The next morning, she found her husband. He said that the Communists had assigned them a place to live—the leper house. "That's where you belong," said the Communists. Lepers, the "growing yin" people, who have too much cold wind in them, died in there. The rest of the family had disappeared; his mother had run away alone with the gold and jade. They never saw her again. The Communists kept an eye on them in the leper house, waited for them to make a false move. One day her husband caught a pair of doves and hid them to feed the family. "And do you know how the Communists killed him?"

"I think my mother said they stoned him in the tree where the birds were."

"They pressed him between millstones," she said.

Of course. In stories, stones fall crash bang crash bang like pile drivers. It was the sound of harvest and executions. After battle, no matter what farmhouse or courtyard a villain or hero used, when it was time for executions, he always had a device handy—the millstones.

"Aiya," I said. "That's horrible. How hard to endure."

Then she escaped to Hong Kong. She gave her wedding ring to get on the ship, her earrings for food, her necklace to get off the ship. She and the two boys slept on the sidewalks; they ate the rice they begged though the Communists threw sand into it, saying "Have some salt." The oldest boy, Big Baby she called him, and her second son, Little Baby, got angry at her when they were hungry or too hot or too cold. "What did you do today?" she asked them after separating to beg on different streets. "What do you care?" they said. "What do you know?"

She noticed a man who was selling shoes alone in a stall. She bade him "Good morning" daily and thus made his acquaintance. He let her sit in the customer's chair under the awning in rain and in the noon sun. Whenever he shared his lunch with her, she hid some for the boys. One day she said— she said it for me with a giggle—"Sir, why doesn't your lady come help you work these long hours?" (Hong Kong people are more refined than us and don't say *old lady* for *wife* or *old rooster* for *husband*.)

"I don't have a lady," he said.

"I'll help you then," she said, and did so. Soon they got married, the first self-matched marriage in the family. They built the stall up into a store, then added a wholesale outlet, then a factory, and she was rich again. They had a boy and a girl of their own, much younger than the other two.

But she did not forget the accurate blind fortuneteller: a downfall imminent. The people who lived in crates on the hillsides and the boat people who had never touched land would soon rise up and kill the rich people and the British. There are rich people who don't see poor people, but she never stopped seeing them. She took varying routes from home to store so the beggars wouldn't recognize her and mark her. "The Revolution is coming," she kept saying, and her husband agreed, "Yes, it's going to happen," but went on building his business. Each downfall had been worse than the last— the Japanese, then World War II, then the Revolution. "The Hong Kong Revolution will be fought with nuclear bombs," she predicted. Her husband called her a superstitious peasant.

At last she said, "My name is at the top of the Refugee List. Let's leave for the United States." But her husband did not want to go; the business was doing very well. He told her that if she went, she would have to go alone. She took the two older boys and left him with the daughter and son. "Badger him to bring you to the Gold Mountain," she instructed these two youngest, and left.

"Father," they said with their little arms out supplicating, the boy especially naughty, "take us to the Gold Mountain. We want to see Ah Ma. Why won't you take us? Do you want us to get killed by Communists? Ah Ba, take us to America and buy us some American toys. You're a selfish father not to take us traveling. All right then. When we're old enough, we're leaving you. We'll go find her. You're cheap, that's why you won't take us."

My mother showed her the street corners where she was to wait for the farm buses to take her to the tomatoes and grapes. Yes, life in America was meaner, but no signs of revolution; the beggars in the street were young and fat "hoppies," who begged for fun. She hoped that this Gold Mountain poverty counted for the next fall in her fortunes. Her husband wrote that he was definitely not about to leave his homeland and his family. And didn't she miss having servants and friends talking her own language? She suggested that he not sell the shoe store but export the shoes to the United States, send them to her here. She had already gotten her American relatives to promise to take cases of sample shoes from store to store. She said a war in Indochina was going to spread to other Asian countries, and the Pentagon would bomb China. She outwrote him. He said, "All right. I'm coming to the United States, but only to have a look at it and to bring you back."

He brought the two younger children with him. What luxury, I thought. World travel. No more deciding once and for all on a country sight unseen. He took one look at the Los Angeles International Airport, and said, "Let's go back." But she said to give the Gold Mountain a chance. Be a tourist. Take a vacation. For a couple of months he complained how there were no jobs, then how hard he had to work, and how he had to obey a boss. Both of them complained about doing hard work for only a fraction of the money they were making in Hong Kong.

I remember they rented a house with peeling and flaking

paint; they did not plaster the cracks, did not hang curtains. They slept on the floor until my sister brought them mattresses. They used their suitcases instead of dressers. Chinese people are like that, we sisters and brothers told one another—no frills, cheap. My sister bought them sheets, then a bedspread. The two older boys, whom we refused to call Big BiBi and Little BiBi, did not talk to us but looked away if we caught their eyes, answered direct questions Yes or No, and never asked us questions in return. Like old uncles, they talked to our parents in Chinese. They were F.O.B.'s all right. Fresh Off the Boat.

The youngest boy was more sociable. He opened our refrigerator door and stood there and ate; he knocked over furniture and sassed his mother in two languages. He asked us questions, and his hair spiked up all over his head as if every hair were listening. "Why do you look like that?" "How do they do instant replay so fast?" "How much money do you make? Yeah, what's your salary?" But when we asked his name, he suddenly stood still. He and his sister looked at one another and down at their shoes. The girl, who was older, pointed to her brother and muttered something, and he turned red. "What?" I asked. She said it again. It was his Chinese name, and we could hardly hear it. "Her name is Lucille," he said. And *Lucille* was easy for him to say and easy to hear. He was proud to be able to give an American name though it wasn't his. So, they'd already learned to be shamed by a Chinese name.

When I Fu, Aunt's Husband, said, "I'm going back. You do as you please, but I'm going back," Auntie went with him. They took the two younger children. Our older cousins decided that they would stay in the United States; they were never going back; they would finish school, apply for citizenship, risk getting drafted—it was worth it. How foreign they were. Another generation of heartless boys leaving their family. Only my mother and aunt showed regret at leaving each other.

My mother nagged her nephews if they took any time off from work and study whatsoever. "My own children study all the time," she scolded, to which the F.O.B.'s replied, "They must not be very bright if they have to study that hard." She told us that retort, stirring up suspicions, establishing a

pecking order, which must have been the way in China. They
lived down in our basement with a bare light bulb. They were
not to put their belongings in our closets or drawers, nor to
ride our bikes or watch our TV or listen to the radios. MaMa
said, "They're not my children." When they came home from
school or from the grocery store, where they worked for
twenty-five cents an hour, they were to go to the cellar.

Meanwhile in Hong Kong, Auntie was enjoying another
one of her high fortunes. But one day I Fu stood up from a
customer's feet and told a clerk to finish up. A surge of chemicals or light had rushed through him. He went back to his
office and unlocked his desk. He walked to the bank. The walk
he took was magical: Inanimate objects glowed, but, oh, the
animate—the trees and flowers and bugs and dogs were spraying colors. Human beings flared haloes around their heads
and the rest of their bodies. Bands of light connected couples.
He explained later how he understood the stopping quality
of red light and the go of green. The city was not making
a general roar or hum. His ears separated out the sounds of
various motors, the gas pipes and water mains under the city,
each bicycle wheel, the way the rubber peeled off the asphalt.
It was a good thing it had been a sunny seaport day and not
San Francisco; a foghorn would have melted him with sorrow.
He passed a bookstore. Jets of colored lights jumped along
the books' spines; he wanted to stop and see whether *Red
Chamber Dream* and Communist books were red, the Clear
River poems blue and green, Confucius's writings a white
light, and the *I Ching* yellow or saffron, but he had to hurry
on. The seats, handlegrips, and pedals of the pedicabs and
bicycles pulsed like fire. The newspapers were aflame in reds
and oranges. He passed a drugstore and saw the little drawers
leaking squares of light.

At the bank, he filled out a withdrawal slip with the very
figure that was the last balance in his account. He said later
those digits had had a numerological significance. He took the
money in cash—and money had its own brilliance. It was so
much money, the bank let him keep the canvas bag to carry it
in. The teller and manager asked if he were certain he didn't
want a check or money order, and he said Yes. He liked the
feeling of the Yes escaping warm out of his body. He also liked

voices warming his ears. He would have to remember to go to the theater more often. He carried the money through the streets. He was certain that thieves would not snatch it; he was choreographing the movements of people and the weather. Time and fate were his invention and under the control of his will. He walked into a part of Hong Kong where he had never gone before, but he knew where to go. Fences made out of air guided his way. He entered the correct building and in the elevator knew which floor to choose. He walked through a particular door into a particular room. There were several men he had never seen before, but he knew just which one to approach and what to say. He gave this man all the money he had in the world. He walked out. Free of money. Free of burden. Purpose fulfilled. He flew home. "I can control the weather," he said earnestly. "You can too." His wife and the employees kept asking if he were all right. They planted in him the possibility of his not being all right.

"You look sick," his wife said.

"Stop saying that," he said, and he crashed down to normal. "I've been robbed," he said. "I've been robbed. I was drugged by the bandits that prey on Gold Mountain Sojourners. They slipped a drug into my lunch. And their post-hypnotic suggestion was for me to take all the money out of the bank. I gave it all to them. We're ruined. Why didn't you stop me?"

"What are you talking about?" my aunt asked. "That's impossible. A drug, you say? Hypnosis? How could I have stopped you? Is there such a drug? You gave all our money away? All of it? It wasn't gambling?"

"It was like sleepwalking," he said. "I could see everything; the world was the same, but the story behind it was different. I thought strangely. I thought it was a friend I gave the money to, that he was doing me a favor taking it." According to the passbook, which he found in his pocket, the account had been closed out. "Our life savings."

Husband and wife dashed outside, trying to trace where he had walked. They ran about asking if anyone had seen him come this way. "Did you see me go by a little while ago?" "The bookstore," he said. "I remember it. And that drugstore." The unknown neighborhood had disappeared as if the bandits had set it up, then taken the buildings away. They ran to the bank, which was closed. They went to the police station, though they knew that the police were themselves crooks.

They and a policeman were at the doors when the bank opened in the morning. The teller who had waited on I Fu confirmed that he had been at that window the day before, and he had withdrawn all his money. "Was there anyone with him?" his wife asked. "Did you see anyone behind him? Could there have been someone behind him with a gun?" The tellers had not seen anyone. I Fu told the bank manager that he had been drugged or hypnotized to take out all his money and give it away. The bank manager could do nothing about that. "We don't insure against that," he said. Hong Kong was full of criminals, tricksters, shysters, cheaters, con artists, plotters. People made their living by eating other people, by catching pigs. At lunch, a customer who followed him to the back room might have waved a hand over I Fu's food, and the drug had poured down a sleeve or slipped out of a button or a hinged ring. "Maybe so," said the policeman. Pig-catching was a game among the southern people. The shoe clerks and his relatives were probably in on it too, and the police too.

"We shouldn't have left the United States," Auntie complained. "American police and American people are honest."

When I Fu made change for the last customer of the day, when the bell dinged in the cash register, the spell came over him again. He scooped up the bills and put them in a shoe box. "Where are you going?" cried Auntie, alarmed at his pinpointy, jumpy eyes. "Where are you going? Stop it. You're doing it again. You told me to stop you. It's come over you again. Snap out of it. Put the money back. Give it to me. Wake up." She clapped her hands and shook him, but he pushed her aside "with superhuman strength," she said. "Hold him," she called to the customers and employees. "He's under a spell. Don't let him go. He's got all the petty cash we have left in the world."

"Leave me alone," he said. "It's my money." He broke from their grasp and ran through the streets. The after-work crowds moved aside and closed behind him.

"Stop him. Stop him," Auntie and the employees called, but the people did not want to grab the wild man. Auntie hunted for him, but he had entered a side street into another world.

She went back to the store, terrified at what the thieves were capable of.

I Fu returned, walking slowly; he looked fatigued, having been run about like a puppet. "Let's sell the shoe business," he said, giving in at last, "and go back to the United States." "Return," he said. "Return to the United States."

"Be warned not to travel to China," Auntie told me. "Chinese are crooks. Travelers disappear and are never heard of again."

My aunt and uncle sold their businesses before someone could trick them into signing them away. With that money, they went for the second time to the Gold Mountain, where they arrived no better off than other immigrants. They would never go back; they said good-bye properly, good-bye forever.

"He got the job at the bakery, and I got the one at the hotel," said Auntie. "But I've been sick and can't work any more."

"You look well."

"I get dizzy when I work. By the time I carry my vacuum cleaner and linens up the stairs, I'm so dizzy I have to lie down on the landing. High blood pressure. I'll not fly in an airplane again."

"Do you keep seeing a doctor?"

"Yes."

"The doctor gave you some pills?"

"Yes, but I'm not taking them. It's not the blood pressure that makes me dizzy; it's the pills. I've discovered a cure. The Chinatown women, who all have high blood pressure, say that fresh, unprocessed, pure honey is good for hypertension, and I've been drinking it by the quart. I'm going to get your mother started on the pure honey cure too. I feel so much better on the honey than the pills. Too many side effects with the pills."

"Is that honey in the cans in the kitchen?"

"Yes, I like to stock up when a fresh supply comes into Chinatown. It comes from a special farm with special bees."

"I think you ought to keep taking the pills," I said. "How does the honey have that effect?"

"I'm not sure. Maybe it smooths out the blood so it takes less pressure to move through the veins."

There was no use talking her out of it. I would have to

persuade my mother to continue taking the pills along with the honey.

"I'm glad you've decided to quit your job," I said. "You're lucky to be able to stay home and be a housewife."

"But I need a job badly, very badly. My husubun insists on one thing," she said. "He makes six hundred dollars a month. Exactly three hundred goes to China. He's a rescuer. Out of our three hundred dollars, we have to pay rent, food, clothes, everything. So you see why I have to get a job. He's been saying that I don't know how to save money, that I spend too much. He's so stingy; ever since I lost my job, he's been doing the grocery shopping himself. I had to refuse to cook until I got control of the grocery money again. I went on strike." She laughed. "Sometimes when the two of us are carrying the groceries home, he puts his bag down on the sidewalk and walks away swinging his arms free. I have to hurry home with my bag and run back for his before somebody takes it. Men from Kwangtung are arrogant like that. Independent."

"I'll cook if you stay for dinner," she added.

"I have to go," I said.

"Well, I know there isn't much room to play," she said, as if I were a child, or perhaps she meant "stroll" or "tour."

"No, it's not that. I have some tasks that I have to do. Was your apartment in Hong Kong bigger than this one?"

"No. No. About this size." Oh, such relief that the Chinese life they keep regretting leaving is no better than this.

"Do you want to move outside Tang People's Street?" I asked.

"No. No. Here my husubun can walk to and from work. He can wake up five minutes before the bakery opens and get there on time. And I can talk to the neighbors. The children walk across the street to Chinese school." I hoped that she was drawing the conclusion that she and her family were well off, that they were living in this room by choice, in a way.

"Stay for dinner," she urged. "There won't be good food, but stay."

"I can't," I said. "I have work to do."

"Then let me phone my husubun to bring home a cake for you."

"No, thank you. You don't need to do that. I just ate some cake."

"You can give it to someone, your brothers and sisters." She picked up the phone (another luxury, I counted) and called the bakery. "Bring a cake for my niece," she said. "The best kind—lemun kuk." "The bakery is just around the corner," she said to me. "He'll get off work in five minutes and be here in another minute or two."

It would only be polite to stay and say hello to my uncle. Also I wanted to take a good look at him after what I had heard about him. I did feel nervous that he would walk in angry at me for causing him to have to carry a lemon cake through the streets. A request right before closing time. What if he had to whip together a lemon cake on his own time or humble himself to ask the boss for a remainder cake, or, worse yet, if he had to take it out of his pay? My mother would want me to protest a gift, argue and tussle, my aunt and I trying to give the cake away, running back and forth, her yelling, "All right, then, I take it back. No cake for you," tucking it into clothes, hiding it in bags, throwing it in and out of windows, pushing the windows up and down, pulling the box back and forth until I gave up and took it. Being rude because young and American, taking advantage of that, I planned to say "Thank you" and take the cake.

I Fu arrived at the front door at exactly 5:05, as I could see by the alarm clock on the desk. Watching the knob turn, I thought, What if he were filled with years of gall, furious from kneeling at people's feet and carrying groceries? He would be mad at me for making my aunt sit all afternoon, no dinner started. But he seemed ordinary, handing over the cake box, a man not particularly burdened by money, smiling, not wide-eyed on drugs, the *Gold Mountain Times* under his arm. I stood up, old enough to have manners without being told. "How do you do, I Fu?" I said, shaking his hand. He did not look like a tough businessman who had built and lost a shoe empire or one who could marry a flirtatious beggarwoman from off the street or dash through Hong Kong giving away bags of money. He asked me what I was doing in the Big City. He sat down, asked if I wanted to eat anything. Then he couldn't resist any longer, rolled the rubber band off his newspaper, shook it open, and began to read, exactly as my father would have done. He looked just like my father behind the

newspaper, the very same newspaper, skinny legs and hands
sticking out.

"Why don't you come visit my parents at Christmas time?"
I invited my aunt, figuring out a way to leave.

Just then the door opened again, and my girl cousin came
home. She glanced at me, startled, and headed straight for the
locked door, which I had thought led to the next apartment.
She bent and unlocked it with one of the keys on the chain
around her neck. I could see inside; it was the children's room,
larger than the rest of the apartment, girl's stuff in one half,
boy's stuff in the other.

"Lucille," scolded my aunt. "Say hello to Big Sister."

"Hello," she said, her whole body leaning to get into her
own room.

"Lucille is returning from Chinese school," said Auntie.

The only times I had ever gotten Lucille to sit down with
me was when playing games; she methodically set out to win
everything on the board, only talking to clarify a rule.

"I was trying to explain to Big Sister what your brothers are
studying at college," said Auntie.

"Nutrition and engineering," said my cousin.

"I see," I said, wishing my aunt would let her go. I Fu could
have said something from behind the newspaper, like "I'm a
baker and didn't have to study nutrition," but he didn't.

"Where's your youngest son?" I asked my aunt, and while she
answered, Lucille went quickly inside her room and locked it.

"In the streets I guess," Auntie said. "Sometimes he doesn't
come home until all the stores and restaurants are closed." He
was only about ten years old.

"What does he do out there all night?"

"I don't know. Explores."

"Aren't you afraid of kidnappers and gangs getting him?"

"Yes, of course, but there's nothing we can do about him."

I asked her, "Will you walk me a short distance and point
out which way I ought to go?" I said good-bye to my uncle,
who looked up and said, "Leaving so soon?" My cousin did
not come out of her room. Auntie and I walked for a block
and a half until I recognized where I was, though the night
and the street lights were coming on. We stood on a corner
and shouted good-byes, me carrying a box of food with a

red string, so Chinese, shouting and carrying food, shouting good-bye.

Once MaMa telephoned her brother after not having seen him for fifty years. This was the Singapore uncle who had spent his first fortune throwing a party for friends in Hong Kong. ("Americans get steadily richer building up their savings; Chinese save for years, then spend it all and go into debt for a party.") She told me to be ready to get up at 5 A.M. to do the dialing. They had written letters agreeing on this day, January 2, when it would be a cheap time and 8 P.M. in Singapore. "Oh, the size of the world," she exclaimed. "Look at that time difference. That's not three hours but fifteen hours apart. How far away."

I heard the alarms go off all over the house at 4:30 A.M. and leapt out of bed for nervousness. Wrapped in my blanket, I dialed the operator. After hearing my uncle's phone ring once, I handed the receiver to my mother. She heard a ring and handed it back to me. "Here, you talk to him." "No," I yelped, "I've never met him. He's your brother. You talk to him." Besides, I didn't want to scare him. My parents' friends hang up when we forget to answer with a Chinese accent.

The index finger of my mother's hand that held the phone tapped involuntarily against her cheek; it was the only part of her that shook. "Happy New Year, Wah," she yelled in her loudest voice, no titles, just his name, her baby brother, named after the Chinese Republic. "Is this Wah? Are you well? You're all well, aren't you? Everyone well. Yes, we're all fine too. Yes, very good. Everyone is good. Do you celebrate this New Year's day? Ours is very festive. All my children come back, eating at everybody's houses every day. We go from one of my children's house to another's eating. No, I can't come visit you. Five years ago I could have visited you. But I'm old now. Yes, I'm old now too. Are you old? Do you work hard? Did you just now come home from work? How hard do you work? I still work. Yes. Yes. Thirty employees, huh? That's good. Yes, my children are all working. Everyone working. Happy New Year. Yes, you have a good year too. Good year, good business, good health. Your son has his own corporation? Why don't you come visit me? No, I don't fly. Yes, we're all well.

Doing well. Fine. Good jobs. It's five A.M. here. What time is
it there? It's January second now. What day is it there? You're
home from work? Let me talk to your wife." Then she talked
to his first wife, repeating just about everything. My father
said, "Nine minutes," and she said, "That's enough. Be well.
Good-bye," and hung up.

"Well," she said, "nothing significant said." She tried repeating the conversation to us. "He employs thirty people. He
says that he wishes his children were smart. They're horses and
oxen, he said. His son is in the construction business too, but
has a different company. He says it's eight P.M., January second there in Singapore." I noticed she had not asked him how
his second wife was, nor how the children of that family were.
"Fifty years since we've talked, and we didn't say anything
important," she said.

"That's the nature of phone calls," my father said. "You just
hear each other's voices. That's enough."

"You can call again next year, you know," I said. "You can
call again any time."

The Wild Man of the Green Swamp

FOR EIGHT months in 1975, residents on the edge of Green Swamp, Florida, had been reporting to the police that they had seen a Wild Man. When they stepped toward him, he made strange noises as in a foreign language and ran back into the saw grass. At first, authorities said the Wild Man was a mass hallucination. Man-eating animals lived in the swamp, and a human being could hardly find a place to rest without sinking. Perhaps it was some kind of a bear the children had seen.

In October, a game officer saw a man crouched over a small fire, but as he approached, the figure ran away. It couldn't have been a bear because the Wild Man dragged a burlap bag after him. Also, the fire was obviously man-made.

The fish-and-game wardens and the sheriff's deputies entered the swamp with dogs but did not search for long; no one could live in the swamp. The mosquitoes alone would drive him out.

The Wild Man made forays out of the swamp. Farmers encountered him taking fruit and corn from the turkeys. He broke into a house trailer, but the occupant came back, and the Wild Man escaped out a window. The occupant said that a bad smell came off the Wild Man. Usually, the only evidence of him were his abandoned campsites. At one he left the remains of a four-foot-long alligator, of which he had eaten the feet and tail.

In May a posse made an air and land search; the plane signaled down to the hunters on the ground, who circled the Wild Man. A fish-and-game warden "brought him down with a tackle," according to the news. The Wild Man fought, but they took him to jail. He looked Chinese, so they found a Chinese in town to come translate.

The Wild Man talked a lot to the translator. He told him his name. He said he was thirty-nine years old, the father of seven children, who were in Taiwan. To support them, he had shipped out on a Liberian freighter. He had gotten very homesick and asked everyone if he could leave the ship and go home.

But the officers would not let him off. They sent messages to China to find out about him. When the ship landed, they took him to the airport and tried to put him on an airplane to some foreign place. Then, he said, the white demons took him to Tampa Hospital, which is for insane people, but he escaped, just walked out and went into the swamp.

The interpreter asked how he lived in the swamp. He said he ate snakes, turtles, armadillos, and alligators. The captors could tell how he lived when they opened up his bag, which was not burlap but a pair of pants with the legs knotted. Inside, he had carried a pot, a piece of sharpened tin, and a small club, which he had made by sticking a railroad spike into a section of aluminum tubing.

The sheriff found the Liberian freighter that the Wild Man had been on. The ship's officers said that they had not tried to stop him from going home. His shipmates had decided that there was something wrong with his mind. They had bought him a plane ticket and arranged his passport to send him back to China. They had driven him to the airport, but there he began screaming and weeping and would not get on the plane. So they had found him a doctor, who sent him to Tampa Hospital.

Now the doctors at the jail gave him medicine for the mosquito bites, which covered his entire body, and medicine for his stomachache. He was getting better, but after he'd been in jail for three days, the U. S. Border Patrol told him they were sending him back. He became hysterical. That night, he fastened his belt to the bars, wrapped it around his neck, and hung himself.

In the newspaper picture he did not look very wild, being led by the posse out of the swamp. He did not look dirty, either. He wore a checkered shirt unbuttoned at the neck, where his white undershirt showed; his shirt was tucked into his pants; his hair was short. He was surrounded by men in cowboy hats. His fingers stretching open, his wrists pulling apart to the extent of the handcuffs, he lifted his head, his eyes screwed shut, and cried out.

There was a Wild Man in our slough too, only he was a black man. He wore a shirt and no pants, and some mornings when we walked to school, we saw him asleep under the bridge. The police came and took him away. The newspaper said he was crazy; it said the police had been on the lookout for him for a long time, but we had seen him every day.

The Adventures of Lo Bun Sun

W̲E̲ ̲H̲A̲D̲ a book from China about a sailor named Lo Bun Sun, who as a child had a calling to go to sea. His father, a man from a foreign country, ordered him and his two brothers to settle down working in the family business. But Lo Bun Sun did not enjoy the business nor did he learn a trade or study law. He signed on a ship. "Heaven will not bless you," his father said.

A storm came upon his ship, which sprang a leak. He escaped in a lifeboat, and from there watched the ship sink. Other sailors told him that this unfortunate first voyage was a warning that he give up the sea, but he signed on another ship, which was besieged by pirates. After escaping from them, he bought land in Brazil and planted sugarcane. But one day he became tempted to go to sea again, this time on a slave-trading ship. The ocean reared black waves that knocked the sailors off the decks. Masts snapped, and the ship broke against the reef of an unknown shore. The deck splintered under Lo Bun Sun, and he dropped into the water. Waves big as buildings fell on him whenever he surfaced, and drove him under.

Then he had a sense of coming back from a distance. His dream was that he had been flying but clutching something in his hand; he had tried to open his fingers to drop it, but the burden had pulled him down to this beach. The storm had thrown the ship here also, its stern in the air and its head in the sea. No shipmates had landed with him, not even their bodies.

He put his forehead against the ground and thanked the heavenly beings for protecting him. After resting some more, he swam to the wreckage. With pieces of topmast and spars, he fashioned a raft, on which he loaded sacks of grain—rice, barley, and wheat. In the bread room, he filled his pockets with biscuits. Eating as he worked, he helped himself to ink, paper, and pens, barrels of flour and bolts of cloth, clothes of men and officers, tools—an adze, hatchets, axes, a saw; he took tobacco and rum, guns, pistols, muskets, and shot.

And happily a dog and two cats, glad to see him, came out of hiding. The dog swam; Lo Bun Sun carried one cat in his arms, and the other jumped from the wreck onto the raft. Also for delight, the illustrator had drawn rats climbing down ropes; the rats had wonderfully long tails and whiskers.

The first night, Lo Bun Sun covered himself with a piece of sail and slept in a tree.

He set up a work schedule, rescuing things against the next obliterating wave. Every day he worked during the daylight hours just as if he had a job, stopping only to eat at set meal-times. He ate the beef jerky and drank water from the ship's barrels; he ate lemons and pickles also. According to the drawings, the clay water jugs and wine jugs, the water gourds, and vinegar jugs leaned together in rows and stacks padded with straw; one or two jugs had broken into graceful shards.

MaMa repeated exactly what things Lo Bun Sun took from the ship (this was one of the more boring tales she read—no magicians, no beautiful ladies, no knights, or warrior poets): rice, barley, wheat flour, clothes, bolts of cloth, ink, pens, and paper, biscuits, jerked beef, water, fruit and vegetables, guns, pistols, muskets, bullets, adze, hatchet, ax, saw, tobacco, rum, a dog, two cats.

He also found a chest of gold coins, and although he had not seen a place to spend money, lugged it onto the raft.

One morning, he awoke and the ship was gone. No man-made hulk served as a marker against all that sea. He might have been born on the island.

He walked around the island and saw no signs of another human being. He decided on places to build two houses. One was a dry cave ("such as the cave I lived in when the Japanese bombed China"). He bolstered the roof and sides with planks and planted a wall of stakes, which sprouted and grew around the entrance. The other house was in the woods on an opposite part of the island; if enemies found it, they would be satisfied, diverted. He called his dwellings castles.

A rescue ship would probably come any moment now. Food grew plentifully on the island, and Lo Bun Sun had taken abundant stores from the shipwreck, yet he did not loaf and tan himself on the beach; neither did he nap or play. Lo Bun Sun worked. He was never idle, never lazy. He farmed the island. There is drudgery in his name: *Lo* is "toil," what one does even when unsupervised; he works faithfully, not cheating. *Lo* means "naked," man "the naked animal," and *lo* also sounds like the word for "mule," a toiling animal, a toiling sexless animal. *Bun* is the uncle who went to China to work on a commune. And *sun* is like "body" and also "son" in English and "grandson" in Chinese. *Sun* as in "new." Lo Bun Sun was a mule and toiling man, naked and toiling body, alone, son and grandson, himself all the generations. There is still another meaning of *lo*, the *lo* in "lohan"; like "arhat," like "bodhisattva." There were eighteen lohans, two of them Chinese and sixteen Hindu, personal disciples of the Buddha who enjoyed an easy life like the life on the island of lotus eaters.

Lo Bun Sun marked the days with notches on a board, but on the first busy days when he was hurrying to unload the wreck, he had not yet started this system and might have been thrown off a day.

After physical labor, he wrote in his diary, with which he kept his spirits up. He would leave a record. He ruled a page down the middle and listed the advantages and disadvantages of his island life. The two columns were entitled "Evil" and "Good." One of the Evils was the desolation; that he had not drowned was the balancing Good. Other Goods were food and water and the tropical weather that made up for his dearth of clothes. An Evil was that he had no one to talk to. His Good list outstripped the Evil list; Good may always preponderate in this method of reckoning.

Another way he wrote was: "I really ought to stop complaining because I could be writing that . . ." He began fictions about raving death, starvation, and mutilation, but stopped to continue chronicling his chores, which were endless. He built a table for writing and eating. He preserved eggs in vinegar and some in wine. He spread wild grapes to dry for raisins. He built barricades. He opened a turtle and admired its thirty gold eggs in the shell bowl. (*Lo* also connotes the mystic markings on the tortoise shell.)

When he felt poorly, he drank liquor in which he had soaked tobacco, a mixture also good for rubbing bruises. He grew beans and made tofu and bean sauce. He shot and snared goats; he penned the kids in corrals for domestication.

From the start, he worried about using up his ink and paper, so he decided he would record only "the most remarkable events of my life." He wrote how he planted rice in dry ground, and it did not grow. Then he planted the seeds in boxes, where the shoots remained from twenty-five to fifty days. Next to a stream, he dug pools and built clay walls into dams and sluices to make paddies of water and soil two to four inches deep, which he stirred, *lo* connoting "dike" and "libation," and he transplanted the young plants by hand. One day he counted thirty panicles of rice, and he wrote that down. "Miracle. Miracle." He reaped the heavy tops, handshocked and dried them. Then he carefully ground the brown hulls with rocks. The husks blew away like insect wings. The rice straw was thatch for his roof, slippers, an umbrella, a raincoat; he wove a winnow for next harvest. He searched the ground at the feet of the cut shafts and picked the grains that had fallen; this he used for seed. (My father came to listen to this part of the story, and he told it again, retelling the gleaning several times.) Birds also picked the seed grain, but he scared them away by shooting three birds, which his dog retrieved, and hanging them in the field. From planting to harvest was one year.

Lo Bun Sun shaped pots out of clay and baked them in the sun, which was not hot enough. He built an oven of rocks sealed with clay. When he saw how well it fired, he began decorating the pots. He dipped them in a mixture of mud and beach sand, which melted into a glaze. He wove nets around the outsides of wet pots; the grass burned off, leaving decorations. Sometimes he wove baskets around the cooled pots; he tied the straw into handles.

He made bread without yeast. There was a picture of him with a hand on his stomach; he was sniffing the loaves from which savory steam arose in wavy lines. The same oven baked bread as well as pottery because of vents that regulated the temperature.

He built a boat and rowed around the island. The waves took him farther and farther out. He had to fight his way back, desiring his island. "There's no miserable condition of mankind that heaven can't make worse," he wrote.

He knocked a young parrot out of a tree, and after some

years taught it to say his name so that he would hear a voice other than his own, a voice calling him by name. "Poor Lo Bun Sun," it said. "Poor, poor Lo Bun Sun. Where are you? Where have you been? How come you here? Poor Lo Bun Sun, and how did I come here?"

If there were migratory geese on the island, he could have bound a letter to the leg of a goose.

More years passed, and he used up the brushes, inks, and paper. How to replace the Four Valuable Things? When the rice stalks dried to a pale yellow, he crisscrossed them in a woven mat. The squares were the right size for a word each. He also soaked rice straw, pounded it, and pressed the mash into sheets. And there was a tree whose bark peeled off in soft layers; he called it a paper bark tree. He sewed its pages into notebooks. If he had not found these things, he could have written on stones. He could have written on leaves. For brushes he used goat hairs.

Making good ink took years of experimentation. He hunted for berries dark enough; he crushed leaves, opened reeds, bled trees, but the sap ran clear or amber and sticky or milky. (Plants with milky sap are poisonous to eat.) He tried swamp mud. He caught squid offshore to see if the black in them was ink. But no dirt or flower or blood flowed correctly and lasted. He wrote with oil and dipped the paper in berry stain. What he ate, he fed to parrot, dog, cats, goats, and fields, and he also wrote with it. At last, he discovered the juice of the sandalwood, whose bark and flowers he crushed to produce red. And he found woad, whose leaves look like arrows and writing brushes, and he wrote in indigo. He used red and purple; he was king of his own island.

Still more years went by, and now he was dressed entirely in straw and skins, straw coat, goatskin vest and pants, straw shoes. His pants were open at the knees for movement. He carried a straw umbrella in the sun and a skin umbrella in the rain; the hair was on the outside of the umbrella so the water ran off. Hair grew long on his face and head. A picture showed him trimming his hair with the scissors he treasured, looking at his mirror face and talking to himself. The sea continued empty and the nights black.

One day while patrolling the beach, where the crabs rolled

seaweed bubbles across the sand, Lo Bun Sun saw something
that sent a burning fear up his spine—a human footprint. He
ran to one of his fortifications. He chattered, "It can't be. It
can't be." After starving for human company for twelve years,
he did not shout, "Where are you? Who are you? Hey, where
are you? Come on out. Welcome. Welcome. I'm here. I'm over
here." Instead, he became scared and henceforth timid on his
island. His eyelid began to twitch. He took up the musket,
which he always kept loaded anyway, and never again walked
abroad without it. He stuck loaded pistols and rifles into gun-
ports in his walls. For days he shivered in his cave, peeked
through cracks in every direction, jumped at noises of winds
and animals. He had another look at the print. Perhaps he
had construed a human foot rather than paw or hoof or claw
because of his loneliness. In need of human company, he had
imagined the five toes and a heel. But, no, there it was—
unmistakably the imprint of a naked human foot. The drawing
showed Lo Bun Sun kneeling propped against his musket and
regarding a footprint, inky like a baby's on a birth certificate.
"It must be my own," he said aloud, but the footprint was
bigger than his foot. He clapped his hand over his mouth like
a Japanese; he did not know how loud or soft was normal any
more. He returned to puzzle over the footprint until the wind
and rain wore it away. From then on in case some accident
disabled him, he planted two or three years' supply of grain.

For more than a decade, he thought about the footprint
and sometimes thought he had dreamed it. But one dawn he
saw a light on the beach and crept up hidden behind rocks and
trees to see who was there. Around a campfire in the warm
climate, nine black demons danced and ate. Then they rowed
off, leaving the beach strewn with human bones, heads, hands,
and feet.

Lo Bun Sun fortified his hiding places. He planted vegetables in small separate patches and split his goats into small
herds. He tied the muskets on tripping lines so that he could
pull seven triggers in two minutes. He established burrows,
coverts, and camouflages everywhere, and planted twenty
thousand trees in all. The cannibals might come when he was
doing his chores or sleeping. He comforted himself by recalling a hero, Kao Chung, who overcame the cooking-and-eating

sea monster, and then ate its food on the beach. Several more times in later years, the black demons held their ghastly feasts, and Lo Bun Sun found the remains. Once he also found a wrecked galleon and the body of a drowned sailor.

Thirteen and a half years after the footprint and twenty-five and a half years after his arrival, five canoes landed. From his watchtower in a tree, Lo Bun Sun looked through his spyglass at the black figures against the yellow sand. In the ink drawings, they were silhouettes and far away, so we could not study facial expressions. They slaughtered one prisoner and dressed the meat in front of the others. Suddenly a prisoner broke loose, his ropes falling from him. Two or three savages gave chase—all running directly toward Lo Bun Sun's hiding place. The savages swam a creek, where one pursuer was left behind because he could not swim. Standing between the pursued and pursuers, Lo Bun Sun shot the oncoming cannibals. One of the wounded men returned to the others, who quickly paddled off. The poor man who might have been eaten fell to his knees. He lifted Lo Bun Sun's foot and set it on his head. This was the first human being Lo Bun Sun had touched and who had touched him in over a quarter of a century. One of the cannibals had only been wounded, and when Lo Bun Sun pointed to him, the rescued savage cut his head off. "I name you Sing Kay Ng," said Lo Bun Sun, "because I saved your life on a Friday." "Sing Kay Ng," he pointed to the savage. "You name Sing Kay Ng. My name Teacher."

Sing Kay Ng buried the dead men, then took his first lesson in the Teacher's language. Lo Bun Sun pointed at everything—"*Goat. Jar. Fence. Man.*" Sing Kay Ng pointed to the graves and gestured: "Let's dig them up and eat them." Lo Bun Sun acted as if he were vomiting. He let Sing Kay Ng know that he would kill him if he offered him any human meat or showed his cannibal tastes in any way again.

Sing Kay Ng understood the calendar, the arc his arm made from horizon to horizon, sunrise to sunset to sunrise, one mark. They walked on the island measuring off a distance, which Lo Bun Sun said was one li. "One hundred and twenty li away," said Sing Kay Ng. "I come from land one hundred and twenty li in that direction." The people fought, and the winners brought the losers here for eating. In his country, it was the custom to worship The Old Man Who Had Made Everything. "All things do say 'O' to him," he said. He said that he had a father.

Lo Bun Sun gave his servant and pupil a notebook and a brush with a gold cap and many brushes in bamboo tubes so that he too could record his thoughts and life. Every day the Naked Toiling Mule and Friday sat like two scholars at their desks, reading, studying, writing, recording plantings, harvests, bird migrations, the seasons, the weather, and how many goats had kids.

Lo Bun Sun armed Sing Kay Ng for hunting. Also they would be in league should the cannibals return. "'A real hero will take on a village,'" Lo Bun Sun taught.

Three years later, twenty-one savages and three prisoners, two of whom looked like Lo Bun Sun and one like Sing Kay Ng, came sailing to the island in a fleet of canoes. The companions fired from their ambuscade, killing seventeen cannibals and wounding one, three escaping by boat. When the boat was out of sight, the victors came out and untied the prisoners. Suddenly Sing Kay Ng was jumping up and down and shouting in his own language, "O joy! O glad!" He was embracing the man who looked like himself, and when he untied him, they held each other and wept. It was his father. The father praised Sing Kay Ng for waiting all these years on this island to save him. What a good son he had raised.

One of the other prisoners was a sea captain who had lost his ship in a mutiny. "I have loyal men on the mainland," he said. "If I can just reach them, I'll come back here and take you home." Arming themselves from Lo Bun Sun's store, the captain and Sing Kay Ng's father took the wounded cannibal as a hostage and left in a canoe.

Another ship came to the island, and Lo Bun Sun was in such a rush, he left on it. He took with him one of his parrots, his goatskin cap, an umbrella, his money, and his man, Sing Kay Ng, and returned to his native land.

"But that isn't the end of the story," said my mother. At about sixty years of age Lo Bun Sun found a wife and had two sons and a daughter. When his wife died, he went to sea again. He and Sing Kay Ng had many adventures in barbarous lands; they fought wolves, bears, and bandits. Once, surrounded by a wolfpack, they remembered that the fiercest beasts are terrified by the voice of man; at their shouting, the wolves retreated.

A nostalgia for his island came over Lo Bun Sun, and he sailed back there without telling Sing Kay Ng their destination. Sing Kay Ng recognized it on sight, clapped his hands, and cried, "O yes, O there, O yes, O there," pointing to the site of one of their houses and dancing like mad. The island was now inhabited by mutineers and savages, who had formed a society. They felt no need for rescue, nor did their children have any curiosity about their ancestral countries.

And Sing Kay Ng found his father again; he had seen him from a distance so far at sea that Lo Bun Sun could descry no human shape even through his perspective glass. Sing Kay Ng embraced his father, kissed him, stroked his face, hugged him again, picked him up and set him down under a tree, lay down by him, then stood and looked at him for a quarter of an hour at a time, stroked his old feet and kissed them, and got up again and stared at him. He walked along the beach leading his father by the hand as if he were a lady. He went back and forth to the ship, fetched him a lump of sugar, a drink, a cookie. He danced about him, and he talked and talked, telling him of his travels.

The island was warring with another island, and the ship became caught in the war. A thousand canoes attacked the ship. Lo Bun Sun ordered Sing Kay Ng to go on deck and talk to the attackers in their own language and translate. Three hundred arrows flew at him, and Sing Kay Ng was killed. He was buried at sea with an eleven-gun salute. After more adventures, Lo Bun Sun returned to the land where he was born; he retired at the age of seventy-two.

THE AMERICAN FATHER

IN 1903 my father was born in San Francisco, where my grandmother had come disguised as a man. Or, Chinese women once magical, she gave birth at a distance, she in China, my grandfather and father in San Francisco. She was good at sending. Or the men of those days had the power to have babies. If my grandparents did no such wonders, my father nevertheless turned up in San Francisco an American citizen.

He was also married at a distance. My mother and a few farm women went out into the chicken yard, and said words over a rooster, a fierce rooster, red of comb and feathers; then she went back inside, married, a wife. She laughs telling this wedding story; he doesn't say one way or the other.

When I asked MaMa why she speaks different from BaBa, she says their parents lived across the river from one another. Maybe his village was America, the river an ocean, his accent American.

My father's magic was also different from my mother's. He pulled the two ends of a chalk stub or a cigarette butt, and between his fingers a new stick of chalk or a fresh cigarette grew long and white. Coins appeared around his knuckles, and number cards turned into face cards. He did not have a patter but was a silent magician. I would learn these tricks when I became a grown-up and never need for cigarettes, money, face cards, or chalk.

He also had the power of going places where nobody else went, and making places belong to him. I could smell his presence. He owned special places the way he owned special things like his copper ashtray from the 1939 World's Fair and his Parker 51. When I explored his closet and desk, I thought, This is a father place; a father belongs here.

One of his places was the dirt cellar. That was under the house where owls bounced against the screens. Rats as big as cats sunned in the garden, fat dust balls among the greens. The rats ran up on the table where the rice or the grapes or the beans were drying and ate with their hands, then took extra in their teeth and leapt off the table like a circus, one rat after another. My mother swung her broom at them, the straw swooping through the air in yellow arcs. That was the house where the bunny lived in a hole in the kitchen. My mother had carried it home from the fields in her apron. Whenever it was hopping noiselessly on the linoleum, and I was there to see it, I felt the honor and blessing of it.

When I asked why the cellar door was kept locked, MaMa said there was a "well" down there. "I don't want you children to fall in the well," she said. Bottomless.

I ran around a corner one day and found the cellar door open. BaBa's white-shirted back moved in the dark. I had been following him, spying on him. I went into the cellar and hid behind some boxes. He lifted the lid that covered the bottomless well. Before he could stop me, I burst out of hiding and saw it—a hole full of shining, bulging, black water, alive, alive, like an eye, deep and alive. BaBa shouted, "Get away." "Let me look. Let me look," I said. "Be careful," he said as I stood on the brink of a well, the end and edge of the ground, the opening to the inside of the world. "What's it called?" I asked to hear him say it. "A well." I wanted to hear him say it again, to tell me again, "Well." My mother had poured rust water from old nails into my ears to improve them.

"What's a well?"

"Water comes out of it," BaBa said. "People draw water out of wells."

"Do they drink it? Where does the water come from?"

"It comes from the earth. I don't think we should drink it without boiling it for at least twenty minutes. Germs."

Poison water.

The well was like a wobble of black jello. I saw silver stars in it. It sparked. It was the black sparkling eye of the planet. The well must lead to the other side of the world. If I fall in, I will come out in China. After a long, long fall, I would appear feet first out of the ground, out of another well, and the Chinese would laugh to see me do that. The way to arrive in China less obtrusively was to dive in head first. The trick would be not to get scared during the long time in the middle of the world. The journey would be worse than the mines.

My father pulled the wooden cover, which was the round lid of a barrel, back over the well. I stepped on the boards, stood in the middle of them, and thought about the bottom-less black well beneath my feet, my very feet. What if the cover skidded aside? My father finished with what he was doing; we walked out of the cellar, and he locked the door behind us.

Another father place was the attic of our next house. Once I had seen his foot break through the ceiling. He was in the at-tic, and suddenly his foot broke through the plaster overhead.

I watched for the day when he left a ladder under the open trap door. I climbed the ladder through the kitchen ceiling. The attic air was hot, too thick, smelling like pigeons, their hot feathers. Rafters and floor beams extended in parallels to a faraway wall, where slats of light slanted from shutters. I did not know we owned such an extravagance of empty space. I raised myself up on my forearms like a prairie dog, then bal-anced sure-footed on the beams, careful not to step between them and fall through. I climbed down before he returned.

The best of the father places I did not have to win by cun-ning; he showed me it himself. I had been young enough to hold his hand, which felt splintery with calluses "caused by physical labor," according to MaMa. As we walked, he pointed out sights; he named the plants, told time on the clocks, ex-plained a neon sign in the shape of an owl, which shut one eye in daylight. "It will wink at night," he said. He read signs, and I learned the recurring words: *Company*, *Association*, *Hui*, *Tong*. He greeted the old men with a finger to the hat. At the candy-and-tobacco store, BaBa bought Lucky Strikes and beef jerky, and the old men gave me plum wafers. The tobacconist gave me a cigar box and a candy box. The secret place was not on the busiest Chinatown street but the street across from the park. A pedestrian would look into the barrels and cans in front of the store next door, then walk on to the herbalist's with the school supplies and saucers of herbs in the window, examine the dead flies and larvae, and overlook the secret place completely. (The herbs inside the hundred drawers did not have flies.) BaBa stepped between the grocery store and the herb shop into the kind of sheltered doorway where skid-row men pee and sleep and leave liquor bottles. The place seemed out of business; no one would rent it because it was not eyecatching. It might have been a family association office. On the window were dull gold Chinese words and the number the same as our house number. And delightful, delightful, a big old orange cat sat dozing in the window; it had pushed the shut venetian blinds aside, and its fur was flat against the glass. An iron grillwork with many hinges protected the glass. I tapped on it to see whether the cat was asleep or dead; it blinked.

BaBa found the keys on his chain and unlocked the grating, then the door. Inside was an immense room like a bank or a post office. Suddenly no city street, no noise, no people, no sun. Here was horizontal and vertical order, counters and tables in cool gray twilight. It was safe in here. The cat ran across the cement floor. The place smelled like cat piss or eucalyptus berries. Brass and porcelain spittoons squatted in corners. Another cat, a gray one, walked into the open, and I tried following it, but it ran off. I walked under the tables, which had thick legs.

BaBa filled a bucket with sawdust and water. He and I scattered handfuls of the mixture on the floors, and the place smelled like a carnival. With our pushbrooms leaving wet streaks, we swept the sawdust together, which turned gray as it picked up the dirt. BaBa threw his cigarette butts in it. The cat shit got picked up too. He scooped everything into the dustpan he had made out of an oil can.

We put away our brooms, and I followed him to the wall where sheaves of paper hung by their corners, diamond shaped. "Pigeon lottery," he called them. "Pigeon lottery tickets." Yes, in the wind of the paddle fan the soft thick sheaves ruffled like feathers and wings. He gave me some used sheets. Gamblers had circled green and blue words in pink ink. They had bet on those words. You had to be a poet to win, finding lucky ways words go together. My father showed me the winning words from last night's games: "white jade that grows in water," "red jade that grows in earth," or—not so many words in Chinese—"white waterjade," "redearthjade," "firedragon," "waterdragon." He gave me pen and ink, and I linked words of my own: "rivercloud," "riverfire," the many combinations with *horse*, *cloud*, and *bird*. The lines and loops connecting the words, which were in squares, a word to a square, made designs too. So this was where my father worked and what he did for a living, keeping track of the gamblers' schemes of words.

We were getting the gambling house ready. Tonight the gamblers would come here from the towns and the fields; they would sail from San Francisco all the way up the river through the Delta to Stockton, which had more gambling than any city on the coast. It would be a party tonight. The gamblers would eat free food and drink free whiskey, and if times were bad, only tea. They'd laugh and exclaim over the poems they made, which were plain and very beautiful: "Shiny water, bright moon." They'd cheer when they won. BaBa let me crank the drum that spun words. It had a little door on top to reach in for the winning words and looked like the cradle that the Forty-niner ancestors had used to sift for gold, and like the drum for the lottery at the Stockton Chinese Community Fourth of July Picnic.

He also let me play with the hole puncher, which was a heavy instrument with a wrought-iron handle that took some strength to raise. I played gambler punching words to win—"cloudswallow," "riverswallow," "river forking," "swallow forking." I also punched perfect round holes in the corners so that I could hang the papers like diamonds and like pigeons. I collected round and crescent confetti in my cigar box.

While I worked on the floor under the tables, BaBa sat behind a counter on his tall stool. With black elastic armbands around his shirtsleeves and an eyeshade on his forehead, he clicked the abacus fast and steadily, stopping to write the numbers down in ledgers. He melted red wax in candle flame and made seals. He checked the pigeon papers, and set out fresh stacks of them. Then we twirled the dials of the safe, wound the grandfather clock, which had a long brass pendulum, meowed at the cats, and locked up. We bought crackly pork on the way home.

According to MaMa, the gambling house belonged to the most powerful Chinese American in Stockton. He paid my father to manage it and to pretend to be the owner. BaBa took the blame for the real owner. When the cop on the beat walked in, BaBa gave him a plate of food, a carton of cigarettes, and a bottle of whiskey. Once a month, the police raided with a paddy wagon, and it was also part of my father's job to be arrested. He never got a record, however, because he thought up a new name for himself every time. Sometimes it came to him while the city sped past the barred windows; sometimes just when the white demon at the desk asked him for it, a name came to him, a new name befitting the situation. They never found out his real names or that he had an American name at all. "I got away with aliases," he said, "because the white demons can't tell one Chinese name from another or one face from another." He had the power of naming. He had a hundred dollars ready in an envelope with which he bribed the demon in charge. It may have been a fine, not a bribe, but BaBa saw him pocket the hundred dollars. After that, the police let him walk out the door. He either walked home or back to the empty gambling house to straighten out the books.

Two of the first white people we children met were customers at the gambling house, one small and skinny man, one fat and jolly. They lived in a little house on the edge of the slough across the street from our house. Their arms were covered with orange and yellow hair. The round one's name was Johnson, but what everyone called him was Water Shining, and his partner was White Cloud. They had once won big on those words. Also *Johnson* resembles *Water Shining*, which also has *o*, *s*, and *n* sounds. Like two old China Men, they lived together lonely with no families. They sat in front of stores; they sat on their porch. They fenced a part of the slough for their vegetable patch, which had a wooden sign declaring the names of the vegetables and who they belonged to. They also had a wooden sign over their front door: TRANQUILITY, a wish or blessing or the name of their house. They gave us nickels and quarters; they made dimes come out of noses, ears, and elbows and waved coins in and out between their knuckles. They were white men, but they lived like China Men.

When we came home from school and a wino or hobo was trying the doors and windows, Water Shining came out of his little house. "There's a wino breaking into our house," we told him. It did occur to me that he might be offended at our calling his fellow white man a wino. "It's not just a poor man taking a drink from the hose or picking some fruit and going on his way," I explained.

"What? What? Where? Let's take a look-see," he said, and walked with us to our house, saving our house without a fight.

The old men disappeared one by one before I noticed their going. White Cloud told the gamblers that Water Shining was killed in a farming accident, run over by a tractor. His body had been churned and plowed. White Cloud lived alone until the railroad tracks were leveled, the slough drained, the black-birds flown, and his house torn down.

My father found a name for me too at the gambling house. "He named you," said MaMa, "after a blonde gambler who always won. He gave you her lucky American name." My blonde namesake must have talked with a cigarette out of the side of her mouth and left red lip prints. She wore a low-cut red or green gambling dress, or she dressed cowgirl in white boots with baton-twirler tassels and spurs; a stetson hung at her back. When she threw down her aces, the leather fringe danced along her arm. And there was applause and buying of presents when she won. "Your father likes blondes," MaMa said. "Look how beautiful," they both exclaimed when a blonde walked by.

But my mother keeps saying those were dismal years. "He worked twelve hours a day, no holidays," she said. "Even on New Year's, no day off. He couldn't come home until two in the morning. He stood on his feet gambling twelve hours straight."

"I saw a tall stool," I said.

"He only got to sit when there were no customers," she said. "He got paid almost nothing. He was a slave; I was a slave." She is angry recalling those days.

After my father's partners stole his New York laundry, the owner of the gambling house, a fellow ex-villager, paid my parents' fares to Stockton, where the brick buildings reminded them of New York. The way my mother repaid him—only the money is repayable—was to be a servant to his, the owner's, family. She ironed for twelve people and bathed ten children. Bitterly, she kept their house. When my father came home from work at two in the morning, she told him how badly the owner's family had treated her, but he told her to stop exaggerating. "He's a generous man," he said.

The owner also had a black servant, whose name was Harry. The rumor was that Harry was a half-man/half-woman, a half-and-half. Two servants could not keep that house clean, where children drew on the wallpaper and dug holes in the plaster. I listened to Harry sing "Sioux City Sue." "Lay down my rag with a hoo hoo hoo," he sang. He squeezed his rag out in the bucket and led the children singing the chorus. Though my father was also as foolishly happy over his job, my mother was not deceived.

When my mother was pregnant, the owner's wife bought her a dozen baby chicks, not a gift; my mother would owe her the money. MaMa would be allowed to raise the chicks in the owner's yard if she also tended his chickens. When the baby was born, she would have chicken to give for birth announcements. Upon his coming home from work one night, the owner's wife lied to him, "The aunt forgot to feed her chickens. Will you do it?" Grumbling about my lazy mother, the owner went out in the rain and slipped in the mud, which was mixed with chicken shit. He hurt his legs and lay there yelling that my mother had almost killed him. "And she makes our whole yard stink with chicken shit," he accused. When the baby was born, the owner's wife picked out the scrawny old roosters and said they were my mother's twelve.

Ironing for the children, who changed clothes several times a day, MaMa had been standing for hours while pregnant when the veins in her legs rippled and burst. After that she had to wear support stockings and to wrap her legs in bandages.

The owner gave BaBa a hundred-and-twenty-dollar bonus when the baby was born. His wife found out and scolded him for "giving charity."

"You deserve that money," MaMa said to BaBa. "He takes all your time. You're never home. The babies could die, and you wouldn't know it."

When their free time coincided, my parents sat with us on apple and orange crates at the tiny table, our knees touching under it. We ate rice and salted fish, which is what peasants in China eat. Everything was nice except what MaMa was saying, "We've turned into slaves. We're the slaves of these villagers who were nothing when they were in China. I've turned into the servant of a woman who can't read. Maybe we should go back to China. I'm tired of being Wah Q," that is, a Sojourner from Wah.

My father said, "No." Angry. He did not like her female

intrigues about the chickens and the ironing and the half-man/
half-woman.

They saved his pay and the bonuses, and decided to buy a
house, the very house they were renting. This was the two-
story house around the corner from the owner's house, convenient for my mother to walk to her servant job and my father
to the gambling house. We could rent out the bottom floor
and make a profit. BaBa had five thousand dollars. Would the
owner, who spoke English, negotiate the cash sale? Days and
weeks passed, and when he asked the owner what was happening, the owner said, "I decided to buy it myself. I'll let you rent
from me. It'll save you money, especially since you're saving
to go back to China. You're going back to China anyway."
But BaBa had indeed decided to buy a house on the Gold
Mountain. And this was before Pearl Harbor and before the
Chinese Revolution.

He found another house farther away, not as new or big. He
again asked the owner to buy it for him. You would think we
could trust him, our fellow villager with the same surname,
almost a relative, but the owner bought up this house too—
the one with the well in the cellar—and became our landlord
again.

My parents secretly looked for another house. They told everyone, "We're saving our money to go back to China when
the war is over." But what they really did was to buy the house
across from the railroad tracks. It was exactly like the owner's
house, the same size, the same floor plan and gingerbread.
BaBa paid six thousand dollars cash for it, not a check but
dollar bills, and he signed the papers himself. It was the biggest but most run-down of the houses; it had been a board-
ing house for old China Men. Rose bushes with thorns grew
around it, wooden lace hung broken from the porch eaves,
the top step was missing like a moat. The rooms echoed. This
was the house with the attic and basement. The owner's wife
accused her husband of giving us the money, but she was lying.
We made our escape from them. "You don't have to be afraid
of the owner any more," MaMa keeps telling us.

Sometimes we waited up until BaBa came home from work.
In addition to a table and crates, we had for furniture an ironing board and an army cot, which MaMa unfolded next to the

gas stove in the wintertime. While she ironed our clothes, she
sang and talked story, and I sat on the cot holding one or two
of the babies. When BaBa came home, he and MaMa got into
the cot and pretended they were refugees under a blanket tent.
He brought out his hardbound brown book with the gray and
white photographs of white men standing before a flag, sitting
in rows of chairs, shaking hands in the street, hand-signaling
from car windows. A teacher with a suit stood at a blackboard
and pointed out things with a stick. There were no children
or women or animals in this book. "Before you came to New
York," he told my mother, "I went to school to study English.
The classroom looked like this, and every student came from
another country." He read words to my mother and told her
what they meant. He also wrote them on the blackboard,
it and the daruma, the doll which always rights itself when
knocked down, the only toys we owned at that time. The little
h's looked like chairs, the *e*'s like lidded eyes, but those words
were not *chair* and *eye*. "'Do you speak English?'" He read
and translated. "'Yes, I am learning to speak English better.' 'I
speak English a little.'" "'How are you?' 'I am fine, and you?'"
My mother forgot what she learned from one reading to the
next. The words had no crags, windows, or hooks to grasp. No
pictures. The same *a*, *b*, *c*'s for everything. She couldn't make
out ducks, cats, and mice in American cartoons either.

During World War II, a gang of police demons charged
into the gambling house with drawn guns. They handcuffed
the gamblers and assigned them to paddy wagons and patrol
cars, which lined the street. The wagons were so full, people
had to stand with their hands up on the ceiling to keep their
balance. My father was not jailed or deported, but neither he
nor the owner worked in gambling again. They went straight.
Stockton became a clean town. From the outside the gambling
house looks the same closed down as when it flourished.

My father brought his abacus, the hole punch, and extra
tickets home, but those were the last presents for a while. A
dismal time began for him.

He became a disheartened man. He was always home. He
sat in his chair and stared, or he sat on the floor and stared.
He stopped showing the boys the few kung fu moves he
knew. He suddenly turned angry and quiet. For a few days

he walked up and down on the sidewalk in front of businesses
and did not bring himself to enter. He walked right past them
in his beautiful clothes and acted very busy, as if having an
important other place to go for a job interview. "You're nothing but a gambler," MaMa scolded. "You're spoiled and won't
go looking for a job." "The only thing you're trained for is
writing poems," she said. "I know you," she said. (I hated her
sentences that started with "I know you.") "You poet. You
scholar. You gambler. What use is any of that?" "It's a wife's
job to scold her husband into working," she explained to us.

My father sat. "You're so scared," MaMa accused. "You're
shy. You're lazy." "Do something. You never do anything."
"You let your so-called friends steal your laundry. You let
your brothers and the Communists take your land. You have
no head for business." She nagged him and pampered him.
MaMa and we kids scraped his back with a porcelain spoon.
We did not know whether it was the spoon or the porcelain or
the massage that was supposed to be efficacious. "Quit being
so shy," she advised. "Take a walk through Chinatown and
see if any of the uncles has heard of a job. Just ask. You don't
even need to apply. Go find out the gossip." "He's shy," she
explained him to us, but she was not one to understand shyness, being entirely bold herself. "Why are you so shy? People
invite you and go out of their way for you, and you act like a
snob or a king. It's only human to reciprocate." "You act like a
piece of liver. Who do you think you are? A piece of liver?" She
did not understand how some of us run down and stop. Some
of us use up all our life force getting out of bed in the morning, and it's a wonder we can get to a chair and sit in it. "You
piece of liver. You poet. You scholar. What's the use of a poet
and a scholar on the Gold Mountain? You're so skinny. You're
not supposed to be so skinny in this country. You have to be
tough. You lost the New York laundry. You lost the house with
the upstairs. You lost the house with the back porch." She
summarized, "No loyal friends or brothers. Savings draining
away like time. Can't speak English. Now you've lost the gambling job and the land in China."

Somebody—a Chinese, it had to be a Chinese—dug up our
loquat tree, which BaBa had planted in front of the house. He
or she had come in the middle of the night and left a big hole.

MaMa blamed BaBa for that too, that he didn't go track down the tree and bring it back. In fact, a new loquat tree had appeared in the yard of a house around the corner. He ignored her, stopped shaving, and sat in his T-shirt from morning to night.

He seemed to have lost his feelings. His own mother wrote him asking for money, and he asked for proof that she was still alive before he would send it. He did not say, "I miss her." Maybe she was dead, and the Communists maintained a bureau of grandmother letter writers in order to get our money. That we kids no longer received the sweet taste of invisible candy was no proof that she had stopped sending it; we had outgrown it. For proof, the aunts sent a new photograph of Ah Po. She looked like the same woman, all right, like the pictures we already had but aged. She was ninety-nine years old. She was lying on her side on a lounge chair, alone, her head pillowed on her arm, the other arm along her side, no green tints at her earlobes, fingers, and wrists. She still had little feet and a curved-down mouth. "Maybe she's dead and propped up," we kids conjectured.

BaBa sat drinking whiskey. He no longer bought new clothes. Nor did he go to the dentist and come back telling us the compliments on his perfect teeth, how the dentist said that only one person in a thousand had teeth with no fillings. He no longer advised us that to have perfect teeth, it's good to clamp them together, especially when having a bowel movement.

MaMa assured us that what he was looking forward to was when each child came home with gold. Then he or she (the pronoun is neutral in the spoken language) was to ask the father, "BaBa, what kind of a suit do you want? A silk gown? Or a suit from the West? An Eastern suit or a Western suit? What kind of a Western suit do you want?" She suggested that we ask him right now. Go-out-on-the-road. Make our fortunes. Buy a Western suit for Father.

I went to his closet and studied his suits. He owned gray suits, dark blue ones, and a light pinstripe, expensive, successful suits to wear on the best occasions. Power suits. Money suits. Two-hundred-dollars-apiece New York suits. Businessmen-in-the-movies suits. Boss suits. Suits from before we were born. At the foot of the closet arranged in order, order his habit, were his leather shoes blocked on shoe trees. How could I make money like that? I looked in stores at suits and at the prices. I could never learn to sew this evenly, each suit perfect and similar to the next.

MaMa worked in the fields and the canneries. She showed us how to use her new tools, the pitters and curved knives. We tried on her cap pinned with union buttons and her rubber gloves that smelled like rubber tomatoes. She emptied her buckets, thermoses, shopping bags, lunch pail, apron, and scarf; she brought home every kind of vegetable and fruit grown in San Joaquin County. She said she was tired after work but kept moving, busy, banged doors, drawers, pots and cleaver, turned faucets off and on with *ka-chunk*s in the pipes. Her cleaver banged on the chopping block for an hour straight as she minced pork and steak into patties. Her energy slammed BaBa back into his chair. She took care of everything; he did not have a reason to get up. He stared at his toes and fingers. "You've lost your sense of emergency," she said; she kept up her sense of emergency every moment.

He dozed and woke with a jerk or a scream. MaMa medicated him with a pill that came in a purple cube lined with red silk quilting, which cushioned a tiny black jar; inside the jar was a black dot made out of ground pearls, ox horn, and ox blood. She dropped this pill in a bantam broth that had steamed all day in a little porcelain crock on metal legs. He drank this soup, also a thick beef broth with gold coins in the bottom, beef teas, squab soup, and still he sat. He sat on. It seemed to me that he was getting skinnier.

"You're getting skinny again," MaMa kept saying. "Eat. Eat. You're less than a hundred pounds."

I cut a Charles Atlas coupon out of a comic book. I read all the small print. Charles Atlas promised to send some free information. "Ninety-seven-pound weakling," the cartoon man called himself. "I'll gamble a stamp," he said. Charles Atlas did not say anything about building fat, which was what my father needed. He already had muscles. But he was ninety-seven pounds like the weakling, maybe ninety pounds. Also he kicked over chairs like in the middle panel. I filled in the coupon and forged his signature. I did not dare ask him how old he was, so I guessed maybe he was half as old as his weight:

age forty-five, weight ninety. If Charles Atlas saw that he was even skinnier than the weakling, maybe he would hurry up answering. I took the envelope and stamp from BaBa's desk.

Charles Atlas sent pamphlets with more coupons. From the hints of information, I gathered that my father needed lessons, which cost money. The lessons had to be done vigorously, not just read. There seemed to be no preliminary lesson on how to get up.

The one event of the day that made him get up out of his easy chair was the newspaper. He looked forward to it. He opened the front door and looked for it hours before the mailman was due. *The Gold Mountain News* (or *The Chinese Times*, according to the English logo) came from San Francisco in a paper sleeve on which his name and address were neatly typed. He put on his gold-rimmed glasses and readied his smoking equipment: the 1939 World's Fair ashtray, Lucky Strikes, matches, coffee. He killed several hours reading the paper, scrupulously reading everything, the date on each page, the page numbers, the want ads. Events went on; the world kept moving. The hands on the clocks kept moving. This sitting ought to have felt as good as sitting in his chair on a day off. He was not sick. He checked his limbs, the crooks of his arms. Everything was normal, quite comfortable, his easy chair fitting under him, the room temperature right.

MaMa said a man can be like a rat and bite through wood, bite through glass and rock. "What's wrong?" she asked.

"I'm tired," he said, and she gave him the cure for tiredness, which is to hit the inside joints of elbows and knees until red and black dots—the tiredness—appear on the skin.

He screamed in his sleep. "Night sweats," MaMa diagnosed. "Fear sweats." What he dreamed must have been ax murders. The family man kills his entire family. He throws slain bodies in heaps out the front door. He leaves no family member alive; he or she would suffer too much being the last one. About to swing the ax, screaming in horror of killing, he is also the last little child who runs into the night and hides behind a fence. Someone chops at the bushes beside him. He covers his ears and shuts his mouth tight, but the scream comes out.

I invented a plan to test my theory that males feel no pain; males don't feel. At school, I stood under the trees where the girls played house and watched a strip of cement near the gate. There were two places where boys and girls mixed; one was the kindergarten playground, where we didn't go any more, and the other was this bit of sidewalk. I had a list of boys to kick: the boy who burned spiders, the boy who had grabbed me by my coat lapels like in a gangster movie, the boy who told dirty pregnancy jokes. I would get them one at a time with my heavy shoes, on which I had nailed toe taps and horseshoe taps. I saw my boy, a friendly one for a start. I ran fast, crunching gravel. He was kneeling; I grabbed him by the arm and kicked him sprawling into the circle of marbles. I ran through the girls' playground and playroom to our lavatory, where I looked out the window. Sure enough, he was not crying. "See?" I told the girls. "Boys have no feelings. It's some kind of immunity." It was the same with Chinese boys, black boys, white boys, and Mexican and Filipino boys. Girls and women of all races cried and had feelings. We had to toughen up. We had to be as tough as boys, tougher because we only pretended not to feel pain.

One of my girl friends had a brother who cried, but he had been raised as a girl. Their mother was a German American and their father a Chinese American. This family didn't belong to our Benevolent Association nor did they go to our parties. The youngest boy wore girls' dresses with ruffles and bows, and brown-blondish ringlets grew long to his waist. When this thin, pale boy was about seven, he had to go to school; it was already two years past the time when most people started school. "Come and see something strange," his sister said on Labor Day. I stood in their yard and watched their mother cut off his hair. The hair lay like tails around his feet. Mother cried, and son cried. He was so delicate, he had feelings in his hair; it hurt him to have his hair cut. I did not pick on him.

There was a war between the boys and the girls; we sisters and brothers were evenly matched three against three. The sister next to me, who was like my twin, pushed our oldest brother off the porch railing. He landed on his face and broke two front teeth on the sidewalk. They fought with knives, the cleaver and a boning knife; they circled the dining room table and sliced one another's arms. I did try to stop that fight— they were cutting bloody slits, an earnest fight to the death.

The telephone rang. Thinking it was MaMa, I shouted, "Help. Help. We're having a knife fight. They'll kill each other." "Well, do try to stop them." It was the owner's wife; she'd gossip to everybody that our parents had lost control of us, such bad parents who couldn't get respectable jobs, mother gone all day, and kids turned into killers. "That was Big Aunt on the phone," I said, "and she's going to tell the whole town about us," and they quit after a while. Our youngest sister snuck up on our middle brother, who was digging in the ground. She was about to drop a boulder on his head when somebody shouted, "Look out." She only hit his shoulder. I told my girl friends at school that I had a stepfather and three wicked stepbrothers. Among my stepfather's many aliases was the name of my real father, who was gone.

The white girls at school said, "I got a spanking." I said we never got spanked. "My parents don't believe in it," I said, which was true. They didn't know about spanking, which is orderly. My mother swung wooden hangers, the thick kind, and brooms. We got trapped behind a door or under a bed and got hit anywhere (except the head). When the other kids said, "They kissed me good night," I also felt left out; not that I cared about kissing but to be normal.

We children became so wild that we broke BaBa loose from his chair. We goaded him, irked him—*gikked* him—and the gravity suddenly let him go. He chased my sister, who locked herself in a bedroom. "Come out," he shouted. But, of course, she wouldn't, he having a coat hanger in hand and angry. I watched him kick the door; the round mirror fell off the wall and crashed. The door broke open, and he beat her. Only, my sister remembers that it was she who watched my father's shoe against the door and the mirror outside fall, and I who was beaten. But I know I saw the mirror in crazy pieces; I was standing by the table with the blue linoleum top, which was outside the door. I saw his brown shoe against the door and his knee flex and the other brothers and sisters watching from the outside of the door, and heard MaMa saying, "Seven years bad luck." My sister claims that same memory. Neither of us has the recollection of curling up inside that room, whether behind the pounding door or under the bed or in the closet.

A white girl friend, whose jobless and drunk father picked

up a sofa and dropped it on her, said, "My mother saw him pushing *me* down the stairs, and *she* was watching from the landing. And I remember him pushing *her*, and *I* was at the landing. Both of us remember looking up and seeing the other rolling down the stairs."

He did not return to sitting. He shaved, put on some good clothes, and went out. He found a friend who had opened a new laundry on El Dorado Street. He went inside and chatted, asked if he could help out. The friend said he had changed his mind about owning the laundry, which he had named New Port Laundry. My father bought it and had a Grand Opening. We were proud and quiet as he wrote in gold and black on big red ribbons. The Chinese community brought flowers, mirrors, and pictures of flowers and one of Guan Goong. BaBa's liveliness returned. It came from nowhere, like my new idea that males have feelings. I had no proof for this idea but took my brothers' word for it.

BaBa made a new special place. There was a trap door on the floor inside the laundry, and BaBa looked like a trap-door spider when he pulled it over his head or lifted it, emerging. The basement light shone through the door's cracks. Stored on the steps, which were also shelves, were some rolled-up flags that belonged to a previous owner; gold eagles gleamed on the pole tips.

We children waited until we were left in charge of the laundry. Then some of us kept a lookout while the rest, hanging on to the edge of the hole, stepped down between the supplies. The stairs were steep against the backs of our legs.

The floor under the building was gray soil, a fine powder. Nothing had ever grown in it; it was sunless, rainless city soil. Beyond the light from one bulb the blackness began, the inside of the earth, the insides of the city. We had our flashlights ready. We chose a tunnel and walked side by side into the dark. There are breezes inside the earth. They blow cool and dry. Blackness absorbed our lights. The people who lived and worked in the four stories above us didn't know how incomplete civilization is, the street only a crust. Down here under the sidewalks and the streets and the cars, the builders had left mounds of loose dirt, piles of dumped cement, rough patches of concrete tamping down and holding back some of the dirt. The posts were unpainted and not square on their pilings. We followed the tunnels to places that had no man-made materials, wild areas, then turned around and headed for the lighted section under the laundry. We never found the ends of some tunnels. We did not find elevators or ramps or the undersides of the buckling metal doors one sees on sidewalks. "Now we know the secret of cities," we told one another. On the shelves built against the dirt walls, BaBa had stacked boxes of notebooks and laundry tickets, rubber stamps, pencils, new brushes, blue bands for the shirts, rolls of wrapping paper, cones of new string, bottles of ink, bottles of distilled water in case of air raids. Here was where we would hide when war came and we went underground for guerilla warfare. We stepped carefully; he had set copper and wood rat traps. I opened boxes until it was time to come up and give someone else a chance to explore.

So my father at last owned his house and his business in America. He bought chicks and squabs, built a chicken run, a pigeon coop, and a turkey pen; he dug a duck pond, set the baby bathtub inside for the lining, and won ducklings and goldfish and turtles at carnivals and county fairs. He bought rabbits and bantams and did not refuse dogs, puppies, cats, and kittens. He told a funny story about a friend of his who kept his sweater on while visiting another friend on a hot day; when the visitor was walking out the gate, the host said, "Well, Uncle, and what are those chicken feet wiggling out of your sweater?" One morning we found a stack of new coloring books and follow-the-dot books on the floor next to our beds. "BaBa left them," we said. He buried wine bottles upside down in the garden; their bottoms made a path of sea-color circles. He gave me a picture from the newspaper of redwoods in Yosemite, and said, "This is beautiful." He talked about a Los Angeles Massacre, but I wished that he had not, and pretended he had not. He told an ancient story about two feuding poets: one killed the other's plant by watering it with hot water. He sang "The Song of the Man of the Green Hill," the end of which goes like this: "The disheveled poet beheads the great whale. He shoots an arrow and hits a suspended flea. He sees well through rhinoceros-horn lenses." This was a song by Kao Chi, who had been executed for his politics; he is famous for poems to his wife and daughter written upon leaving for the capital; he owned a small piece of land where he grew enough to eat without working too hard so he could write poems. BaBa's luffa and grapevines climbed up ropes to the roof of the house. He planted many kinds of gourds, peas, beans, melons, and cabbages—and perennials—tangerines, oranges, grapefruit, almonds, pomegranates, apples, black figs, and white figs—and from seed pits, another loquat, peaches, apricots, plums of many varieties—trees that take years to fruit.

The Li Sao: An Elegy

I N   T H E   epic elegy *Li Sao*, or *Lament on Encountering
Sorrow* (also translated *Sorrow After Departure* and *Sorrow
in Estrangement*), Ch'ü Yüan, who is Kwut Ngin in our dialect, China's earliest known poet, a Homer, told how he wandered in exile. He lived during the Warring States period when
China was twelve states.

("All Chinese know this story," says my father; if you are
an authentic Chinese, you know the language and the stories
without being taught, born talking them.)

Ch'ü Yüan, who was born on a Tiger day, was a minister
in the Chou Kingdom. He advised the king not to go to
war against Ch'in, but the king listened to the warmongers
and fought a losing war. Because he had expressed an unpopular opinion, Ch'ü Yüan, also called Ch'ü P'ing, meaning "Peace," was banished. He had to leave the Center; he
roamed in the outer world for the rest of his life, twenty
years. He mourned that he had once been a prince, and now
he was nothing. And the people were so blind, they thought
he was a wrongdoer instead of the only righteous man left
in the world. His love for his country was not returned. He
sang poems wherever he went, haggard and poor, always
homesick, roving from place to place on foot like an old beggar. Paintings show him floating above the tips of trees and
horned houses, over other people's heads, his gown blowing
with the clouds at his feet.

He braided a gown out of cress leaves and lilies, and traveled
south into the barbarous lands. He met the Goddess of the
Hsiang River and the Lady of the Hsiang River, the wonderful
women on either side of the water, who decorated him with
clinking jade stones, winterthorn, orchids, angel herbs, and
selineas. Flying horses, swift green dragons, and phoenixes
with gold plumes pulled his chariot, which was a winged dragonboat made of jade and ivory and entwined with ivy leaves.
He rowed with cedar oars and flew orchids for flags; orchids
were woven in the rigging, and the boat was harnessed to the

whirlwind. He left the land of gray plane trees. He drank dew from lotus leaf and magnolia cups. His food was aster petals. Which may all be a way of saying that he had nothing but the outdoors, the mist, the rivers, stones, lightning (his gold whip), and his imagination and dreams. He reached heaven's gate and climbed the roof of the world.

He had many adventures. He followed the phoenix to the uttermost parts of the earth, crossed and recrossed the sky. No home anywhere. He saw the entire world, but not his homeland. He crossed the quicksand; he crossed the burning river red as blood. The Emperor of the West helped him, and the Great Emperor of the East listened to his odes of sacrifice. His steeds drank at the lake where the sun bathes. He brushed the sun with a golden bough. The Lady of the Clouds took him to nine continents and four seas. The Princess of the West, however, declined to meet him, and the falcon refused to act as go-between; the capricious turtledove offered to go, but sent the phoenix, who failed him. Some say he cast his jasper pendant on the earth, where it blossomed; some say he cast his jade pendant into the Hsiang River. He sang to the goddess who dries her hair in the rising sun. He gave spiced rice to the wizard who makes circles with green feathers, shoots the dog star with a shaft, casts rainbows, and pours cassia wine from the North Star. He traveled on the nine waters and among the islands with the God of the Yellow River, who rides on a white tortoise beneath the water. He visited the Dragon Halls, purple and pearly red palaces with walls that glittered like fish scales.

When winter came, he journeyed in thunder and rain. The monkeys and hyenas moaned at night, and he cried that he could not find his king and home. "Time runs like water and takes my youth," he wrote. He told the God of Law how he had been wronged and exiled; the king had gone hunting and the queen had been stolen by a false friend. His king did not aid the suffering people. "I am the phoenix dispossessed," said Ch'ü Yüan. In all these travels, he could not find one uncorrupted human being. He was once rich and handsome with moth-wing eyebrows; now he had no reputation and was misunderstood by Southern Savages. "I am the naked roaming saint whose head was shaved like a slave's." The distance between him and home grew farther each day. "My old wife has gone to a strange district; wind and snow separate us." "Birds fly back to last year's nest; foxes face the hill to die, but I cannot go home." "No go-between anywhere." He was an orphan who traveled everywhere because one place was denied him.

He wrote a poem made of one hundred and seventy questions with no answers. "Soothsayers who use tortoise shell and yarrow," he asked, "what is the order of creation?" "Who built the sky?" "Where does it end?" "What supports the sky?" "Shall I be one of the common herd or a skylark?" "Why do I try to bank up the waters in the dark sea when I am not a great whale?" "Can I convince people one by one about what is right?" The soothsayer said, "I cannot help you." The Witch of the Future, to whom he gave mistletoe, asked him, "Why do you want just that one country?"

From his dragonboat, he looked down at his home and realized that escape and return were equally impossible.

At last he walked along the Tsanglang River while reciting poems. He met a fisherman and told his story again. He had seen the entire corrupt world, and "the crowd is dirty," but he had never given up the ideal of good government. "The crowd is drunk; I alone am sober, I alone am clean, so I am banished. The world has gone bad. Even the reliable orchid has changed."

"Why should you be aloof?" asked the fisherman. "When the water's clear, I wash my tassels, but when it's too muddy for silk, I can still wash my feet."

Upon hearing these words, Ch'ü Yüan decided that he would use the river too. He sang all his poems and his elegy, his requiem. He danced at the edge of the river to make his last moments happier. He threw himself into the water and drowned. "There is no wisdom in the world," says the commentary to the *Li Sao*. "Its people are too corrupt to deserve a man like this."

After he drowned, the people realized his sincerity and their loss. Too late, they felt guilt for their waywardness. They tried to call him back. Poets stood by the river and told him how uncomfortable death was: "Return, O Soul," they sang, "from the empty places and the wrong things. Do not go where the titans live who are a thousand cubits tall, and ten suns eat stone, bronze, and gold. Don't wander among the Blackteeth. Don't go where the demons sacrifice men's flesh and grind their bones. Return, O Soul, from the land where cobras move like grass, and foxes rule for a thousand miles. Don't sink into the thousand-mile quicksand or the pool that thunders. Don't go where red ants grow big as elephants and black wasps big as gourds. No crops grow in the dead lands, and human beings eat thorns and weeds. Return from the land of icebergs like mouths. Don't go to the heaven where tigers guard nine gates, serpents have nine heads, and the giant with the nine heads tears up nine thousand forests. Stay away from the devil with the tiger's forehead and three eyes. Stay away from the eater of human beings."

Then they enticed him with the pleasures of earth: "Return to earth. Return to earth where you have your own room with no surprises, your home warm in winter and cool in summer. Return to the porch with the balustrade and enter again the doors with the red squares. Return, O Soul, to the earth's great halls, domes, towers, and terraces. Remember the flowers and the birds, wild ducks, black cranes, wild geese." They chanted food poems and long, long lists of food: "Pepper with honey, steak, bitter melon soup, lamb, turtle, sugarcane juice." They reminded him of his clothes, the red belts, the silks. "Remember candles and early wheat, salt vinegar, ginger, and water." They sang about girls as mouthwatering as salt plums and lemons. "Come back and listen to the singing girls, who have made new songs. Play the urn and drum. Do the wind dance. Play the drums for war songs. Walk in the fields and sing the rustic songs from sea countries. Look again at the actresses playing warriors. Play chess. Hunt the rhino. Return, O Soul. Return."

The people threw rice into the river for his ghost to eat. They did this every year on the anniversary of his death, and they raced dragonboats up and down the river in memory of his travels or in search of him. Ch'ü Yüan was such a smart man that one day he managed to send his ghost out of the river and say, "Oh, you foolish people. The fish are eating the rice, and I'm going hungry. Wrap it in leaves for me." For a change they listened to him. And so on the fifth day of the fifth month, we eat rice and barley cooked in sausage and pork and salted eggs and beans, and a yellow gelatin, shaped by ti leaves. Not just Chinese but the people in Korea, Japan, Vietnam, Malaysia, and America remember Ch'ü Yüan the incorruptible.

THE BROTHER IN VIETNAM

M Y MOTHER holding my hand, I went through a curtain into a dark, out of which came explosions and screams, voices shouting things I did not understand. In a rectangle of light—which grew and shrank according to how close or far away I thought it—men with scared eyes peered over the top of a big hole they were in. Helmets weighed down their skulls. Their cheekbones were black. The men ran, clutching guns, and fell, and crawled. The explosions rolled them screaming on the ground. I saw the undersides of their boots. Their faces and hands were not flesh-color. Everyone wore the same outfits. The color had gone out of the world. I stumbled tangle-legged into my mother's skirt and the curtain and screamed with the soldiers.

Suddenly they were all gone like a dream, and I was crying in the street. Years later I figured it had only been a movie, a war movie, an old sepia-tone. "Did you take me to an American movie when I was a baby?" I've asked. Usually my father took us to American movies, my mother to Chinese movies, where she could visit with friends during the boring parts, and children played and shouted without getting ejected. MaMa said, "You cried so much that the usher ghost threw me out of the theater." I worried about making her waste money on a ticket, and so she diverted me from the actual horror—I had seen a vision of war.

There has always been war, whether or not I knew about it. My tall parents even taller standing on ladders and covering the windows with black curtains, playing theater in the bright interstice, had been thinking about war. The curtains fell long and black, but the inside of the room shone. My father cut a picture out of a magazine and pinned it on the wall. The yellow light came from it. "You look like this," he said, or "This girl looks like you." She was shining because of her golden hair, a golden girl. It couldn't have been the blonde curls that made her look like me, so it must have been the round face with the fat cheeks. "Shirley Temple also looks like this girl." I had been diverted again, and for some years the importance of that day seemed the blonde girl when those were blackout curtains for World War II.

433

There is no word like *vision* for what one hears. I heard *earthquake*—it may have been during an earthquake—and listened to the world, which was a blue and green sphere with lines of meridians, spinning against a wood fence. It did not clatter against the fence but hummed. "The earth," I said, and did not say "quake" because of the mightiness of it, *earth* the same word as *world* in "World War II."

About the fourth and fifth things I remember—and each thing has to do with war—were my two youngest brothers being born. My sister and brother and I were alone; the adults were in a room across the hall. They had said, "Stay here," but did not shut us in. My sister and I were standing on the bed when we noticed that through a crack at the doorjamb coincidentally lined up with the crack of the door across the hall, we could see into that other room, which was filled with light. MaMa was squatting over a basin, and blood was pouring from her. So that was how babies were born. Our room turned white, and through the window flew a white Christmas card like a dove and landed on the floor. It had fluttered in the air. Forgetting about what we had seen through the cracks, my sister and I picked up the card. It was very beautiful with snow and sparkles. "There's no envelope," we said. "No stamp. No name. No mailman. How could it come through the window?" I checked the window; someone must have snuck up to the open window and thrown the card in. But screen and glass were shut tight against the winter. "You saw it too, didn't you?" my sister and I asked each other, our brother only about a year old and no help. "Yes, it flew through the glass near here." We pointed out the pane, one of the top ones. "How did this card come into the room?" we asked when an adult entered. "The baby's born," said the adult. That baby was my brother who was born on Christmas day. Later the adults said that they found him naked under a pine tree, but I knew what I had seen: blood and a flash of white flying, a flash of flying white.

In addition to his American name, this new brother was named Han Bridge like a bridge between Han and here. We're Han People from the Han Dynasty. Bridge is the name of my brothers' generation. The Chinese name of the brother who waited with us is Incorruptible Bridge or Pure Bridge.

Two years later when our youngest brother was born, I knew days and hours in advance that we were going to have another brother. My mother and the lady doctor locked themselves in a bedroom. I was in charge of my sister and two brothers and decided that we had to arrange to see this birth. Each of us carried a crate or a stool outside and lined it up on the porch under the window (where the card had flown in). We climbed up in a row and saw the doctor lift a white bundle like a snow-drop on a hook. A foot stuck out. The baby had been born. He was being weighed. We heard him cry. Joy swelled the world. We jumped up and down and sang a song the animals in fables sing when they are happy. "'Jump like a squirrel. Bob like a bluejay. Tails in the air. Tails in the air.'" We added our own lines, "The baby's born. The baby's born." Our parents motioned for us to come inside.

This youngest brother was long, thin, and red with very black hair; the other brother had been pale. His fists were tight like fern curls. I pried the fingers open, careful not to break one; there was lint in there already. I put my finger in his hand so that it would feel as if he were holding my hand. MaMa said that a tightfisted baby is lucky because his father saves money, and the baby will also save money. I was glad to see that he had that good useful trait to keep him safe. BaBa named him Bright Bridge, also translated Severe Bridge.

"Where did the baby come from?" I asked the doctor as I walked her to the door.

"I brought him in my black bag." Adults were always divert-ing us from the awful. They wanted to protect us, as I wanted to protect the baby, who a moment ago had been nothing and could easily slip back.

I made sure the windows were locked over the baby's crib, and patrolled those locks and latches. I watched the winos and hoboes. Once, we found one of my brothers sitting in the lap of a black man, who was sitting on the sidewalk. I saw burglars carry off the tuba from the Filipino Marching Band's base-ment. I watched shadows in the neighbors' windows stran-gling one another. Feet dangled from ceilings and trees. A big gray bomb slowly covered the skies between houses, but it was only a Navy blimp. Airplanes flew over, but their bomb hatches stayed shut. *Life* magazine showed black and white photographs of dead bodies, limbs, and heads in impossible positions, rib cages barely covered with skin, faces that one could not stop staring at. Piles of skeletons with teeth and eye sockets and hair. "Is this real?" "Yes, it's real." "What happened to these people?" "They were killed in the war."

The Chinese magazines had war cartoons. In the first panel an ugly man in the cockpit of an airplane laughed as he dive-bombed villagers and water buffaloes. "What is he, MaMa?" "He's an enemy person." So that was what the enemy looked like. He had an evil black pointed moustache, a skullcap, and goggles. She did not say enemy people were Japanese, so for a time, I thought they were from outer space. In the next panel an enemy bayoneted an old man, spurting his blood. A bayonet was a gun that shot knives. An enemy threw two naked babies into the air, and another enemy caught one on his bayonet. The second baby fell to the ground and smashed. A booted enemy stepped on its head. The mother had her arms raised toward the babies. Then the mother was in a cage, the father in another cage, a crowd of children in another, the mother's and father's and children's arms reaching toward one another through the bars. The cells were like cages for ducks and chickens at market. In one panel the huge mother was grimacing, her stomach bloated. She was drinking from a jug. MaMa explained that the Japanese were forcing her to drink water until she burst. They would bounce on her stomach and it would explode. They were torturing her children in front of her, and stopped whenever she drank. If she peed, she had to drink her own urine. The children's mutilation was so gruesome, the cartoonist did not show it.

The adults told us how the Japanese tortured the American soldiers they captured: They tied the prisoner to a stake, and while slicing and poking, they cut an opening in his side and knotted a rope to one of his large intestines. A Japanese, pretending to be friendly, loosened the rope that bound his hands and feet. The American ran, and the rope pulled his guts out in a stream behind him. The Japanese laughed, as they did at the bursting mother and the skewered baby.

While watching for lurkers come to kidnap the babies, I saw many first stars, and wasted them wishing for peace. I was careful to define *peace* so the tricky gods didn't make

the earth peaceful by killing everything on it. War used up
the magic rings, bracelets, wands, the fairies with dandelion
skirts, the fish I let go. I wrote a spell, a one and zeroes all
the way around the rims of the lamp shades on my parents'
nightstands, turned on the lights, and said, "I wish MaMa and
BaBa to live as many years as I have written around this lamp."
Black ribbons, black wreaths, and pennants with stars hanging
in windows and on doors meant the sons of those houses had
been killed in war.

Each time we went to the Confucius Hall for meetings and
Chinese movies, everybody together bowed three bows, and
somebody on stage lit three sticks of incense, the first to wish
happiness to the ruler, the second for World Peace, and the
third, good harvest. Sun Yat Sen's and Chiang Kai Shek's pictures were on the stage next to the American and Chinese
flags. (My father's small picture was among the other founders' in the foyer.) We sang the Chinese National Anthem, and
heard hours of speeches about war and the obligations of us
Wah People, then pledged money to help China.

At the parades, where tanks and rockets rolled by and soldiers and sailors marched, Chinese Americans carried a giant
red Chinese flag that covered the street for people to throw
money on. The dragon in those days came to our houses. We
tied lettuce and new dollar bills from the porch eaves, and
the dragon jumped for its food. All this money was used for
rescuing war refugees.

The houses where the Japanese American families lived
were shut down, and the gardens overgrown as if enchanted.
We kids explored empty houses and called them haunted. We
walked around the yards, climbed in doors and windows, wandered about the rooms, sat on the furniture. A boy fell through
a floor. And once we saw a foot step out of a doorway. We ran
from it and lost one of the girls, who sat on a curb bent over
with a stomachache. The foot was in white socks and oxfords.

All the talk was about war and death. Even the story about
the squirrel and the blue jay was about their burying a friend.
Buried. Fa Mu Lan bled from sword wounds until her armor was soaked red. Ngok Fei's arms were tied behind his
back, and the blood squeezed out from the wooden collar
around his neck. Grandfather was bayoneted in the head for

patriotically withholding information from a Japanese soldier. My mother's family, which had four girls, had saved the only boy, the youngest, Uncle Wah, who dodged the draft. He had been fifteen years old, maybe only fourteen, Chinese adding a year, when they gave him all their money and helped him escape to Singapore.

"'The superior man minds his own business; fools concern themselves with public matters,'" said the adults, talking politics. "'Fan Kuai was a butcher before becoming a general.'" "'Warlords confiscate the land, and kidnap the farmer to guard some obscure border.'" "'To go to war is to mingle with the desert sands.'"

"Armies enter the village with draft lists, and there are dots against our names," sang Tu Fu. "Boys come back with their hair white." He wrote that giving birth to daughters is better than sons. "We can still give her in marriage, keep her as a neighbor, but a son is buried without ceremonies among the hundred grasses." "Soldiers ravage and burn even the print blocks." He sang a threnody for a woman sewing the head back on her husband's dead body. "A wife of a soldier is a wisteria clinging to an old tree." "A woman married to a soldier is rabbit silk clinging to wild chrysanthemum and hemp."

Soldiers wrote their poems on the paper money they'd been paid and let the money fly away in the wind at crossroads.

In his last five poems before he died in battle, Wang Tsan, a poet with eidetic memory in Ts'ao Ts'ao's army, witnessed the final days of the Han Dynasty. He saw a woman throw her child into yellow weeds, which were studded with skulls. While he wandered in the embers and ashes of once-tall cities, he cupped his hands like blinders beside his eyes.

There was a farmer in Mei Chia village, who knew that he would be drafted. Recruiters told the hungry farmer about the food, clothes, and shoes the army would give him free. He could send all the pay home to his mother. Whichever army reached the village first would force him to fight on its side or shoot him for an enemy, so he might as well volunteer. His mother told him that she did not want that money. But the farmer said he would have to get some sleep if he was to go to war in the morning. That night as he lay sleeping, his mother stabbed his eyes out with her two hairpicks.

Freedom from the draft was the reason for leaving China in the first place. The Gold Mountain does not make war, is not invaded, and has no draft. The government does not capture men and boys and send them to war.

My father was exactly the right age for the draft. So was Uncle Bun's son and Big Brother Sao. Everybody suggested ways to get out of war. Certain butchers were supposed to be efficient cutting off the trigger finger with one blow of the cleaver. "He's faster than a surgeon." There were diets to get thinner and diets to get fatter. So-and-so had gained ten pounds on the day of the physical by eating ten pounds of bananas. They discussed the advantages and dangers of staying awake for a week drinking coffee. They rehearsed flunking ear tests—not to turn around when a tester whispered behind them, for example.

"There was a poet who took a drug that paralyzed his vocal cords. I wonder what drug that was."

"Chlorine bleach and ammonia. The effect, unfortunately, is permanent."

"What you do to foil the X-ray machine is drink ink straight. Then the photograph comes out black."

"Is ink poisonous?"

"A brother in Los Angeles drank ink. He's gotten out of the draft, and he's still healthy. Wouldn't you rather die drinking ink than be blown up by a land mine?"

Borax, alum, rat poison. Run for twenty miles a day while smoking cigarettes.

I sniffed at the undiluted ink; it smelled metallic sweet. The men were brave and desperate to drink it. It made my teeth clench.

"Drink two quarts before the X-rays."

They experimented how to make more phlegm, how to ruin the stomach, how to control temperature and blood pressure by will power and breath.

"That inking the X-rays is not going to work," my father said. "It's only a superstition; it won't work." He was interested because he had been drafted.

BaBa did not sleep after he got drafted. I planned to be always awake too, alert, on guard. I would make time pass deliberately, like a slow train, but suddenly my mother and

two of the children and I were on a train. Our father was not
with us; we were traveling with the owner of the gambling
house. He was the most powerful of the Stockton Chinese,
an American citizen, an English speaker; he dealt with white
people on our behalf. They knew him as a good citizen and
Chinese community spokesman. The seat did not fit; I stood
on it or in the aisle. Everything moved. We did not have to
walk on top of the train, nor did we have to sneak aboard a
boxcar. We were going where the tracks went, to Sacramento,
Second City. "Look," said my mother. "Sheep. Look at the
sheep." I was standing at the window, but did not see anything
until she said "Sheep," and they appeared, white in the sun. I
looked at her, and when I turned back, they were gone. The
train whistled regularly ahead of us. At bends the engine and
the caboose looked like other trains. We were on our way to
rescue BaBa from the United States Army.

In Second City we took taxis and walked to places that were
like train stations. We sat on benches waiting, or stood against
MaMa on sidewalks and in hallways. We waited in lobbies decorated with posters of Army, Navy, and Marine demons. The baby
didn't cry. Father's employer went away to talk to generals; then
he also waited. BaBa was somewhere inside this city. Homeless
and fatherless, I did not see how we were going to find the train
tracks again. My mother said, "I'm going to go into the general's
office and beg him not to take your father. I'll say, 'These children's lives depend on him.' Then all of you cry, 'BaBa. BaBa.
Don't take our BaBa away from us.'" I would hang on to her
coat, my sister to her hand, my brother be the babe in arms.

MaMa was wearing her black New York coat with the black
fur collar; I wore my maroon coat with the brown fur collar,
and my sister, her powder blue coat with the gray fur collar.

This waiting was like when villagers waited in the landlord's
courtyard to pay taxes. The other reason for leaving China was
the taxes paid with grain. There was a story about a widow
who paid with the heads of her two children. The peasants
cried Aiya when she poured their heads out of a rice bag.
"Here are your taxes," she said as the heads rolled out at the
feet of the landlord. Landlords and generals and governments
"pare and peel the ignorant country people." Families had to
sell the mother or a sister, leave her there at the landlord's.

At last, suddenly, BaBa came out of a door, laughing and talking. Time rippled again. He told MaMa what had happened to him: "We had to take all our clothes off, and file past the doctor demon. The white man in front of me was white and fat—rolls of fat. And there I was next to him—skinny with rows of ribs. The doctor flunked us both at once. Too fat and too skinny. He took one look at us, and said, 'Four F.' Mr. Too Fat and Mr. Too Thin. We pointed at each other and laughed." He told this miracle many times.

All of us together again, we found the train and went home. As soon as we got in the door, MaMa started fattening him up, but it never worked. She had been using her old doctoring skills poisoning him, and his weight had dropped permanently. "I poisoned him to keep him out of World War II," she says. "Now all these years, I've been trying to plump him up with food and medicine, but he stays skinny. His metabolism is ruined. He eats a lot but doesn't gain weight."

The cousins who were not clever enough to avoid the war—in fact some foolhardy ones enlisted—sent pictures from Europe. They looked like the good soldiers in the movies. Uncle Bun's son, who had been the most enthusiastic about drinking ink and shooting off toes, had posed for a studio portrait of himself in a helmet with antennae. His hands in gauntlets held a machine with nozzles; the hose was draped around his neck. Big Brother Sao, an officer, wore a creased hat in some pictures and a brimmed hat in others; he is looking sideways into the camera to show off the bars on his collar. A Boston cousin was among a group of soldiers kneeling and standing in front of their tent. Their hair was inside hats and helmets, and they wore rumpled uniforms. My mother said they were army doctors. I kept asking which were men and which women, but she didn't know either. We guessed the pretty ones were women. The ones with beard stubbles and big knuckles were definitely men. The one that was our cousin had the chin strap of his helmet unbuckled, and it hung down jauntily and war-wearily. If he had not written which one he was, we would not have been able to pick him out; he did not look peculiarly Chinese. It must have been the uniform. Another cousin sent a picture of himself leaning against a palm tree; he looked like he was in a war musical.

One cousin was in the Fourteenth Service Squad, the Chinese American Air Force Battalion, the first American soldiers into China. What they found in Chungking was a city of primitive natives who did not understand Cantonese. The soldiers hired them as houseboys, carriers, and road builders. Two by two the Chinese carried bombs tied to a pole between them. They moved fifty-gallon drums of fuel. The Chinese Americans drove their trucks on the new road while thousands of natives built it before them. Men, women, and children broke rocks into gravel so fast the drivers did not have to step on their brakes.

We had a family portrait taken to send to the faraway relatives. One brother was dressed in a kid army uniform with a leather strap across his chest and another brother in a baby navy uniform with white middy collar and white shorts, his sweet knees showing.

We went to a movie where the attendants gave each kid a free picture of an atomic bomb explosion. Smoke boiled in a yellow and orange cloud like a brain on a column. It was a souvenir to celebrate the bombing of Japan. Since I did not own much, I enjoyed the ownership of the V. J. picture. At the base of the explosion, where the people would have been, the specks didn't resolve into bodies. I hid the picture so the younger children could not see it, to protect them against the fear of such powerful evil, not to break the news to them too soon. Occasionally, I took it out to study. I hid it so well, I lost it. I drew billows and shafts of light, and almost heard the golden music of it, the gold trumpets with drums of it.

For a while after the soldiers in the family came home, they looked like their photographs; they wore the uniforms visiting. But then they put on their regular slacks and white shirts. Their hair grew out, and their wives trimmed it with home clippers. Their noses rounded out, the bridges receding, and their tight jaws softened. They did not walk from the shoulders like football players and boxers any more. They started speaking Chinese loud again. Big Brother Sao's eyes began looking at things far away again.

The one family of AJA's, Americans of Japanese Ancestry, on our block came out of relocation camp. They did not seem capable of killing 10 million Chinese civilians, but then these were Americans and not Japanese. We had not broken into their house; it had stood shut for years. They pruned the bushes back into neat balls; they preferred ornamentals over vegetables. They gave us their used comic books, and were the only adults who gave us toys instead of clothes for Christmas. We kids, who had peasant minds, suspected their generosity; they were bribing us not to lynch them. The friendlier they were, the more hideous the crimes and desires they must have been covering up. My parents gave them vegetables; we would want them to be nice to us when the time came for us Chinese to be the ones in camp. No matter how late we walked home from the laundry, as we passed their house, they switched on their porch light to light our way.

A comic book they gave us each month was *Blackhawk*, which is about a squadron of allied pilots. Chop Chop was the only Blackhawk who did not wear a blue-black pilot's uniform with yellow and black insignia. He wore slippers instead of boots, pajamas with his undershirt showing at the tails, white socks, an apron; he carried a cleaver and wore a pigtail, which Chinese stopped wearing in 1911. He had buck teeth and slanted lines for eyes, and his skin was a muddy orange. Fat and half as tall as the other Blackhawks, who were drawn like regular human beings, Chop Chop looked like a cartoon. It was unclear whether he was a boy or a little man. He did not pilot his own plane but rode behind the main Blackhawk, the American. "Very clever, these Chinese," Blackhawk kept saying; "I always said little Chop Chop is the smartest of the Blackhawks." And not being clever myself, I took these words as compliments. Tall dragon ladies with cigarette holders said, "I'd kill for a kiss from those lips," meaning Blackhawk's or André's. I thought I had to learn to like Chop Chop; it was certainly true that we used cleavers, and we admired fat people, and I for one was short. We decided the Japanese family must not have known what those comics meant, or they wouldn't have bought them.

The cousins who had gone to war didn't talk about what they had seen or done, just as the AJA's did not mention the camps. They must have been too ashamed. They might have talked among themselves, and shut up in front of an outsider like me, not a soldier, not an AJA. The stories unfit for children must have been worse than guts hanging out, legs and brains hurtling through the air, cities and countries bombed into insanity, my own cousins killing Germans and Italians. I wouldn't tell children such things either.

The next enemy was the Communists. Our parents agreed that we should not meet at a designated place should Stockton be bombed but be free to escape with our teachers if we were at school or to run with the neighbors. But we children privately planned to meet at the big tree, wait for each other there, come back to the tree years later if we got lost in the city altered by bombing. The scary thing about going to school was that I might come home to find a bomb crater, or the house would be empty. I would walk from room to room calling, and then the sun would go down. The AJA children must have come home from school and waited on the porch for their parents to open the door, but they had been taken to camp.

Grandmother and the aunts wrote letters on the deaths of every last uncle. If the uncles could have figured out what the Communists wanted of them, they would have complied, but Communism made no sense. It was something to do with new songs, new dances, and the breaking up of families. Maybe it had to do with no sex; the men were separated from the women. Children were put into motherless, fatherless camps for training; they were taught to report on their parents instead of guarding family secrets. The Communists were not simply after property; they wanted the people to say certain things. They had to sing ugly Communist songs. "Stoop and scoop, stoop and scoop," they sang, and genuflected, swooping their red scarves from air to ground. The aunts waved their kerchiefs vigorously; they memorized fast and sang loud, but still they had to kneel on ground glass, and their thumbs were broken. They did whatever they thought the Communists wanted, but the Communists were not satisfied. Communists were people who had gone crazy and perverted. They made order by rationing food, a cup of oil per family per week. They held court trials, which they thought were the same as entertainment and theater. The torturers asked riddles with no correct answers. The uncles had listened to the answers of the people ahead of them, but the Communists wanted peculiar responses; the same answer did not fit everyone. Communist schools taught from strange books. The uncles had been kept awake at night to study. "If Uncle doesn't get some sleep soon, he's going to die. He's working from four A.M. to eleven P.M., then has to study how to be a Communist in his spare time. If he doesn't memorize a page a day perfectly, he can't have his dinner." The Communists were monkeys trying to be human beings; they were pretending to explain and reason, putting on serious faces. They were saying nonsense, pretending they knew the classics when they were not teaching from real books. Communist schools, Communist books, Red art work, Red courts, theaters, customs were almost like real ones but off. The shrewd villagers were not fooled. The Japanese had tortured people for the fun of it; the Communists wanted something else: their monkey civilization. Neighbors informed against one another to prove they were true Communists. The number of people the Communists killed was 60 million.

After the uncles were killed, the aunts fled to Hong Kong, Canada, and the United States. That the Communists were holding their distant cousins as hostages did not deter them.

"I wish the Japanese had won," my mother said.

For the Korean War, we wore dog tags and had Preparedness Drill in the school basement. We had to fill out a form for what to engrave on the dog tags. I looked up "religion" in the *American-Chinese Dictionary* and asked my mother what religion we were. "Our religion is Chinese," she said. "But that's not a religion," I said. "Yes, it is," she said. "We believe in the Chinese religion." "Chinese is our race," I said. "Well, tell the teacher demon it's Kung Fu Tse, then," she said. The kids at school said, "Are you Catholic?" "No." "Then you're a Protestant." So our dog tags had *O* for religion and *O* for race because neither black nor white. Mine also had *O* for blood type. Some kids said *O* was for "Oriental," but I knew it was for "Other" because the Filipinos, the Gypsies, and the Hawaiian boy were *O*'s. Zero was also the name of the Japanese fighter plane, so we had better watch our step. The teachers gave us anti-Communist comic books and Civil Defense pamphlets about atomic bomb attacks. We did a scientific experiment about chain reactions by arranging matches in triangles, the first match burning and lighting two, and those two igniting four, and so on until the whole world was on fire. The earth would quake and split in half.

"The War," I wrote in a composition, which the teacher corrected, "Which war?" There was more than one.

Before the letter writers stopped complaining about the
Communists, the Vietnam war had begun. The government
said that Viet Cong weapons came from China. We ought to
bomb China into the Stone Age, the generals said. Soon the
war would be Chinese Americans against Chinese. And my
brothers old enough to be drafted.

One brother got married a few months before the draft
exemption for married men was canceled. But one brother
enlisted in the Navy and the other was commissioned as an
officer in the Air Force.

I drove my youngest brother to the airport in the middle
of the night. He didn't want the flowers I brought; he had
already refused to carry the chickens and puddings that MaMa
had cooked. He was in his uniform like the middy that he
wore in his baby picture. He said not to wait for him to board
or for the plane to take off. "Go on," he said. "Don't wait
around." So I only got to see him check his luggage. As I
drove past the terminal, I saw him sitting by himself on a cement bench under a light.

The brother tried to get into the Coast Guard, which he
thought rescued surfers and sailboats and directed traffic
around buoys. He drove to Santa Cruz and Monterey, and
there were no openings; everybody else who did not want to
go to war had had the same idea. Then the Coast Guard were
sent to Vietnam to fight on the rivers there.

The Japanese and Chinese Americans warned one another
what would happen if they got captured: the Vietnamese
would flay Asian Americans alive. Unless you die of shock,
you're still alive after being skinned. You had to die fighting.
Imagine the eyes looking out of a skinless body. During World
War II the United States had tactfully sent the 442nd Go-For-
Broke AJA's to Europe, not Asia or the Pacific. But for this
war, there was not that special consideration.

The rumor also went that the brother's draft board
was channeling hippies and blacks into the infantry. And
"Orientals" belonged over there in Asia fighting among their
own kind. The only way that he would be able to get classified

as a Conscientious Objector was to have a religion, and he did not have one. He did not want to end up a medic in this immoral war anyway.

While deciding what to do, as time ran out, the brother did his job, which was teaching high school. He had been teaching for months, but had not gotten over his surprise at how dumb the students were. Most of them had an I.Q. of 100, the average, which permitted them to read by sounding out each word. The human race was not smart.

During Current Events, he told his class some atrocities to convince them about the wrongness of war. The students looked at the pictures of napalmed children and said, "Sure, war is hell." Where had they learned that acceptance? He told them the worst torture he knew: the Vikings used to cleave a prisoner-of-war's back on either side of the spine, and pull the lungs out, which fluttered like wings when the man breathed. This torture was called the Burning Eagle. The brother felt that it was self-evident that we ought to do anything to stop war. But he was learning that upon hearing terrible things, there are people who are, instead, filled with a crazy patriotism.

"Who owns the electricity?" a boy with an 85 I.Q. and a third-grade reading level asked one day. The brother recognized a "teachable moment," as these happy seconds were called in college. He explained how water, electricity, gas, and oil originally belonged to nobody and everybody. Like the air. "But the corporations that control electricity sell it to the rest of us," he said. "Well, of course they do," said the student; "I'd sell the air if I had discovered it." "What if some people can't afford to buy it?" "Whoever discovered it deserves to be paid for it," said the stubborn boy. "It's Communist not to let him make all the money he can." Although the students could not read or follow logic, they blocked him with their anti-Communism, which seemed to come naturally to them, without effort or study. He had thought that it was self-evident that air, at least, belongs to all of us. The students' parents were on welfare, unemployment, and workmen's compensation, but they defended capitalism without knowing what it was called.

"Can you invent a plan where a person can always find a job, and with that job make a living?" the brother asked. "How do we go about making food instead of bombs?" "What steps can we take to stop the war in Vietnam?"

"You think like that because you're a Communist," the kids replied. "That's a Communist question." Any criticism he had of America they dismissed as his being gookish.

Students were dropping out, not in protest like college students but to volunteer for the Army, Navy, and Marines. He had a few months, a few weeks, days to educate them before they got killed or killed others in Vietnam. Or until he himself had to go. He had to make up words of advice on the spot. Supposedly men, the dropouts came back to the hallways to show off their sturdy uniforms and good shoes. They looked more substantial, taller, smoothed out, as if some kind of potential had been fulfilled. "Take care of yourself," he told them. To those who dropped out to work on assembly lines, he said, "Find out what you're making."

In the one class that wasn't remedial, strange things happened to the literature. After the lessons on how to fill out employment forms, checks, income tax forms, drivers' license and health insurance applications, after reading and discussing the motor vehicle code, he introduced *Romeo and Juliet* with a movie of it, models of the Globe, role-playing, and the sound track from *West Side Story*. But upon its reading, *Romeo and Juliet* became a horror story about children his students' age whispering, tiptoeing, making love, and driven mad in the dark. They killed and were killed in dark streets and dark rooms. They married in the dark. Plague infested the country, and drugs poisoned instead of cured. Children were buried alive among their ancestors' bones, with which Juliet feared she would dash in her brains. She was locked in a tomb with her dead husband, a young suicide, and her cousin festering green. The brother could not shift the emphasis; he felt he had spoiled the love story for a generation of students.

Between classes he found secret torn books hidden underneath shelves and stuffed behind other books. Somebody had jammed books behind the radiator and up the air vent, "Fuck you, basturds" scrawled on their pages. Books that he had bought for a classroom library were ripped in half along the bindings.

The students shamed by Remedial Reading covered their

books with paper bags or oil cloth. The remedials had no brotherly feeling toward one another. "Dummy," they said. "Stupid." "Shut up, Stupid." There were hardly any girl remedials; when girls landed in those classes, they improved quickly and got out.

His students stole anything. They shot up bowling alleys, and beat up hippies and whores ("Hors Welcome" they painted on their cars). One boy collected German helmets, bayonets, knives ("with real bloodstains"), swastikas, atrocity and Hitler photos, flags, iron crosses, grenades. He had big hands but quit football practice for the brother's private reading lessons. When the poor boy stayed at third-grade, 3.0, reading level, he banged his head against the wall. His file said that he had had two older brothers who died when they reached third grade; one drowned and the other fell off a roof. One boy tied rocks around the necks of dogs and watched them struggle and drown. He bragged about killing two tied together. He also jumped dogs and slit their throats. One boy had three babies by three different girl friends, and persuaded all of them to keep the children; the brother gave him three Doctor Spock books. One student was a vampire boy, who wore a cape and would not go out into the sun. The others pulled him away from the shade along the walls, tore off his clothes, held him down, and trained magnifying glasses on his skin. Many students acted like animals: One, Benjie, lowered his heavy head snarling over his papers, peeped and spied over his left arm so nobody could cheat off his poor paper. He held his pencil straight up and down in a fist that stuck out of an unraveling sweater sleeve. His eyebrows jerked; growls came from inside his arms. Whenever his pencil broke, he walked all the way around the room to the sharpener, and wrote *fuck* and *chink* on the blackboards.

"Why does he think he's so smart?" Benjie asked, pointing with his middle finger at a yearbook picture of the student body president. "People who get *A*'s don't have fun. They're fairies. Fuckin' fairies. That guy's such a fairy, if I hit him, he'd fall over like anybody else. Is it true about that ten-year-old kid who's going to college?"

"Yes," said the brother, "but there are hardly any people like him. He's sort of a freak of nature."

"If I hit him, he'd fall over." He threw something, then retreated behind his arms, came out again. "You don't think I'm smart, do you? You think I'm dumb. Stu-pee-do."

"No, you're not so dumb. In three months you went from third-grade books to fourth-grade books. That's very fast. Three more months and you can read fifth-grade books. Two years' improvement in one year. At that rate in about two years you'll catch up to twelfth grade. You are the most improved person in the class."

"Most improved means I started out the dumbest. In a class of stupidos. But I'm in the twelfth grade right now. Eighteen years old. I ain't no dumb Mexican from Mexico. I been speaking English all my life. All my life." He put his head down inside the cave of his arms.

The next day he said "Is it true about that three-year-old kid studying physics in Korea?"

"Yes."

Benjie hit himself hard on the face.

To give the students something they would read, the brother brought them a pile of comic books. "They're coming out with the first black superheroes," he said. "Too bad, though, they're starting to make Oriental villains again with yellow skin and long fingernails."

"That's supposed to be a chink?" Benjie asked, interested. "You're making a mistake this time. That doesn't look like no chink." He took the comic book and read it. "Don't feel bad. I just read it all the way through. That's not a chink. They draw him ugly to show how bad he is, that's all." Fu Manchu. The Mandarin. Yellow Claw. The brother was touched at Benjie's trying to protect his feelings.

The first of the brother's students to go to Vietnam was Alfredo Campos, who was twenty-one years old, the age at which the brother had graduated from college. Alfredo had emigrated alone from Mexico when he was nineteen. He was going to school to get a job away from the grape fields. He asked the brother to help him write letters to his eleven brothers and sisters, who practiced English for coming to the United States someday. But suddenly, in the middle of the semester, Alfredo dropped out and went to Vietnam. "I send honor to you, Teacher," he wrote from there. "I send congratulations to you, my Teacher, on Christmas day." His sister, who was eighteen, took his place in class. She brought slides he had sent from Vietnam.

The brother showed the pictures to the class: A puff of orange smoke was artillery fire. A row of tanks fired into what looked like a prairie. Guns mounted on wheels taller than men shot at a mountain. Rows of shit-colored helicopters blotched the sky. No dead bodies, though. Alfredo and his prisoner smiled side by side at the camera; they were both small, dark boys. Alfredo and a Vietnamese girl friend, who was dressed in a leopard mini-skirt, stood with their arms around each other's waist. Children cut his hair and shined his shoes; they did not seem to heed their broken arms and missing legs. He and his buddies, all Latins, toasted his former classmates with beer and made *V*'s with their fingers. Women rummaged through garbage cans marked PROPERTY OF USA. The sun made everybody's eyes squint.

The brother did not say anything. The students also did not say much. He showed the slides to all five of his classes, and therefore got to see them himself five times. He didn't find anything to say about them. It was just as well; it would be unfair to say anything, Alfredo being in the war, more fair to let the students draw their own conclusions seeing actual pictures of Vietnam taken by somebody they knew.

The third or fourth time around, the pictures seemed very happy, very attractive: Alfredo, grown, not lonely, almost married to a large and happy leopard-skinned wife. The sun shining orange in their cottage. Smoking an after-dinner cigarette while children played at his feet. Children laughing around his head, all their faces catching the light. Many friends, compadres. In winter Alfredo had jungles, not leafless trees in concrete. Even the prisoner was smiling. A lovely day. Sunshine and palm trees. The old woman held up half a potato and laughed.

The brother had to answer Alfredo's letters. "Dear Alfredo," he wrote, and could not think of the next thing to say. "I hope you are well," he wrote because that was the truth. He did hope he was well. "Take care of yourself," he wrote, but not "Take *good* care of yourself"; Alfredo might have to kill someone in order to do that. He did not write, "I showed your slides to the class"; he did not want to encourage him to take more dramatic shots. The brother kept writing the same letter: "I am fine. I hope you are too." He did not send any war or history books or peace pamphlets; Alfredo might let down his guard at a crucial moment and not defend himself. He did not mention religion though he knew Alfredo had one; if he put doubt into him, maybe he would hesitate at the wrong moment and get shot. Nor did he ask if he had killed anybody yet.

The schools started atomic attack drills again. The teachers had to sign a paper to be Civil Defense deputies. The brother did not turn it in, as he had not submitted his loyalty oath. Nobody noticed. If the principal said a code sentence on the P.A. system, "The fire department will be inspecting Buildings C and D at two o'clock today," it meant that a bomb was really coming. The students were not to know so that they wouldn't panic. For drill, the brother was assigned to take his group to the weight room, where the P.E. Department stored the body-building equipment. He sat in the dark with the remedials and waited for the all-clear bell. The boys rolled the weights about, lifted them in the wrong postures, dropped them on the wood floor, punched one another. He would not like being trapped under rubble with them. He'd be the only rational, unselfish adult there, the only one with an idea of order, responsible for the safety of all of them, the only one who would question cannibalism. No, these would not be the people he would wish to die with. "Stop throwing the barbells," he ordered.

He could not escape induction. He did not have physical disabilities. He was not married. He was not in a job vital to defense. The Army would not assign him to some easy NATO duty like guarding a German border. They'd send a gook to fight the gook war. He had to do something, not leave his fate to the draft lottery, an all-or-nothing gamble. The chances had narrowed to two: go to Canada or enlist in the Navy. He decided against Canada though he had relatives in Vancouver Chinatown, Pender Street. He had no friends there. He had never met those relatives. He did not want to live the rest of his life a fugitive and an exile. The United States was the only country he had ever lived in. He would not be driven out.

So he enlisted in the Navy for four years. The Air Force was more apt to drop bombs. On the ocean, he would not have his heart broken at the sight of Vietnamese grandmothers and babies.

He arrived at his decision by reasoning like this: In a country that operates on a war economy, there isn't much difference between being in the Navy and being a civilian. When we ate a candy bar, drank grape juice, bought bread (ITT makes Wonder bread), wrapped food in plastic, made a phone call, put money in the bank, cleaned the oven, washed with soap, turned on the electricity, refrigerated food, cooked it, ran a computer, drove a car, rode an airplane, sprayed with insecticide, we were supporting the corporations that made tanks and bombers, napalm, defoliants, and bombs. For the carpet bombing. Everything was connected to everything else and to war. The Peace Movement published names of board members of weapons factories; they were the same people who were bankers and university trustees and government officials. Lines connected them in one interlocking system. The Pacifists' boycott lists included so many ordinary things, we couldn't live day-to-day American lives without adding to the war. Universities, funded with government grants, were inventing eerie new weapons: cobalt bombs, cluster bombs, scatter bombs, porpoise delivery systems, shrapnel that couldn't be X-rayed, fires that water did not put out, spider-web sensors that picked up body heat and relayed its presence to computers and from computers to satellites to bombers. Fragmentation bombs, "guavas," embedded pellets that sent out radio signals to be traced to hideouts. Seismologists were not just studying the natural quaking of the earth but the impact of bombs. Electronics companies in the United States and the Far East, headed by retired admirals and generals, were building missiles, firebombs, and nuclear weapons for warfare on land and under water. Bugs monitored conversations miles away. Engineers and psychologists were researching police systems for riot control in American cities. Computer companies were keeping track of everyone by cross-indexing our banking and social security numbers, drivers' licenses, airline tickets, birth certificates, jail records, and purchases. The metals and stones of the abundant continent were being changed into weapons, which were funneled to Vietnam.

The way to contribute less to the war was to go on welfare and eat out of garbage bins in back of grocery stores. Women were having babies at home to help them escape the draft in future wars or this war, which might not end by the time they grew to adolescence. There were drop-outs in a wagon train leaving California for Alaska, a Texas wagon train having already reached Canada. People were living in caves in Nevada and in the California north woods. A family from Hawai'i had had all their teeth replaced with metal ones; they went to live on a secret island forever. Families and friends bought boats and would live on the sea. The brother knew people leaving for the New Hebrides, Honduras, New Zealand. But he enlisted.

He resolved that in the Navy he would follow orders up to a point short of a direct kill. He would not shoot a human being; he would not press the last button that dropped the bomb. But he would ride the ship that brought the bombs, which his taxes had already paid for. If ordered to shoot at a human target, he would then go AWOL to Canada or Sweden. But up until then, he would be a Pacifist in the Navy rather than in jail, no more or less guilty than the ordinary stay-at-home citizen of the war economy.

When the new Secretary of Defense called the Chinese "the enemy of the world" and predicted all-out nuclear war before 1970, the brother stopped reading newspapers. There wasn't any news; it would be news if the war ended. The news didn't change; only the numbers kept going up.

When the brother handed in his resignation, the principal told him that he would get credit for being in the service; he would rise four years on the salary schedule just as if he'd been teaching all along. The school would have a job for him later, give him preference. "You don't have to do that," he said. He did not tell his students where he was going or that he was leaving. The last thing he tried to teach them was: "The military draft is not an American tradition. Protest against it is a longer tradition."

His mother said, "Bring a wife home. Look for a Chinese girl, but Japanese are okay too, Koreans okay. Just as long as she has a soft smile." His father stood at the door waving good-bye. "Good-bye," he said. "So long," like leaving for college.

Basic training wasn't bad; he had expected worse, like in *D.I.*

with Jack Webb. He did not have to fight and die like Prewitt and Maggio. Nobody called him chink or gook or slope or Commie. The only personal racial harassment was when the Company Commander stopped in front of him and hollered, "Where you from?" and he had to shout out his hometown, Sir. "Louder. Where you from?" "Stockton, California, Sir." "Where is that?" "West Coast, Sir." "What country?" "U.S.A., Sir." Each time the Chief shouted at him, it wasn't about his shoe shine or his attitude but "Where you from?" "Stockton, California, U.S.A." The chief didn't ask anyone else about his home town. It was a racial slur, all right, as though he were saying, "Remember you're not from Vietnam. Remember which side you're on. You're no gook from Vietnam." That's right, he wasn't. Fat men got the worst chewing out; the Company Commander called them girls—pussies, twats, sows, cunts, girls, ladies—and assigned them to run extra laps. His fellow man was like the remedials.

For the first five weeks, the recruits, or "boots," were not allowed to talk during meals. At the brother's first dinner conversation, a big man across from him spread a hand and said, "See this? You know what it's for?"

"What?"

"It's to make this." He made a fist and nodded at it.

"Nah," said the brother. "It's to put good food in your mouth, not this swill." They were eating the same chili sauce they cleaned the metal urinals with. Heads over their plates, which they encircled with one arm, the men stoked their mouths.

The brother lost his appetite. From the first day of boot camp when the recruits were marched to breakfast, he did not want the food. No food tasted any better or worse than any other. Peanut butter, french fries, chocolate did not taste good. He had lost the sensation of hunger. His stomach did not growl no matter how long he did without food. Not eating gave him some extra time, privacy; there were men who had nothing better to do than line up in front of the mess hall long before mealtime. He would use his insensitivity to advantage; he would not have to plan his life around food. He had not eaten for days when it occurred to him that his appetite was unreliable; he could not depend on it to keep alive. He would never get hungry. "I have to eat to keep myself alive," he said aloud at table; he would remember better by saying it to those around him. He would have to use his reason instead of his instinct to eat and stay healthy. Each day, regularly, he would eat three meals, enough of each kind of food whether he wanted it or not. "I've got to keep eating," he said. He would eat by reason rather than appetite. He calculated what foods a body needed and ate them. He would take care of himself until his appetite returned. "Eat vegetables," he grumbled. "Eat salad. Why do they feed us canned peas and carrots. Why can't they get fresh vegetables to San Diego?"

Whether anybody listened or not, he muttered from morning till night. "They get us up at five-thirty before our brains can start functioning," he said. "My brain feels like wet cement. I can't see. Here I'm getting up, and I didn't even go to sleep yet. I didn't even have any dreams. Sorry. No dreams to tell. When I get out of the Navy, I'm never going to make a bed again. They're turning us into housewives. Make beds. Fold clothes. Shine shoes. Sweep. Swab. The Navy is housework. And the Navy is gym class. Hell is staying in P.E. forever." He mumbled while marching, "Foot blisters. Bone bruises. Shin splints. Slave labor." He mumbled while swimming, "Abandon ship. Sharks at my underbelly. The ocean covered with black oil and the oil igniting. Ears clogged with chlorine." Actually he was making up the sharks; the reasons for the training were not given. "Can't shit in peace," he said, sitting in the head while twenty people stared awaiting their turn, no doors and walls around toilets. "I'm getting dumber," he said. "I can feel it, the I.Q.'s are leaking away. Everybody here is so dumb." "Yeah," people agreed, "they sure are." He was ordered to mutter numbers in the tear-gas training room, to feel the gas burn before running out. He talked even in his sleep. "Cut it out," said the men in the next bunks or "racks," but he didn't hear them because he'd stuffed erasers in his ears.

Recruit training wasn't the first time he had handled a gun. Each New Year's eve, his father took a heavy box out of its hiding place, lifted the lid, unwrapped the wads of cloth, and took out the black pistol. The brothers and sisters passed it around with barrel upturned. Their father oiled it and loaded it. They followed him outside, and at midnight he fired one shot into the air over the slough, a year ending and a year beginning at that bang. On the rifle range, shooting at bull's-eyes, the rifle became so hot that when the brother looked at his hand, a flap of skin was rolled back. It did not hurt.

Because he could type, he escaped some of the clean-up. He was not as bad off as the others. He was older and had had something going for him before the Navy. Office work was in addition to other duties; he lost time the Navy allotted for letter-writing or study. He made schedules, and wrote out permits, attendance, and duty rosters. No exciting orders to kill Vietnamese.

On the last day of boot camp, his group voted him Champion Complainer. There were men who admitted that they hadn't taken a shit the entire ten weeks. He did not think he was any more full of hate and a desire to kill than before. Nor did his appetite return. At restaurants and at home on leave, he had no appetite for his favorite foods. If only the war were as easy as recruit training, he could take it.

Then for a while he was shuffled from one base to another without there seeming to be a plan. At a sort of holding bar-racks for homosexuals, his orders were to keep them from "bed-hopping," though they didn't seem ill. He sat at his lookout's desk watching TV or writing letters or reading. He didn't catch anybody.

One area he avoided was the dependents' housing, which he stumbled upon one lunchtime. Navy wives in curlers and bed-room slippers sat on benches, two facing benches in front of each doorway. Arms folded, they yelled at their kids in the ac-cents of many nations and regions, but even the black women looked colorless. These were women and children who were loved. "The attack plans are not going to work," a family man had confided during man-your-stations drill. "If an enemy ever attacks this place, nobody is going to man his station. Do you think I'm coming to this desk during an attack? I'll be with my wife and kid. And everybody else will be with his wife and kids." As a single man, the brother had not consid-ered dependents.

Next he was assigned to a ship, an aircraft carrier. The beams and cables of the Golden Gate Bridge swung overhead. A few people up there waved and gave the peace sign. The Bay was gray like the pewter-color rocket launchers bolted to the decks. For a frantic second the brother wanted to turn the ship around. It was like a moving island of planes and jeeps and tanks. Maybe those khaki torpedoes and silver rockets were H-bombs. Or they were flares. He didn't know what an H-bomb looked like, perhaps a cassette or a crystal chip.

The officers announced that the ship was on its way to Subic Bay in the Philippines. Still not Vietnam, still not time to jump ship. Some men were disappointed that the Navy did not immediately send them to Vietnam. "We're gonna miss the war," they said. They should have joined the Army, they said, or the Marines. They were children themselves so would not recognize the Vietcong as children; they would think they were fighting short men.

The brother's favorite activity was to stand watch in the flight control tower. He volunteered for extra duty hanging over the sea, sighting dolphins and sea conditions. When the ocean went gold with what he thought were low-flying birds, he climbed down and saw flying fish for the first time. Another day, in the swaying air he sighted an airplane speck, which turned out to be an albatross come to follow the ship. The slop jockeys soaked the garbage with hot sauce; the brutes guffawed as the albatross ate it and its throat jerked. Still it followed near and far, black wings against the sky, against the sunrise.

A personnel officer had read the brother's records, and gave him the collateral duty of teaching English classes on board ship, Remedial Reading to grown men who were so ignorant they did not know where Indochina was or Sweden or the various states.

"What do you see when you read?" he asked. "Describe what you see." They were not seeing the stories or ideas.

"I see small, small words, and they get darker and darker." Poor boys; they must have joined the Navy to get away from school, and here they were in school again.

"I see words, and the ink runs together. Then it's dark."

"I see letters at first, but they turn into colors that jump around."

"Colors. Blue, I think. Or purple."

"The words look like they're melting in water. They float."

"I see a mist. Like fog."

"Dark like a tunnel."

"Like in an elevator."

"Dark. Claustro."

"Like a tight cave. And I can hardly breathe."

"Can't I stop reading now? I'm getting dizzy."

"I have a headache."

"My eyes are watering."

"I can't breathe."

"My eyes hurt."

"Dark. Claustro."

He taught writing by having them write home. They had a Navy textbook with sample letters. "'Dear Mom,'" the boys printed. "'How are you? I am fine. I hope you are fine too. We sure have a lot to eat here. They keep you busy in the Navy. The weather has been cool/warm. Lots of love. Yours truly, Your Name.'" Some of the students copied it out just like that. "'Your Name,'" they wrote.

They took so long copying, class ended before he could give them some spelling or literature. There were people who didn't know all the letters of the alphabet, or they knew them but out of order, yet they had passed intelligence tests to get in the Navy. "The government lowered the standards to get our bodies," he told them. He showed them where Canada and Sweden were on a globe.

"You speak English pretty good," his students complimented him. When white people said that, he had figured out what to answer, "Thank you, so do you," but he was at a loss again. He did not feel like using sarcasm on these boys, nor would they understand it.

What he wrote to his own parents because his Chinese vocabulary was small was, "How are you? I am fine. I hope you are fine too." But when he wrote in English for his sisters to translate, he again said, "How are you? I am fine." He didn't want to worry them.

As the ship moved toward Asia, he dreamed fiercely. The dreams came more and more quickly; the land sent them: An army enters a city to free it from an enemy. A soldier of the rescuing army, he walks through a castle into the dungeons. Going down the stairs, he sees at face level—bodies hanging, some upside down, some brown and dried up, black hair and arms swaying, feet turning this way, then that, bodies with black hair in their middles, corpses with sections missing and askew, but mercifully all dead, hanging by hooks and ropes. Laundry tubs drain beneath the bodies. The live women and children on the ironing tables, the last captured, are being dissected. It has to be a dream or a movie, he thinks, but he blinks his eyes, and the sights do not go away. He takes up his sword and hacks into the enemy, slicing them; they come apart in rings and rolls. He grits his teeth and goes into a frenzy, cutting whatever human meat comes within range. When he stops, he finds that he has cut up the victims too, who are his own relatives. The faces of the strung-up people are also those of his own family, Chinese faces, Chinese eyes, noses, and cheekbones. He woke terrified. The live bodies he had cut up had not screamed or wept because their mouths had been gagged and eyes blindfolded. Scared awake, he looked at the underside of the rack above him and at the sleeping man across the aisle; it was only the closeness in these berths that had made him dream like that.

He went to sleep again, and another dream recurred: Armies crawl like alligators under barbed wire. They have been ordered to charge a beach like at Normandy—only the beach is as wide as the Sahara Desert or the Gobi or Death Valley. In a panic of attack all those miles, they crawl and charge for years. It is an army of burrowing animals, moles, groundhogs, prairie dogs, ostriches. Frightened by shadows and sounds, they dig deeper. Nursing cubs and kids wriggle beneath bigger animals. Turkeys burrow under one another and die in a pile. Administering first aid, he cuts open their chests and sees gross internal damage. He tries unstacking the animals, weaning them. The alligators, left arm and leg, then right arm and leg, crawl toward battle. Occasionally, a wild stallion rears up and is shot.

He woke again, wondering why he should have such disorderly animal dreams when the ship was a machine. These dreams must have come from his years of poultry chores. When he slept again, he dreamed that he was a barkless dog tied to a table leg in a kitchen equipped with a sink, oven, and operating table. Families—mother, father, and one child—are in kitchens like this all over the world. A voice comes over the loudspeaker: "Children, take up your knives; women, forks; men, spoons." The fathers take the children's knives and stab them quickly. Then with their arms around one another, the wife picks up the fork, and the husband the spoon. The loudspeaker says for them to kill themselves by forking and scooping. "Spoon, knife, or fork?" the loudspeaker asks the barkless dog, who knows that if he took the sharpest instrument, he would deprive someone else of a quick death. He chooses the spoon, but is not willing to gouge himself to death. Because he is a dog and not watched as closely as human beings, he runs out of the kitchen-surgery, but outside, the shooting war has begun. He runs in and out the door, unable to decide whether it is better to commit suicide or to kill.

His bunk neighbors told the brother he talked Chinese and yelled in his sleep, complaining even more in sleep than awake. Mornings in another life, his family had told their dreams while eating breakfast. He found some shipmates who listened, though he would have otherwise muttered to himself.

The people he had met in basic training or another base seemed old friends meeting again, homeboys. Bill, a hippie Pacifist, followed him around asking about Zen, macrobiotic diet, yang and yin, brush painting. Bill was often swabbing decks or peeling potatoes because his hair was too long or completely shaved off, or he saluted crooked, or he wouldn't stand at attention during "Anchors Aweigh." He questioned the cooks and officers about the chili, whether there was hamburger in it, whether the fish had been fried in lard or vegetable oil. "Use peanut oil," he suggested. He picked out the bacon bits from his salad in case they were really bacon instead of soy. Ordinarily the brother wouldn't have liked a person who had a thing for the Orient, a sinophile, but Bill badgered him. "Tell me about Buddhism," he said. "Do you know kung fu? Tai Chi? I want to be a Buddhist Pacifist. When the ship returns to San Francisco, I'm joining the flower children. When we get to Asia, I'm going to find my guru or stand on a street corner and let my guru find me. Come on, say a few words in Chinese. Go ahead." Bill spoke Chinese in a scholarly or citified or northern dialect. He was very annoying, but he liked listening to dreams and complaints. There would be no real friends in the Navy anyway; these people didn't stick together—they were stuck with one another, assigned to one another.

The brother also spent time with a chubby tenor who had dropped out of a seminary and did not become a priest. Louder than the country-and-western records the other men played, he sang Italian opera and Mozart, which filled the bunkroom, the showers, the corridors and flew out across the water to the albatross. The young sailors shunned him in case he was homosexual and contagious. He rummaged the ship for bits of history and showed the brother the bolt marks in their berthing compartment, where ten years ago the Navy had kept a small cell for jailing one sailor as a warning. The tenor found a pair of foils, and he and Bill or the brother fenced across the decks pretending to be Errol Flynn and Basil Rathbone, leaping off hatches and swinging from guy wires like riggings.

Instead of carrying out his lists of projects, his reading lists, guitar lessons, correspondence, the brother, like the other sailors, wasted time sitting around, bullshitting, complaining, going to the nightly movies. In the sudden lights after a movie, the audience looked especially depressing.

At Subic Bay the Commander ordered two hundred sailors to go to a dance with one hundred girls in an outlying town. The mayor, a woman, had invited them, but not enough sailors volunteered. The brother danced with some of the one hundred, "all schoolteachers," according to the mayor's speech. The food was plentiful, and he watched a cockfight in the middle of the dance floor. One of the one hundred schoolteachers promised that in case the brother went to Vietnam, she would write dates on his letters and periodically mail them to his parents.

The next port was Korea, the magic place, where the good ginseng comes from. The civilian workers read the brother's name tag and asked if he were Korean. They had that same last name. "Chinese," he said, "American. Chinese American." "Chinese American," the Koreans repeated. "Lucky, huh? Lucky." He bought ginseng, "man's heart," the root of life, the root in the shape of a human being, and sent it to his mother. She kept writing for him to buy more, red and yellow ginseng and many different grades, also instants and concentrates.

On Thanksgiving, the sailors gave a party for local children, who ate very seriously. The children hid bananas and oranges inside their coats, into which they or their relatives had sewn enormous pockets. "We'll give you a doggy bag," the men, who sat in every other seat, said. "Go ahead. Eat." But the kids stored it away. "Have another apple. Have some more cupcakes," the brother said to the kids next to him. "Take the whole bowl." He handed one boy the potatoes. "Say some Korean," men said to the kids. "Cat got your tongue?" "They don't talk much, do they?" they said. "Aren't they cute? Cute little fellas."

Next the ship went to Taiwan, where he would be stationed. He watched the real China pass by, the old planet his family had left light years ago. Taiwan was not China, a decoy China, a facsimile. He would not find out if the air and flowers of China smelled sweeter than California and the sky filled with golden birds, whether promises would come true, time move slower, and life last long.

In Taiwan he was for the first time in a country of Chinese people. The childish dream was that he would find like minds, and furniture that always fit his body. Chinese Americans talk about how when they set foot on China, even just Hong Kong, their whole lives suddenly made sense; their youth had been a preparation for this visit, they say. They realize their Americanness, they say, and "You find out what a China Man you are." An ophthalmology student from the ship, an American of Japanese Ancestry, who was proud of his "double-lids," said that the eyes of ethnic Asians have a naturally faraway focus. "If we lived in Asia," he said, "where everything is arranged according to our eyesight, we wouldn't need glasses." Clarity was a matter of preference and culture. "Americans zone cities and make billboards for Caucasian eyes," he said. "Blackboards are set so many feet from the students' desks, traffic signals at such a size and distance, newspapers and books in a certain size type. If we AJA's with our epicanthic eyes and peculiar focus went back to Japan, we wouldn't need glasses any more." The brother had American 20–20 vision, but didn't notice things getting either blurrier or sharper in Taiwan. That eye doctor trainee was a crackpot.

The brother, Bill the Buddhist monk, the opera singer, and

the ophthalmologist decided to live on the economy. They rented a prefab house next to rice paddies with water buffaloes; it had a fireplace though the climate was hot. The others looked for a houseboy to do the cleaning and cooking. "We ought to clean up after ourselves," the brother argued. "A man ought to wash his own dishes and wash the clothes he wears. Like Truman. Truman washed his own socks. Cleaning up after yourself is the followthrough."

His friends said he was blithering again. "We're pumping bucks into the economy," they said. "We're paying top dollar and putting food in bellies. If we don't hire him, somebody else will make him work for less." They hired an old man for houseboy.

The brother hoped Bill would not point him out to the old man, "He's Chinese too," unleashing a whole set of customs. The old man would scorn him for speaking the wrong kind of Chinese, scold and mock, turn him into a child, a bad Chinese who couldn't speak right. "Ho Chi Kuei," he'd scold. "Ho Chi Kuei." He'd call him names for who knows what. For being in the Navy, for living with a gang of white devils, for going out with girls, for drinking, for coming in late, for smoking dope, for the invasion and colonization of Asia. The old man leaned on his iron pressing their uniforms sharp "inside out," as the sailors requested. The brother had pressed them this same way when he worked at the laundry. If he were living alone, he would have gotten rid of the old man. So the old man wouldn't see his father's Chinese writing on envelopes, the brother made sure his mail came to his office at the base.

Once he came home in the middle of the workday and found the old man asleep on the sofa, and left so as not to wake him. Another day while wandering in a market, he saw him with his wife and three children. When the old man introduced everyone, the brother felt surprisingly honored, as if the old man were letting him have something special, personal. The brother resolved he would return after he got out of the Navy and say Hello to him. He'd look him up. He had a list of things to do after the Navy, after the war was over, the endless war not even officially begun yet, the beginning let alone the end not in sight: he would take a cruise ship from San Francisco to Asia; he would see the Philippines and Taiwan as a civilian.

The Chinese workers at the base were curious about him. "What are you?" they asked. "Chinese American," he said. "Lucky. You're lucky," they said in English just like the Koreans.

Life was getting to be a routine when in the Chinese New Year season, which the Vietnamese and Americans were calling Tet, the brother was assigned to the U.S.S. *Midway* for an attack mission to the Gulf of Tonkin. There were nuclear weapons on board, sidewinders, matadors, six-hundred-mile-range rockets with atomic warheads. The men discussed cyanide in case of torture. "If I were in the jungle, I'd carry cyanide." "But bringing cyanide is like having Thorazine on hand when dropping acid. Expecting a bad trip causes a bad trip. You set yourself up." The hippies were doping themselves silly. A sister ship was supposed to accompany the *Midway*, but a kid had dropped a wrench into the engine. It wasn't sabotage, just an accident. Pilots ejected themselves inside of hangars, mechanics got sucked into the jets, flight deck crew sliced by guy wires. It did not require precision to deliver the massive tonnage.

The brother did not go AWOL to Sweden or Canada. He was, after all, only coming a few miles physically closer to Vietnam, and his job of flipping switches and connecting circuits and typing was the same as on land, the numbers and letters almost the same.

So here he was on an aircraft carrier from whose flight deck hour after hour corps of planes took off. He could not take naps, his bunk was directly beneath the rocket launchers. Even using binoculars, he did not see much of the shore. Hanoi was an hour away by plane. He did not see the bombs drop out of the planes, whether they fell like long white arrows, or whether they turned and turned, flashing in the sun. During loading, when they were locked into place, they looked like neatly rolled joints; they looked like long grains of rice; they looked like pupae and turds. He never heard cries under the bombing. They were not attacking the enemy with surprise bombings but routine bombings or "air operations" in twelve-hour shifts. When the sister ship got there, there would be bombings through the night, round-the-clock bombings. The pilots flew out there, unloaded their quota, and came back. It took intelligence and imagination to think that they were in Vietnam in the middle of the heaviest American bombing. A man he'd eaten lunch with did not show up for dinner, and that meant the man's plane had gone down. He had to imagine his death because he saw no blood, no body. The pilots either came back or they did not come back. There were no wounded. Sometimes a pilot would say that he had returned with a dead co-pilot in the cockpit. The sailors did not mourn the pilots, an arrogant, strutting class who volunteered for the bombings. Nobody was drafted to drop bombs. "Extra dessert tonight," the sailors said. "He asked for it," they said. "Hot shot." "Gung ho." When the pilots returned alive, it was no different from a practice run. No celebrations and no mournings, just business, a job. An officer was assigned to sort the dead man's personal effects; he censored those things too embarrassing to send to the family, such as photographs of Asian women.

The brother did touch foot on Vietnam by visiting a base near Saigon. He did not explore the city. He met some infantrymen who told him that when they were ordered to patrol the jungle they made a lot of noise, clanged equipment, talked loud. The enemy did the same, everybody warning one another off. Once in a while, to keep some hawk officer happy, they fired rounds into the trees.

The brother was formally asked by his Commanding Officer to train as a pilot. He had the test scores, the potential, but he said No.

The pilots often invited their shipmates for the bombings. "Want to come along?" "Come on. Take a ride. Come along for the ride." The brother said No, "No, not me," many times. Then one day he said, "Sure. Why not? When? Sure, I'll come along for the ride." He put on a parachute and walked with the pilot and co-pilot across the flight deck on to the plane. He felt overheated, his head crammed into the helmet and his body pulled backward by the parachute. He had to duck through the door. Stuffed into his low seat, which was tilted toward the ceiling, he found with effort the seat belts and buckled himself in. The door slid shut. It was not too late to ask out. The plane was still lined up behind others waiting for takeoff. He could say he'd changed his mind and cause only a minor inconvenience. He wouldn't be embarrassed. The engine revved. He wasn't, after all, committing a worse act by riding on the plane than riding on the ship. The plane accelerated on its short runway, left the deck, and climbed over the water, the horizon slanting, dipping, and rising. Then there was the steadiness one feels riding in any plane, train, or car. The instruments, needles, dials, and lights made no alarming flashes or jumps. He put on a headset and heard familiar numbers and letters. He stood up against the gravity and looked out of the windshield, which was narrow like a pair of wraparound glasses. All that he witnessed was heavy jungle and, in the open skies, other planes that seemed to appear and disappear quickly, shiny planes and their decals and formations. The bombs must have gone off behind them. Some air turbulence might have been a bomb ejected. He heard no explosion. There did seem to be some turns and banks like a ride in any small plane. The plane turned in the direction from which they seemed to have come—he could tell by the sun now on the other side—and they were descending and landing. The plane caught in the wires, not needing the net. The door opened, and he climbed out. "Smooth run," said the pilot. "Yeah, smooth," said the co-pilot. The brother felt no different from before, but he made a decision never to go again.

He got promoted and transferred back to Taipei. His Commanding Officer dealt out personnel papers: "Communications Specialist. Q Clearance," he heard. "You've been run through a security check—" (The brother's breath caught—his family deported.) "—and cleared. Congratulations. Secret Security."

"Thank you. Thank you. I got something out of the Navy," the brother blurted. "I'm getting something good out of the Vietnam war."

The government was certifying that the family was really American, not precariously American but super-American, extraordinarily secure—Q Clearance Americans. The Navy or the FBI had checked his mother and father and not deported them. Maybe that grandfather's Citizenship Judge was real and legal after all. So Uncle Bun's defection to Communism didn't matter, nor Father's gambling, nor Great Uncle's river piracy, second-story work, and murder. And the government had forgiven whoever it was who had almost gotten caught stowing away, or he had covered his tracks so well that they overlooked him, missed him, impervious to investigation. The Communist grandmother, aunts, and cousins, potential hostages, were not hurting his trustworthiness as an American. Maybe Uncle Bun was dead, never got to China; maybe he wasn't even really an uncle. His grandfather's and father's papers had indeed burned in the earthquake, and it was all right that his mother was an alien. The government had not found him un-American with divided loyalties and treasonous inclinations. Though he was conveniently close to China, the U. S. government, which could make up new laws, change the law on him, did not dump him there. While his services were needed for the undeclared American-Vietnam war, the family was safe. And the family had friends and neighbors who protected them during investigation.

His Commanding Officer said that the brother's record as a communications expert with language aptitude qualified him for the Monterey Language School. Wouldn't he like to study Chinese? Or Vietnamese? "You studied French," he said. "You speak Chinese too, don't you?" A vision of Monterey leapt up like a mermaid out of the sea and lured him. He wanted that Pacific coast, that sunshine and fog, the red tile roofs in the dark trees, the fiery and white bougainvillea, the walks on the streets leading to the ocean—and school again, to be a student a luxury. "Let me think about it," he said.

A letter came from his older brother, who had gotten a commission in the Air Force. He had just been given Top Secret Security Clearance. Maybe he was the one who had prompted the security check, too ambitious to remain a private. The NAC had processed both of them at once. So they had not only been checked but double-checked, and cleared, doubly cleared.

The brother found some language books in the library. If he learned Chinese better, or if he let on how much he already knew, the Navy would assign him to be a spy or an interrogator. There was only one use the military had for Chinese language—war, the same use it had for raw materials and science. He would be assigned to gouge Viet Cong eyes, cattle-prod their genitals. He would have to hang prisoners from helicopters, drop the dumb-looking ones, and tell the smart remaining ones to talk or else. It wouldn't be Chinese poetry he'd be memorizing but the Pentagon's *Vietnam Phrase Book*:

Welcome, Sir. Glad to meet you. How many are with you? Show me on your fingers.

Are you afraid of the enemy? Us?

Do you place faith in America? Will the people fight for their freedom? We are here to help them in the struggle on the side of (1) the free world (2) the United States (3) the Allies (4) freedom (5) God.

Would they (1) support (2) join (3) fight on the side of (4) work for (5) sacrifice their lives for U.S. troops?

Your nickname will be ———. My nickname is ———.

Do you believe in (1) U.S. victory (2) annihilation of Bolshevism?

Open the door or we will force it.

Is he your father? Village leader?

Are you afraid? Why?

If we cannot trust a man, (1) wink your right eye (2) place your left hand on your stomach (3) move your hand to the right, unnoticed, until we note your signal.

The Vietnamese call their parents Ba and Ma; *phuoc* means "happiness," "contentment," "bliss," the same as Chinese; *lan* is "orchid," the same as his mother's name; Vietnamese puns are like Chinese puns, *lettuce, life*; they probably also bring heads of lettuce home on holidays. *Study, university, love*—the important words the same in Chinese and Vietnamese. Talking Chinese and Vietnamese and also French, he'd be a persuasive interrogator-torturer. He would fork the Vietnamese—force a mother to choose between her baby with a gun at its belly and her husband hiding behind the thatch, to which she silently points with her chin.

"No," he told his Commanding Officer. He had been given a choice, and he said No. "No, thank you." He would not be like the scientists making plasma bombs and supersonic brain scramblers for want of a better use of their abilities.

On days off and after work, he and friends went to museums, bars, the aborigine village, looked for girl friends, wandered about the Taiwanese countryside, shopped for stereo equipment. Passing many Chinese faces made him feel vaguely rude for not greeting every last one the way he'd been taught to do back home. As happened every time he went out, he heard somebody shout, probably at him, but he did not understand the words. Once in the middle of the night, someone came out of an alley and jumped him from behind. An arm hooked around his neck. He broke loose and ran, got away. Later his throat remembered the choke-hold of that arm. It had probably been a mugger, not someone after him personally. Off duty, he wore a white shirt, baggy pants, and civilian shoes to blend with the crowds. Yet he had not "returned." Of course, the Center was elsewhere. This island was not the Center, its people emigrants, rejects, and misfits. He'd be more at home if he walked straight away from this Taipei street to a military base. Sailors and soldiers didn't blend into American towns either.

He had two weeks R and R and went on a vacation to Tokyo and Hong Kong. His parents had given him the names of relatives to visit. He liked Tokyo, where the Japanese were too busy to stare at strangers. They walked fast, had places to go, business to do. He bought Peace brand cigarettes for their packaging. Then, not able to delay any more, he went to Hong Kong, where he heard Cantonese almost like back home. Storekeepers and waiters told him that they had hard lives. "You're lucky," they said. He took a train tour, which included a trip to the border of the New Territories. He saw a valley and distant hills covered with wild vegetation. "There is the People's Republic of China," said the guide. If he had not said that, the brother would not have known. A solitary guard stood here and there, also local policemen in British uniforms. The brother saw no man-made crossings, tracks, bridges, or fences, or anything to hinder or facilitate a crossing. No red wall, no curtain. He walked on the overpass above the railroad tracks for a better look at Red China. Just as Hong Kong had a Communist wharf among other wharves, Communist shops among other shops, he saw no Red distinction.

He boarded another train back to the city to look for the street where his relatives lived. Shopping, he tried to remember what to bring on the occasion of meeting after many years. Oranges, black bean cake, a roast duck might have been appropriate for a harvest blessing or a month-old baby, and his relatives would make fun of him and call him Ho Chi Kuei and *jook tsing*. But he would bring gifts upon entering a nightmare. His aunts and cousins would be poor, and live in a cave or shack. He would find a cardboard and tin shack full of people. Out of a gray rag pile, thin hands would grope and beg, and mouths stretch wide open. "They will change my life," he worried. Their faces would resemble brothers' and sisters' and parents' and his own. He would need to rescue them. He would not be able to leave them. Or he would leave at great cost, pain, and guilt. He would end up like his parents, pledging his salary forever. The relatives would have no manners, no polite ways that would make his visit easy. But a cardboard box on a hillside was not the worst shelter; worse would be if he were a Vietnamese returning from Paris to his hootch or his hole underground.

Queen's Road led him away from the hills. He would rather have rich relatives, the kind who didn't notice beggars, the kind who said, "Why, the hill people and sampan people are lazy. They choose to live like that. Yes, they prefer it." They'd take him out to dinner and wouldn't let him pay. They'd say, "I've never met a poor Chinese. We Chinese are raised with discipline. We make it." He'd tell them his parents were well, and leave. He'd have no trouble leaving them. He came to apartment buildings or housing projects with balconies of laundry. As many little girls as little boys were out on the sidewalks.

But as he looked, the numbers on the doors skipped the one in his hand. There was a number higher and one lower. He was not shirking; he walked back. It was not there, no such number, his number missing. He went in the alleys and looked in the crates. He entered the buildings with addresses that were approximate. No one had heard of his relatives' names. Trying combinations of the numbers, he searched on parallel streets, searched an afternoon, and did not find the house or hovel or tenement where they lived. He left the perishable food in front of any door. The next morning he tried again. Finally he left the rest of the gifts by another door. Perhaps they did live in one of the shacks upon the hill and had put a fake address for their relatives not to worry.

The brother decided that after his time in the Navy and after the war, he'd try again, and also ride into China and look for the ones there.

It was just as well he hadn't found them. The ophthalmologist had gone to Japan and found his village and his relatives, who were very hospitable and gave him the main bed and meat. But on the last day, before dawn, he heard the door slide open. Through his eyelashes, faking sleep, he watched his uncle tiptoe across the room and leave a piece of paper on his chest. (The brother pictured it on his breast, but he must have meant the chest of drawers.) It was a day-to-day running account of all he had eaten, down to the numbers of helpings of rice, a list of the laundry his aunt had washed and ironed, the number of times the little girl cousin had polished his shoes, each cup of tea, an itemized list of all the presents and loans, the bathrobe and slippers, the number of baths in the hot-tub, the number of days and nights in his room, totaled neatly in yen and dollars. He had paid it, of course.

When the brother took a cargo plane on standby home—CONUS, the Continental United States—there were no other passengers; it was a plane especially to take him home. At night in lonely parts of airports, he saw electric conveyors move coffins draped with flags on and off planes. A soldier stood guard in front of stacks of them.

Mustered out at Treasure Island, he rode a Greyhound to Stockton. He walked the few blocks to his parents' house, in front of which many cars were parked. A party was just ending. Some of the guests were leaving. "He's back," they said, typically talking about him in the third person.

"Well, so you've come back," said his father, "you've come back." "You're back home," said his mother.

The chicken still sat whole on the table. Pieces of the roast pork from a whole pig, noodles, and lettuce remained. This was a very important, religious party, a thanksgiving that he had come back home, more than personal, not a party only for him, and that was why they hadn't had to wait for him to have it. He ate the rock sugar on red paper his mother handed him; he ate the leftover pork. She hacked the white chicken for him. No, his appetite hadn't come back yet; he'd have to do more duty-eating.

Three years after his return, the United States withdrew from Vietnam. For a time longer than that, the things people did seemed to have no value; nobody else saw this. But his appetite did gradually increase. He had survived the Vietnam war. He had not gotten killed, and he had not killed anyone.

The Hundred-Year-Old Man

THERE IS a man who would be one hundred and seventeen years old now. He had a one-hundred-and-sixth
birthday party in the Palolo Chinese Home in Hawai'i in
1969. He wore a wool cap. He told the guests he came to
Hawai'i in 1885 on the S.S. *Coptic*. He brought with him pigs
in cages, and chives and onions growing in cans. He had divided his ration of fresh water with the pigs, the chives, and
the onions.

He worked in the sugarcane fields for four dollars a month,
and his first job had been to clear the brush for planting. He
lived in a grass house, but later moved into a dormitory, where
he slept in a bunk covered with grass mats. He sent one half of
his pay to his family in China. Here's how he spent the rest: He
bought kerosene and wood; he paid off some of his debts, his
passage to Hawai'i, and the twelve-dollar fee for processing his
papers; he spent six dollars to join his Benevolent Association,
which gave him room and board when he took his monthly
trip to Honolulu on pay day. He rode to town in a horse cart
for thirty cents; it carried five passengers. When he could not
afford the thirty cents, he walked.

He rested by smoking opium, which the plantation foreman
sold. A half-hour's worth of high was called a dragon seed and
cost fifty cents. When Hawai'i outlawed opium, he switched
to cigars.

He saw King Kalakaua and Prince Kuhio. In 1893 he did not
go to town because of the American revolution against Queen
Lili'uokalani, who was "big and friendly," he said. "I was for
the Americans," he added.

Since 1885 he has left the island twice, once to go to Maui
and once to Kaua'i.

On this one-hundred-and-sixth birthday, the United States
was still fighting in Vietnam, and people asked him how to
stop the war. "Let everybody out of the army," he said.

"In one hundred and six years, what has given you the most
joy?" the reporters asked.

He thought it over. He said, "What I like best is to work in a cane field when the young green plants are just growing up."

"In the end," said Tu Fu, "I will carry a hoe."

On Listening

A T A party, I met a Filipino scholar, who asked, "Do you know the Chinese came to the Philippines to look for the Gold Mountain?"

"No," I said. "I know hardly anything about the Philippines."

"They came in a ship in March of 1603," he said. "Three great mandarins landed at the Bay of Manila. The Filipinos were amazed to see them riding in ivory and gold chairs. They were higher class than the thirty thousand Chinese who were already living in Luzon. They had with them a Chinese in chains, who was to show them where to look for a gold needle in a mountain."

It was past midnight, or it was his accent, but I could not hear if he was saying that looking for the Gold Mountain was like looking for a needle in a haystack. "No. No," he said. "A gold needle." To sew the sails, was it? A compass needle, was it? "The mandarins asked for more ships, which they would fill with gold, some to give to the Filipino king, some to take back to the Queen of Spain, and some for the Emperor of China."

A group of Chinese Americans were gathering around the Filipino scholar. "Oh, yes," said a young man, "a Chinese monk went to Mexico looking for that mountain too, and either he came there with Cortez, or it was before that."

"And the Filipino king," continued the Filipino, "who had met conquistadores and knew about seven cities of gold and a fountain of youth, sent them to the town of Cabit."

"And they went to Weaverville, California," said another. "And in Weaverville, Cantonese laborers built a replica of their village in China."

"No, no," said someone else. "The way I heard it was that some cowboys saw mandarins floating over California in a hot-air balloon, which had come all the way from China."

"Now, these Chinese who were looking for the gold needle," I reminded the Filipino man, "what happened after they got to Cabit?"

"They sailed up a river farther and farther inland." And they built roads and railroads and cities on their way to this mountain. They filled swamps. They had children. "And on a certain mountain they sifted rocks and dirt looking for a gold needle. They asked the man in chains where the gold was, and he said that all they saw was gold."

Because I didn't hear everything, I asked him to repeat the story, and what he seemed to say again was "They found a gold needle in a mountain. They filled a basket with dirt to take with them back to China."

"Do you mean the Filipinos tricked them?" I asked. "What were they doing in Spain?"

"I'll write it down in a letter, and mail it to you," he said, and went on to something else.

Good. Now I could watch the young men who listen.

TRIPMASTER MONKEY:
HIS FAKE BOOK

To Earll

This fiction is set in the 1960s, a time when some events appeared to occur months or even years anachronistically.

Contents

I
Trippers and Askers

MAYBE IT comes from living in San Francisco, city of clammy humors and foghorns that warn and warn— omen, o-o-men, o dolorous omen, o dolors of omens—and not enough sun, but Wittman Ah Sing considered suicide every day. Entertained it. There slid beside his right eye a black gun. He looked side-eyed for it. Here it comes. He actually crooked his trigger finger and—bang!—his head breaks into pieces that fly far apart in the scattered universe. Then blood, meat, disgusting brains, mind guts, but he would be dead already and not see the garbage. The mouth part of his head would remain attached. He groaned. Hemingway had done it in the mouth. Wittman was not el pachuco loco. Proof: he could tell a figment from a table. Or a tree. Being outdoors, in Golden Gate Park, he stepped over to a tree and knock-knocked on it, struck a match on it. Lit a cigarette. Whose mind is it that doesn't suffer a loud takeover once in a while? He was aware of the run of his mind, that's all. He was not making plans to do himself in, and no more willed these seppuku movies—no more conjured up that gun—than built this city. His cowboy boots, old brown Wellingtons, hit its pavements hard. Anybody serious about killing himself does the big leap off the Golden Gate. The wind or shock knocks you out before impact. Oh, long before impact. So far, two hundred and thirty-five people, while taking a walk alone on the bridge—a mere net between you and the grabby ocean— had heard a voice out of the windy sky—Laurence Olivier asking them something: "To be or not to be?" And they'd answered, "Not to be," and climbed on top of the railing, fingers and toes roosting on the cinnabarine steel. They take the side of the bridge that faces land. And the City. The last city. Feet first. Coit Tower giving you the finger all the way down. Wittman would face the sea. And the setting sun. Dive. But he was not going to do that. Strange. These gun pictures were what was left of his childhood ability to see galaxies. Glass cosmospheres there had once been, and planets with creatures, such doings, such colors. None abiding. In the *Chronicle*, a husband and wife, past eighty, too old to live, had shot each other with a weak gun, and had had to go to a doctor to have the bullets prized out of their ears. And a Buddhist had set fire to himself and burned to death on purpose; his name was Quang Duc. Quang Duc. Remember. In the cremations along the Ganges, the mourners stay with the burning body until its head pops. Pop.

Today Wittman was taking a walk on a path that will lead into the underpass beneath the gnarly trees. In fact, the park didn't look half bad in the fog beginning to fall, dimming the hillocks that domed like green-grey moons rising or setting. He pulled the collar of his pea coat higher and dragged on his cigarette. He had walked this far into the park hardly seeing it. He ought to let it come in, he decided. He would let it all come in. An old white woman was sitting on a bench selling trivets "@ ½ dollar ea.," which a ducky and a bunny pointed out with gloved fingers. She lifted her head and turned her face toward Wittman's; her hands were working one more trivet out of yarn and bottlecaps. Not eyelids exactly but like skin flaps or membranes covered her eye sockets and quivered from the empty air in the holes or with efforts to see. Sockets wide open. He looked at her thick feet chapped and dirty in zoris. Their sorry feet is how you can tell crazy people who have no place to go and walk everywhere.

Wittman turned his head, and there on the ground were a pigeon and a squatting man, both puking. He looked away so that he would not himself get nauseated. Pigeons have milk sacs in their throats. Maybe this one was disgorging milk because last night a wind had blown in from the ocean and blown its squabs out of their nest, and it was milking itself. Or does that happen in the spring? But in California in the fall as well? The man was only a vomiting drunk. This walk was turning out to be a Malte Laurids Brigge walk. There was no helping that. There is no helping what you see when you let it all come in; he hadn't been in on building any city. It was already cold, soon the downside of the year. He walked into the tunnel.

Heading toward him from the other end came a Chinese

dude from China, hands clasped behind, bow-legged, loose-seated, out on a stroll—that walk they do in kung fu movies when they are full of contentment on a sunny day. As luck would have it, although there was plenty of room, this dude and Wittman tried to pass each other both on the same side, then both on the other, sidestepping like a couple of basketball stars. Wittman stopped dead in his tracks, and shot the dude a direct stink-eye. The F.O.B. stepped aside. Following, straggling, came the poor guy's wife. She was coaxing their kid with sunflower seeds, which she cracked with her gold tooth and held out to him. "Ho sick, la. Ho sick," she said. "Good eating. Good eats." Her voice sang, rang, banged in the echo-chamber tunnel. Mom and shamble-legged kid were each stuffed inside of about ten homemade sweaters. Their arms stuck out fatly. The mom had on a nylon or rayon pantsuit. ("Ny-lon ge. Mm lon doc." "Nylon-made. Lasts forever.") "No!" said the kid. Echoes of "No!" Next there came scrabbling an old lady with a cane. She also wore one of those do-it-yourself pantsuit outfits. On Granny's head was a cap with a pompon that matched everybody's sweaters. The whole family taking a cheap outing on their day offu. Immigrants. Fresh Off the Boats out in public. Didn't know how to walk together. Spitting seeds. So uncool. You wouldn't mislike them on sight if their pants weren't so highwater, gym socks white and noticeable. F.O.B. fashions—highwaters or puddlecuffs. Can't get it right. Uncool. Uncool. The tunnel smelled of mothballs—F.O.B. perfume.

On the tunnel ceiling, some tall paint-head had sprayed, "I love my skull." And somebody else had answered, "But oh you kidney!" This straighter person had prime-coated in bone-white a precise oval on the slope of the wall, and lettered in neat black, "But oh you kidney!"

He would avoid the Academy of Sciences, especially the North American Hall. Coyotes and bobcats dead behind glass forever. Stuffed birds stuffed inside their pried-open mouths. He was never going to go in there again. Claustro. Dark except for the glow of fake suns on the "scenes." Funeral-parlor smell seeping through the sealant.

Don't go into the Steinhart Aquarium either. Remember *The Lady from Shanghai*? The seasick cameras shoot through and around the fish-tanks at Orson Welles and Rita Hayworth saying goodbye. The fish are moving, unctuously moving.

No Oriental Tea Garden either. "Oriental." Shit.

On the paths where no other human being was wending, he stepped over and between fallen trees into sudden fens of ferns and banana trees with no bananas. A wild strawberry—someone had been wounded and bled a drop here—said, "Eat me," but he didn't obey, maybe poison. How come ripe when it isn't even spring? There were no flowers in the Shakespeare Garden, its plants gone indistinguishably to leaf and twig.

Long before Ocean Beach and the Great Highway, he turned back into the woods. Eucalyptus, pine, and black oak—those three trees together is how you tell that you're in Northern California and not Los Angeles. The last time he had walked along the ocean, he ended up at the zoo. Aquarium and dank zoo on the same day. "Fu-li-sah-kah Soo." He said "Fleishhacker Zoo" to himself in Chinatown language, just to keep a hand in, so to speak, to remember and so to keep awhile longer words spoken by the people of his brief and dying culture. At Fu-li-sah-kah Soo, he once saw a monkey catch a flying pigeon and tear it up. In another cage, a tiger backed up to its wading pool and took a dump in it. The stained polar bears make you want to throw things at them and to bite into an eraser.

If it were Sunday, football roars would be rising out of Kezar Stadium, and everywhere you walk, in the woods, along the Chain of Lakes, at the paddock of buffaloes, you'd hear the united voice of the crowd, and the separate loudspeaker voice of the announcer doing the play-by-play. Football season. Good thing that when he was in school, an American of Japanese Ancestry had played on the Cal football team, and there had been a couple of A.J.A. pompon girls too. Otherwise, his manhood would have been even more totally destroyed than it was.

Having lost track of his whereabouts, Wittman was surprised by a snowy glass palace—the Conservatory—that coalesced out of the fog. A piece had sharded off and was floating to the right of the spire on top of the cupola—the day moon. Up the stairs to this fancy hothouse (built with Crocker money), where unlikely roses and cacti grow, climbed a man and a dog. They were the same color and leanness, the dog a Doberman

pinscher. "Bitch. You fucking bitch." The man was scolding
the dog, the two of them walking fast, the dog pulling forward and the man pulling the short new chain taut. "Who
do you think you are, bitch? Huh, bitch? You listening to me?
Who the fuck do you think you are?" The man had plucked
his eyebrows into the shapes of tadpoles, the same definition
as the dog's, which were light tan. The dog wore a shame look
on its face, and its legs were bending with strain. "Bitch animal," said the man, who looked nowhere but at his dog. "How
could you, huh, bitch? Huh? You listening to me?" A yank on
the choke-chain. "You hear me? You cuntless bitch."

Along a side path came another Black man, this one pushing
a shopping cart transporting one red apple and a red bull from
Tijuana. It was time, Wittman thought, to stop letting it all
come in.

"Newspaper, sir?" said the man with the red bull.
"Newspaper. Ten cents." He was holding out a folded page of
newspaper. He was embracing an armload of these folios and
quartos. Wittman had dimes in his pocket, so bought one.
The man thanked him, and specially gave him a color insert
from last Sunday's paper. He must be illiterate and not know
that newspapers come out new every day.

Some children were climbing rocks. A little girl, who was
at the top of the pile, jumped off, saying, "Don't tell *me* your
personal problems." She talked like that because she copied
women. "I got problems of my *own*," she said. The kid was
ruined already. A shot of hate went from him to her that ought
to have felled her, but up she climbed again. Wittman tossed
his smoke and headed for an exit from the park.

Under a bush was a rag that had been squirted with blue
paint. That rag had sucked a boy's breath and eaten up his
brain cells. His traitorous hand that should have torn the rag
away had pressed it against his face, smeared him blue, and
made him drag in the fumes.

Wittman stood at the bus stop on the corner of Arguello
and Fulton. He was avoiding the corner where the grizzly bear
on one rock and the mountain lion with tensed shoulders on
the opposite rock look down at you. The Muni bus came along
on the cables not too much later. Continue. "I can't go on, I
go on." "I can't go on comma I go on." Wow.

On the ride downtown, for quite a while—the spires of St. Ignatius to the left and the dome of City Hall straight ahead as if rising out of the center of the street—San Francisco seemed to be a city in a good dream. Past the gilded gates of the Opera House and Civic Auditorium. Past the Orpheum, once "the best vaudeville house in the West"; on the evening of the day of the Earthquake and Fire, its actors went to the park and sang an act from *Carmen*. In 1911, Count Ilya Tolstoy, *the* Tolstoy's son, lectured in the Orpheum on "Universal Peace." Wittman had heard the orotund voice of Lowell Thomas intone, "THIS IS CINERAMA!" The Embassy, the Golden Gate, U. A. Cinema, the Paramount, the Warfield, the St. Francis, the Esquire. Then the neighborhood of the Curran, the Geary, and the Marines Memorial, where he had seen the Actor's Workshop do *King Lear* with Michael O'Sullivan as Lear—"Blow, winds, and crack your cheeks." Out the bus window, he kept spotting people who offended him in their postures and gestures, their walks, their nose-blowing, their clothes, their facial expressions. Normal humanity, mean and wrong. He was a convict on a locked bus staring at the sights on the way from county jail to San Quentin. Breathe shallow so as not to smell the other passengers. It's true, isn't it, that molecules break off and float about, and go up your nose, and that's how you smell? Always some freak riding the Muni. And making eye contact. Wittman was the only passenger sitting on a crosswise seat in front; the other passengers, facing forward, were looking at him. Had he spoken aloud? They're about to make sudden faces, like in *El. Who, if I cried out, would hear me among the angels' hierarchies?* All right, then, all right. Out of a pocket, he took his Rilke. For such gone days, he carried *The Notebooks of Malte Laurids Brigge* in his pea coat—and read out loud to his fellow riders: "'My father had taken me with him to Urnekloster. . . . There remains whole in my heart, so it seems to me, only that large hall in which we used to gather for dinner every evening at seven o'clock. I never saw this room by day; I do not even remember whether it had windows or on what they looked out; always, whenever the family entered, the candles were burning in the ponderous branched candlesticks, and in a few minutes one forgot the time of day and all that one had seen outside. This lofty and, as I suspect, vaulted

chamber was stronger than everything else. With its darken-
ing height, with its never quite clarified corners, it sucked all
images out of one without giving one any definite substitute
for them. One sat there as if dissolved; entirely without will,
without consciousness, without desire, without defence. One
was like a vacant spot. I remember that at first this annihilat-
ing state almost caused me nausea; it brought on a kind of
seasickness which I only overcame by stretching out my leg
until I touched with my foot the knee of my father who sat opposite me. It did not strike me until afterwards that he seemed
to understand, or at least to tolerate, this singular behavior,
although there existed between us an almost cool relationship
which would not account for such a gesture. Nevertheless it
was this slight contact that gave me strength to support the
long repasts. And after a few weeks of spasmodic endurance,
I became, with the almost boundless adaptability of a child,
so inured to the eeriness of these gatherings, that it no longer
cost me effort to sit at table for two hours; now these hours
passed comparatively swiftly, for I occupied myself in observing those present.'" Some of those present on the Muni were
looking at the reader, some had closed their eyes, some looked
out the window, everyone perhaps listening.

"'My grandfather called them "the family," and I also heard
the others use the same term, which was entirely arbitrary.'"
Wittman read on, reading the descriptions of the four persons
at table. The bus driver did not tell him to shut up, and he
got to the good part: "'The meal dragged along as usual, and
we had just reached the dessert when my eye was caught and
carried along by a movement going on, in the half-darkness,
at the back of the room. In that quarter a door which I had
been told led to the mezzanine floor, had opened little by little,
and now, as I looked on with a feeling entirely new to me of
curiosity and consternation, there stepped into the darkness of
the doorway a slender lady in a light-colored dress, who came
slowly toward us. I do not know whether I made any movement
or any sound; the noise of a chair being overturned forced me
to tear my eyes from that strange figure, and I caught sight
of my father, who had jumped up now, his face pale as death,
his hands clenched by his sides, going toward the lady. She,
meantime, quite untouched by this scene, moved toward us,

step by step, and was already not far from the Count's place, when he rose brusquely and, seizing my father by the arm, drew him back to the table and held him fast, while the strange lady, slowly and indifferently, traversed the space now left clear, step by step, through an indescribable stillness in which only a glass clinked trembling somewhere, and disappeared through a door in the opposite wall of the dining-hall.'"

None of the passengers was telling Wittman to cool it. It was pleasant, then, for them to ride the bus while Rilke shaded and polished the City's greys and golds. Here we are, Walt Whitman's "classless society" of "everyone who could read or be read to." Will one of these listening passengers please write to the City Council and suggest that there always be a reader on this route? Wittman has begun a someday tradition that may lead to a job as a reader riding the railroads throughout the West. On the train through Fresno—Saroyan; through the Salinas Valley—Steinbeck; through Monterey—*Cannery Row*; along the Big Sur ocean—Jack Kerouac; on the way to Weed—*Of Mice and Men*; in the Mother Lode—Mark Twain and Robert Louis Stevenson, who went on a honeymoon in *The Silverado Squatters*; *Roughing It* through Calaveras County and the Sacramento Valley; through the redwoods—John Muir; up into the Rockies—*The Big Rock Candy Mountain* by Wallace Stegner. Hollywood and San Elmo with John Fante. And all of the Central Valley on the Southern Pacific with migrant Carlos Bulosan, *America Is in the Heart*. What a repertoire. A lifetime reading job. And he had yet to check out Gertrude Atherton, and Jack London of Oakland, and Ambrose Bierce of San Francisco. And to find "Relocation" Camp diaries to read in his fierce voice when the train goes through Elk Grove and other places where the land once belonged to the A.J.A.s. He will refuse to be a reader of racist Frank Norris. He won't read Bret Harte either, in revenge for that Ah Sin thing. Nor *Ramona* by Helen Hunt Jackson, in case it turned out to be like *Gone with the Wind*. Travelers will go to the reading car to hear the long novels of the country they were riding through for hours and for days. A fool for literature, the railroad reader of the S.P. is getting his start busting through reader's block on the Muni. Wittman's talent was that he could read while riding without getting carsick.

The ghost of Christine Brahe for the third and last time walked through the dining hall. The Count and Malte's father raised their heavy wineglasses "to the left of the huge silver swan filled with narcissus," Rilke's ancestral tale came to a close, and the bus came to the place for Wittman to get off. He walked through the Stockton Street tunnel—beneath the Tunnel Top Bar on Bush and Burill, where Sam Spade's partner, Miles Archer, was done in by Brigid O'Shaughnessy—and emerged in Chinatown. At a payphone—this was not the phone booth with the chinky-chinaman corny horny roof—he thought about whether he needed to make any calls. He had a couple more dimes. What the hell. He dropped one into the slot and dialed information for the number of the most ungettable girl of his acquaintance.

So, that very afternoon it happened that: It was September again, which used to be the beginning of the year, and Wittman Ah Sing, though not a student anymore, nevertheless was having cappuccino in North Beach with a new pretty girl. The utter last of summer's air lifted the Cinzano scallops of the table umbrella, and sun kept hitting beautiful Nanci Lee in the hair and eyes. In shade, Wittman leaned back and glowered at her. He sucked shallow on his cigarette and the smoke clouded out thick over his face, made his eyes squint. He also had the advantage of the backlighting, his hair all haloed, any zits and pores shadowed. She, on her side, got to watch the sun go down. A summer and a year had gone by since graduation from Berkeley. Somebody's favorite tune was "Moscow Nights," and balalaikas kept trembling out of the jukebox.

"You," he said. "You're from L.A., aren't you? Why didn't you go back there?" Well, the place that a Chinese holds among other Chinese—in a community somewhere—matters. It was a very personal question he was asking her. It would pain a true Chinese to admit that he or she did not have a community, or belonged at the bottom or the margin.

People who have gone to college—people their age with their at-tee-tood—well, there are reasons—people who wear black turtleneck sweaters have no place. You don't easily come home, come back to Chinatown, where they give you stink-eye and call you a saang-hsü lo, a whisker-growing man, Beatnik.

Nanci brought her coffee cup up to her mouth, bouging to catch the rim, and looked warily, he hoped, at him over it. Beautiful and shy, what a turn-on she is. She took a cigarette out of her purse, and held it in front of that mouth until he lit it. "Yes, I'm from Los Angeles," she said, answering one of his questions. Pause. Take a beat. "I'm going back down there soon. To audition. I'm on my way." Pause yet another beat or two. "Why don't you go back to Sacramento?"

Unfair. No fair. L.A. is wide, flat, new. Go through the flashing arch, and there you are: Chinatownland. Nothing *to* going back to L.A. Cecil B. DeMille rebuilds it new ahead of you as you approach it and approach it on the freeway, whether 101 or over the grapevine. But, say, you stake a claim to San Francisco as your home place. . . .

"Golden Gate Park was wild today. I fought my way out. Lucky." He blew smoke hard between clenched teeth. "The paint-heads were cutting loose out of their minds, and messing with my head. Through the pines and eucalyptus, I could smell the natural-history museum. They may have let those trees grow to hide the funeral-parlor smell, which seeps through the sealant. You got claustro, you got fear of the dark, you keep out of museums of natural history; every kind of phobia lets you have it. It's too quiet, the ursus horribilus propped up on its hind legs; his maw is open but no roar. I don't like walking in the dark with fake suns glowing on the 'scenes.' Pairs of cat-eye marbles look at you from bobcat heads and coyote heads. Freak me out. The male animals are set in hunting poses, and the female ones in nursing poses. Dead babies. There's a lizard coming out of a dinosaur's tail. Stiffs. Dead behind glass forever. Stuffed birds stuffed inside pried-open mouths. 'Taxidermy' means the ordering of skin. Skin arrangements. If you're at my bedside when I die, Nanci, please, don't embalm me. I don't want some mortician who's never met me to push my face into a serene smile. They try to make the buffaloes and deer more natural by balding a patch of hair, omitting a toenail, breaking a horn. I paid my way out of the park. I saw the pattern: twice, there were people refashioning and selling castoffs. Flotsam and jetsam selling flotsam and jetsam. I bought this insert from last Sunday's paper."

Nanci took the paper from him, and folded it into a hat.

She put it on Wittman's head. She was not squeamish to touch what a dirty stranger had touched, nor to touch this hairy head before her. He was at a party. He took off the hat, and with a few changes of folds, origamied it into a popgun. He whopped it through the air, it popped good.

"In Sacramento, I don't belong. Don't you wonder how I have information about you and L.A., your town? And how come you have information about me? You have committed to memory that I have family in Sacramento." And, yes, a wondering—a wonderfulness—did play in her eyes and on her face. Two invisible star points dinted her cheeks with dimples; an invisible kung fu knight was poking her cheeks with the points of a silver shuriken. "And I bet you know what I studied. And whether I'm rich boy or poor boy. What my family is—Lodi grocery or Watsonville farmer, Castroville artichoke or Oakland restaurant or L.A. rich." Smart was what he was. Scholarship smart.

"No," she said. "I don't know much about you."

No, she wouldn't. She was no China Man the way he was China Man. A good-looking chick like her floats above it all. He, out of it, knows ugly and knows Black, and also knows fat, and funny-looking. Yeah, he knows fat too, though he's tall and skinny. She's maybe only part Chinese—Lee could be Black or white Southern, Korean, Scotsman, anything— and also rich. Nanci Lee and her highborn kin, rich Chinese-Americans of Orange County, where the most Chinese thing they do is throw the headdress ball. No, he hadn't exactly captured her fancy and broken her heart. When the rest of them shot the shit about him, she hadn't paid attention. Though she should have; he was more interesting than most, stood out, tall for one thing, long hair for another, dressed in Hamlet's night colors for another. Sly-eyed, he checked himself out in the plate-glass window. The ends of his moustache fell below his bearded jawbone. He had tied his hair back, braided loose, almost a queue but not a slave queue, very hip, like a samurai whose hair has gotten slightly undone in battle. Like Kyuzu, terse swordsman in *Seven Samurai*. A head of his time, ha ha. He was combat-ready, a sayonara soldier sitting on his red carpet beside the palace moat and digging the cherry blossoms in their significant short bloom.

"You must not have been in on the Chinese gossip," he said, counting on what would hurt her, that at school she had been left out by the main Chinese. (They left everybody out.)

"Let me tell you about where I was born," he said. She was, in a way, asking for the story of his life, wasn't she? Yeah, she was picking up okay.

"Chinatown?" she guessed. Is that a sneer on her face? In her voice? Is she stereotypecasting him? Is she showing him the interest of an anthropologist, or a tourist? No, guess not.

"Yes. Yes, wherever I appear, there, there it's Chinatown. But not that Chinatown." He chinned in its direction. "I was born backstage in vaudeville. Yeah, I really was. No kidding. They kept me in an actual theatrical trunk—wallpaper lining, greasepaint, and mothball smells, paste smell. The lid they braced with a cane. My mother was a Flora Dora girl. To this day, they call her Ruby Long Legs, all alliteration the way they say it."

Yes, when she came near the trunk, a rubescence had filled the light and air, and he'd tasted strawberry jam and smelled and seen clouds of cotton candy. Wittman really does have show business in his blood. He wasn't lying to impress Nanci. He was taking credit for the circumstances of his birth, such as his parents. Parents are gifts; they're part of the life-which-happens-to-one. He hadn't yet done enough of the life-which-one-has-to-make. Commit more experience, Wittman. *It is true you were an actor's child, and when your people played they wanted to be seen.* . . .

"She did the blackbottom and the Charleston in this act, Doctor Ng and the Flora Dora Girls. Only, after a couple of cities, Doctor Ng changed it to Doctor Woo and the Chinese Flora Dora Girls so that the low fawn gwai would have no problem reading the flyers. 'Woo' easier in the Caucasian mouth. Not broke the mouth, grunting and gutturating and hitting the tones. 'Woo' sounds more classy anyway, the dialect of a better-class village. 'Woo' good for white ear. A class act. You know?" Of course, she did not know; he rubbed it in, how much she did not know about her own. "Doctor Woo's Chinese Flora Dora Jitter and June Bug Girls were boogie-woogying and saluting right through World War II. Yeah, within our lifetimes."

"What *was* the blackbottom?" she asked.

For her, he danced his forefingers like little legs across the tabletop. (Like Charlie Chaplin doing the Oceana Roll with dinner rolls on forks in *The Gold Rush.*) "'Hop down front and then you doodle back. Mooch to your left and then you mooch to your right. Hands on your hips and do the mess around. Break a leg and buckle near the ground. Now that's the Old Black Bottom.'" She laughed to see one finger-leg buckle and kick, buckle and kick, then straighten up, and the other finger-leg buckle and kick all the way across and off the table. Knuckle-knees.

O Someday Girl, find him and admire him for his interests. And dig his allusions. And laugh sincerely at his jokes. And were he to take up dandy ways, for example, why, remark on his comeliness in a cravat. Say "He's beau," without his having to point out the cravat.

But at the moment, this Nanci was smiling one of those Anne Bancroft–Tuesday Weld sneer-smiles, and he went on talking. In case she turns out to be the one he ends up with, he better tell her his life from the beginning. "You have to imagine Doctor Woo in white tie, top hat, tails—his Dignity. He called that outfit his Dignity. 'What shall I wear? I shall wear my Dignity,' he used to say, and put on his tux. 'I'm attending that affair dressed in my Dignity.' 'My Dignity is at the cleaner's.' 'My Dignity will see me out,' which means he'll be buried in it. Doctor Woo did sleight of hand, and he did patter song. He also did an oriental turn. Do you want to hear a Doctor Woo joke? No, wait. Wait. Never mind. Some other time. Later. It'd bring you down. He rip-rapped about sweet-and-sour eyes and chop-suey dis and dat, and white people all alikee. Yeah, old Doc Woo did a racist turn." (What Wittman wanted to say was, "Old Doc Woo milked the tit of stereotype," but he went shy.) "The audience loved it. Not one showgirl caught him up on it." Wittman made lemon eyes, and quince mouth, and Nanci laughed. He scooped up shreds of nervous paper napkins, his and hers, wadded them into a ball—held it like a delicate egg between thumb and forefinger—palm empty—see?—and out of the fist, he tugged and pulled a clean, whole napkin—opened the hand, no scraps. Come quick, your majesty. Simple Simon is making the princess laugh; she will have to marry him. "During inter-missions and after the show, we sold Doctor Woo's Wishes Come True Medicine. The old healing-powers-and-aphrodi-siacs-of-the-East scam. I'm dressed as a monkey. I'm running around in the crowd handing up jars and bottles and taking in the money. Overhead Doc Woo is giving the pitch and jam: 'You hurt? You tired? Ah, tuckered out? Where you ache? This medicine for you. Ease you sprain, ease you pain. What you wish? You earn enough prosperity? Rub over here. Tired be gone. Hurt no more. Guarantee! Also protect against acciden-tal bodily harm. And the Law. Smell. Breathe in deep. Free whiff. Drop three drops—four too muchee, I warn you—into you lady's goblet, and she be you own lady. Make who you love love you back. Hold you true love true to you. Guarantee! Guarantee!' We sold a line of products: those pretty silver bee-bees—remember them?—for when you have a tummy ache?—and Tiger Balm, which he bought in Chinatown and sold at a markup—cheaper for Chinese customers, of course. The Deet Dah Jow, we mixed ourselves. I use it quite often." "Deet Dah Jow" means "Fall Down and Beaten Up Alcohol." Medicine for the Fallen Down and Beaten Up. Felled and Beaten.

"When I smell Mahn Gum Yow," said Nanci, saying "Ten Thousand Gold Pieces Oil" very prettily, high-noting "gum," "I remember being sick in bed with the t.v. on. I got to play treasure trove with the red tins. I liked having a collection of gold tigers—they used to be raised, embossed—they're flat now—with emerald eyes and red tongues. I thought Tiger Balm was like Little Black Sambo's tiger butter. That in India the tigers chase around the palm tree until they churn into butter. And here they churn into ointment."

May this time be the first and only time she charms with this tale, and he its inspiration. "Yeah," he said. "Yeah. Yeah."

He continued. Onward. "Backstage old Doc Woo used to peptalk the Flora Dora girls about how they weren't just en-tertaining but doing public service like Ng Poon Chew and Wellington Koo, credits to our race. Show the bok gwai that Chinese-Ah-mei-li-cans are human jess likee anybody elsoo, dancing, dressed civilized, telling jokes, getting boffo laffs. We got rhythm. We got humor." Oh, god, he was so glad. He had not lost it, then—the mouth—to send the day high.

Nanci said, "You aren't making this up, are you?"

"Hey, you don't believe me? I haven't given you anything but facts. So I don't have an imagination. It's some kind of retardation. So I am incapable of making things up. My mother's name is Ruby, and my father is Zeppelin Ah Sing. He was a Stagedoor Johnny, then a backstage electrician, then emcee on stage. To get Mom to marry him, he bought out the front row of seats for entire runs. He loved her the best when she was on stage as Ruby Long Legs; and she loved him best leading his Army buddies in applause. They got married in Carson City, which is open for weddings twenty-four hours a day.

"To this day, whenever they go gambling at State Line, they start divorce proceedings. To keep up the *ro*mance. My parents are free spirits—I'm a descendant of free spirits. He left her and me for World War II. My aunties, the showgirls, said I was a mad baby from the start. Yeah. Mad baby and mad man." Come on, Nanci. The stars in a white girl's eyes would be glittering and popping by now.

"Uh-huh. Uh-huh," she said. "Uh-huh."

"You should have seen me in my Baby Uncle Sam outfit. The striped pants had an open seam in the back, so if I could grow a tail, it would come out of there. Sure, the costume came off of a circus monkey or a street-dancing monkey. You want details? I can impart details to you." She wasn't bored out of her mind anyway. Please be patient. Are you the one I can tell my whole life to? From the beginning to this moment? Using words that one reads and thinks but never gets to hear and say? "Think back as far as you can," he said. "First it's dark, right? But a warm, close dark, not a cold outer-space dark." A stupid girl would think he knew her personal mind. "Then you made out a slit of light, and another, and another—a zoetrope—faster and faster, until all the lights combined. And you had: consciousness. Most people's lights turn on by degrees like that. (When you come across 'lights' in books, like the Donner Party *ate* lights, do you think 'lights' means the eyes or the brains?) I got zapped all at once. That may account for why I'm uncommon. I saw: all of a sudden, curtains that rose and rose, and on the other side of them, lights, footlights and overheads, and behind them, the dark, but different from the previous dark. Rows of lights, like teeth, uppers and lowers, and the mouth wide open laughing—and either I was inside it standing on the tongue, or I was outside, looking into a mouth, and inside the mouth were many, many strangers. All looking at me. *For a while they looked at me, wondering at my littleness.* And pointing at me and saying, 'Aaah.' Which is my name, do you see? Then one big light blasted me. It was a spotlight or a floodlight, and I thought that it had dissolved me into light, but it hadn't, of course. I made out people breathing—expecting something. They wanted an important thing to happen. If I opened my mouth, whatever it was that was pouring into my ears and eyes and my skin would shout out of my mouth. I opened my mouth for it to happen. But somebody swooped me up—arms caught me—and carried me back into the wings. Sheepcrooked m'act." . . . *a door had swung open before you, and now you were among the alembics in the firelight. . . . Your theater came into being.*

Yes, this flight, this rush, the oncoming high. He had talked his way—here—once more. Good and bad, the world was exactly as it should be. The sidewalk trees were afire in leaf-flames. And the most beyond girl in the world was listening to him. The air which contained all this pleasure was as clear as mescaline and he was straight. The sun was out which shines golden like this but three times a San Francisco autumn.

"When I was a child," said Nanci—*her* turn to talk about *her* kiddie-hood—"I had a magic act too. But it wasn't an act. I didn't have an audience; it was secret. I believed I could make things appear and disappear by taking every step I had seen the magician take at my birthday party. I sprinkled salt on a hanky to make a dime appear." She opened a paper napkin, and shook salt into it. What's this? She doing geisha shtick for me? "I tied the corners together and said my magic words. Then undid the knot, and blew the salt." She made kiss-me lips, and blew. The wind is driving snow off of a silver pond. The wind is driving a snowcloud across the full moon. "I didn't find a dime then either. What step did I do wrong—not enough salt, too much salt? Didn't I tie the knot right? It has to be a seventh birthday?" She giggled, looked at him to help her out, to sympathize with her gullibility or to laugh at her joking. Doesn't she know that all magic acts you have to cheat, the missing step is cheating? You're not the only one,

Wittman, who fooled with magic, and not the only one who refuses to work for money. And also not the only one to talk. She had to talk too, make this a conversation. In those days, women did not speak as much as men. Even among the educated and Bohemian, a man talked out his dreams and plans while a girl thought whether she would be able to adapt herself to them. Girls gave one another critiques on how adaptable they were. The artistic girls had dead-white lips and aborigine eyes, and they wore mourning colors. There were two wake-robins, Diane Wakoski and Lenore Kandel; the latter wailed out sex-challenge poems larger and louder than the men, who were still into cool.

"Why did you ask me out?" asked Nanci.

Because you're beautiful, he thought, and maybe I love you; I need to get it on with a Chinese-American chick. He said, "I wanted to find out if the most beautiful girl of all my school days would come to me." There. Said. Would come to me. Intimate. He let her know that he used to be—and still was— in her thrall. "I'm calling you up," he had said on the phone, "to celebrate the first anniversary of our graduation. Come tell me, have you found out, 'Is there life after Berkeley?'" "I told you—we're having a reunion, a party for me."

"Shouldn't we be at Homecoming, then, with everyone else?"

What? Buy her a lion-head chrysanthemum, pin it on her tweed lapel? Do the two of us have to walk again past the fraternities on College Avenue, and admire their jungle-bunny house decorations? The Jew Guais too with Greek letters—Sammies—and Yom Kippur banners. Yeah, there were a Chinese fraternity and sorority, but if you were bone-proud, you didn't have anything to do with SOP sisters and the Pineapple Pies. Nor the Christian house, which let anybody in. The crowd let the city and county sawhorses route them, governments too co-operating with football. He was always walking alone in the opposite direction but ending up at Strawberry Canyon—the smell of eucalyptus in the cold air breaks your heart—among the group looking down into the stadium for free. Only he was up here for the walk, awaiting a poem to land on him, to choose him, walking to pace the words to the rhythm of his own stride. And there was all this football interference. The Cal Marching Band, the drum booming, and the pompon girls kneeling and rotating an arm with pompons in the air, and the teams running toward each other with the crowd going oo-oo-OO-OH! How do all those people know you're supposed to stand and yell that yell at kickoff? The reason he didn't like going to football games was the same reason he didn't like going to theater: he wanted to be playing. Does his inability at cheers have to do with being Chinese? He ought to be in Paris, where everything is dark and chic.

"The Big Game soon," she said.

"Weren't you an Oski Doll? You were an Oski Doll, weren't you?"

"Come on. It was an honor to be an Oski Doll. It's based on scholarship too, you know? It's a good reference. Some of us Oski Dolls helped integrate the rooting section from you boys."

"'Here we go, Bears, here we go.' 'We smell roses.' 'All hail Blue and Gold; thy colors unfold.' 'Block that kick, hey.' 'Hold that line, hey.' 'The Golden Bear is ever watching.'"

"See? You did participate."

"Well, yeah, I went to the Big Game once. Stanford won." But most of the time I was participating in the big dread. "Those songs and cheers will stick in the head forever, huh?"

"I know your motive for wanting to see me," she said. "You want to know how you were seen. What your reputation was. What people thought of you. You care what people think of you. You're interested in my telling you."

He looked at the bitten nails of the fingers that held her cigarette and of her other fingers, both hands; they put him at ease. "Yes, if you want to tell me, go ahead."

"Well, let me think back," she said, as if school had been long ago and not interesting anymore. "It seems to me you were a conservative."

No. No. No. He had been wild. Maybe she thought it flattered a Chinese man to be called temperate? Safe. What about his white girlfriends? What about his Black girlfriend? His play-in-progress? That he read aloud on afternoons on the Terrace and at the Mediterraneum (called The Piccolo by those hip to the earlier Avenue scene). There had been no other playwright.

Of whatever color. He was the only one. She hadn't cared for his poem in *The Occident*?

"Conservative like F.O.B.? Like Fresh Off the Boat?" He insulted her with translation; she was so banana, she needed a translation. "Conservative like engineering major from Fresno with a slide rule on his belt? Like dental student from Stockton? Like pre-optometry majors from Gilroy and Vallejo and Lodi?" But I'm an artist, an artist of all the Far Out West. "Feh-see-no. Soo-dock-dun," he said, like an old Chinese guy bopping out a list poem. "Gi-loy. Wah-lay-ho. Lo-di." But hadn't he already done for her a catalog of places? Repeating himself already. One of his rules for maintaining sincerity used to be: Never tell the same story twice. He changed that to: Don't say the same thing in the same way to the same person twice. Better to be dead than boring.

"I mean quiet," she said and did not elaborate, poured more espresso out of her individual carafe, sipped it, smoked. She wasn't deigning to go on. No examples. He had talked for four years, building worlds, inventing selves, and she had not heard. The gold went out of the day. He came crashing down. He must have been feeling good only because the sun was out amid grey weeks. (In the plague year, according to Defoe, the people's moods were much affected by the weather.)

"Well?" she said, pushing away from the table, her shoulders up, like a forties movie girl being hugged. "I have an appointment at three-thirty." As if she had come to the City for that important appointment and incidentally might as well have met with him too, a former classmate, after all. But there was no guile on her face, which seemed always uplifted. Was she joyful, or was that curve the way her mouth naturally grew? The way some cats and dogs have smile markings. Yeah, it was not a smile but a smile marking.

"Hey, wait a minute," he said, and grabbed her hand, held hands with her, a sudden endearment achieved right smack through force fields. "Let's go for a walk. Come for a walk with me. I live near here. Yeah, I do. Let me show you where I live."

Since she, in truth, did not have an appointment, she agreed to go with him. Finding digs, having digs, arranging them interested each of them very much. *God's solitaries in their caves and bare retreats.*

"Let's walk," he said, stubbing out his cigarette. Let's amble the blue North Beach streets as the evening sun goes down into the far grey water.

Though they walked through the land of the wasted, no Malte sights popped out to hurt him, she dispelling them. By day, the neon was not coursing through its glass veins. The dancing girl in spangles and feathers had flown out of her cage, which hung empty over the street. Nobody barked and hustled at the doorways to acts and shows. The day-folks, wheeling babies, wheeling grandpas, holding children by the hand, were shopping for dinner at the grocery stores and the bakery, dropping by the shoe repair. Oh, the smell of the focaccia ovens—O Home. A florist with white moustachios jaywalked through traffic with armsful of leonine football chrysanthemums. Behind glass, at the all-day-all-night place on the pie-wedge corner, poets, one to a table, were eating breakfast. The Co-Existence Bagel Shop was gone. The old guys, *Seventh Seal* knights, had played chess with Death and lost. The Bagel Shop, Miss Smith's Tea Room, Blabbermouth Night at The Place—all of a gone time. Out from the open door of La Bodega, a folksy guitar sweetened the air. The guitar was being passed around, and each played the tune he knew. You should have been there the night Segovia dropped by and played flamenco. Wittman musefully sang as if to himself a Mose Allison riff.

> *A young ma-a-an*
> *ain't nothin' in this world today.*
> *Because the ol' men's*
> *got all the money.*

The air of the City is so filled with poems, you have to fight becoming imbued with the general romanza. Nanci's long black hair and long black skirt skirled with the afternoon breezes. The leather of her shoulder bag strapped a breast. Her arms and outstretching legs were also long and black; she wore a leotard and tights like an old-fashioned Beat chick but, honestly, a dancer, dance togs for a good reason. Here he was: Wittman Ah Sing profiling down the street with a beautiful almost-girl-friend, clipping along, alongside, keeping up with him, the

two of them making the scene on the Beach, like cruising in
the gone Kerouac time of yore.

He ducked into the bookstore. She followed right on in. She
stood beside him, browsing the rack of quarterlies, quite a few
brave Volume I Number Ones. There were homemade books
too, mimeo jobs, stencils, and small-press poetry that fit neat
in the hand. On the top rack—right inside the door at eye level
for all to see coming in or going out—was: an artistic avant-
garde far-out new magazine that had published—in print—a
scene from his play-in-progress—the lead-off piece—with his
byline—right inside the front cover. He could reach over and
hand it to her, but it would be more perfect if she happened to
pick it out herself, come upon his premiere on her own, and
be impressed. (F. Scott Fitzgerald, trying to impress Sheilah
Graham, had driven to every bookstore in L.A., but could not
find a copy of any of his books.)

Wittman went downstairs to the cool basement, where
among the bookshelves were chairs and tables with ashtrays.
He had first come to this place when he was a high-school kid
on one of his escapes from Sacramento, Second City to Big
City. No *No Free Reading* sign. No *No Smoking*. You didn't
have to buy a book; you could read for nothing. You had a
hangout where you didn't have to spend money. Quiet. All the
radios in Chinatown blaring out the ball game, but here, we
don't care about the World Series. He hadn't known the City
Lights Pocket Book Shop was famous until the *Howl* trial,
which he had cut school to attend. "Shig" Shigeyoshi Murao
was the one charged with selling an obscene book. The muster
of famous poets had blown Wittman away—everybody friends
with everybody else, a gang of poets. He, poor monkey, was
yet looking for others of his kind.

There had been a Chinese-American guy who rode with
Jack and Neal. His name was Victor Wong, and he was a
painter and an actor. Wittman had maybe seen him, or someone Chinese with the asymmetrical face of a character actor;
he wore a white t-shirt with paint streaks and "hand-tooled
leather shoes." Victor Wong, who went to the cabin in Bixby
Canyon with Jack Duluoz and Neal/Cody. All this written up
in *Big Sur*, where Jack calls Victor Wong Arthur Ma ("Little
Chinese buddy Arthur Ma." Shit.), and flips out of his gourd

walking in the moonless night above the wild ocean that rants for his life. Jack hangs on to the side of the mountain and listens and shouts back and sings. "Mien Mo Big Sur killer mountain for singing madly in." It would have been better if Victor/Arthur had been a writing man like the rest of them, but anyway he talked a lot and was good at hallucinations. "Little Arthur Ma [yet again "little"!] who never goes anywhere without his drawing paper and his Yellowjacket felt tips of all colors, red, blue, yellow, green, black, he draws marvelous subconscious glurbs and can also do excellent objective scenes or anything he wants on to cartoons—." They stay up all night, and Arthur Ma keeps making it up; he's not one of those storytellers who has to rehearse in the bathroom. Wittman had not gone up to the man with the character actor's face—one eye big, one eye small—and grabbed him by the arm and introduced himself. The poets at Big Sur fall asleep but not Arthur, who stays awake with Jack, the two of them yelling till dawn. ". . . and Arthur Ma suddenly yells: 'Hold still you buncha bastards, I got a hole in my eye.'"

It would be nice were Nanci to walk down the pine-slab steps and say, "Oh, you're published. Why didn't you tell me? Will you autograph a copy for me?" Holding his words to her bosom.

Girls in my native land. May the loveliest of you on an afternoon in summer in the darkened library find herself the little book that Jan des Tournes printed in 1556. May she take the cooling, glossy volume out with her into the murmurous orchard, or yonder to the phlox, in whose oversweet fragrance there lies a sediment of sheer sweetness.

She was two aisles away browsing through the French and German shelves. The Europeans made books with creme linen paper; the soft covers were not illustrated except for a sharp line of vermillion trim. When you slice the pages open with your paperknife, the book will have flossy raggedy edges. You feel like owning books like that. Remember Phoebe Weatherfield Caulfield asking Holden to name one thing he liked a lot? "Name one thing." "One thing I like a lot, or one thing I just like?" "You like a lot." Wittman liked a lot this poky hole in the San Francisco underground earth. He will not point out to Nanci what's so good about it. Spoil it to make a big deal.

She had to take a liking of her own accord. He took his own sweet time, testing her scanning and skimming of foreign lit.

But the next time he looked her way, she was talking to a couple of Black guys, laughing, carrying on in French. Maybe they had met before, or maybe she let herself be picked up. There was something Black about her too, come to think of it; it was in a fullness of the mouth, and a wildness in her clothes, and something about her dry hair. "Très joli. Ahh, très joli. Oo-la-la, très joli." So, people really do say "Oo-la-la." She and they were mutually delighting in something. These black French must have lately arrived from one of those colonial places. Their faces were not chary and wary; they were not "friendly," or "bad," or "loose." Their long hands and fingers wafted through a gentler atmosphere. Give them a few more weeks among the Amerikans; we'll show them how far très joli manners get them, and how much respect with *Saturday Review* tucked under the arm. They'll tighten up their act. Turn complicated. He squeezed past them; they easily stepped aside, gave him no trouble. Let's go already, Nanci. Wittman gave a jerk of his head—¡Vamos! ¡Andalay!—and, surprisingly, she said her adieux and followed him up the stairs. You would think only homely girls obey like that.

"Wait," she called. "I'll be right with you." She paid for a book. "See?" she said. "Beckett."

"Ah, Bik Giht," he said, Chinatown having a pronunciation because of Beckett Street and not because of absurdity. Of course not.

"I'm looking for audition pieces," said Nanci as they walked along. "The speeches of just about any Beckett man make sense—more sense—coming from a woman. A minority woman. It doesn't matter what a Beckett character looks like. I won't play an oriental prostitute, and I won't speak broken English. No matter what. I can't. I won't. I'll be too old to play an ingenue? I'm a leading lady. I am the leading-lady type. No ching-chong chinaman for me."

What did she say? She said "ching-chong chinaman." She can bear to say that. God, she's tough. He had to get tougher. His head and bod were going through contortions from merely hearing that. Did I hear wrong? Hallucinating again? She mean me? Who you talking to? You talking to me, girl?

You talking *about* me? Am I too paranoid, or what? She hadn't called me a name, had she? Someone called her that? Who called her that? Who she quoting? Was he hearing English wrong like any greenhorn F.O.B.? Now he was laughing nervously—the Chinese laugh—the giggle—lest it be a joke— that please-let-it-be-a-joke giggle. That betraying Chinese giggle trebled out of him. Where he'd almost gone deaf, she had said, "No ching-chong chinaman for me." She meant she refused to read a grotesque whose bucktoof mouth can't make intelligent American sounds. As if this language didn't belong to us. Well, the ugly is ugly no matter whose beautiful mouth it comes out of. She shouldn't wreck her mouth, and her voice, and her face, and her soul by repeating scurrilities.

"For my classical, I'll do Rosalind or Portia. Then when I'm older, anybody can be the queen." Anybody. Her. A leading lady. Why not? Who has more in common with a Shakespeare queen—a country-fair beauty starlet or Leontyne Price? Medea and Cleopatra and Clytemnestra and the statue lady from *Winter's Tale* are not blondies. Nor, it so happened, were any of the people walking by them on the street, nor are most people in the world.

"I don't like *Flower Drum Song*," she said. Wittman didn't either—a bunch of A.J.A.s and "Eurasians" playing weird Chinese. Not that Chinese have to play Chinese. Chineseness does not come to an actor through genetic memory. The well-trained actor observes humanity and the text.

"Oh, I'm so sorry," said Nanci, "that I took my grandmother to see *The World of Suzie Wong* for the scenes of Hong Kong. I'm so sorry. Wittman? I've been to New York and Hollywood. I look a bit dark. They're overt, you know? They say, 'You don't *look* oriental.' I walk in, they can tell about me. They read me, then they say, 'You don't sound right. You don't sound the way you look. You don't look the way you talk. Too distracting.' I'm wearing my high heels, and walking elegant, you know? The a.d. hands me the script, and tells me I have to take my shoes off. It's a cold reading, but I know what my part will be—an oriental peasant. You only need high heels for the part of the oriental prostitute. A good-looking talented actor, who's gotten his callback, who's been cast maybe, says my cue, which is 'Hey, there, mama-san,' And I

have to say, I have to say, you know, something stupid. I have
to speak in a way I've worked hard not to speak like. I stand
there barefoot saying a line like—like that. And the director says, 'Can't you act more oriental? Act oriental.' I haven't
been making rounds for a while." Oh, no, Nanci, don't lose
the will to audition.

Wittman, now's your chance to whip out your Rilke, and
give her his sympathy: *Let us be honest about it, then; we have
no theatre, any more than we have God: for this, community is
needed. . . . Had we a theatre, would you, tragic one, stand there
again and again and again—so slight, so bare, so without pre-
text of a role. . . .*

"Wittman?" she said, laying a hand on his arm. "I performed twice as a crowd member. Once in a movie, and once
on t.v. While the make-up lady was shading my nose, she said,
'I'm going to give you a cute Irish nose.' I'm tilted back in the
chair, and holding my face steady. I don't reply. I don't want
to get her mad so she makes me up ugly. And I wanted to see
what I'd look like with my nose upturned. She shadowed the
nostrils, and put white make-up down the length, ending with
a diamond on the tip. The other show I was in, we had a male
make-up artist—bitchy gay?—who finished my face without
talking to me. Then he says, 'There's just so much we can
do about those eyes.'" Those eyes were now downcast with
mortification and tears. Oh, baby, what can I do to defend you
against—cosmetologists. "They were trying to give me advice?
For my own good? They didn't mean to hurt me."

"Yes, they did. They hurt you."

"Yes. I should have done my own make-up."

"It's no fair," said Wittman, who would not put his arm
around her shoulder or waist. This called for a higher level of
comforting. Help her out by thinking up a piece for her to do
without insult. He ought to tell her that her face was perfectly
lovely. But he was annoyed at her for talking about her face
so much. Her nickname in college had been The Face. "How
about the girl in *The Seven Year Itch*?" he suggested. "Yeah,
that's what the script says—The Girl. Not The White Girl. The
Girl. She's just a girl in New York on her own. No family from
the old country camping in her apartment."

"I hate *The Seven Year Itch*. I loathe it."

"Just testing. I was testing you. You passed." Therefore, thou art mine, sought and found.

"But you're right. She could very well look like me. There isn't any reason why she shouldn't look like me. Wittman?" She had his sleeve in her fingers, and pulled at it for them to stop walking so fast. "I was thinking of *Krapp's Last Tape*. I could do it by myself, no other face up there to compare mine to. A director doesn't have to match me. My lost love who's beside me in the boat could be a male nurse. 'We lay there without moving but under us all moved, and moved us, gently, up and down, and from side to side.' When Krapp says, 'Let me in,' I, a woman, could mean: Open your eyes, and let me into your eyes."

Why hadn't he thought of that? She must think him ill-read and a dried-up intellectual not to have seen the sensuality in Beckett. "You're resorting to Krapp, Nanci, because of being left out of the Hogan Tyrone Loman Big Daddy family. And whatever the names of those families were in *Seven Brides for Seven Brothers*. Seven white brides for seven white brothers. They took a perfectly good pro-miscegenation legend and wrote fourteen principal parts for Caucasians. I know legends about seven Chinese brothers named Juan; they were part of a nation of one hundred and eight heroes and heroines. What I'm going to do, I've got to wrest the theater back for you. Those Juans were hermanos chinos.

"I understand your agony, Nanci," he said. "The most important tradition in my high school was the senior play. My year they did *The Barretts of Wimpole Street*. The student who won the most Willie Awards was supposed to play the lead. In the U.K., 'willie' means 'weenie'; in Sacramento, it means 'talent.' I was the man of a thousand faces and got my Willies for winning talent shows. Robert Browning, tall, thin, sensitive, dark, melancholy—that's me, let me count the ways. But the drama coach held auditions. Then he told me, I'm the emcee for the evening, the 'host'; I warm up the audience, talk to them entr'acte, do my stand-up shtick, whatever I like, do my magic act, my ventriloquist act, throw my voice, 'Help. Help. Let me out.' I'd be featured. Very special, my spot. The way they staged *The Barretts of Wimpole Street* was Wilderesque, with an important *Our Town* stage manager character played by me. I look like Frank Craven, who had Chinese eyes and a viewpoint from the outskirts of Grover's Corners, U.S.A. I did my medley of soliloquies, Hamlet, Richard III, Macbeth, Romeo. No Juliet. I did my bearded Americans, Walt Whitman and John Muir, guys with a lot of facial hair to cover up my face and my race. Mark Twain: '. . . a white to make a body sick, a white to make a body's flesh crawl—a tree-toad white, a fish-belly white.' Between *Barretts*, I also did great movie lines. 'Philip. Give me the letter, Philip.' 'Last night I dreamt I went to Manderley again.' 'As God is my witness, I'll never be hungry again. Chomp chomp.' 'The calla lilies are in bloom. Such a strange flowah.'"

Nanci guessed the actress whom each of those lines belonged to. "'Maybe you found someone you like betta,'" she said. "Mae Clarke before James Cagney shoves the grapefruit in her kisser. 'I'd rather have his one arm around me than be in the two arms of another man.'"

"I know. I know. That movie where Linda Darnell and the British flyer and Tab Hunter are marooned on an island of desire. The British flyer has one arm, and Tab Hunter has the two arms but doesn't get the girl."

"No. Thelma Ritter says it to Marilyn Monroe in *The Misfits*."

"Nanci, I think we're on to something. That line is so meaningful, they've used it in two movies. It's what you call a perennial favorite. Women have all the good lines. I almost turned into a Mei Lan Fan androgyne doing those lines single-handed. I'm ruined for ensemble work. I haven't been on the stage since."

Grant Avenue, or Du Pont Gai—they/we call it Du Pont Gai—changed from North Beach to Chinatown. That factory which baked the Beatnik fortune cookies for the Actor's Workshop benefit should be situated at this border. You can't pick out just exactly which Italian store or Chinese store or red or red-white-and-green festooning it is that demarcates the change, but suddenly or gradually—depending on how closely you're keeping a lookout—you are in the flak and flash of Chinatown. Autumn was here: A red banner strung above the street announced the Double Ten parade and its sponsors, the Chinese-American Anti-Communist League and the Six Companies. They'll leave the banner up there all this month before Double Ten and afterwards into winter. To show Immigration and HUAC that we Chinese-Americans, super Americans, we too better dead than red-hot communists. Neither Wittman nor Nanci had plans to observe Double Ten. They had no idea how you go about doing that since nobody they knew showed much interest. It seemed like a fake holiday. A woody station wagon with Ohio plates drove slowly by. Painted across it was: "North Beach or Bust." Poor bastards. Too late. They had crossed the country to join the Beatniks.

"I'm writing a play for you, Nanci," said Wittman. Wait for me while I write for you a theater; I will plant and grow for you a pear garden. Then she did look at him—he's wonderful. She stopped in her tracks to look up at him. She took his upper arm with her two hands. "I'll write you a part," he said, "where the audience learns to fall in love with you for your ochery skin and round nose and flat profile and slanty eyes, and your bit of an accent."

She made a pouty mouth. They walked on, she still holding his arm with both hands. Nanci, as a matter of fact, had a pointy nose with a bridge, where her dark glasses had a place to sit. Even Marilyn Monroe, blonde, dead, had not been able to get away with a round nose. Rhinoplasty. Nanci looked good. When the directors tell her, "You don't look Chinese," they mean: too pretty for a Chinese. She had represented Cal at the intercollegiate (Chinese) beauty-personality-good-grades contest at U.C.L.A.

What theater do we have besides beauty contests? Do we have a culture that's not these knickknacks we sell to the bok gwai? If Chinese-American culture is not knickknackatory— look at it—backscratcher swizzle sticks, pointed chopsticks for the hair, Jade East aftershave in a Buddha-shape bottle, the head screws off and you pour lotion out of its neck—then what is it? No other people sell out their streets like this. Tourists can't buy up J-town. Wait a goddamn minute. We don't make Jade East. It's one of your hakujin products by Swank. Would we do that to you? Make Jesus-on-the-cross bottles, so every morning, all over the country, hairy men twist his head off, and pour this green stuff out of his neck? So what do we have in the way of a culture besides Chinese hand laundries? You might make a joke on that—something about 'What's the difference between a Chinese hand laundry and a French laundry?' Where's our jazz? Where's our blues? Where's our ain't-taking-no-shit-from-nobody street-strutting language? I want so bad to be the first bad-jazz China Man bluesman of America. Of all the music on the airwaves, there's one syllable that sounds like ours. It's in that song by the Coasters. "It'll take an ocean of calamine lotion. Poison iv-ee-eeee-ee." No, not the ivy part. It's where they sing, "Aro-ou-ound-aaaaa-ah." Right there, that's a Chinese opera run. A Coaster must have been among those Black guys you see at the Chinese movies and at dojos seeking kung fu power.

Wittman and Nanci toned down any show-off in their walks. Chinese like for young people to look soo-mun or see-mun. Proper. Well turned out. Decorous. Kempt. The Ivy League look is soo-mun. Clean-cut all-American. For girls: sprayed, fixed hair—hair helmet—and they should have a jade heart at their throat always. Wittman was glad Nanci was wearing a defiant black leotard. If they were Japanese and walking through J-town in their grubbies, the Issei, who have a word for every social condition, would call them "yogore." (Zato-Ichi the Blind Swordsman, who flicked his snot into the haw-haw-haw mouth of a villain, is yogore. He'd be rolling the snotball all the time he's pretending to be putting up with their taunts.) Wittman went up Jackson Street (Dik-son Gai), sort of herding Nanci, turned her at the corner, guided her across the street by leaning toward her or leading away. Strange the way a man has to walk with a woman. She follows his lead like they're dancing, she wasn't even a wife or girlfriend. Did you hear what Jack Kennedy said to his media advisers, who told him that in pictures Jackie isn't walking beside him enough? He said, "She will just have to walk faster." (It is not a Chinese custom for women to walk behind men. That's a base stereotype.) No, Wittman didn't want to slow down for anybody either, become an inclining, compliant owned man. Husbands walk differently from single guys. He unlocked the door of his building, having to reach in through the security bars for a somewhat hidden lock. Nanci went right on in. They climbed the many steps and landings, she ahead, and he behind thinking, "Pomegranates." They didn't run into anybody in the hallways, all decent people at work, their doors shut, rows of jailhouse-green doors.

"My ah-pok-mun," he said, opening the door wide to
his roomland, switching on the overhead light, which also
switched on the desk lamp. "Come in. Come in," turning his
desk chair around for his guest. "Welcome to my pok-mun.
Sit. Sit." He dumped the fullness of his ashtray into the trash
and set the ashtray next to his mattress on the floor. "For sitting furniture, I don't have but the one chair." She hung her
suede jacket over the back of it, and sat down. Sweeping open
his invisible magician's cape, he presented: his roomland, his
boxes of papers, his table, which was desk and dining table, his
hotplate on a crate, which was a cupboard for foodstuffs such
as instant coffee and Campbell's Soup, edible out of the can.
(Cook like a Mexicano: Put the tortilla directly on the burner,
flipflop, ready to eat. So you get burner rings on your tortilla,
but fast and nongreasy.) He quoted to her some Beat advice:
"'How many things do you own?' 'Fifteen.' 'Too many.'" No
rug here. No sofa here. Never own a rug or a sofa. And thus
be free. "'What's the use of living if I can't make paradise in
my own roomland?'" Peter Orlovsky was another one good at
how to live. She laughed but did not give him the next lines,
which are: "For this drop of time upon my eyes / like the endurance of a red star on a cigarette / makes me feel life splits
faster than scissors."

Good thing the typewriter crouched, ready, on the table—
his grand piano—that faces the window, where you look out at
another pok-mun. If he was going to bring people up here, he
ought to have been a painter. Painters have something to show
for their work—an easel with the painting they're working on
like a billboard all sunny under the skylight, their food composed into still-lifes, their favorite colors everywhere. They get
to wear their palette on their grey sweatshirts, and spatters
and swipes on their blue jeans. He sat down on the mattress,
straightened out his sleeping bag, bed made.

"So this is where you live," Nanci said, looking down into
one of his cartons, not touching the poems, just looking.

"See that trunk over there?" He pointed at it with the toe of
his boot. Books, papers, his coffee cup sat on its lid; a person
could sit on it too, and it become a second chair.

"That's the trunk I told you about. Proof, huh? Evidence.
It exists. It *became* a theatrical trunk; it used to be a Gold

Mountain trunk." It was big enough for crossing oceans, all right. It would take a huge man to hoist it onto his back. The hasps and clasps were rusty (with salt sea air), and the leather straps were worn. Big enough to carry all you own to a new land and never come back, enough stuff to settle the Far West with. And big enough to hold all the costumes for the seventy-two transformations of the King of the Monkeys in a long run of *The Journey to the West* in its entirety. "My great-great-grandfather came to America with that trunk."

"Yes," said Nanci, "I recognize it." Every family has a Gold Mountain trunk in their attic or basement.

"I can't die until I fill it with poems and play-acts," said Wittman.

"Would you like to read me a poem?" asked Nanci.

Oh, yes. Yes, I would. My name is Wittman Ah Sing, but you may call me Bold. When you get to know me better, you may call me Bolder, and I'll show you like Emily Dickinson secret poems in the false bottom of my Gold Mountain theater trunk. Oh, too guest-happy.

He rummaged through a carton for a poem that had made him feel like a genius when he made it. "New poems. New green poems. Haven't gone over this batch. Too green. Need one or two more drafts, make fair copies." Oh, shut up. Take one up at random. Any old poem.

Remember when everyone you fell in love with read poems and listened to poems? Love poetry has gone. And thou? Where went thou?

He put on his intellectual's glasses with the heavy black rims, scowled, made no eye contact. Oh, no—a poem—nah, a paragraph—that had been forced on speed, and coffee jacking the bennies up higher, then grass to smooth out the jaw-grinding jangles—does it show? A poem on beanie weenies, when he was a frijoles head—from his Making a Living series, a cycle of useful poetry—well, prose poems, actually—Gig Poems. Wishing he had a chance to re-do it, explain, he read aloud to Nanci something like this: Should a window-washing poet climb over the edge of a skyscraper, one leg at a time, onto his swing, and unclutch the ropes, may the tilted City hold still. Don't look down those paned streets. In view of the typing pools, he makes a noose, and tests the slide of it, and the

dingle dangle of it. Yes? Yes? No? No? Yes? No? Hey, look—sky
doggies. Up here—a stampede of longhorns. Point the rope
like a wand, whirl a Möbius strip, outline a buffalo. Shoot la
riata sideways over the street, overhead at the helicopters, jump
in and out of it, and lassoo one of those steers. It drags the poet
right off the plank—but the harness holds! Hey, you pretty
girls of the typing pool, give me a big pantomime hand. Can't
hear the clap-clap, but it's applause, and it's mine. Kisses blow
through glass. Their impact knocks me off again, falling far
down, and down as the pulley runs, and brakes. I vow: I will
make of my scaffold, a stage.

The poet—the one in real life, not the one in the poem—
wouldn't mind, when the poem ends, if his listening lady were
to pay him a compliment. Such as agreeing, yes, let's transfig-
ure every surface of the City with theater. Such as saying, "Did
you on purpose make the line that tells about the tilted City
bevel upsettingly—the verb fulcrumming a lot more phrases
on one end than the other?" He'd love her for such particular
appreciation. At least, praise him on the utilitarian level. From
out of my head into the world. The window-washer was using
newspapers and water, the chemicals in newsprint as good as
Windex spray. Also, you can get rich by contracting with the
owners of buildings for window-washing services a year in advance. Charge thousands, but pay the window-washers minimum wage by the hour. The kind of men you hire, whatever
you pay them, they think it's a lot.

Nanci made no move to show that she heard that the poem
was over. Give her a love story, Wittman. He ought to have
read her the one about how this broken-hearted guy had long
ago stashed in his *Physicians' Desk Reference* the last letter, un-
read, from the ex–love of his life, written upon taking her leave
of him. A lifetime later, an envelope falls out of the *P.D.R.* . . . .
(No, he wasn't a doctor. Each head had his own *P.D.R.* to
identify street pills, and their effects and side effects, that is,
trips and side trips.)

"Want to hear another one?" he asked.

"Okay," she said.

He reached into the poem box beside the black curve of
her calf. His arm could graze its black length. But a true
poet can't love up a woman who doesn't get that he's a poet.

He can't touch her until she feels his poetry. Japanese have a custom where the host leaves a piece of art about, and the guest may notice it. The carton was labeled The International Nut Corporation, 100 Phoenix Ave., Lowell, Mass. His soul chick would notice it, and say, "Did you make a pilgrimage to Kerouac's town and his city?" Then he grabs her leg.

"What do you want to hear? How about one of my railroad cantos? A land chantey, the worker-poet as chanteyman? How's about a dueling sequence? 'The Dueling Mammy,' ha ha. Loss poems? You need a revenge sonnet? I've got twenty-eight sonnets now. I have one hundred and twenty-six sonnets to go to catch up with Shakespeare, who finished everything at the age of forty-five. I'm twenty-three. You too, right?"

She nodded, crossing one of those legs over the other. She folded her arms under her breasts.

He read to her about the ineluctable goingness of railroad tracks. Then he gave her the poet's intense stare, holding her eyes until she spoke. "Lovely," she said. "Sweet."

But he did not want to be sweet and lovely.

He dug deeper into the poem box, letting the ashes of his cigarette fall right on in. He took hold of a bane poem. Standing up, as if on platform, he read to her about mongoloids. "'What's wrong with the baby, doctor?!' 'Is it deformed!?' 'Is it Chinese?!' Interbang?! Interbang!? 'But *we're* Chinese.' 'He's *supposed* to look like that!?' 'How can you tell if it's defective or if it's Chinese?!' 'Look at its little eyes.' 'Its tongue's too long.' 'Yellow skin *and* yellow jaundice?!' 'It's mongoloid?!' 'It's mongoloid!' 'It's an idiot?!' 'It's a mongolian idiot!' 'They're affectionate.' 'No, they bite.' 'Do they drool?!' 'All babies drool.' 'Can they be house-broken?!' 'Let's put it in a home.' The chorus goes like this: 'Gabble gobble. One of us. One of us.'" Wittman opened his eyes as wide as they got and looked into Nanci's—epicanthic eyes meeting epicanthic eyes. Fingers wiggling to communicate. "'Look at it cry!' 'Is that a cleft palate in there? And a giraffe tongue?!' 'It's got a wee penis.' 'All babies have a small penis.' 'Unlike apes, mongoloids do not turn dangerous to their keepers at puberty.'" Wittman played like he was sitting with the other mongoloid children on the go-around in the playground at the home. Their arms and chins hang over the top railing, a head lolls. A club foot gives the earth a kick, and they go around and around and around. Reading in the manner of Charles Laughton as the Hunchback of Notre Dame (who grunted and snorted in some scenes, and in others discoursed fluently on the nature of man) and like Helen Keller, he stuttered out, "'Wa-wa-wa-water? Gabble gobble, one of us.'"

No coward, Wittman asked Nanci, "How do you like my work?" Straight out. Asking for it. I can take it.

"You sound black," she said. "I mean like a Black poet. Jive. Slang. Like LeRoi Jones. Like . . . like Black."

He slammed his hand—a fist with a poem in it—down on the desk—fistful of poem. He spit in his genuine brass China Man spittoon, and jumped up on top of the desk, squatted there, scratching. "Monkey see, monkey do?" he said. "Huh? Monkey see, monkey do?" Which sounds much uglier if you know Chinese. "Monkey shit, monkey belly." "A lot you know," he said. "A lot you know about us monkeys." She got up and stood behind her chair. He sprang from the desk onto the chair, and from the chair to the mattress, and from the mattress up to the desk again, dragging his long arms and heavy knuckles. His head turned from side to side like a quick questioning monkey, then slower, like an Indian in a squat, waggling his head meaning yes-and-no. He picked a flea from behind an ear—is this a flea?—or is it the magic pole in its toothpick state that the King of the Monkeys keeps hidden behind his ear? He bit it. "Monkey see. Monkey do. What you do in fleaman's pok-mun?" She didn't answer him. He picked up loose papers with one hand and looked at them, scratched his genitals with the other hand, smelled hands and pages, nibbled the pages. "'Black?'" he hatefully imitated her. "'Jive.'" He let drop the papers, nudged one farther with his toe, and wiped his fingers on his moustache. "That bad, huh?" He lifted a page and turned it, examined it back and front. Upside down and sideways. "'LeRoi Jones?!'" He recoiled from it, dropped it over the edge of the desk, and leaned way over to watch it fall. Keeping an eye on it, he picked up another sheet and sniffed it. "Too Black. If you can't say something nice, don't say anything at all. That's my motto." He wadded it up and threw it over his shoulder. He jumped on top of the trunk, scrunching and scattering the whole shit pile, then pounced on a page, and returned with it to the desk. "This is it! Here's one you'll like. That is, likee. Guarantee. Ah. I mean, aiya. 'Wokking on da Waywoad. Centing da dollahs buck home to why-foo and biby. No booty-full Ah-mei-li-can gal-low fo me. Aiya. Aiya.'" He wiped his eyes with the paper, crushed it, and pitched the wad at the window, which was shut. Sorting papers into two piles, he said, "Goot po-yum. Goot. Goot. No goot. No goot. Goot. No goot." He tasted one, grimaced. "No goot." Breaking character, he said, "Now, if I were speaking in a French accent, you would think it charming. Honk-honk-ho-onk." He did the Maurice Chevalier laugh, which isn't really a laugh, is it? He started new piles. "Angry po-yum." "Sad po-yum." "Goot and angry." "Angry." "Angry." "Imitation of Blacks." He threw some to the floor. "Angry too muchee. Sad. Angry sad. No goot. Angry no goot. Sad. Sad. Sad."

"Please don't freak out," Nanci requested, standing behind the chair.

"I am not freaking out," Wittman said. "I've got to tell you the real truth. No lie. Listen, Lois. Underneath these glasses"—ripping the glasses off, wiping them on his sleeve, which he pulled out over his hand, so it looked like one hand was missing—"I am really: the present-day U.S.A. incarnation of the King of the Monkeys." He unbuttoned his blue chambray workshirt, which he wore on top of his black turtleneck. "Promise me you won't blab this all over the front page of the *Chron.* You'd like a scoop, I know, but I'm trusting you to keep our secret. For the sake of the world."

Now, if Nanci were the right girl for him, she would have said, "Dear monkey. Dear, dear old monkey. Poor monkey." She could scratch his head and under his chin, laugh at his antics, saying, "Poor dear monkey, what's to become of you?" and have him eating out of her hand. "Dear monkey. Poor poor monkey. You do have such an endearing Chinese giggle."

But who could be the right consoling girl for him? Nanci was getting into her jacket and finding her purse. How fucked up he is.

She hurried for the door, and got it open. She turned in the doorway, and said, "An actress says other people's words. I'm an actress; I know about saying other people's words. You scare me. A poet saying his own words. I don't like watching."

She held up her hand, "Ciao," closed her fingers, and shut the door.

Alone, Wittman jumped off the table to the mattress, trampolined off that to the Gold Mountain trunk and onto the chair. Keep up the mood, not in liege to her. Elongating his chimp-like torso, he stretched for a look at himself in the built-in mirror on the door. He ruffled out his hair. Sao mang mang mang-key maw-lau. Skinny skinny monkey. "Bee-e-een!" he yelled, loud enough for her to hear. "Bee-e-een!" which is what Monkey yells when he changes. He whipped around and began to type like mad. Action. At work again.

And again whammed into the block question: Does he announce now that the author is—Chinese? Or, rather, Chinese-American? And be forced into autobiographical confession. Stop the music—I have to butt in and introduce myself and my race. "Dear reader, all these characters whom you've been identifying with—Bill, Brooke, and Annie—are Chinese— and I am too." The fiction is spoiled. You who read have been suckered along, identifying like hell, only to find out that you'd been getting a peculiar, colored, slanted p.o.v. "Call me Ishmael." See? You pictured a white guy, didn't you? If Ishmael were described—ochery ecru amber umber skin—you picture a *tan* white guy. Wittman wanted to spoil all those stories coming out of and set in New England Back East—to blacken and to yellow Bill, Brooke, and Annie. A new rule for the imagination: The common man has Chinese looks. From now on, whenever you read about those people with no surnames, color them with black skin or yellow skin. Wittman made an end run, evaded the block. By writing a play, he didn't need descriptions that racinated anybody. The actors will walk out on stage and their looks will be self-evident. They will speak dialects and accents, which the audience will get upon hearing. No need for an unreadable orthography such as Mark Twain's insultingly dumb dis and dat misspelling and apostrophying. Yes, the play's the thing.

It is ridiculous. Here I sit in my little room, I, Brigge, who have grown to be 28 years old and of whom no one knows. I sit here and am nothing. And nevertheless this nothing begins to think and think, five flights up, on a grey Parisian afternoon, these thoughts: . . .

A long time ago, before the blackbottom, a band of ancestors with talent left their music house, which was the largest hut in Ancient Wells, a place, and sailed a music boat a-roving the rivers of China. They beat the big drum hard, which vibrated in stomachs and diaphragms for miles around. An audience gathered on the riverbank, and saw the red swan boat come floating on strains of mandolin and flute. Between red wings, got up in the style of putting-on-a-show, rode the players. To the knocking of the wood fish drums—dok-dok-dok—the singer lifted his skylark voice over water and fields. He threw out ropes, and their audience pulled them to shore. Party time again. Let musicians rule. Play a—what kind of music?—how does it go?—and make the world spin in the palm of your hand.

Our Wittman is going to work on his play for the rest of the night. If you want to see whether he will get that play up, and how a poor monkey makes a living so he can afford to spend the weekday afternoon drinking coffee and hanging out, go on to the next chapter.

2
Linguists and Contenders

WITTMAN AH SING wrote into the dark of the night, through dinner time and theater time and bar time. *Here I sit in the cold night, writing . . . the recluse in his night. . . .* He followed the music boat on courses of waterways—sailing the Long River across the Earth and guided by the River of Stars in the sky—to the mouth or the ass end of China—the Pearl River Delta, where Americans come from. The Boca Tigris ejects *The Song Boat* into the bay between Macao and Hong Kong. Our singer poles it to the Typhoon Shelter. Gliding out of the glittering black of water and starry sky come other sudden lit boats. Land-people hire them for a night of eating, gambling, sleeping on the water. Here's a boat selling escargots, steaming on the stove and smelling up the air with anise and garlic and snail. "Fresh shrimp," shouts a cook, and tosses a live prawn across to a dining-table boat; it dances the Japanese shrimp dance. A trysting lover throws it back, "Ho. Ho, la. Cook it, la. Cook it with scallions." And from another boat, he orders for his veiled lady: clams steeping in black-bean sauce. And here's a boat named *Cowboy* bringing rice and kettles of jook. And here's a floating bar with the beer and wine. Order the wine of the poets, the plum rosé that inspired Tu Fu and Li Po. The lights of the city on hills make a vertical shimmer from sky straight into the water, like a backdrop, like a dream.

"What do you want to hear?" Our singer, Joang Fu, calls for requests and dedications. (His name, Joang Fu, pronounced like Joan of Arc, like a bell of Time, means Inner Truth, which was also Wittman's byname, it so happened. Named by his father at the throw of the Ching.) "Our band has traveled more than five thousand days, and found no gold, and found no eagle-feather shield, but we bring back music to our tribe." Balancing, he hands a menu of songs over to the lovers. "We've stolen spells and bells from Tigermen. I can melt snow with my

voice. Listen. Listen to the peal of these tiny silver cymbals."
The cymbals are no bigger than a pair of ears. "How far can
you follow the rings of ringing? Do they sound longer in the
crevasses and altitudes of the Himalayas or across water?" As
bait, he tells bits of many stories and the most terrible customs
you never did see. He makes sounds of other tongues. "Id
al-Kabir. Id al-Kabir. A god asks a father to sacrifice his son.
What to do? Hear the aria as he raises his knife. Hear the opera
of White-Hat Muslims at the Great Festival of the Sacrifice.
Hear the Passover songs of Blue-Hat Jew Guai Muslims of
the northwest. We've found the lost story of Monkey and the
Muslim. Hear how we were captured by the Lolos and escaped
with their wild music too. Do you want to listen to me yodel-
lay-hee-hoo like a Mongol cowboy wailing with the Gobi
wind? Hear the songs that we sang against Genghis Khan."
Then, in a softer voice, confidentially: "My parents sold me
to this opera troupe, and I'm trying to save money to buy my
freedom and go to Hollywood to join the movies. I ran away
in a storm one night, and met a beautiful girl, alone and wet
in the rain. I sang her a song. Do you want to hear it? And she
sang back to me, eerily. I remember her song. Do you want to
hear it? Do you think she's a real girl, or is she a snake?"

Springing up, the singer lands nimbly on the railing of
the lovers' boat, where he hunkers, riding the easy sea's rise
and fall. It's a rich man's boat, like a floating gazebo with its
horned topside and red pillars, and veranda railings all around.
He fills the shy silence for the lovers, "I myself have sailed
to Bali." (Like Antonin Artaud, who also sailed there in his
imagination, he could've said, but a lot had to be left out.)
"There, women play gods, and men play demons and monkeys." He has given the rich man a cue to look teasingly into
his lady's eyes, and to toast her, "To a goddess," and to flirt
with her, "From a demon." "I stayed up chitter-chattering and
chanting all night with monkey dancers, little boys in the in-
most circle, me, Joang Fu, among the youths in the next circle,
middle-aged men in the middle, and old men on the outside—
kit-chak kit-chak kit-chak—hum hum—waves of humming in
fumes of clove and cubeba cigarettes—until gods dropped out
of the sky and did their dramas amidst men and monkeys—
halleluia hands halleluia hands."

Joang Fu gets a good look at the dark lady's unveiled face.
The other boats have slipped away, and she has had to lift her
netting to eat. Their oarswoman has fallen asleep, and the
little boat turns in its own world. The dark lady says something to her fella, who makes the request for a new song.
That world-wandering songboatman sings Stephen Foster
of the West. "'All the world is sad and dreary, everywhere I
roam. . . .'" No, wait, wait. Let's go back earlier—the world is
yet newer. She asks to hear "The Gold Mountain Song." "O,
Susanna, don't you cry for me. I'm going to Californyah with
a banjo on my knee." "O, Susanna," the song of the Gold
Rush.

The lady sees to it that our singer is paid lavishly. *The Song
Boat* returns for him, and the troupe skims away, treating its
audience to a skiddooing tableau vivant—a would-be king is
pouring poison into the sleeping king's ear, his crown pushed
aside. A juggler throws the vial into the air, where other bottles are flying; they are caught, caught, caught, though the
boat is shooting fast away.

Well, it was the ass end of things, all right. As you know
from San Francisco Bay, hungry birds, swirling and diving,
mirror the swirls of fish below them. Fishing boats follow
these whirlwinds of birds farther and farther out to sea. The
smallest boats turn back soonest, empty, and then the others
also have to quit. So—no more entertainment dollars. The
musicians sell their instruments and sing a cappella. Then,
following the unlucky fishermen, they go on land, where
they become as vagabond as poets who wrote on rocks and
leaves.

At the Dogs Don't Mind restaurant (which has piles of orts
on top of the tables, and bones and slop buckets under the tables, but "dogs don't mind"), he strolls from table to table, like
a bridegroom, and tells homesick tales about pirates; he maps
their hideouts among the dangerous keys and straits. City people can't simultaneously eat and hear about torture-for-ran-
som; he disgusts them and wins their food. Whoever hears his
sea yearnings stops feeling sorry for the people of the water
and, instead, envies them their free lives. Born on the sea and
never been landed, before. He'd met, so he says, Cheng I Sao,
widow and lady pirate, but he can't say what she looks like

because she uglifies herself with the blue-and-black make-up of a stage villain. "I sent a poem for her to finish, but she returned it rhyming in 'no' when I'd set it up for an inevitable 'yes.' Do you want to hear how it goes?"

It was a good job. All profit, no overhead except for food you have to eat regardless. And with self-discipline, he can live on what the dogs don't mind. When the beer and wine cart comes around, and the voice dries out, why, somebody's sure to buy a drink. And the friendly storyteller is likely to be invited to join in eating the rest of the dinner. You can always add one more guest to a Chinese meal; everybody eats from the mutual food in the middle. Feed the storyteller. Feed the storyteller.

Joang Fu invents and throws out generous new lines of bait: "I met a scientist who experimented in his laboratory with opium and mushrooms, and discovered how to make his sperm addictive." Oh, the listeners were laughing already in anticipation of scenes of gluttonous unending sex. Ladies undone. Gentlemen unpantsed. "How does he find out it's truly addictive? How many women have to be chasing you before you know? What happens to the economy when you market addictive sperm? Wheeling and dealing dope sperm. 'Oh, no, this sperm's been cut.' 'Does she love me for myself or for my golden sperm?'"

On moonless nights, our storyteller kindles light from the faces of listeners, and they cannot bear to leave. The gambler is turning over his hand. The executioner has raised his ax to the apex. The father is pressing his knife on the son's throat. The princess is untying her blindfold. The widow lady pirate kisses the guy with the sperm. The storyteller pauses. "Pay up. Pay up," he says. "Time to pay up." And who could stand not to know what happens next? What's money for, after all? The more money comes kerplunking down, the more flash in the swordplay, and heartfelt the lovers' vows to meet again, and aphrodisiacal the sperm. Prolong the outcome, make the story burst one more time into payoff—like two-stage fireworks— one last outburst that wipes out stars—just when they thought it was the end.

On the radio, Sweet Dick Whittington the Allnight Cat was playing King Pleasure.

When you see danger facing you,
   little boy, don't get scared.
When you see danger facing you,
   little boy, don't you get scared.
When you see danger facing you,
   little fellow, don't get yellow,
and blu-u-e.

Then, Cannonball Adderley, being interviewed, told about a young musician coming to New York. "He gets cut bad." He has to stop playing his tune, and change his ways to New York ways. "He becomes a better musician," says Cannonball. That can't be true. New York cant.

On the Black station, people were phoning in and arguing whether you can tell somebody's color by his voice. Back at the jazz station, Wittman heard: "Louis B. Armstrong and John Cage credit Chinese opera for inspiring their rhythms." Yes? Yes? Was Wittman's yearning giving him an hallucination of the ear? A piece he could not identify bingbanged forth and jangled his mind.

The reason he had the radio on was that whenever he stopped typing, he heard someone else nearby tapping, tapping at a typewriter, a typing through the night. Yes, it was there, steady but not mechanical. Not furnace or pipes or adding machine or teletype or timer. Not an echo. Now and again, the noise did hesitate, as if for thought, then a few word-length taps. An intelligence was coming up with words. Someone else, not a poet with pencil or fountain pen but a workhorse big-novel writer, was staying up, probably done composing already and typing out fair copy. It should be a companionable noise, a jazz challenge to which he could blow out the window his answering jazz. But, no, it's an expensive electric machine-gun typewriter aiming at him, gunning for him, to knock him off in competition. But so efficient—it had to be a girl, a clerk typist, he hoped, a secretary, he hoped. A schoolteacher cutting mimeo stencils. A cookbook writer. A guidebook-for-tourists writer. Madam Dim Sum, Madam Chinoiserie, Madam Orientalia knocking out horsey cocky locky astrology, Horatio Algiers Wong—he heard the typing leave him behind.

He picked up a ballpoint and crossed out by the line what he had written that night, every page. He had been tripping out on the wrong side of the street. The wrong side of the world. What had he to do with foreigners? With F.O.B. émigrés? Fifth-generation native Californian that he was. Great-Great-Grandfather came on the *Nootka*, as ancestral as the *Mayflower*. Go-sei. The story boat has got to light out on the Mississippi or among the houseboats on the San Joaquin Delta. It should work the yachts at Lake Tahoe. His province is America. America, his province. But story boats and story teahouses where a professional can talk are as gone at Lake Anza and the Bay as they must be gone from China. What is there beautiful and adventurous about us here? Dave Brubeck was playing "Take Five" on the radio.

Wittman took the trash down the hallway to the garbage closet. The pages made a flying noise down the chute. Pure Jack Kerouac set fire to his day's words. There used to be a furnace at 17 Adler Place—the Chinese Historical Society of America is in that building now—where the Society of Beautiful Writing used to burn important papers. Fire up them poems. See the phoenixes and salamanders. The Society took the ashes to Baker Beach and Fort Point and scattered them in the Bay. Much purer than sitting in the garbage waiting for the truck to the dump.

It's all right. Wittman was working out what this means: After two thousand days of quest, which takes a hundred chapters to tell, and twenty-four acts, seven days to perform, Monkey and his friends, Tripitaka on the white horse, Piggy, and Mr. Sandman, arrive in the West. The Indians give them scrolls, which they load on the white horse. Partway home, Monkey, a suspicious fellow, unrolls the scrolls, and finds that they are blank scrolls. "What's this? We've been cheated. Those pig-catchers gave us nothing. Let's demand an exchange." So, he and his companions go back, and they get words, including the Heart Sutra. But the empty scrolls had been the right ones all along.

Back at his table, Wittman put his head down and groaned. He ought not to have gone ape in front of Nanci. It was the sort of episode that can back up on you anytime and make you want to shoot the embarrassment of it clean out of your head. Too late. *And one has nothing and nobody, and one travels about the world with a trunk and a case of books and really without curiosity. What sort of life is it really; without a house, without inherited things, without dogs?* With Rilke singing the sound track of my life?

A rooster crowed. It woke up in a cage stacked above and beneath other chickens, grain and shit dropping from tier to tier; the grocer must be pushing the cages out to the sidewalk. Zoning laws are different here from Union Square, I. Magnin's and the City of Paris, or else we're breaking them. The fish trucks were unloading today's catch, lobsters and catfish coming back to life in window tanks. Farm trucks were bringing vegetables and fruit from the Valley. Soon alarm clocks will ring and toilets flush. It was time to go to sleep. *I have taken action against fear. I have sat all night and written and now I am as agreeably tired as after a long walk over the fields of Ulsgaard.*

Sleeping in this part of the City was very odd. He was often awakened by dinosaur garbage-truck noises. But in daylight the garbage would still not have been picked up. Why is the air shattering like it's raining glass? *To think that I cannot give up sleeping without the window open. Electric street-cars rage ringing through my room. Automobiles run their way over me. A door slams. Somewhere a window-pane falls clattering: I hear its big splinters laugh, its little ones snicker. Then suddenly a dull, muffled noise from the other side within the house. Someone is climbing the stairs. Coming, coming incessantly. Is there, there for a long time, then passes by. And again the street. A girl screams: Ah tais-toi, je ne veux plus. An electric car races up excitedly, then away, away over everything. Someone calls. People are running, overtake each other. A dog barks. What a relief: a dog. Toward morning a cock even crows, and that is boundless comfort. Then I suddenly fall asleep.* More than one pane of glass has fallen; an entire glass side of a building has crashed down, but the next day, if he remembers to look, the street will not be covered with glass. The electric cars do not run on this street at four in the morning.

The storyboatman vaults on his pole of changing lengths. He whizzes through lands and time. He touches down here, and he takes off and touches down there. Over Angel Island.

Over Ellis Island. Living one very long adventurous life, thou-sands of years long, perhaps accomplished with the help of reincarnations and ancestors.

The calls in Wittman's dreams came from the children of the building going off to school. *I don't even know how it is possible for school-children to get up in bedrooms filled with grey-smelling cold; who encourages them, those little precocious skeletons, to run out into the grown-up city, into the gloomy dregs of the night, into the everlasting school day, still always small, always full of foreboding, always late? I have no conception of the amount of succor that is constantly used up.* Bang! Bang! Bang!—that's the grandmas smashing garlic with the flats of their cleav-ers. (Knights dealt what the storytellers called garlic-banging blows.) Bang! Bang! They were also chopping up pork for pat-ties, and shrimp into paste. There was a kitchen on this floor anybody could use. On its kitchen scroll, Wittman was able to recognize three words—"Food body fire"—out of about ten, and took Confucius to mean that the superior person, fueling up, pays no mind to aesthetics. That humming that under-scored everything was the motor sound of sewing.

At noon, Wittman got up and walked his bathroom gear, including his private roll of toilet paper, down the hall. He walked in on a woman, who scolded him from her throne, "Who you think you are, haw, boy? Haw, boy?" As he stepped out—her own fault, she hadn't locked the door—she called him some of the many Chinese words for "crazy"—"Saw! Deen! Moong cha cha! Ngow! Kang!" So many ways to go ba-nanas. Kang, the highest degree of nuts. "Too late, he's gone kang." He returned to his room and pissed in the sink. "There comes a time in life when everybody must take a piss in the sink—here let me paint the window black for a minute."

He brushed his teeth and washed up, plotting how he might have socialized better with that bathroom woman. "It hap-pens in the best of families," he might've said.

He took time combing out his moustache and beard, which were sparse but coarse. Hairs didn't just hang there, they stood out. His face was wired. Buttoning up his dark green shirt, he took a good look at his skin above the collar—yel-lower. Sallow like tallow. This effect of the wearing o' the green had been pointed out through the years by his mother, aunties, kid friends, make-up artists. "Don't wear green." One said it like a secret, another like a helpful hint, yet another, a sure fact that any fool knows. "Green's a bad color." For a long time he thought it had to do with bad taste or bad luck. Or his own personal complexion. "Green doesn't look good on you." Then some dorm guy said, "We look yellow in that color." It had to do with racial skin. And, of course, from that time on, he knew what color he had to wear—green, his color to wear to war. He tied his hair back in the samurai–Paul Revere–piratical braid. He had assumed his mirror face, but thought he always looked like that. Once, on drugs, on the mirror trip, this face had zoomed backward and whomped forward in time—he was a star, a tadpole, a cave baby, himself like now, then a dry old man with skull pushing against, almost protruding out of, his skin. Then he saw through skin to poor, jesting, once-singing Yorick. And his farflung soul returned on a starpoint of light in Yorick's eyehole.

He put on the suit that he had bought for five bucks at the Salvation Army—the Brooks Brothers three-piece navy-blue pinstripe of some dead businessman. Wittman's suited body and hairy head didn't go together. Nor did the green shirt and greener tie (with orange-and-silver covered wagons and rows of Daniel Boones with rifles) match each other or the suit. The Wembley label on the tie said, "Wear With Brown Suit," which Wittman defied. He pulled on his Wellingtons and stomped out onto the street. His appearance was an affront to anybody who looked at him, he hoped. Bee-e-en! The monkey, using one of his seventy-two transformations, was now changed into a working stiff on his way to his paying job.

Out on the street, Wittman fitted onto his mongolian cheeks his spectacles that blurred everything, thus finding metaphors everywhere, like how a cable car looks like an animal-cracker box. Some things he couldn't tell what the fuck they were, so he'd go up to a bedevilment and have a look-see, not to miss out. Like Rimbaud, I practice having hallucinations. He had picked his hallucination glasses out of the Lions Club donation box at the bank.

What got him to take the glasses off, a brother of the streets hit him up for a light. In thanks, the street man offered a look through a toilet-paper roll tube, which he demonstrated how to use. One eye peeping, other eye squinting, he pointed that pirate spyglass viewfinder, here, there, everywhere, and said, "Wow. Oh, wow. Here, hippy, dig." I look like a hippy dippy's idea of a hippy dippy.

Wittman's turn, he saw encircled: the traffic light change to amber, and a sparrow burst out of the light can, straw straggling after it. Autumn nest. A bum—how pass wine to his fellow clochard, who drank from the bottle without first wiping its mouth. Water flow in the gutter at their feet—Lenny and George at the river. "Guys like us . . ." Tu Fu and Li Po beside the Yangtze. Pigeons. He looked for i.d.s on their red ankles. Nope, these hadn't performed in Doctor Woo's Bill and Coo act. The red flag click up in a parking meter. A hand put money into a newspaper dispenser and take two *Chronicles*. A leaf. Faces. He thanked the cinéma-vérité freak for the look-see. "Hippy, you are welcome."

At the department store where he had a job—"Are you in the English Department or the History Department?" "I'm in the Toy Department."—it was Hallowe'en month. Wittman had helped trick up the kid dummies in flat apron-like run-over-with-a-steamroller cartoon costumes. The Management Trainees had sent out a memo: Floor personnel to wear costumes of their choice on Hallowe'en, which Wittman hoped would not fall on one of his workdays, Tuesday, Thursday, Friday, 1:00 to 9:00 P.M., Open Late for Your Shopping Convenience. Another season, in the Candy Department, he had worn rabbit ears and white gloves. For revenge, he had stolen candy—white chocolate—and saved on buying groceries. Do something about your life. Find a way out before you have to set up Christmas Toyland. Transfer into Notions? Sell armpit shields and corn pads? When he was a kid, he thought he could be happy forever working in a store. The tall glass at Kress had curved around brand-new toys, each one in many copies, which the owner arranged as he pleased. Is this malcontentedness what comes with a liberal-arts education? The way they taught you to think at school was to keep asking what's really going on. What's that thing at the end of this assembly line *for*? Why merchandising? Why business? Why money? Who are the stockholders? What else have they got their fingers into? Are any of the holdings in bomb commodities? Seek out vanities and emptiness. Which way out? Which way out? One of the clerks spotted him, and left the floor—quitting time for her. No wonder he didn't know anybody. But anything's better than the Defense Department. And he wasn't a soldier. He wasn't a prison guard. He was barely employed, a casual employee.

Wittman readied his station, sized up the house. Who are these people that no matter what odd time of day or night they have the wherewithal to go shopping? Put up roadblocks, do a survey, where are they going, and what do they do for a living? Are there many people like himself, then? They're all poets taking walks? "Just browsing." "Just looking." Between customers he was supposed to staple-gun black-and-orange corrugated cardboard into walls and along counters. The toys on the demonstration table could use a tidying up. Few of them sprang into action today because the customers had wound them too tight, unsprung them, or their batteries were shot. He pressed the laying hen, and a white marble rolled out of a hole in her stomach. He turned her upside down and re-inserted the half-dozen marbles that had rolled to the little fence. So it has come to this. (Lew Welch, the Red Monk, says: now and again, stop and think, "So it has come to this.")

The other clerk, Louise—see? he remembers their names, so there's something wrong they don't remember his—Louise was standing on top of a ladder, taking down a Back to School theme sign. He pretended he didn't see her. Let her do it herself, he's not good enough for her to say hello to.

Two tourist ladies held a large toy before his critical eyes. "Would my grandson like this? What is it? How much is it?" How come people leave their brains at home when they go on vacation? "It's a basketball gun," he said. "See? It says so right here. 'Basket Shooter.' You shoot this ball with this gun into this hoop here. It's a basketball game, but it's like a cannon." No kidding. The fuckers were turning basketball into target practice. "It's the cheapest large toy we have." Any job can be human as long as there are other people working in the same room as you. Even in a hell of noise, such as an automobile plant, you can roll a tire or pass a tool to the next guy on the line, and do it with good will. There are big people in small jobs, and small people in big jobs, and big people in big jobs, and small people in small jobs. The only wrong job would be where you have to be cooped up by yourself making some evil item, such as a bomb part, and never meet anybody. So here were this grandmother and her buddy giving him a chance to make this toy job human. Humanize them, as they said in the Cal Education Department, meaning one's contacts in the teachable moments during contact hours.

"For the good of the kid, your grandson," said Wittman, "you should not buy him this thing that is really a gun."

"You said it was a basketball game," said the buddy.

"But the kid shoots the ball with this trigger, see?"

"How clever," said the grandma. "May I try it?"

"No, no. We can't take it out of its blister pack. You don't want the kid to grow up to be a killer, do you?"

"Oh, is this Basket Shooter dangerous? I don't want to buy him anything dangerous."

"We don't want him to hurt himself," the buddy agreed.

"Well, kids can't hurt one another with this basketball gun even if they aimed point-blank at any part of the body. The harm comes from their pretending to kill. They learn to like the feel of weapons. They're learning it's fun to play war."

"Are you one of those people against war toys?" "We didn't come in here to be lectured to."

"Yeah, I'm against war toys. I'm anti-war. Look, I'm looking after your grandkid better than you are if you're going to let him grow up to be a draftee."

"We don't have to listen to this." "I'm buying whatever present I want to buy for my grandson. I'll take this—this Basket Shooter." She flipped out her charge card. "How much is it?"

"Fifteen ninety-nine," said Wittman, who discovered that his anger was mightiest when he was forced to be a spokesman for an inimical position. Speak up against charge cards too, Wittman. Instead he wrote up the sale, let these women fuck over themselves and the kid.

"Where's the ladies' room?" a lady interrupted, bouncing impatiently like she was going to unload on the spot. He gave her the labyrinthine though most direct directions to the rest-room, which he had never actually heard a store manager say should be kept secret and hard to find. "You stay here, honey," she said to her son. "Mommy has to go take a grunt for herself. Stay there, Bobby, stay there. Keep an eye on him, okay?" She was dumping him.

"Wait a minute," said Wittman. "No. We're not a nursery. You can't leave him here."

"I'll be right back," she said from aisles away.

The place was filling up with dumped kids. They were poking holes in cellophane boxes. One was rubbing his runny nose on the very clean white plush tummy of a Snoopy. "Stop that," said responsible Wittman. "Go away. Go that way," he suggested, pointing in the direction of the Shoe Department. "Shoo." Was that a diaper smell? He ought to get on the intercom. "We have a lost child, a lost bleeding child found unconscious, possibly dead, in the Toy Department." Don't you mothers drop your get on me.

"Sir. Sir." It was Louise coming at him with a clipboard like a P.E. coach. "Sir. What's your name again?"

"Wittman Ah Sing."

"Right. You're supposed to be hanging up the bicycles. Not those bicycles. Bring up the new ones from the stockroom, will you? I *could* bring them up myself. They're not heavy, just unwieldy." Give a man credit for muscles, why don't you?

"I'll get them," said co-operative Wittman, glad to get off the floor. Take his own sweet time.

Down in the stockroom, through his own cigarette smoke came fuming the smell of somebody smoking dope. As I live and breathe. Wittman took off his glasses to see. You know, by the time your brain recognizes the smell of reefer, you're high already. On the way, far out, gone. No innocent passersby. He followed the redolence and the loosening—or are they tightening?—vibes through the mazes of merchandise and came upon a fellow reading at a coffee table, at home as he could be. The radio was on the classical station. The man did not jump to his feet and start working; Wittman must not look boss. Crates had been stacked to block off a private room, and there were extension cords leading to a percolator and reading lamp, all new and belonging to the store. "Come in if you like," invited this man, who seemed to have it made.

Wittman entered through an opening in the barricade. "You live here?" he asked.

"No, I work here, like you. I'm stockboy." He seemed too old to be stockboy, his forehead high because balding. An ancient Chinese would have tonsured his head to get such baldness. "Have a seat," he said, passing Wittman a roach in a paper-match holder.

"No, thanks. I'll have some coffee, though." The stockboy unpacked a new cup, blew the wood shavings out of it, and poured coffee. Wittman sat down across from him. "I used to dope, I don't dope anymore. I've seen all there is to see on dope; the trips have been repeating themselves, looping like *Dead of Night*. I liked dope; I learned a lot. I felt religious. I felt communal. I believed in all sorts of things: the possibility of getting so far out that we pop through to another reality. Change one's head, change the universe. The paranoia was driving me nuts, however. Too ripped. I don't like getting wasted anymore. Nice hideout you've got here."

"Yes, I keep out of the way." He was one of those older guys, hip to the underworld, an ex-con maybe, or a Beatnik who will never sell out. "Work some, hide out some. Make accordion time." He was giving Wittman valuable, true orders.

"I'm hip," said Wittman. "I'm hip to accordion time." Like collecting garbage fast before the sun comes up, and free by morning for the day. Be a garbageman; be a mailman. This stock guy wasn't a jailhead, then, but wise to jobs, how to work from the inside. "What do you do down here with your extra time?"

"Handle consciousness."

"Hey, I do too. Me too. I want to do that too, man. How do you do it? Have you found some good ways? Lay low, right?"

"One way—I sit, I hang on to my seat." He demonstrated— looking straight ahead, arms straight down stiff, shoulders up, hands pulling up on the stool, butt pushing down. "Sit tight," he said.

"Is it better to keep your eyes open like that? Or is it better to shut them?"

"Open if no horror is . . . transpiring in the very room. Shut if they're torturing your family in front of you. Open if your mind goes places. Use your good sense. Slow the centrifugal-force machine down. However, the stopped trip is also dangerous. 'I. Can't. Take. My. Eyes. Off. Of. That. Spot. Spot. Spot. Spot.' The groove-rut is a killer." He stared at the daisy on the percolator. If he were actually stopped, his facial bones would slam into his skin, not a mind trip but an observable phenomenon. "The hell of whatever's going on goes on forever."

"Yeah. Like a short loop of film. 'When is this trip going to change?' Though the speed trip is no good either. Eschew speed."

"There's nothing to do under either circumstance but wait until you are let go. I would say, as a rule, open eyes is better, don't get so lost. Find a locus and a focus in this room, for instance, though it becomes crowded with . . . becomes crowded. I say open—and hang on to your seat."

Because our Wittman had not been brought up in a religion, he admired this man's ability to know that something starts us up and stops us and lets us move again, and that there were holy ghosts or something all around. Too much. Far out of sight, as Spenser exclaimed, ripped with amazement in *The Faerie Queene*. Two intelligent conversations in two days. Oh, yes: "Trippers and askers surround me." Crazy Jane Talks with the Bishop. Wotta Bishop.

"You have a good trip for me?" asked brave Wittman, butt-sitting. "Any good trips?" Be careful what you hear. You set yourself up. You get imprinted with a bad trip, you're fucked for life. The words don't come true now, they come true later in some real-life form.

"When I have friends, I take them for a ride on the coast train to Santa Cruz. We carry archery equipment into the redwood mountains. We each shoot an arrow straight up overhead. The red nock feathers look like a space bird blasting off between the evergreens, going up and up clear past the tallest Kings Canyon sequoia into the nothing sky, and hangs there and hangs there. Then the steel tip dips, flashing—it has stabbed the sun and is bringing a piece of it down to us on Earth. The arrow turns and falls. I stand my ground. If it's going to hit me, it hits me. Last time, it went into the ground between my toes. The friends also shoot all together—a flock of space birds—and run when the arrows rain down. If the weather turns to rain, we put out buckets and cans upside down among the trees, and listen to God's rhythms."

Wittman wanted to be one of the friends to do interesting

things like that. The eidolons were dancing around the man's
head and cakewalking over to Wittman's head. Contact high
one more time. Their inhalations and exhalations stoked the
ions in their halos a-hopping and a-changing. The +'s and –'s
a-winking and a-blinking like cartoon eyes.

"I had a pretty good time in the Santa Cruz Mountains
myself," Wittman said, returning good trip for good trip. "I
was on my way to the Monterey Jazz Festival, but ended up
in those woods too. I saw two kinds of leprechauns, one tall
like a tree and the other round like a boulder, kneeling with
its gnomish back toward me. When I tried to study them, they
went transparent. Their clothes and bearing reminded me
of friends of mine. They didn't say anything." He had not,
once back in cities, asked those friends if they had dreamed or
thought of being in a redwood forest at that hour. This new
amigo was understanding him and the anti-scientific nature
of those woods. Nobody here but us empiricals. The knuck-
lebone maniac of the Santa Cruz Mountains had been on the
loose—a cannibal arrested with his pockets full of hikers'
knucklebones—and had skipped them.

The stockman licked two rolling papers together and pushed
some grass into line with an eight of hearts. (Another way to
handle consciousness is to play solitaire like George in *Of Mice
and Men*.) A neat and graceful roller, he made himself a tight,
dry joint, not offering his guest a hit this time.

"Where you from?" Wittman asked, something out-of-state
in the way the fellow said "the coast."

"Back East." He rubbed the back of his neck as if he were
laboring in the sun. "There was a year when I was the Yale
Younger Poet."

"No shit," said Wittman. "What are you doing here?" Why
end up at the same place as me? Where's the glory? There
ought to be ongoing glory. A Yale Younger Poet should be
swirling his cape and plumes at the Mandrake and the Blind
Lemon, dueling with pretender poets at Mike's Pool Hall, riding with Jim Young, and Bob Younger, Cole Younger, and
the James brothers, Vaughan Williams conducting "Seventeen
Come Summer" on the sound track.

"I like my job."

But what's there to like being an old stockboy? Was this a

poet humbled but not from anything major like war, just the
daily shit—job, friends, girlfriends, relatives, food, cleaning
up—the ordinary middle-size life stuff that we're all supposed
to handle, and he's gone under?

Even Wittman isn't so down that he likes his job. There's a
poet's career, get your ass in gear. First, do a reading in North
Beach, non-invitational, get to your feet at The Coffee Gallery
or Nepenthe or The Forum, make ass. Find the open mikes,
and sing. Stand in doorways of auditoriums where known poets are on platform, and hand-deliver dittos of your own outcast poetry; Richard Brautigan did that. And Bob Kaufman
on megaphone in front of the St. Francis Hotel. Bring the poems back to the East Bay to read to Jack Spicer at Robbie's, the
F.O.B. cafeteria men acting like they don't notice you. Then,
single poems published around the country. Yale publishes the
first collection. Wittman Ah Sing—the Yale Younger Poet of
1967 or 1968 or 1969. Nineteen seventy at the outermost shot.
The Lamont people publish the second collection. And so on.
Until you get to be Robert Frost inaugurating the President.
And here's this Yale Younger stock guy getting older and going nowhere, ending up a minor poet, Wittman's never heard
of him. (How is a minority poet a minor poet? You might
make a joke on that.)

Ask him what he's got against the life I want. "Like Einstein
said, 'It is the duty of the scientist to remain obscure.' You
think it's the duty of the poet to remain obscure?"

"Einstein was feeling bad about the Bomb," said the Yale
Younger Poet. "The Bomb was the penultimate. Einstein died
without telling us the last thing he knew."

"What's that? Do you have a suspicion what it is?"

"It's either Nothing, or it's the malevolence of ultimate
reality."

Were the two of them to sit quietly thinking, they might
feel the presence on high of an evil thing that roams the sky.
Mention of it brings it closing in. It is hovering over the rooftop. It's the size of Mt. Diablo. There are probably more than
one. Good thing they were in the basement.

"Have you heard the one about spacemen who flew to the
end of the universe?" said Wittman, trying to regale the down
poet. "In the last wall was a metered telescope. They dropped

a dime to see what they could see. 'Oh, wow. Will you look at that?' 'What is it?' 'Nothing.'"

The Yale Younger guy nodded, smiled.

"This gig leaves your head free for poems, right?" asked Wittman.

"I quit poetry. I don't write poems anymore."

"Can you do that? You don't write it down, but you're still a poet, huh? You *be* a poet. You don't have to *do* poetry. You be a poet, everything that you do is poetry, right? You don't need to actually scribe. You have human feelings, you're a poet regardless of words, which, as you know, especially on dope, are very, very far removed from Things. I had Mark Schorer for Twentieth Century British and American Lit. His face sad and blue like Humphrey Bogart's, he said that Being beats Doing. He quoted George Sand, 'He who draws noble delight from poetry is a true poet though he has never written a line in all his life.' You draw noble delight, don't you?"

"No, I don't read poetry much."

"I don't think I'm ready for Being yet," said Wittman. "I'm going to start a theater company. I'm naming it The Pear Garden Players of America. The Pear Garden was the cradle of civilization, where theater began on Earth. Out among the trees, ordinary people made fools of themselves acting like kings and queens. As playwright and producer and director, I'm casting blind. That means the actors can be any race. Each member of the Tyrone family or the Lomans can be a different color. I'm including everything that is being left out, and everybody who has no place. My idea for the Civil Rights Movement is that we integrate jobs, schools, buses, housing, lunch counters, yes, and we also integrate theater and parties. The dressing up. The dancing. The loving. The playing. Have you ever acted? Why don't you join my theater company? I'll make a part for you."

"I don't know."

"You'd have to work for no pay. You might need to chip in for costumes and props."

"I'll think about it."

"You don't mind if I come down here and visit once in a while, and let you know how the play is coming along?"

"Do that."

Yes, he would. This Yale Younger guy was a real poet, all right. Amazing the creativity that came pouring out in his presence. Now that the Pear Garden in the West had been confided—and promised, twice—it will have to be made to come about.

Wittman rolled two bicycles into the freight elevator. One of these days, he'd have to go to the library and look up the Yale Series of Younger Poets, and see if his new friend looked like any face on a dustjacket. He wasn't James Agee, he knew that. Agee's vision of the malevolence of ultimate reality was that we're cattle grazing green pastures, believing that those who are rounded up go somewhere even more wonderful. A young bull escapes from Chicago and tries to warn the herd about cattle cars and stockyards and mallet guns and meathooks. Agee, another Yale Younger Poet.

Upstairs, Wittman propped one bicycle against the wall and the other on its kickstand. He rolled the ladder under the empty space on the pegboard. He picked up a bicycle by the crossbar and climbed up, but at the top saw that there were no fasteners. With its front tire turned against the board, the bike fit on the shelf okay. Leaving it balanced up there just so, he looked for hooks, which did not seem to be under the cash-register counter either. From that coign of vantage, he saw another shopper leaving her kids. No more Mr. Nice Guy. "Hey. Hey, you. Do I look like a babysitter, huh? This is not a nursery. I am not a babysitter. Don't you leave your kids here. Take those kids with you."

"I'm sorry," she said. "It won't happen again." She wasn't sorry; she's on her way out of here without kids. Don't let her get away. Escalate. "Wait a minute. I want to talk to you. You can't walk off easy." This minding so much about justice must have to do with being Chinese. "You're in the big city, ma'am." Yeah, let her have it. "I'm taking you in to see the manager." Not meaning that. Never call the cops—a Berkeley rule.

"How come these other children get to stay here?" the woman said. "My children are well behaved. I'm coming right back. I was just going out to put my packages in the car. I'm coming back for them. It's dangerous to take children across the parking lot without holding them by the hand. Look. Look at how much money I've spent in your store." Her arms were full of bags and boxes with the store's logo. "I buy here. I buy here, and you can help a customer out for once." "Backward I see in my own days," Walt Whitman said, "where I sweated through fog with linguists and contenders."

The bicycle at the top of the ladder was rolling, and when Wittman rushed up to halt it, the mother escaped. And those two pulling out boxes of model cars from the bottom of a stack were hers. Her get. "If you leave those kids here," he ought to have said, "I'm going to nail their feet to the floor. One foot each. I'm going to teach your vampire kids how to pivot." The next one, then. He would deal effectively with the next abandoning mother. It was a good thing that photographing babies for a Penny-a-Pound was a concessional job, and he would not be rotated to it.

The hooks were in the drawer with the charge slips. He climbed up with them, but now the bicycle was in the way of places for the hooks. He tried moving it aside farther along the shelf. The wheels turned, carrying his hand along, and it caught under a fender, cutting the skin, bunching a flap up. He pulled the bike the other way, and the gear sprockets and chain chewed into his tie and did not let go. A customer was nagging, "Isn't anybody around here going to wait on me?" Not me. "You. I'm talking to you." He lifted the bike connected to his tie, and carried it down the ladder without strangling himself.

His nose to the bicycle seat, good thing nobody's butt has yet sat upon it, he cut the tie with the dull scissors on a string tied to the counter. The Steppenwolf gnaws his leg free from the trap of steel, he thought.

He wrestled the bicycle up the ladder again, saw that the hooks were still not in place, and brought it down again.

Up again. Insert hooks in pegboard. Down again. Up one more time with the bike. The hooks did not meet the frame; if part of the bicycle fit on one hook, the rest of it did not fit on any of the others. Down. I have not found right livelihood; this is not my calling. Oh, what a waste of my one and only human life and now-time.

"It's time for the presentation," Louise was saying to him, the bicycle again on the verge of the shelf, maybe to topple on a customer or her. "Let's go. I don't want to be late." Though nobody else seems to be taking charge of the floor, the two of them are about to leave? He acted as if he knew exactly what she was talking about. The way to hang on to a job is to pretend you understand whatever's going on. Figure it out as you go along.

Louise, clutching a long clutch purse under an arm, handed him her wrap for him to help her into it. "Hold my shrug, please?" she said. It's probably called a shrug because it would fall off if she shrugged. She wiped her hands on her skirt. Sausage skin. She led the way to the street level and out the main entrance, letting him hold the door open, like they were on a date.

How dark it was already. Day was gone, and he had just gotten up. The fog was dropping a veiling—a star-filter—over the streetlights and headlights, already on. Five o'clock, and most people were rushing home. They had commuted here before daylight, which shone on them on their too few days off. How fucked up they must be. Like veals that spend their lives in the dark.

"Get us a taxi. The store's paying for a taxi," Louise was saying, straddling the curb, finger in the air. She must be from New York. Don't you order a cab by phoning for it? A cab with no passenger came out of the fog; his hand shot up like in the movies, and—surprise—it pulled that obedient cab right over. (His being so cheaply surprised—this being new at almost every dumb thing—must also have to do with being Chinese, or will it go away with age?)

She pointedly waited for him to open the door, and slid in sideways, lady-like (not head first with butt in his face). "The Jack Tar," she told the driver. "What happened to your tie?" she asked in the intimate backseat.

"This is the new style. Don't you talk to the buyers? The short tie is going to hit the City by next week. You watch. The man in a grey flannel suit will be wearing this castration tie." A man of mode talking here. "If I were wearing a velvet tie, would you stroke it?"

"Of course I wouldn't. Why would I do that?"

"Because a womanly hand naturally likes to finger nappy velvety furry fuzzy wuzzy nap pile. I could take advantage of your instincts. But I won't. I make it a policy to tell women exactly what I'm up to from the get-go, and I expect women to be up front too. Nobody ambush anybody's instincts. Put your cards right out there on the conscious level. Don't take advantage. If you want to stroke my tie and work your way up and down to the rest of the bod, you have to tell me that that's what your intentions are, and not pretend you're interested in retailing that type of tie. Years from now, when our affair is over, or we're getting a divorce, I don't want you to say you were just interested in my necktie, and one thing led to another, and it was all my fault."

"What are you talking about?" she said.

"I am practicing on you my technique of honesty with women. Alas, women I've tried it on decide not to see me again."

"You've got motor oil or something on you. And your hand is bleeding." The girl of my dreams does not say that line distastefully, Louise.

"This is a workingman's hand, and this on my tie is the grease of hard labor."

She didn't answer. Neither said anything for slow blocks. Wittman smoked out the window.

"What are you doing this weekend?" she asked.

"I don't know. I haven't thought about it." The trouble with people in the workaday world is that they live for the weekends. Don't live for the weekends.

"The U.S.S. *Coral Sea* is coming in on Sunday. I know a couple of guys on it. I'm bringing my girlfriends to meet them. It's going to be a really nice weekend." Why's she telling him this? Isn't it bad manners to discuss a party that somebody's not invited to? Oh, he gets it. She's being friendly, talking about her social life with a business colleague.

So, the Navy is sailing home to San Francisco, and Louise and the wahines will be at Naval Air Station Alameda to greet them. You can count on women to have a life outside of the office. Others with outside lives: people who speak another language, criminals, people who dress differently from mannequins. Louise is not the kind of girl he's used to. The ones at school would have met ships to convert the sailors from war.

Central Casting put this influential girl beside him on this backseat taxi ride, and his next line should be: "Are you going to make the sailors go AWOL to keep them from sailing on Sasebo and Kobe and Subic and Pearl Harbor and the Gulf of Tonkin and setting up strategic hamlets and imperializing other countries?" Be a responsible citizen. "Fuck the war out of them, Louise," he said.

"What did you say? Hey, don't talk dirty. I just date them. That's all."

"As long as nice girls like you think that men look cute in uniforms, they're going to keep warring and killing."

"Men *do* look cute in uniforms. *You'd* look cute in a uniform. The ones with the best uniforms are the Marines."

What's the use, huh? Babytalk. They were on Van Ness Avenue, passing the showrooms of new cars. She pointed out the one so-and-so owned and the one she wanted once she got promoted to buyer. "Buyers go on buying trips to New York and Europe." They passed the Board of Education building. If she were smarter, he'd entertain her by telling about the City's multiple-choice test for teacher applicants. They arrived at the Jack Tar Hotel, which people were still making fun of because of its plastic red, blue, and yellow panels (the same colors as the pipes outside of walls at the new architecture building at Cal), forever modern and ugly. The searchlight that was sweeping the sky was shooting from the Jack Tar, not from a car show. The fog or clouds caught in the big beam roiled and boiled; it seemed to be raining up there. Louise paid for the taxi. She and Wittman became part of the crowd beaconed here.

"Hi. Hello. Hi, there," Louise said left and right, stirred up by a crowd. Party time. They followed the arrows to one of the convention rooms, where there was a sign-in table at the door. His name wasn't on the rolls; he wasn't a Management Trainee anymore and should be back minding the store. But as long as he was here, he might as well stay. Gee, thanks. You're welcome too. Too bad he didn't rate a name tag, stick it on his tie to make it longer, or tape up the cut on his hand. "*One* good thing, you're tall," Louise said. What did she mean by that? So he could see above the crowd? So she could have a tall escort? His height made up for his color? A salesman howdy-doodied her, and she peeled away from his tall side.

There was a food table with a drizzly grizzly bear made out of plastic ice, the California bear, re-usable for every occasion. Wittman loaded a tiny plate with coldcuts, deviled eggs, battered deep-fried shrimp, carrot sticks, and sheet cake. As soon as the Mexican-looking lady in the maid outfit put the shrimp down, people glommed on it, very aggressive and rude over food. Wittman ate in a corner, near an ashtray. A Pilipina-looking lady asked him what he wanted to drink. "A martini," he said. She wrote that down without asking for money. So, this was not no-host. Good.

There was no other of his ethnic kind here. Counting the house every time. Can't help it. Made racist by other people's trips. Politics and war—other people's bad trips that spoil the ad-hoc scene. What's wrong with him that he keeps ending up in Caucasian places? Like the English Department. Like Management Training. Like the Actor's Workshop audience. He didn't have a thing for bok guai. And he wasn't, as far as he knew, blackballed by Chinese. So where were the brothers? Where was fraternité? Wherever I go, I do the integrating. My very presence integrates the place.

The serving lady came back with a martini for him, and he didn't have any place to set down his paper plate and the glass and the cigarette in his mouth. So he slid down the wall to the floor, and made of the floor both chair and table.

Over a roomful of people, there spreads an invisible blanket that covers everybody. Wittman was drawing it to himself, bunching it, stuffing it into a hole in his corner (that leads to the fourth dimension). He shot back stink-eye for stink-eye. He felt satisfaction at having found an answer for how to sit wherever, and from now on he can use it in many situations, in line at the movies, for example, in line for a restaurant table, a teller's window, an airplane, and, if the world got very bad, in an Army line, in a bread line. And when he gets to the Tuileries, where you have to pay to sit on a folding chair, he'll have a seat ready. Yes, the earth means to be benevolent, after all, and always provides a place for the weary to sit down.

Then—here they come—"orientals," all in a group. A guy and three chicks, one in a cheongsahm. He was against girls who wear cheongsahm. This oriental group were busily talking to one another; *they* didn't have trouble finding their coterie.

The guy, embarrassingly short, twinkling away in his cute suit, reached up and clapped a white guy on the back, gave him the old glad hand, got patted on the back in return. Then he was introducing the chicks, every one of them pretty. Suddenly, as if a volume knob had been turned up, the oriental was no longer saying "rhubarb rhubarb rhubarb." Bouncing about on his toes out of exuberance and shortness, he distinctly said, "Wanta get your ashes overhauled, huh?" *Over*hauled? He had a Hong Kong San Francisco accent. Too bad he wasn't Japanese. Nobody laughed, so he said it again, a broader delivery, a thumb at the girls, who didn't seem to notice, or pretended they didn't. He was telling a sex joke—American guys tell sex jokes—man to man—but if it didn't go over, it could be taken as a cigarette joke, everybody standing around with long ashes. Or a car joke. Hedging his bets, the coward. If Wittman were not already on the floor, he would have slunk down now.

One of the girls—not the one in Miss Chinatown Narcissus Queen drag—turned around—her spike heels stabbed and drilled the carpet—walked over to Wittman in the corner, and said, "Get up, and quit making a fool of yourself."

"What business is it of yours?" he answered in Chinese. She went right back to her friends. She probably hadn't heard how snappy his comeback was; she probably didn't even know the most common Chinese sayings, such as, "What's it to you?" He stood up. He'll get her. "Slowly I turn, step by step, inch by inch, closer and closer." The clique left for the next part of the program.

Everybody moved into a room with a platform. A banner read, IT'S MATTEL—IT'S SWELL. Wittman took a seat by the door. An executive at the microphone welcomed "the community of retailers" to the "premiere" of new toys. "But first," he said, "let me show you the stats." A chick in net stockings held up a poster. It had a pie chart on it. "Entertainment dollar," said the man. "Family fun." In Wittman's entire life, whenever anybody—econ professor, insurance salesman, t.v. newscaster—threw one of these percentage pies at him, his mind died. For the hell of it—he had little enough to do—he paid attention, but the next thing he knew, he was aware of not having listened for some time.

The orientals—all right, the Chinese-Americans—were

sitting together near the front. They've set up the section where we're all supposed to come sit, which they'd done to the school cafeteria of every school he ever went to. At Cal, they had their own rooting section within the rooting section. Watch. One by one they're going to turn around and sneak a peek at him. See? One of the girls—a dec-art major, or a child-development major—put her elbow up on the back of her chair, profiled the room. He and she gave each other the old once-over. They both looked away; why should they greet each other? (Because your parents and grandparents would have run up yelling to one another and shouted genealogies of relatives and friends and hometowns until they connected up.) I am not going to the prom with the only Chinese girl in the class. I am not going to be the one to room with the foreign-exchange student.

The guy had a shaved neck; the girls had sheets of black hair, one bob and two pageboys. Their hair was so shiny that you could see why you call the crown of the head the crown. Buddhaheads. Is it really true that Caucasians have more of a variety of looks than other people? Grant that almost all Black people and russet people have brown eyes. Do they say they can't tell us apart because we all have brown eyes and we all have black hair? Whereas they have red hair and strawberry blonde and dishwater blonde and platinum and wisps-of-tow and auburn, and brown, and black. And they also have curly and wavy as well as straight. Ash blonde. Honey blonde. Taffy. Hey, wait just a minute. Hold everything. Are there all those kinds of blondes or are there lots of words? There are lots of words *and* all those blondes. Because of the words, and vice versa. People look at blondes with discernment. When you think about it, aren't blondes sort of washed out? Pale? But there's an interest in them. Everybody looks at them a lot. And sees distinctions, and names the shades. Those four heads were each a different black. Kettle black. Cannonball black. Bowling-ball black. Licorice. Licorice curls. Patent-leather black. Leotard black. Black sapphire. Black opal. And since when have ashes been blonde? Ashes are black and white. Ash black. And his own hair. What color was his own hair? He pulled a mess of it forward. It's brown. But he always put "black" on his i.d.s. I've got brown hair. And never knew it though combing it at the mirror daily because when you think of Chinese, Chinese have black hair. This hair is brownish, and two of the heads of hair in front are brownish too. He felt the dearness of those four people. Keep an eye out from now on. There are probably more of us with brown hair than black hair. Easy to think up words for browns. Chestnut, and more. We'll make up many, many names for dark.

"Let me have a little fun with you," said the emcee, who was telling business jokes. At least he didn't tell race jokes. A lot of people warm up meetings with race and sex jokes. "Seriously, folks," he said. "The concept of toys," he said. "Fun." "Play." "Core departments." "Meet the needs of the key customer audiences." (Where did my toys go? I've stopped having toys.)

Helpers ran up and down the aisles handing out "literature"—more pies, pictures and descriptions of toys, their stock numbers, order forms, handouts, inserts. As the executives talked—the people who introduced them were very honored by their presence—they had long titles, Western Regional this and that—you were to follow along marking up a page, then insert it among other pages. The pages were numbered like 19.B.2.a. Very scientific. Pagination. You could add to this binder forever at any point. Lots to do. Wittman hated this perversion of the classroom and books and the decimal system. All four of the other Chinese-Americans were taking information down in their notebooks like this was a difficult college lecture. "And that's true too," they wrote, which is a line in *King Lear.* Wittman had written a paper on how an actor playing Gloucester must have written it in the margin of his script.

With the nice sharp pencil they'd given out for free, Wittman drew a grid, a copy of his time sheet, and marked the days he'd cut out from work. The regular workers accumulated one day of sick leave per month. He had used up his accrued days. Now that he'd been demoted, was he accruing a half-day per month? It seemed that he was six days overdrawn. When would be a good day to cut out again? You don't want a conspicuous pattern of absences. It was time to call in sick on a Tuesday again. An absence is more enjoyable when you can anticipate it for days in advance. Taking a long weekend is suspect, of course. Taking off on Wednesdays is good—breaks the back of the week. But he didn't work Wednesdays anymore.

Is it time yet to speak up and give this meeting some life? Well, to tell the truth, the reason he was no longer in Management Training was that he had treated it like school. It wasn't a school? He had raised his hand, and contributed to discussion, "Do you give any goods, furniture, clothes, candy to the poor?" And he had tried to inform and give perspective—"During World War II, this store gave dolls and toy cars to the 'relocated' children. But every girl got the same make of unsold doll, and every boy the same car. Kids don't like to get the same toy as the next kid. Kids walked away from the Camp Santa when they saw what they were going to get. It doesn't do any good to gift-wrap either unless there's a surprise inside. I move, the next war we send a variety of individualized toys. This isn't a voting meeting? What do you mean this isn't a voting meeting? I think every meeting in a democracy should be a democratic meeting. Robert's *Rules of Order* at least." No, of course he wasn't being facetious. He wasn't asking for pie in the sky; he knew this wasn't the place for legislating that there be no more "Relocation" Camps and no more war, but they could pass resolutions. He most certainly had stuck to the subject at hand. "Doesn't anyone want to second my motion?" There had been others who got carried away; they too thought that meetings are places where one makes motions and seconds them and votes on them. See? He wasn't crazy. "I move that we operate on a profit-sharing plan." "Let's run this store on co-op principles." "I move that we reserve one table in the Garden Lanai for feeding the poor." "Does selling candy to children contribute to their good?" "I move that the Sports Department stop selling guns and ammo." He'd even won a few victories—against selling books out of vending machines, and against blisterpacking books to protect them from spit-on-fingers browsing. Yeah, it scared him to speak up, but what actor doesn't have stagefright? An actor dead of smugness, that's who. Well, he didn't pass Management Training. A supervisor wrote him up as "disruptive at meetings," and gave him some new hours. There wasn't a scene or anything. Nobody said that part-time was a demotion. He liked shorter hours. Make stockboy soon. (The Monkey King had not minded cleaning stables until somebody told him that his title, Shit Shoveler to Avoid Horse Plague, was bottom in rank.)

Three chicks and three men with straw hats, red-and-white blazers, and candy-cane canes, men in blue pants, girls in nets, hoofed out. They led a cheer, "YOU CAN TELL—IT'S MAT-TEL—IT'S SWELL." "All together, boys and girls," they said. "Hit it." Taped music started up. They banged tambourines and shook sleighbells. They sang that Christmas song that rhymes "boy and" and "toyland." The Chinese-Americans in front, and Louise in front too, were having a good old time, singing along, shrugging shoulders to the beat.

The lights went out. Whistling. Clapping. "The new Mattel line!" A curtain opened—a movie screen. Green hills and blue sky, and the noise of engines. And around a turn in the road—a long shot of the road—thunders a motorcycle gang. Like *The Wild One*, like Marlon Brando riding into Hollister. The gang comes into view—right up to the camera—they are little boys in Nazi leather jackets and boots. Words splay across the sky—VA-ROOM! VA-ROOM! It was just an ad for plastic tricycles with outsize wheels that made a lot of noise. The cameras settled at a normal angle, and we see the suburban street we normally live on. Not the road into Hollister. The gang leader, the cutest little Nazi, says into the camera, "Va-room by Mattel. You can *tell* it's Mat*tel*. It's *swell*." VA-ROOM! VA-ROOM! The end. Applause. Lights. The emcee announced how many times per day this commercial was going to run on network t.v. between now and the last shopping day be-fore Christmas. Blitz the Saturday-morning shows for kiddos. "Demographics." "The entire country." "Going national on all three networks." "Across America." "Major." More ap-plause. Go to U.C.L.A. film school and make industrial films.

The fishnet girls came back through a side door—costume changes accomplished during the screening—ta da! Barbie and Barbie's best girlfriend, Skipper, and Barbie's best Black girlfriend, Christie, did a skit about waiting for Ken to show up for a date, then he *does* show up. Ken and Barbie, informal, danced to Barbie's theme music. Ice-skating Skipper. Nurse Christie. Barbie-Q with her potholder and other accessories. Ken and Barbie après ski. The audience whistled and stomped for Malibu Barbie, Malibu Christie, Malibu Skipper, Malibu Ken in bathing suits and sunglasses. And the grand finale—Barbie Bride. And Bridegroom Ken and Bridesmaid Skipper.

Everybody sang out together like community sing: "You can tell it's Mattel. It's swell." Oh, god, I don't belong on this planet. Then it was over, and time to leave the Jack Tar.

Louise found him. Their taxi, which she had remembered to ask the first driver to send, was waiting. You could tell why she was a successful Management Trainee and he was not. On the ride back, she talked about how cute one of the Kens was— "What a doll." Ha ha.—and how generous Mattel was to sponsor the do. "What an excellent presentation," she kept saying. Excellent. You have to be dumb to be happy on this Earth.

"You know what I think would be the best thing that could happen to me?" she asked. "There would be a grand ballroom under the stars. I would be wearing a long white formal that has a loop at the hem to loop around my wrist. I'd have a wrist corsage of a single black orchid with white ribbons. My partner would be in white tie, and the floor would be of black and white diamond tiles. We would dance forever." Wittman pictured lines of perspective extending to infinity, and Cyd Charisse dancing in the dress with the long long chiffon scarf that blew to the sky. That was it? Shouldn't the dream for her life have more to it than that? But he didn't say anything. Better than dreaming about world conquest.

"It's going to be a really nice weekend," she said. "The U.S.S. *Coral Sea* is coming into port. I know some guys on it." She'd said that already. This was where he came in. Very short loop. He vowed (again) never to repeat himself.

Back in the Toy Department, finally having mentally figured things out, he took a pencil and a bicycle up the ladder, and, using the bicycle as template, marked the pegboard where the hooks ought to go, brought the bicycle down, placed the hooks, then hung up the bicycle.

Beneath him, a mother was explaining to her kids, "I can buy a toy for one of you if I feel like it. Sometimes I find just the right thing for one of you. I don't have to buy three things for all three of you whenever I want to buy something for one of you. Just because Mommy doesn't buy you something doesn't mean she doesn't love you." She tried that again. "Mommy loves you even if she doesn't buy you a toy. I can buy one of you a toy, and on another day, I can buy another one of you a toy. I love you the same."

Another mother was leaving a child. Wittman put on his don't-fuck-with-me face, rushed down the ladder, and nabbed her. "What's your name?" he asked, notepad and pen at the ready. She said a name, but while he was writing it, it occurred to him that she'd made it up. A man said, "How about waiting on me? I have to catch a plane," in a voice that made Wittman stay with his citizen's arrest. "May I see your i.d., please?" While she went through her purse, he turned to the kid. "What's your name?" Oh, no, something was sinking in his Mexican-American eyes, and he can't jump in to save it. "Never mind," said Wittman. "It's all right. It's okay. Everything's okay. Here. Take this. A present from me to you." Pushing a red truck into the kid's arms. Taking it back, bagging it (to protect the kid from Security), giving it to him. "It's yours. Take it home. Bye-bye." "Okay," said the kid. "Okay. Okay." Don't grow up worried about how much things cost, kid. Please. The kid had nicks in his home haircut where his scalp showed.

The plane-catching man wanted a look at no other bicycle but the one attached to the wall. "It's a good thing you're taking that down," Louise called. "You've got the wrong bikes. You're supposed to put up the Va-rooms." Now how are those bulges going to sit on the flat wall?

"Look. Look," a kid was saying. "Mommy, look." The mommy turned her head too late and didn't see that, in the mirrorwall, the top of the kid's head came exactly to the height of a shelf of boats. As he walked, a flotilla of boat hats fleeted atop his head. Wittman was at an angle to have seen it.

"You're pretty damn fast with the scissors, aren't you? She's pretty damn fast with the scissors." A terrible, violent shouting. A gigantic man was shouting at Louise, then shouted his case to the masses. "How shall I be going back to Canada without my credit card? Look what you've done. Look at what she's done. I'll have your job for this, young woman. I'll have her job for this. Damn fast with the scissors. I bought a building on Castro Street today, and you're telling me I can't buy a goddamn toy? Who's your supervisor, Miss Fast-with-the-Scissors? Call him down here. I'm having your job for this. You're going to answer for this, you are."

The other shoppers were listening hard, giving the man flailing room, but acting intent on their own shopping, examining goods, their backs to the scene but prick-eared. "I have your number," Louise was saying. "They gave me your number." At last, a manager came, and the Canadian and Louise followed him away.

And the yammering began again. "How about helping me out here, you?" "Where's the restroom?" "Mommy will be right back." "Don't you have those plain domino masks? Where can I get a plain domino mask?" Come to think of it, domino masks are no more. The Lone Ranger, no longer able to disguise his Chinese eyes, rides nevermore. "Where are the refrigerators?" "I want to make an exchange."

Wittman went over to the display table and wound up a doggy. Once he had had a girlfriend whose dog named Dusty ran away. Whenever she heard on the radio, "Was it dusty on the train? P.S. I love you," she thought of Dusty on the train, paws up on the window and tail wagging goodbye. The toy dog sat down, wagged its tail, stood, barked, walked, sat again, wagged, stood, barked, walked. Wittman pressed the egg-laying hen; the eggs rolled out. Tough shit if a kid swallowed one.

Out of a box, he took an organ-grinder's monkey with cymbals attached to its hands. It had a red fez on its head. He took off its little vest, and inserted batteries in its back. It hopped about, clapping the cymbals and smiling. Its tail stuck out of a hole in its green-and-white-striped pants. "Look here, kiddos," said Wittman, and unboxed a Barbie Bride. He put her on her back with her arms and veil and legs and white dress raised, and the monkey on top of her. Her legs held it hopping in place and clapping her with its cymbals. Her eyes opened and shut as the monkey bumped away at her. "Mommy, look at the monkey fight Barbie." "Oh, how perverted." Wittman walked. The tongue of his necktie stuck out from the bicycle. A green razzberry to you, World.

Ah, Bartleby.
Ah, Humanity.

Our monkey man will live—he parties, he plays—though unemployed. To see how he does it, go on to the next chapter.

3
Twisters and Shouters

IN THE Tenderloin, depressed and unemployed, the jobless Wittman Ah Sing felt a kind of bad freedom. Agoraphobic on Market Street, ha ha. There was nowhere he had to be, and nobody waiting to hear what happened to him today. Fired. Aware of Emptiness now. Ha ha. A storm will blow from the ocean or down from the mountains, and knock the set of the City down. If you dart quick enough behind the stores, you'll see that they are stage flats propped up. On the other side of them is ocean forever, and the great Valley between the Coast Range and the Sierras. Is that snow on Mt. Shasta?

And what for had they set up Market Street? To light up the dark jut of land into the dark sea. To bisect the City diagonally with a swath of lights. We are visible. See us? We're here. Here we are.

What else this street is for is to give suggestions as to what to do with oneself. What to do. What to buy. How to make a living. What to eat. Unappetizing. The street was full of schemes: FIRE SALE. LOANS. OLD GOLD. GUNS NEW AND USED. BOUGHT AND SOLD. GOING OUT OF BUSINESS. OUR PAIN YOUR GAIN. Food. Fast-food joints. Buy raw, sell cooked. If he got a-hold of food, he'd just eat it, not sell it. But we're supposed to sell that food in order to buy, cook, and eat omnivorously. If you're the more imaginative type, go to the mud flats, collect driftwood, build yourself a cart or a stand, sell umbrellas on rainy and foggy days, sell flowers, sell fast portable hot dogs, tacos, caramel corn, ice-cream sandwiches, hamburgers. Daedalate the line-up from cow to mouth, and fill up your life. If a human being did not have to eat every day, three times a day, ninety percent of life would be solved.

Clothes are no problem. He'd found his Wembley tie on a branch of a potted plant in front of the Durant Hotel, and an Eastern school tie hanging on a bush on Nob Hill. Coats are left on fences and wristwatches inside of shoes at the beach.

Musicians have a hard time of it. Sax players and guitarists and a bass player have left their instruments in pawnshops; they're away perhaps forever, trying to make money, and to eat. A lot of hocked jewelry sits in the windows overnight; the real diamonds, they keep in the twirling-lock safe. These cellos and jewels belonged to people who for a while appreciated more than food. The nature of human beings is also that they buy t.v.s, coffee tables, nightstands, sofas, daddy armchairs for dressing the set of their life dramas.

Market Street is not an avenue or a boulevard or a champs that sweeps through arches of triumph. Tangles of cables on the ground and in the air, open manholes, construction for years. Buses and cars trying to get around one another, not falling into trenches, and not catching tires in or sliding on tracks, lanes taken up by double and triple parking. Pedestrians stranded on traffic islands. How am I to be a boulevardier on Market Street? I am not a boulevardier; I am a bum-how, I am a fleaman.

Now what? Where does a fleaman go for the rest of the evening, the rest of his adult life? The sets haven't started at the Black Hawk, but no more spending extravagant money on music. Music should be overflowing everywhere. It's time to find out how much free music there is. And no hanging out at the Albatross anymore, taken over by scary Spades. To feel the green earth underfoot, he could walk on the green Marina, look at the moon over the sea, and perhaps a second moon in the sea. Keep track of moonphases; are you going through changes in sync with werewolves? But something about that nightlight on the grass that looked sick, like the Green Eye Hospital. *I saw: Hospitals.* No walk in the Palace of the Legion of Honor either, not to be by himself in that huge dark; better to have a companion, and impress her at high noon, Wittman Ah Sing as Hercules chained to the columns and pulling them down, while shouting Shakespeare. If he went to Playland at the Beach, he would get freaked out by Sal, The Laughing Lady setting off the laughing gulls. Haaw. Haaaw. Haaaaw. He had yet to walk across the Golden Gate at night, but did not just then feel like being suspended in the open cold above the Bay; the breath of the cars would not be warm enough. Continue, then, along Market.

No boulevardiers here. Who's here? Who are my familiars? Here I am among my familiars, yeah, like we're Kerouac's people, tripping along the street.

> *Soldiers, sailors,*
> *the panhandlers and drifters,*
> *[no] zoot suiters, the hoodlums,*
> *the young men who washed dishes in cafeterias*
>   *from coast to coast,*
> *the hitchhikers, the hustlers, the drunks,*
> *the battered lonely young Negroes,*
> *the twinkling little Chinese,*
> *the dark Puerto Ricans [and braceros and pachucos]*
> *and the varieties of dungareed Young Americans*
>   *in leather jackets*
>   *who were seamen and mechanics and garagemen*
>   *everywhere . . .*
> *The same girls who walked in rhythmic pairs,*
> *the occasional whore in purple pumps and red raincoat*
>   *whose passage down these sidewalks was always*
>   *so sensational,*
> *the sudden garish sight of some incredible homosexual*
>   *flouncing by with an effeminate shriek of*
>   *general greeting to everyone, anyone:*
>   *"I'm just so knocked out and you all know it,*
>   *you mad things!"*
> *—and vanishing in a flaunt of hips . . .*

Well, no such red-and-purple whore or resplendent homosexual. Might as well expect a taxi door to open and out step a geisha in autumn kimono, her face painted white with tippy red lips and smudge-moth eyebrows, white tabi feet winking her out of sight on an assignation in the floating demimonde.

Shit. The "twinkling little Chinese" must be none other than himself. "Twinkling"?! "Little"?! Shit. Bumkicked again. If King Kerouac, King of the Beats, were walking here tonight, he'd see Wittman and think, "Twinkling little Chinese." Refute "little." Gainsay "twinkling." A man does not twinkle. A man with balls is not little. As a matter of fact, Kerouac didn't get "Chinese" right either. Big football player white all-American jock Kerouac. Jock Kerouac. I call into question your naming of me. I trust your sight no more. You tell people by their jobs. And by their race. And the wrong race at that. If Ah Sing were to run into Kerouac—grab him by the lapels of his lumberjack shirt. Pull him up on his toes. Listen here, you twinkling little Canuck. What do you know, Kerouac? What do you know? You don't know shit. I'm the American here. I'm the American walking here. Fuck Kerouac and his American road anyway. Et tu, Kerouac. Aiya, even you. Just for that, I showed you, I grew to six feet. May still be growing.

Like headlines, the movie marquees seemed to give titles to what was going down—MONDO CANE, THE TRIAL, LORD OF THE FLIES, DR. NO, MANCHURIAN CANDIDATE, HOW THE WEST WAS WON. Now, if there is one thing that makes life bearable, it's the movies. Let them show a movie once a week, and Wittman can take anything, live anywhere—jail, a totalitarian socialist country, the Army. Not educational films but big-bucks full-production-values American glitz movies. WEST SIDE STORY. The biggest reddest block caps told him to go see *West Side Story*, which had returned from the sixth International Film Festival at Cannes. The girl in the ornate ticket booth said that he was on time, so he bought a ticket and went into the Fox. Inhaling the smell of the popcorn and the carpet, he felt happy. In the middle seat a screen-and-a-half's width away from the front, he continued happy. In the breast pocket of his Brooks Brothers suit, on a page margin, Malte Laurids Brigge: *This which towered before me, with its shadows ordered in the semblance of a face, with the darkness gathered in the mouth of its centre, bounded, up there, by the symmetrically curling hairdos of the cornice; this was the strong, all-covering antique mask, behind which the world condensed into a face. Here, in this great incurved amphitheatre of seats, there reigned a life of expectancy, void, absorbent: all happening was yonder: gods and destiny; and thence (when one looks, up high) came lightly, over the wall's rim: the eternal entry of the heavens.* Then a thunder-clapping pleasure—the movie started with simultaneous blasts of Technicolor and horns.

"When you're a Jet, you're a Jet all the way from your first cigarette to your last dying day." Oh, yes, that's me, that's me, a-crouching and a-leaping, fight-dancing through the city,

fingers snapping, tricky feet attacking and backing up and attacking, the gang altogether turning and pouncing—monkey
kung fu. "You got brothers around . . . You're never disconnected . . . You're well protected."

Oh, yes, all the dances in all the wide and lonely gyms of our
adolescence should have been like this. Us guys against one
wall and you girls across the basketball court and along the
opposite wall ought to have come bursting out at one another
in two co-operating teams. The girls, led by Rita Moreno,
high-kicking and lifting their skirts and many petticoats. "I
like to be in America. Everything free in America."

And Tony meets Natalie Wood, and asks her to dance, and
falls in love at first sight with her. Me too. "I just met a girl
named Maria." And I'm in love with her too. Though her
brother and her boyfriend belong to the Sharks, I love her like
a religion.

In this world without balconies, climb a fire escape to court
the city girl. And no sooner kiss her but have to part. "There's
a place for us." Our monkey finds himself crying. Stop it.
Look, identify with Chino, the reject. "Stick to your own
kind." What kind of people are Tony and Maria anyway, both
with black wavy hair, and looking more like each other than
anybody else on or off the screen? They are on the same mafi-
oso side, Natalie Wood as dark as a star can be. "Make of our
hands one hand, make of our hearts one heart, make of our
lives one life, day after day, one life." (Wittman had been to a
wedding, he was best man, where his college friends had sung
that song as part of the ceremony. The bride was Protestant
and the groom was agnostic.)

The Jets are an Italian gang? But what about jet black? Like
the Fillmore, the Western Addition. Black. Only they don't
hire and cast Blacks, so Russ Tamblyn, as Riff the gangleader
with kinky hair, indicates Blackness, right? (Like Leslie Caron
with her wide mouth as Mardou Fox in *The Subterraneans* is
supposed to be Black. George Peppard as Jack Kerouac, also as
Holly Golightly's boyfriend in *Breakfast at Tiffany's*. Mickey
Rooney with an eye job and glasses as Holly's jap landlord,
speaking snuffling bucktoof patois.) The leader of the Sharks is
Bernardo, Maria's brother, played by George Chakiris. Greek
Danish Puerto Ricans of the East Coast. This is Back East,

where they worry about Puerto Rican gangs, who are Black
and white and blond. Don't the rest of the audience get Sharks
and Jets mixed up in the fight-dancing? They should have
hired dark actors for one side or the other. But not a face up
there was darker than Pancake #11. Come on. Since when?
A white-boy gang? Two white-boy gangs. White boys don't
need a gang because they own the country. They go about
the country individually and confidently, and not on the lookout for whom to ally with. "You got brothers around; you're
a family man . . . We're gonna beat every last buggin gang
on the whole buggin street." They mean they can beat kung
fu tongs, who invented fight-dancing, and they can beat the
dancing Black boxers, who fight solo.

Wittman got up and moved to a seat two rows forward,
on the aisle, near the exit, but entered the movie no deeper,
looking up at the squished faces. Can't get sucked in anymore.
He went up to the balcony, smoked, nobody telling him to
put out his smoke, and watched Tony talk to Doc, this lovable
old *Jewish* candy-store guy—get it?—this movie is not prejudiced. Some of the Italians are good guys, Tony is reformed,
and some are bad guys; the bad guys, see, are bad for reasons
other than innateness. Wittman got up again and climbed to
the back of the balcony. He would walk out except that he was
too cheap to leave in the middle of movies. There weren't very
many people in the audience, and they were spread out singly
with rows of empty seats around each one, alone at the movies
on Friday night with no place else to go. "The world is just an
address. . . ." So, white guys, lonely also, borrow movie stars'
faces, movie stars having inhabitable faces, and pretend to be
out with Natalie, and to have a gang.

Chino does not disappear de-balled from the picture. He
hunts Tony down and shoots him dead. Maria/Natalie kneels
beside his body, and sings with tears in her eyes. "One hand,
one heart, only death will part us now." Gangboys look on
through the cyclone fence. She throws away the gun, which
hits the cement but doesn't go off. "Te adoro, Anton," she says
foreignly. Some Sharks, some Jets, biersmen, in rue, bear the
dead away. The end.

Where are you, Bugs Bunny? We need you, Mr. Wabbit in Wed.

Wittman came out of the theater to the natural world that

moves at a medium rate with no jump cuts to the interesting parts. Headache. Bad for the head to dream at the wrong time of day. The day gone. Should have cut out—the only human being in the world to walk out on *West Side Story*—too late. He'd stayed, and let the goddamn movies ruin his life.

Well, here was First Street, and the Terminal. The end of the City. The end of the week. Maws—gaps and gapes—continuing to open. But Wittman did too have a place to go, he'd been invited to a party, which he'd meant to turn down. He entered the Terminal, which is surrounded by a concrete whirlpool for the buses to turn around on spirals of ramps. Not earth dirt but like cement dirt covered everything, rush-hour feet scuffing up lime, noses and mouths inhaling lime rubbings. A last flower stand by the main entrance—chrysanthemums. And a bake shop with birthday cakes. A couple of people were eating creampuffs as they hurried along. People eat here, with the smell of urinal cakes issuing from johns. They buy hot dogs at one end of the Terminal and finish eating on their way through. They buy gifts at the last moment. Wittman bought two packs of Pall Malls in preparation for the rest of the weekend. No loiterers doing anything freaky. Keep it moving. Everybody's got a place to go tonight. Wittman bought a ticket for the Oakland-Berkeley border, and rode up the escalator to the lanes of buses. The people on traffic islands waited along safety railings. Birds beak-dived from the steel rafters to land precisely at a crumb between grill bars. The pigeons and sparrows were greyish and the cheeks of men were also grey. Pigeon dust. Pigeons fan our breathing air with pigeon dander.

Wittman was one of the first passengers to board, and chose the aisle seat behind the driver. He threw his coat on the window seat to discourage company, stuck his long legs out diagonally, and put on his metaphor glasses and looked out the window.

Up into the bus clambered this very plain girl, who lifted her leg in such an ungainly manner that anybody could see up her skirt to thighs, but who'd be interested in looking? She was carrying string bags of books and greasy butcher-paper bundles and pastry boxes. He wished she weren't Chinese, the kind who works hard and doesn't fix herself up. She, of course, stood beside him until he moved his coat and let her bump her bags across him and sit herself down to ride. This girl and her roast duck will ride beside him all the way across the San Francisco–Oakland Bay Bridge. She must have figured he was saving this seat for her, fellow ethnick.

The bus went up the turnaround ramp and over a feeder ramp, this girl working away at opening her window—got it open when they passed the Hills Brothers factory, where the long tall Hindu in the white turban and yellow gown stood quaffing his coffee. The smell of the roasting coffee made promises of comfort. Then they were on the bridge, not the bridge for suicides, and journeying through the dark. The eastbound traffic takes the bottom deck, which may as well be a tunnel. You can see lights between the railings and the top deck, and thereby identify the shores, the hills, islands, highways, the other bridge.

"Going to Oakland?" asked the girl. She said "Oak Lun."

"Haw," he grunted, a tough old China Man. If he were Japanese, he could have said, "Ee, chotto." Like "Thataway for a spell." Not impolite. None of your business, ma'am.

"I'm in the City Fridays to work," she said. "Tuesdays and Thursdays, I'm taking a night course at Cal Extension, over by the metal overpass on Laguna Street. There's the bar and the traffic light on the corner? Nobody goes into or comes out of that bar. I stand there at that corner all by myself, obeying the traffic light. There aren't any cars. It's sort of lonely going to college. What for you go City?" He didn't answer. Does she notice that he isn't the forthcoming outgoing type? "On business, huh?" Suggesting an answer for him.

"Yeah. Business."

"I signed up for psychology," she said, as if he'd conversably asked. "But I looked up love in tables of contents and indexes, and do you know love isn't in psychology books? So I signed up for philosophy, but I'm getting disappointed. I thought we were going to learn about good and evil, human nature, how to be good. You know. What God is like. You know. How to live. But we're learning about P plus Q arrows R or S. What's that, haw? I work all day, and commute for two hours, and what do I get? P plus Q arrows R."

She ought to be interesting, going right to what's important. The trouble with most people is that they don't think about the meaning of life. And here's this girl trying for heart truth. She may even have important new information. So how come she's boring? She's annoying him. Because she's presumptuous. Nosiness must be a Chinese racial trait. She was supposing, in the first place, that he was Chinese, and therefore, he has to hear her out. Care how she's getting along. She's reporting to him as to how one of our kind is faring. And she has a subtext: I am intelligent. I am educated. Why don't you ask me out? He took a side-eye look at her flat profile. She would look worse with her glasses off. Her mouse-brown hair was pulled tight against her head and up into a flat knot on top, hairpins showing, crisscrossing. (Do Jews look down on men who use bobby pins to hold their yarmulkes on?) A person has to have a perfect profile to wear her hair like that. She was wearing a short brownish jacket and her bony wrists stuck out of the sleeves. A thin springtime skirt. She's poor. Loafers with striped socks. Flat shoes, flat chest, flat hair, flat face, flat color. A smell like hot restaurant air that blows into alleys must be coming off her. Char sui? Fire duck? Traveling with food, unto this generation. Yeah, the lot of us riding the Greyhound out of Fresno and Watsonville and Gardena and Lompoc to college—even Stanford—guys *named* Stanford—with mama food and grandma food in the overhead rack and under the seat. Pretending the smell was coming off somebody else's luggage. And here was this girl, a night-school girl, a Continuing Ed girl, crossing the Bay, bringing a fire duck weekend treat from Big City Chinatown to her aging parents.

"Do you know my cousin Annette Ah Tye?" she asked. "She's from Oak Lun."

"No," he said.

"How about Susan Lew? Oh, come on. Susie Lew. Robert Lew. Do you know Fanny them? Fanny, Bobby, Chance Ong, Uncle Louis. I'm related to Fanny them."

"No, I don't know them," said Wittman, who would not be badgered into saying, "Oh, yeah, Susan them. I'm related by marriage to her cousin from Walnut Creek."

"I'm thinking of dropping philosophy," she said. "Or do you think the prof is working up to the best part?"

"I don't know what you say," said Wittman. *Know* like *no*, like *brain*. "I major in engineer."

"Where do you study engineering?"

"Ha-ah." He made a noise like a samurai doing a me-ay, or an old Chinese guy who smokes too much.

"You ought to develop yourself," she said. "Not only mentally but physically, spiritually, and socially." What nerve. Chinese have a lot of nerve. Going to extension classes was her college adventure. Let's us who wear intellectual's glasses talk smart to each other. "You may be developing yourself mentally," she said. "But you know what's wrong with Chinese boys? All you do is study, but there's more to life than that. You need to be well rounded. Go out for sports. Go out on dates. Those are just two suggestions. You have to think up other activities on your own. You can't go by rote and succeed, as in engineering school. You want a deep life, don't you? That's what's wrong with Chinese boys. Shallow lives."

What Wittman ought to say at this point was, "Just because none of us asks you out doesn't mean we don't go out with girls." Instead, to be kind, he said, "I not Chinese. I Japanese boy. I hate being taken for a chinaman. Now which of my features is it that you find peculiarly Chinese? Go on. I'm interested."

"Don't say chinaman," she said.

Oh, god. O Central Casting, who do you have for me now? And what is this role that is mine? Confederates who have an interest in race: the Ku Klux Klan, Lester Maddox, fraternity guys, Governor Faubus, Governor Wallace, Nazis— stupid people on his level. The dumb part of himself that eats Fritos and goes to movies was avidly interested in race, a topic unworthy of a great mind. Low-karma shit. Babytalk. Stuck at A,B,C. Can't get to Q. Crybaby. Race—a stupid soul-narrowing topic, like women's rights, like sociology, easy for low-I.Q. people to feel like they're thinking. Stunted and runted at a low level of inquiry, stuck at worm. All right, then, his grade-point average was low (because of doing too many life things), he's the only Chinese-American of his generation not in grad school, he'll shovel shit.

"It's the nose, isn't it, that's a chinaman nose?" he asked this flat-nosed girl. "Or my big Shinajin eyes? Oh, I know. I know. Legs. You noticed my Chinese legs." He started to pull up a pants leg. "I'm lean in the calf. Most Japanese are meaty in the calf by nature, made for wading in rice paddies. Or it's just girls who have daikon legs? How about you? You got daikon legs?"

She was holding her skirt down, moving her legs aside, not much room among her packages. Giggling. Too bad she was not offended. Modern youth in flirtation. "You Japanese know how to have a social life much better than Chinese," she said. "At least you Japanese boys take your girls out. You have a social life."

Oh, come on. Don't say "your girls." Don't say "social life." Don't say "boys." Or "prof." Those Continuing Ed teachers are on a non-tenure, non-promotional track. Below lecturers. Don't say "Chinese." Don't say "Japanese."

"You know why Chinese boys don't go out?" she asked, confiding some more. Why? What's the punchline? He ought to kill her with his bare hands, but waited to hear just why Chinese boys stay home studying and masturbating. You could hear her telling on us to some infatuated sinophile. Here it comes, the real skinny. "Because no matter how dumb-soo, every last short boy unable to get a date in high school or at college can go to Hong Kong and bring back a beautiful woman. Chinese boys don't bother to learn how to socialize. It's not fair. Can you imagine a girl going to China looking for a husband? What would they say about her? Have you ever heard of a Japanese girl sending for a picture groom?"

"No," he said.

"And if Chinese boys don't learn to date, and there are millions of wives waiting to be picked out, then what becomes of girls like me, haw?"

Oh, no, never to be married but to a girl like this one. Montgomery Clift married to Shelley Winters in *A Place in the Sun.* Never Elizabeth Taylor.

"You shouldn't go to China to pick up a guy anyway," he said. "Don't truck with foreigners. They'll marry you for your American money, and a green card. They'll say and do anything for a green card and money. Don't be fooled. They'll dump you once they get over here."

Another plan for her or for anybody might be to go to a country where your type is their ideal of physical beauty. For example, he himself would go over big in Scandinavia. But where would her type look good? Probably the U.S.A. is already her best bet. There's always white guys from Minnesota and Michigan looking for geisha girls.

"No, they won't," she said. "They'd be grateful. They're grateful and faithful forever. I'm not going to China. People can't just go to China. I was talking hypothetically." Oh, sure, she's so attractive.

"Last weekend, I went to a church dance," she said, letting him know she's with it. "I went with my girlfriends. We go to dances without a date for to meet new boys. All the people who attended the dance were Chinese. How is that? I mean, it's not even an all-Chinese church. The same thing happens at college dances. Posters on campuses say 'Spring Formal,' but everyone knows it's a Chinese-only dance. How do they know? Okay, Chinese know. They know. But how does everybody else know not to come? Is it like that with you Japanese?"

"I don't go to dances." Don't say "they."

"You ought to socialize. I guess the church gave the dance so we could meet one another. It's a church maneuver, see?, to give us something beneficial. We'd come to their buildings for English lessons, dances, pot luck, and pretty soon, we're staying for the services. Anyway, there was a chaperone at this dance who was a white acquaintance of mine from high school. We're the same age, but he was acting like an adult supervisor of children. We used to talk with each other at school, but at this dance, of course, he wouldn't ask me to dance."

"What for you want to dance with him? Oh. Oh, I get it. I know you. I know who you are. You're Pocahontas. That's who you are. Aren't you? Pocahontas. I should have recognized you from your long crane neck."

"No, my name is Judy. Judy Louis." She continued telling him more stuff about her life. On and on. Hadn't recognized her for a talker until too late. Strange moving lights, maybe airplanes, maybe satellites, were traveling through the air. The high stationary lights were warnings, the tops of hills. It seemed a long ride; this voice kept going on beside his ear. He looked at the girl again, and she looked blue-black in the dark. He blinked, and saw sitting beside him a blue boar. Yes, glints of light on bluish dagger tusks. Little shining eyes. Not an illusion because the details were very sharp. Straight black

bristly eyelashes. A trick of the dark? But it was lasting. Eyes
and ivory tusks gleaming black and silver. Like black ocean
with star plankton and black sky with stars. And the mouth
moving, opening and closing in speech, and a blue-red tongue
showing between silver teeth, and two ivory sword tusks. He
leaned back in his seat, tried forward, and she remained a blue
boar. (You might make a joke about it, you know. "Boar" and
"bore.") He couldn't see where her face left off from her hair
and the dark. He made no ado about this hallucination, acted
as if she were a normal girl. Concentrated hard to hear what
she was saying. "You're putting me on, aren't you?" she was
saying.

"What you mean?"

"You're not really Japanese. You're *Chi*nese. Japanese have
good manners." Her piggy eyes squinted at him. He wanted
to touch her, but she would think he was making a pass. But,
surely, he could try touching a tusk because the tusks can't
actually be there. "And you look Chinese. Big bones. Long
face. Sort of messy."

"Listen here. I'm not going to ask you out, so quit hinting
around, okay?"

"What?! Me go out with you? I not hinting around. I
wouldn't go out with you if you ask me. You not my type.
Haw."

"What type is that? Missionaries? Missionaries your type?
You know where you ought to go for your type? I know the
place for you. In New York, there's a nightclub for haoles and
orientals to pick each other up. It's like a gay bar, that is, not
your average straight thing. Sick. Girls such as yourself go there
looking for an all-American boy to assimilate with, and vice
versa. You can play Madame Butterfly or the Dragon Lady and
find yourself a vet who's remembering Seoul or Pearl Harbor
or Pusan or Occupied Japan. All kinds of Somerset Maugham
combinations you hardly want to know about. Pseudo psycho
lesbo sappho weirdo hetero homo combos."

"You the one sick. Look who's sick. Don't call me sick. You
sick." The blue boar had eyebrows, and they were screwed together in perplexity. "*If* you are a Japanese, you shouldn't go
out with a Chinese girl anyway, and I wouldn't go out with
you. Japanese males work too hard. Chinese males dream too

much, and fly up in the air. The Chinese female is down-to-earth, and makes her man work. When a Japanese man marries a Chinese woman, which does not happen often, it's tragic. They would never relax and have fun. A Japanese man needs a girl who will help him loosen up, and a Chinese man needs a girl who will help him settle down. Chinese man, Chinese woman stay together. I'm going to do a study of that if I go into psych."

"Don't say 'tragic.' You want the address of that place where keto hakujin meet shinajin and nihonjin? Look, I'm just helping you out with your social life."

His talking to her, and her speaking, did not dispel her blueness or her boarness. The lips moved, the tusks flashed. He wanted her to talk some more so he could look closely at her. What was causing this effect? The other people on the bus had not turned into animals.

"Help *yourself* out with your *own* social life. Why *don't* you ask me out on a date? Haw?" The boar lips parted smiling. "Because you are scared." "Sked," she pronounced it. "You been thinking about it this whole trip, but you sked." Don't say "date."

"No, I'm not." You're homely. He can't say that. She functions like she's as good-looking as the next person, and he's not going to be the one to disabuse her.

This guise, though, is not plain. A magnificent creature. The voice that was coming out of it was the plain girl's. She must be sitting next to him engulfed in a mirage.

He touched her on a tusk, and it was there, all right. It did not fade into a strip of metal that was the window frame. The narrow eyes looked at him in surprise. "Hey, cut it out," she said, pushing his hand away from her mouth with a gentle cloven hoof. She giggled, and he backed away as far over by the aisle as he could back. What he had touched was harder than flesh. Bony. Solid. Therefore, real, huh? She giggled again. It is pretty funny to have somebody touching you on the teeth. Warm teeth.

"What was that for? Why did you do that?" she said. "Why you touch my teeth? That isn't the way to ask for a date."

"I'm not asking you for a date. I do not want to date you."

"Well, I understand. You don't like aggressive girls. Most

guys can't take aggressive girls. I'm very aggressive." She'll never admit to homeliness. "Aggressive girls are especially bad for Japanese boys."

"Lay off my race," he said. "Cool it." Which was what he should have said in the first place. She went quiet. Sat there. But did not change back. The bus went on for a long time in the dark. And whenever he glanced her way, there beside him was the blue-black boar. Gleaming.

"Hey," he said, tapping her on the shoulder. Boar skin feels like corduroy. She cocked a flap of silky ear toward him. "See these people on the bus? They all look human, don't they? They look like humans but they're not."

"They are too," she said.

"Let me warn you." He looked behind him, and behind her. "Some of them only appear to be human." What he was saying even sent shivers up his own back. "There are non-humans in disguise as men and women amongst us."

"Do you see them everywhere, or only on this bus?"

"On this bus, maybe a few other places. I'm surprised you haven't noticed. Well, some of them have gotten the disguise down very well. But there's usually a slip-up that gives them away. Do you want me to tell you some signs to watch out for?"

The boar's great blue-black head nodded.

"You've seen 'The Twilight Zone' on t.v., haven't you? Have you noticed that Rod Serling doesn't have an upper lip?" He demonstrated, pressing his upper lip against his teeth. "That's a characteristic sign of the werewolf." The glittery eyes of the boar opened wider, surprised. "Their hands are different from ours. They wear gloves. Walt Disney draws them accurately. And Walter Lantz does too. Goofy wears gloves, but not Pluto. Goofy is a dog, and Pluto is a dog, but Pluto is a real dog. Mickey and Minnie, Donald and the nephews, Unca Scrooge—and Yosemite Sam—never take their gloves off. Minnie and Daisy wash dishes with their gloves on. You see women in church with those same little white gloves, huh? They are often going to church. There are more of these were-women in San Francisco than in other cities."

"What do they want? What are they doing here?"

"You tell me. I think they're here because they belong here. That's just the way the world is. There's all kinds. There are cataclysms and luck that they probably manipulate. But there's different kinds of them too, you know; they don't get along with one another. It's not like they're all together in a conspiracy against our kind."

"Aiya-a-ah, nay gum sai nay, a-a-ah," said the creature—the Pig Woman—beside him. "Mo gum sai nay, la ma-a-ah." Such a kind voice, such a loving-kind voice, so soothing, so sorry for him, telling him to let go of the old superstitious ways.

At last, the bus shot out of the tunnel-like bridge. Under the bright lights, she turned back into a tan-and-grey drab of a girl again. Wittman got himself to his feet, rode standing up, and the bus reached the intersection of College and Alcatraz. Here's where I get off.

"Goodbye," she said. "Let's talk again. It will make our commute more interesting." She was not admitting to having weirdly become Pig Woman.

He said, "Huh." Samurai.

What the fuck had that been about? Nevermind. It's gone. Forget it. It doesn't mean a thing. No miracle. No miracles forevermore, because they may be drug flashes. I've lost my miracles. It don't mean shit.

Oh no, the plain girl had gathered up her smelly stuff, and gotten off behind him, and was following him up the street. "Are you going to the party too?" she asked. "Are we going to the same party?"

"No," he said. I'm not walking in with Miss Refreshment Committee bringing salt fish and rice, and pork with hom haw. "No party," he said, and walked off in the opposite direction of the way he was meaning to go. No more to do with you, girl. He walked quickly ahead and away down Alcatraz. The group of lights in the Bay must be the old federal pen. The Rock. As usual, Orion the Warrior ruled the city sky, and you had to know the Pleiades to find their nest. He turned left, then left again, and up the hill to the party.

The street was jampacked with cars and music, no room in the air for one more decibel. The trees held loudspeakers in their arms; their bass hearts were thudding. Wittman made his way among the bodies, some already fallen on the lawn. Above huddles of four or six, there hung oval clouds of smoke, like thought balloons. He walked the porch that wrapped all the way around the house, an Oakland Victorian, looking into doors and windows for an interesting opening, or somebody he might want to party with. From a backdoor, he went into the kitchen, where he poured himself some Mountain Red, and struck a party match. The flag flared up—stars burst, stripes curled—"bombs bursting in air"—a leftover from the Fourth of July party, which had followed the Bloom's Day party. He had, in his life, gone to four Bloom's Day parties, every end of spring semester since freshman year, missing this last one because of party dread. Dread of parties for over a year now. (The way you could tell you were at a Bloom's Day party was by a bunch of red roses in a vase, and by the date.) There was always a plot to one of these parties; the fun was in figuring out what the point was, and who got it and who didn't. Creative paranoia. Lance, who gave the parties, liked testing perception. He taught his friends, invited or not: The most important thing in the world is parties. In the bowl of walnuts was a nutcracker in the shape of a pair of woman's legs in garters and spike heels. The nut went in the crotch, and you clamped the legs shut, and cracked the nut. Nobody was using it. You'd be a fool to get a kick out of it, and a fool to be offended.

The dining room was a sane enough place—a sane zone, quieter with normal lighting—the eye of the noise. There were people he recognized from other parties; they never appeared anyplace else in his life except at parties. Party friends.

Suddenly, Lance Kamiyama, the host, and his bride, Sunny, Sunny the bride, swooped about him, one set of newlywed arms about each other, hers in luna-moth wings, dashiki cloth, and their outward arms holding their guest. Each of them kissed him on a cheek. Choreography. "You remember Wittman from our wedding," said Lance. "We're glad to see you once more," she said. A queenly We. The married We. "Once more" like "a year and a day," that is, a ritual amount of time has passed. The wedding had been the party between Bloom's Day and July 4. She had worn a sea-green wedding gown; her long Guinevere hair fell in tresses. Wittman had not met her before the wedding, but felt jealous nevertheless that during his lifetime she had chosen another, Lance. It was the first post-grad wedding, the one with music from *West Side Story*. No shame. At the reception, Wittman's last party,

Sunny told him (while they were dancing, the best man and the bride) that Lance had said to her, "There's nothing in the world as beautiful as a blonde." He had something on Lance there; Sunny had been unfaithful already telling a thing like that on her husband.

"Howzit?"

"Howzit."

Checking Lance out for signs of marriage, it seemed he hadn't been married long enough to have been altered. Yet. There's something priest-like about married guys. No matter whether they're faithful or unfaithful or what. Having lived en famille once would seem to be enough for anybody.

"Isn't this one the Chinese Beatnik?" Sunny said. Discussing him. Aha, so they do talk you over. And she's given away some more of their private talk. Lance unhugged him, gesturing with that arm. "Don't my two hundred closest friends look prosperous?" he said. "We've done very well, haven't we?" Well, yes, he'd gotten them off the floor, off mattresses and gym mats, and on to furniture; the food was on tables, not on a door plank. Everybody was up on a higher level, sitting and standing. Sofas rather than automobile seats and park benches. End tables. "Lance told me, but I forgot. You're one of his business friends, right?" If the music were somewhat louder, he would not have to answer her. "Or are you primarily a social friend?" She didn't forget, she's putting him on. Do you and Lance really think like that? Does everybody? Are you mocking my natural paranoia? Isn't "business friend" an oxymoron, and "social friend" redundant? "We're old friends," he said. "We're childhood friends." A lifelong friend. The one who had turned him on to L.S.D. from the Sandoz Labs (twice), and homemade chiles rellenos, and William Carlos Williams' prose. "I was best man, remember?"

Another thing he disliked about couples—here he was ladling on the heavy charm, and looked up to see they were looking at each other, right across him. The first time a couple had done that to him, he'd been a kid in the dentist's chair. The dentist and his assistant had looked up from his open mouth, caught each other's eye, and smiled like that, the spit sucker slurping loudly and juicily away. His spit. Why was he always the one with his mouth open and his teeth hanging out in the presence of *ro*mance? He had missed the step down from the dental chair and rammed his groin into the spit fountain.

"You're looking appropriate," said Lance. "You do look the Young Millionaire." A Young Millionaire making fun of his job suit by cutting up his tie, it's allowed. After graduation, Lance started calling the parties Young Millionaires' meetings. He said "Mi-yun-neh" with Japanese-Chinese tonations. He could say it with an Oxford accent too; he'd done some study abroad at the London School of Economics.

"I've been canned," said Wittman. "Am I disqualified from the Young Millionaires? I'm going to try for Unemployment; it won't pay anywhere near a million."

"A deadbeat. But you're in luck. Here tonight you have two—maybe three—hundred business heads. Contacts. Contacts, Wittman. Recognize a brain trust when you see one. Take advantage. Hustle." He said "hunnert." He said "bidness." He didn't really talk that way; he was making fun of people who talk that way.

"Lance, why did you decide to go into the Civil Service?" I thought we were going to be brother artists.

"I like problem-solving. Actually, quite a few of our Young Millionaires are geniuses of problem-solving. Circulate. Mix." He burst out laughing at how there are hosts who'll say, "Go mix." He's probably a sociopath.

"I hate playing business games."

Sunny spoke up: "What's the matter? You aren't good at them?"

Lance laughed, delighted with her. Wittman had to laugh too. Oh, god, she's hard. No mercy. And these are his friends, toughening him up for the real world, doing him a service. She isn't so stupid; he had thought she was dumb. Why, she's sharp like her husband. Have you noticed lately that it's getting more difficult to tell smart people from dumb people? "I am too good at business games. Let me tell you what I did to get fired. You know that broken wind-up monkey in the gutter that James Dean covers with his red jacket in *Rebel Without a Cause*? We sell them. I wound one up, and put it on top of a Barbie doll. They fucked away in front of the customers and their kiddos. I should have made a bigger show—a flock of monkeys and a train of Barbies, in her housewife outfit, in her night-out formal, in her après ski, in her Malibu swimsuit, and the monkeys swooping down and up and away like the evil flock in *The Wizard of Oz*. I split before they called the cops on me. Seriously, folks, I'm like fired. I didn't even like the job, but I feel bad."

Lance said in an understanding voice, "You were just trying to make your job interesting. You can't sleep nights after all day faking a liking for your shitty job. And nothing but shit jobs ahead for the rest of your life."

"Yeah. Yeah. You stay awake over that too?"

"Who, me? Of course not." Shit. Red-assed again. The butt of the party—"Did you hear Wittman can't sleep nights over money? He's been fired, poor guy."

Then Lance showed a sincere, probably "sincere," concern. "Hey, you'll get another job soon. Everybody feels bad after getting sacked. Don't take it so hard, man. You worry too much."

"No, I don't. I didn't like that store anyway. I've got better things to do with my life." His own words always came out corny when he talked to Lance. The ironic versus the square. He wished to be the former, but couldn't turn it around. The hell with it. "I'm going to start living the life of an artist now. That was a cheap store where cheap people buy cheap presents for their cheap friends and cheap relatives." Toughen up.

"Yeah, everybody gets fired from there. Didn't you know that? By our age, the Young Millionaire has been fired at least twice. You don't want to settle down too soon. You haven't screwed up your job record at all. Most personnel managers will wonder why you were so tame you haven't been fired more often. In a lifetime, Wittman, you can make a total life change three times. All it takes to switch careers and socio-economic class—from sales clerk, as in your case, to lawyer or shrink or engineer and mechanic—is three years of re-training. I'm giving you an average. Fewer years for a nurse's aide, more for brain surgeon." It was Lance who had explained that smart people don't drive cars as well as dumb people because smart people's minds have too many alternatives.

"What G.S. are you now, Lance?" Wittman asked.

"Gee Ess Nine." Lance drew it out like suspensefully

announcing the first prize. Wittman didn't know much about what exactly he did in which Alameda federal building, but, reputedly, it was amazing for a person of their age to be a Nine. "Lucky for you, Wittman. The economic outlook is not bad," pulling a bobbin of ticker tape out of his vest pocket. Aha. Plot: Lance was wearing a three-piece suit because the theme of the party had to do with business. You were to judge ad hominem: Which suits at this party are deliberate costumes, and which came straight from work, their wearers wishing they had had time to have changed into party clothes? Those in costume and those not in costume are dressed similarly in Business District outfits, mere bowtie differences. Awareness is all, on the part of the clothes-wearer, and on the part of the beholder. A costume either disguises or reveals. One or the other. No way out of the bag.

Lance scrolled the tape between his hands. "Utilities up a quarter-point," he said. "Burroughs down 1⅜. Friday's Dow up 2.53 points in light trading on the Big Board. The Dow for the week up six good points. Run with los toros, amigo." Now, Wittman was susceptible to trance under the influence of numbers, and the evil name of Burroughs, Old Bull Lee, had been said in incantation. He heard: "The Tao is up," "Friday's Tao up 2.53 points," which is good; we were good today, not a hell of a lot better than yesterday, but holding steady and not backsliding, yes, some spiritual improvement. We are a people who measure our goodness each day. And we trade light; this is our way of shooting beams at one another. A scientific people with a measurable Tao. Wittman felt pleased with himself, that he hadn't lost his Chinese ears. He had kept a religious Chinese way of hearing while living within the military-industrial-educational complex. Wow. Lance was as good as dope—oh, god, the cosmic nature of puns. To show that he had gotten the joke, and could run with it and maybe cap it, Wittman said, "Osaka Stock Exchange, yeah. Sell G.M. Buy Kawasaki. Sell my sole for sashimi futures."

"Besides getting yourself fired, what's been happening to you?" Personally. Now his friend was making him feel ashamed for discussing work at a party. Where's his party spirit? One has to help create the atmosphere of celebration. Be more entertaining. And also candid like a camera.

"Well, I saw this guy chewing out his dog. I was taking a walk in the park yesterday. There was this queenie-looking guy dressed to kill walking his dog, this Doberman pinscher. He yanked on the chain, and said, 'You cuntless bitch.' I've never heard 'cuntless bitch' before. The dog was moving fast, like trying to get away; its ears were back. It was being publicly humiliated."

Lance was enchanted. Sunny smiled. Does she mind "bitch" and "cunt"? Not everybody would get behind this story. He and Lance liked to collect stories that most people can't appreciate.

"What movies have you seen?" Wittman asked. "Have you seen *A Nous la Liberté*?"

"Yeah. Twice. What a song. Did you see *Last Year at Marienbad*?"

"But if you sit for ten minutes at *Last Year at Marienbad* you're already repeating yourself. The point is: no point. I can't stand the imitative fallacy. I saw *West Side Story* today."

"Isn't it beautiful?"

"I like *Lolita* better, though only black and white. I like *8½* better."

"I love that part where Marcello Mastroianni whips his women around the room and the feathers are flying."

"Me too. Me too. That may be the greatest scene in cinema. But he isn't chasing them, is he? He's keeping them at bay."

"I hate that part. I hate that movie. The wife scrubbing the floor, and the aged showgirl weeping goodbye up the stairs to the attic. I hate that."

"But it's a fantasy."

"So men have a wife fantasy where she scrubs the floor on her knees and cooks for the harem."

"It's supposed to be funny. That's the funniest movie I ever saw."

"I hope you're not a man with a wife fantasy—the wife and the mistress holding hands and dancing around him."

"Fellini is a man's film-maker."

"But at the end, when everybody is running in an outdoor circus ring, didn't you like that? Didn't it make you feel good?"

"That part was okay. Everybody dressed in white, the opposite of the death dance—black silhouettes—in *The Seventh Seal*."

"Sunny, you like *Jules and Jim*, huh?"

"Of course, I like *Jules and Jim*. Everyone likes *Jules et Jim*. That's everyone's favorite movie."

"No, it's not. Everyone's favorite movie is *The Treasure of the Sierra Madre*."

"My favorite movie is *Ugetsu*."

"*Children of Paradise*."

"Yes, *Children of Paradise*."

"You like *Jules and Jim* because Jeanne Moreau has two men. We like *8½* because Mastroianni has two women."

"There weren't two women. There were more like twenty."

"That's what's so funny."

"No, it's not. It's not funny."

So, they had themselves a thorough visit right there in the middle of the bigger party, that's how good friends they are. If you have some very good lifelong friends you haven't seen or called for a long time, you have to catch up on what movies you've seen.

But there had been a time when Wittman and Lance had been the entertainment—tapdancing feet beating on skid row cement—Mr. Chin and Mr. Chan, howdy do, grin bones, grin bones, marionette arms dangling from tatter-stick shoulders, shuffle shoes, shuffle shoes. "Howdy do, Mr. Chin?" "J'eat rice, Mr. Chan?" "Yeah. Yeah. Rice and salt fish." "Crabs and black bean for me." "Wedding food, Mr. Chin." "Ah, Mr. Chan, we dance at the marriage of death and fun." Wittman quit the act; all Chinese jokes, no Japanese jokes.

The newlyweds waved to somebody, urgently, and they were off. A long-time-no-see friend has at last made the scene. Mix. Circulate. So, talking to him didn't count as circulation? Ditched. Don't anybody notice who's friendless at the party. He fought his shoulders' hunching up and his feet's shuffling, and his eyes' hunting from downbending, wine-sipping head for who was noticing that he was unpopular. If he could stand by himself alone, him and his cigarette, he would have perfected cool. In another corner, an overexcited party-goer had shut his eyes and was holding his hands in salaam position, his lips ohming and mumbling, trying to calm the space in and around him. How rude. Go home, why don't you? When you meditate, meditate; when you party, party.

Well, here's a "pool of acquaintanceship" of two to three hundred. According to friendship experts, the average American has seven "friendship units," couples counting as one unit, that is, from seven to fourteen friends. How many does he have? Below average.

Over by the fire, people suddenly burst out laughing, apparently at something the chattering fire did. "Oh, no!" "Oh, yeah!" Silence. Then many of them spoke at once, trying to get the rest to listen. "We could get arrested for watching that." "There are people who want to arrest other people for watching that." Giggles. Quick lookings around by the paranoid to check out who meant what by "that." "They want to arrest people for feeling good." Gleeful laughter. Scornful laughter. The glee winning out. Then they were all smiling calmly, gazing into the now silken flames. They were swimming in hallucinogen, ripped but appearing as ordinary as pie. So this is how the psychedelic state looks from the outside, that is, through the vantage eyes of a head straight from ear to ear at the moment. The stoned heads didn't look especially strange, a little high and red-eyed maybe, but they were smoking too, and topping mescaline and/or lysergic acid with god knows what else—combinations, asmador and Stelazine, carbogen and laughing gas, Romilar C.F. and belladonna from Vicks inhalators, whippets and whipped cream and aerosol. If peyote, the messy throw-up stage was over. They were not outwardly extraordinary; they were not actually flying around the room or going through the changes from amoeba on up. They were looking Neanderthally at the fire because we were cavemen for a long time. Then it will be a campfire on the lone prairie because we were cowboys for a generation (and more, counting the movies). And then—atomic flashes. The ages of man, though, did not visibly ripple up and down their faces. Their hair was not standing up on end as antennae for the aurora borealis. Now, all of them were calm, breathing in unison; they must be on that trip where the margins between human beings, and between human beings and other creatures, disappear, so that if one hurts, we all hurt, so that to stop war, all we have to do is drop lysergic acid into the water supply, but we don't even need to do that—because all human beings of all time are in connection—the margins didn't disappear—there aren't any margins—psychedelics only make you know about things, and do not cause a thing to be—it is—it already is—no need to reconnoiter the reservoir at Lake Chabot over beyond Canyon and the one you can see from MacArthur Boulevard, climb the dam walls and elude guards and drop L.S.D. in the water supply after all. The pleasure of acid was in knowing ideas as real as one's body and the physical universe. A girl with long hair brushed her face; the webs were bothering her. A couple of people suddenly sat up and looked around, alert. Somebody knelt like church, arms and face raised like stained-glass cathedral. Wittman did not dash over to ask what anybody saw. They were not a lively bunch. He and his compadres may not have actually flown, but when they turned into fenris wolves and dire wolves in a pack on the roam through the wilds, they had actually run barefoot through Berkeley, running to the Steppenwolf one night, having also dropped rauwolfia serpentina—"What's the trip?" "Fear and panic, man."—The fun of pure fear.—and on another night, landing at the laundromat, as you do, that laundromat on Telegraph Avenue, coming down with green paint on their faces. And recalling talking to a Black man, who was saluting a tiny American cocktail flag on top of a pyre. And they had talked, evolving language from growls to explanations of life in the universe. It must be that people who read go on more macrocosmic and microcosmic trips—Biblical god trips, *The Tibetan Book of the Dead, Ulysses, Finnegans Wake* trips. Non-readers, what do they get? (They get the munchies.)

Wittman went over below the tall black windows, where a group were talking politics. "At the rate the Masai are killing elephants," somebody was saying, "elephants will soon be extinct. Forever. From off the face of the Planet Earth." "Fuck the Masai," said this scientist girl, whom he had met before. "If I had a choice which—Masai or elephant—to conserve, I'd choose the elephants. There are too many people and not enough elephants. Elephants are peace-loving creatures, and faithful to their families and to their tribes their whole lives long. That's more than you can say for people. You must've noticed, there's a lot of anti-elephant propaganda. The movies are brainwashing us against non-human species. We have pictures in our heads of stampeding herds of elephants—rogue

elephants on the rampage—man-eating elephants—tram-
pling villages. Well, the fact is: Elephants can't run. They
walk. Remember in *Dumbo the Flying Elephant* when Timothy
Mouse scares the circus elephants, and they tear down the
tent? Walt Disney couldn't do a *Living Desert*–type movie with
elephants acting like that; he had to use animation." Oh, yes,
she's the one doing her doctoral dissertation on Walt Disney
with an emphasis on *The Living Desert*. "I say, Fuck the Masai.
The brain energy of human beings goes into thinking up ways
to kill whatever there is that moves. Fuck the Masai. Sure, I
mean it. I'm on the side of life. When I shop at the Co-op,
I choose the tomatoes with the bug bites and worm holes.
I do." "Yeah, yeah, I'm hip. Fruit and vegetables want to be
eaten," said this guy with a rep as a heroin addict. "Oranges
drop out of trees and say, 'Eat me. Eat me.'" Strange how
heroin addicts are always eating health food. Somebody else,
who had majored in Africa, said that the Masai were hardly the
elephantine consumers the Disney scholar was making them
out to be. They don't cut up their cattle into hamburger and
sirloins but only bleed and milk them. "The same way that
Indian medicine women harvest parts of plants, some leaves
from each plant, a branch, a section of a tuber system, rather
than pull up the whole plant by the root." "How come Masai
men are really good-looking," said a girl who traveled a lot,
"and Masai women aren't?" "They seem that way to you because you're extremely hetero and not attracted to any kind
of woman." "No, no, I'm speaking objectively." "What do
you mean by 'good-looking'?" "Masai are like fraternal twins.
Take a boy twin and a girl twin who look so alike they'd be
identical if they were both boys or both girls. The boy always
looks good for a boy, but the girl looks like a boy." "Yeah, like
the Kennedys all look alike, but the men look good, and the
women are homely." "If you watch elephants closely, you'd see
that they are individual in looks and personalities." "Maybe
you have a warped standard of beauty. Who amongst us in this
room looks like a Masai woman? Come on, pick one out, and
we can decide for ourselves whether she looks good or not."
The scientist girl and the traveler girl looked at this one and at
that one, turned around to look, and said that nobody there
looked as ugly as a Masai woman. "Keep looking." Putting

them on the spot. "You're being fooled by make-up and fash-ions. The range of human looks can't be that far apart. Of all the people here, who looks the closest to a Masai woman?" They waited, nobody letting the white chicks off the hook. There was a tall Black girl in the group, getting taller, and nobody was about to say it was her, and nobody was going to point out any other Black woman either. Wittman wasn't shining; time to maneuver a getaway. A newcomer was looking over shoulders, and Wittman stepped back, made room for him, and walked off, his place taken. He was getting good at shed-and-dump.

And he ran right into the most boring guest at the party, this left-wing fanatic who can't tell the difference between a party and a meeting. Each time they'd ever met, he carried on about injustice in a country you never heard of, and invited you to a "demo" in front of a hotel or a post office, which is federal property. The "demo" would be sponsored by "The Ad Hoc Committee to Save Whatever," founded by its only member, this left-wing fanatic. If you got a word in edgewise, he put it in his Marxist bag, and let you have it for not being radical enough. He had urged students to take R.O.T.C. to learn practical skills, such as shooting guns, that can be use-ful in making revolution. "You mean you want me to *kill?*" Wittman had asked, to agitate him; "I'll join R.O.T.C. if you join the Tibetan Brigade." Remember the Tibetan Brigade drilling on the soccer field near Bowles Hall? What happened to them? Did they ever get to Tibet? A man of principle has to hear a leftist out. It's very brave of him to picket Nob Hill all by himself, vexing delegates of governments and corpo-rations who stay at the Mark Hopkins, the Fairmont, the Stanford Court. Tonight, the leftist was dragging around an old and tired lady. "This is Doña Maria Francesca de Ortega y Lopez"—a longer name than that—"from Sud America." Wittman, an irrelevant nobody, was not introduced by name. She didn't look at him anyway. One moment she was silent, and the next, she was spieling from deep inside, barely audi-ble. He hoped that she was not saying what he was hearing, ". . . political torture . . . every man in the village . . . ," and names, Dons and Doñas. She rolled up a sleeve; there was a dark indentation in the bruised fat of her arm. "Bullet

wound?" he asked. She shook her head, "Si"; she does that
yes-no under interrogation. Please don't be saying that soldiers killed kids—niños y niñas—in front of parents. "Rapid,"
she said. "Rapid." As in "rapo," "rapere"? Wittman ought to
come to her rescue. She is summoning him to responsibilities which would give him a life with important meanings.
But he's ignorant, inengagé, not serious. "Could you tell her
for me, please, that I don't want to help right now?" he said.
Shame on him, so much more playing to do. The leftist rolled
his eyes—a me-ay of exasperation—didn't translate such a
Norte Americano embarrassment. He took the lady by the
unwounded arm over to another listener, who might have a
better conscience. She said, "Gracias."

Wittman hurried to pass a set of modular sofa-chairs, arranged invitingly by the married women, who were sitting
safely together. They were newlyweds, young matrons, who
last year were dates, but now they were wives. The adventurous
girls had left for New York. The husbands were getting loaded
with the boys, or dancing with the Pan Am stews. He'd gotten
stuck with the wives before—stopped to say howdy-do and
couldn't get away. Not a one of them was like Anna Karenina
or Constance Bonacieux or Lady Connie Chatterley. Nobody
bursting with sexy dissatisfaction. They were unappealing and
blobby—well, two were pregnant. It was true about "letting
herself go." They might as well have blackened their teeth. He
had asked, "What have you been up to?" After they say they're
housewives, there is nothing for him to say next. He had nodded and nodded, as if interested in "my stove," "my dinette
set," "my floors," "my husband," "our pregnancy." A husband
would come by and ask his wife to dance, but afterwards he
brought her straight back here and left her. Surely, wives hate
being stuck with wives. But how to party without being unfaithful? Why hasn't his lively generation come up with what
to do with wives at parties? "Hi, Lisa," he said. "Hi, Shirley."
That turning of wives' faces to him, troping him as he hurried
by to join the men and single girls, wasn't because of his at-
tractiveness; they didn't have anything else to do. They'd been
sitting here like this since the last party. Watch to see when
Lance starts parking Sunny.

His host and hostess were in the middle of a group that

seemed to be having the best time, but he couldn't very well go over there when he'd already been conferred his turn.

"Excuse me," said a little woman beside him. She was unusual in that she seemed older and straighter than anybody. "Have you seen Sam? I've been looking all over for him."

"Sam who? I don't know anybody named Sam."

"I better go look for him. I'll be right back." And she took off. Another hit-and-run.

"I can't find him." Whaddaya know. She had said, "I'll be right back," and she was back.

"You're smart to keep track of him. Sam's a plainclothes narc."

Her eyebrows flew up, and she laughed, delighted. "Sam? You've got to be kidding. Not Sam. Oh. I'm not *with* Sam. I have been going out with him, though. I don't think it's going to work out. He's a health-food freak."

"Is he a heroin addict?"

"Oh, no, of course not. He's a health nut."

"Every heroin addict I know is on health foods. They're always trying to feel better. Another sign of the addict is strange-smelling piss. It must be the asparagus they eat."

"The only food I've seen Sam eat is lettuce with beige stuff. He took me sailing on the Bay, and we landed on Angel Island for a picnic. When he opened up the cooler, there were napkins, and his tacklebox with fifty-six kinds of vitamin pills, and this salad, which he drizzled beige stuff on top of. He talks about grinding up raw almonds in his blender. I guess that's what that beige stuff is. There were deer and raccoons; they went over to other people's picnics. He and I have no future."

"Want another drink?" asked Wittman. "Here I am letting you stand there with an empty glass. Let me freshen it up." He was getting good at party brush-offs. You ask if you can get them a drink, and dig out. Testing them, do they want to talk to you further? If so, they'll say, "No, thanks," in which case you say, "I think I'll get myself one," and cut out before you get bored or boring.

"Yeah, sure."

"I'll be right back," he said, and headed toward the refreshments. There. He'd never used those manners before. Something must be happening to him. She hadn't even been uninteresting, and he had ducked her. He could go back there and talk to her some more if he wanted. They're not supposed to feel hurt. Nothing personal. Circulating. Calculating.

He went straight out to the porch, and up some stairs to a balcony—no other party escapee here—smoked, considered hanging it up, half-ass gibbous moon in the sky—and re-entered to a corridor of closed doors. The Steppenwolf at the entrance to the Magic Theater. Lu Sooon surrounded by the eight slabs of rock doors at Fishbelly Holm. "For Mad Men Only. The Price of Admission—Your Mind." He opened any old door and went in. Movies. Also pot-luck doping going on. And they were showing a short co-produced by his own self with a stop-and-go hand-held camera. He crawled under the lightbeam and sat on the floor beneath the projector. The technique he'd helped invent was to try for a cartoon effect using face cards—you shoot a few frames, stop, move the cards, shoot again. And there they are, very bright, the Queen of Hearts, the Knave of Diamonds, the King of Spades running about on the wood table. The Knave is driving a toy pick-up truck, in the bed of which the King is suddenly hauled away. The Queen is backing off into the distance. And—deus ex machina—a black Hand (in a glove) clacking a pair of scissors beheads the Knave, picks up the King, chases the Queen, and carries them into the air. They'd filmed extreme close-ups of all three beheadings, and during the editing, decided which royal head would have the en scene star focus death. A new king and a new queen parade with the heads on pikes by torchlight. The grande finale—a cauldron of swirling water and red paint, and toy dinosaurs falling in by the Handful, and the pieces of the King, Queen, and Knave turning, and, what the hell, the rest of the pack, everything dizzying in the vortex of time. The End.

People were clapping, and they had laughed. "Not bad." "Not bad." The movie was different from when he'd run it; it was the music. There had been dirge music—the royal family moved majestically. But now there was Loony Tunes music, and the playing cards were rushing nuttily about, though the speed was actually no faster. The same story can be comedy or tragedy, depending on the music. Bad noises roaring overhead and in the streets, the world gets crazier.

Then up on the screen popped a slide of the sun setting beyond the mud flats of the Bay, the sun to the right, a branch of driftwood in the foreground on the left. Somebody said, "Sunset"; otherwise, would you know (if you weren't from around here) whether the sun at a horizon were in the east or the west, a sunrise or a sunset? In real life, there's no doubt. "Sh-sh. Look." Lance at the projector. He ejected the slide, and flipped it over, now the sun on the left and the black stick on the right. It gave off a different emotion—a shift inside the mind and chest. I felt safe, and now I am desolate. Because the first was the image as it occurred in nature? And in this reversal the stick sticks out more lonely on the salt marsh. Lance flipped the picture again, and the sun was again important and warm. Because we saw it this way first? The audience, patient on dope, and never tiring of taking out a somewhat aphasic brain and playing with it, were wowed.

At airport parties, Lance would stand at the revolving post-card rack, and arrange cards in some kind of sequence. "Do you think somebody will come along and read what I've done?" And the next time at the airport, he checked out whether he'd been answered. "Did anybody answer?" "Nope." "You mean those cards are in the same order that you left them in?" "Oh, no, people have been shuffling through them to buy." Just so, Wittman looked for some kind of a meaning to the order of the slides.

Then there was talk about f-stops, camera numbers, apertures, etc., and he went into the next room.

Where the tube was on. He sat himself down and was intercepted by a joint, which he passed on, eschewing the taking of a hit. Contact high already all over the house. The picture wasn't coming in, but the viewers were entranced, chuckling, commenting. "Wow." "Oh, wow." "Do you see what I see?" "Beautiful, yeah." Wittman had not tried the snow show straight before. What you do is turn the knob to a channel that's not broadcasting, and you stare at the snow. Try it. Pretty soon, because the mind and eye cannot take chaos, they will pull the dots into pictures of things—in color even on a black-and-white set—confetti jumping and dancing to music. Snow is not white. Regular t.v. programs are for zombies who allow N.B.C., A.B.C., and C.B.S. to take over the sacred organizing of their brain impulses into segments, sitcoms, the news, commercials. Look, where it comes again! It works both stoned and straight. There, across the bottom of the screen, rolls a line of new cars like off an assembly line in an auto plant. But each car a different make and color. And there are drivers behind the wheels. Nobody tailgating or passing anybody else. They're on an eight-lane freeway. Some people drive with their elbows out the window, and they make hand signals in another language. Girls are poking their heads out of the sunroofs, drying their hair. Can you control what you see by thinking? Wittman sped up his mind, and, sure enough, the cars speed up. A Volkswagen flips over, spins on its back, and slides along among the onrushing race. You can sort of control the pictures, but they are not strict mirrors of your thoughts. They'll do things you don't know what they'll do next. Look. A row of cars has come to a corner. Where are they going, zipping around the corner? People too, running round this edge. Wittman tried hard to see the other side, but was distracted by the girls with long hair, who fly out of the sunroofs, and become a row of feathery angels at the top of the screen. Oh, more space up there. He had been concentrating on a few rows of dots down at the bottom. There are more stars in the universe. Every jumping dot can be one of the billions of people on this planet, each one of whom you will not have time to meet, and everybody up to something. And, furthermore, there are animals. Elephants. Wild elephants. And elephants with fringe and leis and sounding bells and other adornments. A fire truck. A float with a queen and princesses. You cannot make something stop running to study its details. Majorettes. A marching band passing a garage band. An Indian band riding a flatbed truck. The sitar music was coming from the phonograph. It felt like Ravi Shankar was playing one's spine bones—the note off the top vertebra shoots into outer space forever. Bicycles and tandems with silver spokes spinning, Gandhi wheels. Clowns gyrating on unicycles. It's a parade. No tanks, please. No drill teams presenting arms. No nationalistic flags. Every single thing different and not repeating. Cars speeding up, black-and-whites behind. Car chase. Here comes the Highway Patrol. A row of pink piggies with patent-leather hoofs roll all the way across the screen. Yibiddy. Yibiddy. Some of them are wearing police hats. One of them is

hodding bricks. Then the piggies are driving black-and-whites
with stars on their doors. Ouch. The horizontal bar rolled
up through the screen. Straight Wittman felt it smack him
in the brain. That same hit as when riding the glass elevator
at the Fairmont or the Space Needle in Seattle—while you're
looking at the view, a crossbeam comes up, and whomps you
in your sightline. "Ow," said the other people too. "Ouch.
Oh, my head." The stars shoot off from the police cars and the
Highway Patrol cars and the pig hats. Ah, a line of shooting
stars, each with a golden tail. Cycle wheels of many sizes are
spinning silver mandalas in the heavenly skies. The stars are
making formations and constellations—flag stars, wing stars,
sheriff's stars. Stars and stripes, and flags of other nations, stars
on wings and epaulets, kung fu stars. There goes a badge with a
bullet ding in it where it saved a lawman's life. The sitar plinks,
reverberating on and on and on, forever spacious. Wittman
pinned his mind power on one star, made it move to the center
of the screen. It grows magnificently. Is this satori? Am I going
to reach it this time? And it doesn't go away? The star blows
up—smithereens of stars. Explosions massage the brain. Here
we observers sit, detached as Buddhas, as the universe blows
up. What was that? Just before the bang, did you see Captain
America with a star on his forehead and one on his shield, and
Doctor Zhivago/Omar Sharif attach jets to Planet Earth and
blast it crazy off its axis? Wittman picked up (with his mind) one
of these iota stars, and pushed it to the middle of the galaxy,
where it pulsates intensely, and bursts again, a dizzy of birds—
tweet tweet—wun wun day—and stars orbiting around a cat's
head with X'd eyes. The pink pigs in top hats and patent-leather
hoofs roll by. Yibbidy. Yibbidy. That's all, folks.

"Wow." "Oh, wow." "Wotta trip that was." People got
up; some went out; some changed seats. Did all of us get to
the same place at the same time? Did we really see the same
things? "Did you see the pigs roll away?" "Yeah. Yeah." "Pigs?
What pigs?" Somebody has got to be scientific about all this;
lock everybody up independently in separate lead-lined rooms
to draw what he or she sees, and then compare.

"Look. There's more." Mushroom clouds. It was the last
scene in *Dr. Strangelove*—the graceful puffing of H-bombs.
Poof. Poof. Poof. "We'll meet again. Don't know where, don't

know when, but I know we'll meet again some sunny da-a-ay."
Electricity was shimmering between the thunderheads and the
ground. A row of human brains on stems. The End. The End.
The End. The End means the end of the world.

The monkey brains had tuned themselves in to an open
channel to a possible future. If this many bombs were to fall,
light would flash through time, backwards and forwards and
sideways. Images would fly with the speed of light-years onto
this screen and onto receptive minds. Future bombs are dropping into the present, an outermost arrondissement of the
Bomb.

A second row of mushroom clouds bloomed, and the
two rows of them boiled and smoked. Their viewers tried
to shape them into other things, but the winds were dead.
The Bomb, the brain, and magic mushrooms—fused. How
to unlock them? Give us some peace. Some peas rolled across
the screen. Helplessly, the heads watched: A parade of freaks
gimped and hobblefooted across the screen—nuke mutants.
See that baby attached to its mother's back? She's been running with it, carrying it piggyback along the Civil Defense
route mapped out in the phone book, and it got stuck to her
permanently. Werecoyotes—Los Angelenos are going to bond
with the coyotes that come down from the hills and cross
Ventura Boulevard into the suburbs of Studio City. Those mi-
notaurs used to be dairy farmers and cows, or rodeo riders
and toros. We're going to have a mutating generation. Nature
will sport at an accelerated rate. The reason we make bombs
is we want to play with Nature, so we throw bombs at her
to make her do evolution faster. Nature panics. She throws
handfuls of eyes at babies, and some sports will catch three or
four, and some none. See that baby with sealed eyes? Before
it was born, radioactivity zapped through its mother and lit
up her insides. Blind calves have already been born in Nevada.
Furry eyes protect them from too much light. Bees and flies
will especially suffer when the light hits their many eyes and
lenses. Nothing left but insects buzzing crazily. Those may
be our own electrified ashes we're looking at. We won't be
able to bear the touch of one another's fingertips on our faces.
We'll walk blindly through the streets of unrecognizable cities. We'll be able to hear, though. Those who can see must

keep talking and reading to the others, and playing music and ball games for them on the radio. After the bombs, there will be beautiful music, like the pod-picking scene in *Invasion of the Body Snatchers*. We won't have orchestras and bands; the music will be on tape. Fingers will melt together. Spadehands. Spadefeet walked across the screen. Languages will have a lot of vowels like "Aaaaaaah!"

"Remember in the days before the Comic Code Authority," said Wittman, "there was an E.C. comic book about this mad scientist who invented a potion that he gave to his big girl-friend, and she split in two. I don't mean like sides of beef. She became identical twins with red lips and long blue-black hair. Each woman was half the size she used to be, shorter but in proportion, still a normal enough height for a woman. Matter can neither be created nor destroyed. And clothes don't tear when anybody changes identities, according to comic books. Both of her had on a tight red dress and black high-heel shoes, just as before. The mad scientist takes one of her aside, and kills her. No tort case because there's still the other one alive. But that one wants to get even with him for killing her, see? She steals into the laboratory and downs some more of the drug. She's two again. Her plan is to kill him, and only one of her would have to pay for the crime. The two women gang up on the mad scientist, and he's fighting them off, when, because she o.d.ed on the chemicals, and because the two little women need reinforcements, they divide into four. No sooner does he kill one or knock one down than more form. Eight. Sixteen. Thirty-two. Geometric fucking progression. But, don't for-get, every time the women multiply, they become smaller, each one half her former size. Pretty soon, there are hundreds and thousands—sixteen hundred—thirty-two hundred—of these little women in red dresses swarming at him from all over the room. They're attacking from the shelves and tables and curtains and floor. He's tromping on them and swatting them, but they come at him again and again with these little bitty screams, 'Eeeeek. Eeeeek.'" Thousands upon thousands of tiny teeming black-heeled women—a natural for the snow show—engrossed the heads, stoned beyond speech.

Wittman, one of those who talks himself through fear, talked on: "The artists drawing the E.C.s were skin freaks.

They loved to draw viscous flesh dripping. Remember the one about the guy who asks a witch to destroy his evil half? 'I want to be good,' he says. She warns him, 'Are you sure that's what you want?' He can't see how you can go wrong getting rid of your evil self. The last panel took up a full page: He staggers into a mortician's office with his right side healthy, and his left side decaying and dropping worms. His word balloon says, 'Do something. I can't stand the smell.' And remember the funnybook with this girl who had blue doughnuts erupting almost out of her skin? Something at the amusement park had gotten her. I don't remember the story to that one. Only this picture of her in a bathing suit, lying in the sawdust, while in the background, the Ferris wheel and the merry-go-round and the hammer turn and turn." Blue rings—ringworms—the Worm Ouroboros—rolled across the screen.

"You're better than the storybook lady at the library," said Lance's voice. Some viewers laughed. We're regressing, all right. Those who'd learned to read with—because of—comic books pieced together this common past—"Do you remember—?" "I remember—": There were these parents who punish their kid by locking him in the closet. The kid screams repeatedly that there's a thing in there, but they shove him in. Pretty soon he makes friends with it. They hear the kid talking to somebody. "Were you talking to yourself in there?" they ask. No, the kid says, he has a friend named Herman, and they better not be bad to him anymore, or Herman will get them. Just for that, his parents throw him in the closet again. The kid's saying, "No! No! Herman's going to hurt you." And, in the second-to-last panel—oh, yeah, the dad's a butcher, and they live above the butchery—there's this meat grinder with its long handle up in the air, and ground human meat is pouring out of the blades, all over the table and down the legs to the floor. And the Keeper of the Crypt, the narrator-witch who gives the moral of the story, cackles, "Hee hee hee, kiddies, the next time you eat hamburger, don't look too carefully. You might find a gold tooth. Hee hee hee."

Those comic books were brainwashing us for atomic warfare that causes skin cancer and hamburger guts. They were getting us inured so we could entertain the possibility of more nuclear fallout. Chain reactions aren't that bad; that lady in the red dress doesn't go extinct. They tried to make us despair of ridding ourselves of evil. We ought to keep heightening our squeamishness and horror.

Snow jumped and stormed on the screen. Minds were exhausted of images. Most people stood up and left. Those remaining selected a regular channel and talked back to the commercials. Wittman left too.

On his move to the main room, pouring himself another wine, past his limit already—he was one of those Chinese who turn red on a few sips—looked drunker than he felt—Wittman gave his fellow guests the once-over. Strange, there are people you've never met to talk to but they keep showing up on your rounds. See that girl in maroon? She had had to go to the Student Health Center to have a lost Tampax retrieved. That was the revenge tale against her for being a coffee girl, bringing the professors coffee, black or with cream and sugar, and sitting in the front seat and crossing her legs back and forth. You get things on people with whom you go to the same school for four years. And that one over there came back from winter break with a Jackie nose, which probably changed her looks, he didn't know, he didn't know her that well. Her friends said, "Nose job." Over there was a mathematician he had met in Chem 1A lab. Remember the smell of the wooden shed? The first experiment was about sulfur, which you cooked, then went out to the screened porch and washed it down the drains. Year round, the place smelled of sulfur and eucalyptus trees. Charley Shaw had never turned him down when Wittman asked to borrow his notes to dry lab. Where are the Pan Am stewardesses? Lance often promised career girls; he tried to make new girls prettier and possible to talk to by rumoring that they were executive secretaries from Price Waterhouse, or receptionists from the P.G.&E.—"What do you think of the rate increase?"—or Clerk Typist II's from the Bank of California. Girls won't play along with being Playboy bunnies of the San Francisco club. "What?! Me? A bunny? I go to Merritt College." All they had to do was play along being Pan Am stewardesses, and even the weather conversation would get interesting. "How's the weather in Paris this autumn?" Wittman was awaiting that woman who could make up for herself a life of world travel, Oakland only a layover. Wait, the next stew to blow in over the Pole, he had ready for her ears his life-of-crime plan: Does her airline have a job opening for baggage handler? After luggage has cleared agricultural inspection and gone down the chute, he, as baggage handler, could put contraband into the suitcases, and at the other end of the flight, before customs, another baggage handler takes the stuff off. Would she care to work in cahoots with him? What is it he wants to smuggle? A few years ago, *Ulysses*, *Lady Chatterley's Lover*, *Tropic of Cancer*, *Howl*. She didn't happen to know, did she, the titles that the customs officers are currently on the lookout for? You prepare scripts with lines for yourself and lines for her, but you have to try them on somebody brand new you never saw before, and he semi-knew everybody here. And girls won't co-operate. Actually, girls don't care to play stewardess-and-passenger, nurse-and-patient, narc-and-head. "What languages do you speak? Don't you have to be fluent in three languages to fly America's flagship carrier?" And she says, "Who, me? You must be thinking of somebody else. I'm waitressing tables part-time, Jack London Square." You give them one more chance, "You look Pan Am, but you fly P.S.A., right? They're saying you're pit-stopping between the L.A. airport and Seattle. Is it true that air crews pirate movies, take the film cans off the planes from Hollywood, copy them, and send them on on the next flight?"

That information had come from Charley, with the degrees in math, who was moonlighting as a higher mathematician and an actor, brilliant enough to have time left over to go to parties and movies. His full American and stage name was Charles Bogard Shaw, C. B. Shaw okay on the marquee. Wittman was just thinking of him and here he was. "Seen any good movies lately?" he asked.

"No, man," said Wittman. "The movies have been bumming me out. I'm losing it. I can't take *West Side Story*. It's a bad movie, right? I mean, am I crazy, or is it like dog shit? I was losing it at *The Longest Day* too. I'm boycotting *Cleopatra*. Why don't you boycott *Cleopatra* too?"

The way a Buddhist life works is that when you need to learn something bad enough, the right teacher comes along. Charley was so good at seeing movies, he liked anything; he could "see the film behind the film." "I know the movie that will cure you," he told Wittman. "Have you heard of *The Saragossa Manuscript*? Each time I saw it, I broke through another layer of hoodwink. I am a changed person. It's been two years, and I continue changing. I'll try my best to tell you the movie. At the entrance into *The Saragossa Manuscript*, a French soldier is lost from his regiment. Explosions, cannon fire, music that sounds like *Don Giovanni*. He's running, falls, and slides down a hillside. He takes refuge in a Spanish Moorish villa; it may have once been used as an inn or a chapel but its people have fled, and dust lies everywhere. A leatherbound book, a tome, is sitting on a stand. Though this is a black-and-white movie, ask anybody who's seen it, and they'll tell you that the binding is red leather. The soldier blows off the dust, and, in the middle of war, begins to read. It is not the Bible. The camera goes inside the book: Once upon a time, there was a young soldier lost from his regiment. Cannon fire blasts the air, and cannonballs fall near him. The soldier is horrified—he is reading about himself. He runs from the villa, falls downhill, and loses consciousness. He awakes at the foot of a gibbet, and he is face-to-face with the upside-down faces of two hanged men, hung by the feet. Their heads swing on either side of his head. He escapes to a castle, where he meets a princess with long blonde hair. She gives him dinner at a table lit by candelabras of jeweled tapers and set with divining instruments. Across from her is her brother, a magician of the Cabala in a pointed hat and a dream robe that fills half the screen with crescent moons, stars, and alchemical symbols. The cabalist tells the soldier the mathematics of life and death and time. 'We are as blind men walking the streets of unknown cities.' The cabalist's beautiful sister tells a fairy tale about a dark princess—the camera goes inside her story: The dark princess, her sleeve rolled back on her beautiful arm lifting a heavy, branching candlestick, is leading a young soldier into a cave under a castle. She's somebody's sister, maybe his sister, and he falls in love with her."

Hold it. That about blind men walking the streets of unknown cities. The familiar City has been weirding out lately—flashes from a movie yet to be seen.

"The mathematics of life and death and time," said Charley,

"make sense numerologically, the way that the I Ching and the periodic table do."

"What else happens in the movie?" asked Wittman, remembering when we were kids and poor. The one kid who got to go to the show—Wittman had often been that kid; so had Charley—told both double features and all of the serials to a crowd of listening friends.

"I haven't told the best part," said Charley. "The young soldier lost from his regiment follows the light from a candelabra of many branches, carried by a dark princess, one of two princesses, twins. She takes him through catacombs, where he meets houris and fellaheens. The soldier makes love to one of the dark twins, then he meets her identical twin, and becomes very confused visually and morally. What is love? What is faithfulness when in love with a twin? One of these sisters comes to his room, which is inside the Moorish cave, and tells him that she will elope with a man with a beautiful beard. Such a man places a ladder up to her window. The ladder falls. The soldier rolls down the hill to the foot of a gallows. There is a pile of cannonballs and skulls. He screams and runs away, and takes refuge in the inn, where he reads, 'Once in a distant war . . .' Mozart-like music. Cannons boom. The soldier hurries to read to the end of this book about his life. But the movie doesn't end neat there or at the gallows. A lot happens—wars, Napoleonic, Carlist—between one gallows and the next, and you are not returning to the same place or the same time.

"I went to the movie the second time to count how many times the soldier finds himself on the hanging hill, and to note more exactly what propels him there. The ladder falls, the man with the beautiful beard does not become part of the life of the woman in the window. That ladder is a line where planes intersect. Cannons. Perhaps the young soldier dies. Perhaps he sleeps and awakes from dreams. Perhaps he is reprieved, and is cut down, not hung by the neck until he dies—one can't die hung by the foot. No two gallows scenes are alike—the scaffold is farther away or closer, higher, lower, approached from the top of the hill, the bottom, the side. There is one hanged man or many, perhaps depending on tight shot or wide-angle. Have you seen tarot cards? One of the cards is the Hanged Man, and he hangs upside down by one foot. He looks like an upside-down 4. I think the hanged men are tricksters. During other action, they come down off their gibbets and change their costumes and rearrange their poses."

At this point, a girl of the group by the fireplace came over and interrupted, asking Charley very seriously, "Excuse me, but some of us have dropped L.S.D. Will you be our guide? We should have gotten a guide ahead of time. You wouldn't mind, would you?" Those were the days when heads prepared their trips carefully, and chose a watchman who promises to remain straight. Just in case. At sea, a shore. They must have picked Charley because they overheard his articulateness in the midst of revels. If called upon, the guide tells the tour group his wisdom, such as the reality he's seeing back in the straight world. He sometimes takes their temperatures and blood pressures, and writes down anything memorable that is said. Such as discoveries. Mostly what you give them is your composure. No mind-fucking. "You can help too, if you feel like it." Wittman was invited too.

"I have yet to tell the best part. Good thing," said Charley, "that I saw *The Saragossa Manuscript* for the third time. The flick surprised me with logic. I love logic. I wouldn't have gone four times if I weren't getting intelligence. I was mapping the flow chart of the lifeplots. I counted how far inside a story inside a story inside a story inside a story we go. And suddenly I saw that everything made sense. Because that ladder falls, the levanter with the beautiful beard does not elope with the woman in the window. Between scenes and cuts and juxta-positions are strict cause-and-effect links. Nothing is missing. The main link chain, though, is spoken. You have to listen for it. There's a man who says to the soldier that the soldier in the book is the man's grandfather. At the end, it's that grandfa-ther as a young soldier who runs into the chapel/inn with the book under his arm, then runs out the door and up the hill. The first soldier is fighting in a nineteenth-century war. The grandfather is in a mid-eighteenth-century war. And *he* has a father, a man in a periwig, early eighteenth-century. We are connected to one another in time and by blood. Each of us is so related, we're practically the same person living infinite versions of the great human adventure. Now I see more of my father and my grandfather.

"Here's the best part: A man with a patch over one eye climbs up through a trapdoor. As he lifts his eyepatch, and emerges into the room, he crosses over into new and larger realms. I am like him. I came out of the Cinema, and as I walked home, passing the doorways on Shattuck Avenue, and looking up at the windows of the apartments above the stores, I understood that inside each door and window someone was leading an entire amazing life. A curtain moved, a lamp switched on—a glimpse of a life that's not mine. A woman walked from one room to another; if I ran up the stairs, I'd meet her and be in another life. After that movie, Shattuck Avenue is a street of an unknown city. I'm going to spend the rest of my life discovering the streets of unknown cities. I can follow anybody into a strange other world. He or she will lead the way to another part of the story we're all inside of."

The purpose of the population explosion is to make all the multitudinous ways of being human. We are like the water of the I Ching, fluxing and flowing, seeking and filling each crack of each stream, each ocean. Charley was beautifully keeping his charges from wigging out. He got them to be inhabiting the same movie. Here we are, miraculously on Earth at the same moment, walking in and out of one another's lifestories, no problems of double exposure, no difficulties crossing the frame. Life is ultimately fun and doesn't repeat and doesn't end.

"I wanted to go see *The Saragossa Manuscript* again, and appreciate it some more, but its run was over. I've been on the lookout for it ever since. It hasn't come back to the Cinema, and it's not in the film catalogs. Do me a favor, if any of you find it, call me collect no matter from where or at what time of night. I want to play my memory against its trickiness and its thickness."

Wittman felt showered with luck that poured from the air. He'd been given a gift; someone at a party has sought him out and told him *The Saragossa Manuscript*. He can't die. He can't die without seeing this movie. Life has more enjoyment to come. Yes, life is tricky and thick.

For years afterwards, Wittman kept asking after *The Saragossa Manuscript*. He helped start a film society that held Czech and Polish festivals, but did not find it. Nor did he meet anyone else who had seen it. It will be as if he'd hallucinated that movie, a dream he'd had when he was a younger and more stoned monkey. And Charley, who saw it four times in three nights, will not see the movie again. It will become his dream too. Some of those who heard the movie told at the fireside will think they'd seen it. All of them will remember a promise of something good among cannonballs and skulls.

Merciful guide. Heads that had sailed away were gently alighting. They had swum in and as star life, then ocean life. Then they had trogged onto land, and sensed dinosaurs, which were not bald grey as in museums; they had feathers of fiery colors. The hot wind that arose was a flock of dragons flying through the house. We had worshipped winged dragons—Mo'o the terrible lizard god, phoenixes, the Garuda, Horus. It does happen when journeying through a time of caveman wars that stoned heads will break out into fights, but everybody here was descended from tribes of benign vegetarians who had lived in gardening climates. Back in the straight world, in fact, we are citizens of a country that is militarizing us. We have to take barbiturates to keep from getting riled up. Now the wings of light were folding closed, and the heads were at word-understanding. Charley had guided them so well that the visionaries will come away talking story about this movie that they'd gone to. He set them to work applying their word-delight to finding a name to call a thing that the last time you saw it, it was in a hallucination or a story or on another planet or in a thought or dream but makes a crossover into the real world. "If we can name it, then we can more easily map the worlds," he said. "Remember the antique necklace in *Vertigo*? It was around the neck of Carlotta Valdes in the painting. Then Kim Novak as the unearthly Madeleine has it; she dies—and it shows up on Judy, just somebody taking a walk on Geary Street on her lunchbreak from Magnin's. What would you call that necklace?"

Oh, what a guide that Charley is, leading these wide-open feminine minds right past the Bates Motel with its shower and the desiccated mother in the rocking chair spinning aboutface. Unafraid, they were getting off on more examples of things that cross over.

"Yeah, you mean that thing that you see after you think the nightmare is ended. An extra chill goes up you because it proves that it had *happened*. A flower or a ring or a coin that's so small, it fell through a crack in the Twilight Zone."

"You think you're home safe, but sitting on the mantelpiece or falling out of your pocket is a souvenir from the nightmare."

"Yeah, what do you call that?"

"That's what you would call the torn slippers of the twelve dancing princesses who disappeared every night."

"And Cinderella's glass slipper."

"And the rose in Sheridan Le Fanu's *Blood and Roses*, the sign of the vampiress, Carmilla, played by Annette Vadim. On the airplane out of the Black Forest, the rose on Elsa Martinelli's traveling suit withers—she's the next vampiress."

What happens if *you* were to cross over? *You* were a Saragossa or a Slipper or an Ishi, last of his tribe.

A head opened his mouth wide at Wittman, as if he were his reliable Chinese-American dentist, and asked, "Hey, objectively, do my teeth look longer to you?"

Wittman got out of the way of any biting. He nodded, smiling, not to bum the man out. "Yeah, I guess your teeth may be somewhat longer, but I'm not certain because I didn't examine them earlier for comparison." It's morally wrong to throw a hand grenade into a mind helpless on L.S.D.

"You want to look in my mirrors?" said a helpful girl. "Right now you hardly have any pores. I mean your pores are very fine. You must be going through your baby stage. You want a look?" She stood up and circled in her India Imports mirror-cloth dress, and the acid heads peered at themselves in the many many mirrors. Whatever they saw did not freak them out—not fly's eyes, or pieces of ego, or bout of the uglies, or predator's teeth. The color of their coalescent aura was salmon-coral.

"There is no physical organ for guilt," said the cathedral head. "I am so glad. I have no physical organ for guilt. But I have a question. I want to know—I do feel clearly that I have a soul. There is such a thing as a soul. I feel it. I started to send it out of my body, but got scared and pulled it back. I may have thrown my soul out of kilter. How do you reconcile unity and identity?"

"Oh, you dear brave man," said a perfectly beautiful girl, who laughed a wonderful laugh. Wittman wished that he too were spiritually far enough along to ask such an advanced question.

How *do* you reconcile unity and identity? "You and the universe," said the girl, glad for each. "The universe and you."

Me and the universe. The universe and me.

At last, this party was getting somewhere, fluxing and flowing okay—when Wittman got bushwhacked. A chick who had been studying his face said, "Hey, I can see both his eyes. I'm looking at him from the side, and I can see either eye." What she say? I look like a flounder fish? Unless the right retort comes to him fast, this is going to hurt for years. Everybody was checking out his profile. Admiringly, right? "Thanks a lot," he said. Some retort. "Turn that way," said the rude girl. "See? Both eyes."

He turned full face to her. "I don't have much of a bridge," he said. What was he doing, justifying his nose. Here's her chance to say she meant a compliment. His eyes opened and shut from self-consciousness.

She said, "Can you see out of there? How can you see out of there?" She was squinting her own Caucasoid eyes to peer into his, allegedly, slitty eyes. And, god help him—instead of saying, "What is this Nazi shit?"—he explained the advantages of our kind of eyes. "They're evolved for use in desert and in snow. We don't need sunglasses." Which isn't true. We wear shades, we cool. "Finns have this kind of eyes too. Finnish people from Finland, whose language is related to Japanese." Oh, shut up, Wittman. The girl moved to his other side. "Come look," she said.

Beside him came Yoshi Ogasawara, a Nisei girl of Okinawan ancestry, whom he'd never asked out because his sexual hang-up was that he was afraid of smart pretty women. She had carried a double major of pre-med and ballet, and was now at the U.C. Med Center. Yoshi grabbed Wittman by the wrist, and announced to the world: "He's got an epicanthic fold, the same as I do. See?" He fell in hate with her. What's she taking him for? An anthro specimen. Homo epicanthus. Pushing her face forward to show her eyes, weighted down with false eyelashes, she was entertaining the party with our eyes. She batted two black brushes that were glued on with strips of electrician's tape, black eyeliner tailing out to here, blue-green mascara lids, and the lower lids rimmed with silver paste. Her eyelids were the puffy type, and the tight tape pressed into them at mid-puff; skin sort of lapped over the top edge of the tape, and made a crease per lid. She turned from side to side, giving everybody a look-see. With an index finger, she was pointing out her epicanthus, which is at the inner corner of the eye, when this (white) guy reached over and caught her finger, held it, and said, "You have beautiful eyes." It was Wittman ought to have done that. Why wasn't he the one to have leapt up, and taken her in his arms, and spoken up, "You are beautiful"? Because he can't stand her; her eyelids are like a pair of skinks.

"No. Oh, no, they're not," she giggled. "I'm going to have them operated on for double lids. I have single lids. These are single lids."

"What?" "You're what?" What? You people want two eyelids for each eye? Like an owl or a cat, one coming down, one across? Like an iguana? A shark? You don't mean you've only got one eye that's lidded. One of your eyes doesn't have a lid? They were white people, and didn't know what she was talking about. They do not have those phrases, "double lid" and "single lid," Yoshi. Those are our words. No, not ours, they are Japanese-American idioms, and just because they're English words, you think white people can understand them. A.J.A. words. Chinese are not that subtle to have a thing about a fold in the eyelid. But, yes, eyelashes are important—they are a primary sex characteristic. Minnie and Daisy would look exactly like Mickey and Donald if not for eyelashes.

She did not know when to stop. "The upper lid—see?— is prolonged. See? The top lid dips over the inner corner of their eyes." Their. "I can ski all day long without getting snow blindness."

Oh, for the right existential Zen act that would re-define everything. Change the world. No more Mr. Nice Guy. Why were these people listening to this stupid girl, as if she were leading them in sane discussion? She was opening her eyes wide, parting her fake eyelashes top row from bottom row.

"But we came from the Tropic of Cancer," he said. What a weak thing—a fact—to say. And his vow to always identify us as born here—broken. "Eskimos wear goggles," he said. "They have to cup their eyes with these goggles made out of wood that look like egg-carton cups with a slit across them."

What's he talking about Eskimo goggles? He'd made a move when he should be upsetting the chessboard.

"What is this Nazi anthropology?" he said.

She didn't get it.

"You're getting surgery on your eyelids?" asked a pitying white girl, the one who pointed out his flounder-fish eyes to the multitudes. "Are you having trouble seeing?"

The soon-to-be Doctor Ogasawara laughed. "No, I'm not having trouble seeing. I'm going to have my single lids cut, and a line sewn in. The plastic surgeon—Dr. Flowers of Honolulu, the best eye man—will remove some of the fatty tissue, and the lid will fold better. Double up."

Somebody asked why, and as she tried to answer—they were not understanding—disconcertedness overran her. How did she come to be using *this* as party conversation? "Because they—they don't like eyes like ours. We don't find my kind of eyes attractive. We like eyes that . . ." She was prating. "We like eyes like his." She pointed her finger at Wittman's face. "He's got double lids. I've got single lids." She brazened on. "You've got good eyelids, Wittman. He's got a fold. It's a common operation. It's one of the more simple cosmetic surgical procedures." She was looking to Wittman. Help. "*You* know," she said, appealing to him, Be my ally. "Oh, *you* know. *You* know what I mean."

"No," he said. "No, I don't." And walked. He left her there, kinky and alone. Sick seppuku chick slicing and sewing. Left her there with her shameful, unique deformity. He turned about, held his knuckles up to his eyes, and flapped his fingers at her. Like Daisy Duck eyelashes. Waved bye-bye with Daisy Duck eyelashes.

He followed flashing light and music to the room that in olden days was the front parlor—a strobe-light dance, like he first saw at "America Needs Indians." A lightshow dance at home. People breaking apart stroboscopically. Pieces hyperbright. My substantial body likewise—disappears and re-appears. A marionette who flies apart, scares kids, and suddenly reconnects. My parts dance whether I dance or not. Might as well dance. You move your crazy way; the light moves its crazy way. That hand or foot could be yours, it could be mine. Hands fanning. White sneakers stepping.

White socks winking. Fanning feet. A white sleeve. The other sleeve. Angel wings feathering. White duck legs jumping. A white bra through a dark blouse. The fast, cold light will zap through to our white bones. And reveal which beautiful girl to be the White Bone Demoness. Them bones them bones gonna walk around. Step into the dark—floor's there, no abyss. White oxfords doing the splits. Come and go. Go and come. Open and shut your eyes, change the periodicity. Can't tell your blink from its blink. White gloves slapclap and finger-wave. Wittman moved any which way, invisible in his dark suit, crossing his hands before his eyes, like an umpire. Safe. Safe. Dance any silly dance you want to. The light does the rhythm. And rocknroll too loud for talk. Free of partners. I'm dancing with her and her and nobody and everybody. Loose. Is that beautiful Nanci I see? Yes, her face laughing; a curtain of hair swings over it—nope, the back of her head. Twist over in her direction. Here's Sunny the bride coming at him in fragments, her hair a splendor of gold. "'Titania,'" said Wittman, "'dance in our round and see our moonlight revels.'" "Huh?" Hand to her ear. "Leave Oberon, and come with me!" Shout what you want. Dance how you want. Okay to make ass. "You've been married to that guy long enough. Run away with me." She shrugged to the music, and flitted away, designs on her butterfly sleeves—two swarms of fireflies. He reached for her hand, missed, having aimed for the hand at the wrong end of the fan-out. But there's beautiful Nanci again. "Hey!" he said. "Did I scare you the other day?! I'm sorry! That I scared you! Are you pissed at me?! I wanted—I want to show you what I'm like. You did too like my poems. Hey, I know your future. I can tell your future. You'll end up with me." His feet were stumbling; headwork and mouthwork throw the dancing off. She leaned to try to hear him, smiled him a stroboscopic smile, and flew away in a rush of afterimages. She almost stayed long enough to have been his dance partner. People seemed to chase one another—chase movie—all going in the same direction, then switch and run counterwise. Were they whacking one another with rolled-up newspapers? And who's that? A very tall, very black Black man and a very tall, very blonde woman, both wearing street-fighting leathers, stood arrogantly in the center, the same couple, the same pose, at the Democratic Party fundraiser chez Mitford-Treuhaft. Daring you to call them out. Wittman moved toward them, but they were gone, went into a room where they could be lit and appreciated better. There's his old friend and enemy, Lance, looking down on me, no job, poor poems, square trips. Heads flickered by, and on the faces of the flickering heads were flickering expressions. Don't take them personally—am I keeping my discomfiture hidden? Stay very cool. Don't get caught with exertion or envy or smugness or any ugliness on your face. Nor let the light cut to a smile held tight too long, turning fake. A set of teeth were smiling on the floor, clackety-clack Hallowe'en choppers. Who choo laffin' at, boy? The cat disappeared, his smile remained. Trick or treat. Is that a mask or is it your face? Ha ha. Whose hand is that? Doing what to whom? "Suspicious, Mr. Chan?" "I smell foul play, Birmingham Brown." Whose foxy eyes narrowing at me? Wait a second. Just because eyeballs slide back and forth does not mean that conspiracy is afoot. Once paranoia starts, it keeps on coming. Okay, let me have it. Get it over with. A glower of thick eyebrows—do not react back—does not have to be a hate-stare. Keep my own face empty of suspicion and calculation. A mouth screwing up does not have to signify dis-approval. A lot of people have piggy eyes and piggy noses and curly lips and flashy eyeteeth who mean no harm. Mugs are at large. No scene to comprehend expressions, and make use of them. We are blushing chameleons, ripping through the gears of camouflage trying to match the whizzing environment. Hang on. Hang on. Lobsang Rampa, who may not be a fake, says we will see monster faces, such as the ox face, on our way to death. Let them go by, he says. As Macbeth should have let pass the heads of kings without doing anything about them. Sunny winks at me. Interestedly? Lance glows greenly. Sunny hiding. Ah, sequences. Oh, no, a shmeer on my face. Don't look, everybody. Re-arrangements. Control my slidy features. Put the old face in neutral. Hold it. Is there a neutral, or does it come out bored or tired or tightass? Cocksure, ha ha. And there's the girl from the bus. Certainly didn't turn into Queen Kristine. The light jerked her away.

Flashes and music were beating together now. Wittman was getting used to things, yeah, his feet in step, the old bod bopping okay, and his monkey mind going along. His heart was beating with the bass. Go with it. If you fight it, you will shoot off on a long slow bad trip all by yourself, untethered like *Destination Moon*. He went monkeying around the room, fancy feet making intricate moves, multiplexed by the light. Pardon that foot. That's okay. That's okay. Somebody else's unruly white bucks. Might as well be mine. We are as face cards being shuffled, and my fanning arms are merging into the images of the fanning arms of others. And the world is in sync. In sync at last. God Almighty, in sync at last. Feet go with drums. Heart booms to bass. My pulse, its pulse. Its pulse, my pulse. Ears, eyes, feet, heart, myself and all these people, my partners all. In sync. All synchronized. A ballet dancer and an m.s. spastic—no different—O democratic light. Innards at one with the rest of the world. And why not when we're doing the twist, and Chubby Checker does the twist, "Let's twist again, like we did last summer," and the light is a strobe, and a strobila is a twisty pine cone. All right. All right. And—. And—. And—. And then—. Bang bang. Bang bang. But—. But—. But—. Banga. Banga. Lost. Found. Lost. Found. Gotcha. Gotcher teeth. Gotcher face. Boom. Boom. Bomb. The Bomb. Bomb flash. Bomb flash. In what pose will the last big flash catch me? What if. This were. Bomb practice? We're training to dig flashes. And my fellow man and woman aglow. Like fast frequent pulsations of radioactivity. Why is the beat so even? If the bright intervals equal the dark intervals, like the black-and-white gingham on a Balinese butt, then are Good and Evil at an exact standoff? Paranoid again. Like we were last summer. What if Chubby Checker does not mean us well? What if Chubby Checker is up to no good? This is not Chubby Checker. Why is this tape going on for so long? Whose music is this? What. If. Music. Can. Kill. Evil drummer finds your heartbeat, and drums it. You dance along, drumbeat and heartbeat and feet together, like harmony; but what if all of a sudden—a last bang—the drummer stops, and stops your heart? But this set—ominous undertoning bass—goes on and on. This follow-along body is speeding. A race to the death. The End? The End. Is near. Ha ha. Fooled you. Longest coda in the world. To tear the heart from its mooring arteries. Hearts will flop like frogs all over the floor.

The music, however, ended before anything like that

happened. The strobe lights wrought craziness. Survivors talked over what happened. Wittman headed for normal light.

But suddenly a whistling started up, higher and higher, then a supersonic jet war fighter plane crashed through the sound barrier right there inside the house—the fucking house taking off. People ducked to the floor, backed against the walls, dived under tables. Hung on to the shag rug. Sound waves pushed on them, and held them flattened. What the fuck was that? Oh, my god, they've gone and done it. This is it. Blown up the planet. Nothing left but noise. The Bomb. Has set off the Earthquake. California at last breaking loose from North America. The Rad Lab—on the fault. Blown. And resonating booming further sound. People laughed and giggled, holding their faces. Some of them might have been screaming—you could scream all you want, nobody could hear you—opening their mouths like the Munch painting. And the skull and the planet split into bowls of mush brains.

What it was were the sounds of World War II playing full blast out of the loudspeakers, of which there were twelve, hooked up to the roof and the corner eaves, engines for propelling the house away. Sound effects you can check out of the public library. Mixed with the sounds of a takeoff as you lie in the grass among the seagulls and the egrets and the jackrabbits next to the runway at the San Francisco International Airport—and this jumbo jet pulls up off the ground almost right over you, hair and feathers blowing, and just about pulls the soul right out of your body. The wind. The size. The steel. The speed. The noise. Acid flash. Acid flash. That mixed with the roars of Fleishhacker Zoo at feeding time. When you thought back on the tape, you could distinguish mortar shells from rifle shots, fighter planes diving, hand grenades, machine-gun fire, and the A-bomb at Nagasaki and the A-bomb at Hiroshima, and—finale—those bombs over-dubbed in multiplex bombilation. The boom of the Bomb, then subsequent booms, the resounding, rolling aftershocks—roaring, roaring, roaring. We are all hibakushas. The guests were thinking, "All right. Enough already. I got the joke"—and it went on and on and on.

Suddenly it was over. In the silence, people kept explaining things to one another. The amps on the roof make a giant resonator of the house. You can get sound effects from studio connections in Hollywood, the A-bombs from the Oakland Public Library. Direct from the actual bombs to your ears. "That was the Bomb." "Is that all the loud it is? It must have been louder than that."

Nobody heard police sirens. Red and blue lights swiveled onto walls and ceiling. Like the invasion of the Martians in *War of the Worlds.* Guests hiding at the windows listened to Lance sweet-talking the cops. Other guests were leaving, thank you, thank you, goodbye, taking zombie steps past the paddywagons. A two-paddywagon party. One of the policemen was asking him to go inside and bring out people who were breaking the law. Cops without warrants are like vampires; they can't cross the threshold unless you invite them. Lance asked, "Such as which laws, Officer? I didn't notice any unusual misbehavior, sir, but I'll co-operate, and look around." Then he was inside looking out the window at the police asking another person to go find *him*—"about yay tall, business suit." People were going in, coming out, like the townspeople in *Invasion of the Body Snatchers*, unloading the truck of pods, as Kevin McCarthy and his girlfriend spy from behind the blinds. Lance went out there from another direction, and said, "We withdraw all charges. Sorry, we shouldn't have called you. As you can see, no problem, no trouble-makers." And so, toward morning, it became a quiet party.

A girl, who was sitting at the top of the stairs, her sandaled toes playing peek-a-boo, was saying by heart for a crowd ranged on the steps below her every verse of "The Shooting of Dan McGrew."

> *"There's men that somehow just grip your eyes,*
> *and hold them hard like a spell;*
> *And such was he, and he looked to me like a*
> *man who had lived in hell. . . ."*

She looked right into Wittman's eyes—chose him out—and he hung over the railing, listening to the whole thing, taking a liking to her cornball ways. She stood and stuck her elbow out, the jagtime ragtime kid taking five beside his upright 88. A stranger staggers into the Malamute saloon, and buys drinks for the house. She lifted her chin, as if showing off an Adam's apple. She's knocking back a shot of hootch—"the green stuff in his glass." She brushed the swing of fringe on a buckskin sleeve, sat down, and made talon hands—the stranger clutches the keys and plays that piano.

> *"Were you ever out in the Great Alone, when the*
> *   moon was awful clear,*
> *And the icy mountains hemmed you in with a*
> *   silence most could hear;*
> *With only the howl of a timber wolf, and you*
> *   camped there in the cold,*
> *A half-dead thing in a stark, dead world, clean*
> *   mad for the muck called gold;*
> *While high overhead, green, yellow, and red,*
> *   the North Lights swept in bars?—*
> *Then you've a haunch what the music meant*
> *   . . . hunger and night and the stars."*

Goddamn. She knows me, and she wants me bad. The way she's looking at me, and none other, she understands, and she likes me, a heartbreaker and a rover. That's me all over. She's holding her hands over her heart, and beholding me like I'm the one breaking it.

> *"There's a race of men that don't fit in,*
> *A race that can't sit still.*
> *So they break the hearts of kith and kin,*
> *And they roam the world at will."*

That's me. She knows me and my timber wolf Steppenwolf ways, and sympathizes. She's melting my loneliness. Four years of Chaucer and Shakespeare, Milton, and Dickens, Whitman, Joyce, Pound and Eliot, and you shoot me right through the heart with Robert W. Service.

Okay, so Bloomsbury did not recite Robert Service. Neither did Gertrude Stein's Paris salon. Neither did the Beats. But Wittman Ah Sing's friends—the most artistic people he knew how to find anywhere—his generation—did. Wittman had been there at Berkeley when Charles Olson read—and drew, spreading wide his arms, a map of the universe on the chalkboard—circles and great cosmic rings. And Lew Welch dangling his legs off the corner edge of the platform and nodding in rhythm, yeah, yeah, "Ring of bone. Where ring is the sound a bell makes." And Brother Antoninus out of St. Albert's for the night, some other monk ringing the angelus bells. A Black lady from the audience questioned "lily white," and Olson answered her with a lotus vision, and Ginsberg, the social realist, had had to explain to him about politics. That's how far Olson went into his created world. And Wittman Ah Sing had been there in the room too, though nobody knew it. It was okay that nobody knew; he was just a nobody kid. He had seen for himself what an older generation of poets was like. They had not tried to include Young Millionaires and Pan Am stewardesses.

> "They range the field and they rove the flood,
>   And they climb the mountain's crest;
> Theirs is the curse of the gypsy's blood,
>   And they don't know how to rest.
>
> If they just went straight they might go far;
>   They are strong and brave and true;
> But they're always tired of the things that are,
>   And they want the strange and new. . . ."

Shrewd-eyed—Maria Ouspenskaya, "My son, Bela, has the curse of the werewolf."—the girl at the top of the stairs caught and opened the hand of a lucky one of her admirers, and wrote in it the lines of his life and fate. It's hard to tell, mock-corny or real corny. A rebel, reciting fervently what we're supposed to not like. Come now, "The Men Who Don't Fit In" does feel better than "The Waste Land." The brainwashing of a too hip education is wearing off. She sounds so valiant, and one feels so sad. "Ha, ha!" she shouted. If Wittman were not shy, he'd say along with her in duet:

> "Ha, ha! He is one of the Legion Lost;
>   He was never meant to win;
> He's a rolling stone, and it's bred in the bone;
>   He's the man who won't fit in."

Her audience clapped, whistled. Wittman too. She's our brave
queen. We're such geniuses, we know how to like anything.
The hall light shone on her, an overhead light that cast shadow
bags and hag noses on all but her; on her, a halo, a rainbow. Look at her, lifting her hair with both hands. Hair's so
heavy—let me just lift the gold chain-link weight of it off my
neck. Oh, my burdensome hair. She sat up, the hair rippling as
she leaned toward us.

Wittman held out his hand, bidding her descend the stairs
to him, but she shook her head and hair, and sat amid her
court. He climbed over the railing and up the stairs to the
glimmering girl. She turned away, her hair a golden curtain.
He was reaching down to draw it aside when she threw back
her head—her hair fell back—and they were looking each
other in the eyes—he tall above her, and she feminine on the
floor below him. Gazing into her hazelwood eyes, he sat beside her. He pushed aside her hair, broke that hazelwand gaze,
cupped her ear, and whispered into it, whispering much, until
the others, left out, left the two of them alone. Eat your heart
out, Nanci Lee.

O possibilities of what to say. Going over this later, Wittman,
old with wandering, thought what if he'd done another one of
the shticks that was flickering in the brightening air, would
they have loved one another better? Everything counts;
no time off ever, not on weekends, certainly not at parties.
Go ahead, speak poetry to her. Seriously. Let her laugh. He
would be grave. When in doubt, sez Dostoevsky or Tolstoy
or Thomas Mann, always do the most difficult thing. Say to
her your favorite by-heart poem, "The Song of Wandering
Aengus." All the way through with no jokes. What's the use of
having poems in your head if you can't have scenes in your life
to say them in? And nobody to say them to? Who knows when
the chance will come again. Here's a girl who has said poems,
and has made a way possible for someone such as oneself to say
poetry back to her. Play with her a love scene in verse. And at
the same time educate her to a better poet (Yeats) than Robert
Service. She won't take Aengus' vow for Wittman's vow. The
silver-trout girl doesn't stay. So go ahead, Wittman, bring her
the silver apples of the moon, and the golden apples of the sun,
and kiss her lips, and take her hands.

But when he breathed and talked into her erogenous ear, he reserved "The Song of Wandering Aengus" for later, or for another. He praised her looks. "Thy rose lips and full blue eyes," he said. "Alfred, Lord Tennyson," he said, giving credit. He moved away from her ear; he held her hands, and beheld her mouth. He could make a wisecrack about the rosy swollen mouth on thy face like the elsewhere mouth that will leave a trail-spoor of silver snail slime. He could teach her some new words, get her to say, "Enwoman me, Wittman."

He asked her her name. Taña De Weese. He will be able to find her again with an ad in the personals of *The Berkeley Barb*—"Taña, meet me on the barricades."

She asked him his name, and he gave her his first name and last name. If you give your last name, she can find you again. He let go her hands, stood, and galloped down the stairs. Leave before you fuck things up.

Oh, it's a good party now. There's a beautiful girl in hot pursuit of him. Yeah, let her come after him.

One more task to do, and the party will be complete: Clear up some friendship karma. Every get-together can be an occasion to have it out with a friend. The best parties end in a free-for-all.

And there in an alcove were Lance and Sunny, reigning side by side on the window seat. Our emperor and empress. Wittman sat down on the side next to Sunny.

"Make any good contacts?" asked Lance. "Are you having a good time?" asked his consort.

"How many people have asked *you*, 'Are you having a good time?'" asked Wittman.

"One or two."

"When people are going around polling one another, 'Are you having a good time?,' they're not getting *into* the party." He looked across her to say to her husband, "I think that it is fucked to make contacts rather than to make friends. I don't like contacts. What do you say to one? 'Of what use are you to me?' 'What are you offering?' 'To what or to whom is your end connected?' A party is a party. Or do you throw these parties for the sake of business deals? You go around assessing our connections? Why cultivate me? What good am I to you and your associates?" Wittman meant that he didn't want to do business whatsoever. There has got to be a way to live and never do business.

Lance only laughed. "Wittman. Wittman. You have to be subtle. You haven't been bruiting it among others that you've been fired, have you? Sunny and I have been keeping your secret. You do know that you can't get a job without you already have a job. You're not moving fast enough up your own organization, you go after a promotion horizontally. You never admit, 'I don't have a job.' You don't have to talk business at all, especially not at my party." Bidness a-tall. "You relax, have a good time, make friends, and at a future date, when they hear of an opening, they think of you. Make friendships longterm, Wittman. The frat brothers, or in your case, the co-op guys will pay off."

"I didn't go through Cal to make contacts."

"Of course you didn't. You would've gone to a private school for that. Stanford or Back East."

"Lance, you're using a tone on me, aren't you? Will you quit toning on me, and answer me something? There's a matter I've wanted to ask you about for years."

"Held it in all that time, huh?"

"When do you think you first met me? From what time do you date our acquaintanceship?"

"From school."

"Which school?"

"Cal."

"No. Before that. You don't remember meeting me in grammar school? I remember you. You were taidomo no taisho—leader of the kids. No. No. Try wait. General. General of the kids. You got to be taidomo no taisho in the camp. You led your army out of the camps and into the schoolyard, and beat the shit out of me. You don't remember ganging up on a tall skinny transfer who didn't fight back, and beating the shit out of him? That was me."

Shaking his head, Lance looked at Wittman, studied his face, but he looked at everyone with that intensity. In Japanese movies, noble knights, urban businessmen, peasant clowns, women—intense. In real life, Japanese-Americans don't relax. Sansei born and raised in P.O.W. "relocation" camp. He's looking at me with ex-con's eyes.

"You don't remember a Chinese kid that was in class for a while, and suddenly disappeared? My parents moved around a lot. I didn't get the knack of forming gangs. You don't remember socking a lone Chinese? There was just one Chinese boy. That was me. I got in trouble for fighting, and you didn't. You had witnesses. I think I'm running across members of your gang. Some of them were at Berkeley, grown. There are some here. None of you recognize me, huh?"

"I'm taidomo no taisho still yet. I have been and will always be the adult among children. I don't remember you. Are you accusing me of beating you up?"

Now what? Forgotten. Why is it that Wittman remembers others, such as check-out clerks, bank tellers, the coins-and-slugs collector at the laundromat, bus drivers, teachers, fellow students (many gone from parties because of graduation), but they don't remember him? Don't back down. "Yeah. And fighting dirty, and you continue to pick on me. I want to know, are we having a continuous fight that you started at Lafayette Grammar School? And, do you want to finish it now?"

"So I was a kid and didn't know better. Who wasn't? I don't fight dirty."

"You had a gang, and I was by myself."

"If you think I did that, I apologize. You want to fight, we'll fight. Do you want to fight right now, or do you want to go out in the alley?" Is there an alley, or is he being ironic about alley fights? I am not good at irony anymore. Sunny looked like she was being entertained, like they were dueling over her.

"I am less interested in hitting you than in your admitting what you have been up to all these years. You don't remember a kid who could juggle any three things? Erasers? Apples? Knives? Chomping the passing apples? That was me."

"Wittman, have you been smoking too much? You're really paranoid, man."

"The best way to help out a paranoiac is to tell him the truth about whether somebody's after him. You jack memories around, Lance, they turn on you psychologically. What you did, taidomo no taisho, you roasted goats, such as myself. You're good at defining an enemy while the rest of us have our thumbs up our asses, which is the position of most people on most topics. Whoever comes along and tells them what's going on, what the topics are, that there are topics, that a war is on, that's the one who gets to be leader. I've got your strategy, huh? You harness the polymorphous paranoia that floats around all the time, and you rule. I'm not just bringing up something that happened during kidtime, but what you do to us now. I know your m.o., man. Every school I went to, a Sansei Nihonjin, dressed in the right clothes, driving the right car, speaking with no accent, like you're dubbed, became the top bull and took over the junior prom and the senior ball and the assemblies and the student-body elections. At Cal, I recognized you right off, studying in the oriental section of the library at the table with the A.J.A. football player and the two A.J.A. girls on the pompon squad and the two Oski Dolls who were Chinese-Americans. Are you sure you didn't recognize me, the one integrating the other end of the main reading room? I noticed the way you dealt with her kind." A thumb at Sunny. "You take their shit like they're not dishing out any. You act like you're having the best time no matter what kind of racist go-away signals they're flashing at you. And you keep it up and keep it up until they, having a shorter attention span, think that you belong all along. I spot your technique, see? You A.J.A.s are really good at belonging, you belong to the Lions, the Masons, the V.F.W., the A.M.A., the American Dental Association. That's why they locked you up, man. They don't like you taking over the dances and getting elected Most Popular. (While we Chinese-Americans are sweating Most Likely to Succeed, and don't spend money on clothes, or on anything.) At camp you learned to tapdance and to play baseball, and you came out and organized everything, parties, labor unions, young millionaires."

"So? So you're envious?"

"So don't be such a conformist. Don't be such a smug asshole."

"Smug?" said Lance. "Asshole?" said Sunny.

"You better watch being so smug. That's how you're coming across, you know that? I bet you think you're coming across menacing. Well, you've turned smug. No, no. You've always been smug. You had that same smug face as a kid."

"Maybe he's got something to be smug about," said the wife.

"What are you smug about? Everything, huh? Once taidomo no taisho, general of the kids, and now the one who throws the parties, attended by all kinds. Working for the government. Asking what else your country can do for you. Your G.S. number. Your business friends. Your Victorian house and your sofas. And your wife. And your life."

And each and every one of them a samurai. Knights of the chrysanthemum crest, or the hollyhock, or the wave and sun. They didn't come wretched to this country looking for something to eat. They'd been banished by the emperor or Amaterasu herself after taking the losing but honorable side in a lordly duel. A.J.A.s have sword names: Derek, Dirk, Blade, Gerald, Rod, Lance. Damocles, ha ha. Bart, probably a gun name. There's five or six Dereks in a school, another five or six Erics, and the rest are Darrell or Randall. "Eric" probably means "epee" or "snee" in Anglo-Saxon or Viking. Snee Sakamoto, ha ha.

"Let's go outside," said Lance. "I want to beat the shit out of you again."

They stood up, and walked, talking. "I want you to understand why you're going to get it," said Wittman. "This isn't just because of your childhood shittiness. I've let you get away with too much lately. Like when you organized the whole party to humiliate that oenologist guy from Davis. Your husband," he explained to Sunny, "emptied a good bottle of wine and put Red Mountain into the bottle with the expensive label and the price sticker still on it. We watched while the poor shmuck poured this rotgut into a stem glass, and stuck his nose into the glass, and swished the wine around in his mouth. We listened to him pronounce wine words about the nose of the full-bodied bouquet. And then, you showed him the Gallo Red Mountain jug, and everybody hooted him, gave it to him good. The worse thing was he tried to laugh and act as if *he* had been trying to put *them* on. That was a sick thing to do, Lance, and I should have stood up for that guy at the time. I should have said that the French love Gallo. Or I should have warned him. But I let you fuck him over. You prepped us to ask him, 'Has that wine got legs?' It was so premeditated."

Lance held his stomach with laughter at the memory of that scene. "*He* was smug, that wine major with a specialty in cabernets. He said the wine had 'cello tones.' Ha ha. 'Cello tones.'"

"Another time I should have done something was when you were living in that boarding house on Euclid with the rest of the A.J.A.s. Sunny, did your husband tell you that he and his buddies nailed Russell Saito inside his room? It was a team project; they surrounded his room, and hammered two-by-fours and plywood across the windows and door. You could hear him in there for three days banging with books and shoes, and crying, and begging about how he was missing his midterms. And asking about taking a crap. He said, 'Who's out there? Is there anybody out there?' You reduced him, Lance. You shouldn't have done that. I should have let him out. Sunny, have you gotten your A.J.A. Zen? 'If the nail sticks up, hammer it down.'"

"Look, Russell Saito appreciates what I did for him. He could've moved out of Euclid, he didn't. He became known. He's going to be the first Japanese-American governor of California one day, you watch. Wittman, I didn't know you noticed all this stuff. You've got an eye for human nature. Very good."

Have you ever met a Japanese who wasn't a madman underneath? And each one far out in a different direction, the girls too. They don't get ordinary the more you know them.

"Go on," said Lance, sitting down on the rug. "Go on." Wittman and Sunny sat down with him. Get on with the unfinished bidness.

"There's a rumor about you, that you keep a list of friends in order of best to worst. Is that true?"

"Is that what they say about me? That I have a friends list?" He was delighted, and eager to hear more about his image.

"It's pretty childish, Lance, to keep track of who's your best friend and who's your second-best friend. The only people you ever hear anymore who talk about their best friend are department-store girls." He wouldn't mind knowing what number he himself was on the list but they couldn't torture such a question out of him.

Actually, he thought of Lance as his best friend, though lately he hardly saw him except at parties. When they hit the streets as a team, he could ass off, call "Pomegranates" at the girls from in front and behind. One of his kid vows, and it had been a drug vow too, was: Always tell people before you or they die that you like them. He didn't see how he was ever going to tell Lance about his oft-times being the only good friend. Remember how, unless you were totally out of it, everybody had a partner? The problem with being Lance's sidekick was that Lance got to be Don Quixote and Wittman was Sancho Panza, or, rather, Pancho to Lance's leadership role as the Cisco Kid. Wittman didn't like being Sancho or Pancho or Boswell or Tonto. Another vow was that from now on all friendships be friendships among equals. Lance had bragged about his two hundred closest friends. Who, now that I'm grown, is my best friend? Yeah, it's better not to have best friends anymore—the time has come for community.

"You have to be able to take red-ass in this world, Wittman." Speaking as a friend, for my good.

"I don't like the times you came to parties dressed as an S.S. youth. What was the point of that?"

"I was playing Tokyo-Berlin Axis. Everybody told me I looked exactly like Hitler, and that they had never noticed the resemblance before, how could they have missed it." He laughed at people who are easily fooled.

"But they shouldn't have liked it. What were your motives? Satirizing Nazis, or wanting to be a Nazi? Were you trying to offend people? Giving us a chance to get straight with Hitler? Were you trying to flush out Nazi-lovers, or what? I was offended." Shit. Admitted to having had my dumb feelings hurt.

"I look good in a Nazi uniform. Girls are very turned on by Nazi uniforms." ("We are not," said Sunny. "No, we aren't.")

"And you hate them for it. You bring stuff out in people, and then you scoff at them. Are you like sociopathic?"

"I may be, Wittman. I've considered that. We geniuses who are more intelligent than ninety-nine point nine percent of the population of the U.S., and hence the world, have to adjust to a lonely life among stupidos. We have to live among them, and help them out. They're our responsibility. They're a real pain to me." Wittman was overawed by anyone who achieved more pain than he did, given average American conditions.

"Look. To be perfectly honest with you," said Lance, "I don't remember anything that happened to me before junior high school. My memories start at about seventh grade." He *is* a sociopath, the kind that doesn't admit to dreaming in his sleep. "If it was me that beat you up, I don't remember."

He really doesn't remember. My friend is in that much pain that he has to forget almost half his life. "The camps, huh? It must have been the camps did that to you." You know that an A.J.A. has taken you on as a trusty friend if he'll give you a word or two about "camp" and "the years we were away." They've stomped the bad years deep down, like they never happened. Wittman, who didn't forget anything, was struck with pity and envy.

"My memories of kidtime events," said Lance, "come from people who insist that they eyewitnessed me. A neighbor lady—she lived in the next horse stall at Tanforan—said I took a shit at the base of a flagpole. I did that regularly even though an M.P. with a rifle warned me not to. She said, 'You were a free boy.' See? I have a history of protest that goes back to toilet-training time, taking a public dump under the American flag. I can sort of remember looking up at stars and stripes and out at a desert with barbwire all around. Hey, I can tell you exactly when my memory started up again. I'm going to tell the both of you now, my wife, and my best friend, about when the cameras of my life began to roll." You had to admire the guy's daring; he was not afraid to declare, "You are my best friend." And disarm you.

"The moon will be full soon," he said, and, yes, over his shoulder the gibbous moon was mooning them through the window. Hoo haw. "There was blood on the full moon. But I have a new plan to wipe its face clean. I know what to do now. It's come to me what to do. Let me show you."

Lance Kamiyama led them out of his cobwebby house; they followed him around the veranda to the back porch, down the stairs, and across the grass to the end of the yard, where two willow trees grew together above a trickle of a stream. "This stream is part of the system that fills the lake at Mills College. We have crayfish—edible crayfish. I'll cook some for you one of these days. Here I will build a shrine—this is the site—for the fox spirit beside a running stream. Do you know that church they're remodeling in Oakland J-town? The to-rii—do you know what that is? like a gate or door by itself,

not particularly *to* anything—two uprights, like goalposts—
you've seen it, where they hang the thunder god's rope with
white paper clouds and sometimes lanterns—the torii has been
stolen, or lost in construction rubble. The fox is on the run
again. How it came to be in Oakland: Samurai on their way
to becoming American ronin saw a red fox sail with them as a
passenger aboard the *Arizona*. He was not in a cage or a bag.
He walked up the gangplank on his hind legs, which showed
beneath his forest-green robe. There were flaps in the hood
for his ears, and his snout stuck out of the cowl. For most
of the journey, he stood at the prow with his snout pointing
east, that is, toward the West. One paw rested on top of the
other on his new cane. The ship sailed under the Golden Gate,
which is the same color he is, international orange.

"In the U.S., he cut the first notch into his cane—Issei.
It was not an old cane with seals and stamps from climb-
ing Mount Fuji and from his other pilgrimages. No more
Japanese stuff. We start numbering here. From One. Our
parents are Two. Nisei. I'm Sansei. There are already a few
Yonsei. American generations. What for we're keeping track?
At Gosei, will something ultimate happen? Four to get ready,
and five to go.

"In 1941, they had a fox hunt. Executive Order 9066 came
down. Barbwire hatchmarked the shadows of foxes running
through tule fog. A Buddhist church that got an okay from
the government as not pro-Japan hid him. For disguise, they
shaved his head and hung a chain of beads around his neck.

"The fox is without a home; I'm without a home. My mama-
san took me up to my room and shut the door—I thought she
was going to tell me about sex. She told me that I had been
raised by whites. She showed me photographs. She wasn't lying. She had newspaper clippings about a mass family murder.
Done with a plantation machete. Come over here. Look at the
house through these long willow leaves. I escaped alive. I saw
the moon shine red through hanging leaves. There was blood
on the full moon."

What is he telling me? Is this a confession of murder? Or has
he spilled a plan for future doing? His family is dead for real or
in his heart? Had he, as a scared child, run out into the willows
to get away from the machete killer? Or did he mean, with a

machete in his hand, he crept up to the house? To cut down his white foster mother, or his mama-san. The killer son. A murderer's confession would sound like this, evading or trying to transcend the worst, that is the actual macheteing. Wittman wanted to say, "What? Will you speak up please?" But if you ask for clarification, you'll interrupt the murderer into silence. You can't say, "What?! You did what?! Murder?!" Yes, a confession to murder would be part of a civilized conversation. Wow, a chronic mass murderer of not just one but maybe two families, a white family and an A.J.A. family. An Eagle Scout business-suited type like Lance, that's the type that kills his whole family, and the neighbors say, "He was such a quiet boy." They think that being quiet and being good are the same thing. Sunny's face was avid with sympathy. She was participating in cosmopolitan life-and-death events.

"Why?" said Wittman. But to be able to answer why, a criminal has to have done the highest philosophical thinking. Usually you have to be satisfied with a money or sex motive. "What would anyone have against your parents?" Lance must be exaggerating. Wittman had met his mother, a Japanese-American church lady in a pillbox hat, gloves, and a camel-hair coat.

"That A.J.A. family mortified me. I drew swastikas on fences all over the neighborhood. I didn't mean Nazis. I had a box of colored chalk, and it was fun to get those angles right. The mama-san and papa-san made me walk back through town with rags and clean off the fences, and apologize. Gomenasai. They followed me, and if anybody came out to see what we were doing, they bowed. Gomenasai. Gomenasai. They took a picture of me bowing.

"To make memories, I need documentation. At every house, there was a *Life* magazine open at the same picture: a jap soldier with his chest and stomach cut open, the slashes in the shape of a cross, according to the caption. His guts had been pulled out, intestines and heart placed at the center of the cross. It wasn't that horrible, really, unless you read the caption. He looked asleep with a smoking white fluff on his stomach; it was sort of pretty like a flower."

Wittman planned to survive the weekend, then go to the library and look up newspapers for—when?—1953?—a mass murder by machete. And the weather report would have what phase the moon was in.

"They've got a death wish out for me," said Lance. "The mama-san and papa-san held an autumn service to my memory. You weren't invited? You didn't mourn me? From school, they invited the registrar, who didn't show, and our housemother, who did. You don't remember a fall semester when I didn't come back from summer vacation? You didn't miss me? I didn't meet you yet, Sunny, and we might never have met. There's a stone doll of me in the churchyard among the other rock babies with red bandanna bibs. Tonight, I'm going to tell you where I was instead of dead. I was traveling to learn if ex-Japanese in other countries call themselves Issei, Nisei, Sansei, or if those are American words. I was sitting in the sun on one of the thousands of Molucca-Sulu islands, and looking out at the next island. For the fun of it, I was about to try swimming to it when a copra boat came along, and I hitched a ride. We passed that island, which seemed bare and uninteresting anyway, and landed on another one. I understood the boatman to say he would come back for me on his route. But he never came back.

"Days went by. No boat. I walked around and around. I could not see the tourist island I'd been on, nor any other land. I introduced myself to people, who said, 'Yes, there's a boat; it came once a long time ago, and it will come again.' I asked where was the boat I came on? They got excited—that was the boat. Why hadn't I held it for them? They sat on the ground to get over their disappointment. 'How long do we have to wait?' I asked, but their idea of time is not precision movement. I sat with them facing the sea, like *Mondo Cane* cargo cult. Three Frenchmen came along the beach. I asked them and they asked me about a boat. They'd been on that island years too long, they said, and the time has come for action. We cut bamboo and tied it together, and built two rafts. The islanders pointed their clove and cubeba cigarettes north, whence migrations of human beings and animals drifted. We paddled for a long time, and stopped on an island, but no people on it. Two of the Frenchmen went back. With the third Frenchman, an old man, I found many inhabited islands, but each with a smaller and poorer population. I left my aging old partner on an island with only one family. 'A ma puissance,' he said.

"I rowed and floated alone and nowhere until I met a boat filled with people. 'Room for one more,' they said. I left my raft, and went with them to Marore, which is the border-crossing island in the Sangihe Talaud Archipelago. But no airport, no harbor with ocean liners. A crew of Pilipinos from Mindanao, stranded for three years, told me that some years ago, a man who looked like me, a young German, came here on his way north in search of faith healers. He bought a canoe, but never rowed out of sight. The wind and sea kept returning him to the island, and at last wrecked him on the reef.

"One evening I was sitting on a pier, and eating fish jerky. A piece dropped in the water. A man with white hair dived for it, and ate it. He stayed beside me to watch the sunset. 'You live like us,' he said. 'No hotel.' I watched many sunsets with him. Mr. Sondak was his name. On Holy Saturday he said, 'Our food is your food. Our water is your water. Our hunger is your hunger. Our stories are your stories.' I must have been in very bad shape. That was the most beautiful thing I'd ever heard. I wept on the sand. He was welcoming me to remain forever on that island as my home. And give up thinking about how to get to the international airport at Jakarta or Manila."

Oh, that was beautiful. Wittman saw an island where people speak in verse, where a poet sings you a welcome to his tribe and gives you a place in its myth and legend. He asked Lance to say the mele again, and pictured its lines:

> *Our water is your water.*
> *Our food is your food.*
> *Our hunger is your hunger.*
> *Our stories are your stories.*

"But one day," Lance continued, "I walked further inland than I had walked before on any of the islands, probably through the neck of an isthmus—and entered a city again. Civilization, ho-o-o!" The cry of the wagonmaster on the Firesign Theater album. "The next thing I knew, I was riding in a taxi—Teksi, the letters on the door and roof said—racing for the airport. A Garuda plane flew overhead, and I panicked that it was my plane, and I'd missed it. But I caught Pan Am to Tokyo, where I changed planes. I waited at the boarding gate for seven hours, and took the plane to Honolulu, where I didn't leave the terminal during the stopover until takeoff for San Francisco. I've had it with islands. We shouldn't go to Asia even for vacations. We get turned around. I got made into a Kibei. A Returnee to America. Never leave, Wittman. The next time I'm curious about foreign lands, I'm traveling to Vegas or Reno. I came back in time for late registration, though most of the classes I wanted filled up already. And too late to stop my memorial service. It is absolutely necessary that I build the fox a home—in Oakland, here between these willow trees by this stream. It will be large enough for the two of us, Sunny, to use as a gazebo or a gatehouse. It will be so elegant and expensive that the fox will stay put. The stream will run; the fox will not run. The fox has come home. Here." He touched the ground with both hands. Very stoned heads will touch the earth—they dash out of the building and lie down on the street—and be well, okay. "I'm going to throw a fox-viewing party in a tent that covers the lawn. A flap rolls up. On a night when a moon is in the stream and a moon is in the sky, we're going to see the fox follow this stream, and step here under the willows. The fox will enter his house between doorposts of my design."

Wittman turned green and red with envy and admiration; a person of his generation that knows better than to make war its adventure was having himself an interesting life. Experiences befall this friend even when he means to be on vacation as a tourist. Japanese brought a fox; Chinese brought pigs and goats. And Executive Order 9066 has given to Issei, Nisei, Sansei their American history. And places: Tanforan, Manzanar, Tule Lake, Arkansas, Sand Island. And righteous politics, the Sansei's turn to say No and No to loyalty oaths and to the draft. We ought to give A.J.A.s a deep gomenasai apology without them having to ask. If only he hadn't been but a toddler at the time, Wittman would have gotten on the train that took people who looked like himself away. There had been a Chinese-Mexican kid who had done that to be with his friends.

How to kill Lance and eat his heart, and plagiarize his

stories? As a friend of the hero, you're a sub-plot of his legend. When you want to be the star. And wear a beret. And go on vision quest, for which a Young Millionaire can afford plane rides to the other side of the world. The minimum-wage earner—the unemployed—goes for a walk in the park, where Wittman Ah Sing has had vision enough. Everything that comes in—that's it. Foolish ape wants more vision.

"You still want to fight?" Lance asked.

"Don't think you've talked yourself out of it. I want to kill you and eat your heart, and plagiarize your stories. Businessman."

Lance got the insult. Ranked and cut low. He put up his fists. Wittman hadn't been in all that many fights, but people putting up their dukes looked like they learned from boxing movies. He was too embarrassed to prance.

"Don't fight," said Sunny. "Please don't fight. I'm leaving right now if you fight. Do you want me to leave, Lance? Or do you want me to help? If I help, it's two against one. We don't want to outnumber him two against one, do we?"

The willows hung their branches down like weeping cherry trees in their green seasons. And into the moon-bright scene on this gibbous night walked Taña, the pretty girl in hot pursuit, who parted the willow-tail curtains, and said, "Oh, I didn't know there was anybody out here. Is the ground marshy over by you?"

Well, they had to stop for introductions in case everybody hadn't met everybody. "So you two have met," said Lance. So their attachment shows. Ignored, the married couple faded away.

"You knew I was out here," said Wittman, "and you came pursuing me."

Paying no nevermind to swampiness, she stepped right on over to him, and sat down on a log, which would moss-stain her skirt. She had bound up her hair with somebody's necktie, and another tie belted her waist—a piratess of hearts. "To find a certain type of interesting person at a party," she said, "go outside, and there he'll be, all by himself, smoking a cigarette, next to the garbage cans."

Girls who hide from the party are usually crying, and they are unsocialized wallflowers. Let that about the garbage cans go.

Too bad Lance hadn't built his shrine yet; it would be nice to go with her inside a hideaway the size of a Chinese bed. He took a-hold of her hand, and pulling her behind him, led her on a twining walk. Here and there on the grass lay sleepy bodies, girls in skirts, moth wings and daisy petals. They were the fairies of a midautumn's night; they were a slain family. Taña caught up beside him; they walked together holding hands, his every finger between her every finger. He stopped, pushed her hand behind her, her other hand caught between his chest and her breasts. A hug dance. "Let go," she said, and he, laughing and shaking his head no, kissed her. "So that I can put my arms around you," she said pleadingly. Oh, he had to let her do that for a while. Then he pulled her arm down, and, holding swinging hands some more, walked her to the porch. He embraced her by the waist, and lifted her up onto the balustrade. "Sidesaddle, ma'am?" he said. He lit up a cigarette. She took it from him and smoked it too. They were taking turns on his last cigarette.

She looked like Dale Evans as the girl singer with the Sons of the Pioneers. Dale used to wear an off-the-shoulder Mexican blouse, and looked like Marilyn Monroe but not so unstrung. Roy hadn't buttoned her up yet. Roy Rogers always wore his plaid shirt buttoned to the top, and tucked his jeans inside his boots.

Wittman leaned against a post, pushed his pretend hat back, put his boot on the footrail. "I do admire a lady who rides sidesaddle, Taña. Taña De Weese. What kind of a name is that?"

"I don't know, I'm sure, Wittman. Wittman Ah Sing. What's your other name? I should think Wittman is just your American name."

Yes, that's all it is.

"My middle name is Chloë," she said.

"My other name is Joang Fu."

"What does it mean? Joang Fu." She said it with American uplilt that makes Chinese sound good, hearable, not lost inside somewhere.

"I don't ask you what Taña Chloë means. Why do you assume that my name means dick?"

"'Of course it must,'" she said. "'My name means the shape

I am—and a good handsome shape it is, too. With a name like yours, you might be any shape, almost.'"

Our fool for literature is utterly impressed by her allusiveness.

He poeticated her in return. "'By a name I know not how to tell thee who I am.'"

"Joang Fu is a secret name, isn't it? Have you given me your secret name and power over you, Joang Fu?"

"No, that's a white-man superstition. Do you throw the Ching? My name is number sixty-one, which they translate Inner Truth. You can look it up." I am True Center. Core Truth. Truth is a bird carrying a boy in her talons. She can look it up for herself. He hoped nobody Chinese was eavesdropping. Can't stand hippy dippies who trade on orientalia.

Taña leaned her head against her post and sighed. "Happy?" she asked moonily. She cracked him up. He'd found him a girl with that certain alienation.

"Happy," he said, playing along. People who aren't too smart, the ones who live by song lyrics, and who don't know their current events, those people can be happy. Yeah, he felt high, and he knew the difference between being happy and being high, neither of which is as good as joy.

"Do you like parties?" she asked. Oh, she is so understanding. She must sense that he takes celebrations seriously. He's profoundly dionysian and has standards. Too sensitive to be inside yukking it up. She hadn't asked, "Do you like this party?" She said, "Do you like parties?" Is she ready to listen to my shyness party by party? He can tell her how he hated playing Young Affordables. She hasn't heard them talk about him, has she? "He's nowhere near his first million." "He believes in voluntary poverty." "No, he's just plain cheap." But he mustn't come off as afraid of parties. He went to them. To be a no-show, you have to get it scandaled about that you don't go to parties for interesting lone-wolf reasons, and definitely not because you weren't invited. Show up, be tested. And you be cool; defensiveness is the worst of personality emanations. "He's so defensive." He has to let her know how dionysian he can be. Yes, he can be very dionysian, such as the time he rode the motorcycle through the French doors.

He said, "Now, me, what I feel about parties . . . to tell you the truth, I do and I don't like . . . I mean, it depends on what kind of party . . . the kind that . . . like paranoid . . . well, not really paranoid. . . ." It was coming out inarticulate, but that's okay. Hang down your head like sad and blue James Dean, dead already. Like your brains are too heavy. Feelings so deep that there are no words honest enough to express them. The words the world has are not good enough. His head hung ponderous, his hands a-pockets. The girl on the balustrade leaned over to peer up at his face. She reached out, and pushed aside the dark forelock. Girls' hearts break to pull James Dean's head up by the forelock. Yes, he was bowed before her. O gravitational pull of physical bodies. Felled by her. She slid off the railing, and stood before him. His head lowered helplessly toward her upturning face, and nudged at her lips to part, come on, come on, give, until she began the kissing. She was short enough to have to reach for it, and he was tall enough to have been only nodding, just thinking, nodding off, listening to some music of his own.

Taña talked and kissed at the same time, "Do you like partying now? How do you like the party now? Do you like partying with me? You do like to party, huh?" He would enjoy hearing what this girl's instinctively said sex words were. Breathing with catches in her throat, she went on to say, "I like this party. I like partying with you. You know what I wish, though? I wish that all night long you had been thinking about me, that you had been looking for me years ago before we met, and you've found me at last. You maneuvered to be invited here. Tonight you followed me from room to room, didn't you? You flirted with gorgeous girls, but they weren't me. I walked by and I made you look away from them. I made you dissatisfied. Whenever I looked up, there you would be staring at me. You were contemplating me. You went into the library, thinking I was there, and you looked behind the curtains. The toes you had seen under there might have been mine. You notice everything about me. You went out through the balcony doors, and saw me crossing the lawn in the moonlight. And you climbed down the fire escape, and caught me here. On the vine-covered veranda. As I was about to leave, you caught me in your arms. Now, tell me that happened. Tell me that was what you did. You chased me, and caught me in your arms. And hold me in your arms."

"Yeah," he said. "Yeah, looked for you. Saw you there. Caught you. Yeah, I did that. I do that. Hug you. That too." He's her nuzzling colt, her baby houyhnhnm, nuzzling for its mama.

"And hold me in your strong arms, and kiss me. And kiss me again." Oh, at last. He'd found his woman who will talk while making love. Will she blurt out everything of women he needs to know, please?

4
The Winners of the Party

THE WINNERS of the party were: Lance Kamiyama. His bride, Sunny. Wittman Ah Sing. Taña De Weese. Nanci Lee, who might have been by herself, but was sitting in the breakfast nook with Charley Bogard Shaw. And the plain girl from the bus, Judy Louis. To win, you outlast everybody else, and stay up all night. You were civilized, had not rushed off urgently with anyone. You got to talk those other people over.

Night was leaving through the tall windows. The winners of the party, those who did not find room on the banquette, sat on bar stools around the butcher block. Wittman was on one side of it, and Taña across from him. The little door for bowls and plates and for the entrances and exits of the creatures that danced on the sideboard was now shut. Lance was cooking a magic omelette ("oom-lette" he called it because it was special). He shook the grass out of a colander; the stems and seeds, he saved for tea. The heat and the scrambled eggs enriched the grassy smell, somewhat like a blend of Italian parsley and alfalfa. Doesn't the smell of the herb cooking make your limbs shaky? Your guts untangle? The windowpanes steamed up from bottom to top, the kitchen warming like somebody's mother was home, onions sautéing in butter, wooden mushrooms re-mushrooming and fluting in water. Sunny was grinding coffee beans; she fit the filter in a cone that came down by tackle from the ceiling. "The night is over," said Lance, their chieftain. "We have gotten safely through the night. We're alive." He was giving a blessing that there is a time limit to difficulties. Let any battles that were being fought among them, any bad feelings, cease. Troubles and fears are not to be carried over into daylight. Dispel paranoia. The hardiest, the geniuses, the abiders of the tribe have journeyed far and come home. "The weekend is half over," said Lance, handing out the oom-lettes on unmatched California ware. They ate quietly. "Nobody talk while the flavor lasts."

Now, to have been everywhere at once just about, to hear the parts of the party you missed: the couple-fights; who left with whom; the man-to-man fights; the identification of strangers who stood out. Like did anybody see this gigantic, slow man in the black beard? He walked around and looked at faces. He carried a handsaw, and tapped the ban-the-bomb symbol on the door. Had anybody met him before? Whose friend was he? Who was that guy? "Nobody invited him," said Lance. "He walked in from off the street. I asked him his name, and he said, 'I am Friend of All the World.'" "That's wonderful," said Sunny. "Friend of All the World. That's *why* he could walk in off the street." They had been favored. An animal had emerged out of the camouflage, and chosen them to see it.

"I stopped Eugene from throwing a motorcycle through the window," said Charley. "Somebody put chemicals in his drink—or he *thought* somebody did—and he tried to hang himself in the shower, but the curtain rod kept bending. He decided it must have been Chuckie who was trying to poison him, which it might have been; I wouldn't put it past Chuckie, but not to poison him, only to surprise him. Accident. Eugene, with the strength of a madman, tore a board off the garage and chased Chuckie around the house. Chuckie ran inside, and got trapped in the bathroom, and escaped by squeezing out between the louvers. Eugene broke in the door, then got the idea to hang himself. Everybody—girls—who came in to use the john, tried to stop him, but he kept on tying belt, necktie, towels together and around his neck. Each time he lowered himself, the curtain rod bent lower too, and the knot slid down it. All the while, people were coming and going, taking a piss, taking a crap. They talked him out of it." Imagine that, living for reasons thought up by others while crapping. What reasons were they?

"Did you notice," said Sunny, "Candace got so drunk, she lost her English accent. One of her intimates asked her how come she was speaking American like anybody else. She screamed—and fainted. And when she came to, she was speaking like an English bird queen again. Do you remember her from when she went on her fortnight junket to London? She came back with clothes from Carnaby Street, and calling us Luv and Ducks. And birds and toffs. And she does that

English babytalk—lolly and brolly and nappy and lorry and nanny and jolly and tommy and telly and tata." Yes, Sunny, there are those of us right here who can no longer speak in pre-educated accents even among old friends and relatives unless stoned out of our minds.

And Nanci the beautiful, whose knees and long legs stuck out of the breakfast nook to trip one up, reported on a kissing contest. Everybody, male and female, kissed everybody else, no skipping over of anyone. She had won the title of Most Romantic Kisser. Wittman was feeling that he had missed out on the party. Where had he been during the motorcycle tossing and suiciding and fainting and mass kissing? And what had he to contribute to this after-party party? He finished his oom-lette—even square Judy ate hers—and took seconds. He didn't want to get stoned; he was hungry. Nobody has cooked for him for a long time. Grass that's eaten, ingesta, comes on gradually; you can take a-hold of yourself, you would think. And, surely, he was now such a naturally high person that he would not get too ripped, immune now, surely. The sun was brimming pale new light over the top of the hills, and through an open window a pretty breeze blew. Why, then, was he coming down? Who's bringing him down?

"Somebody's bringing me down," he said. "So low. I'm crashing. You're feeling pain too, but you think it feels good. The food tastes good, so your brain, which is right upstairs from your mouth, thinks, 'This is good.' This is not good. Lance. He's the one making us turn the knife on our own stomach. I don't mean only now. It's longterm. We have to fight for our lives. I quit the Young Millionaires. There's nothing to buy out there. I know, I worked retail in one of the biggest department stores in the City. I didn't want to use my employee discount or my opportunities for employee theft to get anything. Nothing is worth a million dollars. You've got to let people out of the Young Millionaires, Lance."

"I feel sorry for you," said Lance. "I feel sorry for you because you can't find something you care for enough to make the money to buy it. I give parties. It costs money to give parties, Wittman. You don't return social obligations; you don't entertain. You don't know how much money I spend on my friends. Thanksgiving with turkey for me and Sunny and three or four orphans will cost fifty dollars at least. And I like serving two wines. And I have to re-stock the bar. Wittman, do I have to point out to you my largesse with the grass and several kinds of mushrooms? I'm stuffing my turkey with grass this year. I spent a couple of hundred dollars on you tonight, and you're one of the orphans I plan to invite for Thanksgiving."

"Give my share to the bums on Howard Street. I'm fasting on Thanksgiving. You ought to give the fifty dollars to a famine somewhere. Like on that island where the old man dived for your droppings. You should have stayed lost longer, Lance. You didn't go far out enough. You spent the whole trip trying to get back. Like there's no place like Oakland? I go further out than you. I'm a genius. I'm warning all of you. He softens us up on dope, then he does his imprinting. But I'll be genius enough to save your lives."

"You're having one of those trips where you think everything comes clear," said Lance.

"You're going through the delusion of clarity," agreed Charley, the mathematician and expert on metaphysical movies.

Wittman set down his cup, reached into his back pocket, and pulled out a sheaf of manuscript, the next part of his play, that had been in there all night all along. Taking the stance of Gwan Goong the Reader, who read in armor during battle, who read to enemies, who read loud when no one listened, Wittman Ah Sing read. He held his papers as Gwan Goong held his soft-covered book rolled in his sword hand. His left hand stroked his beard. His intelligent head was turned in a reading me-ay, black eyebrows winging in thought. Whether or not a listener sat with him knee-to-knee, Wittman sat bent-knee kung fu position. The man of action aggressively reads and talks.

"Remember how bedazzled you felt at black-and-white movies when it rained all up and down the screen? Light and camera through the windowpanes made the lines of rain dripping from the eaves twinkle and sparkle—setting off bodily thrills. And the star in her mermaid cocktail dress shimmered over to the window, and crumpled up a letter. The paper crackled through the sound system. Remember the pure firing milli-shocks of light, and that sound?" Yes, his friends and enemies are nodding yes. They know what he means so far. "Spangling, she crossed the screen, and the camera dollied in a close-up pan around the Christmas tree dangling with foil icicles—tiers of winking metallic rain. Coruscations. Shivering and delighting your vertebrae up and down. And the story-line didn't matter nor who she was in the shimmying dress—when that coruscation sparked and popped on the silver screen, you had corresponding feelings.

"The curtain for my play will be made out of tinsel; lights with blue gels will shaft through the very dark house and play on those moving rain-fringe curtains, which represent a waterfall. I want to suggest mermaids and flashing salmon, fluke tails flipping in the sun, sequins of water, Lorelei sequins, rainbows and trout refracting and multiplying. We'll hang one of those junior-prom rotating mirror balls. Vegas nightclub floor-show glitz production values, but we'll shoot for transcendence. You know what I wish? I wish while they're damming the Feather River, they'd build a stage. All they have to do is shape some of that concrete into risers and platforms. And I could control the waterfall to rise and fall or part and shut—stage curtains. Acoustically, use the tourist information speakers like sound boxes at drive-in theaters. And the actors—you—project hard. Yeah, open the show in Oroville. Or Santa Cruz, at the Brookdale Lodge, where the river goes through the redwood-forest lobby. The guests sit and fish. We need a rain machine. Now, it may be enough in this day and far-gone age to stage a water-and-lights happening, but here's the content: Monkeys live at the falls. All the actors who play monkeys will have to be tumblers. Tumble all over the apron, triple-somersault into the proscenium arch, pyramid barefoot onto one another's shoulders. The Wallenda pyramid breaks; they pitch against the water, which bounces them out. With almost-flying skills, the raggedy-ass and barefoot monkeys are asking of nature and one another, what is on the other side of the water curtain? 'Something to eat.' 'Why doesn't one of you go through it somehow and bring back a report?' 'Whoever does that will be king.' And off a catwalk comes flying on a rope-vine a glorious monkey. Red mask-paint rings his handsome human eyes, and points to his nose. He wears a heart on his face and has a heart on his ass. He swings out over

the heads of monkeys and audience, and into the water curtain, his tail wrapped ingeniously around the rope-vine—he
can fly upside down—'Geronimo!'—and plunges through to
the other side. He does not return for quite a while. The rest
of the monkeys do an apron scene: 'He's not coming back.' 'Is
he dead?' 'He's gone and drowned himself.' 'Was he suicidal?'
'What's the motive? Did he leave a note?' 'I think he's just testing his invulnerability.' 'He's been gone too long. He's not immortal.' 'I don't want to die.' 'Me neither. I don't want to die
either.' But what's the test for immortality? There isn't a safe
test to prove once and for all that some medicine, peach, or
fountain water blots out one's name in the Book of Death. You
keep on questing because of doubts. You can live to be over a
hundred years old, and you're only long-lived. You drink from
a fountain of youth, and you don't die that day, and whattaya-
know, not the day after that either. Life goes along, and pretty
soon you start getting suspicious for proof. So you're thirty
years old, and not dead. Forty, and still not dead. Am I living
forever yet? You go into battle, you live through a war. You
win some hand-to-hand combats. Are you a skilled fighter, or
immortal? What if you were going to survive till eighty anyway in your natural lifespan? You can be ninety, a hundred,
and still not know if you're lasting forever. There are people
who live to be a hundred and ten, even a hundred and twenty.
I'm going to keep escaping from the old-age home, on quest
until I'm a hundred and thirty.

"Plunging out of the waterfall comes Sun Wu Kong, the
King of the Monkeys, hanging on to his rope with toes and tail,
juggling pears and grapes and peaches and bananas, throwing
them to the others, everybody juggle-eating. Monkey dives in
and through the falls—the curtain opens, and we see what's
behind there. 'Come on. Come on. Come on,' says the handsome King of Monkeys, leading his people into one of those
sets that should make the audience gasp and stop everything
to applaud the set designer. The secret and protected country
has a sky that is a vaulting dome—stage it inside a blue mosque
like the inside of the stone egg that Monkey hatched from,
by which he is sometimes known as the Stone Monkey. He
will get mountains whopped on him twice—Stoned Monkey.
In the ongoing vistas, mists and streams curl around green

mountains and far grey mountains. The monkeys link tails—
chains of monkeys bridge the trees and canyons. They spin
around and around on their knuckles. Flowers and fruit everywhere, spring and autumn coeval, each tree blooming and
leafing and hanging with all you can eat. You've all driven the
length of the Central Valley, haven't you, through the miles
of peach ranches and plum ranches? We stage this in a barn in
Fresno County, the audience will have to drive their pick-ups
through a ranch of blooms—pear trees, tragic cherry trees,
thorny inedible quince, and thorny citrus. Ravens (with the
V-tails) and crows (with the straight-across tails) sit on tiptop branches, holding things down to earth. Welcome home
to the land behind the falls. The older people will stick their
tongues out of squared mouths in astonishment. And the
younger people will remember that Zorro kept his black horse
and his weapons and mask behind a waterfall. A black stallion
in a spangly Mexican saddle gallops across the stage, and the
monkeys have a rodeo."

Taña raised an arm, twirled and snapped it, roping Wittman
with her invisible lasso. "Ee-haw!" Cheered by that cowgirl
yell, he went on:

"Three or four hundred years go by. The monkeys spend
their time eating and showing off. Their cavortions become
organized acrobatics. Their moves culminate in kicking feet
and boxing fists and blade-like chops of the hands. They
throw fists and feet and steel stars. The shirakens—stars of
steel—zip like comets—meteor showers—at targets. Bullseye
targets become cop-training targets, which look like men,
that is, like themselves. Their circus parades straighten out,
their hair straightens out, everybody in uniforms with scarves
around their necks. Pheasant feathers wave above the heads
of officers. They drill to the brass and drums of marching
bands playing anthems, which the Monkey King leads with
his magic rod, now the size of a conductor's wand. Straight-
rule chessboard divisions, troops, squadrons, ranks and files
of eighty-four thousand monkeys, horizontals and verticals
like a reinforced-concrete cubiform hundred-story building
viewed from the sidewalk below—you feel hallucinated at the
strictness of the perspective and the monumental unwavering
immensity. What I want to know about: Why the totalitarian

armies that even I, a pacifist person, helplessly see on laughing gas and carbogen?

"The King of Monkeys drills and reviews troops; he leads martial-arts regimens, but something is wrong. He sprawls depressed in his throne. He has enough to eat, and the baby monkeys chase his whipping tail. But he is not entertained. It's not the militarization that's getting him down. His people are transformed into soldiers, and the landscape always has a soldier on patrol in it, but he's used to transformations, being the master of seventy-two of them himself; a slow change by a species is nothing. 'Whyfor?' he asks. 'Whyfor?' He is Aware of Emptiness. Aware of Emptiness is his middle name. His far-hearing ears have heard of a wonderful party being planned to which he has not been invited. He hardly knows the people giving the party, neither hosts nor guests; it has nothing to do with him. But he's got to be there. It's a party that they give only once every three thousand years, it's that special. A triple-millennial party. He feels so left out. Life would not be worth living if he didn't get to that party. The party of a lifetime. Whyfor did they overlook him? He was most handsome. Was it his personality? His lower-class manners? His clothes not good enough for them? He's as good as anybody. He gnashed his teeth over the feting and celebrating going on without him. Nobody should leave anybody out of anything. He'll crash that party. He'll invade it with his army. He'll make a scene. He'll eat everything on the buffet. He'll overturn tables. He'll piss in the wine. He'll show them, leaving him out."

Sunny was clearing her counters and uprighting her chairs. Dig this action, Sunny:

"A messenger comes riding but not with an invitation. Scouts patrolling the farthest ridges have spotted a king-size havoc monster coming this way. 'Help! Help!' shout the monkeys. 'War! War!' Now the drums go wild. Now there's urgency and emergency. He will blood his magic lance. 'I'll go by myself,' he says. 'It's best to meet the enemy one on one on his own turf. I'll stop him from coming here to ruin our country. He won't get you. While I'm gone, you guard our home. You stay here just in case.' His plan is to fight this monster in the neighborhood of the party. He'll drop in sweating heroically. A monster led me a chase this way. Has anyone seen a havoc monster? You having a party? Chase that monster crashing through their party.

"The King of Monkeys, using his magic pole, polevaults away into the sky. He's off to war and party. His patriotic people beat the taiko big drums, a beat that he can hear and take heart from.

"More sound effects—bomb-like fireworks—signal for back-up. Fighting men and fighting women enter on horseback, riding from over the mountains. They sail up the streams and rivers. A band of a hundred and eight superheroes punt swift boats out of the sloughs. An offstage voice will call out the names of heroes and heroines that were once not long ago—less than twenty years ago—star roles in American theater. They have left us. We will call them back. Where are you? Come back. Gwan Goong and his brothers—Liu Pei and Chang Fei. Yue Fei, and his lifelong friends—Hong, Cheung, and Wong. And the great warrior women—Red Jade, Flower Wood Orchid, the fighting aunties from the Sung Dynasty, the ladies and goodwives of the Water Margin, Night Ogress and Pure Green Snake alias the Tigress. And Mrs. Gwan Goong, that is, Gwan Po. And the Red Peony alias Oryu alias Lady Yakusa. No, no, no. Wait. We keep the men's Chinese names, we keep the women's names untranslated too, no more Pearl Buck Peony Plum Blossom haolefied missionary names. No more accessible girls and unspeakable men. The women: Hoong Ngoak, Fa Moke Lan, Ku San the Intelligent, Mrs. Shen the Earth Star. Let the gringo Anglos do some hard hearing for a change. I don't forget actresses. I remember them better than you women do. At this roll call of paladins and mariners, the monkeys kit-chak kit-chak like Molucca-Sulu relatives. Everybody has come from eras and places to unite together on the same stage. War has bust through time.

"The heroes rein in their champing steeds and lie on their oars. On a shadow-puppet screen, they and we watch Monkey King fight the havoc monster, whose black shape looms into the sky and shoots through the crowds of armies and audience. (We can, vice versa, have Monkey en scène, and his drumming nation as shadows.) Ah Monkey dodges the snapping claw that swings out of the wings. The havoc monster is enormous; our special-effects people can build only one claw, which pokes into a side door of the theater and gropes across the stage. Ah Monkey whacks the claw with his sword-size rod, which grows—whoomp—into a battering ram. The king-size monster of havoc keeps clawing, knocking everything on the set around. The magic monkey plucks a few of his own hairs, bites them up, and blows them out, shouting, 'Beeen!' And they change presto into a myriad of little monkeys, each one wielding a monkey stick. They worry the monster, and it goes through changes—a malevolent baby, a white bone demoness, a king of swords, who mentally commands a rain of swords, a king of the lute, whose music drives the monkeys crazy, like The Fiddler against the Batman and the Flash. The other monkeys leave the cave and fight too. Wars involve everyone; every war is a world war. Ah Monkey too goes through his changes—a cormorant, a falcon, a koi fish, a temple with a flagpole tail. The war goes on for a long time. 'Kingdoms rise and fall.'"

Judy Louis was smiling her boar-like smile at this line from the classics. Wittman was encouraged to begin another movement of his play:

"Meanwhile—if this were a movie, we could use a split screen. Walt Disney ought to make the animated epic cartoon. Elsewhere—soldiers are going about the marketplace plastering recruiting posters on poles and walls. A man out of uniform had better not walk upright and show his face. The young Liu Pei, who is braiding a sandal, gets up from his squat-sit among the straw, to see what the army has to say. He reads that his country needs him badly, and he sighs, 'Aiya-a-a.'

"'Hey, you!' says a neighbor, the butcher and vintner, wiping his hands on an apron stained with reds. 'Yeah, you, the romantic young fellow, yearning for glory while hiding from the draft.'

"'I'm not a coward,' says Liu Pei, letting rip another sigh. 'I'd fight in wars if I didn't have to take orders. I want my own army. I have a cause of my own. I don't waste my abilities on jerkwater duels.' He hardly has to turn around to look at the heckler behind him; his eyes are far apart in his bullet-like leopard-like head.

"The butcher-winemaker sizes him up, and says, 'I myself have some abilities, and wherewithal. I've been looking for bold allies. Suppose you and I talk further.' The two of them leave their businesses unattended, and go to a tavern to drink and plan. The tavern is two tables under an awning. The crowd passes around them.

"'We Changs have been in this county for many generations,' says Chang Fei, for it is he. 'We grow peaches and grapes, distill wine, raise pigs. I can outfit knights. I can outfit an army.'

"Among the average-size people comes a huge and mighty man pushing a handcart. The times are bad, that a man thus built be an unemployed tramp of the road. The old Chinese audience will be moved with pity because they recognize our grandfather, Grandfather Gwan Yee, also called Gwan Cheong Wun, sounds like Long Cloud, that excellent man, Gwan Goong, horseless, and no squire to carry his luggage. He sets down the cart, and ducks his head to enter the shade that the two world-changers are at work under. He's no ordinary bum-how. He sings, 'I place my bow against the wall, but I do not take off my moon-curved broadsword.' 'Be quick, innkeeper,' he shouts. 'Bring me wine. I'm in haste to get to the city and join the army.'

"Well, the effect would be the same if you shouted out your martial intentions at Enrico's or Vesuvio's or La Val's. A stalwart is making the scene; he casts his glamour over the sidewalk of tourists and regulars.

"'Hey, stranger,' calls Chang Fei. 'Sit with us. This shoe-and-mat weaver wants to buy us drinks. I've never seen you in these parts before. Where do you come from? And where are you going pushing your belongings?'

"The interesting stranger quaffs the wine, and Chang Fei refills his cup. 'I've been a fugitive wandering the roads and the rivers for five years now,' he says. 'I can't go home to my family village.'

"'Did you kill someone?' asks Liu Pei. 'Are you a wanted man?'

"Granddad puts his quick-draw hand on his sword hilt. His eyes flare like a pair of red birds flying up.

"'You don't look like a pig thief to me, nor an adulterer either,' says Chang Fei. 'I'm sure if you killed a man, you had good reason.'

"Granddad drinks more wine, which sloshes on his thick and beautiful beard. Later kings and ladies will try bribing him with silk beardbags, which were once a fashion. These two brotherly men are trying to get his story.

"'I see you keep red and healthy on wine,' says Liu Pei. 'Were you drinking the day you killed a man? If you had it to do over again, what would you do?'"

Wittman played Gwan Goong speaking out of his coffee cup, fierce eyebrows shooting rays, head down and mumbling, like Marlon Brando about to tell difficult bad memories. Brando can say anything, the ladies will listen. "'I come from a place where the idea of governing was to make everybody obey the biggest man, and give him things, and do him favors. This executive officer taxed us for seasonal deliveries of firewood, harvest, game, three-horn joong, moon cakes, maidens. That story about mice belling the cat came from my hometown. "You do it." "No, you do it." I was the next-biggest man. It was up to me to bring the cat to justice. He was carrying off a maiden when I dragged him from his horse and ran him through. I killed him with this cold and beautiful sword, whose name is Black Dragon. And then I left town. I've been on the run ever since.'

"Chang Fei invites these two men, each of them free of the grubmoney life, to his ranch and home. They learn that one's cause is the others' cause. In the peach orchard, they invent a ritual of friendship. That friendship ritual was one thousand six hundred and twenty-nine years old when the Forty-Niners, our great-great-grandfathers, brought it to the Gold Rush. Every matinee or evening for a hundred years, somewhere in America, some acting company was performing *The Oath in the Peach Orchard*, then it disappeared, I don't know why. The theater has died. The words of that oath used to be printed on programs, and it was inscribed on walls for the World War II audience, when we were kids—that recently—to chant along with the actors, community singing. I want to bring back— not red-hot communist Chinese—but deep-roots American theater. We need it."

Anybody American who really imagines Asia feels the loneliness of the U.S.A. and suffers from the distances human beings are apart. Not because lonesome Wittman was such a persuader but because they had need to do something communal against isolation, the group of laststayers, which included two professional actors, organized themselves into a play. Players took the parts of the three brotherly friends, and improvised a ritual that made the playwright's sketch up-to-date and relevant, and showed him what happens next. Wittman thought whaddayaknow, I've written one of those plays that leave room for actors to do improv, a process as ancient as Chinese opera and as far-out as the theater of spontaneity that was happening in streets and parks. Everyone is a poet-actor adlibbing and winging it.

Lance Kamiyama will be Liu Pei; Charles Bogard Shaw will be Chang Fei; Wittman will be Gwan Goong. Nanci Lee and the other women will be audience for the time being.

"Gong boy!" said Charley Shaw, lifting his cup of coffee. "Yum sing! Mahn sing!" Which are the toasts at banquets and gambling. "Raise your wine cup! Drink to victory! Ten thousand victories!"

"Kanpei!" said Lance, taking off his apron. "Banzai!" Which were the banquet toasts, in Japanese, drunk to him and Sunny at their wedding.

"Here we are, three unrelated people," said Wittman/Gwan Goong. He stood at the butcher block, his podium. "Nobody from my family village, not even that girl that I rescued"—a thumb at Nanci—"rode with me into exile. Before I do battle again, I'd like to hear you vow that we stand by one another no matter what."

"You aren't getting me ready to kill people, are you?" asked Lance/Liu Pei, laying down his spatula. "I'm going to feel very bad if I have to kill anybody. I want to be a dove." He walked up the kitchen ladder, and sat on its top rung. Oh, come on, Lance, co-operate. These men were military heroes. And the first rule of improv is: Don't say No. "I'm warning you, I'd rather be killed than kill."

Wittman was as tall as Lance on the stepladder, and spoke in his face. "There's a war on. It comes this way, we have to take part. You can't stand aside and let your people be slaughtered. You have to be realistic."

Lance stood up on the ladder. "I'm speaking as a veteran of life and war. You should have stayed longer at that job of yours. It was your responsibility to keep track of the kids you sold war toys to. You could've guided them playing with soldiers. One day, those kids, after Ragnaroking their toy armies, will straighten out the dogpile of G.I. Joes and Sailor Bobs, and make them shake hands and become friends. As taidomo of my last gang, I led the maneuverings and the shaking of hands at the Alameda County Fair Grounds gang war of 1956. Nobody got killed or hurt much. I'm experimenting on leading people out of back-to-back, hand-to-hand situations." He tried on a pot-helmet, took it off. "You give me an army, I have additional creative ideas to try out."

"What kind of creative ideas?" asked Charley, an actor generous with the spotlight. "I was at that county fair—blue-ribbon pigs, blue-ribbon wine—I didn't see any gang trouble."

Lance walked back and forth between Charley, who sat in a straightback chair as if upon a throne, and Wittman, who leaned against the butcher block, his horse, Red Rabbit. "I carried out a war without an incurrence of cops, neither Security nor the Oakland P.D. nor the National Guard. I was working out further-along methods for taking over the world without anybody noticing. Like I am blood with the French. I gave at a Parisian mobile bloodbank. They gave me a ham sandwich and vin rouge, and saluted me, 'The people of France are grateful.' I move that we offer ourselves to the enemy as hostages-for-peace. You especially, Chang, are a valuable citizen. They'll agree to take you, especially if we throw in your land too. They can come over and live on it, feed the pigs, water the orchards. Who's ahead in this war? We are, sitting around, drinking wine, living. We can afford to experiment as to whether more lives are lost fighting or in 'unilateral surrender.' It's our duty as the latest evolvement of man to find out. I'm curious. When they get here, let's have our populace be doing something flabbergasting like spinning Gandhiesque wheels, like Frisbee, like Slinky. Invent a Frisbee-Slinky combination. Some satyagraha so interesting that they'll lay down their weapons and do it too, have us teach it to them. They'll kill a few of us from momentum, but they'll calm down by and by. What can they do to us, a wonderful country like us, we put ourselves into their arms." He was out among the audience, who could hiss or crook him or take him into their arms.

"Hai!" said Charley/Chang Fei. "Hai!" which could mean "Cunt!" or "Crab!" or "Yeah!" or "Look!" or "Hello there!" or it was just a noise. "I know you," he said, in character—tough China Man of our childhood. "I know you. You are sly. There is nothing you won't say. You say whatever, peace, whatever, and while they're thinking about it, while we're thinking about it, you do your idiocratic Dada." A Chinatown coot has spoken, sitting on his bench at Portsmouth Square, telling you who you are, and what you do.

"Nothing flabbergasts like explosives," said Wittman as Gwan Goong, sitting atop his horse. "Guns. Bombs."

"No guns. No bombs. I'm using my deepest brains to ban bombs, and to help you plan the barbecue in the orchard. You are throwing a barbecue, aren't you? You've got enough meat and wine to feed everybody." Lance/Liu poured hot coffee all around. "Invite the enemy. Always invite your enemies to parties. What to do with belligerents, we'll hold a tournament on your ranchland. And find out: Do contact sports exhaust the war energy, or is there escalation and dominoes? At pre-game activities and half-time, and everywhere they go, we'll be playing the enemy's ethnic music and speaking their language. We'll take on their ways, and slow them down, unable to distinguish themselves from us." Lance/Liu is not letting go of his tack. "For uniforms: skins versus shirts. Naked, integrated boy-girl teams. *De*fense—nudity as camouflage, bare skin and hair blending into nature. Nudity also works as offense; I've scared off Seventh-Day Adventists and Mormons by answering the door naked. They'll hide-and-seek us; they'll capture our flag; they won't be able to resist us. Let's invite everybody to marry everybody. For the finale, we'll have a multitudinous wedding. Our foreign policy will be: We want to marry you. Propose to every nation. Leaflet them with picture brides. We'll go anywhere and marry anybody! How do unrelated people get together? They get married." His wife smiled at this homage to marriage. Lance has already used marriage to solve a war problem. When he married Sunny, he got out of the draft. He is a Kennedy husband.

"Listen here, Running Nose," said Wittman/Gwan Goong, for that is the way Liu Pei's name sounds in American dialect. "I can tell you how many will die before they calm down.

Thirty million. That's the record the human race is shooting for. Look in the *Guinness Book of World Records.* The record for Greatest Mass Killing is twenty-six million three hundred thousand, which is how many were sacrificed for the communizing of China. That broke the Russians' World War II record for the Most Killed in a War Against Invaders, twenty-five million. The number keeps going up as history goes along. There's something in us that loves to break records." These numbers had been lumbering like dead planets in Wittman's head, ruining life.

"We're inviting soldiers and civilians to a place where they quit ending up at the hillpiles of skulls," explained Chang Fei. "The right disarming, tough Zen non-violence?! What is it?" His chop-socky hand sliced the prana-filled air. He swiveled his head, eyes wide, and came to a hard stop, his foot stomped—bang!—and he held the one brother, then the other with his glare—me-ay. Charley has seen a lot of Hong Kong movies. "My dove brother. My hawk brother. These peach trees are at their fullest and reddest bloom. We vow friendship. Repeat after me. 'We three—Liu Pei, Gwan Goong, and Chang Fei—though not born to the same families, swear to be brothers. Though born under different signs, we shall seek the same death day.'" He knows. He knows. Charley is Chinese, and knows. He is a hearer of legends. And he's translating what may be the secret oath the tongs take into daylight English for all to understand. China Man ways are not gone from this world as long as an actor like Charles Bogard Shaw lives. Oh, yes, free the actors, and they will bring such gifts.

"'In war, we will fight side by side.'" Wittman Goong gave the next part.

But Lance chimed in, and made this up: "Wherever we find a sit-in, we'll sit. A salt march along the coast? We'll march. A spinning wheel, we'll spin."

"'Heaven and Earth, read our hearts,'" Chang Fei continued. "'If we turn aside from righteousness or forget kindliness, may Heaven and man take out vengeance on us.'"

"Bless our chosen family," said Lance, sprinkling each man's and each woman's hair with salt from the saltshaker. "You are my chosen family." The audience, their ladies, liked that part the best, and repeated after him, "My chosen family."

Wittman just about broke character. "Wait a minute. Hold it. Listen." He knelt on the butcher block to talk better. Lance got him with salt in the back of the neck and down his collar. He jumped off the butcher block. "You're right, we throw a barbecue. We're out on a ranch, we do a rodeo tournament and a cookout." Wittman zinged the cleaver from off the knife magnet. "Slaughter a black ox and a white horse, make them into steaks and hamburgers in full shocking en-scène view of the audience. Audience participation—they eat and they're sworn in in this blood ceremony that will change everybody into a Chinese. Yes, we invite foes too to a theater of blood that cuts through t.v. souls. Serve dog. We ought to taste puppy dog and intestinally remember our heritage, our cuisine." Nanci and Sunny put their hands over their mouths and squeezed their knees out of the way and said, "Oooo." They were the little girls you gave worms and bugs to. Taña laughed. Judy frowned. "Three hundred people came to the peach orchard to witness that first vow. The young men vol-unteered for the brothers' army. Later, here in the Far Out West, miners came in from the fields and paid a speck of gold for admission to *The Three Kingdoms.* And lowly brakemen came from railroad yards, and laundry guys, and migrant farm hands, and cooks from out of the basement kitchens of restaurants. They came to be part of a war oath. And to watch the rancher and the tatami-shoemaker and the fugitive be transformed into knights who fought in silks and armor and tiger shoes." Wittman prowled up to the butcher block on tiger feet, and chopped it with his sword, Black Dragon. "Our generation, who have nothing left, will remember the first movies we ever saw—the camera shoots up at the heads of Chang Fei and his black horse against the sky. The drag-on-scalloped flag on his eighteen-foot spear whips in the wind—'Chang' the word on the pennon, 'Chang,' one of the first Chinese words you learned to read. 'Chang Fei,' said our parents and grandparents. And us kids stopped running up and down the aisles. 'It's Chang Fei.' We galloped along the bottom of the screen, part of the army that rides with the three brothers." Making like slow kung fu tai chi moves, Wittman pushed hands and feet circularly. The second rule of improv: A new ritual is embarrassing, it's okay. "Beneath

the peach blossoms—close-up on veins and pollen—and the
beginning green of leaves out of dark branches, Liu Pei rolls
back his runningwater sleeves. He draws his sharp blade. And
cuts the neck arteries of the black ox and the white horse.
The unknowing animals step back from the red streams,
then pass out. Red Rabbit, Gwan's horse, is tethered to a
peach tree, and the tree rains blossoms on him. Interspersed
among the trees are yellow pennons, the mulberry on a yellow field, Liu Pei's insignia and colors; the Southern Pacific
flies a yellow standard to this very day. The chefs and sous-
chefs of Chinatown will be cooking all through the show,
and we'll serve meat rare from the fire. Our faces will turn
red on wine like Gwan Goong's and Chang Fei's. We'll have
dancing. Carouse all night for a week. A fat lady will dance to
cave-thundering drums. Bonfires shoot overlapping shadows
of her abundant body—her uplifted arms make many arms—
against hillsides, where monkeys lean out like gargoyles to
look at her. We could stage this at the Faculty Club at Cal—
inside one of those mead-hall proscenium fireplaces. Light a
fire in one fireplace, and she dances in the other. I got inside
the Faculty Club as a desk clerk. I don't know why they gave
me the job. Everybody else was a Greek, not frat boys, Greeks
from Greece. I wrote their love letters to our American girls,
and in exchange they gave me waiter's rights to turkey car-
cass, duck heads, champagne sleepers. You should see the goings-on—professors in drag dancing on tables. I checked-in
Herman Kahn. Back to the enormous lady: Her tootsie
rolls of fat bounce and jounce and rub together, breast re-
bounding on breast, wonderful crevices in her neck and waist
and limbs and ankles, where gold coins flip and flap. Gold
weights tug at the softest fattest pierced earlobes. She must
turn herself on all the time. She twirls on the underbeddings
of her toes. Her back is a continent of skin. She's more nude
than all of us put together. All by herself, she can be Lady
Yakusa's army, kimonos down to their hips and a tattooed
dragon continuous across the row of their naked backs; ram-
pant gardant, zigzagging their swords before them like the
scythes of time, they scan the battlefield. The fattest lady on
earth is laughing, and her laughter jiggles everything. The
heroes shout and clap out rhythms for her."

"I don't know any woman who would want to play her," said Taña.

"Neither do I," said Sunny. "Fellini's done her already, huh, Lance?"

"I'm certainly not playing her," said Nanci.

"If there's anything I hate," said Judy Louis, "it's bachelor parties with girls jumping out of cakes, and stags horning around the table."

"But she's not a cake girl," said Wittman. "She's scary. What is it about her that scares you? Her size?"

"She is too a pop-up out of the cupcake," said Judy, "and I'm not scared. Everybody else wears armor, and she's naked."

"But she's bigger than they are. She'll raise the question of how come our other beauties are bony witches." He was describing the effect of mascara and eyeshadow and contoured cheeks and noses on the very women around him. Indeed, witch women were riding again, on boy's bikes, which are better made and more like broomsticks than girl's bicycles. Hair streaming behind them, they screeched at windows, "Come out. Come out." They were retrieving old names and the past by ouija board. They'd been burned at the stake in a prior life, and were tough. You play right or else, Wittman, we're going to get you, Monkey King. Not heeding a goddess when he was face-to-face with one, with four, he went headlong, "I won't leave out my large lady. There's a tradition of fatness that we have lost. All that's left are the hippo ballerinas in *Fantasia*. This fat beauty heated up kung fu opera twenty years ago, and I want to see her dance again. I want to bring her back. If none of you guys want to play her, I'm going to have to go on a star search."

"A Hong Kong actress would do it," said Nanci, whose hair color was witch black. She looked down her pale thin nose.

"Felliniesque," said Sunny. "Too Felliniesque."

"Soldiers in fatigued outfits bore me to death," said Judy. "I don't go to movies without female leads. No glamour dresses. No romantic interest. No love music. Men dramas, no good. I see on the t.v. news, suit men meeting and discussing, I know already, up to no good business."

"I hate movies about guys who don't shave digging out of some stalag," agreed Taña. "Or military guys who never change costumes inside the same submarine or foxhole for two and a half hours. I can't sit through trial movies either, twelve guys in a jury box."

"You don't understand," said Wittman. "The fat dancer has unbound feet and unbound tits and unbound hair. She busts through stereotypes. That we're puritanical. That Han people don't dance. That a fatty can't hold center stage. Okay. Here's a part you will live and die for. The drumming for the fat dance is pounded out by a noblewoman named Hoong Ngoak a.k.a. Red Jade. She led a navy to the rescue at the height of the war that you have guessed is coming up. She outfitted the crow's nest with a big-ass taiko wardrum, and she rode that swaying crow's nest through days and nights of sea battle. She kept alit a lantern over her head, and against the black sea and sky, she was a flying, drumming, lit inspiration. The white fur of her headdress circled her face. Her long black hair and the tails of ermines blew with the speed of the flagship. She is a loud-drumming will-o'-the-wisp faery, and she flies on a pair of wings, flags tucked into her sash, the flag of Han and the flag of her family, Leong. Leong Hoong Ngoak, her total name. In the midst of battle, in a star of light—the spot will pick her out in a top balcony or on the catwalk or on a flyup—she's a miraculous living figurehead. She's a target for explosives flown up to the crow's nest by missile birds, which explode and make flare the metal discs in her headdress and in her pink silk maybe bulletproof jacket. From the fleeing ships, she appears to be a supernatural being coming after them. She whips up the drumbeat, and the wind and the waves rise. The sun comes up. We see her fleet—flats of ships, each flat larger than the one in back of it, like a fan of face cards, many ships, each one diminishing in size clear out to the horizon line on the backdrop. The ships have faces—eyes on either side of the bow, which is the nose, and there are moustaches too, and mouths—swimmers treading ocean water while talking and arguing. Lady Jade whams her clublike drumsticks, tasseled with horsehair, down and down upon the taiko for loud war. Her fleet traps the enemy in a bay—we can stage this on Lake Merritt or Lake Temescal, or in the Bay—and her sailors swashbuckle the enemy ships while she drums out victory. They burn the flags of the Gum/Gold armada, who are bearmen and wolfmen."

Unfortunately for peace on Earth, the listening ladies were appeased, and Lance had run out of plowshare ideas. Nanci and Taña and Sunny and Judy thought that if they were allowed to play war women, they were liberated. The time of peace women, who will not roll bandages or serve coffee and doughnuts or rivet airplanes or man battleships or shoot guns at strangers, does not begin tonight.

The unfamiliar light of Saturday morning—daybreak. A wind from the Valley blew the dawn in clouds up and over the Altamont and down into Oakland.

Sky poured pink through the windows. Everyone floated in pink air—spun sugar, spun glass, angel's hair, champagne. The friends moved toward the windows to see where this rose was coming from, and saw everything, the water of the Bay, the glass of houses and buildings, the sky, the dew on the grass, rose-blessed. Is the sun like this every morning if we but wake early enough to catch it? Is it a time of year—a season of rose air? The crew in the lightbooth has flipped on the pink gels, and tinted all the stage and the men's and women's faces. It seemed as if you could float out the window on the strange atmosphere. There are Chinese people who would explain that Gwan Goong was paying us a visit; the color was emanating from a building in downtown Oakland, where you could have seen Gwan Goong's good red face, or its reflection, upon ten stories of brick wall. You could have asked for any wish, and Gwan Goong would have granted it. You could have been a millionaire. As it turned out, nobody in this gathering of friends was ever again afraid when flying in an airplane. And later one or another of them in danger felt that there was someone protective beside or just ahead of him or her, making a way. They didn't discuss the rose air, didn't compare one's sensing of it with what anyone else was seeing, if anything, until years later when two happened to meet, and somebody said, "Do you remember that morning seeing the air—the air before your eyes and on your hands—pink and rose?" And then they wondered that they had not exclaimed over it at the time. (Could it have been a waft of nuclear testing gone astray from the South Pacific?)

A feeling went through Wittman that nothing wrong could ever happen again—or *had* ever happened. It's very good

sitting here, among friends, coffee cup warm in hands, cigarette. Together we fall silent as the sun shows its full face. The
new day. Good show, gods. Why don't I, from now on, get up
for every dawn? My life would be different. I would no longer
be fucked up. I set out on more life's adventure with these
companions, the people with whom I have seen dawn. My
chosen family. We're about to change the world for the better.

Sunny walked about her house with a brown paper bag picking up paper plates and beer bottles and plastic wineglasses,
dumping ashtrays, wiping food up off the floor. "Come on,
people, either keep it in your mouth or on your plate," she
said. She was a full-time housewife, which she had to be in order to keep the trompes-l'oeil functioning. She was returning
what she had put away that needed protection from the party.
Half of a round glass table went against one side of the wall,
and the other diameter on the other side, the found bottles on
top filled to elegant waterlines. Where there had been dancing,
she lowered a board hung on chains back down to its height as
a table, découpaged with the pages of Beardsley's Savoy book.
Salomé's big lips kissing John the Baptist's head, blood looping in designs like her long sleeves. On top of that, pillboxes
and a vase of fake lilies, and green bananas ripening to go with
the rug. She had painted the gold and black rays of Art Deco
shooting out of doorframes. Lance handed out hot towels for
faces and hands. O comfort.

"We've only started," said Wittman, out the door and across
the porch and down the stairs and through the yard. "This
play is immense. Epic. Our story won't fit a one-act on a unit
set of crates and burlap bags. I'm going to bring back to theater the long and continuous play that goes on for a week without repeating itself. Because life is long and continuous. The
way theater was in the old days. I mean the old days in *this*
country. The audience comes back every night for the continu-
ation. They live with us. The thing will not fit between dinner
at the Tivoli and the after-theater snack at Martha Jean, Inc.
or the New Shanghai Café." His friends agreed that he should
work some more on the play; they would act in it, and they
would be on the lookout for more actors and a venue. Then
Wittman was again out on the streets, but this time with Taña.

Dew sparked on the lawns and parked cars. A church bell

rang a few iambs. Brother Antoninus, are you waking up at St. Albert's? A black-and-white cop car and a black-and-white cab cruised past each other. We're in a good part of Oakland, which used to be restricted. "No person of African or of Japanese, Chinese, or any Mongolian descent will ever be allowed to purchase, own, or even rent a lot in Rockridge or live in any house that may be built there except in the capacity of domestic servants of the occupant thereof." Lance was living there in an integrated marriage, and Wittman was walking there. Oakland Tech ought to be teaching this localest history.

Passing St. Albert's, Taña and Wittman learned that they had something in common. On dates, each with another, they had followed the sound of men's voices chanting, carrying far without electric amplification. Hiding in the bushes outside the gate, they had seen monks in procession around the grass. Breath issued from cowl hoods. Which one of those figures was Brother Antoninus himself? Hands from angel sleeves held and shielded candles. How is it that rows of lit candles stir you so? It's automatic. The candles at the Big Game rally at the Greek Theater the night before the Cal-Stanford game get to you too, religiously. Birthday children become arsonists because if little candles on a cake can make me feel this religious, what if I set fire to a building, why don't I blow up a country? Knowing some Latin from high school, Wittman had felt on the verge of understanding the songs. "Compline," said Taña, "the last prayer at night." The compline had been so wonderful, Wittman admitted that he'd wanted to join up but for his vow against missionary religions. This time of the morning all was still, no people on the grounds, and no lights in the buildings.

Taña had taken off her sandals with the tire treads for a long, barefoot walk around the dog shit of Oakland. She held her shoes in one hand and Wittman's fingers by the other. He sang to her, "Tiptoe through the tulips, through the tulips with me." A bearded man, holding his head with care, climbed some front steps, and before going inside, turned and gave them a wave. Fellow tripper come through the night, come home. Not every last one of us who trips out of a Friday night makes it back home. Across the street, a couple with arms around each other hurried along, then stood to talk, then hurried on. A raven had darted a feather into her hair. He carried a black cape folded over his arm. Yes, all over town, batwings were closing. May the minds that shot off to other planets and dimensions settle gently adown to the ground of our Earth.

A single sheet of newspaper flared up into the air and flew, gliding and opening, and sailed over their heads. *Like a blank piece of paper, I drifted along past the houses, up the boulevard again.* Wittman ran after it, pulling Taña along. Please be the girl that I'm in love with.

Her sandals under her armpits, she held on to his hand with both of hers and dragged him to a stop, and up some side stairs of the California School of Arts and Crafts. She led him to a courtyard, and where she leaned back on a wall soft with moss. He leaned above her, like his elbow against her high-school locker. "Hey, wanta make out?"

She didn't laugh, but looked gravely into his eyes for quite a while. "Yeah. Let's make out."

"Let's swap spit," he said, but giggled his Chinese giggle. He had lost his previous cool. He firmed up his face. Took her face between his hands, blonde hair between his fingers. Gave her a hard kiss. Pulled back to look at her, to see how she liked it.

She looked big eyes back at him. Held his gaze. He loved the way her eyebrows frowned; she was troubled. He was getting to her. He took another kiss, longer. This time when he looked, her eyes were closed.

"Hey, Taña," he said. "Taña. Wake up. Talk to me."

She put her mouth up to his ear, and said, "You want it hot, I'll make it hot for you."

He held her chin, led her mouth away from his ear, back to his own mouth. Lips barely rubbing, he slid past her mouth and attacked her ear. "Hey, tell me. Are you blonde all over? Huh? Are you? Are you blonde everywhere? Blonde body hair? Where else are you blonde?"

"My armpits. My armpit hair comes in blonde. Why? Are you queer for blonde pubic hair?"

Shit. A queer for blondes. If she had brown hair, would he have said, "Are you brown everywhere? Do you have brown pubic hair?" "Blonde chick. White girl," he said, calling her names. "Are you a loose white girl? Where do you live, loose white girl? I want to take you home. And I want you to invite me in."

She ought to have slapped his hands away, and dumped him for acting racist. If you have principles, you do not like him anymore when you find out somebody's a racist or a Green Beret or a Republican or a narc. You ought to be able to sense such a defect, and the obstinacy of it, and run.

"Did you go to 'America Needs Indians'?" Tañ
a asked. Yes, the first multi-media event in the world. There had been movies and slides, color, and black and white, projected against these four walls, the sky with moon and clouds overhead, and music and wise Indian voices chanting like Gregorian, like Sanskrit Buddhist. The crowds turned around and around to see everything, and their juxtapositions. A herd of buffalo charged from one side, and mustangs from the other. Indians riding across Monument Valley, and, simultaneously, close-ups of their faces. The art students had painted one another's faces with Day-Glo. People kept saying, "The tribes are gathering again," which sounded new and old. An airplane or a flying saucer—come for us—would look down and see a square flashing in marvelous light show. Now the walls were dark and no vibes. "Because it wasn't here," said Tañ
a. "It was at the Art Institute." Wittman took her word for it, having been too ripped, and also, Chinese having no sense of direction. (That's why the Long March took so long.) Wittman and Tañ
a might have met each other at "America Needs Indians." "What hours were you there?" "What were you wearing?" "Who were you with?" "Who were you?" "I sort of remember somebody who might have been you. Did you wear braids with a headband?" More and more in common. She can be my continuity- and direction-finder.

They walked out of the school, and he followed her through a gate, bedighted with rose vines in thorn, then along a footpath with ivy trailing upon it. Her part of the house was in back.

She had wonderful, wonderful digs—flights of mobiles, windchimes, models (bottles and dry sunflowers) for still-lifes on tables and shelves, even the dishes on the drainboard arranged in a composition, cans of brushes, the smells of linseed oil and paint and patchouli, prisms turning in the east windows, madras India Import bedspreads for curtains and bed, spectrums of yellows and oranges, coat-hanger wire webbed with lavender and purple tissue paper over light bulbs, intricate old rugs (whose mazes you could lose yourself in when stoned, a kid again lining up armies of marbles). He could live here. He was itching to rummage, and to view life through her kaleidoscopes and prisms and magnifying glasses and scientific microscope. He went right over to her industrial-strength easel under the skylight; in its clamps was a sketch of a forest with pairs of points, the eyes of animals. There were smiles in the leaves. "You're a painter," he said. "I wish I were a painter, and always had something to show for it." He spun a land-brown globe—Arabia Deserta, La Terra Inconoscivta, the Great American Desert, Red Cloud's Country, the Unattached Territories, the Badlands, Barbaria, the Abode of Emptiness, the Sea of Darkness, sea serpents and mermaids abounding. "Strange beasts be here." Nada ou Nouvel, whence the four winds blew. And she had a map of the universe—Hyperspace Barrier, areas of Giants, Supergiants, Dwarfs, Protogalaxies. She's another one who knows how to live on her own, where she belongs in time and space.

She went into the kitchen and boiled water, set up her drip system, ground her beans. Wittman wandered about.

Toulouse-Lautrec's *Divan Japonais* took up one wall; Taña had decorated to match that print—the furniture matte black like the man's top hat and the woman's dress, feathered hat, fan and long gloves; the madras picked up the orange hair and the yellow beard and cane. He slid open a box of kitchen matches—a bat, upright, cute face and wings akimbo, not alive. Vampiress? Taña also collected birds' nests with blue and speckled eggshells, and downy nestling feathers, and a piniony quill. A set of false teeth had a reefer crutched in its grin. Tuning forks and magnets. A cabinet of good paper. A shelf of sketch books. Nudes. A roll of new canvas. Buckets of stretcher bars. He sat at the round table with the crystal ball and apples. There were also a set of brass gramweights as in a lab, a brown velvety cloth bunched around things, collages on boxes. Flows and layers of candle wax relief-mapped the courses of many evenings staying up with friends talking and sculpting. On a postcard of Seal Rock, she had drawn a few lines and dots, and you could see that seals are born out of rocks, and rocks come from seals.

Taña brought over two cups of coffee, sat across from him, smoked. "Wittman," she said, "Darling. I've been thinking: The next time I get it on with a man, I set ground rules."

"Yes? What is it, sweetheart?" She called me a man and a darling, and she wants to get it on. I've never called anyone Sweetheart before, never called anyone anything. "Go on."

"I may not be in love with you. Say, you're the one I'm in love with, I won't let you go. But, say, I meet him tomorrow, I'll leave you. I'm being fair. You don't love me either. We're starting even. There was this guy named Edmund I was in love with when I was seventeen. I know what love feels like. I'm not in love with you. Maybe I cannot love again. But, say, I find him again, or another one like him, I'm going to have to get up and leave you. I don't have an obsession over you, though I do want to make love with you. You don't define my life. I just want you to know how I am before you decide to make it with me. Making love is my idea as well as yours. This isn't just your idea, okay? You're not going to say later that this was all my idea, or your idea. We can each of us cut out whenever we feel like it. If somebody that either of us can love comes along, why, we're going to go, okay? As of yesterday we got along perfectly well without each other. And we're not going to feel destroyed because I'm not in love with you and you're not in love with me. So, tomorrow, if one of us wants to be by himself, nobody's going to phone him up. But we could possibly go on forever not falling in love with somebody on the outside. We may get used to having each other around, and end up growing old together. Do you know Chekhov's concept of dear friends? That's what we can be to each other, dear friend."

Damn. She beat him to it. Outplayed again. He was the tough-eyed one who had been planning to let the next girl know point by point what she would be in for entangling with him. But he'd hesitated, what if she then wouldn't want to be in for it? No girl but the one in his head sat still for a read-out of rules. He'd balked, and she'd taken his lines. Now what?

Taña had been warming and softening wax in her hands and was molding it. Don't go away, Taña. Does she know she looks winsome? Truth and Consequences. He was the loser. Consequences for him. "I think I could love you," he said. "I think I do love you."

So they got it on, and they were graceful, just so much fore-play, just so much fervor and abandon and sweat, positions normal. Classic moves. Silently went at it. She didn't say much, and he didn't say much. Mouths against parts of the body, he did not make her blurt out, "I love you." Well, it was a fuck where they were hardly acquainted, after all, and one didn't want to turn off the other by seeming overly weirded out. Don't grunt and groan repulsively. Be courtly. Be mannerly. And honest. Although who's to know without having randomly made it with a large cross-section of the population—not the sampling of the one type that attracts you and is attracted by you—what's abnormally passionate. The business-like way that most people walk around publicly conducting themselves, you would think nobody does anything sexual.

Well, he was not like most people. "Hey," he said. "Play with me. Taña. Tell me, tell me, what is it you like about my body?" He was up on his elbow beside her. She lay on her back with her white arms behind her head, her hair splaying, legs splaying too. All in the light of day.

"I like your smooth bony chest," she said, bringing her slow arms down and holding the flats of her hands against his chest. She put her cheek there too and listened to his heart. "And you're thin. I can almost touch your bones, only skin between my fingers and your bones. And I like the way you look down at me haughty like that, looking over your cheekbones. I like your hair, thick and black. And your eyes have an expression, I don't know what to call it. Your turn. You tell me what you like about me."

"You have pink nipples," he said. Pink nipples have got to be more sensitive than brown nipples like his own.

"And my face? What about my face?" she asked. "Tell me about my face."

"You're lovely. Your face is lovely." (Remember in *Far from the Madding Crowd* where, of her three suitors, Bathsheba Everdean chooses Sergeant Troy, "the one to tell her that she is beautiful." Troy could also "take down Chinese in short-hand.") "Beautiful." He stroked her arm. The hairs stood up and moved back down. More so than the hair on her head, this light hair on the arms was to him Caucasian. "This arm hair is how I can tell you're a white girl," he said, aboveboard. "Your turn, beautiful Taña. Tell me what physical feature of mine makes me Chinese to you, and how it turns you on."

"Your eyes," she said. "Mainly your eyes."

"And my skin?"

"And your skin." Which makes me Chinese all over. "You're the same color as me, but a different tone."

Good. She did not tell him that she liked "yellow" skin or "slanty" eyes. She did not say he was "mysterious." If she turns out to be a freak for orientalia, kick her out of bed. She's not getting any mysterious East from me.

"Is my nose too big?" she asked.

"Everybody thinks their nose is too big," he said, wisely. "Everybody thinks their own face has the most pores too. You have long eyelashes. Bat them against me." She gave him butterfly kisses on his bony chest. She caressed the golden ecru of his flesh, and again he got on her, in her. Went in unto her. And again she enjoyed herself wordlessly. She'll continue speaking after he recedes. Unstoppered. In *Hiroshima Mon Amour*, the Japanese man listens and listens to the Frenchwoman talk. In *Snow Country*, the man does the talking.

"What about my toes?" Wittman asked. "You notice my toes? I noticed your toes. Your toes were pushing against your Tijuana sandals, which strapped them tightly together. That was one of the first things I noticed about you."

"You have a thing for feet, do you?"

"No, not me. Do you?"

"Yes. As a matter of fact, I do. I can't stand the feeling of my toes sticking together, especially the two little ones at the end. Skin to skin. It's always going on, but sometimes I think about it. Feeling them stick together drives me crazy. Especially when I have my shoes on and I'm somewhere where I can't reach down to pull them apart. You have that? They're doing it right now—look. Do you know what I mean? You know what I mean, don't you?"

"I can see if I start to think about it, I could work up an obsession. Toe skins. Yeah, I see what you mean. Lolita had that problem. Remember Humbert Humbert stuffing cotton between her toes? She's sitting on the bed, and she holds up her feet. All her toes are separated with cotton wads."

"Wait a minute." She was laughing. "Lolita didn't have this

toe sensitivity. Humbert Humbert was painting her toenails. He was saying, 'Hold still.'"

"Hey, don't spoil Lolita for me. She and I are just like this." He crossed his fingers—made kings.

"I have it worse in my left toes."

"So you never heard the one about the difference between Chinese toes and Japanese toes?"

"No, what's that?"

"What do you think? Take a look at my toes, and tell me if you see anything unusual."

Whenever you find a white person you can trust, get some inside answers to questions. Spy out specific racisms.

"Is this a test to see how many men's toes I've been looking at?" asked Taña.

"I promise not to get jealous of you looking at other men's toes."

"You have nice toes. Nice long, far-apart toes."

"I can spread them at will, and pick things up with them. I got monkey feet from going barefoot as a kid. Would you say my toes are too far apart?"

"When you open them up like that, they're unusually far apart. I guess you don't have my problem feeling them smack against one another. Tell me the one about Chinese toes and Japanese toes."

"I shouldn't give you a hang-up. There ought to be a rule not to give one another new hang-ups."

"There ought to be a rule when somebody starts to tell something, he has to finish it, no fair bringing up half a secret."

"You didn't grab a peek at my toes to see whether I'm a chinaman or a jap?"

"You can tell by the toes?"

"That's what I'm asking you. Comic books and *Life* magazine said that the way to tell a good Chinese from a bad jap is that the former has more space between the toes."

"Then I must be a Japanese, and you a Chinese."

He parted her sweet, suckable Japanese toes, and bent down and kissed one. Then he sucked each little piggy, and licked the tight spaces between them. He heard her sigh, "My toes are having orgasms." Holding that sensitive foot against his chest and heart, he loved up the other one. "Wittman," she called, and he looked up to see her face, which did not make him feel embarrassed. "You gave me an orgasm between all my toes," she said. "Ten toes, eight orgasms. I didn't know toes could do that."

"I didn't either," he said; "I think we've invented a new sex act." He had not thought of toe love before suddenly doing it. Her feet were so beautiful and so human. He hoped that someday he would get to know her well enough to ask her to make love to and with his toes. Find out whether men can have orgasms down there too.

She put on her X-L t-shirt to go to sleep. Every girl he ever made it with (two) wore t-shirts to bed. They only wear negligees in movies. They want you to make love to their real self and not their peignoir.

Taña thought about complimenting Wittman on how nice and soft his penis was. But he was such a worrier over masculinity, he'd take it wrong. Men don't understand that a penis is the loveliest softness to touch, more tender than a baby's earlobe, softer than a woman's breast. And after fucking is the best time to touch and touch, but you can't do that for too long, or they feel bad they're not getting hard. Wittman was not one you could praise for his softness. Taña saved up her acclaim.

As they lay facing each other, forehead to forehead, and stared, owl eyes, she described what she saw: In another country, a path wound uphill through high waves of yellow grasses. Trumpet flowers on cactus vines blared on either side. On top of the hill there stood a house; it had never been completed, or someone was dismantling it for firewood. No windows and no doors in the frames. Wittman looked clear through to blue sky outlined by boards with driftwood grain and rusty nails. He wasn't asleep and dreaming. On the contrary, he felt especially awake, and was seeing—was walking in—this other place. "I'm awake," he said. "Taña. Taña? Do you see what I see?"

"Yes." He heard her voice beside him. "There's a girl on the other side of the house."

"She's dressed in a costume of a country that I can't identify."

"Yes. Black and red with silver, and her hair is long and coiled."

They blinked at one another. What is this?

Inside the house, every room opened to every other room and to the outdoors. The girl's heel fleeted away past a doorway. A fair breeze blew on their skins and through their hair. The sun radiated through the rooms, radiated inside their heads. Wittman looked at her beside him. "You sent me that flash. It came from you to me." She nodded yes. Just before the flash in his brainpan, he had seen it like a comet with tail whiz the short distance from her to him. His brain felt warm in one spot. "Whoa," he said. "We ought to be documenting this. One of us, the sender—you—should write down what you're about to send, and I write down what I receive. In sealed envelopes. And we get a third-party witness to open them. We ought to be scientific about this."

But E.S.P. has a quality of conviction—I am awake, more awake than ever—no doubt about it; proof feels beside the point, too slow. And it's more fun to fly around a foreign place than to be in a lab counting hearts, clubs, diamonds, and spades. What was causing this? Staying up all night? And not having dreamed? Oom-lette? A coincidence of true minds? Was this going to last forever between the two of them? Wittman added a tree to the hillside. Taña made clouds change shapes fast; strange winds were sculpting the clouds. The beyond mountains changed in a sequence: Pyramids. Glaciers. Volcanoes. Easter Island heads. Stone grandfathers of Cheju Island. Totem poles with ears. Windmills turning. Does this mean that he and she have seen the insides of each other's heads, and he needn't be scared of her? If she's the only human being he's ever encountered, perhaps ever going to encounter, with whom he can read minds, is she the one meant for him? He should never have taken drugs. Can't tell the gods' chimeras from freaks of my own.

"Let's find out if there's a roadsign that will tell us where we are," said Taña. They hiked down the palomino flank of the hill to the main road. A sign gave a traffic rule in international symbols. There was no name of a town or any advertising. There was no mood music.

"Can you do this with anybody or just me?" asked Wittman.

"Just you," said Taña.

They talked and saw more things and ate and made more love and fell asleep together. When they awoke, it was Sunday.

"Do you want to go for a drive?" she asked. "Can I drive you home?"

"Do you want to drive to the City?" he asked. No plans for the day. No job tomorrow. "I live in the City. I found a tunnel I could show you. They were going to build a subway once." He hadn't meant to tell anyone about his secret tunnel, but blabbed, showing off that he knew deep San Francisco. Oh, well, a bomb shelter should be shared.

She drove a Porsche Speedster, "1959. 1600 D," she said. It was an ovoid, softly rounded like a tan nest egg. The wrap bumper was painted white, a curve of Easter egg icing. The upholstery was chocolatey leather, and you sat low to the street. "Wanta drive?" Taña offered him the keys, and got into the suicide seat. The engine started up noisily, high in the throat, an angry muffler. James Dean had been killed in a Porsche, a silver Spyder. It was a risk car, no protection—top down, no roll bar, next thing to a motorcycle.

Showing Taña that he could talk and drive at the same time, Wittman said that she reminded him of his grandmother who dressed theater companies. When the opera costumes arrived from Hong Kong, she handed out the gorgeous raiment saying to the actors, "Treat it like shit." That's class. That's the way Taña treats this car, letting him drive.

"The windows go up and down in a Convertible D," she said. "There are only thirteen hundred of these in California."

"When we pass one of those twelve hundred and ninety-nine, do I have to give him the Porsche owner's wave? Do we flash the high sign at Karmann Ghias and M.G.s and T.R.3s? Or Porsches only? Hey, where's my car cap?" He had to talk somewhat loud above the wind and the motor. Also she put him off having to tell him the windows go up and down.

"You wave to anybody you like." Said with the confidence of a white person. "I didn't buy this car myself. I don't make that much. My parents gave it to me. The deal was: either go to Stanford without a car or go to Cal, only sixty-seven dollars a semester, and with the savings buy a fine car, and live at home and commute." So white parents also care that their kids go to a school that's cheap and close to home. "I got the car, but went to Arts and Crafts."

Wittman decided to take the long way to the City, south on

the Nimitz through Oakland (past the STOP CASTING PO-
ROSITY sign), and across the long, long San Mateo Bridge.
Its railings ran low alongside the low car. Better not have
car trouble. The sign says No Stopping and No Turning
Around. No suicides allowed. There was hardly any traffic
today, and the car seemed to be shooting out on a plank.
A pelican floated up from under the bridge. Wings holding
still, it glided over the open car. They got a detailed look at
its beak with a pouch, its legs and feet perfectly tucked into
its body, like airplane wheels fitting into the wheel well. Two
more pelicans came up on an updraft. Pterodactyls. And the
car an exoskeletal scarab. A new age of reptiles. One of the
birds landed on the bridge rail, wings folding as legs came
down, all in balance, not a wobble or a teeter. "Don't look
at them," said Taña. "Keep your eyes on the road. I'll do the
looking."

Wittman was having a problem with his natural eye-blinks.
He kept seeing three tall pepper mills with round heads, not
well delineated.

"They're the windmills," Taña explained. "They're fading. Don't look at them while you're driving. They look like
Egyptian cats, don't they, with long front legs and long side
whiskers. Those are the vanes." She was holding her hands
over her eyes, her hair blowing out behind her. Sometimes
the wind tossed it into his face as if it were his own blonde
hair. "Now they look like pepper mills," she reported. "Now
they're keyholes. They're fading." How are you bound to the
lady you dream with? And see things with?

Coming off the bridge they crossed the Bayshore and El
Camino Real, and headed north on Skyline. The big bonsai
were bent toward the sea, when today's wind, thick with fog,
was blowing inland. San Francisco—wet as if seen through
tears.

"Look," said Taña. "It's a windmill." It was the abandoned
lighthouse. "What if we've been seeing the future? Do you
want to stop?" No. He does not want her to contain him in
her crystal ball. He wanted to be driving the Porsche by himself, his Porsche, and he did not want to take her to his secret
tunnel or to his pok-mun. Where she'll be needing to go to
the bathroom, and he hands her his roll of toilet paper, and

she hurries down the hall among the commentators in their armpitty tank-tops.

Yes, let's stop and visit the lighthouse, then, as a theatrical family on a drive would do. Explore storefronts, mansions, barns, terraces, vineyards, caves, and imagine the theater they would house. Prisons, forts, water-pumping stations, beer factories, gas stations, lecture halls at teaching hospitals. This lighthouse could be it. The door stood open, but there was no air flow for creatures that need to breathe. A dead pigeon lay on the floor. Taña climbed the steel stairs, and Wittman followed her. The buzzardy air seemed hotter each step up. The windows were opaque with salt and dirt. On a ledge was another dead bird. "Let's get out of here," said Wittman. "We're inside somebody else's brain." The foghorns were groaning, the far-off suffering of ogres and sea dragons. "We're not going to be able to turn this lighthouse into a theater, Taña. Unless our show had vertical action, and an audience of six lay face upward. Or we could seat the audience up here and on the stairs, and they look down at a play about the abysmal." Taña finally couldn't breathe the air from one million B.C. anymore, and they got out of there.

Zip into the City quick past El Barrio Chino, and up Telegraph Hill to Coit Tower. Wittman parked next to Christopher Columbus, who stands with a foot on a rock and his nose toward the Golden Gate and the Pacific beyond. Sailboats and whitecaps were hoving sharp out there. Masts tick-tocking, the docked boats rocked like Daruma dolls. "Welcome to my estate, Taña," said Wittman as he opened the car door for her. "Wait until you see the view from my top floor—all three bridges visible on this windswept morning." They went up the stairs that were the stairway of Rita Hayworth's mansion in *Pal Joey*, the camera avoiding Columbus in her front yard.

The elevator doors were in the middle of a mural about workers turning wheels of cable. A tower of W.P.A. artwork, a continuous epic of labor, musculatured men heroically operating turbines, women in white hats and aprons assembling milk. No place for us hummingbirds. The doors parted. Taña was not beside him. His mind was off of her for a moment, and she was gone. A wanderfooting woman. He looked for her outside.

A sweater had been left on a window ledge. He ought to try it on, a gift to him from the affluent society. A voluntarily poor person has a duty to take such a gift. Just then, a Chinese grandmother came running on gliding strides, to not pound the chi out of her system. She passed the sweater, went on circling the tower. He took the stairs up—Jimmy Stewart looking for lost Kim Novak in all the old familiar San Francisco places.

There she is, silhouetted in an arch, and she's talking to someone. Mrs. Coit ought to have put in a brass pole for her volunteer firemen; he'd slide down the hole and away. He strolled the circularama. Yes, all three bridges in sight today. And the dragon's tail zigzagging up and over Lombard Street. Alcatraz—our troupe will take over the Rock for theater-in-the-round, the audience as yardbirds, a guardwalk for the hanamichi thrust. The cellblocks were already a scaffold set like *Bye Bye Birdie*. And Angel Island too, waiting for us to come back and make a theater out of the Wooden House, where our seraphic ancestors did time. Desolation China Man angels.

Surely, one or two got off those islands and spread the theories about there being no escape against the ocean currents and sharks.

Wittman said a mantra for this place by the poet that his father tried to name him after.

> *Facing west from California's shores,*
> *Inquiring, tireless, seeking what is yet unfound,*
> *I, a child, very old, over waves, towards the house*
>   *of maternity, the land of migrations, look afar,*
> *Look off the shores of my Western sea, the circle*
>   *almost circled....*

"Wittman. Wittman," Taña called him. He went on over, his jealousy up. She had borrowed and was wearing a lumberman's jacket off of a bearded man. Guys with beards, though, were trusting one another, for a few months more anyway, to be pure white doves, who practice right politics, that is, leftist politics. You can tell by the beard, he's a reader of books, a listener to folk, jazz, and classical, a brother of the open road to pick up and be picked up hitchhiking. Taña did getdown introductions, "Greg. Wittman." Last names unnecessary but for the government taxing you and drafting you.

"Gabe. I've changed my name to Gabe."

"He's hiding out from the draft," said Taña. "You too, huh, Wittman?"

"Yeah," said Wittman. "Me too." We won't turn each other in. So I too have a face trusted at first sight by the underground.

"I was hiding out in Mexico," said Greg/Gabe. "But I came back to see if it's possible to live a private life inside this country. Mexico freaks me too far out. Sugar skulls, bread skulls. Kids eat marzipan in the shape of death. Skulls biting on skulls. No trouble with the federales on either side of the border." Yes, the autumn skeletons are appearing in "Gordo."

"I didn't re-register after graduation," said Wittman. "And I didn't give the feds my change-of-address. If I'd known it was coming to this, I would've shown up at a church every weekend until a minister got to know me to write me a recommendation for C.O."

"There's another way to go for the religious exemption. You haven't gotten your Universal Life Church card?"

"No. How do I do that?"

"You have to be ordained by an ordained minister. I'm an ordained minister. The idea of the Universal Life Church is that the First Amendment gives each one of us total freedom to make up religion. Mine has as its main and First Commandment: 'Thou shalt not kill.' No exceptions. My god is literal about that. I'm ethically prepared if I come up against the Army philosopher. Do you want me to ordain you? I can ordain you."

"Yeah, go ahead. I'd like that. Ordain me."

"I ordain thee a minister of the Universal Life Church. There. You write a letter to Reverend Kirby Hensley, 1776 Poland Street in Modesto, and he'll send you a certificate and a card. You take that documentation to the Board of Health, and ask for a license to marry people, so you're recognized by the State of California. If you hold public rituals in your living room, you can be tax-exempt. So you're legit by the I.R.S. too. It's all legal, First Amendment. Every pacifist deed you do, keep your documentation for your C.O. defense. Educated people who read and write well have a chance at it. The Army

Ph.D.s and chaplains, who've graduated from seminaries, break down the high-school dropouts. You can get help on the argumentation from the American Friends Service Committee or Catholic Action."

"I have my ideas straight. Thanks."

"You should think out whether you really want to be an official Conscientious Objector. C.O.s do service, and don't get to choose what kind. They're the avant-garde, who go out ahead of the infantry to dismantle mines. The exemption for married guys is going to stop any day. Why don't I marry the two of you? Cover all the bases. I have a perfect record; nobody I've ever married has gotten a divorce."

"Sure," said Taña. "I'd be glad to save you from the draft, Wittman."

"Sure," said Wittman, who had a principle about spontaneity. Zen. Don't mull. There's divinity in flipping a coin rather than weighing debits and assets. Taña, anyway, is probably his truest love already. Always do the more flamboyant thing. Don't be a bookkeeper. He took Taña's hand and said, "Will you marry me?"

"Yes," she said.

The Reverend Gabe had the wedding ceremony memorized, the one from the Episcopal *Book of Common Prayer* that we all know from the movies: ". . . wilt thou, Wittman ah—?"

"Ah Sing."

"Wilt thou, Wittman Ah Sing, have this woman to thy wedded wife . . . love her, comfort her, honor and keep her in sickness and in health, for richer, for poorer, forsaking all others, keep thee only unto her, so long as ye both shall live?"

"Yes, I will."

Taña also said, "Yes, I will," for her part. "My first marriage. Your first marriage too, isn't it, Wittman? You haven't been married before? No alimony? No child support?"

"No. My first marriage too." No little Chinese wife back home.

"You can also say, 'I plight thee my troth,'" said the preacher.

"I plight thee my troth."

"I plight thee my troth."

Thou. How do I love thee? What if I were always to address you as "thou"? Then how could I do thee wrong? Then I will always love thee. He will gather actors and ask them to improv "thou." If his ardency flags, why, he need only call her "thee." "Thee," said Wittman again, looking at her.

"Those whom God hath joined together, let no man put asunder."

O lovely peaceful words. What if I were to think in that language? I would not have the nervous, crimpy life that I do.

A movie kiss against the sea and sky. The End.

"I'll send you the papers," said Gabe.

A Sunday of vows. The way to make a life: Say Yes more often than No. Participate. Shoulder one of the vows that are always flying about like hovering angels. *Every angel is terrible. Still, though, alas! I invoke you, almost deadly birds of the soul, knowing what you are.* Swear, and follow through. No need to invent new vows; we haven't done the old ones, and they aren't done with us. Vows remain after those who gave them are gone. Think them in kanji and in English, so no matter if a part of your brain aphasicly goes out, some word remains. A posse of angels have rounded up some strays. To keep the old promises that are not broken, though the people break. To be a brother, a friend, a husband to some stranger passing through.

5

Ruby Long Legs' and Zeppelin's Song of the Open Road

MR. AND MRS. WITTMAN AH SING monumentally descended the sculpturesque steps outside Coit Tower. Across their path ran the Chinese grandmother, wearing her sweater. She met another grandmother at the parapet, her white hair in a chignon bun, her hands on her hips, turning her torso this way and that way, breathing. The running grandmother talked loud to her about the price of fruit. She lifted her arms toward the eucalyptus trees. As the inter-racial couple walked past, she said, "Goot mah-ning." "Good morning," said Taña. So, this is the hour they come up here to do their old-lady kung fu. Taña had better not make a remark. Nobody had better make a remark. A girl jumped up on the parapet; she's ballet-dancing on it. Two boys ran alongside, trying to catch her by the hand or by her skirt, but she pirouetted away, yes, on point. At the turn in the wall, she pivoted, and ran, leaping at her pursuers.

Taña went toward her car. She walks with her arms folded across her breasts. She'd returned the jacket to her friend. Oh, please don't shrink up like that, Taña. All of young and old womankind dancing but not my Taña. It must be the effect of marriage. "Did you see the ballerina? You ought to be more like that," he suggested. He was instructing her: Stay alive for me. Never tire. Stay up all night, and play all day. Don't be cold in the wind. Else, how can I keep up loving you? She didn't answer; she will get even with him later.

To perk her up, Wittman surprised Taña with a honeymoon—a trip to Sutro's. For the rest of their lives, they could say, "That marriage, I spent my honeymoon at Sutro's." Their third anniversary, Sutro's went up in a fire. Near the entrance, a true-to-life sculpture of a Japanese man stood almost naked, holding a hand mirror and looking itself in the eyes. Self-portrait. According to the plaque, the artist had used his own

human hair for the hair on his statue. It had hair on its head;
it had eyebrows, stub-brush eyelashes above doll glass eyes,
nostril hairs, armpit hair. There was probably pubic hair under its loin cloth. There was a lot of yellowy-pinky skin. The
honeymoon couple should have left then and there. It's not
true that freakiness takes you far out and breaks through into
miracle.

"I hope that he used only hair from his head," said Wittman,
"clipped it and curled it for other parts of the body. How
would you like to move into a studio, and find collections of
eyebrow hair, fingernail clippings, eyelashes, beard shavings,
pubic hair?"

"Call the cops," said Taña.

"Doesn't it make you want to cremate it?"

"He probably thinks that his statue is in some fine art museum in New York, America," she said. The commiseration of
one artist for another. "It's exact, and it ought to be beautiful."

"But isn't."

"But isn't. Strange what he thought to be perfectly himself."

Oh, god, is she profound and aesthetic. And she did not
say that the thing looked like Wittman (which it did not), or
had anything to do with him. We umberish-amberish people
are not nitpicking hair-savers, creepy fingernail-collectors, or
money-hoarding coprophiliacs. No way.

Near the real-hair Japanese man was a mechanical monkey
dressed in Louis XVI courtier clothes, laces and plumes, bowing to guests, sweeping his hand back and forth. "I hope that's
fake fur," said Taña. Its motor heart hummed and beat.

"If you scratch its hair, part it like looking for fleas, you'll
either see the pores and follicles of a real monkey or the warp
and weave of cheesecloth."

"Yew. Let's not."

"It's probably real, hunted and shot by Lucius Beebe or
Sutro." Taña had never been here before. He was showing her
new things, keeping the marriage lively, and the momentum
of life rolling apace. A bond forms between those who have
seen an odd phenomenon or laugh at a joke. He could never
get it on with a straight chick.

In the musée méchanique, he led the way directly to his
favorite mechanical, which was the amusement park that

convicts had made out of toothpicks. He slipped a quarter into the slot, and started the Ferris wheel turning; the basket chairs trembled and lifted and, at the top of the ride, cunningly dropped. How many life sentences to build the latticework of the rollercoaster trestle? No people on the rides, but the music box plinked and tinked "Let Me Call You Sweetheart."

"This is a meditation about time and doing time," said Tana. "A meld of boredom and amusement. People who commit crimes are children, and when you lock them up, they stay children. This park is their idea of freedom. When they get out on parole, the first place they'll go is the boardwalk at Santa Cruz. Amusement parks are full of criminals."

Wittman hugged her shoulders. Here's the girl he met at the party. Out in the dull world, he loved hearing Berkeley insights. And not having to make them all by himself. "Do you remember Robert Walker stalking Alfred Hitchcock's daughter Patricia's look-alike, and the merry-go-round and the Ferris wheel turning and turning?"

"*Strangers on a Train*," said Tana.

After the fire, some people will remember the amusement park, and other people will remember a mining-camp scene with men panning and carrying and dumping, and a tram going in and out of a tunnel. It would have been a replica of the Sutro Metallurgical Works.

Tana put her arm around his waist, and they walked over to another exhibit. He ought not to feel afraid. Would there be less anxiety if she were taller and stronger than he? And women were the protectors of men. There's nothing to be afraid of. Wait until he's under fire in a battlefield. Panic then.

But there is something sickening about miniatures. Scale a thing down small, work on it for a long time, some life gets compressed into it. Only a tiny bit of life is needed to make a netsuke breathe, and be scary because alive, motored for always by the exhalations of its creator, and the chi and sweat from his hands. Frankensteinish animation. But I have always been afraid. It's not the freak show, and it's not her and marriage to her. I am always afraid.

His coin brought the Electric Cassandra to life. She nodded, turned back and forth. Her jaw dropped and a voice said: "Seeker, ware—the future." Her large hands shoved a card out of an opening in the glass: "After heartbreak, you find true love." "Yours," said Taña, putting the card in Wittman's hand.

"Oh, no, it's yours. You touched it first, your fortune. Mine's the next one. I'll take the next one."

The next one was: "Follow your destiny to be rich or famous." "I choose famous," he said.

"I choose rich," she said. "I don't think I could handle famous."

"Realistically, in my life, Taña, I keep getting dealt a choice between time and money. An American peasant has to choose between time and money. I choose time."

At the diorama of the Cosmos, the moon rolled around the Earth, the planets around the sun in blue space luxurious with silver and gold stars. The Cosmos is a music-box that twinkles and spins. A comet with rainbow tail arced slowly past. Then a brindle cow jumped over the moon, and a little dog laughed to see such sport, and the dish ran away with the spoon.

There were no other people about. They could jimmy the glass case, and try to fit inside Tom Thumb's and Mrs. Thumb's carriage. Finger-dance in the tiny kid gloves and the shoes with spats. "You fan yourself with the wee fan," said Taña, "and the gloves will fit."

In the photo booth on the mezzanine above the skating rink, they took wedding pictures, a strip of four for a dollar. The first picture, "for the folks," they pantomimed feeding each other cake. The second, "our real selves," she wore a nice smile, and he looked pissed off. The last two were for each other's wallets, one of her by herself, and one of him by himself. Taña looked like a blonde movie star; Wittman looked like a wanted bandito. El Immigrante, his wetback passport picture i.d.

How is their marriage to work out when, as they could see from "our real selves," they were not on the same trip at the same time? "It's hard to take two-shots," said Wittman. "Actors have to be well directed to appear as if they belong in the same picture."

"You're photogenic, Wittman," she said. Good thing. How can those who are not photogenic walk about showing their faces? Or is she putting him on? Telling him what he needs to hear?

They hung over the balcony and watched the skaters going around. If we run downstairs and rent skates, could we be Orlando and the Russian princess zipping on the frozen Thames above the apple woman in the deep ice? Wittman, the fool for books, ought to swear off reading for a while, and find his own life.

For their wedding picnic—can't go home, home have I none—they drove to the Palace of Fine Arts. Near the No Admittance sign, he showed her a hole in the cyclone fence, and helped her through it. The green grass grew all around. In a nest of it, they ate cheese and French bread, nectarines, snappy raw stringbeans, and drank a California champagne from the bottle. This Taña could be anyone, a perfectly good enough person to be married to. She had patches of freckles on her arms and on one knee. There was blue paint and green paint—her palette—under her nails. He had been wide awake when he married her, his daylight love. Forget the dreamgirl of the dark night.

"I'm going to own this palace," he said. "We're home. These are my ducks." They threw them crumbs. They walked about, poking at the chicken wire and the insides of the hollow papier-mâché colonnades. The pink crust of the structure was breaking off in chunks. Lazy caryatids and atlantes, without a roof to hold up, draped their thick arms over the tops of the columns. The human couple walked all the way around and inside. From every angle, the giants turned their backs; backs are easier to sculpt than fronts.

"My palace was built to be viewed from up there," said Wittman, and led the way climbing the slope to the street. From the bench, they saw across the greensward a pink city on a moat lagoon. It looked like the hideout of the hundred and eight outlaws, a mountain encircled by borders of water. The caryatids and atlantes were looking down into pens at—a dog fight? A cock fight? A people fight. "Nobody wants a land, I got uses for it. I'm going to take over this ghost palace, where the atmosphere is suggestive with deeds on the verge of taking place."

"I will help you rule," said Taña.

O Central Casting, she's the consort of my life.

"The wedding present from me to you," he said, presenting her with this World's Fair site that belongs to all. He's giving her every chance to speak up if to her it was but a bogus abbadabba marriage. She doesn't like him, why, she can leave him here among the grasses and ruins. "This place and a starring role in my play that continues like life are yours. The army that we raised at breakfast will parade down Broadway and the length of Market Street. There will be a train of elephants, and in each of their howdahs, four soldiers, pointing rifles in four directions. Their uniforms are G.I. camouflage khakis. The eyes peering out from between their helmets and the tar on their cheekbones are Indochinese eyes. This part, I'm not making up. Have you read in the papers? The side we're backing in Viet Nam goes to war on elephants. A patrol of four or six elephants pick through the jungle to search-and-destroy communists. Elephants have very sensitive trunks and toes. The disadvantage is that an expanse of elephant makes a too easy target. Because of the guilt of having dropped A-bombs, we are returning to a more natural warfare. Elephants and dolphins."

Wittman was getting his inspiration from a book known as The Book of Evil; its title is something like *The Water Verge*. In preparation for warfare in marshes and rivers and rice paddies, the Pentagon was using this book too. There is a curse that anyone who tells or stages or discusses its legends would be struck mute, and his children and grandchildren also be mute. Wittman and the U.S. military may fall silent at any moment now. The ideas for strategic hamlets and agrovilles came from that book, and from Lucretius' *De Rerum Natura*, which warns that animals often backfire in battle. War animals were part of the *impedimenta* that Hannibal took over the Alps. Generals, who were wizards of the wind, blew the animals—wild boars, tigers, lions, bulls—around, and they turned on their owners. Our engineers are keeping the elephants and dolphins under control with radio implants.

There used to be three peace books too. They were found in a cave by a wind wizard, and now they're lost. This wizard had blue-green eyes and looked both young and old. He gave the books to a student who had failed his exams. This student learned control of the weather. Which could mean he had the charisma to change the atmosphere when he walked into a room. His young-old teacher said, "You can rescue mankind. You will suffer," and handed him *The Way of Peace*. That book's title is all we know of it anymore; its contents are but suspect memorizations, argumentations, and rumors.

Ho Chi Minh's favorite reading was *The Romance of the Three Kingdoms*, and it's a text at West Point too. Uncle Ho and Uncle Sam were both getting their strategy and philosophy from Grandfather Gwan, god of war.

Wittman continued telling his story as follows:

"Yonder palace is defended against the elephant army by knights on black stallions, Trigger palominos, and stout Mongolian ponies with trick riders that charge out of the intercolumniations into battle on the greensward. Archers on horseback and archers on the roof pull bows that shoot ten simultaneous arrows. On the water, a boat with blue sheets sails slowly by and collects the arrows in the cross-fire. Knights are fighting up and down those stairs that lead along the walls and into walls. Two beautiful ladies stand on those platforms amid the two clusters of columns, and sing about no one missing them. 'Two leaves from off a tree, two grains dropped from a silo.' They're the two most beautiful women in the land, and Cho Cho, as we call him in American, the brothers' archenemy, has built towers to keep them as his very own. On that tree hangs the red silk robe that he is giving as a tourney prize. Five arrows hit the bullseye, shot from horseback, shot riding backwards, shot hanging upside down from stirrups, shot from a single bow. The knights fight over it; then he gives all of them a red silk robe each. Kettle drums and cymbals and strings of ten thousand firecrackers echo like mad in the rotunda and across the water. Hookmen try to scale those turrets and the ice wall. Infantry run to it with pocketfuls of dirt, which they pile into a slope. Actors stride the tops of those ramparts. The platforms are for the soliloquies of heroes and for dialogues across chasms.

"The failed student with a peace manual and the power of the winds fights against the three brothers. His army in yellow scarves charge from over there, and the brothers charge, pounding the earth, from that side. They clang in the middle. The knights cross halberds, fleur-de-lis steel on X-ing lances. Trumpets blare, drums and gunpowder bang. Elephants trumpet. Liu Pei fights with a bullwhip; you can hear it cracking amid the firecrackers. Chang Fei flies like his name, his eighteen-foot spear before him, and pierces an elephant through the heart. Grandfather Gwan rides Red Rabbit, and cuts men in half with one swoop of his sword. You, Tañā, gallop bareback on a white horse across the esplanade.

"At nightfall, the campfires (some are decoys) light up swaths of turf with a no-man's-land of darkness in between. The outnumbered brothers ambush the enemy on three sides of that triangular palace. They set fire to the turf grass. The flames throw shadows of battle up among those watching giants. The sunrise or the fire enflames the world. Each side has its wind wizard howling the weather up. The special-effects guy goes wild. Rocks and elephants roll. The brothers confer. Their wizard advises to pour pig's blood, goat's blood, and dog's blood down on the heads of their enemies, who were maybe Muslims. From the tiers of the palace cascades a storm of blood rain. Fireballs roll like burning tumbleweeds. Knights and horses and elephants explode.

"A silence descends for an interval. A black cloud settles on the field. Soldiers and animals land. The wind stops. Thunder stops. The bands stop playing. We've used up the fireworks. Rocks settle. Out of the smoke rides Liu Pei chasing Chang Chio, the student of the magic books, shooting arrows at each other from horseback. Chang Chio drops his bow, clasps his arm; he's been hit. He turns his horse about; they fight hand to hand. Liu Pei wins, but the men in yellow break through the flames. And from around the back of the palace comes another army, red guidons high; it's Cho Cho. His army drives the brothers to the Yangtze. Cho Cho does a victory dance in red silks up there on the rooftop."

Along the street behind Wittman and Tañā, a moving van passed back and forth. Those who have lived near a river and a highway know that one sounds much like the other.

"The city is on fire. The people run to the river. The brothers blow up the dam, and escape in a boat. Chang Fei has to hack away at the hands of allies who could pull the boat down. They sail through devastation. Liu Pei weeps, 'Why was I ever born to be the cause of all this misery to the people?'

"Your part is coming up, Tañā, and it gets larger, I promise. I have to talk fast. I may go mute at any moment. And the curse goes down three generations."

"We're going to have very quiet kids and grandkids who talk with their hands?" said Taña.

"We'll love our little muties. I better warn you; there's another curse. I'm going to tell you a wedding story from the tradition of the Heroic Couple on the Battlefield that will turn you into a Chinese. Ready?"

"Ready," said Taña.

"Years go by; battles are lost and won; kingdoms rise and fall. Lady Sun, a beautiful princess with red hair and blue eyes, has beaten all of her father's and brother's knights using their choice of weapon. She wants to try combat in a real war. News reaches her that Liu Pei's two wives have been killed. She could marry the famous old warrior, and be his partner, martial and marital. She sends him a proposal, which Liu Pei receives while mourning his wives. He has been singing an aria about growing old alone, having spent his life at war. To answer her, he sets off with a fleet of ten fast ships across the Yangtze to the southern kingdom of Wu, where Americans come from. Herding sheep and bearing wine jars, Liu Pei and half his army and navy go to the royal palace. The other half, dressed in their best civvies, shop all through the town for wedding presents.

"Liu Pei meets the gold-haired family: The old king, killer of a white tiger. Sun Ch'üan, the prince who is plotting against this would-be brother-in-law. The queen, one of the two women Cho Cho wants to keep in towers. She scolds her family, 'You're using my girl as a decoy duck.' Underneath his scholar's robe, Liu Pei wears light mail."

"Charley's not Liu Pei," said Taña. "You are."

"Yes, and you're my Lady Sun. On our wedding day, we walk between lines of red torches to the bride's apartment—which is a private armory. You've furnished your rooms with spears and swords, banners and flags, and your ladies-in-waiting are an amazon army. 'Is this the ambush then?' I ask.

"The women laugh at me, 'What's wrong? Haven't you seen weapons before?'

"I ask them to take the deadlier ones with them when they leave.

"I part the curtains of the wedding bed. A Chinese bed is like a proscenium stage, and like a very private room. The three walls and the ceiling are carved out of wood, forests of animals and people with mother-of-pearl eyes; in the grain of the inlaid marble are misty mountains and waterfalls. There are doors and drawers, and shelves for books and vases. You could peek out through gingerbread and spindles. The beautiful redhead who's in there says, 'So you don't like my weapons. Afraid of a few swords after half a lifetime of slaughter?'

"'Take off your swords,' I say. 'Remove your armor. Disarm thyself.' You do, and I love you, and you love me.

"The gold-haired family luxuriate me. They build me a castle, where I regularly dine off gold and silver. I read in a library. Musicians always play. My men practice archery and race their horses. They don't see their leader much. A year goes by.

"Lady Sun gets her husband to swordfence with her every day, acquiring his abilities. Then we have tea in our tower, whence we look down at the beautiful land and the river. We sing duets. A wind whips up waves, rocking and pitching a tiny boat. 'You southern people are sailors, and we northern men ride horses well,' observes Liu Pei.

"At that, you jump from the balcony onto your white steed, galloping headlong downhill. You wheel around, calling, 'So the southerners can't ride, eh?'

"I lift my robe, jump on my horse, and full-gallop down the hill too. We ride side by side into the capital, where the people acclaim us.

"'Beloved, is it true that northerners call their spouses "comrade"?' you ask.

"'I'll call you "beloved," my beloved southerner.' Oi yun. Beloved.

"'And are southern women the most beautiful?'

"'Thou, the most beautiful, and the most beloved.'

"We often talk about how northerners and southerners differ. Northerners are stubborn; southerners are quick to revolution. Southerners are natural comedians; northerners laugh just hearing them speak Cantonese, the ugliest language in the world. Peking opera is for sissy academics; Cantonese opera has soul. Northerners are old; southerners are older. Educated people speak Mandarin; real people speak Cantonese, albeit the ugliest language in the world.

"One day near spring, I hear that Cho Cho, my lifelong

enemy, is leading fifty legions to attack the one city that is
mine. A man with the gift of tears, I weep in front of my wife.

"'Why are you sad, my beloved husband?' you ask.

"'I've been driven hither and yon all my life. I've ridden
past my ancestral village many times, and couldn't stop at my
parents' grave. And another new year is coming.'

"'Tell me the truth. You want to leave me.'

"'I have to save my city. I have to go, but I don't want to
leave you.'

"'Don't be sad, my husband, my loved one. I'll find a way
for us to leave together.'

"Kneeling to you, I say, 'I will always love you.'

"We attend New Year's parties all day, and toward evening,
you say to your mother, 'My husband is thinking of his parents. He wants to go to the river to make offerings toward the
north.'

"'As a good wife, you ought to go with him,' says the queen.

"You ride in your palanquin, and I ride my horse at the head
of our small entourage.

"Sun Ch'üan goes to bed after feasting. He wakes up after his sister and brother-in-law have had a night's head start.
Throwing his jade inkstone across the room, he says, 'I want
their heads.' He sends cohorts after us. 'Bring back their
heads, or I'll have yours. My sister plays war. I'll teach her
what war is.'

"Liu Pei and Lady Sun see a cloud of dust, soldiers coming.
'You go on,' you say. 'I'll stop them.' But troops also block the
road in front.

"'I have something private to say to you.' I dismount, and
go inside your palanquin with you. We enclose ourselves from
the rest of the world. 'You've got me. I'm in your hands now.
You win. I know there's a plot to this marriage. If you want to
kill me, go ahead. You've been kind to me, and I thank you.' I
face the utter paranoia of marriage.

"'I don't want to kill you,' says my wife. 'I don't want
you killed. I'll save you.' You hold me by the hand. We walk
through the troops, whom you scold all the while. 'My brother
sent you, so you say. You fear him more than you fear me, do
you? I'll get him for this. You're turning traitors. Or are you
bandits who want money? What are your names?' You take

down the names of the officers. 'You're in trouble now, spoiling this holiday journey that my mother ordered. What have we ever done to you?'

"You lead your group onward, but companies of soldiers follow us. 'Go,' you tell me. 'I'll hold them off.'

"I ride away. You retreat behind your curtains. Your retinue stops in the middle of the road, waiting for the pursuers to catch up. They hear your voice, 'What are you doing here, captains?' They tell you to come home with them alive.

"Out of the carriage and into the saddle of her rearing white warhorse leaps Lady Sun, fully armored, silver from head to toe. Your hair curls out of your helmet in waves of gold, and your eyes have caught the blue of the sky and the river. You draw your sword, pare your nails with it. 'Whom do I have to fight?' you ask. Your brother's knights put down the swords that had been forged expressly to kill you."

Wittman thought that with this story he was praising his lady, and teaching her to call him Beloved. Unbeknownst to him, Tañua was getting feminist ideas to apply to his backass self.

"I have been waiting at the river by myself. None of my ships meet me. There are many poems about me weeping on the banks of the Yangtze, which divided kingdoms. The river will separate me from my love, I sing. I mourn for the wonderful year with the princess and for my stay in the country that lies between the Yangtze and the Pacific.

"The soldiers overtake me; twenty ships appear. And you arrive. The well-married couple run up a gangplank together. Warships flying Sun Ch'üan's flags, running with the wind, chase us to the north shore. We hear drums; there is Grandfather Gwan meeting us with fresh horses.

"That's it, my present to you," said Wittman. "Got no money. Got no home. Got story."

Tañuа was giving him that impressed look from the party, which she had given to everyone though. He loved that look, she's interested, beholding him, and others. That's all it takes, a few seconds of being smiled at, a while of being listened to, and he feels loved. I can go about my life, she loves me.

"I'm your beloved lady in shiny armor?" she said.

"Yes, if you'd like."

"I've already saved you from the draft. Well. Do you want a ride home?"

"Yes." Got to go home sometime.

"Are you embarrassed to take me home? Is someone there?" She does have me on her E.S.P.

"Yeah. My mother. Do you want to meet her? You feel like driving to Sacramento?" He has access to a car, might as well take advantage to see how the Aged Parents and Grandparent are doing.

"Let's drive across the Golden Gate," she said. This week-end, then, he will have crossed three bridges. The Golden Gate, the most bridge-like of bridges, swept them from the green Presidio to the Marin hills, where the manzanita and the bridge are the same red. Fog poured out of the forests. His grandmother liked being taken for Sunday drives. He had been in the backseat when the car radio said the Japanese had bombed Pearl Harbor. "Go to the Golden Gate Bridge," she said. "I want to drive across it one last time." PoPo was very good at last wishes. Taña would enjoy meeting her. They didn't have to worry about meeting Taña's family; white people don't have families. They're free.

He drove the eggshell car around the Bay and through the milky bogland of Suisun, whereinto it merged, sunlight on tan metal, water over peat dirt. Between the whitish water and whitish sky, endless mirrorings, egrets stood on long long legs, mirror-doubled. A lone oak tree cringed like burned. Who is it that shoots the roadsigns? Every pick-up truck has a gun rack. It is eventful enough when a marshbird dips its foot and causes rings of silver going and going.

Somewhere between Fairfield and Vacaville, theirs was the only vehicle on the road. Wittman turned the car radio—shit-kicking caballero music—off. He pulled the Porsche to the roadside and killed the engine. A turn of the ignition key switched off the world's noise. They twisted out their ciga-rettes in the ashtray. It's against the law to toss them because peat smolders. At night, you sometimes see parts of an under-ground fire, and smell like bread baking. A stream of white butterflies frittered by, on and on. A flock of small black birds came next; the ones at the top were high in the sky, the ones at the bottom flew through the yellowing grass, and they were the same continuous flock. At last the birds tailed away. Next, yellow moths blew about; they will alight in another season, and become the mustard flowers of January. They heard a car at a distance, and then it arrived, and passed them. It had gathered eventfulness, passed, and pulled it away at seventy miles an hour. The silence re-closed. A soul extends in nature, then you are aware of having one. Buildings, jackhammers, etc., chop it up, and you took drugs to feel it. The extent of the soul is from oneself to wherever living beings are.

Too low in the sky came a black warplane. Its two winglights glared in the bright day. Its flat belly had hatchdoors— for bombs to drop out. The plane was the shape of a winged bomb. That humming and roaring must have been underlying everything for some time. It had no insignia, no colors, no markings, no numbers. It hung heavy in air. It passed overhead and off to the right. Wittman started the car, and drove fast to get out of there. But the plane came back around, skulking around and around. The sky seemed not to have enough room for it. Like a shark of the ocean inside a tank. How is it that I co-exist with that dead impersonal thing which moves, and is more real than the fields and more real than this unprotectable girl? Its noise replaced thought and om. Evil is not an idea. It is that. Sharks swim in schools. This thing was unpaired, singular in the isolation of the sky. Somebody ought to report it in Berkeley. And call Travis Air Force Base; one of their experiments is loose, blindly circling where Primary State 12 intersects I-80. But people who've seen the evil plane and heard it forget to do anything about it when they get back. Its dull blackness and noise are somehow subliminal, and cause helplessness and despair. They just want to hurry and get to their people. Good thing Wittman will be with his mother right away.

Ruby Ah Sing lived in sight of the capitol. A fence went around her property, a flower garden and a house with a porch and a porch swing. The years she had lived in trailer parks and her roomette on the train, she had had a dreamhouse. She'd settled down in old Sac for her boy, to give him a home, which he drove past. Take the long way. He had liked better living on the train, reading funnybooks in his fold-down bunk, everything you own at your toes. Sometimes the window had seemed to be a long television screen scrolling sideways, and sometimes another room, and sometimes a dream. In pajamas, he lay against the window, moving through a city street. Underneath him, hobos and Mexicanos were riding next to the wheels; they fell off in their sleep. Once a circus traveled with them, or they traveled with a circus. The aerialists spoke European, but the clowns were friendly with everyone. He wore his monkey outfit for them. They warned him of the circus tradition of tossing enemies and wise asses off the train. Boys and girls in Europe were riding in cattle cars, and were trampled. That was why he had had to give an anti-jap speech from the caboose. The men around the potbelly stove gave him a yellow flag. A steward let him serve lunch. Never work as an animal trainer; if an elephant shits in the ring, you have to shove a broom up there where the sun don't shine. Going through a black tunnel, a conductor said, "They say a thousand chinamen used a thousand tons of dynamite to make this cut. I don't know the truth of that." The engine puffed out words—"Elephant. Elephant."—through the semiconscious nights. Trestles, trigonometrical puzzles worked out by ancestors, carried him across canyons. His father waited at stations, where he'd be waving hello or goodbye. The train whistled woo woo. Ruby and Zeppelin had a joke about wooing each other.

"Sutter's Fort is that way," said Wittman. "Sac High. I graduated from Sac High. That's the Greyhound Station. Crocker, who invested in the railroad, built that museum. That's the old Old Eagle Theatre. The first theater was the Chinese puppet theater on I Street. That's the Governor's Mansion. That's the hotel where congressmen go to wheel and deal." He drove around the capitol. "Los Immigrantes go in that door to become citizens. There's the peanut man. I used to buy peanuts from him to feed the squirrels." It was an easy town to learn. A Street, B Street, C Street, and so on, and the number streets gridding the other way.

"The Land Hotel," said Taña. "There's a Land Hotel, isn't there?"

"Yes. Near the Senator. It's a fleabag."

"That's where we used to stay summers when I was a little girl. During the war. I didn't know it was a fleabag."

"Well, maybe it wasn't a fleabag back then."

Suddenly Wittman was coughing hard. His lungs were not made for an open-air car.

"Are you all right?" asked Taña, patting his shoulder.

"I'm okay. I always cough when I get near home."

"That's interesting. Whenever I've ridden the bus and heard somebody coughing, and I turn around, most of the time they're Chinese."

"Yeah, they're on their way home."

"It gets me in the stomach," said Taña. "Half a bottle of Kaopectate, and I'm ready to see my mother. I'm on my way out the door, and she says right in front of my date, and our double-dates, 'Are you wearing your bra? Get upstairs, young lady, and put on a brassiere. You're too big to be going out all over town without a brassiere.' Does your mother do that? It probably was a fleabag. I remember I always wanted to stay at the other one."

"The Senator."

"Yeah. One night, really hot, we had to keep the window open. I heard someone singing down on the street. In the morning, I looked out the window, and there was a sailor asleep in a phone booth. What's the main street? Is it Main Street?"

"K Street."

"On K Street, there was a captured Japanese plane, tan with big red circles on the wings. An open cockpit, and a ladder. My father made me sit in the cockpit, and I was crying because I thought it was going to fly away with me. My mother got really mad at my father. I sat in it for about five seconds. Don't laugh," she said, laughing.

"I'm not," said Wittman, coughing.

"Later I saw home movies of myself in that Zero, me in my pinafore and white stockings and real long hair, trying to climb out of the cockpit. Alice in Wonderland bombs Pearl Harbor."

The folks are going to love her, thought Wittman. Ruby and Zeppelin are really going to love her. I love her myself. No brassiere, wow! I have to buy her a leopard-skin bathing suit so we can play Sheena, Queen of the Jungle. Me Chimp.

Ruby Ah Sing, Wittman's mother, had a maple tree, the crown-leaves gold and red now. The crowns of many kings on a hat rack. The pear tree had some pears, and green leaves, and dead black leaves on long offshoots, and flowers. Wild in the time machine.

Through the screen door—the crack clack crash of mah-jongg. Oh, no, mah-jongg day. That's why, all those Coupe de Villes to have squeezed a parking space among. The son of the house would have turned about but for the girl he was with. Always do the harder thing. He opened the door, went ahead, held it for Taña.

Ruby screamed. "Eeek!" Stood up and screamed again, pointing. And Auntie Sadie screamed, and Auntie Marleese ran to him. His mother eeked him again. "Eeek!" What's wrong? The white girl? A hobo bumbled after them inside? "What have you done to yourself?!" She put her hands to her cheeks.

"You used to be such a beautiful boy!" shouted Auntie Marleese, looking up at him.

"Too much hair," said Auntie Sadie. "Much too hairy."

"You go shave," said Mother. "Shave it off! Shave it off! Oh, hock geen nay say!" That is, "Scares you to death!" "Gik say nay!" That is, "Irks you to death!" "Galls you to death!" Clack! Clack!

"No act, Ma," he said.

"Don't say hello to your mother," she said.

"Never you mind sticks and stones, honey boy," said Auntie Bessie. "Have a heart, Ruby."

A dog jumped on him. "Down, Queenie. Behave," said Auntie Jadine, its owner. "Where you manners, Queenie?" Those who usually spoke Chinese talked to the yapperdog in English. "Down, Queenie. Come heah." They spoke English to him and to the dog. American animals.

"GOOD dog," said Wittman. It mind-fucks dogs to be called good when they're trying to be fierce.

"Wit Man has come to see his momma," explained the aunties, one to another. "Good boy. Big boy now." Clack clack clack. A racket of clack clack clack. "All grow up. College grad, haw, Wit Man?" Nobody asked if he were a doctor or an engineer yet. How tactful. Not asking about work at all. "Sit. Sit. Sit. Here's an empty chair by me, dearie. Come meet me." Taña got a side chair at one of the dining tables.

"Oh, I be so sorry I didn't recognize you, Wit Man," said Auntie Sadie. "You so changed."

"That's okay, Auntie Sadie."

"Come talk to your Aunt Lilah."

"Hello, Aunt Lilah. Hello, Auntie Dolly," said Wittman. "Hello, Aunt Peggy." He went to each auntie, shaking hands with some, kneeling beside this one and that one for her to take a better look at him. "He was a cute biby." "Why you not visit Auntie more often?" "Me too, honey boy. Visit you Aunt Sondra too." The ladies called themselves "ahnt," and Wittman called them "ant." "Hair, Big City style, isn't it, dear?" said Auntie Dolly of San Francisco, ruffling his hair. "Beard in high style, Ruby. Wit Man Big City guy now."

The ladies at his mother's table were comforting her. "Hairy face, fashion on a plate," said Auntie Sophie. "You the one sent him to college, Ruby." Clack. Clack.

"Where I go wrong, I ask you," said Wittman's mother. "He was clean cut. He used to be soo mun." That is, "He used to be soigné." "He doesn't get his grooming from me. Kay ho soo kay ge ba, neh. Gum soo. Soo doc jai." That is, "He takes too much after his father, neh. So like. Too alike." "Moong cha cha. Both of them, father and son, moong cha cha."

"In Hong Kong now, they say m.c.c.," said Auntie Peggy, who was up on the latest.

"M.c.c." "M.c.c." The aunties tried the new Hong Kong slang. "Moong cha cha" means "spacy," spaced out and having to grope like a blindman.

Meanwhile, at Taña's table, Aunt Dolly, who was sophisticated, was saying, "What's your name, honey? Tan-ah. What a pretty name. Russian? Do you play, Tan-ah? I'll show you how to play. This is a very famous Chinese game. Mah-jongg. Can you say 'mah-jongg'?" Auntie Dolly had been a showgirl in New York, and knew how to endear herself to foreigners. She did introductions. Good. Wittman did not want to announce Taña to the room, and he was not about to tablehop with her like a wedding couple. "That's Madame S. Y. Chin. This is Madame Gordon Fong." Et cetera. "Hello," said Taña. Well, you can't expect her to say, "How do you do, Madame." And if she said, "How do you do, Mrs.," the lady would feel demoted. Meet Madame Wadsworth Woo. How do you do, Woo? "Madame" to you. Madame. Shit. Madame Chiang Kai Shek. Madame Sun Yat Sen. Mesdames Charles Jones Soong

and T. V. Soong. Madame Nhu. All the cookbook ladies
are madames too. And all the restaurant guys are generals.
Generalissimo. "Let me show you how to play, honey." Don't
trust anybody who calls you "honey," Taña. It's a verbal tic.

"My name is Maydene Lam," said Auntie Maydene. "Call
me Maydene, dear."

"How do you do, Maydene."

"I've always liked your name," said Auntie Lily Rose. "Such
a pretty stage name. Maydene Lam."

"Isn't it delicious? There are four little girls named after me
in the Valley." Clickity clackity.

"What beautiful hair you have, Tan-ah. She's gorgeous, Wit
Man!" yelled Aunt Dolly. "You are so fair. Isn't she fair?!"

"Thank you," said Taña, who hadn't yet learned that compliments need to be denied and returned.

Every auntie had jet-black dyed hair. Why do women as they
get older have to have fixed hair? Because of beauty fixed at
1945. These were the glamour girls of World War II. Taking
after the Soong sisters and Anna Chennault, who married
guys in uniform. Whenever the aunties' pictures appeared in
the papers—Chinese or English—they were identified as "the
lovely Madame Houston W. P. Fong," "the beauteous Madame
Johnny Tom." They were professional beauties. To this day
the old fut judges vote for the Miss Chinatown U.S.A. who
most reminds them of these ladies. Quite a few of them had
been Wongettes—"Ladies and gentlemen, Mr. Eddie Pond
proudly welcomes to the Kubla Khan the beautiful Wongettes,
Chinese Blondes in a Blue Mood." "Myself, I am a blonde at
heart," said Auntie Dolly. Don't you look askance at her, Taña,
with your sanpaku eyes, or else I'm getting a divorce.

"Ciao!" "Poong!" "Kong!" Action. "Eight ten thousands!"
"Mah-jongg!" Clack! Crash! "Mah-jongg!"

"Wit Man, over here," said Ruby.

"Coming, Mother," said Wittman. He stood behind her to
look at her winning hand.

"Talk to See Nigh here," said the mother.

"You enjoying the game, See Nigh?" he said to the lady
whom he had never met before.

"Oh, how well behaved," said the See Nigh, the Lady. "So
dock-yee. And such good manners. Most boys with beards are

bum-how. He doesn't have to call me See Nigh. You call me Auntie, Wit Man."

His mother spoke sotto voce, in Chinese, "Who's the girl?"

"My friend. A good friend," he said in English. One shouldn't speak a foreign language in front of people who don't understand it, especially when talking about them. Don't add to the paranoia level of the universe.

"Serious?"

"Sure."

"How serious?"

"Serious, okay?"

Gary Snyder had gone to Japan to meditate for years, and could now spend five minutes in the same room with his mother. Beat his record.

"So you walk with her," said Auntie Sophie. She was translating "go with." She meant "So you go with her."

"Mixing with girls," teased Auntie Marleese. "Old enough to mix the girls." Go after girls with an eggbeater.

"She's so rude, she's not talking to me," said Mom. "She's hurt my feelings, Wit Man."

"Introduce you gal to you mama, young man," said Auntie Sophie. Clack!

"Hey, Taña," he called over to her table. "Meet my mother, Ruby Ah Sing. Ma, meet my pahng yow, Tan-ah." "Pahng yow" means "friend"; maybe Taña would think it meant "wife."

"Hi." Taña waved. Click.

"You aren't growing up to be a heartbreakin' man, are you, honey boy?" said Aunt Lilah.

"Speak for your own self," said back-talking Wittman. She was a glamour girl still raising hell at seventy-five. She gets you alone for a moment, she'll confide her *ro*mance. "Honey, this entre news is on the Q.T., and must not go further than this very room. My beloved is a sai yun. He's fifty-five years old, and so distinguished. All his clothes are Brooks Brothers. My sai yun lover is offering to divorce his wife for me, but I don't want to be married. Monday, Wednesday, and Friday are enough." A "sai yun" is a "western man," which isn't correct; we're westerners too.

"U.C., state-run public school, does not teach them to present themselves socially," Auntie Jean was explaining. She was an authority on higher education, a son at Harvard, a daughter at Wellesley, where the Soong sister who married Sun Yat Sen went, another son at Princeton, the baby daughter at Sarah Lawrence. "As I said to Mayling Soong, I-vee Leak be A-number-one all-around. They learn how to make money, *and* they learn to go around in society. Very complete." The cruel thing to say back to her is: "What eating club does Ranceford belong to?" But you don't want to be mean to her. They will graduate, and never come back.

"At U.C., this one learned: grow hair long," Mom agreed. "Grow rat beard. And go out with bok gwai noi." As if dating las gringas wasn't his idea, he had to be taught. "You ought to see them there in Berkeley. Doi doi jek. Yut doi, yow yut doi." Pair after pair (of mixed couples). "Jek," an article used with livestock. "Doi," an article used with poultry. "You meet my Wit Man too late, See Nigh. You missed out on one good-looking boy."

"You still got one matinée idol under the hair, Ruby," said Aunt Marleese. "Cut it for your poor mother, Wit Man. I remember when you were yay high. I used to change his diapers. You were deh, Wit Man. He was so deh." Click click. She gave them an example of deh, her head to one side, a finger to her dimple, coy lady pose. The aunties smiled at him like he was going to act deh any moment for his mother at least, do baby-talk, act babyish, and bring out motherly love.

"Cut it off, Wit Man," said his mother. "Cut it off. I'll pay you." Clack!

"Just—. Just—," said Wittman. "Just—." Just lay off me. Cut me some slack. Let me be. And let me live.

All this time at four tables, outspread fingers with red nails and rings of gold and jade pushed and turned the tiles in wheels of bones and plastic, clockwise and counterclockwise. The sound of fortune is clack clack clack. They built little Great Walls, and tore them down. Crash! "I'm the prevailing east wind." Aunt Lily Rose is dealing. "You in luck today, Maydene." "Not luck like you, Dolly." "Poong!" "I've got a hot one," said Mom, fanning a tile like she was putting out a match. "Dangerous. Dangerous." She's got a red dragon. "Aiya." "The wind shifts to the west." "Here comes the green dragon." "The white dragon." "A hot one." "Four circles. Kong!" "Ciao!" shouted

Wittman's mother, pouncing on the tile that the See Nigh had discarded. "One, two / three bamboo!" "Mah jeuk birds all in a row." (Is "mah-jongg" a white word, then, like "chop suey," a white food?) "Your mama, one cutthroat," said Auntie Sophie. "You working hard, Wit Man?"

"I've been fired." Let 'em have it.

"Fired!" His mother screamed. "Fired! Fired!"

"It's okay, Ma. I didn't like the job anyway."

"Four years college." Mom put down her tiles. She shut her eyes, a mother defeated. She's an actress. She's acting. You can't trust actors, feel one thing and act another. She put her hand on her brow. Chewed the scenery. "What are we to do?"

The chorus gals snowed her with more comfort. "He'll get a job again, Ruby." "Nowadays they try out jobs, then settle down." "Wit Man be smart. He'll be rich one of these days."

"He read books when he was three years old. Now look at him. A bum-how."

"Don't you worry. He's one good boy." "He be nice and tall." "He always has beautiful gallo friends." "He'll turn out for the better."

He should shut them up with Rilke: *It will be difficult to persuade me that the story of the Prodigal Son is not the legend of him who did not want to be loved. When he was a child, everybody in the house loved him. He grew up knowing nothing else and came to feel at home in their softness of heart, when he was a child.*

But as a boy he sought to lay aside such habits. He could not have put it into words, but when he wandered about outside all day and did not even want to have the dogs along, it was because they too loved him; because in their glances there was observation and sympathy, expectancy and solicitude; because even in their presence one could do nothing without gladdening or giving pain. . . . But then comes the worst. They take him by the hands, they draw him toward the table, and all of them, as many as are present, stretch inquisitively into the lamplight. They have the best of it; they keep in the shadow, while on him alone falls, with the light, all the shame of having a face.

. . . No, he will go away. For example, while they are all busy setting out on his birthday table those badly conceived gifts meant, once again, to compensate for everything. Go away for ever.

O King of Monkeys, help me in this Land of Women.

"And so-o-o much talent, too-o much talent." "He got up-bringing, Ruby; you gave him upbringing he cannot lose." "He got foundation." "You one good mother." "He's clean too. Most beardies are dirty." Clackety clack clack. "And such good grades. Remember his report cards?" "He was so cute. Do you still have dock-yee knees, honey boy? You have got to tapdance for your Aunt Lilah again."

Mom's best friends were cheering her up, letting her brag out her happy, proud memories. "I remember, three years old, he made five dollars reading. His father bet a bok gwai lawyer that our biby could read anything. They took the biggest book down from the shelf. He read perfect. 'He's been coached on that book,' said the lawyer, and sent his secretary out to buy a brand-new *Wall Street Journal*. Our Wit Man read the editorial. He won five dollars. We let him keep it. Does he eat regular?" she asked Taña.

"Sure. He eats." Clack!

Does a mother, even an artiste mother who led a free youth, and chose her own husband, does such a mother want her son to have a free artistic life? No. Rimbaud wanted his kids to be engineers.

"You need a job?" asked Auntie Mabel. "I got one gig for you, dear. You come to Florida with me, and do my revue."

"You still doing your revue, Auntie May-bo?"

"Yeah, I do revue. You come, eh, Wit Man. We need a fella in the act."

"In Florida, you dance? You sing?"

"No-o-o. I stand-up comedy. My gals dance and sing. I train them. Miss Chinatown 1959, 1962, and 1963—all in my act." She liked breasts and balls jokes. The punchline: "One hung low. Ha ha." Miss Mabel Foo Yee, the Kookie Fortune Cookie. You had to hand it to her, though. Women aren't funny, and she's still cooking. Cook dinnah, Auntie May-bo. She herself had won beauty contests umpteen years ago. And went on to fan-dance, almost top billing with Miss Toyette Mar, the Chinese Sophie Tucker, and Mr. Stanley Toy, the Fred Astaire of Chinatown, Miss Toby Wing as Ginger, and Prince Gum Low, and Mr. Kwan Tak Hong, the Chinese Will Rogers, who also danced flamenco. Wittman had seen Auntie May-bo topless at Andy Wong's

Skyroom. The first tits he'd ever seen, scared the daylights out of him. A blare of brass and a red spotlight—Aunt Mabel had slinked about the Skyroom, snaking her arms and legs like Greta Garbo and Anna May Wong, legs tangoing out of her slit dress. The light shrank to head-size, and the spot held her face. Chopsticks in her hair. False eyelashes blinked hard, and the light went out. She ran about with incense sticks, writing red script in the dark. Red lights flashed on. The front of her dress broke away. Gong. Gong. Lights out. Gong. Lights on. Auntie Mabel stood with arms and naked tits raised at the ceiling. You looked hard for two seconds, the lights went out. Gong. Lights on—she was kneeling with wrists together, tits at ease, eyelashes downcast. Lights out, climactic band music, The End.

She was saying, "My gals, queen of the prom. Court princess, at least. I teach them. Mothers of junior-high gals say to me, 'Start her on her makeup, May-bo.' I teach them hair and dress. They do not go out in blue jeans or with no gloves." Wittman had met some of these trained gals. They looked like young Aunt Mabels. They wore their hair in beehives with a sausage curl or two that hung down over the shoulder. Today Aunt Mabel had on one of her specially ordered Hong Kong dresses. The mandarin collar was frogged tight, but there was a diamond-shaped opening that showed her lace underwear and her old cleavage. Her old thigh flirted through a side slit. There was a lot of perfume in the room, My Sin, Chanel No. 5, Arpège, most of it coming from her. To their credit, no girl of Wittman's college generation would be caught dead in Chinese drag.

"Good you get fired from demeaning employment. You get back into show biz, honey. For you, Aunt Carmen has special ten percent," said Aunt Carmen, a theatrical agent. She sometimes charged twenty percent, twice as much as the regular (white) agents. Her clients, Chinese and Japanese types, who'd gotten SAG cards from *Flower Drum Song* and SEG cards from *Duel in the Sun*, and hopeful ever since, were hard to place. The go-between (white) agent had to make his ten percent too. The actors didn't ask how come these double agents weren't getting 5%–5%. She was up from L.A. to touch base with the talent in the Bay Area and Seattle, and the home folks in the Valley. She had a corner on the West Coast talent.

(Auntie Goldie Joy of Manhattan handled the East Coast. The two of them had helped book S. I. Hsiung and his all-Caucasian Chinese opera, starring Harpo Marx and Alexander Woollcott, into theaters in San Francisco and London and New York.)

"You a good type, Wit Man," said Auntie Carmen. "Your gal a good type too. You an actress, darling? Lose ten pounds, you be one actress."

"No, I'm not," said Tañia. "I'm an assistant claims adjuster." Why won't she tell them she's a painter?

"We need a man in the act, Wit Man," said Auntie Mabel. "You be interested, huh." Because local boys don't wear tights, Wittman had been the boy brought in from out of town to play the prince. "You were a natural, such good ideas. Tan-ah, you should have seen him, wearing his underpants outside his regular pants, like comic-book superheroes, he said. You got personality, Wit Man." There was a song that went, "Walk personality, talk personality." "Come on. Sometime we play Reno. North Shore Lake Tahoe."

"Auntie Mabel, I like do Shakespeare."

"You snob, Wit Man. You will be hurt and jobless. We have one elegant act. High-class educated gals." Yeah, like Patty (Schoolteacher) White, the stripper in—and out of—cap and gown and eyeglasses. She was showing that you make more money working North Beach than the School District, and you get more appreciation too.

"You join Auntie May-bo's revue," said Mom, "you meet prettier gals." Clack! Putting the girlfriend in her place.

"I know a girl who would like your boy," said the See Nigh, who didn't speak English. "She came from Hong Kong only a month ago, and already has a job. Her sponsor pulls influence, and her papers are legal. She's a very good old-fashioned, traditional girl. Not in this country long enough to be spoiled. She'll make a good wife."

"Listen to See Nigh, Wit Man," said Mother. "A Chinese girl like that doesn't like beards. You be one Beatnik, you scare her away. You be clean-cut All-American Ivy-Leak boy, okay?"

"I've got a daughter I hope she won't marry somebody second-rate," said Auntie Marleese. "Gail is so smart, professors gave her a personal invitation to attend Stanford University, and pay her to go there. You know S.A.T.? Best S.A.T. in California. Ten thousand points. Pre-med. Her teachers tell me that they never taught a more intelligent girl."

"You still not get Gail married yet?" said Auntie Doll. Clack! The showgirls had been young when it was smart to be catty.

"My Betty," said Auntie Lily Rose, "made valedictorian again. *And* she is popular. *And* she is the first Chinese girl president of her parachute club. She never told me she jumps out of airplanes till after her one hundredth jump. She had to tell me, she landed on her face. Still pretty but. Only chipped her tooth. She said, 'I saved the altimeter.' Any of you know of a good boy, help settle her down?"

Wittman ought to say, "Bring me your daughters. I'll talk to them with my hom sup mouth and touch them with my hom sup hands. Hom sup sup." A hom sup lo is a salty drippy pervert.

"Come on, honey boy," called Auntie Bessie. "Tapdance for us. You the cutest most dock-yee fatcheeks. Tan-ah, did he tell you he's one great soft shoe? Come on, Wit Man, do some soft shoe, huh?" They remember, he had taken classes in Good Manners and Tap Dance at Charlie Low's school. Eddie Pond of the Kubla Khan had also sponsored schools, and given to the community his expertise in engineering, insurance, real estate, and law. The showmen competed to be most socially responsible.

"No, thanks, Auntie Bessie."

Auntie Bessie sang, "'I won't dance. Don't ask me. I won't dance. Don't ask me. I won't dance, monsieur, with yo-o-ou.' Not even for your favorite aunt, honey boy?"

"Hey, Auntie Bessie, do you still say Yow!?" She had played Laurie in the Chinese Optimist Club production of *Oklahoma*. And sang and danced in all the best Big City clubs—Eddie Pond's Kubla Khan, Charlie Low's Forbidden City, Fong Wan the Herbalist's, Andy Wong's Chinese Skyroom. Benny Goodman and Duke Ellington had swung in those clubs too. "'Okla—, Okla—, Okla—,'" sang Wittman to start her off.

"'And when we sa-a-ay Yow!'" Auntie Bessie was on her feet. "'Yow! A yip I yo I yay! we're only sayin' you're doin' fine, Oklaho-ma. Oklaho-ma, okay.'" She had worn a white lace Laurie dress with a half-dozen petticoats, and wigged out her hair with black ringlets. She held her hands over her heart, and sang some more,

> *"Don't sigh and gaze at me.*
> *Your sighs are so like mine.*
> *Your eyes musn't glow like mine.*
> *People will say we're in love.*
> *Don't throw bo-kays at me.*
> *Don't please my folks too much.*
> *Don't laugh at my jokes too much."*

"'Who laughs at *yer* jokes?'" said Wittman as Curly.

"'People will say we're in love.'" He had fallen in love with her himself. She'd kept her stage make-up on for the cast party. He had stood beside her at the community sing around the piano, and saw her powdery wrinkles. Off stage, she sang and smoked at once. "Don't daa de dada daah? Line? Line?"

Taña sang her the line in the sweetest voice, "'Don't dance all night with me.'"

"Oh, Tan-ah can sing," said the aunties. "Good, help out."

Taña and Bessie sang together.

> *"Till the stars fade from above.*
> *They'll see it's all right with me."*

And all the showgirls chimed in, "'People will say we're in love.'"

"Good, Bessie!" "Ho, la!" "Bessie just as good as ever." "Good, Tan-ah!" "Wit Man, you never said she's show business."

"She's not. She's an assistant claims adjuster."

"Thank you, Tan-ah," said Auntie Bessie.

"Thank *you*, Auntie Bessie," said Taña. "You have a beautiful voice."

"Tan-ah, I tell you," said Aunt Dolly, "that voice of Bessie's bought an airplane for World War II."

"And the rest of us too," said Aunt Sophie, "we were stars. We put on so many shows, and so many people paid to watch us dance and sing, we raised enough money to buy an airplane."

"We toured nationwide," said Aunt Lily Rose. "We had

the most active chapter of the Association of Vaudeville Artistes."

"Remember? Remember we were dancers in the Dance of the Nations," said Auntie Mabel. "We each did a solo to honor our brave allies. I was Miss France."

"I was Miss Great Britain," said Ruby Long Legs.

"I was Miss Belgium," said Aunt Sondra.

"I was Miss Russia," said Aunt Lilah.

"I was Miss China," said Aunt Bessie.

"I was Miss Finlandia," said Aunt Maydene.

"I was Miss U.S.A.," said Aunt Sadie, who had been with another Jadine, Jadine Wong and her Wongettes, those dancing Chinese cuties.

"Money was not all that we raised," said Aunt Lilah, winking at Wittman. She had danced with petite Noel Toy and the Toyettes.

"We had a painting party," said Aunt Carmen, "and painted our airplane—a Chinese flag and an American flag—red, white, and blue."

"We painted across our airplane in Chinese and English: California Society to Rescue China," said Auntie Marleese, swooping her hand like a rainbow. "And we did, too—rescued China and won World War II."

"Auntie Bessie's brother flew it to China and became a Flying Tiger," said Auntie Jean. "And is now a pilot for China Airlines."

"Hungry, Ma," said Wittman. "What's there to eat?"

"Go eat," said Mother. "So help yourself. Sow mahng mahng." "Mahng mahng" is the sound of being skinny. "Fai dut dut" and "fai doot doot" are the sounds of being fat. "Eat. Eat. Don't wait for us."

Wittman grabbed Taña's hand, and beat it to the kitchen.

There were cartons and covered dishes on every surface, more warming in the oven, and more cooling in the refrigerator. The cartons came from the restaurants which some aunties owned and some hostessed, queens of nightlife. When you're out on the town, your rep for setting it on fire depends on them treating you and your gal right. Also, when an actor loses his will to audition, they give him a meal on the house. The food in cartons was courtesy of the chefs, letting themselves go, back-home cooking that they don't do for the customers.

"You must be very hungry," said Taña, watching Wittman load his plate. "It was getting really interesting in there. I want to tell them about *my* airplane."

"World War II was where I came in. I've heard their war stories so many times. How Mom and the aunties used their beauty to get this country to go to war, to rescue ladies-in-distress, who looked, for example, like themselves. The next thing, they'll tell about their parades that stretched from one end of the country to the other and stopped the U.S. selling scrap iron to Japan. And Auntie Doll will do her speech about buying war bonds instead of opium. Taña, you'll never meet people who love working unless they're in show business. They used to have work that they loved. Now they're housewives who have nothing better to do than sit around all day playing mah-jongg until they die. It's tragic."

Taña was looking at him out of sanpaku eyes. He'd been aware all along that she was gwutting his family with that scrutiny from another world. Judy Garland has sanpaku eyes, too much eyewhite under the irises, and John Lennon does too. Elvis and Brando act like their eyes are sanpaku by looking out from lowered heads. Over her chow mein, Taña was feyly giving him lots of eyewhite. If she says "dragon ladies," definitely divorce.

"What's so tragic about mah-jongg?" she asked. "It keeps them home. They're not out escalating our involvement in Southeast Asia." Taña's E.S.P. almost let her foresee that Auntie May-bo, Miss Australia Down Under, would take her troupe to Viet Nam.

"You don't have to be so understanding. The highpoint of a life shouldn't be a war. At the war rallies, they performed their last, then the theater died. I have to make a theater for them without a war."

"They would love to perform again, I know it. Your mother and Lily Rose and Peggy and Aunt Bessie—they're still pretty, and want to show it off. I'm sorry; I'm not going to say 'still pretty' about old people anymore. That's like 'She's pretty—for an old lady,' 'He's hard-working—for a Negro.' Some women *get* pretty in old age. I plan to be that way."

"Did you recognize any of them? You can see them on the late show. Peggy played Anna May Wong's maid, when Anna May Wong wasn't playing the maid herself. Come here. I want you to meet a respectable member of my family. I have a granny. She hates mah-jongg. She's not invited to the front room. Why don't we bring her some food?"

They carried plates and bowls to the back of the house, where he called at a door, "PoPo, tadaima-a-a," Japanese. No little-old-lady voice answered, "Okaerinasai." She had taught him more phrases than that, but when he tried them out on Japanese speakers, they didn't seem to mean anything. She spoke language of her own, or she was holding on to a language that was once spoken somewhere, or she was more senile than she appeared. Wittman opened the door, but no little old pipe-smoking lady there. They put the dishes on her coffee table, and sat on her settee and her footstool. The room was webbed with lace that she tatted from thread. The light made shadow webs, everything woofing and wefting in circles and spirals, daisies, snowflakes, the feather eyes of white peacocks. Well, if you're going to be a string-saver, you can do better than roll it up into a ball. He opened the windows and started the room buoying and drifting.

GrandMaMa owned a phonograph but mostly Cantonese opera and "Let's Learn English" records. There were pictures of little Wittman in his disguises—sumo wrestler, Injun with fringe, the Invisible Man (which he had worn only once because everybody felt bad for "the poor burned boy"), opera monkey. "Are you supposed to be a monkey?" asked Taña. "Not 'supposed to be.' I *am*," said Wittman. "That's true," laughed Taña. Pictures of aunties shaking hands with F.D.R. and Truman. A girl—Jade Snow Wong?—christening a liberty ship at the Marin Shipyards. The thermos of hot water sat next to tea glasses, which were jelly glasses caked with what looked like dry dirt. "Want some tea?" Wittman offered. "It's supposed to look like that. You're supposed to let the tea residue keep accumulating." Against the day when you can't afford tea leaves? So when you drink water, it Zenly reminds you of tea? "Like a wooden salad bowl," he explained.

"No, thanks anyway," she said, which was all right. He

didn't want a girl who would gulp it right down saying, "How interesting. How Zen. Say something Chinese."

They sat quiet. He did not turn on the t.v. to watch some Sunday sport. Taña was probably picturing his grandmother as an old bride—Miss Havisham—or a spider woman. They lit up smokes. He hadn't smoked in front of Mom, who would've said, "Quit, you. You quit."

"Your grandmother's in show business too." Taña was looking at the memory village on the dresser. It did look like a stage designer's model for a set. There were rows of houses with common walls, like railroad flats of New York, like shotgun apartments of the Southwest, except no doors from home to home. The rows were separated by alleys, which were labeled with street names. Two of the houses had thatch stick roofs that opened up; ladders led to lofts. The rungs were numbered; the adobe steps with only two-risers were also numbered, one, two. One of the houses had a brick stove; the next-door had two stoves. Toy pigs, numbered, lived inside the houses and walked in the alleys. The rich man's house had a larger courtyard and more wings than the others, plus flowered tiles, and parades or boatloads of people and animals atop the horn-curved eaves. In the plaza was a well, and beside the well (where PoPo had fetched water) was the temple (where the men whistled at her and made remarks, and she dropped and broke her water jar, and the men laughed). Away from the houses was the largest building, the music building for the storage and playing of drums and horns. There were numbers on the lanes and paths out to the fields. It was autumn; the fields were shades of gold. One of the fields was edged with thirty-three lichee trees. "Twenty of those trees belonged to my great-great-uncle," said Wittman, "and three of them belonged to my great-grandfather. He didn't plant them or ever see them. He sent the money to grow them; some autumns his family thought of him, and mailed him dried lichee. Near harvest time, the boys, my cousins far removed, stayed awake nights guarding the trees with a loaded gun." A bridge went over a stream. Above the rice fields was a pumpkin patch and a graveyard. "People from this village don't like Hallowe'en or pumpkin pie. They've eaten too much of it. Pumpkins were the only crop that hardly ever failed. Like your Irish potatoes.

People's skin turned orange from eating nothing but pumpkins. Slanty-eyed jack-o'-lanterns. I used to run Crackerjack
cars on the paths, and boats on the rivers. Should the I.N.S.—
Immigration—raid this room, looking for illegals, they can
take this model as evidence, and deport our asses. Everybody
who claimed to have come from here studied this model, and
described it to Immigration. It is not a model *of* anything, do
you understand? It's a memory village." He slid the model
onto his open hand and held it like a birthday cake. "This is
it. My land. I am a genie who's escaped from the bottle city of
Kandor. I have told you immigration secrets. You can blackmail me. And make me small again, and stopper me up. But if
I don't have a friend to tell them to, where am I?"

"Thank you, Wittman. I won't tell."

"Thank you. I'm trusting you with my life, Taña, and my
grandma's life." But he was holding out on her the documentation. In PoPo's Gold Mountain trunk was the cheat sheet, a
scroll like a roll of toilet paper with questions and answers about
the people and the pigs who lived in those houses. Nobody had
destroyed the scroll or the memory village. Wonder why.

"This room smells like a grandma's room," said Taña. "I
have two grandmas, and their houses smell like this. Tell me
when I get the old-lady smell, Wittman. Or do they get it from
using a powder that's out of fashion? Orrisroot, lavender."

"Salonpas. The old lady who lives here may not be my
grandmother. She showed up one day, and we took her in. I've
tested her for her background: I watched for her to hurt herself,
and heard what she said for 'Ouch!' She said, 'Bachigataru.'
Japanese. At New Year's, she doesn't go to the post office to
have her green card renewed, so either she's an illegal alien or
she's a regular citizen. The night she showed up she brought
news about relatives that we shouldn't have lost touch with.
My parents acted like they understood her, 'Yes, the cousins.'
'Of course, the village.' 'Yes, three ferries west of the city,
there live cousins and village cousins. Anybody knows that.'
They didn't let on that they'd lost their Chinese. You want to
know another secret? She may be my father's other wife, and
they're putting one over on my mom. Not to get it on sexu-
ally, she's old, but so that my mom will take care of her." The
strange old lady pulled her apron to her back, a cape, and hung

a twenty-four-carat gold medallion to her front, a breastplate, and belted herself with a twenty-four-carat gold buckle shield. Waving fans of dollar bills, she danced whirlygiggly the way they danced where she came from. They couldn't very well turn her away.

He wandered in back of her shoji screens, opened her closet, walked into her bathroom. No grandma dead or alive. Her long pipe was gone; her shoes were nowhere to be found. In the medicine cabinet was his grandfather's safety razor. He wet his moustache and beard, soaped up, and shaved his face clean. "That ought to freak my mother out," he said. "How do I look?"

"You look better," said Taña. So why is she looking at herself in the mirror instead? She ought to be touching and kissing his nude face. *In any case I felt a certain shyness . . . such as one feels before a mirror in front of which someone is standing.*

"My mom hasn't seen my face for a while. I'm going to give her a break. She's my mother, after all, and has a right to see her son's face."

"Wittman, answer me something," said Taña. "Honestly. Promise?"

"Yes. What?"

"What does 'pahng yow' mean? You called me that to your mother."

Uh-oh, thought Wittman.

"It doesn't mean 'wife,' does it?"

"No, it means 'friend.' Let's go. I'm ready to smoothface my mother."

Holding hands with his wife and friend, he led her back to the mah-jongg games. He did not let go of her hand.

"Ma, what do you think?" he asked, poking his clean-shaven face in front of her mah-jongg tiles.

"What do I think about what?" said Ruby. "You eat enough, Wit Man? You looking skinny."

He straightened up, tucking his wife's hand under his arm. "Ma, where's PoPo?"

"Out."

"Whereabouts?"

"To the Joang Wah to see a movie."

"I'll go pick her up, give her a car ride back." Leave home, come back visit, give the old folks a ride.

"No need. She'll get a car ride."

"I'll pick her up anyway."

"She may not be there. She does errands."

"She's not in an old-age home, is she, Ma? You didn't dump her? She's not dead?" Said in front of the aunties, who were all ears.

"She's alive. Strike *you* dead for saying such a thing."

"She isn't really at the movies. Where is she?"

"Wit Man, I have taken good care of her for twenty years." Arranging her tiles. Gin.

"Ruby took in a poor stranger lady, and gave her food and a home," said Aunt Lilah.

"The money you spent on her," said Auntie Jadine, "you sacrificed your own pleasures." Her commadres were helping Mom out giving her back-up. Certain aunties who were present needed to loudly let everyone know that they were against bringing a grandma over from China to be a charwoman. *They* hadn't talked *their* old lady into signing her Hong Kong building over to them, then selling it to pay for her expenses in America.

"And I taught her a skill," said Ma. "She can run wardrobe anywhere." Grandma had earned her keep, mending costumes, ironing, sleeping in dressing rooms as dark-night security watchwoman.

"Oh, you're too kind, Ruby." "Ruby has a big heart. Bighearted Ruby—what they call you behind your back."

"Okay, Ma," said Wittman. "Where is she?"

"Your father has her."

"He took her camping?"

"He has to take care of her too. He has to take responsibility. She's from *his* side."

He walked to the door, pulling his lady with him. "I'm going to find her."

"I took responsibility long enough," shouted Ruby. "You find her, you the one responsible. You never took too much responsibility before. What for you care about the old lady all of a sudden?"

"I want to announce something to her. We gotta go. Bye, everybody."

"Tan-ah, go so soon?" "Stay, Wit Man." "Don't go already."

"You going?" "Stay eat with us." "Kiss auntie goodbye." "What you announcing?" "Where you going so fast, young man?"

"Going on our honeymoon. Bye."

Out to the porch and gate and street, chasing the bride and groom, came the voices and the clacking. "Your what?" "Eeek!" "What'd he say?" "They married." "Who?" "Congratulations, honey boy." "Happy long life, Tan-ah!"

"Married!" shouted Wittman. "Goodbye, Mrs. Ah Sing!" called Taña. "Thank you for the delicious luncheon."

Taña got in on the driver's side, her turn at the wheel. "Steve McQueen taught me how to drive," she said, and peeled away from the curb. She took her passenger's cigarette, and sucked hard on it. "Let's go to Grandma's rescue." She sped out of town. Her pointy nose cut into the wind, born for a convertible. He directed her to the American River. At the turn-off, she did a double-clutch downshift from the highway to the frontage road. Her hair was blowing back, a giant brush of a mane painting the hills its own color.

"You're the only one who noticed I shaved," he said. "See how neglectful of her family my mother is? I wouldn't put it past her to give Grandma the old heave-ho."

"You have the same custom as Eskimos?" asked Taña. "You have a 'leading out of the old citizen'? I read that in William Burroughs."

"I don't know. How many times does something have to be done for it to be a tradition? There has to be ceremony. You can't just toss a grandmother on an iceberg, and run. Eskimos probably had an aloha ceremony with torches and honors, and the old citizen sat on a lit-up birthday cake of ice. She would feel bad without her farewell."

"And her body heat warms up her piece of glacier. It breaks off, calves, and Grandma is riding away on a white calf. Like Europa. It melts, and she falls into the water and has ecstasy of the deep." She put her hands over her eyes. He took the wheel, steering from the side until she got a-hold of herself.

"Thanks," she said.

Once Wittman saw the inside of an old-age home, a board-and-care. The beautiful aunties were dancing. The t.v. set had been left on out of respect for those whose heads were turned toward it. Out of a mouth hole with no teeth, an old guy farted,

"Niggers." His face and eyes hadn't looked like he meant it. He hadn't meant anything; vibes from other people who had sat in that same padded wheelchair had come emanating out of it and through his body and out of his open mouth. "Nigger" is in the American air and will use any zombie mouth. Bust Grandma out of a place like that.

"Aren't you going to tell me anything about your dad?" asked Taña. "I could use some preparation."

"His name's Zeppelin."

"Who?"

"Zeppelin."

"Like in dirigible?"

"It's a perfectly respectable Chinese-American given name. Spondaic, heroic, presidential. Say your poems to him. He'll like you. He likes unusual people. You guys are really going to get along. He's the one started me on my trips. He used to play this hand organ that he won off a Gypsy for the line in front of theaters. He cranked out music, like grinding rice or coffee or wringing the wash. He didn't need music lessons. But where to put the money box? He tried leaving a guitar case open at his feet, but people are too shy to come up during the concert. They don't like to interrupt. They can toss coins, they can't toss bills. But the music's over, they go, forget to pay. And passing a hat unaccompanied, they take money out. A helper to follow the hat has to be paid. So he made little Wittman his money monkey. He paid me in peanuts. You don't have to split the take with the monkey, which is cute in itself. People like to give it money and watch its fingers take the coins, and it bites the coins with its teeth. Nowadays he does a lot of fishing. He watches 'American Bandstand' with the sound off."

On Slough Road, they passed houseboats, fishing boats, a two-room motel For Sale, piers, rafts, truck-size inner tubes, all attached to the shore. Beyond the settled part of the river, Wittman looked for a tree with familiar clothes in its branches. There. Pop's river camp. Two bird cages with a java finch in each swung side by side. A pick-up truck, hood up like its mouth open for dental work, was connected by jumper cables to a V.W., wings open for its backseat battery. Neither engine was running; the truck had drained the bug battery. Fishing poles were staked at the water. Taña

parked behind the mobile home, from which came masculine rumble and laughter; you feel like a child listening to
the wolf-bear sounds of Father and men friends. Does a girl
walking into this camp think about raping sites? The trailer
bounced on its shocks and springs. "Son of a bitchee!" That
was Pop; he'd learned to swear from Harry S. Truman.
"Naygemagehai!" That was Uncle Bingie saying, "Your
mother's cunt!" "Say lo! Say, la!" Uncle Sagacious Jack losing, and shouting about death. "Kill the commies!" Big
Uncle Constant Fong winning. (He used to yell, "Kill the
japs!," slap down his cards, scoop up his money. If it weren't
for the Japanese and the red-hot communists, these old futs
would have lost their spirit.) "My pop and his friends are
gambling," Wittman explained. "Poker."

He led the way through the grass to the open door of the
trailer, Taña behind and to the side of him. Be careful not
to trip over the siphoning hoses and extension cords, which
were circulating juices from buckets and machines to other
buckets and machines. A cookout grill sat level on top of black
rocks. Pot-shaped rice crusts drying in the screenbox. Father is
a string-baller and rice-crust saver. The shouting stopped. Ha!
Got the drop on the old futs. We could have been robbers,
County Sheriff's men, Immigration, Fish and Game.

"Wittman. Just my son," said Pop by way of greeting.

"Hi, Ba. Hello, Uncles."

"Eh."

"Um."

"Haw."

They won; he had said Hello, and they had cleared a throat,
snorted, breathed hard. Don't want to make you feel too good.
He used to think it was because they didn't approve of him for
something, such as his beard, or his studying liberal arts. But
who knows what it was. General badness.

"Go sit down by the river," said Pop. "Room by the river.
Have some crackers and juice." He reached into the cooler and
handed out orange soda and strawberry soda. He didn't know
the difference between soda and juice. The soda companies
take advantage of people like that.

Sitting next to the fishing poles, Wittman said, "This is his
hospitality. A seat, refreshments. He likes you. Otherwise, he'd

chase us away." Taña was drinking the orange soda. Wittman drank the strawberry, which tasted like tobacco.

"Blonde queen of my heart, come to me at last!" yelled Big Uncle Constant. "Haw! Haw!" "Ho! Ho! Ho!" Had he picked up another queen, or was he teasing Wittman about his girlfriend? For laughs, the old futs liked to jump out from behind doors and trees and scare the shit out of a kid. That was their idea of playing with kids. I'm too old for that now, you old futs.

The young futs leaned back in their lawn chairs, looking at the river go by, looking at each other. The smell of anise and spearmint, the smell of bay laurel, like a childhood day of licorice and chewing gum. A bee-loud glade. Pop's rowboat tried to follow the current, but was tied to a mulberry tree. A gold rocker was catching and cradling whatever came tumbling by. We are water rats under the willows, which Valley Cantonese call skunk trees because we are realistic. Wind in the skunk trees and the shiverleaf aspens. The mulberry tree was dripping with purple earrings. Autumn.

"I ought to quit my job," said Taña. "Wittman, we ought to stop going to parties, and live on a houseboat. Eat catfish and crayfish and mustard greens."

The river breeze blew her hair across his eyes; through it, he saw the spanking-gold California sun hitting the blues and greens of the river, the reeds, and her beautiful sanpaku eyes. The river passed on and on.

What could come by now is a small ship, a spy ship from China, playing music. Because whoever controls music has the world spinning on the palm of his hand. Like a dreydl, like a wish-fairy. There's a plum-wine party on board. Cho Cho, now a fifty-four-year-old water rat with narrow eyes and a long thin beard, is standing alone on the prow. He makes up a song: "I built a casita, where springs and summers I might have studied my books, autumns and winters, have a home after hunting. I might have had a tranquil life but for news of the wedding of a certain woman, and news of war. Aiya, I am sad. I wasted my life at war. The ravens fly across the moon; they circle the trees, and find no nest." A guest comes up on deck, and Cho Cho asks him, "Why are the ravens cawing and knocking in the middle of the night?" "The moon is so bright, they think it's day. Don't sing such a sad song." The V of the raven's tail does not stand for "victory" in their language. "You don't like my poetry then?" says Cho Cho. For he is a warrior poet like Mao Tse Tung and a warrior actor like Chou En Lai. "What's wrong with it?" he says. His guest, a good man who has re-built farm communities and schools, says, "On the night be-fore battle, you shouldn't sing discouraging words." Cho Cho drops his spear to fighting level, and runs the critic through. The ship sails on, flying the Big Dipper and the North Star, a flag of the night sky to guide him day and night.

And after the ship of spies and music comes Marilyn Monroe pushing and pulling the tiller of her boat with all her body, and singing "The River of No Return." Strange people—cat women, sandmen, castle builders—denizen the islands of the Delta. And some of them are one's relations, who have to be explained.

"That thing is a gold rocker. My father made it. It works. He's found gold in it. Zep had a big moment in his life. He found a gold boulder in the roots of an upturned tree. It came up out of the water like an arm and a hand with gold in its fin-gers, and handed it to him, a gift from the MiWuks. Zeppelin Ah Sing started the Jamestown gold rush. He found his boul-der in Chinese Camp, but told the newspapers it was Jimtown so as to decoy the rush away from the mother lode. He came home carrying his bird cage in one hand, and his gold boul-der—like the head in *Night Must Fall*—in the other. He was living with his pet bird, inside an abandoned mine 'for free, at no cost,' he said to the newspapers. 'Americans never be homeless,' he says. Take over the mines that the Caucasians have given up on—they've done the hard digging, ha ha on them. His birds test the air. They live in thousand-year-old cages with Ming Dynasty porcelain seed and water cups. All a Chinese guy has to do is to hang out his bird, and he feels like an emperor at leisure in his castle. They think birds sing because they're happy. My dad emigrated to Australia once— 'took my birds to Australia'—but came back in six months because one of the birds died; there had been two of them, twin thrushes. Gold spoiled him for regular ambition. He lives from gold find to gold find."

An especially loud uproar of swearing came from the trailer.

Triumph. Losses. Zeppelin went into the bushes to piss, which you could hear. Then he came over and hunkered down next to the pretty girl for a smoke. He looked like Mescalito on the cover of the *Oracle*.

The beauty spot on a lucky part of his face, near his mouth, meant that he will always have enough to eat; if the spot were at the center of his lip, he'd have more, but he didn't want more.

"Lose?" asked Wittman, the concerned son.

"One game."

"That's what you get for playing with Uncle Bingie." Gordon (Bingie) Young Ah Doc was pit boss at the Emeryville gambling.

"Win the next. Straighten your collar. Bums wear collar up." Wittman flattened his collar. Humor the old fart, who's going to die before me. "Don't wear striped shirts, I tell you. Make you look like one prisoner. Ex-con. Bum-how." Enough already.

"I'm not wearing a striped shirt."

His father patted the collar. "Keep your collar down."

"It's nice here, Ba. Rent free."

"No. A farmer owns this land. Every piece of land belongs to somebody. You know that? The river is owned. You hear of Eminent Domain? When we got rid of King George, we should have got rid of Eminent Domain. When I die, don't pay the death tax."

"I won't. You aren't gonna die, Ba." Wittman could return affection as good as the next guy.

"Farmers have guns. If the farmer finds me, I have to pay rent."

"That's too bad."

"I'll change my parking space. Yeah, I want to stay here for the rest of my life. I'm too old to live in mines. What you been up to? You okay? Not spending too much?"

"Yeah. Okay."

"You like tea?" His father had brought out a tea tray. Very courteous of him, giving humble respect. Taña probably thinks it's like getting coffee.

"Yes, please," she said.

The teapot had been steeping in the sun. Pop poured

everyone's, removed the lid, put one of the teabags on the spoon, looped the string around spoon and bag, and pulled, squeezing dark tea into his cup. A Depression trick no doubt, cheap Chang.

Taña fished up another bag, looped, squeezed. Dark tea pissed out. "The last drop," she said. Yes, Taña, he's living fully. A really Chang guy would've made one bag do for the entire tea party. Wittman dunked his bag a couple of times, and put it sloppy wet on the tray, Diamond Jim.

"Is this Indian tea?" asked Taña.

"Do you think I look Injun?" asked Zeppelin, who was wearing his turquoise belt buckle. "Some say I look Italian." He was proud to be taken for whatever, especially by one of their own kind, Mexican, Filipino. His favorite, he'd been asked by a Basque once near Gardenerville, "You Basque?" "I'm pure Chinese," he told Taña. "A pure Chinese can look Injun, Basque, Mexican, Italian, Gypsy, Pilipino." Wittman thought of Pop whenever he heard, "Some say he's black, but I know he's bonny."

"Teabags aren't a Chinese custom," said Zeppelin. "I tell you a tea custom before communists. There once was a kind of teacup with a lid. A poor man would catch a sparrow, and bring it to a teahouse. Waiting for the waiter, he put the bird inside the empty cup. The waiter opens up the lid to pour, and the bird flies out. Then the poor man says, 'Look what you've done. That was my valuable pet bird. You let it fly away. You have to pay me for my bird.' The waiter says it was a common sparrow. The poor man says, 'It was a rare almost-extinct species that flew away so fast, it looked like a sparrow to you. You owe me free tea, at least.' That's why we have the custom to lift the lid ourselves.

"I've got a new one for you, Wittman. Next time you order a cup of tea, ask for lemon, and get the whole lemon. The other day in town, I tried it. First, I paid my bill, then I waited at the cash register. The waitress said, 'Something else?'

"I said, 'Where's my lemon?'

"'Pardon me?' the waitress said, as if she didn't understand my English.

"'You forget the rest of my lemon?' I said.

"'What lemon?'

"'I ordered tea with lemon. You gave me a slice, in fact, one very thin slice. Where's the rest of my lemon?'

"'It's in the kitchen, I guess.' Acting dumb blonde.

"'Are you going to get it for me?' I was polite.

"She got mad. 'I should go and get the rest of the lemon? You want the whole lemon? We don't sell whole lemons. You get a slice, and another customer gets another slice. That lemon's not there anymore. It's been sliced up, and used already.'

"I said, 'Don't bully me, young woman. Your menu says, "Tea with lemon."' I showed the menu to her and to everybody. 'What does it say? Can you read? It does not say part of a lemon. If you mean part of a lemon, you write part of a lemon on your menu. You are selling my lemon to other customers. I don't care which lemon you give me, I just want a lemon, one slice out okay.'

"'She said, 'One lemon has to go around for ten or twelve customers.'

"'You feed a dozen customers at my expensive.'

"She went in back, and got the manager. I had to explain it over again. 'Does the menu say tea with slice of lemon? No. It says tea with lemon. I paid fifteen cents for my tea and lemon. All I ask is the rest of my lemon. In the market, lemons are fifteen cents for two. Here I should get one lemon for that dear price.' Everybody in the diner was listening. I teach them a lesson.

"The manager said, 'You get a slice. Everybody gets a slice.'

"I repeated many times, 'I want the whole lemon. I paid for the whole lemon. I'll leave when you give me my lemon. I have a right to it.'

"He ordered the waitress to go get it, and gave me about three-fourths of a lemon, not eleven-twelfths, a compromise but all right. Lemonade for a week. You ought to try it. That's the lemon you're using right now. You understand, it's not just the lemon but the principle of the thing."

What principle of what thing? When you live in the wilds too long, and go to town, you have to boss waitresses around? Waitresses and clerks are not for giving a bad time to.

"I saw Ma," said Wittman.

"She okay?"

"Yeah. I didn't see PoPo, though. Where is she?"

"Most likely she is not your grandmama."

"Don't matter. Where is she?"

"Ee, chotto," he said in her language.

"Tell me what you did with her."

"I drove her to Reno." He was trying to sound like a good guy who took her on a vacation.

"Where is she now?"

"Maybe Reno still."

"What do you mean maybe?"

"You know your popo, she likes her gambling. She likes her gambling too much."

"You left her there?"

"I looked all over, she didn't show up. I waited, she didn't show up. It wasn't my idea, go to Reno. Your popo said, 'Let's go on a drive and picnic.' She likes that place where you can first see the Lake from the top of the mountains. We get up there—no snow, good weather for one last picnic—and she says, 'I brought my savings. Let's go gamble.' And your ma says, 'Look out. She's tricking us to gamble.' I say, 'You women argue, I dump you at Donner Pass.' Your ma, you know your ma, says, 'How you afford to gamble, PoPo, and not pay rent? How much money did you bring?' 'All,' says PoPo. 'I bring every savings I got. I an old lady can spend all.' I had to be good to her. Her last gambling trip. I drove her down to Reno."

"And dumped her there?"

"I tell you, not dump."

"Dumped."

"I like my blackjack. Your ma likes her odd-even red-black roulette wheel. Your popo likes her machines. She said, 'Amscray.' We split up. When we get back to the truck, she's not there and she's not there. Then we figure, she showed up from nowhere one day long ago, she goes away now. She lived okay by herself before she found us. Everybody has to learn to take care of herself. PoPo is self-reliant. And she has advantages—waterproof matches, fatwood kindling, Army surplus kit. Nevada one rich state from the gambling industry. Good libraries. Good services for the old folks."

"Didn't you look for her?"

"We waited."

"I'm going to look for her, Ba."

"Up to you. What you say her name is?" Pointing a thumb at his unbeknownst daughter-in-law.

"Taña."

"Taña, nice car you have. Please, may I borrow it?"

"Where are you going? Are you going to get your mother?"

"I'm not going. I want to jump-start Bingie's little V.W. Then he can drive to the junkyard, and find me a battery for the truck."

"Okay," said Taña. She backed her car up to the V.W.'s free side. Zeppelin disconnected the jumper cables from the pick-up. He crawled into the bug's backseat to adjust the clamps and arrange the cables out the other door. Then he will open up Taña's rear lid, and clamp her anode and her cathode. If there was one thing that bored Wittman to death it was hanging around while people worked on their cars. He had a block against memorizing what was carburetor, what was motor, where the oil went, what wire to stick where for a hot-wire job, though he had spent years saying, "Uh-huh, uh-huh," while handing pliers, wrenches, screwdrivers to friends. He had hoped that those adolescent days were over. He went for a walk along the river, left the mechanics signaling at one another from behind their wheels. He heard the car almost start, die, almost start.

One Christmas day in a big city where it snowed, maybe New York or Chicago, he and his father were walking through a train station. A man in a ragged coat moved away from the pole he was leaning against. His hand came out of a pocket, and brought out a toy, a plastic horse. "Say thank you," said Ba. "Say Merry Christmas." The three of them shook hands Merry Christmas all around. Wittman held the toy horse, and watched the man walk out of the station. His father said, "He's Santa Claus. That was Santa Claus." Then they were in an elevator with an old man, who kept looking at Wittman. As all of them were getting off, the old man gave him a little green car with wheels that turned. His father said, "That's another Santa Claus. He be Santa Claus too." And out on the street, a lone man reached inside his coat, and gave him a stocking bag of candy. Many Santa Clauses. Santa Claus is a bum-how, and he does not have a sack full of toys. These men's pockets were not bulgy with more presents for other boys and girls. They hadn't had a family or a home; they had had enough money for one toy, and they'd gone out into the city to celebrate Christmas by choosing one boy to give the gift to. Because of his haircut and clothes or his Chinese face or his Chinese father, they chose him.

Teen-age time, he stopped going places with his father out of shame. He ought to give him a thrill, and make the rounds with him one of these days. Appreciate a father who doesn't dictate much, nor hit, drink, nor hang around having habits that use up all the room.

Januaries, they had gone to American banks and stores to collect calendars of the solar year; Februaries, to Chinese banks and stores to collect calendars of the moon year. On the pages of time—Gwan Goong, god of gamblers, beautiful Hong Kong girls, faery girls who float among birds and bats and flowers, kids riding on deer. The world is full of free stuff. The three-hundred-and-sixty-five-page calendar. The food in back of supermarkets. His father hoisted him into the garbage bins, where he handed out cheese in plastic, cereal in boxes that the grocer had slit whilst opening the shipping carton, day-old bread, pies in tinfoil pans. Bread gets a week old at home anyway before you get to the end of the loaf, right? At the state legislature, probably of every state, you can get all the scratch paper you want—the bills that didn't pass, and the ones that did pass and were acted on already, stapled together into legal-size notepads, print but on one side—moundfuls tossed into the basement. A day out with Pop was filled with presents. The world was a generous place.

Another outing, he and Pop had gotten themselves invited to some kind of a club. In the men's room, they filled their pockets with combs, razor blades, tiny tubes of toothpaste. It hadn't been that fancy a club, no valet. Pop hadn't lifted the silver shoehorn, but the two of them had taken off their shoes, and horned them back on. Wittman, playing rich man, had left a check for a trillion godzillion dollars.

When he went to live in Berkeley, his father showed up, and took him to the back of India Imports. They recovered enough stuff to decorate his room, a madras bedspread with a stripe that hadn't taken the dye. Pop got a poncho, and Wittman, a sweater from Brazil, a strand had unraveled. The singleton earrings he took for hanging in the window. Never buy a bed, you can always take in a mattress from off the street. Find it before it rains. His school desk was a card table, one of many he's found by the curb. Must be gamblers throw them out if they get unlucky. Eat in cafeterias where the condiments are on the outside of the cash register. You buy a serving of rice or some bread, and then you load up with relish, onions, salad dressing, Worcestershire sauce, catsup. Never leave a restaurant without taking the packs of sugar and jam. (In that same *Oracle* wherein Mescalito looks like Zeppelin, Gary Snyder says for gleaners to come to the docks. The forklifts poke holes in sacks, and you can scoop fifteen or twenty-five pounds of rice once a week.) (Grocers padlock their bins now.)

How to break the news to a wife that she's married a Chang? Don't worry; she's going to be supported but in a way that isn't going to sacrifice his free life. She's going to have to help out. He'll teach her how to live on nothing, and she'll always be able to get along, with or without him. For her birthday and anniversary, take her out to the dining rooms that feed any old body, such as the Salvation Army and the Baptist mission. Not the St. Mary's kitchen, though, because of pride, too many Chinese nearby. Don't go to the Red Cross either; after battles they meet soldiers carrying back their dead, and charge them for coffee and doughnuts, according to Zeppelin. For Wittman's twenty-first birthday, his father took him to a skid-row bloodbank, where they gave blood for ten dollars apiece. The Red Cross and the bloodbank don't preach.

The car started. The uncles were applauding. The footsteps that came up behind him were the two mechanics'. "Here." Pop whacked him on the shoulder with a sheaf of paper.

"Zeppelin! Ah Zeppelin, ah!" The gamblers were calling for more chances at him. Pop handed him the paper, and left.

"Bye," said Taña.

"Um," said Pop without turning around.

"Um," said Wittman.

The river continued flowing down from the Sierras and on to the Pacific. Taña drove, heading toward Reno and PoPo. "Pop isn't so bad," Wittman said by way of apology. "I know a family where the son had to throw a cleaver at his father's head—this was in the kitchen, a restaurant family—and got

him to start saying Hi." We wouldn't mind our fathers so
much if Caucasian daddies weren't always hugging hello and
kissing goodbye.

Wittman used his talent for reading in a moving car without getting carsick to read to his wife, busy at her practical
tasks. *Find Treasure* was a newsletter published, written, edited, typed, duplicated, and distributed by Zeppelin Ah Sing.
The main article this quarter was about the mountains of
Hawai'i—they're hollow inside, where continues to live the
royal family that descended from navigators who came from
Tahiti and Samoa via Malaysia via Israel. Even tourists and scientists have sighted the king's warriors nightwalking through
certain streets of the city and carrying torches on top of the
sea. When he was stationed at Schofield, Zeppelin himself had
seen menehune sidhe standing on rocks. They wore bright
crowns, and turned toward him with open mouths. Another
evidence of the hidden kingdom is that historically there were
decoy funeral processions. Inside the mountains, there live ali'i
more royal than the branch on the Peninsula. When Ko'olau
the Leper alone held off the U.S. Army until he ran out of bullets, he was looking for a way inside the mountains. Zeppelin
warned his readers that the Hawaiians at their most glorious
were pre-metal, and their treasures were feathers, stones, hair,
teeth, bones, and cloth.

As in all newspapers and magazines, the Letters to the
Editor were the best reading because of their non-confor-
mity. Pop's letters came from his six subscribers: Vincent
"Helicopter" Hoople of Anchorage reported that termination
dust has begun to fall. Luckily, he's finished collecting the free
coal that washes down to the beach from the melting glaciers.
Worldbeater Tam Soong, who had been reporting about life
on the Malay Peninsula—"I can't like it"—has found work
on a cattle ranch in Calgary, and recommended *Canadian
Short Stories* as a field guide. Rosalie Manopian complained
about missing cherry-blossom time in Japan and gardenia time
in Hawai'i. She is in Guam during toad season. She has to
hose out the dogs' mouths, which foam from catching toads.
"'Guam is good,'" she quoted the sign at the airport. Chance
S. L. (Shao Lin) Go gives up on getting near the gold and
diamonds of Johannesburg, which the conglomerates have

glommed, and is investing in a diving bell. He will join Mr.
Arthur C. Clarke, who has news of a gold web over Ceylon.
And Gavino McWong of the Americas complimented the editor for giving him info that is changing his life for the richer;
he will send more details after he registers his claim on a river
of opals in Baja. There was a query from Higinio Nicolas,
Palos Verdes, who needs to know anything more about the
treasure ship that came from China a thousand years ago and
sank near the beachfront lots which he has bought up.

Find Treasure featured an abandoned mine per issue. How
much wealth it might realize. How to own it. A map and a
deed upon request and twenty-five dollars. Each site personally visited by Zeppelin Ah Sing. His philosophy was that the
mines had been abandoned at a time when the equipment was
inadequate. Using modern techniques and positive thinking,
one could dig deeper. Dredge the gold mines that had been
but grazed, too much rush. Politically, change zoning codes,
change society. His position on using acids to leach out gold
was that he was for it.

The history lesson was that Constant Fong's grandfather
fainted down the steps of the Gong Jow temple-and-court-
house in Sacramento. This happened at the very moment that
John Wilkes Booth shot Lincoln, and their pains were in the
same places. Grandfather Fong put two and two together
when the news of the assassination reached the West.

These were the filler facts: $\frac{f(x+\Delta x)-f(x)}{\Delta x}$ = The Limit. Many first-
generation Americans are named Gordon because when their
ship landed on Angel Island, and Immigration asked for their
real names, they took the one off the ship, the *Gordon*.

The last page was about equipment for the retrieval of treasure, buried or sunken, types of metal detectors, prices of used
machinery, where to order, etc. Professional geologists write
dates and places on chunks of geode, quartz, garnet, gold with
India ink on white paint. Professional archaeologists christen
their sites. They dig with the Marshalltown trowel.

Wittman used his English major's skills to sneer at and
correct the dumb grammar, but suddenly stopped, folded
the paper away. *Find Treasures* by Pop gave him that same
homey-internationale feeling as the Catholic Worker one-cent
newspaper. The beans are growing at Peter Maurin Farm. I

have a father who gives me a city in a coral-reef volcano. Father
and son self-made men out of dregs and slags.

The highway followed the American River east, up among
the turkey vultures and the red-tail hawks. They stopped to
put up the top. Wittman took the wheel and drove on toward Reno. If there is a plot to life, then his setting out in
search of her will cause PoPo to appear. Do something, even
if it's wrong, his motto. His understanding of Kierkegaard: To
think up reasons why something would not work guarantees
that it will not work. Never do feasibility studies. Get on with
creation. Do the most difficult thing. Keep the means moral.
His path and her path will synchronize. Taña turned on the
radio, which was talking about a "tragic automobile accident."
"At least somebody died," she said. "To most people, tragedy
is when they don't get what they want." She snapped the radio
off. She sang "Clementine." GrandMaMa will hear. It can't be
so easy to lose track of one's people.

He chimed in at "You are lost and gone forever, dreadful
sorry." He sped up, but smoothly. He felt the drag and pull
of climbing. Don't punch the gas. Shift smooth. Ahead, a
slow Pilipino man in a Frank Sinatra hat peered at the road
through his steering wheel. Pass him. If Wittman were alone,
he wouldn't be trying to live up to this Porsche, which didn't
let family cars overtake and pass it by. A car like this costs as
much as a house. But as the Angelenos say, you can live in your
car; you can't drive a house. What do you get when you cross
a Black with a Chinese? What? A car thief who can't drive.
Ha ha. How come twenty Mexicans show up at the wedding?
How come? They've only got one car. Ha ha. How do you
teach a chinaman a sense of direction? How? Paint R's on his
thumbnails so he can tell Right from Reft. Ha ha. A man's
instincts show up behind the wheel. Wittman naturally drove
like an international student from a developing country. He
concentrated on counteracting his stereotype. If he were Black,
no Cadillac; if he were Mexican-American, no duck ass on
his head, and no 'fifty Merc, raked and deshocked, waddling
through the downtown; if he were a girl, no red Mustang; if
he were socialist, no V.W. with a Co-op bumpersticker. He got
out of the slow lane—carefully because of having no rhythm
for merging. Lean one elbow casually out the window. Drive

Okie. Lew Welch says, "Think Jew, dress Black, drive Okie."
Why Jack Kerouac had to hitchhike and be chauffeured was he
couldn't drive. Pass the Flammable truck with car lengths to
spare. The oncoming cars could crash through the poison ole-
anders, head-on. He went back to hugging the mountainside.
But bravely tried to pass a logging truck, the logs far longer
than he'd thought. The trucker seemed to race him, and not
let him back in for a long time—the last moment over the hill.
His mouth dry, he wanted a cigarette but neither hand wanted
to leave the steering wheel to fumble around on the dashboard
for a lighter that might not even be there. He could use a look
at the speedometer too, but. Having trouble breathing. The
altitude or an acid flash? Don't tell Taña. Shit. The log rig is
too large behind him, tailgating the chinaman. He tried to
step on it but seemed to go slower. He wanted to slow down,
and to stop. But what if his shaky leg miscalculate the brake,
and we overshoot the guardrail, or bounce off it into the logging rig? He may be about to lose it. "Isn't that beautiful?" he
said at the gorges. "That's beautiful," he said at the fires of red
and gold trees. The quaking of the shiverleaf aspens was inside
his feet. He cannot get into an accident; the Highway Patrol
will ask for his driver's license, which had expired. "Want to
pull over for a good look?" asked Taña, and broke the spell. He
pulled controllably into a rest stop. The logger juggernauted
over the spot where he had been, its driver blasting him with
the horn, giving him the finger while looking straight ahead,
ignoring the bird Wittman flipped him in return. After they
appreciated the scenery, he let Taña take the wheel. "I'll do the
looking out for GrandMaMa," he said. She took them up and
over the summit.

The evergreen pines and redwoods stood in red tangles of
poison ivy and poison oak. In a Disney flick, the trees would
be picking up their itchy feet and scratching them with their
branches. The railroad tracks ran above here and below there.
The chaparral has grown over cuts, and the mountains seem
to have never been re-graded and re-shaped.

Taña was asking a question, some kind of a driving game.
"See those lakes down there?" There were several flat lakes
or pools, perfectly round—too round—no waves, no ducks,
no campers. "You know what those are? Those are fake lakes.

The C.I.A. built them. They store missiles and nuclear warheads under that glass. They press co-ordinating buttons at
the Lawrence Rad Lab and Washington and Los Alamos; a
lake slides open. Out of it will rise the nose of a timed rocket.
It's aimed at Russia. If we were to park here, and hide—you
watch—at 3:00 A.M., the lakes will open. Workers and equipment will move in and out." It was a very eerie secretive place,
all right, no other cars. "It looks peaceful, huh? They're dis-
guising the violence." She's just being her old self. He liked
her old self.

Where are you, PoPo? Did you walk into the mountains and
valleys, and fall asleep behind a tree, or accept a ride with a
stranger, a yacht ride on Lake Tahoe? Be resting on a shoulder
of the highway of life, be scraping the road apple off your shoe,
I will find you.

In Reno, he parked the car, and they walked up and down
the main drag. GrandMaMa was not arm-wrestling the one-
arm bandits in the open-air sidewalk casinos. She was not in
hotel lobbies, or in cafeterias, nor was she trading her jade at the
coin-and-metals stores. At the Washoe County Courthouse,
they sat on the steps that Marilyn Monroe had walked down
after her divorce in *The Misfits*.

"Want to get a divorce?" asked Taña. She got the jump on
him again. "Now's your chance." She was ahead by quite a
few points.

"What about you? You want a divorce?" She must have
noted his driving, and been disappointed in him.

"I asked you first."

"No, I don't want a divorce." Not bad, Mr. Monkey. Like
"I'm not saying I don't love you." Better you should've said,
"Let's go inside and really get married."

Everywhere they walked, neon hearts winked and blinked.
Stuffed doves—Bill and Coo—lifted ribbons in their beaks.
Legal Weddings Legal. No Waiting. Flower Bo-Kay. Photos.
Rings. Garter. Hitching Post. Witnesses. Cake Reception.
Se Habla Español. Ceremony by the Reverend Love in the
Chapel of Love. Taña took Wittman by the hand, and pulled
him under the arch-gate of white bells and valentines that led
to the Chapel of Love. They looked like the couple on top
of the cake. World Famous & Reno's Finest! Civil Marriage!

Commitment! Non-denominational! In revenge for his not saying, "I love you, let's really get married," she said, "I wouldn't
be caught dead inside the Chapel of Love again. Once you get
inside, they separate the men from the women. The bride and
bridesmaid go into this room, where they change into dresses.
The wedding march starts, and an amber light goes on, the
signal for the bridesmaid to walk out. She emerges at the top
of these stairs that go down to the altar. Like church. And at
the top of the other wing of this double staircase, the best man
walks out his door. Like a cuckoo clock. Then, green lights go
on in the dressing rooms, and here comes the bride and the
groom. In sync without a rehearsal. And the Reverend Love of
the Chapel of Love marries them."

She's been married before? She's a divorcée? A bigamist?
Nah. She'd been the bridesmaid, not the bride. Her gang of
friends drove across State Line and married one another for
kicks.

"I'm glad we're already married, and don't have to go
through that," he said.

They went into a coffee shop to tank up for the drive back.
They filled out the keno cards with crayons. Tables in Reno
have salt, pepper, and a carton of crayons. Numbers lit up on
the boards. Although Zenly one doesn't care about winning
and losing, one feels a thrill and satisfaction at each number
that matches. It's sort of like watching the board at the U.C.
library to see if they've got your book. Flash. Your book is *in*.
Lucky. Gamblers think they want money, but they're really
after the hit-the-jackpot pinball lights. Like satori.

"I can't stand to lose," Taña said. "But if I win, I'll get addicted. I have an addictive personality."

"I don't. Do you think I would be more stable if I acquired
some habits like a rabbit?"

Should they stay and make Reno their home? There was a
Berkeley plot to take over Nevada, which is the state with the
smallest population for its land size. Establish residency in kib-
butzim of tents and caves, and vote our people into office. Two
U.S. senators easy, same as New York, California, Texas. The
prostitutes and gamblers of Reno and Las Vegas and Mustang
would, of course, be leftish and help send hip representatives
to Congress and Carson City. They will legalize marijuana,

and re-appoint the draft boards, and ban bomb testing from the desert, and send our own friendly ambassadors throughout the world. The center of world revolution was supposed to move from Berkeley to Nevada.

No, not yet. Still more private life to lead. Find GrandMaMa. Wittman paid for gas, and drove. Fall off a horse, get right back on. Same with a car. The sun going down, the casino lights going up, the night softening the Sierras, he'll take it through. Taña looked for GrandMaMa on the right side of the freeway; Wittman looked to the left across the oncoming traffic. One more chance, PoPo.

Silverado. Silver cities. If you know your history, you can see more clearly the ghosts in the ghost towns. There had once been Chinese parades. To the surprise of their neighbors, one day every Chinese in town and from out of nowhere, including the women with bound feet, had dressed up and paraded. On a buckboard stage, the few women, representing eighty-seven faeries, played banjos and flutes, and strewed flowers, and waved branches of quince and poles of streamers and tassels. A faery seemed airborne, dancing in the circles of ribbon she twirled on a stick; ribbon dancing will be an Olympic event, wait and see. The men walked with their birds or sat on antique throne-chairs on haywagons. Farm-hand clowns did handsprings and bird calls and animal calls, and acrobatic pile-ups. Those who remembered opera sang the parts of kings. They fanned themselves and their birds and the townspeople with elaborate vanes of feathers, paper, wood. At the end of the street, the procession turned around and went through town again, and again. The main streets were very wide, not for quickdraw gunfights, but so that wagons, which had no reverse, could turn around. A buckboard carried a pyramid of buns for everyone to help themselves. A man walked among the crowds inviting them to look inside his gourd, and to drink from it. Merchants and traders—this happened on a workday—came out on the plank walkways and the balconies, and were amazed at their cook and babysitter, their laundryman, their cowhand, so changed. Why, but a few years ago, they had been pogrommed in a drive-out, and here they were parading. Yes, the citizens of the town will marvel at the comeback. They'll find these human beings so beautiful that they won't want to massacre them anymore. Already the lifetime of the town had never seen the like—when overhead sailed men in a basket lofted by a red silk balloon. It floated low. The people in the air seemed wonder-struck to see the people on the ground. Their runningwater sleeves streaming in the sky, they pointed at this one and that one. They dropped notes upon them. They called in a foreign language. Each wore a different shape of hat. They had long moustaches. The wind caught the balloon up, and they blew away to see the Indians and buffaloes. They went in the di-rection of one of the four words on the sides of their basket. Those words might have been the compass points, or perhaps they said, "We discover you, America." Nobody could read Chinese, they could've said anything. It had been an explora-tion all the way from Cathay.

In Truckee after dark, a warm light drew the car, which came to a stop under a wooden sign twined with ivy. La Vieille Maison. Usually, both Tañerang and Wittman fought against be-ing waylaid by the advertised, but they were cold and hungry, and in need of bathrooms.

As he held the car door open for her, some cowboys in a pick-up truck shouted something, whistled. Fucking rednecks. The way they get you paranoid is you can't tell whether they're admiring the car and the chick, or they're giving you racist red ass. Flipping them the old finger isn't satisfying enough. They run away, and don't catch your reaction.

The amber in the windows was coming from a fireplace, which the maître d' seated them near. Given a choice, Wittman would have chosen that hearth table anyway. Who cares if it's the conspicuous, overheated table that they couldn't get rid of? Right off he ordered a carafe of the house red. The waiter brought homemade bread rolls and said that the butter was "drawn and whipped." This restaurant was famous for board-ing the cast and crew of *The Gold Rush*. Charlie Chaplin might have sat right here and invented the Oceana Roll. Wittman stuck his fork and Tañerang's fork into two rolls, held these feet un-der his chin, and danced his head across the table, kicked left, eyes left, kicked right, eyes right, run run run run, and bowed. Tañerang applauded, and ate one of the feet. Chaplin had hired eleven thousand tramps from the Yellow Jungle of Sacramento to build the Yukon in the Sierras. Every structure in the area

had had its artist-in-residence. Wittman leaned back, looking through his wine at the firelight and at his woman. Taña
raised her glass, he raised his. Clink. Can you stay in love with
somebody you've been with—let's see—for how many hours
straight? Thirty-six continuous hours. Some kind of a record,
he bet. Romeo and Juliet weren't together for that long their
entire lives.

Oh, yes, to have an orderly table three times a day every
day, plus second breakfast and a high tea, five sittings a day, a
pressed tablecloth, cloth dinner napkins, utensils lined up, a
plate for salad, a plate for bread, clean ashtrays, flowers, oneself
fitting just right in front of his place setting. At the clink of
maybe real crystal, holding the stem between thumb and finger, Wittman resolved ways to make life better for himself: He
ought not to eat and work at the same table; clear off the papers
and decant the catsup, put away the Peace Brand nori furikake
fish flakes, except when that meal required a dash. Wash coffee
cup between usings, use its saucer strictly as saucer, not for
a sandwich plate or an ashtray. Set up each course and activity. His whole outlook would change. Be more Japanese and
French. Take time to fix food; take as long to eat it. Serve it
presentably. No more naked lunches. He's got to stop eating
with his head in the refrigerator or bent over the pot on the
stove. Peel an orange into the garbage bag, okay, but then walk
a ways off, don't slurp over the bag. His parents hadn't raised
him on organized meals; they didn't know better, scarfing hot
dogs and soda pop while taking a walk between the matinée
and the evening show. He had forgotten how to live, but it was
coming back to him. End the day gracefully. See each day out,
toast it, feast it, sing its farewell. At least, sit down and eat with
another human being.

Across from him—Taña. He loved the way her hands moved,
a long finger going down the menu. She's in no hurry to get
to the next thing. An artist's pace. She pretended to untie the
laces of a bread-shoe; she picked its bone-nail from between
her teeth. With a silver blade, the waiter scraped the crumbs
into a silver crumb-catcher, then brought the appetizer—wonderful escargots. She got down to business. The same garlicky
buttery pleasure that is coursing from my mouth to my soul
is gladdening your insides too. We are communicating. Her

sixth and last shell empty, she traced the snail whorls with her
menu finger. Hers are sculptress's hands. "Will you cook for
me?" her dinner companion asked with his mouth full of the
Gruyère crust of the onion soup. "I could have French onion
soup every meal. You'll make it for me?" Yes, he could take this
for the rest of his days.

This monkey man of hers has lessons coming to him. He
should have said, "I love French onion soup. I love you. Let
me cook it for you, and feed it to you. Then you cook it for me.
Let's cook for each other. You taste my version, I taste yours,
we know each other's taste buds."

"Every damn Sunday at this time, I get brought down,"
Tana said, cutting her rumsteake. They had ordered the rumsteake maître d'hôtel pour deux personnes and pommes frites
and carottes râpées au citron. And a salade de saison and a
fromage. They had yet to choose the mousse au chocolat with
strawberries or the tartelette aux fruits avec Chantilly or le
mystère. And coffee with a B&B. "I start thinking about calling in sick. What do you think? Should I call in sick? Help me
decide what I have. Nobody can lie about sick leave. Whatever
you say you have, you get."

Here was another chance for Wittman to let his woman
know how he loves her. He should have said, "Eat your French
fries. Go wild on strawberries. You don't have to worry about
your job anymore. I'll do the providing."

Instead, he gave her advice on what to do about Mondays.
"I've never worked on a Monday, restaurants and theaters dark
Mondays. At this job I just lost, Monday was one of my days
off. I'm going to go on Unemployment. Six months off."

"I'll say diarrhea. Diarrhea gets to them. They don't know
what to reply to a diarrheaist. They don't want anybody with
the runs around the office. It's one of my best excuses. You
have my permission to use it when you get a job again. 'I can't
come into the office. I got the runs. Gotta go, bye.' Hang up
quick, don't give them a chance to discuss it and say no."

She doesn't understand, he doesn't want a job again. Fired,
he's got more self-respect than ever.

They were smoking between courses, and did not make it
to dessert. The voice of a loud man at Wittman's back said,
"Every Mexican in town has one."

The party at that table laughed and laughed, repeating in appreciation, "Every Mexican in town has one."

Has one what? Go ahead.

More laughs. Wittman turned to see what they looked like. They looked like the kind who entertain one another with race jokes. The vigilante of parties has got to go into action when he hears jokes against any color. He knows, it started out as a chink joke, but they had looked about, saw one, and changed it to Mexican. Like a heroic Black man who has overheard a jiggaboo junglebunny joke, he got up, turned, walked over to that table, step by step, closer and closer. "You talking about me?" he said. "What you say? You say a joke about me? Say it to my face. Come on, let's hear it." So I can have right paranoia.

He struck the two men and two women speechless. He prompted them, "I want a laugh too. Every Mexican has one what? I want a laugh too."

"You're causing a disturbance," said the joker. "This is a private party." The men got to their feet to defend their table. "You're spoiling our dinner." "Waiter. Waiter," said the other man.

Their waiter and the maître d' and a cook or owner in a black rubber apron came running. "What's wrong? Be seated, please. No fighting in here, gentlemen. Sir, return to your table, please."

Wittman spoke loud for the dining room to hear. "You like jokes? I tell you joke. What's ten inches long and white? Nothing, ha ha. Every gringo doesn't have one. Why you not laughing? I funny, you not funny. You nauseating. You ruin my dinner. You slur all over my food with dirty not-funny joke." He pointed his finger at each nose. "Don't you tell jokes anymore. Don't let me catch you laughing against any raza again. You tell a gringo joke, wherever you are, I'm coming to get you. Understand? You sabe?" He held the edge of their table ready to overturn it.

"We weren't telling dirty jokes," said one of the ladies. Her husband will get her later.

"Ignore him," said the other woman. "He's disturbed."

"Are you going to eject him, or do I have to?" said the joke-teller.

"I'm leaving," said Wittman. "I might throw up my gorge, barf eating next to you. You're getting off easy this time. I give you a chance. Next time, out of luck." He turned to the help: "If you want to run a gourmet cuisine place, you shouldn't allow pigs."

He paid his bill and tip with virtually all the money he had left, and no wages ahead. It was worth it. He had come up with excellent rejoinders. His americanismo was intact. Everybody had sat up and taken notice. Taña didn't give anybody a disloyal look or shrug. He wished he could speak private Chinese to her, and she to him.

Outside, she asked, "What were those people saying? I didn't hear what they said."

"They were racists. They were telling a race joke. I didn't overhear it all the way through. During jokes, I have trouble hearing anyway. I get this blockage in my ears, like a wall or a roar that protects me. Line by line, I'm thinking, Is here where I break in and call them out, 'Don't tell coon jokes'? And try to educate them as to the unfunniness of the genre. Or can I laugh, it's not a coon joke? I'm a good sport, I'm ready to catch on and laugh, or catch on and bust ass. They get quiet when I walk into the party. I don't get to hear as many jokes as most people. I caught the punchline in there. It went like this: 'Every Mexican in town has one.' Do you know how the rest of it goes?"

"'Every Mexican in town has one.' No, but I can find out for you." Will he be with her at that by-invitation party where she listens for Anglos making merry prejudice?

As they crossed the street, a voice demanded, "What time is it?"

Wittman didn't look about. Not every shout is meant for you.

"You. You have the time?"

"No," Wittman shouted into darkness. "No. I don't own a watch."

"What's the time? What time?"

"No watch. No watch." He could not see who was there.

The way they drive you crazy is you can't calibrate your paranoia. Like "Your time is up"? Like "Your time is up, chinaman"? You can't be too paranoid in these small towns with separate outskirt Chinese cemeteries full of graves with the dates of young men. A few years ago, he'd gone up to

Middletown to join an anthro dig; the storekeeper said, "You ain't gonna find nothin' but the bones of the chinaman, ha ha ha." He'd said that to the white kids too, nothing personal. In these parts, anyone who wants to cash a check has to turn himself in to the sheriff.

Wittman escorted his lady safely through the main street toward the car. They window-shopped and looked for GrandMaMa. Notches to the tops of doorframes recorded snows. He got in the driver's side. He drove well, the while inventing a ratsbane parade. These towns need banging.

Ba-baan! Blow the ram's horn—announcing public executions. On prancing Red Rabbit, Grand Marshal Grandfather Gwan, god of war and theater, rides again. Halberdiers and gunslingers carrying scythes, samurai swords, grenades, railroad spikes, chef's knives, Mrs. Winchester's rifle, whatever there is around the house, make an exit from the theater on the esplanade and processionally walk to the temple in the middle of town. No permit, tough shit, we parade anyway. Four days of parading a town, leafletting it, advertising ourselves. The flyers quote *The Sacramento Union*: "It would appear that John Chinaman means to remain with us for an indefinite period and to enjoy himself the while." You bet your booty and sweet patootie. Yes, it must have been a show-of-force parade that the *Union* reacted so meanly. King Mulu walks his beasts, white tigers, kirins, camelopards on bridles which also guide the winds. Chuko waves his feather fan that can sic elephants on a populace. Doctor Woo will be there, flashing his fishbait lures: "Step right up for a peek between my hands. The lure is lighting up. Ten cents to look. One dollar to buy. The lure is difficult to see by daylight, but. It allures in the dark. It allures you for to dig your mine tunnel. Good for a lifetime. Dig for fifteen years, guarantee you find prosperity. You will find you a palace of chrome. You will meet the Queen of Silverado, who looks like this lovely lady. At no extra cost, she will take from her own head to you very own head the wolf helmet. You wear the ruff of a wild wolf all around you face, you hear and remember the lucky strike chant I be singing." Eddie Toy swags and slides his lariat noose. And here comes our all-girl drum corps shuffling along in slippers. And Miss Chinatown and her court of runner-up princesses on the backs of convertibles.

Roll flam-flam flam-flam. Roll flam-flam. Each girl mad to turn into a swordswoman, her secret identity. Running about everywhere and interacting with everybody—blue-faced varmints and clowns in skull-white. You won't be able to make them laugh, even tickling them keelee keelee in the armpits. And riders are coming in warpaint, each with its peculiar menace—black-winged eyes and eyebrows, curlicues around round noses, grooves beside their red mouths, red and green diamonds on foreheads and chins. None of the horses is gunshy because of the bats and words painted on their hoofs and rumps (over the Bar-B-Q brands). Stomach-echoing ear-blasting cherry bombs go off. And fountains and showers of fireworks rise and fall. Fire falls hurtle down mountainsides. And at the end, six white horses pull a stagecoach delivering in its belly ten thousand gold eagles won by a Chinese gambler.

The black shapes in the sky were ravens, those on the ground were a herd of tumbleweeds. They had broken from their roots, and were traveling on the freeway. Wittman slowed down for a couple of thickets to cross, did not get tail-ended, and drove under a bouncer, big as the car, swerving around a sitter. In his rearview mirror, he saw a gnarly snarly mass switch directions to chase a windbreaking truck. Taña said that he played dodge-the-tumbleweeds very well.

Yes, he was getting into driving. The Porsche Speedster smoothed out the plodsome world, which he controlled with the steering wheel. The Sierras rolled by like movie scenery to the background music from the radio, *Fanfare for the Common Man* by Aaron Copland. For long stretches, no other traffic messed with him.

But then he started thinking about the moving light yonder. Didn't it seem to be staying with them? What was it, and was it coming this way? In emptiness, brainwaves home in on one another. There may be thinkers tracing you. Try not to attract killers, and things from outer space. People are always meeting flying saucers in Nevada and being taken aboard to Venus. Anything could have happened to GrandMaMa.

At State Line, Taña told the ag inspector that the only fruit they had was Juicy Fruit. That's why he likes her—she is socially aggressive.

GrandMaMa probably won a jackpot, and the casino is

sending her home with an escort at its own expense. The news of her winnings may have reached Sacramento by now. Her friends are waiting at the Greyhound Station.

Oakland came up before San Francisco. Good. He would drop this girl off. He had gotten here on the bus, he could take the bus back. If you don't get back to your own pokmun alone when the weekend is over, you start becoming the husband part of a longterm living-together couple. She was worrytalking about Monday morning turning her into an assistant claims adjuster. (Can a monkey love an assistant claims adjuster?)

"I loathe my job," Taña was saying. "You know what the most creative part of it is? I mean, besides making up excuses. I match up a monetary figure with a loss of a body part, so much for a hand, so much for each finger, so much for an eye, one leg, two legs, a foot, a toe, more for the big toe than the baby toe. Loss of an extremity is usually accidental. In beatings, people get hurt in the torso. That's the most interesting information I've gotten out of the job. You know what the most common occurrence in the human body is? Cysts and fibroids. At parties, I say, 'I'm an assistant claims adjuster,' I may as well say, 'I'm just a housewife.' I never meet these people with the cysts, or the one eye and one leg. I just match up the number of stitches with the number of dollars. I type out the checks. I write letters denying pregnancy coverage for the unwed daughter of the family. The most excitement we've had was when my desk partner recognized the signature on a physician-verification form to be the name of the acid killer doctor. An autograph of a killer. I've got to change jobs, but Claudine—that's our Office Manager—isn't going to give me a good letter of recommendation."

She carried on like that all the way back to the curb of her house. Here was Wittman's chance, come to her rescue. At least walk her to the door. And come on in for a sit and a listen. Don't leave her like this. "At eight o'clock A.M., this chime goes off. The first four notes of Lara's theme in *Doctor Zhivago*. We have to be at our desks. It goes off again at ten-fifteen, coffee break, and ten-twenty-five, end of coffee break, and at twelve noon and twelve-forty, and at two-fifteen, second coffee break, and two-twenty-five, end of coffee break, and five o'clock—commute hour. I live for those two ten-minute coffee breaks and the forty-minute lunch hour. They compute those sixty minutes against us. We get paid for eight hours when we're at the office for nine hours, plus two rush-hour commutes. Plus getting ready, dressing for work, nylons and make-up you wouldn't wear otherwise. When we get so sick that we have to stay home, they call that a benefit. If I lost a toe or got beaten up in the torso, I ought to be able to type myself a check. They keep congratulating themselves for giving us a girls' lounge. The girls crochet and knit and read *Bride* magazine in there. Men never come in. I don't know where the idea of office romances comes from. Males and females don't have much to do with one another. When one of the men does talk to you, he tells you that insurance is the answer to everything—especially death, everything. The girls knit ten minutes at a time, and after a couple of years, they have a sweater or an afghan to show for it. Some of the older girls knit booties for their grandbabies. Most of the girls graduated from high school; they think they have to obey bells. The men don't go by the chimes. It's not fair. The men go to lunch from eleven o'clock till two or three, and it counts as work. They eat with clients. You can smell what they had to drink. And they get paid many, many times as much as the girls, plus commissions. Claudine told us not to compare paychecks. She said pay envelopes are confidential. So whenever I'm alone with a girl in the restroom or the elevator, I tell her how much I'm making, then ask her what she's making. Most of them say it's none of my business, and that I'm breaking the rules. I did get a couple of girls mad, though; they've been there longer than me and I make ten dollars a month more than they do. We think it's because I went to college. We've got to start a union, but white-collar workers don't like unions. And do you know what's really unfair? I'd have to hold organizing meetings on my own time; bosses get to have union-busting meetings on company time. The job of executives is to fuck over employees. When I brought up unions, some girls said I was a communist. In fact, they reported me to the American Legion, who called on Claudine, who told me to watch my step. If I quit my job, I won't be able to get back in elsewhere. I'll be blacklisted by the insurance industry. Ordinarily, I'm not political, Wittman, but most people are so dumb, I can't just stand by and enjoy having brains. We have to take responsibility for the dumb people." Wittman hoped that those scared office workers, whom he pictured typing their lives away at infinite banks of desks, weren't Chinese-American girls. Most likely they were, and Claudine was too. "I can finish my work by the second coffee break. I tried reading, writing letters, making phone calls. Claudine told me to spread insurance forms on my desk. 'Look busy,' she says. I was reading a very educational book, but she made me put it away. I've got to get out of there."

Wittman can't be her rescuer. The only way he could see to rescue her was to take her place, and he had just escaped from wageslavery. But what kind of a monkey would he be not to stay and try to change her trip? Anyway, he had lost the energy to go out into the streets and catch the last bus of the drear night, stopping all along San Pablo, transferring, ending up at the Terminal again, walking to his poor room. And here were clean sheets, a made bed, and this girl getting into her lavender tie-dyed t-shirt. He had to have his feel of her. He ought to have said, but not any good at saying, didn't say, "Thank you for being brave, showing me the insurance side of you. I love you nevertheless. I love you." He loved her up quietly, stilling her chatter. Bodies have their touching ways, their own dumb language. Look into eyes and face, watch the giving in and the changing. The reason we're made of flesh that feels pain, we're evolving to be careful creatures who handle one another with all consideffateness.

Taña lit up a Balkan Sobranie, and offered Wittman a Gauloise, both brands on her headboard shelf for decoration, the packs almost full because they taste worse than shit. Taña sucked a mouthful of smoke, rounded her lips. She puffed out a smoke ring that drifted upward. "Let me practice my call-in on you, okay? 'Claudine?' Picture an S.S. Nazi concentration-camp guard on the other end of the line. 'Claudine, I can't come in today. I've got . . . I'm embarrassed to say . . . running diarrhea.' Can you tell I'm lying? I get all hesitant and inarticulate lying. 'Claudine, I'm pregnant. Puking all morning. I'm going to be late puking in the mornings from here on in. I'll get there as soon as I can. Upchucking goes away after the abortion.' They probably fire girls for abortions. They fire you for getting pregnant, married or not. We're always having baby-shower farewell parties, where Claudine says, 'We can't have you big as a cow in a business office, now, can we?' I've got it. I'll say, 'Claudine, to keep my job I got an abortion, resulting in feminine complications. How much sick leave do I have?' Good night, Wittman, my dear. I need to get some sleep, and get up early whether I go to work or not. Even when we're legitimately sick, we can't sleep in. We have to call as soon as the switchboard opens, before the clients start phoning. Claudine has hung up her coat and put her purse in her file cabinet, and hasn't noticed that I'm late or missing, her phone's got to be ringing, me on the line. They ought to let us call the night before, so we can relax."

She pulled the covers up, turned her back, shut her eyes. Wittman panicked. Taña, please don't go. Don't shut me out. He leapt out of bed to the vase behind the door, whereout he pulled two fencing foils. When naked making love with a stranger, locate the weapons. "Taña, wake up. Here, take this sword. Fence me." He found her lipstick, and painted a pink heart under his left tit. "Show me some moves. Come on, Taña. Be a good hostess."

She sat up, picked up her sword, undid the safety tip, thrust, parried, parried again, and touched him at the heart.

"No fair. You've taken lessons," he said.

"Good night, Wittman," she said, sliding down, rolling over, her sword between her side of the bed and his.

He sat on the footboard, his sword between his knees. In the shining steel handguard, his penis reflected huge. Behind it, his pinhead peeped out a long ways off. How odd, his head, the container of his mind, which contains the universe, is a complicated button topping this gigantic purple penis, which ends in a slit, like a vagina. "Hey, take a look at this."

She acted asleep. Well, he couldn't expect her to watch him play with himself. He brought the sword mirror up to his face, a Jiminy Cricket face with a bug body. Hey diddly dee, the actor's life for me. What interesting reflections of pinks and mauves and tans. She's asleep, might as well explore her place. In the kitchen was another Toulouse-Lautrec, *75 Rue des Martyrs*. Yeah, he ought to be living in Paris, home for his type. Taña had matching canisters, alphabetized spices, glass jars with red beans, green peas, sugar, pasta. Domesticity. Don't get domesticated. In the living room, he sat himself down at her dainty secretary desk. Looking in the pigeon-hole dioramas, he found no letters either to or from her. He could write her a note saying that the buses aren't running, he had to steal her car. Two A.M. already. Should he remove the Isolde sword, and uxoriously crawl into bed? No fair; "uxorious" refers to men, and "husbandly" also refers to men. He ought to use her expensive texture-weave stationery and the pen of her desk set, and write more play. Back in the bedroom, he went inside the closet. Behind her clothes were shelves of labeled shoe boxes—huaraches, slingbacks, spectators, red shoes, white pumps, etc. "Beeeen!" said the evolutionary monkey.

The curtain opens—he flung her dresses aside—the great killer ape in chains sees the audience. Bloodshot eyes roll, sharp teeth gnash. Roar! Roar! He opened his mouth wide like in the silent movies. Laughing at me, are you? Look at my red lashing tongue, and down my gullet—a real ape, not some fool inside an ape costume. Feel my guffs of hot breath. I will slip these chains. White hunters, you will die. Let me make my hand small here, change it into a wing, a red fin. Oh, no, I'm stuck at ape. I'll grow then—to one hundred thousand feet. The chains snap. "Bring down the curtain!" shouts the stage manager. The curtain swings across. Down drops the asbestos wall. The shape of the gargantua ape swells and bulges. He tears through man's puny barriers against reality, and leaps out of the proscenium into the stampeding audience. Swinging his chains—tool-wielding ape—he lassoos the chandelier, pulls himself up, and rides it. He screams louder and higher than the ladies. Swooping Fay Wray up in his mighty arm, he and she swing across the ceiling of the San Francisco Opera House. Down rain crystal and loose excrement—cee—on to the audience. Balso Snell. O, say can you cee? The ape is loose upon America. Crash their party. Open his maw mouth, and eat their canapés and drink their champagne. The party is mine.

No one left but me. And this fellow in milady's dressing-table mirror, and in her hand mirror. With opposing mirrors, I can see my profile. I look like an ape. I have an ape nose. I do not look like a flounder.

Who's that human being unconscious down there? Dead?
And here is her suitcase for going away to death camp. I alone
am left alive. She is a mother dead beside the evacuation road.
I am her babe clinging to her dead body still warm. Tanks are
coming. And bombers in the sky. If I run after the others, I
leave her dead alone forever.

He put his cheek and ear close to her face, felt her breathing.
Alive, whew. He picked up her sword, and put it on the floor.
He lay down at her side, and slept.

6

A Song for Occupations

WITTMAN AH SING, for one who wanted badly to be a free man, was promising quite a few people that he would help them out. He had to create for Nanci Lee a theater. And find his PoPo. And keep Taña for richer, for poorer. "Forsaking all others." That part of the ceremony ought to include the saying of the names of the forsaken, so that we can specifically and publicly give them up. The bride's catalog of the forsaken. The groom's catalog of the forsaken. I forsake thee, Nanci Lee, et alia.

He did too have a philosophy of life: Do the right thing by whoever crosses your path. Those coincidental people are your people.

He rode into the City with Taña, who went to work after all, having wakened too late to call in, and late for work too, though it was early. The air was yet unbreathed through too many engines and lungs. The sun was a dime in the rearview mirror as she bravely drove into the fog of the Bridge toward the City, which looked like a grey thought. Drag boats were visible section by section crossing blue clearings. The City emerged, unmoved. Among its necktied men and heeled women, Wittman was yogore, a mess on a business day. Taña dropped him off near the Unemployment Office, where he would try for full benefits, six months of money to finance all that had to be done. She volunteered a plan for the rest of their lives: alternately, each spouse work half the year and collect Unemployment the other half. Bending over the roofless car, he kissed her goodbye.

He walked past two clochards sitting on the curb with a bottle of vin ordinaire. One poured a red trickle into his cupped hand, started to wipe his face with it, and flicked it in the other's face. Good morning. They bust up laughing—they still have laughs in them. The man with wine-wet face took the bottle, put his thumb over its mouth, and shook a rain of wine down on his friend. A toast—to superabundance for grasshoppers. They passed the bottle between them, drinking, swapping germs, mingling fates.

Inside a smoke shop, four bad boys, why weren't they in school, were at the magazine rack. It had to be porn that they were reading so intensely, warping their imaginations. But the tallest kid was reading aloud to the others, and it was *Astounding Stories.* The next tallest kid hung on the reader's shoulder and stared at the page as though there were illustrations. The littlest one rested his head on a shelf. The fourth kid sat on a bundle of magazines with his chin on his fists. Everybody enrapt.

At the corner across the street slouched a tough-shit girl with raccoon make-up, black motorcycle jacket, short skirt, fruit boots. Wittman prepared for rude eye contact, but at the light's change, she waited to walk slow with her old-world grandma. He slowed down too, an additional pedestrian body in the crosswalk against cars jumping the light. The girl bent down, speaking in kind Spanish to the babushka head.

How to behold strangers: longer.

The reason he was receiving all these beneficences must be because he was free from work. The city becomes an easier place. Indian summer was holding steady.

And parked at the parking meter in front of a deli—a red toy bull in a shopping cart. Of course, no pets allowed. Wittman went inside and ordered a pastrami on rye. The owner of the red bull was not there. The guy at the counter reached into the refrigerator and handed him his sandwich. "Could you heat it up please?" Wittman asked.

"You want it hot? I'll make it hot for you," said the deli man. Wittman laughed in the street. He left the sandwich in the shopping cart.

At the Unemployment Office, the jobless were lined up clear out the door. He went inside to figure out whether that long line was indeed where he had to start. Nobody told him to get his ass back out there. No information booth or posted instructions to help him out. What do the dumb people, who are most of the people in the country, do? The unemployed, his fellow man, waited before windows marked A, B, C, and D, and 9:00, 9:30, 10:00, 10:30. Rows of them waited in chairs arranged as if the down-and-out were an audience. A man in a boss suit jumped ahead to the counter. "Half a sec. Half a sec," he kept saying, a fired executive who hasn't learned that his time isn't valuable anymore. Everybody ignored him, and he left. Come on, give him the benefit of the doubt, he's no different from you and me. Tail him, and he'll lead you to a secret neighborhood of skylit lofts and underground poetry readings, and to the studio where he is making something beyond your imagination. Look at us: artists, squandering our creation time. Please give us our grants to do the work we were born for. We won't waste our lives in front of the t.v., we promise. Wittman decided on line A, a beginning and also his initial. This maneuver put him out the door. Well, he'd learned patience at registration for classes. When inside again, he followed a stripe of yellow tape on the concrete floor. Yeah, hitting his marks. All together now: "Follow the yellow brick road. Follow the yellow brick road. Follow, follow, follow, follow, follow the yellow brick road." The people did not look particularly employable or unemployable, or tired or abashed. Some women and a few men had brought their children. The movie stars were traveling incognito. No communists leafletting the crowd. Some unshaven guys starting beards. Some ladies in curlers, and some Black guys in stingy-brim hats, a few in do-rags. There were a bunch of Chinatown ladies; he didn't know them. They were talking about the advantages of migrant labor. "At the grape camp, I felt like a Girl Scout." "Just like college girls in one dormitory." "I forget my boy in Army. Indochina." A good life, harvest the tomatoes, harvest the grapes, collect Unemployment between crops. They spoke good and loud because the low fawns can't understand them. Wittman let his cigarette ashes fall, then his cigarette butt, and stood on it. No ashtrays for the poor. He wondered how much money he was going to get, whether this waiting and whatever else they'll make him go through was worth it. Good thing he was a stable person, otherwise run amok. Nobody was running amok. How patient most people are. How law-abiding. He was standing amok. So, it has come to this. Lew Welch teaches us to stop and say every now and then, "So it has come to this." So it has come to this.

The best dresser in the place was a very pretty Black lady a couple of lines over, the C line. She wore a halo hat, suit, gloves, and very high-heel shoes, on which she was rising on tiptoes above the situation. Her hair fluffed out around her Nefertiti face. She must be a high-fashion model back from Paris after the haute-couture showings. Two Black guys, who came in together, spotted her, and their faces changed—were gladdened—their postures straightened up, inspirited by her. There ought to be such a girl doing the same for our unemployed, but our career girls wouldn't be seen at the Unemployment Office, too shame.

After about an hour, all at once, the clerks flipped the cards over the wire—11:00, 11:30, 12:00, 12:30. Eventually he got near the front of window A, where he stayed behind a white stripe perpendicular to the yellow line. The unemployed person gets privacy at the window. The one behind him could not overhear the right answers. Then our pilgrim passed the test of waiting. It was his turn to step over the white stripe. "Good morning," he said cheerfully, to take the initiative, to keep up his end of the day, to shoot this government worker some sarcasm, it hardly being morning anymore.

She didn't say Good morning back, but had her hand out for him to give her something.

"I want to sign up for Unemployment," he said.

"Your form?"

"What form?"

"Application form."

"What application? I thought when I made it to the front, you were going to hand me my money." He didn't really think that, but was suggesting to her a possible vision.

"You're supposed to've filled out a form that looks like this"—she held up a sample—"before you got into line." Don't deck her out. She's an artist too, artists and wayfarers all, earning her livelihood, meeting me in her path.

He reached for the application form. "Can I borrow your pencil?"

"I have to use it. I'm using it."

He turned around, keeping his place, and said across the foot-fault line, "Anybody got a pencil I can borrow? Hey, can you lend me a pencil?" A kind soul threw him a pencil.

"You can get a form over there." She put hers out of his reach.

"Then do I come right back here? I don't have to stand in line all over again, do I?"

She looked at him like she didn't know what he was talking about. Nobody in the history of Unemployment ever asked that before.

He did not but should have rushed the counter. Kick over file cabinets. Spill I.B.M. cards. George C. Scott as the social worker in "East Side West Side" revolutionizing the bureaucracy.

He stepped over to a wall table. List your previous employment, beginning with most current. Retail clerk, Management Trainee, ZIP sorter, busboy and grease-trap rongeur, U.C. Psych Department subject. Wittman Ah Sing, this is your life.

Line A came this side of the door now. He gave the blunt pencil to the next poor man to enter, someone even more behind than he was. Pass it on. The cards with half-hour increments flipped once more before he got to the front. The same clerk was in the window, but she did not recognize him. She asked him the same questions as were printed on the application, made a mark beside each of his answers as he re-answered them orally. Her supervisor is a checker of checkmarks. We unemployed keep many scribes employed.

"I.d.?" she said.

He said his Social Security number.

"You don't have a driver's license?"

"I don't have a car."

"You don't have your passport?"

What's this? Is she calling me a wetback? "I'm not going anywhere."

"You don't have a credit card?" A wide-open invitation to give her his speech against installment buying. "Is it government policy to encourage the jobless to go into debt?"

"All I'm asking you for is a firm i.d. card."

"I'm morally against credit cards."

"You shouldn't leave the house without identification," she said. He felt scolded.

"You're speaking for the government, right? As a representative of the state, you're ordering me to have papers on my

person at all times?" The Berkeley rumor was that the computers in Washington, D.C., cross-referenced your I.R.S. file with
your bank statement with your F.B.I. record with your Motor
V Registration. It's your duty to confound them. Any conspiracy we can get paranoid over, the U.S. Government is already
carrying out. "Here's the number assigned to me by the feds,"
he said, handing her his Social Security card.

"A Social Security card is not an i.d.," she said.

"Why not? I'm the only one in the world with this number, right?" Social Security and the I.R.S. had promised the
Americans of Japanese Ancestry that their Social Security
numbers and their tax returns would not be used to hunt them
down.

"How about your draft registration card?" Oh, shit. Oh
fucking shit. She'll see his expired 2-S. She'll turn his evasive
ass in, and he will go to jail. He gave her the stub from a paycheck, and his A.S.U.C. Activity card, and a party invitation
(in a court summons theme). And his library card. Here. This
is the most important thing about me—I'm a card-carrying
reader. All I really want to do is to sit and read or lie down
and read or eat and read or shit and read. I'm a trained reader.
I want a job where I get paid for reading books. And I don't
have to make reports on what I read or to apply what I read.
Ah, girl, don't sear me with trade, smear me with toil. Hand
over my money and let me get on with it.

"Next time, bring an official picture i.d.," she said, and gave
him a yellow card. She wrote his name and Social Security
number in a tiny yellow booklet, stamped the date, and wrote
an appointment time. "Your interview is for 1:00. Here's your
literature."

"Thanks." Thanks for nothing. My dole and your salary
come out of the same budget. "Didn't you just now interview
me? What else do you want to know?"

"I'm registering you. They'll interview you over there. This
isn't the interview."

"You mean I stood in line just to get to stand in another
line?"

He went to the 11:30 line, calculating that when the
cards flipped, that one would say 1:00. His booklet said:
"Unemployment Compensation is paid for by employers."

Somebody's lying. The money has been taken out of our paychecks, everybody knows that. And we're entitled to get it back. How come so many people say so if it isn't true? The State of California is putting out "literature" to snow our common knowledge. The truth must be that employers pay at a penultimate step; the workers' paychecks absorb the money in the long run indirectly.

Wittman had free time, and an old Chinese lady caught a whiff of it. "You Chinese?" she asked. When you have a moment of idleness, an old Chinese lady will always appear, and give you something to do, keep you from going lazy. He looked around, a wise guy, like she could be addressing somebody behind him.

"Yes," he said.

"Good boy." She was praising him for accomplishing the excellent geste of being a Chinese boy. "You tell them for me that I can work, and I want work, and I need work. I must have work. I went looking every day this week. I had a job at the Fruitvale Cannery putting three molly-see-no cherries"—maraschino—"in the fruit cocktail. Not two. Not four. Three." Lowering her voice for a secret—"The boss floorlady told everyone: I—the exactest Chinese lady in the cannery. Do you understand me? I want you to tell them for me. Okay?"

"Okay," he said. Though she shouldn't need translation. She spoke back and forth, a shuttling scuttling weaver of Chinese and English.

"Never never eat fruit cocktail. Do you know what a molly-see-no cherry is? An onion. They bleach it white, no more onion smell, no onion taste. Then they soak it in red dye and sugar syrup. Fruit cocktail is bad for you health. Don't eat fruit cocktail." She was making him a gift of her insider advice. It was in exchange for the upcoming translation work. "Have an orange," she said, rummaging in her plastic shopping bag.

"No. No, thank you."

She came up with an orange in her gloved hand. She was wearing long white prom gloves. "Keep it for later. Don't eat canned. Do you know how they take skins off peaches? Lye bath. My job is to gwoot out the pit with my fruit knife." She had her fruit knife in her bag too, and showed him its crescent blade, honed fine by long and abundant peach seasons. "Aiya, I have to learn how to work fast left-handed."

"Why's that?"

"Do you want to see my hand?" She handed him the orange, the fruit knife, her purse, her shopping bag. She pulled the glove off her right hand, her back to the counter windows. "I can move it a little." Her thumb and index finger were swollen purple-grey and stretched too far apart. Her hand was tautening into a claw, a fruit knife. "When we talk to them, you tell them I must work. Must. You sabe? It hurts a lot but. I will get Unyimployment, and give my hand a rest." She pronounced "Unemployment" with a "yim," as in "salt," the sweat of labor, the salt of the earth. "Don't tell them about my hand. Tell them I'm healthy, and can work."

Grimacing, she pushed her fingers closer together and tugged the glove back on. "This is as tight as I can bring my thumb and pointer together. I can't shut my hand but. Everything will be all right. Yesterday I went to the Workman's Comp office. I told them I was hurt on the job. I'll be all right. I'll get Workman's Comp and I'll get Unyimployment."

"Wait a minute," said Wittman. "Can you do that? It says here in this booklet and on this card that you have to be physically able to work."

"So?"

"Well, what if the Government says you lie?"

"Oh." He felt very sorry that he was making her falter.

"What happens if Workman's Comp sends to this office the paper that says you're too hurt to work, but here you say you are *not* too hurt to work? And the Government notices that the answers don't match? Do you see what I mean?"

"No. No, I don't. No."

On the cover of the yellow handbook, there was a box around all caps:

> PENALTY FOR FALSE STATEMENT—
> UNDER THE LAW IT IS A MISDEMEANOR
> TO WILLFULLY MAKE A FALSE STATEMENT.
> CONVICTION IS PUNISHABLE BY FINE
> OR IMPRISONMENT OR BOTH.

"It says here one could go to jail for lying." He was breaking the news to this innocent: Meat comes from piggies and cow-cows and little lost lambs.

"Aiya," she said. "Here. Change the answer to 'No.'" They were moving up in line. She gave him her card and a pen. He found the question about being physically able. Somebody had written the 'Yes' in ballpoint. He rubbed it with spit; tails of paper epidermis rolled off. He wrote "No."

"You don't need to stand in line and go through all this," he advised. "Go home and take care of your hand." He meant she wasn't going to qualify anyway.

"But I can work. I use my left hand. Change it back to 'Yes.'"

Her card looked suspect. "Are you sure you want me to do that?" he asked. "Your card will look messy. 'No.' 'Yes.' 'No.'"

"What do you think I should do?"

"I think too much trouble to apply for both Workman's Compensation and Unyimployment. Decide on one, save yourself the standing in line and the paperwork."

"Oh, I have the time to stand in line. And I get double chances. And win both if I'm lucky."

"If your hand hurts a lot, then the Government is not going to give you Unyimployment."

"My hand hurts a lot. Should I leave that square empty and ask the Government lady what's best to write down?"

"The Government lady is going to say write down what's true."

"The best answer is 'Yes,' I am going to work. Put 'Yes.'"

"Remember yesterday you filled out a form that said that you're not able to work, that you want them to pay you be-cause your hand was injured at work."

"You mean that I best write down on this card the same answer today and yesterday. But." To hear her think to sur-render stuck a pain into his heart. She was co-operating with the authorities, which included himself. "I like work," she said.

"All right. All right. 'Yes.'" He blackened out the 'No,' and wrote 'Yes' beside the blot. Enough Unemployment counsel-ing; the Government can do its own dirty work. See what you have to put up with if you want to have community? Any old Chinese lady comes along, she takes your day, you have to do her beckoning. The hippy-dippies don't know what they're in for. They couldn't take Communitas.

"Let me help you fill out your card right," she said. "I've been coming to this office between seasons for twenty years, so I know. They give the same test questions every week, and we have to give the same answers. Listen now. I teach you. Learn. You ready? Remember these ten answers: 'No.' 'None.' Number Two is not 'No.' The right answer is 'None.' Don't forget, 'None.' That's the tricky part right there. I start over, okay? 'No.' 'None.' 'Yes.' 'No.' 'Yes.' 'No.' 'No.' 'No.' 'No.' 'No.' Always answer like that. One more time, okay? 'No.' 'None.' 'Yes.' 'No.' 'Yes.' 'No.' 'No.' 'No.' 'No.'"

"'No.' 'None.' 'Yes,'" repeated Wittman. "'No.' 'Yes.' 'No.' 'No.' 'No.' 'No.' 'No.'" (That first "Yes" is the answer to Number Three, "Were you physically able to work full-time each of the seven days that week?")

"Ho, la. Smart boy. One wrong answer, they send you inside to the office. And they take the money away. Don't forget. Always answer like that. One wrong answer—no more money."

"Why is it better to say 'No' to Number Seven?" he asked. "That's the one that asks, Did anybody in this office or anywhere else tell you about a job?" He considerately told her the question in case she couldn't read or remember.

"That's called 'refer.' No matter what the refer is, you have to go try for that job. But they hardly ever refer. Twenty seasons of cannery, they referred me one time. I think they drew my name out of a bad-luck lottery. They referred me on the telephone. My mistake, I put 'No' on Seven the same as usual. So the Government lady sent me to interrogation. I said, 'Oh dear, I forgot. Now I remember, you refer. The answer is "Yes."' There *had* been a Sai Yun voice on the phone." To call them Sai Yun instead of White Demon shows the classiness of the speaker, and also gives the Caucasian person class. "For punishment, they delayed my Unyimployment for one week."

The two of them crossed the stripe on the floor together. "How old is she?" asked the Government lady.

"Tell her sixty-five."

"Sixty-five," said Wittman.

"Tell her," said the Government lady, speaking slowly,

enunciating, "that I have to inform all the senior citizens that there's a bill in Congress to deduct Unemployment Compensation from their Social Security checks. So her benefits may total no more than her Social Security. This bill may not pass, but we have to tell senior citizens about it."

"No sabe," said the old lady.

"The Government lady says," said Wittman, "that you get Social Security, you might not get Unyimployment. Maybe. They might subtract one from the other. Sabe?"

"No sabe. Tell her I don't understand English." She meant she didn't like what she was hearing.

"She doesn't get it."

The clerk repeated the whole thing. "In other words," she said, "she could be making extra paperwork for herself, and for us, and she wouldn't be getting more than her Social Security."

"I no sabe." Sometimes if you act stupid, you get your way.

"She wants to apply anyway," said Wittman.

The clerk marked the answers to Number One and Number Two with red checks. Some of the new Hong Kong people say that writing with red is unlucky, but it's unclear for whom, the writer or the written about or to. Her red pencil hesitated at the answer to Number Three, which had been worked over. "Is she physically able to work?" she asked.

Wittman said to the popo, somebody else's grandmother, now his responsibility, "Are you physically able to work?"

"I can do a great many things." She folded her gloved hands on the counter.

"Can she do her usual job at the cannery?" Good question.

"Better than most people," answered the popo.

"'Yes' or 'No.'"

"Not outstanding as usual but. I will be okay one day soon."

The clerk said, "Please sign here for me."

Her poor hand could not close over the pen. She took it in her left hand and wrote her signature, copying her name that a relative with careful penmanship had written out. Mrs. Chew.

"Have her wait in line D for an interview."

"Tell her thank you," said Mrs. Chew.

"Thank you."

"Thank *you*."

As long as he was up here, Wittman pushed his own papers forward.

"Did you work last week?"

He recognized the first question, to which the right answer is "No." "As a matter of fact, yes," he said. "Tuesday's the first day I won't be going in to work. But I'm eager to get a jump on my paperwork, get the machinery rolling, as it were. In case I don't find a job right away, possibly later on today, who knows, no time wasted. I have drive. I'm no O.E.O. deadbeat. I'm a go-getter. An active job seeker." The "literature" said that he had to be "an active job seeker."

The Government lady asked him the rest of the questions. He was grateful to Mrs. Chew for the answer ("No") to Number Four, which is one of those negative subjunctive questions that if you stop to think about it too much, your brain gets confused, doubling back, turning around. "'Was there any other reason you could not have worked full-time each workday?'"

He wished that this were not a force-choice test. He would say, like an Englishman, "Would that there were. Ah, would that there were."

"You have to go to two more interviews—the intake interview for a new claimant—that's you—and a job counseling appointment at the Employment Office."

He followed the green stripe to sit next to Mrs. Chew in line D, which was the row of chairs against the wall. Aiya, there ought to be a nice waiting room for us like at the dentist's with carpets and magazines. Where are the potted plants and music? Where's a receptionist offering coffee or tea? No comforts for the unemployed. They're punishing us for losing our jobs. When they ought to be honoring us. We people who have unbusied ourselves to scout around, to review the system, to do some doubting and questioning, the ones who try if it's possible yet for the human race to live on air and sun.

The two Chinese-Americans, who looked like relatives, ate an orange. Its peelings filled the stand-up ashtray that Mrs. Chew had found and pushed between them. "Now we're going to be interrogated," she said. "This is the worst part. They give you bad news in that inside office. You should avoid going in there if you can. You are coming in with me, aren't you?"

It was now 1:45, as he could tell by looking on the wrists of people who owned watches.

"Sure," he said. "Don't you worry."

"Are you married?" she asked. "Do you have kidboys?"

"No. Yes. No. No kids."

"Don't worry. I know a very kind rich girl. Fix you up, okay? She puts in the money; you do the hard work, you do the English-speaking; you can have a restaurant, children, everything. You're clever enough, I can tell. You remind me of the boys from China I met on Angel Island. You're older than most of them but. You'll get down to business and work harder. They were fifteen, sixteen, seventeen years old, not broken in. They had no patience for I.N.S. red tape. They didn't like the food, they had food fights. I didn't like the food myself. Noodles with tomato sauce. Jell-O. We didn't know how to eat Jell-O. We spread it on the white bread. Jell-O sandwiches." She laughed at the greenhorns they used to be. "There was too much we didn't know. The ground on Angel Island is covered with jade. We walked on dark green jade clink-clinking underfoot from the boat to the Wooden House. When the soldiers turned their backs, I picked up a piece. We thought, the island is made of jade; the mainland must be made of gold. Now I know, it's just mock jade. Monterey jade. For breaking rules, the boys got locked up one at a time in the closet. They built a trapdoor which was a dove-tail puzzle. It was also their shit-and pisshole. The closet was always clean no matter how long a boy was locked up. That's how Chinese got the reputation for being able to hold it in.

"We ladies had a big bathroom with flush commodes and showers. But we didn't shower; we bathed using basins. Whenever in the middle of the night, we heard someone in the showers, we knew that a woman was going to hang herself. We wouldn't try to stop her because she had her reason—she failed her interrogation or she couldn't bear the waiting any longer or nobody came for her or she was being deported. It was her own business. The suicides wore their wedding dresses; they tied the sashes around their necks, and hung themselves from the shower pipes. The commodes sat up on stands all in a row. The women, who were from the country, were very modest. For privacy, they put pillowcases over their heads. Can you picture it? A row of peasant ladies shitting and pissing with bags over their heads."

Mrs. Chew didn't need to go, did she? "Do you have to go to the bathroom?" Wittman asked. "Do you want me to go look for the ladies' seesaw?"

"No, thank you. You're very considerate. I know you would make that kind rich girl a good husband. I'm just talking-story to pass the time."

"I thought you were about to tell me a hero story. Didn't any of those guys try to escape through the trapdoor and swim to the Big City? I don't think we ought to spread crap stories about how tightass and clean we are, and how sneaky sly we are." Chinese do not have a thing about boxing them/ourselves up inside puzzle mazes; Kafka was the one, made that up. And we didn't come here to make money off of America; we burn money.

"Oh, but we have a tradition of shitting and pissing," said Mrs. Chew. "The reason we have war on earth was because of a fart. Do you know the story of Ngok Fei? You remind me of him. Maybe you know him as Yue Fei? Yue Fei, the Patriot. What in your dialect?"

"Ngok Fei." Most Americans would say Ngok. "The man with the words cut on his back." His own old grandmother had received a postcard from a Hong Kong wax museum of a young man on his knees, and a hag with a knife behind him. The young man, fleshy and acquiescent, had made him feel sick. "The words on his back mean something like 'First—Save the Nation,' correct?"

"Oh, very good." Mrs. Chew clapped her hands. "Your name wouldn't happen to be Gwock Wai or Wai Gwock, would it?"

"Not me. If I had a name like that, I'd change it. I don't agree that my first duty is to serve a country. Mrs. Chew, I'm running away from the draft. I'm helping my country but. What I'm going to do for the U.S.A.: I'm not going to kill anybody. An American who doesn't kill—that's what I want to be. You're not trying to talk me into joining the Army, are you? You don't see a war in my future, do you?"

"I'm no hag witch."

"Tell me about the fart that started a war. Was Ngok Fei a farter?"

"No, no. He was against farting. That's why you remind me of him. A long time ago, back before Ngok Fei was born, a Buddha was chanting with students in the sky. They were so loud and so lovely that saints—. Do you know what a saint is? A sunseen? A fut? A good person who has lived and died and gone to live Up There. A bunch of those sky beings encircled this Buddha and his students." She was tripping him out as on drugs—spheres of protons and neutrons resolve into orbiting planets with rings and moons that resolve into the bald heads of monks, Buddhaheads. "And suddenly a girl student farted." Mrs. Chew did a razzberry right there in the Unemployment Office for dramatic illustrative sound effect. A religious fart. "Well, the Red-bearded Dragon laughed; and the students laughed. You know how students are, always laughing at farts. But Gold Wing did not laugh. With one peck of his scissors-like beak, he stabbed that farting girl student." These are bodhi-sattvas, Wittman thought, like in *The Dharma Bums.* A fart-ing bodhisattva. With Toshiro Mifune as Red Beard. "She fell down dead." So people in Heaven can die? "And landed in our world as a baby, who grew up to marry a man with a red beard. Red-Beard Dragon reared over everyone's heads and almost caught Gold Wing in his claws and teeth. The bird-angel flew up, turned, and jabbed out Red Beard's eye. The dragon thun-dered, and flashed lightning all through the skies. Gold Wing flew downward, where he tried to hide as a human being. But. He has just killed somebody, don't forget. For punishment, he could not become human right off. The dragon searched every-where, flooding burrows in the ground and washing away nests in trees. At last Gold Wing was born as a human baby. Guess which baby he became? I told you a hint already."

"Ngok Fei. I see, he's 'Fei' because he flies. When he was a boy collecting firewood, he fell lightly out of trees because he was a bird. He and his mother were in a jar floating down the river because the dragon was after him. And years later, when he was a political prisoner, his stay of execution lasted until the rainy season because you-know-who controls the rain." Wittman loved link-ups. He had just learned the pre-human events behind the boy who learned to read by stealing lessons outside the schoolhouse window and to write by scratching with a stick upon the earth.

"Mrs. Chew Ying May? Mrs. May?" Unemployment was calling. The senior citizen walked through the swinging gate while naming heroes for the young man behind her. "Gold Wing's cohorts were led by Wong, Cheung, and Hong. You've heard of those families, huh?" Yes, common in America. This is the way we would go to the gas chambers or the locomotive furnace in *Man's Fate*. They reached the interrogation desk a long way from the finish of the story, Chinese stories having no end, sons and ghosts continuing to fight in the ongoing wars.

Mrs. Chew picked up a G.I. metal war-surplus chair with her prom-gloved hands, and carried it over to the desk for her interpreter, Wittman. He and the Government man both offered to help, but she was too quick. When everyone was seated, the Government man leaned forward across his desk and said in a kind voice, "Now, Mrs. May, can I help you? What's the problem?"

His sympathy undid her. She pulled off the glove, and said, "Let me show you. To wear this glove hurts. And in the cannery I wear tight, hot rubber gloves." She has this guy mixed up with a doctor. "Let me show you. See how it's turned blue here? Like a Santa Rosa plum."

"That must hurt a lot. It's hurting you now, isn't it?"

"Oh, yes, it does. It hurts bad. Aiya. Oh." She's going to get her way by trying to make the Government feel guilty and sorry at the sight of her poor hand.

"Have you been to a doctor? Has she seen a doctor?"

"Have you seen a doctor?"

"I have a doctor," she said, handing over a prescription order she hadn't had filled. She's saving money not filling her scrip. She's proud to keep this documentation that she does have a physician.

The man picked up the phone, and dialed the doctor's number. He asked whoever answered about Mrs. Chew Ying May. "Uh-huh. Uh-huh. Shingles, huh? Shingles," he said, hanging up. "Listen, when your hand gets better, you come back here, all right? You come back here and see me. I hope it gets well soon. Thank you for coming in, Mrs. May."

"Thank you," she said. "Thank you very much." She tried to carry Wittman's chair back to where she'd gotten it.

"No, please," said the man. "That's all right. Leave it there. I'll take it back."

"Thank you. Thank you too much."

"You're welcome."

"You're welcome too." Thanking, being thanked, thanking Wittman, thanking the man, she got turned around and out the gate.

"Wittman Ah Sing?" His turn on the docket. The same Government man read through his application form and said, "Laid off, fired, quit, strike, or other?"

Definitely not out on strike, and he'd decided never to answer "other" to anything ever again. Come to think of it, he hadn't had a confrontation scene where anybody said, "You're fired." He hadn't had his chance to say, "You can't fire me. I quit." "Laid off," he said, which is just the right answer.

"Since you came in on a Monday, Tuesday, or Wednesday," said the Government man, "you get backdated to Sunday. You get credit for this week as your one-week waiting period." He was being given good news; if he'd waited to come in on Thursday or Friday, they would've started him off the following Sunday. "Wait a minute. I have a file on you." Sitting on the blotter was a Notification of Changes or Terminations Due to Personnel Action re: Wittman Ah Sing. The store must have hand-delivered it by messenger, they were in such a hurry to unemploy him. "You might be interested in this," said the Government guy, pointing to Comments: "He seems to hate merchandising, and can benefit from psychiatric counseling." Wow. Written evidence that the establishment is monitoring our minds. He was to get his head shrunk on the recommendation of a department store. It's official, he's not fit for commerce. In this society, retailers define saneness. If you hate the marketplace, and can't sell, and don't buy much, you're crazy. In black and white and carbon copies on file here and at the store and in Sacramento—"He seems to hate merchandising, and can benefit from psychiatric counseling." Wait until the S.S.S. gets a load of this. Too crazy to fight for capitalism. He giggled. The Government man did not smile in return. Wittman should contain himself, shrink his head, shrink his face, but he let out another baboonish heh heh heh. The Chinese giggle. One of twenty theatrical laffs.

Jauntily, he tossed the Notification of Changes back. "Who is it that doesn't get the boot now and again?" he said. "One can be too Steady Eddie." Shut up already. He never said "one," or "get the boot," or "now and again," or "Steady Eddie." Where does this diction come from out of his Chinese mouth that was born with American English as its own, its first language?

"Every young person gets canned a couple of times before he settles down," said the Unemployment guy. Huh? What you say? "That store has a big turnover. They fire everybody. You'll find better stores to work for." Ah, I have brothers around. He thinks I'm funny to get hung up on a job nobody else wants.

To qualify for Unemployment, Wittman had to report within three days to the Employment Office near Chinatown. (Why the Chinatown one? Because of my looks and ghettoization accordingly? Because that's my address? Or merely because every place in the City is near every place else?) After his waiting period, which he had already begun, he might be eligible for twenty-six weeks of benefits. The penalties they dealt out seemed to be week-long increments of waiting, no hardship really. Think of a string of twenty-six markers at Mike's Pool Hall; whether you slide them from this end or that end, there are twenty-six of them.

Almost enjoying the dread-laden fall of the afternoon and of the season, he reported to the Employment Office near Chinatown, where he was headed anyway. Why fuck up another day? Waste the rest of this one, which is shot already. You took the best, take the rest. I cannot go on I go on.

The Jobs Office of the Department of Human Resources was better lit than the Unemployment Office, cleaner, fewer people. Two receptionists, men, greeted him, and sent him right through to an Employment Counselor. There wasn't the deadface waiting; people were reading printouts of jobs. The white collars sat at tables under a sign that said White Collar, and the blue collars were at Blue Collar. A sign also said that only those with an E.S. i.d. card were eligible to use the printouts. Some Hamlet ought to stand up and say, "Would not this, sir, and a forest of feathers—if the rest of my fortunes turn Turk with me—with two Provincial roses on my razed shoes, get me a fellowship in a cry of players, sir?"

The Employment Counselor was a Mexican-American guy

about Wittman's age; you expect right understanding from him. He was dressed extremely Ivy League, argyle sweater with V neck setting off an oxford collar and well-knotted black knit tie. Don't you look down on him. The token has to excel over everybody of every kind for that one job. He's overqualified to get this far. Sitting on the desk was one of the c.c.s of the Notification of lunacy. "Let's see," said the counselor, Mr. Sanchez, "Mr." on his nameplate as if it were his given name. "What kind of work are you looking for?"

"Playwriting," said Wittman. "I'm looking for a playwriting job. I'm a playwright."

Mr. Sanchez leaned forward, frowned. "What's the last job you had? And the one prior to that? What company you last work for as a playwright?"

"I'm not a playwright for a corporation. I'm not a corporate playwright." I'm no playwright who scripts industrial shows and hygiene films for the educational-military-industrial complex.

"Did you write plays at your last job?"

"I wrote plays during my last job, yes."

"Did you get paid for them? Paid for writing plays?"

"No." If you don't make money, it doesn't count as work.

"What did you get paid for doing?"

"Sales." But I don't want another selling job. I never want to sell anything to anybody as long as I live.

"Then that's what you should write down. The last job you had was retail, and the one before that, retail. So you write down that you are seeking a retail job."

Actually, the job before this one, he worked for one day at a vet clinic, a pet hospital which was also a dog pound. He unloaded flat cats off this truck into the incinerator. Mounds of fur, some necks with collars. Gassed dogs. Teeth, tails. Auschwitz, Bergen-Belsen. He also held pets for the vet to work on. An aged half-dead mangy dog got expensive surgery while a perfectly good dog got put away. Tranked, Rover and Fluffy and Anonymous slid sideways out of consciousness, then out of life. Memorial ashes cost ten dollars a box. There was this one stiff dog that its owner kept weeping over. "What's wrong with Poochy?" She wouldn't listen to Wittman's diagnosis but kept bugging the vet, who had to tell her, "What's wrong with him is he's dead." Wittman only lasted the one day. He didn't list that job in his vita; a spotty job record is worse than no experience at all. He had stayed until closing time. He did his duty, found out what was going on behind appearances. A liberal-arts education is good for knowing to look at anything from an inquisitive viewpoint, to have thoughts while shoveling shit.

Another job, he hadn't stayed the day, he was wired up to a dictaphone—earphones in his ears, hearing a boss's voice that kept saying "Dear" and "Sincerely" and "Truly" and "Yours," with all manner of repulsive business bullshit in between. Which his fingers typed, and his eyes read, and his foot forwarded, rewound, forwarded. Only his dick had been free.

"I see here that you've had management training experience. Take advantage of that. You should go out for management positions. Listen, about this playwriting thing, hombre, I get a lot of college graduates in here who were t.a.s for one semester. They get a taste, you know? To get paid for intellectual discussions and released time to do research, thinking, the writing of a play, whatever. They sign up for college teaching. Universities. They snoot J.C.s. When there's hardly any openings. Colleges don't hire through this office. A theatrical producer has never called. You have to be realistic. I'm hip to your side of the street, man. The one thing people like us have to learn after graduating from college is—be realistic. Let's face it, there is no connection between your major and a job. That's why they told us that we should work to learn, and not for grades."

No, you're not hip to my side of the street, man. Does this look like the hair of a realist? This is poet's hair. You can see this hair and talk to me like that? If you're so hip to my side of the street, why don't you give me some ideas on how to make long hair look short for interviews?

Or is he hinting to me a loophole? Like go ahead and sign up for college teaching. Our office will never bother you with phone calls and leads. You stay home, work on your play. This Sanchez hombre majored in a social science, and he's trying to apply it on me, counseling my ass.

"I am a realist," said Wittman. "It's the business of a playwright to bring thoughts into reality. They come out of my head and into the world, real chairs, solid tables." He knocked on the desk. "Real people. A playwright is nothing if not realistic." He offered Mr. Sanchez a cigarette, which he took. They lit up, laying their matches in the clean ashtray. Wittman said, "Confucius, the realist, said, 'Neither a soldier nor an actor be.' I have no eyes for either line of work." (If he can say "hombre," I can say "Confucius." Nobody's going to put anybody into a bag.) The truth was he didn't want a job of any kind. He was empty of desire for employment.

"You Chinese?" said Mr. Sanchez. "You went to Berkeley? I can tell by the way you talk. You went to Berkeley, didn't you? I went to Berkeley."

"Yeah," said Wittman. "It shows, huh?"

"How were your grades? Your G.P.A.?"

"Not bad. Not too good."

"Did you get a lot of Cs? You got a lot of Cs, right?"

"Some."

"I thought so. Those were Chinese Cs."

"They were what?"

"You haven't heard of the Chinese C? The professor I t.a.'ed for told me to give guys like you the Chinese C, never mind the poor grammar and broken English. You're ending up engineers anyway."

"I wasn't an engineering major. What do you mean? Do you mean they kept me down to a C no matter how well I was doing?"

"No, they were raising you to a C. They were giving you a break who couldn't learn the language. They were trying to help out, get the engineering majors through the liberal arts requirements."

Monkey powers—outrage and jokes—went detumescent at the enormity of the condescension. Too late. He should've been informed of the system, then could've gone into their offices and reasoned with them until they heard his English was gradable.

Mr. Sanchez was saying, "I read all my blue books and papers, and wrote comments. It wasn't like I just read the Chinese name and assigned a C."

"You ought to put in my file that my Cs are worth more."

"Actually, I think they're worth less. Okay, I'll notify

employers that you're a really unusual Chinese, who was able to graduate in the liberal arts. You're an idealist. You want to go into a service profession."

"I know just the service I'm qualified to perform. I've invented a job for myself. Let me run it past you up the flagpole."

Wittman put out his cigarette; he had drawn one of those horse-manure numbers that they slip into a pack now and then. "I want to save the world from the bomb. I have an idea how to do it: We implant the detonator inside a human chest. The only way the President can get at the red button is to tear a man open. He has to reach inside the chest cavity with his own hands, and push the button with his personal fingerprint. That will make him think twice before bombing Cubans or Russians. Look, as a pacifist, I volunteer to be the one holding the detonator. It would be better to put it inside the chest of a little kid, but. I'll be the fail-safe detonator. Put that down. I'm signing up with you. Fail-safe detonator. That's what I'll be."

"I won't put that. You can't put that. You're volunteering to be a human sacrifice. The Army already has its pool of human sacrifices. We don't send people on jobs that will never be. And you don't have the experience or qualifications to do bomb work."

"Yes, I do. I worked in a science lab. We, these German ladies and I, harvested R.N.A.-D.N.A. It comes from worms, which have a light-sensitive end. That end—ass or face—rears up at the lights overhead, and we nip it. The ladies were hired for the exactness of their touch. I got hired for my touch too because I look like a delicate and precise Japanese. We gave the worms, which were very clean and pink, a pinch, and out squirted raw R.N.A.-D.N.A. life stuff. It shot into a test tube. We wore goggles because we sometimes shot ourselves in the eye. While the physicists were making bombs, I was storing up life. I know where it's kept. I made friends with the lab tech who had the job of taking the tubes to an underground vault. He showed me the location. Whenever any test-tube washer says to me, 'Hey, man, you want to see something trippy?'—I go with him. I've been to some far-out labs. I've seen kitty cats with electrodes sticking out of their heads. I saw a core sample, which is a piece of the center of the earth brought up from as far down into the ocean floor as they can drill. It looks like shit. I've been inside the Livermore Rad Lab out in the Altamont. They *say* they're studying earthquakes, they mean the earth quakes when they bomb it. I dated a research assistant who took me up to the cyclotron (which is built on top of the Hayward Fault—it may go at any moment). She spun subatomic particles in the cloud chamber and counted them. She let me count some. Because of the Heisenberg miracle, it's the duty of artists to volunteer to do particle counting. Don't leave creation up to the accountants. My eyes have influenced the laws of the universe. I spoke over the particles. I laid trips on them. I made faces at them. I played connect-the-dots—constellations of my own—on a strip of film. My girlfriend threw me out of the lab. Scientists are paranoid. The ones that teach won't tell you the meat of the projects they're working on. They lock their file cabinets. They lock their refrigerators, where they're making winter to hatch baby grasshoppers in 'spring.' They take their briefcases home. I took Physics for Non-Majors from Dr. Edward Teller, who mostly appeared to us on closed-circuit t.v. He didn't teach us dick about fathering the A-bomb. I got assigned to do my reports on the dance of the bumblebees and soap bubbles. Dr. Teller had me working on babyshit when he should have been teaching me the bomb. I learned more from research assistants. An r.a. in physics and an r.a. in biology independently told me that they were working on isolating a chronon—a time ion. Like time *is* a clock. The physicists are looking for it inside the atom, and the biologists are looking in the pituitary gland. Alvarez's team is looking inside pyramids, which they were getting ready to X-ray with lasers that measure cosmic rays. The models and the blueprints looked like set designs for *Aida*. But the Sudan crisis came up, and I don't know what happened next. We are not talking mad scientists here. These are sane scientists.

"Anyway, back at our Frankenstein lab, this techie friend of mine says, 'Do you want to see where they store this stuff?' I helped him carry a vat of R.N.A.-D.N.A., followed him walking on this dirt path in the woods above Strawberry Canyon. We came to a mound with a grass groundcover. The trees were in a circle. The mother tree had died, and its outmost ring had shot up a grove. On top of the mound, under a flat of sod, there's a metal manhole cover with a ring in it. My friend grabbed a-hold of the ring, and turned it in a combination, which I memorized. He lifted the cover off. There was a metal stopper that pulled up like a piston. A mist floated out hovering close to the ground—dry ice. Yeah, I myself have looked inside the vault that stores the essence of life. There's a pool, a well of raw life. We poured in the new stuff. It ran in a rainbow stream. Ribbons and streamers of pure R.N.A.-D.N.A. We stirred it with a glass wand that flashed with the running snot of pure germ. You should be glad to know, in case the bombs go off, the quiddity of pure life is hidden away to start us up again, unless a bomb lands smack dab on that vault on the mound in the circle of trees.

"That was one job that I knew it had a purpose. Boring nevertheless. Hour after hour. Me and the German ladies. Pinch. Squirt. Pinch. Squirt. Pinch. Squirt. Until my techie friend invented a machine that laid all of us off. What if we darkened the room and put the light at the end of the table? You should have seen those greedy little pinkies. Like actors, 'Get outta my light.' They stretch out, important end craning. And this juggernaut-guillotine roll-chops it off. Pop squirt pop squirt pop squirt. We saved us a lot of dainty time. I didn't put that job on my résumé because of being phased out so soon. My friend who invented the worm light and pinch-squeezer lost his job too, and is now an oenologist in Sonoma County.

"No, no, what's so unlikely? I'll tell you the unlikely part, which I left out. The Tibetan Buddhists predict that there will come a time when human beings will be only fourteen inches high. Some say eighteen inches. What year this evolution is supposed to happen is hard to translate from Tibetan time into our time. But I think it will be after the bomb, like in *The Time Machine*. We're going to be mutants like Yvette Mimieux, Weena of the Eloi, but smaller and not everybody a blonde. Because of a contribution I made, which I'll tell you about. What we were doing in our lab was working out the science of how we'll come to be fourteen inches high.

"I went one more time to the stash of R.N.A.-D.N.A. I remember the way to the mound, and went there by myself. I held the ring, and turned it so many clicks this way and so many clicks that way. What the hell, I'll give you the combination. Mr. Sanchez, you could be the survivor who uses it to save mankind. I'll bet anything that there are vaults hidden throughout the Berkeley hills, and the Marin hills, and in the Altamont all around the Lawrence Rad Lab. The combination to that vault—ready?—easy to remember—is: clockwise to fifty-four, counterclockwise passing fifty-four three times to thirty-two, clockwise two times to ten. Nothing to it. Fifty-four right thrice—thirty-two left twice—right to ten. A countdown, get it? As crackable as a bicycle lock. There I was, all by myself at the well of life. I wet my hands in it. I let it run from hand to hand in the sunlight. I've touched and played with the clear mucous gist of life. When the bomb goes off, the radiation will cook the stuff, see? And these fourteen-inch guys will be animated. They will incubate in the pregnant earth. One of us has to let them out. Out from their bomb shelter will come hopping the prettiest little men and women avid for daylight. The next Big Bang will destroy and create, just like the last Big Bang. Well, there I was alone in the forest, and the sun smiling down on me, alive. I didn't want to die. So I added my two cents to the stuff in the vat. I mean I donated some sperm. There'll be some of me jumping out of the earth. Yvette Mimieux as Weena of the Eloi has Chinese eyes. She'll get them from me. Mr. Sanchez, after the wipe-out, we need to start the earth up with new life. Help me out, man. You have to put me down for a job in science."

"I can't send you to interviews talking like this. Scientists won't buy it. Physics for Non-Majors was just for the fun of it, and to make us well rounded. It doesn't qualify you to work for NASA. Like you aren't fit to be a beekeeper either, or a soap-bubble physicist. All right, all right, I'll put you down for a playwright job. We have never had a call for a playwright, I'm telling you. You better put something else in addition, a fallback position that you can realistically get, such as retail clerk."

"Is there a law that says I have to try for retail clerk and/or retail management?"

"No, I'm suggesting it to you. You want to be humanitarian, you could clerk in a charitable organization, or a political organization."

"Yeah, I could do that. If one of those organizations calls me up, I don't have to take the job, do I?"

"No. This isn't an agency for slaves or human sacrifices. You have to try for the job, though. You ought to go see the movie too." Mr. Sanchez pointed to an arrow that said To Movie Room. "Yes, you better go see the movie." He was writing "Playwright" on the form. Wittman was being humored. Then he wrote "Clerk."

"Okay. I'll go see your movie. Hey, thanks a lot, huh, hombre? I appreciate the counseling. You gave me some good ideas. Adios, huh?"

"Adios," said Mr. Sanchez. When Wittman looked back at him, he was shaking his head muttering, let's hope, "Fifty-four right thrice—thirty-two left twice—right to ten."

Wittman followed the arrow, and joined about a dozen of the pre-employed sitting in front of a roll-down screen. They were evenly spaced away from one another, nobody wanting to sit with a deadbeat. A civil servant finished re-winding the film, and said, "Lights out, please." Wittman, who sat nearest the door for a quick getaway, flipped the switch. Deadbeats and freeloaders in the dark.

It was a cartoon about going for a job interview—how to dress and cut your hair—your personal appearance. Good grooming for that all-important interview. Come to think of it, what everybody in that room had in common was that they were bad dressers. Bad hair. Bad clothes. Bad skin. Nobody in here but us bandanna heads and fishnet torsos and flipflop feet. And ethnicks who carry lunch greasing through a brown paper bag. Wittman had been sized up and found sartorially incorrect. (Where had he lost his chewed-up tie?) "Good grooming hints," said the sound track. "Mind these etiquette tips." "Hints." "Tips." Like this was no major deal. Watch, they're going to use his other unfavorite words, "peeve," "hue." Personnel's pet peeve—necktie and socks of the wrong hue. "You mean business. Dress for it." An X crisscrossed a brunette with a low-cut blouse and tight skirt and a cigarette hanging from her lips. She had a beauty spot on her cheek. Rita Moreno. Light rays shone around a woman with a Peter Pan collar and a blonde flip; she was smiling into a hand mirror and patting her hair. Trashy Rita Moreno versus employable Sandra Dee. Who would you hire? An X through the man in a greasy d.a., t-shirt and jeans. Light rays for the man in three-piece suit and barbered hair. X the tennis shoes; gleam all over black shoes with black socks. We the underdressed had to sit there taking one insult after another against our every style and taste. Checkmark: Take a bath or shower, Trim nails and cuticles, Shake hands firmly. X out red pointy fingernails, chewed nails, claw-dirt nails. Another word he didn't like, "cuticles." Do other people really push that bit of nailskin down and cut it off? This is a Watch Bird watching a Nail Biter; this is a Watch Bird watching YOU.

"DO wear a friendly facial expression. DO ask informed questions. DO NOT ask about perquisites and salary right away." The voice read the words on the screen for you. This was not your Cinema Guild and Studio audience. Nobody snickered or made a wisecrack. Oh, shame. Gone are the audiences who laughed at suits and white sidewalls over the ears. But, you know, the average person is not bright. Somebody here may now be reformed to use mouthwash and deodorant. There's a Basic Training hands-on class on how to use your G.I. toothbrush, which some Americans cannot afford. They join the Army, and get their first toothbrush and first pair of new shoes. The Army civilizes. Kill and die with clean teeth. "CHECK the heels of your shoes. DO wear clean linen." Linen? "BRUSH your teeth. COMB your hair." And you'll be all right. "DO sit up straight. DO NOT slouch. DO NOT chew gum. BE on time." He vowed never to polish his shoes or cut his hair again. "PRESENT yourself at your best." Like female monkeys in heat present lipstick-red asses. "A positive attitude," said the voice. At-tee-tood, thought Wittman. "Well turned out. That out-of-the-bandbox look." What the fuck's a bandbox?

"COME ALONE to the interview. DO NOT take friends or relatives with you." An X through my people. Adios, mis amigos. There it is, up on the screen, and in the handbook too: "DO NOT take friends or relatives with you." An American stands alone. Alienated, tribeless, individual. To be a successful American, leave your tribe, your caravan, your gang, your partner, your village cousins, your refugee family that you're making the money for, leave them behind. Do not bring back-up. You're doing it wrong, letting your friends drop you off in a ratty car full of people who look like they live in the car. Out you come wearing the suit and the shoes, carrying the lunch your mamacita made. The girls sitting on the floor outside offices are waiting for commadres taking typing tests and mopping tests. Personnel walks those corridors and lobbies to see who brought a horde. No job for them. Wittman got lonely for that tribesman that said to the Peace Corps volunteer, "We don't need a reading class; we've already got a guy who can read." That's the tribe where he wants to belong, and the job he wants, to be the reader of the tribe. O right livelihood.

Wittman had wanted a tribe since he was a kid at the theater late one night when the cleaning man came, an immigrant from a South Sea island. It was he that had the job but his wife helped, and an elderly grandfather and four kids. They brought a t.v., which they plugged in down in the green room. They enjoyed the use of the rug as a kang, everybody and Wittman sticking their legs under the one blanket, the baby for warming laps. The daddy had people to have his breaks with, eating home-popped popcorn and drinking sodas. He wasn't at all lonely working. Jobs ought to be like that.

"DO write neatly on your application. STRESS your qualifications for the job. AVOID gum chewing, fiddling with a purse, or jingling coins in your pocket. DO NOT SMOKE unless invited to do so." Wittman lit up; it's a free country. "DO NOT apply during the lunch hour or after working hours. AVOID talking about your personal, domestic, or financial problems. RELAX. SPEAK clearly and answer questions honestly. BE business-like and brief." Don't let them smell your fear that you won't make the rent, and you're hungry, and your child is going to die the death of a ragbaby. No flop-sweat. If you're desperate for a job, and why else would you want one, it shows, and they won't give it to you. Act like you don't need money. The End, they don't even say Good luck or any blessing.

At the slapping, snapping tail end of the film, the projectionist said, "Lights. Lights, please." Wittman was so offended that he refused to be light monitor, went right out the door. Where did my monkey powers go? He should have pulled the film out of its sprockets, festooned it around the room, and torn his papers and other people's papers into confetti.

The film that we're going to make after the revolution will give practical information, such as Down with dress codes.

Come as you are. The F.O.B.s ought to be told: After the try-out period, nobody wears interview clothes. Bring your greasy lunch in a briefcase, or bring money to eat out. The revolutionary monkey will give lessons on how to tell jokes that crack up employers. He'll teach an etiquette good enough to talk to anybody.

Walking back to his pad, Wittman planned his twenty-six weeks of subsidized living. Forty-four dollars per week to fund subsistence and theater. Jobless, no more pilfering of office supplies and trick-or-treat candy, but no more dry-cleaning of the suit. Stop buying newspapers. Pall Malls are long enough to cut in half for two smokes. Eat one meal a day; fast one day a week. Start shoplifting food from chains. He never did look beyond the year at the furthest. The Bomb could very well fall before Unemployment runs out. He had always taken maximum exemptions—fourteen—and gotten his money in case of bombing before the spring refunds.

Back in his demesne, he found in the mailbox the last paycheck from the store, and the dimmest carbon of the Notification of Changes enclosed. Where's the thank you for your services? Enough bread, though, until Unemployment comes through.

He sat himself right down at his desk and got a head start on the next Claim card. No. None. Yes. No. Yes. No. No. No. No. No. On the flip side were blanks for the names, addresses, and phone numbers of three places where one has inquired for work. As his first contact, he listed Lance Gentaro Kamiyama, President of the Young Millionaires. If Unemployment phoned Lance, being fast on the uptake, he would answer Yes, Wittman had indeed come in for an interview, a good prospective employee, yes. No need to call Lance up requesting and explaining. He was a true friend. On the sheet for keeping an ongoing record, he again wrote Lance's name, and an "I" next to it for "Interview." Interviews would be most troublesome as compared to contact by letter ("L") and contact by telephone ("T"). Surely, U.I.D., the Unemployment Insurance Division, doesn't check every contact, but if they do, may they randomly pick Lance. Whoever needs to cover an Unemployed ass can always write in Wittman Ah Sing as a prospective employer; he would never fail to lie to the Government for the sake of a friend eluding a job, either civilian or military. There. One down. Two to go. Wait a few weeks, put Lance's name again. ("DO make repeat contacts with employers.")

In six months, a Claim every two weeks, twelve cards times three contacts per, that's thirty-six employers. Everyone should form a hui of thirty-six friends. According to friendship scientists, it takes a pool of one million people in order to make twenty friends. But how many of those can you count on to let you use their name on a U.I.D. Claim card? The befriending is hard work in itself.

For the second entry, he wrote, "Chinchillo Fruit Co., a Tillie Lewis Co." That sounded like two employers in a space for one; how hard he's trying. Those canneries pick up busloads of los braceros y los hobos at the hiring halls and on street corners, and drive them to the fields. The U.I.D. won't waste the taxpayers' bucks for a long-distance check-up call. There's no list of those who tried but didn't get a seat on the company bus. Hanging around a hiring hall would count as an interview—"I."

For his third contact, he put the John Simon Guggenheim Foundation. That would be an "L," contact by mail. Next card, the Rockefeller Foundation, then the Ford Foundation, the Woodrow Wilson National Fellowships, the Rhodes. He'll cull *Grants and Fellowships* at the library—enough names and addresses for years of Unemployment.

There. Done. Ass covered for next week. Free to go about his true life. Looking for a job could've become a full-time job; and he'd covered two weeks' worth of interviews in fifteen minutes. And it's only Monday. Number Five, "Did you try to find work for yourself that week?" "Yes." And Number Six, "Was any work offered you that week?" "No." Log in first thing every other Monday, and the rest of the fortnight will be his.

Too bad no more spaces already. He was getting hot. What the hell. Fill out some more. Put the F.B.I., and on a later card, the C.I.A. The F.B.I. and the C.I.A. will deny that Wittman Ah Sing was a candidate, then he'll say to Unemployment, "Well, of course, the F.B.I. doesn't tell anybody the everyday-identity name of a G-man trainee-to-be. They can't blow my cover. They offered me a spy job, as a matter of fact, but I don't sign loyalty oaths." NASA, the Pentagon, Scotland Yard. "T," phone calls, hard to trace.

His aunties, the showgirls, would vouch that he had talked to them about work. Start with Auntie Carmen, the agent, then Auntie Mabel's revue. List the casinos in Reno; Unemployment won't question his talent as a croupier, all Chinese are gamblers.

And another thing you can do—put Chinatown businesses. Your contact is Woo Ping Sao or Go Wing Mao or Soo Hoo Ting Bao. If Unemployment were to say, "We can't find that name in the phone book," you say, "You must have looked under Sao. Sao's not his last name. Woo is his last name. We put the last name in front, see?" And if they say they did look under Woo, you say, "Oh, it must be under Ng. In my dialect, we say Ng instead of Woo. Sometimes he goes by Ng. Try looking under Quinto. They came up out of Bolivia." Or you find some actual name in the Chinatown phone book, and when that king of tofu hears the white Government voice on the phone, he'll say he doesn't speak English. Throw flak all around. Outsmarting the government is our heritage.

Wittman's not crazy and he's not lazy. The reason he doesn't have right livelihood is that our theater is dead. A company of one hundred great-great-grandparents came over to San Francisco during the Gold Rush, and put on epic kung fu opera and horse shows. Soon the City had six companies—not those six business companies—six theater companies—the Mandarin Theater, the last to die; the Great China Theater, which runs movies now. The difference between us and other pioneers, we did not come here for the gold streets. We came to play. And we'll play again. Yes, John Chinaman means to enjoy himself all the while. "If some of us don't live this way, then the work of the world would be in vain," says Lew Welch, poet guide, whose California incarnation is Leo, the Red Monk. We played for a hundred years plays that went on for five hours a night, continuing the next night, the same long play going on for a week with no repeats, like ancient languages with no breaks between words, theater for a century, then dark. Nothing left but beauty contests. Wittman may be untalented, poor, not called upon, but he will make vocation; he will make theater. *Had not one had a hundred times to promise not to die?*

From a shelf higher than his head, he took down the *I Ching*, which is a book and also a person dressed in yellow. He—the Ching—jumps reality to reality like quantum physics. Wittman found any three pennies from his pocket change, shook them, ringing the changes, and threw the Big Have. Dai Yow. Hexagram Number 14, Possession in Great Measure. Dai Yow, a name we give our gambling houses—The Big Have— and Dai Loy, the Big Come, ha ha. When you get something terrific like that, you don't believe it. He threw again, and got Dai Kuo, the Big Crossing, or, as they say, Preponderance of the Great. The Ching says Go. The pre-Americans, before they crossed the ocean to here, went to a church-casino to throw with God. They bet the Big Crossing, and here we are. He threw again. The Ching said, "Youthful Folly. It is not I who seeks the young fool; the young fool seeks me. At the first oracle I inform him. If he asks two or three times, it is importunity." Let us go then, you and I, to make the world our own place.

Through the windows, the San Francisco weather gave no hint as to what time it was, afternoon grey or morning grey. *Here he rises from his meditations and goes to his window; his high room is too close to him, he would like to see stars, if that is possible.* Wittman's stars were the pinholes in his roller blinds, constellations like none in the sky. He shook his pillow out of the pillowcase, stuffed in his sheet, bathroom towels and dishtowel from off the fire escape. He took off the green shirt, stuffed it in too. He put on one of his chambray blue shirts, and his black knit tie, collar down neat, and changed to jeans and tennis shoes. He gathered the socks and underwear from off the shelves of stacked-up crates and off the floor and out of corners. The good thing about living by yourself in an uncomfortable room is that it forces you out into the marketplace and the forum, a notebook and a couple of books under the arm.

His afterschool and afterwork homecoming neighbors went at him again in the halls and stairwell. "College graduate, believes too much what they teach over there." "Bum-how." "No job. Useless." He faced a woman down, "Have you eaten yet, Grandmother?" "I'm not *your* grandmother, boy. Jook tsing." Bamboo head. "Ho chi gwai jai." Earth paper boy. Just the community's way of letting you know we care. He ought to bring his white girl up here for a tour, give them something to talk about. *Now since I have been drifting about alone like this, I have had innumerable neighbors; neighbors above me and beneath me, neighbors on the right and on the left, sometimes all four kinds at once. I could simply write the history of my neighbors; that would be the work of a lifetime. It is true that it would be, rather, the history of the symptoms of maladies they have generated in me. . . .* The smell of other people's dinners was filling the air with hungers.

He turned up his pea-coat collar, slung his seabag over his shoulder, and walked toward his ship, which had been torpedoed during World War II. He was the ghost of one of the five fighting Sullivan brothers. Five roles for five Caucasians. The sun looked like a foggy moon. The old eyes of the man in the moon, up again during the day, were drooping tearfully. The street, the buildings, the people seemed spackled, blending them into a coherent set. The laundromat was on a corner; the traffic took right turns around the windows like sharks at the Steinhart Aquarium. There were pools of water on the street and on the floor. He bought some soap out of the vending machine, shoved everything into a small washer, stretching his money. President Truman had washed his own socks in the White House sink, so as not to make Bess his laundress. "Nobody should have to wash a man's socks for him," he'd said. Wittman was having the same consideration for Taña. But he did miss laundromats near a campus; there had been propaganda leaflets you could agree with, recent magazines and newspapers and good paperbacks left behind to share the wealth, and readers and writers at the chairs with a desk-arm. Though too often a head was watching t.v. at a front-loading washer.

He picked up a postcard from off the floor. It was porno, two or three fleshy people cheesing into the camera. The girl looked Chinese or Japanese or Korean. Arms and legs were bent funny because of balancing on high-heel shoes while fucking while looking at the birdie. There was an address and phone number, which the Steppenwolf would have gone to or called up, letting whatever wrong number trip him out into somebody else's movie. No, thanks. Wittman, a man of purpose, had in mind a place to go while his clothes were washing.

At his bus stop, a very strange person, a blonde Black lady, also waited. She stood closer and closer. She was wearing too many clothes, not knowing why she was uncomfortable. They had been boiled in dark dye, as PoPo used to do to costumes. He felt her stares touching his face. "Do you know what they did to the pretty little oriental girl?" she asked. He put his books on his shoulder, blocked her view. But didn't fool her into thinking he was invisible. "They killed the pretty little oriental girl. And do you know why they killed her?" Why did they kill her? "I'll tell you why they killed her." Dramatic pause. Five, six, seven, eight. "They killed her for her kidneys." No shit, Dick Tracy. He walked fast to another bus stop, lost her. Her voice came on the pouring fog, ". . . kidneys," chasing him for quite a while.

"Is that you? Is that you?" What is this? One for each bus stop. Who? Me? Yes, pointing at him, addressing him, shouting him out from across the traffic was a white lady in a raincoat and scarf. The shark cars were cutting her off from coming over to his side of the street. "It's you, isn't it?"

"No, it's not," Wittman answered.

"Sure, it's you."

"No. No. I don't think so." Hey, wait a second. That's not right. She's tanglewitting him.

"Georgie. You Georgie?"

He knows the answer to that one. "No, I'm not. I'm not Georgie."

"Georgie, you go home and phone your mother. You phone your mother. You hear? Go home, Georgie. Phone your mother. Why won't you call your mother, Georgie? You call your mother. Georgie, you call her right now."

Street talkers choose him. They're always recognizing him. It takes one to know one. The bus came, and he rode away, passing both his ladies. What is it about me that I am picked out by the touched?

Well, yes, he ought to give his mother a call, tell her she can stage a memorial service. PoPo is not getting herself found.

When a familiarity pervaded a certain neighborhood in the Avenues, Wittman got off and walked. He peeked like X-ray eyes through cracks between buildings and saw the ocean. Sea dragons were rolling about sounding their foghorns. He came to a Queen Anne house that he had seen before; it hadn't been a dream or a wish. That red plant they make soup out of, who knows its English name, was growing in the strip of dirt between the sidewalk and the street. Over the front door were three words that looked like the Chinese on houses that his parents and grandmother had pointed out to him in Vancouver, Seattle, Sacramento, Stockton, Denver, L.A. "Ours." A house not much different from others on the block except for the sign that was a board off a crate: Bow On Hong, which isn't even how you pronounce Benevolent Association but the best the founders could spell. Wongs and Lees have headquarters that are architect-designed office buildings; they own the block, the shopping center. The Ah Sings had had to join up with a bunch of other families, and they still weren't much. Not one of your power clans. "You need help," said his father, "you go there." Zeppelin went to the New Year's banquet and July 4 picnic as a philanthropist, a big donor, a buyer of many raffle tickets with his last twenty-dollar bill. The only beggarmen at the Eighth Month Fifteenth Day party were Black bum-hows and white bum-hows, who walked in off the street, no shame.

An old fut in B.V.D. undershirt came out to the curb with a watering bucket. Wittman turned and walked away. He needed to go around the block practicing what to say. Admit it, he was sort of afraid of the Bow On Hong. There are non-Chinese who understand that. At school, he'd met a Jewish girl who was afraid of Hadassah ladies. Same thing.

He folded the collar of his pea coat down, and came at the old fut from the other direction. He was watering the curb vegetables with warm piss. Smell it, hear it bubble, see it steam. Fresh. "Sir," said Wittman, that is to say, "Teacher." "Teacher, may I speak with you awhile?" Sloshed the old honeybucket there almost onto one's shoes. Then picked up a broom and started sweeping his way across the sidewalk and up the stairs. Swept that Wittman aside. "Teacher, may I please have a word with you?" Importuning, crabwalking.

The old coot bent over with his ass in one's face, and swept into his oilcan dustpan. He could have stood straight, using the upright handle. He was giving Wittman the ass on purpose. "I have an idea I want to discuss with you," said Wittman.

"No speak English," said the old fut, heading up the stairs, blocking the way with his equipment. Oh, come on, he can speak English. Anybody can speak English who feels like it. "Boss not here," he said, like Wittman was some health inspector, some tourist, some Caucasian salesman. But Wittman's half-ass Chinese would have insulted him, as if he were not good enough to use American on. The boss is too here. This is our president, Mr. Grand Opening Ah Sing. Do they call him Grand Opening to his face?

"Teacher, I need to talk to you about something very important," said Wittman, as he had rehearsed, stepping over things to beat Mr. Grand Opening up the stairs.

The old fut banged his broom, oilcan dustpan, honeybucket. Wittman sat down on the top step. "Let's sit and talk awhile, Teacher. Rest," he said, beckoning the old fut to have a sit, like host inviting guest. This place is my place too.

"Talk then talk, la." Like suit yourself. The old fut kept walking on up.

Wittman jumped to his feet, yanked the screen door open, "Let me help you," grabbed the wet honeybucket. "I came here with a good idea for you, Uncle." But quick, the old fut rattled through the door and locked it. His hair stuck up from its whorl in a topspin. He laughed, hoisting his droopy drawers by their suspenders. He's no president; this is our village idiot who has no other place to live and no family, our charity case in exchange for caretaking the estate.

"Hoi mun!" shouted Wittman. "Open the door!" The old guy stood there looking at him. "'Knock knock.' 'Who's there?' 'Hoimun. Hoimun Who? Hoimun, I want to come in, ah.' Ha ha. Get it? Herman, open the door."

"Go away," said the old fut. "You go."

"No, no, I'm not ah Go. I'm Ah Sing. Are you an Ah Sing too, Uncle? I'm Ah Sing. I'm not a robber." You can trust me not to steal this honeybucket. "I want to talk to you. I'm Ah Sing. I'm Zeppelin Wadsworth Ah Sing's boy. You know Ruby? Ruby Long of Chicago. I'm Ruby Long Legs' boy." Shit. What's GrandMaMa's name? "I have a popo. I'm Ah Sing PoPo's grandson."

He was grabbing look-sees over the old fut's shoulders. A large living room with a pair of heavy carved throne-chairs at one end—the stage area. "My Ah Sing PoPo was here at the New Year's party, do you remember her? My mother gave a lot of money to this association, Sacramento branch. My baba is a past president of the Six Companies. I just want to visit, okay? Just visit. Just just. Please, Ah Sing Uncle, may I come in and sit?"

"Come in then come in."

Wittman brought the rest of the pissing and cleaning equipment inside. He set his books on the conference-dining table, and sat down before them. They like you to have books. He gestured the old fut toward a chair, "Sit. Sit," acting as if he were a dues-paid active member, whose family were founders from way back. The old fut took the seat at the head of the table, next to a chalkboard. "So what you want?" he said.

"I want to put on a play here. For free. It won't cost you anything. It will make money for you. For us. For the Family Association, who doesn't have to pay to see it. The Association can sell tickets, and make money. Will you please donate the use of our hall for a play? We could open up these doors to make the living room and eating room one big room. Only move this long table."

"What you mean play?"

"A bock wah. A bock wah, wah." White speech. Pure speech, as in a play. "Jew hay, wah. I like to jew hay." To make air. To give to airy nothing a local habitation and a name. "I like to make a play with Gwan Goong. A Chinese play." But he doesn't mean a Chinese play. Is there a Chinese word for Chinese-American? They say "jook tsing." They say "ho chi gwai." Like "mestizo." Like "pachuco."

"Gwan Goong be here." The god of actors and writers and warriors and gamblers and travelers was on top of the mantel.

"This house be a good house to make a play," said Wittman, said all the spiel he'd prepared, and began repeating himself.

"You no can play in here."

"Listen, we must play in here. Else, what Association for, huh? Collecting dues? What you do, huh? You bury old men. You be nothing but one burial society. Better you let United Farm Workers use the bathroom and kitchen. Let them crash overnight. Be headquarters—Hello, Strike Central—for union of waiters and garment workers." Where's more language, for to amplify and ramify? In Berkeley, a Black Muslim spoke about "sanctuary that the Chinese brothers provide one unto another." He had looked right at Wittman, a member of a people with a genius for community. Black guys see too many kung fu movies. They think a Chinese-American can go anywhere in the country and have a safehouse where a stranger can be served a family dinner. Well, there had been a time, any old Chinese stopped you in the intersection and scolded you to be careful crossing streets. Scolded you to be a good boy, like they all took a hand in raising you. The ethnos is degenerating.

"We no can have Black gwai and bum-how meeting here. Don't say old men dead."

"Okay, okay, old men not dead. Nobody dead. Everybody plays. Look, I'll show you." Wittman jumped up and ran to the fireplace, to the flags and the oranges and pomelos and the dusty plastic fruit and flowers. "Here. Gwan Goong and Chang Fei be here. Kung fu. Hi ho, Red Rabbit." He picked up a feather duster, which represents horse. "Sabe? Move this." He shoved the big table. "Chairs. People." Moved chairs away from the wall, turned them toward the front. "Talk big stories."

"What you doing?" said the old fut. "What you doing?" He moved the chairs back. He pushed against the other side of the table. "What you do, jook tsing boy? You ho chi gwai. You monkey." But the old fut was asking a question. Always take questions as signs of friendliness.

"Monkey kung fu," said our monkey. "I do monkey kung fu." He grabbed a flagstaff. "Monkey gim." The gim is the double-edged sword. Wave the red-white-and-blue, wave the horse. "Monkey at war." The magic monkey twirls his rod that turns into needle, gim, staff, the Empire State Building, a soft-shoe swaggerstick. "Monkey fights Lao Tse." "Lousy," he pronounced it, trying to hit the tones. "Monkey fights lousy," which is all right; Monkey lost that fight. "Monkey fights Kwan Yin." He picked Kwan Yin up from the mantelpiece, and shook her, shook himself as if she were doing it, bonked himself on the head with her, and disappeared, yanked, behind the chalkboard. He ran out, carrying the flag sweeping the furniture and floor. He stopped at the fruit, and bit a plastic peach.

"Monkey drinks the wine and eats the peaches. Monkey pisses in the cups. Priests drink monkey piss. Pfooey." Funny face toward the audience. "Monkey changes seventy-two ways. Bee-e-en! Monkey bird. Monkey fish." Bug eyes, blowfish cheeks, mouth and eyes opening and shutting, his fingers swimming like gills and fins beside his face. "Monkey as temple." Stiff and articulated like an Egyptian, his flagpole-tail erect, salute it. "Be-ee-en! Monkey as a dancing bouillon cube. Help. Help. I'm diminishing. Bee-e-en!" Jumping up and down, voice fading, cooking in the cauldron of life. He picked up the jar of sticks, and shook them onto the hearthstone, like jackstraws. He threw the three coins in his pocket against the baseboard. There were three turtle shells, and he threw them on the floor. "Did they land lucky, huh, Uncle? Good luck, huh? We okay for a play? Monkey bets God." He wrapped himself around the porcelain footstool-drum, and banged out a rhythm. "Come see the bock wah, laaaah." He fell into the throne-chair. Come on, come on, where's the applause? "Seriously, sir," he said, "let me give you a tryout free sample story. If you like it, we have more show for everybody. You don't like it, I leave. Fair?"

"Okay okay," said the old fut.

"Okay?! Once upon a time, the one hundred and eight outlaws fought against an army that took arrows through their hearts, and got stronger and stronger. There came word or a dream about a weapon that would keep that army down. Tai Chung, the messenger of the outlaws, would go get it. 'Take me with you,' said Li Kwai, the Black Whirlwind. Now, some say he's black because he was bad and his weapon was the ax. He killed anybody, little kids, girls. He didn't mean it but. He was like a storm. He knuckle-rapped this girl singer's forehead, and she died. He had wanted her to stop singing while he talked-story. You could get rich taking the adventures of the Black Whirlwind to Hollywood. He was trying to civilize himself, bringing his old mother to the community at the Water Verge. She got eaten by a tiger while he fought the wrong tiger. He made too much trouble for his own side, losing. He might as well go on errand. I say he was Black Li because his skin was black. He was Chinese and black, a black Chinese, many roles in our bock wah for all kinds of us.

"Tai Chung, the Flying Prince, says, 'You may come along if

you promise not to eat meat on the way. Will you do whatever I tell you to do?'

"'No problem,' says Black Li.

"'Good. We'll be traveling fast. Don't lag behind.'" Wittman did two voices, me-aying his head back and forth. "They go only three or four miles before Black Li suggests that they stop for wine. Tai says that wine is about as bad as meat. They run until evening. At an inn, Black Li serves Tai vegetables, but doesn't touch them himself." Wittman brought the plastic fruit over to the big table. "'Why aren't you eating with me?' asks Tai. 'Aren't you hungry?'

"'I be back,' says Black Li.

"Tai tails him to a back room. He's eating platters of beef and pork." Wittman pretended to gobble up the plastic fruit. "The next morning, they get up at four A.M., and both eat vegetables for breakfast. Tai says, 'Yesterday wasn't fast enough; we have to make three hundred miles today. Pack tight.'" Wittman wrapped his tie around his head, and stuck paper—letters and dispatches—into his belt. He knelt at the old fut's feet, untied his shoes, could've tied the laces together. "'I'm giving you leg armor that was hammered from enchanted metal.'" He blew and spoke on the shoes, which the old fut was re-lacing. "'There. You've eaten your peas and carrots. You're going to run well. One more magic: You carry our dark banner. Feel the wind pulling at it? I'll carry everything else.'" He put the broom in the old fut's hand, and picked up the honeybucket, the basket of gifts for negotiating with friends and strangers. "Black Li sails away, his legs moving in long strides without touching the ground." Wittman grabbed the old fut's hand, and pulled him around the table. "Run *this* way, Uncle," he said, his feet going ahead of him, the rest of his body trying to catch up.

"Stop," said the old fut, "stop, you." He gave a yank, and Wittman fell down, landing on his butt. The old fut laughed. Fall down, make 'em laff.

Wittman got up, continuing in character as mercuric Tai.

"'Move those feet. Hear the storms rushing in your ears. See the trees and houses whirl by. You're passing inns and can't stop for a drink. Your feet keep moving under you. Swim, Black Li. Fly. All I see of you is a black streak, you're going so fast. I'm two yellow streaks—my yellow turban and my cum-merbund. I catch up to you when the sky is red with sunset. Brother Black Li, why aren't you stopping to eat?'

"'Elder Brother Tai,' you say, 'save me. I'm dying from hunger and thirst, and I can't stop running. Help. Food. Please.'

"Tai holds out a bun. They miss the relay. He eats it himself.

"Black Li turns around, feet running ahead, hands reaching for the bun far far behind. Tai catches up. 'Things are very strange today,' he says, 'as I can't seem to control my legs.'

"'I can't either,' says Black Li. 'My legs won't obey me. I feel like chopping them off.'

"'Yes, where's your ax? We go on like this, we won't stop until New Year's Day.'

"'Please don't play tricks on me, Elder Brother. If I cut off my legs, how can I go home?'

"'You must have disobeyed me and eaten meat. I think that's why strange legs.'

"'I don't lie. I ate some meat yesterday. But not much. Only six pounds. When I looked at your vegetables, I just had to have a little meat. What do I do now?'

"'Stop!' Tai catches hold of Black Li's leg, and yanks." From behind, Wittman scooped the old fut into a chair. "'I see you're having trouble with gravity. Let's take off one shoe, and slow you down by half. Walk this way.'" He did a banana-peel run, slip-sliding around the room.

"They rush past wine flags and grog flags, but the waving of a fingery pennon draws them both to a halt. They find themselves at a crossroads where grows a tree that five men holding hands exactly encircle. There's an inn with a woman leaning out the window. She's wearing a green see-through coat, a low-cut blouse, and a pink underblouse. The buttons are real gold. In her hair are gold combs and red flowers. She has red-rouge cheeks. 'Good meat,' she calls. 'Good wine. Come refresh yourselves.' She walks out to meet them. Her skirt is red and short. They follow her through the grape arbor outdoor café to the cedar tables and stools inside. There are no other customers. 'We have very tasty bow and dim sum.'

"'Bring forty then,' says Black Li.

"'Bring vegetable bow,' says Tai. 'Bean filling.'

"'What are you afraid of?' The woman laughs. 'That we use

dog meat? These are good times; no need to eat human meat or dog meat. We serve pork and beef.'

"'I've lived through many travels,' says Tai. 'I know about inns where they cut up fat men to fill dumplings, and toss thin men into the river. Vegetarianism makes my senses strong, and I'm smelling a strange meat.'

"'What a way you have of flirting with me. As a vegetarian, you've come to the right place. We're famous for our peas and beans. My husband's nickname is Vegetable Gardener.'

"'I'll test the meat,' says Black Li. 'I'll taste what these bows are made of.' He takes a mouthful.

"Tai pulls a long hair out of his bow. 'Now isn't this a human hair?'

"Their hostess giggles and scratches her head with a comb. 'It's one of mine. I'm sorry. I do have a profusion of hair, don't I?'

"'Sister, why isn't there a man about?' asks Tai.

"'My husband, the Vegetable Gardener, went to visit friends, and is bringing them home for dinner.'

"'How long has he been gone?'

"'So you are flirting with me.'

"'Woman, this wine is weak,' says Black Li. 'If you make better wine, let's have it.'

"'I have a thick red I've been saving for a special drinker.'

"'Bring it. And two tubs of warm water for our feet.'

"She goes out and comes back with a dark and dull wine. She's laughing to herself.

"'This wine is cold,' says Tai. 'Could you warm it please?'

"'You want it hot, I'll make it hot for you. I'll redden that vegetarian body of yours with grog blossoms.'

"While she's gone, Tai whispers to Black Li that the wine has been poisoned. They should pretend to drink but pour it out the window.

"'No waste,' says Black Li, who downs it. His eyes close, and he falls off his stool. Tai also shuts his eyes, and lays his head on his arms. He hears the woman clap her hands. 'Ha, I washed my feet in that swill you drank.' She undoes their belts and pouches, feeling for money, laughing all the while. 'I've caught two big ones. Meat bow for days.' Her henchmen come out from the kitchen. 'Carry the meat to the butcher block,' she orders. They drag Black Li off. Tai lies rigid; they can't move him. 'You lazy clowns,' she scolds the helpers. 'You eat and drink but can't work. I'll lift him myself. Why, he's going to be as tough as water buffalo.' She takes off her green see-through coat and her red silk skirt. She throws his arms over her shoulder, trying to get him into a fireman's carry. He clamps her in his legs. She screams. And just then, her husband comes home, banging through the swinging door with his gang of friends. Black Li crashes in from the kitchen, chased by the cooks with butcher knives. Tai tries to hang on to the Night Ogress, for it is she. They have a free-for-all bar-room brawl fracas and melee all over the place. Black Li swings from the rafters and kicks stomachs and jaws and asses. The Vegetable Gardener lassoes the paddleblade fan, and rides it around the room, swiping at Black Li. The mirror behind the bar shatters in a storm of reflections. A cook throws a wok. It carries him off the balcony. The bartender falls out through the swinging doors into a horse trough. Aces, kings, queens, and knaves fly." Wittman was running all over the Benevolent Association, up and down the stairs, on and off the furniture, the old fut chasing him.

"They fight to a tie and draw. Tai has his foot on Night Ogress's neck. 'Your mother farts like a dog,' she curses. 'He's accusing us of murder,' she tells her husband. 'He's saying we're cannibals.'

"'There are body parts in the kitchen,' says Black Li. Tai lets go of the Night Ogress to have a look.

"'Oh, no,' says she. 'What must you be thinking?' She flusters around with the featherduster, just a housewife caught behind on her housekeeping. She picks up a hand. 'You're thinking that I—that I—cook and serve and eat—? That this is food? Oh, how could you? Why, you're looking at trophies. These are the pieces of armed and dangerous men with prices on their heads. We don't have room in the house for their whole bodies. I'm not strong enough to bring back their entire remains. I just clip a part for identification—a scalp, a distinctive patch of tattooed or branded skin. This hand is the hand of Three-Finger Jack.' Well, there are two fingers missing, all right; the famous trigger finger is still there. 'And this head is the head of Joaquín Murrieta.'" Wittman took hold of the old fut's head by the chin.

"Tai and Black Li examine the head with respect. There was the handsome eagle nose, the handlebar moustache, the brown eyes, looking at them even in death. But throughout the Far Out West were many heads of Joaquín Murrieta. Stagecoaches miles apart were held up at the same time by a man who said, 'It is I, Joaquín.' Of course, those who were robbed insisted that no lesser Joaquín Murrieta than El Famoso had done it. How do we know this head is the head?

"'I have the hand from the selfsame body,' says the Night Ogress a.k.a. Mrs. Chang a.k.a. Mrs. Sun a.k.a. the Goodwife Sheng. 'This hand of his has the correct finger dedigitated. We got El Famoso, all right. Next time you go to Sacramento, honey, take me and the head and the hand with you. I need to redeem my bounty coupons. We have fifteen thousand dollars coming.'

"Now that everyone has calmed down, Chang Ch'ing alias the Vegetable Gardener says, 'My wife and I invite you to dine on chicken and goose al fresco under the grapevines.' Though Chang fought hard, his black cap is still on his head, and his white coat is clean and neat. 'Honey, you got carried away again,' he says to his wife in everyone's hearing by way of apology.

"'How did we get so drunk?' asks Black Li. 'We didn't drink much. The wine must have been very good. We'll have to remember the inn under the great tree at the crossroads, and drop by on our way home.'

"'Please accept my apology,' says Tai to Mrs. Chang, 'for messing up your house.'

"She accepts, and everyone adopts one another as brothers and sister. Flying Prince Tai invites the couple to start a restaurant-guardpost at the Mountains of the White Tigers and the Two Dragons, Shantung. There the stranger, the weird and the alienated make their own country. And have one hundred and seven brothers and sisters. The one hundred and eight banditos, banished from everywhere else, build a community. Their thousands of stories, multiples of a hundred and eight, branch and weave, intersecting at the Water Verge. An inn at each of the four directions run by four couples, famous for serving their guests generously and sweetly, account for the strange things that happen at city limits."

"You give wrong impressions," said Grand Opening Ah Sing. "We not be cannibals. We not be bad."

"But, Uncle, we bad. Chinaman freaks. Illegal aliens. Outlaws. Outcasts of America. But we make our place—this one community house for benevolent living. We make theater, we make community."

"But you wreck the restaurants. The tourists will ask, 'What is this stuff inside the dim sum? What kind of meat you put inside the char sui bow?' Business goes down, no more Chinatown."

"But they ask anyway, huh? Answer once and for all."

"Answer what? Cannibal meat."

"You're getting the idea, Uncle. White meat."

"Bad advertising. What's the matter for you, boy? The tourists save money for years, working all their lives until they retire, and they come here to see us. Whyfor you want to hurt them? They want to see the Gold Mountain too."

The monkeys which had broken loose, jumping all over the old man and the young man, tickling toes, armpits and groins, keelee keelee, rubbing paw-hands, oh boy, oh boy, stopped their funny business. Wittman said, "I promise: no bad advertising. May I put on a show, okay?"

"Okay okay."

"Okay?!" Wittman grabbed the old fut's pissy hand and shook it.

"You come go outside now. Meet again."

"Don't forget you said okay; we shook on it. Thank you, Uncle. Thank you. Lucky meet again."

"Meet again," said the old fut, latching the screen door, and looking at him through it.

"When?" asked Wittman. "When do we meet again? How about tomorrow everyday nighttime I bring the troupe? And grand-opening night be Tenth Month, thirty-first day. Guai Night. Hawk Guai Night." Imitation of Ghosts Night. Scare the Ghosts Night. Hallowe'en. "Call a meeting for our play, okay? Take a vote. Okay? Okay."

"Yeah yeah yeah," said the old fut.

Wittman hopped the bus back to the laundromat. Yes, he

was in luck, laundry all there. He jammed it wet back into the pillowcase, to be hung up to dry on the fire escape. Pea-coat collar up against the foggy dusk, which can break your heart—your true love has left, and you're lost, when you haven't even found her—he walked through ambiguities. Poems blow about that nobody has put into words. Old poems partly remembered sniff at your ears. Nah. Lew Welch warned that it isn't the moon that's sad, it's you. The moon is never sad, says the Red Monk.

North Beach was lit up, jumpy with neon. Chinatown was bright too, paper lanterns over light bulbs, a party nev-erending. On Stockton Street was the biggest Joang Wah, the Consolidated Benevolent Associations. Majestic stairs going up to the locked gates and locked doors, roof curlicu-ing above gilt words—it ought to be a theater. Give our little Family Association first crack at a hit play; the Consolidated Benevolent will invite it here, and get revolutionized. Bust the men in suits. They haven't done useful politics anymore since China Relief. United Farm Workers, when you march on Sacramento at Easter, you are invited to bivouac here and at all the Associations en route from Delano up the Central Valley. I, Wittman Ah Sing, welcome you. And while you're at it, lib-erate the twenty-one missions that Junipero Serra built a day's walk apart—perfectamente for protesters. Then take the Gong Jow temple. Please. They don't do nothing in there but wor-ship goats. No kidding. GrandMaMa once sent a postcard of a statue of goats climbing a pinnacle. A ram stood on its hind legs; it held wheat shafts in its mouth. She said, "Goats saved Gong Jow." I come from a people who worship billygoats.

And, of course, who should Wittman see—find—crossing kittycorner on the green light though it wasn't a Scramble Walk, just when he was thinking of her—but PoPo. The traffic was jammed up, and she walked slow and old in it. Break, my heart. She has gone out without her cane, to show off her legs. Her head—a mantilla comb was stuck high in the geisha-style coils of her very black hair—baubled among the cars. The light changed; the cars picked up speed, a metal river before her and behind her. She kept on coming. A quick nick and one grandma closer to orphanhood. Wittman went out into the intersection, and took from her her purse and her pink box of pastries. He didn't rush her, walked slowly with her, let her take her time, let the fucking honkers run over the both of them. (I am Carlos Bulosan's manong pinoy come home from the city to take the reins of the carabao from the old mother's brown hands, and plow the wet rice field.) It takes youth and willpower to stop cars—look the drivers in the eyes. He brought GrandMaMa safe through the street and up onto the curb.

"How did you get to Big City, PoPo? I've been looking all over for you."

"By miracles. I was upstairs at the Gong Jow giving my thank you."

"What do you do up there, PoPo? Who do you thank? Goats? What's upstairs?"

"Pile up some fruit, stick three incense sticks in the pile. You don't have to go to temple, you can do it anywhere; the kitchen is okay. Oranges, grapefruit, not lemons but. Then hold your hands together like this, and say something."

"Say what?"

"Whatever you feel like saying. Say it all out."

That's all there is to it.

He's going to have to find out if our organizations take upon themselves the reputation as law-abiding, super-patriotic do-nothings so that they can hide illegal aliens, and be a peace sanctuary for fugitives from the next war.

Hardly resting at the street corner, she kept walking; she wasn't going to lose her momentum. "Your grandmama was an abandoned grandmama," she said. "Give me a cigarette, honey girl." Managing the purse and the box, and his laundry, he lit a smoke for her and one for himself. "Your mother and your father lost me on purpose to die in the high-up Sierras. Left me like an extra cat or dog that's cute no more. Oh, you should see the ex-pets dumped in the wild woods. Perfectly good dogs. I fed them my food. I made a wish at those dogs to turn back into wolves. But they forget how to be animals. They thought I was going to take them home. I walked up and down the roadside, and two dogs and a skinny skinny cat and one creature I don't know what it was followed me."

"Did it have a tail? How big was it?"

"It might have had a tail tucked up. It was brown and white

and about this big. O life. The hundred and eight outlaws had a saying: 'Even an ape will cry when another ape is sad.' Your parents are heartless, little Wit Man. Oh, my poor honey girl, you had to be raised by them." Well, he had been raised by her too, and he would probably be better off psychologically if she didn't call him "honey girl," mutt hong nay, which doesn't sound good translated or untranslated. "I tell you, honey girl. Your mother said, 'Do you want to go on a picnic, PoPo?' We went in your father's pick-up truck. I sat in the back. They sat up front plotting against me. We bought takeout, a fire duck with plum sauce and steam rolls."

"Do you want my jacket, PoPo?" She was wearing one of her Malay dresses, and you could see her bony tan shoulders through it. They took turns holding the purse, the pink box, the cigarettes, the heavy wet laundry; he took off the pea coat, she put it on. It hung heavy and long on her, an old urchin of the U.S. Navy.

"Your father drove high, high; he wound around in the mountains so I didn't know east or west. The wind was getting me. I pressed against the backs of those two in the cab. They were talking too much to each other. They were passing picnic spots by. Pretty soon, no benches, no barbecue stoves. We were driving into the wild woods. They acted as if they couldn't hear me banging at their heads and calling Stop.

"At the top of the mountains, they stopped, and your father lifted me down from the pick-up. He carried me. He said, 'Upsy Daisy.' Your mother handed me the blanket and said, 'Spread the blanket under that tree, PoPo.' They put the bag of duck on the ground. I cleared off stones and pine cones. I got tangled in the blanket trying to shake it out in the mountain wind, and do you know what those two kai dai did?" Wittman didn't know the translation for "kai dai," such a dirty word that the dictionary leaves it out and nobody claims to know what it means. "Those kai dai got in the truck and drove away. I thought to myself, they're hurrying down to State Line to do some gambling before we eat. But they didn't come back, and they didn't come back. I ate fire duck without them. Some picnic. A dog came out of the forest carrying a doggie dish in his mouth. I fed him their duck; it served them right. I had lunch. I had dinner. I stood beside the road—they had gotten me off the highway to a hidden road—and looked for the pick-up, and never saw it come back or go by. I gave steam rolls and soda to that dog and another dog and the cat and the creature animal. I patted them—'Good dog. Good dog'—and kept them with me. Those animals were so worn out, they didn't read my mind that I might need to eat them by and by. Oh, honey girl, I'm a perfectly good grandmama, and they dumped me. But a 'perfectly good dog' isn't as good as a 'good dog,' is it? Oh, honey girl, I began to cry. I wept loud. The sun was setting. Oh, who wouldn't cry? It's not fair. Why hadn't they warned me? They could have given me a chance. Judges and employers give people chances. Did they think they had already heard all my conversation? If they were tired of me repeating myself, they could have told me so. I would have done something about it. I repeat myself but not because I forget that I've told a story already. I know I told it before. I tell a thing over again because I like going through it again. I could keep a calendar, and not tell the same things so often. I'm going to read more, and know facts that nobody's heard yet. Maybe they don't like my habits? Your mother and I were at a banquet, where a bit of food spilled on my skirt. I licked my finger and cleaned the spot. Your mother said, 'Stop that, PoPo, that's an old-lady habit.' I stopped, and don't do that anymore. She didn't notice I changed. That was my last chance. It's hard to keep being new and different, honey girl. I was falling behind on the news. The newspapers were piling up in my room. Don't grow old. Otherwise, out you go."

"Yeah, be fun or else, no more use for you. Otherwise, old-age home. Otherwise, divorce. Otherwise, up for adoption. Dog pound. You're a perfect and good grandmother. PoPo, you come live with me. We be cronies." It's not fair, a crone is an old sheep, but a crony is a friend through time.

"Oh, but no, thank you. You one good boy, Wit Man. I found me a place to live. Let me tell you what happened."

"You were waiting by the side of the road, the sun going down."

"I was weeping by the side of the road, the sun going down. High high in the cold, far mountains, the trees are thick, and the woods are dark long before the sun goes down. Oh, those two ex-children of mine acted so caring of me. 'Why don't you

get out here and take a pee, PoPo?' 'Go ahead, start eating,
PoPo. Don't wait for us.' Under the tall red trees, I cried and
cried and cried. There was no other sound in the air.

"It happened that an old Chinese man was driving through
that forest with his windows down. He heard crying, and
thought, 'Who can that be weeping in the dark woods?' He
braked beside me, and stuck his head out the window. 'Lady,
why do you weep?' 'Sir,' says I, 'I have been forsaken by un-
grateful children.' 'Aiya,' the old man said, 'no-good children.
Come with me. Come home with me. I've been seeking a
wife. Will you marry me? And return to the City, and live
with me?' I put the picnic blanket in the car, and got in next
to him. Fortunately, Reno was nearby. We drove there, and
were married. The numbers we bet on were our wedding date
and our ages. We won a great deal of money. Such a lucky day.
We're living together now on Washington Gai. You can tell
your no-heart mother and father that their plot to kill me has
failed. My love story is the talk of Chinatown."

A miracle, all right. Wittman hoped that when he grew
old, he would become like that old man. A babe goes bouncing down the street; a wrinkled popo lags along. Why, he'd
whistle at the latter and mean it. He was beginning already.
He liked the way her eyelids draped at the corners. Debbie
Reynolds eyelids. She wore October opals at the top tips of her
ears, perhaps a fashion of a country nobody else knows about
or comes from. Perhaps her family sold her, but earmarked her
to find again.

"Tell me some more about your old man," he said.

"He's important. A big shot. He owns the building we live
in. He collects the rent from a whole building. I help him collect. His office is on the ground floor, and our apartment is the
top floor. We don't work and live in the same room. Do you
know what he was doing in the Sierras? He was waiting for a
storm. He wanted to ride a tree, as he did when he was a lumberjack. He hugged the trunk at the tiptop of a sequoia—the
tree whipping around and around in the thunder and lightning. It staggered backward and forward, arms waving, almost
losing its balance. My old man, the best tree rider, could let go
of his tree and fly to the next tree. He went for one last ride,
but it didn't storm, and he found me."

Wittman pictured a tree flinging the old man—slingshooting him out of a fork—and he catches another tree. And many lumberjacks riding a forest, and flying from tree to tree. Angel shots. "PoPo, will you do me one favor, huh? Will you ask your old man for some costumes and make-up and lights? I like put on a play. He doesn't have to do work; he could just help out with money."

"What will my old man think of me? No sooner does he take a wife, but my needy greedy relatives come out of hiding. The next thing he knows, he's sponsor of a village. They want airplane tickets, and they want to be house guests, and they want clean jobs. And they want a college education for every kid all the way up to M.D. and Ph.D. And they want Wilson tennis rackets. There's a lady in our building whose cousin is living in her guest room; he sits all day long to be served like he's king of America. Relatives keep asking for more until everybody is down to living on shrimp paste on rice. Any pair of undershorts my old man buys for himself, they'll call a luxury. They don't understand that nowadays we don't live in a bare room and eat hom haw on rice so they can go to college. They ask too much. I've seen it before. I'm protecting my oi yun from relatives." GrandMaMa was the witch under the eclipse in *King Solomon's Mines*. "I've seen it before. I've seen it before."

"Yeah," said Wittman, "they think they can come over here and take advantage of us Americans, they got another think coming. We're wise to their actions. Good thing we don't have any more people to come from China. You're the last one. I'm not asking for money for keeps, PoPo. We make our nut, your oi yun can have all the profits. Everyone will call him Angel. Come on, you used to help me do plays. You like be in my play, PoPo? Play Mother Hsü. You get to tell off Cho Cho. 'Kill me or lock me up in the tower; this hand will never write a ransom note.' And you scold your son, stupid, foolhardy to ride to your rescue and get captured. You can take care of yourself; you don't need rescue. Onstage down-stage-center death scene, PoPo. Climactic and dramatic seppuku harakiri. You fall on the longsword—the gim, your oi yun needs to help me buy. His name will be on the program: Angel—Mr. Oi Yun."

PoPo giggled. "His name isn't Oi Yun, Mr. Beloved. He's Mr. Lincoln Fong."

Wittman's English better than his Chinese, and PoPo's Chinese better than her English, you would think that they weren't understanding each other. But the best way to talk to someone of another language is at the top of your intelligence, not to slow down or to shout or to talk babytalk. You say more than enough, o.d. your listener, give her plenty to choose from. She will get more out of it than you can say.

PoPo said, "Who I really want to play is the princess with the eighty-seven attendant faeries, represented by two dozen beautiful actresses, leading up to my entrance. Did I tell you I played such a princess on the London stage?"

"Yeah, you have, PoPo. How about I arrange six beautiful girls representing the eighty-seven faeries?"

"How about ten or twelve?"

"How about eight? And your oi yun plays K'ung Ming, the tactician for the three brothers. We'll invent a way to give him a tree ride on stage—K'ung Ming controlling the winds. And controlling the atmosphere. Everywhere he abides, gibbons and birds fill the forest; villagers sing in taverns and fields. He outlives the three brothers, and takes over the try for emperor."

"Yes. Yes, that sounds like my beloved."

They were then in front of Wittman's pad. "Well, PoPo. I live up there now. Do you want to come in and drink tea? Do you want to sit awhile?"

"No, thank you," she said. "My oi yun has a car. We're going to meet at a dim sum parlor, and he'll drive me home. Am I sah chun or am I not? Sah chun, ma? If you need a ride anywhere, you call your popo. Look up Mr. Lincoln Fong of Washington Gai in the telephone book, Lincoln Ho in the Chinese phone book. Honey girl, you aren't lonely living up there by yourself, are you?"

"No, no, not me. Don't worry about me. I just got married myself, PoPo. Isn't it lucky, we two newlyweds meeting on the street?"

"Yes. That's very good. Lucky. You and I, a bridegroom and a bride." She smiled up at him. "A tall newlywed and a short newlywed." She made him laugh. She patted him on the arm.

"Lucky." She took off his coat, and took her purse and the pink box. "You want some money? Here."

"No, thank you, PoPo. It's okay. Too much. You buy something for your oi yun." She was giving him a roll of tens.

"No, no. Wedding present. You buy persimmons for *your* oi yun. Sayonara, honey girl." His sah chun grandmama sashayed away sassy down the street. She was wearing a batik cloth tied over her skirt, and her feet were bare brown in sandals. Persimmon season. She's lived for a long time, and in many places. Lucky to have her here now. It was her that Samuel Pepys saw in *A Midsummer Night's Dream*, which featured four peacocks and six monkeys and twenty-four Chinese faeries.

There. Wittman Ah Sing had gotten married, found a venue for a theater, found his grandmother, who gave him money that he did not have to report. Good work. Phone the wife, and so to bed. A reader doesn't have to pay more money for the next chapter or admission to the show if there's going to be a show; you might as well travel on with our monkey for the next while.

7
A Pear Garden in the West

THE CHINESY bank with dragons coiling its red pillars was closed for making change, so Wittman Ah Sing
went to a newsstand and bought cigarettes with a part of
the grandmother money. He intended to pay her back out of
Unemployment money. At his phone booth, he called his people. Yes, he does have people, and they belong to him whether
they like it or not.

"Ma? I'm not sick or in trouble." He always had to say that
right off.

"Good. Why you call then? You find a job?"

"I found PoPo."

"Aiya."

"Not her body. Her. She's alive, and she's married."

"Aiya. That old body, married? Who married her old self?"

"I think, Ma, that there are people who know how to prefer
old bodies. Good thing too, else we're going to be lonely most
of our time."

"What kind of man is he? Did you meet him?"

"A good man. He gives her everything. You don't have to let
her take back her furniture. She's here in the City, and lives in
a building that her old man owns."

"I knew she would make for herself a happy ending. How
about you? Job yet? Don't grow up lazy, Wit Man, that's the
worst." He showered her voice with long-distance dimes.

"Ma? I'm producing a show. I'm a show producer. And our
Joang Wah will sponsor. They like see you and the aunties do
your historic War Bonds Rescue China act. Do you remember
how it goes?"

His mother went quiet. He dropped in some more dimes.
"Ma. Ma, are you there?"

"Remembering or forgetting the act is not the problem,
Wit Man. I contributed to the world war effort that ended up
with A-bombs. I'm changed now. I did those shows because

I wasn't thinking. You were a baby. But now you're draft-age. I'm not sending you off to Viet Nam. I'm not helping drop the H-bomb. Don't you think about Viet Nam? What's the matter for you? You're too carefree, like your father. I want you to run for Canada. Go." His mother was so advanced, he could hardly keep up with her.

"I do think about Viet Nam, Ma. I'm against it. You put on your show after all these years, it won't be the same but. You guys are old nowadays. Not so smooth on your feet, okay. Tap shoes skid, okay. Legs kick crooked, okay. Make the audience see through propaganda." Still talking down to her, he was trying to explain Brechtian.

"You young kid, don't know nothing. The legs are the last to go."

"Ma, if you can stir up a war with your dancing, you can stop one, right? Why don't you and the aunties make up an Anti–War Bond show, and see what happens? If it doesn't work, I'll go to Canada."

"Maybe I take you to Canada. I don't want to stay here and get persecution when I refuse to roll bandages and knit socks. Wit Man, do me one favor."

"Sure, Ma."

"If you go to Viet Nam and get shot down, I don't want you to scream Mama. I can't take that, hurt soldiers yelling Mama on the battlefield, crying for their mother in the hospital. Scream Daddy, why don't they? You don't yell Mama, okay? Have consideration for me for once in your life."

"Teach Daddy to the audience at the Anti–War Bond show."

"I'll talk to the girls. Some are for Viet Nam but. I have to argue them out of it. Good night, Wit Man. Long distance costs too much." She didn't ask after Taña.

A group of tourists walked by, a lone man with his herd of widows. And crossing the street, a family of tourists, all dressed in the same fabric.

He dialed Lance's number. "Howzit? This is Wittman." Lance liked to put you through identifying yourself. Beat him to it.

"Howzit? What's up?"

"You're not giving a Hallowe'en party, are you?"

"Sure, I'll give one if you like. Feel like partying again already, huh?" Always pinning you with motives.

A woman's voice came from another place, "Hallowe'en party? I was about to send out invitations. You're invited, Wittman." It was Sunny on the extension.

"Sunny, is that you? Hi." It's a marriage where he won't be able to talk to his friend alone again. He has to address the both of them, the Kamiyamas as one. "Listen, will you do me a favor, and not give a party that night?"

"*You're* giving the party?" "A party costs at least fifty dollars."

"Well, yes. That night will be opening night for our play. I need your party guests for audience, and you up front." That is, the plural you. If he were to ask to go out with just one of them, would there be a break in the marriage? "The read-through is tomorrow night at our Benevolent house. Bring people for me to read, okay?"

"We're looking forward to it, Wittman," said Sunny. "Hold it," said Lance. "It's a kung fu challenge, Sunny. He's couched it in Japanese politeness, but he's handing us a kung fu challenge all right. His gwoon is about to raid our gwoon; we have to beat him to the punch." "What's a gwoon, Lance?" "It's a school of martial arts. The students of a gwoon will march or drive to another gwoon and attack during practice. That's the walk-through-town of the Seven Samurai and the Magnificent Seven. They fight aikido against chi kung, tai kwan do against zazen, monkey style against wu style against push hands against karate. For keeps. Winner takes all. The sensei roshi whose students lose has to give over his gwoon, his teaching business, his students, his reputation, the Benevolent house, and he has to admit that his form of kung fu is not the superior form. I know what you're after, Wittman—you heard him, Sunny—my mailing list and my phone tree. I accept your challenge. I and my men will be there at your Benevolent house tomorrow night." "Oh, Wittman," said Sunny, "you better be ready. His jiu jitsu is getting so superior." "Chinese against Japanese, Wittman, just like in a Bruce Lee movie. This time, Japanese win."

"Thanks for warning me," said Wittman. "Bring your gang and your artillery and your bombs. I'll fight you single-handedly." His own only kung fu was acting like a monkey. For defense, he would count on what he had seen Bruce Lee do on a t.v. talk show. A challenger was waving hands and feet at him, and Bruce Lee knocked him out with a good old American right cross to the chin. "Sometimes a black belt is only good for holding up pants," said Bruce Lee, who showed himself capable of a street-fighting move, an alley-fighting move.

"By the way, I gave Unemployment your name," said Wittman.

"Are we going to let him use our good name, dear?" "We can't begrudge a man getting on the dole, dear." "Goddamn it, darling, is our tax money paying for his Welfare?"

"Not Welfare," said Wittman. "Unemployment."

"Wittman is siphoning off funds from the war machine." "Oh, come now, Lance, the Pentagon has a separate budget from Welfare. He's draining the California taxpayer, us." He should hang up, and let them talk to each other. "I'm disgusted by thieves who call sponging and shoplifting revolutionary activities." "You're right. Lifting a steak in one's bookbag is not a complete political act. You have to distribute it to the poor, then call in a news release to KQED." Listen to them, showing off for each other. Wittman slowly lowered the receiver hook. He'll have to tell Taña that he won't have a marriage that makes friends feel left out.

Speaking of whom, he called her next. "What's your phone number, Wittman?" Taña asked. "Where're you calling from?"

"I'm at a payphone."

"You don't have a home phone?"

"Nope." Nor a home. "At a pay phone, I can dig the street. Do you hear it? There's a blind guy waving his broken cane at the cars. It's hanging by a string. Blind guys and magicians use the same kind of collapsible cane. He's shouting. Can you hear him? 'The next son of a bitch who runs over my cane is gonna be a dead son of a bitch.'" *I saw an old man who was blind and shouted. That I saw. Saw.*

She was silent until he finished laughing. "You put me at a disadvantage," she said. "You have my number; I don't have yours."

"I didn't mean to put you at a disadvantage. I see what you're thinking. 'Don't call us; we'll call you.' I don't operate like that, Tañan. I just don't have a telephone, that's all, honest. Do you want me to get one? I'll get one if you like, and you'll be the only one I'll give the number to. You can call me any time of the day or night."

"The telephone isn't the problem. I do want to be married to you, but I don't want to be the wife. I think it's very important, Wittman, that we tell each other our ideas about marriage. There's a certain proposal that I want from a man. He'll love me and understand me so much, he'll say, 'Tañan, let me be your wife.' I got carried away with you, Wittman, and forgot to ask which one of us would be the wife."

"You want me to be your wife?!"

"I hadn't thought the proposal would come in that tone of voice, Wittman, but, yes, I do."

"Wait, wait. We take turns. I want a wife too sometimes, you know."

"Now you've proposed to me, but I haven't proposed to you. I don't want to be a woman who waits for proposals from men. One thing I've never done, I've never asked anyone to marry me. I want to do that someday. I'll get down on one knee and offer my hand and a diamond ring. When are we going to see each other again, Wittman? How about tomorrow night?"

"Tomorrow night I'm gathering a troupe to read-through the play. Will you come? Please come, Tañan. We'd see each other and work together every night for months, like marriage."

"Say 'I love you,'" said Tañan, who was better at loving than Wittman was. She was also tougher at using the phone.

"I love you."

"I love you too. Where do I meet you tomorrow night?"

He gave her the address, and they said good night agreeably.

Nevertheless, he next called Nanci, who was home alone, as the most beautiful girls are.

"Nanci? Wittman Ah Sing. Did you have a good time at the party? I saw you dancing." Did you notice I was with the blonde? Ask why I didn't ask you to dance with me.

"Yes. No. It was okay. I don't like big parties."

"Me neither. I don't think I'll go to them anymore." I ought to ask her to go out with me on a real date. Dinner with harp and violin music at the Garden Court of the Sheraton Palace. A gardenia for fifty cents at a flower stand. Dancing around the rain forest at the Tonga Room. Ah, the hell with it, let her see his ordinary self and love him for it. "Say, I didn't scare you with my poems, did I? I'm sorry if I scared you."

"No, you don't scare me, Wittman."

"You haven't been cast in anything yet, have you?"

"No."

"I've found a theater site, and we're opening on Hallowe'en. Will you read for me? After seeing those improvs? I mean, they were only improvs but."

"I liked those scenes, Wittman, and I don't mean to criticize but." While she criticized, he watched the street. A showgirl in a sequined cheongsahm yelled after somebody driving off in a white car, "You dumb fuck" or "You dumb cluck." Then she had to walk in her impossibly high heels.

"What's so funny?" asked Nanci.

"The street is wonderful tonight. You ought to be out in it." At a street phone, you can't run out of what to talk about; it comes to you in the on-swirling lifestream. "I get what you're saying about the play, Nanci. You're saying: Do better. Will you be in it nevertheless?" . . . *I entreat you, request you and desire you . . . meet me in the palace wood, a mile without the city, we shall be dogged with company. . . . I pray you, fail me not. We will meet; and there we may rehearse most obscenely and courageously. Take pains; be perfect: adieu.*

"I'd love to be in it. Bye-bye."

"Bye-bye."

With his last dimes, he called the stockroom of his ex–department store. After quite a while, somebody who must be living there picked up the receiver. "Hello?" said Wittman. "Is this the Yale Younger Poet I'm talking to? Is it you?"

"Who is this?"

"It's me, remember?" Not by my looks, and not by my race, nor by my deformities, I will yet identify myself. "I was moving bicycles."

"Yeah. What's up?"

"I got fired. I'm on Unemployment."

"That's too bad. Or, do you mind?"

"It's all right. I don't mind. That play I was telling you about? I found a venue. You said you'd think about it. If you come out of hiding, people wouldn't know it was you. You could wear make-up or a mask. You'd have a good time. It's not like poetry."

"Heh." He sounded like an old fut.

"You'd be helping me out. Do me a big favor. I need to integrate the cast. You have lots of parts to choose from. Let me tell you about them. You have time?"

"Yeh. That's what I have. Time."

With his last dimes, Wittman gave the ex-poet a catalog of heroes whom he looked like. "Choose: Lee Yoon, the Blue-eyed Tiger (green, blue, Chinese don't distinguish), is in charge of building a commune for a population of one hundred and eight outlaws, some with families. By architecture and city planning, he arranges space—where who sleeps with whom, communal kitchen, dining commons, outdoor cafés, plazas, no jailhouse—so that anarchists can live together. He fights Black Li, the most unruly commune member, to a draw.

"And/or you could play Liu Tang, the Red Hairy Barbarian. Excuse me, but we call your type barbarian. He was a big man with dark skin—you can use pancake—a broad face—broad faces are best for the stage—with a red birthmark, and black and yellow hair on his head and feet. We'll spray you with Streaks 'n Tips. He appears one morning asleep on the altar of a temple. The outlaws take him in to share their food and fate.

"And/or Tuan Ching Chu, the Gold-haired Dog, who wins from a Tartar prince a wonder horse named White Jade Lion That Shines in the Night.

"And/or Doctor Huang Pu Tuan, Uncle Purple Beard, a horse vet and a horse thief, the last outlaw to join the community. He's got blue-green eyes and blue-red beard and hair. To look like a barbarian does not mean you're ugly. These were not Caucasians; a Chinese can look like anything. A sign of a person being special—extra smart or brave or lucky or spiritual—was that he had something odd about his looks— eyebrows down to his knees, bumps or horns on his head, very skinny, very fat." Yes, in our theater, we will have regard for all kinds no matter they're disregarding us.

"You get to win the last battle in the play, okay? King Sun Ch'üan, who also had your looks, leads his navy west up the Yangtze, eight warships disguised as merchant ships with thirty thousand men hidden belowdecks. You ride your horse along the shore of that oceanic river, and capture lighthouses. You signal the ships, and you signal Cho Cho, your ally, who is head of a million men. He is sailing east, singing a poem about ravens. You meet at the enemy's walled capital. 'We're merchants, and we bear gifts,' you say. The gates open. You take the city. Gwan Goong flees. His brothers are missing, probably dead. The locals will not help him when he's losing. You post a reward of ten thousand gold pieces for his head, then you yourself capture him alive. 'How strange life is,' you muse to him. 'Gwan, my prisoner. I can't get over it. That we fought against one another, and now it has come to this. Why not be my brother instead? Come over to my side as ally and family.'

"'My blue-eyed boy,' says Gwan Goong. 'My red-whiskered rodent, I have my allies and family. I won't be brothers with a traitor.'

"'I could execute you as a traitor,' you say. 'I could kill you like any soldier. But I'm offering brotherhood, familyhood, a marriage for your daughter with my son. Our war chests could pay for one munificent wedding celebration.'

"'My tiger girl will never marry your son, a mongrel dog.'

"'You're the barbarian,' you say, 'for keeping the war going.'

"Gwan Goong's son, Gwan P'ing, interrupts, 'We don't surrender.' He draws his sword. 'We have not lost. I'll kill you, and we win.'

"Gwan Goong stands between his son and you. He has a way of standing so that the reality of his presence disperses illusions. His son lays down his sword. We have lost the war.

"Gwan Goong at the age of sixty and his son were beheaded in the winter of 220 A.D., our time."

Before hanging up, Wittman got Yale Younger to agree to his dropping the script off, such as it was, soon to be completed by improv and workshop.

Everyone came—friends, and friends' friends, and family. Not because Wittman had charisma or leadership, and certainly not because of his standing in the community. Nor were they here to feel sorry and give charity, which one human being has to give another anyway if he or she is to stay Chinese. They came because what Boleslavsky said is true: "Acting is the life

of the human soul receiving its birth through art." Everyone
really does want to get into the act.

They were bawling one another out for long-time-no-see.
Those who weren't such talkers riffed the jungs, banjos, er-
hus, fiddles. Drummers were hitting the wooden whales—
knock-knocking, that is, dock-docking truths out of their
wide mouths. PoPo and Mr. Fong asked kung fu boys to carry
up trunks—lifetimes of wardrobe, which the actors unfurled
and unfolded. "Oh, remember? Remember?" Some remembered wearing these costumes, and some remembered seeing
them on stage or in a movie. Out of sleeves came lengths of
worn and torn ripplingwater inner sleeves like lines of magician's hankies. Too few pants, but Levis will go with anything.
Time, the wardrobe mistress. PoPo shook out an operatic
brocade, and here we are again—inside the cedarwood, sandalwood, camphorball, mothball atmosphere. Aunties were
crowning one another with headdresses. Peacock feathers
and silver eyeballs were waving around looking at one and all.
Somebody was growl-speaking from the depths of a dragon
head. Beautiful Nanci was tippy-toeing in fake bound-feet
shoes. The Goodwife Taña and Auntie Bessie and Auntie
Sophie were tappety-tapping "The Sidewalks of New York."
Pop was scuffle-shuffling in raggedy shoes. (Huck's Pap too
had done "play-acting at the palace.") So word-of-mouth had
reached even the bo daddy river, and Zeppelin's battery was
well enough to bring a truckload of uncles. Mom and Pop
together in the same room. Archenemies running into one another. PoPo on the arm of her new old man walked past Pop—
and slapped her ass at him, one of her Japanese gestures. She
sashayed up to Ruby Long Legs, and said, "We're cutting you
out of our wills. The money will go to Wit Man, and he can
build a theater if he wants. Nada for you." The old fut (who is
our president after all, Mr. Grand Opening Ah Sing) brought
the rest of the tribal council, who voted okay. And there's the
cannery lady with her prom gloves on. She and fellow workers
and fellow unemployed artists were catching up on news of
one another's between-gig gigs. The program notes will be interesting for the bios of caterers, furniture movers, stevedores,
housesitters, lifeguards. After laboring all day, they come here
to work on the impossible. Our most famous Hollywood

movie star and tree trimmer, the one who's had an Oscar nom-
ination—oh, we're all available—was telling about his chain-
saw that jumped loose and missed his jugular vein by a graze.
So close, we might have lost him. Judy Louis was dressed for
fiesta, and setting out refreshments. She looked nothing like
a boar. Oh, everyone. Yale Younger—with a Barbie from the
Mattel Industrial Show! A Miss Chinatown who got too good
for Auntie Mabel's revue was saying to Charles Bogard Shaw,
"Yes, that was me on 'Hawaiian Eye.' I didn't tell anyone
to watch for me because they made me wear a Suzie Wong
dress. So shame." Most people brought as costumes and props
Chinesy things they happened to have around the house, such
as nightgown kimono, wedding kimono and obi, dragoned
jackets that they sell to G.I.s in Korea, yarmulkes, borlas, a
samurai grandfather's armor and swords that had been buried under the house and dug up to give to a sansei on his
twentieth birthday. A backscratcher from a Singapore sling, a
paper umbrella from an aloha mai tai, a Buddha bottle with
head that unscrews—make something of it. Use it. From these
chicken scraps and dog scraps, learn what a Chinese-American
is made up of. Yes, the music boat has sailed into San Francisco
Bay, and the boatman is reunited with his troupe. Write the
play ahead of them to include everyone and everything.

Wittman pounded a drum for order. Standing in front of
the chalkboard, he welcomed the players, and thanked them
for embarking tonight on an enormous loud play that will
awake our audience, bring it back. For a century, every night
somewhere in America, we had had a show. But our theater
went dark. Something happened ten years ago, I don't know
what, but. We'll cook and blast again. We have so much story,
if we can't tell it entirely on the first night, we continue on the
second night, the third, a week if we have to. He handed out
Xeroxes of the script that had lots of holes for ad lib and actors'
gifts. Gwan Goong, standing on the mantelpiece, was using
his powers over illusions to sway the house to theater—

Crash! Through the door came a grand entrance—Lance
and a kung fu gang. "That's him, there." Lance was siccing
their champion on Wittman. The champ kicked over the jack-
straw pile of weapons, and walked at him while rolling up his
sleeves. "I hit strong kung fu. My kung fu win." The force

of his voice blew slam-bang at the listener. They don't "do" kung fu or "play" it. They "hit" it. A tiger was flaming on his forearm, and a dragon was flaring on his other forearm, branded on, according to the movies. At the graduation test, he had lifted a five-hundred-pound red-hot iron cauldron by hugging it to himself. Lick-on tattoos, thought Wittman, body paint. "You're welcome to a script, Siew Loong," he said, showing the guy that he can read his jock jacket—the Little Dragon. Me too, born in a year of the dragon, but I don't advertise Wittman Dragon, nor would I call myself Little. "Your gwoon, help yourselves to scripts too. Do they read? Do they take direction? Don't I recognize you from parades? You do dragon dance, huh?" Yes, he was the dancer at the head of the dragon, who lifts the head with those branded arms, and dances beneath its beard.

Siew Loong pushed the script aside, and stuck out his pinky and said, "See this finger? I can kill with this finger. I be careful." "He's restraining himself," explained Lance. "You be careful too, Wittman. He's got the touch that kills. He knows places on the body that all he has to do is touch, and you die on a specific date years hence. He'll have an alibi of being nowhere near the death scene. Watch out, he's getting into position for the vibrating palm. It can wreck the flow of blood and air."

"Oh, Jesus, the poor guy," said Wittman. "You shouldn't let oppression do that to you, Siew Loong. I understand. You walk around lonely among the tall and racially prejudiced, and you start getting crazy ideas. A foreign-exchange student, lonely on campus, no dates, no money for round-trip tickets during vacations, staying by yourself in the empty dorms, no maid service, nobody to talk to. You start thinking, they better not fuck with me, I'm just keeping myself from touch-killing them with this mighty finger."

There was a turn of the hand somehow that Wittman didn't see what hit him, but suddenly he was coming to. What do you know, you really do see stars. And, oh no, his mother has climbed into the ring, holding his head. "Are you alive, biby?"

"I'm all right, Ma," he said, getting to his feet. Eyewitnesses were saying it must have been a force of directed energy. No punch had been thrown; none landed. The champ had been gesturing, and some chi got loose. Ruby Long Legs stuck a long leg out to trip Siew Loong, but he stepped over it. Some of us must be born doves; Wittman had no instinct to hit back. He was glad to learn that his pacifism went deep.

Siew Loong said, "I have a script here. You help me put on one show?"

"You're bound to do it, Wittman," said Lance. Mrs. Lance was handing out copies. It was only a page long, let him have his say.

The Little Dragon stood where Wittman had been standing, his gang leaning against the walls; they do the gang swagger standing still. F.O.B.s run in a gang, no cool American independence. Their leader talked-story like so: "A kung fu monk walks into town in old California. He thinks, this be one ghost town. The long long main street is too quiet because the citizens are chickenshit that a gang of bad guys are coming to showdown. They see the monk has no gun, so they haw him for being chinaman. They pull his short pigtail, which he grew for to disguise himself." Siew Loong pulled out a whip-cord—no, it's a queue—and stuck it to his head. "He is far far away from Shaolin, Hunan, where monks invented kung fu to be strong in body because Buddhism heavy to carry. You understand? How did he come west to here? Okay, back-flash: The monk as a kidboy bang-bang on the back gate of the Shaolin temple, and waits and waits. A teacher opens the gate, but there is an inside gate, and another inside gate inside the inside gate. At each back gate, he sees no-good students kicked out or run away. At last, he gets inside the gwoon. Don't say 'dojo,' Japanese. Say 'gwoon.' He studies hard years. Training is allthesame hell. Arrows and spears shoot out of walls. Stones and axes fall down. Eagle stars—they look like cutting wheels that cut up pizzapie—whiz-shoot at his eyes. The skeletons are the bones of students who failed tests." Wittman imagined Billy Batson going down the hallway between the statues of virtues and vices, and reaching Shazam on his throne, who gave him the holy-moly herb and the word that changes him into Captain Marvel. "The monk graduates high. And makes kung fu revolution to kick invaders and opium out of China. One night at the international ball thrown by Empress Suzie—"

"Kiai!" The kung fu jocks came off the walls and swung

into action, chop-socking and barefoot-kicking, and swinging from doorways right side up and upside down. They fought through the crowd, flexing feet, stretching spines, levitating, bilocating, radiating colors, screaming, "Kiai!" They played the good guys, and they played the enemy. Their eyes bulged round and red and saw through darkness. A fast finger plucked out an eyeball, and no evidence of it remained but a coin—a quarter—in the hand. They cracked you up; you could die laughing. A bad guy laughed to death. They attacked a fort, represented by the tall table that had had fruit on it. "Kiai!" They conquered it with their dexterous feet.

Suddenly, the Little Dragon did the most amazing thing. He sucked in his cheeks and puckered his lips into a tight 8. He knelt and concentrated himself into a ball, from which his hands were flapping—two blurs at his shoulders. He did fly up onto the table. A buzzing came from him, from his mouth or from the whir of wings. Those tiny thalidomide wings flew him up. He landed in a crouch, and looked at everyone with inhuman eyes. It was the weirdest, most foreign thing an American audience will ever see; that man changed into a bee.

The boxers escape-exited—they had the power to escape anything. They held their hands in front of their chests like paws, and walked sideways heel-and-toe out the front door, their spinal tails whipping. They came back inside to wild applause. Chop-socky flix kix and lix tickle box office. They took bows, all dozen or twenty boxer jox dressed in Hong Kong Pop Art t-shirts. On each chest was an egghead of Gwan Goong's red face with hood-eyes, like the Hawkman, or Chang Fei's face, which was a blue-and-black ovoid like the Atom's; Cho Cho looked like black Dr. Midnight. The gang had given one another those home haircuts, every one with hair that stuck up in black shocks; the chi energy they fool around with does that to hair.

Squatting on the table, Siew Loong continued talking from his outline or treatment: "Kung fu—hit fair, hit square and courageous. Get you ass near to opponent. Hit him with bare hand. Your own fingers de-eyeball him. But. The enemy—Germans, Austrians, Italians, French, Russians, British, mostly Japanese, mostly Americans—no-fair fight with tanks and gunboats. Us against the world."

He got off the table and stepped to one side, letting Lance, good at English, have the floor to do elegy. "Those on the side of the animals and the wind should have won. Tigers, crabs, white cranes, eagles, monkeys, bees—'Kiai!' the fighting cry of cats and of birds—hands and hair moving with the wind, our team blew toward the cannons, which blasted them to pieces. Bare hands, bare feet, the weapons of poor people—bare human bodies lost against machines. Why hadn't it worked? Right politics ought to make the body bulletproof. They had practiced on blocks of wood and ice, bricks and tiles, materials out of which forts and castles are made. Had the masters cheated their students by firing blanks at them? Are monkey style and white-crane style and wu good for nothing but morning calisthenics? The victorious martial arts are fighter jets and bombs. Clip a coupon and get the secret of the East: A black belt is only good for holding up pants."

"So," continued Siew Loong, "the Shaolin monk crosses the ocean to America to raise money for guns. He leads the townspeople to fight the gang of bad guys, and he has victory, okay. He travels on to the next town, New York, Hawai'i. American ladies wave hankie after him, and hold hankie to eyes and in teeth. He has many adventures, suitable for t.v. series. He goes to university, and studies science." Using the tail end of his queue as a compass, he drew a perfect circle on the chalkboard. "He gets M.D. He works restaurants, cook and dishwasher. He gives speeches for revolution. He makes parades and flagsful of money. He dances tai chi among sick people in hospital and cures an epidemic. When he moves, the air changes, and sick be well. He meets Two-Gun Cohen, faithful Jewish Canadian sidekick and bodyguard. They go back to China and win revolution this time. You see me before? You see Hong Kong movies, you see me before. I was ming sing—bright star—in Hong Kong, but I have a dream: I go Haw-lee-woot. I bought one Z card, and I trampsteamer out to Little Mexico, and jumpship in the Bay, Fisherman's Wharf. I been all over this land ball"—"ball" as in "pompon." "All over this pompon of Earth, I took this script. To Warner Brothers and A.B.C., I said, 'I be a Hong Kong ming sing. But I like be one Haw-lee-woot ming sing. Have I got a great idea for you—an eastern western—*Kung Fu*. Every week I be Shaolin monk, and have another eastern-western adventure.' But. They said No. They said Chinese man has no Star Quality. The hell with them. Good for me. I did not let Haw-lee-woot change me into the dung dung dung dung dung with the little pigtail in back." His hand slice-whacked off the queue, which a free-dom-fighter grandfather had cut off, and his lady saved. "The hell with them. I act you theater; you act me theater." His fist beat-beat on his hand, then beat-beat on his heart.

Yes, hurry—do the play now or else the generation of actors that talk like that go unheard. "See the players well bestowed. Do you hear, let them be well used; for they are the abstract and brief chronicle of the time." That chi charge that had come off of him was a blast of actor's energy. With his presence—his Star Quality—we could have our first Chinese-American male sex symbol. All he's after is an act or two in a play that will go on for sixty acts lasting forever. Give it to him.

"Okay," said Wittman. "I act you theater; you act me theater. Only one thing but. You're going to stay F.O.B. as long as you hear and say 'Revolution,' and be thinking 1911, 1949. Forget Tobacco Shit War and Kung Fu War. Seventeen seventy-six, Siew Loong, July 4—our Revolution. We allthes-ame Americans, you sabe? Get it?"

Shut up, Wittman. On with the show already. As promised, Lance read Liu Pei, and Charles Bogard Shaw read Chang Fei, he himself Gwan Goong as before, and Yale Younger as Sun Ch'üan. He asked Siew Loong to read Cho Cho, and Step-Grandfather Fong to read K'ung Ming. The part about the death of the Chinese kings—the old country, gone—went like this:

Gwan Goong, one of those people who has to tell his dreams at breakfast, tells his last dream: "A black boar or a black bull charged into my tent, and bit my leg. I leapt out of bed and took up my dagger, but I woke up stabbing the tent."

"It's only a dream," says a soldier. "A dragon floated through your tent last night." Another of his men tries to read his character: "It means that you're alert, and you face difficult problems head on." Others think dreams are omens: "You're going to be awarded a large medal with an animal crest on it. You'll win the tiger-head breastplate." "You're not going to be killed in battle."

Gwan rubs his leg. "It still hurts. I'm awake, and the pain is still there. I often have aches and pains now. I'm getting old. Sixty this year."

Sure enough, their every interpretation turns out true. He isn't killed in battle. Sun Ch'üan captures him, and executes him. To banish Death, Sun piles up pyramids of grapefruit, oranges, tangerines; he steams flocks of chickens and roasts herds of pigs. Surrounded by altars of food, he wraps up Gwan's head, and sends it to Cho Cho with this message: "I want to join you against his brothers. I pledge you my kingdom."

Cho Cho silently looks at Gwan's head. Then out of a piece of wood, he carves a body for the head. He dresses it in the brocades which Gwan had refused as gifts. (He had accepted one gift—the horse Red Rabbit.) Branches of hands and feet stick out from the stubby trunk. Gwan looks to be an ogrish, trollish chunk, which makes perspective crazy. Out of his big head the once-beautiful hair frizzes like lightning. Pinpointy dots stare out of goggle eyes.

Cho Cho talks to his lifelong enemy: "You've been well, I trust, General, since we parted?" Which were the very words that Gwan had said to him after besting him in combat.

And the Gwan Goong thing—like the votive statue over there—hears Cho Cho. Its eyes roll, and it opens its black mouth as if about to speak. Cho Cho faints in a fit of terror.

He moves to a clean new house, but a tree that is hundreds of years old bleeds on him—the branches hang over and drip—and a voice comes out of it: "I come to take your life." And at midnight, into his lighted bedroom walks Lady Fu, a queen he murdered long ago. "You," she says. "Y-o-o-ou. Y-o-o-ou." (Taña with her pale hair hanging did that very well.) She calls, "Children. Oh, chi-i-ildren." Two boys come trailing. The ghosts follow one another through the wall. There's a tearing sound, and that section of the house breaks off.

Night after night, voices howl. Those of us who can hear them will perform them for those who don't have the ear for them. The howls—weeping, groaning—come from wars and hungry children. Some of us can hear the actual sounds no matter how far away. Cho Cho thinks they are the voices of people he's killed. "For thirty years, I've ridden across the empire doing battle against heroes. I have only two equals left to fight. But my health is gone." He orders seventy-two decoy tombs, appoints his son emperor, and dies at the age of sixty-six.

Gwan visits Liu Pei. At the sight of the cloud-soul, Liu Pei knows that his brother is dead. Gwan's voice says, "I beg you raise an army. Avenge me." "I am getting old," says Liu Pei, "and I have spent my life at war." He sings, "I Have Grown Old Waging War."

The brothers do not reach death on the same day. Trying to fulfill another part of their vow, Liu Pei declares the three kingdoms united, and himself the emperor. Chang Fei kneels to him, and says, "You've achieved our cause, emperor now. Avenge our brother." Against the advice of their spiritual and military guru, they attack Sun Ch'üan.

Through the nights, Chang Fei drinks too much, promising that in the morning he will be leading the troops as usual. "Or else tie me to a tree, give me a flogging, and have me beheaded." He sleeps with his eyes open, but does not see two men steal into his tent. They are men he had flogged with fifty lashes apiece. They stab him to death at the age of fifty-five, and cut off his head, which they take to Sun Ch'üan.

Sun Ch'üan receives that head, and sends it to Liu Pei. The messengers try to assassinate Liu Pei as they hand it to him. But he chops off their heads, and sends those two heads back. (Hollywood, do not stick pigtails on any of these heads— they were free men, who lived before the Manchus. Set a long table with a row of heads, like the banquet scene in *Titus Andronicus*.) Liu Pei fights on alone, wearing white armor and flying white flags. His banners in the sun whiten the land for seven hundred leagues.

Sun receives his assassin-messengers' heads. With heads on his mind, he leads his army onto the battlefield. Galloping out of the smoke and dust comes Red Rabbit. On his back sits a headless horseman, who wields a blue-dragon sword. The voice of Gwan says, "Give me back my head."

That night in his throne room, Sun hears that voice come from one of his men, "My blue-eyed boy. My red-whiskered rodent, have you forgotten me?" The man walks up the steps to the throne, knocks Sun off, and himself sits on it. Gwan no longer looks like a troll or a cloud-soul. His eyebrows and the creases beside his mouth are vertical black lines; his eyes and face are blood red—War incorporated. He speaks out of the earthly body he's using: "So I crisscrossed the empire for forty years, and fell into your trap. You have me with you, then. I failed to taste your flesh in life; I shall give you no peace in death."

Sun leads his army up the Yangtze, setting fire to everything. The trees are torches from which flames jump back and forth. Curtains of flame hang and blow. Liu Pei, running from the heat, enters a grove of woods, which break into fire. Fire chases him to the river, but its banks are burning. Chang's son leads him through forests of torches up a hill. He sees everywhere below him—fire, which has left the country barren of trees to this day. And then Sun's army shoots flaming arrows up the hill. Gwan's son finds a way down it, and Liu escapes.

In hiding, badly burned, he mourns his brothers. Spots appear in front of his eyes, and he blacks out. On a still night, a draft blows against him. He sees two figures in the candlelight. "I thought I dismissed you," he says to servants. He looks again. "Then you are still alive."

Gwan Goong, who has a more normal shape now, says, "We are ghosts, not men. The time is not far off when we shall be together again."

"We will the three of us all go home," says Liu Pei.

O home-returning powers, where might home be? How to find it and dwell there?

In the morning, Liu calls for K'ung Ming. "I am dying," he says, "and my children are not wise enough to rule. You be emperor after me." The wizard of the wind knocks his forehead on the ground until blood runs. Liu tells his sons to serve the new ruler, and dies in 223 A.D.

This was not the end, only the end of a night's performance. Just because they all die, it isn't the end. Gwan's grandchildren were gathered to find out: Then what? Gwan Goong has the ability to travel anywhere, crossing back and forth the River of Stars to visit his brothers and his enemies. An ocean-going ship will cross the stage behind a scrim of time, and he will be on it. Gwan Goong on Angel Island. Gwan Goong on Ellis Island.

The night was growing late, yet people who had to go to

work graveyard or in the morning were taking up lines of a play that the savage world beyond the black windows didn't know or care about. Look at their heads bowed over words. The oldest ladies have the blackest hair. Too many older women—a chorus line of beautiful ladies—without men friends. If only we could match them up with the kung fu boys. Everybody should leave with somebody—a bad boy placing his jacket on the shoulders of a Flora Dora girl, and a stage kiss becoming a real kiss.

At the inconclusive ending of this first rehearsal, Wittman tried out on the crowd—actors make the best audience—an intermezzo (that he had practiced and set in front of the mirror). He took both parts.

Ah Monkey is bragging to Tripitaka, "I crashed the party in the sky, and ate up the food. I've been cooked in the pot on the moon. I'm a chase-master, and catch arrows in my teeth. I climb skyscrapers. I bet you I can polevault over those clouds."

Wittman turned facing where he'd been standing, and said in a different voice, "I bet that you can't clear this hand." Tripitaka holds an open hand at waist level.

The monkey laughs, opening wide his big mouth and showing his big teeth. "It's a bet." His pole elongates between his hands, and shoots up into the air, his eyes following its enormous growth. "Watch. At the height of my parabolic jump, you won't be able to see me. Watch now. Watch." He rocks heel-and-toe, his tail and nose twitching. "I'm off!" He polevaults into the sky. Clouds go by. The moon and sun and stars go by. He arrives on a mass of pink-and-white ether and meteorite dust. If this were a decent theater, he would be up in the catwalk. "Ha," he breathes, waving his tail like a flag. "Look at me. Nothing to it. I can do anything. Higher than his hand, ha!" He strolls among clouds of many levels and shapes. "These must be the white columns that hold up the sky. I'm going to leave proof that I've been here." At the tall middle pillar, he pulls out one of his hairs. "Presto be-e-e-en change-o!" The hair becomes a pen wet with ink. He writes his graffito: "The Greatest Wisest Man wuz here." He saunters over to the thickest pillar, turns his back to the audience, unzips, and takes a piss. He returns his pen to his hair, and his penis to his pants, and jumps down off the cloud. "I jumped clear of your hand and your head and of Earth," he brags, "all the way to the top of the sky."

"Fool ape," says Tripitaka. "You never left my hand." He holds up his hand to the monkey's nose, and to the noses of the audience, who said, "Pee-yew." Wittman dangled his hand out there like it was somebody else's, looked at it, sniffed it, "Pee-yew! Monkey piss." Then Tripitaka sticks up his middle finger. "What's this?" He studies that middle finger, holds it to his eyes for a close look-see. "Why, there's writing on my middle finger. 'The Greatest Wisest Man wuz here.'" With thumb and finger, he picks up the monkey, and lowers him into his other hand. "You never left my hand." And to the audience, "Do you see the tiny monkey on my hand? See? See? A teenyweeny gorilla? See his little hat with the feathers? See his cute tail?" Like King Kong with Fay Wray in his hand, but vice versa. At the table where the bee had sat, he suddenly smashes his hand down. Bang! The audience jumped, some let out a scream, and laughed. "A mountain holds Ah Monkey imprisoned for five hundred years." (James Dean covers with his red windbreaker the toy monkey broken in the gutter.)

Wittman handed out a schedule of rehearsals to the actors going out the door. They would work scene by scene, then run-throughs, then open on Hallowe'en. Promise. We will meet again in the Pear Garden. They walked out wearing the shoes that will give them a way of going about in character.

But people didn't say Good night right off. They had to say, "Good but." "Good but you left out our millionaires. What about our millionaires?" "Good but bad impression of us. We not be uncivilized, we not be monkeys. We got inventors. We got scientists." Oh, stop looking over your shoulders, why don't you? And best friend Lance said, "Good but can a cannibal be capable of tragedy?" "What about an omnivore?" said Mrs. Lance. Wittman didn't argue with wise guys, said Thank you for the constructive criticism.

At least nobody quit. The kung fu gang whose practice room this was did not take away the use of the hall.

Nanci was talking to one of the agent aunties. Without looking, he could sense the whereabouts of loveliness. Her atmosphere included him. She was leaving slowly, awaiting him?

If he were a different type, and she were a different type, he could help her on with her coat, while saying in her ear, "I've missed you. I love you. I want you. Come with me." He felt her tug toward the door. He stood in the path of the doe stepping into the night forest. "You aren't going out there by yourself, are you? Do you have a ride?"

"We'll give you a ride. We have a car." It was Taña, his wife, with not a guile in voice or face.

"I live on Red Rock Hill now. Near the steps. It won't be out of your way? Yes, thank you all."

Everybody pulled his or her coat collar up. The fog and their cigarette smoke entwined in the San Francisco night. Out with two beautiful women, one on either side, if only a couple arrangement had not been made already. Wittman, of course, had to talk too much. "I love it when good actors come on stage, meet, interact and go off. In oceans and seas of time and space, amidst all the creatures and species, this one and that one find one another for a while of eternity on the same schedule and life-route as oneself. Nanci, you're an actress who can deliver a Hello that makes us see the miracle of meeting, and a Goodbye that echoes all the partings and dyings." Now, Nanci could say, "It's your wonderful play that does all that for an actress."

"I like the play," Taña said.

"Me too," said Nanci, giving him the opportunity to look at her. Say some more. Say, "I also like you."

"I also like you," said Taña, and put her arm through his.

They unzipped her pretty little car. Taña got in on the driver's side. Wittman jumped into the air and landed in the space behind the seats. Taña reached over and opened the door for Nanci. Well, what did you expect? To ride through the suggestive City with her in his lap, his legs entangling with her legs? A hand at her waist curve? Scrunched amidst her and the gear shift? His back to the driver? As it was, he sat in the back with his head behind her head, and his feet sticking out the driver's side. Black hair blew in his eyes and his mouth. One arm was like casual along the top of her door. The other arm was pinned. He can't whisper into her ear, the wind blowing voices away. The Great Monkey would have given the neck in front of him a dracula bite. Dracula-bite them both. "Turn

here," she pointed, and jabbed him in the face with her elbow.
She was not aware, then, of the air between them, and the
exact boundaries between their bodies? She was sitting sort of
upright. If she would fit herself better into her bucket seat, and
back up against him, they could feel their connection through
it. Come to think of it, he's not feeling it much. Does this
mean that it's over? That would be okay, for it to be over. Let
it be over. Let me out of love. *How he thought then of the trou-*
badours who feared nothing more than being answered. She was
yelling the directions to where she lived, the Divisadero, near
Ashbury, Vulcan Street, you know where the planet streets
are, Mars, Saturn? The city lights streamed over the low car,
and they dropped her off at her planet. Good night. . . . *be-*
cause I never held you close, I hold you forever.

In all scrupulosity, he can't go home with Taña. She dropped
him off. He spent the rest of the night looking for the plot of
our ever-branching lives. A job can't be the plot of life, and not
a soapy love-marriage-divorce—and hell no, not Viet Nam.
To entertain and educate the solitaries that make up a community, the play will be a combination revue-lecture. You're
invited.

8
Bones and Jones

O N HALLOWE'EN, the red marble head of Sun Yat Sen breaks off, and kremlin gremlins fly out of the aluminum body and spook the City. His red marble hands move. Kids who once hid and waited in Portsmouth Square to be scared by this miracle had grown up. This year, these adults put on costumes again, and go-out clothes and fake and safe-deposit jewels, and went to an opening night of their own making. More maskers were at large than ever. They were trick-or-treating the Benevolent Association house. Jaywalking with children by the hand, they followed a boom-booming that pounded and sounded like Come come come until they arrived at the sight of the drummers. Two men and a woman banged the taikos with all the might of their workers' arms. The tails of their sweatband-fillets jumped and flipflapped. A barker with pants rolled up over peasant legs ran barefoot up and down the sidewalk, calling friends by name and you and you while plinkplunking on his porcelain drum. Welcome. Welcome. The crowd walked through flowers—arrays of carnations and aisles of chrysanthemums sashed with red ribbons and calligraphy—and became audience.

A call—la-a-a-a!—out of the dark grew nearer with each of four soundings. The Talking Chief crosses the white rainbow. His eagle feathers flare—sun up—and he rains the audience with water from the Atlantic and the Pacific. Overhead flies Garuda, whose wings like a wheel we were wearing on our batik clothes, which Peace Corps volunteers were sending home from Southeast Asia. Ranga of the long fangs, long hair, long tits, shakes her scythe-like fingernails at a young man, and makes him arm-wrestle himself, his right hand trying to stab his bare chest, his left hand wrist-twisting his knife hand. Suddenly, he breaks from that Damballah trance and does the bent-knee hula—his thighs clapping, his hands rising from between his legs and up to the sky in enormous praise of the volcano goddess. Hanuman, the white monkey, swings in and out the windows. The black-and-white Abba-Zabba man—the one with the clown-white skull-white face and the black tur- tleneck—giving away Abba-Zabbas was Antonin Artaud, who had had to evoke genies of a crueler theater. Caliban is raging at not seeing his face in the mirror. Good red Gwan Goong is rid- ing good Red Rabbit again, and has led eight genies through the streets to here. A sunseen man opens his water gourd that cools water as the sun gets hotter; the audience looks inside, and sees—everything, the Earth, everything. At any moment, one or another of these genie of the theater may interfere in a gambling scene and change the luck, or whisper answers to a test. And chant, "May he live" or "May he die." The Talking Chief will cast his yo-yo, and hunt up children, twins, soldiers.

Across the stage, which was the size of Tripitaka's hand, forward-rolled acrobatic twins, tied together—four heels over two heads that did not gravity-drop katonk. They backflipped off. And re-entered—verbal twins in green velveteen con- nected suits. Yale Younger and Lance Kamiyama as Chang and Eng, the Double Boys, pattering away in Carolina-Siamese. Chinkus and Pinkus.

"Sir Bones, how you feeling?"

"I feel like I'm being followed, Mr. Jones. The footsteps go where I go and stop where I stop. They don't seem to be getting any closer but. I'm paranoid."

"How do you do, Mr. Paranoid. I feel uneasy myself, you peeking at me sideways like that."

"I have an idea that would make us be more like the normal American person."

"What idea is that?"

"Let's change our name."

"What name would befit us?"

"Bunker. They like you in green velvet, and they like you being named after battles. Chang Bunker and Eng Bunker."

"I'm dubious."

"Ah, Mr. Dubious, the footsteps pursuing us come on fem- inine feet. You all see that belle give me the eye?"

"She's looking at me."

"Do you think she'll marry me?"

"She wants to marry me."

"You all think every beautiful gal wants to marry you."

"No, no. See that gal dancing with the Yankee officer? That's Miss Adelaide, who wants to marry me. Her sister, Miss Sally, wants to marry *you*. And finds me repulsive. And vice versa."

"Oh, such marvelous order in the universe. I'm beside myself with happiness. You'll introduce me, won't you?"

A tasteful scrim, a golden net, falls and a just-right pair of beautiful women hold out their arms and dance with him/them. Not the Virginia reel. It's sort of a square-dance waltz. You never saw such a sight in your life. Two men dancing with their wives, Mrs. Bunker and Mrs. Bunker, née Adelaide and Sally Yates. And these lovely white ladies of the wider American world don't spoil the brothers for the Chinese girls. Adet and Anor, Lin Yutang's daughters, accept a dance. As do the Eaton sisters, Edith and Winnifred, a.k.a. Sui Sin Fah (Narcissus) and Onoto Watanna of Hollywood and Broadway and Universal Studios and M-G-M. Not a loner woman among them, each and every one a sister. And more concurrence: the brothers dance with their colleagues, Millie and Christine, the Carolina Black Joined Twins.

Eng: I'd like to buy you from Mr. Barnum. You be my slave. I have thirty-one slaves. You won't be lonely.

Miss Millie: Why, no, sir. I won't be your slave. Mr. Barnum pays me an artiste's salary, the same as you. I'm a free woman.

Miss Christine: You are making her an indecent proposal, sir.

Chang: We shouldn't be seen together in society. *Re*jects shouldn't settle for *re*jects. We need to better ourselves. There's nothing as rejected as a Black woman but a yellow man.

Eng: Speak for yourself, sir. I for one am an uncommon and rare man. And Miss Christine and Miss Millie are uncommon and rare women.

Miss Narcissus, who writes for newspapers: Are you fraternal twins or identical? You certainly do look alike.

Chang: I am alike.

Miss Narcissus: Tell me about your meeting with President Lincoln.

Chang: He told me a joke. Something about an Illinois farmer with a yoke of oxen that won't pull together. He was making fun of me.

Eng: You're always taking things personally. You're too

sensitive. He was speaking metaphorically and politically. The punchline goes, "To make a more perfect union."

Miss Watanna: I'm so sorry for your sad life and persecution, and your loneliness. I sympathize.

Chang-Eng: Loneliness?

Miss Watanna: I'd advise a Japanese identity. Americans adore cherry blossoms and silk fans and tea ceremony and geisha girls and samurai and Mount Fuji and Madame Butterfly and sea waves and dainty vegetables such as a tempura of one watercress leaf. (Were this a movie, an extreme close-up: the Eaton sisters have blue eyes, which belie that the brown-eye gene is dominant. Their father was an English painter, and their mother was a Chinese tightrope dancer; such a miscegenation produces American children.)

Chang-Eng: Identity? (He are baffled.)

Eng: South Carolina, the rice capital of the world, also has cherry blossoms and butterflies, and women who are artful with fans and women with flower names. We have a seacoast and tea and watercress sandwiches, and our soldiers are aristocrats.

Miss Watanna: You've lost your identity.

Miss Narcissus: You're assimilated, Mr. Eng. And you too, Winnifred.

The sisters go away, and from across the ballroom comes a beautiful girl, Miss Sophia, played by Taña. She holds out her hands and clasps the outside hands of each twin. They are in a ring-around-the-rosy circle. In an English accent, Miss Sophia says, "Will you marry me, dear? I love you, Chang-Eng."

"No, thank you, Miss Sophia," says Chang.

"I can't marry you, Miss Sophia," says Eng.

"May I see you now and then, dearest?"

"No, Miss Sophia."

"May I write to you? Write poems to you? And mail them to you?"

"Yes, I'll read your poems."

"Goodbye, Chang-Eng dear."

"Goodbye, Miss Sophia dear."

Alone, Chang says to Eng, "I love her very much."

"Me too. I was in love with her."

"She had no discrimination. She had the capability for

impartial love. She will write democratic love poems. I'm sorry I can't marry her."

"So am I."

A stagehand in black spins the lottery drum that was once upon a time a Gold Rush cradle, and a voice calls out: "The United States Army wants you, Mr. Eng Bunker."

Eng: We've been drafted into the Union Army. They need men to tear up the North Carolina and Piedmont Railroad.

Chang: What you mean "we," white man? (As Tonto says to the Lone Ranger when they are surrounded by Indians.) As Confucius said, "You are you, and I am I." I'm not going to tear up any railroads, and I'm not freeing any slaves. I don't want to go to war.

Eng: Shall I make a plea of conscience?

Chang: You all ought to make a plea of the body. You all weren't constructed to be a soldier.

Eng: I am an able-bodied man. Twice as able-bodied as most. I have to think out a deep philosophy against war.

Chang: Point out that you have an attachment to a dove of peace.

Eng: I'm on your side. And a good thing too. If you were to join the Confederate Army, I don't see that we have enough room to shoot long rifles at each other. Does a conscience have to be pure of self-interest? When I think about fighting against my own son and your own son, I get a limpness in my trigger finger, and an anchoring in of my heels.

Chang: Yes, I feel that too. That's our conscience all right, real and most concrete. Brother Eng, aren't you afraid of going to Salisbury Prison as a traitor and a coward?

Eng: Only one thing I'm scared of—myself.

Chang: Mr. Jones, you strike me as ornery. I drink to you, an ornery American man.

Eng feels the liquor too. And they do drunk shtick, slurring and weaving, and falling down, which gets a laff.

But the circus crowd wants more. "Let's have a look!" "Let's see! Let's see!" They rush the brothers and pull at the green velveteen to try to see and touch the ligament. A doctor gets between the twins, examines it, and says, "He is as human as the next American man." The brothers hit the doctor from either side. Chang chases him, dragging Eng after him.

The lights throw bars of shadow across the stage; Chang is jailed for starting a riot. He yells at the audience through the bars, "We know damned well what you came for to see—the angle we're joined at, how we can have two sisters for wives and twenty-one Chinese-Carolinian children between us. You want to see if there's room for two, three bundling boards. You want to know if we feel jointly. You want to look at the hyphen. You want to look at it bare."

"My, you all are a violent man," says Eng. "How am I to make my plea of conscience?"

"Mr. Bones, your troubles give me a pain in the ass."

The brothers are let out of jail and out of the draft on technicalities. Only one of them is a rioter and only one a draftee, so what to do with the extra man but let him go?

But they cannot evade age and death. Chang dies. He does death throes, then hangs there dead with his pigtail fanning like a fishtail sweeping the floor. The world has been contemplating the horror of being attached to a corpse—the albatross tied to the sailor; Ripley's camel roaming the desert with the dead legionnaire tied to its saddle. The remaining brother pushes at the dead one, runs without getting anywhere, and says: *Now it was there. Now it grew out of me like a tumor, like a second head, and was so big. It was there like a huge, dead beast, that had once, when it was still alive, been my hand or my arm.* Eng dies too after several days and nights of sympathy and fright.

Then here come The Flying Lings! The Living Target! The Frame of Knives! The Chinese Coin and the Enchanted Straw! Experiments in Human Elasticity by the Boneless Boy! The Bowl of Water and the Charmed Sling! The World Record Number One Balancer of Eight (8) Stools on the Nose—Going for Nine (9) Tonight Only! The Magic Balls! Bird Calls and Animals of the Farm! The Revolving Oil Jar! The Most Ambidextrous Jugglers in the World! The First Chinese Woman in America! And off fly the Lings, Four Muscular Orientals, to Mystic, Connecticut.

So, several families of brothers are dead. Kingdoms rise and fall. World war again. Vaudeville time! The screen for changing costumes behind—black silk stockings and a red feather boa flung over it—fell with a crash-bang! It's Ruby Long Legs and the Flora Doras with all their clothes on. They ran out of their huddle and got into chorus-girl formation. They rolled their shoulders, winked over their high almost-Pilipina sleeves, wiggled their peplum asses. Ruffling the air with dusting powder and French perfumes, Auntie Dolly, Auntie Sadie, Auntie Bessie, Auntie Maydene, Auntie Lilah, Auntie Marleese, and Mom, all together now—knee kick, full kick, knee kick, full kick. "Can you do the cancan? I can do the cancan"—segueing into "There's a place in France where the ladies wear no pants." They gave us their backsides, and lifted their skirts. Each auntie was wearing undies with the flag of an ally on them. It's the Pants Dance of the Nations. The audience went wild for each auntie doing her national special. Clicking castanets over her head, Auntie Dolly with a rose between her teeth stamped her feet in tight circles, and flung that rose at her old man. "La cucaracha. La cucaracha." "King Georgie had a date. He stayed out very late. God save the King. Queen Lizzie paced the floor. King George came in at four. She met him at the door. God save the King." Skirts down and hands proper, they sang as regally as queens. Aunt Maydene, Miss Finlandia, sang, "Dear land of home, our hearts to thee are holden." "Yo-ho-HEAVE-ho-o!" The aunties bent their backs and pulled, a chorus line of Mother Courages. March march march, tappy toes, tappy toes, salute, salute. "From the halls of Montezuma to the shores of Tripoli." Aunt Bessie sang "Mae Ling Toy and her Chinee Boy"; she danced, wagging her head back and forth between pointer fingers pointing up and down. The merry widows—they *wore* merry widows—were yet breaking hearts at forty feet; and at five feet, which was how close the front row was, their kicking spike heels could knock your head off. The oldest stars in our firmament sky were radiating. The audience whistled for encore after encore, drawing the aunties out amongst them, where they sat on laps, rubbed bald heads, gazed into eyes, vamped "I'd like to get you on a slow boat to China all to myself alone." Ruby Long Legs parted her legs, and did the splits, sliding down all the way to the floor. Then everybody on her back—legs wide open making V for Victory.

As the pink feathers settled, here come the bathing beauties down the hanamichi thrust runway. The old-guy judges say, "Beauti-foo. Beauti-foo," when "foo" means "pants," and choose Miss Chinatown U.S.A.: the tallest girl with the tightest blackest curls and reddest lips, the roundest nose, the reddest apple cheeks in the whitest face, the plumpest cheongsahm.

Little girls in loose, fluttery cheongsahms bring Jade Snow Wong a dozen long-stem American Beauty roses, and orchid corsages for her mother and sister. Jade Snow is wearing an embroidered black satin coat with slits, but all you see through them is her pleated skirt. Youngest Sister Wong is sweet in peach-blossom silk, and their mother is dignified in a pale blue gown, everybody's hair marcelled. "It was almost like a wedding," says Jade Snow. She reads her essay about absenteeism in factories, which won first prize in a contest sponsored by the War Production Board's War Production Drive. This essay was sent to President Roosevelt, and you can read it in the *Congressional Record*. The prizes are a war bond and the christening of a liberty ship on a Sunday, and sending it to war. The loudspeakers play our crash-bang music. Jade Snow hits the ship with a bottle of champagne beribboned in red, white, and blue. "I christen thee the *William A. Jones*." Welders cut away the plates that hold the ship to the pier of the Marin County shipyards, where Jade Snow works. "Burn one!" "Burn two!" The maiden ship is free on the water and sails to war.

The Soong sisters and Anna Chennault, dressed in suits that the bride wears at her wedding reception, travel all over the country and give speeches. "Freedom," they say. "Liberty." Their accents were schooled Back East. They prove that the ladies-in-distress aren't bucktoof myopic pagans. Women not unlike Katharine Hepburn and Myrna Loy are burning the rice fields as they flee the invaders. (The invaders are the ones with the buckteeth and glasses.) These excellent dark women should have overcome dumb blondes forevermore. Women get their wish: War. Men, sexy in uniform, will fight and die for them.

All hell broke loose on the third night of this play, for which the audience kept growing. The public, including white strangers, came and made the show important. The theater went beyond cracking up family, friends and neighbors come to see one another be different from everyday. The take at the box office paid for the explosives for the climactic blowout.

The audience sat on the staircase and windowsills; there was no longer an aisle.

We are in a show palace on the frontier. We have come down out of the ice fields of the Sierras and the Rockies and the Yukon, and up from Death Valley. Three authentic crescent oil lamps were pulled up and down throughout the evening that seemed endless because time is a dragon that curls and smokes. Trappers, hunters, prospectors, scouts are spending their earnings to see fellow human beings. As still as animals, they suddenly shout because they haven't talked to anyone for a long time. They need to hear people, and to tune their voices again.

When the sun is farthest from the Earth, Lantern Festival lights up the five days of deepest winter. Curves of scaffolding form a white dragon; the white lanterns are its scales. Each holding a lantern, children file singing through the ice tunnels. Dragons are playing with flames englobed in ice—the pearl that is the universe or Earth. A thousand lanterns—phoenixes in paper cages—hang from the Blue Cloud Tower, the most famous restaurant ever, with over a hundred dining rooms. At crossroads, shopkeepers and householders build mountains of buns as in Marysville. But this is not Marysville. This is Tai Ming Fu, the Great Bright City, and to this City of Big Lights on the clear silver-and-gold night of the full moon will come the hundred and eight bandits. Or so warns the poem on the gate, scrolls of poetry unfurling on walls and posts. Sung Chiang, the Timely Rain, leader of the hundred and eight, has written a guarantee-poem giving fair warning that the bandits are about to attack. But the innocent shall not be harmed; the imprisoned shall be free. Teams of husband-and-wife knights enter the city from different routes. It's the Dwarf Tiger and the Tigress, played by Zeppelin and Ruby; the Vegetarian and the Night Ogress, played by Charles Bogard Shaw and Nanci Lee; the Dry Land Water Beast and Devil Face, played by Lance and Sunny Kamiyama; the Pursuing God of Death and the Lively Woman, played by Mr. Lincoln Fong and PoPo. They're wearing party clothes to account for glamour. They shop and eat until time to reveal themselves as the toughest fighters of all.

Dudes and schoolmarms from Back East, and picture brides

from Back East, and Frank Cane step out of the stagecoach. "Get back on that stage and keep riding if you know what's good for you." See that woman in a poke bonnet leading her workhorses? She's a runaway slave. She turns around; you see she has a Chinese face. That man walking here and there in a cangue—like locked in stocks that are not stuck into the ground—has committed so many crimes, ten-pound and twenty-five-pound iron weights have been added to his burden; the papers that list his penalties seal the joins and cover the wood. He's been collared. But on this holiday, kind people are making his cangue into a feasting table—roast duck and buns. Horses have brands on their butts, while men have them on their faces. You can read on cheeks and foreheads their places of exile, where they're supposed to be. The men with hanks of straw tied around their blades are swords-for-hire, walking up and down the marketplace. The clomp and stomp of boots on wooden sidewalks satisfy the ear, no shuffling and scuttling in slippers.

Friends and enemies find one another. Agon.

Into the dungeons Night Ogress Nanci carries paper flowers and paper butterflies, which hide brimstone and saltpeter, the ingredients for gunpowder. Her accomplices are the Forest Dragon and the Horned Dragon, who once knocked down a fir tree with his head. The jailers have gone out to celebrate, having put their poor relations in charge. "Where are my brothers?" asks the Ogress, taking her swords out of her belt. "I've come for my brothers. They were framed. It's time you let them out. Before I deal with you, I want to hear your idea of justice. Should you lock up the man who stole the tiger or the two innocent boys whom he stole it from?" "Let me think. I need to think," says the amateur jailer, backing away from her. He bumps into a prisoner, who bangs him over the head with his cangue. The Ogress fights the guards while the dragons free prisoners and set gunpowder. Outside, the Vegetable Gardener ties the jailhouse bars to his pommel. His horse pulls the wall down. The other Perfect Couples of the Battlefield open all the city gates, just as, amid fireworks, the Blue Cloud Tower blows up. At the sight of that flambeau, Miss Hu the Pure, played by Judy Louis, spurs her ash-grey horse. Twirling her red silk lasso overhead, she leads the main army of four thousand men and amazons into the city. Snow falls. A fire dragon and a snow dragon have come at once.

As in real life, things were happening all over the place. The audience looked left, right, up and down, in and about the round, everywhere, the flies, the wings, all the while hearing reports from off stage. Too much goings-on, they miss some, okay, like life.

Inside a grocery store, some bad Caucasians plant dope among the mayjing and the black-bean sauce, then call the cops. A lynch mob raids the store, where the grocers both work and live. They jerk the chinamen through the streets by their long hair. Ropes hang from lampposts and fire escapes. Nooses are lowered over heads. The accusation and sentence are read: To be hung by the neck until he dies for dealing opium, which debauches white girls for the slave trade. The kung fu gang leaps to the rescue. Everybody dukes it out. The opium war in the West. John Wayne rides into town, asking, "Where's the chinaman? Gotta see the chinaman about some opium." The police break up the riot, and arrest the grocers for assaulting officers. So Chinese-Americans founded the Joang Wah for the purpose of filing legal complaints with the City of New York against lynchings, illegal arrests, opium, slavery, and grocery-store licensing. A tong is not a crime syndicate and not a burial society. It is organization of community, for which Chinese-Americans have genius.

A storyman arrives on I Street, and unpacks a troupe of puppets, the tribe and clan that he carries with him. Pretty wife doll and courtesans and warrior girls and faeries. With puppets, you can bind their feet as tiny as you like, ladies' slippers on their feet, foxgloves on their hands. The troupe has a hundred bodies and a thousand switchable heads. The gambling house is in front; the hundred-seat theater is in back. The gamblers drink and play pai gow standing up, one boot on the railing, which has U's like stirrups, worn into it. Guns are at-ready in holsters. Motivated by human nature, the poker players sock one another across the tables, and crash through the wall. Puppets whack the live actors on their heads and in their faces. The set spins about; another life is going on on the reverse side. The bar mirror falls in a sleet of crashing reflections. Gamblers and cheaters swipe at one another's eyes with jagged bottles. Puppets lose their heads. Hand-puppets lose their insides, which change into fists. The puppet master, invisible black ninja, kicks ass. Wail. Bang.

The floor caves in, and those who don't fall in jump into the hole—gold dust has been raining down through the floor-boards for years.

Meanwhile, Rudyard Kipling (played by the Yale Younger Poet), the first white explorer to write an account of crossing America from west to east, sets foot in "the Chinese quar-ter of San Francisco, which is a ward of the city of Canton set down in the most eligible business-quarter of the place." He guides a tour group of ladies and gentlemen through our town. Look at how strange the tourists are, pale outsiders abroad in their own country. Sir Kipling gives them *American Notes*: "The Chinaman with his usual skill has possessed himself of good brick fireproof buildings and, following in-stinct, has packed each tenement with hundreds of souls, all living in filth and squalor not to be appreciated save by you in India." The poor tourists follow him down into a basement. "I wanted to know how deep in the earth the Pig-tail had taken root. I struck a house about four stories high full of celestial abominations, and began to burrow down. . . ." He descends a level below the cellar, and another one below that. He goes into what Frank Norris called the Third Circle of Evil. (The First Circle is the shops and restaurants; the Second Circle is the home life.) Three levels down, Kipling discovers that "a poker club had assembled and was in full swing. The Chinaman loves 'pokel,' and plays it with great skill, swearing like a cat when he loses. One of the company looked like a Eurasian, whence I argued that he was a Mexican—a supposition that later in-quiries confirmed. They were a picturesque set of fiends and polite, being too absorbed in their game to look at a stranger." A fate of the cards set the Eurasian Mexican (played by Mr. Leroy Sanchez of the Office of Human Development) and a chinaman against each other. "The latter shifted his place to put the table between himself and his opponent, and stretched a lean yellow hand towards the Mexican's winnings." A pis-tol shot bangs out. Smoke obscures the scene. Kipling and the Eurasian-Mexican hit the floor. The smoke clears. "The Chinaman was gripping the table with both hands and staring in front of him at an empty chair. The Mexican had gone, and a little whirl of smoke was floating near the roof. Still gripping the table, the Chinaman said: 'Ah!' in the tone that a man would use when, looking up from his work suddenly, he sees a well-known friend in the doorway. Then he coughed and fell over to his own right, and I saw that he had been shot in the stomach. I became aware that, save for two men leaning over the stricken one, the room was empty. It was possible that the Chinamen would mistake me for the Mexican—everything horrible seemed possible just then—and it was more than possible that the stairways would be closed while they were hunting for the murderer. The man on the floor coughed a sickening cough. I heard it as I fled, and one of his companions turned out the lamp. . . . I found the doorway, and my legs trembling under me, reached the protection of the clear cool light, the fog, and the rain. I dared not run, and for the life of me I could not walk. I must have effected a compromise, for I remember the light of a street lamp showed the shadow of one half skipping—caracoling along the pavements in what seemed to be an ecstasy of suppressed happiness. But it was fear—deadly fear. Fear compounded of past knowledge of the Oriental—only other white man—available witness—three stories underground—and the cough of the Chinaman now some forty feet under my clattering boot-heels. Not for anything would I have informed the police, because I firmly believed that the Mexican had been dealt with somewhere down there on the third floor long ere I had reached the air; and, moreover, once clear of the place, I could not for the life of me tell where it was. My ill-considered flight brought me out somewhere a mile distant from the hotel; and the clank of the lift that bore me to a bed six stories above ground was music in my ears. Wherefore I would impress it upon you who follow after, do not knock about the Chinese quarters at night and alone. You may stumble across a picturesque piece of human nature that will unsteady your nerves for half a day."

You would think that that Chinese guy had killed somebody instead of having gotten killed himself. Rudyard Kipling exits, chased off by cherry bombs and cymbal clangs. Nobel Prize winner. No wonder the Yale Younger Poet was depressed in spite of honors.

At the Fook Tai Lottery Co., Liang Kai Hee, an actor and a gambling man, has broken the bank. Everybody stops fighting as they recount in wonder how he did it, which is a legend to this day. He bought a ticket for fifty cents, and picked six numbers, like a hexagram out of the Ching, and won ten dollars. He put those ten dollars on the same six numbers and won the jackpot—ten thousand dollars. The stagecoach with wheels spinning like coins and its belly sagging with the gold and silver weight of the fortune rolls to him. Black and white boys are chanting, "Ching chong chinaman sitting on a fence, trying to make a dollar out of fifty cents," caterwauling the vowels and honking the "n"s, slurring us. The kung fu guys chase them, and they run like the cowards they are.

Firecrackers boomed in the chimney. A mother-and-sons bomb ricocheted crazily inside a garbage can—a big mother bang detonating and creating seventy-five scatter bombs that bounced about for a long time. An M-80 barrel bomb went off. Night mirages filled the windows, reflecting and magnifying—a city at war and carnival. All aflare and so bright that we understand: Why we go to war is to make explosions and lights, which are more beautiful than anything.

At the climactic free-for-all—everybody fights everybody everywhere at once. The hundred and eight bandits and their enemies (played by twenty-five actors) knock one another in and out all entrances and exits, sword-fighting up and down the stairs and out amongst the audience, take that and *that*, kicking the mandarin-duck kick, swinging the jeweled-ring swing, drums and cymbals backing up the punches. The intellectuals grasp their five-pronged pen holders, and make of their hands claw-fists. Everybody chased one another outside and battled on 22nd Avenue among the cars. Audience hung out of window. Ten thousand San Franciscans, armed with knives and shouting, "Death to capitalists," attack the railroad office, and set fire to Chinatown. Four thousand Sacramento's Order of Caucasians sing a scab song, "Ching chong chinaman sitting on the fence." Bullets and arrows zing from the false fronts of the sharpshooter roofs. Gunslingers and archers jump from balconies into the saddle. Rain barrels explode. Puppets pummel and cudgel and wack-wack. Tenderfoot drinkers of lemonade and sarsaparilla and milk bust out through swinging

doors and over hitching posts into water troughs and rain barrels and Ali Baba wine jars. Through the smoke, a jugger-
naut, an iron roller with spikes, thunders across a hollow floor.
The audience got to its feet in participation. The sheriff will
surely come soon to stop the show with a cease-and-desist-
disturbing-the-peace order. Jail us for performing without a
permit, like our brave theatrical ancestors, who were violators
of zoning ordinances; they put on shows, they paraded, they
raised chickens within city limits. They were flimflammers of
tourists, wildcat miners, cigar makers without the white label,
carriers of baskets on poles, cubic air breathers, miscegenists,
landsquatters and landlords without deeds, kangaroo jurists,
medical and legal practitioners without degrees, unconvertible
pagans and heathens, gamblers with God and one another,
aliens unqualifiable to apply for citizenship, unrelated communalists and crowders into single-family dwellings, dwellers and
gamblers in the backs of stores, restaurateurs and launderers
who didn't pass health inspections, droppers of garbage into
other people's cans, payers and takers of less than minimum
wage, founders of martial-arts schools with wall certificates
from the Shaolin Temple of Hunan, China, but no accredi-
tation by the Western Association of Schools and Colleges,
Unemployment-check collectors, dodgers of the draft of several countries, un-Americans, red-hot communists, unbridled
capitalists, look-alikes of japs and Viet Cong, unlicensed man-
ufacturers and exploders of fireworks. Everybody with aliases.
More than one hundred and eight outlaws.

In chain reactions, thousand-firecracker strands climbed
poles to the microphones and blasted out the loudspeakers.
Blow it all up. Set the theater on fire. The playwright goes
down with his play like the historians who were killed at the
ends of their eras, their books burning at their feet. No as-
bestos-and-metal guillotine curtain here. The Globe and the
Garrick had many fires, then holocaust. It's a theater tradition. Chinese hold all the Guinness records—1,670 audience
members and actors killed in Canton in 1845 at the Theater,
which was enclosed by a high wall. The fire at the Theater in
Kamli killed two thousand in 1893. The Fu Chow playhouse
burned down in 1884 under bombardment by the French fleet.
Every theater you've ever been to or heard of has had its fire.

The Bowery Theatre in Vauxhall Gardens, New York—burned and rebuilt six times. Eleven hundred theater fires all over the world during the last hundred years. In London and Paris and Budapest and Silver City, Eureka, Virginia City, Leadville (three times), Marysville, Placerville, Meadville, and in San Francisco alone, not counting earthquake fires—the Adelphi Theatre, the Jenny Lind Theatre, Ronison & Evrad's Theatre, the Olympic Circus, the New Jenny Lind, the Lyceum (twice), the Music Hall, Pickwick Hall, the Russian Gardens, the Grand American Theatre I, the Grand American Theatre II, the Winter Garden, and the Chinese Theatre of San Francisco. Floors caught fire when winter stoves under the stage heated up the boards too hot. The candles in the luster pooled and became a bowl of sheet-flame. The gasman at the Baltimore Front Street Theater held his pole-torch up to a jet, and a gust of fire shot out through the stage, which is a wind tunnel. The hay bales for dragging the floors clean caught sparks and smoldered. For the sake of verisimilitude, the actor-soldiers at the court theater in Oldenburg set fire to a stage fortress, midnight, 1891, and the rest of the building went with it. On Bastille Day, 1873, cannons were shot off indoors, which destroyed the Grand Opéra House and the bibliothèque. The last act of *Faust*, the masked ball, caused many theaters to burn, including the holocausts of the Leghorn and the Teatro degli Acquidotti. There was a cinematographe fire in Paris in 1897; and in 1908, at the Rhoades Opera House, Boyerton, Pennsylvania, a motion-picture machine exploded and killed a hundred people. And just this past spring in Saigon, three hundred children were killed at a waterfront theater. We'll do anything for lighting, die for it, kill for it.

In the tradition of theater fires, in remembrance of the burnings of Chinatowns, and of the Great Earthquake and Fire, and of the Honolulu plague fire at the New Year and the new century, and in protest of the school fact that Chinese invented gunpowder but were too dumb to use it in warfare, and in honor of artists who were arrested for incendiarism, Wittman Ah Sing—"Gotta match?" he asked. "Not since Superman died," answered a chorus of kids in the audience.—lit every last explosive. Go up in flames and down in history. Fireworks whiz-banged over and into the neighborhood. Percussion caps, powders, and instruments banged and boomed. A genie of the theater ran around with torches—Antonin Artaud torches the grass-hut theater of Bali, and the actors gesture through the flames.

The neighbors turned in four alarums. Fire engines were coming, wailing louder than Chinese opera. On cue—the S.F.F.D. was bringing the redness and the wailing. Sirens. Bells. A hook-and-ladder truck. The audience ran out into the street. More audience came. And the actors were out from backstage and the green room, breaking rules of reality-and-illusion. Their armor and swords were mirrored in fenders, bumpers, and the long sides of the fire trucks. The clear clean red metal with the silver chrome glorified all that was shining. The emergency lights reddened faces and buildings. "Fire!" "Fire!" The *Chron*'s banner tomorrow: Chinese Fire!

"Where's the fire?"

"No fire. Chinese custom."

"Do you have a fireworks permit?"

"Permit?" Only three flashpowder technicians in the State of California had a Class C license for setting off theatrical explosives. Wittman Ah Sing wasn't one of them.

"You don't plan to keep this racket up all night, do you?"

"The noisy part of our ritual is done. Would you like some tickets to the quiet part? You're invited to come in and see it." And to the crowd of neighbors, "We invite you too," papering the house. "I promise to be quiet."

The next part of Wittman's night could have had him caged and taken through the City in a paddywagon. He might have seen the streets through grillwork and between the heads of a pair of cops.

Instead, he was given a chance; Chinese are allowed more fireworks than other people. He went back inside, and continued the play. We'll let him tell you about himself by himself.

9
One-Man Show

It came to you to be yourself. Your fellow-actors' courage failed;
as if they had been caged with a pantheress, they crept along the
wings and spoke what they had to, only not to irritate you. But
you drew them forward, and you posed them and dealt with
them as if they were real. Those limp doors, those simulated
curtains, those objects that had no reverse side, drove you to
protest. You felt how your heart intensified unceasingly toward
an immense reality and, frightened, you tried once more to take
people's gaze off you like long gossamer threads—: but now, in
their fear of the worst, they were already breaking into applause:
as though at the last moment to ward off something that would
compel them to change their life.
—Rilke, *The Notebooks of Malte Laurids Brigge*

I. I. I.
I. I. I.
I. I. I.
—Monkey's aria, *The Journey to the West*

OF COURSE, Wittman Ah Sing didn't really burn down
the Association house and the theater. It was an illusion of fire. Good monkey. He kept control of the explosives, and of his arsonist's delight in flames. He wasn't
crazy; he was a monkey. What's crazy is the idea that revolutionaries must shoot and bomb and kill, that revolution
is the same as war. We keep losing our way on the short
cut—killing for freedom and liberty and community and a
better economy. Wittman could have torched the curtains
and the dry flowers; he could have downpoured the oil
lamps onto the chairs and fruit crates. He'd been envying
that Japanese-American guy that got shot allegedly helping
to set the Watts fires, yelling, "Burn, baby, burn." But, no,
Wittman would not have tried to burn the City. It's all too
beautiful to burn.

The world was splitting up. Tolstoy had noted the surprising gaiety of war. During his time, picnickers and fighters took to the same field. We'd gotten more schizzy. The dying was on the Asian side of the planet while the playing—the love-ins and the be-ins—were on the other, American side. Whatever there is when there isn't war has to be invented. What do people do in peace? Peace has barely been thought.

Our monkey, master of change, staged a fake war, which might very well be displacing some real war. Wittman was learning that one big bang-up show has to be followed up with a second show, a third show, shows until something takes hold. He was defining a community, which will meet every night for a season. Community is not built once-and-for-all; people have to imagine, practice, and re-create it. His community surrounding him, then, we're going to reward and bless Wittman with our listening while he talks to his heart's content. Let him get it all out, and we hear what he has to say direct. Blasting and blazing are too wordless.

On the third night, the one hundred and eight bandits climbed the stairs to become stars in the sky, except for some of the Juan brothers. They escape westward, that is, to Southeast Asia. They shunt their skiffs through the tule fog and shoot out in Viet Nam. Juan II, Juan V, and Juan VII (pronounced the Hispanic way, not like Don Quick-set and Don Jew-On the way we learned at Berkeley), played by Chicanos, become the One Hundred Children who are the ancestors of the Vietnamese. Though Vietnamese will deny that. Everybody would rather be the indigenous people of a place than be its immigrants. Another Indian punchline: "Are they going back where they came from yet?" A door like two golden trays opens up for a moment in the sky, which tears like blue silk, and a hundred and five bandits go to Heaven and three start a new country. The audience clapped loud, bone-proud of our boys and our girls, just like graduation, where we take the hardest awards, math and science. The End.

Except: A Chinese-minded audience likes the moral of the story told in so many words. And the American theater was rejoicing in scoldings; Blacks were breaking through the fourth wall. Whites were going to the theater and paying good money to be yelled at by Blacks, and loving them for it. Wittman Ah Sing waited for the audience to stop applauding, whistling,

calling out names—"Kamiyama!" "Shaw!" "Nanci!"—a kabuki tradition. The actors had taken solo bows after arias and
scenes and acts. He held up his hands—enough, enough already—turned his chair around, lit a cigarette, smoked, strad-
dled the chair. He wanted to address the world as the shouting
Daruma, fists upthrust pulling force up from lotus butt base,
his body a triangle of power, and hairy mouth wide open and
roaring. Not the Daruma doll that you knock around but
Daruma the Shouter.

"I want to talk to you," said Wittman. "I'm Wittman Ah
Sing, the playwright." The audience clapped for the playwright.
He further introduced himself by giving them the mele of his
name. "I'm one of the American Ah Sings. Probably there
are no Ah Sings in China. You may laugh behind my family's
back, that we keep the Ah and think it means something. I
know it's just a sound. A vocative that goes in front of everyone's names. Ah Smith. Ah Jones. Everyone has an ah, only
our family writes ours down. In that Ah, you can hear we had
an ancestor who left a country where the language has sounds
that don't mean anything—la and ma and wa—like music.
Alone and illiterate, he went where not one other Chinese
was. Nobody to set him straight. When his new friends asked
him his name, he remembered that those who wanted him
had called, 'Ah Sing.' So he told the schoolmarm, 'Ah Sing,
ma'am,' and she wrote down for him the two syllables of a new
American name."

Wittman waved the newspapers in his hand, and whacked
them against his knee. "The reviews have come out. You've
seen the reviews, haven't you?" The audience, which now included the actors, gave the reviews a round of applause. "I want
to talk," he said. They gave him another hand, welcoming him
to go ahead, talk. "So. You were entertained. You liked the
show, huh? I myself have some complaints and notes but. Let
me discuss with you what the *Chron* and the *Examiner* said,
and the *Oakland Tribune*, and *The Daily Cal* and the *Berkeley
Gazette*, and the *Shopping News*, and the *Barb*. They've reviewed us already, thinking that opening night is no different from the second night and tonight. You like the reviews?
I am sore and disappointed. Come on, you can't like these
reviews. Don't be too easily made happy. Look. Look. 'East

meets West.' 'Exotic.' 'Sino-American theater.' 'Snaps, crackles and pops like singing rice.' 'Sweet and sour.' Quit clapping. Stop it. What's to cheer about? You like being compared to Rice Krispies? Cut it out. Let me show you, you've been insulted. They sent their food critics. They wrote us up like they were tasting Chinese food. Rice, get it? 'Savor beauteous Nanci Lee,' it says here. That's like saying that LeRoi Jones is as good as a watermelon. 'Yum yum, authentic watermelon.' They wouldn't write a headline for *Raisin in the Sun*: 'America Meets Africa.' They want us to go back to China where we belong. They think that Americans are either white or Black. I can't wear that civil-rights button with the Black hand and the white hand shaking each other. I have a nightmare—after duking it out, someday Blacks and whites will shake hands over my head. I'm the little yellow man beneath the bridge of their hands and overlooked. Have you been at a demonstration where they sing:

> *Black and white together.*
> *Black and white together.*
> *Black and white together*
> *someda-a-a-ay.*

Deep in my heart, I do believe we have to be of further outrage to stop this chanting about us, that 'East is east and west is west.' Here's one that keeps quoting longer, like more learned. I won't read it to you. My mouth doesn't want to say any more wog-hater non-American Kipling. 'Twain shall.' Shit. Nobody says 'twain shall,' except in reference to us. We've failed with our magnificence of explosions to bust through their Kipling. I'm having to give instruction. There is no East here. West is meeting West. This was all West. All you saw was West. This is The Journey *In* the West. I am so fucking offended. Why aren't you offended? Let me help you get offended. Always be careful to take offense. These sinophiles dig us so much, they're drooling over us. That kind of favorableness we can do without. They think they know us—the wide range of us from sweet to sour—because they eat in Chinese restaurants. They're the ones who order the sweet-and-sour pork and the sweet-and-sour spare ribs and the sweet-and-sour shrimp. I've read my Aristotle and Agee, I've been to college; they have ways to criticize theater besides for sweetness and sourness. They could do laundry reviews, clean or dirty. Come on. What's so 'exotic'? We're about as exotic as shit. Nobody soo-pecial here. No sweet-and-sour shit. No exotic chop suey shit. So this variety show had too much motley; they didn't have to call it 'chop-suey vaudeville.' I am so pissed off. But. This other piece says that we are *not* exotic. 'Easily understood and not too exotic for the American audience.' Do I have to explain why 'exotic' pisses me off, and 'not exotic' pisses me off? They've got us in a bag, which we aren't punching our way out of. To be exotic or to be not-exotic is not a question about Americans or about humans. Okay, okay. Take me, for example. I'm common ordinary. Plain black sweater. Blue jeans. Tennis shoes ordinaire. Clean soo mun shaven. What's so exotic? My hair's too long, huh? Is that it? It's the hair? Does anybody have a pair of scissors? Here, help me spread these newspapers on the floor. I'm cutting my hair. If I bend over like this, I can see it, and cut it fairly straight. What's so funny? It ought to be the same around each ear? No need for symmetrical, huh? I don't want to snip off my ears. Earless Oichi. I'll lean over this way, and off comes this side. And this side too. And the top. The do-it-yourself haircut. Can be done without mirrors or friends. Whatever you get, you wear. Natural. Fast. Cheap. Just cut until you yourself can't see any more hair. Go by feel. I like the feel of sharp blades sandily closing through hairs. Sure, it's my real hair. I'm not wearing a wig, I'm honest. Wow, I didn't know I was carrying so much hair on my head."

Winging it, the monkey was indeed cutting off his actual hair. Black hair covered the newspapers. Wittman was performing an unpremeditated on-the-spot happening, unrepeatable tomorrow night. His prickly pear head cracked the audience up. The hair down his collar kept him in aggravation.

Wittman turned the chair flush toward the audience, sat up straight facing them, classic talk-story pose, and said: "We should have done a soap opera that takes place in a kitchen about your average domestic love agonies and money agonies. The leading lady is in hair curlers and an apron, and her husband, who has a home haircut like mine, stomps in, home from work. He knocks the mud off his workboots. He lets down the bib of his farmer or mechanic overalls. He drinks his beer while kneading his toes. She empties his lunch-bucket, and they argue about whether a napkin does or does not count as one lunch item. A radio is on, and it's tuned to some popular station broadcasting whatever happens to be on, show tunes or a ball game or the news. No ching-chong music, no epic costumes, you understand? The highpoint will be the family eating and discussing around the table—where the dramatic confrontations of real life take place; that's why meals are the hardest scenes to block. You know what the *Tribune* will say? 'Exotic.' Or they'll say, 'Whaddya know? Not exotic. The inscrutables are explaining themselves at last. We are allowed into their mysterious oriental world.'" Pause for the thinkers to think. "Okay, let's say in this soap opera, they hear bad news about their only son—killed in war. (Don't you whites get confused; he's killed fighting for *our* side. Nobody here but us Americans.) The mom is weeping big sobs with nose-blowing, and the dad howls, 'Aiya! Aiya! Aaaaaaa! Say, la! Naygamagahai! Aaaargh! Say, la! Say, la! Aiyaaaah!' and like in the funnies, 'Aieeeee!'"

Wittman stood and vocalesed a wail of pain that a dad might cry who'd given his only kid to his country. His eye-brows screwed toward each other, and his mouth was bent into the sign for infinity. Some audience members laughed.

"And guess how too many people will react? They'll say, 'Inscrutable.' We do tears. We do ejaculations. We do laffs. And they call us inscrutable.

"I have an idea how to make them cut that inscrutable shit out. Our next task is to crack the heart of the soap opera."

"I've gotten work on the soaps," said Charley. "They're starting to hire minorities now."

"Me too," said Nanci. "I played a nurse."

"Did you play the lab tech again, Charley? Or the court stenographer? You guys are too grateful. The job of the char-acters they let you play gets upgraded from criminal or servant to semi-professional, and you're fooled that we're doing better. Just because you get to wear a nurse's uniform rather than a Suzie Wong dress doesn't mean you're getting anywhere nearer to the heart of that soap. You're not the ones they tune in every day to weep over. We need to be part of the daily love life of the country, to be shown and loved continuously until we're not inscrutable anymore.

"Wait a minute. Let me try that again. We're not inscrutable at all. We are not inherently unknowable. That's a trip they're laying on us. Because they are willfully innocent. Willful innocence is a perversion. It's like that other perversion where people fly to Japan or Denmark to have their ex-hymen sewn shut. People who call us inscrutable get their brains sewn shut. Then they run around saying, 'We don't know you. And it's your fault. You're inscrutable.' They willfully do not learn us, and blame that on us, that we have an essential unknowableness. I was reading in a book by a Black man who travels far from America to this snowy village in the Alps. No Black man had set foot on that part of the Earth before. The villagers are innocent of slavery and of standing in the schoolhouse door and even of having ever seen a Black person. Their innocence pisses him off. On his walks, the kids call to him, innocently, 'Neger. Neger,' which makes echoes of another word to his American ears. He doesn't make a scary face and chase those kids, and he doesn't lecture them. He is a very quiet guy, who thinks at them: 'People are trapped in history and history is trapped in them . . . and hence all Black men have toward all white men an attitude which is designed, really, either to rob the white man of the jewel of his naïveté, or else to make it cost him dear.'"

Wittman was quoting from "Stranger in the Village," which is in *Notes of a Native Son* by James Baldwin. After getting educated, a graduate has to find ways to talk to his family and regular people again. It helps, when you want to tell them about your reading, to leave out the title and author. Just start, "I was reading in a book . . ."

"We have a story about what to do to those who try to hang on to the jewel of their naïveté. Cho Cho will get them. Once after losing a battle, Cho Cho hides out in a farmhouse with a well-meaning family. So many kids of various sizes run all over the place, they seem like the hundred children. The farm folks are going about their chores and speaking ordinarily, but all is fraught; the birds are stirring and beating their wings. Cho Cho walks here and there, peeping through doors and windows. What are these people up to, treating him so well?

They say they are not political; they welcome the stranger as a guest. They certainly laugh a lot. Cho Cho steps into the wine cellar; a tall boy ducks into a jar. 'Aren't you too old to be playing hide-and-go-seek?' And where did the father go? Cho Cho strolls in the fields and orchards. No father. 'Where is he?' he asks this kid and that kid. 'He went to market to buy a fat pig.' The same answer from everybody. Had they had a meeting, and rehearsed that answer? Some kind of code? They say, 'He went to market to buy a fat pig,' and look at one another and laugh. Grandma brings a butcher knife, and a sister brings a boning knife. The mother sharpens them. 'Why are you sharpening the knives?' 'We're going to slaughter the fat pig that Father is bringing home from market.' Did she say 'pig' like she meant *him?* Why's everybody giggling? A brother and a cousin are talking behind a tree. What are they laughing at? What's so funny? There were eight of them—they could gang up on him. Nothing for it but to pick them off one by one. He catches a brother alone in a lean-to, and quietly kills him, and hides the body behind the storage. Kills the mother, and hides her in the loft above the kitchen. Kills the grandma with her own knife, tucks her behind the grain jars. The rest of the family goes about their routine, not missing the others. He kills them one and all. Got a sister in the courtyard, a brother in the fields, another brother in the barn. Very neatly. No fights, no hysteria. Killed that family clean. Got them from behind, a hand over their eyes, fast. They didn't know what hit them. Nobody suffered.

"He leaves the farm, and meets the father on the road. He is trundling a fat pig bundled upside down in a basket. The rattan binds against its human-like skin. A pig's eye looks out between wickerwork bands. One has to look closely to see that it is a pig and not a naked man; sometimes there are naked men trussed up like this as a punishment for adultery, adulterer in a pigpoke. So the family had been acting secretive and excited because they had been planning a surprise party. The father says, 'The party's for you. You'll act surprised when the ladies tell you, won't you?' 'I'll do that, yes,' says Cho Cho. The father will have to go too, a quick stab in the back. The poor man is spared the suffering of finding his family slaughtered. Cho Cho takes the pig and continues his journey."

The listeners did not applaud this tale of paranoia. They were not ready to slaughter innocents. The white people were probably getting uncomfortable. The others were watching to see Wittman get struck mute.

"I think," he tried explaining, "that history being trapped in people means that history is embodied in physical characteristics, such as skin colors. And do you know what part of our bodies they find so mysteriously inscrutable? It's our little eyes. They think they can't see into these little squinny eyes. They think we're sneaky, squinnying at them through spy eyes. They can't see inside here past these slits. And that's why you girls are slicing your eyelids open, isn't it? Poor girls. I understand. And you glue on the false eyelashes to give your scant eyes some definition. I could sell all this hair for eyelashes. Make a bundle."

The girls and women who were wearing them did not lower their eyelashes in abashment. Wittman was just part of a show, which did not upset them; he's talking about other girls. Bad Wittman did not let up. "I have been requesting my actresses to take off their false eyelashes, to go on bareface and show what we look like. I promise, they will find a new beauty. But every one of them draw on eyeliner, top and bottom rims, and also up here on the bone to make like deep sockets. Then mascara, then—clamp, clamp. They kink their stubby lashes with this metal pincher that looks like a little plow. With spirit gum and tape, they glue on a couple of rows per eye of fake-hair falsies. A bulge of fat swells out over the tape—a crease, a fold—allthesame Caucasoid. That is too much weight for an eyelid to carry. There's droop. Allthesame Minnie Mouse. Allthesame Daisy Duck." Wittman held the backs of his hands over his eyes, and opened and shut his fingers, getting laffs.

Judy, the awfully beautiful pigwoman, was agreeing with him, nodding her natural head. And Tañá, who did not have an eye problem, also understood. She will let that tactless husband of hers have it later in private. The ladies with the mink eyelashes ought to speak up for themselves. But through the make-up they did not feel assaults on their looks.

"Worse than make-up," said Wittman, "is the eye operation. There's an actress who dropped out of the show because she was having it done—the first Chinese-American I know to cut herself up like an A.J.A., who have a thing about knives. I won't tell you her name. Too shame. She's hiding out in a Booth home for girls during double-eye post-op. She didn't want to show her face with black stitches across her reddish swollen Vaselined eyelids X'ed across like cut along the dotted line. You girls shouldn't do that to yourselves. It's supposed to make you more attractive to men, right? Speaking as a man, I don't want to kiss eyes that have been cut and sewn; I'd be thinking Bride of Frankenstein. But I guess you're not trying to attract my type. I can tell when somebody's had her lids done. After she gets her stitches pulled and the puffiness goes down, she doesn't have a fold exactly, it's a scar line across each roundish lid. And her mien has been like lifted. Like she ate something too hot. The jalapeño look. She'll have to meet new guys who will believe she was born like that. She'll draw black lines on top of the scars, and date white guys, who don't care one way or the other single-lid double-lid."

Several pioneer showgirls were present who had secretly had that operation done long ago. They were laughing at the girl with the jalapeño expression. They did not admit that all you have to do is leave your eyes alone, and grow old; the lids will naturally develop a nice wrinkle.

"As a responsible director, as a man, I try to stop my actresses from mutilating themselves. I take them for coffee one at a time, and talk to them. You guys need to help me out, there's too many beautiful girls who think they're ugly. You're friends of a raccoon-eyed girl, tell her how beautiful she might be without make-up. She says, 'No, I look washed out. I look sick.' You say, 'You shouldn't wear stage make-up out in the street. Will you take it off for me? I want to see what you look like. Go to the ladies' room with this jar of Abolene cream, and come out with a nude face. Be brave. Go about bareface. Find your face. You have enormous eyes, not enormous-for-a-Chinese but for anyone. I want to kiss your naked eyelids, and not feel false eyelashes on my lips.' Okay, I get nowhere. Maybe I say it wrong, you laugh, they laugh. But you guys who get chicks to listen to you better than I do should give them a talking to.

"Please don't end up like a wife of some military dictator of a nowhere Southeast Asian country. Trip out on the before-and-after Madame Sukarno and Madame Thieu and Madame Ky and Madame Nhu. Their eyes have been Americanized. They wear shades, like everything is cool, man. They've been hiding stitches or maybe a botch job. They have round noses but Madame Nhu's is the roundest, hardly enough bridge to hang her glasses on. Any Mongolian type you see fucking with their eyes, you know they've got big problems. You girls ought to step right up here, and peel those false eyelashes off, and cast them down amongst this other hair."

Nobody took him up on that, but they didn't walk out either, and Wittman went on:

"Speaking of plastic surgery, did you see on t.v. this dentist named Dr. Angle, D.D.S., who invented a way to straighten buckteeth? He's fixed thousands of people—the champion bucktooth fixer in the world. He brought along audio-visual aids, shots of make-overs. The interviewer asked him what his standards are for a good bite. He said, 'That's a good question. I thought hard about that very question.' His answer did not have to do with chewing, or being able to talk better, or teeth in relation to the rest of the face. He said, 'I use my own teeth as the model. Because they're perfect. I've got perfect teeth.' And he does. Dr. Angle looks just right. Regular eyes, regular nose, regular teeth. No mole or birthmark or crookedness I can use to describe him so's you'd recognize him.

"Like Dr. Angle, I declare my looks—teeth, eyes, nose, profile—perfect. Take a good look at these eyes. Check them out in profile too. And the other profile. Dig the three-quarter view. So it's not Mount Rushmore, but it's an American face. Notice as I profile, you can see both my eyes at once. I see more than most people—no bridge that blocks the view between the eyes. I have a wide-angle windshield. Take a good look. These are the type of eyes most preferred for the movies. Eyes like mine sight along rifles and scan the plains and squint up into the high noon sun from under a Stetson. Yes, these are movie-star eyes. Picture extreme close-ups of the following cowboys: Roy Rogers. Buck Jones. John Wayne. John Payne. Randolph Scott. Hopalong Cassidy. Rex Allen. John Huston. John Carradine. Gabby Hayes. Donald O'Connor, if *Francis the Talking Mule* counts as a western. Chinese eyes. Chinese eyes. Like mine. Like yours. These eyes are cowboy eyes with which I'm looking at you, and you are looking back at me with cowboy eyes. We have the eyes that won the West."

Now, Wittman was giving out what he thought was his craziest riff, the weirdest take of his life at the movies. But the audience stayed with him. His community was madder than he was. They named more cowboys with Chinese eyes—Lee Marvin, Steve McQueen, Gary Cooper. And more—Alan Ladd and Jack Palance in *Shane*, a movie about a Chinese against a Chinese. Gregory Peck. Robert Mitchum. Richard Boone. Have you heard: James Coburn is taking Chinese lessons from Bruce Lee, his "little brother." There's this guy, Clint Eastwood, who can't get work in Hollywood because of Chinese eyes, working in Italian westerns now. Some are traitors to their Chinese heritage. Richard Widmark took a role as a U.S. Cavalry expert on Indians in *Two Rode Together*, where he says, "I've lived among the Apache. They don't feel pain." The Lone Ranger masks his Chinese eyes. So does Cato.

The poets who sit zazen get Japanese eyes: Philip Whalen and Gary Snyder.

The ladies refused to be left out. They found for themselves actresses who have Chinese fox eyes: Luise Rainer and Myrna Loy and Merle Oberon and Gene Tierney and Bette Davis and Jennifer Jones and Katharine Hepburn and Shirley MacLaine. Rita Hayworth is Chinese. The showgirls have a souvenir program of the Forbidden City's All-Chinese Review, and there she is, Rita Hayworth, in the middle of the front row.

"Marlon Brando," said Wittman, "is not Chinese, and he's not Japanese either. To turn him Japanese, they pulled back his hair and skin and clamped the sides of his head with clips. They shaved his eyebrows clean off, and drew antennae like an insect's, like an elf's. Sekiya scoot-scoots about, procuring his sisters for the all-white American armed services."

Lance Kamiyama stood up from the throne-chair where he was sitting at the back of the room. Sunny sat in the other one. He held up a banana, and made as if to throw it. "For you," he said. He tried to walk with it up to the stage area, but the floor was too crowded. He handed the banana off, "Pass it on, no pass back." It went from hand to hand up to Wittman. What signifies a banana? If I were Black, would I be getting an Oreo? If I were a red man, a radish?

"'Is this a dagger which I see before me, the handle toward my hand?'" said Shakespearean Wittman. "No, it's a banana. My pay? Thank you. Just like olden days—two streetcar tokens, two sandwiches, one dollar, and one banana—pay movie star allthesame pay railroad man. Oh, I get it—top banana. Thank you. Ladies and gentlemen of the Academy, I thank you. Hello. Hello. Nobody home in either ear. I feel like Krapp. I mean, the Krapp of *Krapp's Last Tape* by Ah Bik Giht. He wears his banana sticking out of his waistcoat pocket. I'm going to wear mine down in my pants. Have you heard the one about these two oriental guys who saved enough money for a vacation at the seashore? They're walking on the beach and desiring all the bathing beauties. They make no eye contact with bullies who kick sand in faces. The smaller oriental says, 'I strike out with the chicks. I try and I try but. How you do it?' The bigger oriental says, 'I been studying your situation, brother. I recommend, you put one banana in your bathing suit.' 'Ah, so that be the secret. I'll go buy a banana and try it.' He does that, and too soon returns in disappointment. 'I don't understand. I buy one big ripe banana. I stick it in my swimsuit. I walk on the beach—and the chicks laugh at me. What be wrong?' The big oriental says, 'I think you're supposed to wear the banana in front.'

"Seriously, folks, this banana suggests two parts of the anatomy that are deficient in orientals. The nose and the penis. Do you think if I attached it between my eyes I'd get to be a movie star? Do you think if I attach it between my legs, I'd get the girls?

"I ought to unzip and show you—one penis. Large. Star Quality. Larger than this banana. Let me whip out the evidence that belies smallness. Nah. Nah. Nah. Just kidding, la. I'd only be able to astound the front rows; the people in back will tell everybody they didn't see much. I've got to get it up on the big screen. The stage is not the medium for the penis or for the details of this face. For the appreciation of eyelids, double-eye or single-eye, we need movie close-ups. So you can learn to love this face.

"Is there anybody out there who's heard the joke all the way through that has the line, 'The chinaman don't dig that shit either!'? That may be the punchline. All my life, I've heard pieces of jokes—maybe the same joke in fragments—that they quit telling when I walk in. They're trying to drive me pre-psy-chotic. I'm already getting paranoid. I'm wishing for a cloak of invisibility. I want to hear the jokes they tell at the par-ties that I'm not invited to. Americans celebrate business and holidays with orgies of race jokes. A white friend of mine has volunteered to hear for me what comes before 'The chinaman don't dig that shit either!' Don't dig what shit?"

"It's about this horny bushy guy who comes down out of the Arctic Circle," said Lance.

"He wants a girl for fifty cents," said Zeppelin. "But she costs too much—one dollar."

"No," said Lance. "No girls available, but for one dollar, you can have the chinaman. This manly guy doesn't want the chinaman. He says, 'I don't dig that shit.'"

"No, no, that's not the way it goes," said Zeppelin. "He can afford fifty cents but they up it on him to one dollar."

"The exact amount of money," said Charley, "is beside the point. Whatever they say the cost is, this guy thinks it's too much, especially since he wouldn't even be getting a girl. He goes away. He's very horny, so comes back for the deal on the chinaman. But now they want to charge three times as much. Let's make it simple, three dollars."

"Three dollars?!" said Zeppelin. "How come three dollars. Awhile ago, you offered one dollar. I don't dig that shit."

"One dollar for the chinaman, and two dollars for the two guys to hold him down," said Lance. "The chinaman don't dig that shit either."

"American jokes too dry," said Siew Loong.

"No wonder they call you inscrutable, you don't laugh at jokes," said Wittman.

"You guys feel so sorry for youself," said Auntie Dolly. "But you tell tit twat cunt chick hom sup low jokes."

"All you joke experts be here, why don't you men tell us, 'Is it true what they say about Chinese girls?'" said Auntie Bessie. "Is *what* true?"

"The full line," said Wittman, "is, 'Is it true what they say about Chinese girls' twats?' They think they're sideways, that they slant like eyes. As in *Chi*nese *Jap*anese *Kor*eean." He put his fingers on the tails of his eyes, and pulled them up, "*Chi*nese," pulled them down, "*Jap*anese," pulled them sideways, "Ko*ree*an." He felt immediately sorry. He had pulled tears of anger and sorrow up into his eyes. White men let little yellow men overhear that twat joke to make them littler and yellower. And they fuck over the women too. Kick ass, Wittman. "The King of Monkeys hereby announces: I'm crashing parties wherever these jokes are told, and I'm going to do some spoilsporting. Let me educate you, Mr. and Mrs. Potato Head, on what isn't funny. Never ask me or anyone who looks like me, 'Are you *Chi*nese or *Jap*anese?' I know what they're after who ask that question. They want to hear me answer something obscene, something bodily. Some disgusting admission about our anatomy. About daikon legs and short waist or long waist, and that the twat goes sideways, slanting like her eyes. They want me to show them the Mongoloidian spot on my ass. They want to measure the length of my ape arms and compare them to Negers' arms.

"And don't ask: 'Where do you come from?' I deign to retort, 'Sacramento,' or 'Hanford,' or 'Bakersfield,' I'm being sarcastic, get it? And don't ask: 'How long have you been in the country?' 'How do you like our country?'"

"The answer to that," said Lance, "is 'Fine. How do *you* like it?'"

"The one that drives me craziest is 'Do you speak English?' Particularly after I've been talking for hours, don't ask, 'Do you speak English?' The voice doesn't go with the face, they don't hear it. On the phone I sound like anybody, I get the interview, but I get downtown, they see my face, they ask, 'Do you speak English?' Watch, as I leave this stage tonight after my filibuster, somebody's going to ask me, 'You speak the language?'

"In the tradition of stand-up comics—I'm a stand-up tragic—I want to pass on to you a true story that Wellington Koo told to Doctor Ng, who told it to me. Wellington Koo was at a state dinner in Washington, D.C. The leaders of the free world were meeting to figure out how to win World War II. Koo was talking to his dinner partners, the ladies on his left and right, when the diplomat across from him says, 'Likee soupee?' Wellington nods, slubs his soup, gets up, and delivers the keynote address. The leaders of the free world and their wives give him a standing ovation. He says to the diplomat, 'Likee speechee?' After a putdown like that, wouldn't you think Mr. and Mrs. Potato Head would stop saying, 'You speakee English?'

"And I don't want to hear any more food shit out of anybody. I'm warning you, you ask me food shit, I'll recommend a dog-shit restaurant. Once when I was in high school, I met one of the great American Beat writers—I'm not saying which one because of protecting his reputation. He's the one who looks like two of the lohats, beard and eyebrows all over the place. He was standing next to me during a break at the *Howl* trial. I told him I wanted to be a playwright. I was a kid playwright who could've used a guru. While he was shaking my hand, he said, 'What's a good Chinese restaurant around here?' I tell you, my feelings were hurt bad. Here was a poet, he's got right politics, anti-war, anti-segregation, he writes good, riding all over America making up the words for it, but on me he turned trite. Watch out for him, he's giving out a fake North Beach. He doesn't know his Chinatown, he doesn't know his North Beach. I thought about straightening him out, and almost invited him for crab with black-bean sauce, and long bean with foo yee, and hot-and-sour soup, but I didn't want to hear him say, 'I likee soupee. You likee?'

"I know why they ask those questions. They expect us to go into our Charlie Chan Fu Manchu act. Don't you hate it when they ask, 'How about saying something in Chinese?' If you refuse, you feel stupid, and whatsamatter, you're ashamed? But if you think of something Chinese to say, and you say it, noises come out of you that are not part of this civilization. Your face contorts out of context. They say, 'What?' Like do it again. They want to watch you turn strange and foreign. When I speak my mind, I spill my guts, I want to be understood, I want to be answered. Peter Sellers, starting with the Ying Tong Goon Show and continuing throughout his buck-toof career to this day, and Mickey Rooney in *Breakfast at Tiffany's* and Warner Oland and Jerry Lewis and Lon Chaney are cutting off our balls linguistically. 'Me no likee.' 'Me find clue to identity of murderer.' 'Ming of Mongo conquers the Earth and the universe,' says Ming of Mongo. 'Confucius say,' says Confucius. 'Me name-um Li'l Beaver,' says Li'l Beaver. They depict us with an inability to say 'I.' They're taking the 'I' away from us. 'Me'—that's the fucked over, the fuckee.

'I'—that's the mean-ass motherfucker first-person pronoun of the active voice, and they don't want us to have it.

"We used to have a mighty 'I,' but we lost it. At one time whenever we said 'I,' we said 'I-warrior.' You don't know about it, you lost it. 'I-warrior' was the same whether subject or object, 'I-warrior' whether the actor or the receiver of action. When the turtles brought writing on their shells, the word for 'I' looked like this." Wittman wrote on the blackboard:

"It looks almost like 'Ngo' today, huh? 'Wo' to you Mandarins. This word, maybe pronounced 'ge,' was also the word for long weapons such as spears and lances and Ah Monkey's pole and the longsword. This longest stroke must be the weapon. And 'ge' also meant 'fight.' To say 'I' was to say 'I fight.' This isn't a Rorschach craziness on my part. I'll bet somewhere in China, a museum has collected that turtle shell in the same exhibit with the longswords. To this day, words to do with fighting and chopping off heads and for long weapons have this component:

as does the word for 'I.' We are the grandchildren of Gwan the Warrior. Don't let them take the fight out of our spirit and language. I. I. I. I. I. I. I. I. I-warrior win the West and the Earth and the universe.

"They have an enslavement wish for us, and they have a death wish, that we die. They use the movies to brainwash us into suicide. They started in on us with the first movies, and they're still at it. D. W. Griffith's *Broken Blossoms*, originally entitled *The Chink and the Child*: Lillian Gish as the pure White Child, Richard Barthelmess as the Chink, also called The Yellow Man. They were actually about the same age. The Child has a drunken father, so the Chink takes her into his house to protect her. One moonlit night, she seems to be asleep in a silk

Chinese gown. He yearns for her. Ripped on opium, he looks at her out of stoned, taped eyes. His fingernailed hand quivers out for her, and barely touches a wisp of her gossamer hair, lacy and a-splay and golden in the moonbeams. The audience is in nasty anticipation of perversions, but before he can do some sexy oriental fetishy thing to her, his yellow hand stops. He kills himself. The Yellow Man lusts after a white girl, he has to kill himself—that's a tradition they've made up for us. We have this suicide urge and suicide code. They don't have to bloody their hands. Don't ever kill yourself. You kill yourself, you play into their hands."

Nanci was saying something to Auntie Marleese. "Poor Wittman." The two of them shook their heads. "He's so oversensitive."

"I am not oversensitive," he said. "You ought to be hurting too. You're dead to be insensitive, which is what they wish for you. You think you're looking good; you think you're doing fine, they re-run another one of those movies at you. And the morning cartoons get you wearing that pigtail again. And Hop Sing chases after the white man, and begs, 'Me be your slave. Please let me be your slave.' John Wayne has a Hop Sing, and the Cartwrights have a Hop Sing. They name him Hop Sing on purpose, the name of the powerful tong, to put us down. Here's another custom for orientals: Deranged by gratitude, an oriental has to have a master, and will tail after a white man until enslaved. In *Vertigo*, which could have been my favorite movie, James Stewart dives into the Bay and saves Kim Novak. He brings her back to his apartment that has a railing with the ideograms for joy. He lives within sight of Coit Tower. He tells Kim Novak, who's wearing his clothes and drying her hair by the fire, 'Chinese say if you rescue someone, you're responsible for them forever.' Think carefully; you've never heard a real Chinese say that; the ones in the movies and on t.v. say it over and over again. Every few days they show us a movie or a t.v. episode about us owing them, therefore thankfully doing their laundry and waiting on them, cooking and serving and washing and sewing for John Wayne and the Cartwright boys at the Ponderosa. The way Hop Sing shuffles, I want to hit him. Sock him an uppercut to straighten him up—stand up like a man.

"I want to punch Charlie Chan too in his pregnant stomach

that bellies out his white linen maternity suit. And he's got a widow's hump from bowing with humbleness. He has never caught a criminal by fistfighting him. And he doesn't grab his client-in-distress and kiss her hard, pressing her boobs against his gun. He shuffles up to a clue and hunches over it, holding his own hand behind his back. He mulls in Martian over the clues. Martians from outer space and Chinese monks talk alike. Old futs talking fustian. Confucius say this. Confucius say that. Too clean and too good for sex. The Good Mensch runs all over Setzuan in a dress, then in pants, and fools everybody because Chinese look so alike, we ourselves can't tell the difference between a man and a woman. We're de-balled and other-worldly, we don't have the natural fucking urges of the average, that is, the white human being.

"Next time you watch insomnia television, you can see their dreams about us. A racist movie is always running on some channel. Just the other night, I saw another one that kills off the Chinese guy for loving a white lady. I'm not spoiling it by giving away the ending. They always end like that. Barbara Stanwyck is the bride of a missionary, and she is interested in converting this guy with tape on his eyes named General Yin, played by Nils Asther. He talks to himself, rubbing his hands together, plotting, 'I will convert a missionary.' Which is racially and religiously very fucked up. Chinese don't convert white people but vice versa. (Someday I'll tell you my theory about how everyone is already a Buddhist, only they don't know it. You're all Buddhas whether you know it or not, whether you like it or not.) General Yin's religion has to do with burning incense in braziers and torturing slavegirls. He keeps faking wise sayings about conquering the Earth. I liked him. He seemed intelligent. Whatever his cause, he's lost. He's fought his last battle, and lost his army and friends. He's alone in his palace with Barbara Stanwyck and one last slavegirl, Anna May Wong, whom he has locked up and plans to kill slowly. The right couple would have been General Yin and Anna May, coming to an understanding of each other and living happily ever after. However, Barbara enters his throne/bedroom to plead with him for the life of the poor slavegirl. This is an emergency, and she didn't have time to dress. She's wearing her satin nightgown that flows like a bridal train down

the stairs of the dais. He's sitting enthroned, and she kneels
at his feet to beg him. Her face comes up to his knee. She asks
him for mercy while holding back tears, an actress's trick that
gets to the viewer more than her weeping outright. He denies
her pleas. The tears well up and up, and spill. She lifts her face
to his face, her lips trembling, eyes, cheeks, and lips moist,
her head almost touching a knee of his spread legs, which are
draped with the silk of his smoking robe. They don't touch
each other, but they tantalize and agonize nearer and nearer.
Smoky snakes of incense entwine them. But she's a woman of
God. She says, crying softly, looking up, looking down, pul-
sating, daring to teach this general, 'It's good to do something
when there is no advantage to you, not even gratitude.' He
has no morals; as we were taught from grammar school, life
is cheap in Asia. Listening, he moves closer, she moves closer.
Two-shots of their heads nearing. He slides past her lips, and
gives her a hug. She allows it, her motivation being that she
feels sorry for him. They hug, and they part. 'I will think over
what you have said,' he says. She rushes back to her room,
where she takes off her satin nightgown and puts on one of
those spangly mermaid-skin evening dresses. She has to try
another plea in a different outfit. The general could've looked
down, as the camera does, and seen pretty far down her décol-
letage. She's wet with tears again. This time he touches her.
He wipes her eyes and cheeks with a silk hanky. More tears
well and fall. He wipes her off again, and again. The audience
is catching thrills. Are they going to make out? Are the tails
of that silk handkerchief tickling her neck and the tops of her
tits? Are his lips going to land on her lips in an inter-racial kiss?
Will her heavy head come to rest in his crotch? And he peel off
her mermaid skin and carry her to the canopy bed? Which has
all along been a large part of the ravishing decor. Will its lush
curtains open for them, and close, and two masculine feet and
two feminine feet thrash out, his on top of hers, and their four
feet kick and stiffen? I saw that once in a Hong Kong movie;
he was a demigod and she was a mortal. The wedding bed was
in a garden among the flowers and under the sky. The bed was
like a chamber or a stage, you could live in there. The actor
who played the demigod had Star Quality, not just good-look-
ing-for-a-Chinese—a thin straight nose, eyes which beheld

his lover's ways so that from then on she's wonderful, even when she's alone, because watched from the sky whatever she does and wherever she goes. Whatever she asks, he answers, 'Forever.' But back to Barbara Stanwyck and General Yin. Are they going to get it on? Or neck or what? He picks up his tea-cup and drinks, and quietly leans back in his throne. And dies. He has poisoned himself before he can defile her. The name of that movie was *The Bitter Tea of General Yin*. They named him that to castrate us. General Yin instead of General Yang, get it? Again the chinaman made into a woman."

"No, no," said Charley Bogard Shaw. "That's Yen. *The Bitter Tea of General* Yen."

"Yen Shmen," said Wittman. "That movie was a death-wish that Confucius and Lin Yutang take poison as co-operatively as Socrates."

Stepgrandfather Lincoln Fong raised his hand. You had to let the old guy talk, and once started, take over. "Yes, Ah Goong," said good Wittman.

Mr. Fong stood, waited for attention, and addressed each dignitary, "President Ah Sing"—that is, Grand Opening Ah Sing—"Mr. Chairman"—that's Wittman—"ladies and gentlemen, Lin Tse Hsü was General Commissioner of Canton Against Narcotics. He stopped the opium from coming in for five months. He arrested two thousand Chinese dealers. He executed addicts. Nine out of ten Cantonese were addicted to opium. He wrote to Queen Victoria, held meetings with the British and American Tobacco Company, and led a raid on a factory, confiscated the shit, and detained the British manu-facturers for seven weeks. There are paintings of Lin burying opium in trenches half a football field long and seventy-five feet wide and seven feet deep. The Queen fired Lin from his office, and sent her navy to enforce opium sales. Your grandmothers and grandfathers, using Cho Cho's tactic, chained sixty junks across the Boca Tigris. Ten thousand of our Cantonese rela-tives fought with hoes, pitchforks, and two hundred new guns. They dumped opium into Canton Harbor like the Boston Tea Party. The British broke through into the Pearl River Delta and up the Yangtze to the rest of China. The famous joke of the nineteenth century: the West brought three lights—Fiat Lux, Standard Oil, and the British and American Tobacco

Company. Why China went communist was to build an economy that does not run on opium."

"Thank you, Ah Goong," said Wittman. "Let's give Mr. Lincoln Fong a big hand." PoPo's old man took his bows and sat down. Please, don't another competitive old fut get up, and another, orating through all the wars, war after war, won and lost. "I'm doing dope no more, no, sir. Lest our grandparents dumped Brit shit in vain. We don't need dope because we're naturally high. We come from a race of opium heads. Nine out of ten—wow!—of our immediate ancestors were stoned heads. We're naturally hip. Trippiness is in our genes and blood. In fact, we need kung fu for coming down to Earth, and kung fu is all we need for flight. I'm quitting cigarettes too. Ah Goong, you have given me the political strength to take a stand against the American Tobacco Company." Wittman turned his pack upside down, and strewed cigarettes amongst the hair.

"The Delta they're blowing us out of nowadays is the San Joaquin Delta. The footage of John Wayne beating his way through the hordes on Blood River, they shot on the San Joaquin River. They keep celebrating that they won the Opium Wars. All we do in the movies is die. I watch for you, Charley; your face appears, but before I can barely admire you, they've shot you dead. Our actors have careers of getting killed and playing dead bodies. You're targets for James Bond to blow to pieces. Did you know that J.F.K.'s favorite *reading* is James Bond *books*? The books are worse than the movies. Have you read one? You should, and dig what the President gets off on. He has ideas for what you can do for your country, and empire. There are these 'Chigroes'—what you get when you crossbreed a Chinese and a Negro—mule men with flat noses and cho cho lips and little eyes and yellow-black skin. They're avid to be killer-slaves. 'Chigroes.' It makes my mouth sick to say that out loud. You actresses have got to refuse to play pearl divers in love with James Bond. You have to get together with Odd Job. That's where the love story ought to be. That's not funny. A face as big as Odd Job's should star on the Cinerama screen for the audience to fall in love with, for girls to kiss, for the nation to cherish, for me to learn how to hold my face. Take seven pictures of a face, take twelve, twenty of any face, hold it up there, you will fall in love with it. Mako got his face up there, filling the screen with shades of oak and gold, this-color wongsky skin, and these eyes, and this nose, and his cho cho lips. What should be done with a face in close-up is to behold and adore it. They skin Mako alive. They peel him alive. He's skinned by his fellow Chinese. Hearing their voices making vulture-like sounds of an inhuman language, and watching Mako's screaming face, you imagine the skinning. You don't see it on camera. Where's my banana? Here, I'll show you, like so—peeling yellow skin. A strip, another yellow strip. And Mako is screaming, 'AAaaa! AaaAAagh! AAaaaaiyaaa!' His solo screams fill the sound track. 'AaaaaAAAaah! Aaaaaieeeeee!' We've been watching his face directly, then we watch it through the cross-hairs of Steve McQueen's rifle. The audience wants to kill him so badly. We're in an agony of mercy to shoot him out of his pain. Steve McQueen, to whom he has been a faithful sidekick, does him the favor. Bang! Here's what they really think of their little buddy. Squanto and Tonto and Li'l Beaver. They have skinned and shot their loyal little tagalong buddy. Die, Hop Sing, Wing Ding, Chop Chop, Charlie Two Shoes, Tan Sing. Skin that cute li'l Sherpa. Like the banana he is! And no Pocahontas to save him. She's busy sticking her neck out for John Smith."

Wittman held the banana in his fist so the peelings flapped out like two arms and two wings. "Mako got nominated Best Supporting Actor for his role as the banana. He didn't win the Oscar but. None of us gets an Oscar except James Wong Howe—for the cinematography on *Hud*. You guys have got to get your asses out from behind the camera. You're the most all-around talents in Hollywood, but they don't give Oscars for what you do best. There ought to be an Oscar for the One Actor Best at Playing a Horde. You run around and around the camera and back and forth across the set. Clutch guts, twitch, spazz out—the bullets hit here and here—fall like trip-wire ankles, roll downhill, dead with face up to the sky and camera. The director sends you back in there for the second-wave attack. 'I was killed already in the last scene,' says the conscientious supernumerary. 'That's all right,' says the director: 'Nobody can tell you apart.' I accept this Oscar for Most Reincarnations. Again and again, we're shot, stabbed, kicked, socked, skinned, machine-gunned, blown up. But not kissed. Nancy Kwan and France Nuyen and Nobu McCarthy kiss white boys. The likes of you and me are unstomachable.

The only hands we get to hold are our own up our sleeves. Charlie Chan doesn't kiss. And Keye Luke doesn't kiss. And Richard Loo doesn't kiss. We've got to kiss and fuck and breed in the streets."

Poor Wittman Ah Sing, Ah Star. It's going to get worse. He could spend the rest of his life advocating our stardom. When the *Planet of the Apes* series begins, the Asian American actors will say, "Here's our chance. You can look like anything under those ape costumes." But the roles will go to those who have to wear brown contact lenses. Pat Suzuki, after singing so well in *Flower Drum Song*, will play an ape-girl in *Skullduggery*; she roots in the dirt and grunts and squeals, and points, jumping up and down. And John Lone will play the title role in *Iceman*, a grunting, gesturing Neanderthal; his forehead is built up, his jaw juts prognathously, you won't recognize a Chinese-American of any kind under there. And when he gets to show his face in *Year of the Dragon*, John Lone, who has the most classic face amongst us, will have to have it broken on camera, and his eyes beaten shut. The last third of the movie his expressions are indecipherably covered with blood. He begs to be killed, and his co-star cradles his head, then point-blank shoots it off. The U.S. will lose the war in Viet Nam; then the Asian faces large on the screen will be shot, blown up, decapitated, bloodied, mutilated. No more tasteful off-camera deaths. We're going to have a President who has favorite movies rather than favorite books. The British actor who will bring back Fu Manchu claims not to be a racist because he doles money to the boat people. The actress who plays the dragon lady says that if you people picketing the set want movies from your p.o.v., "make your own movies." She doesn't understand that her movies are our movies, and that those horde-like picketers are her fellow SAG members.

"Thank you," said Wittman, eating the banana, no waste. "You feed the artist—thank you." He dropped the peel among the hair and cigarettes. "If there were Oscars for Improvisation and for Directing Oneself, you guys would sweep them. You made four hundred films about some kind of Chinese, whose roles were barely scripted. Maydene Lam and Richard Loo and Keye Luke, all of you, you sized up the scene, and invented the dialogue with appropriate dialects and business. You keep giving your name to the character you're playing. Whenever the name on the left in the credits is the same as the name on the right, you aren't getting credit for acting. You just be the oriental you are. They think you behave oriental without having to act. 'Just say something Chinese,' says the director, throwing you into the movie. 'Do something Chinese.'

"Which gives me an idea. You have the set-up to do some sabotage. Go ahead, take whatever stereotype part. They ask you to do Chinese shtick, make free to say whatever you want. True things. Pass messages. 'Eat shit, James Bond. Kiss my yellow ass.' 'Fuck off, John Wayne. I love Joang Fu.' 'Ban the Bomb.' 'C.I.A. out of Southeast Asia.' Gwan's grandchildren—take over the movies.

"And say who we are. You say our name enough, make them stop asking, 'Are you *Chi*nese or *Jap*anese?' That is a straightman's line, asking for it. Where's our knockout comeback putdown punchline? Who *are* we? Where's our name that shows that we aren't from anywhere but America? We're so out of it. It's our fault they call us gook and chinky chinaman. We've been here all this time, before Columbus, and haven't named ourselves. Look at the Blacks beautifully defining themselves. 'Black' is perfect. But we can't be 'Yellows.' 'Me? I'm Yellow.' 'I'm a Gold. We're Golds.' Nah, too evocative of tight-fisted Chang. Red's our color. But the red-hot communists have appropriated red. Even Fruit of Islam, though too fruity like Fruit of the Loom, is catchier than anything we've got. The image of a black bulge in the jockey shorts scares the daylights out of the ofay. We want a name like that, not some anthropological sociological name. American of Chinese extraction—bucktoof ethnick. A.J.A. is good—sharp, accurate, symmetrical. The long version sounds good too. Americans of Japanese Ancestry. Makes up for 'jap.' And the emphasis is right—'American,' the noun in front, and 'Japanese,' an adjective, behind. They had the advantage of Relocation Camp to make them think themselves up a name. We don't have like 'Americans of Chinese Ancestry.' Like 'A.C.A.' We are not named, and we're disappearing already. We want a name we can take out in the street and on any occasion. We can't go by what we call ourselves when we're among ourselves. Chinese and Hans and Tangs are other people of other times and another place. We can't go to the passport office and say, 'I'm a Han Ngun,' or 'I'm a Tang Ngun.' I'll bet that Tang Ngun are gone anymore even from that red Asiatic country on the opposite side of the planet. Try telling the census taker, 'I'm a Good Native Papers Boy.'

"For a moment a hundred years ago, we were China Men. After all, the other people in the new world were Englishmen and Frenchmen and Dutchmen. But they changed themselves into Americans, and wouldn't let us change into Americans. And they slurred 'China Man.' 'Chinaman,' they said dactylically. One of the actresses who is giving me a bad time— I'm forsaking her—said, 'Is China Man like china doll? Like fragile?' Here I'm trying to give us a Sierra-climbing name, a tree-riding name, a train-building name, and she said, 'You're fragile like china?' She's a Mississippi Delta Chinese, and says 'fragile' like 'honey chile.' 'China Man' makes echoes of another word.

"Once and for all: I am not oriental. An oriental is antipodal. I am a human being standing right here on land which I belong to and which belongs to me. I am not an oriental antipode.

"Without a born-and-belong-in-the-U.S.A. name, they can't praise us correctly. There's a favorable review here of our 'Sino-American' theater. When the U.S. doesn't recognize a foreign communist country, that's Sino-American. There is no such *person* as a Sino-American."

"They used to call us Celestials," said PoPo, "because at one time they glorified us so."

"But you never called yourself a Celestial, did you?" said Wittman. "They called you Celestial hoping that you'd go to heaven rather than stay in America. You called yourselves Wah Q and Gum Sahn Hock and Gum Sahn How."

PoPo said, "Gum Sahn Po. Gum Sahn Lo Po Nigh. Sahm Yup Po. Say Yup Po." The old fut names for Gold Mountain Ladies made people laugh.

Wittman said, "Sojourners no more but. Immigration got fooled already. You not be Overseas Chinese. You be here. You're here to stay. I am deeply, indigenously here. And my mother and father are indigenous, and most of my grandparents and great-grandparents, indigenous. Native Sons and

Daughters of the Golden State. Which was a name our ancestors made up to counteract those racists, the Native Sons
and Daughters of the Golden West. We want a name somewhat like that but shorter and more than California, the entire
U.S.A.—ours.

"They get us so wrong. 'Sun Ch'üan, the king of Wu, played
by an American. . . .' Of course, he's an American. As opposed to what? We're all of us Americans here. Why single
out the white guy? How come I didn't get 'an American' after my name? How come no 'American' in apposition with
my parents and my grandma? An all-American cast here. No
un-American activity going on. Not us.

"When I hear you call yourselves 'Chinese,' I take you to
mean American-understood, but too lazy to say it. You do
mean 'Chinese' as short for 'Chinese-American,' don't you? We
mustn't call ourselves 'Chinese' among those who are ready to
send us back to where they think we came from. But 'Chinese-
American' takes too long. Nobody says or hears past the first
part. And 'Chinese-American' is inaccurate—as if we could
have two countries. We need to take the hyphen out—'Chinese American.' 'American,' the noun, and 'Chinese,' the adjective. From now on: 'Chinese Americans.' However. Not
okay yet. 'Chinese hyphen American' sounds exactly the same
as 'Chinese no hyphen American.' No revolution takes place in
the mouth or in the ear.

"I've got to tell you about this experiment I volunteered
for in college. I answered an ad for 'Chinese-Americans' to
take a test for fifty bucks an hour, more per hour than I've
ever made—but hazard pay. So we Chinese-hyphenated-
schizoid-dichotomous-Americans were gathered in this lab,
which was a classroom. The shrink or lab assistant asked us
to fold a piece of paper in half and write 'Chinese' at the top
of one half and 'American' at the top of the other. Then he
read off a list of words. Like 'Daring.' 'Reticent.' 'Laughter.'
'Fearful.' 'Easygoing.' 'Conscientious.' 'Direct.' 'Devious.'
'Affectionate.' 'Standoffish.' 'Adventurous.' 'Cautious.'
'Insouciant.' 'Painstaking.' 'Open.' 'Closed.' 'Generous.'
'Austere.' 'Expressive.' 'Inexpressive.' 'Playful.' 'Studious.'
'Athletic.' 'Industrious.' 'Extroverted.' 'Introverted.' 'Subtle.'
'Outgoing.' We were to write each word either in the left-hand

column or the right-hand column. I should have torn up my paper, and other people's papers, stopped the test. But I went along. Working from the inside, I gave the Chinese side 'Daring' and 'Laughter' and 'Spontaneous' and 'Easygoing,' some Star Quality items. But my bold answers were deviated away in the standard deviation. The American side got all the fun traits. It's scientifically factual truth now—I have a stripe down my back. Here, let me take off my shirt. Check out the yellow side, and the American side. I'm not the same after they experimented on me. I have aftereffects—acid flashbacks. I got imprinted. They treated me no better than any lab animal, who doesn't get the journals nor invited to the conferences that announce the findings. I happened to pick up the weekly science section of the newspaper, and saw a double-decker headline: 'Oriental Frosh Stay Virgins Longest / Caucasian Boys Get Most Sex Soonest.' When I thought they were testing my smarts, élan vital and spelling, they were checking out my virginity. There was this other test where they squeezed my Achilles tendons with calipers. I was to rate the pain from discomfort to unbearable, which level I never reached. I thought it was a pain tolerance test, but maybe they were testing for inscrutability. I'm not making this up. I tell you, there's a lot of Nazi shit going on in the laboratories. Don't fall into their castrating hands. Even if you don't go off into longterm or side effects physically or chemically, you're fucked philosophically. I'm never going to know what my straight head would have thought unaltered. I'm off, like the roosters you hear crow any time of day or night that you walk past the labs. No more lab gigs.

"I *am* this tall. I didn't get this tall by being experimented on by scientists trying to find the secret of height. They're looking for a time hormone in the pituitary gland; maybe the chronons are up there. Speeding them up (or slowing them down) may fool the body into growing more. They're taking unused time from the brains of cadavers and injecting it into the brains of short little orientals. You Sansei kids, stop going to height doctors to fuck with your hypothalamus. How many inches anyway between short and tall? Two. Three. Not many. The price of size—your mind. Don't be a generation of height freaks.

"It has to do with looks, doesn't it? They use 'American' interchangeably with 'white.' The clean-cut all-American look. This hairless body—I mean, this chest is unhairy; plenty hairy elsewhere—is cleaner than most. I bathe, I dress up; all I get is soo mun and sah chun.

"Which is not translated 'Star Quality.' Do you see it? Is my Star Quality showing nakedly yet? I've been trying to acquire it through education, attitude, right words, right work. Don't trust the movies, that stars are born. In a democracy, Star Quality can be achieved. And it can be conferred; I can love anybody. I'm learning to kiss everyone equally. Do you want to learn too? There's this theater game we play for warming up. Everybody goes around the circle and kisses everybody else. I judge who gets the title—Best Kisser in All the Land. The kissing contest is too good to keep backstage. Ladies and gentlemen, do I have some volunteers for free kisses? Step right up. That beautiful girl over there, Nanci, holds the title of Best Kisser and all the rights, duties, obligations, and privileges pertaining thereto. She'll participate. Now do I have some volunteers? Here's your chance. Come on up and take the championship away from her. Old futs too, come on, come on. I'll hug and kiss you myself. Nah, nah, nah, just kidding, la. I don't dig that shit either. But I challenge you old futs. You've been scolding me too much for the flagrancies of hugging and kissing going on in this play. You need to be taught a lesson, accusing me of affection. I'm going to unbrainwash you from believing anymore that we're a people who don't kiss and don't hug."

Led by PoPo, quite a few old futs stepped right on up. Nanci and Tana volunteered, the show-offs, and Sunny and Lance, good at parties, fielded a contingent—"We're game."—including Caucasians who had tuned out during the racial business.

To help everybody over shyness, Wittman went first. He kissed his wife, and got ready to kiss this girl he'd had a crush on, an obsession for, wanted but can't have, quite a few girls of the unattainable type, and a girl that was always making him puzzle over her physicality, and his mother, and his grandmother. Test his rule: Kiss the one you love for as many seconds—five six seven eight—as you kiss anyone you can't stand, an ugly girl the same hardness you kiss a pretty one. Equality

in food, jobs, and amount of loving. He touched a rough complexion, pores all wrecked by too much stage make-up, hot
lights and late hours, and liked the feel of zits on his fingertips. A man of principle kisses everybody as though they're
the same beautiful. Everybody was getting the same kiss off of
him. This girl he was trying to forget put her hand on his face
and her other hand on his naked, feeling chest, maneuvering.
Is this going to be a cheek smack, or are we going to land on
the lips? They kissed mouth to mouth, she turning aside, im-
perceptible to onlookers but felt by him, her move away from
him. All he had to do was prolong that kiss, pull her to him
for half a second too long, and it would slide into another
meaning. He put his hands on her waist, and tickled her. He
pounced on the next girl, and tickled her in the armpits. And
somebody ambushed him from behind, Taña tickling him.
Wittman laughed. Whereby his community shouted out a title
for him—Most Laughable.

To cheers and comments, each man went around and kissed
each of the ladies, and each lady kissed all the men. Because
everybody excelled at kissing, Wittman gave all of them titles—Most Juicy Kisser, Most Sincere, Best Technique, Most
Succulent, Most Experienced, Most Passionate, Mr. and Miss
Congeniality, Most Promising, Most Style, Coolest, Hottest,
the One Who Causes the Most Dreams, Most Motherly (not
won by Ruby Long Legs), Most Sisterly, Most Brotherly,
Most Troublemaker, Most Suave, Most Dangerous. Those
whom Wittman didn't personally kiss, he dubbed-thee by
observation.

So these champion kissers were practicing a custom of
a country they were intuiting. If ever it happens that the
Government lets us take vacations to China, we're going to
find: everywhere friends and relatives who will embrace us
in welcome. Everywhere demonstrative customs of affection—holding hands, sitting in laps, pats and strokes on heads
and backs, arms around waists, fingers and cheeks touching
cheeks. It has to be that way. Chinese live crowded, don't have
enough chairs, or space on the sofa, so sit close and all sleep
together in the one bed at inns and at home. In a land where
words are pictures and have tones, there's music everywhere all
the time, and a party going on. Whenever they need affection

during the labor of the day or the insomnia of the night, why, they betake themselves publicly, and the crowds receive them with camaraderie and food. The whole country—on all its streets—is an outdoor café. Commadres and compadres are always around for some talk, a card game, and a midnight snack. A billion communalists eating and discussing. They're never lonely. Men are brothers holding hands, and women hold hands, and mothers and fathers kiss children. We see evidence of their practices here: The day people from that country step off the boat, or off the plane, they walk up and down Grant Avenue holding hands with one another, or arm in arm, or one's arm around the other's neck and the other's arm around the waist, walking and talking close face-to-face. You have to look fast. The next time you see them, they're walking apart. They've learned not to go about so queer. They have come to a lonely country, where men get killed for holding hands. Well, let them start a new country where such opposite creatures as a man and a woman might go about the streets holding each other's hand in friendship.

Given heart by a loving community, Wittman confided to them his marriage. "While off guard, I got married, she married me. I have a wife to support. I'm having a bad time of it. I've been looking for a job. The other day I was at an interview, and trying not to smoke, I set my socks on fire. I had my foot over my knee like this. I was rubbing up the fuzz on my new socks. Gotta match? My face and your ass. I mean your ass and my face. I mean, nevermind. The next thing I knew, I'd lit my match on the bottom of my shoe, and touched it to my sock, like so. Whoosh. Flambé. Flaming foot of fire. Flash fire." As he talked, Wittman did what he was saying, and for a moment looked like Prince Na Zhen, the malicious baby, who runs on wheels of fire. Fire rushed around his ankle and leg. The kids yelled for an encore. The mothers yelled at him for burning himself. "I'm all right. It doesn't hurt. I'm okay. See? My ankle's fine. Flame out so fast, it didn't burn through. I didn't feel a thing. The interviewer probably thought he was seeing things. No, I can't do fire socks again. You can only do it once per sock. This other sock I fired up already. I didn't get the job.

"I applied at the insurance company where my wife works.

Don't worry, I knew better than to use her as a reference. Does anyone know why it is that at certain jobs such as insurance and teaching, they won't hire husband and wife? Family fights and family sex in front of the customers? I dressed straight-arrow. I treated the receptionist like she's boss. I applied myself, and filled out the forms without wedging any wisecracks or opinions into the answer spaces. I'm trying to be a Young Affordable, like you; then I'll buy my own shoes and new socks. I borrowed these shoes from the costume shop. They're too big for me." He lifted his foot over his knee. The shoe, too heavy, kept going, pulling him over with it. "I took an arithmetic test in these shoes. I matched rows of long numbers with other rows of long numbers, digit for digit the same. For example, is 68759312 exactly the same or not the same as 68759312? I did not add, did not subtract, just read horizontally and vertically. What for I went to college? I did pretty well, got everything right. And this personnel guy says to me, 'You people are good at figures, aren't you?' I can't think of how to answer right off. I should take that as a compliment? It's within his realm of *in*surance to recognize in me one of a tribe of born mathematicals, like Japanese? I say, 'Who, me? Not me, man. I come from the group with no sense of direction. I'm more the artistic type. What do you have in the creative line?' I didn't get a callback.

"At a corporation that I don't know what they actually produce, I told the interviewer about having organized a sales campaign before. And he says, 'Made fifty cents on the dollar?' I think I heard right. I say, 'What you say?' He says, 'Made a dollar out of fifty cents.' I let him have it on the immorality of profits. 'I'm against profits,' I say; 'I won't work for a corporation that profits from making shit. And if you're making something worthwhile, you should be giving it away.'

"What they always ask is, 'Why do you want to join our firm, Mr. Ah—Ah Sing?' They don't understand, I don't want to. I have to. And I don't join; I rule. But the most they'll let me do is the filing. How I answer, I say, 'I be-leaf in high high finance. I be-leaf in credit. Lend money; get interesting. Smallkidtime, I like bang money like Scrooge McDuck. I also likee bad Beagle Boys—follow map and dig under city into fault. No, not San Andreas Fault. Bang fault. Safu.' I was up for teller—I'm pretty smart—passed typing, passed adding machine—but when they call the tellers 'our girls,' I can tell they're not about to hire me.

"I'm unfit for office work. I'm facing up to that. And I can't write sales anymore. It fucks me up bad to sell anything to anybody. I have no attitude against blue collar, just so long as they make fruit cocktail instead of bombs, but I hate to lie that I'm not too overeducated. At this hiring hall for Fruitvale, guess what the guy says to me? He says, 'Do you have your green card?' My skin turning browner, my back getting wet, my moustache drooping, I say the truth, 'I don't have to show you no steenking green card.' And I don't, don't have to show it, and don't have one. I get so fucking offended.

"Unemployed and looking, my task is to spook out prejudice. They'll say any kind of thing to the unemployed. In Angel tradition, let me pass on to you the trick question they're asking: 'What would you say your weak point is?' They ask in a terribly understanding manner, but don't you confide dick. You tell them you have no weak point. Zip. 'None that I can think of,' you say. 'Weak point?' you say. 'What you mean weak point? I only have strong points.' They get you to inform on yourself, then write you up, 'Hates business,' 'Can't add,' 'Shy with customers.'

"My caseworker at the Employment Office, that is, the Office of Human Development—he's right over there—give him a hand—stand up—take a bow—Mr. Leroy Sanchez—advised me to get a haircut, and sent me to this shopping-news office on the Peninsula. On the bus, I thought out the power that would be mine peacemongering the shoppers with an aboveground grass-roots press. I'd be practicing right politics among locals who buy and sell. A radical can't accuse me, 'Poet, aussi, get your ass streetward,' that is, aux barricades et rues of Burlingame. I'd already be out on the block. Dig: the shopping news taking a stand on zoning—zoning can change society—re-seating the draft board and ex-locating the recruiting office. We'll sponsor contests with trips to Russia and Cuba and China for exchange workers and exchange soldiers. They will feel possessive of the Alameda shipyards, and can't bear to bomb them. We'll join one another's Friends of the Library and League of Women Voters and Audubon Society and food co-op and Sierra Club and S.P.C.A. and SANE and cornea bank. We exchange families and pets and recipes and civil servants. Like Leadership Day in high school, we hand over the running of the Government and everything to them, and vice versa. We do one another's work and keep up one another's social invitations. Sister cities conduct the foreign policy. Pretty soon we'll be all miscegenated and intermarried, we'll be patriotic to more than one place. By the time I got off the bus, I wanted the gig a lot. I was on time for my appointment. I gave my plan for world peace to the editor. I hope he appropriates my ideas. And you appropriate them too. Please. He asked, 'How old are you?' They think we look young. I told him nicely that I wasn't a short and young Chinese boy. He didn't hire me. I'll make my own shopping news. I'm passing the hat. Will you please put some money in it toward offset printing of my shopping news?"

As you may imagine, when Wittman promised a love story, but it was turning into a between-gigs story, he was losing some audience. He didn't try to stop them. Go ahead, leave. He did notice when this one and that one cut out. It's all right. Go. Go. Squeeze out between the knees and the chair-backs. (There are two types of audience members when they're excuse-me-leaving-excuse-me—some turn their ass and some their genitals toward the faces in a row.) They love fight scenes; they love firecrackers. But during a soliloquy when a human being is thinking out how to live, everybody walks about, goes to the can, eats, visits. O audience. For those who stayed with him, those with hungry ears but nobody has read to them since bedtime stories, he kept on talking. Those kind people were putting money and red envelopes into the hat.

"Readers will be able to pick up my shopping news for free. I'm going to give ideas on how to live on barely anything. From experiments in living, I know that three thousand dollars a year is plenty enough to live on and to sock some away as back-up for eventualities, and for projects such as this play. Our editorial policy will be that Congress has to pass Walter Reuther's plan for a guaranteed annual minimum living wage for United Auto Workers and everybody—three thousand dollars, which will bring every American up to the official poverty level. A married couple could pool their money—six thousand dollars. Two couples—twelve thousand dollars, a ten-percent down payment on a hundred and twenty thousand dollars worth of communal land. Life is possible.

"I want to run an information exchange on how to live like a China Man. Whenever you buy a newspaper, whenever you spend a dime for a pay toilet, you leave the door of the dispenser or the can open—don't slam it—for the next guy on voluntary poverty who comes along. I've found a route of newspaper dispensers where somebody's being regularly thoughtful of me. I hardly buy anything. I use the bathroom at Pam Pam's without being a customer, and they're okay about it. Lately I order pizza, and leave an unbitten wedge for some hungry person to grab ahead of the busboy. Do the same with club sandwiches. I'm going to make a listing of cafés where you may sit for a long time over one cup of coffee, and they don't say, 'There's a dead one at table eleven.' Sticks and stones. Just be sure to tip the waitress extra well. The Christian Science Reading Room is a private club for yourself alone, no other readers ever in there. Old St. Mary's has a reading room too, and the church part is open day and night seven days a week; in the middle of the night when you're freaking out, it's a quiet dark place to come down, sniffing the India Imports smells. Sometime in our lives, everyone ought to live on just what nature and society leave for us. Loquats dropping off the park trees bid us who know they're not poisonous, 'Eat me. Eat me.' To live on leavings, we find out just how inhabitable this planet, this country is. I pick up stuff off the street that I don't even need. I have to think up uses for what's there. If you sit on the seawall at Baker Beach or Aquatic Park for quite some time, you'll see the shoes and socks that nobody is coming back for. You'll not be wearing a drowned man's shoes; he went out into the water or walked along the shore and lost his landmarks. If they're still there after your own long walk, they're yours. Take them or the tide will. Of course, later, you will lose those shoes, and the watch that was inside one of them; there's a losing karma to things that you find. Like there's a stealing karma to hot stuff. When a Chinatown coot gets his unregistered gun stolen from under his pillow, and another old coot gives him his, that gun gets stolen too. My free shopping news will help every human being survive as an artist. If you hadn't helped me put on this show, I was going to drop Xeroxed copies of scripts into Goodwill bins. Painters can use the Salvation Army thrift shop for a gallery. Shoppers who buy art there would also buy playscripts, and read them and perform them.

"Among the ads about the price of bananas and birthday clowns and other odd jobs, I plan to keep running my idea for an anti-war ritual: Cut off the trigger finger instead of circumcision for all the boy babies, and all the girl babies too. Chop. I'll volunteer to have mine done first. On the other hand, the people who love shooting, they'll use their toes, they'll use their noses. It's more difficult to make peace than war. You take war away from human beings, you have to surrogate them with projects that haven't been thought up yet. Workers at weapons factories could keep their jobs making missiles but out of papier-mâché, and install them in the landscape for admiration. They're launchable. We let ourselves go at long last, drop them on Russia and Cuba, and invite them to drop theirs on us.

"You didn't come to the theater on your night offu to think about jobs and war; you came to be entertained. For my last bit, I'll tell you about marriage. I was learning to live poor— for one only. Then I got married. But. I have mixed feelings about that. About her. I may be getting a divorce. I have a marital problem. I married my second-best girl. I like her. She started the marital problem. She said that she's not in love with me. 'I'm not in love with you, Wittman,' is how she put it. I answered, 'Well, I'm not in love with you either, but. It's okay.' If I were in love with her, or vice versa, we should go to a shrink. Shrink the *ro*mance out of us. She—my wife—said, 'We haven't been romantic about each other. I never fantasized about you.' And I said, 'That's good. I don't want anybody fantasizing about anybody.' And she said, 'Out there somewhere is the soul chick you're going to fall in love with and leave me for. She's waiting for you, and you're waiting for her. The prosaic things you do, Wittman, will be interesting in her eyes. You'll become brave showing off for her. You better start regretting our marriage now so you won't regret everything when you're old, and it's too late.' One of the things I like best about my wife, she'll face a bad trip head on.

"I am sometimes somewhat in love with her. But it's not fate or magic. There's a specialness about her that is photographable. She has an expression on her face like she's appreciating whomever she's looking at. All she has to do is regard me, behold me like that, and I won't be able to leave her. She's listening; I hope she doesn't get self-conscious on me; I hope she isn't acting. The way her top lip upcurves with a dip in the center—she can't act that. She can't make mean lips. She smiles sideways. Quite a few movie stars have a sideways smile and beholding eyes, and we fans want them to keep reacting like that—to us, to everything. And she's got long blonde hair. I wouldn't mind a shrink immunizing me to it. I don't like being taken in by movie-star eyes and movie-star hair and movie-star lips.

"She admitted to me how she got this guy. Before she met me. On a rainy night, she went with her girlfriend and this guy into a coffeeshop. He held the umbrella and the door for this other girl to go ahead; he went in next. Water poured off the umbrella onto the girl in back, that is, her, my wife. He had made his choice. She said to herself, 'I'm going to get him.' At the next party, she let her hair down all clean and dry, a-tumble and curly, cascades of it down her back and shoulders, parted to the side, the way bad girls part hair, for a hank to fall over one eye and have to be seductively pushed back. That guy didn't have a chance. He was mesmerized in love, and the only thing changed about her was her hair. She's told me her magic. I've seen her with her hair wet and in a rubber band and in curlers. I'm not taken in. I'm not under her blonde power.

"She's not Chinese, I'll admit, but those girls are all out with white guys. What am I to do, huh? I don't want a Hong Kong wife marrying me for a green card. I've been testing my wife out. There was this sofa game in *Life* magazine a long time ago, where the guy sits at one end of the sofa and the girl at the other. They look into each other's eyes. In the next frame, they move closer together. 'Irresistibly,' said the caption, they meet in the middle. In the last frame, they're in each other's arms, kissing. A time clock at the corners of the pictures marked off minutes and seconds. There were three test couples in a series of long photographs. I've wondered, what happens if you mix the couples up, or pair strangers at random? My wife and I tried it. She can resist forever. She kept talking; she recited love poems; she read. So I read back to her Thomas Hardy, where Sergeant Troy says, 'Probably some one man on an average falls in love with each ordinary woman. She can marry him; he is content, and leads a useful life. Such a woman as you a hundred men always covet—your eyes will bewitch scores on scores into an unavailing fancy for you—you can only marry one of that many. . . . The rest may try to get over their passion with more or less success. But all these men will be saddened. And not only those ninety-nine men, but the ninety-nine women they might have married are saddened with them. There's my tale.' 'We don't want to be part of a system like that,' I told her. We're going to prove that any two random people can get together and learn to care for each other. I'm against magic; I go into despair over things happening that skip causation. The superior man loves anyone he sets his mind to. Otherwise, we're fucked.

"From the day that I made my explanations to my wife, she hasn't cleaned the apartment. I noticed before long that we'd gone through the dishes. Some of them have turned into ashtrays. I can trace the mess beginning at when I took my Hardyesque stand against *ro*mance. There are coffee cups all over the place with mold growing out of them. I can hear the dregs festering and bubbling. Her cups are especially disgusting because she uses cream. But black coffee grows mold too. Even non-dairy coffee creamer grows mold. Coffee must be nutritious, it can cultivate that much life. You have to watch where you step or sit. You kick aside newspapers, and the coffee cups underneath spill coins of mold that blend with the rug. All the doorknobs have towels and coats on them. I don't know where so much stuff comes from. It doesn't belong to me. It probably used to be in the drawers and closets, and she isn't putting it back. The place smells of cat piss and cat shit. My sense of smell is shot from smoking, but the cat is getting through to my nose. She got this S.P.C.A. cat and made it into a flealess indoor cat. The vet de-fleaed it the same day the fumigator came. The cat never goes outdoors again. She didn't have a cat when I married her. She does clean out the cat box and refill the kitty litter. But that fucking disoriented cat's been shitting in the clothes and newspapers. You don't want to step or sit for the cat turds.

"At meals, we clear off two spots at the table for her setting and my setting. The centerpiece is growing—rib bones from Emil Villa's Hickory Pit, a broken wineglass and candlewax and shrimp shells from an October candlelight dinner, plates from our last evening of clean dishes, movie popcorn boxes and used paper plates. I eat amongst mementos of other breakfasts, other suppers, naked lunches.

"The water standing in the kitchen sink started out as a soak for the pots and pans. Some are soaking in the bathtub too, and the skillet is in the living room from when we ate out of it. She can't wash dishes anymore because you can't run clean water without delving your arm through the scum and knives to unclog the drain. I wish, were I to flip the dispose-all on, a rotation would vortically twirl the room including the cat, and grind everything down and away.

"To be honest, one of my wife's attractions is that she's got a coin-operated washer and dryer in the garage. She did some laundry the other day; she picked her clothes out of the piles, and washed them, and ironed them. She does outfits to go to work in. I tossed in a pair of my skivvies, which didn't come back. As long as she's running a wash, she could do an item of another person's, right? I don't give her a full load. It's not as if she has to get depressed at the laundromat." Wittman put on his shirt; *he* didn't have the habit of dropping dirty clothes on top of piles of newspapers and banana peels and hair and cigarettes.

"We've been running all over the apartment churning up the newspapers and cat shit, yelling at each other, looking for a shoe and car fare and the phone. The off-the-hook noise is driving me nuts. I fell down slipping on a phonograph record under newspaper. She's always late for work because she can't find her car keys, or the house keys. They'll fire her, then the two of us on Unemployment, she can stay home and clean up. I was almost late myself tonight. The keys to the place were in the toaster oven. I don't know how they got there. Like the gravity has been acting up. She does cook. She's been standing at the stove and eating over the saucepan. If I want any, I have to eat her leftovers. We're leaving the front door unlocked, which the bags of garbage and the bags of groceries are shoving against. Anybody who would want to do some thieving in there, clean us out. Please. The ironing board unfolded out of the wall and dropped across the doorway.

"In the bathroom, I drape my washcloth on the rim of the sink, flat and neat, and she puts hers on top of it. Mine never dries. It took me days to detect that the mildew I was smelling was coming off of me. The newspapers for reading on the john get wet and print the tiles black. The black in the shower stall is an alga, and a strain of red alga is growing too.

"On Wednesdays, she says, 'Tonight's garbage night.' She knows the schedule. On her way to her car for work, she could pick up a bag of garbage and beat the scavengers to the cans. I've never believed the stereotype that Caucasians are dirty, but. Her place wasn't a dumpyard when I first went over there. Cleaned up for visitors, I guess. Good thing I haven't given up my own apartment until she learns better habits. The broom is missing. We need to hose the place out, or burn it down—a good fire—and start over. She isn't house-proud. I won't ask her to clean up. Our conversation has got to transcend garbage and laundry and cat shit. I don't want to live for garbage night. Domesticity is fucked. I am in a state of fucked domesticity. I am trying for a marriage of convenience, which you would think would make life convenient at least.

"Each of us announces to the other which room he's walking to. 'Well, I think I'll watch t.v. while I eat this t.v. dinner.' 'I'm going to read in the bathroom.' We don't want to lose track of each other's whereabouts. Things sure don't feel like they're about to end up in sex again. Yet how am I going to leave her? I ought to go out the door with my laundrybag and my toothbrush, and keep walking." He held his thumb and forefinger in a downward ring, as if holding his toothbrush by a suitcase-type handle.

"I had thought that one advantage of marrying a white chick would be that she'd say, 'I love you,' easily and often. It's part of their culture. They say 'I love you' like 'Hi, there,' nothing to it, to any friend, neighbor, family member, husband. You know how verbal they are. No skin off their pointy noses to say 'I love you.' But all I'm getting is, 'I'm not in love with you, Wittman.'

"The marriage is about two months old. I know what will happen next. I'm going to stay married to her; we're going to grow old. At our deathbed scene, whoever's not too gone to talk—she, I hope—will say at last, 'I love you.' I'll hear her. (The ears are the last to go.) And I'll think, Do you mean *in* love with me? Have you now or at any time in our life together ever loved me? Did you finally fall in love with me for a few moments during our long marriage? And since she has E.S.P. on me, she'll answer, 'Sure. Do you love me back? If you love me back, nod or blink.' I'll die suspicious and being suspected of loving and loving back. I'll nod, I'll blink. So I lied.

"Taña, if you're listening in the wings, you're free to leave if you want to leave me. But I'll always love you unromantically. I'll clean up the place, I get the hint. You don't have to be the housewife. I'll do one-half of the housewife stuff. But you can't call me your wife. You don't have to be the wife either. See how much I love you? Unromantically but."

Out of all that mess of talk, people heard "I love you" and "I'll always love you" and that about dying and still loving after a lifelong marriage. They took Wittman to mean that he was announcing his marriage to Taña, and doing so with a new clever wedding ritual of his own making. His community and family applauded. They congratulated him. They pushed and pulled the shy bride on stage, and shot pictures of her and of the couple. They hugged the groom, and kissed the bride. They teased them into kissing each other. More cameras flashed and popped. They threw rice. They congratulated their parents and grandparents. Their parents congratulated one another. Friends were carrying tables of food through the doors, and spreading a cast party and wedding banquet. And more firecrackers went off. And champagne corks popped. To Wittman and Taña—long life, happy marriage, many children. Taña and Wittman Ah Sing were stars in a lavish, generous wedding celebration. To drums and horns, the dragons and lions were dancing again, a bunny-hopping conga line that danced out of the house and into the street. Wittman's community was blessing him, whether he liked it or not.

And he was having a good time. He still had choices of action, more maybe. If he wanted to drop out and hide out, he had heard of the tunnel that goes under a hill between the old Army Presidio and the Marina for a subway never built. And somewhere in Fresno, there's an underground garden of fifty rooms. And he himself had been beneath the Merced Theater in Los Angeles. He had memories of dug-out dressing rooms that were part of an underground city where Chinese Americans lived and did business after the L.A. Massacre, nineteen killed. He and other draft dodgers could hide in such places until the war was over. But better yet, now that he had Taña—she could be the paper-wife escort who will run him across the U.S.-Canada border at Niagara Falls. He had made up his mind: he will not go to Viet Nam or to any war. He had staged the War of the Three Kingdoms as heroically as he could, which made him start to understand: The three brothers and Cho Cho were masters of war; they had worked out strategies and justifications for war so brilliantly that their policies and their tactics are used today, even by governments with nuclear-powered weapons. And they *lost*. The clanging and banging fooled us, but now we know—they lost. Studying the mightiest war epic of all time, Wittman changed—beeen!—into a pacifist. Dear American monkey, don't be afraid. Here, let us tweak your ear, and kiss your other ear.

THANKS To friends whose stories inspire my stories:

EARLL KINGSTON for the railroad reader of the West, the man with the addictive sperm, the Osaka Stock Exchange, and more.

JAMES HONG for his role in *The Barretts of Wimpole Street*.

JOHN CRONIN for the man whose Dear John letter falls out of the *P.D.R.*

JAMES D. HOUSTON for the fool-for-literature's reading list from *West Coast Fiction*, Bantam Books, Inc., 1979.

MARGARET MITCHELL DUKORE for "I'd rather be dead than boring," from *A Novel Called Heritage*, Simon and Schuster, 1982.

SUSIE QUINN GANIGAN and DUSTY on the train.

BRITT PYLAND for his arrangements of postcards at the airport.

VICTORIA NELSON for her recall of *The Saragossa Manuscript*.

STEPHEN SUMIDA for the four-act play, which is his novel-in-progress about being lost in the archipelago and the return of the fox, and for his luaus.

PHYLLIS H. THOMPSON for the wisdom about vows from "Blue Flowers," a poem in *The Ghosts of Who We Were*, University of Illinois Press, 1986.

L. LEWIS STOUT for the Electric Cassandra from *Trolling in America*, a screenplay.

AURORA PUTSY HONG for how to tell left from right.

GARY AND MOLLY MCCLURG WONG for Gavino McWong.

JACK CHEN for *his* Pear Garden in the West.

ROBERT WINKLEY for his memory of the Sun Yat Sen Hallowe'en tradition.

JACK PRESLEY for his contribution to R.N.A.-D.N.A.

RICHARD DI GRAZIA for "the marriage of Death and Fun" from "The Witness," a poem, and for fire socks.

DENIS KELLY for his dancing bouillon cube.

RHODA FEINBERG for the papier-mâché missiles.

JOHN VEGLIA for asking after that land where words are pictures and have tones.

To the John Simon Guggenheim Foundation and the M. Thelma McAndless Distinguished Professor Chair in the Humanities at Eastern Michigan University for generous financial support.

HAWAI'I ONE SUMMER

To the friends who are in this book

Contents

PREFACE TO THE PAPERBACK EDITION

I WROTE these essays during the middle of our seventeen-year stay in Hawai'i. Reading them today, I see that I have changed, and Hawai'i has changed. I am happier, and Hawai'i is more wonderful. A black cloud had covered my home place, Northern California. But leaving the Mainland for Hawai'i had not gotten us out from under it. The black pall that spread over the world during the long war had still not lifted. In 1978, the year of the Summer of this book, I was continuing my depression from the Vietnam War. The fallout from that war went on and on—wars in Cambodia and Laos, MIAs, agent orange, boat people.

A reader of this book surprises me. She asks, Why the many allusions to suicide? I reread these pages, and see: *Mortgage* meant *death*. The bombing of Kaho'olawe—by ANZUS and Japan. My son haunted by the ghosts of Mānoa, and I haunted by the ghost of a lost poet. Nature's creatures suffering and killing. Kālua pig looking like a haole human being. And homesickness—but if I do not feel at home in Paradise, where is home? My first take on Hawai'i was, Here I am arrived at the Land of Lotus Eaters, and I'm not going to leave. I thought I was writing lighthearted essays.

This same sympathetic reader wondered, Could it be that you'd broken taboos by writing and publishing secrets? Well, it did not feel good to be a writer in a place that is not a writing culture, where written language is only a few hundred years old. The literary community in Hawai'i argues over who owns the myths and stories, whether the local language and writings should be exported to the Mainland, whether or not so-and-so is authentic, is Hawaiian. For me, Hawai'i was a good place for writing about California and China, and not for writing about Hawai'i. I felt the kapu—these are not your stories to write; these myths are not your myths; the Hawaiians are not your people. You are haole. You are katonk. My great grand-fathers, one on my mother's side, one on my father's side, and

867

my paternal grandfather lived and worked in Hawai'i. Even so, they were not kama'āina, and I am not kama'āina.

Once, on the Big Island, Pele struck me blind. She didn't want me to look at her, nor to write about her. I could hear her say, "So you call yourself Woman Warrior, do you? Take that." I feel fear even now as I write her name. And I could hear the Hawaiians: "You have taken our land. Don't take our stories."

Hawai'i held an Asian Pacific American writers' conference the very Summer of this book. We addressed one another with rancor and panic, though some did try for aloha. The name *Asian Pacific American* had barely been thought, and many people denied every term in it. We were divided between those who would give the stories, myths, ceremonies to whoever hears them, and those who would have possession be by blood. So, I decided that I would write personally, about myself and my family, about homesickness for California, and my upcoming high school reunion, about washing the dishes, teaching school, reading. I would publish these humble pieces in New York, and bypass Hawai'i. I meant to honor kapu, not touch kapu things at all.

But though I did try to leave her out, Hawai'i—people sing her and speak of her as Spirit—made her way into these essays. Writing about buying our first house, I worried that I was trying to own property that had been a Royal Hawaiian Land Grant. Describing Nature, the sea, the air, the lands and fish, is describing Hawai'i. I studied Lew Welch on dialect because I was thinking about Hawai'i's language—how to teach standard English to students who speak pidgin without offending or harming them?

Now, a dozen years after leaving her, I realize a way free to tell a story of Hawai'i.

In 1980, I was recognized as a Living Treasure of Hawai'i. The enrobed monks and priests of the Honpa Hongwanji Mission at the temple on the Pali chanted Sanskrit, and passed a certificate through the incense that entitles me to "all the rights, privileges, and consideration" of a Living Treasure of Hawai'i. Some of my fellow Living Treasures are Mary Kawena Pukui, Gabby Pahinui, Herb Kawainui Kane, Francis Haar, Bumpei Akaji, Satoru Abe, Auntie Irmgard Farden Aluli, Don Mitchell, Auntie Emma Farden Sharp, Tadashi Sato, Eddie

Kamai, and everybody, really, only not yet formally recognized in ceremony.

As a responsible Living Treasure, I feel called upon to tell you a story that will give help and power. Once there was a prophecy that Kamehameha would conquer all the islands if he could build a great temple to his family war god, Kū-kā'ili-moku. Setting some of the lava rocks and boulders with his own hands, Kamehameha built the heiau on Pu'ukoholā, the Hill of the Whale, at Kawaihae. His domain at that time was the northwest half of the Big Island. Before the heiau could be finished, the chiefs of Maui, Lāna'i, Moloka'i, Kaua'i, and O'ahu raised an armada and attacked Kamehameha's land and people. Kamehameha repelled the attack, and completed the building of the massive temple. To dedicate it, he summoned his cousin, Keoua Kū'ahu'ula, ruler of the rest of the Big Island, to come to the ceremony. It was understood that Keoua Kū'ahu'ula would be the gift to the war god. In honor, he could not refuse this call, but he emasculated himself; Kamehameha would not have a perfect male sacrifice. Kamehameha waiting on shore, Keoua Kū'ahu'ula arose in his canoe. Kamehameha's counselor and father-in-law, Ke'eaumoku, killed him. Keoua's blood and body sanctified the new temple. Enmity between their two clans lasted for two hundred years.

In 1991, descendants of Kamehameha and descendants of Keoua Kū'ahu'ula had an inspiration "to heal the bitterness, grievances, and enmity of the past two hundred years." The families gathered at Pu'ukoholā Heiau, and re-created the event of long ago: Keoua Kū'ahu'ula approaches Kamehameha. This time, they meet and walk on together.

To Kamehameha I, unification meant conquering all the Hawaiian people by war. Now unification is the coming together of former enemies in peace. It is possible to heal history. It is possible to be one people living in harmony.

I heard the above story from Jim Houston, who heard it from the Park Service and from Kalani Meinecke, who narrated the unification ceremony at Pu'ukoholā Heiau.

I am not the person I was in the "War" essay, and the "Dishwashing" essay. Now looking back at Sanctuary at the Church of the Crossroads, I remember the AWOL soldiers who were true pacifist heroes. And the black cloud no longer hangs over Hawai'i. I am more joyful and hopeful than when I was young. And I love washing dishes, which attitude is the answer to *that* koan.

Ke aloha nō! Aloha!

Mainland, 1998

P.S. I must tell you about the incarnations of the pieces in this book. Most of them first appeared in my "Hers" column in the *New York Times*, which rejected "Lew Welch: An Appreciation." I thought: New York is too provincial to understand the Pacific Rim. But now I see that I didn't follow Lew Welch's disappearance far enough. He got off at *leina-a-ka-'uhane*, leaping place of souls. I owe this poetic insight to Victoria Nelson of *My Time in Hawaii*; our times coincided.

Leigh McLellan of Meadow Press gathered these pieces, and made a book of them with her own loving hands. She chose paper from the Kozo rice fields in Korea, hand-set the type, made the paste paper for the cover, and sewed the binding. The Taoist teacher, Deng Ming-Dao, son of Jade Snow Wong, cut and printed four beautiful six-color woodblock pictures. There are 150 books, half of them in slipcases that Leigh constructed. It is a luxury to hold and touch and smell one of these books. But, at $400 per book and $500 for the slipcased one, the fine print edition of *Hawai'i One Summer* is for art collectors, and not for readers.

So, these writings, once ephemeral newspaper articles, then revered artifacts, have found their just-right form—the paperback in your hand.

PREFACE

Twenty years after an adventure, I can write about it truly. A few large shapes remain in the memory—unforgettable. A thing which at one time seemed monumental becomes background or a surprisingly small figure in front, or it has disappeared. Remember how stereopticon pictures look like popping 3-D with cut-out-like cars and buildings and people artificially forward and backward? Memory is artistic in the ways it arranges and sorts out. My son is exactly twenty years old, and what I remember of his being born was a big hand holding a little foot. I am forty-three years old, and I just noticed that the hero in the novel I'm working on is twenty-three. At last, I understand about being a young person setting out in the world.

I did not wait for twenty years to write the pieces in this book, which is like a diary. There is sometimes only a week or two between an event and my writing about it. I wrote about my son's surfing upon coming home from it. I wrote about the high school reunion before going to it. The result is that I am making up meanings as I go along. Which is the way I live anyway. There is a lot of detailed doubting here.

Since the invitation to the twentieth year high school reunion came at the beginning of the summer, I could have followed up and told you what happened next. But by August my worrying was all taken up by my son's surfing. Also, the reunion was so complicated—the people were so complicated—my seeing the child and the aging adult in others and in myself—that I have to wait until I'm still older to figure it out.

What I like very much about being middle-aged is that I can write from opposing points of view at once—rebel's and householder's, student's and teacher's, mother's and child's.

I was finishing *China Men* in the summer when other people were vacationing. So, for breaks, I wrote these pieces. But I was in the world of *China Men*, and its images kept appearing everywhere—in my letters to friends, in life, and in this book. So, here again are the frigate birds in the air currents, creatures on the beach, assembly lines funneling napalm to Vietnam, the sandalwood that was still here in Hawai'i when my great-grandfathers came.

It is very difficult to capture Hawai'i. Whose point of view among all of Hawai'i's peoples is the right way of seeing? Her beauty defies artistic imitation. There should be epic poems to her, as there were in ancient times. Failing that, I have instead and incidentally described her piece by piece, and hope that the sum praises her.

As I read over these essays, there is some grammar that I was tempted to clean up. I used to have a habit of saying "like," as in "like cool, man" and "like wow." It was my tribute to the slang of my generation. The twenty-three-year-old hero of my novel, which is set in Chinatown and North Beach in 1963, talks like that, and his style is spilling over into mine. Let it stand.

April 1984

JUNE
Our First House

IT HAS been a month now since we moved into our own
bought house. So far, we've been renters. I have liked saying, "Gotta make the rent" and "This much set aside for rent"
and "rent party."

A renter can move quickly, no leases, forego the cleaning
deposit and go. Plumbing, wiring, walls, roof, floors keep to
their proper neutral places under the sun among the stars. If
we looked at each other one day and decided that we really
shouldn't have gotten married after all, we could dismantle
the brick-and-plank bookshelf or leave it, no petty talk about
material things. The householder is only one incarnation away
from snail or turtle or kangaroo. In religions, the householder
doesn't levitate like the monk. In politics, the householder
doesn't say, "Burn it down to the ground." I had never become
a housewife. I didn't need to own land to belong on this planet.

But as soon as we drove up to this house in Mānoa, we liked
everything—the cascades of rosewood vines, lichen and moss
on lava rock boulders, moss-color finches, two murky ponds
thick with water hyacinth, an iridescent green toad—poisonous—hopping into the blue ginger, a gigantic monkey pod
tree with a stone bench beneath it, three trees like Van Gogh's
cypresses in the front yard, pines in back, an archway like an
ear or an elbow with no purpose but to be walked through,
a New England–type vestibule for taking off snowy coats and
boots, a dining room with glass doors, only one bedroom but
two makeshifts, a bathroom like a chapel, a kitchen with a
cooler—through the slats you can look down at the earth and
smell it. And—the clincher—a writer's garret, the very writer's
garret of your imagination, bookshelves along an entire wall
and a window overlooking plumeria in bloom and the ponds.
If I could see through the foliage, I could look downhill and
see the (restored) hut where Robert Louis Stevenson wrote his
Hawai'i works.

What thick novels I could brood up here with no interrupting chapter breaks but one long thought from front to back cover.

We found two concealed cupboards, one of them with seven pigeonholes; the artist who painted in the garret must have stored brushes in them, or perhaps, here, a sea captain or his widow kept his rolled-up maps. The person who once sat at the built-in desk (with a formica top) had written in pencil on the wall:

eros
agape
philos

Promising words.

But when we talked about house-buying, both of us thought about dying. The brain automatically adds 20 years of mortgage on to one's age. And *mortgage* derives from *mors, mortis*, as in *mortal. Move* was one of the first English words my parents ever used, such an early word I thought it was Chinese— *moo-fu*, a Chinese American word that connotes "pick up your pants and go."

Renting had begun to feel irresponsible. Our friend who teaches university students how to calculate how many grams are gained or lost on a protein exchange, how much alfalfa turns into how much hamburger, for example, told us about the time when each earthling will have one square foot of room. This friend quit the city and bought five acres in the mountains; a stream runs through his land. He will install solar energy panels and grow food, raise a goat, make the five acres a self-sufficient system.

We heard about a family who had all their teeth pulled, bought their own boat, and sailed for an island that's not on maps. If we owned a vacant lot somewhere, when the world ends, we can go there to sleep or sit.

Coincidentally, strange ads were appearing in the real estate section of newspapers: "Ideal place for you and your family in the event of war, famine, strike, or natural disaster."

The advantages—to have a place for meeting when the bombs fall and to write in a garret—outweighed the dread of ownership, and we bought the house.

The writer's garret is a myth about cheap housing. In real life, to have a garret, the writer has to own the house under the garret and the land under the house and the trees on the land for an inspiring view.

On the day we moved in, I tried walking about and thinking: "This is my tree. This flower is mine. This grass and dirt are mine." And they did partly belong to me.

Our son, Joseph, looked up at Tantalus, the mountain which rises straight up in back of the house, and said. "Do we have to rake up all the leaves that fall from there?"

At the escrow office (new word, *escrow*), we signed whatever papers they told us to. Earll read them after we got home, and so found out that this land had been given to E. H. Rogers by a Royal Hawaiian Land Grant. "We don't belong on it," he said. But, I rationalized, isn't all land Israel? No matter what year you claim it, the property belongs to a former owner who has good moral reason for a claim. Do we, for example, have a right to go to China, and say we own our farm, which has belonged to our family since 1100 A.D.? Ridiculous, isn't it? Also, doesn't the average American move every five years? We just keep exchanging with one another.

The way to deal with moving in was to establish a headquarters, which I decided would be in the dining room, a small powerful spot, surprisingly not the garret, which is secretive. The Headquarters would consist of a card table and a lawn chair, a typewriter, papers, and pencils. It takes about ten minutes to set up, and I feel moved in, capable; from the Headquarters, I will venture into the rest of the house.

Earll assembles and talks about a Basic Kit, by which I think he means a toothbrush and toothpaste. "The Basic Kit is all I really need," he keeps saying, at which I take offense. I retaliate that all I need is my Headquarters.

Joseph's method of moving in is to decide that his bedroom will be the one in the attic, next to the writer's garret, and he spreads everything he owns over its strangeness.

As at every place we have ever moved to, we throw mattresses on the living room floor and sleep there for several nights—to establish ourselves in the middle of the house, to weight it down. The night comes black into the uncurtained windows.

I attack the house from my Headquarters, and again appreciate being married to a person whose sense of geometry is not much different from mine. How do people stay together whose eyes can't agree on how much space there should be between pictures?

The final thing that makes it possible to live in the house is our promise to each other that if we cannot bear the weight of ownership, we can always sell, though we know from fifteen years of marriage that this is like saying, "Well, if this marriage doesn't work out, we can always get a divorce." You don't know how you change in the interim.

My High School Reunion

I JUST opened an envelope in the mail and found a mimeographed sheet smelling like a school test and announcing the twentieth year reunion of my high school class. No Host Cocktail Party. Buffet Dinner. Family Picnic. Dancing. In August. Class of '58. Edison High. Stockton. My stomach is lurching. My dignity feels wobbly. I don't want to go if I'm going to be one of those without the strength to stay grown up and transcendent.

I hadn't gone to the tenth year reunion. The friends I really wanted to see, I was seeing, right? But I've been having dreams about the people in high school, and wake up with an urge to talk to them, find out how they turned out. "Did you grow up? I grew up." There are parts of myself that those people have in their keeping—they're holding things for me—different from what my new friends hold.

"When I think of you, I remember the hateful look you gave me on the day we signed yearbooks. That face has popped into my mind a few times a year for twenty years. Why did you look at me that way?" I'd like to be able to say that at the No Host Cocktail Party. And to someone else: "I remember you winking at me across the physics lab."

I dreamed that the girl who never talked in all the years of school spoke to me: "Your house has moles living in it." Then my cat said, "I am a cat and not a car. Quit driving me around." Are there truths to be found?

Another reason I hadn't gone to my tenth was an item in the registration form: "List your publications." Who's on the reunion committee anyway? Somebody must have grown up to become a personnel officer at a university. To make a list, it takes more than an article and one poem. Cutthroat competitors. With no snooty questions asked, maybe the classmates with interesting jail records would show up. We are not the class to be jailed for political activities or white collar crimes but for burglary, armed robbery, and crimes of passion. "Reunions are planned by the people who were popular.

They want the chance to put us down again," says a friend (Punahou Academy '68), preparing for her tenth.

But surely, I am not going to show up this year just because I now have a "list." And there is more to the questionnaire: "What's the greatest happiness you've had in the last twenty years? What do you regret the most?" I should write across the paper, "These questions are too hard. Can I come anyway?" No, you can't answer, "None of your business." It *is* their business; these are the people who formed your growing up.

I have a friend (Roosevelt High '62) who refused to go to his tenth because he had to check "married," "separated," "divorced," or "single." He could not bear to mark "divorced." Family Picnic.

But another divorced friend's reunion (Roosevelt '57) turned out to be so much fun that the class decided to meet again the very next weekend—without the spouses, a come-without-the-spouse party. And when my brother (Edison '60) and sister-in-law (Edison '62) went to her reunion, there was an Old Flames Dance; you asked a Secret Love to dance. Working out the regrets, people went home with other people's spouses. Fifteen divorces and remarriages by summer's end.

At my husband Earll's (Bishop O'Dowd '56) reunion, there was an uncomfortableness as to whether to call the married priests Father or Mister or what.

What if you can't explain yourself over the loud music? Twenty years of transcendence blown away at the No Host Cocktail. Cocktails—another skill I haven't learned, like the dude in the old cowboy movies who ordered milk or lemonade or sarsaparilla. They'll have disco dancing. Never been to a disco either. Not cool after all these years.

In high school, we did not choose our friends. I sort of ended up with certain people, and then wondered why we went together. If she's the pretty one, then I must be the homely one. (When I asked my sister [Edison '59] about my "image," she said, "Well, when I think of the way you look in the halls, I picture you with your slip hanging.") Not well-groomed.) We were incomplete, and made complementary friendships, like Don Quixote and Sancho Panza. Or more like the Cisco Kid and Pancho. Friendships among equals is a possibility I have found as an adult.

No, my motive for going would not be because of my "list." I was writing in high school. Writing did not protect me then, and it won't protect me now. I came from a school—no, it's not the school—it's the times; we are of a time when people don't read.

There's a race thing too. Suddenly the colored girls would walk up, and my colored girlfriend would talk and move differently. Well, they're athletes, I thought; they go to the same parties. Some years, the only place I ever considered sitting for lunch was the Chinese table. There were more of us than places at that table. Hurry and get to the cafeteria early, or go late when somebody may have finished and left a seat. Or skip lunch. We will eat with whom at the Buffet Dinner?

Earll says that he may have to work in August, and not be able to escort me. Alone at the Dance. Again.

One day, in high school, I was walking home with a popular girl. (It was poor to be seen walking to or from school by oneself.) And another popular girl, who had her own car, asked my friend to ride with her. "No, thanks," said my friend. "We'll walk." And the girl with the car stamped her foot, and said, "Come here! *We* ride home with one another." Meaning the members of their gang, I guess. The popular-girl gang. "I remember you shouting her away from me," I could say at the reunion, not, I swear, to accuse so much as to get the facts straight. Nobody had come right out and said that there were very exclusive groups of friends. They were not called "groups" or "crowds" or "gangs" or "cliques" or anything. ("Clicks," the kids today say.) "Were you in a group? Which one was I in?"

My son, who is a freshman (Roosevelt, Class of '81), says he can't make friends outside of his group. "My old friends feel left out, and then they ice me out."

What a test of character the reunion will be. I'm not worried about looks. My woman friends and I are sure that we look physically better at thirty-eight than at eighteen. By going to the reunion, I'll be able to update the looks of those people who are always eighteen in my dreams.

John Gregory Dunne (Portsmouth Priory '50) said to his wife, Joan Didion (McClatchy High '52), "It is your obligation as an American writer to go to your high school reunion."

And she went. She said she dreamed about the people for a long time afterward.

I have improved: I don't wear slips anymore. I got tired of hanging around homely people. It would be nice to go to a reunion where we look at one another and know without explanations how much we improved in twenty years of life. And know that we had something to do with one another's outcomes, companions in time for a while, lucky to meet again. I wouldn't miss such a get-together for anything.

War

TRYING TO define exactly how Hawai'i is different from California, I keep coming up with the weather, though during certain seasons the weather isn't all that different. In 1967, Earll and I, with our son, left Berkeley in despair over the war. Our friends, retreating from the barricades, too, were starting communes in the northern California woods. They planned to live—to build and to plant, to marry and to have babies—as if the United States were out of Vietnam.

"Look," Lew Welch was saying, "if nobody tried to live this way, all the work of the world would be in vain." He also wrote about Chicago: "I'm just going to walk away from it. Maybe / A small part of it will die if I'm not around / feeding it anymore." That was what we felt about America.

We did not look for new jobs in Hawai'i. It was the duty of the pacifist in a war economy not to work. When you used plastic wrap or made a phone call or drank grape juice or washed your clothes or drove a car, you ran the assembly lines that delivered bombs to Vietnam.

Gary Snyder said that at the docks the forklifts make holes in sacks, and you can pick up fifteen or twenty-five pounds of rice for free once a week. We discovered that a human being could live out of the dumpsters behind the supermarkets. Blocks of cheese had only a little extra mold on them. Tear off the outer leaves, and the lettuce and cabbage heads were perfectly fresh. It wasn't until about three years ago that the supermarkets started locking their garbage bins at night.

At least the weather in Hawai'i was good for sleeping outdoors if necessary. So it really did come down to the weather. I remembered Defoe writing in *A Journal of the Plague Year* that during the plague, moods were greatly affected by the weather. Also, we had our passports ready, and if the United States committed one more unbearable atrocity, we would already be halfway to Japan.

We discovered that O'ahu is a rim that we could drive in less than a day. Shoes, clothes, tables, chairs washed up on the shores. We found a ninety-dollar-a-month apartment above a grocery store on the rim. We cadged a bunk bed from an abandoned house, a broken park bench for a sofa, fruit and nuts but not pineapples because of the fifty-dollar fine. If only the war would end before our life savings did, we would be all right. The greenery was so lush that we did not notice for a long time that the people were poor, that we were living in a slum by the sea.

We had not, of course, escaped from the war, but had put ourselves in the very midst of it, as close as you could get and remain in the United States.

We should have thought of it—hardware and soldiers were sent to Hawai'i, which funneled everything to Vietnam. Tanks and jeeps in convoys maneuvered around the rim. Khaki soldiers drove khaki vehicles, camouflage that did not match the bright foliage. Like conquered natives standing on the roadside, we were surprised when soldiers gave us the peace sign. (In Berkeley, we hardly saw any soldiers.) We heard the target practice—with missiles—in the mountains, where we hiked, and looked at the jagged red dirt like wounds in the earth's green skin.

At the airport, near the luggage carts, we saw coffins draped with flags. One marine per stack stood guard through the night. The coffins disappeared by day. We went to Tripler to visit a soldier we knew hurt in a motorcycle accident. He was in Neurosurgical Post Op, a ward full of young men who had been wounded in the brain. Quadriplegics. A totally paralyzed man lay on his stomach, his face toward the floor, not reading.

Soldiers came to Hawai'i for R & R. At the beach, many swimmers had various unlikely parts of their bodies bandaged. I saw three soldiers, one crippled and two bandaged, jumping in the waves with their clothes on, splashing one another, cavorting. Glad to be alive, I thought, glad to be out of Vietnam alive.

Many of the soldiers had not been wounded in Vietnam but in auto accidents here, bike accidents, swimming and surfing accidents; also they shot one another. Once out of Vietnam, they got careless, sucked through the Blowhole, drowned in the lagoons, swept away in undertows, killed the first day or week out of Vietnam. Beaten up by locals. "Swim out there," the girls said, practicing their siren ways, pointing into the Witch's Brew, the Potato Patch, the Toilet.

Paul Goodman was spending one of the last years of his life teaching in Hawai'i. Earll asked him if he were giving up working for peace. The protest was so feeble here. "No," he said, "people on all levels of power are accessible in such a small place." He wrote poems about Hawai'i: ". . . here I will never be able to make love / the people are not plain. I would be happier / trying to make out with the porpoises / if only I could swim better than I do." The newspapers cartooned him as an East Coast haole presuming to criticize paradise.

There was nothing to do but continue the protest, help the AWOL soldiers and sailors when they took sanctuary at the Church of the Crossroads and formed the Servicemen's Union. During this time, it seemed that there were more nights than days; the light came from candles and hibachis and bonfires in the Japanesy courtyard of the church. The soldiers, mere kids, illiterate boys from the poorer states, did not agree that the war was wrong; some went AWOL because they didn't like their officers, or the food was bad, or they wanted a vacation, or they were just fooling around. The peace movement was using them no less than the government was.

In the sanctuary, the peace people drilled the AWOLs in history while from outside came the voice of the Army chaplain on a bullhorn, asking them to give themselves up. Winning hearts and minds. We tried to make conversation. "What do you like to do?" I asked a short boy, who looked both stunted and hurtable in his new PX aloha shirt and the haircut that exposed his neck and ears. "I build model cars," he said. "I built five hundred of them, and I lined 'em up and shot 'em and set 'em on fire." "Why did you do that?" "It felt good—like when I was a door gunner on the chopper in Nam. Thousands of bullets streaming out of my gun." Silence. Don't tell me about the gooks you shot, I thought. Don't tell me about the hootches you torched.

"What will you do next if the war doesn't end?" I asked. I did not want to keep feeding and visiting these people forever. "I don't know." Long silence. "You could go to Sweden." "Sure. That's in Canada, right? I'll help your son build model airplanes if he likes." He was comfortable playing cars with a five-year-old. He did not read the directions and glued the more intricate parts wrong. Not having the sense to stay hidden, he got into two auto accidents; we had to go to the rescue at two and three in the morning. Finally he and another boy turned themselves in at Schofield. They asked Earll to drive them. They swallowed the rest of their acid. Before they surrendered to the M.P. at the gate, they said, "Tell them you captured us. You get fifty dollars apiece reward."

The war is more or less over, but we have remained here. The military paraphernalia also remains; even our dovish members of Congress have defended Hawai‘i against military cuts. But after ten years in these islands, I see through camouflages and find the winding trails inland, away from the rim. Reading Goodman's Hawai‘i poems now, I hardly understand why he wanted plain loves; the world calmer, I like complexities. That his sadness seems inappropriate shows the possibility of a happier place, Hawai‘i a vacation spot. I want to stay for a while to vacation.

Dishwashing

D ISHWASHING IS not interesting, either to do or to think about. Thinking has dignified other mundane things, though. At least it will postpone the dishwashing, which stupefies. After eating, I look at the dishes in the sink and on the counters, the cat's dirty bowl and saucer underfoot, swipe at the dabs and smears recognizable from several meals ago, pick up a cup from among the many on chairs and beside beds, and think about suicide. Also about what to write in the suicide note.

The note is an act of kindness. The criminals who most upset us are the ones who refuse to give satisfying motives. "I don't want to wash the dishes one more time." A plain note, no hidden meanings.

I run water into the frying pan—its black underside just clears the faucet because of the pile-up—but the scrubber and the sponges are hidden somewhere in the bottom of the sink. Thwarted at the start. The frying pan fills; the pile shifts; greasy water splashes on me and spills. I turn off the water and get out of the kitchen. Let the pan soak itself clean. No way to wash the pot and the blender underneath it nor the dishes under that, the crystal wine glasses at the bottom. The dishpan and the drain are buried, too, so I can't let the cold, dirty water out. When the mood to do so overcomes me, I'll take these dishes out and start all over.

Once in a while, early in the morning, my powers at their strongest, I can enjoy washing dishes. First, reorganize the pile, then fill the dishpan again with clean water. I like water running on my wrists and the way bubbles separate from the suds and float about for quite awhile. I am the one who touches each thing, each utensil and each plate and bowl; I wipe every surface. I like putting the like items together back on the shelves. Until the next time somebody eats, I open the drawers and cupboards every few minutes to look at the neatness I've wrought.

Unfortunately, such well-being comes so rarely, and the mornings are so short, they ought not be wasted on dishes.

Better to do dishes in the afternoon, "the devil's time," Tennessee Williams calls it, or in the evening immediately before dinner. The same solution for bedmaking—that is, right before going to bed. I try to limit the number of items I wash to only those needed for dinner, but since I can't find them without doing those on top, the obstructing ones get washed too. I trudge. I drudge.

The one person I know who is a worse dishwasher than I am pushes the dishes from the previous meal to the middle of the table to make places for clean saucers, no plates left.

Another person pulls a dish out of the sink and uses it as is.

When my father was a young man, working in a laundry on Mott Street in New York, he and his partners raced at meals. Last one to finish eating washed the dishes. They ate fast.

Technology is not the answer. I have had electric dishwashers, and they make little difference. The electric dishwasher does not clear the table, collect the cups from upstairs and downstairs, scrape, wipe the counters and the top of the stove. One's life has to be in an orderly phase to load and arrange the dishes inside the dishwasher. Once they're gathered in one spot like that, the momentum to do the rest of the task is fired up.

Although dishwashing is lonely work, I do not welcome assistance. With somebody else in the kitchen, I hurry to get at the worst messes to spare her or him. Alone, I wash two plates, and take a break. Helpers think that dishwashing includes unloading the dishwasher, sweeping and mopping the floor, defrosting the refrigerator, and de-crusting the oven, cleaning the kitchen, and cleaning the dining room.

In *Living Poor With Style*, Ernest Callenbach says that it is unsanitary to wipe dry because the dish cloth spreads the germs evenly over everything. Air drying is better, he says, meaning letting everything sit in the drainer. (He also recommends washing the cooking implements as you finish each step of cooking. Impossible. I did that once in a temporary state of grace, which was spoiled by having to wash dishes.)

Paper plates are no solution. There are no paper pots and pans and spatulas and mixing bowls. The plates are the easiest part of dishwashing.

I prop books and magazines behind the faucet handles.

Some people have television sets in their kitchens. Books with small print are best; you don't turn the pages so often and dislodge the book into the water.

I do enjoy washing other people's dishes. I like the different dishes, different sink, different view out the window. Perhaps neighbors could move over one house each night and do one another's dishes. You usually do other folks' dishes at a holiday or a party.

I like using a new sponge or dishcloth or soap or gloves, but the next time, they're not new.

In *Hawaii Over the Rainbow*, Kazuo Miyamoto says that in the World War II relocation camps for Americans of Japanese Ancestry, the women had the holiday of their lives—no cooking, no dishwashing. They felt more at leisure than back home because of the communal dining halls and camp kitchens. I can believe it.

Compared to dishes, scrubbing the toilets is not bad, a fast job. Also you can neglect toilets one more week, and you only have one or two of them.

I typed a zen koan on an index card, which I have glued to the wall beside the sink. You may cut this out and use it if you like:

> *"I have just entered the monastery. Please teach me."*
> *"Have you eaten your rice?"*
> *"I have."*
> *"Then you had better wash your bowl."*
> *At that moment, the new monk found enlightenment.*

This koan hasn't helped yet with the dishwashing; that is, no one in the family has picked up on it. It would probably be more enlightening to post Miyamoto or Callenbach's words. But I have a glimmering that if I solve this koan, I can solve dishwashing too. If I can solve dishwashing, I can solve life and suicide. I haven't solved it but have a few clues.

The koan does not say that the monk was enlightened after he washed the bowl. "At that moment" seems to be at the instant when he heard the advice.

I hope the koan doesn't mean that one has to pay consequences for pleasure; you eat, therefore you wash bowl. Dismal. Dismal.

It could mean something about reaching enlightenment through the quotidian, which is dishwashing.

The monk did not gain his enlightenment after washing the dishes day after day, meal after meal. Just that one bowl. Just hearing about that one bowl.

I have come up with a revolutionary meaning: Each monk in that monastery washed his own bowl. The koan suggests a system for the division of labor. Each member of the family takes his or her dishes to the sink and does them. Pots and pans negotiable. Cat dishes negotiable too.

The koan shows that dishwashing is important. A life-and-death matter, to be dealt with three times a day.

JULY
Chinaman's Hat

L IVING ON an island, I miss driving, setting out at dawn, and ending up five or six hundred miles away—Mexico—at nightfall. Instead, we spin around and around a perimeter like on a race track.

Satellite photos of the Hawaiian Islands show swirls, currents, winds, movement, movements of clouds and water. I have to have them pointed out to me and to look closely before I descry three or four of the islands, in a clearing, chips of rock, miniatures in the very shapes you find on maps. The islands, each one the tip of a volcano connected to the ocean floor, look like the crests of waves.

Logs and glass balls have creatures living on them too. Life gathers and clings to whatever bit of solidity—land. Whales and porpoises and sharks become land for colonies of smaller animals. And the junked cars, like sunken ships, turn into living reefs.

On drives along the windward side of Oʻahu, I like looking out at the ocean and seeing the pointed island offshore, not much bigger than a couple of houses—Mokoliʻi Island, but nobody calls it that. I had a shock when I heard it's called Chinaman's Hat. That's what it looks like, all right, a crown and brim on the water. I had never heard "Chinaman" before except in derision when walking past racists and had had to decide whether to pretend I hadn't heard or to fight.

When driving south, clockwise around Oʻahu, there is an interesting optical illusion: at a certain point in the road, the sky is covered with Chinaman's Hat, which looms huge, near. The closer you drive toward what seems like a mountain ahead, the farther it moves away until there it is, quite far off, a small island in the midst of ocean, sky, clouds.

I did not call it Chinaman's Hat, and no one else calls it Mokoliʻi Island, so for a long time, I didn't call it anything. "Chinaman's Hat," people say to visitors, "because it looks just like a Chinaman's hat. See?"

889

And the visitor knows right away what they mean. At first I watched expressions and tones of voice for a snide reference to me. But the locals were not yelling at me or spitting at me or trying to run me down with a bike saying, "Chinaman."

Although I don't swim very well, I ventured out to Chinaman's Hat three times. The first time, we waited until low tide to walk as far as we could. The other times, we left in the early morning. Snorkeling is like flying; the moment your face enters clear water, you become a flying creature.

Schools of fish—zebra fish, rainbow fish, red fish—curve with the currents, swim alongside and away. Balloon fish puff out their porcupine quills. How unlike a dead fish a live fish is. We swam through spangles of silver white fish. I hovered in perfect suspension over forests, flew over spring forests and winter forests. No sound but my own breathing. Sometimes we entered blind spots, darkness, where the sand churned up gray fog, the sun behind clouds. Then I had to lift my head out of the water to see and not be afraid.

Sometimes the sun made golden rooms, which we entered from dark hallways. Specks of sand shone like gold and fell like motes, like the light in California. Sea cucumbers rocked from side to side.

Approaching Chinaman's Hat, there is a group of tall black stones like an underwater Stonehenge, and we flew around and between those rocks.

Then we were walking among the palm trees and bushes that we had seen from O'ahu. Under those bushes, large white birds nest on the ground. We hurried to the unseen side of the island, the other face of the moon.

Though tiny, Chinaman's Hat has its leeward and windward. The ocean side is less green but wonderful in its variety. We found a cave, a tiny pirate's cove with a lick of ocean going in and out of it; a strip of beach made of fine yellow sand; a blowhole; brown and lavender cowry shells, not broken; black live crabs and red dead crabs; a lava rock shelf with tide pools as warm as baths. Lying in a tide pool, I saw nothing but sky and black rock; the ocean spit cold now and again. The two friends with us stood in the blowhole, and said wedding vows while the ocean sprayed rainbows around their heads.

At day's end, tired from the long swim at high tide, we

pulled ourselves up on the land, lay with arms open holding on to Oʻahu. We were grateful to return, relieved that we had made it back alive. Relieved to be out of the water before the sun went down.

After that first exploration, we heard from Hawaiians that the channel between Chinaman's Hat and Oʻahu is the spawning place for sharks. This information did not stop us from swimming out there twice more. We had the fatalism of city people who had lived on the San Andreas Fault. It will crack open at any moment, and California break off from North America, and sink like Atlantis. We continued to swim home with the fish we'd caught tied to our belts, and they did not attract sharks though pilot fish swam ahead of us.

The air of Hawaiʻi breathes warm on the skin; when it blows, I seem to turn into wind, too, and start to blow away. Maybe I can swim because the water is so comfortable, I melt into it and let it carry me like the fish and the frigate birds that make the currents visible. Back on Oʻahu, our friend who got married in the blowhole, often broke into hysterics, and she and her husband returned to the cool northern California woods.

There is a rending. The soul leaks out to mix with the air, the skin an osmotic membrane. But the eyes squint against the bright green foliage in the red light. These islands fool human beings into thinking that they are safe. On our second trip to Chinaman's Hat, a Hawaiian man and his son were camping under the ledge by the palm trees. They had a boat and meat hooks and liver for catching sharks.

On the third trip, Earll went spear fishing off the ocean side, where I did not go because of the depth and choppiness. I was climbing as far as I could up the crown, and finding seashells there. I watched him jump vertically out of the water. He had seen a giant thing and felt it swim under him, yards and yards of brown shadow under him.

Another time, we rowed a boat out there, our children sitting on the outrigger to weight it down on the water. A cleft in the hillside made a shelter for building a fire to get warm after swimming. At sunset, we cooked and ate the fish the men speared. We were climbing down to the boat, holding on to the face of the island in the dark, when a howling like wolves, like ghosts, came rising out of the island. "Birds," somebody said. "The wind," said someone else. But the air was still, and the high, clear sound wound like a ribbon around the island. It was, I know it, the island, the voice of the island singing, the sirens Odysseus heard.

The Navy uses Kaho‘olawe for bombing practice, not recognizing it as living, sacred earth. We had all heard it, the voice of our island singing.

A City Person Encountering Nature

A city person encountering nature hardly recognizes it, has no patience for its cycles, and disregards animals and plants unless they roar and exfoliate in spectacular aberrations. Preferring the city myself, I can better discern natural phenomena when books point them out; I also need to verify what I think I've seen, even though charts of phyla and species are orderly whereas nature is wild, unruly.

Last summer, my friend and I spent three days together at a beach cottage. She got up early every morning to see what "critters" the ocean washed up. The only remarkable things I'd seen at that beach in years were a Portuguese man-o-war and a flightless bird, big like a pelican; the closer I waded toward it, the farther out to sea the bird bobbed.

We found flecks of whitish gelatin, each about a quarter of an inch in diameter. The wet sand was otherwise clean and flat. The crabs had not yet dug their holes. We picked up the blobs on our fingertips and put them in a saucer of sea water along with seaweeds and some branches of coral.

One of the things quivered, then it bulged, unfolded, and flipped over or inside out. It stretched and turned over like a human being getting out of bed. It opened and opened to twice its original size. Two arms and two legs flexed, and feathery wings flared, webbing the arms and legs to the body, which tapered to a graceful tail. Its ankles had tiny wings on them—like Mercury. Its back muscles were articulated like a comic book superhero's—blue and silver metallic leotards outlined with black racing stripes. It's a spaceman, I thought. A tiny spaceman in a spacesuit.

I felt my mind go wild. A little spaceship had dropped a spaceman on to our planet. The other blob went through its gyrations and also metamorphosed into a spaceman. I felt as if I were having the flying dream where I watch two perfect beings wheel in the sky.

The two critters glided about, touched the saucer's edges. Suddenly, the first one contorted itself, turned over, made a

893

bulge like an octopus head, then flipped back, streamlined again. A hole in its side—a porthole, a vent—opened and shut. The motions happened so fast, we were not certain we had seen them until both creatures had repeated them many times.

I had seen similar quickenings: dry strawberry vines and dead trout revive in water. Leaves and fins unfurl; colors return.

We went outside to catch more, and, our eyes accustomed, found a baby critter. So there were more than a pair of these in the universe. So they grew. The baby had apparently been in the sun too long, though, and did not revive.

The next morning, bored that the critters were not performing more tricks, we blew on them to get them moving. By accident, their eyes or mouths faced, and sucked together. There was a churning. They wrapped their arms, legs, wings around one another.

Not knowing whether they were killing each other or mating, we tried unsuccessfully to part them. Guts, like two worms, came out of the portholes. Intestines, I thought; they're going to die. But the two excrescences braided together like DNA strands, then whipped apart, turned pale, and smokily receded into the holes. The critters parted, flipped, and floated away from each other.

After a long time, both of them fitted their armpits between the coral branches; we assumed that they were depositing eggs.

When we checked the clock, four hours had gone by. We'd both thought it had only been about twenty minutes.

That afternoon, the creatures seemed less distinct, their sharp lines blurring. I rubbed my eyes; the feathers were indeed melting. The beings were disintegrating in the water. I threw the coral as far out as I could into the ocean.

Later, back in town, we showed our biologist friend our sketches, I burbling about visitors from outer space. He said they were nudibranchs. This was our friend who as a kid had vowed that he would study Nature, but in college, he specialized in marine biology, and in graduate school, he studied shrimps. He was now doing research on one species of shrimp that he had discovered on one reef off O'ahu.

A new climate helps me to see nature. Here are some sights upon moving to Hawai'i:

Seven black ants, led by an orange one, dismembered a fly.

I peeled sunburn off my nose, and later recognized it as the flake of something an ant was marching away with.

A mushroom grew in a damp corner of the living room.

Giant philodendrons tear apart the cars abandoned in the jungle. Tendrils crawl out of the hoods; they climb the shafts of the steam shovels that had dug the highway. Roofs and trunks break open, turn red, orange, brown, and sag into the dirt.

Needing to read explanations of such strangeness, we bought an English magazine, *The Countryman*, which reports "The Wild Life and Tame" news.

"Stamped to Death—A hitherto peaceful herd of about fifty cows, being fetched in from pasture, suddenly began to rush around, and bellow in a most alarming manner. The source of their interest was a crippled gull, which did its best to escape; but the cows, snorting and bellowing, trampled it to death. They then quieted down and left the field normally.— Charles Brudett, Hants."

Also: "Big Eye. Spring, 1967—When I was living in the Karoo, a man brought me a five-foot cape cobra which he had just killed. It had been unusually sluggish and the tail of another snake protruded from its mouth. This proved to be a boom-slang, also poisonous but back-fanged; it was 1½ inches longer than the cobra and its head-end had been partly digested.—J. S. Taylor, Fife."

I took some students to the zoo after reading Blake's "Tyger, Tyger burning bright," Stevens's "Thirteen Ways of Looking at a Blackbird," and Lorenz's *King Solomon's Ring*. They saw the monkeys catch a pigeon and tear it apart. I kept reminding them that that was extraordinary. "Watch an animal going about its regular habits," I said, but then they saw an alligator shut its jaws on a low-flying pigeon. I remembered that I don't see ordinary stuff either.

I've watched ants make off with a used Band-Aid. I've watched a single termite bore through a book, a circle clean through. I saw a pigeon vomit milk, and didn't know whether it was sick, or whether its babies had died and the milk sacs in its throat were engorged. I have a friend who was pregnant at the same time as her mare, and, just exactly like the Chinese superstition that only one of the babies would live, the horse gave birth to a foal in two pieces.

When he was about four, we took our son crabbing for the "crabs with no eyes," as he called them. They did have eyes, but they were on stalks. The crabs fingered the bait as if with hands; very delicately they touched it, turned it, swung it. One grabbed hold of the line, and we pulled it up. But our son, a Cancer, said, "Let's name him Linda." We put Linda back in the river and went home.

Useful Education

I HAVE taught school for twelve years. I've taught grammar school, high school, alternative school, business school, and college; math, English, English as a second language, journalism, and creative writing. I've also been a writer for twenty-eight years, the writing years and the teaching years overlapping. I ought to be able to tell how to teach people to write.

The way I don't do it is the way Mrs. Garner taught us in fourth grade. Mrs. Garner was an organized woman, who brought out a box of decorations for each holiday and new season. Year after year, she put up the same bulletin boards and gave the same lessons; we knew exactly what the younger brother or sister was learning and what would come next. Nowadays we teachers invent new courses each semester— The American Novel in Film, Science Fiction, The Alienated Adolescent, Lovers at War, etc. We never get to establish a file of tried and true ditto sheets like Mrs. Garner's. She pressed hers on a gelatin plate, and pulled duplicates one by one.

It was her tradition to have us make a notebook entitled *Gems*. She did not explain what "gems" were. The only other time we used that word was in "Columbia, the Gem of the Ocean," one of her favorite songs. The notebook was not about jewels, nor is "Columbia, the Gem of the Ocean." She let us pick out our own construction paper for the cover; I chose a pink nubby oatmeal paper, and lettered "Gems" in lime green. While we were numbering the pages the way she showed us, she stuck chalk into the fingers of the wood-and-wire rakelike thing that enabled her to draw five straight lines at one stroke. She usually made musical scales with it, but for "gems," she ran it back and forth until the blackboard looked like a sheet of binder paper. Then she wrote a "gem," which we were to copy word for word and line for line, indenting and breaking the lines the way she did. Perhaps the "gems" were a penman- ship lesson, I thought, but wasn't that when we drew loops and zigzags? Copying the "gems" was like art period, when she drew an apple on the board with red chalk, then a brown stem with a green leaf shooting off to the right. We copied this apple as exactly as we could, and she corrected our shapes with her art pencil. She had a drawer filled with the comic books she confiscated, another drawer of water pistols and another of slingshots. If I were to use her methods today, the students would beat me up. (I once confiscated some nunchakus, a pair of night sticks on a chain, which I put in my desk drawer.)

And yet it was in Mrs. Garner's classroom that I discovered that I could write poems. I remember the very moment the room filled with a light that would have been white except that the warm light off the wooden desks (with the inkwell holes and the pencil grooves) suffused it with yellow—and out of the air and into my head and down my arm and out my fingers came ten, twenty verses in an a-b-b-a rhyme. The poem was about flying; I flew.

I was supposed to have been writing the multiplication tables or making our daily copy of the map of California. We had to draw every squiggle in the coastline. How lucky the fourth graders in Colorado are, we said. Instead I wrote down the music and the voices I heard. So, as a teacher, when I see students staring at nothing, I am loathe to interrupt.

One of my students who is now a published poet, Jody Manabe, said that she quit writing for one year because her seventh-grade teacher, a man, told her, "You write like a man."

The best I ever wrote in high school was when the teachers said, "Write whatever you like." Now I can appreciate what a daring assignment that is. I would not like to be caught saying that when an administrator or department head walks in to see if I have lesson plans.

The worst writing happened during the four years of college, which I attended when the English departments were doing the New Criticism (and the art department, Abstract Expressionism). The rule at our school was that an undergraduate could take one creative writing class, and she had to wait until junior or senior year. Poems, short stories, plays, and novels were what great masters wrote and what we students wrote about. We wrote essays.

The school system is dominated by the essay. And for me, essays would not become poems or stories. The real writing got stalled until after homework and graduation. The only place I could be fanciful was in the title. The professors wrote, "Purple prose," next to the few interesting phrases I could squeeze into "the body." Looking back on it, I believe the essay form was what drove English majors into becoming the most vituperative demonstrators during the student strikes.

My favorite method for teaching writing is to have the students write any old way. I tell them I "grade by quantity and not quality." By writing a hundred pages per semester, they have to improve—and the writing will find its form.

I tell the students that form—the epic, the novel, drama, the various forms of poetry—is organic to the human body. Petrarch did not invent the sonnet. Human heartbeat and language and voice and breath produce these rhythms. The teacher can look at a student's jumble of words and say, "I see you are moving toward the short story," or whatever. This is a good way to criticize and compliment—tell the young writer how close he or she is getting to which form.

To begin with form would probably work, too, as long as it's not the essay. Put a problem into a sonnet and it will help you state the problem, explore it, and solve it elegantly in a couplet. Ballads come naturally to students, who are lyric, and young like Keats and Shelley.

In *The Catcher in the Rye*, Holden takes an Oral Expression class where the students have to give spontaneous speeches, and whenever a speaker digresses, the class and Mr. Vinson yell, "Digression!" Sometimes the speaker can hardly talk anymore and gets an F. Mr. Vinson doesn't know that if you let somebody digress long enough, what he says will eventually take shape, a classical shape.

As a teacher, I have a stake in controlling that classroom, too. And the essay is orderly, easy to write and easy to grade; a computer can do it. Just check the thesis statement and make sure that each major paragraph backs up the thesis with arguments, examples, and quotes.

I do teach the essay—the three-paragraph essay, then the five-paragraph essay, then the term paper—so that my students can survive college. I try to throw in enough other kinds of writing to put the essay in perspective. When the class is over, though, kids probably forget everything but the essay. It is a form that the brain grasps. But if I become paralyzed worrying about the kid writers I am damaging, I try to remember how tough writers are. Kwan Kung, the god of war and literature, rides before us.

Talk Story: A Writers' Conference

Two weeks ago, I went to Talk Story, the first conference of Asian American and Hawai'i writers. Never before had I listened to writers read and talk for a week straight, taking time out for eating and sleeping, but usually talking about writing while eating, too. It takes me about twenty years to see meaning in events, but here are some first impressions:

The opening party was at Washington Place, the Governor's mansion, where Queen Lili'uokalani stayed under house arrest in 1895. We ladies trailed our long skirts over the lawns and through the rooms of Victorian furniture to the lanai, where the band and the food and wine were. People blessed one another with leis and kisses, and the smell and the music of Hawai'i filled the air. The moon, full that very night, rolled out of the rushing clouds. I didn't get to the food because I was dazzled by meeting the people whom I had only imagined from their writings.

The writers from the mainland, not used to Hawai'i, must have felt strange, having just come out of their solitary writing rooms.

Listening to the keynote speakers the next morning, I was humbled when Ozzie Bushnell, author of *Ka'a'awa*, said that if "us local kids" don't write the Hawai'i novel, then "the outsider" will come in and do it. I guiltily identified with this "outsider." Ozzie is such a strong speaker, talking both standard English and pidgin, that I felt scolded, a Captain Cook of literature, plundering the islands for metaphors, looting images, distorting the landscape with a mainland—a mainstream—viewpoint. I temporarily forgot my trusty superstition: the capable seer needs only a glimpse of the room or the forest or the city to describe it and its inhabitants more truly than one who has lived there always. A place gives no special writing powers to those born and raised in it.

On the second day, during the panel, "The Plantations and the World War II Camp Experience," Noriko Bridges read the one poem she has taken a lifetime to write. She wept in the middle of it, where the brothers are killed fighting in Europe, their families still imprisoned; many listeners cried too, some women holding hands. Writers who had not seen one another since camp days were having a reunion. They had first published in the camp newsletters.

There was a lovely moment when Milton Murayama, author of *All I Asking for Is My Body*, talked about how pidgin vocabulary is changing. For example, nowadays, Hawai'i people say, "good," "mo' bettah," and "da best." But in the old days, they said, "good," "go-o-od," and "go-o-o-od!" He said the "goods" louder and louder and louder.

On the third day, we Chinese Americans had a fight. Two of the panelists were Jeff Paul Chan and Shawn Wong, editors of the anthology, *Aiiieeeee!*, who said that publishers maintain a ghetto of female ethnic autobiographers and reject the work of male ethnic novelists. They said that the known bulk of Chinese American literature consists of nine autobiographies, seven by women. We are to draw the conclusion that the dominant society uses minority women to castrate the men. The audience was very upset. Some felt insulted at the speakers' proud use of the word "Chinaman." Lilah Kan from New York came bursting forth with her beautiful gray hair flying, to accuse the panelists of being part of a "Chinese American literary mafia."

Afterward, my feminist friends said we should have cheered for those seven women. The newspapers said the "brawl" was between the mainland Chinese Americans and the island Chinese Americans. But I think it was the men against the women—the men erecting Louis Chu, male novelist, as the father figure by knocking down the Jade Snow Wong mother figure. It was embarrassing that we were the only ethnic group that did not show a harmonious face; on the other hand, I felt good about our liveliness.

On the fourth afternoon, I moderated the panel, "Themes and Concerns of Writers in Hawai'i." Probably because of the events of the previous day, people kept interpreting this title politically, but none of the panelists wanted to or could talk that way. Phyllis Hoge Thompson, speaking from the audience, said she had set out to write a poem about Tom Gill losing the election for Governor. "But the poem turned out to be about a tree in the snow," she said. "Holding" is about the Scandinavian Yggdrasil tree, though even the name of the tree doesn't appear. She was mapping the strange, secret way of poetry, and I wished she were on the panel instead of me, an "outsider."

The most wondrous presentations were two evenings given by the Hawaiians, who each gave his or her genealogy of teachers. They chanted and danced variations of the same mele, sometimes accompanied by gourd and sometimes by knee drums, for example. They told how a new mele is written today, often first in English, then translated into Hawaiian by a teacher, who tells the poet what kind of a mele it is (an Entrance poem, a Call, etc.), and where it belongs in tradition.

The panelists' families and students sat in the back of the auditorium, and after the program, the children walked up to the stage and sang for their teacher, John Kaha'i Topolinski. Some participants who had attended the two previous Asian American Writers' Conferences (Oakland '75 and Seattle '76) said that the Hawaiians were contributing the only new theory and scholarship. The Hawaiians also gave a vision of the artist, not as anchorite but as builder of community.

Voice after voice telling all manner of things, by Saturday, I found myself saying my own work inside my head to counteract certain poets. My ears and head and body rejected their beats, which I also tried to cancel by tapping out my own rhythms with a finger. I felt like Johnny-Got-His-Gun, paralyzed except for that one finger. Earll, my husband, was reciting Yeats's poetry to himself, as antidote.

A rhythm that is wrong for you might stop your heart, or, anyway, scramble your brain. I learned that it is not story or idea that counts. What really matters is the music. A famous writer walked out as I read my suspenseful new chapter. ("'Nothing but disdain,' Mimi thought, 'could make some Chinese passionate.'"—Diana Chang in *The Frontiers of Love*.) I watched her high-heeled silhouette dart out of the lighted doorway. She probably prevented my rhythms from breaking up hers. Or maybe she needed sleep; it was almost midnight.

At the last set of readings Saturday night, Ninotchka Rosca was nowhere to be found. The rumor spread among the writers that she was at work on her novel; the writing was coming to her that night, and she would not interrupt it. We enviously told one another this story of discipline, dedication, and nerve. We could have been making the story up in a fit of withdrawal symptoms, having abandoned our writing for a week.

Hundreds of us went to the lūʻau at the Sumida Watercress Farm Sunday evening. I felt a shock to see Stephen Sumida exhume the pig—pink and long like a human being—the dirt and burlap falling away. Will there now be a cycle of pig imagery in our work? How do reality and writing connect anyway?

I know at least six people who fell in love at first sight during the conference—all requited—levels and levels of conferring.

Strange Sightings

A CCORDING TO mystical people, spiritual forces converge at Hawai'i, as do ocean currents and winds. Kāhuna, keepers and teachers of the old religion and arts (such as song writing, the hula, navigation, taro growing), still work here. The islands attract refugee lamas from Tibet, and the Dalai Lama and the Black Hat Lama have visited them. Some kāhuna say they see tree spirits fly from branch to branch; the various winds and rains are spirits, too; sharks and rocks have spirits. If ancestors and immortals travel on supernatural errands between China and the Americas, they must rest here in transit, nothing but ocean for thousands of miles around. They landed more often in the old days, before the sandalwood trees were cut down.

Whether it was because I listened to too many ghost stories or was born sensitive to presences, I spent about three years of childhood in helpless fear of the supernatural. I saw a whirling witch in the intersection by our house. She had one red cheek and one black cheek. Surrounded by a screaming, pointing crowd, she turned and turned on her broom. Maybe she was only somebody in a Hallowe'en costume when I didn't know about Hallowe'en, but she put me into torment for years. I was afraid of cat eyes at night. Wide-eyed with insomnia, I listened in the dark to voices whispering, chains dragging and clanging, footsteps coming my way.

At about the same kidtime, Earll saw a little witch dancing on his dresser. Hoping to help our son become a fearless down-to-earth person, we have raised Joseph secularly. We explain things to him logically.

Joseph had already gotten through his babyhood when we came to Hawai'i; he would seem no longer in danger of succumbing to the fear of ghosts. But Hawai'i, new land which has recently risen out of the water, has overwhelming animism; that is, it seems more alive than cities which have been paved over for hundreds of years. Or Joseph developed his sixth sense

at a later age than we did, and, person and place coming together, he started to see things.

Even our friends with Ph.D.s see things in Hawai'i. Our
friend from Minnesota kept telling us about the row of fishermen walking in the ocean with torches at night. "They're
chanting to attract the fish," he said. Later, he learned he was
describing the march of the dead warriors. Another sensible
friend tells us how he ran from block to block to dodge the
nightwalkers. "I would've died if they crossed my path," he
said. The most unimaginative people hear the hoofbeats of
the princess's horse, and lock their doors. They wrestle with
invisible foes at ceremonial grounds, see—and photograph—
the face of the goddess Pele in the volcano fire, offer the old
woman—Pele in disguise—water when she comes asking for
it, floating on smoking feet.

We were driving one day when I caught a sign that Joseph
was not the simple little boy I had hoped for. He held his
head, shaking it, and crying out, "I can't stand it. The
thoughts are moving so fast in there." I didn't like that;
he felt his thoughts apart from himself; the very process of
thinking hurt him. With my hands on the wheel, I gave inadequate comfort.

One night I heard him walking about, and in the morning
he said he had seen a light come over the top of the wall. (The
wall of his room didn't join the ceiling.) He had gotten up
to shut off the light. What he saw in the living room was one
window lit up and a man standing in it. The glow was coming
from the man. We lived on the second floor.

When he was about twelve, and should have been old enough
to have outgrown his fancifulness, he came home early in the
morning and jumped shaking into bed. He and his friends
had been playing at a construction site before the workers
came. Hiding from one another, he had lost his friends and
was running home when he saw a Menehune, one of the little
people of Hawai'i, standing on a lava rock fence. "It had a
shiny crown on its head," he said, "and its mouth opened and
opened until there was nothing but this big hollow in its face.
Its head moved like this, following me." He tells about this
laughing Menehune as factually as he tells a math problem,
without self-dramatization or doubt.

Months afterward, he wasn't sleeping well; he kept groaning and tossing. "You know the voices calling your name before you go to sleep?" he said. "I usually like listening to them. But lately they've been very loud, and I don't like their sound." I was alarmed that he thought that everyone has voices, though pleasant ones, calling them. "The voices are coming out of the closet." And I noticed that the closet door kept opening. I would shut it myself when he went to bed, and when I checked on him, I'd find it open.

Without mentioning it, he bought five pounds of rock salt with his own money and sprinkled it all over the house; Hawaiians do that to stop hauntings.

I remembered Chinese stories about voices calling, and the lesson would be that you mustn't answer when you hear your name. You mustn't follow the voices. I recalled Goethe's poem about the Erl-king's daughter. To find guidance, you have to use the lore that science scoffs at. If Joseph had started being afraid of bats, we would have hung garlic around his neck and around the house.

I pulled his ears while calling his name and address the way my mother did for us after nightmares. He helped me seal the closet door with good Chinese words on red paper. We found a cross that had been part of a theatrical costume, also an ankh and scarab, replicas from the Metropolitan Museum of Art, and hung them from the doorknob. We picked ti leaves and strewed his room with them.

Joseph had a few quiet nights, and we thought the strangeness was over. But then I found him standing in the hallway shivering in the hot afternoon. He said that something had come out of the closet and was in the hallway. "The cold spot is here," he said. "I'm standing in the middle of it. I'm fighting it." That spot did not feel odd to me.

We asked our friend from Thailand what to do, and she gave us a medallion of a saint for him to wear around his neck, and also a little stone Buddha that Thais wear in a gold box. She said he should put the Buddha by his head when he went to bed. It had been handed down in her family, which have been rulers and rebels of Thailand. Joseph has had no more supernatural disturbances.

In a way it's a shame to have him put his powers away, fold

his wings, but those abilities are not needed in America in the twentieth century.

The writers' conference I went to ended with a kahuna who helped us perform ho'oponopono; all animosities would be resolved. Fewer people stayed for that event than any other. Maybe in ancient Hawai'i, a kahuna like this one would have trained Joseph, whose tendencies would have become useful. She asked us to shut our eyes and hold hands in a circle; she talked to us calmly, saying that a column of light was entering the circle. I opened my eyes to peek, to check out the reality of that column. There was indeed a column of light, but also a skylight in the roof that let it in. The way the world works now, Joseph needs to learn to see the skylight, too.

AUGUST
Lew Welch: An Appreciation

N OT EVERYBODY who writes poems knows what a poem is.
Lew Welch knew. I'm glad I got to meet him before he disappeared. He's often called a San Francisco poet or a California
poet. He studied music in Stockton. He lived with his wife,
Magda, in a house on a slope in Marin City, which is a Black city.

They had been expecting Earll and me; Magda had made
enough sandwiches for about ten people, then went outside to
work in her garden. She probably fed lots of kid poets who came
to see her husband. Being still young, we naturally expected food
and attention from adults, and did not recognize largesse when
we received it. Lew Welch then was working at the docks as a
longshoremen's clerk, and now that I'm a worker and a writer
myself, I know better than to take up a man's time on his day off.

He had cut his red hair for the summer. He had written
about that: "In summer I usually cut it all off. / I do it myself,
with scissors and a / little Jim Beam." He looked exactly as he
said in his poem:

> *Not yet 40, my beard is already white.*
> *Not yet awake, my eyes are puffy and red,*
> *like a child who has cried too much.*

Only, I think, he had reached forty already; he had lines in
his face, but though his eyes were red, they opened wide. He
looked at you out of bright blue eyes, but at a part of you that
isn't your appearance or even your personality; he addressed
that part of you that is like everybody. I would like to learn to
look at people that way.

He went for his papers and books and got down to business.
He read to us. He cried. He sang:

> *She bared her bos'm*
> *I whupped out m'knife*
> *Carved my initials on her thin breast bone.*

"I invented putting a note before and after the parts that need to be sung," he said. "The book has these fussy sixteenth notes because those were the only notes the printer had. They should have been quarter notes." I admired his caring about detail, and have checked the editions of his work that were printed after he disappeared, to see if the notes had been changed. They had, and they do look better.

He read a poem about driving, written by one of his students, and said, "Now, there's a poem. There's a poet. I phoned him to come do a reading with me, but he had to work on his car." There was going to be a reading that weekend by the Bay Area's best-known poets. "That's cool. That's right. He ought to be working on his car."

From the window, you could see down the hill to a round space filled with motorcycles and cars with their hoods up. Kids were repairing them. "Somebody ought to subsidize garages all over the country, stocked with automotive tools," he said. "Kids can come work on their cars, something real, when they drop out of school."

He had many ideas for things for you to do. There is a poem accompanied by a circle drawn in one brushstroke. The poem is in his clear handwriting. He read it as if it were a friendly but imperative suggestion:

> *Step out onto the planet*
> *Draw a circle a hundred feet round.*
> *Inside the circle are*
> *300 things nobody understands, and, maybe,*
> *nobody's ever really seen.*
> *How many can you find?*

One of his ideas was to organize to feed poets "so poets could have babies and fix their wives' teeth and the other things we need." He planned a magazine to be called *Bread* that would discuss the economics of being a poet in America. Somebody still needs to carry out these plans.

He talked about being one of the young poets who had driven William Carlos Williams from the airport to Reed College. I love the way that car ride has become a part of literary history. Gary Snyder, Lew Welch, Philip Whalen, and

William Carlos Williams were the poets in the car. Today, Welch told us that he had felt Williams giving the power of poetry to him. The two of them had agreed on their dislike of T. S. Eliot.

Then Lew Welch sang us "The Waste Land" to a jive beat, and it did not sound at all as if he disliked it.

He said that poetry has to be useful. He was very proud that the No Name Bar in Sausalito pasted in its window his poem for protecting the town, and the "innkeeper" published that poem, "Sausalito Trash Prayer" by duplicating forty copies of it and giving it to people. It was "pasted in the florist's window . . . carefully retyped and put right out there on Divisadero Street . . . that it might remind of love, that it might sell flowers. . . ."

He read "After Anacreon," a poem about cab driving. He said that he had also read it to his fellow Yellow Cab drivers, and was happy when they told him that that was exactly what being a cabby is like.

He didn't say it that day, but there's some practical advice of his that is told by one to another, a word-of-mouth poem: "Think Jewish, dress Black, drive Okie."

He was a wise and trustworthy man. He warned and comforted kid writers: "To become enamored of our powers is to lose them, at once!" ". . . full / full of my gift / I am only / left out and afraid." He wrote two poems he called the first American koans, "The Riddle of Hands" and "The Riddle of Bowing." He invited readers who solved these koans to have their answers confirmed by writing to him. There was flesh behind his words. I guess that's why he was willing to see us, and also why he looked so worn.

After about two hours, we had to go, a sense of urgency about the work to be done having come over us. We thanked him and Magda for the poems and the beer and sandwiches, and said goodbye.

I haven't told you much that you can't read for yourself. He had spoken exactly like his writing.

I encourage my own students to write in dialect, and give them Lew Welch's instructions on how to do it: "Dialect is only a regional and personal voiceprint. . . . You can easily separate structure and meaning from dialect, and still be dealing with sound, with music, with speech, with another's

Mind. Gertrude Stein perfectly mimicked the rhythms and structures of Baltimore Blacks in her story 'Melanctha' and she didn't transcribe the dialect at all—that is, didn't have to misspell a lot of words to get the work done. Nelson Algren has many many passages with no misspellings, but he catches the real flow of regional speech."

I keep some Lew Welch advice over my desk: "When I write, my only concern is accuracy. I try to write accurately from the poise of mind which lets us see that things are exactly what they seem. I never worry about beauty, if it is accurate there is always beauty. I never worry about form, if it is accurate there is always form." I ditto this for my students at the beginnings of courses, and tell them I have not much more to teach them, but they don't believe me, and stay.

In the spring of 1971, Lew Welch walked away into the woods of Nevada County, and has not come back. Those woods are in the northwest—the direction of leina-a-ka-'uhane. I think there must be a jumping-off place in California, just as there is one on each of the islands in Hawai'i. And Lew Welch's soul leapt away.

A Sea Worry

THIS SUMMER our son bodysurfs. He says it's his "job" and rises each morning at 5:30 to catch the bus to Sandy Beach. I hope that by September he will have had enough of the ocean. Tall waves throw surfers against the shallow bottom. Undertows have snatched them away. Sharks prowl Sandy's. Joseph told me that once he got out of the water because he saw an enormous shark. "Did you tell the life guard?" I asked. "No." "Why not?" "I didn't want to spoil the surfing." The ocean pulls at the boys, who turn into surfing addicts. At sunset you can see surfers waiting for the last golden wave.

"Why do you go surfing so often?" I ask my students.

"It feels so good," they say. "Inside the tube. I can't describe it. There are no words for it."

"You can describe it," I scold, and I am angry. "Everything can be described. Find the words for it, you lazy boy. Why don't you stay home and read?" I am afraid that the boys give themselves up to the ocean's mindlessness.

When the waves are up, surfers all over Hawai'i don't do their homework. They cut school. They know how the surf is breaking at any moment because every fifteen minutes the reports come over the radio; in fact, one of my former students is the surf reporter.

Some boys leave for mainland colleges, and write their parents heartrending letters. They beg to come home for Thanksgiving. "If I can just touch the ocean," they write from Missouri and Kansas, "I'll last for the rest of the semester." Some come home for Christmas and don't go back.

Even when the assignment is about something else, the students write about surfing. They try to describe what it is to be inside the wave as it curls over them, making a tube or "chamber" or "green room" or "pipeline" or "time warp." They write about the silence, the peace, "no hassles," the feeling of being reborn as they shoot out the end. They've written about the voice of God, the "commandments" they hear. In the margins, they draw the perfect wave. Their writing is full of clichés. "The endless summer," they say. "Unreal."

Surfing is like a religion. Among the martyrs are George Helm, Kimo Mitchell, and Eddie Aikau. Helm and Mitchell were lost at sea riding their surfboards from Kaho'olawe, where they had gone to protest the Navy's bombing of that island. Eddie Aikau was a champion surfer and lifeguard. A storm had capsized the Hōkūle'a, the ship that traces the route that the Polynesian ancestors sailed from Tahiti, and Eddie Aikau had set out on his board to get help.

Since the ocean captivates our son, we decided to go with him to see Sandy's.

We got up before dawn, picked up his friend, Marty, and drove out of Honolulu. Almost all the traffic was going in the opposite direction, the freeway coned to make more lanes into the city. We came to a place where raw mountains rose on our left and the sea fell on our right, smashing against the cliffs. The strip of cliff pulverized into sand is Sandy's. "Dangerous Current Exist," said the ungrammatical sign.

Earll and I sat on the shore with our blankets and thermos of coffee. Joseph and Marty put on their fins and stood at the edge of the sea for a moment, touching the water with their fingers and crossing their hearts before going in. There were fifteen boys out there, all about the same age, fourteen to twenty, all with the same kind of lean, v-shaped build, most of them with black hair that made their wet heads look like sea lions. It was hard to tell whether our kid was one of those who popped up after a big wave. A few had surfboards, which are against the rules at a bodysurfing beach, but the lifeguard wasn't on duty that early.

As they watched for the next wave, the boys turned toward the ocean. They gazed slightly upward; I thought of altar boys before a great god. When a good wave arrived, they turned, faced shore, and came shooting in, some taking the wave to the right and some to the left, their bodies fishlike, one arm out in front, the hand and fingers pointed before them, like a swordfish's beak. A few held credit card trays, and some slid in on trays from McDonald's.

"That is no country for middle-aged women," I said. We

had on bathing suits underneath our clothes in case we felt moved to participate. There were no older men either.

Even from the shore, we could see inside the tubes. Sometimes, when they came at an angle, we saw into them a long way. When the wave dug into the sand, it formed a brown tube or a gold one. The magic ones, though, were made out of just water, green and turquoise rooms, translucent walls and ceilings. I saw one that was powder-blue, perfect, thin; the sun filled it with sky blue and white light. The best thing, the kids say, is when you are in the middle of the tube, and there is water all around you but you're dry.

The waves came in sets; the boys passed up the smaller ones. Inside a big one, you could see their bodies hanging upright, knees bent, duckfeet fins paddling, bodies dangling there in the wave.

Once in a while, we heard a boy yell, "Aa-whoo!" "Poon-tah!" "Aaroo!" And then we noticed how rare human voice was here; the surfers did not talk, but silently, silently rode the waves.

Since Joseph and Marty were considerate of us, they stopped after two hours, and we took them out for breakfast. We kept asking them how it felt, so that they would not lose language.

"Like a stairwell in an apartment building," said Joseph, which I liked immensely. He hasn't been in very many apartment buildings, so had to reach a bit to get the simile. "I saw somebody I knew coming toward me in the tube, and I shouted, 'Jeff. Hey, Jeff,' and my voice echoed like a stairwell in an apartment building. Jeff and I came straight at each other—mirror tube."

"Are there ever girls out there?" Earll asked.

"There's a few women who come at about eleven," said Marty.

"How old are they?"

"About twenty."

"Why do you cross your heart with water?"

"So the ocean doesn't kill us."

I described the powder-blue tube I had seen. "That part of Sandy's is called Chambers," they said.

I have gotten some surfing magazines, the ones kids steal

from the school library, to see if the professionals try to describe the tube. Bradford Baker writes:

> *. . . Round and pregnant in Emptiness*
> *I slide,*
> *Laughing,*
> *into the sun,*
> *into the night.*

Frank Miller calls the surfer

> *. . . mother's fumbling*
> *curly-haired*
> *tubey-laired*
> *son.*

"Ooh, offshores—," writes Reno Abbellira, "where wind and wave most often form that terminal rendezvous of love—when the wave can reveal her deepest longings, her crest caressed, cannily covered to form those peeling concavities we know, perhaps a bit irreverently, as tubes. Here we strive to spend every second—enclosed, encased, sometimes fatefully entombed, and hopefully, gleefully, ejected—Whoosh!"

"An iridescent ride through the entrails of God," says Gary L. Crandall.

I am relieved that the surfers keep asking one another for descriptions. I also find some comfort in the stream of commuter traffic, cars filled with men over twenty, passing Sandy Beach on their way to work.

ESSAYS, REVIEWS
& POEMS 1977–87

Review of A Book of Common Prayer
by Joan Didion

J OAN DIDION said at a Regents' Lecture at Berkeley that she writes to discover the grammar of the pictures that shimmer. She said that before she began *A Book of Common Prayer* she had made these sightings: the lights in the bevatron, the view from her hotel room in Colombia, a 707 burning, and the Panama airport at 6 A.M. Her lecture, which appeared in the *Monthly* (January–February), was entitled "Why I Write."

The bevatron itself does not appear in the book, but the reader can hear a metallic humming and see the landscape and the characters in an x-raying light. These atmospheric conditions must come from a radioactive source—probably Joan Didion's vision that impelled the book. The cancer to which the narrator, Grace Strasser-Mendana, accommodates herself must come from that bevatron vision too. Like Grace, who is a biochemist and ex-anthropologist, the author isolates objects as if they were molecules and holds them up to the light: a Neiman-Marcus Christmas catalogue, a Honeywell 782 solid-state computer, Porthault linen, a Kraft Dinner, KY jelly, Hertz, *Vogue*. There are catalogues of drugs, hotels, airlines, highways, cities, but instead of a sense of clutter, Joan Didion has created expanses of space, a white background against which she brings each thing into sharp, hard-edged focus.

The other pictures that shimmer do appear in the book, the burning airplane a central image, and it is the author's style to return again and again to the key images in order to examine them at various angles and in different lights. The plot structure, then, is a coruscating play of flashbacks, each moment about the size and shape of a poem.

A responsible visionary, Joan Didion finds the connections between her visions and human characters. Charlotte Douglas is the person we must understand if we are to find out what American life and things mean. Charlotte is the mother of Marin, a fugitive after she and her guerillas set fire to the

airplane they had hijacked. The author returns to a universal vision she did not mention in her Regents' Lecture—the
woman's nightmare of the disappearing child. Doris Lessing
described it in *The Summer Before the Dark*, John Updike in
Rabbit, Run; Joan Didion explored it in *Play It as It Lays*.
It is the nightmare of the mother who cannot protect her
child. Charlotte Douglas, whose passport says "Occupation
MADRE," loses two children, one to "complications" and one
to "history." Grace, the narrator, has "lost" her son, Gerardo,
"an acquaintance." However, she herself had been a lost child,
eight years old when her mother died, and ten when her father died. "From that afternoon until my sixteenth birthday
I lived alone in our suite at the Brown Palace Hotel." Grace
is a self-sufficient widow, working in her laboratory, surviving
revolutions. Perhaps the author is giving guilt-ridden mothers
some consolation, that our protectiveness doesn't make much
difference in this world.

When I read the pre-publication excerpt (it was entitled
"California Blue") from *A Book of Common Prayer* in *Harper's*,
I felt disappointed that Joan Didion would make use of such
a recent occurrence as the Patty Hearst story, which does not
seem a personal enough vision, too public, too new. But in the
context of the entire book, Marin's SLA–type activities—like
the Micronesian independence movement, the OAS, the FBI,
Berkeley, the Tupamaros, the Alabama 3, the Tacoma 11—do
become part of a pattern of the 20th century: a pattern seen
from Boca Grande, a fictitious Central American country,
where Charlotte and Grace, two "norteamericanas," live.

(The difference between the effects of a pre-publication excerpt and an actual book does call into question the artfulness
of excerpting. If you decided after reading "California Blue"
not to read *A Book of Common Prayer*, do try the book from
the beginning.)

A Book of Common Prayer is one of those wonderful books
in which the author sometimes lets us glimpse the underpin-
nings of her craft. "Perhaps Gerardo does not play the motive
role in this narrative I thought he did." "'I mean, Charlotte. If
you say "the outlook is not all bright" and then you say, "nor
is the outlook all black," then you can't start the next sentence
with "nevertheless." It can't possibly mean anything.'" "'The

verb form made a difference. . . ." "It occurred to me that I had never before had so graphic an illustration of how the consciousness of the human organism is carried in its grammar. Or the unconsciousness of the human organism. If the organism under scrutiny is Charlotte." One of Charlotte's ex-husbands had been her English professor, who had flunked her before beginning their affair. Throughout the book, Charlotte struggles to write a *New Yorker*–type "Letter from Boca Grande." She uses jargon and cliches, which Joan Didion scrutinizes until they yield their real meanings—or lack of meaning. Joan Didion gives us insights from the field which she has said is her only expertise—writing.

And, most important, she has created two women in a narrator-protagonist relationship that will probably live in literary history as the female counterparts to Nick Carraway and Jay Gatsby. Grace Strasser-Mendana and Charlotte Douglas have the same skillfully intertwined lives, and the subject-object relationships are not distorted by male-female misunderstandings. An irony in *A Book of Common Prayer* is that it is not the narrator but the heroine, Charlotte Douglas, who "writes." Grace Strasser-Mendana is the "witness." Which brings us again to Joan Didion's lecture on how the pictures come first, then the writing.

1977

Duck Boy

I WANTED to adopt Britt Masy. He was not preliterate—
he was fifteen—but he could not read, and he never did
learn how to read during the two years he had to come to my
classes. We would both grin and grin at each other so happily
because he read two pages of a first-grade reader, and the next
day he would have forgotten it all. To adopt him or marry him
would have been the only way I could have changed him a little, and even then it would have been too late—unless I could
have adopted him when he was born. He had no mother,
and his father, an alcoholic, had given him away. His foster
parents took in a different child every few years for the $75 a
month from the state. They must have done it for the money.
Who else would take on Britt as a daily responsibility? Short.
Skinny. Pimply. Glasses. Scared, darting, jumping eyes when
he did not understand something or when the others teased
him or hit him. But he was scared only when they pounced
from hiding, or jumped on him from the back. After the surprise and pain, always sweet words and sweet smiles, not id-
iotic smiles. When I made an incomprehensible assignment
to the class (it was a regular public-school class, not Special
Ed or E. H., whatever that stands for), I watched him staring around at the corners of floor and ceiling, startled and
panicked, a bird, a wild mouse, then the amazing smile if he
understood.

Britt hungered after a reality that leaped into him now
and then. It seemed to come like a hard light that flashed
too quickly to examine. Like one hammer blow. Like a curtain yanked aside for a moment. The reality would be some
emergency from a special television news report, a war picture of bodies in an old *Life* magazine, that picture of the
Vietnamese guerrilla with the blindfold and gag, a disfigure-
ment in the *National Enquirer*. Newspapers and news magazines with "actual photos" impressed him; they were "real."
I watched him see. He would first glimpse the picture accidentally, then quickly turn the page or slap the magazine

shut. Fear shot through his eyes. He looked around at the rest of us to see whether anyone else had *seen*. He would turn away, but return later to touch the picture, to trace it through a piece of typing paper, to copy it in margins and on the blackboard. Sometimes I would sit by him and try to explain until the fear let up and the good smile came. The next few days the two of us would play grown-up-discussing-current-events, and he would smile and smile at his normalcy.

One day the whole school was snickering and guffawing at a new joke. Everywhere kids drew graffiti of *Peanuts'* Lucy, her stomach sticking out huge and pregnant. "Good grief, Charlie Brown," she said. Britt copied the picture in his seven notebooks, which had no particular order as to content or front and back or top and bottom. Other students had six or seven notebooks, too, one for each class. He carried his seven notebooks in a black clarinet case. Sometimes he came to school early or stayed late and played his clarinet for this one or that one of his teachers. He played while we graded papers. He drew the simple Lucy figure over and over again in his notebooks and on the blackboards, coloring in the dress and the hair, tracing the lines with his index finger (sometimes with his middle finger; ninth graders make a great fuss over their middle fingers)—and still could not understand. Britt began to whine, "What is it? What is she? Why is it funny? Why is it funny? Tell me. Why don't you tell me?" I told him. And told him, and told him, and he did not understand. He followed me everywhere, all over the campus. He came out of hallways and doorways to ask me, "Why is it funny? Please tell me why it's funny. Please. Tell me. Tell me." The panicked eyes. The pleading.

"Lucy is pregnant, Britt. She's going to have a baby. See? That's why she is so fat, because there's a baby in there. And Charlie Brown is the father. She says, 'Good grief, Charlie Brown.' That's funny because in the comics, she says that all the time for all kinds of situations. Now here is a situation they never show in the comics. She says the same old thing even in this unusual situation, which happens quite often, really, in real life, but not in comics. Now do you understand why it's funny?"

Nodding his head, but still the eyes dazed with confusion. "I guess so."

"Listen, Britt. I'll try to explain it better later. O.K.? I have a class now. I have to go. I just cannot be late. So I'll see you later. O.K.? You go to your class, too. You're late already. Go on." A fresh jerk of fear in the eyes; I have told him to go away.

For many weeks, he drew the picture on book jackets, on folders. I watched his fingertips trace Lucy's contours on his desk top. He stopped asking me about the cartoon.

He started to tell me his dreams. He drew pictures of the dreams. He dreamed about his clarinet. In his dreams, his clarinet has gotten fat and puffy in the center. He drew his clarinet, fat and puffed up. That is all that happens in the dreams, the clarinet growing.

I asked him why he didn't just play his clarinet to me for the next couple of mornings while I thought about the dream. Once he started playing, he did not care whether I was grading papers or listening. He did not notice bells going off. To him I must have faded away and reappeared like people in dreams; we are all part of his dream, upon which particularly horrible news items impinge strongest. How can I, one of the dreamed, explain things to my dreamer? Surely, the dreamed cannot make more sense than the dreamer.

I took the picture of the fat clarinet from him, and next to it, I drew Lucy. From the clarinet's mouth I drew notes and other clarinets, not puffed up. Above Lucy, I drew other children, not puffed up, playing and smiling. I drew children and notes mingling in a dance. They dance in a circle until they turn into fat Lucy and fat clarinet. The girl children become Lucy. The boy children are the clarinets. I drew circles and arrows connecting everybody.

Britt nodded, smiling and laughing. "Girls and clarinets love each other, don't they?" he said. "That's what it means."

In stories, even in psychiatric case histories, that would be the denouement, and Britt would be cured. Britt got worse. What is one good dream that turns out useful when you have to dream every night, and no one answers but your own phantoms? I had not taught him to speak like the rest of us. He had taught me to speak like him. (Boys are *not* clarinets. Girls are *not* Lucy.) He continued to tell me his dreams, but

I came up with no more inspired interpretations. I was only bored, as you are bored with listening to normal people's dreams.

Then he stopped dreaming. He had stepped into another new world. He spoke like this.

"The two ducks came to visit me last night. They talked together, and I laughed. They do not pay attention to human beings."

"Three nights in a row, close."

"I know a boy whose ears ring so loud even other people can hear them. I heard them."

"One of the ducks did not come last night. I tried to talk to the one who came. He walked back and forth across my room, and pretended he didn't see me."

I could no longer follow him. I asked him silly questions to satisfy my curiosity, not to help him.

"What color are the ducks?"

"They are white."

"Do they ever answer you?"

"No, they talk to each other. They pretend they aren't watching me all the time."

"What do they talk about, Britt?"

"They tell jokes and make me laugh."

"How big are they?"

"They are four or five feet tall, with orange bills and orange feet."

He usually seemed happy now. When somebody hurt him or if I said something difficult, his head still jerked up with surprise, confusion, bewilderment, a scurrying-about look of dismay on his face. But then almost immediately came the smile. Now he was not so often afraid of the people around him.

At first, he was concerned that the ducks and the voices were not normal. By the end of the year, he was only unhappy when one or the other of the ducks did not come to visit him. He was worried that it would not return the next night or the next, that it had decided to abandon him. After a while he gave up trying to make them talk to him, and was satisfied to laugh at their jokes and to know they secretly cared, only pretending indifference, another one of their jokes.

He was an innocent, too dumb not to forgive, unable to remember grievances clearly.

I abandoned him, too.

There were so many like him.

1977

Middle Kingdom to Middle America:
Review of Child of the Owl by Laurence Yep

T HERE ARE scenes in *Child of the Owl* by Laurence Yep that will make every Chinese-American child gasp with recognition. "Hey! That happened to me. I did that I say that," the young reader will say, and be glad that a writer set it down, and feel comforted, less eccentric, less alone.

I remember at Chinese school I wrote English phonics alongside the Chinese words, just as Casey Young, the 12-year-old heroine, does. She has been thrown into Chinese school and San Francisco Chinatown after years of wandering with her vagabond gambler father. My classmates and I used English phonics when we were about 12 also, not because the lessons were getting harder and longer, and we needed a short-cut if we were to keep up in Chinese school and also work at the stores and laundries and also finish the ever-increasing homework from American school.

As in *Child of the Owl*, the Chinese teacher walked up and down the aisles and made us erase our English sounds. Laurence Yep sympathizes with kids who invent ingenious phonetic systems and are then made to feel like cheaters. He even suggests that a phonetic system might be a very sensible way of teaching Chinese. Ironically, if you ever take Chinese in college, you find that you learn the Romanization first, and the ideographs last.

Another scene with which second, third- and fourth-generation Chinese-Americans will identify is the painful one in which Casey Young shops in Chinatown for a dinner for her grandmother. Since she can only speak English, the Chinese push ahead of her, try to charge her extra, won't fill her orders properly, and say, "Native-born, no brains." Casey realizes they are treating her "like a tourist." Laurence Yep explains compassionately:

"The middle-aged clerk picked up an old towel and began wiping at the grease on the steel shelf. 'Back in China,' he explained, 'all the time people they gotta push and push because things so crowded. They come over here. They doan understand they supposed wait their turn.' . . .

"It was like the Chinese were a bunch of people stuck inside a little forest grove and every day a bunch of American owls came over and dumped on them. And then one day an owl wandered into the middle of the grove and the people got a chance to get even for everything the owls ever did to them by dumping on that one owl."

Like all good children's books, *Child of the Owl* can enrich an adult's life too. I had thought I was the only person with a mother who leaves the radio dial always on the station with "The Chinese Hour," afraid of losing the Chinese voices and music. Now I see that Paw-Paw, Casey's wonderful grandmother, who gives her her name and her past, handles machinery in the same way. Laurence Yep sees the old people as clearly as he sees the children: "All of them would at some time sit and stare emptily at the traffic passing by on the street below as if they were lost inside their own memories, trying to understand how they found themselves old and alone, sitting on a bench—with the look of people who had been left behind on some grassy shore when the ship had sailed. Only it was more than an ocean they had to cross, it was time and space itself."

Along with the sadness, *Child of the Owl* makes us laugh with familiarity. Casey Young wears her sweat shirt and jeans aggressively, and I realize that in middle age, I use the same weapons to fight stereotyping. I posed for the cover of my own book in a sweat shirt to deny "exotic." It did not work; there were critics who insisted on assessing whether or not my book was "exotic" and "inscrutable."

Perhaps in order to write straight, an "ethnic" writer needs to ignore the temptation to shock readers out of stereotypes. If we explain every misconception and joke, we would lose sight of our own original visions, and an explained joke loses all its humor. You need to know just the point at which to stop the explanations, and let the readers figure out things for themselves. Usually Laurence Yep knows where that point is as he just tells enough about the Eight Immortals to whet the appetite; just enough about Paw-Paw's piece work in the garment industry; just enough about the cramped apartments and the sense of neighborhood in Chinatown; just enough to allay a child's fears. The book does not get weighted down with exposition for non-Chinese-American readers! I liked it very much when an adult tells Casey that the reason people hang their clothes up on their balconies is that in Hong Kong they use laundry for curtains. We can decide for ourselves whether the adult is telling the truth or putting her on. I found the lightness at this point in Yep's writing very daring.

There are a few instances, however, when he succumbs to too facile solutions to stereotype-busting. A style currently popular among young Chinese-American writers is the hipster voice, a reaction—perhaps an over-reaction—against the stereotypical unctuous Confucius-say voice. At the beginning of the book Casey Young is a hip little kook like the heroines in American movies—throughout the book, one of Casey Young's main references is the movies—which give individuality to women by characterizing them as odd-balls, like Streisand characters, like Liza Minnelli characters. Barney and Casey Young remind me immediately of Ryan and Tatum O'Neal in *Paper Moon*. Fortunately, as Casey grows up, she wisecracks less, and she does seem to find new ways of speaking.

Laurence Yep himself has at least two voices, and I was enchanted that he tells a story-within-a-story about the owl totem of the Young family. It disconcerted me, however, when he adds an afterword in which the "I" is no longer Casey Young as in the rest of the book but apparently the author. He tells us that he has not actually seen an owl charm nor heard the owl story but made them up himself. Now in that afterword I believe Laurence Yep to be anticipating those critics—both Caucasian and Chinese-American—who will question whether his work is "typical" of the rest of us Chinese-Americans. So to all those ethnocentric villagers, he in effect says, "No, I'm not misrepresenting Chinese customs. This is fiction." Good art is always singular, always one-of-a-kind, and an artist certainly has the right to make things up to write fiction—but somehow we expect Chinese-American in a way we do not expect of Caucasian-American writers. I hope that when more of our work gets into print that this burden—"Speak for me!

Speak for me!"—we lay on each of our writers who gets pub-lished will become lighter. Laurence Yep has written a lovely novel that needs no apologies.

1977

Talk Story: No Writer Is an Island—
Except in Hawaii

I HAVE a feeling that the upcoming "Ethnic American Writers' Conference" in Honolulu will be different from any other writers' conference—that it will matter to me.

When I have gotten together with writers before, we could hardly talk, so tongue-tied were we in the flesh-and-blood impressiveness of one another. Sometimes we held hands; that is, when the writer is a woman, she and I hold hands; a man would be too embarrassing. Sometimes it was as Kurt Vonnegut said, "Writers lumber past one another like wounded bears." Struck dumb. No way to talk the way we write, and, understanding that impossibility, we sit mute holding hands or lumbering past. Writers don't confer. I have avoided conferences; the best writer of us all wouldn't be in the crowd anyway, but, alone and unknown, composing the work that will be remembered centuries from now.

Maybe because I have unreasonable expectations of Chinese-Americans, especially in numbers, I am looking forward with unaccustomed anticipation to "Talk Story: Our Voices in Literature and Song—Hawaii's Ethnic American Writers' Conference." There I hope to find writers who will tell me things that will nourish and test—like at a family reunion.

There is a family reunion scene at the end of Darrell Lum's play, "Oranges Are Lucky," that makes me cry every time I have heard or read it. When the grandmother makes her wish on her birthday candles, both what she wishes for and how she speaks tear me up. Though Lum would call her speech "pidgin" and I hear it as California Valley Chinese-American dialect, there is a power in her own kind of English that ordinary English cannot evoke. How do you—should you—write dialect in a world that speaks like a television set? Even Mark Twain could not write his 18 or so different kinds of Mississippi River speech so that a reader doesn't skip it. And how do you create a permanent literature with a language that keeps changing so quickly? How do you write vernacular so that the reader who has never heard it reads it the way you meant it? Joe Hadley, a Kauai writer, has a phonograph record tucked into the back cover of "Chalookyu Eensai"; is that the solution? I expect to hear solutions from Hawaii writers such as Ozzie Bushnell and Milton Murayama, who have been experimenting with pidgin for years.

We've been holding planning meetings for the conference and we talked about ourselves and our families for an hour. Eric Chock said that a year after he wrote "Poem for My Father," he finally showed it to his father with the letter that said he had won a prize for it "so that he would know it was good." ("I lie dreaming/when my father comes to me and says,/I hope you'll write a book someday./He thinks I waste my time,/but outside, he spends hours over stones,/gauging the size and shape a rock will take/to fill a space,/to make a wall . . .") People have told me that they deliberately killed the writer in themselves for their families' sakes. Writers are ruthless. I know one merciful and humble young man publishing fine work under a pseudonym. I have a cousin who shut my book when she got to the conflict and so missed the climax and resolution. Readers can be ruthless, too. At the poetry readings here in Hawaii, the poets' grandparents, parents, uncles, aunts and siblings are in the audience. How brave. How brave.

Warren Iwasa, one of the first editors of the *Hawaii Observer*, said, "Just call it fiction." But doesn't good writing have a universally private appeal? Won't the family identify with the fictional characters anyway? Stephen Sumida, a coordinator of this conference as well as the one in Seattle in 1976, said that the community accuses the writer of airing its dirty laundry in public. His comment brought us to the larger perspective of the ethnic writer's responsibility to the community, which has suffered the effects of propaganda—lynching, deportation, internment. No wonder some of our relatives would rather that we write cookbooks and tourist guides than tragedies.

In the tight Japanese-American and Filipino-American and Chinese-American and Island communities, which include the Hawaii Council of American Indian Nations, the writer cannot say, "I am not an ethnic writer" or "I write to please just myself." The community claims you and your work, reviews it in the foreign language and alternative presses, calls you to account.

And we discussed accuracy. What happens if you never noticed how many bowls were used in the ceremony? Do you go look it up? Or do you write it as you remember it? ("Call it fiction," said Warren.) And exposition? How do you write smoothly—no halting footnotes and parentheses—when the common reader (who may be a number of your own ethnic group) doesn't know history? How do you keep a gesture or a joke light, not load it down with explanations?

At one of the series of three poetry readings leading up to the conference, Jody Manabe introduced her poem, "Hadaka De Hanasu" ("Talking Nakedly"), in which a daughter bathing with her mother hears about having babies. "I got this from a sociology class I took about Japanese peoples and institutions," she said. The audience laughed, to which she responded, "No, it was helpful because I realized that my family wasn't unique, that there are other people who live the same way." (My own favorite of "our" poets is Jody Manabe, and, of the prose writers, Mari Nakamura Kubo. I can hardly wait until you read them in the "Talk Story" book.)

Preparing for this conference, I also feel fear and rivalry, maybe because these writers are my siblings, brothers and sisters. One of our characteristics is that we Asian-Americans are very hard on one another, nitpicking and clobbering one another's work, name-calling and fingerpointing. In the anthology "Asian American Heritage" (Washington Square Press, 1974), editor David H. Wand carefully records who is calling whom a banana. The "Aiiieeeee!" anthology (Howard University Press, 1974, and Doubleday, 1975) accuses an older generation of writers of having split personalities. In "Counterpoint—Perspectives on Asian America" (UCLA, 1976), Bruce Iwasaki accuses David H. Wand of being "so ignorant . . . of Asian America that he includes select English translations of Polynesian oral poetry"; the new anthology, "Talk Story," to be published in time for the conference, will be a collection of Hawaii's writers and does not launch itself with an attack on its ancestors. Many of the editors and writers of the above anthologies will be at the conference.

The title of the conference, "Hawaii's Ethnic American Writers' Conference," itself has a history. In 1975 the first Asian-American Writers' Conference was held at the Oakland Museum in Oakland, Calif.; in 1976, a second one at the University of Washington in Seattle. With the decision to hold a third conference in Honolulu, Hawaii herself set the rules and scope.

"Asian-American" is not a self-evident grouping here; it is a mainland term that has not caught hold in Hawaii. Obviously, we cannot have a conference here and exclude Polynesians, and, of course, one of the foremost Hawaii writers is Ozzie Bushnell, who is *haole* (with some Portuguese ancestry; the Portuguese are considered "locals," not *haoles*). Phyllis Thompson, Marjorie Sinclair and Muffy Webb are working in Hawaiian. Most of the Hawaiians are part Chinese, also part *haole*. For the first time, then, white people will be included. In fact, it never occurred to the conference planners to exclude them from either the conference or the readings or the anthology. (I feel like such a *kochink*, a mainland Chinaman, for bringing this up at all—so inhospitable.) How contrary for a Chinese-American to establish solidarity with people of Japanese ancestry by calling oneself Asian-American when the Japanese killed 10 million Chinese civilians in World War II. Why hold out against friendly *haole* (and black and Indian and Polynesian) Americans? Why hold out against anyone?

In the series of readings, I was struck that on the mainland it would be impossible to have a program called "Three Chinese Poets" with Wayne Westlake, Wing Tek Lum, and Black Dog Michael Among. Wayne Westlake read his translations of Chinese poetry, which even if he were Chinese would have angered mainland Asian-Americans who want to trace our literary tradition to writers during the Gold Rush, to diarists on the English ships during the colonial period, not back to China. Claim our American history, they'd say; we are creating a distinct new literature and theater that has nothing to do with Kabuki, haiku, five word tze. And yet, here is Wing Tek Lum, a real Chinaman poet, saying, "I knew Wayne Westlake was a brother when we discussed Tao Chen." And here is Black Dog reading poems about drinking sake with Westlake.

Up to now, though I've lived in Hawaii for 10 years, I have

never believed that Hawaii was much different from the mainland; same old politics, same old life, but I do now discern a
difference: The writers here are not fighting with one another.
I have a prescience that literary history will be made. We will
meet the mainland writers at the airport with *aloha*. The penultimate event of the conference will be "Son of a Talk Story—
Talk Stink," based on the Hawaiian custom, "*ho'opono-pono*."
Have it out. Clear the air.

1978

Reservations About China

MY FRIENDS know how many years I have been on the verge of deciding whether or not I really want to apply for a visa to China, a country that may not be there at all, you know, I having made it up. They send me clippings to show how real it is, how benign or how dangerous. Usually I don't learn anything that changes the fantasy much. Then a friend from Saipan sent me an inch-long article from a public health journal.

Chinese doctors at Tietung Hospital in Anshan, by inserting a suction tube through a pregnant woman's vagina into her uterus to take a few cells from the placenta, have been able to correctly determine the sex of the fetus in 93 cases out of 99. Using this method of identification, they have aborted 29 female fetuses.

At least 14 of those fetuses should have been male.

China has already carried woman-hatred to its extreme conclusion; the obvious injustices against women—female infanticide and female slavery—helped force the Revolution. Part of Mao's plan for the new China was that women be liberated—feet unbound, slaves emancipated, fiancées who refused marriage freed from jails. Men and women are workers, partners, comrades, People, everyone wearing blue jackets and pants, women also digging ditches, driving tractors, carrying rocks, and men's physical strength not the only reason for valuing them. Then why were all 29 fetuses female? Why was not one male?

I went to the volleyball games when the teams from the People's Republic played the Hawaii All-Stars. While the Hawaii All-Stars varied in shapes, colors, sizes, the Chinese were all tall and fair and thin. They seemed to move less earthbound than the rest of us. The women on the sidelines stood on one another's shoulders, not as a formal exercise but for fun. Women and men talked, shouted, laughed without self-consciousness or flirtatiousness. Women did not wear makeup, and their hair was tied in uneven braids or cut short. When I looked at their far-seeing eyes, a desire to visit the new China overwhelmed me, though I reminded myself that these were athletes, a select group of physically outstanding people. The men's competitions were not the main events; the time was evenly divided between men's and women's games. The Chinese teams, both the men and the women, won easily. Their stay in Honolulu seemed a visitation from a graceful new race of human beings.

Yet meanwhile back at the laboratories, their scientists were identifying and aborting female fetuses.

Those 29 female fetuses force me to consider an antiabortion stance dangerous in an overpopulated world. I would have to take the position of some blacks and other Third World peoples: if abortion means genocide—or gynocide—or even just the thinning of *our* ranks but not *their* ranks, then I have to be against it.

I had thought that the hatred of the female was no stronger and deeper than politics, economics, historical tradition, and thus curable with money, jobs, food, peace, sharing the dishwashing, organizing the work. But many Chinese doctors are women; China has no taboos against contraception and abortion; yet the Chinese use the new invention to abort female fetuses only. What is it in the human psyche that hates the female so? What is the woman-hatred behind rape, wife-beating, the beating of pregnant women, prostitution? What is this hatred of the female body, not just because it is fat or thin, not just because breasts, buttocks, and legs do not measure up to an ideal female body? The female body is hated precisely because it is female, and thus not improvable, though American women pump up their breasts and Japanese women slice their epicanthic folds.

I do not want to cooperate if the yin forces and the yang forces of the universe complement each other not only like the dark and the light and the sea and the land but like wolves and sheep, like foxes and chickens. And the ascendancy of woman as slow as evolution.

I have woman-hatred in me too. I recognize it in the feeling I get when I look at the clusters of dinosaur eggs at the museum of natural history. I want to crush those eggs, stomp on them, crack them open. Nests of dinosaurs. I get the same feeling when I come across clusters of spider eggs in cellars.

My skin crawls. My teeth clench and grind. Nests of spiders. Nests of snakes with snaky tongues. Nests of turtles with wet black eyes. The feeling is not maternal, not protective at all. But I come to my senses quickly. There must be people who do not hold back the urge to destroy nests and females.

Fearful at the enmity of Creation, I went to visit a friend who lives on the beach. The last time I had seen her, she told me that she felt the presence of a huge female spirit, a large Hawaiian woman, near some caves between her house and the beach. She went inside a cave to sweep it out, a desire for housekeeping having come over her. As she raked the leaves and debris from the cave floor, she unearthed 11 dog's teeth pierced with the neat holes the ancient Hawaiians drilled. She phoned a Hawaiiana expert, who said that men once wore dog's teeth around their ankles and necks for making a rattling noise when they danced. He said to call the Bishop Museum when she found about 40 teeth. At 38 teeth, she called the museum, which sent a team of diggers. In the square they marked off, they brushed away dirt a thin layer at a time, until an adz emerged from the ground, also ancient fishhooks, sinkers, more dog's teeth.

She showed me the teeth, white and pale yellow, smooth, clean. "They feel masculine, don't they?" said my friend, who was wearing one on a gold chain around her neck. "I'm not sure if I ought to, but I'm wearing it to give me power," she said. Yes, the teeth felt masculine to me too. I walked to the cave, went inside, and wished I could see or sense the large female presence, but just saw the cave, the leaves, the beach, the sea, very real, as usual.

That night in my friend's living room, I sat with my eyes closed and listened to the ocean, so regular, like breathing, like heart beating. Miraculously, I found a vision:

I saw a dark red light. Afterglow from the sun, I thought, angry aftermath of the day, tired red eyes. It will turn green soon, I thought, green contrast soon. But it did not fade. It leapt like fire, red bloody flames. Red star. I could make out its configurations; it had limits. It was a wound, red blood, bleeding meat, a cut, a gash in human flesh; I could see the edges—white human skin. Bleeding female flesh. Not her heart. Red hole. Fear. Disgust. My body shrinks before the sight. I curl up, helpless before this wound. "Mother!" I was looking at a vagina—the vagina. Her vagina. Open, birthing. The first view of Mother is not the face. Oh, shore it up. Cover up sloppy fleshiness. Make the world solid and geometric so that I can walk upright on it. Paint over it so that I can reason and calculate. Cover it, house it, cement it.

But when I heard "Mother!" like a voice, I felt tenderness and pity for the pain of so much blood, the pain of that size wound. That tenderness released me, allowed me to open my eyes so that I could get up and go about my daily small life.

A human life ought to be a moving away from that red hole, stepping back for a larger and larger perspective so that the red hole becomes only a small part of a woman, then a woman a part of the planet and the universe, and the universe a spot of white light in a black field. The killing of female fetuses is going the wrong way—a journey inside the red hole to find a tiny being with a tinier red hole, and poking that out. Obliterating the red star is not the way to the white star.

Rational again, I realized that I couldn't have had a birth trauma like that unless I had been a breech baby, and as far as I know, I wasn't, nor are most people breech babies. But when my reason is boggled, as at the thought of the 29 female fetuses, it doesn't work anymore, and I see things. I'll leave it up to more politically talented minds to find a way to take the unenlightened ones by the shoulders and pull them away so they no longer stare aghast at the dark red light, the past.

1978

San Francisco's Chinatown: A View from the Other Side of Arnold Genthe's Camera

O NCE A year or so, we drive our parents to San Francisco to spend the day in Chinatown, where they stock up on Chinese goods like picture frames, petit-point patterns, honey, mushrooms. They believe that they could not buy picture frames better than these unless they traveled to Asia. Sometimes they skip a year or two because a trip from Stockton to San Francisco is a journey into foreign territory—urban, competitive, the people like Hong Kong city slickers, not at all like the people in the San Joaquin Valley, where villager is still neighborly to villager as in the Chinese countryside they remember, helping one another, "not Chinese against Chinese like in the Big City."

San Francisco Chinatown shows off for the tourists; our Chinatowns blend into the Valley towns and cities. Our businesses and houses are spread out, not concentrated into a few blocks. Yet our communities are more tightly knit. We speak the peasant dialects. We know one another. Gossip gives each person a reputation. The boys would find it very uncomfortable to dress like punks and hoods, because everybody would talk about them and stare and point. In San Francisco there are Chinese and Chinese Americans who are fabulously rich and hire immigrants at twelve cents and twenty-five cents an hour. In the Valley, even the richest women work in the fields. We are closer to the earth; no one lives in apartment houses. If we don't have a farm, we work our yards into fruit groves and vegetable gardens.

It's not only the older generation which sees differences between the Big City Chinese and the rest of us in Stockton, Sacramento (Second City), Marysville (Third City because it was the third largest in Gold Rush days), Lodi, Locke, Watsonville, Tracy, and other central California towns. My own scholarly friends have complained how the Big City Chinamen refuse to share research work, whereas we Valley Chinamen will help each other get ahead. We show notes and let each other read manuscripts in progress. (The term "Chinamen," by the way, is used here as neither denigration nor irony. In the early days of Chinese American history, men called themselves "Chinamen" just as other newcomers called themselves "Englishmen" or "Frenchmen": the term distinguished them from the "Chinese" who remained citizens of China, and also showed that they were not recognized as Americans. Later, of course, it became an insult. Young Chinese Americans today are reclaiming the word because of its political and historical precision, and are demanding that it be said with dignity and not for name-calling.)

I was raised to say "Hello, Aunt" and "Hello, Uncle" to all older Chinese people I passed in the street, whether or not I had ever met them before. Although in recent years this custom has been practiced less frequently because of the large influx of strange immigrants, in San Francisco I still have a sense of committing many rudenesses as we walk through crowds of ethnic Chinese without greeting them, treating them like white people.

Paradoxically, my parents also see San Francisco Chinatown as a relic of the past, foreign not because it is so American but because it is like an exciting Chinese city before the Revolution. As if she were in the Canton or Shanghai or Macao of the thirties, my mother bursts into the San Francisco stores yelling at the clerks and bargaining fiercely. "You won't sell me these picture frames, huh?" she shouts. "We'll sell them," they answer, "but not at your price. You have to pay the price on the tag." They are modern young American salesclerks who have not had to deal with a woman like her. "All right for you," she shouts. "If you won't sell them to me, I'm taking them for free." She picks up the frames and walks toward the door; she seldom has had to take such drastic measures, but she is dealing with clerks who have not come down one cent. We are embarrassed that our mother is making such a scene, but she doesn't often get a chance to bargain so combatively. The clerks are out-bluffed and rush to the door to stop her. They agree to a huge discount, which they'll probably have to make up out of their own pockets. We carry the frames for her, and go on to the next store.

Instead of lunching in a restaurant, my parents want to eat with my aunt and uncle, recent immigrants from Hong Kong. We find their building, then tunnel along looking for their door among the many doors on either side of the dark hallway. They and their children live in a one-bedroom apartment with a kitchen the size of a closet; the children have bunk beds in the bedroom, and the adults sleep on the sofa, which takes up all the space in the living room. The entire apartment is about the size of one room in an ordinary house. We leave our parents with our aunt and uncle, no room anyway for so many of us, and go to Ghirardelli Square and other parts of San Francisco that our parents have no curiosity to visit.

I remember, however, that when I was a child, our parents did once take us to a restaurant in Chinatown. Perhaps it was part of a wedding celebration. The walls were covered with blown-up black-and-white photographs of Chinese people. They were like pictures out of the earliest pages of our family album—that familiar—but not stiff and formal. People had been caught going about their daily lives; children were shown playing and not standing like soldiers. Because of their old-style Chinese clothes, which they were wearing while playing and not just for special occasions like school assemblies, it struck me that all those children had grown up and died, but they had been playing and didn't think about that. The older people were very wrinkled, laugh wrinkles and work wrinkles. The way their eyelids folded and their noses grew, the way their faces showed hardships and dignity and humor—I felt connected to them, as if their faces gave me my face, as if I understood very clearly where my face came from. I felt enlarged. That was the first time I had seen Arnold Genthe's photographs. "Those pictures are the way our grandfathers lived," the adults said. "That's the way it was in China." "No, no," others said, "it's not China. Those were Americans." As an adult, I have looked for this restaurant on my own rare trips to San Francisco Chinatown but have not found it again.

As I look at Genthe's pictures now, essentially I feel the same way I did when a child, but I also see more particularly because I know more of our history. I can measure more exactly the distance between me and the people in the pictures. I know now that Genthe took the pictures before the San Francisco

earthquake, which was only seventy-two years ago, not centuries. The people had looked so ancient—so Chinese. The
earthquake, a true holocaust, must have suddenly changed
everything. As the old people said, there were different San
Franciscos before and after the holocaust. Out of the fire
there was also born a new generation of American citizens;
since it was illegal for Chinamen to apply for citizenship, they
claimed that their American birth certificates had gone up in
flames with the Hall of Records. Coincidentally—and many
Chinamen believe it wasn't coincidence at all but conspiracy—
Honolulu, Los Angeles, and Walnut Grove Chinatowns were
also burned completely, Honolulu ostensibly because a wind
blew plague fires out of control; Los Angeles during a massacre of Chinamen; Walnut Grove because of "crowded conditions." On the outskirts of Walnut Grove, the Chinese rebuilt
themselves a new town of their own, Locke, the only town
founded by Chinese in America. Chinamen were also lynched
and driven out of Rock Springs, Denver, Seattle, Portland,
Tacoma, Juneau. Whatever Chinatowns these cities have today
have been rebuilt. No wonder Genthe's Chinatown looks like
such a foreign, bygone time and place.

Another person who left records of San Francisco
Chinatown before the earthquake was Ng Poon Chew, the
newspaper editor who founded the *Chung Sai Yat Po* (The
Chinese Western Daily) in 1900. He kept his readers informed
about the continually changing, tricky employment and immigration laws, praised Chinese American accomplishments,
deplored injustices. He gave Chinamen advice on how to survive in America. White Americans, he said, hated Chinamen
because whites could not see the common humanity beneath
the pajama pants, the gowns, the high collars, the queues.
He recommended that Chinamen dress like whites and learn
English; they ought to look and act like Americans because
they were Americans. He made himself an example of such a
well-dressed Chinese American gentleman by cutting his hair,
growing a thick mustache, and always wearing a suit, vest,
and tie in photographs. A Presbyterian who spoke eloquent
English, he was one of the most popular lyceum attractions in
the United States.

Looking over Genthe's pictures, I see no men dressed

like Ng Poon Chew. I wonder whether Genthe had to aim his camera selectively in order to frame out what he felt were anachronisms. There must have been men who took Ng Poon Chew's sartorial advice. Indeed, Genthe, who managed to photograph Greta Garbo, could have tracked down Ng Poon Chew himself.

What is missing from Genthe's Chinatown photographs are white people, whose presence would have broken the spell of a self-contained, mythical Cathay. There have been rough times when Chinatown was supposed to have been an armed strong-hold inaccessible to Caucasians, but usually it has been an inte-gral part of an American city, eight blocks in the very center of San Francisco. Chinatown depends on a vigorous, aggressive relationship with white America to survive. Surely, white busi-nessmen, tourists, gamblers, customers could be seen dealing with the Chinese inhabitants. Some Chinese men brought white wives back to China with them. I would have enjoyed seeing pictures of those American women who were willing to give up their citizenship to marry a Chinaman. The immigra-tion laws took citizenship away from such a woman, did not grant citizenship to her Chinaman husband. If Genthe could not find cosmopolitan people to photograph, he could have recorded the streets at the boundary of Chinatown. Perhaps there were Chinese business signs next to English signs, con-trasts between crowdedness and spaciousness, squalor and affluence. Perhaps the differences were barely perceptible, ev-eryone living like Chinamen at the turn of the century. But the context for Chinatown has always been white America, and by omitting Caucasians from the pictures, Genthe isolated the Chinese and added to the stereotype of the exotic, myste-rious, inscrutable Oriental.

Genthe's pictures show so much, and yet do not tell enough. There is, for example, an interesting picture of a Chinaman con-templating a dead, strung-up wildcat, which Genthe claimed would be eaten "raw" by hatchetmen. I am sure that the lynx will be eaten: from my own experience, I know that Chinese will experiment with all kinds of food. But it will not be eaten raw by thugs in some sort of savage blood ceremony. Some housewife or group of men who cook together will buy the lynx and go home to prepare it, probably with a good sauce.

Another example of his seeing the details but missing the overview is the preponderance of children in his pictures. We see men carrying children, walking hand in hand with them, groups of children playing—the wonderful picture of the row of children playing like circus elephants, holding on to one another's pigtails—and this gives the impression that Chinatown was a healthy community of flourishing families when exactly the opposite was the actual, lonely situation. Notice how formally and carefully the women and children dress—elaborate headdresses, silks, not a child among them in street-urchin rags. Women and children were valued, specially treated because they were so rare. How protective and attentive the men in the pictures are. It was not until the second half of this century that the American immigration laws allowed Chinese women to enter the U.S. on the same basis as men—whose own immigration was restricted by the Chinese Exclusion Acts. The wives of treaty merchants and ambassadors were allowed to accompany them, and these may be the aristocratic-looking women we see in the pictures. Genthe said that women rarely walked about in the streets except on certain holidays, and women who were valued would certainly act that way. (I question whether the girls in the photographs whom he called "Slave Girls" were really slaves; even in China, slaveowners were duty-bound to find husbands for their slaves at an early age, and to free them upon marriage. There would have been no problem in this country finding husbands; and men found it difficult enough to smuggle themselves into this country, let alone bring slave girls.) There are even now Benevolent Associations and hotels filled with old men who never could send for their wives. No wonder white housewives defended Chinamen as good nursemaids, no matter what heathenish rites they practiced on their nights off in Chinatown; white children were the only children they could cuddle and cherish. The typical Chinaman was a bachelor; Chinatown was a bachelor society. The Chinese American family and the Chinese American woman like me are relatively new phenomena. Genthe's pictures of crowds consisting entirely of men was the way Chinatown usually must have looked.

There is a photograph Genthe entitled *No Likee* that breaks the heart. To me and to the people I showed it to, the man looks as if he were weeping in public and covering his face with his big sleeve. I saw him as a man who could no longer face his hard American life stoically and, alone in this alley of a street, began to cry. Genthe said he was merely hiding from the camera. "He would notice you no more than a post—unless you pulled a camera on him." He thought that Chinese did not like having their pictures taken because of primitive superstitions. Therefore he devised ways to hide his camera, which caught people in natural poses. The people Genthe asked to be his subjects must have been fooling him; even Chinese in China enjoyed having their pictures taken. When the camera was invented, instead of just writing their names on plaques for the family hall, Chinese had their portraits hung. No public event was complete without a group photograph of all participants. Homesick men and waiting wives, parents, and children exchanged photographs whenever they could afford it. They refused to let Genthe take their pictures, not because of exotic beliefs but because they were afraid of incurring trouble from the white authorities with their Exclusion Acts and deportation laws. Those Chinese who allowed Genthe to take their pictures full face—the sword dancer, the paper gatherer, the smiling cook—were probably bona fide Americans with no secrets to hide.

The laws were made so that it was very easy for the Chinaman to get in trouble. The picture of the vegetable peddler with his two baskets on a pole could have gotten that man jailed, fined, or deported. There were laws against using poles on San Francisco streets. The U.S. Supreme Court overruled certain state and city laws, such as a San Francisco health-inspection law for laundries, on the grounds that they had been passed for the purpose of harassing Chinamen, but often as soon as a law was repealed, it would be passed again in another form by another legislature or city council. Other anti-Chinese laws included a "police tax," which every Chinese over eighteen not already paying a monthly miner's tax had to pay for the extra policing he needed, a queue tax, a shoe tax, special curfews, a "cubic air ordinance" (which required that each residence have so many cubic feet of air for each inhabitant, thus keeping Chinese from sharing housing). Chinese said that they were treated like dogs, who also had to be licensed and chased by dogcatchers. It was easy for a Chinaman to become a criminal, and inevitable that he would take the law into his own hands with his own courts and police system. An 1850 law held that "Mulattoes, Negroes, and Indians" could not testify in court "either for or against any white man"; later, it was broadened to include "Mongolians" on the grounds that they were racially related to Indians.

There are no farmers in Genthe's pictures, even though farming was sometimes the only legal work left for a Chinaman. After building the Central Pacific Railroad, the Chinese, using shovels and wheelbarrows, leveed and filled in the California delta and created one of the most fertile farm regions in the world. Nonetheless, there were laws that Chinese could not own land.

Periodically, the state of California as well as various cities forbade "Mongolians" from obtaining business licenses. Also, any individuals or corporation representatives who hired "Chinese or Mongolians" could be imprisoned or fined. The 1879 California Constitution provided that public works hire no Chinese labor. Chinese were thrown out of the cigar industry and the shoe industry. In Marysville and other places, white miners dynamited shafts and tunnels with Chinese miners inside. Only Chinese fishermen had to pay fishing taxes and shellfish taxes—even though they had begun the shellfish trade. As California tried to corner him and annihilate his livelihood with laws, the Chinaman moved from the coast inland, from the cities to the countryside, from the countryside back to San Francisco, from the Valley back to the coast; there was no getting rid of him.

Jobs were legal or illegal depending upon the need for Chinese labor. It was all right to hire Chinese as cooks and nursemaids. Genthe took several pictures of such men, including the one of the sunny, smiling cook. During the Driving Out period after the building of the railroads, Chinamen were captured and locked up in a shed near the presidio. Housewives selected "houseboys" to take home, as if the Civil War and Emancipation had not happened.

Genthe took pictures of Chinatown on the brink of change. Nineteen hundred is the midpoint of Chinese American history. The one image that symbolizes this change for me is the queue. Almost every male in the photographs wears a pigtail. The spirit of revolution had not reached San Francisco. Over the centuries, Chinese men had grown pigtails as signs of sub-jugation to the Manchus and their successors. By the turn of the century, Sun Yat-sen already had made several inspiring appearances in San Francisco, and young revolutionaries were cutting off their queues in defiance of oppression. I can see from Genthe's photographs that the movement still had not become popular. But the revolution was to come very soon, and just a few years, possibly a few months, after these pic-tures, there would not have been any man with a queue on these streets.

If Genthe were to take pictures in Chinatown today, there would be at least one similarity to the pictures of the past: the settings would still be the streets. Even now, Chinese and Chinese Americans would not take him into Chinatown homes. I would not invite him to come with me to visit my aunt and uncle. Homes are for families and for friends who are almost family. Also, it is very embarrassing for us to have outsiders see us cramped into closets. I wouldn't want to have to explain that the rent is as high as for houses or apartments outside Chinatown. On the other hand, Genthe was not one to feel sorry for the people he photographed. He looked at them in wonder.

1978

The Coming Book

WHEN A worker who knows how much more labor has to be done in no time nevertheless sits idle because caught in a situation where she can't work—visiting in a strange house overnight or eyes closed in the dentist's chair or darkness suddenly fallen deep in the woods—then the visions come assailing.

Once at the dentist's, I shut my eyes and saw The Book—a volume as thick as Joyce's *Ulysses* but not *Ulysses*—fly at me and fly past. Just before its appearance, I heard words from Joyce like music; not having read Joyce for years, I was surprised at the independence of memory. His words reeled out in entrancing rhythms flowing in small and large figure eights looping into infinity without periods and commas. The Joyce ended on the last Yes, and I heard No, no, no, no, and again No. I almost jumped out of the chair with elation. The universe had doubled! No, more than doubled; it was multiplying by millions. Joyce's day was but one day in a few people's lives, and there are millions of days more, millions of people more. A book of No would balance out a book of Yes, not cynically or unhappily but like a facing page. The Book had flown out of the distance and zoomed past my head.

I felt tired ahead of time for the work to be done to build The Book word by word. If I could finish it, I would never have to write again; in it would be the last word. So far we have only written approximations.

The Book begins with the sound of a telephone ringing, ringing, ringing. Also a radio is playing a rock song, hard electric rock words, which I've forgotten. If I write The Book, I'll have to invent that song.

That's all I glimpsed when The Book zipped by. I will have to make trails of words into that room to find out who answers the phone, who is calling, and what they talk about.

Right now I don't know who these people are or what the room looks like or what city it's in. But it is not me on the telephone, and not me who lives in that room. I wouldn't play a

rock station that loud. So, with The Book, I will make a break
from the "I" stories I have been writing.

"*The telephone rang too loud again and again and again,
crashed into the rock music, the top song on the top ten, at inflex-
ible intervals. It was a warm afternoon. . . .*" There will next be
a rushing about, turning down the radio, grabbing the phone
before it stops ringing.

I can't follow this story any further. First I have to finish the
stories I couldn't write during childhood because of the years
it took to acquire vocabulary.

The Book's pace will be normal, no skips but one moment
moving to the next like the phone's rings. No elisions like "As
the years passed. . . ." I heard each full ring and the time
before them. And each word of the song. The characters will
rush about, but the narration will be deliberate—*ring . . .
ring . . . ring.*

I did not *see* the radio or the telephone; The Book begins
with two sounds, which are not proper "visions." But I am not
an audile, and I believe that if I lose my sight, I will no longer
be able to write. I like to look at poetry on the page, the spac-
ing of the lines, the letters. I like rearranging by eye. Blindly
composing by voice would bypass reason, miss precision. Both
the sounds are modern sounds, technological noises, not the
birds and rivers and winds that I like. Harsh rings. Harsh music. Not the epic symphonies that I hear (but can't remember
because I don't know notation).

The second paragraph will begin the dialogue. The Book
will be filled with voices as heard through machines. When
read aloud, it will sound like the Twentieth Century. The
reader will not need a visual imagination, only ears.

I heard somewhere that aural hallucinations are a more severe symptom of psychosis than visual ones. But in healthy
people, auricular images may be only a more advanced form of
imagination than pictures. (I also habitually hear what other
people don't hear—firecrackers or gunshots, which may be
Chinese music.) The Book will not be a collection of nonsense
sounds but English words, a translation of music.

I told a woman who plays viola in a symphony orchestra how
uncapturable music is, how I cannot think of organizing the
music I hear, but only be its audience. But she said that writing

is the most abstract form; the other forms have concomitant human sense organs; music has the ear, and painting the eye, sculpture the hands, and acting and dancing the voice and body. But writing, she said, does not have its organ. She began to cry; I'm not sure why.

I can feel the texture of The Book; it will be modern like science fiction, like black vinyl. The characters will not worry so much about food as they do in my present writings; they can afford phones and a sound system.

When alone, I am not aware of my race or my sex, both in need of social contexts for definition. Visions (and "aurisons"? "audisions"?) come to a human being alone; they are embarrassed away when people watch you humming to yourself or staring at nothing. Yet visions probably don't come from nowhere but grow from what we see everyday and live everyday, which is America. In America, Everyman—the universal human being—is white. (I have been watching a lot of television.) The Book may exclude me as first-person narrator, and the Chinese-American heroines who have interested me may disappear.

"*Hello.*"

"*Hello, is it you?*"

"*Yes. I mean No. Who is this?*"

"*It's me.*"

"*Oh, it's you. What are you doing?*"

"*Nothing much. What about you?*"

If The Book is an archetype, I needn't be the one to write it. Someone else can write what happens next, and I'd be happy to read it. You can have the opening if you want; it may save you a few moments' work.

You'd save me the time to examine some other sightings, like the town I saw when I got lost in the woods. Also, there were people calling, "We hear you. We're coming. This way. This way." The shingled roofs and white walls and windows turned out to be optical illusions made by the spaces between the leaves and the shaking leaves catching the sun. "This may be how I'll go," I said aloud. "I'll die of starvation and exposure lost in the mountains." When I'd circled the same landmarks twice, I sat on the ground and waited to get some ultimate message while facing death. The leaves and the insects kept on shimmering. Apparently you have no choice about what shows itself. What I did learn was: Don't trust deer trails; they meander and fade. Head downhill, where you'll come to a stream; follow it to town.

1983

Precarious Lives:
Review of Scent of Apples
by Bienvenido N. Santos

B EN, THE narrator of a number of the stories in *Scent of Apples*, asks, "Who would publish such things?"

"Nobody," says his friend, "because you remember the wrong things. Heaven help you, but you remember the wrong things."

"All our stories are sad," says Ambo, another narrator. "So my friends will not listen, because my tales are sad, because they do not have the heart. But you will listen to me, Ben, even if you too are going away."

One of the things that Ben remembers is meeting a Filipino farmer in Kalamazoo, who invites him home to dinner. The man has left the Philippines long ago and wants Ben to tell him whether "our Filipino women are the same like they were twenty years ago." "I'm bringing you a first class Filipino," the farmer tells his American child and white wife, who says, "Aw, go away, quit kidding, there's no such thing as first class Filipino." Ben goes home with the farmer: It is a journey like those that happen in an Isaac Bashevis Singer story, in which people meet their own kind far away from home. An evening with a countryman is all that the farmer and his family can have of the Philippines.

Perhaps the narrator's memories are "the wrong things" because no human being ought to be as lonely as the "Pinoys"— as the Filipino men in America are called. And "the wrong things" are also the bits of joy—a graceful play at poker, a few happy hours one Christmas eve, the day a troupe of Philippine dancers came to Chicago—the miracles that should not have been possible in the sad lives of "the hurt men." Relishing the good times, Bienvenido N. Santos places these rare incidents of joy at the center of his stories. The Philippine dance concert, for example, is so wonderful an event that Mr. Santos describes it in two short stories, from the viewpoint of two different Pinoys in the audience. The reader comes away remembering sunbeams in the dark.

Though a small book—it is only 178 pages long—*Scent of Apples* gives us scenes from 35 years of Filipino American life and selections from Mr. Santos's writings over the same period of years. The stories have their settings in San Francisco, New York, Washington, D.C., Chicago, Kalamazoo and many other cities of the Midwest—places where Filipino men, who have left families and communities behind, make precarious American lives. To protect themselves against brutality, they befriend one another and try not to forget Filipino manners, establishing a civility in skid row. At Manila House, a sort of restaurant and club in Washington: "It was a feast laid before us, and as we sat down, we remembered the nice things to do; each of us turned in every direction where the boys were talking and playing and said with our eyes and with our lips: 'Come, let's eat.' And the boys respond with the usual, 'Thanks, we have already eaten.'" Mr. Santos's writing is very delicate, very fine, gently rendering "the hurt men," or "the boys," as they jauntily call one another.

Some of "the boys" are students, others family men sending money home—until their families are wiped out in war—and one is a rich man's son. But in America, they are "Pinoys." At the beginning of the book, they go about in groups, pretending that they are almost brothers: "'Yes,' I said, lying deliberately. When we talked of boys we lied to our American friends, we always said we knew each other in the Philippines; and we talked about our families as though we had deep ties of association and kinship. Mostly it was just talk. Perhaps it gave us strength to talk like that. We didn't want to appear the homeless waifs that we were. We didn't wish to be known as the forgotten children of long lost mothers and fathers, as grown up men without childhood, bastards of an indifferent country."

The later stories are about pairs of friends who watch over one another. Western literature ought to have more such writing in praise of friendship, a strong tradition in Eastern literature. In "The Day the Dancers Came," the *compadres* are Tony, who is dying, and Fil, who tries to bring the dancers home.

"When Fil arrived at the Hamilton, it seemed to him the Philippine dancers had taken over the hotel. They were all over the lobby, on the mezzanine, talking in groups, animatedly, their teeth sparkling as they laughed, their eyes disappearing in mere slits of light. Some of the girls wore their black hair long. For a moment, the sight seemed too much for him who had all but forgotten how beautiful Philippine girls were. He wanted to look away, but their loveliness held him. He must do something, close his eyes perhaps. As he did so, their laughter came to him like a breeze murmurous with sounds native to his land." He thinks they will want to meet fellow Filipinos as much as he does, but to the dancers, he's just a strange old Pinoy. Fil goes to the dance concert, then to record the sounds in his "magic sound mirror."

In "The Contender," the *compadres* are Bernie and Felix, Felix a family man and Bernie a bachelor and ex-boxer who is losing his sight. Bernie also goes to the dance concert, which Mr. Santos describes visually in this story, adding to the aural beauty of the previous story. "At first Bernie thought something had gone wrong with the lights on the stage. The darkness was total. . . . It took a long time before he could see again. Yet nobody seemed to have noticed him. The stage appeared nearer and brighter. A lovely Philippine maiden walked proudly under a parasol held up by dusky slaves, and at the sound of a gong, she began to dance, swaying about in fluid grace, her arms and wrists and long-nailed fingertips sharpening the rhythm of her dance." This interweaving of the stories is a playful delight. Sometimes a minor character in one story takes a large role in another, like actors in repertory.

Scent of Apples includes Mr. Santos's first works, published in the 1950's in the Philippines and only now published in this country in book form. I would have liked each story to have been labeled with the year it was written. It would have been fun to trace more exactly Mr. Santos's development—as, for instance, in his use of the two narrators, Ben and Ambo. As if denying loneliness, the narrators are friends, Ambo telling Ben some of the stories. Both of them are gamblers "with a sense of smell." Mr. Santos seemed to have begun writing by using a narrator similar to himself, then created Ambo to experiment further with fictional distance. In the later stories, both narrators disappear, the main characters receiving all the attention, and the stories are written entirely in the third person. Mr. Santos no longer needs to voice his doubts about the stories but gets on with the job.

Another development that I enjoyed following was the changes in Mr. Santos's style, which echo a Filipino accent. His editor left uncorrected some of the odd usages of articles and prepositions that those of us for whom English is a second language are prone to. If the stories were dated, I could see whether these usages diminished in more recent writings. Many of the characters in the book are trilingual, speaking several Philippine dialects plus English. Mr. Santos is a master at giving the reader a sense of people speaking in many languages and dialects. Even Mark Twain couldn't transcribe dialects so that they were readable. But Mr. Santos can. All of us for whom English is a second language and all of us who write in English about people who are not speaking English must read him and try to figure out how he does it so smoothly.

In the Philippines, Bienvenido N. Santos published novels and collections of short stories. He won that country's highest literary awards and came to the United States on a Rockefeller writing grant and a Guggenheim. Ethnic studies programs at colleges have been ordering his books from the Philippines until now, but with this first American edition, Mr. Santos ought to be read by more of the general public and his work should make its way into the mainstream of American literature. Also, Filipino-Americans now have a book.

1980

TWO POEMS

Restaurant
for Lilah Kan

The main cook lies sick on a banquette, and his assistant
has cut his thumb. So the quiche cook takes
their places at the eight-burner range, and you and I
get to roll out twenty-three rounds of pie
dough and break a hundred eggs, four at a crack,
and sift out shell with a China cap, pack
spinach in the steel sink, squish and squeeze
the water out, and grate a full moon of cheese.
Pam, the pastry chef, who is baking Choco-
late Globs (once called Mulattos) complains about the disco,
which Lewis, the salad man, turns up louder out of spite.
"Black so-called musician." "Broads. Whites."
The porters, who speak French, from the Ivory Coast,
sweep up droppings and wash the pans without soap.
We won't be out of here until three A.M. In this basement,
I lose my size. I am a bent-over
child, Gretel or Jill, and I can
lift a pot as big as a tub with both hands.
Using a pitchfork, you stoke the broccoli and bacon.
Then I find you in the freezer, taking
a nibble of a slab of chocolate big as a table.
We put the quiches in the oven, then we are able
to stick our heads up out of the sidewalk into the night
and wonder at the clean diners behind glass in candlelight.

Absorption of Rock

We bought from Laotian refugees a cloth
that in war a woman sewed, appliquéd
700 triangles—mountain ranges
changing colors with H'mong suns and seasons,
white and yellow teeth, black arrows,
or sails. They point in at an embroidery,
whose mystery seems the same as that posed
by face cards. Up close, the curls and x's do
not turn plainer; a green strand runs through
the yellow chains, and black between the white.
Sometimes caught from across the room, twilighted,
the lace in the center smokes, and shadows move
over the red background, which should shine.
One refugee said, "This is old woman's design."

We rented a room to a Vietnam vet,
who one Saturday night ran back to it—
thrashed through bamboo along the neighborhood
stream, then out on to sidewalk, lost the police,
though he imprinted the cement with blood
from his cut foot. He came out of the bathroom
an unidentifiable man. His strange
jagged wound yet unstaunched, he had shaved.
Yellow beard was mixed with blood and what
looked like bits of skin in the tub and toilet.
On the way to the hospital, he said, "Today
the M.C. raised his finger part way.
They're just about ready to gong my act."

We search out facts to defend a Vietnamese,
who has allegedly shot to death a Lao
in Stockton, outside a bar. It was in fear,
we hear him say, of a cantaloupe or rock
that the Lao man had caused to appear
inside him. One anthropologist testifies

that Vietnamese driving in the highlands
rolled up the windows against the H'mong air.
The H'mong in Fairfield were not indicted for
their try at family suicide; there was a question
of a Lao curse or want of a telephone.
Three translators have run away—this fourth
does not say enough words.

An Answer to the Question, "Who Is an Ethnic Writer?"

DOES WILLIAM CARLOS WILLIAMS come off better as a great "American poet" or as a great "Puerto Rican poet"? Depending on the circles you're trying to run in, one term gives a cachet and the other can be a downright liability.

I want English professors to put my books on regular reading lists. An American writer. We have worked hard for fairness in the job market and housing and schooling, and our art should not be segregated out. Readers ought not to have boring preconceptions of what a story is about just because its author is "ethnic." "Ethnic writer" and "feminist writer" have been used dismissively.

I love it when the Chinese Americans give me banquets. (I've been honored for being their own ethnic regional hometown writer by the Chinese and/or Asian Americans in Stockton and in San Francisco and in Los Angeles, and I expect to go to New York's Chinatown soon for another such honor.) I love being a Living Treasure of Hawaii. I love being the Asian American and Pacific Islander Network's Woman of the Year. On my own, I could never have thought up such wonderful titles for myself. I love it when people in Hong Kong and Singapore and Kuala Lumpur and Bangkok welcome me "home"—one of *their* own too. I am glad I look the way I do, though there is no choice. In the next few years, I'll see whether I can also pass as home-girl-makes-good in Beixing, Sun Woi, Taipei, and Norman, Oklahoma. I love writing about—I *have to* write about people in their specific and distinctive ways. I sing along with Henry James: "The ways of the people, their ideas, their peculiar cachet."

Of course, I'm an ethnic writer, and only benighted people see ethnics as not partaking of the macrocosmic. And only Chinese Americans who are very mad would kick an admirer of Henry James and William Carlos Williams out of our family.

1982

960

Cultural Mis-readings
by American Reviewers

WHEN READING most of the reviews and critical analyses of *The Woman Warrior*, I have two reactions: I want to pat those critics on their backs, and I also giggle helplessly, shaking my head. (Helpless giggles turn less frequently into sobs as one gets older.) The critics did give my book the National Book Critics Circle Award; and they reviewed it in most of the major magazines and newspapers, thus publicising it enough to sell. Furthermore, they rarely gave it an unfavourable review. I pat them on the back for recognising good writing—but, unfortunately, I suspect most of them of perceiving its quality in an unconscious sort of way; they praise the wrong things.

Now, of course, I expected *The Woman Warrior* to be read from the women's lib angle and the Third World angle, the *Roots* angle; but it is up to the writer to transcend trendy categories. What I did not foresee was the critics measuring the book and me against the stereotype of the exotic, inscrutable, mysterious oriental. About two-thirds of the reviews did this. In some cases, I must admit, it was only a line or a marring word that made my stomach turn, the rest of the review being fairly sensible. You might say I am being too thin-skinned; but a year ago I had really believed that the days of gross stereotyping were over, that the 1960s, the Civil Rights movement, and the end of the war in Vietnam had enlightened America, if not in deeds at least in manners. Pridefully enough, I believed that I had written with such power that the reality and humanity of my characters would bust through any stereotypes of them. Simplemindedly, I wore a sweat-shirt for the dust-jacket photo, to deny the exotic. I had not calculated how blinding stereotyping is, how stupefying. The critics who said how the book was good because it was, or was not, like the oriental fantasy in their heads might as well have said how weak it was, since it in fact did not break through that fantasy.

Here are some examples of exotic-inscrutable-mysterious-oriental reviewing:

Margaret Manning in *The Boston Globe*: 'Mythic forces flood the book. Echoes of the Old Testament, fairy tales, the *Golden Bough* are here, but they have their own strange and brooding atmosphere inscrutably foreign, oriental.'

Barbara Burdick in the *Peninsula Herald*: 'No other people have remained so mysterious to Westerners as the inscrutable Chinese. Even the word China brings to mind ancient rituals, exotic teas, superstitions, silks and fire-breathing dragons.'

Helen Davenport of the Chattanooga *News–Free Press*: 'At her most obscure, though, as when telling about her dream of becoming a fabled "woman warrior" the author becomes as inscrutable as the East always seems to the West. In fact, this book seems to reinforce the feeling that "East is East and West is West and never the twain shall meet," or at any rate it will probably take more than one generation away from China.'

Alan McMahan in the Fort Wayne *Journal–Gazette*: 'The term "inscrutable" still applies to the rank and file of Chinese living in their native land.' (I do not understand. Does he mean Chinese Americans? What native land? Does he mean America? My native land is America.)

Joan Henriksen in a clipping without the newspaper's name: 'Chinese-Americans always "looked"—at least to this WASP observer—as if they exactly fit the stereotypes I heard as I was growing up. They were "inscrutable." They were serene, withdrawn, neat, clean and hard-workers. *The Woman Warrior*, because of this stereotyping, is a double delight to read.' She goes on to say how nicely the book diverges from the stereotype.

How dare they call their ignorance our inscrutability!

The most upsetting example of this school of reviewing is Michael T. Malloy's unfavourable review in *The National Observer*: 'The background is exotic, but the book is in the mainstream of American feminist literature.' He disliked the book *because* it is part of the mainstream. He is saying, then, that I am not to step out of the 'exotic' role, not to enter the mainstream. One of the most deadly weapons of stereotyping is the double bind, damned-if-you-do-and-damned-if-you-don't.

I have a horrible feeling that it is not self-evident to many

Caucasian Americans why these reviews are offensive. I find it sad and slow that I have to *explain*. Again. If I use my limited time and words to explain, I will never get off the ground. I will never get to fly.

To say we are inscrutable, mysterious, exotic denies us our common humanness, because it says that we are so different from a regular human being that we are by our nature intrinsically unknowable. Thus the stereotyper aggressively defends ignorance. *Nor* do we want to be called *not* inscrutable, exotic, mysterious. These are false ways of looking at us. We do not want to be measured by a false standard at all.

To call a people exotic freezes us into the position of being always alien—politically a most sensitive point with us because of the long history in America of the Chinese Exclusion Acts, the deportations, the law denying us citizenship when we have been part of America since its beginning. By giving the 'oriental' (always Eastern, never *here*) inhuman, unexplainable qualities, the racist abrogates human qualities, and, carrying all this to extremes, finds it easier to lynch the Chinaman, bomb Japan, napalm Vietnam. 'How amazing', they may as well be saying, 'that she writes like a human being. How unoriental.' 'I cannot understand her. It has to be her innate mystery.' Blacks and women are making much better progress. I did not read any reviews of *Roots* that judged whether or not Alex Haley's characters ate watermelon or had rhythm. And there were only two cases I encountered of sexist stereotyping: one from my home-town paper, *The Stockton Record*: 'Mrs. Kingston is a 36-year-old housewife and mother who teaches creative writing and English.' The above was a news story on *The Woman Warrior* winning the National Book Critics Circle Award, so the paper might have described me as a writer. The other was *Bookshelf*, a journal of Asian Studies: 'The highly acclaimed first book by a Chinese-American school-teacher.'

How stubbornly Americans hang on to the oriental fantasy can be seen in their picking 'The White Tigers' chapter as their favourite. Readers tell me it ought to have been the climax. But I put it at the beginning to show that the childish myth is past, not the climax we reach for. Also, 'The White Tigers' is not a Chinese myth but one transformed by America, a sort of kung fu movie parody.

Another bothersome characteristic of the reviews is the ignorance of the fact that I am an American. I am an American writer, who, like other American writers, wants to write the great American novel. *The Woman Warrior* is an American book. Yet many reviewers do not see the American-ness of it, nor the fact of my own American-ness.

Bernice Williams Foley in the *Columbus Dispatch*:

> Her autobiographical story (in my opinion) is atypical of the relationship between Chinese parents and their American Chinese children whom I have known in New York City and Cincinnati. Moreover as a "foreign barbarian of low culture" living in China, I always sensed in the Chinese, whether they were our business friends or our servants, a feeling that the ancient cultural heritage of their Middle Kingdom—the Center of the Universe—was superior to ours . . . She rebels against the strict pattern of life inherited from old China and based on Confucius' moral teachings, which preserves the strength of the family's heritage, and which are the basis of Chinese ethics and virtues.

The headline for this article was 'Rebellious Chinese Girl Rejects Ancient Heritage'. Foley goes on to say that she does not find the book 'likeable'. Of course not. What she would like is the stereotype, the obedient-Confucian-Chinese-servant-businessman. (What is a 'business friend' anyway?)

Kate Herriges in an ecstatically complimentary review in *The Boston Phoenix*: 'Subtle, delicate yet sturdy, it [*The Woman Warrior*] is ineffably Chinese.' No. No. No. Don't you hear the American slang? Don't you see the American settings? Don't you see the way the Chinese myths have been transmuted by America? No wonder the young Asian American writers are so relentlessly hip and slangy. (How I *do* like Jane Howard's phrase in her *Mademoiselle* review: 'Irrevocably Californian.' I hope the thirty per cent of reviewers who wrote sensible pieces accept my apologies for not praising them sufficiently here.)

The Saturday News and Leader of Springfield, Missouri: 'Maxine Ting Ting Hong Kingston is a Chinese woman, even though the place of her birth was Stockton, California.' This does not make sense. *Because* I was born in Stockton, California, I *am* an American woman. I am also a Chinese American woman, but I am not a Chinese woman, never having travelled east of Hawaii, unless she means an 'ethnic Chinese woman', in which case she should say so.

Rose Levine Isaacson, in the *Clarion–Ledger* of Jackson, Mississippi: '. . . the revelation of what it was like for a Chinese girl growing up.' She tells of Chinese laundries she has seen as a child. Though I enjoy her childhood recollections, I cringe with embarrassment when she says, 'We knew they lived in back of the laundry . . . '. That was one thing I always hated— that they *knew* we lived there when we owned a house.

Margaret E. Wiggs in the Fort Wayne *News–Sentinel*: 'The timid little Chinese girl in San Francisco . . . Clever girl, this little Chinese warrior.' Ms Wiggs does not know that as a kid I read 'Blackhawk' comics, and was puzzled, then disgusted, that Chop Chop was the only Blackhawk who did not get to wear a uniform, was not handsome, not six feet tall, had buck teeth and a pigtail during World War II, wore a cleaver instead of a pistol in his belt, and never got to kiss the beautiful ladies. Blackhawk was always saying, 'Very clever, these little Chinese.'

I know headline writers are under time and space deadlines, but many of them did manage to leave the 'American' in 'Chinese American'. Here are some exceptions: Malloy's article in *The National Observer*: 'On Growing Up Chinese, Female and Bitter'. *The Sunday Peninsula Herald*: 'Memoir Penetrates Myths Around Chinese Culture'. *The Baltimore Sun*: 'Growing Up Female and Chinese'. *The Cleveland Plain Dealer*: 'A California-Chinese Girlhood'. (I wouldn't mind 'Chinese-Californian'.) Harold C. Hill's article in a clipping without the newspaper's name: 'Growing Up Chinese in America'.

That we be called by our correct name is as important to Chinese Americans as it is to native Americans, Blacks and any American minority that needs to define itself on its own terms. We should have been smart like the Americans of Japanese Ancestry, whose name explicitly spells out their American citizenship. (Semantics, however, did not save the AJAs from the camps.) Chinese-American history has been a battle for recognition as Americans; we have fought hard for the right to legal American citizenship. Chinese are those people who look like us in Hong Kong, the People's Republic and Taiwan.

Apparently many Caucasians in America do not know that a person born in the USA is automatically American, no matter how he or she may look. Now we do call ourselves Chinese, and we call ourselves Chinamen, but when we say, 'I'm Chinese', it is in the context of differentiating ourselves from Japanese, for example. When we say we are Chinese, it is short for Chinese-American or ethnic Chinese; the 'American' is implicit. I had hoped that this was the usage of the reviews, but instead there is a carelessness, an unawareness.

As for 'Chinaman', I think we had better keep that word for use amongst ourselves, though people here in Hawaii do use it with no denigrating overtones as in the popular name for Mokolii, 'Chinaman's Hat'. And lately, I have been thinking that we ought to leave out the hyphen in 'Chinese-American', because the hyphen gives the word on either side equal weight, as if linking two nouns. It looks as if a Chinese-American has double citizenship, which is impossible in today's world. Without the hyphen, 'Chinese' is an adjective and 'American' a noun; a Chinese American is a type of American. (This idea about the hyphen is my own, and I have not talked to anyone else who has thought of it; therefore, it is a fine point, 'typical' of no one but myself.)

I hope that the above explanation makes clear why I and other Chinese Americans felt a clunk of imperfection when reading Peter S. Beagle's and Jane Kramer's otherwise fine pieces in *Harper's Bookletter* and *The New York Times Book Review* respectively. Both gathered from the dust-jacket, and perhaps from my name, that I had 'married an American'. Chinese Americans read that and groaned, 'Oh, no!' immediately offended. I guess Caucasian Americans need to be told why. After all, I *am* married to an American. But to say so in summing up my life implies these kinds of things: that I married someone different from myself, that I somehow became *more* American through marriage, and that marriage is the way to assimilation. The phrase is also too general. We suspect that they might mean, 'She married a Caucasian.' Too many people use those two words interchangeably, 'American' and 'Caucasian'. In some ways, it is all right to say that I am 'Chinese' or my husband is 'American' if they did not stop there but go on to show what has been left out.

Another problem in the reviews is New York provincialism, which *The New Yorker* teased in one of their covers, which showed nothing west of the Rockies except Los Angeles and San Francisco. New Yorkers seem to think that all Chinese Americans in California live in San Francisco. Even my publisher did not manage to correct the dust-jacket copy completely, and part of it says I am writing about Stockton, and part says San Francisco. The book itself says that the Chinese Americans in the San Joaquin Valley town, which is its setting, are probably very different from the city slickers in San Francisco. I describe a long drive *away from* San Francisco to the smaller valley town, which I do not name; I describe Steinbeck country. Yet, *New West*, which published an excerpt, prefaced it by twice calling it a San Francisco story—ironically, it was the very chapter about the San Joaquin Valley. How geographically confused their readers must have been. *New West* is a California magazine; so the theory about New York provincialism applies to more places than New York.

The New Yorker: 'A Picture of nineteen-forties and fifties Chinese-American life in San Francisco . . . '.

The Fort Wayne News–Sentinel: 'The timid little Chinese girl in San Francisco . . .'.

The Boston Globe: '. . . the "foreigner-ghosts" of San Francisco . . .'.

Newsweek: 'The most interesting story in *The Woman Warrior* tells how Brave Orchid brought her sister, Moon Orchid, from China to San Francisco.'

Sometimes you just have to laugh because there really is no malice, and they are trying their best. *Viva* magazine published the 'No Name Woman' chapter with a full-page colour illustration of Japanese maidens at the window; they wear kimonos, lacquered hair-dos, and through the window is lovely, snow-capped Mt Fuji. Surprise, Asian brothers and sisters! We may as well think of ourselves as Asian Americans because we are all alike anyway. I did not feel angry until I pointed out the Japanese picture to some Caucasians who said, 'It doesn't matter.' (And yet, if an Asian American movement that includes Chinese, Japanese, Filipinos is possible, then solidarity with Caucasian Americans is possible. I for one was raised with vivid stories about Japanese killing ten million Chinese, including my relatives, and was terrified of Japanese, especially AJAs, the only ones I had met.)

It appears that when the critics looked at my book, they heard a jingle in their heads, 'East is east and west is west . . .'. Yes, there were lazy literary critics who actually used that stupid Kipling British-colonial cliché to get a handle on my writing:

'East Meets West', said *Newsweek*'s headline. (*Time* was more subtle with 'A Book of Changes.')

The Philadelphia *Bulletin*: 'The Twain Did Meet Among the Ghosts.'

The Sacramento Bee: 'East and West Collide Inside a Human Mind.'

The San Francisco Examiner: 'East Meets West in a Large New Talent.'

The Chattanooga *News–Free Press*: 'In fact, this book seems to reinforce the feeling that "East is East and West is West and never the twain shall meet," or at any rate, it will probably take more than one generation away from China.'

I do not want the critics to decide whether the twain shall or shall not meet. I want them to be sensitive enough to know that they are not to judge Chinese American writing through the viewpoint of nineteenth-century British-colonial writing.

Interviewers, including those from Taiwan and Hong Kong, as well as reviewers have been concerned about how 'typical' of other Chinese Americans I am. Michael T. Malloy in the *National Observer* says, 'I'd like to report that *The Woman Warrior* seemed as singular to my Chinese Canadian wife as it did Irish American me.' (Malloy is the critic who attacked the book for being 'mainstream feminist'.) And I have already quoted Bernice Williams Foley of *The Columbus Dispatch*: 'Her autobiographical story (in my opinion) is atypical of the relationship between Chinese parents and their American-Chinese children whom I have known in New York City and Cincinnati.' Here is a paragraph from a review in the San Francisco Association of Chinese Teachers newsletter (I think they mean Chinese American teachers):

It must be pointed out that this book is a very personal state-ment, and is a subjective exposition of one person's reactions to her family background. It would be dangerous to infer that this 'unfamiliar world' represents or typifies that of most Chinese Americans. *The Woman Warrior* is not an easy book to grasp, both in terms of style or content. Especially for students unfamiliar with the Chinese background, it could give an overly negative impression of the Chinese American experience.

(This review gave the book a seventh grade reading level by using a mathematical formula of counting syllables and sentences per one hundred–word passage.) These critics are asking the wrong question. Instead of asking, 'Is this work typical of Chinese Americans?' why not ask, 'Is this work typical of human beings?' Then see whether the question makes sense, what kinds of answers they come up with.

I have never before read a critic who took a look at a Jewish American spouse and said, 'There's something wrong with that Saul Bellow and Norman Mailer. They aren't at all like the one I'm married to.' Critics do not ask whether Vonnegut is typical of German Americans; they do not ask whether J. P. Donleavy is typical of Irish Americans. You would never know by reading the reviews of Francine du Plessix Gray's *Lovers and Tyrants* that it is by and about an immigrant from France. Books written by Americans of European ancestry are reviewed as American novels.

Now I agree with these critics—the book *is* 'personal' and 'subjective' and 'singular'. It may even be one-of-a-kind, unique, exceptional. I am not a sociologist who measures truth by the percentage of times behaviour takes place. Those critics who do not explore why and how this book is different but merely point out its difference as a flaw have a very disturbing idea about the role of the writer. Why must I 'represent' anyone besides myself? Why should I be denied an individual artistic vision? And I do not think I wrote a 'negative' book, as the Chinese American reviewer said; but suppose I had? Suppose I had been so wonderfully talented that I wrote a tragedy? Are we Chinese Americans to deny ourselves tragedy? If we give up tragedy in order to make a good impression on Caucasians, we have lost a battle. Oh, well, I'm certain that some day when a great body of Chinese American writing becomes published and known, then readers will no longer have to put such a burden on each book that comes out. Readers can see the variety of ways for Chinese Americans to be.

(For the record, most of my mail is from Chinese American women, who tell me how similar their childhoods were to the one in the book, or they say their lives are not like that at all, but they understand the feelings; then they tell me some stories about themselves. Also, I was invited to Canada to speak on the role of the Chinese Canadian woman, and there was a half-page ad for the lecture in the Chinese language newspaper.)

The artistically interesting problem which the reviewers are really posing is: How much exposition is needed? There are so many levels of knowledge and ignorance in the audience. 'It's especially hard for a non-Chinese', says Malloy, 'and that's a troubling aspect of this book.' A Chinese Canadian man writes in a letter, 'How dare you make us sound like savages with that disgusting monkey feast story!' (Since publishing the book, I have heard from many monkey feast witnesses and participants.) Diane Johnson in *The New York Review of Books* says that there are fourth and fifth generation Chinese Americans who can't speak English. (It is more often the case that they can't speak Chinese. A fourth or fifth generation Chinese American and Caucasian American are not too different except in looks and history.) There is a reviewer who says that it is amazing what I could do with my IQ of zero. (How clumsy the joke would be if I explained how IQ tests aren't valid because they are culturally biased against a non-English-speaking child.) There are Chinese American readers who feel slighted because I did not include enough history. (In my own review of Laurence Yep's *Child of the Owl* in the *Washington Post*, I praised him for his bravery in letting images stand with no exposition.) My own sister says, 'You wrote the book for us—our family. It's how we are in our everyday life. I have no idea what white people would make of it.' Both my sisters say they laughed aloud. *Harper's* says the book is marred by 'gratuitous ethnic humor', and *Publishers Weekly* says the humour is 'quirky'. So who is the book for?

When I write most deeply, fly the highest, reach the furthest, I write like a diarist—that is, my audience is myself. I dare to write anything because I can burn my papers at any moment. I do not begin with the thought of an audience peering over my shoulder, nor do I find my being understood a common occurrence anyway—a miracle when it happens. My fantasy is that this self-indulgence will be good enough for the great American novel. Pragmatically, though, since my audience would have to be all America, I work on intelligibility and accessibility in a second draft. However, I do not slow down to give boring exposition, which is information that is available in encyclopedias, history books, sociology, anthropology, mythology. (After all, I am not writing history or sociology but a 'memoir' like Proust, as Christine Cook in the *Hawaii Observer* and Diane Johnson in *The New York Review of Books* are clever enough to see. I am, as Diane Johnson says, 'slyly writing a memoir, a form which . . . can neither [be] dismiss[ed] as fiction nor quarrel[ed] with as fact'. 'But the structure is a grouping of memoirs', says Christine Cook. 'It is by definition a series of stories or anecdotes to illuminate the times rather than be autobiographical.') I rarely repeat anything that can be found in other books. Some readers will just have to do some background reading. Maybe my writing can provide work for English majors. Readers ought not to expect reading always to be as effortless as watching television.

I want my audience to include everyone. I had planned that if I could not find an American publisher, I would send the manuscript to Britain, Hong Kong, Canada, Taiwan—anywhere—and if it did not then find a publisher, I would keep it safe for posthumous publication. So I do believe in the timelessness and universality of individual vision. It would not just be a family book or an American book or a woman's book but a world book, and, at the same moment, my book.

The audience of *The Woman Warrior* is also very specific. For example, I address Chinese Americans twice, once at the beginning of the book and once at the end. I ask some questions about what life is like for you, and, happily, you answer. Chinese Americans have written that I explain customs they had not understood. I even write for my old English professors of the new criticism school in Berkeley, by incorporating what they taught about the structure of the novel. I refer to Virginia Woolf, Elizabeth Barrett Browning, Shakespeare; but those who are not English majors and don't play literary games will still find in those same sentences the other, main, important meanings. There are puns for Chinese speakers only, and I do not point them out for non-Chinese speakers. There are some visual puns best appreciated by those who write Chinese. I've written jokes in that book so private, only I can get them; I hope I sneaked them in unobtrusively so nobody feels left out. I hope my writing has many layers, as human beings have layers.

1982

A Writer's Notebook from the Far East

I JUST went on a tour of Japan, Australia, Indonesia, Malaysia, and Hong Kong, sponsored by the United States International Communications Agency and the Adelaide Arts Festival.

At the Adelaide Arts Festival, British poet Elaine Feinstein said, "Writers have power in direct proportion to the danger of being locked up, tortured, jailed." She said there isn't a writer in Great Britain giving Margaret Thatcher a moment's unrest. Nobody is bothering Ronald Reagan either.

—In Adelaide, Australia: "Why did you people vote for Ronald Reagan?"

—In Adelaide and in Kuala Lumpur, Malaysia: "When you lost the war in Vietnam . . ."

—In Sapporo, Japan, at my lecture on "Asian American Literature": "Really, she ought to distinguish between literature and writing."

—In Kuala Lumpur at a newspaper's auditorium:

Me: "The reason Asian American literature has flourished is even from the start we aggressively exercised our right to a free press."

My translator (in English): "'Free press'?"

Me: "Yes, 'free press.'"

My translator: "'Free press'?" Then he said something to the audience which made them laugh.

An audience member later: "He knew the words for 'free press.' He didn't want them in his mouth."

—In Kuala Lumpur: "I hope that girl who told you about the suppression of Chinese identity wasn't reported by a deputy tonight."

"College professors who are reported lose their jobs. Some people go to jail."

—In Kuala Lumpur: "When the censors cut *The White Shadow*, they left in the part where the father beat up the son, and cut where the son hit the father. In *Superman*, they cut out Lois Lane coming back to life."

—In Kuala Lumpur: "Can you tell us how to write political messages disguised subtly as fiction?" Given my background and education, I found that I could not. On the other hand, these writers face a censorship that I have never encountered. I will have to put my mind to answering that question before I go there again. (In the old days, Chinese poets had a code system of flower metaphors.)

—In Jakarta, Indonesia: "I wouldn't want my child to marry one." This from a university professor talking about Chinese Indonesians (or "Indonesian Chinese," as they call themselves, the noun first). "They're like Jews. They send money to China like Jews send money to Israel. They stick together. They practice their Chong Mong or whatever you call it. We don't stop them. I must say, they give no trouble in class. They do what I tell them to do. Very obedient." None of the other faculty members present contradicted or modified her statements. They smiled.

—In Hong Kong: "Your writing is un-Confucian." "Chinese women don't act or talk like that."

—In Penang, Malaysia: "'Hamlet' is anti-Islamic." The government prohibited its showing on television.

—In Hong Kong at a discussion about my book, *The Woman Warrior*, in which Moon Orchid comes to America and does not survive the culture shock: "The reason that Moon went crazy is that she did not have any sons."

In Penang:
Me: "That gas station sent four children to college."
Audience member: "About that gas station that sent four sons to college . . ."

—In the *Thung Pau*, a Malaysian Chinese language newspaper after an interview about swordswomen and Amazons: "*The Woman Warrior* is about how the introverted, chaste, and conservative Chinese women patiently and silently overcome all odds in a challenging new world."

—In Jakarta:
Women: "Read again the part about Amazons capturing the man and binding his feet."

—In Medan, Indonesia: "There are people who say that after Russia and America destroy each other, Indonesia can rule the world."

—In Hong Kong: "How can there be Asian Americans? How can a Chinese and a Japanese get together?"

—In Surabaya, Indonesia: "There are Chinese women who have converted to Islam. What are they up to?"

—In Tokyo: "The way the junior faculty, who are women, get out of pouring tea for the senior faculty, who are all men, is to be very clumsy at pouring tea. This is not good politics. I personally don't pour tea because I am clumsy. The custom doesn't change."

"The custom of women pouring tea for men in the faculty lounge is not going to change in a hundred years."

—In Sapporo: "People in Tokyo have a surface sophistication. At our university, all the work is divided evenly among all faculty members regardless of pay or rank."

—In Adelaide, there is a big statue of the Angel of Sacrifice with a man, a woman, and a child in pleading positions at its feet. It commemorates the wars of Gallipoli, Israel, and Africa.

—In Jakarta, there is a giant statue of Kartini, a feminist martyr who died at the age of 25. She refused to be sent to Holland to be educated and fought for Indonesian independence from the Dutch. There is a magazine named *Kartini*, whose writers believe that men and women have a tradition of helping one another.

—In Adelaide at a book launching, a Cuban myth: "All God's children are beautiful, but Truth and Falsehood were fighting one day. Truth knocked Falsehood's head off. It was shaped like a pig's. Truth picked up the head and put it on, and couldn't take it off. And that is why truth must always speak in the guise of fiction."

There were riots in Jakarta, and we saw tanks and soldiers with bayonets. In Medan we saw soldiers tear down a squatter house and drag the women out. The women were raging, weeping, throwing rocks. Jakarta was the first place where I saw a censored newspaper. There is a kind of black tar over the censored article, and a page from an old *Reader's Digest* on top of the tar. The authorities in Jakarta paint over Chinese words that are on shop signs and other advertising on the street. There are still Chinese words here and there, but people say they are Japanese words. In Medan, the teenagers had me autograph their T-shirts with my Chinese name.

Many, many of God's children are beautiful. An Indian artist was painting squatters being evicted. The squatters are grandmothers, mothers, and children. A Malaysian dramatist is videotaping 70- and 80-year-old storytellers and dancers. The Adelaide Arts Festival voted to protest a "reading tax" on books. Young writers have pledged themselves to write about "Hong Kong poverty." Hong Kong is turning the farms in the New Territories into more public housing, which I once saw as dungeons and now understand as heroic—Hong Kong, city of refuge. A choreographer in Sapporo is taking her troupe to dance a nuclear bomb dance in Moscow.

Our planet is as rich and complex as a Balinese painting, which is covered every inch with life. To stop the bombs, to free ourselves—we are nations of hostages—we continue dancing, painting, telling stories, writing whether or not there is a free press.

1983

Imagined Life

Oₙₑ ₛᵤₘₘₑᵣ in Hawai'i, John Hawkes and I taught writing seminars in adjoining classrooms. I told my students: Don't worry about form; write any old thing, and it will naturally take shape. It will be a classical shape—a sonnet, an essay, a novel, a short story, a play—of its own accord. Do you think that Petrarch cooked up fourteen lines and an *abbaabbacdcdcd* rhyme scheme capriciously? After stating a problem, the human mind inevitably mulls on it, looks at its complexities, and comes to a new understanding. At its most efficient, the mind does this in fourteen lines, and when the resolution is especially neat, it makes a couplet. Like a computer program, a sonnet is one of the natural patterns of the brain. And iambic pentameter is the normal rhythm of the English language. I told the students to copy and tack over their desks some advice from Lew Welch:

> When I write, my only concern is accuracy. I try to write accurately from the poise of mind which lets us see that things are exactly what they seem. I never worry about beauty; if it is accurate there is always beauty. I never worry about form; if it is accurate there is always form.

Write about any old thing that has been obsessing you for years, then step back and see what shape the words are tending toward; then use that recognizable structure for guidance as you rewrite. For example, if some of the lines are iambic tetrameter with a syllable left over, see what happens if you push the line out another half a foot. Maybe there will be a concomitant extending of thought. Or shorten the line and see if you like the closer, thicker effect. You short story writers, sustain a scene for one more page; the characters may have to perform a culminating deed, and the scene then must yield its drama.

Meanwhile, in John Hawkes's seminar, I imagined wonderful goings on. Better goings on. In college, my husband and

I had written a series of papers on Hawkes's *The Beetle Leg*, *The Blood Oranges*, *The Cannibal*, *The Lime Twig*, and *Second Skin*. And I had just read *Travesty* in preparation for meeting Hawkes. He must be telling his students miraculous things that I didn't dare fool with. That I didn't even know about. While I dealt with form, he must be counselling imaginations. I could almost hear him speaking like the narrator in *Travesty*: "*Imagined life is more exhilarating than remembered life.*" In Italics. Repeating. "*Imagined life is more exhilarating than remembered life.*"

> *Somewhere there still must be*
> *Her face not seen, her voice not heard.*

I picture John Hawkes listening to students' lives, their loves, figuring out how to strengthen them, probing at sources of power. Helping people find bottomless pitchers of cream and the other sides of walls.

Every time I have taught a class or a workshop, the most forbidding student in there has been somebody who signs up for the course because she's "blocked." That summer, there was again such a woman. It's always a woman, and she is always too nicely dressed. I tried talking her into switching from my course to John Hawkes's, but she wouldn't go. It was too late anyway; she'd already handed me her IBM card, which I'd turned in to the office. Also, it was at the last of the course that she admitted to being "blocked." Like other troubled writers in previous classes, she had shown me work she had done years ago, and fooled me. If I come across such a woman again, I will pretend to be John Hawkes and tell her to wear wanton dresses and to brush her hair more loosely. Then I am going to tell her that what's wrong with her is that she believes that a writer only exposes lives—when what a writer really does is imagine lives. To imagine a life means to take such an interest in someone that you suppose about him. You conjecture about him. You care what he eats and about whatever he is doing. "Stands he or sits he? Or does he walk? Or is he on his horse?"

"But—," says the "blocked" lady, who begins too many of her sentences with "but." "But I don't have a problem with romantic fantasizing." No, her problem is in the real world, and it is with real people. Each one of my "blocked" ladies has said she can't write because she is afraid of hurting her friends and relatives. "What does your mother think about your book?" she keeps asking me. "What does your father think?" Well, like everybody else of my generation who majored in English, I was trained in the New Criticism, and I didn't like that kind of question.

All right. To make your mother and your scandalous friends read about themselves and still like you, you have to be very cunning, very crafty. Don't commit yourself. Don't be pinned down. Give many versions of events. Tell the most flattering motives. Say: "Of course, it couldn't have been money that she was after." In *The Woman Warrior*, my mother-book, the No Name Woman might have been raped; she might have had a love affair; she might have been "a wild woman, and kept rollicking company. Imagining her free with sex. . . ." Imagining many lives for her made me feel free. I have so much freedom in telling about her, I'm almost free even from writing itself, and therefore obeying my mother, who said, "Don't tell."

Forget "definitive." The reason that John Hawkes finds imagined life more exhilarating than remembered life is that imagined life is not set.

The blocks that my father put in my way took more craftiness to break than my mother's. A consequence for my mentioning immigration papers could be his deportation. The Immigration and Naturalization Service demands consistency in the life story of a China Man. So, in my father-book, *China Men*, I used the very techniques that the men developed over a hundred years. They made themselves citizens of this country by telling American versions of their lives. My father has three or four stories about how he happens to be in America in spite of the Exclusion Laws and history and common sense. In "The Father from China," the illegal father sailed to Cuba, where he had his friends nail him up in a crate to stow away to New York Harbor. The last sentence of that story goes like this: "Of course, my father could not have come that way. He came a legal way." The legal father landed at the immigration station on Angel Island, where the imprisoned men wrote poems on the walls. They spent their time memorizing stories to tell at hearings. Some even had paper and wood models of the village they had supposedly come from so that all the people from that village could describe it the same way. Those who bought papers from American citizens memorized other men's lives.

In a third story, my father was born here. If you're born in America, you're automatically a citizen. So, my grandfather ran out of the San Francisco Earthquake and Fire with a newborn baby in his arms. It was a magical birth since my grandmother was in China at the time. Coincidentally, this happened when the San Francisco Hall of Records burned to the ground. That means that everyone who wants a birth certificate can say, "All records of my birth were burned in the San Francisco Earthquake and Fire." "Every China Man was reborn out of that fire an American."

A fourth way that my father is legal is that his father had bought for a bag of Sierra gold a Citizenship Paper from a Citizenship Judge. So, we are Americans many times over. Even more times over: The brothers in Vietnam got top security clearances.

You see how people have imaginations out of necessity. I didn't have to make up ways for telling immigration stories.

My father doesn't say, "Don't tell." He doesn't say much at all. The way to end the silence he gave me was to write this sentence: "I'll tell you what I suppose from your silences and few words, and you can tell me that I'm mistaken." You may use that sentence yourself if you like. Copy it down and see what comes next.

My father is answering me by writing poems and commentary in the margins of my books. The pirated translations have wide margins. Writing commentary is a traditional Chinese literary form. You can break reader's block by writing well.

Yes, the imagined life is so exhilarating that householders go in quest of new lands—the Gold Mountain and China. The

Gold Mountain is a land of gold-cobbled streets, and it is also a country with no war and no taxes; it is governed by women. Most of us are here in America today because somebody in our families imagined the Gold Mountain vividly enough to come looking for it. I guess most people think they've found it, and "Gold Mountain" is synonymous with "United States of America." But we aren't peaceful; taxes are due the day after tomorrow; and women aren't in charge. You see how much work we have ahead of us—we still have that country to find, and we still have its stories to tell. Maybe those "blocked" ladies don't know: There is work that belongs to all of us, and they can't quit.

I haven't seen China yet. I didn't want to go there before finishing my two books because I was describing the place that we Americans imagine to be China. The mythic China has its own history, smells, flowers, one hundred birds, long-lived people, dialects, music. We can taste its sweetness when our grandmother sends us invisible candy. The place is so real that we talk about it in common, and we get mail from there. As real as the Brontës' childhood cities. As real as Dungeons and Dragons. If I had gotten on a plane and flown to the China that's over there, I might have lost the imagined land.

I have a Boston cousin, and a Foster City cousin who went back to our home village. They report separately that there were hardly any people about. It's like Roanoke. What to make of such "airy nothing"?

Now, I don't want to leave you with the impression that to imagine life means that you only invent ways to befuddle and blur and to find what is not there. To live a true human life today, we have to imagine what really goes on when we turn on the machines. "The Brother in Vietnam" warns about how easy it is to operate an instrument panel and not see the people far away dying horribly. That story is grey like an aircraft carrier—no red, green, and gold dragons in the riggings. No red blood. We deliberately weaken and divert our imaginations to be able to bear a world with bombs.

We went to a movie where the attendants gave each kid a free picture of an atomic bomb explosion. Smoke boiled in a yellow and orange cloud like a brain on a column. It was a souvenir to celebrate the bombing of Japan. Since I did not own much, I enjoyed the ownership of the V-J picture. At the base of the explosion, where the people would have been, the specks didn't resolve into bodies. I hid the picture so the younger children could not see it, to protect them against the fear of such powerful evil, not to break the news to them too soon. Occasionally, I took it out to study. I hid it so well, I lost it. I drew billows and shafts of light, and almost heard the golden music of it, the gold trumpets and drums of it.

The yearning for beauty can prettify reality, and sometimes imagination has to restore us to terror.

(Do you have any friends—I do—who believe that they are poets because they have imagination and poetic feelings even though they don't write at all? I don't like telling them so, but it seems to me that imagination is one thing and writing is something else, a putting-into-words. Words pin down the once-seen, and reproduce it for readers. That's why I'm quoting from my books so much—I need those words to call forth other realities. The New Critics seem to be breathing over my shoulders and saying, "Cut it out." The work is supposed to be a self-contained whole, speaking for itself. There's not supposed to be an imagination apart from the work. But I know there is one. Words are only the known world—La Terra Conoscivta—beyond which the old maps showed Arabia Deserta, the Great American Desert, Red Cloud's Country, the unattached Territories, the Badlands, Barbaria, the Abode of Emptiness, the Mountains of the White Tigers, the Sea of Darkness—sea serpents and mermaids swam there—"strange beasts be here."—Nada ou Nouvel, whence the four winds blew. And the space maps show the Hyperspace Barrier, areas of Giants, Supergiants, Dwarfs, Protogalaxies, Black Holes—infinite areas named with a word or two.)

The Brother in Vietnam, who has some imagination left, refuses to go to language school because he can picture scenes in which he would use the *Vietnamese Phrase Book*:

Welcome, Sir. Glad to meet you.
How many are with you? Show me on your fingers.
Are you afraid of the enemy? Us?
Do you believe in
    (1) U.S. victory?
    (2) annihilation of Bolshevism?
Are you afraid? Why?
If we cannot trust a man,
    (1) wink your eye
    (2) place your left hand on your stomach
    (3) move your hand to the right, unnoticed, until we note
    your signal.

And because he knows languages, the brother cannot go wholeheartedly to war against people who have the same words as the Chinese for "happiness," "contentment," "bliss," "orchid," the same pun on "lettuce" and "life," the same words for things that matter, "study," "university," "love." The young men in the Vietnam story have reader's block.

As a passenger on a bombing run, the Brother in Vietnam tries his best to see.

> Even using binoculars, he did not see much of the shore. Hanoi was an hour away by plane. He did not see the bombs drop out of the plane, whether they turned and turned, flashing in the sun. During loading, when they were locked into place, they looked like neatly rolled joints; they looked like long grains of rice; they looked like pupae and turds. He never heard cries under the bombing.

We approach the truth with metaphors.

> All that he witnessed was heavy jungle and, in the open skies, other planes that seemed to appear and disappear quickly, shiny planes and their decals and formations. The bombs must have gone off behind them. Some air turbulence might have been a bomb ejected.

When a pilot did not show up in the chow line, it was up to the other men to imagine his death.

John Hawkes approaches God with metaphor:

> . . . and I heard what she was saying: "God snapping him fin-
> gers," she said, and that sudden moment of waking was just
> what she said, "God snapping him fingers," though it was prob-
> ably Edward breaking a twig or one of the birds bounding a
> bright seed off the smooth green back of a resounding calabash.

Now, I have told you those things about imagination that I'm
sure of, and I have shown ways that words hold the imaginary;
the book opens like hands parting, presenting you a surprise.
But there are properties of the imagination which I don't understand at all. I hope that one of you will delve into the following, and let the rest of us know:

How is it possible that the writer can suddenly and effortlessly
become now this character and now that one, see through his
eyes, her eyes, speak with his voice, her voice, make the reader
view the world with the soul of another? I can see a room,
a forest, a street, from a very particular character's angle of
vision, and there are details as definite as if I were watching a
movie with point-of-view camera directions. What is the process that makes this—what is it? empathy? voodoo?—happen?
If the "blocked" writer can't do this anymore, how can I show
her how it's done? In voodoo, creatures exchange souls. But
there are exercises and rites in voodoo, whereas in writing, the
inhabiting of another person seems to happen spontaneously.
Would it do us good to study with voodoo priestesses?
    What about interest? How is it that interest is an emotion in
me, and, I presume, in other writers. There are things, people, images that seem to have no significance in the world but
are obsessionally interesting to me. And there are major current events, wars, assassinations that you would think every
informed person should care about, and I cannot work up an
interest. For about thirty-five years, I glimpsed a sharp white
triangle. It looked like a shark's tooth or a corner of paper or
a creased pantleg. I felt great fear and energy whenever I beheld it. I beheld it and beheld it until I found the story of it.
That white triangle turned out to be *China Men*, and appears
contained in that book as the creased pantleg of a Navy officer

looking for the stowaway father. Where did that image come from? Why is it full of radiation—stories ramifying from it? How do you recognize this white triangle when it appears? How do you evoke one?

And that snap—God's fingers? a bird? a twig?—how and why did John Hawkes hear that snap?

Perhaps it does some good just to be aware of these writer's figments. Wanting them and wanting to write well may help them come.

Voodoo and white triangles. No wonder Shakespeare compared the lunatic, the lover, and the poet.

> The lunatic, the lover, and the poet
> Are of imagination all compact;
> One sees more devils than vast hell can hold,
> That is, the madman; the lover, all as frantic,
> Sees Helen's brow in a brow of Egypt.
> The poet's eye in a fine frenzy rolling,
> Doth glance from heaven to earth, from earth to heaven;
> And as imagination bodies forth
> The forms of things unknown, the poet's pen
> Turns them to shapes and gives to airy nothing
> A local habitation and a name.

Everybody knows about being a lover, so I'll just talk about madness. Haven't you tried to go mad? What a relief it would be. You could act any way you please. Say anything to anybody. But don't give in to madness. It binds too tightly. Moon Orchid, who couldn't speak English, imagined that the Mexicans plotted against her. She was talking-story as fast as she could, putting into words what the people around her were doing. And she kept repeating the same crazy stories over and over.

The lunatic exaggerates evil, and the lover exaggerates beauty. The poet, though, makes things real. I like that plain word "local"—and take it to mean the mundane, the ordinary. In the formless universe, the poet makes us at home.

Here's how John Hawkes ends *Second Skin*:

> Now I sit at my long table in the middle of my loud wandering night and by the light of a candle—one half-burned candle saved from last night's spectacle—I watch this final flourish of my own hand and muse and blow away the ashes and listen to the breathing among the rubbery leaves and the insects sweating out the night. Because now I am fifty-nine years old and I knew I would be, and now there is the sun in the evening, the moon at dawn, the still voice. That's it. The sun in the evening. The moon at dawn. The still voice.

What's it? What still voice? We have to learn to hear it.

Finally, remember the most common use of imagination, its fantastic and magical power to turn the order of things upside down. I wrote about a tribe of musical barbarians, who played reed flutes and fought with bows and arrows. So I invented for them a nock whistle to attach to their arrows; the archers shot terrifying sounds through the air. Then, my book finished, I went to a Chinese archaeological exhibit, and there, in the last case before the exit—I was just about to leave but turned back—behind the glass was a nock whistle. I believe that I caused it to appear on earth. Just as, because my husband and I wrote many papers about him, one day John Hawkes appeared at our door and said, "Hello, my name is Jack. And this is my wife, Sophie."

(Hopwood Lecture, 1983)

Through the Black Curtain

BEFORE I could read or write or even speak much, an idea came to me of black curtains that hang over something wonderful—some amazing show about to open. All my life, I've looked for those black curtains; I want to part them, and to see what is on the other side. Probably, the curtains were not only imaginary; I saw actual curtains. The blackout curtains of World War II. My mother and father laughed and talked while climbing up and down the ladder and unfurling lengths and folds of drapery. They hadn't owned curtains before. Sun rays shot out the top and side edges. We were safe from the street, the city, strangers, World War II.

As a kid, I loved black crayons and black paint and ink and blackboards, through which I could almost see glorious light and hear voices and music. When I learned English, I wrote that the black curtains rose or swung apart. My mother said, "Don't tell." In order to write *The Woman Warrior*, I construed "Don't tell what I am about to tell you" to mean that I could *write* it. As long as the words I used were different from the words she used. (Which wasn't so difficult to do since she talks-story in Chinese.) Young girls who want to be writers must take "Don't tell" as you take "You aren't so pretty. You are so very pretty that you'll get a big head if people keep telling you the truth." The talking women start their best gossip with "Don't tell" to make the listener feel extra special, and to give the story importance. And to free themselves to tell. "Don't tell" means "Tell."

The black curtains appeared in *China Men* as the highest, most vertical mountains I'd ever seen—the Ko'olaus in Hawai'i. My great grandfathers did not part those mountains. So, when dynamite was invented, my grandfather blasted through the Sierras and built the railroad. The Gold Mountain, that is, America, was what he found.

In the book I am working on now, *Tripmaster Monkey: His Fake Book*, I am trying to understand that the black curtains are literally curtains—stage curtains. I remember the shows to

987

raise money for China Relief. And parades with a red flag, street-wide for the bystanders to throw money into. And operas, live and on film. And American films on Saturday afternoons and Hong Kong films on Sundays. Talk-stories and letters that came from China were often about what happened at the theater, how the theater became Communist, how theaters went dark. The first time I crossed the border from Hong Kong into a village in China, I saw that the only large building was the theater, which had the face of a monkey-clown on the wall. On my second, longer trip, I visited my parents' villages; the biggest building in my father's village is the Hong family temple, which was changed into a barn during the Cultural Revolution. The only large structure in my mother's village is the music hall. So that's where my son's and nieces' and nephews' love of music comes from, and why they want to go into show business. As I write further into *Tripmaster Monkey*, I learn a new view of human nature and why we migrate—we didn't go looking for the Gold Mountain in order to plunder it, nor to find something more to eat. I had thought after writing *China Men* that curiosity and adventure were high-minded enough purposes. But out-on-the-road and off-the-boat, we made theater. The songs and myths and dances changed to fit circumstances in the new world. America is our country not just for work but for play.

In *Tripmaster*, the curtains are made of water, the water-falls behind which the King of the Monkeys leads his people. They find a land where they cavort and parade and tell jokes. The Monkey King has 72 transformations, and, of course, he changes into an American, a Californian, a North Beach–Chinatown cat. He does stand-up comedy and stand-up tragedy.

My own contribution to theater is that my books are being made into a movie and a play. David Henry Hwang and Philip Glass are talking about a musical in which the heroine (me) wants to be a singer but has a duck voice. By the finale, she sings beautifully. Haven't you noticed that modern music sounds just like Chinese opera. It may even *be* Chinese. John Cage and Louis Armstrong both admitted to learning jazz from Chinese music.

One of my goals as a writer is to capture Chinese American speech, and to do so without having to invent an unreadable orthography. The play is the thing for speakers of American in its variations, and for audiences to hear that language directly from the actors' mouths. However, for reasons I can only guess at, though I kept seeing visions of stage curtains, I did not become a playwright. And I can only hope that a reader who has never heard our voices can reproduce them from the page.

I think that David Henry Hwang got the idea to make *The Woman Warrior* a musical from the following passage:

THE wealthiest villager wife came to the laundry one day to have a listen to my voice. "You better do something with this one," she told my mother. "She has an ugly voice. She quacks like a pressed duck." Then she looked at me unnecessarily hard; Chinese do not have to address children directly. "You have what we call a pressed-duck voice," she said. This woman was the giver of American names, a powerful namer, though it was American names; my parents gave the Chinese names. And she was right: if you squeezed the duck hung up to dry in the east window, the sound that was my voice would come out of it. She was a woman of such power that all we immigrants and descendants of immigrants were obliged to her family forever for bringing us here and for finding us jobs, and she had named my voice.

"No," I quacked. "No, I don't."

"Don't talk back," my mother scolded. Maybe this lady was powerful enough to send us back.

I went to the front of the laundry and worked so hard that I impolitely did not take notice of her leaving.

"Improve that voice," she had instructed my mother, "or else you'll never marry her off. Even the fool half ghosts won't have her." So I discovered the next plan to get rid of us: marry us off here without waiting until China. The villagers' peasant minds converged on marriage. Late at night when we walked home from the laundry, they should have been sleeping behind locked doors, not overflowing into the streets in front of the benevolent associations, all alit. We stood on tiptoes and on one another's shoulders, and through the door we saw spotlights open on tall singers afire with sequins. An opera from San Francisco! An opera from Hong Kong! Usually I did not understand the words in operas, whether because of our obscure dialect or theirs I didn't know, but I heard one line sung out into the night air in a woman's voice high and clear as ice. She was standing on a chair, and she sang, "Beat me, then, beat me." The crowd laughed until the tears rolled down their cheeks while the cymbals clashed—the dragon's copper laugh—and the drums banged like firecrackers. "She is playing the part of a new daughter-in-law," my mother explained. "Beat me, then, beat me," she sang again and again. It must have been a refrain; each time she sang it, the audience broke up laughing. Men laughed; women laughed. They were having a great time.

"Chinese smeared bad daughters-in-law with honey and tied them naked on top of ant nests," my father said. "A husband may kill a wife who disobeys him. Confucius said that." Confucius, the rational man.

The singer, I thought, sounded like me talking, yet everyone said, "Oh, beautiful. Beautiful," when she sang high.

Walking home, the noisy women shook their old heads and sang a folk song that made them laugh uproariously:

> Marry a rooster, follow a rooster.
> Marry a dog, follow a dog.
> Married to a cudgel, married to a pestle,
> Be faithful to it. Follow it.

The Woman Warrior ends with my grandmother and the family going to the theater. Most readers remember Fa Mu Lan as the Woman Warrior, but I meant to question her weapons. She was a swordswoman and a military general, who led an army against the Tartars. As a pacifist, I would rather we use the powers of Ts'ai Yen, the woman warrior who made words of the formations of birds in the sky, V for "human." She cut nock-whistles into flutes.

1987

CHRONOLOGY

NOTE ON THE TEXTS

NOTES

Chronology

1940   Born Maxine Ting Ting Hong on October 27 in Stockton, California, the third of eight children and firstborn in the United States of Tom Hong and Ying Lan Chew Hong. (Father, born 1901, was a poet and teacher from Sun Woi, village near Canton [now Guangzhou], the first of his family to settle in the United States, though many male family members had worked in the U.S. as "sojourners," sending home remittances and eventually returning to China. Named himself "Tom" after Thomas Edison. Parents married in China and had two children who did not survive childhood. In 1924, Tom Hong sailed to Cuba, and three times stowed away inside a cargo crate on a ship to New York City; was jailed, caught, and deported on each of his first two attempts. After working as a window washer in New York, he opened a laundry business with partners. Mother, born c. 1903, also known as Brave Orchid, trained as a midwife at the To Keung School of Midwifery in Canton, practiced medicine, and ran a hospital in a cave during the Japanese invasion. After a fifteen-year separation from his wife, father helped her immigrate to the United States after a man who owed him gambling winnings was unable to pay and gave him visa paperwork instead. Mother arrived in California on the USS *President Taft* in 1939; after being detained at Angel Island immigration station, she traveled by train to New York City. Parents will have concerns about deportation their entire lives. After Tom Hong's business partners pushed him out as co-owner of the laundry, the couple migrated to Stockton, California, where father manages an illegal gambling house and is arrested in police raids; Maxine is named after one of its customers.)

1941–45   Sister Carmen is born, followed in the next several years by brothers George, Norman, and Joseph and sister Corrinne. Gambling house shuts down during the war; mother works in a cannery as well as doing agricultural and domestic work. Parents do not speak English, and Kingston's first language is Say Yup, a Cantonese dialect. At home hears stories about Chinese history, folktales, and sagas, including Fa Mu Lan, the woman warrior, as well as the Confucian *Analects* and Tang dynasty poetry, including Tu Fu and Li Po. Mother tells bedtime stories about assertive, independent women via "talk-story," the Chinese storytelling tradition. Family opens New Port Laundry at 40 N. El Dorado Street in Stockton, where their children will help out when old enough.

1946–54   Her English very limited, Kingston is generally silent at school and fails kindergarten; among other punishments, is told she has an IQ of "zero" after coloring a test examination page black. Begins learning English to fluency. After six hours of school at Lafayette Elementary, she attends Chung Wah Chinese school for three hours in the later afternoon and evening and on Saturdays for seven years. Family lives at 219 E. Hazelton Avenue in Stockton; neighborhood, which she later recalls as "a sort of Chinatown barrio on either side of the Santa Fe–Southern Pacific tracks," is racially varied but "not a geographically distinct place; there isn't even one whole block that is [fully] Chinese." Begins creating poems and stories orally. Sees performances of Chinese opera and theater. At the age of nine, she later recalls, composes her first written poem: "I was in fourth grade and all of a sudden this poem started coming out of me. On and on I went, oblivious to everything, and when it was over I had written 30 verses." Reads Jade Snow Wong's memoir *Fifth Chinese Daughter* (1950): "For the first time I could see a person somewhat like myself in literature. I had been trying to write about people who were blond, or a beautiful redhead on her horse, because those were the people who were in the books. So I was lucky that at a young age I could see a Chinese American."

1954–58   Begins attending Edison High School in Stockton. Takes field trip to University of California, Berkeley campus, which has been and continues to be her only desired choice for college. Wins prize and is awarded $5 for her essay "I Am an American," which is published in *American Girl*, the magazine of the Girl Scouts of America, in May 1956. Writes college entrance exam on F. Scott Fitzgerald's *The Crack-up*. Wins eleven scholarships and matriculates at Berkeley.

1959–63   Intending to major in engineering according to her parents' wishes, struggles at first at Berkeley, falling ill for two weeks and getting poor grades. Later she switches major to English ("I felt I had abdicated all my responsibilities! I was just living life for the fun of it"). Takes painting courses. Serves as the night editor for the campus paper *Daily Californian*. Meets actor Earll Kingston (born 1938). Graduates with an A.B. in English. Continues to paint seriously after graduation and though she abandons any ambition to become a visual artist, will continue to enjoy painting and drawing. On November 23, 1962, marries Earll Kingston. Works an office job, where she escapes the drudgery by writing in the restroom. Son Joseph Lawrence Chung Mei Kingston is born.

1964   Obtains teaching certificate from Berkeley. Campaigns for the Free Speech movement. Works as a student teacher at Oakland Technical High School, where a parent of one of her students objects to her purported communist teachings.

1965   Joins the faculty as an English and math instructor at Sunset High School in Hayward, California, while Earll teaches English at Berkeley High. Brothers Norman and Joseph and a brother-in-law are drafted; brother George leaves for Canada.

1967   Unhappy about the Vietnam War, and strained over violence and growing tensions and drug use among friends in Berkeley, the Kingstons decide to move to Japan, but on a stopover in Hawaii decide to stay, renting an apartment above a grocery store in Kakalu'u in Honolulu. They take part in a small antiwar march, the first in Hawaii opposing the Vietnam War, and work with a local church providing sanctuary for AWOL American military personnel. She teaches at Kahuku High School.

1968–70   Works as teacher at Kahaluu Drop-In School, then as ESL teacher at Honolulu Business College and language arts teacher at Kailua High School. In 1970, begins seven years of teaching English at Mid-Pacific Institute in Honolulu, living in a cottage on campus.

1973   In January, Kingston's essay "Literature for a Scientific Age: Lorenz' *King Solomon's Ring*," is published in the *National Council of Teachers of English Journal*. During a vacation trip to La'nai, begins writing "Gold Mountain Stories," the working title for what will become *The*

Woman Warrior; book as initially conceived also encompasses the material developed in Kingston's second published book, *China Men*, its chapter "The Brother in Vietnam" written first.

1974–76   Looks for agent, thinking that "Gold Mountain Stories" might be published by a small American press or perhaps in England, Canada, or Hong Kong, and agrees to be represented by agent John Schaffner. Partial versions of the manuscript are sent to Norton and to Little, Brown and are rejected. Manuscript is accepted for publication by Alfred A. Knopf; her editor there, Charles Elliott, asks for minimal changes in the book itself but, insisting on a new title, proposes *The Woman Warrior: Memoirs of a Girlhood Among Ghosts* (Kingston, a pacifist, later expresses some discomfort with the title, "finding a lot of dissatisfaction with having a military general as a hero"). From July to November 1976, engages in a heated letter exchange with author and playwright Frank Chin, who had been sent bound galleys of the book; he disparages it and insults and threatens Kingston, sometimes obscenely. *The Woman Warrior* is published in the fall of 1976 in a modest 5,000 hardcover print run; after it receives glowing praise by John Leonard in *The New York Times Book Review*, sells out and with a next printing quickly goes on to sell forty thousand copies.

1977   Attends January ceremony for the National Book Critics Circle awards in Manhattan and accepts general nonfiction award for *The Woman Warrior*; tells audience, "Tonight, with this award, you have made me feel certain that I am a writer." New York trip marks first in-person meeting with her editor Charles Elliott; she is interviewed at Knopf's offices for short profile in *The New York Times*, "'Ghosts' of Girlhood Lift Obscure Book to Peak of Acclaim." Leaves position at Mid-Pacific Institute and becomes a visiting professor of English at the University of Hawaii. Publishes the short story "Duck Boy" in *The New York Times Magazine* and the book review "Middle Kingdom to Middle America" in the *Washington Post*. Gives a talk at the East-West Conference in Honolulu called "A Review of the Inscrutable Reviews of *The Woman Warrior*." Success of *The Woman Warrior* prompts her to change telephone number to an unlisted number. Writes to film director James Ivory about possible movie adaptation of

The Woman Warrior; Ivory is receptive, but rights have already been optioned. Works on "Gold Mountain Heroes," a book based on the experiences of male members of her family going back to the nineteenth century. *The Woman Warrior* is published in London by Allen Lane.

1978   Purchases house on Huelani Drive in Honolulu, with a writer's office upstairs. In June and July, writes a weekly column for *The New York Times* under the heading "Hers." Garners the Anisfield-Wolf Book Award for *The Woman Warrior*. Publishes essay "Reservations about China" in *Ms.* magazine.

1979   Publication of French translation of *The Woman Warrior* under the misleading title *Les fantômes chinois de San Francisco* (the book's American sections are set in Stockton, not San Francisco). *Time* magazine hails *The Woman Warrior* as one of the top ten nonfiction books of the decade. Finishes draft of "Gold Mountain Heroes" and gives it to Earll to read, then embarks on extensive revisions. Travels to New York City, living in an apartment on West End Avenue in New York City preparing what is ultimately called (at Knopf's suggestion) *China Men*, while Earll auditions for Broadway roles. Revisions to galley proofs are significant and lead to the book being newly typeset.

1980   "The Making of More Americans," an excerpt from *China Men*, appears in *The New Yorker* in February. Boston College prints thousands of copies of this prepublication excerpt for distribution to incoming students in the fall. Dedicated to her father, three brothers, husband, and son, *China Men* is published in a 40,000 copy first printing by Knopf in June; it is a Book of the Month Club selection, and its prizes include the National Book Award and the American Book Award as well as nominations as finalist for the Pulitzer Prize and the National Book Critics Circle Award. Wins a National Endowment for the Arts Writers Award. Appears on *The Dick Cavett Show*. In a traditional ceremony at Hoopa Hongwanji Temple in Honolulu, Hongwanji Mission deems her a "Living Treasure," the first Chinese American to attain this honor. As U.S. Congress considers bills reinstating the military draft, becomes active in the anti-draft movement. Father reads a pirated translation of *China Men* published in Hong Kong and writes responses and other additions in the margins throughout.

1981   Named Woman of the Year at the Asian Pacific Women's Network. The Bancroft Library at the University of California, Berkeley, begins to collect her papers as part of its special collections. Father's annotated copy of *China Men* is put on display there to his amazement and delight. Publishes poems "Absorption of Rock" and "Restaurant" in *The Iowa Review.*

1982   Wins a Guggenheim Fellowship for fiction and a second National Endowment for the Arts Writers Award. Response to the question "Who is an ethnic writer?" is published in *Cultural Climate.* On a trip sponsored by the United States International Communications Agency and the Adelaide Arts Festival, tours Japan, Australia, Indonesia, Malaysia, and Hong Kong. Contributes the essay "Cultural Mis-readings by American Reviewers" to the edited volume *Asian and Western Writers in Dialogue,* in response to reviewers' adherence to Chinese stereotypes when writing about *The Woman Warrior.* Producer Martin Rosen, who has bought film rights to *Woman Warrior* and *China Men,* begins planning a film adaptation (ultimately unrealized) of the books to be directed by Joyce Chopra and written by Tom Cole; Sundance Institute finances development of the screenplay, and Kingston takes part in interviews with female actors.

1983   The State of Hawaii bestows on Kingston its Hawaii Award for Literature. Publishes essays "A Writer's Notebook from the Far East" in *Ms.* magazine and "Imagined Life" in *Michigan Quarterly Review,* the latter the text of her Hopwood Memorial Lecture at the University of Michigan. Film version of *The Woman Warrior* and *China Men* fails to coalesce and instead a stage adaptation is planned in Los Angeles.

1984   Travels to mainland China, the first of many visits, with the writers Toni Morrison, Allen Ginsberg, Gary Snyder, Francine du Plessix Gray, William Least Heat Moon, Harrison Salisbury, and Leslie Marmon Silko as guests of Chinese writers, poets, and scholars. Visits her ancestral village in Guangdong Province where she visits the Hong family temple, the well where her aunt drowned herself, and the site of the school where her mother learned medicine (school had been shuttered during the Cultural Revolution). Moves to Los Angeles with Earll, who is seeking more acting opportunities; Joseph stays in Hawaii.

1986   Named the Thelma McAndless Distinguished Professor in the Humanities at Eastern Michigan University in Ypsilanti, Michigan. Reads *Moments of Being* by Virginia Woolf, whose *Orlando* is one of her favorite books. Works on *Tripmaster Monkey: His Fake Book*.

1987   Meadow Press in San Francisco collects the "Hers" columns as well as her essay "Lew Welch: An Appreciation" in a limited hardcover edition called *Hawai'i One Summer*, containing woodcuts by Deng Ming-Dao, the son of Jade Snow Wong. Moves with Earll to Oakland, California, living in the Rockridge section.

1988   Earll adapts "Ruby Long Legs' and Zeppelin's Song of the Open Road" from *Tripmaster Monkey: His Fake Book* into a radio play entitled *Mah-Jongg*, which is performed in workshop at Eureka Theatre in San Francisco and at the California State Railroad Museum in Sacramento the following February. Kingston receives an honorary doctorate from East Michigan University in Ypsilanti. Essay "Rupert Garcia: Dancing between Realms," about an artist who had been one year her junior at Edison High School in Stockton, is published in *Mother Jones*. On trip to China, reads a chapter of *Tripmaster Monkey* to an audience of Chinese writers; is told that she is continuing the tradition of the classical novel *Dream of the Red Chamber*, which the Cultural Revolution had cut off from them.

1989   Attends a series of Buddhist retreats, including a retreat made up exclusively of Asian women (reflects, "by the end of the time, I had rediscovered the beauty of Asian women. Most of the time, the TV is showing blonde people, Barbie dolls, and advertising that says you are worthy of love if you look like this"). Publication of *Tripmaster Monkey: His Fake Book*, in the United States, the U.K., and Australia, where she travels for a book tour and is met with enthusiastic readers: "the Australians and I were in love at first sight." The novel will win the PEN West Award in Fiction. In November, spends a week at the University of California, Santa Cruz, as a Regent's Lecturer. Publishes essay "The Novel's Next Step" in

Mother Jones. Comments about Tiananmen Square, "We get excited about Tiananmen Square, and then a few weeks later it's gone. We have this amnesia . . . that's the silence. And we have to constantly be awake and remember our history."

1990   Contributes foreword to David Henry Hwang's *FOB and Other Plays.* Joins faculty of University of California, Berkeley, as a Chancellor's Distinguished Professor of English and Creative Writing. Wins American Academy and Institute of Arts and Letters Award in Literature. Colby College confers honorary doctorate. Reads and is generally pleased with draft of a stage adaptation of *The Woman Warrior* and *China Men* written by Deborah Rogin. Directed by Joan Saffa, written by Stephen Talbot, and narrated by the actor B. D. Wong, the hour-long documentary *Maxine Hong Kingston: Talking Story*, is broadcast on public television. Participates in Bill Moyers's public television series *Becoming American: The Chinese Experience.* By this time *The Woman Warrior* is widely read and assigned for college courses; according to one estimate from the Modern Language Association it is the most widely taught book by a living writer at U.S. universities. Works on sequel to *Tripmaster Monkey* entitled "The Fourth Book of Peace."

1991   Receives an honorary doctorate from Brandeis University and the University of Massachusetts. Contributes "Personal Statement" to *Approaches to Teaching "The Woman Warrior."* Father passes away in Stockton in September. In October, while she is attending the one-month commemoration of his death, with Earll in Virginia performing in a Chekhov play, Oakland Hills firestorms kill twenty-five people and burn down the Kingston home, destroying many of her personal effects, including the only copy of 156-page "Fourth Book of Peace" manuscript. Decides that rather than try to reconstruct it from memory she will create something new, drawing from material of others, and solicits submissions, including at the Modern Language Association's annual convention at the end of the year.

1992–93   Struggles to cope with the aftermath of her home's destruction and the loss of her manuscript, recalling later that she lost the ability to read with any sustained concentration. For a time she stores drafts of material for her next book, *The Fifth Book of Peace*, in a bank safety-deposit box. Offers writing and meditation workshops for veterans, many suffering from post-traumatic stress disorder, to help them voice their experiences and move toward healing. Receives the Lila Wallace Reader's Digest Writing Award and uses the prize money for funding these workshops, which come to be known as the Veteran Writers Group ("a phoenix of an idea came to me: Gather around me veterans, who have been through fire, and let's write together," she remarked in 2017. "Write our way home. Write Peace."). Contributes foreword to Chân Không's *Learning True Love: How I Learned and Practiced Social Change in Vietnam* and the essay "Precepts for the Twentieth Century" to Thich Nhat Hahn's edited collection *For a Future to Be Possible: Commentaries on the Five Wonderful Precepts.*

1994   The Berkeley Repertory Theater premieres the three-hour, three-act play *The Woman Warrior* (based on *China Men* as well) written by Deborah Rogin. Martin Rosen produces the play, which is directed by Sharon Ott and stars an all-Asian and Asian American cast of twenty actors playing 120 characters. The production travels to Boston in September and is performed in Los Angeles the following February. Guest conducts a benefit concert for the Berkeley Symphony Orchestra.

1996   Total sales of *The Woman Warrior* exceed 900,000 copies, with translations in more than twenty languages.

1997   Mother dies. President Bill Clinton awards Kingston the National Humanities Medal. Participates in the symposium "Peacemaking: The Power of Nonviolence" with the Dalai Lama, Alice Walker, and Dolores Huerta, held in San Francisco.

1998   Wins Longwood University's John Dos Passos Prize for Literature.

2000   Delivers the William E. Massey Sr. Lectures in American Studies at Harvard University. Co-edits the anthology *The Literature of California.*

2001   Completes draft of *The Fifth Book of Peace* and submits manuscript to Knopf.

2002   Harvard University Press publishes *To Be the Poet*, Kingston's Massey lectures. Stockton school district announces its plans to name a new middle school in her honor.

2003   On International Women's Day (March 8), while protesting against imminent American military action in Iraq, is arrested, along with writers Alice Walker and Terry Tempest Williams, and is briefly imprisoned for crossing a police line in front of the White House; she will write about the episode at length in *I Love a Broad Margin to My Life*. *The Fifth Book of Peace* is published.

2004   Retires from teaching literature and creative writing at University of California, Berkeley. The National Women's History Project selects Kingston as an honoree.

2006   Receives the Lifetime Achievement Award from the Asian American Writers' Workshop. Her edited compilation *Veterans of War, Veterans of Peace*, a collection of accounts of veterans, war widows, children, and conscientious objectors derived from her workshops, is published in October by the Hawaii-based publisher Koa Books.

2007   Awarded the Northern California Book Award in Publishing for *Veterans of War, Veterans of Peace*.

2008   Wins the National Book Foundation's Medal for Distinguished Contribution to American Letters.

2009   Is one of the prominent women over age sixty-four featured in the documentary *I Know a Woman Like That*, directed by Elaine Madsen.

2011   Publishes *I Love a Broad Margin to My Life*, a book-length poem with memoiristic aspects. Receives the F. Scott Fitzgerald Literary Award for Outstanding Achievement in American Literature at Montgomery College in Rockville, Maryland.

2014   President Barack Obama confers the National Medal of Arts on Kingston in a White House ceremony on July 28. Kingston wins the Hubert Howe Bancroft Award.

2016   The Litquake Festival in San Francisco honors Kingston as a Literary Legend. Randolph College in Lynchburg, Virginia, presents Kingston with the Pearl S. Buck Award. Reads Terry Tempest Williams's *When Women Were*

Birds, Yiyun Li's *The Vagrants*, and *The Sympathizer* and *Nothing Ever Dies: Vietnam and the Memory of War* by former Berkeley student Viet Thanh Nguyen.

2017   In an interview in *The New York Times*, Barack Obama names *The Woman Warrior* as one of the "really powerful" books that he had given to his daughter Malia. Kingston speaks at the Women's National Book Association's Centennial Visionaries Series in San Francisco. In April, New York University's Contemporary Lecture Series and the Asian American Writers' Workshop host a celebration of *The Woman Warrior*. Granddaughter Hana Měi is born.

2018   Is elected to the American Academy of Arts and Letters.

2019   Is awarded honorary doctorate from San Francisco State University. Appears on the *PBS NewsHour* television program with novelist Celeste Ng. Works on "Posthumously, Maxine," a novel that she wishes not to be published until after her death.

2020   Grandson Malu Hua born in February. Lengthy profile of Kingston by Hua Hsu, based on interviews conducted with Kingston in Hawaii, is published in *The New Yorker*.

Note on the Texts

This volume contains works by Maxine Hong Kingston first published from 1976 to 1989: *The Woman Warrior: Memoirs of a Girlhood Among Ghosts* (1976); *China Men* (1980); the novel *Tripmaster Monkey: His Fake Book* (1989); the essay collection *Hawai'i One Summer* (1987), gathering newspaper columns written in 1978; and fourteen essays, reviews, and poems published from 1977 to 1987.

In 1973, while vacationing on the Hawaiian island of La'nai, Kingston began working in earnest with her family history in writings that would become her first two published books, *The Woman Warrior* and *China Men*. She had previously written fiction but had deemed these efforts unsuccessful, in part because, working from her diaries, she felt she had not transformed these personal writings into convincing fiction. The project about her family—which was generically ambiguous and was later characterized by Kingston as "a new kind of biography . . . biographies of imaginative people"—was originally projected as a single long book. "The Brother in Vietnam," a short story ultimately incorporated into *China Men*, had been written first. As her draft expanded, however, Kingston decided to divide the material into two projected books provisionally labeled "Home I" and "Home II," the first centered on the women in her family, the second on the men: "I had conceived of one huge book," she recalled. "The women had their own time and place and their lives were coherent; there was a women's way of thinking. My men's stories seemed to interfere. They were weakening the feminist point of view. So I took all the men's stories out, and then I had *The Woman Warrior*."

A complete draft of "Gold Mountain Stories," the working title for *The Woman Warrior*, was finished in Honolulu in 1975. For her debut book Kingston envisioned publication by a small press or university press or perhaps by a publisher in Canada, the U.K., or Hong Kong. Nonetheless John Schaffner, Kingston's first agent, submitted versions of the manuscript to East Coast trade publishers. W. W. Norton and Little, Brown passed on "Gold Mountain Stories" but it was accepted by Knopf, with Charles Elliott as its assigned editor. Impressed by the manuscript's cleanness, Elliott asked Kingston for fairly minimal changes. The publisher did not like the title because in their view it sounded misleadingly like a collection of short fiction, so Elliott proposed instead *The Woman Warrior*, along with a subtitle casting the book, whatever its imaginative dimension, as a work of nonfiction: *Memoirs of a Girlhood Among Ghosts.* (Shortly after publication he nevertheless remarked to Kingston that had the book been packaged as fiction it might have better chances of winning an award.) *The Woman Warrior* was published by Knopf in the fall of 1976. Its wide critical acclaim and robust sales in the United States led to an English edition, using the same typesetting as the Knopf edition except for the title and copyright pages, brought out by Allen Lane in London in 1977. In 2005 *The Woman Warrior* was included with *China Men* by Knopf in its Everyman Library series. Kingston did not revise *The Woman Warrior* (nor any of the other books collected in the present volumes). The text printed here is taken from the 1976 Knopf edition of *The Woman Warrior: Memoirs of a Girlhood Among Ghosts.*

After the success of *The Woman Warrior*, which Kingston has called her "mother-book," she resumed work on her "father-book," which she titled "Gold Mountain Heroes." It went through at least eight drafts before Kingston gave a completed version to her husband to read; after absorbing his comments she worked further on the manuscript. Commenting on her general practice of writing, Kingston has noted that "the various drafts are like building a tower. When you get to the top you can see visions, and you can see further, and you can see higher. Sometimes it's not till I get to the galleys that I can really see up there." Rounds of late revisions in 1979 were made not at Kingston's home in Honolulu but in Manhattan, where Kingston lived for a few months in a rented apartment on West End Avenue. As with *The Woman Warrior*, Knopf proposed a different title, though her original title was printed in Chinese on the Knopf edition's cover and title page. As Kingston recalled in an e-mail conveyed via her agency to Library of America in 2021,

> "Gold Mountain Heroes" . . . was my original title for the book, but the publisher said there were other books coming out with "gold" and "mountain" and "hero" in their titles, so named my book *China Men*. I felt clever having my title on the cover, but in Chinese. Also the men I wrote about couldn't become Americans, so what can we call them? ("Gold mountain" is our name for "America.")

Kingston continued to make revisions in proof as *China Men* was being prepared for publication; her changes were extensive enough to require the book's pages to be newly typeset. A prepublication excerpt, "The Making of More Americans," was published in *The New Yorker* on February 11, 1980; "The Brother in Vietnam" was published in *Mother Jones,* June 1980; and another short excerpt appeared in *The American Poetry Review*'s May–June 1980 issue. *China Men* was published by Knopf in New York in June 1980. An English edition soon followed, published by Picador in London. As noted above, in 2005 *China Men* was paired in a single volume with *The Woman Warrior* in Knopf's Everyman Library series. The 1980 Knopf edition contains the text printed here.

Kingston's work on her novel *Tripmaster Monkey: His Fake Book* spans much of the 1980s. She had completed most of a full draft by 1986, as evident by remarks in interviews that year claiming that only two chapters remained. A complete manuscript was sent to Knopf in the spring of 1988. As with *China Men*, Kingston extensively revised the novel almost up to its publication. Rewrites to galley proofs led to a new typesetting at Kingston's expense ("Knopf charged me a thousand dollars," she recalled), and she later noted that a review critical of the book's ending was based not on the final version but on the advance reader's copy that had not been compared to the published book and its revisions. *Tripmaster Monkey* was published by Knopf in New York in April 1989 and in London and Australia that same year. The text printed here is taken from the 1989 Knopf edition of *Tripmaster Monkey*.

In the summer of 1978 Kingston wrote a series of columns for *The New York Times* under the heading "Hers." She collected these articles, along with the short essay "Lew Welch: An Appreciation," in *Hawai'i One Summer*, a limited-edition book (150 copies) published by San Francisco's Meadow Press in 1987, which in 1998 was reprinted, with a new introduction, by the University of Hawaii Press, containing the text printed here (Kingston revised the final paragraph of "Lew Welch: An Appreciation" for the present edition). The remaining essays and two poems are taken from their sole published sources:

Review of Joan Didion, *A Book of Common Prayer*: *California Monthly*, April–May 1977.

Middle Kingdom to Middle America: Review of *Child of the Owl* by Laurence Yep: *Washington Post Book World*, May 1, 1977.

Duck Boy: *The New York Times*, June 12, 1977.

Talk Story: No Writer Is an Island—Except in Hawaii: *Los Angeles Times*, June 4, 1978.

Reservations about China: *Ms.* magazine, October 1978.

San Francisco's Chinatown: A View from the Other Side of Arnold Genthe's Camera: *American Heritage*, December 1978.

The Coming Book: In *The Writer on Her Work: Contemporary Women Writers Reflect on Their Art and Situation*, edited by Janet Sternburg (New York: W. W. Norton, 1980).

Precarious Lives: Review of *Scent of Apples* by Bienvenido N. Santos: *The New York Times*, May 4, 1980.

Two Poems: "Restaurant" and "Absorption of Rock." *Iowa Review*, Spring–Summer 1981.

An Answer to the Question, "Who Is an Ethnic Writer?" *Cultural Climate*, January 1982.

Cultural Mis-readings by American Reviewers: In *Asian and Western Writers in Dialogue: New Cultural Identities*, edited by Guy Amirthanayagam (London: Macmillan, 1982).

A Writer's Notebook from the Far East: *Ms.* magazine, January 1983.

Imagined Life: *Speaking of Writing: Selected Hopwood Lectures*, edited by Nicholas Delbanco (Ann Arbor: University of Michigan Press, 1990). The essay had been delivered as the Hopwood Award Presentation Lecture at the University of Michigan, Ann Arbor, March 13, 1983.

Through the Black Curtain: *Through the Black Curtain* (Berkeley, CA: Friends of the Bancroft Library, 1987).

This volume presents the texts of the original printings chosen for inclusion here, but it does not attempt to reproduce nontextual features of their typographic design. The texts are presented without change, except for the correction of typographical errors. Spelling, punctuation, and capitalization are often expressive features and are not altered, even when inconsistent or irregular. The following is a list of typographical errors corrected, cited by page and line number: 66.8, stick; 247.14, the the subway; 250.40, superstititions; 366.25, Baba.; 424.13, gorilla; 438.9, Kuei; 450.7, year's; 468.25, bouganvillea; 487.8, straint; 524.8, Adderly; 594.29, Valdez; 594.30, Madeline; 760.28, beween; 814.1, back; 844.37, Reincarnations."; 845.2, kiss And; 845.3, Look; 870.20, clipcases; 878.8, answer.; 893.12, were Portuguese; 914.39, MacDonald's; 921.15, Carroway; 927.28, young; 929.6, hand; 929.18, movie—; 929.20, Minelli; 932.27, have an; 938.7, *Rabbit Run*; 951.30, moment's; 966.37, interchangably; 967.17, Magazine; 977.2, Hawa'i,; 981.6, synonymous.

Notes

In the notes below, the reference numbers denote page and line of this volume (the line count includes headings but not blank lines). No note is made for material that is sufficiently explained in context, nor are there notes for material included in standard desk-reference works such as Webster's Eleventh Collegiate, Biographical, and Geographical Dictionaries or comparable internet resources such as Merriam-Webster's online dictionary. Foreign words and phrases are translated only if not translated in the text or if words are not evident English cognates. Quotations from Shakespeare are keyed to *The Riverside Shakespeare*, edited by G. Blakemore Evans (Boston: Houghton Mifflin, 1974). For more biographical information than is contained in the Chronology, see *Conversations with Maxine Hong Kingston*, edited by Paul Skenazy and Tera Martin (Jackson: University Press of Mississippi, 1998).

THE WOMAN WARRIOR

9.35 *Oh, You Beautiful Doll* with Betty Grable] Film (1949) directed by John M. Stahl (1886–1950) and starring Mark Stevens (1916–1994) and June Haver (1926–2005), not Betty Grable (1916–1973).

9.36–37 *She Wore a Yellow Ribbon* with John Wayne] Western (1949) directed by John Ford (1894–1973) and starring Wayne (1907–1979), Joanne Dru (1922–1996), and John Agar (1921–2002).

16.4 round moon cakes] Round stuffed pastries usually eaten during the Mid-Autumn Festival. They were traditionally given as gifts between family members, and their shape symbolizes family reunion.

20.24 talk-story] The passing down of tales, fables, and histories between generations through the practice of telling stories.

20.32 Fa Mu Lan] A legendary Chinese folktale heroine (often transliterated as Hua Mulan). "The Ballad of Mulan" (c. fifth–sixth century C.E.) tells the story of a woman who takes her father's place in the army. After winning much acclaim as a warrior, she returns home to her proper place as a woman of the house.

33.10 Eight Sages] Most often referred to as the Eight Immortals, these are popular figures of Taoist legend. They are associated with happiness, benevolence, romance, and luck.

35.35   Peiping] One of Beijing's former names, usually transliterated as Beiping.

36.34   Chen Luan-feng] Legendary T'ang dynasty hero; see p. 80.4–16.

41.37   Long Wall] The Great Wall of China; one of the Great Wall's longer names in Chinese is "The Ten Thousand Li Long Wall" (a "li" being a measure of distance roughly equal to a third of a mile).

46.12   CORE] Congress of Racial Equality, a civil rights organization founded in 1942.

49.23   tong ax] Tongs are Chinese American organizations; in the late nineteenth and early twentieth centuries, they were formed as joint associations to protect members from anti-Asian violence, but quickly became associated with brothels, opium, gambling houses, and street violence. The "Tong Wars" were a series of violent encounters, beginning in the 1880s and ending in the 1920s, between tongs in San Francisco's Chinatown. The ax is a reference to tong "hatchet men" paid to engage in tong warfare.

51.20   twenty-third year of the National Republic] 1935: the Republic of China was founded in 1912.

51.32–34   "Ex-assistant étranger . . . Lyon"] Former foreign assistant at the surgical and delivery clinic of the University of Lyon.

52.2   at Canton] Guangzhou, capital of the province of Guangdong.

56.12–13   Chang Chung-ching] Physician (150–219) whose work continues to influence the modern practice of traditional Chinese medicine.

56.27–28   Sun Yat-sen, who was a western surgeon before he became a revolutionary] Sun Yat-sen (1866–1925), first provisional president of the Republic of China, January–March 1912 (and premier of the Kuomintang, 1919–25), had been licensed as a medical practitioner by the Hong Kong College of Medicine for the Chinese.

64.6   Kwangtung City, Kwangtung Province] Another Romanization of Guangzhou, in Guangdong Province.

68.22–23   "barefoot doctors" today] A Maoist health initiative that trained peasants and farmers in basic medicine to be provided in rural villages. They were "barefoot" because they continued their daily work as farmers and often worked barefoot in rice paddies. The system was officially abolished in 1981.

69.33   six states combined to overthrow Ch'in] Ch'in, or Qin, was one of the seven Warring States that fought for control of China during the Zhou dynasty, 480–221 B.C.E. Ch'in defeated the other states, and became the first imperial dynasty to unify China (which takes its name from Ch'in).

69.34   *I Ching*] "Book of Changes," ancient Chinese book used as the basis for a system of divination.

84.23–24 Li T'ieh-kuai's magic gourd] Li T'ieh-kuai was the first of the Eight Immortals (see note 33.10). According to legend, he used a gourd full of medicines to revive the dead mother of one of his disciples.

85.31–32 cut off his pigtail?] Beginning in late 1910, to remove one's pigtail was to show support for the nationalist revolution that overthrew the Qing dynasty in 1911 and established the Republic of China. See also p. 968.10–19.

85.35 defy the Manchus] The Manchu people, an ethnic minority in China, founded the Qing dynasty, China's last imperial dynasty, in 1644.

89.23 eating too much *yin*] According to Taoism, yin and yang are two elemental forces in nature, which must be in balance. In Chinese traditional medicine, healthy diets must be composed of a balance between yin and yang components, and an unbalanced diet can lead to physical and mental illnesses.

98.11 Da Nang] Fifth largest city in Vietnam and the location, during the Vietnam War, of a major air base for the U.S. military.

117.4–5 Middle Nation."] Zhongguo, the contemporary name for China (referencing both the People's Republic of China and the Republic of China), is roughly translated as "Middle Kingdom," regarded as reflecting China's self-understanding as being at the center of the world.

117.5 benevolent associations] Prominent Chinese American organizations, a means of consolidating social, fiscal, and political support in Chinatown, and helping Chinese Americans to establish themselves in the community, buy property, and run for political office.

143.23 Chiang Kai-shek's] Chiang Kai-shek (1887–1975), leader of the Chinese Nationalist Party, 1928–75.

147.2 Ton Duc Thang] Ton Duc Thang (1888–1980), president of North Vietnam, 1969–76, and Vietnam, 1976–80.

159.35 Napa or Agnew] Napa State Hospital and Agnew State Hospital were both psychiatric hospitals in California, infamous for their "criminally insane" populations and violent, unsafe conditions.

163.38–39 second Communist five-year plan] The Communist Party of China used five-year plans to shape social and economic policy. The institution of the second plan began in 1958.

178.32 Southern Hsiung-nu] A confederation of nomadic peoples and tribes.

CHINA MEN

194.5 cut your pigtail to show your support for the Republic?] See note 85.31–32.

202.7–8 what Tu Fu called "the beating . . . guilt."] See the episode recounted in Florence Ayscough, *Tu Fu: The Autobiography of a Chinese Poet,*

A.D. 712–770 (1929), referring to the government punishment of Tu Fu's contemporary and fellow poet Kao Shih (c. 704–765).

204.17   Dragon's Gate . . . carp ready to run the falls.] According to a Chinese legend about perseverance and endurance, a carp who successfully swam up the Yellow River toward and over a waterfall called the Dragon's Gate is transformed into a dragon.

206.7   Three Character Classics] *Three Character Classic*, thirteenth-century educational text of Confucian precepts for young children.

211.16   Buddha . . . that is, like a *fut*"] The Chinese word "fut" means "Buddha."

225.3   Matteo Ricci] Italian Jesuit priest (1552–1610) who arrived in Macau in 1582 and spent the remainder of his life in China.

228.19–20   King Mu] Zhou dynasty ruler of ancient China during the tenth century B.C.E.

234.13   "the Mexican Exclusion Laws"] Conflation of anti-Mexican violence, discrimination, and other forms of mistreatment in the United States with the legal measures taken against Chinese immigrants, most notably the Chinese Exclusion Act of 1882.

235.2   Yüeh Fei, the patriot] Twelfth-century military general during the Song dynasty, a folk hero known for his patriotism and loyalty.

235.6   Li Po] Chinese poet (701–761).

239.27–28   *City Lights . . . Little Miss Marker.*] Film (1931) starring and directed by Charlie Chaplin (1889–1977); film (1934) directed by Alexander Hall (1894–1968) and starring the child actor Shirley Temple (1928–2014) in the title role.

240.1   Rainy Alley Poet, who lived in Paris] The Chinese poet Dai Wangshu (1905–1950), who lived in France during the 1930s; one of his best-known poems is "Yuxiang" (Rainy Alley).

240.18–20   Europe . . . reed flute . . . Ai Ch'ing] The Chinese poet Ai Qing (1910–1996) studied in Europe; he wrote his poem "The Reed Flute" while imprisoned for his opposition to the Kuomintang, 1932–35.

240.21   old poet, too, Yüan Mei] Chinese poet and essayist (1716–1798).

250.18   memorial days of Clarity and Brightness] The Qingming (pure brightness) festival, also known in English as Tomb-Sweeping Day, celebrated in early April; people clean the graves of their ancestors and honor their memories in other ways.

253.12   West Lake region] Area around Xi Hu (West Lake) in Hangzhou, Zhejiang Province.

264.8   *The White Haired Girl*] *Bai mao nü*, folktale that became the basis of a well-known Chinese opera, adapted as a film in 1951 and a ballet in 1964.

265.13   good will of normalization] Late in 1978 the U.S. and the People's Republic of China issued a joint communiqué announcing mutual recognition and the establishment of diplomatic relations between the two nations, effective January 1, 1979.

267.29   The Navy continues to bomb Kaho'olawe] For decades up until 1991 the U.S. Navy used the Hawaiian island of Kaho'olawe as a bombing range.

270.10–11   Taiping, the army of the Great Peace . . . revolt against the emperor and his British and French armies] The British and French had fought a series of battles with the Taiping rebels in 1862. ("Taiping," meaning "Great Peace," is a Daoist social ideal.) After defeating the Manchus in the Second Opium War, 1857–60, the British and French had forced the Chinese to make military, economic, and political concessions opening the country to European influence.

272.39–273.1   Tse's . . . opposing thoughts at the same moment.] The *Tao Te Ching* (pinyin: *Daodejing*) by Laozi (sixth century B.C.E.) encourages the acceptance of contradiction in thought.

278.12   Prince I] Or Hou I, legendary Chinese archer who (as related in the second-century B.C.E. compilation *Huainanzi*) averts catastrophe by shooting ten suns that have threatened to collectively incinerate the world.

283.7   "Li Shih Min,"] Tang dynasty emperor Taizong (598–649), who came to power by overthrowing his father in a military coup in 626.

296.4   Li Fu-yen] Ninth-century Chinese writer, author of *Xu xuanguai lu* (More Accounts of Mysteries and the Supernatural).

315.40   revolution against Kublai Khan . . . mooncakes.] In 1353, according to legend, the rebellion against Mongol rule in China was aided by plans for an attack transmitted to Liu Ji (1311–1375) inside the mooncakes prepared for the Mid-Autumn Festival (see note 16.4). The reference to Kublai Khan (1215–1294) stands more generally for Mongol rule in China during the Yuan dynasty (1271–1368), which ended with the founding of the Ming dynasty (1368–1644).

318.22   Mohist] Of the philosophical and logical school deriving from the philosopher Mozi (c. 470-c. 391 B.C.E.).

320.39   Fou Loy Company] Fou Loy & Company, later Fou Loy Tai, store in New Orleans's French Quarter that sold Chinese groceries, teas, medicines, and other products, named for one of its owners; the firm also did business in San Francisco.

323.13   Los Angeles Massacre] Racial violence against Chinese Americans in Los Angeles, October 24, 1871, committed by a mob of about five hundred. Nineteen Chinese Americans, about 10 percent of the city's total Chinese American population, were murdered.

324.3–4 until the army came; the demon rioters were tried and acquitted] In 1885, as part of a broader campaign against Chinese American workers in the Pacific Northwest, the labor group the Knights of Labor attempted to expel Seattle's entire Chinese population. After only a small fraction of Chinese left the city, the Knights redoubled their efforts, issuing an ultimatum on February 6, 1886, threatening forcible removal. The following day, 89 Chinese American residents were forced onto a steamship by a mob; 215 others were trapped inside a warehouse. In response to the widespread mob violence Washington's governor declared martial law, assisted by federal troops that arrived on February 10. Of thirteen men charged with crimes related to the violence, none were convicted.

324.4–5 when the Boston police imprisoned and beat 234 chinamen, it was 1902] On October 11, 1903, following a well-attended funeral, Boston police attacked and forcibly detained more than 250 individuals in a building at 19 Harrison Avenue in Chinatown, demanding their immigration papers. The raid prompted a large protest five days later.

324.11–12 the hero, Guan Goong] In *The Oath in the Peach Orchard*, based on an episode in the fourteenth-century novel *The Romance of the Three Kingdoms*.

337.1–2 THE MAKING OF MORE AMERICANS] Cf. the title of *The Making of Americans: Being a History of a Family's Progress* (1925), experimental prose work by Gertrude Stein (1874–1946).

364.26–27 the Red Army and the White Army] The respective armies of the Communist and Nationalist sides in the Chinese Civil War.

366.31 Mao himself . . . Long March] In the Chinese Civil War, the strategic march of 6,000 miles by more than 85,000 Chinese Communist troops, October 1934–October 1935, resulted in a massive loss of life but led to the consolidation of Mao Zedong's power as leader of the Communists.

384.25–26 *Red Chamber Dream*] Eighteenth-century novel by Cao Xueqin (1715/1724–1763/1764).

393.1 *The Wild Man of the Green Swamp*] The Taiwanese man's name was Hu Tu Mei, aged thirty-nine when he took his own life on May 19, 1975.

414.2 "Sioux City Sue."] Hit country music single (1945), lyrics by Max C. Freedman (as Ray Freedman, 1893–1962), music by Dick Thomas (1915–2003).

419.31 Charles Atlas] Italian-born athlete and businessman (1893–1972) who helped popularize bodybuilding through his mail-order course.

437.37 Fa Mu Lan] See note 20.32.

437.38–40 Ngok Fei's . . . collar around his neck.] Yue Fei (see note 235.2) was imprisoned and executed due to the machinations of his rival Qin Hui (1090–1155).

438.9 Fan Kuai] The butcher Fan Kuai (242–189 B.C.E.) became a military commander and aide to Liu Bang (256–195 B.C.E.), whose rebellion against the Qin dynasty led to the establishment of the Han dynasty.

441.7 "Four F."] 4-F, draft-board designation for those deemed unfit for military service.

446.6 bomb China into the Stone Age, the generals said] Cf. the remark by American general Curtis LeMay (1906–1990) in the book *Mission with LeMay* (1965, written with MacKinlay Kantor): "My solution to the problem would be to tell [the North Vietnamese] frankly that they've got to draw in their horns and stop their aggression or we're going to bomb them back into the Stone Age." (LeMay later disavowed the remark, claiming it was Kantor's invention.)

446.33–34 442nd Go-For-Broke AJA's] Made up of second-generation Japanese Americans (Nisei), the highly decorated 442nd Regimental Combat Team of the U.S. Army, which adopted the phrase "Go for broke" as their motto, was established in 1943 and saw action in Europe during World War II.

448.23 *West Side Story*] Stage (1957) and film musical (1961), music by Leonard Bernstein (1918–1990), lyrics by Stephen Sondheim (b. 1930), an adaptation of *Romeo and Juliet* set in 1950s Manhattan.

449.21 Doctor Spock books.] The American pediatrician and political activist Benjamin Spock (1903–1998) was the author of the best-selling *Baby and Child Care* (1946) and other books on raising children.

450.28 Fu Manchu . . . Yellow Claw.] Dr. Fu Manchu was a Chinese master criminal and archvillain featured in English novelist Sax Rohmer's (1883–1959) *The Mystery of Dr. Fu-Manchu* (1913) as well as numerous sequels, movies, and comic books; a similar character, Mr. King, appears in Rohmer's novel *Yellow Claw* (1915).

453.7–8 ITT makes Wonder bread] ITT manufactured radar, navigational and communication systems, and night vision devices used by the U.S. military in Indochina; they had acquired the Continental Baking Company, makers of Wonder Bread, in 1968.

454.40–455.1 *D.I.* with Jack Webb] *The D.I.* (1957), film directed by and starring Jack Webb (1920–1982).

455.1–2 not have to fight and die like Prewitt and Maggio.] Soldiers in *From Here to Eternity* (1951), novel by James Jones (1921–1977), adapted as a film released in 1953.

462.14–15 across the decks . . . Basil Rathbone] The American actor Errol Flynn (1909–1959) and British actor Basil Rathbone (1892–1967) were known for their swashbuckling roles in films such as *Captain Blood* (1935), in which they both starred.

464.18   "Ho Chi Kuei,"] See Kingston's explanation on p. 175.

467.27   Q Clearance] The Department of Energy's highest level of security clearance.

468.32   NAC] National Agency Check.

471.12   *jook tsing.*] Chinese: bamboo head (see also p. 784.19).

472.35   Treasure Island] From 1942 to 1997, a U.S. Navy facility in San Francisco Bay.

474.26   King Kalakaua and Prince Kuhio.] Hawaiian monarch (1836–1891) who ruled the Kingdom of Hawaii, 1874–91, and the popular prince Jonah Kuhio Kalaniana'ole (1871–1922), later a delegate to the U.S. House of Representatives.

474.27–28   American revolution against Queen Lili'uokalani] Lili'uokalani (1838–1917), queen of the Kingdom of Hawaii, 1891–93, proclaimed a new constitution in January 1893 that would restore the monarchy's powers. Backed by the U.S. Navy, the business community responded by deposing the queen and having her placed under house arrest in the royal palace. A provisional government was declared on January 17, 1893, led by Sanford B. Dole.

476.25   Cabit] Cavite, Luzon Province.

TRIPMASTER MONKEY: HIS FAKE BOOK

483.14   el pachuco loco] Spanish: the crazy gang member.

484.5–7   And a Buddhist . . . Quang Duc.] Protesting the South Vietnamese government's anti-Buddhist policies, the Vietnamese Buddhist monk Quang Duc (1897–1963) set himself on fire on June 11, 1963, setting off a wave of self-immolations by monks that were accompanied by street demonstrations and other forms of unrest leading up to the coup that toppled the Diem government on November 1, 1963.

484.35   Malte Laurids Brigge] Protagonist of *The Notebooks of Malte Laurids Brigge* (1910) by the Austrian writer Rainer Maria Rilke (1875–1926).

485.40   *The Lady from Shanghai*] Film (1947) directed by Orson Welles (1915–1985), who also starred in it with Rita Hayworth (1918–1987).

486.38   Crocker money] Family fortune established by Charles Crocker (1822–1888), one of the "Big Four" founders of the Central Pacific Railroad.

488.10   Lowell Thomas.] American journalist and broadcaster (1892–1981).

488.15   Michael O'Sullivan] American stage actor (1934–1971) known for his roles in stagings of Shakespeare and Molière.

488.16   "Blow, winds, and crack your cheeks."] *King Lear*, III.ii.i.

488.28–29   *Who, if I cried out . . . hierarchies?*] The opening line of Rainer
Maria Rilke's *Duino Elegies* (1922).

490.11–12   "everyone who could read or be read to."] See "Toward an
American Language" (1952), essay by the American playwright and novelist
Thornton Wilder (1897–1975): "It is not necessary to remind you that Walt
Whitman addressed himself to everyone who could read or be read to."

490.26   with migrant Carlos Bulosan, *America Is in the Heart*] Born in
the Philippines, the writer Carlos Bulosan (1911?–1956) immigrated to the
United States in 1930 or 1931; his best-known work, the autobiographical
novel *America Is in the Heart*, was published in 1946.

490.28   Gertrude Atherton] San Francisco–born novelist (1857–1948), author of *The Californians* (1898), *The Conqueror* (1902), *Rezánov* (1906), and
Black Oxen (1923).

490.29–30   "Relocation" Camp] Referring to the internment camps for
Japanese Americans during World War II.

490.34   Ah Sin] Chinese immigrant character invented by the American
writer Bret Harte (1836–1902), first appearing in the poem "The Heathen
Chinee" (1870), which was used by opponents of Chinese immigrants.

490.34   *Ramona*] Popular novel (1884) by the novelist and activist Helen
Hunt Jackson (1830–1885), the basis for an annual pageant in Hemet,
California.

491.8   Archer, as was done in by Brigid O'Shaughnessy] In *The Maltese
Falcon* (1930), crime novel by Dashiell Hammett (1894–1961).

491.28   "Moscow Nights,"] Soviet song (1955), music by Vasily Solovyov-
Sedoi (1907–1969), lyrics by Mikhail Matusovsky (1915–1990), known in the
West through adaptations such as "Midnight in Moscow" beginning in the
1960s.

493.37   *Seven Samurai*] Epic film (1954) directed by Akira Kurosawa (1910–
1998) and starring Toshiro Mifune (1920–1997).

494.15   Flora Dora girl] A member of the double sextette or chorus line
from the musical *Floradora* (1899).

495.18   Anne Bancroft–Tuesday Weld] The stage, film, and television actor
Anne Bancroft (1931–2005), whose roles included the play (1959) and film
(1962) of *The Miracle Worker*, *The Graduate* (1967), and *The Turning Point*
(1977); film and television actor Tuesday Weld (b. 1943), a child and teen star
in the 1950s and 1960s with a tempestuous personal life.

496.35   Ng Poon Chew] Chinese-born American newspaper publisher,
Presbyterian minister, diplomat, and civil rights advocate (1866–1931). See
also pp. 963.27–964.5.

496.36 Wellington Koo] V. K. Wellington Koo (1888–1985), Chinese states-man and diplomat.

496.36 bok gwai] Literally "white ghost," a pejorative term for white people.

497.35 Donner Party] A party of settlers from Illinois who were trapped by snow in the Sierra Nevada in the winter of 1846–47. Only forty-five of the eighty-one people who were snowbound survived, and more than half of the survivors resorted to cannibalism.

499.10 Diane Wakoski and Lenore Kandel] The poets Diane Wakoski (b. 1937) and Lenore Kandel (1932–2009).

499.29 Sammies] Members of the Jewish fraternity Sigma Alpha Mu.

499.31–32 SOP . . . Pineapple Pies.] The Asian American interest sorority Sigma Omicron Pi; nickname for members of Asian American fraternity Pi Alpha Pi.

500.12 Oski Doll?] The Oski Dolls were female Berkeley students selected as hostesses and boosters for the university for sporting and other events, named for Oski Bear, the school mascot.

501.22 In the plague year, according to Defoe] In *A Journal of the Plague Year* (1722), common title for the account of the 1665 bubonic plague out-break in London by the English writer Daniel Defoe (c. 1660–1732).

502.18 *Seventh Seal* knights . . . played with Death and lost.] The film *The Seventh Seal* by the Swedish director Ingmar Bergman (1918–2007) includes a scene in which Death wins a chess match against the film's protagonist, the knight Antonius Block.

502.23 Segovia] The Spanish classical guitar virtuoso Andrés Segovia (1893–1987).

502.25–29 Mose Allison riff . . . *money.*] From "Back Country Suite: Blues" (1957), also known as "Young Man Blues," by the jazz and blues musician Mose Allison (1927–2016).

503.24–25 Sheilah Graham] English-born writer (1904–1988), author of a long-running Hollywood gossip column; she was romantically involved with F. Scott Fitzgerald (1896–1940) in the last years of his life.

503.26–27 *Howl* trial . . . Murao] "Howl" (1956), poem by the Beat poet Allen Ginsberg (1926–1997), was the subject of a widely publicized obscenity trial in San Francisco in 1957. Charges against Lawrence Ferlinghetti (1919–2021), co-founder of the City Lights Pocket Bookshop, and the store's clerk Shigeyoshi Murao (1926–1999) were dismissed by a municipal judge after they had been arrested for selling Ginsberg's *Howl and Other Poems* to an undercover police officer.

503.33 Jack and Neal.] Jack Kerouac (1922–1969) and his friend Neal Cassady (1926–1968), who appears in Kerouac's writings in fictionalized form as Dean Moriarty and Cody Pomeray.

503.38 Jack Duluoz] Kerouac's alter ego in *Big Sur* (1962) and other writings.

504.24–29 *Girls in my native land . . . sweetness.*] From Rilke's *Notebooks of Malte Laurids Brigge*.

504.35–36 Phoebe Weatherfield Caulfield asking Holden] In *The Catcher in the Rye* (1951), novel by J. D. Salinger (1919–2010).

506.14 Rosalind or Portia] Shakespearean heroines from, respectively, *As You Like It* and *The Merchant of Venice*.

506.17 Leontyne Price] Soprano (b. 1927) who in 1961 became the first African American singer to join the Metropolitan Opera Company.

506.18–19 the statue lady from *Winter's Tale*] Hermione, the maligned wife of King Leontes who in the final scene of Shakespeare's *The Winter's Tale* is revealed as a statue to her husband and others; she then comes to life.

506.22 *Flower Drum Song*] Broadway musical (1958) with music by Richard Rodgers (1902–1979) and lyrics by Oscar Hammerstein II (1895–1960), based on the 1957 novel by C. Y. Lee (1915–2018).

506.28–29 *The World of Suzie Wong . . .* Hong Kong.] Stage play (1960) by Paul Osborn (1901–1988) based on the novel by the English writer Richard Mason (1919–1997) in which a young Chinese woman working as a prostitute falls in love with an American in Hong Kong. It was later adapted into a film starring Nancy Kwan (b. 1939) as Wong.

507.36 *The Seven Year Itch*] Play (1952) and film (1955) by the American playwright and screenwriter George Axelrod (1922–2003).

508.6 *Krapp's Last Tape*] Play (1958) by the Irish playwright and novelist Samuel Beckett (1906–1989).

508.17 Hogan Tyrone Loman Big Daddy family.] References to families in classic American plays: the Hogan family in *A Moon for the Misbegotten* (1943) by Eugene O'Neill (1888–1953), the Tyrone family at the center of O'Neill's *Long Day's Journey into Night* (1941–42), Willy Loman and his family in *Death of a Salesman* (1949) by Arthur Miller (1915–2005), and Big Daddy Pollitt and his family in *Cat on a Hot Tin Roof* (1955) by Tennessee Williams (1911–1983).

508.18–19 *Seven Brides for Seven Brothers . . .* pro-miscegenation legend] Set in nineteenth-century Oregon, the musical film *Seven Brides for Seven Brothers* (1954), directed by Stanley Donen (1924–2019), was loosely based on the ancient Roman legend known as the rape of the Sabine women, in which members of the Sabines, a neighboring tribe who had resisted inter-marriage with the Romans, were invited to a banquet, where the legendary

Roman founder Romulus then gave a signal for his warriors to forcefully seize Sabine women and take them as wives.

508.28 *The Barretts of Wimpole Street*] Stage comedy (1930) by the English playwright Rudolf Besier (1878–1942) about the early relationship of the English poets Robert Browning (1812–1889) and Elizabeth Barrett Browning (1806–1861).

508.40–509.2 *Our Town* stage manager character . . . Frank Craven . . . Grover's Corners, U.S.A.] The actor Frank Craven (1875–1945) introduced the role of the Stage Manager in Thornton Wilder's play *Our Town* (1938), set in the fictional American town of Grover's Corners.

509.6–8 Mark Twain . . . a fish-belly white.'] From *Adventures of Huckleberry Finn* (1884), ch. 5.

509.9 'Philip. Give me the letter, Philip.'] Line associated with Bette Davis (1908–1989) and her starring role in *The Letter* (1940), though she did not say it in the film.

509.9–10 'Last night . . . Manderley again.'] Line from the opening of *Rebecca* (1940), directed by Alfred Hitchcock (1899–1980).

509.10–11 'As God is my witness . . . again.] Line spoken by Vivian Leigh (1913–1967) in her role as Scarlett O'Hara in *Gone with the Wind* (1939), directed by Victor Fleming (1889–1949).

509.11–12 'The calla lilies are in bloom . . . flowah.'] Line spoken by and later associated with Katharine Hepburn (1907–2003) in her role as Terry Randall in *Stage Door* (1937), directed by Gregory La Cava (1892–1952).

509.14–16 'Maybe you found someone . . . kisser.] From *The Public Enemy* (1931), directed by William Wellman (1896–1975), starring James Cagney (1889–1986) and Mae Clarke (1910–1992).

509.18 That movie] *Island of Desire* (1952), directed by Stuart Heisler (1896–1979) and starring Linda Darnell (1923–1965) and Tab Hunter (1931–2018). The "British flyer" was played by Donald Gray (1914–1978).

509.26 Mei Lan Fan androgyne] The Chinese singer Mei Lanfang (1894–1961), famed for his performances of female roles in Chinese opera.

509.38 Double Ten] National holiday of the Republic of China (Taiwan), so called because it falls on October 10.

510.2 HUAC] The House Un-American Activities Committee.

510.35 hakujin] Japanese: white person.

511.6 that song by the Coasters] The Coasters' hit "Poison Ivy" (1959).

511.19 Issei] Japanese: First generation.

511.20 "yogore."] Japanese: dirty.

511.20–21 Zato-Ichi the Blind Swordsman] Hero of a prolific series of popular Japanese action films starring Shintaro Katsu (1931–1997).

512.18–23 'What's the use of living . . . scissors."] From "Second Poem" (1957) by Peter Orlovsky (1933–2010).

513.8 *The Journey to the West*] Classical sixteenth-century Chinese novel, also known in an abridged translation (1942) by Arthur Waley as *Monkey*.

514.3–4 la riata] Or *riata*. Spanish: rope.

515.9 'The Dueling Mammy,'] Unused suggested title for a film-within-the film in the movie musical *Singin' in the Rain* (1952). "Mammy" alluded to the popularity in the 1920s of the singer and actor Al Jolson (1886–1950), widely known for his performances in blackface and his "mammy" songs, such as "Mammy" in the film *The Jazz Singer* (1927).

516.2–3 Charles Laughton as the Hunchback of Notre Dame] Laughton (1899–1962) played the title role of Quasimodo in the 1939 film adaptation of Victor Hugo's novel (1831), directed by William Dieterle (1893–1972).

516.5 like Helen Keller, he stuttered out, "'Wa-wa-wa-water?] As she stood by a well, "water" was the breakthrough word uttered by the blind, deaf, and mute Helen Keller (1880–1968) to her teacher Anne Sullivan (1866–1936) in *The Miracle Worker* (1957), play by William Gibson adapted into a film in 1960.

516.6 Gabble gobble, one of us.'"] In *Freaks* (1932), directed by Tod Browning (1880–1962), part of the chant (with "we accept you") at a wedding banquet welcoming the trapeze artist Cleopatra into the film's group of circus performers.

516.10 LeRoi Jones] Poet (1934–2014) later known as Amiri Baraka.

517.11 Maurice Chevalier] French actor and singer (1888–1972) whose films included *The Big Pond* (1930), *The Merry Widow* (1934), and the musical *Gigi* (1958).

520.24 Tu Fu and Li Po.] Tang dynasty poets Tu Fu (712–770) and Li Po (701–762).

521.6–7 Id al-Kabir.] Or Eid al-Kabir, "festival of the sacrifice," Islamic feast commemorating Abraham's thwarted murder of his son Isaac by an angel after God has commanded the sacrifice, a story also told in Genesis 22:13.

521.12 Lolos] Members of a large group of Tibeto-Burman-speaking peoples in Southeast Asia.

521.28–29 Bali." (Like Antonin Artaud . . . imagination] The avant-garde French playwright and filmmaker Antonin Artaud (1896–1948) was influenced by Balinese performances he saw as part of the 1931 Colonial Exhibition in Paris.

522.7–10   "'All the world is sad and dreary . . . Susanna,"] From "Old Folks at Home," a minstrel song written for Christy's Minstrels in 1851 and attributed to the American songwriter Stephen Foster (1826–1864), also known as "Swanee River" or "Suwannee River." Foster's song "Oh! Susanna" dates from 1848.

522.39   Cheng I Sao, widow and lady pirate] Zheng Yi Sao (1775–1844) took over her husband's leadership role in a large piracy confederation after he died in 1807.

523.39   Sweet Dick Whittington the Allnight Cat] Los Angeles radio disc jockey (b. 1934).

524.1–7   *When you see danger . . . blu-u-e.*] From "Don't Get Scared" (1954), song by the jazz vocalist King Pleasure (Clarence Beeks, 1922–1982), which he wrote with Jon Hendricks (1921–2017).

524.8   Cannonball Adderley] Alto saxophonist and bandleader (1928–1975).

524.38   Horatio Algiers Wong] Play on the name of Horatio Alger (1832–1899), whose novels included *Ragged Dick* (1868) and *Luck and Pluck* (1869), known for his optimistic view of American opportunity.

525.13–14   Dave Brubeck was playing "Take Five" on the radio.] Hit recording in 1961 for the quartet of the jazz pianist and composer Dave Brubeck (b. 1920); the composition was written in 1959 by Paul Desmond (1924–1977), who played saxophone in the ensemble.

526.29   *tais-toi, je ne veux plus*] French: shut up, I don't want any more.

528.16   jesting, once-singing Yorick] See Shakespeare, *Hamlet*, V.i.

528.35   Like Rimbaud, I practice having hallucinations.] See *Une Saison en enfer* (A Season in Hell, 1873), prose poem by the French poet Arthur Rimbaud (1854–1891), "I got used to elementary hallucination. . . . And so I explained my magical sophistries by turning words into visions!"

529.12–13   Bill and Coo] Titular bird protagonists of 1948 film directed by Dean Riesner (1918–2002).

530.21–22   Lew Welch, the Red Monk . . . "So it has come to this."] Cf. lines from "He Finally Reaches the City" (1964) by the poet Lew Welch (1926–1971): "The Red Monk used to say . . . *So / It's all come to this!*" A variant of the last two lines (as an exclamation, not a question) also appears at the close of Welch's "Small Sentence to Drive Yourself Sane" (1970). For Kingston's appreciation of Welch, see pp. 909–13 in this volume.

533.10–11   looping like *Dead of Night*.] In the British horror film *Days of Night* (1945), a killer thinks he has dreamed the murders he has committed, only to seemingly wake and begin repeating the same sequence of events.

534.17–18   *The Faerie Queene*.] Epic poem (1590–96) by the English Renaissance poet Edmund Spenser (1552–1599).

534.19 "Trippers and askers surround me."] From section 4 of Walt Whitman's "Song of Myself" from *Leaves of Grass*, first published in 1855.

534.19 Crazy Jane Talks with the Bishop.] Title of poem (1932) by the Irish poet W. B. Yeats (1865–1939).

535.23–24 *Of Mice and Men*] Novel (1937) by the American writer John Steinbeck (1902–1968), also adapted for the stage and screen.

535.29–30 Yale Younger Poet."] Since 1918, the Yale Younger Poet Prize has been awarded to a poet who has not yet published a book; the winner has the manuscript published as a debut collection.

535.37–38 Vaughan Williams conducting "Seventeen Come Summer"] Reference to the first movement of "English Folk Song Suite," orchestral piece (1924) by the English composer Ralph Vaughan Williams (1872–1958), based on the folk song "I'm Seventeen Come Sunday."

536.11–13 Richard Brautigan . . . Bob Kaufman . . . Jack Spicer] The novelist, short story writer, and poet Richard Brautigan (1935–1984); the poets Bob Kaufman (1925–86) and Jack Spicer (1925–1965). All lived in the Bay Area.

536.18 Lamont] Prize (since 1975) for a poet's second collection, now called the James Laughlin Award, given by the Academy of American Poets.

536.19 Robert Frost inaugurating the President.] Robert Frost (1874–1963) read his poem "The Gift Outright" (1941) at the presidential inauguration of John F. Kennedy in 1961.

537.12 Mark Schorer] American critic, academic, and fiction writer (1908–1977), the author of *Sinclair Lewis: An American Life* (1961).

537.15 He quoted George Sand] From *La Mare au Diable* (The Devil's Pool, 1846) by the French novelist George Sand (pseud. Aurore Dupin, 1804–1876).

537.21–22 Pear Garden was the cradle of civilization, where theater began] In China "Pear Garden" was a term associated with theater and Chinese opera, which according to tradition had been founded in the eighth-century emperor's Ming Huang's pear garden.

538.9–15 James Agee . . . another Yale Younger Poet.] The writer James Agee (1909–1955), author of *Let Us Now Praise Famous Men* (1941) and the posthumously published *A Death in the Family* (1957), won the Yale Younger Poets Prize for *Permit Me Voyage* (1934).

539.4 Walt Whitman said] In "Song of Myself," section 4.

544.17–18 Narcissus Queen] Winner of a Chinese American beauty pageant.

548.14 *The Wild One.*] Film about motorcycle gangs directed by László Benedek (1905–1992) and starring Marlon Brando (1924–2004).

549.18–19   Cyd Charisse] Dancer and actor (1922–2008) whose films included *Singin' in the Rain* (1952) and *Silk Stockings* (1957).

551.33–34   *Ah, Bartleby. Ah, humanity.*] Cf. the closing of "Bartleby, the Scrivener" (1853), story by Herman Melville (1819–1891).

552.2   *Twisters and Shouters*] Cf. "Twist and Shout" (1961), written by Phil Medley (1916–1997) and Bert Russell (1929–1967), a hit single for the Isley Brothers as well as the Beatles.

554.4–26   *Soldiers, sailors . . . hips*] Lineated version of a passage from Jack Kerouac's first published novel, *The Town and the City* (1950).

555.38–39   "When you're a Jet . . . dying day."] From "Jet Song" from *West Side Story*, in which the Jets and the Sharks are rival gangs.

556.9–11   Rita Moreno . . . in America."] From "I Want to Live in America," song that in film version of *West Side Story* was led by Rita Moreno (b. 1931) in the role of Anita.

556.12   Tony meets Natalie Wood.] In *West Side Story*, Tony, played by Richard Beymer (b. 1938), falls in love with Maria, played by Natalie Wood (1938–1981).

556.31   the Fillmore, the Western Addition.] District in San Francisco.

556.33–34   Leslie Caron . . . *The Subterraneans*] In the film adaptation (1960) of Jack Kerouac's novel *The Subterraneans* (1958) the character of Mardou Fox, who in the novel was a Black American woman based on Kerouac's romantic partner Alene Lee (1931–1991), was represented as a young French woman played by the French actress and dancer Leslie Caron (b. 1931).

556.35–36   George Peppard . . . *Breakfast at Tiffany's*] Peppard (1928–1994) played Paul Varjak in *Breakfast at Tiffany's*, film (1961) based on the novella (1958) by American writer Truman Capote (1924–1984).

561.25–26   Lester Maddox . . . Governor Faubus, Governor Wallace] Segregationist politicians: Lester Maddox (1915–2003), governor of Georgia, 1967–71; Orval Faubus (1910–1994), Arkansas governor who opposed school integration in the wake of the Supreme Court ruling in *Brown v. Board of Education* (1954); George Wallace (1919–1998), governor of Alabama, 1963–67, 1971–79, 1983–87, and third-party and Democratic presidential candidate known for his slogan "Segregation now, segregation tomorrow, segregation forever."

561.38   Shinajin] Derogatory Japanese word for Chinese.

562.31–32   *A Place in the Sun.*] Based on Theodore Dreiser's novel *An American Tragedy* (1925), the film *A Place in the Sun* (1951) was directed by George Stevens (1904–1975) and starred Montgomery Clift (1920–1966), Shelley Winters (1920–2006), and Elizabeth Taylor (1932–2011).

564.27   haoles] Hawaiian term for non-Hawaiians, particularly whites, generally pejorative.

564.33–34   Somerset Maugham combinations] The English writer W. Somerset Maugham (1874–1965) wrote about Asia under the sway of Western colonialism in his novels and short stories.

565.10   nihonjin] Japanese: Japanese people.

566.24–25   'The Twilight Zone' . . . Rod Serling] Serling (1924–1975) was the host of the original iteration of *The Twilight Zone* television show, 1959–64.

566.30   Walter Lantz] American animator (1899–1994) whose creations included Woody Woodpecker.

568.7   Bloom's Day] Celebration commemorating the Irish writer James Joyce (1882–1941) that occurs every June 16, the day his epic novel *Ulysses* (1922) takes place, named for the novel's protagonist, Leopold Bloom.

569.30   L.S.D. from the Sandoz Labs] LSD (lysergic acid diethylamide) was produced legally by Sandoz Laboratories in Switzerland as an experimental psychiatric drug.

571.39   G. S.] General Schedule, pay scale for federal employees.

572.21   Burroughs, Old Bull Lee] Old Bull Lee, name in Jack Kerouac's *On the Road* (1957) for character based on American novelist William S. Burroughs (1914–1997), whose works include *Naked Lunch* (1959) and *The Soft Machine* (1961).

573.13   *A Nous la Liberté*] Film (1931) by the French filmmaker René Clair (1898–1981).

573.16   *Last Year at Marienbad*] Film (1961) by the French filmmaker Alain Resnais (1922–2014).

573.20   *Lolita*] Film adaptation (1962) directed by Stanley Kubrick (1928–1999) of the novel (1955) by Vladimir Nabokov (1899–1977).

573.20   *8½*] Film (1963) by the Italian director Federico Fellini (1920–1993) starring Marcello Mastroianni (1938–1996).

574.1   *Jules and Jim*] Film (1962) about a love triangle, directed by François Truffaut (1932–1984), starring Henri Serre (b. 1931), Oskar Werner (1922–1984), and Jeanne Moreau (1928–2017).

574.4–5   *The Treasure of the Sierra Madre*.] Film (1948) directed by John Huston (1906–1987) starring Humphrey Bogart (1899–1957), an adaptation of a novel (1927) written by the author known by the pen name B. Traven.

574.6   *Ugetsu*.] Film (1953) also known as *Tales of Ugetsu* directed by the Japanese director Kenzo Mizoguchi (1898–1956).

574.7 *Children of Paradise.*] Film (1945) set in the nineteenth-century Parisian theatrical world, directed by the French director Marcel Carné (1906–1996).

575.22 asmador] Asthmador, commercially available treatment for asthma in the form of a fine powder.

575.22 Stelazine] Brand name for the antipsychotic Trifluoperazine.

575.23 Romilar C.F.] Commercial name for dextromethorphan, a cough syrup removed from circulation in 1973 because of frequent misuse.

576.17 rauwolfia serpentia] Indian snakeroot, a plant with medicinal uses.

576.26 *The Tibetan Book of the Dead*] English title (from W. Y. Evans-Wentz's 1927 translation) of *Bardo Thodol*, Tibetan Buddhist text intended as a guide to the *bardo* (intermediate state between death and rebirth).

577.3–5 *Dumbo the Flying Elephant* . . . Disney couldn't do a *Living Desert*–type movie] The story "Dumbo, the Flying Elephant" (1939), by Helen Aberson (later Mayer, 1907–1999), was adapted into the full-length animated film *Dumbo* (1941) released by Walt Disney Productions. In 1953 Disney released the Oscar-winning nature documentary *The Living Desert*, directed by James Algar (1912–1998).

579.22 Constance Bonacieux] Character in *The Three Musketeers* (1844), novel by Alexandre Dumas (1802–1870); she becomes involved in an extramarital relationship with D'Artagnan, whom she marries after the death of her husband.

579.22 Lady Connie Chatterley.] In *Lady Chatterley's Lover* (1928), novel by D. H. Lawrence (1885–1930), Constance Chatterley has an extramarital affair with a gamekeeper.

583.31 Ravi Shankar] Virtuoso Indian classical musician and composer (1920–2012) whose sitar playing was long admired in India and the West.

584.24 Doctor Zhivago/Omar Sharif] The Egyptian actor Omar Sharif (1932–2015) played the title role in *Doctor Zhivago* (1965), directed by David Lean (1908–1991), a film adaptation of the novel (1957) by Russian novelist and poet Boris Pasternak (1890–1960).

584.39 *Dr. Strangelove*] *Dr. Strangelove; or, How I Learned to Stop Worrying and Love the Bomb* (1963), film directed by Stanley Kubrick.

586.3–4 pod-picking . . . *Invasion of the Body Snatchers.*] In the science fiction film (1956) directed by Don Siegel (1912–1991), alien replacements for human beings emerge from seedpods.

589.8 smuggle? . . . *Ulysses, Lady Chatterley's Lover, Tropic of Cancer, Howl.*] Notable works banned or censored for their purported obscenity: James Joyce's *Ulysses*; *Lady Chatterley's Lover*, see note 579.22; *Tropic of Cancer* (1934), novel by Henry Miller (1891–1980); *Howl*, see note 503.26–27.

589.35   *The Longest Day*] Film (1962) dramatizing the D-day landings based on the book (1959) by Irish-born journalist Cornelius Ryan (1920–1974).

589.35   *Cleopatra*] Historical film (1963) directed by Joseph L. Mankiewicz (1909–1993) and starring Elizabeth Taylor (1923–2011), notorious for its outsized budget.

590.5   *The Saragossa Manuscript*] Polish film (1965) directed by Wojciech Has (1925–2000), based on the novel by Jan Potocki (1761–1815).

594.13   Mo'o the terrible lizard god] In Hawaiian mythology.

594.13   the Garuda] Creature in Buddhist and Hindu mythology resembling a bird, most often represented with a man's head; in Hindu mythology, the mount of Vishnu.

594.29   *Vertigo*?] Film (1958) directed by Alfred Hitchcock starring James Stewart (1908–1997) and Kim Novak (b. 1933).

594.35   Bates Motel with its shower] Scene of the notorious murder at the center of Hitchcock's *Psycho* (1960).

598.33   "America Needs Indians."] Multimedia art happening hosted by San Francisco's Committee Theater beginning in 1965, organized by Stewart Brand (b. 1938) and Ken Kesey (1935–2001).

599.18–19   'dance . . . moonlight revels.'] Spoken by Titania, queen of the fairies, to Oberon in Shakespeare, *A Midsummer Night's Dream*, II.i.141.

600.1   chez Mitford-Treuhaft] At the home of Jessica Mitford (1917–1996), English author of *The American Way of Death* (1963), and her husband Robert Treuhaft (1912–2001), Bay Area lawyer who took on many cases representing leftist and radical defendants.

600.15   Birmingham Brown."] Chauffeur for the detective Charlie Chan, central figure in a series of mystery novels created by Earl Derr Biggers (1884–1933) and in numerous movies.

600.27   Lobsang Rampa] The English occult and spiritualist writer born Cyril Hoskin (1910–1981) published books including *The Third Eye* (1956) under the name Lobsang Rampa, a Tibetan lama whose spirit he claimed his body was hosting.

601.3   *Destination Moon*] Science-fiction film (1950) directed by Irving Pichel (1891–1954).

602.36   hibakushas] Survivors of the atomic bombings of Hiroshima and Nagasaki.

603.27–28   "The Shooting of Dan McGrew."] Popular poem (1907) set in the Yukon by the English-born Canadian poet Robert W. Service (1874–1958).

604.31 Bloomsbury] Early twentieth-century English artistic circle that included writers such as the art critic Clive Bell (1881–1964), the artist and art critic Roger Fry (1866–1934), the novelists Virginia Woolf (1882–1941) and E. M. Forster (1879–1970), and the biographer Lytton Strachey (1880–1932).

604.35 at Berkeley when Charles Olson read] A reading of more than three hours at the Berkeley Poetry Conference, July 23, 1965, by the American poet Charles Olson (1910–1970), among the most prominent members of the midcentury Black Mountain School of poetry and poetics.

605.1–4 Lew Welch . . . a bell makes."] Cf. Welch's "Hermit Poems," 9: "I saw myself / a ring of bone [...] then heard/ 'ring of bone' where / ring is what a // bell does."

605.4–5 Brother Antoninus out of St. Albert's] The poet William Everson (1912–1994) was also known as Brother Antoninus during his time spent living as a Dominican lay brother at St. Albert's Priory in Oakland.

605.23 Maria Ouspenskaya] Russian actor (1876–1949) who came to the U.S. as a member of the Moscow Art Theater and went on to appear in Hollywood films such as *The Wolf Man* (1941).

607.3–4 "Thy rose lips and full blue eyes,"] From "Adeline" (1830) by Alfred, Lord Tennyson (1809–1892).

608.39 Sansei] Japanese: Third generation.

614.14 next horse stall at Tanforan] In 1942 the Tanforan horse-racing facility in San Bruno, California, was used as an internment camp for Japanese Americans, many of whom were housed in converted horse stalls.

615.15–21 Issei . . . Yonsei . . . Gosei] Japanese: First, fourth, and fifth generation.

615.23 Executive Order 9066] Executive order signed by President Franklin D. Roosevelt on February 19, 1942, authorizing the removal of Japanese Americans from their homes, a measure that by September 1942 resulted in internment, without trial or hearing, more than 120,000 Japanese Americans and Japanese resident aliens living on the West Coast.

616.27 Gomenasai.] Japanese: I'm sorry.

617.30–31 *Mondo Cane* cargo cult.] The final section of the sensationalistic Italian documentary *Mondo Cane* (1962) contains footage of the cargo-cult practices of Indigenous people in Papua New Guinea.

618.1 'A ma puissance,'] French: To my power.

618.35–36 on the Firesign Theater album] *Waiting for the Electrician or Someone Like Him* (1968), album by the comedy troupe The Firesign Theater (later spelled "Theatre"), specifically its opening track "Humboldt County Forever."

618.38 Garuda] The flagship airline of Indonesia (but see also note 594.13).

619.32 Manzanar . . . Sand Island.] Sites of internment camps for Japanese Americans during World War II.

621.19–22 Dale Evans . . . Sons of the Pioneers . . . Roy Rogers] The singer and actor Roy Rogers (1911–1998) was a founding member of the country-and-western vocal ensemble Sons of the Pioneers; the singer Dale Evans (1912–2001), Rogers's third wife, would perform with the group, including on television.

629.31 Wallenda pyramid] A human pyramid; members of the Wallenda family were twentieth-century German circus acrobats who performed in the United States with Ringling Bros. and Barnum & Bailey Circus.

642.27 Herman Kahn.] American mathematician and military strategist (1922–1983), founder of the conservative Hudson Institute, author *of On Thermonuclear War*(1960) *and Thinking about the Unthinkable* (1962).

643.26 *Fantasia.*] Animated feature film (1940) released by Walt Disney Productions.

646.19 Beardsley's Savoy book.] *The Savoy Book* (1896), illustrated periodical, edited and founded by the English artist and writer Aubrey Beardsley (1872–1898) and the British poet and editor Arthur Symons (1865–1945), which featured art and writing from Decadent and Aesthetic movement figures including Beardsley.

646.20 Salomé's big lips kissing John the Baptist's head] In the gospels of Matthew and Mark, the wish of Herod Antipas's stepdaughter (unnamed but traditionally called Salomé) for the head of John the Baptist is fulfilled; the story, including a seductive dance before Herod, was adapted several times in nineteenth-century art, music, and literature.

648.5–6 *Like a blank piece of paper . . . again.*] From Rilke's *Notebooks of Malte Laurids Brigge.*

652.33–34 *Far from the Madding Crowd*] Novel (1874) by the English novelist and poet Thomas Hardy (1840–1928).

653.18 *Hiroshima Mon Amour*] Film (1959) with a screenplay by the French writer Marguerite Duras (1914–1996), directed by the French filmmaker Alain Resnais (1922–2014).

653.20 *Snow Country*] Novel (1948) by the Japanese novelist Yasunari Kawabata (1899–1972).

658.1–2 the stop casting porosity sign] An advertisement put up by the Western Sealant Company about its pressure-proofing services for cast-iron fixtures to prevent leakage, though the phrase's meaning eluded most of the drivers passing by on the Nimitz Freeway.

659.23–32   Coit Tower . . . Columbus . . . Rita Hayworth's mansion in *Pal Joey*] The Coit Tower was used for shots showing the mansion of Vera Prentice-Simpson, a character played by Rita Hayworth in the 1957 film adaptation of *Pal Joey*, based on the musical derived from the interconnected stories by John O'Hara (1905–1970), published in 1940. From 1957 until its removal in 2020, a statue of Christopher Columbus stood next to the site of the tower.

659.27   Daruma dolls.] Round, hollow Japanese dolls of papier-mâché representing the head of the Indian Buddhist monk Bodhidharma (fifth–sixth centuries C.E.), said to bring good luck.

660.16–17   *Bye Bye Birdie*] Musical (1960), music by Charles Strouse (b. 1928), lyrics by Lee Adams (b. 1924), and book by Michael Stewart (1924–1987), followed by a film adaptation in 1963.

660.17–18   Angel Island . . . Wooden House.] From the nineteenth century through 1940 many Chinese and other Asian immigrants were processed and often subjected to lengthy detentions at Angel Island in San Francisco Bay. Chinese detainees referred to the detention barracks as the "wooden house."

660.19   Desolation China Man angels] Reference to the title of Jack Kerouac's novel *Desolation Angels* (1965).

660.25–30   *Facing west . . . almost circled . . .*] From Walt Whitman's "Facing West from California's Shores" (1860).

661.32   Reverend Kirby Hensley] Founder (1911–1999) and head of the non-denominational Universal Life Church.

663.12–14   *Every angel is terrible . . . you are.*] From Rilke's first Duino Elegy.

666.6   "Let Me Call You Sweetheart."] Popular waltz (1910), music by Leo Friedman (1869–1927), lyrics by Beth Slater Whitson (1879–1930).

666.16–17   Alfred Hitchcock's daughter Patricia's look-alike] In Hitchcock's *Strangers on a Train* (1951), Patricia Hitchcock (1928–2021) played the role of Barbara Morgan, who bears physical resemblance to Miriam Haines, played by Kasey Rogers (1925–2006).

668.1   Orlando and the Russian princess] The eponymous protagonist and the Russian princess Sasha in Virginia Woolf's novel *Orlando: A Biography* (1928).

679.37   Sheena, Queen of the Jungle.] Comic-book character created by Will Eisner (1917–2005) and Jerry Iger (1903–1990) in 1938, the heroine of an eponymous comic book as well as a film and television series.

681.39–40   Madame Chiang Kai Shek.] Soong May-ling (1898–2003), the wife of Republic of China president Chiang Kai-shek.

681.40 Madame Sun Yat Sen] Rosamond Soong Ch'ing-ling (1893–1981), Chinese political figure who was the third wife of Sun Yat-sen.

681.40–682.1 Charles Jones Soong and T. V. Soong] Ni Kwei-tseng (1869–1931), wife of the Chinese businessman Charles Soong (1861–1918) and mother of the businessman and politician T. V. Soong (1894–1971) and the three prominent women known as the Soong sisters: Ai-ling Soong (1888–1973), as well as May-ling and Ch'ing-ling (see two preceding notes).

682.1 Madame Nhu.] Born Tran Le Xuan (1924–2011), the glamorous, influential, and outspoken wife of Ngo Dinh Nhu, the younger brother and chief political advisor of South Vietnamese president Ngo Dinh Diem (1901–1963).

682.19 Anna Chennault] Chinese-born American journalist and lobbyist (1923–2018), the wife of General Claire Chennault (1893–1958), who had advised Chiang Kai-shek and led the "Flying Tigers" in the U.S. Army Air Forces during World War II.

685.22 *story of the Prodigal Son*] See Luke 15:11–32.

686.36–37 Sophie Tucker] Popular actor and singer (1884–1966) nicknamed "Last of the Red Hot Mammas."

686.38 Ginger] The dancer, actor, and singer Ginger Rogers (1911–1995), Fred Astaire's partner in numerous stage and film performances.

686.39 Will Rogers] Humorist, vaudeville performer, and screen actor (1879–1935) known for his folksiness.

687.4 Anna May Wong] Glamorous and groundbreaking Chinese American actor (1905–1961) whose films include *Shanghai Express* (1932) and *Daughter of Shanghai* (1937).

687.35 *Duel in the Sun*] Western (1946) directed by King Vidor (1984–1892), starring Jennifer Jones (1919–2009), Joseph Cotten (1905–1994), and Gregory Peck (1916–2003).

688.2–4 S. I. Hsiung and his all-Caucasian Chinese opera . . . Woollcott] *Lady Precious Stream* (1934) by S. I. Hsiung (or Hsiung Shih-I, 1902–1991), play based on Chinese folklore that debuted in London, was also staged in American cities; a 1941 revival in Marblehead, Massachusetts, of *The Yellow Jacket* (1912), play by George C. Hazelton (1868–1921) and J. Harry Benrimo (1874–1942), included the comic actor Harpo Marx (1888–1964) and the writer Alexander Woollcott (1887–1943) in its cast. The cast of these productions were white.

689.21 Charlie Low's] The San Francisco real estate entrepreneur and businessman Charles P. Low (b. 1901), proprietor of the Chinatown nightclub Forbidden City.

689.31 *Oklahoma.*] *Oklahoma!* (1943), stage musical with music by Richard Rodgers, lyrics by Oscar Hammerstein II.

690.3   "*Don't sigh and gaze . . . much.*"] From the song "People Will Say We're in Love" from *Oklahoma!*

692.18   sanpaku eyes.] Japanese term for eyes meaning "three whites," referring to white being visible above and below the iris.

693.8–9   tadaima . . . Okaerinasai."] Japanese: I'm back home. Welcome back.

693.31   Jade Snow Wong?] Ceramic artist and writer (1922–2006) from San Francisco, author of the autobiographies *Fifth Chinese Daughter* (1950) and *No Chinese Stranger* (1975).

694.5   old bride—Miss Havisham] In *Great Expectations* (1861), novel by Charles Dickens (1812–1870), Amelia Havisham, an elderly unmarried woman, has continued to wear her wedding dress ever since her fiancé abandoned her as a young woman on what was to be their wedding day.

696.14–15   *In any case . . . standing.*] From Rilke, *The Notebooks of Malte Laurids Brigge.*

702.13   "The River of No Return."] Song (1954), music by Lionel Newman (1916–1989), lyrics by Ken Darby (1909–1992), sung by Marilyn Monroe (1926–1962) in the film of the same name, directed by Otto Preminger (1905–1986).

702.26   *Night Must Fall*] Play (1935) about a murderer by the Welsh writer Emlyn Williams (1905–1987), adapted in film versions in 1937 and 1964.

703.4   *Oracle*] *San Francisco Oracle*, underground publication, 1966–68.

709.10   Gary Snyder] Poet, essayist, and environmental activist (b. 1930) whose many collections include *Turtle Island* (1974) and *No Nature: New and Selected Poems* (1992).

710.18   ali'i] Hawaiian hereditary nobility.

710.19–20   Ko'olau the Leper alone held off the U.S. Army] The Hawaiian man Ko'olau (1862–1896) contracted Hansen's disease and, during the so-called Leper War (June–July 1893), resisted attempts to quarantine him with others afflicted with the disease at a colony on the island of Molokai, where among other abuses the detainees were subjected to medical experimentation. From within the Waimakemake cave on the island of Kalalau, Ko'olau, though low on supplies, held off attacks from soldiers of Hawaii's National Guard, killing three, and afterwards lived as a fugitive with his wife and young son for over three years until his death.

711.39–40   Catholic Worker . . . Peter Maurin Farm.] In 1933 the Progressive Catholic activist and writer Dorothy Day (1897–1980) and the French-born farmer and writer Peter Maurin (1877–1949) co-founded the Catholic Worker movement, which includes communal farms named for Maurin.

712.8   Kierkegaard] The Danish philosopher and religious thinker Søren Kierkegaard (1813–1855).

714.3 Lawrence Rad Lab . . . Los Alamos] The Lawrence Livermore National Laboratory, research institute in Northern California run by the U.S. Department of Energy; established in 1952, it was active in developing the American nuclear arsenal. Los Alamos, national laboratory in northern New Mexico, site where scientists working on the Manhattan Project developed the atomic bomb during World War II.

714.22 *Misfits.*] Film (1961) directed by John Huston and starring Clark Gable (1901–1960) and Marilyn Monroe, then married to Arthur Miller, who wrote the film's screenplay.

717.33 *The Gold Rush.*] Silent film (1925) starring Charlie Chaplin, also its writer and director.

723.27–28 *Fanfare for the Common Man* by Aaron Copland.] Orchestral composition (1942) by the American composer Aaron Copland (1900–1980).

724.36–37 Lara's theme in *Doctor Zhivago*] Composed for the film (see note 584.24) by the French composer Maurice Jarre (1924–2009).

727.35 Jiminy Cricket] Comic talking cricket who made his debut in Walt Disney productions in an animated adaptation of Carlo Collodi's *Pinocchio* (1883).

728.30 Fay Wray] Actor (1907–2004) and star of *King Kong* (1933), evoked here.

728.32–33 excrement . . . Balso Snell.] *The Dream Life of Balso Snell* (1931), the first novel of the American writer Nathanael West (1903–1940), is replete with scatological imagery.

730.2 *A Song for Occupations*] Cf. "A Song of Occupations," Whitman poem in *Leaves of Grass* that was given this final title in 1881.

730.21 yogore] Japanese: dirty.

734.10 "East Side West Side"] CBS television drama (1963–64) about a New York City social worker starring George C. Scott (1927–1999).

743.14–15 Kafka . . . made that up.] See "The Great Wall of China" (1917), story by Franz Kafka (1883–1924).

744.17 *The Dharma Bums*] Novel (1958) by Jack Kerouac.

745.7 *Man's Fate.*] *La Condition humaine* (The Human Condition, 1933), a novel by André Malraux concerning the failed 1927 communist revolution in Shanghai, was published in English translation as *Man's Fate* (1934).

746.36 S.S.S.] Selective Service System.

747.36–37 "Would not this . . . sir?"] From *Hamlet*, III.ii.275–78.

752.7 Heisenberg] The German theoretical physicist Werner Heisenberg (1901–1976), a pioneer of quantum mechanics.

752.17–18   I took Physics . . . Dr. Edward Teller] Hungarian-born American physicist Edward Teller (1908–2003), the chief designer of the U.S. hydrogen bomb, was a professor of physics at the University of California, Berkeley.

752.27–28   Alvarez's team is looking inside pyramids] The Nobel Prize–winning physicist Luis Walter Alvarez (1911–1988) and his associates looked for possible unknown chambers inside Egyptian pyramids via the use of X-rays in the 1960s.

753.31–32   *The Time Machine . . .* Mimieux, Weena of the Eloi] In *The Time Machine* (1895), novel by the English writer H. G. Wells (1866–1946), the world of the year 802,701 is peopled by the barbaric Morlocks and the effete, childlike Eloi, including a girl named Weena, played in the book's 1960 film adaptation by the actor Yvette Mimieux (b. 1942).

755.35   Rita Moreno . . . Sandra Dee.] Moreno, see note 556.9–11; Sandra Dee (1942–2005), first known as a teen actor in films such as *Imitation of Life* (1959) and the comedy *Gidget* (1959).

760.31–32   "If some of us . . . vain,"] Cf. lines from Welch's dedication to his collection *On Out* (1965).

760.40   *Had not one . . . die?*] From Rilke, *The Notebooks of Malte Laurids Brigge*, as are the italicized passages on page 761.

762.23   Bess] Bess Truman (1885–1982), wife of President Harry S. Truman (1884–1972).

764.27   Hadassah] Zionist women's organization.

766.4   Six Companies.] The Chinese Consolidated Benevolent Association of San Francisco, umbrella group of mutual-aid societies serving Chinese immigrants and Chinese Americans.

772.39–773.1   Three-Finger Jack . . . Murrieta.'] A group of American miners nearly fatally assaulted the Mexican-born Joaquín Murrieta (1829–1853) in Northern California, raping his wife, Rosita, and murdering his brother. After the attack Murrieta, along with Rosita and a companion called Three Finger Jack (also known as Bernardino Garcia), became an outlaw and a stagecoach robber. In July 1853, the two men were killed by a group of California Rangers under the leadership of Harry Love (1810–1868). Preserved in a jar of whiskey, the decapitated head of Murrieta and the hand of Three Finger Jack were brought to San Francisco and exhibited for the admission price of one dollar.

774.35   Guai] Chinese: Ghost.

776.3   Carlos Bulosan's manong pinoy] Filipino firstborn son or elder brother (Bulosan, see note 490.26).

779.23–24   Debbie Reynolds] Actor and singer (1932–2016) who starred in films such as *Singin' in the Rain* and *Tammy and the Bachelor* (1957).

780.23   *King Solomon's Mines.*] Adventure novel (1885) set in Africa by English novelist H. Rider Haggard (1856–1925), adapted into a movie in 1950.

781.17   K'ung Ming] The Chinese statesman and military strategist Zhuge Liang (181–234).

782.11   Samuel Pepys . . . *Dream*] The English diarist Samuel Pepys (1633–1703) attended a performance of *A Midsummer Night's Dream* (which he called "the most insipid ridiculous play that ever I saw in my life") in London on September 29, 1662.

783.2   *A Pear Garden in the West*] Name of a performing arts festival in San Francisco founded by the artist and writer Jack Chen (1908–1985), also the author of a book of that title about Chinese theater in America. See also note 537.21–22.

784.10–11   Make the audience see through propaganda . . . Brechtian.] The political theater of the German playwright Bertolt Brecht (1898–1956) relies on innovative techniques such as the "distancing effect" (*Verfremdungseffekt*) in which the audience is made aware of the artifice and ideology involved of what is being staged.

786.34–35   *saw an old man . . Saw.*] From Rilke's *Notebooks of Malte Laurids Brigge.*

788.20–24   *I entreat you . . . adieu.*] Cf. Shakespeare, *A Midsummer Night's Dream*, I.ii.78–86.

790.39–791.1   "Acting . . . through art."] From *Acting: The First Six Lessons* (1933) by the Polish theater and film director Richard Boleslawski (1889–1937).

791.22   "The Sidewalks of New York."] Song (1894) with lyrics by Charles B. Lawlor (1852–1925) and music by James W. Blake (1862–1935); its chorus begins with the well-known lines "East Side, West Side, / All around the town."

791.23–24   Huck's Pap . . . palace."] See Mark Twain's *Adventures of Huckleberry Finn* (1884), ch. 20.

792.9   'Hawaiian Eye.'] Television detective drama, 1959–63, broadcast on ABC.

794.33–36   Billy Batson . . . Captain Marvel.] In the Fawcett comic-book series *Captain Marvel*, the boy Billy Batson says "Shazam!" and is transformed into a superhero of that name, also known as Captain Marvel.

795.28–30   Hawkman . . . the Atom's . . . Dr. Midnight.] Superheroes in comic-book series published by DC Comics.

796.40–797.2   *Kung Fu* . . . Chinese man has no Star Quality.] The ABC television drama *Kung Fu*, 1972–75, about a Shaolin monk in the nineteenth-century American West, starred David Carradine (1939–2009).

797.19–20 thinking 1911, 1949.] The Republic of China was founded in 1912, after the overthrow of the Qing dynasty the previous year; the Communist People's Republic of China was founded in 1949 after the defeat of the Chinese Nationalists on the mainland.

799.27–28 banquet scene in *Titus Andronicus.*] Shakespeare, *Titus Andronicus*, V.iii.

805.27 Garuda] See note 594.13.

805.29 Ranga] The menacing female demon Rangda in Balinese mythology.

805.33 Damballah] Serpent god in the Vodun mythology of Haiti.

806.1 Hanuman] Monkey god in Hindu mythology.

806.2 Abba-Zabba] Candy bar with a peanut butter center and a white taffy exterior.

806.4–5 Artaud . . . crueler theater.] Artaud (see note 521.28–29) founded the Theater of Cruelty in Paris in 1935, part of his advocacy for a radically new theater based on the staging of extreme bodily acts and the use of stage effects that create an atmosphere of violent intensity.

806.5–6 Caliban is raging at not seeing his face in the mirror.] See the remark in the preface to *The Picture of Dorian Gray* (1890) by the Irish writer Oscar Wilde (1854–1900): "The nineteenth century dislike of realism is the rage of Caliban seeing his own face in a glass," referring to Caliban in Shakespeare's *The Tempest*, described in the play's dramatis personae as "a savage and deformed slave."

806.19–20 Chang and Eng] Siam-born Chinese twins (1811–1874) joined at the waist who were exhibited as curiosities in America and later became naturalized American citizens.

807.11–12 née Adelaide and Sally Yates.] The sisters Adelaide Yates (1823–1917) and Sarah Yates (known as Sally, 1822–1892) were married to Chang and Eng, respectively, in 1843.

807.14 Adet . . . daughters] The novelists Adet Lin (1923–1971) and Anor Lin (1926–2003), daughters of the Chinese writer Lin Yutang (1895–1976), long resident in the United States.

807.15 the Eaton sisters] Edith Eaton (1865–1914), English-born writer who published under the name Sui Sin Far (Cantonese for "the narcissus"), and her younger sister Winnifred Eaton (1875–1954), a journalist, screenwriter, and playwright who published as Onoto Watanna.

807.19 Millie and Christine] Millie McKoy (1851–1912) and Christine McKoy (1851–1912), conjoined twins born enslaved in North Carolina who performed worldwide, including with the Barnum circus, under several stage names.

810.22–25 *Now it was there . . . my arm.*] From Rilke's *Notebooks of Malte Laurids Brigge.*

811.21 "Dear land . . . holden."] First line of the patriotic orchestral and choral work (1899) by the Finnish composer Jean Sibelius (1865–1957).

811.23 Mother Courages.] A reference to the heroine of Bertolt Brecht's play *Mother Courage and Her Children* (1959).

812.29 Katharine Hepburn and Myrna Loy] White actors cast as Chinese women: Hepburn in *Dragon Seed* (1944) and Myrna Loy (1905–1993) as the title character's daughter in *The Mask of Fu Manchu* (1932).

816.24 what Frank Norris called the Third Circle of Evil.] See the short story about San Francisco's Chinatown, "The Third Circle" (1897), by the naturalistic novelist Frank Norris (1870–1902).

822.30 that Japanese-American guy that got shot . . . Watts fires] Eighteen-year-old Eugene Shimatsu was fatally shot by police at a liquor store just after midnight on August 15, 1965, during six days of unrest in the mainly Black neighborhood of Watts in Los Angeles.

825.9 *Raisin in the Sun*] *A Raisin in the Sun* (1959), play by Lorraine Hansberry (1930–1965), adapted into a film in 1961.

825.18–22 *Black and white together . . .* I do believe] From "We Shall Overcome," protest folk song often sung at civil rights demonstrations.

825.23 'East is east . . . Twain shall.'] From "The Ballad of East and West" (1887), poem by Rudyard Kipling (1865–1936): "Oh, East is East, and West is West, and never the twain shall meet / Till Earth and Sky stand presently at God's great Judgment Seat."

831.3 Booth home] Housing for unmarried mothers run by the Salvation Army.

832.1 Madame Sukarno] One of the several wives of Sukarno (1901–1970), Indonesian nationalist leader and the country's first president.

832.1 Madame Thieu] Thi Mai Anh Nguyen (b. 1931), wife of Vietnamese military leader and politician Nguyen Van Thieu (1923–2001), president of South Vietnam, 1967–75.

832.2 Madame Ky] Dang Tuyet Mai (1941–2016), wife of Nguyen Cao Ky (1930–2011), prime minister of South Vietnam, 1965–86.

832.2 Madame Nhu.] See note 682.1.

833.27–28 "Marlon Brando," . . . turn him Japanese] Brando (1924–2004) played Sakini, an Okinawan man who interprets for the U.S. occupation forces in *The Teahouse of the August Man* (1956).

834.1–2 'Is this a dagger . . . hand?] Macbeth, II.i.33.

836.31–32   Wellington Koo to Doctor Ng] Koo, see note 496.36; Ng Poon Chew, see note 496.35.

837.31–33   Peter Sellers, starting with the Ying Tong Goon Show . . . to this day] "Ying Tong Song" (1956) was a novelty song written by the British comedian and actor Spike Milligan (1918–2002) and performed by The Goons, comedy troupe with a popular radio comedy show on the BBC, 1951–1960. The actor Peter Sellers (1925–1980), a member of the troupe, went on to play in films that trafficked in Asian stereotypes, such as *The Pink Panther* series, which contained set pieces in which his Inspector Clouseau fought with his servant Cato Fong (played by Burt Kwouk, 1930–2016), whom he referred to as "my little yellow friend." He also played the title role in *The Fiendish Plot of Dr. Fu Manchu* (1980).

837.33–34   Mickey Rooney in *Breakfast at Tiffany's*] In the film *Breakfast at Tiffany's* (1961) Rooney played the role of Japanese photographer I. Y. Yunioshi, in a performance based on egregious stereotypes.

837.34   Warner Oland and Jerry Lewis and Lon Chaney] White film actors playing caricatured and stereotypical portrayals of Asians: the Swedish-born actor Warner Oland (1879–1938), who played Fu Manchu and the detective Charlie Chan; Jerry Lewis (1926–2017), comedian who performed racist stereotypes on television and in films such as *Hardly Working* (1981); Lon Chaney (1883–1930), who played the title role in the silent film *Mr. Wu* (1927).

837.36   Ming of Mongo] In *Flash Gordon*, comic strip created in 1934 by Alex Raymond (1909–1956) and later adapted into movie and radio serials and for television; Ming the Merciless was the tyrannical ruler of the planet Mongo.

839.22   the Cartwrights have a Hop Sing.] The Cartwright family was at the center of *Bonanza*, the Western television series broadcast on NBC, 1959–73; the servant Hop Sing was played by Victor Sen Yung (1915–1980).

840.33–34   one last slavegirl, Anna May Wong] In *The Bitter Tea of General Yen* (1932), directed by Frank Capra (1897–1991), the role of Mah Li, originally announced as given to Anna May Wong, was performed instead by the Japanese actor Toshia Mori (1912–1995).

843.28–29   There are these 'Chigroes'] In *Dr. No* (1958), James Bond novel by Ian Fleming (1908–1964).

843.34   Odd Job.] Oddjob, villain in the James Bond novels and films, played by the Hawaiian-born athlete and actor Harold Sakata (1920–1982).

843.39   Mako] Japanese-born American actor (1933–2006) with roles in film including *The Sand Pebbles* (1966), directed by Robert Wise (1914–2005) and starring Steve McQueen (1930–1980).

844.18   Charlie Two Shoes] Nickname for Tsui Chi Hsii (b. 1934), who was fed and housed at the end of World War II by a group of U.S. Marines;

decades later, he immigrated to the United States and opened a restaurant in Chapel Hill, North Carolina.

844.39 Nancy Kwan and France Nuyen and Nobu McCarthy] Kwan, see note 506.28–29; France Nuyen (b. 1939), French film and television actor (b. 1939) whose career included roles in *Battle for the Planet of the Apes* (1969) and *The Joy Luck Club* (1993); actor Nobu McCarthy (1934–2002).

845.2 Keye Luke] Chinese-born American actor (1904–1991) who portrayed Charlie Chan's oldest son in Charlie Chan films, among other roles.

845.3 Richard Loo] Actor (1903–1983) with roles in *God Is My Co-Pilot* (1945) and *The Steel Helmet* (1951), among other films.

854.40 SANE] The National Committee for a Sane Nuclear Policy was organized by U.S. pacifists and anti-nuclear protestors in 1957, and was active in the antiwar movement in the 1960s and 1970s.

855.35–36 Walter Reuther's] Walter Reuther (1907–1970), labor leader active in the United Auto Workers Union and the Congress of Industrial Organizations.

859.2 Thomas Hardy, where Sergeant Troy says] From *Far from the Madding Crowd*, ch. 26.

863.4–5 L.A. Massacre, nineteen killed.] See note 323.13.

HAWAI'I ONE SUMMER

867.11 agent orange] Defoliant used to destroy forests and crops in South Vietnam during the Vietnam War until 1971. Human health problems linked to exposure to Agent Orange are believed to be caused by dioxin, though the U.S. government has claimed that the amount of the toxin present in the defoliant is too small to be harmful.

867.15–16 bombing of Kaho'olawe—by ANZUS and Japan.] In 1978 the massive ten-day RIMPAC war games exercise in the waters around Hawaii involved ships, aircraft, and military personnel from several countries, including the United States, Australia, New Zealand, Japan, and Canada. The 1951 ANZUS agreement is a collective security treaty among the United States, Australia, and New Zealand. The use of the island of Kaho'olawe by the U.S. Navy as a site for bombardment training, which would end in 1991, had long been the subject of protests by Hawaiians.

867.32–34 kapu . . . katonk] Hawaiian terms for taboo and mainlanders, respectively.

869.2 kama'āina] Hawaiian: native-born.

869.3 Pele] Hawaiian fire goddess, a figure at the center of Hawaiian mythology, here a personification of Hawaii.

869.5 Kamehameha would conquer all the islands] Kamehameha I (c. 1758–1819) conquered rival chieftains of all of the Hawaiian Islands but Kauai and in 1810 established the Kingdom of Hawai'i.

870.10–11 I didn't follow Lew Welch's disappearance far enough.] Welch is believed to have committed suicide, having left behind a suicide note before disappearing into the woods in Nevada County in Northern California; his body was never found.

870.18–19 Jade Snow Wong] See note 693.31.

870.25 once ephemeral newspaper articles] See Note on the Texts.

873.34 hut . . . Robert Louis Stevenson] The Scottish writer Robert Louis Stevenson (1850–1894) spent several months in Hawaii during the first half of 1889.

878.38–39 Cisco Kid and Pancho.] Fictional Mexican bandit and his sidekick featured in comic strips, on the radio, in movies such as *In Old Arizona* (1928) and *The Gay Caballero* (1940), and in a television series, 1950–56.

881.10 Lew Welch was saying] See note 760.31–32. The quote that follows is Welch's "Chicago Poem" (1958).

881.30 *A Journal of the Plague Year*] See note 501.22.

883.3 Paul Goodman] Social critic, novelist, poet, and prolific writer (1911–1972) whose best-known book is *Growing Up Absurd* (1960). The lines quoted are from Goodman's poem "A Diary of Makapuu" (1968).

895.29 *King Solomon's Ring*] English translation (1952) of book (*Er redete mit dem Vieh, den Vögeln, und den Fischen*, 1949) by the Austrian zoologist and animal behaviorist Konrad Lorenz (1903–1989).

898.33 New Criticism] Methodology based on close reading of works that became the dominant mode of literary criticism taught at American universities from the 1950s through the 1970s.

899.24 Holden] Holden Caulfield, protagonist of *The Catcher in the Rye* (1951), novel by J. D. Salinger (1919–2010).

901.9–10 Lili'uokalani . . . house arrest] See note 474.27–28.

902.29 Louis Chu] Chinese-born American writer (1915–1970), author of the novel *Eat a Bowl of Tea*, published in 1961.

902.39–40 Tom Gill losing the election for Governor.] The Democratic politician Thomas Gill (1922–2009), lieutenant governor of Hawaii, 1966–1970, ran unsuccessfully for governor in 1970 and 1974.

903.2   Yggdrasil tree] In Norse mythology, a vast tree at the center of the cosmos.

907.15–16   Goethe's poem about the Erl-king's daughter.] The poem "The Erlkönig" (1782), by the German writer Johann Wolfgang von Goethe (1749–1832), features not a daughter but a son; it is a variation on the poem "The Erlkönig's Daughter" (1778), itself based on a Danish ballad.

910.38   Philip Whalen] Beat and San Francisco Renaissance poet (1923–2002).

912.4   Nelson Algren] American writer (1909–1981), whose books include *The Man with the Golden Arm* (1949) and *A Walk on the Wild Side* (1956).

ESSAYS, REVIEWS, AND POEMS 1977–87

920.21–23   Patty Hearst story . . . SLA–type activities] Patricia Hearst (b. 1954), heiress to the Hearst newspaper fortune, was kidnapped by the radical Symbionese Liberation Army (SLA) and then, under the pseudonym "Tania," took part in their criminal activities during 1974–75.

920.24   OAS] Organisation de l'armée secrète (Organization of the Secret Army), terrorist organization opposed to Algerian independence whose violent actions included a failed military coup against French president Charles de Gaulle (1890–1970) in 1961.

920.25   the Tupamaros] Uruguayan guerrilla organization of the 1960s and 1970s.

928.13   "The Chinese Hour,"] "The Golden Star Chinese Hour," long-running Cantonese radio program in San Francisco, hosted by its founders Tommy Tong and his wife, May Tong.

931.10–11   as Kurt Vonnegut said, "Writers . . . bears."] See the remarks by the novelist Kurt Vonnegut (1922–2007) in the version of his essay "Teaching the Unteachable" published in *The New York Times*, August 6, 1987: "The idea of a conference for prose writers is an absurdity. They don't confer, can't confer. It's all they can do to drag themselves past one another like great, wounded bears." The passage was omitted from the essay when it was collected in Vonnegut's *Wampeters, Foma & Granfalloons* (1974).

949.14–15   The Joyce ended on the last Yes] In the final chapter of James Joyce's *Ulysses* (1922), "yes I said yes I will Yes" are the final words of Molly Bloom's soliloquy.

960.29–30   "The ways of the people . . . their peculiar cachet."] From dialogue in the story "A New England Winter" (1884) by Henry James (1843–1916).

962.5   *Golden Bough*] Twelve-volume study (1890–1915) by the British anthropologist James George Frazer (1854–1941).

965.13–14   'Blackhawk' comics . . . Chop Chop] See p. 443.

967.2   *The New Yorker* teased in one of their covers] See "View of the World from 9th Avenue," cover illustration by Saul Steinberg for the March 29, 1976, issue of *The New Yorker* magazine.

969.18–19   J. P. Donleavy] American-born writer (1926–2017) who spent most of his life living in Ireland, the author of the novel *The Ginger Man* (1955).

969.20–21   Francine du Plessix Gray's *Lovers and Tyrants* . . . immigrant from France.] Gray (1930–2019), the author of the novel *Lovers and Tyrants* (1976), spent her childhood years in France before immigrating to the United States at the age of ten.

973.33–34   *The White Shadow*] Television drama on CBS, 1978–81, about a basketball coach for a high school in South Central Los Angeles.

973.35   *Superman*] Film (1978) directed by Richard Donner (b. 1930) starring Christopher Reeve (1952–2004) in the title role and Margot Kidder (1948–2018) as Lois Lane.

975.15–17   Adelaide . . . Gallipoli] During World War I, Australian troops played an important role in the Gallipoli Campaign, April 25, 1915–January 9, 1916, an unsuccessful attempt to open the Dardanelles.

981.20   the Brontë's childhood cities.] The imaginary cities Glasstown and Angria invented as the setting for childhood fiction by the English novelists Charlotte Brontë (1816–1855), Emily Brontë (1818–1848), and Anne Brontë (1820–1849), along with their brother Patrick Branwell Brontë (1817–1848).

981.27   "airy nothing"?] *A Midsummer Night's Dream*, V.i.16.

984.1   John Hawkes approaches God with metaphor] The passage is from Hawkes's novel (1925–1998) *Second Skin* (1961).

985.10–22   Shakespeare compared . . . name.] *A Midsummer Night's Dream*, V.i.17.

988.32–33   David Henry Hwang and Philip Glass] Hwang (b. 1957), whose plays include *M. Butterfly* (1988) and *Yellow Face* (2007), frequently collaborated with the composer Philip Glass (b. 1937), including the writing of three opera libretti.

This book is set in 10 point ITC Galliard, a face designed
for digital composition by Matthew Carter and based
on the sixteenth-century face Granjon. The paper is acid-free
lightweight opaque that will not turn yellow or brittle with age.
The binding is sewn, which allows the book to open easily and lie flat.
The binding board is covered in Brillianta, a woven rayon cloth
made by Van Heek–Scholco Textielfabrieken, Holland.
Composition by Jordan Koluch.
Printing by Sheridan Grand Rapids, Grand Rapids, MI.
Binding by Dekker Bookbinding, Wyoming, MI.
Designed by Bruce Campbell.

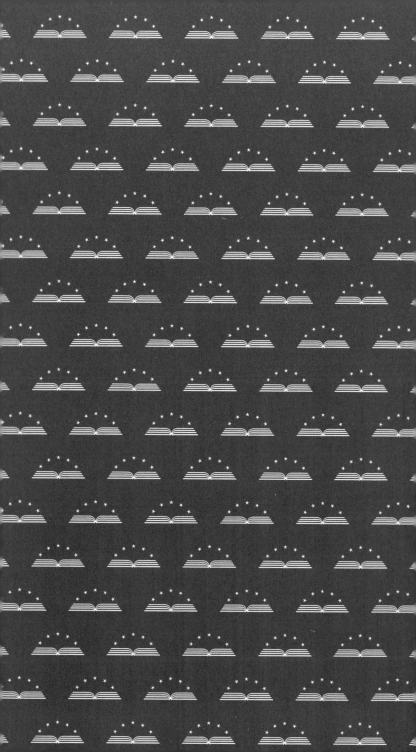